THE LONESOME CROWN

Also by Brian Lee Durfee

The Five Warrior Angels
Book 1: The Forgetting Moon
Book 2: The Blackest Heart

BRIAN LEE DURFEE

THE LONESOME CROWN

THE FIVE WARRIOR ANGELS

BOOK THREE

SAGA PRESS

LONDON SYDNEY NEW YORK TORONTO NEW DELHI

✝ ✝ ✝ ✝ ✝

SAGA PRESS
AN IMPRINT OF SIMON & SCHUSTER, INC.

1230 AVENUE OF THE AMERICAS, NEW YORK, NEW YORK 10020

FOR ALL

THE BRAVE WOMEN WHO MADE THE HEARTRENDING DECISION TO GIVE UP A CHILD FOR ADOPTION—SPECIFICALLY MY BIOLOGICAL MOTHER, **Shayla Sanders**, WHO BROUGHT ME INTO THIS WORLD. MAY YOU ALWAYS KNOW THAT I MADE SOMETHING OF THIS LIFE YOU GAVE ME. AND FOR ALL THE BRAVE WOMEN WHO ADOPTED THE CHILD OF ANOTHER AND LOVED THAT CHILD AS THEIR OWN—SPECIFICALLY **Maxine Durfee**, WHO RAISED ME IN ALL THE RIGHT WAYS.

INTRODUCTION AND ACKNOWLEDGMENTS

In the introduction to *The Forgetting Moon*, I mentioned that I was adopted and that I had never met a blood relative. I talked of how I related to all the movies and books about clichéd orphan farm boys like Luke Skywalker, Rand al'Thor, Jon Snow, etc. Those stories meant a lot to me as a kid and still do. I reckon that's why my own fantasy series is full of parentless children trying to find their way in a harsh world and accomplishing great things on their journey.

Well, the introduction to this book is a bit different. See, nowadays, all you gotta do is spit in a tube, place your spit in the mail, and *BOOM!* Through the sorcery of DNA, you can find your long-lost relatives! Right? Actually, it is about that easy. In fact, I did just that a few years ago and located my birth mother through Ancestry.com. It was a dream come true, a mystery solved, and one of the major highlights of my life. It was also interesting to discover that my birth mother was but a lonely sixteen-year-old living in Las Vegas on that glorious day on which I was born. And clearly my beloved Oakland Raiders moved to Las Vegas in honor of the event, thank you very much.

All kidding aside, as you saw on the previous page, I dedicated this book to both my biological mother and my adoptive mother. And, alas, before I proceed further, I must now apologize for dedicating such an R-rated book to such fine and wonderful women.

Again, never-ending gratitude goes out to **Matt Bialer**, the best literary agent in the universe, and to **Stefanie Diaz** for foreign sales. Thanks also to Klett-Cotta in Germany and Canelo in the UK. My editor at Saga Press, **Joe Monti**, still deserves all the credit for drafting me into the big leagues and creating such wonderfully designed books. Please read my afterword at the end of this book to learn how truly awesome he is. Thanks also to **Valerie Shea** and Simon & Schuster for all the heroic, time-consuming, and precise editing. She deserves all the praise and thanks. A big thanks also to production editor **Alexandre Su**, managing editor **Caroline Pallotta**, editorial assistant **Jela Lewter**, VP deputy publisher **Jennifer Long**, and **Chloe Gray** in production along with **Kayleigh Webb** in publicity and marketing. A huge shout-out also to **Alexi Vandenberg** at Bard's Tower for promoting *The Forgetting Moon* and *The Blackest Heart* at conventions around the country. Mapmaker **Robert Lazzaretti** still deserves a big thanks, as does designer **Lisa Litwack** and illustrator **Richard Anderson** for creating such great covers. And I cannot forget thanking voice narrator **Tim Gerard Reynolds** and Recorded Books for making both *The Forgetting Moon* and *The Blackest Heart* Amazon/Audible.com bestsellers.

Thanks also to **Stephen King**, **Mötley Crüe**, and the **Las Vegas Raiders**.

CONTENTS

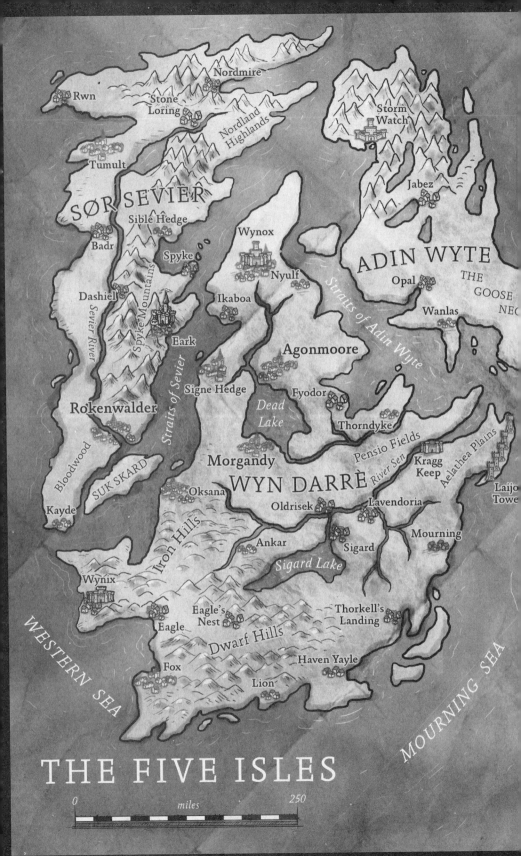

Rwn

Nordmire

Stone
Loring

Nordland
Highlands

Storm
Watch

Tumult

Jabez

SØR SEVIER

Sible Hedge

Wynox

ADIN WYTE

Badr

Spyke

Nyulf

Opal

THE
GOOSE
NEC

Dashiel

Ikaboa

Wanlas

Sevier River

Spyke Mountains

Eark

Agonmoore

Straits of Adin Wyte

Signe Hedge

Fyodor

Rokenwalder

Bloodwood

Dead
Lake

Thorndyke

Pensio Fields

Aelathea Plains

Straits of Sevier

Morgandy

River Sen

Kragg
Keep

Laijo
Towe

SUK SKARD

WYN DARRÈ

Kayde

Oksana

Oldrisek

Lavendoria

Iron Hills

Ankar

Sigard

Mourning

Wynix

Sigard Lake

Eagle's
Nest

Thorkell's
Landing

Eagle

WESTERN SEA

Dwarf Hills

Fox

Haven Yayle

MOURNING SEA

Lion

THE FIVE ISLES

0   miles   250

THE LONESOME CROWN

Only through silver and blood and the green elixir of life can the dead rise again.
So I ask, would summoning the demons up from the underworld be a dread or
glorious thing? For in the end it is life renewed. And that is true Absolution.
—THE MOON SCROLLS OF MIA

CHAPTER ONE

STEFAN WAYLAND

6TH DAY OF THE FIRE MOON, 999TH YEAR OF LAIJON
WROCLAW, GUL KANA

Scorch and blood and the cold taste of terror hung stark in the air. "Who are you?" the frightened girl asked, shivering on the rocky slope below Stefan Wayland and Mud Undr'Fut. However, the question was not meant for Stefan or the small oghul in ragged leather armor crouching behind the lichen-covered boulder, hidden from view. Instead, the girl's fright-filled eyes danced between the five whip-wielding Aalavarrè Solas and the black saber-toothed lion on the crimson-splattered hillside directly above her.

There were a total of six dead fishermen strewn between the Aalavarrè and the girl, six innocent men cut down by silver whips of scorch, their mounts cut down too. The Aalavarrè had wasted little time in killing. And Stefan could tell that Mud's fangs were in dire need of quenching. The oghul's pursed gray lips concealed gums that were aflame and swollen, and his eyes were aglow at the sight of so much human blood. Mud gripped a small curved dagger in his gnarled fist, his entire body itching to go down and slake his thirst on the dead. Stefan put forth a hand, holding the small oghul back.

1

His own gaze was focused on the white sailboat bobbing in the quay below and the four familiar castaways: Nail, Val-Draekin, the broad-faced oghul who had taken the black angel stone, and the girl with the white feathers tied in her hair who had stolen Gisela, the bow he had carried from Gallows Haven.

"Where do you come from?" the girl repeated, panic and pleading in her voice.

"We come from a place far from here," Icelyn the White, firstborn of the blood cauldrons of Hragna'Ar, answered. The Aalavarrè's voice was silky and hollow, her pale white face hidden behind a silver mask of Skull, white dragon-scale armor shimmering under a long black cloak. Her scorch whip dripped quills of hissing silver into the grass.

Behind Icelyn were four other Aalavarrè Solas, also known as the Cauldron Born: Raakel-Jael the Green, Basque-Alia the Blue, Sashenya the Black, and Aamari-Laada the Red, all of them in colorful dragon-scale armor and similar black cloaks, silver eyes roaming the dismal landscape behind their own silver masks of Skull.

The black saber-toothed lion moved down the slope toward the girl, its own silver eyes naught but flat blank slates as it sank its cruel silver teeth into her ribs. The girl slumped to the ground, straining hands clawing at the sunbaked soil. A silent scream—and she tried to blink away the pain. Her slender body writhed as her terrified gaze searched the barren hillside for help that would never come.

"For a human, she had such soft, beautiful eyes," Mud whispered, still crouching behind the rock. Stefan watched the girl's lungs cease their heaving under the lion's long teeth. "And she bleeds so red." Mud licked his lips.

The white handkerchief tied in the girl's hair was soaked red now, her white dress, too. With silver claws, the large black cat tore open her stomach, exposing purple guts. The lion's previously flat silver eyes now glinted shards of warm sunlight as its long teeth bled the girl colorless.

Stefan was certain that once the five whip-wielding Aalavarrè were gone but before reporting back to Sledg H'Mar, Mud would creep down the slope and greedily sate his thirst on the fresh pallid neck of the girl, draining her of what blood was left. Though it would not be a pure bloodletting, what nourishment Mud could glean from the recently dead would be better than the squirming gutter rats and field gophers he usually complained about. Besides, *One must partake in the blessed miracles of Hragna'Ar,* Mud was fond of saying.

Stefan was also one of those miracles, born again of scorch and blood and Hragna'Ar sacrifice, or so Mud had told him. But Stefan was confused about a lot of things Mud related. Supposedly he had been fed the green elixir of life by the Cauldron Born, eyes once again opened, shattered legs fully healed, born anew of the blood cauldrons of Hragna'Ar. And like Mud Undr'Fut, Stefan was now a servant of the Aalavarrè Solas, beholden to them and the return of the Skulls. He had been appointed as such by the Hragna'Ar high priest, Sledg H'Mar, the most menacing oghul Stefan had ever seen, the one they reported to daily. Mud Undr'Fut liked to sneak around when dealing with the Aalavarrè, he liked to remain hidden. But Stefan was under no illusion that the Aalavarrè were being fooled. They were lucid and aware at all times. They knew exactly where Stefan and the oghul hid.

"Harsh and vibrant these humans are in this sacrament of death," Icelyn the White said, watching the black cat sift through the innards of the girl.

Stefan watched the cat feast. He felt a kinship to the large cat that he could not explain. Mud claimed the cruel lion had also been reborn through Hragna'Ar, pulled from the same sacrificial cauldron of scorch and blood as Stefan.

"Vibrant in life and then so pale in death," Basque-Alia the Blue, third-born of Hragna'Ar and the blood cauldrons, agreed. "Humans die beautifully, their smell in death like a perfume."

"Everything is so vivid and bright and clear in this new world, the Great Above," Icelyn went on. "The very landscape has been carved as though with a magical instrument, the water so crystal clear and full of silver fishes that sparkle in the sun. Not like the Great Beneath, the underworld, where the water pools so dark and dead."

Stefan had a vague memory of listening to a traveling Vallè minstrel sing tavern songs in the Grayken Spear with the same pleasant, poetic verse as these five Aalavarrè. Their talk soothed him, though it was often talk of death and blood. Mud always reported to Sledg H'Mar what the Cauldron Born said. That was why he and Stefan were here with them today. Hidden. Observe and report. Even though the faces of the five Cauldron Born were veiled behind silver masks of Skull, Stefan could still discern their individual voices.

"My eternal soul now quivers with life and purpose," Aamari-Laada the Red, fifth-born of Hragna'Ar and the blood cauldrons, said. One long hand gripping his own scorch whip tight, Aamari-Laada reached his other hand up to the red dragon-scale breastplate covering his chest, fingers tracing the myriad of circles, squares, crosses, crescent moons, and shooting stars that decorated his armor.

"We are roaming, stalking, hunting once again with Viper," Icelyn agreed. "And an enthralling hunt it is, to make extinct the race of men, to avenge the genocide visited upon the Aalavarrè so long ago, to erase the memory of the War of Cleansing, to make right that Vicious War of the Demons, to rid ourselves of all memory of the underworld and its black, colorless depths, to serve again the Dragon, to bring about Fiery Absolution, to worship again at the feet of our Immortal Lord."

"For I am no demon," Aamari-Laada said, "and dragons are no curse."

"This is what the eternal soul was created for," Icelyn said, motioning to the girl and the six dead fishermen on the slope, "To become one with Viper in the long hunt. For it is a hunt uncultivated and raw, shrieking with fiery pain. The song of Viper. And the severed bodies on the hillside below have sung that song. Their lifeless crimson bodies are shrieking it still, their sacred melody doing Viper honor."

"And I myself can hear that pure cry of the human dead sail high and loud toward starshine and moonlight," Aamari-Laada the Red agreed. "It sails high toward the eternal God of open blue sky, toward Viper, the one who carved out the underworld."

Icelyn said, "And that song also leads us toward the dreamer of dreams, the maiden with the wrought-iron soul, toward the Dragon, wherever he may be, the ones who shall guide us back to that cross-shaped altar and our Immortal Lord."

They were all alike, the five Aalavarrè Solas, all of them speaking in mysterious verse, all of them in their dragon-scale armor of red, green, black, blue, and white, all of them with their silver masks of Skull. Yes, they were all similar, they were like Stefan and the black saber-toothed lion, Mud claimed, all born of the sacrificial blood cauldrons of Hragna'Ar, all awaiting the arrival of the Dragon and his vast armies of Vallè, all of them born to usher in Fiery Absolution, all of them preparing for the cross-shaped altar and the return of their Immortal Lord. They seemed to worship some God they called Viper.

Mud Undr'Fut had explained it all to Stefan repeatedly. The diminutive oghul had also claimed he had helped the high priest, Sledg H'Mar, in the Hragna'Ar births of all five Aalavarrè. A task that did Mud and his long-dead kin great honor. As for the Aalavarrè Solas themselves, the killing of both humans and animals did Viper great honor. And, as Mud explained, Hragna'Ar was all about the sharing of honor and bringing about the return of the Skulls. And Stefan was part of that plan. Found dead some half-moon ago, he had been gathered up from the woods and born again with the saber-toothed lion. Stefan and the large cat had been a "test" for a greater Hragna'Ar resurrection yet to come.

Stefan recalled only some snippets of Gallows Haven and his life before, but through a haze darkly. The memories were all there, but covered over in smoke and mist. What he did remember of his last day alive was the Vallè maiden, Seita, betraying him, stealing *Afflicted Fire* and *Blackest Heart* and the red angel stone from him. He recalled clenching the black angel stone tight in his fist until a strange girl in a green cloak and white feathers tied in her hair appeared from the woods with a burly oghul and stole even the black stone and his precious longbow named after his lost love, Gisela.

Now he was here with Mud and the five Cauldron Born, watching as the two thieves drifted silently free of the quay in a small white fishing boat. And Nail and Val-Draekin sailed with them. *Has everyone been born anew of scorch and blood?* Stefan had watched Nail and Val-Draekin die in the glacier. He had watched the boiling river of ice suck them down into its murderous depths and kill them.

Or am I still trapped in Deadwood Gate? Is the curse of the mines still warping my brain as Culpa Barra said it would? Or has everyone been resurrected like me?

His mind was in turmoil as he watched Nail and Val-Draekin sail away. In some ways he wanted to call out to them. But he remained hidden behind the boulder with Mud, sweating under his leather armor, watching as the white vessel carrying his precious longbow and the four castaways sailed away, not quite knowing what to think of his new life, not quite knowing if any of what he was experiencing was real. "You have new friends now," Mud had told him not long ago. "Those who brought you back to life, the Aalavarrè Solas."

But were his new friends really these cold and merciless killers? Icelyn the White was clearly the leader of the Aalavarrè Solas. She was the firstborn, and like Sashenya the Black, a female. Icelyn was also the coldest of the Aalavarrè, pure venom living within her eternal soul. 'Twas Icelyn who had slain every single horse on the slope below with her barbed scorch whip of dripping starlight. 'Twas Icelyn who allowed the saber-toothed lion to feast on the flesh of the human girl, its long silver teeth now scarlet with death, silver eyes now shining and cruel.

On the barren knoll just below Stefan and Mud's hiding place, Icelyn removed her silver mask of Skull, revealing the stark white face and silver eyes of a Cauldron Born. Her metallic gaze traveled down the boulder-strewn bluff toward the small port nestled within the windy inlet. The other four Aalavarrè followed Icelyn's cold stare, all of them watching as the boat carrying Nail and Val-Draekin floated away. It was a relatively small vessel with a tall mast and an unfurled sail that now set out over the choppy bay.

"Are we to allow them such easy escape?" Sashenya the Black, fourthborn of the blood cauldrons of Hragna'Ar, said. Her voice was a hollow, silken echo from behind her mask of silver. "Death and decay. I feel the power of the black star stone goes with them. It calls to me."

Stefan could also feel the black stone's distant call. *I should never have touched any of those cursed stones.* Death and decay was what they were. *One of the star stones killed Gisela. One of the stones likely killed me!* He looked down at his own hands. *Yet I live when I should not!* Hovering at the edges of his memory was that image of a broken boy sitting against a white aspen tree, a thick oghul arrow lodged in his chest, red butterflies drifting up all around. The oghul riding in that boat with Nail and Val-Draekin had taken the black stone.

"Those on yonder vessel are of no matter to us now," Icelyn said. "For the Dragon, our master, watches over the black stone now. Do not fall into despair, Sashenya, for all the star stones will make their way into the hands of our Immortal Lord at Fiery Absolution."

"But the Aalavarrè Solas have arisen anew." Sashenya turned to Icelyn. "We should not be so passive. While human, oghul, dwarf, and Vallè seek their 'salvation' underground, we Aalavarrè Solas have already spent a thousand years trapped there. Do you not remember the underworld was a vast and deep purgatory, oceans and rivers and cities unseen, the lifeless dead in need of an awakening, in need of blood sacrifice and the cauldrons of Hragna'Ar? I do not wish to return to such a state. The star stones are part of *our* keys to salvation, the keys to the marble quarry and the salvation of our lost and buried kin, the keys to the resurrection of our Immortal Lord. We should go after them."

Icelyn was swift to answer. "We must live with patience but a while longer. The star stones will be gathered when the Dragon arises to answer the Call of the Burning Tree. It is written in crystal vision, starshine that used to be silver. We have heard the stars whisper as much in the deepness of our long sleep, in the infernal depths and cavernous haunts of our underworld. Do *you* not recall? Our souls have spent an eternity living in both dreams and chains, forever moving through a silent windstorm of invisible dark, shattered, broken, and lost. But no more. For one by one we have all awoken, clawing our way from the infinite blackness of the underworld by the power of Viper, woken again through pure scorch and blood harvest and sacrifice in the cauldrons of Hragna'Ar, woken again by the only true and everlasting life—Blood of the Dragon. So patience but a little longer, Sashenya. Patience before the fullness of the light."

Sashenya bowed her head in acquiescence.

Icelyn hooked the coiled scorch whip back onto her silver belt, then drew a long silver dagger from the folds of her dark cloak and eyed the ravaged body parts scattered about with an eagerness and hunger. She stepped over a pile of horse entrails and crouched over the nearest dead fisherman. Her white dragon-scale armor creaked softly as she sliced away both of the human's ears with the dagger, then quickly moved to the next. Stefan drew back farther behind the boulder, for these strange knights were brutal in all they did.

"'Tis an ancient ritual the Aalavarrè perform," Mud whispered. "'Tis the ancient oghul way. Mutilate. Disfigure. Taking the ears of the enemy so as to make it hard for anyone to tell if the dead are human or Vallè. Those severed ears are then collected and later used in the Blood Cauldrons of Hragna'Ar. 'Tis quite normal, really."

Normal? Stefan listened to the oghul in cold fascination, figuring every corpse looked the same once the maggots had done their job, ears or no ears. The dead were dead. The rotting were rotting. *And I am born anew!*

As for the five Cauldron Born, one thing Stefan knew for sure: within the heart of their leader, Icelyn the White, firstborn of the blood cauldrons of Hragna'Ar, there clearly lived a need for revenge, for a devouring, for an absolution. And the heart of Icelyn had infected the heart of the other four Aalavarrè. For they were all savage killers.

Icelyn knelt on the hillside, face seemingly etched in joy, silver eyes squinting against the harsh sun as she cut the ears from the dead. She cast her gaze out to sea several times during her task, watching as the boat carrying Nail and Val-Draekin and the black angel stone sailed away. *And my bow, Gisela,* Stefan thought. *Gisela goes with them, stolen by the girl with two white feathers tied in her hair.*

In that final day of Fiery Absolution, the grand vicar shall
take a bride most beautiful and young.
—The Way and Truth of Laijon

CHAPTER TWO
TALA BRONACHELL

6TH DAY OF THE FIRE MOON, 999TH YEAR OF LAIJON

AMADON, GUL KANA

The Val Vallè ambassador, Val-Korin, and his bodyguard, Val-So-Vreign, escorted Tala Bronachell into the king's bedchamber. Val-Korin's daughter, Seita, followed them. All three Vallè bowed low to Jovan Bronachell upon entry.

Tala did not bow. She would not bow. She planned never to obey any of Jovan's wishes again. In fact, under her tattered cloak she wore simple leather leggings and a black shirt—boyish clothes that were sure to displease the king. She let the cloak fall open just enough that her brother could see her offensive garb.

"Where has Lawri gone off to now?" King Jovan fired the question, his voice deep and accusing. He eyed Tala and her ragged clothes with distaste.

She'd known the king's summons was going to be full of questions about Lawri Le Graven. Every time Tala thought of her cousin, she couldn't help but shudder. *Her missing arm! And those ever-glowing eyes of green!*

Jovan stood upon the thick bearskin rug set before his four-post

9

mahogany bed. He was wrapped in a luxurious red-trimmed black velvet cloak fastened with a brooch of Vallè-worked silver. Under the cloak he wore black leather pants and a decorative black leather tunic festooned with red gems up the center. Silver necklaces draped his neck and silver bracelets circled each wrist. His wavy brown hair fell just past his shoulders and was confined by a silver band—the royal crown. Sky Reaver— the sword that used to belong to the White Prince, Aeros Raijael—hung at his hip.

"You know where she is, sister." His eyes narrowed. "Mona Le Graven hasn't seen Lawri since early this morning. Her daughter went off with a wicker basket and two Silver Guard escorts. The escorts say they lost track of her. Those escorts are now being dealt with for their gross failure. I know you had something to do with her disappearance. Just as you facilitated her disappearance before."

"I told you, I had nothing to do with Lawri's disappearance the first time," Tala countered, her back growing rigid. "I thought we already went over all that."

Truth be told, Tala was just as confused that Lawri Le Graven had vanished. She was probably more worried than her brother was. *Where have you gone this time, Lawri?*

Her cousin wasn't hiding in Jovan's bedchamber, that was certain. The place was well-lit from the large open window to the east, though low-hanging clouds blanketed the sky, dimming the room some. Sconces lined gray stone walls draped with brilliant velvet tapestries and decorative swords, opulently shined blades with bejeweled and sculpted crosspieces that glittered dully in the light. Also casting a dull shine were the numerous golden trinkets, goblets, and Laijon statuettes atop the various scrollworked armoires and cabinets in every corner. Jovan's room was always too fancy for Tala's tastes.

"May I interject, if it please Your Excellency?" Val-Korin spoke in his peculiar taut voice, bowing respectfully as he did so. "Perhaps you accuse the wrong sister for Lawri's disappearance this time."

"You think Jondralyn is behind this?" The king's brow furrowed even more as he met the Val Vallè ambassador's cool eyes. Val-Korin was clothed in just as much finery as Jovan. He wore a long black robe, and the red brass pendant of his rank dangled from a slender, gem-studded chain about his neck.

"She acts most suspicious," Val-So-Vreign added.

Jovan's gaze fell on the ambassador's bodyguard, a green-eyed Vallè with coal-colored hair. He then glanced at Val-Korin's daughter.

Seita bowed, then said, "Jondralyn has not been seen in the castle since Lawri went missing." Her round green eyes were ever watchful and did not stray from those of the king. The Vallè princess looked stunning as always. She wore tanned leather breeches laced up the sides, a black belt, and a dark umber tunic under a shimmering white cloak. Her hair was the glowing hue of fine silk, hanging sleek and loose over the sides of her face and tapered Vallè ears and even over her forehead.

Does her hair cover a bruise? Tala fixed her eyes on the delicate pale skin of the Vallè's forehead, but she couldn't tell for sure if there were any flaws there. *If she is bruised, she's not only covered it with her hair but likely some ashy makeup, too.*

"Jondralyn had nothing to do with Lawri's disappearance," Tala said with a trace of strained conviction in her tone. She gave both Val-Korin and Seita a flat stare.

Val-Korin's thin hand rose to his chest. He held her eyes a moment. "What makes you so sure Jondralyn is not hiding Lawri?"

"Jovan is paranoid, and you two are only feeding into that," she answered without hesitation, coldness in her voice. "He thinks both Jondralyn and I are out to betray him at every turn, when in reality—"

"Oh, hold your tongue," Jovan cut her off, voice dropping to a threatening whisper. "You and Jondralyn are both full of mischief and betrayal. That is known. We've had this pointless conversation numerous times already."

"I have never betrayed you," Tala fired back. "And neither has Jondralyn."

"Nonsense," Jovan said. "The answer to this vexing problem has now been made simple. You shall be watched at all times, Tala Bronachell. You shall be held under guard until further notice. You shall be held in Mother's old chamber, where it will be easier for the guards to keep track of you. You are not to be allowed back into your own chamber. In fact, you are not allowed anywhere without permission from me."

"What?" Tala's heart beat furiously under her ribs. "Why?"

"You shall be watched," he repeated. "Watched and watched and watched until you confess all your sins and betrayals against me, until you tell me exactly where Lawri Le Graven is. Only then will you be free."

"This is not fair!"

"It is beyond fair in the eyes of the Silver Throne!" Jovan shouted back at her. "I wouldn't put it past you or Jondralyn to have been instrumental in Lindholf's escape from the arena. Think about that, Tala. Think about where *both* of your cousins lie hidden, both Lawri and Lindholf. Only when you have the answers to those mysteries will I allow you to roam free."

**

"This is a day long overdue." Glade Chaparral had a cocky sneer pasted on his smug face as he strolled up the corridor toward Tala. "Given to all manner of mischief and sneakiness and betrayal, and now our king *finally* sees fit to place you under guard, to lock you away. Indeed, it is long past time."

Tala stood with Val-Korin, Val-So-Vreign, and Seita in the corridor just outside Swensong Courtyard. She felt her whole body stiffen at Glade's approach, for he had the knack of making even the most horrible of situations worse.

Glade was clothed in polished Dayknight armor, helm in the crook of his left arm, long black sword dangling at his belt. His three rakish Dayknight lackeys strode casually behind him—Tolz Trento of Avlonia, Alain Gratzer of Knightliegh, and Boppard Stockach of Reinhold. All three were tall and imposing and good-looking, their own polished helms in the crooks of their arms, swords girted at their hips. Ser Boppard was so casual in his approach, he actually had a half-eaten chicken leg in one greasy hand, tearing at it with his teeth as he walked.

In Tala's estimation, Tolz, Alain, and Boppard were the scoundrels who had helped Glade frame Lindholf Le Graven for the murder of Sterling Prentiss and implicated him in the assassination attempt on Jovan. They were now assigned to escort Tala from the courtyard to her mother's bedchamber and then help the Silver Guard set up a twenty-four-hour watch rotation outside her door.

"I'll escort the princess from here?" Glade bent his knee to the Val Vallè ambassador.

"Then we shall take our leave." Val-Korin bowed in return. With another bow to Tala, he whirled and strode down the corridor, Val-So-Vreign following, their boots clicking loudly on the tiled floor.

Seita did not go with her father. She lingered, eyeing Glade suspiciously.

"What's this?" Glade's gaze darted between Tala and the Vallè princess. "Two girly lovers not willing to part?" He laughed. The three Dayknights behind him laughed too, Boppard's thin lips sucking at the chicken leg now, grease around his mouth.

"How's our delicate Vallè flower today?" Glade's laughing eyes met Seita's. The Vallè princess did not answer, just stared, not even a trace of anger sparking in her eyes. Just calm. "Cuddling up to Tala, cuddling up to the king's sister, I see," Glade continued. "Don't think the entire court hasn't seen the doe-eyed looks you two girly lovers give each other. Tala and the delicate Vallè flower."

"You're not the first to call me a delicate Vallè flower," Seita said flatly. "I'm just here to make sure you get Tala to her chamber safely, make sure there are no side trips, make sure nothing . . . untoward happens."

Glade turned to his companions, grinning wildly. "To make sure Tala gets to her chamber safely, she says." He looked back to Seita. "You don't think we can do the job?"

"Oh, I'm sure four Dayknights could do the job all right." Seita yawned, hand up to her mouth as she looked around. "But I don't see four Dayknights here, do you?"

Glade's face darkened.

"Leastwise not any *real* Dayknights," Seita finished.

Glade, Tolz, Alain, and Boppard had been knighted full-fledged

Dayknights by Jovan under less-than-deserving circumstances. During their initiation, Tala had detected many disapproving looks amongst some of the older Silver Guard and even a few of the Dayknights present.

Glade quickly recovered, not letting Seita's jibe affect him. He carried on with his lame joke. "We've all been making bets on whether you two were lovers. Seems that we've found out. Took forever for confirmation, though, or so it seems."

"Well." Seita stared at him blankly. "Any conversation with you, Glade Chaparral, is enough to make us all know what forever feels like."

"What is that supposed to mean?"

"Means whatever you want it to mean." Seita shrugged.

"Whatever." Glade shook his head in feigned disgust. "Dumb bitch."

"Well, I'm done then." Seita cocked her head. "It just can't possibly be worth it, intellectually sparring with one as unworthy as you. Ridiculous, even."

"You think I'm ridiculous?" Glade's helm dropped from the crook of his arm to the floor with a clatter. He balled up his fists, stood in a mock fighting stance. "I'll box your fragile Vallè face in, you call me ridiculous again." He flashed a sly grin and laughed. The three knights behind him chuckled too.

"When does your boorishness ever end, Glade?" the Vallè princess asked.

Tala noticed a subtle skulking darkness deep set behind Seita's eyes now.

"And who is gonna stop my 'boorishness'?" Glade asked. "You? Always strutting about this castle like a man, not a princess. Makes one wonder, do you have hairy balls and a thin Vallè cock under those leather pants? Is that your secret? Is that why you and Tala get along so famously?"

Glade grinned madly at Tala. "So have you let Seita dip the ol' noodle yet, Tala? Let her go down on that sweet little honeypot twixt your legs?"

Boppard actually giggled, taking another loud chomp out of his chicken leg.

Glade continued, bolstered by Boppard's laughing. "Is Seita's wee Vallè noodle gonna just get lost up in there, Tala? Or did some blood-sucking oghul-faced loser like Lindholf already loosen you up good?"

Glade reached for Seita's crotch. "What exactly is under them pants?"

Seita blocked his hand, eyes throwing off sparks now. "Just stay clear of me and shut the fuck up."

"Shut the fuck up, you say?" Glade laughed. Boppard giggled too.

Seita continued, "Every bully I've ever known could never keep their hands to themselves or their fucking mouth shut."

"Oh, really." Glade moved toward her, hand reaching for her crotch again. "Feisty."

Seita thrust the palm of her hand forcefully into Glade's chest plate, sending him awkwardly tumbling backward, his flailing arm knocking the chicken leg from Boppard's hand. Boppard didn't giggle at that.

Glade's rear smacked the floor with a thud. "Rotted angels!" he raged, scrambling to stand, slipping on the smeared grease from the chicken leg, awkwardly falling face-first to the tile floor. "You savage elf bitch!"

"What did you just call me?" Seita's eyes were narrowed and sharp.

"An elf bitch." Glade was on hands and knees, glaring up at her.

"Say that again and I'll poke this right into your mouth." Seita smoothly produced a thin black dagger from a hidden pocket some-where in her leather pants. The black blade in Seita's hand reflected no light. Tala was instantly on guard, afraid. The weapon looked like a Bloodwood dagger.

Glade scrambled back across the tile on his butt, reaching for his sword. Tolz and Alain already had their weapons drawn. Boppard stared at his chicken leg on the floor.

"Kill her!" Glade shouted.

"I'll gut the bitch like a wet herring!" Tolz cried out, attacking.

Seita ducked under his wild swing and answered with a powerful strike of her own, disarming the knight. She whirled and aimed straight at Glade still on his haunches, back against the wall. He threw up his blade, but a fraction too late. The quickness of Seita's blow knocked the sword from his hand. Worry lined Glade's face, but Seita allowed him no respite, and her dagger slashed a swath of wavy hair from the top of his head.

Alain struck at her from behind. Seita kicked out backward. Alain's left leg buckled as her kick landed square against the front of his knee. He jerked away and went down awkwardly to the hard stone floor.

Tolz struck again, having gathered up his weapon. But with a flick and twist of her blade, Seita sent his sword spinning away a second time. Tolz fell back to the stone floor, landing hard on his back.

Boppard drew his sword last, chicken leg now forgotten. He lunged at Seita's exposed back. Tala threw herself between the Dayknight and the Vallè princess. Boppard's heavy rushing bulk knocked her aside, sending her sprawling to the floor. She slid on her back helplessly in the opposite direction of the fight.

Boppard swung his sword at Seita's back again. But she spun away, knocking the knight's sword from his hand with seemingly scant effort. Boppard scrambled to grab it, tripping over Tolz and Alain. All three of them were piled up on the floor now in a tangle of arms and legs.

"You must have forgotten our dagger lessons in Greengrass Courtyard." Seita knelt and put the point of her black dagger to Glade's throat. "Or did you think this delicate Vallè flower was just playing games that day?"

Glade shrank away from her, for it was clear Seita was just toying with them, that she could have slain them all easily. He was scared.

Seita sneered, "I ought to kill you now, you small-minded little asshole." She pressed the tip of the blade into his skin, drawing blood.

"Leave him be, girl." Grand Vicar Denarius' hand was suddenly on Seita's shoulder, his fleshy jowls red with anger. "Just leave him be."

Seita rose to her feet and faced the grand vicar, black dagger hidden behind her back in one hand. Glade swiped the droplet of blood from under his quivering chin.

Denarius wore the burnt-orange cassock of his station, silken priest-hood robes underneath. His chest was hung with jeweled necklaces of gold. He was bald as ever, sweat beading up on his head.

The five archbishops crowded the corridor behind the vicar in

16

their most garish robes and priesthood finery—Vandivor, Donalbain, Spencerville, Leaford, and Rhys-Duncan. Leaford and Donalbain did the three-fingered sign of the Laijon Cross over the chains of silver and gold covering their hearts. Spencerville folded his arms over his own round gut. Vandivor and Rhys-Duncan glared at Seita contemptuously.

Tala stood, brushing herself off.

"It's no wonder you're so insecure, Glade Chaparral," Denarius said, "if a wisp of a girl like Seita can knock you and your three cronies right over."

The vicar stepped back from Seita, large sandaled foot smashing Boppard's fallen chicken leg into the tile floor, mashing it flat. Boppard looked sick to his stomach at the sudden horrible fate of the chicken leg.

The vicar's face darkened when he noticed that Seita was trying to hide the dagger behind her back. "Give me the knife," he motioned.

Seita slid the black blade into a hidden fold in her pants, eyeing the man coolly.

Denarius' twin beady eyes roamed over Glade and the other three Dayknights. "You're lucky I don't just demote you all."

Then his eyes fell again on Seita. "And I ought to have Jovan banish you back to Val Vallè."

"Do what you must," Seita answered cordially.

"Just shake hands with Glade and end these childish disagreements," Denarius ordered, glaring at the Vallè princess. "You know better than this, Seita." He glowered at Glade, too. "All you kids know better than this."

The Vallè shrugged, thrusting her hand down toward Glade, if somewhat reluctantly. Still, it was an offering of truce. Glade's scowl was immense; still, at length he reached up and shook Seita's hand. In the moment of silence that ensued, Denarius appeared mighty pleased with himself.

"Don't look too happy," Glade said to the vicar. "If I ever corner the bitch alone, she will pay."

Tala stepped cautiously back, knowing the confrontation was far from over.

"My dear girl," Denarius gasped, noticing her again. "Worry not."

And before Tala knew what was happening, the vicar had stepped forward, pulling her tight to his body in an engulfing hug. Tala tried to squirm away, feeling as if the very breath was being squeezed from her lungs. But he clenched her tight.

"We've had the queen's chambers cleaned just for you," he said. "And at Jovan's behest, we even lit a fire under the baths, set the water to running." He loosened his hug and held her by both shoulders now, staring deep into her eyes. "You must use the baths. And you must consider using your time wisely in the purification of both your body and your mind and your soul."

Denarius had bad breath. He was fat, he was lecherous, and he was ugly. All Tala could think of were the words of her cousin Lawri: *In my dream you were betrothed to the grand vicar, Tala. I attended your wedding.* Anger, livid and raw, filled her.

Being handled by this man whom she loathed unleashed a rage within that she had not known existed. Tala raised her leg and stomped down with all her might, the heel of her foot connecting with the bridge of the vicar's.

Denarius let out a sharp shout of pain and released her, doubling over. Tala's knee came up hard, connecting solidly with the vicar's heavily jowled face. The huge man folded to the floor. All five archbishops reacted at once, rushing to his aid.

Tala fled down the corridor, bursting out into the humidity and cloud-covered light of Swensong Courtyard, legs churning as she sprinted through the gardens and milling people. "Get her!" Glade yelled, frantic. "She can't be allowed out of our sight!"

Tala headed straight for the black iron gate along the yard's southernmost wall. There was an escape route to the hidden ways in a lone passageway not far away. *If I can reach it!* She ran, that one goal in mind. Escape. But she wasn't fast enough.

Glade tackled her before she was halfway across the courtyard.

**

There was only one thing good about being sequestered in her mother's abandoned chambers. And that was the queen's bath chamber. The chamber had an air of grandeur about it unlike anywhere else in the castle. It was situated just off the bedroom—a splendid two-story-high columned gallery of five baths fashioned of Riven Rock marble, large open windows streaming in light high above. The baths were carved right out of the marble floor: one long row of baths in a room lined with numerous arcades and alcoves all recently festooned with sumptuous fresh flower arrangements. The steamy bath chamber had also been recently swabbed clean. Fires had been lit somewhere under the floor beneath the two furthermost baths; the other three baths were always left at room temperature.

Naked, Tala Bronachell luxuriated in one of the cooler stone baths, her head propped against the tub's marble rim. She had initially tried sitting in one of the warmer, deeper tubs, but found the water far too hot.

Her gaze roamed the room, moving past her folded white towel to the smooth surface of the clean pale floor to the steam-filled room beyond. She lay on her back, the garden-scented water covering her stomach and chest, her chin floating above. Occasionally she would dip her mouth down into the water. It tasted of bright spring foliage and crisp spring air.

She had to admit that after today's events, it was nice to soak in her mother's baths. She had not been inside Alana's chambers since the queen had died bearing Ansel. In fact, despite everything she had never felt so relaxed in all her life.

She took a breath and closed her eyes and let her head slip below the skin of the water, trying her best to think of absolutely nothing, trying her best to feel the presence of her mother, her father. After a while, she felt herself dozing.

Then she heard muffled footsteps against the marble floor and her head burst from the water, startled gaze sweeping the room.

Jovan approached, his hard leather riding boots thudding loudly with each step, light ring-mail armor jingling, long black cape swirling in his wake, Dayknight sword at his hip.

"What are you doing in here?" Tala jerked to her feet, her entire body adrip. She snatched the nearby towel, covering her naked body. "You shouldn't be here! I'm not properly dressed!"

"You're rarely properly dressed." Jovan drew near, within arm's reach. "Naked or dressed like a man, what is the difference? You are uncouth in every way, sister."

Tala backed away, "Please leave," she pleaded. "You've no right to be here."

"Oh, stop your blubbering, or I'll punish you far worse than I've a mind to."

"Just leave." She felt so vulnerable before him. She clung to her towel more tightly.

Jovan shook his head. "No sister of mine is going to tell me what to do. No sister of mine is going to act the way you do." He pointed at her. "And no sister of mine is going to go about this castle talking of the Ember Gathering in such blasphemous ways."

Tala's mind spun with fear. "What are you talking about?"

"Oh, don't act so innocent," Jovan said. "Before she went missing, Lawri Le Graven told the grand vicar all you said of the Ember Gathering, how you spoke to our cousin of sacred things, challenged her on sacred things. And now Lawri is gone. As is Lindholf. Both of them disappeared."

"We already went over this. I am not responsible—"

"A king's sister ought not act in such ways!" He cut her plea short, eyes burning with a crazed fervor she had seen all too often as of late. "And it *is* your fault!"

"It is not my fault."

"It is, and you must soon purify yourself before Laijon or perish!"

Tala was angry. And scared. But mostly angry. Jovan's last words had sparked a fury in her. She spoke in a rush. "You are acting like a bully because you know you have no power over me. Just like you have no power over Jondralyn or anyone in this kingdom."

"Watch your tongue or I'll wash your mouth out with soap." His flaring eyes circled the steam-filled room. "I imagine there is some soap around here someplace. For I ought to purify your mouth before the vicar purifies your body and your soul. Denarius is most displeased with you, Tala Bronachell. Most displeased, as you shall soon find out."

"And why should I care what pleases the vicar?" Fear raced up her spine.

"You should love your king and your vicar and obey their bidding in all things!"

"Why should I listen to you?" She gripped the towel tighter around her body. He had stripped her of her clothes before, and she would not let him get his bloody foul hands on her again. "You have never loved me or Jondralyn or any of us. You only love the church, and the vicar, and Leif Chaparral! You only love your sisters if they do as you say, believe as you do, but all you are is full of lies!"

"Stop saying such things!" Jovan fired back. "All lies! Evil lives within you, Tala Bronachell, and needs to be rooted out of your soul. You are the sister of a king! You need to act like a lady!"

"It's always about me acting like a lady! Why can't you love me for who I am? Why does it always have to be about your own precious identity as the king? Why does it always have to be about my allegiance to the vicar and the church?"

"Because the gospel of Laijon is the only thing that brings us happiness in this world, my sister. Can't you see that? Or do the wraiths have such a firm hold on you? When you speak against the vicar and reveal secrets of the Ember Gathering, the spirit of Laijon disappears and the wraiths move in. They must now be purged. And you must now be purified."

That dread chill settled over her again at the mention of purification. "But you can't prove any of what the vicar accuses me of. I have said nothing to Lawri of the Ember Gathering." She knew that part was a lie, but cared not. "I've not yet even seen Lawri's Ember Gathering beads. Nor her Ember Gathering cross. I don't even know where she is at—"

"I've heard enough!" Jovan's crazed eyes again roamed the steamy room as if searching for someone. "Have you heard enough, Your Grace?"

"Yes," a voice sounded from out of the mists. "We all have."

Six ghostly apparitions emerged from the billowing steam behind her brother. Grand Vicar Denarius and the five archbishops of Amadon. Denarius limped, his foot still injured from where she had kicked him. Archbishop Spencerville carried a leather-bound bedroll in the crook of his left arm. The goose-down-filled bedroll was typical of the ones Tala had seen some of Leif Chaparral's Dayknight warriors tie to the backs of their war chargers before leaving for Lord's Point. Most Dayknights called their bedroll a "sleeping bag," for it was sewn shut on three sides like a sack, leaving just an opening at the top for a man to slip into feet-first and sleep.

Seeing the sleeping bag in Spencerville's clutches, Tala's heart hammered.

"Our venerated archbishops and grand vicar have already offered up alms in your name," Jovan said. "And they shall now offer up your own purification before Laijon."

Denarius nodded. His fat jowls looked freshly shaved and glowed pale and slimy as a wet oyster in the steamy baths. His beady eyes were brimming with a rigorous and pointed lust. And the matching looks on the faces of the five archbishops froze Tala solid.

"My sister is to become a lady," Jovan stated. "She is to become a lady and do lady things." He nodded to the vicar. "And you've the Silver Throne's permission to do what you want with her ladyship to make that happen." With that said, Jovan bowed to Denarius and strode through the mists and out of the queen's baths, leaving Tala alone with the grand vicar and five archbishops, both of her hands still gripping the towel about her body, fingers straining in the effort.

She wanted to back away from the six men, run away from them, but she could not. She was rooted in place. It was as if her every anxiety and fear were pressing her down against the marble floor like a thousand-pound weight.

"You must tell us where Lawri Le Graven has gone off to," Denarius said. "You have hidden her before, and I know you hide her now."

"I do not *hide* her," Tala croaked, hoping that something would release her from the spell holding her to the floor.

"You confronted Lawri about her Ember Gathering, no?" the vicar asked. "You falsely accused me and the archbishops of doing horrible things to her during the Ember Gathering, did you not?"

"Leave me alone." Tala shuddered, mind churning. *These men are monsters! I saw you molesting her!* she wanted to scream.

"Wickedness never was happiness," Denarius said. "And wickedness consumes you. I can feel it. I can feel the wraiths working within you."

"I am not wicked." She was shivering under the towel now, feeling so very exposed to his roaming eyes. "I am happy." Her voice was weak.

"You only think you are happy," the vicar said. "As most ripe and youthful and beautiful girls do. But you shall never know full joy until you embrace the gospel of Laijon, until the wraiths have been purged from your soul and your young body has gone through its purification."

Tala turned and bolted away from him, bare feet uncertain on the mist-coated marble. Denarius gave chase. She slipped. Denarius fell on her from behind. They both thudded face-first onto the hard stone floor, Tala's teeth biting into her lip. She tried to wrestle free, her hands letting go the towel, her flesh now exposed. She fought. But Grand Vicar Denarius was heavy. He pinned her to the ground with the bulk of his body as the other five archbishops held down her squirming arms and legs. Then the vicar sat upon her chest, the palms of both his hands covering her forehead as he began muttering an indecipherable incantation.

Tala could barely breathe under his weight. But through her gasping breaths the vicar's prayer came into focus. "In the name of Laijon I expel the wraiths from within you, Tala Bronachell. I command what nightmares and conjurations of evil are in your mind to cease this instant. You have a heritage, my young princess. Honor it. I command you to turn your life around and live according to the teachings within *The Way and Truth of Laijon*. May you regain health in the mind, marrow, and bones, and may the power in the priesthood be upon you throughout eternity and your coming purification. Amen."

Then she was released. The vicar climbed off. The other five arch-bishops backed away. Tala remained on her back, hands fumbling to wrap the towel once again around her nakedness, embarrassed that they had seen so much of her, feeling powerless beneath them. Archbishop Spencerville began undoing the leather straps around the goose-down bedroll he'd carried in. Then he unrolled the Dayknight sleeping bag before her.

The vicar tore away her towel with a swift jerk. Then the five arch-bishops were lifting her up, stuffing her headfirst into the open end of the sleeping bag, tying the leather drawstrings at her feet closed. Captive in the bedroll, Tal felt herself being dragged across the floor. She heard the grand vicar's muffled voice through the fabric: "Only your faith in Laijon can save you now, Tala Bronachell. Best pray to him now."

And then they rolled her into the hottest of the marble baths. In that moment Tala swore she would die before she prayed for Laijon's help, especially considering it was Laijon's own vicar causing her torture. But as death closed in like a thick, hot blanket, she had second thoughts. It was a searing heat at first, wet and suffocating. She struggled to free herself from the Dayknight sleeping bag, but surrounding her naked body was naught but blackness and boiling heat. *And nothing to breathe!*

Yet, as she felt herself sink to the bottom of the hot bath, Tala felt herself become acclimated to the temperature. She came to rest on the floor of the pool in her goose-down bedroll coffin, feeling the hot marble floor under her.

She knew she could hold her breath for maybe a minute or two. *But I won't pray for them! I won't believe what they believe! I'd rather die!* At the moment belief in Laijon was a prison no less torturous than this drowning, this fight for air. . . .

She kicked. Nothing. She struggled to move her arms. *Am I truly going to die?*

Panic set in. The sleeping bag clamped around her like a forger's vise, the weight of the water pushing her flat. The more she struggled, the more she felt the pain. She gasped for air. Water rushed into her mouth. She choked. She gagged. She thrashed wildly, biting at the inside wall of the bedroll. It tasted gritty, chalklike. Still Tala kept the fabric clenched between her teeth, slowly sucking in water. *I need air. . . .*

Then one of the men was in the pool with her, clutching the bag, pulling, lifting. Tala felt herself float up, up, her stomach pressed against the fabric, then *air!*

And she was dumped onto the edge of the marble bath like a soggy sack of potatoes, pain digging into her lungs.

She coughed up water and spat. Then sucked in more sweet *air!*

All was darkness until the bag was untied and light crept in around her feet. She struggled to find the light, but the bedroll was too heavy and wet, still constricting around her like a tight glove.

"You didn't pray for Laijon to save you," the vicar said.

Then the bag was tied shut again and Tala was dumped into the hot bath a second time. *I won't pray for them!* Her mind was flushed with terror as she sank to the bottom of the pool again. She struck the bottom, awaiting the pain to form again in her lungs, biting the side of the bag, readying herself for the involuntary breathing reflex she knew was coming, figuring if she was going to choke to death, perhaps the fabric of the bag would act as a filter, so the rush of water to her lungs wasn't so sharp, so sudden. The sleeping bag closed in around her again. She could feel the pressure build. *But I won't pray to their Laijon!*

She wanted to scream. But even if she screamed, no one would hear. *If I could stand up, maybe . . .*

Earlier she had judged the heated baths to be about five feet deep. *And I'm taller than that, taller by six or seven inches.* She bit into the bedroll and kicked. She felt her foot slip free of the leather thongs. She tried to slide her other foot free, but the drawstrings were still too tight.

Air!

Her lungs gave out and she heaved in a mouthful of water. She gagged. Involuntarily sucked in more water. It hurt so much. She felt herself slipping away toward death. She kicked wildly one more time. Failed to free her legs.

Once again one of the men was in the water with her, hauling her up, dumping her onto the side of the pool.

Air!

She breathed. She felt the drawstrings loosen around her foot and she strained to push herself from the bag. Firm hands grabbed her exposed ankles and held them fast. Then her feet were stuffed into the bag once more and the leather thong cinched tight.

"Don't fight it, Tala," the vicar said. "Do yourself a favor and accept your purification. If you just pray to Laijon, he will deliver you from this death and I won't have to save you a third time. It is now up to your *own* faith. This shall be your last chance. Even your brother was not given this many chances. None of us wishes for you to die. Not even Jovan wishes for that."

And she was rolled into the pool again. This time the water was not so hot—she was growing used to it. But when she nestled against the bottom of the bath, the burning in her lungs felt like shards of glass. She wished for death now. Wanted it. *But wishes are like prayers—and I shall never wish again.*

But had she ever given up so easily?

Tala searched for a seam in the bedroll, a loose thread, anything to pull on. There was nothing. She tried to sit, struggled and thrashed. She sucked in water—it tasted like hot blood. She gritted her teeth and fought, then choked, lungs filling, the pain like a spear jabbing into her chest. *Oh, Laijon, please help me!* her mind screamed.

She clutched the inside of the sleeping bag. Dug at it. Clawed at it. Panicked. Wild with fear, she lost control. *Oh dear Laijon, I'm dying, please do not let this happen. I haven't even really lived yet. I am so young. Oh, dear Laijon, please.* As she sucked in more water, Tala wished her hands were knives like Baron Jubal Bruk and she could rip through wood and iron and Dayknight bedrolls. *But wishes are like prayers!* As the darkness took her, she fought and fought, tearing and clawing and pulling and ripping and *losing.* The battle was over. *No, please, Laijon, save me, please, Laijon, dear Lord in heaven, I am too young. . . .*

Be at peace, she heard a deep voice say. *Laijon!* It was the voice of the great One and Only. *It was Laijon!*

Forgive me of my doubts, my questioning, she prayed to him. *Take me in your arms, dear Laijon. Give comfort to my sinful soul. Forgive me for mocking the Ember Gathering, for I know it is a sacred thing. . . .*

Be at peace, the voice repeated.

And then she saw the light. *White powder and light.*

She saw the Atonement Tree. She saw fire and flame and Lawri Le Graven sailing through the clouds and sitting on the Silver Throne. She saw a silver gauntlet and the Riven Rock slave quarry and five black holes punched into the glowing marble . . . and there was something awaiting her beneath those holes . . . someone . . .

And then Tala felt herself floating heavenward. And her mind was at peace. As she flew above the castle she looked down, seeing a colossal set of wide marble stairs rising up the side of the castle mount not far from Sunbird Hall. The Long Stairs they were called. Seldom used. A wide staircase that rose some two hundred feet up the slope of Mount Albion, at the top a flat marble platform and long stretch of tall marble columns. As she looked down, those stairs ran thick with blood below her now, a cascading stain of red. The pain in her chest eased and the vision of bloody stairs vanished. She could see the light, the white light. And she felt so weightless, as if she was no longer in her body, but a spirit, rising to meet Laijon . . .

. . . and everything was beginning to fade. She *was* dying. It didn't feel so awful. Nothing was awful but for Lawri's two glowing green eyes staring at her . . .

. . . then her head burst from the water.

A sharp shock of cold air slapped her face and blasted her into wakefulness. She sputtered and spat. Then her head went under again. Her toes touched bottom and she thrust herself up. Another gasp for air. She paddled to keep her head above water.

Then the vicar was in the pool with her, fully garbed. He grabbed her around the waist and lifted her onto the edge of the bath. She stomach slapped the cold marble floor like a wet herring, and she flopped over onto her back.

She couldn't deny it. She *had* prayed to Laijon near the end.

The floor was hard, frigid, unforgiving, and Tala felt the sting of cold air bite into her naked flesh. She sat up, watching the bloody water run in rivulets from her skin.

Am I bleeding?

All five of the archbishops were leering at her.

She shivered, trying to cover her nakedness with thin arms. Then she saw the slash marks on her flesh; arms, chest, stomach, hips, and thighs. It was as if some savage beast with paws the width of a saber-toothed lion had clawed her. The wounds were not deep, mostly just scrapes, and only a few bled. But what was terrifying about the wounds was their shape and width and ferocity, for she knew her own small hands and fingernails could not have produced them.

It was as if some beast had been down there in the water with her.

She turned toward the pool for answers, but the vicar was down below, the water covering him calm above, but for the rising tendrils of steam.

At length Denarius' bald head emerged from the pool. He was dragging the bedroll behind him, amazement on his round face, head bobbing above the swirling mists. "You prayed for Laijon's help this time, didn't you?"

Tala stared at him blankly, shivering even more. *I did pray! I groveled and begged forgiveness!*

"Proof that Laijon has purified you." The vicar climbed from the pool with the help of Archbishop Spencerville. Denarius pulled the Dayknight sleeping bag out of the water behind him. "You cannot deny it now. No sister of the king can deny it now. Laijon saved you. Laijon hath purified you!"

The bedroll was shredded, slashed like a demon from the underworld had hacked it away with tooth and claw. Strips of the bag lay along the sides of the marble pool, tangled and mutilated. Then the bedroll slid back into the hot water like a ragged animal hide and sank. Feathers of down floated on the water like a thin blanket of snow.

Tala knew her small hands and nails could not have created such carnage. She scrambled away from the vicar and five archbishops.

"Aren't you happy now?" Denarius reached down and seized her by the arm. "You've passed your test, your purification. Only by full immersion in water can one become pure in heart."

Tala tore away from the vicar's strong grasp. She stood. She ran. The pain from her beastly wounds was stinging and intense. She ran naked through the swirling mist toward her mother's bedroom. The men behind her were too slow to follow this time, and she did not slip. She reached the door and had it open, then closed, then locked and barred behind her. *Escape! Escape! Escape!* her mind screamed.

There was bound to be a way to get into the secret ways from her mother's chamber. And she would find it; she would find that way to escape.

And once she did, Tala vowed she would never step foot in the castle again.

CHAPTER THREE

GAULT AULBREK

6TH DAY OF THE FIRE MOON, 999TH YEAR OF LAIJON

WEST OF AMADON, GUL KANA

The two Dayknights rode their horses from behind the copse of trees with a soundless ease. Both were mounted on dun-colored destriers, their polished black armor silhouetted against the edge of the willowy bank, the small hazy river just a ghost of gray movement behind them. Wisps of humidity threaded through the glade and through their horses' legs. Neither knight wore a helm. One of the knights was blond, the other dark-haired. They drew up with confidence some twenty paces in front of Gault Aulbrek and his two fellow fugitives.

Gault held the long white sword named *Afflicted Fire* loosely at his side, the damp grass of the dell brushing against his thighs. His companions, Lindholf Le Graven and the barmaid, Delia, came to a stop on either side of him. The boy carried the shield, *Ethic Shroud*. The girl held the crossbow, *Blackest Heart*. None of them were mounted.

"What have we here?" The blond knight's fog-muffled voice echoed through the clearing. He sat tall and straight atop his stout horse, black helm and black shield secured on his saddle behind him. He drew his Dayknight sword with a rasp that cut the stillness of the glade.

The dark-haired knight pulled his own blade too, pointing its sharp black tip at the slave brand on Gault's neck. "Those with the slave brand are seldom seen this far from Riven Rock. And you three all bear the mark."

The knight was right. It was hot and humid near the river, and Gault ofttimes let the dark cowl of his gray cloak slide from his bald head, exposing the RR of Riven Rock Quarry on his neck. He had found a sharp hunting knife at the bottom of the skiff they had escaped Rockliegh Isle in. He had been using it for shaving daily, a ritual that soothed him. Lindholf and Delia traveled with the hoods of their own cloaks pulled back, their slave brands also visible. *I've grown complacent with these two fools as companions. I should rid myself of them.* Cursing himself, Gault gripped the hilt of *Afflicted Fire* tighter in hand, set his stance firm in the long grass. *You're better off alone than with Lindholf and Delia.*

The long white blade seemed to glow, its crescent-moon hilt-guard too.

The two knights sensed Gault's tenseness, eyes narrowing when he lifted the bright sword. Gault's cloak covered the bulk of his Sør Sevier armor, but in raising the blade, the armor was now revealed. An observant knight would know exactly what it was he wore. The colors of the enemy.

I'll have to fight them! There was no escape. He had no horse. A dense forest of oak loomed on three sides, black ravens roosting in the branches above, watching. Willows nuzzled the grassy riverbank to Gault's left. The bells of sheep and bickering hens could be heard in the far distance to his right. He judged that the gap between himself and the two Dayknights had now closed to less than ten paces.

He had never used *Afflicted Fire* in real battle before. He had swung it only once, but that was at the Vallè Bloodwood, Seita, on Rockliegh Isle. He did not know how it might perform against blades the quality of Dayknight swords. In the short time he had been lugging it about, *Afflicted Fire* had seemed a light and flimsy thing one moment, hard and heavy the next. The three angel stones were in the leather pouch tied at his belt under his cloak. The very thought of them weighed him down. *More burdens I must rid myself of, these weapons and stones.*

"What are your names?" the blond knight demanded. "And what is the strange sword you wield, and the strange white shield the boy carries? They look unnatural."

Yes, the weapons are more of a liability than anything. To Gault's left, Lindholf's jittery hands gripped the strap of the shield. *Ethic Shroud* seemed to glow with some white light, illuminating the clearing around the boy, its sleek surface pearly and bright. The barmaid, Delia, carried the crossbow in one hand. Black as midnight, it was half-hidden behind her right hip.

"Your names?" the blond knight pressed. "You fit the descriptions of those we seek: Ser Gault Aulbrek of Sør Sevier, Lindholf Le Graven of Eskander, and a barmaid from the Filthy Horse Saloon in Amadon."

A tense hush filled the humid air. Nobody spoke.

"I've never heard of any of them." Lindholf's voice finally split the silence. He looked scared. He was an ugly boy with a languid manner and a frail, unpleasantly fretful air about him at all times. His short blond curls were plastered to his deformed head. Burn scars covered one cheek up to his forehead and back down his neck. Both of his ears were mangled wrecks of deformed flesh too.

"You've never heard of the three most famous fugitives in the Five Isles?" the blond knight asked.

Lindholf gulped. "I'm but a lone hosteler traveling home. News oft escapes me."

"A lone hosteler traveling home?" the blond knight scoffed. "A lone slave-branded hosteler wearing prison garb under his cloak and wielding an ivory-colored battle shield unlike anything I've ever seen. Just a lone hosteler traveling with a slave girl in similar prison garb and some poor sod doing an even poorer job of hiding Sør Sevier armor under his cloak."

The dark-haired knight said, "I wager our reward from the Silver Throne will be great for finding just such a lonely hosteler."

"Just let us go," Delia pleaded, fear in her voice. She was a pretty girl. Gault had seen that much from the first. But she was less confident and sure of herself than Lindholf, and ofttimes a bit more dense. "We've harmed no one. Just leave us be."

The two mounted knights exchanged glances, gray destriers shuffling in the grass, one horse snorting and chuffing as if he could sense the building tension of its rider. For all their bravado, Gault could tell, these knights were as unsure of themselves as Delia was. He had a knack for sizing up an opponent, and these men were inexperienced. *Perhaps they were in the arena when I beheaded the Prince of Saint Only,* he thought. *Perhaps they know I am a cold killer.*

It had been less than a week since Gault had faced death in the center of the arena, hangman's noose around his neck. The throng had wanted to see him die in his Sør Sevier armor, and that was why he wore it now, rather than the prison raiment. Seita's rescue had been a spectacle, swift bloody chaos and fire, three cut nooses. Gault, Delia, and Lindholf freed. The executioner's platform dropping straight down into the floor of the arena. The Vallè had killed the Dayknights under the arena with *Afflicted Fire*, the sword drinking their blood. Then Seita had guided Gault, Lindholf, and Delia through the myriad of tunnels, gathering the white angel stone and *Ethic Shroud* from a cellar under the Filthy Horse Saloon, and had marooned the three fugitives on Rockliegh Isle for days. That was until Gault had taken the stones and weapons and fled with his two current travel companions.

He judged they were maybe ten miles northwest of Amadon now. The highest spires of the city's castle could still be seen in the far distance, just over Lindholf's shoulder, Mount Albion naught but a dwindling outcrop of blackness set against the far eastern horizon. They had spent that first day off Rockliegh Isle afloat in Memory Bay. The day of their escape, Gault had rowed them as far north of Amadon as his weary arms would allow. They snuck ashore during the darkest watches of the night. Since then, even the smallest pathways were subject to the random knight on horseback, searching.

Though Gault had studied many maps of Gul Kana, he didn't know the landscape hereabouts all that well. The three of them had spent today wandering afoot westward through farm fields and smaller hamlets, always wary, avoiding all people, hiding in forests, hedgerows, and abandoned barns when the need arose. What food they scrounged was quickly gone. They'd made scant headway, finally locating this small river, using it as a guidepost for their journey west.

Toward Saint Only and Ava Shay. Thoughts of the Gallows Haven girl had consumed Gault with every step he took. Now here he was, two mounted Dayknights blocking his way.

"I don't know who you think we are." Gault's voice was hard, stern. "But it would be best for everyone if you do as the girl asked and leave us be."

Both knights glared at him now, what trepidation they'd once had replaced with bravado. "That sword you carry, it will soon be mine," the blond knight said.

"Just leave us be, as my friend has asked," Lindholf said. "Truth is, we are no strangers to danger."

"Strangers to danger." The dark-haired knight laughed, gleeful eyes cast toward his companion. "A poet and a bard this one, make no mistake. No strangers to danger."

The other knight also laughed. "Strangers to danger indeed—"

Gault struck with a speed reserved only for battle. The keen white tip of *Afflicted Fire* whistled high through the air, opening wide the dark-haired Dayknight's throat. The man's eyes widened as his voice was instantly cut short, gauntleted hands suddenly clutching at his neck. Blood spewed between his fingers.

Gault was already swinging at the blond knight, whose startled destrier had jumped to the side. Despite the horse's sudden leap, the white blade caught the bigger knight across the left arm, slicing through both armor and bone with a cleanness of ease that astonished even Gault. The knight cried out, blood gushing from the stump of his arm as his horse leaped back once again. Gault was quick to silence the knight's cry, *Afflicted Fire* swooping back around, taking the man's head off just under the chin.

The fight was over that swiftly, both knights toppling from their mounts simultaneously, the blond one headless, the dark-haired one writhing on the ground, clutching at his neck. Blood, crimson and thick, slithered between his black-gauntleted fingers. The man grimaced, and his lips opened without speech. Gault placed the tip of the white sword into the fellow's earhole and pushed down hard. The man's legs kicked and spasmed in death. *Just another cruel casualty in a sad and cruel world.* Gault pulled *Afflicted Fire* from the knight's ear and the man went still.

Despite having just cut through Dayknight armor, *Afflicted Fire*'s gleaming white blade still appeared sharpened to an impossibly fine edge. And the blood of the two dead men seemed to simply fade into the sword, as if being devoured by the strange metal. Soon the surface of the blade was clean of all stain, yet under its ivory sheen pulsed faint ribbons of red glowing light, as if the sword had a heartbeat all its own.

"What do we do now, Gault?" Delia's soft voice calling out his name woke him to the matter at hand. His gaze roamed the landscape once more sizing up the scene: a river, a grassy bank, a forest of oak, bells of sheep in the distance beyond, two dead Dayknights in the knee-high grass at his feet. One of the two destriers had galloped away. It was breathing heavily about thirty paces from Gault, eyes wide; the other horse calmly nibbled the grass at Gault's feet. "What do we do now?" Delia asked again.

Gault rammed the white sword into the turf and examined both corpses. "What do we do now, indeed." He stepped toward the body of the headless knight first and knelt in the grass. He unstrapped the bucklers of the man's shoulder-plate armor. "I'm not a man to sneak about for long," he said. "The two horses should speed our journey, and this Dayknight armor just might grant us passage anywhere we please."

He met Lindholf's startled face. "Strip the other knight," he ordered the boy. "You're about his size. His armor should fit well enough, any-way."

"But these men are dead," Lindholf muttered.

"Indeed they are. The perfect time to strip their armor."

"Me?" the boy asked, incredulous. "Strip their armor? I cannot don the Dayknight black, no matter how well it fits. I have not been sworn in."

"If you want to live, you'll don that man's armor and strap his sword to your side," Gault said. "And you need to do it quick. No telling what farmers or other folk might wander down here by the riverside. We need to shove the bodies into the water as soon as possible and hope they sink."

Lindholf appeared still in a daze. "You can't just go around killing people and putting them into rivers to get what you want."

The boy's statement made Gault remember Salisan Lusk. The young Rowdie had been wounded in Wyn Darrè, somewhere between Oldrisek and Lavendoria. Salisan had asked Gault to deliver a copper trinket to his girlfriend back in Sør Sevier in case he died in the war. Salisan did die. And Gault had tossed the copper trinket into the River Sen. *Would I deliver the copper trinket for the boy now?*

Lindholf remained silent, and Gault was left alone with his own thoughts. *Angel stones! The Chivalric Illuminations* of Sør Sevier only hinted of the stones, vague rumors that they were cursed, but those rumors also stated that the stones—along with the famed weapons of the Five Warrior Angels—would somehow return to the hands of the last heir of Raijael before Fiery Absolution. As a child, before his parents Evalyn and Agus had died, Gault had dreamed of the angel stones— dreamed that the myths and legends of the Five Warrior Angels were somehow part of his own destiny. Most in the Five Isles grew up believing that the angel stones and weapons of the Five Warrior Angels had been translated into heaven at the time of Laijon's death. But not Gault; he had been taught differently by his mother, a secret adherent of the tenets of Mother Mia, a faction of religious worshippers who believed the angel stones and weapons were still upon the land, still part of the living fabric of the Five Isles.

Afflicted Fire, Ethic Shroud, Blackest Heart, the three angel stones, Lindholf and Delia, all of them combined were slowing him down, becoming a burden. *And were the weapons and stones even real?* The milk-white sword with its crescent-moon hilt-guard was certainly magnificent and mysterious. *And it greedily drank the blood of the Dayknights. But what do I trust? Who do I trust? The weapons? The stones? It could all just be some Vallè witchcraft.*

His life entire he had dreamed of finding the lost weapons and stones of the Five Warrior Angels. *And now that I possibly possess them . . . they just weigh me down and make me question my own sanity.*

Am I part of the Illuminations' *prophecy?* Aeros Raijael claimed all the weapons would come to him. *Am I just an instrument of the gods, fulfilling a prophecy by bringing the weapons back to Aeros in my own foolish effort to save Ava Shay?* Yes, they were just one more burden on his way to Ava Shay. As was Delia. And Lindholf. In fact, the dough-faced boy wished to murder him. Gault knew Lindholf carried a Bloodwood blade under his clothes. It was wrapped in the hem of his ragged slave shirt, tucked beneath his belt. Gault knew the dagger was likely poisoned, knew that Seita had given it to the boy with instructions to use it on him. *And it's only a matter of time before the boy grows brave enough to stick me with it.* Gault had to be wary.

"Do as I said," he ordered the boy with some distaste. "Strip the armor from that knight. And be quick about it too."

"You are a bad person, Ser Gault Aulbrek," Lindholf said boldly. "Naught but a man who coldly kills to get what he wants."

"I kill to survive." Gault glared at him. "It is what I do. It is what I have always done. What of it? And my cold killing just saved your hide, I wager. Delia's, too."

The boy just stared stupidly. His spider-black eyes stuck out so prominently against the pallid, deformed flesh of his face that it was startling. *Who does he remind me of?*

"Gault is right, Lindholf," Delia said. "Take the armor. You two can pass as Dayknights. Nobody knows my face. It will be better than sneaking about."

"Where is he even taking us?" the boy asked. "Or why do we even follow him? We should have stayed with Seita."

"The Vallè girl isn't here. Gault is our only chance of survival. Can't you see, Lindholf? Just do as he says already."

"You always favor him," Lindholf muttered sourly. "Seita saved us from the gallows. And look how Gault repaid her. He nearly killed her. He stole the weapons and stones from her. You should not trust him, Delia."

"Just do as he says," Delia repeated. "Get that knight's armor off, and hurry."

Lindholf set *Ethic Shroud* in the grass and knelt near the dead knight. He slowly began unhooking bucklers and plate. It wasn't long before Gault smelled the vile reek of the dead fellow's shit-filled armor.

"This man's crapped himself." Lindholf backed away from the half-naked corpse. "It's all over the armor."

"People shit themselves when they die," Gault said matter-of-factly. "It happens. You'll just have to deal with it."

"*Deal* with it?" Lindholf whined, doing the three-fingered sign of the Laijon Cross over his heart.

"Wash it in the river."

"But your knight didn't shit himself."

"And yours did," Gault snapped, knowing that he himself would never wear previously shit-upon clothing of any kind. It wasn't his way. He'd risk traipsing about as he was—in his Sør Sevier armor—before he put on another man's previously befouled armor. But what did Lindholf know of such things? Gault had to admit there was a dark side to his involvement in Aeros' ten-year crusade. *Am I a bad man, as Lindholf accused?* He almost felt guilty surviving for as long as he had when so many others had died. *Yes, I should have saved Salisan's copper trinket and taken it to his girl.*

Gault thought of his own place in *The Chivalric Illuminations of Raijael*, realizing there would be no honorable place for him in the *Illuminations* now. He would be forever known in Sør Sevier as a failure, a betrayer of Raijael. Aeros, Enna Spades, Hammerfiss, all the people and powers that he had trusted were so far from him now.

He found himself thinking of his wife, Avril, and the day he had first met her. She was naught but a lone, cloaked figure on the dusky plains north of Stone Loring, carrying a babe in swaddling clothes—a small bundle of innocence. Krista.

There was only one place in all the Five Isles where Gault had ever felt true joy, and it had been on that very spot he had first laid eyes upon Avril and Krista—his family. They were the only love and comfort he had ever known. And when he died, he wanted it to be on that very plot of land, that very dusky plain, that very rocky slope.

Or at least someone lay my body there when I die. But not before I see Krista again. Hold my daughter in my arms. He thought of the blue ribbon he had gifted her upon their last parting. *Does she still carry it? Where is she now? What will Aevrett do with her once he hears of my fate, my disgrace?*

Within his soul arose an unanticipated turmoil contrary to the whole tenor of his life. He wanted to save Ava Shay more than anything. He also wanted to kill Aeros Raijael for betraying him. And he wanted to live happily ever after with his daughter. But it was all wretched reasoning, bound to get him killed. And what confusion and disgust such wretched reasoning would have normally caused in him was absent. But he would not give up on those goals. And the faster he could accomplish them the better.

But there was no urgency in Lindholf Le Graven. The boy just knelt there in the grass, staring at the befouled corpse under him in revulsion.

"Strip the armor off the man and clean it in the river," Gault growled. "And put it on. It won't kill you. We've a long way to go yet."

"I don't know if I can," the boy said.

"I will help." Delia knelt next to him.

"And we might want to think of finding some kind of sack to carry the shield and crossbow in," Gault added. "The sword too, for that matter. They all three stick out like shining stars, just waiting to be noticed, just waiting to get us in trouble."

CHAPTER FOUR

AVA SHAY

6TH DAY OF THE FIRE MOON, 999TH YEAR OF LAIJON
SAINT ONLY, ADIN WYTE

Ava Shay's wants and needs had been as simple as the wind that blew over Mont Saint Only. She had only ever wanted a home and a family. But Jenko was dead now and her hopes had drifted away, lost. She stood weak-kneed on the lofty terrace overlooking the Saint Only Channel, gripping the balcony's chest-high stone railing with trembling hands, the dark entry to Bruce Hall and bulk of the fortress looming just behind her.

To her right was Ser Edmon Guy Van Hester, the former king of Adin Wyte. To her left was Edmon's young servant, Leisel, the girl's freckled face as white as the seagulls circling far below. Her tawny hair and tan shift rippled softly in the balmy breeze. *She can't be more than fifteen,* Ava surmised. The small girl sniffed at the flowers circling the nearest trellis but seemed to take no joy in the act.

For there was no joy to be had. Ava wondered if the tall towers and trellised balconies of Mont Saint Only had ever rung out with the sound of children playing and lovers' laughter. Or had the soaring stronghold always been naught but a gray mass of gloom and despair? Yesterday the savage sounds of war had drifted up the rocky crags of the Mont like the lonely baying of a million hounds. And today the sandy floor of the channel below was a velvety carpet of red, dark and plush and florid with blood, stretching to the north and south between Saint Only and Lord's Point as far as her eyes could see.

The tide had receded an hour ago, revealing the hundreds of thousands of dead knights from both Sør Sevier and Gul Kana in the ten-mile-wide channel below. It was a tide that seemed to breathe in and out one long, deep breath daily, sucking water from the channel, then exhaling it back in every day. And today that tide had laid bare a vast expanse of glittery corpses strewn over a red-streaked battlefield of the dead; men, horses, sharks, and merfolk. It was an endless field of armor and weaponry glinting like silver stars under the morning's raw sun, shrieking seagulls stark and white and gleefully afloat over it all. *And Jenko Bruk was one of those sparkling dead knights.* By merely asking herself the question, sadness and fear again poured over Ava in a frigid wave.

She shivered, never more confused and unsure in her life. She shook uncontrollably, despite the humid air that clung to her, warm and damp. Despite her sorrow and fear and unease with it all, at least she was sober. There was that one brightness to her life, even though Aeros' spirits could be glorious in their ability to numb. But the truth was, she'd stopped imbibing Aeros' wine days ago, sick of always feeling bleary-eyed with drink. She no longer needed to chase away the wraiths. No longer needed to chase away the horrors of war. Now she met those horrors with clear eyes. Frightened eyes. But clear.

"We're all liable to be put to death today, m'lady." Edmon's voice croaked hoarsely as he shaded his eyes with one dirty hand, gazing down onto the bloody channel far below. The old king wore filth-covered breeches and a tattered, ill-fitting cloak several sizes too small for his already stooped and bandy-legged frame. His ratty gray hair and beard were gummed with filth and soot, his bushy eyebrows, too.

"Our Lord Aeros is most displeased." He cackled then, the sound of his dry laughter like pebbles grinding in the surf. "Our lord is most displeased with how yesterday's battle turned out."

Yes. Ava knew how displeased the White Prince was. Nearly his entire army lay dead in the bloody, sunbaked sand below. So high up the face of the Mont, she could just make out the tiny forms of people beginning to walk out there in the channel amongst the dead, scavengers from Gul Kana sifting through the corpses, looting the dead of weaponry and armor before the tide rose up again and swallowed it all whole.

The Autumn Range and the Lord's Point castle and cathedral loomed in the east beyond the red battlefield. To the west Ava could just make out the cliffs of Wyn Darrè and the five Laijon Towers. She had stood atop this vantage point many times before, soaking in the spectacular view of both Gul Kana and Wyn Darrè, the grandest vista of all in the Five Isles. But not today. Today her lofty perch offered naught but a view of the bloodiest battle the Five Isles had likely ever seen.

"Will you not speak, m'lady?" Edmon dipped his head to her. "I do like conversation, and Leisel has never been one for that sort of thing—talking, I mean. Yet I am one for talking. But only if it please you, of course, m'lady . . . er, I mean, your ladyship, um, I mean princess."

He bent his knee to her then, face flushed with embarrassment.

"Why name me princess?" she asked.

He stood. "That is what my lord Aeros calls you."

"I know nothing of that," she answered, though she had to admit the White Prince had been referring to her as his princess more and more of late.

"He does say you are his princess?" Leisel added softly, still sniffing at the flowers. "He says it to everyone."

"Yes," Edmon said. "He does at that."

"Well," Ava lied, "I've never heard him."

"And perhaps it matters not," Edmon said. "For I believe Aeros will slay us all in his rage. He will slay us today."

Leisel's gentle round eyes met Ava's, deep with concern. "I must go to him," she said. "He will be mad if I linger up here too long." Then the servant girl took her leave of the balcony and scampered to the great hall below.

Ava watched her go. Leisel was clad in such simple garb. But not Ava.

Not anymore. Upon their arrival at Saint Only, Aeros had gifted Ava with many fine brocaded dresses, lacy shawls, shiny bracelets, and lovely jeweled necklaces of every kind, ordering her to wear them always. Even today she wore a long gown of a deep maroon color that clung tightly to her body. Her neck was hung with a long necklace of pure white pearls. But watching Leisel bound down the stairs in her tan shift, Ava couldn't help but think back to something the White Prince had said during their first meeting in his tent just outside Gallows Haven, haunting words she would never forget: *As a prince, one grows used to stripping the finery off the noblewomen. Not much excitement in that after a while. What I desire most is to rip the simple, coarse, filthy raiment off the peasantry, particularly the fetching young peasantry.*

And last night, when Aeros had returned from battle, angry, bloodied, and weary, he had insisted Ava retire with him to his bedchamber. There she had tended to the wounds on his arm, bathed and massaged him, and listened to his mad ramblings. "Ten years and a thousand battles and never injured until today." He'd made the statement with pure incredulity in his voice.

She had cleaned and wrapped the deep gashes on his flesh as he spoke. "'Twas a damn dog that got me. Of all things, a fucking dog. Sharks in the water. Sea serpents and merfolk. Knights and swords slashing all around. Spades lost. Mancellor lost. Jenko and Spiderwood gone. All of them likely dead. My entire army vanquished! *Forgetting Moon! Lonesome Crown!* The angel stones! All of them gone! 'Twas a fucking large raggedy gray mutt of a dog floundering in the water that got to me. A floundering shepherd dog drew first blood. First fucking blood! A fucking dog!"

And his bemoaning of the battle had continued throughout the night. He'd spoken of *Forgetting Moon* and *Lonesome Crown* lost at the bottom of the channel, lost to the filthy Gul Kana scavengers who would surely loot the bloody sand once the tide rolled off.

"Unless I can search the seabed myself, recover them myself." He'd gripped Ava's arm as he spoke; then his face had drooped and his hand had fallen away. "No. The battlefield is too large. Too close to Lord's Point. Not enough time before the tides will cover it again. And I've no idea how many soldiers I have left alive to guard me, to guard you, my princess. How will I ever find the weapons again?"

Aeros crawled into his large bed, still babbling about his defeat at the hands of the incompetent Leif Chaparral, growing more and more despondent over the loss of the ax and helm and the angel stones. He had eventually fallen asleep, Ava on one side of the bed with him.

Ivor Jace and Hammerfiss—Aeros' only two remaining Knights Archaic—had stood guard on the other side of Aeros' bedchamber door throughout the night as the White Prince soundly slept.

Now, standing on the balcony with Edmon, Ava felt all hope for herself fade. *I have to escape. I can't go on living like this.* She felt as despondent as Aeros Raijael. *Am I already pregnant?* The thought scared her. Filled her with dread. The only good thing about it was she knew the idea was likely real, not some foul conjuration of the wraiths. The wraiths had left her alone for some time now. *Pregnant. I cannot have a baby. What if it looks nothing like Aeros and everything like Jenko....*

But Jenko Bruk was already dead!

What will happen to me? Her mind returned to the present, the balcony, the old man standing beside her.

"I can help in your escape." Edmon gave her a sooty wink, as if he had known what she was thinking this whole time. "I know every nook and cranny and secret passageway in this castle. Secret doors that lead to secret places. Secret doors that once shut will never again be opened. I can help you find a way to flee. In fact, I can help you with anything, if you wish."

**

"Enna Spades was the type of woman who will haunt you, even in death." Hammerfiss lifted the tall goblet and drank deeply. "And I for one shall miss her numerous cruel charms and glorious wickednesses. Today I drink to her death." He slammed the goblet down hard atop the wooden table, mead sloshing over the rough oak.

Leisel was there to wipe it clean.

A dozen Knights of the Blue Sword sat at the long table in the center of Bruce Hall with Hammerfiss, all having listened for the last hour in rapt attention as the red-haired giant regaled them with tales of Enna Spades and her bloody exploits.

"Aye, she shall be missed most deeply," Hammerfiss carried on, tear-filled eyes looking toward Aeros Raijael, who stood alone in front of the cold hearth at the western end of the large chamber, his back to the table of knights.

"I suppose I shall also miss Mancellor Allen, for that matter," Hammerfiss continued, swiping at his eyes. "A stout warrior was he. And the boy from Gallows Haven, Jenko Bruk, that one also had potential for sure." The giant man's skin was flushed with both drink and sadness beneath the blue Suk Skard clan tattoos spanning his face. There was anger growing there too. And he was drunk.

"But the Spider, that one can rot in the underworld for all I care." He belched loudly. "I pray that both the Bloodwood and his demon horse are lying face-first and dead in the bloody sands of the channel, their corpses baking in the sun, fetid bodies bloating with foul stink. It's only what they deserve, rank reeking creatures."

"It's all my doing," Ser Edmon cackled.

"Huh?" Hammerfiss looked at the old man, bleary-eyed.

"It's all my doing." From his place at the foot of the Throne of Spears, drooling dogs of various breeds gathered around him, Edmon continued to cackle like a madman.

"It's all my doing," he said a third time. The throne was but a blocky wood-carved chair draped in red velvet, a large brown dog curled on the seat. "This whole mess is my doing."

"You're crazy." Hammerfiss tossed his goblet at the former king of Adin Wyte. The small fetishes tied in the tangled mass of his red hair and beard jingled and jangled at the abrupt motion. The goblet lit in the pile of dogs, splashing mead everywhere. None so much as moved in irritation, though one raised his ears slightly and another one began lapping up the mead. Hammerfiss snarled, "Just keep your yapper shut, old man!"

"This whole mess, it's all my doing," Edmon repeated, grin wide. "As Aeros has said many times since his arrival, most messes around here are my fault. And now you all wallow in your defeat, much as I once did."

Hammerfiss grunted. "Your babbling is hurting my ears."

Edmon laughed. "I only speak the truth."

"Do not speak at all!" Hammerfiss stood and moved toward the throne. "Worthless scum! Our entire army was drowned yesterday, and I imagine you're hardly even aware of the ramifications in your docile senility! I ought to stab a knife in your throat now and rid us all of your prattle, then let your dogs lick up the mess, let them show you their love!"

At seven feet, Hammerfiss towered over everyone in Bruce Hall. With a thick build and barrel chest and powerful massive arms and shoulders, he had the look of a man who could bring the entire stone castle down around the former king of Adin Wyte with his bare hands if he so wanted.

But Ser Edmon only pretended to cower under Hammerfiss' cold stare. He looked away from Hammerfiss and curled himself up amongst the dogs gathered at the foot of the throne. "I only speak the truth," he repeated. "'Tis you who understand nothing."

"Shut up!" Hammerfiss roared, kicking one of the dogs near Edmon. The dog yelped and scurried off. The dozen knights left at the table with Ava looked on with some amusement, all of them likely wondering when the bigger man would snap Ser Edmon's neck once and for all.

"Leave the old man be." Aeros Raijael turned from the hearth, a dour look on his pale face. His skin appeared so ashen in the dim light of the hall it seemed to bleed into the white of his tunic and cloak. His eyes, black as spilled ink, were fixed on Ser Edmon as he approached the throne, cradling his injured and bandaged arm as he walked.

"Please, Hammerfiss, I beg of you, just leave the old man be," the White Prince said. "I can't take the negativity. The place is mostly cleaned up now. Just look around, will you? He is merely an old man, doing the best he can in his infirmity."

"Such compassion from our lord?" Hammerfiss leaned back as if he couldn't believe what he was hearing. "Cleaned up, perhaps." His eyes roamed the hall. "But none of it Ser Edmon's doing, that I assure you, my lord."

Upon Ava's arrival, Bruce Hall had been naught but a dog-feces-strewn and soot-covered chamber of filth and broken-down furniture. But the floor, fashioned of large flat stones laid in squares, once scuffed and stained, was now scrubbed clean. The hall's sculptures and other such finery were no longer tipped over and scattered about. Mosaics, tapestries, and many banners, red with white crossed spears, lined the walls. The massive hearth sat in the center of the western wall, its stone-carved mantelpiece no longer covered in grit and melted wax, nor its innards stuffed with debris. Above the hearth, a stone-railed gallery encircled the entire hall, accessible only by a set of recently swept stairs along the northern end. Above the gallery were many stained-glass windows, now scrubbed free of soot and shimmering with colorful light. The newly shined gallery led to the ivy-trellised balcony Ava, Leisel, and Ser Edmon had stood upon earlier that morning.

"On second thought, it's not clean enough," Hammerfiss growled. He turned to Leisel. "Scrub it all again, girl. Every inch."

"The whole chamber, Ser?" Her soft eyes widened.

"Leave the girl be," Aeros said. "Just leave everyone be, Ser Hammerfiss. Let's sit, my good friend. Finish our drinks. Get drunk. Or drunker. Lament our lamentable state with gallons of wine."

"But we lost the war," Hammerfiss growled. "And my horse is dead. How can I be happy when Battle-Ax is dead? That beast carried me through every battle across the breadth of Adin Wyte and Wyn Darrè. Laijon bless his soul."

"My stallion perished too," Aeros said. "'Twas eaten by a shark, eaten right out from under me. They all perished, all of our stallions, all but for Gault's mount, that is. Spirit lived. 'Twas Ivor Jace who carried me back to shore on the back of Spirit. A stout beast, is Spirit. We should at least be glad of that, glad that one of our glorious fighting stallions survived."

Hammerfiss dismissed Aeros' words with a groan. "If you say."

The massive wooden double doors to the grand hall swung wide, startling them all. And as if he knew he was the center of the conversation, Ser Ivor Jace strode into the chamber, garnering the attention of both Aeros and Hammerfiss. Ivor was Aeros' newest Knight Archaic, bold and tall and fair-haired. And Ava had always felt more than just a little uncomfortable around the handsome blond knight.

Upon reaching the table, Ivor bent his knee to Aeros with a natural grace, stood again, and spoke with a steady self-assurance. "We've counted the survivors as best we can. Of the two hundred and fifty thousand we went to war with yesterday, we've some twenty thousand squires, some twenty thousand Hounds, some twenty thousand Rowdies, and some thirty thousand Knights of the Blue Sword, and two Knights Archaic, Hammerfiss and myself, for a total of ninety thousand. Or thereabouts."

"That many?" Aeros seemed to brighten at the news.

Ivor went on. "And I'd guess about twice as many horses as men were able to swim back to Adin Wyte. In fact, more are probably wandering in Lord's Point, and I imagine a lot of our own knights swam there too, as it was immeasurably closer. More of us may have survived than we first thought. Maybe more than half."

"So I still have an army?" Aeros asked.

"It's all my doing," Edmon cackled from his spot on the floor near the throne. No one paid him any mind but for a few dogs who wagged their tails. "All my doing."

Aeros seemed to take Ivor's news with some measure of happiness. But Ava knew he was still confused, and quite possibly even scared. It was those subtle differences in his overall manner that gave him away, the slight angle of his chin, tip of his head, tilt to his posture, an extra dip of his Adam's apple, his want to get drunk and lament things suddenly out of his control. She had spent too much time with him. Knew him too well. Normally his bearing was naught but beautiful, unwavering confidence. But ever since the battle, he looked more bloodless than usual, ill and desperate.

"There has still been no sighting of Enna Spades or Mancellor Allen," Ivor continued. "The Spider has also not been seen. They are all feared dead."

"Unless they are in Lord's Point." Aeros swallowed hard as he spoke. "As you said, some of my fighters may have swum there. Which leads me to give unto you another task, Ser Ivor. Launch a boat and messenger south, or send one of your pigeons with a note. We must get word to our armies we left there waiting: the fifty thousand soldiers we left camped south of Lord's Point. They must be instructed not to attack Lord's Point, for I fear losing them, too. Perhaps we should have them completely move away from the city, retreat farther south to a safer distance until we can recount our decimated forces. We do not know how many of Leif's troops survived. We dare not risk any more of our men until we have fully regrouped."

Ivor bent his knee to Aeros. "A messenger shall be sent within the hour, and your orders will reach the commanders there by evening."

"Splendid," Aeros said, sitting down next to Ava, his body almost melting over the stone bench in exhaustion. The bandages on his arm were faintly red with seeping blood. "Splendid," he repeated. "Perhaps all is not lost."

Ava wondered if anyone she knew—other than Jenko Bruk—had been in the battle yesterday. Had Nail been down there? Or Liz Hen? Stefan Wayland? Dokie Liddle? *Where are they all now? Alive? Worrying about me as I worry about them? Or are they dead like Jenko?* She thought of the Grayken Spear and happier times. She recalled her joy in serving meals to all the Gallows Haven conscripts after arms practice. She remembered her wood carvings. Nail's drawings.

The door to the chamber creaked wide again. All the knights at the table rose as one, hands on the hilts of their swords. The ears of every dog perked.

Silhouetted against the bright rays of the late morning streaming into the hall was a tall black stallion with glowing red eyes, hooves echoing loud and sharp. The Bloodeye horse clomped its way heavily into the chamber, led by the Bloodwood assassin called the Spider, black cloak around his body. Everything about the dark-haired man and his demon-eyed steed seemed dangerous, and dark. And Ava found that she was glad to see them both.

A large bulging and bloody canvas sack was strapped to the stallion's back. The canvas sack dripped a thick trail of blood down the horse's lathered flanks, trailing over the cold stone floor. The Spider dipped his head in calm greeting as he reached the center of the hall and stepped into their midst. His close-cropped hair was black as a crow's feather, brows dark and sharp. He looked straight at Aeros through icy, vaporous eyes—eyes that were bloodshot.

"And the one we least wanted to survive has returned." Hammerfiss grunted his displeasure as he stood. "Alas, the man who just won't die."

Spiderwood spoke directly to Aeros. "I've brought you a gift from the battlefield." He quietly reached around the back of his Bloodeye steed and untied the leather thongs binding the canvas sack closed.

From the large bloody sack spilled an umber-colored hunk of scaled flesh the size of an ale keg. The bloody-scaled lump slid to the floor with a strong wet thud, a dark red pool forming under its ragged end. Two large, glassy eyes stared up vacantly on either side of the pile of scales. Twin black holes for nostrils were set just forward of the eyes, a long slit of a mouth below that. Two sharp dagger-sized teeth extended from the front of the mouth, scraping the floor as the scaled puddle of flesh settled. A forked tongue lolled from between the two long teeth, unfurling flat against the floor.

Hammerfiss took a startled step back. Leisel squealed in horror. Ava's heart thundered in her chest. *What new horror is this?*

"The severed head of the sea serpent that sought to drown me," the Bloodwood announced. "Mount it above yonder fireplace, Lord Aeros." The Spider pointed to the large cold hearth against the western wall. "It will be the only trophy of its kind in all the Five Isles. I killed it for you."

"You likely killed it to save your own skin." The White Prince's black-pupiled eyes drifted from the head of the serpent on the floor to Spiderwood. "I would rather you have brought me back *Forgetting Moon* and *Lonesome Crown*."

The Spider's gaze cut though the darkness of the chamber, straight through Aeros. "Hang my gift above the hearth as I say." His voice was fraught with menace. "For it shall serve as a reminder to you to always heed the warnings of a Bloodwood."

"And what warnings are those?" Aeros asked.

"Spies," the Spider hissed. "The spies I warned you of here in this castle, the very spies who warned Leif Chaparral of our attack. The spies that I advised you to station in Lord's Point. The spies who would have alerted us to Leif Chaparral's trap."

"I heed my own counsel," Aeros said. "Not the counsel of a Bloodwood."

"You forget yourself," the Spider said. "That you did not heed the counsel of Black Dugal and myself and station spies in every corner of Gul Kana long ago will likely be the downfall of Sør Sevier and the very end of your place in Fiery Absolution. That is the truth of the matter. You know it and I know it and Black Dugal knows it."

The White Prince's eyes seemed to retreat deeper into their sockets. He did not even glance at the Bloodwood. Was it pain Ava saw there in Aeros? Humiliation? A recognition of the truth? She had never witnessed anyone in the army speak so harshly to the Angel Prince. She could not see Spiderwood living out the day. *Aeros will surely have him killed for this insolence—*

"I told you, 'twas all my doing." Ser Edmon's voice broke the silence between Aeros and the Spider. The old king was standing now, dogs gathering at his feet, the gravel and strain now gone from his voice. "Oh, but you arrogant fools would not listen." He grasped hold of the hound dog lounging on the seat of the Throne of Spears by the scruff of the neck and yanked it from off the seat with a strength Ava did not know was in the man.

The dog now gone, Ser Edmon sat down on his throne, settling himself comfortably into the plush velvet, raising his head with pride. "'Twas me and my little birds who warned Leif Chaparral of the exact time of your attack, Lord Aeros. 'Twas I who was the spy. 'Twas I who destroyed your armies." His voice rose in timbre. "'Twas I, Ser Edmon Guy Van Hester, Lord of Saint Only, High King of Adin Wyte, who came up with the plan that brought down the mighty army of Sør Sevier."

The old king pulled forth a thin-bladed dirk from the folds of his tattered garb and looked directly at Ava Shay. "I would have saved you myself, sweet girl. But alas, things have changed and I must now depart. But do not despair, for I did leave you a clue on how best to save yourself."

Aeros looked at her in complete confusion.

"My work here is done," Edmon said, settling back into the throne, lifting his chin, sliding the tip of the knife up under his throat. "Let them know 'twas me who helped defeat the armies of Aeros Raijael, Ava Shay. Let them know I was the spy who undid him." Then he looked directly at the White Prince. "Have it recorded in your precious *Illuminations* that it was Ser Edmon Guy Van Hester who helped destroy the armies of Aeros Raijael."

Then, to the sudden howling of the dogs that surrounded him, the king of Adin Wyte pushed on the pommel of the dirk, the slim blade sinking swift and hard into his brain.

If ye be honest and kind, your woman may deceive you. Be honest and kind anyway. If ye be good unto her, that good will quickly be forgotten. Be good anyway. If ye do all things right by her, she shall surely leave. Do all things right by her anyway, for you shall remain a man, and happy. Do all things wrong by her and she shall most assuredly stay by your side and true. And there lies misery.
—The Way and Truth of Laijon

CHAPTER FIVE
MANCELLOR ALLEN

6TH DAY OF THE FIRE MOON, 999TH YEAR OF LAIJON

LORD'S POINT, GUL KANA

B loody rotted angels, you've been cut open somethin' fierce," Jenko Bruk said, muffled voice scarcely above a whisper. His tense amber eyes were fixed on Mancellor Allen's injured arm. "Not sure my handiwork will do much. I'm no Vallè sawbones."

"Just tie that last stitch and wrap it lest I vomit from the pain." Mancellor gritted his teeth as Jenko pulled the thread through the torn flesh and tied it off. They had scavenged the thread from a dusky old drape pulled from the wall behind the abandoned tavern's bar. Enna Spades had been no help in the effort. She'd slept until noon, waking naught but an hour ago.

The warrior woman now stood watch some fifty paces away, peering through the rotted wood slats and grit-stained glass of the broken front window of the abandoned tavern they were camped in. The door of the tavern was open just a crack and Spades' hair was silhouetted like a ring of fire against the light streaming in. She was barefoot and wore absolutely none of her Knight Archaic armor, all of it abandoned at the bottom of the channel, same as Mancellor's and Jenko's armor. Spades was clothed in naught but leather breeches and a torn and bloody undershirt, leather belt and thin sheathed dagger at her hip. Mancellor had survived the battle with just his undershirt and pants. Jenko too. Among the three of them, Spades was the only one without a slave brand burned into her flesh. It set her apart. And she knew it. She had stayed away from both Mancellor and Jenko ever since their arrival here.

Jenko tied the thread tight and Mancellor nearly fainted. Yes, he desperately wanted to vomit from the pain. But he was so hungry he doubted he could spew anything up anyway. The jagged wound along his right bicep stretched from the back of his elbow around the front of his arm and almost up under his armpit—a half inch deep at the deepest, slicing through naught but skin and muscle, missing all important arteries. Still, the injury had rendered his arm nearly immobile from the stiffness and pain. The wound bled scant little now, but last night it had oozed dark and red into the soily old bar rag he had kept it wrapped in.

Jenko sat back, seemingly satisfied with his stitching job, eyes roaming the dank tavern. The two of them sat in the middle of the room, the gloomy place a-litter with overturned stools and tables and random piles of trash. Mugs and dishes were strewn about everywhere, everything blanketed in a thick layer of dust and cobwebs and mold. This abandoned building had become their hiding place in the city of the enemy since reaching shore early last evening. From the faded and crooked sign above the tumbledown bar, in better days the place had been called the Patriot Sly.

"There's scarcely anyone moving around outside today," Spades announced from her lookout at the front of the tavern. "Perhaps we should make our move. Find a boat and row ourselves back to Saint Only."

Returning to Saint Only was the last thing Mancellor wanted. Whenever he looked at Enna Spades, he couldn't help but recall those first few years as Aeros' captive, when she had worked to seduce him, same as she had worked to seduce Jenko Bruk and countless others. She was not to be trusted. Her freckle-faced innocence could turn deadly or seductive at a moment's notice. It had been Spades' smoky stare and conniving ways that Mancellor had finally given in to, though he felt she had forced herself on him that first time. But he had to ashamedly admit, he went to her bed willingly thereafter, until she tired of him, that is. It was Enna Spades who had turned Mancellor Allen into a cold killer. *And one day I will kill her for making me into someone I never wanted to be. I will kill her for that initial rape.* But would today be that day?

Mancellor stood, bare feet tender against the rough wood flooring. Pain shot through his arm with every slight movement. Even from his vantage point in the middle of the room, he could see one of the many stone wharves that stretched from Lord's Point into the Strait of Saint Only—the lofty fortress naught but a blurry dark blotch in the distance through the window.

The bay itself was a haze of red grimness and death, hundreds of seagulls circling above, screeching and white, their maws red-stained from feasting on the grim carnage of human debris that spoiled the sands between Lord's Point and Saint Only. Last night's tide had clearly washed some of the bodies and armor away, but not all.

Jenko groaned and stood too, fidgeting with the sleeves of his tattered shirt, leaning against the tavern's bar. He snatched the thin spear off the bar top, the spear he had carried from yesterday's battle. Mancellor was unarmed. Jenko had that spear, Spades the dagger at her hip. Jenko examined the spear briefly, then leaned the weapon up against the bar next to him. He looked nervous. Mancellor felt the same way. It seemed he couldn't concentrate on any one thing for long. Truth be told, despite Jenko's help with stitching his arm, Mancellor had detected tension in the Gallows Haven boy all morning, tension directed at him, at Enna Spades, at their situation in general. He did not trust Jenko either, for Jenko's greedy eyes eventually fell on the battle-ax, *Forgetting Moon*, and the war helm, *Lonesome Crown*. Weapons that belonged to no one. Weapons that had no master.

Both the ax and helm had been hastily and unceremoniously plopped down amid the abandoned tavern's dust and junk upon their arrival, so weary the three of them had been. Mancellor didn't want to recall yesterday's savage battle in the bloody channel. It was the first battle he had ever fled. Early last night they eventually reached Lord's Point in their small boat, disembarked, and with zero fanfare stumbled across the stone wharf and into the city, bootless, armor-less, and wearing naught but rags, Spades carrying both the battle-ax and the helm. Mancellor and Jenko had followed the red-haired woman through the bleak dock district, weaving through the wailing chaos of the injured and dying. They had eventually found the ruined inn, slipping through the cracked-open door, finally collapsing in exhaustion and shock, the ax and helm tossed in the middle of the room, forgotten. And there they had rested ever since. Untouched. Both relics now just an arm's reach from Jenko Bruk. The blue and green angel stones were still hidden in the leather pouch tucked away in the pocket of Mancellor's pants—the one secret he kept from his two companions, the one secret he would never reveal.

Mancellor knew Jenko Bruk also desired the ax and helm, but the weapons were meant for him, and him alone. The weapons were a clear sign from Laijon, as were the two angel stones. They had provided him hope, they were the great One and Only's answer to his many prayers. And with that hope had come a slow trimming back of the nightmare of his long captivity. He knew for a surety that his destiny was tied to the ancient weapons. And he knew for a surety what Laijon's plan was for him. Freedom was finally so near. And *Forgetting Moon* and *Lonesome Crown* were coming with him.

Jenko helped him rewrap his injured arm in the dirty bar rags from last night. Mancellor was worried the rags would cause infection. But there was naught else to use. He'd already searched the tavern for whiskey—or liquor of any kind—to clean the wound. But there was nothing. In fact, during the search he had nearly fallen through the decaying wood-plank floor near the back of the inn. His foot had busted through the rotted wood, leaving a jagged black hole in the floor. He imagined some dank cellar below. The wooden floor creaked under their feet no matter where they stepped, and Mancellor wondered how safe they really were within the abandoned Patriot Sly.

When he was done wrapping the wound, Jenko leaned in and whispered, "What now?"

Mancellor stole a quick glance toward Enna Spades. She was still at watch near the slatted window. Hatred toward Spades was building anew within Mancellor by the moment. The vile redhead had been the source of much torment and pain over the years. Mancellor had remained a virgin up until the day Aeros Raijael had captured him in Wyn Darrè, until that day Spades had raped him. Yes, at first she had forced him. And yes, as time wore on, he had allowed their coupling to become consensual, ofttimes seeking her out himself—much to his shame. But in the end, those humiliations Spades had heaped upon him were the very reason he refused to partake in similar spoils of war.

And now here she was, weaponless and armor-less, with her back turned to him.

"We cannot let her find a boat and row it back to Saint Only," Mancellor said. judging the distance between himself and Spades and the battle-ax on the floor.

"I know you want me to help you kill her," Jenko said. "But I will not."

"We cannot let her take the ax and helm back to Saint Only, back to *him.*"

"We know not if Aeros even survived."

Yesterday's bloody horrors came rushing back, stark and harsh. Flashing swords. Blood. Sharks. Serpents. Horse entrails swirling in the seawater. Sharks. The mermaid that had nearly drowned him in her grim grip and slithery cold scales. Visions in the water. *Horrors in the deep.* He had seen skull-faced knights and a green dragon. A city boiling in silver and blood and an ancient broken abbey full of thieves. He'd seen himself falling from a tower and meeting a dark-haired queen whom he loved. And lastly, he'd seen himself fighting in an empty gladiator arena with Jenko at his side. *We are bound, the two of us, two captives, two slaves, two victims of Enna Spades.*

"We have to stick together," Mancellor hissed, voice harsh in the dim room.

Spades looked back into the tavern, eyeing Mancellor and Jenko coldly.

Mancellor lowered his voice. "She can't hear us."

Jenko pulled away. "I must go back for Ava."

"Ava?" Mancellor questioned.

"She belongs to me," Jenko said. A darkness had crept up into his eyes.

"How does she 'belong' to you?"

"Aeros wanted her," Jenko said. "Gault, too. And the Spider. Hammerfiss. Even Spades. And you, too, Mancellor Allen. Everyone has always wanted Ava Shay." His face was fixed in anger. "But she belongs to me. I will go back for her. She is mine."

"Ava belongs to no one," Mancellor said. "You must let her choose who she wants. That's if she even still lives."

"She lives," Jenko said.

Spades was watching them still. "What are you two going on about, whispering like that? Do you share secrets?"

"Ava is likely dead," Mancellor kept whispering, his voice a low hiss.

"She lives," Jenko hissed back at him. "And I will rescue her." His eyes were on *Forgetting Moon* and *Lonesome Crown* now. "That is why I dove into the water and pulled the ax and the helm from the sea when Aeros lost them. I saved the weapons, for I knew that the weapons would help me save Ava. *Forgetting Moon* will make anyone who wields it invincible. I have felt its magic."

Mancellor's blood turned to ice. "If you think Spades will let you just *take* that ax, you are a fool."

"Will *you* let me just take it, Mancellor?"

"I . . ." Mancellor paused. "Don't put that choice before me."

Jenko's eyes narrowed to daggerlike slits. "The ax and helm have come to me for a reason. I can feel them. They *speak* to me."

"They *speak* to you?" And Jenko lunged for the battle-ax.

Mancellor rammed his good shoulder into Jenko's side, sending the Gallows Haven boy flailing away. Mancellor grabbed the weapon first, pain screaming though his arm as he hefted it up in both hands, fingers curled around the hilt. It was surprisingly weightless in his hands, shockingly weightless.

He whirled to face Jenko. But Jenko was sprawled on his back on the floor. Enna Spades had her dagger drawn, eyes cold pricks of rage. Barefoot, she strode toward Mancellor. Jenko scrambled toward the thin spear leaning against the bar. Pain raged though Mancellor's wounds as he set his stance.

Pain is but temporary! Deal with it and stay in the fight!

His eyes met Spades' cold orbs, and he knew this would be the most dangerous foe he had ever faced. But the battle-ax felt like it belonged in his hands, weightless as a feather and simple to hold. Some familiar spirit inhabited it as faint wisps of blue mist crawled over its surface and double-bladed shine.

"You are a dead man, Mancellor Allen." Spades' voice was laced with poise and certainty. She stalked forward undaunted, slim dagger a shimmering shard in her grip. "And I will enjoy carving your eyes right from your skull and crushing them 'neath my toes."

Jenko struck at him first, spear tip aimed right at his face. Mancellor blocked the blow, *Forgetting Moon* effortlessly slicing the spearhead in twain, sending Jenko's weapon spinning off in two separate pieces and sending Jenko reeling against the bar.

Spades attacked. Mancellor whirled to meet her, the battle-ax a blur of silver light and blue smoke. Spades deftly ducked the blow and rolled, knocking over bar stools, her momentum carrying her toward the dark rear of the tavern. Gathering her feet, she snatched one of the overturned bar stools with her free hand and hurled it through the air toward Mancellor. *Forgetting Moon* shattered the stool in midair, and splinters rained over the floor. Spades launched her next attack. And there was a thunderous loud *crack!*

The rotten floorboards split open and dropped out from under the red-haired warrior woman. Enna Spades instantly vanished into the darkness below in a clamor of wood and jagged debris.

Mancellor scrambled back as the entire rear of the tavern floor and bar continued to peel from the walls, all of it plummeting into the darkness atop Spades. A horrendous billow of dust boiled upward. Jenko was crawling away from the ever-plunging chaos of the expanding hole, eyes frantic and wide. Mancellor darted away too, barely keeping his feet as the building shook under him. Gripping *Forgetting Moon* in one hand, he seized *Lonesome Crown* in the other. He headed straight for the shuttered front window choking on the dust-filled air, injured arm a flaming knot of pain.

Behind him, the tumult of crashing wood and debris came to an abrupt halt.

"B-bloody Mother Mia!" Jenko stammered, slowly climbing to his feet. "She's gone." His startled gaze met Mancellor's. "Do you think she's dead?"

Mancellor couldn't hear any sounds coming from the ominous gaping hole that had consumed nearly half the tavern.

"Spades!" Jenko yelled, moving toward the blackness, swiping at the swirling dust blocking his path.

"Don't!" Mancellor yelled. "That hole will swallow you, too, and you'll find yourself down in that cellar with her."

Jenko turned, cold eyes fixed on Mancellor. "So the ax and helm are yours?"

"They are now." Mancellor moved toward the tavern door, ax and helm gripped comfortably in each hand, knowing he was finally free of Enna Spades, free of the White Prince, finally free of the armies of Sør Sevier.

"You can't just take them for yourself," Jenko said.

"It is divine providence that Spades vanished without a trace," Mancellor said. "Some strange magic is at work with these weapons, Jenko, especially when they are in my hands. The ax and helm are meant for me. They always have been."

"How can you be certain they are for you?" Jenko asked. "For I am also sure they belong to me. I too have felt their magic."

"Then escape with me now that Spades is finally gone," Mancellor said. "Now that we are finally free of them all, escape with me. Our destinies lie together, Jenko. Come with me."

"To where?" Jenko asked, face a mask of dust and fear.

"Anywhere," Mancellor answered. "What does it matter? We are free. We can take *Forgetting Moon* and *Lonesome Crown* to Amadon. Take them to the grand vicar. He shall know what to do with them."

"We'll be captured as soon as you leave this building."

"Nobody knows who we are. Our Sør Sevier armor is at the bottom of that channel. And I imagine that enough armor and clothing and weapons washed up along these shores last night that we can scavenge something up from the sands. We can soon be fitted as knights of Gul Kana. We can take the ax and helm to Amadon. Present them to Grand Vicar Denarius before Fiery Absolution. Present them to King Jovan. We would forever be hailed as heroes. What other choice could we possibly have?"

"*Forgetting Moon*? *Lonesome Crown*? Take them both to Fiery Absolution?" Jenko looked at the ancient artifacts in Mancellor's hands. "We are not men of legends, Mancellor. We are just two insignificant slaves."

"Well, I'm sick of feeling insignificant," Mancellor said. "I'm sick of killing just to save my own skin. Sick of this crusade I never once believed in. Sick of feeling full of vileness and sin for all the slaughter I have partaken in. Sick of all I do just to keep myself alive."

"We did what was necessary to survive," Jenko said. "And ofttimes what is necessary ain't pretty. We did what we had to, but we were never beholden to Aeros Raijael."

"I want to do something good and right for a change." Mancellor stepped back into the room toward Jenko, holding *Forgetting Moon* out for the Gallows Haven boy. "Come with me. For I call you friend, Jenko Bruk. Come with me to Amadon. 'Tis Laijon who guides us now, not Raijael."

Jenko took the ax, hefted it in his hands, testing its weight, eyes wide in awe of the weapon once again in his grasp. "It feels so light."

Mancellor glimpsed his own reflection in the ax's shiny surface. It was a face that seemed to be his, but also that of a stranger, mayhap some distant relation. He could not reconcile the changes, both within and without, that now gazed back at him. His eyes were deep pools of both sadness and grief that seemed to scarcely even belong to him. He did not like what he saw. He did the three-fingered sign of the Laijon Cross over his heart and stood taller, straighter, braver, realizing this was the first time he had ever done the sign of the cross before the eyes of another since his capture five years ago.

But his sacred ritual seemed to have the opposite effect on Jenko, as the Gallows Haven boy's face seemed to darken. "I would not take *Forgetting Moon* to Amadon," Jenko said, handing the battle-ax back to Mancellor.

"What do you mean?"

"I would not hand either the ax or the helm over to the grand vicar. It's futile worshipping Laijon and the church in Amadon. If there is one thing I have learned, it is to place scant faith in the gods. They will only betray you."

They stared at each other at length, neither moving, Mancellor with the ax and helm again in hand. The pain of his injured arm was almost forgotten, as if just holding the weapons was a healing balm.

"Jenko!" Spades called out, startling them both. "Jenko, are you there?"

"Go now." Jenko's voice was quiet, reserved, *resigned*. "Go. I've made my decision. Take the ax and the helm wherever you so wish, Mancellor. I will not try to stop you."

Jenko's faraway gaze was fixed on something beyond Mancellor and the two weapons he carried, something out beyond the dusty window and wooden slats covering it. "You let me hold the ax again," Jenko murmured, almost to himself. "And that was enough. I now know my destiny lies elsewhere, separate from those weapons. I must go back for Ava Shay. I cannot leave her to some unknown fate."

"Jenko!" Spades' voice called again. "Are you still up there?"

Mancellor looked out the tavern window too. Even from afar, and despite the brightness of the sun, he could see the twinkling yellow beacon atop the Mont Saint Only fortress. "If Ava Shay is still there, then save her you must."

"She is my heart," Jenko said. "I love her."

"Then go to her," Mancellor said.

Jenko reached out and grasped him by his uninjured shoulder. "Go in peace, Ser Mancellor Allen, and may you find whatever glory you are searching for."

Mancellor nodded, a lump growing in his throat. Just moments before they had been willing to kill each other over the possession of an ancient battle-ax and war helm. Now they were looking into the other's eyes as friends.

"Jenko!" Spades called again. "Are you up there?" Mancellor could hear the clanking and clattering of wood from below, Spades moving around in the hole.

"Farewell, my brother," Mancellor said. And without looking back, he kicked open the rickety front door of the Patriot Sly and stepped out into the sunlight, *Forgetting Moon* and *Lonesome Crown* gripped in either hand.

**

The sun seethed over the corpse-littered channel, stark and raw and hot, pulsing golden red off the sands. They were bright sands that seemed lit from within, luminous with rivers of blood, sparkling with the armor of the dead, alive with the movement of screeching gulls. Now that the tide had fully receded again, there were scavengers of another sort—citizens from Lord's Point. They scoured yesterday's battlefield by the hundreds, moving like ants amongst the tens of thousands of stiff and lifeless knights, rotting horses, bloated sharks, and dead merfolk.

Mancellor abandoned his plan of searching the sands for armor, knowing he would never—could never—venture back onto that savage seascape. Instead he struggled away from it with the bulk of both *Forgetting Moon* and *Lonesome Crown* his burden. They weighed him down now. So heavy when they had been so light. Now his injured arm could scarcely bear the weight of either. He had to carry the ax in his left hand, the helm in the crook of his left arm just for some measure of relief.

Wandering the docks for no more than ten minutes and everyone was already starting to take note of him, alone, bare of foot, dressed in naught but his underclothes, two shining magnificent weapons in hand. Mancellor knew he had to find shelter soon, hide the weapons. He angled away from the shoreline and its myriad of busy wharves and headed toward the nearest cluster of buildings. He needed a saddlebag, a canvas sack, a horse, boots. But what he needed most was to be off the streets. Yet the door to every building he tried was shut, locked, windows shuttered.

He eventually found a gated courtyard, the gate open wide. The well-worn yard beyond led to the back door of an abandoned inn. A horse stable was situated along one side of the yard; a row of empty weapons racks lined the other. Mancellor slipped through the open gate and collapsed against the outer wall of the stable, ax and helm tumbling to the ground at his side, resting in the dirt. He breathed a deep sigh of relief, weary arms finally rid of their burden.

He studied the weapons in the dirt. *Are they worth it?* He was already doubting himself. *Forgetting Moon* was a sight. It had a thick steel haft swaddled in black leather interwoven with Vallè runes fashioned of silver thread. Its curved double blades gleamed with razor-sharp edges. And the ox-horned helm, *Lonesome Crown*, was burnished a glorious bronze color, with intricate gold and silver inlays. It sparkled, and the two pale horns sprouting from it seemed like something from another world.

Mancellor heard the snort of a pony. The sound came from the stable behind him. He stood and turned, setting his eye between the wood slats of the barn. There were three ponies. He slipped around the stable and cracked open its wood door. All three ponies were healthy piebalds, and all three were saddled and provisioned. There were two piles of strange-looking armor at their feet, helms and shortswords too. Mancellor did the three-fingered sign of the Laijon Cross over his heart, thanking the great One and Only for this sudden good fortune.

"Bloody rotted angels, I know that ax!" An excited voice rang out loud and clear from the courtyard behind him. "What do you think it's doin' here at the Turn Key Saloon, Dokie?"

Heart pounding, Mancellor backed out of the barn. He was met by two familiar faces: the plump red-haired boy from yesterday's battle and his diminutive companion. They were the two Gul Kana knights who had almost killed Aeros Raijael. The smaller of the two boys carried a huge canvas sack over his left shoulder. He had a pinched look of concern on his thin face, brows furrowing under dirt-colored hair. The larger boy carried a stumpy shortsword, hand gripped fiercely around the hilt, red hair cropped short, his round face covered in both freckles and purple bruises.

"Just who the fuck are you?" the redheaded boy demanded. "A thief trying to steal our mounts?" The tip of the boy's sword rose. "I'll jab this blade into you twenty different ways from Eighth Day if you so much as think about taking one of them ponies. Don't think I won't."

Mancellor quickly began to suspect that the plump knight threatening him might not be a boy, but rather a girl instead. Girl or not, the shortsword the redhead carried, though dull-looking, could still poke holes in him. Plus, he'd seen these two fight in battle. Determined and ferocious they were.

His eyes drifted to *Forgetting Moon* and *Lonesome Crown*, still lying in the dirt where he had so carelessly dropped them. He cursed his own foolishness.

"What you doin' with that ax?" the redhead asked, an impatient edge to her voice. "It belongs to Nail. It belongs to *us*."

"*Nail?*" Mancellor asked, the name jogging his memory. Jenko had taken the ax from a boy named Nail in Ravenker.

"You knew Nail?" the girl asked.

"No."

"Well, you said his name as if you did."

The smaller boy pointed. "That helm there, it looks like what the White Prince was wearin' fore it got knocked off his head."

"Who are you?" Mancellor asked. "I saw you both fighting in the channel yesterday."

"We saw you, too," the big girl answered, suspicion still etched on her wide, bruised face. "We saw you fighting in the colors of the enemy."

"But I am not your enemy." Mancellor held up his hands. "Never was."

"I'm Dokie Liddle," the small boy said. "We traveled with Nail from Gallows Haven. But we got separated somewhere up north by the Sky Lochs—"

"Bloody rotted angels," the big girl cut the boy off, glaring. "Don't give up your name so easy to strangers."

"I just assumed he was a friend of Nail's, hauling that ax about and all. He said he wasn't an enemy." The boy named Dokie looked crestfallen. "Sorry, Liz Hen."

"You clodpole," the girl exclaimed. "You absolute daft-headed clodpole."

"What did I do?"

"Now he knows my name too."

"Sorry."

Liz Hen faced Mancellor. "We've a history with Nail, true that. But what of it?"

Mancellor didn't answer.

"Is it really Nail's ax?" she asked.

"Yes, it was once Nail's," Mancellor admitted. "I'm returning it to him. If you know where he is."

"Returning it to Nail?" Liz Hen stepped nearer to the ax and helm, but gave Mancellor a wide berth as she examined them, the tip of her sword still angled between them. "Why would you return the ax to Nail?" she asked.

"I've got to take it somewhere," he answered.

"Are those tattoos under your eyes?" Dokie asked, his own eyes a-squint as he stepped closer for a better look at Mancellor's face. "You really are the man with tattoos who I saw fighting beside Aeros Raijael yesterday?"

"As you said, I was in yesterday's battle." Mancellor nodded. "And I saw you two fighting against the Angel Prince."

"You mean the White Prince," the girl corrected him.

"Aye." He nodded again. "The White Prince. My mistake." In fact, he promised himself right then and there never to make that same mistake again. Aeros would forever be known as the White Prince to him.

"Wasn't there an old man with you?" he asked the pair. "An old man who fought with you, and a dog, too, if I'm right?"

"They're both dead," Dokie mumbled, hiking the canvas sack up higher on his shoulder, a dark look crossing his face. "And we're going home now, to Gallows Haven."

"That's right, Gallows Haven," the girl confirmed. "We've provisions enough for the journey."

"We looted the inn," Dokie added, as if he was proud of the fact. "You won't find nothing of worth left."

"So get out of our way," Liz Hen ordered. "'Twas us who saddled those three ponies in the stable, and we aim to leave now. You won't be stealing them from us."

"Gallows Haven?" Mancellor questioned. "I would not head south if I were you. The White Prince still has an army of near fifty thousand soldiers camped south of Lord's Point. You won't make it past them."

"We didn't ask your advice," the girl said, a hint of bitterness souring her tone. She pointed her sword right at him again. "Who are you anyway?"

"I am Mancellor Allen of Wyn Darrè." He showed them the Sør Sevier slave brand on the underside of his wrist. "And I am not your enemy. And it is true, I aim to return the battle-ax to Nail. I stole it from Aeros Raijael for just that purpose. I shall give the helm to Nail too, for it is also most priceless."

"Who is Nail to you?"

"I was there when Jenko stole the ax from Nail in Ravenker," Mancellor said. "I only aim to return it."

Liz Hen was clearly not buying any of it. "You must understand, those tattoos under your eyes make you look like trouble. It's all very suspect, is what it is. Everything you say is suspect, showing up with Nail's ax and that horned helm the White Prince wore in battle. It's all very suspect."

"Very suspect," Dokie agreed.

Liz Hen motioned to *Forgetting Moon*, saying, "That ax is cursed. I'll have you know that at least."

"You may be right," he agreed.

"Was there a blue stone with the ax?" Dokie asked.

Mancellor's heart lurched. The two angel stones in his pants pocket were the one secret he'd vowed to keep. He'd cut them free of Aeros' belt himself. But for some reason, he wanted to be as honest as possible with these two, for though they didn't know it yet, they offered him possibly his only means of escaping Lord's Point.

"I have the blue stone with me too," he admitted. "And a green one. The White Prince believed that that battle-ax is *Forgetting Moon*, ancient weapon of the Warrior Angels, straight out of legend. He believed the helm he wore to be *Lonesome Crown*."

"So we've heard others also say," the girl grumbled, with a hint of trepidation.

"Can you spare one of those three ponies in the stable?" he asked. "And some of that armor you piled up near them, perhaps some food, too?"

"It's gaoler armor," Liz Hen said. "And we've not much to spare. The third pony is to carry our provisions. We certainly cannot spare it. We are going back to Gallows Haven. Truth is, we want nothing to do with that battle-ax. And as for you yourself, you needn't worry about us stealing the ax from you. You can go your own way. But you won't be taking one of our ponies with you, nor any of our foodstuffs."

Mancellor knew if it came to it, in a fight he could easily take what he wanted from these two. But he did not want to take anything by force again. These two youths were innocent. He looked toward the channel. The courtyard of the Turn Key Saloon abutted the docks along the northwest edge of Lord's Point and gave him a clear view of Adin Wyte ten miles away.

Atop the lofty seven-hundred-foot-high pinnacle of rock called the Mont was the Fortress of Saint Only. *Ava Shay could very well still be alive, looking over the ghastly channel herself.* He hoped Jenko Bruk truly did go back for the girl. *But what is my purpose?* He knew he needed to get out of Lord's Point fast.

He let his gaze fall on the sunny haze of the ocean channel itself and the silver sparkle of the dead soldiers in their glistening armor, knights that would again soon be covered up by the swelling tide. The deep gloom and despair of the bloody channel seemed to physically press down upon the city and the stable yard he stood in, holding him in place, shrinking him.

"Do not make for Gallows Haven," he said. "I beg of you. Only death lies to the south."

"And I said we don't want no advice," Liz Hen said.

"As I said, a great portion of Aeros' armies are still camped south of here," Mancellor repeated, feeling like it would take forever to convince this girl of the folly of her plan. "You'll not make it past them. They will kill you."

"He raises a valid point," Dokie said. "He's warned us twice now."

Liz Hen glared at her friend. "What do we do then, Dokie? Answer me that."

"We could go with him," Dokie answered. "I think that's what he is hinting at, after all. And I do like adventure. And if he takes the ax back to Nail, then we can see our friend once more. Perhaps Stefan Wayland, too. And Val-Draekin and Rogue—"

"You blabber too much," Liz Hen cut him off, her attention returning to Mancellor. "Dokie is by nature both distractible and impractical. That's what he means when he says he likes adventure. But him liking adventure is also an example of his impractical thinking. I honestly don't know what to do. I never was much of a leader, truth be told."

She looked back at the boy. The two stared at each other, confidence draining from the girl's face by the second. "What do we do, Dokie?"

"We do our best to survive," Dokie said. "We should join together with Mancellor here. We've a better chance to survive with him, I think."

"I don't know . . ." Liz Hen trailed off, her face a tortured mask of uncertainty.

"There is strength traveling in numbers," Mancellor said. "I could use two stout companions like you, real warriors like myself."

Dokie's face brightened. "You truly think we are real warriors?"

"Aye." He nodded, meaning it. "The fiercest. Anyone who fought in that battle yesterday is more than just a warrior, but a hero."

"Do you have any Blood of the Dragon on you?" Liz Hen asked, almost breathless.

"No," Mancellor answered, detecting the faint trace of red in her eyes, realizing the girl was likely addicted to the stuff. "But I've a knack for locating those who do."

The girl exhaled. "Then we shall follow you until you find Nail."

"Bless you." Mancellor dipped his head in a short bow to her. "I could use the company of good companions for a change." He did the three-fingered sign of the Laijon Cross over his heart.

Liz Hen scowled. "I do not believe in prayers and such anymore."

"I believe in prayer," Dokie piped up. "For having a stout fighter like Mancellor with us is an answer to mine."

*Beware, for he who seeks knowledge finds only pain, for ofttimes truth is
more cruel than the lie. For the key to Absolution shall come down to
those lonely two who finally believe in one truth shared.*
—The Way and Truth of Laijon

CHAPTER SIX

NAIL

7TH DAY OF THE FIRE MOON, 999TH YEAR OF LAIJON
MEMORY BAY, SOUTH OF WROCLAW, GUL KANA

Nail woke. Cramped. He had somehow become jammed uncomfortably under the bench just below the sidewall of the boat. He rose. Standing. Stretching. Aching. Weary gaze roaming east over the vast expanse of Memory Bay, locating the dark haze of the Gul Kana shoreline in the far distance.

He was also hungry. There were a few foodstuffs under the sidewall, left by the fishermen. But most were rotten. Cromm Cru'x had caught a red salmon late last night with one of the leftover fishing nets. But Nail had not partaken. The salmon was raw. They'd had nothing to cook it with. The oghul ate it alone.

Bronwyn Allen was sitting on the center bench under the billowing white sail next to Cromm. She was stringing her black bow. The oghul was sharpening one of his many daggers with a whetstone. The Vallè, Val-Draekin, sat near the rear of the boat. His dark eyes had not even glanced up when Nail woke. Ever since setting sail from Wroclaw, the dark-haired Vallè had grown overly contemplative, taciturn, scarcely speaking to anyone.

They had been sailing one night and a day since Wroclaw, and Nail still couldn't shake the horror of witnessing the five colorful knights in silver masks slaughter the fishermen who had traded this very boat for a few measly horses. With scant effort, the white knight's silver whip had sliced the men and the horses right in half.

And the saber-toothed lion and the poor young girl—Nail didn't even want to think of that. *Skulls*, Val-Draekin had called the five creatures. *An ancient race of Vallè. The Last Demon Lords.* The marks on Nail's flesh burned with a deeper intensity now than ever before. He knew the renewed pain had something to do with the five skull-faced knights.

He yawned, just wanting to go back to sleep, the motion of the boat so soothing.

"The marked one thinks he can sleep all morning," Cromm Cru'x commented gruffly, not looking up as he continued sharpening one of the many stilettos he pulled from his leather boot tops. The oghul also had daggers tucked into hidden pockets within the wrist sheaths strapped around his forearms. He had another collection of knives hooked to the buckler at his hip and a square-headed war hammer strapped to the thick leather baldric over his shoulder.

"Useless for one to sleep so much," the oghul grumbled, sucking vigorously on the black rock he ofttimes kept between his lower lip and gums. Nail knew that oghuls were apt to suck on rocks to stave off their hunger for human blood. But this oghul sucked on that rock constantly. Cromm's gums were swollen, and Nail wondered how long before the beast would need another bloodletting.

"Is Cromm growing disappointed in the marked one?" Bronwyn asked, not looking up from her bow.

"True, Cromm is growing disappointed in the marked one," Cromm grunted.

Nail suddenly felt disappointed in Cromm's disappointment. He didn't want the oghul to think less of him just because he had fallen asleep again, the third time that day. But what could he do?

Cromm Cru'x was a flat-nosed and keen-eyed oghul—the largest Nail had ever seen. The broad sheets of battered iron plate armor buckled to

Cromm's chest, thighs, and forearms made him look even larger. Two long teeth protruded from both the top and bottom of his thick lips like daggers. Sparkling jewels were embedded in those teeth and also in each of his knuckles. Cromm was a fearsome-looking monster capable of brutal violence at a moment's notice.

And as long as he referred to Nail as the marked one, Nail wanted to at least live up to the name.

"He sleeps too much," the oghul reiterated.

"Leave the boy be, Cromm." Bronwyn glanced up at Nail, winking. Her green cloak, shortsword, and quiver of black-hafted arrows rested on the floorboards of the boat at her feet. She smiled. "Like an Avlonian court girl, Nail needs his beauty sleep."

Nail flicked strands of blond hair from his eyes and glared at the copper-haired girl. He did not want her to think ill of him any more than he wanted the oghul to.

Bronwyn Allen wore black pants and a leather vest laced up the front over a black shirt. Her leather boots rose up to mid-calf, dark leather thongs twining the rest of the way clear up to her knees. Her blue eyes were always harsh and wary beneath the two dark tattoos on her face. The black ink stretched from underneath each sharp brow down over each of her eyelids and over her cheekbones. Two white feathers were tied onto her dark hair just below her left ear.

Those two feathers had bothered Nail for some days now. They had vexed him ever since meeting the girl. It wasn't until a few days ago that he realized why. The last time he had seen a girl with two white feathers tied into her hair, it had been in Gallows Haven at the Mourning Moon Feast. Ava Shay had danced around the bonfire that night, two white feathers in her hair. She had also kissed Jenko Bruk that night. And Nail had followed them clear to Jubal Bruk's manor house, spied on them through the slats of the barn, seen private things between them that he wished he could erase from his mind.

"Beauty sleep." Bronwyn still smiled as she shook her head in distaste. She held her black longbow up, plucking confidently at the newly strung string. Nail had noticed long ago that the bow was similar in

shape to the Dayknight bow Bishop Godwyn had carried, akin to the
bow Shawcroft had gifted Stefan Wayland. The only difference was that
Bronwyn's bow was painted as black as the tattoos over her eyes.

The Wyn Darrè girl eyed her oghul companion. "You've every right
to be a little disappointed in the marked one you've searched your whole
life for. He is a lazy sleepyhead."

Cromm stashed the stiletto he'd been sharpening into a hidden fold
of his leather boot then looked back up at Nail. "A little disappointed,
maybe. Makes Cromm question the marked one's destiny. Makes Cromm
question Cromm's own destiny."

Nail tried his best not to break the oghul's gaze as he said, "I don't
know who you think I am, but I am not part of your destiny."

Cromm sucked on the black rock. "You are the marked one. You are
part of Cromm's destiny." Then the oghul craned his neck, looking toward Val-Draekin in the rear of the boat. "Seeing five knights in silver
skull masks so soon after finding the marked one, if that is not confirmation enough for Cromm that the marked one is the marked one, then
Cromm does not know what is."

"And there's no arguing that logic," Bronwyn said flatly. "For those
knights sure looked to be born of some foul oghul witchcraft."

"Born of Hragna'Ar," Cromm said. "Not foul witchcraft. Cromm is
devoted to Hragna'Ar."

"But you killed Hragna'Ar oghuls to save both Val-Draekin and me,"
Nail said.

Bronwyn answered, "Cromm hunted down and killed those particular Hragna'Ar oghuls for sinking the *Ja Tr'all*."

The oghul grunted his agreement. "Cromm does not like all Hragna'Ar
oghuls, and he hated those oghuls that sunk his ship. Was destiny that
Cromm also found the marked one when he found those foul oghuls
that sunk Cromm's ship."

Nail was mostly confused by the oghul's insistence that he was
the marked one tied to oghul legend. He was also mostly confused by
Cromm's stance and beliefs in Hragna'Ar altogether and his convoluted
relationship with his own fellow oghuls.

All things considered, Bronwyn Allen and Cromm Cru'x were still mysteries. Over time, Nail had gleaned only a few sparse details of their previous lives. Bronwyn was a year older than he. Her father—before he died when the armies of Sør Sevier attacked Wyn Darrè—had been a trader from north of Ikaboa, a dealer in rare oddments and mind-altering drugs mainly sought by oghul pirates. Cromm had been one of the oghul pirates Bronwyn's father had traded with. After Bronwyn's family had been killed, she had taken up with the oghul, raiding the Bloodwood Forest for Blood of the Dragon to sell, until Cromm's boat was sunk and they began traveling through Gul Kana intent on exacting revenge.

The odd pair had been avenging the death of Cromm's sailing partners when they had found Nail and Val-Draekin hanging in the oghul cages north of Deadwood Gate. Cromm had insisted on rescuing Nail, claiming he was the marked one. And now here they all were on a boat bound for Amadon.

The boat rolled gently in the waves as Val-Draekin stood, winds whistling by overhead. The sails were full and the boom of the vessel creaked and groaned as the Vallè moved from the back of the fishing boat to the prow and sat near Nail.

Val-Draekin faced Cromm. "You claim the skull-faced knights we saw yesterday were an omen?"

"They are the Cauldron Born," Cromm said, sucking on his black rock hungrily. "Their rebirth before Absolution is well-known in oghul legend. Something not written down in your *Way and Truth of Laijon*."

"Would you tell me what you know of them, Cromm?" Val-Draekin asked.

"You seemed to know plenty about them when we sailed away from that dock yesterday," Bronwyn said. "You named them the Aalavarrè Solas. Perhaps you should be the one telling us about the Cauldron Born."

"I must plead as much ignorance as you." Val-Draekin nodded to the girl. Then his dark-eyed gaze fixed on Nail. "As Nail knows, I am always wary of ancient prophetic writings and ancient legend. But Seita was different than I on topics of a mystical nature. She dreamed of the silver-faced knights. She dreamed of the Skulls. I do know that *The Moon Scrolls of Mia* mentioned them. They were a race made extinct at the time of the great War of Cleansing, an ancient race of Vallè banished to the underworld. They were the ones who helped the oghuls tame the dragons. If dragons ever were real." He paused, contemplative, looking at Nail.

"Cromm knows not who this Seita is, but he suspects the great Val-Draygin knows more than he claims," the oghul said, shrugging. "Cromm only knows what Hragna'Ar legends and prophecy Cromm has been told. Cromm's great-grandfather told Cromm's grandfather, who told Cromm's father, who told Cromm. This is Hragna'Ar legend, handed down mouth to mouth, not written down in books. Oghul beliefs are never written down. Oghul beliefs can never be corrupted. Hragna'Ar is truth. And Cromm is surprised that a Vallè who would call himself Val-Draygin would not know these things."

Val-Draekin shifted, looking uncomfortable. "And you truly believe that Nail is the marked one, important to Hragna'Ar?"

"Cromm has said so numerous times. Has *Val-Draygin* not been careful in listening?" The oghul produced another hidden knife from under his armor and began sharpening it with his whetstone. "Or does Val-Draygin think he can play games with Cromm?"

Val-Draekin shifted in his seat but remained stone-faced.

"Oghul legend can be convoluted in its own way," Bronwyn said. "Just like *The Way and Truth of Laijon*. For instance, Cromm has also mentioned to me that Hragna'Ar prophecy speaks of the marked one as having a burnt head."

"A burnt head?" Nail questioned.

"Aye." Cromm nodded in confirmation. "Cromm has been thinking of setting fire to your face for some time now."

"Set fire to my face?" Nail found himself scooting farther away from the oghul. But the boat was only so large. He was about as far away as he could get.

"I've asked Cromm to lay off burning your face, for now," Bronwyn said. "I've advised him that your head will likely be sufficiently burnt at Fiery Absolution."

"But Cromm can be impatient." The oghul met Nail's concerned gaze. "Cromm has yet to decide what to do about that detail. Should Cromm burn you now or wait?"

"I won't let you burn me," Nail said.

"Cromm does what Cromm wants," Bronwyn laughed.

The oghul finished sharpening the dagger he was working on and shoved both it and the whetstone away into his leathers. He then pulled forth another dagger, this one as black as polished coal. He used the tip of it to pick at his teeth.

And Nail felt his body continue to shrink back against the sidewall of the boat, feeling the rolling of the ocean waves acutely under him, the smell of the surrounding seawater making him nauseous. He didn't know whether Bronwyn and the oghul were serious. He could feel the scars he already carried burning; he could even feel the turtle carving Ava had given him burning against his flesh. He ran trembling hands through his hair.

"Don't look so worried, Nail." A rueful smile spread across Bronwyn's face. "As I said, Hragna'Ar legend is a bit convoluted, with some parts left open to interpretation."

She is as dangerous as the oghul, Nail thought. *Not to be trusted.* He knew Bronwyn could easily slay him with that black bow in her hands. Nail had come to the realization that he had been taught his whole life that women were less than men. But Seita and Bronwyn Allen had easily proved that notion wrong. Bronwyn Allen's eyes were stark and blue against the smears of black tattoos from her brows to her jawbone. He could see she was beautiful under all that ink. Still, the look of her sent a chill up his spine. Before him was a female who was tough and who was deadly, who would kill without compunction or hesitation, a girl who would murder another man over a horse.

Val-Draekin had made mention that Princess Jondralyn Bronachell was also a strong-willed woman, her younger sister, Tala, too—though they probably weren't cold killers like Bronwyn. He ofttimes wondered what this girl, Tala, might be like. He tried to picture her in his mind but had no reference to go upon other than the image of her sister, Jondralyn, that he had seen on a coin. *Pretty.* It was silly to think of someone like Tala, though. *Even if I was to meet a princess, what of it?* A bastard certainly had no place near royalty of any kind. *Unless I am royalty myself.*

Hawkwood claimed that Nail's mother was Cassietta Raybourne, younger sister to King Torrence Raybourne of Wyn Darrè. *He claimed my father was King Aevrett Raijael of Sør Sevier. Hawkwood claimed that I was the true Angel Prince!* Nail had never much trusted Roguemoore or Culpa Barra on the subject. The dwarf was dead now, anyway. And who knew where Culpa was? But had Hawkwood told him the truth? Val-Draekin had also made mention that Hawkwood had been in the mining town of Arco when his mother was killed. And that was the question. *Was Hawkwood speaking the truth about my heritage? Or was it merely the power of suggestion?*

There were things Nail wished were true, things he *wanted* to be true. But that didn't make them true. He recalled explaining to Val-Draekin how it had felt to wield *Forgetting Moon*, how he had felt its magic. The Vallè claimed he had experienced naught but some natural phenomenon, attributing his experience to the power of suggestion. Val-Draekin had claimed that Shawcroft had planted into his mind the seeds that the ax was special, that he himself was special. Val-Draekin had pointed out that the scars on his body were just random coincidence, that any number of folks could have similar markings. It still seemed the first honest and real evaluation of his situation that anyone had yet offered. For the Company of Nine had journeyed to find Blackest Heart and Afflicted Fire. He had no idea the true fate of the others in his company. But Roguemoore was dead! If there was any proof that Laijon was not watching over them, that was it.

With that thought, he wondered where everyone now was: Seita, Culpa, Bishop Godwyn, Liz Hen, Dokie, Stefan. Val-Draekin was the only friend he had left, Nail realized. Through mines and glaciers they had traveled, saving each other time after time along the way, relying on each other for survival. *He is the only one I dare trust, the only one who has been honest with me.* Nail always wanted to believe there was something extraordinary about himself, that there was a great destiny awaiting them somewhere. But Val-Draekin had convinced him that the reality was far removed from that fantasy. *It will not be self-righteous blind faith in Warrior Angels that will save the Five Isles,* the Vallè had said, *but rather those with humble doubt, those who take it upon themselves to hone the strength of their own will and intellect and fight against the power of suggestion, fight against faith and blind belief.*

Nail would never forget that conversation. *When it comes to faith, what men fear most is the truth they already know in their heart, yet deny. They know it is all false. Their beliefs. The fanciful tales and fables and miracles of the past written down in ancient texts. They know deep down it is all nonsense. Yet still they believe. . . . The truth is, there will likely be no miracles or saviors in the end.* And yet even simple oghuls like Cromm Cru'x held steadfast belief in Hragna'Ar and Absolution and marked ones. *He even wants to burn my face so I match his oghul legends perfectly!*

A strange thought struck him then. Something Val-Draekin had said earlier about if dragons ever were real. He voiced his opinion. "If there were once nameless beasts of the underworld, wouldn't there be some remnant of their existence left lying about the Five Isles? Bones? Teeth? Scales? All the holy books and even oghul legends hint of their existence. Yet we've no physical evidence of these beasts other than what is written in those ancient texts and what is carved onto a few rocks and altars and what was handed down mouth to mouth from oghul-kind."

"Well, aren't you just the dour one with all your sudden philosophizing about the nameless beasts of the underworld?" Bronwyn was frowning at Nail, her black bow gripped in both hands. The sea breeze lifted a lock of her copper-colored hair and swept it over her eyes.

"It was just a question," Nail said.

But Val-Draekin did not answer.

The boat rolled on the sea. And Nail felt suddenly sicker than before. The rays of the sun lent glitter to the waters of Memory Bay. But that flickering light combined with the chop of the waves against the hull of the boat just made him feel worse and worse.

The Wyn Darrè girl brushed the hair from her face with the end of the bow. "I might be a skeptic regarding a lot of things myself, but I've always felt that those who completely deny the existence of dragons are a dismal lot. It's as if their very souls have been stolen from them and locked away somewhere. That *The Way and Truth of Laijon* tells us not to even speak their name, or carve their likeness into stone, lets me know that the men who wrote the words in that book of scripture were hiding something. And I believe they were hiding the fact that oghuls like Cromm, with their foul ritualistic beliefs in Hragna'Ar blood sacrifice, might have been more right than they were willing to acknowledge. The fact that those who penned the scriptures wished to bury the true name of the beasts meant they also wanted to hide much, much more about themselves."

"Is that why you painted that bow black?" Val-Draekin said, dark eyes narrowing in suspicion. "To hide something about yourself?"

Nail studied the bow in Bronwyn's hands, immediately taking some comfort in its familiar lines. For it was a Dayknight bow, just like Godwyn's, just like Stefan's.

"And where did you get that dagger?" Val-Draekin stood. His bearing was now tense and coiled like a serpent as he stared at the black dagger Cromm was using to pick his teeth. "That's a Bloodwood dagger, familiar to me."

Cromm stood too, clenching the black dagger in his grip.

"Easy, Cromm," said Bronwyn, still gripping her black bow tightly in hand. "We do not want to kill this 'Val-Draygin' yet."

Nail noticed the faintest of carvings under the black paint on the stock of Bronwyn's bow, a carving he was all too familiar with, a carving he had seen a thousand times, a carving created by his dearest friend, a carving of a name he well knew. . . .

Gisela!

How did I not see the carving in the bow before now?

A glacial chasm of pain yawned open inside his chest, tearing at his very soul, as he realized that what he saw was indeed real and that he did not need a closer look, realized what seeing Gisela's name on the bow really meant. The fact that the Wyn Darrè girl now carried the Dayknight bow with Gisela's name carved into it could mean only one thing: Stefan Wayland was dead.

"Where did you get that bow?" His voice cracked, eyes now fixed on Bronwyn.

"And the Bloodwood dagger?" Val-Draekin added, his dark orbs on the dagger in the oghul's hand. "How did you come by that dagger?"

"Cromm took both the dagger and the bow from a dying boy," Bronwyn said.

"What dying boy?" Nail asked, heart in his throat.

"A boy we found propped against an aspen tree near Deadwood Gate," Bronwyn continued. "We came upon him not long before we found you two hanging in those Hragna'Ar cages."

Cromm added, "The boy was killed by the same Hragna'Ar oghuls we chased."

"Stefan?" Nail looked at Val-Draekin. "It had to be him. They have his bow."

He faced Bronwyn and Cromm again. "What about Culpa Barra? Seita? Was there a knight with Stefan, a Dayknight in black armor? And a blond Vallè maiden?"

"Not that I saw," Bronwyn answered. "Though we did see some cloaked figure huddled over this boy, Stefan. But I did not get a good look at that person, for they ran off at the approach of the oghul fighters. 'Twas the oghul fighters who ended up shooting an arrow into the boy, the boy you believe is Stefan."

"And that was when Cromm took the dagger and the bow from the dying boy," the oghul added.

"Stefan wasn't dead?" Nail asked, hope springing into his voice.

"He was breathing when we came upon him," Bronwyn said. "But his injuries were dire; arrow-shot, legs broken, a hole above his heart from some previous wound. Yet he still breathed. But faintly."

"We have to go back for him," Nail blurted, his pleading gaze now focused on Val-Draekin. "We have to go back for Stefan."

But by the look on the Vallè's face, Nail knew the request was futile.

They would not be going back. Unfathomable loss and pain over-whelmed him.

Stefan Wayland was dead.

And how do I trust these strangers in the boat with me? The girl would happily kill me for a horse. The oghul would burn my face to fulfill a prophecy.

And it was becoming more and more obvious every day: Val-Draekin was a deep well of secrets.

Either it has all happened before, or none of it has happened yet. All these histories and scriptures and bards' tales are perhaps prophecies of the future, or warnings of the past. Or so the unbeliever would want you to think.
—THE WAY AND TRUTH OF LAIJON

CHAPTER SEVEN
TALA BRONACHELL

7TH DAY OF THE FIRE MOON, 999TH YEAR OF LAIJON

AMADON, GUL KANA

I t was a summer day, hot and drear. Putrid refuse and filth clogged every nook and cranny of Amadon's grim dock district, and it disgusted Tala Bronachell in every way. But she would never go back to the castle. She had finally escaped those confining stone walls that had become her prison. She had spent one whole day of searching her mother's chamber until she finally found it, her way out—a loose stone in the floor beneath the Avlonia-sewn throw rug under her mother's red velvet couch.

The secret ways. She thanked those who had built them. Her escape from Amadon Castle had led her beneath her mother's bedchamber and through many winding dark passages, and then straight on to her own bedchamber. Once safely there, she slipped on her favorite boots and leather leggings, and donned a sturdy black shirt and belt. Lastly, she stuffed a dark cloak under the crook of her arm. Hawkwood's sword was still hidden in the hearth, and she grabbed that too.

She gripped the hilt tightly in hand now, the spiked hilt-guard and long, curved blade hidden under her cloak, realizing that this dirty, sweltering neighborhood might now be her home, the sword her only possession. She stood alone on the muddy cobbled street in front of the Filthy Horse Saloon, cloak and hood concealing her identity. But the cloak and hood also caused her to sweat profusely. The beastly injuries to her flesh—a dozen or so tender scabbed wounds left over from the grand vicar's purification in her mother's baths—stung fiercely. Tala didn't know exactly what had caused her injuries, but she had clawed her way free of the Dayknight sleeping bag and left it shredded. It was that one singular sacrament that had made up her mind to flee the castle for good. She feared Jovan. And she feared Denarius and the quorum of five even more. She had to learn to protect herself. If she could cleanse the church and its leaders from the Five Isles, she would. They were altogether evil in her mind.

Just return my sword to me, Hawkwood had said when he'd cornered her in the red-hazed room where Glade Chaparral had murdered Sterling Prentiss. *And how will I find you?* she'd asked. *The Val-Sadè,* he'd answered before taking his leave. He had promised that if she found him, he would teach her to be an assassin.

And now that was what she sought—the Val-Sadè. Be it man, woman, child, or place, she did not know. She had escaped the castle. Yes. And that was the first step. But as she gazed up at the Filthy Horse's crude sign hanging on rusty hooks over the door, she couldn't shake the feelings of gloom and utter loneliness. Her life had turned to shit. And now she was naught but a vagabond, a gypsy traveler. *"In all your darkest hours, have you ever heard gypsy melodies, such soft melodies that can only stir deep sorrows in your heart?"* The lyrics of her favorite bard's song came suddenly into her head. *"How long shall you wait for the sound of your own awakening gypsy's soul?"*

The grand vicar had actually tried to drown her! And Tala still could not wrap her mind around that. *"Deep sorrows in your heart."* Her vision swam with tears as she tried to focus on the dirty saloon in front of her. Her life was now her own, and all she did now was for herself and herself alone. She wanted to find answers to Lindholf's whereabouts. She wanted to find answer to Lawri's whereabouts. She just wanted answers. She wanted to find Hawkwood. And Jondralyn. And the Val-Sadè.

Or is this all still just part of the Bloodwood's game? The assassin had certainly hinted that everything was connected. It was all so maddening and confusing. But Tala realized then and there that any emotion or danger she might soon face was better than the boring security of Jovan's court and her Silver Guard escorts and Dame Mairgrid's constant scrutiny and being locked away in her mother's cold bedchamber.

The Bloodwood's game was just a continuation of a game Tala had been involved in all her life—escaping Mairgrid's supervision, escaping Glade and Tolz and Alain and Boppard and Seita, escaping the grand vicar and all five of the archbishops and their cruel priesthood prayers and dark rituals. Yes, perilous adventure intrigued her. And she would carry on. The determination buried deep within her own soul bolstered her. Three deep breaths later, fingers of her right hand clenching the hilt of the sword at her belt, she stepped toward the saloon door and pushed.

It opened wide, and she stepped inside to the familiar sights and smells: darkness, smoke, burnt food, pine-pitch, and tar. The Filthy Horse Saloon looked the same as it had before, grim and filthy and buzzing with flies. With a stained rag, the dour-looking barmaid with fair-colored hair wiped down the bar along the left-hand wall. Only a few sailors hunkered over tankards at the dusky tables to the right. Dust trickled from thick timber rafters overhead as one of the burly sailors stood from his drink and approached her immediately. "I know you," he said.

Indeed, she recognized him too, for he was the same cranky sailor who had confronted Glade and Lindholf when they had all come into the saloon before.

"You're that little princess from the castle." He grinned, revealing rotted brown teeth.

"Geoff, you know this lassie?" the barmaid asked, wringing water from the soily brown rag in her hand.

"Aye." The sailor's grin vanished, his uninviting eyes hardened. "Ever since this lassie come in here, there's been naught but trouble for our Delia."

"Still, best we not speak Delia's name again," the serving girl said warily, going back to wiping the bar "'Specially not in front of strangers."

Geoff reached a rough hand forward and shoved the hood back from Tala's face. Tala stepped back a pace, letting her cloak fall open down the center, letting the sword clenched in her fist show now. He chuckled at the sight of the blade. "What is it you want, girl?"

"Well, have you seen Delia of late?" Tala found that her voice shook as she spoke. "Delia would be traveling with a friend. You saw him before, a blond boy with a scarred and burnt face—"

"Best you just turn and march right on out of here, girl," Geoff said, a bleak tone in his voice, a hard tone that brooked no argument. "You speak of things that happened in the arena, things best not spoken of in dockside taverns. If you take my meaning?"

"Have you ever heard of Val-Sadè?" she asked.

"Nope." Geoff's eyes widened slightly, both thumbs now hooked in his belt. "Ain't ever heard of such a thing," he grunted.

"Bollocks," the barmaid said, still scrubbing the bar down. "The *Val-Sadè*? We've both heard tell that ship was haunted."

"Hush!" Geoff barked. "Just hush it up and keep your yapper shut before I ram that disease-ridden rag right down your gullet."

He turned his wrath back on Tala. "And I'll hear no more—"

But Tala was already out the front door and into the streets again, searching.

A light rain fell over the wooden docks and tall riggings of the ships like a sodden blanket. Tala soon feared she would suffocate under her cloak, so damp was the air. Still, she kept the cowl up as she hustled her pace.

The barmaid had mentioned a ship—a *haunted* ship.

But along the length of the dock district's scores of wharves and quays there were hundreds—if not thousands—of ships afloat in the water. The bay was vast, stretching miles in either direction. Some vessels were tied to the docks, but most were moored hundreds of feet out to sea. And as far as she could tell, none of them looked even remotely haunted. Memory Bay was well protected from the tides; every ship bobbed and dipped gently in what few small waves there were, the boats at the docks thumping dully against worn timber, creaking against the boardwalks and straining at their ropes.

Tala headed down one of the longer wooden jetties for a closer look at some of the ships moored farther out in the bay. As her leather boots clapped hollowly against the wood planks, her mind wandered. Hawkwood had offered to train her in his craft, and that was ultimately why she was here. And after making the offer, he had left her alone in the red-hazed room with the cross-shaped altar—alone but for the silver liquid dripping from the ceiling. She had touched that silver. The strange liquid had burned away the very tip of the pinky finger on her right hand. Mad at herself for having acted so recklessly, she chalked the silver up to some foul Vallè alchemy. After all, everything about the Vallè was suspect.

She thought of her conversation with Seita about the secrets of Lawri's Ember Gathering—a vexing conversation, to be sure. It was as if Seita had played a game of words and deception like the Bloodwood. All meant to *confuse my mind.* And Seita had wielded a black dagger against Glade in the corridor. A Bloodwood dagger. *Or is Seita's father, Val-Korin, the Bloodwood who stalked me?* That cold thought had followed Tala for some time now. *Can he be using his daughter against me? Is that why the Vallè princess desired to be friends one day and then disappeared the next, only to return again?* These thoughts plus a hundred others pooled in her mind, creating an ever-growing puddle of confusion and suspicion.

"From afar she looks like a skeleton, no?" a voice said from behind her.

Tala's heart failed a beat as she turned. The stooped figure on the quay behind her was a frightful sight—a rickety old man in ragged and moldering brown clothes that smelled of salt water and brine. A thin gray beard and stringy gray eyebrows covered the fellow's leathery, sun-wrinkled face. And the most disturbing thing about him—he had only one good eye, the other naught but a dark, empty socket, cavernous and hollow. One of the man's crooked fingers pointed out into the bay. "Like a skeleton, that ship, no?"

Tala followed his one-eyed gaze. Several hundred feet from the end of the dock was a half-sunken ship of wind-scarred timber listing sideways in the bay. From the intricate wooden scrollwork on the starboard railing and masthead, it looked like an old Vallè pirate ship, a very large old Vallè pirate ship. It was rolled halfway onto its side in the water, its mainmast, mizzenmast, and fore lancing out above the water at three separate but precarious angles. Tattered sails, ratlines, and bowlines dangled limply into the water like torn cobwebs from every crosspiece and spar.

The Val-Sadè! Tala's eyes were fixed on the half-drowned wreck. There were no other ships anchored near this skeleton ship. It had to be the place she sought.

"That boat be cursed," the old man said, his voice sounding from a distance now.

"Do you know the name of the ship?" she asked, turning back toward the one-eyed old man behind her.

But nobody was there. Tala's heart failed another beat. Other than the gentle waves lapping against the dock, the sea was calm, the quay on all sides empty.

She looked back into the bay at the sunken ship. *Does my own mind play tricks on me now?* She felt her body grow heavy with sweat. Tala shed the dark cloak, glad to be rid of it. She kept hold of Hawkwood's sword. It was heavy in her grip. Yet she would not leave it behind. Her mother had taught her to swim at a young age, but could she swim two hundred feet gripping a sword in hand? And after her experience in the baths with the grand vicar and archbishops, the thought of water filled her with no small measure of terror.

Still, she kicked off her boots and wasted no time in diving headfirst into Memory Bay.

**

The journey proved about as arduous as she'd imagined. Every injury on her flesh stung, salty water clawing at the wounds. And by the time she reached the ship, both her arms and wrists were weary, fingers numb and nearly unusable from the pain of gripping the sword so tightly. She had managed to switch the weapon from hand to hand as she swam. And she had made it. Another baptism of a sort, another purification, but this one of her own volition, a purification not meted out by the grand vicar.

The ship was rolled nearly halfway onto its side. The hull of the ship jutted from the water but offered nothing but slippery rough wood and barnacles. She swam around the prow of the vessel. The slanted deck of the ship dipped far into the water and was lined with all manner of ropes and chains dragging in the swells around her. She swam toward the center of the deck, pulling herself along with help of the ropes and chains. Soon the thick mast of the ship angled out above her, tattered sails a-flutter in the breeze. She spotted an open hatch in the canted floor of the deck not far above. The opening was near the base of the mast.

Bobbing in the water against the slippery, angled deck of the ship, she carefully slid the tip of the sword's blade deep into a crack in the wood and took a moment to just hang on to the hilt and rest. She breathed hard. It had been a difficult swim.

Then one of the ropes smacked into the side of her face.

"Grab ahold," a familiar voice urged. "Grab ahold now. Hurry. And don't forget the sword." It was the one-eyed old man from the dock.

Tala still struggled against the slanted deck clinging to the hilt of the sword. She looked up at the wooden slope looming above, following the trail of the rope. The raggedy old man was up there. His wrinkled, one-eyed face was staring down at her from the open hatchway above. His leathery hands gripped the other end of the rope that dangled near her face. "Grab ahold," he urged. "I will pull you up."

Tala knew she could either founder against the deck, or grab the rope and climb. She wrapped her hand in the rope, gripping it tight. "And don't forget the sword," the old man urged again.

Tala yanked the blade free of the wood. And then she felt herself half climbing, half being pulled up the pitched banking of the deck, the man hauling on the rope from above. When she reached the rim of the hatchway, she grabbed ahold. But the one-eyed man had disappeared be-lowdecks somewhere. Pulling herself up into the opening of the hatch-way, Tala peered down. She could see nothing but blackness.

"Drop the sword," the man said from the dark. "Drop the sword to me, yes." Tala dropped the sword down into the blackness below. "Good. Good," she heard the one-eyed fellow say. Tala swung her own legs up and over the lip of the hatchway and then lowered herself carefully down into the darkness, feet dangling as she clung to the frame of the hatchway above. Maneuvering without the sword was easier.

"Just let go of it," the old man urged. "The floor is flat and only just below you."

Tala let herself drop, and landed safely on a flat surface as promised. Brushing herself off, she cursed herself for being so foolishly trusting. *What are you doing here, you silly, silly girl? Have you learned nothing?*

"The ship is tilted on the outside," the old man said from somewhere in the darkness, "Though the walls lean weirdly, rest assured the floors are level and safe. Now follow me."

"I can't see you," Tala said to the shadows.

There was a loud clapping sound and a small flame appeared. The flame rested in the palm of the one-eyed man's right hand, his face cut and wrinkled with dark shadow in the flickering light. He scurried off into the gloomy bowels of the vessel. Tala followed him, noticing he still had Hawkwood's sword gripped in his left hand. He led her down a crooked narrow passage, glancing back at her twice to make sure she still followed.

But when he turned back to her the third time, the face she saw was not that of an old man, but rather the shimmering ashen image of her sister, Jondralyn, one eye missing, the eye socket a foreboding black hole in her head.

Tala stopped, her feet refusing to move, her mind screaming in grave warning. *The* Val-Sadè? she remembered the barmaid saying. *We've both heard tell that ship was haunted.*

"Follow me, Tala," the man said. His voice even sounded like

Jondralyn's. He was naught but a shadowy form in front of her now. "Nothing to fear down here. You are safe, Tala. Trust me."

"Who are *you*?" Tala asked. "How do you know my name?"

The ghostly visage of her sister returned, drifting toward her quickly. There was a black eye patch over her missing eye now and a familiar scar running the length of her beautiful pale face. "It is me, Tala. Your sister, Jondralyn. Do you not recognize me?"

Tala backed away, aching hands fumbling for the sides of the crooked corridor, hoping to grasp hold of something, anything that would help her whirl around and flee this cursed place. But everything was so slanted and out of place. *You silly girl, following a stranger into a haunted ship. These wraiths will kill you in here and nobody will know!*

There was another flash of light to her left. A hand gripped hers, viselike, yanking her sideways through an open door and into a room of lantern light. Tala found herself standing in a small, well-lit galley with tilted walls that smelled of strong pine-pitch and heavy timber. And she was standing face-to-face with Hawkwood.

Under dark locks of hair, the Sør Sevier man's piercing eyes bit into hers. Then the corners of his mouth curled into a mischievous, but sly grin. "I see Jondralyn's disguise was sufficient enough to fool even her own sister."

Jondralyn stepped into the room and sidled up next to Hawkwood. "She brought your sword." Jondralyn held up the weapon. "I knew she would."

"Splendid." Hawkwood took the blade.

When his gaze returned to Tala it was once again severe, his voice now humorless. "Your training in the art of subtly, surprise, and death begins today, Tala Bronachell, for as Jondralyn has proven, a Bloodwood relies on illusion to survive."

Hawkwood took her hand and led her into a more expansive chamber empty of all furnishings. This new room's timbered floor was also strangely level and flat, though its walls and bulkheads were all still canted to the side, lanterns dangling.

"Tala?" Lawri Le Graven's unmistakable voice sounded from behind Tala, soft and lilting. "Is that you?"

Tala whirled and faced her cousin. Lawri stood in a black dress in the darkest corner of the room, one shoulder leaning against a tilted bulkhead. A dagger was clutched in Lawri's good hand. Her ashen face and tawny hair appeared almost ghostlike in the dim light of the ship's bowels. Her left arm was hidden in the shadows of the corner.

"What are you doing here?" Tala asked in a breathless gasp.

"Don't you know?" Lawri tilted her head to the side. "I'm training to be a cold-blooded assassin, like Jondralyn, like you."

Cold-blooded assassin. Tala's mind froze with fear.

"Look what's happened to me now, Tala." Lawri stepped out from the shadowy corner and into the light. The white bandages that typically covered the stump of Lawri's left arm were gone, and in their place was an exquisitely polished silver gauntlet.

Tala sucked in a rushed gasp of breath. The scaled arm bracers of the gauntlet appeared *molded* to the flesh of Lawri's arm just below the elbow. And red glowing light seemed to pulse and flow in rippling waves over the gauntlet's intricate leaf-shaped scales. There were holes in each of the gauntlet's fingertips, as if something was meant to be screwed into them . . .

. . . or as if something were meant to grow out of them . . .

Tala felt the beastly claw marks on her own flesh burn.

And then cold horror coiled itself around her heart when the fingers of Lawri's gauntlet creaked to life and began to move.

Scripture is naught but insanity and contradictions: love and hate, peace and war. For any man who claims to speak for god is insane. All the time. Every time. Thus religion is naught but allegory and fable, and in the end answers nothing, leaving the mind and soul bereft and empty when it thinks it is full.
—THE BOOK OF THE BETRAYER

CHAPTER EIGHT

CRYSTALWOOD

8TH DAY OF THE FIRE MOON, 999TH YEAR OF LAIJON

WYNIX, WYN DARRÈ

Chains rattled as the sailboat thudded against something solid, jolting Krista Aulbrek awake. The first thing she noticed was that the sickness from the poisons on Hans Rake's daggers had mostly dissipated. Borden Bronachell and the dwarf, Ironcloud, had kidnapped Krista, trying to conceal her gagged and bound at the bottom of their boat during their escape from dungeons of Rokenwalder. She had initially thought Hans had come to the wharf to rescue her. He had tried to murder her instead. Bleary-eyed and blinking, Krista raised her head as the portside of the sailboat scraped against a long wharf of thick timber that stretched out before her into the distance. Prison garb still clung to her sweaty, unwashed body. She could smell herself, and she did not smell good.

Both her travel companions, Borden Bronachell and the dwarf Ironcloud, steadied the boat as it eased into the quay. *"Squateye,"* she hissed under her breath, cursing the dwarf who now called himself Ironcloud.

Hans Rake still rode in the small white skiff behind Krista's. Their two boats were still connected by a length of chain. The bulldog, Café Colza, was in the boat with the dangerous Bloodwood. They had been traveling across the Straits of Sevier for sixteen days now. Land was a welcome sight.

Rising up against the gray horizon beyond the long dock was a tree-studded hill town of haphazardly placed stone buildings and houses, all with matching umber-colored roofs of tile. Atop the emerald hill of tree, grass, and shrub, silhouetted against the clouded sky, was a squat castle seemingly hewn of one solid piece of giant gray stone. Krista had never been off the island of Sør Sevier. But if this was Wynix she looked upon, then Wyn Darrè was a much greener place than her homeland, and a much less populace place too, for there was nobody around but for one lone blond boy at the end of the deserted wharf. There weren't even any other boats tied to the quay. Still, the brilliance of the foliage crawling up the hill and buildings behind the boy was so green it almost hurt her eyes.

She continued to blink away the sleep, orienting herself properly in the boat. Her hands were still tied with rope, feet also bound, but she was soon standing. She just wanted a bath more than anything. Well, maybe she wanted to run a dagger across Squateye's fat neck more than anything.

The blond-haired young man at the far end of the wharf held the reins of five roans in hand. The tall horses stood round-eyed and alert behind him, all five saddled, all five geared up with bedrolls, leather packs, and weapons. Krista could see the cross-shaped silhouette of a black Dayknight sword jutting up over the back of one of the horses. A thick-hafted battle-ax was strapped to another one of the roans.

Ironcloud's voice cut the silence. "I told you, Borden, Culpa's cousin was dependable. Tyus Barra is the truest of friends. I knew he would be waiting here for us, mounts packed and ready."

The boy in the distance waved, hitched the five horses to the nearest rail, and hurried up the long wooden dock toward them.

"Bear in mind," Ironcloud continued, "Tyus Barra cannot speak. He had his tongue cut out by two of Aeros Raijael's henchmen, Enna Spades and Hammerfiss, at the Battle of Kragg Keep. Spades offered him a deal and he lost. Leastwise that's what Seabass claims. Never did get the whole story from the boy himself, as he can't talk that well anymore. Mostly hand motions or written notes. And he never was that talkative to begin with. Plus, he was never very well educated, so his writing can be spotty. Just know that he is loyal, though he cannot speak."

"The most loyal kind of friend is the silent one," Borden said softly. "I'm just glad he is here. Let's make sure we secure what weapons Tyus Barra brought us before we pull the Bloodwood's boat to the dock."

Krista didn't know much about Seabass. At least there was nothing she could remember. The poison on Hans' daggers had muddled her memory on some things. From what she could recall, Seabass was a dwarf with important information and Tyus Barra would be guiding Borden and Ironcloud and their two captives to him. How far away he lived she did not know.

Hans Rake and the bulldog were perched at the prow of their own boat now, both poised and ready. Hans still wore his Bloodwood leathers, stark and black against the horizon as his skiff bobbed in the light surf some twenty feet away, the chain connecting the two boats now drooping into the water.

Borden leaped onto the dock and tied the sailboat to the nearest piling.

"Borden Bronachell," he introduced himself to Tyus Barra. They shook hands upon greeting. Tyus carried a double-edged shortsword of his own in a sheath at his hip. He was clothed in simple woolen pants reinforced with boiled leather armor at both the knees and thighs. His shirt was long-sleeved and black under a leather-armored jerkin of stiff elk hide studded with dull gray iron loops draped over each shoulder. Under his mop of curly blond hair was a round, boyish face. He did not look a day over sixteen, though she knew from Ironcloud's previous description that he was nearly twenty.

"Run back and get the sword from off that horse if you will," Borden instructed the boy. Tyus headed back up the dock toward the horses.

Krista knew why Borden wanted the sword. She looked back at Hans Rake and Café Colza. She detected relief on Hans' face, relief that they were again near dry land. She felt that same relief. But she was worried about other things now. *Will he launch another escape attempt? Do I help him if he does? Or will he try and stab me again?*

She did not know whose side her Bloodwood partner was truly on. *Once I was known as Crystalwood. But do I call myself that now? And do I call him Shadowwood?* Together Black Dugal had called them his most dangerous weapons. But whose side she was on now? It all came back to her in a rush of pain. Her murder of King Aevrett Raijael. Her time in the dungeons of Rokenwalder. Her betrayal by Black Dugal and Hans Rake. Her Sacrament of Souls.

Krista had worked it out early in life, how to mask whatever pain she felt, how to dig a hole in both her heart and head to bury any pain beyond bearing. For five years she had hidden within Dugal's Caste, taking on another persona. Playing the role of Crystalwood in her Sacrament of Souls had been the perfect way to hide who she truly was and what she truly felt. Still, she'd had no notion of the cost it would exact. *Am I a good person or bad?* And that not knowing was the worst.

Not knowing where her father was. Not knowing who she was. Not knowing how she had felt about her first-ever murder. In fact, she didn't know which murder *had* been her first. Dugal had nailed a row of corpses to a fence line in a cornfield south of Badr, a dozen dead men and women. He then had her pull the fingernails and toenails from each corpse, had her remove them as slowly and deliberately as she could, just for practice. And then he had her scoop the eyes from each and remove their tongues. Then he had her stab each in the heart a half-dozen times whilst reciting some ancient prayer to Dashiell Dugal, the patron god of all assassins.

Dugal had told her only later that day that three of the corpses had actually been healthy living humans when she had started on them, drugged to seem dead. *Did they feel every manner of torture I performed on them?* Krista had never asked that question. She had killed that day without even feeling a thing, and then she had paid alms to Dashiell Dugal.

Her master's subterfuge had at first shocked her, then numbed her. And she had mostly buried those events as deep into her soul as she could and kept them there.

A Bloodwood must become fatherless!

Borden Bronachell had hinted at her heritage. And the evidence that Gault Aulbrek was not her real father kept mounting. *Or is it all a lie?* She still kept the blue ribbon Gault had gifted her tied around her ankle. *Because he* is *my father!* Feelings she could not quite understand raced through her simply by looking at Hans Rake on the skiff tied behind hers. She could still feel traces of the poison from Hans' blades working within her, stirring her brain. *Get control over yourself if you aim to survive.*

When Tyus Barra returned, he came bearing a thick-handled battle-ax with a leather-wrapped handle and the large black longsword with the black opal-inlaid pommel that Borden had requested. Tyus Barra handed the latter weapon to Borden, and the sword seemed to fit easy and perfect in his grip, like he was born to wield it. Tyus Barra gave the battle-ax to the dwarf.

Borden stepped back into the boat. With a flick of the sword tip, Borden sliced the rope binding Krista's ankles. With one hand he motioned her out of the boat. Reluctantly she assented, stepping stiffly onto the dock, legs now free, but sore to the point that she could scarcely move. She stumbled. Tyus Barra reached out to help her. She jerked away from him. His blue eyes met hers, then glanced away bashfully. Krista felt herself scowling over the exchange.

Still in the sailboat, Borden leaned over the gunwale and began hauling on the chain, pulling Hans' skiff slowly toward them. The Dayknight sword was leaning against the side of the boat within arm's reach.

The Bloodwood's hair, shaved above his ears on both sides of his head, was an inch-high row of blond spikes, limp, matted, and dirty from the long journey. The Suk Skard clan tattoos that blanketed both sides of his scalp were a dull blue in the cloudy atmosphere. Still, his lithe figure cut a swaggering air as it always did.

"Make any attempt to fight us and I will not hesitate to spill your guts all over into the bay." Borden's sharp gaze was hard as flint.

"Your energy is wasted on idle threats, old man." Hans held out his arms in supplication. "I have no wish to fight you."

Ironcloud stepped into the boat next to Borden, the thick haft of his ax in both hands. "Why should we believe anything you say?" the dwarf asked. "You jumped into shark-infested waters to try and kill us some seven days ago."

Hans' smile was soft and smooth. "I'm a changed person. I now see life differently."

Hans was calm, but the drooling bulldog next to him looked ready to jump straight onto the dock at any moment. His stumpy tail wagged with anticipation.

Once the boats were side by side, Borden lifted the sword and put the tip of it up to Hans' throat, saying, "Hold out your hands and let the dwarf secure you before you take one step off that boat."

Café Colza didn't listen or hesitate. In two bounds, the dog was off the small skiff, scrambling over the sailboat and onto the dock, his powerful little legs churning toward Wynix. The rusted spiked collar around his neck matched the umber-colored roofs of the town he was barreling toward.

"Damned dog." Ironcloud set his ax aside and grabbed a length of thin rope.

"Tie me up if you wish." Hans held out his hands for the dwarf. "That rope won't hold me, but you can go through the motions if you'd like. Like I already told you, I've no wish to fight you."

"Trust no one." Ironcloud bound the Bloodwood's wrists together with the rope.

Hans stepped calmly from one boat to the next and then up onto the dock without incident, Borden's sword tip at his back the entire way. Hans looked at Krista, his cold gaze faintly streaked with red. Then he smiled. "I doubt they have any Blood of the Dragon awaiting me. I surely could use some." His smile did not soften his harsh, thin face.

Tyus dug through his pocket and handed Ironcloud a folded note. The dwarf read it, then chuckled. He glanced up at Borden and then read it aloud. "'I've waited here from sunup to sundown daily for the past moon.'"

"He is the truest of friends." Borden grasped Tyus Barra congenially by the shoulder. "How long did you have this note prepared for us and waiting in your pocket?"

Tyus Barra shrugged, bashful blue eyes falling on Krista again.

"He thinks you're pretty," Hans laughed. "You might have a new suitor."

Tyus looked away from her swiftly, face flushed with red.

"How is Seabass?" the dwarf asked the boy. "Still squirreled away in that tree house near Sigard Lake? Still feeding crops to the goats and chickens on that farm?"

Tyus Barra nodded.

"Then we've a long way to travel, if we wish to join him," the dwarf said. "We needn't tarry." Ironcloud led the group up the dock. Tyus Barra fell in on the right side of Tala, Hans on the left. Borden walked behind them, sword ready. Café Colza Bouledogue came running back down the dock, slobbering and waddling to a wheezing stop next to Hans. Then he too followed the group.

As they walked, Hans looked at Krista. "You stink worse than the dog."

Krista winced. She knew how she smelled. "Unless you know of a warm soapy tub nearby, shut up."

"If there's a tub where we're going, I'm sure Tyus would happily bathe you."

"And I'll happily gut you." She glared.

Still walking step for step with Tala, Tyus was blushing even more now. The boy might be mute, but he could hear well enough. And Hans was back to his old self. Annoying. Tala asked him, "So why will you not fight Borden and the dwarf now? Why so sudden a change of heart, Hans?"

His smile did not fade. "The question you should be asking, Crystalwood, is why are they keeping us alive?"

She *had* wondered about that.

Borden prodded the tip of the sword into Hans' back. "When we reach the horses, you will each be tied to a mount of your own. And those mounts will both be tied to mine. Though you will be mounted, you will not escape."

"So there's to be no bath for Crystalwood?" Hans drawled. "She stinks."

"Just do as I say," Borden ordered.

"I wouldn't mind a bath myself," Hans went on, eyeing the horses. "Oh, and thanks for the horses. At least you're not gonna force us to walk clear across Wyn Darrè."

"I'd force you to walk," the dwarf turned. "But speed is of the essence now, so fortunately, you ride."

Hans bowed to him, smiling. "Most gracious of you."

"Hush it already." Borden again prodded Hans forward with the tip of his sword.

"And what exactly will you do if I continue to talk?" Hans asked, trying to wiggle away from the sword. "What if I do nothing but jabber and jabber the entire journey? Will you cut my tongue out?" He then opened his mouth wide and waggled his tongue at Tyus Barra, licking his lips, making a show if it.

Tyus would not meet Krista's gaze, holding his eyes to the dock, as if truly embarrassed by Hans' cruel jest. But Hans didn't even acknowledge the boy's embarrassment. He was again focused on Borden. "Fact is, I'll talk all I please, Borden Bronachell, for I know very well you won't kill me. You won't kill Crystalwood. You won't even slice out our tongues."

Borden continued prodding Hans with the tip of his sword. "And why don't you think we will kill you?" he asked.

"Because you need both of us alive," Hans answered. "Because you need us to assassinate Aeros Raijael before Fiery Absolution."

Timeless is the creature in disguise. Five Cauldron Born shall arise, leading the way through blood and sacrifice toward the Dragon, their master. For only the hottest fires of the deep can purify the Skulls. Only then shall Absolution be made one with Viper. Only then shall one speak through crystal vision and crack open the world, only then shall one speak through the Claw and raise those trapped in the underworld up and over the bones of the human dead.
—THE ANGEL STONE CODEX

CHAPTER NINE
LINDHOLF LE GRAVEN

9TH DAY OF THE FIRE MOON, 999TH YEAR OF LAIJON
EAST OF SAVON, GUL KANA

I t was near dusk. Gault Aulbrek rode one of the stolen horses. Lindholf Le Graven and Delia shared the other. Together they wended their way through a thicket of oaks and out into the fields above. There were sheep gathered in the distance, white and fluffy, bells tinkling, a lone farmer stacking bales of hay. Seeing the farmer, Gault guided them back down into the dark ravine below before they were spotted.

It had been three days since Lindholf had watched Gault slay the two Dayknights with *Afflicted Fire*. Three days since the men's corpses had slowly sunk into the river. Three days since they had stolen the dead men's dun-colored destriers. It had also been three days since they had stolen the dead men's Dayknight armor—foul armor that one of the knights had stained with shit when he died. Lindholf had cleaned and polished the armor over and over. But he still smelled its fetid stench.

He needed relief. He needed something. How many days had he been without Shroud of the Vallè? He could not remember. But it was almost more than he could bear. The addiction clawed at his mind daily. He thought of the white powder more than he thought of his own parents, or his own sister. He only wondered where Lawri was part of the time, whereas he wondered where Shroud of the Vallè was all the time. *What would they think of me now? Naught but a pathetic, drug-addled fugitive following an enemy knight.* And onward they had traveled toward Savon, journeying over rolling hills and flatlands, skirting farms bordered with hedgerow and rock, crossing roads both straight and crooked and powdered with dust—dust he could not snort up his nose.

In the last three days they had run into no other Dayknights or Silver Guards. They had only garnered the cursory glance of the occasional journeyman or farmer. They camped at night in forests of dark oak or old abandoned barns, eating what ample foodstuffs the two dead Dayknights had fortunately left in their saddlebags. Being clad in Dayknight armor had its advantages in that most folks generally wished to avoid them. Gault cut a fine figure in the armor, sitting tall and stern on his destrier. Whereas Lindholf looked utterly loutish, or so he imagined. He knew he was a slouch on the horse, Delia clinging to his back.

At least now they had a plan. A destination. An inn and tavern called the Preening Pintail in Savon. It was a little inn at the base of a square stone tower, where Delia claimed they could find safe lodgings. It was an inn her father did trade with from time to time. The barmaid claimed to have stayed there many times. She claimed the owner, a man named Rutger, was desirous that she move to Savon and work for him.

"Rutger always had a bit of a thing for me," Delia had mentioned on more than one occasion. "Ever since I was a little girl."

They were still some days away from Savon, though. Their journey had gone slowly, despite the addition of their two mounts. Gault preferred to take a meandering path over hills and through wooded areas rather than stick to the roads. But the landscape between Amadon and Savon was well populated. No matter where they traveled, they always seemed to come upon some small farm or woodsman's lodge.

Just now Gault led them along a crystal clear brook that skirted the low ridgeline of the shady ravine. A tumbledown wooden barn leaned against the rough outcrop of rock ahead. The barn and its surrounds looked long abandoned.

Gault reined up at the dusty barn, dismounted, and removed his black Dayknight helm, hooking it to the saddle horn. He strode cautiously toward the broken-down structure, the long white sword, *Afflicted Fire*, firmly in hand. He left the black Dayknight sword clanking at his hip. "We'll stay here tonight," he announced after nosing around the place and finding it clear.

"Maybe we can still make it to Savon tonight," Delia said, worry in her voice.

"Savon is days away," Gault answered.

"But we've been traveling for days. We should already be there."

"Yet we are not," Gault said. "Besides, I don't like the sound of this Preening Pintail you keep talking about. I don't think it wise to stay in taverns and inns full of people who could recognize us."

Delia lowered herself from the saddle behind Lindholf, the slanting rays of the sun catching fire to her face and auburn hair. The crossbow, *Blackest Heart*, was strapped to her back. Lindholf carried the shield, *Ethic Shroud*. Gault kept the three angel stones with him. He was their leader. And Lindholf didn't like it. *Seita wants me to kill him!* But he didn't even know how to do that.

Delia followed the Sør Sevier knight toward the barn. Lindholf couldn't help but think back to their time together in her bedroom in the back of the Filthy Horse Saloon, a room that had glowed so softly with yellow light. How Delia had undressed him and called him *my love*. How she had pulled him down onto her bed. How she had promised him Shroud of the Vallè. How it had all been a lie.

The backs of her fingers had so tenderly stroked his face. *I knew you before we met,* she had said. *I knew we would become lovers.* And her wide blue eyes had glowed back at him with frank interest. She'd kissed him on the cheek, brushed her tongue over his ear, her voice a sultry whisper. Her body melted into his as she pressed down with her hips, moving ever so slowly atop him. *But it was all a lie!* Still, even in acting, she had filled a void within him, cured a loneliness, if only for a moment. *If only for a false moment, I would give her the world. . . .*

Lindholf slid from the saddle and removed his helm, letting the cool breeze of early evening flow over his face, letting it wake him from his utter stupidity of thought.

He secured *Ethic Shroud* to the saddle and followed his travel companions toward the barn, feeling the hilt of his own Dayknight sword. Though it had been just a few days wearing the black-lacquered armor, Lindholf was growing used to wearing another man's clothes, a dead man's clothes. Though the fit was wrong. The armor was large for him. He felt like he was drowning in it. And it still smelled of shit. But Gault had been right: stealing it had been the correct thing to do. It was all that would keep them safe.

The barn itself was a hollow plank-wood structure and empty—though a lone rabbit bounded from in front of the strange building and dashed between Gault's legs as he swung open the rickety door. All three of them stepped into the dusty gloom, surprised to find a second wooden door across from them. The second door was of a more solid make, its frame fashioned of rough masonry and set directly into the rock face of the cliff wall. It was connected with two rusted iron hinges on the left, and a small iron lock on the right was fastened shut.

"A cellar of some sort carved into the cliff." Gault's voice echoed in the dim barn, coarse and deep. "Perhaps there's tack and rope we can use within. Even a burlap sack to carry these cumbersome weapons would help." He turned to Delia. "Grab a torch and flint from my saddlebag, would you?"

The barmaid scampered from the barn and back to Gault's horse as ordered, eagerness in her step. Her enthusiasm to fulfill any task the Sør Sevier man set her to stuck in Lindholf's craw like rotten apples. Delia practically doted on Gault nightly, preparing his food by campfire, laying out his bedroll in the smoothest of spots, making sure her own bedroll was always nearer his and not Lindholf's.

Fact was, Gault was the reason they were still alive and free, and both

Delia and Lindholf knew it. And Delia had been making herself more amiable to the bald man ever since he had saved her from rape at the hands of the dirty slaves in the bowels of Riven Rock Quarry. But her behavior was almost to the point of blind worship now. And Lindholf feared where the barmaid's worship of the man might eventually lead.

Delia returned with both torch and flint. Gault struck the pitch swiftly to light, and Delia held the burning torch aloft. The Sør Sevier man then pried the small iron lock from the door with the hard white tip of *Afflicted Fire*. The lock made a clicking sound and the door in the cliff swung open, its two rusted hinges screeching.

Gault thrust the torch into the dark opening.

"Oh," Delia exclaimed softly at what she saw.

It wasn't the simple storage cellar cut into the cliff Lindholf was expecting, but rather an entire room of stone as large as Tala Bronachell's bedchamber. It was also full of old furnishings. Lindholf followed Gault and Delia into the chilly space, sizing it up with a wary eye. *Who lives here?* With what pallid light came streaming into the room from the open door, combined with Gault's torch, Lindholf could see most every corner of the room just fine. There was a dust-covered four-post bed against the far wall, an even dustier divan just in front of that. Several wooden crates lined the left wall, along with a wooden table and many overturned stools. In the back corner were stacks of farming equipment: saddles, harnesses, iron buckets, and several busted wagon wheels. With so much dust covering everything, it was clear the room hadn't seen use in moons, if not years.

"Oh," Delia exclaimed again, blue eyes dancing at the sight of an iron tub sitting over a cold stone fire pit carved into the middle of the floor. Her dimples accentuated a hidden little smile at the corner of her mouth. "Oh, my. A hot bath is in order now."

Lindholf felt his heart plummet at the girl's gleeful reaction to the tub. For some unexplainable reason, he felt nothing good could come of a tub.

"Place hasn't seen use in ages," Gault grunted. "I reckon it's safe. Yes, we'll hole up here for the night. It is a good spot. We can secure the horses inside the barn and bring all the weapons and supplies in here with us." His hard eyes met Lindholf's. "But one of us shall have to stand guard outside the barn at all times."

"I can take first watch," Lindholf said in an attempt to be of some use, any use.

"No, I'll take first watch," Gault countered.

"And we can build a fire under that tub," Delia said, wide eyes still focused on the iron tub. "And take a hot bath."

**

By the light of a torch they found, their dinner of radish, jerky, and sourdough bread was eaten in silence. Then Gault stepped outside to stand first watch of the night, the Dayknight sword at his hip his chosen weapon. He left *Afflicted Fire*, *Ethic Shroud*, and *Blackest Heart* inside the cave with Delia and Lindholf. He left the pouch with the angel stones with them too. It was the first time the Sør Sevier man had left the weapons and stones alone with anyone but himself. Gault had also found a fairly large canvas sack, announcing it would be used to haul the weapons in from now on. And that was where they all now rested.

Once Gault was outside, Delia cleaned out the dusty iron tub with an old blanket she found stuffed in a crate, polishing it until it nearly sparkled. She then began gathering up all the wooden chairs and stools she could find and broke them apart, then stuffed them into the stone fire pit under the tub.

With nothing else to do, Lindholf took all the weapons out of the canvas and spread the angel stones out on the stone floor in front of each weapon. For the longest time he had been trying to plumb their secrets, daring not to touch them, keeping each stone safe within its black silk. In fact, neither Gault nor Delia had ever laid a hand on the stones. It was as if something in their very essence was screaming, *Do not touch!*

As for the weapons, he knew where the shield had come from. But he oft wondered how Seita had come upon the other two—the sword and the crossbow.

Afflicted Fire was a spectacular item indeed. The sword was as long as Delia was tall, with a ruby of deep red color set into its white pommel.

The weapon's hilt and crescent-moon-shaped hilt-guard were both carved of one solid piece of ivory or walrus bone—Lindholf couldn't tell which. He knew that the tusks of the walrus were where most ivory came from. But it would have taken one huge walrus to produce a cross-piece so astonishing. The blade itself seemed forged of some mysterious silver-and-ivory mix, for the translucent white veins twisting and twining in the silver depths seemed to pulse with some faint red glow.

Blackest Heart was even more vexing. Over the last few days, Lindholf had marveled at its elegant beauty and perfect mechanisms. It too seemed to be carved of one piece of mysterious solid black wood. On Rockliegh Isle, Gault had made mention that the crossbow was carved of a type of wood he had never before seen, yet it was the finest bow he had ever laid eyes upon. Gault also said he could not imagine what type of quarrel or bolt fit its foreign mechanisms. Lindholf hadn't a clue either. Seita had claimed that only Vallè quarrels would fit it.

Ethic Shroud was the strangest of them all. Again, like *Afflicted Fire*, the glorious white shield appeared to be fashioned of the most brilliantly large chunk of walrus tusk Lindholf had ever imagined existed. *Or some ancient monstrous otherworldly bone!* A pearl-colored inlay in the shape of a gleaming cross covered the length and breadth of the shield. The inlay was even more mystifying than the shield itself. Lindholf doubted even the most polished Riven Rock marble could produce such brilliance. Like undulating waves of water, the peculiar substance that made up the cross inlay was pure magic, alive with light.

And when Lindholf picked each of them up, they each seemed to vary in weight at any given time. It had been like that since the beginning, depending on who held which item and when. They never weighed the same. Gault seemed most comfortable with the sword, Delia the cross-bow, and Lindholf the shield.

In fact, with *Ethic Shroud*, Lindholf felt some essence of wondrous magic within it, as if the artifact was trying to speak to him. It was a feeling that often stole over his body when he touched the shield, a feeling that caused every bone in his body to shudder and every muscle to tighten, the scars on his body to burn. He was becoming as obsessed to the shield as he was to the white powder Val-Draekin and Seita had gotten him addicted to. Eventually he wouldn't be able to live without either.

As for the three angel stones themselves, the white and red were warm and full of life and continually stole his breath, whereas the black stone was cold and lifeless. The red stone was a precious ruby gem of flaming red power. The white stone was like a pure stream of light, as if made of stardust and fire. And the black stone was dusty, dull, and dead. It seemed to want to swallow his soul and never give it back. It seemed wrong.

In the secret ways, he had overheard Roguemoore and Hawkwood talking about the angel stones and the weapons. He recalled them mentioning that Jondralyn was the Princess and that she would one day wield *Afflicted Fire*. He wondered if he shouldn't take the weapons and stones back to Amadon, back to Jondralyn. But he'd have to kill Gault before he could ever do that.

"Will you do me a favor, Lindholf?" Delia asked.

The sound of his name on the barmaid's lips was bright as a dove's call in the darkness, bright as an angel stone. He looked at her, the weapons all but forgotten now. She looked so pretty in the dull light. *If only for a moment with her, I would give her the world.*

"Will you grab two of those buckets"—she pointed—"and help me take them down to the stream and fill them with water?"

"For a hot bath?" he asked.

"I'll even let you take the first bath, if you help me."

The thought of finally getting out of his armor did sound splendid. But that ominous feeling washed over him again when he looked at the tub. He felt his face darken. "I don't think so," he said.

"Please." Her eyes met his pleadingly. "I've cleaned the tub. We can light a fire under it with the wood I gathered, warm up the water. I so want a hot bath."

"It'll take several dozen bucketfuls to fill that thing," he said, shaking his head. "And you can't build a fire in here. Where would the smoke go?"

"Through that hole in the roof." She pointed straight up to a small black hole in the rock above. "Same as where the torch smoke goes."

"Gathering water is just too much work."

Her brow furrowed in anger. "I'll just do it myself then."

Gault Aulbrek stepped back into the stone room, heading for the pile of farm equipment in the corner, Dayknight armor creaking as he moved. "I'll help you," he said, snatching up all three of the buckets. "I need to water the horses anyway." And he marched back out of the room with the buckets in hand.

Lindholf couldn't fathom the man's sudden gallantry in gathering water for the girl. But Delia's face practically glowed. She started breaking up more of the wooden stools, stuffing them under the tub. Lindholf was sick of the way her blue eyes sparked to life whenever the bald man talked to her. Almost as if her heart beat in wild pleasure at his every word, be it curt or nice. Gault was a cold killer and the enemy of their kingdom. A man they soon needed to be rid of. A man Lindholf needed to kill. He reached under his armor, and his fingers curled around the small bundle that held the poisoned black dagger Seita had given him.

He watched Delia ready the firewood. Then let his gaze fall on the weapons of the Five Warrior Angels, ruminating. "Do you feel anything when you touch the crossbow?" he asked Delia, hoping to find a connection with her.

"The crossbow does nothing but frighten me." She did not look up from her task.

They sat in silence. At length, Gault returned with his first two bucketfuls of water. Lindholf figured he must have watered the horses with the third. He dumped them into the tub and retreated from the room again, buckets in hand, heading toward the stream for more.

"You should help him, you know," Delia said.

"I don't want no bath," Lindholf shot back.

"You're useless."

Her words cut deep. He turned away from her. He would not let her see the pain he felt. Gault soon returned with two more bucketfuls of water and poured them into the tub. He then grabbed the torch and jammed it into the fire pit. Flame shot up from the wood gathered under the iron basin. The smoke rose straight up into the hole above the tub, just as Delia said it would.

"Oh," she exclaimed, hand over her mouth in wide wonder as she dipped her hand into the tub. "It will be so warm and cozy soon."

Gault again left the room to fetch her more water. *She's always so demure with the evil Sør Sevier man, yet always guarded and mean with me.* Lindholf almost wanted to puke. *Gault is a bad man. He's a cold killer. He's a villain. Can't she see that I am the nice one? Can't she see that I deserve her more?* Gault soon returned with two more bucketfuls and dumped them into the tub. And the sultry look Delia gave the Sør Sevier man curdled Lindholf's blood.

Before he left for more water, she said, "You should take a bath with me, Ser Gault. I'll be as fresh as a spring flower. And you too will feel oh so much better."

"I'd rather not feel anything, if it's all the same to you," Gault responded, and walked away, buckets in hand, to fetch more water from the brook.

The fourth time he returned to dump water, Delia continued on with her quest. "Even though you think you don't want comfort of any kind, I can make you feel better. I know you, Gault Aulbrek."

"You know nothing of me." He headed for the door again. "You do not know who I am."

"I know you are a killer," she said. He hesitated in the doorway. She went on, "You are a killer, Gault Aulbrek, a killer who finally knows what it's like to be human. All it takes is one look to know that about a man. And though you don't know it, you gave me that look once. And I saw it."

He did not respond, merely stepped through the door and out into the darkness. She looked crestfallen. She wouldn't even look at Lindholf. "I just want someone to soothe me," she said, staring at the back of the closed door.

After a moment, she finally did look at Lindholf. "I still dream of being hung. Every night I dream of it. And I can't escape the feeling of that noose around my neck. I'm so afraid that is how I shall die. I just want someone to hold me. Make the evil dreams go away. Why does he have to be so cruel?"

"He will not *hold* you," Lindholf scoffed. "He clearly hates you."

"He doesn't *hate* me," she said.

A dozen more trips to the stream by Gault and the iron tub was full and heating up swiftly from the fire, steam rising into the room. Gault stood in the doorway, staring into the fire. Delia's fingers traced lazy swirls through the water as it grew warmer and warmer. "A girl always bathes in private," she said, her voice throaty and deep, impatience and longing glinting off her eyes—eyes that were still focused on Gault. "I shall need some time alone, some solitude. You two boys shall have to leave."

A lump of regret immediately formed in Lindholf's gut, and he suddenly wished he could stay and watch her bathe. He stared at Delia, unmoving, until he felt Gault's hand clamp down on his shoulder-plate armor, turning him.

"Leave us," the bald man said sternly, his tone devoid of emotion. "Now."

"Leave you?" Lindholf questioned.

Gault's eyes sharpened. "Stand watch outside the barn until I come to relieve you."

"But I thought—"

Before Lindholf could finish the sentence, Gault grasped him under the armpit and shoved him through the door and then closed it shut behind him.

**

Middle of the night and Lindholf still stood guard just outside the old barn, gazing sullenly into gloom and darkness, grappling with both hurt and anger. Miserable in his own humiliation, he had listened to the Sør Sevier man and the barmaid bathe each other and then make love, each pleasurable sound like a dagger in his heart.

He had polished his armor to take his mind off their coupling. It still

stank, and he couldn't rid himself of its rank odor. But he could only
polish and clean the armor so much before he grew restless. *She only pretended to like me.* That harsh fact he had known for some time now. But
it had never been more evident than tonight. He felt a scathing hate for
Delia. And for Gault. And for himself.

Frustrated, he dragged his fingers through his tangled mass of dirty,
unwashed hair and felt the top of his deformed ears and the side of
his scarred face, wishing he were anyone else but who he was—a misshapen freak. He recalled the Temple of the Laijon Statue and the magnificent marble statue of the great One and Only. A deformed statue,
pointed fey ears chiseled smooth. And yet people traveled the length of
the Five Isles to worship at its feet. And it was a fraud. Or was the flaw
on the altered and deformed ears of the statue just some cruel joke on
the part of the original sculptors? Just as the world had played some
cruel joke on him. The thought filled him with more anger and pain.
And with each heartbeat, it seemed the rage grew. *The world is full of
secrets and deception! Nobody is honest with anyone, least of all honest with
me.* He felt the tears streaming down his cheeks, wet and accusing. He
wiped the wetness away with stiff fingers, cursing his own weakness.
One thing was certain: he could carry on in the self-pity of his own
suffering and disappointment, or he could finally act on his own behalf
and take action.

But do I have it in me to do what I must? He knew he had never been
very brave, very strong. With some trepidation, he reached into his
armor and pulled out the small bundle he had carried since Rockliegh
Isle. He unfolded it carefully, revealing the black dagger Seita had given
him—a dagger that seemed to swallow what little starlight shone from
above. *You must go with him,* the Vallè princess said as she'd handed him
the black blade. *It's a rare gift. So keep it safe. Bring the weapons and angel
stones back to me. This task has fallen to you.* But could he truly murder the
enemy of Gul Kana?

The fact that he now doubted himself was infuriating. It was a lifetime of being around those like Glade Chaparral, Tala Bronachell, King
Jovan, and Sterling Prentiss that had filled him with such uncertainty

about himself. Even his own mother had forsaken him in the end. Even Delia had.

Nobody has ever believed in Lindholf Le Graven.

As he gazed down at the black blade, he mustered what courage he could. *I am a thief,* he told himself, *trained by Seita and Val-Draekin. They believed in me.* And Seita was a Bloodwood. She had taught him stealth, silence, caution, patience.

Gault and Delia had finished with their lovemaking over an hour ago. He could hear Delia's muffled snores even from where he stood outside the barn.

Mind made up, he silently eased open the door to the barn, dagger in hand. He proceeded softly and carefully with each step, slowly moving into the warm cavern Gault and Delia slept in. The room carved of rock was faintly hazed in scarlet, coals still aglow beneath the iron tub.

Delia lay on her stomach under a thin blanket in the center of the four-post bed against the far wall. She snored and mumbled in her sleep, the sound of one distressed with bad dreams. Gault was alone on the divan just in front of Delia's bed. The Sør Sevier knight was on his back, lying in naught but his underclothes, hands folded over his stomach. The Dayknight sword lay at the foot of the divan, next to his Dayknight armor and helm.

As Lindholf crept silently through the room, the scars on his flesh began to burn anew. He desperately wanted to claw away the heat. But whenever the scars flared in pain, he felt it was some great omen. *Embrace the pain.*

That Gault did not share Delia's bed angered Lindholf. She had just made love to him. Numerous times. And still he slept alone. *Had she made love to me even once, I would have held her all through the night and never let go.*

His stomach was a boiling cauldron of nerves. Seita's dagger was still clenched in his hand. *It is poisoned,* the Vallè princess had said. *Stick Gault with it, and he will die within moments.* Standing directly over the sleeping form of Gault Aulbrek, Lindholf felt the sweat that had beaded up on his forehead crawl down into his eyes, stinging. He blinked the moisture away and set his feet solid on the floor, raising the dagger in one curled fist. He watched the man's chest rise and fall to the sound of calm breathing.

The dagger was suddenly shaky in his hand. *Why be afraid? I need but scratch him anywhere with the blade: the stomach, the arm, the top of the head. And with the poison, it will all be over. Why hesitate, you fool?* One deep, silent breath to calm himself, and Lindholf settled his gaze on the bald knight's tranquil pale face.

Then he plunged the knife straight down toward the man's chest.

And Gault's hand shot forth, catching Lindolf's wrist, the tip of the black dagger a hairsbreadth away from his flesh.

Sharp pain shot through Lindholf's entire torso as his arm was twisted to the side, the motion forcing his whole body to the floor in the process, forcing him straight onto his back on the cold stone ground.

Gault's free hand was suddenly pressing down over Lindholf's mouth. "Shhh," the man whispered, kneeling on Lindholf's chest, their faces mere inches apart. Another painful twist of the wrist and the dagger slipped from Lindholf's grip, sliding noiselessly to the floor. "Listen carefully." Gault's quiet voice was harsh and incisive as he picked up the dagger with his free hand. "If you make even the slightest of sounds and wake the girl, I will slice off your cock and boil it in that tub."

Lindholf felt the dagger he'd just wielded pushing down against his own throat, the man's hand still clamped against his mouth. "I'm going to stand now." The knight's whisper was almost soundless. "And when I do, you won't make a peep. Do we understand each other? Even one sound from you and I slice you to ribbons."

Lindholf did his best to nod, head held to the floor by the strength of the man's cold hand. Gault stood, releasing Lindholf, the knife blade no longer at his throat. Lindholf wanted to gasp for breath, but he controlled himself. The bald knight set the Bloodwood dagger on the divan where he had been sleeping, then silently gathered up his Dayknight armor, his sword and helm, too.

Cradling the armor, Gault cast a long glance down at the angel stones and weapons of the Five Warrior Angels spread about the floor where

Lindholf had left them. He spoke quietly, a whisper. "I suggest you take the weapons and stones back to Amadon, make sure they get to Jondralyn Bronachell and no other."

"You're not taking the weapons and stones with you?"

"I've other matters to attend to."

"You're leaving us?" Lindholf asked. "You're not going to kill me?"

"Take care of Delia," Gault said, nodding to the barmaid snoring away on the bed. "She's under your care now, Lindholf Le Graven. She still has nightmares of being hung, of being raped by Glade and his friends, of a lot of things. She's a tender soul and needs your protection."

"But I don't know how to protect anyone," Lindholf said, panicking now.

"I'll leave you with one of the horses," the bald man said. "And you still have the weapons and stones."

Then Gault Aulbrek slipped from the room, the door closing silently behind him.

*War is willful madness and pain. But make no mistake, the demons
of the underworld are real. And they must be slain. For they are at
battle within the living man's mind, more than oft feeding upon
his soul. For only the dead have truly seen the end of war.*
— THE WAY AND TRUTH OF LAIJON

CHAPTER TEN

TALA BRONACHELL

9TH DAY OF THE FIRE MOON, 999TH YEAR OF LAIJON

AMADON, GUL KANA

The wind crooned over the *Val-Sadè*, and waves lapped against the ship's timber all around. The eerie combination of echoing sounds from outside the hull sent a chill through Tala's heart as Hawkwood approached her through the tilted vessel's galley, black daggers twirling in each hand. In the lantern light, the man's dark eyes glinted like shards of ice.

"From a distance, anyone can shoot a longbow and slay their foe with scant effort or feeling," he said. "Swords and axes are a different matter altogether, cold and clean and personal in the killing."

Tala nodded, letting him know she was listening, sweating profusely under her leather pants and tunic. Lawri Le Graven stood not far away, watching with interest.

"But few have it in them to use a knife against another human," Hawkwood continued, daggers still spinning in his hands. "For it is an even more profound thing, a close and intimate way to kill. In just an instant, a dagger can enter a soft belly, slicing through fat and muscle and meat and stirring the vitals to jelly. A small blade makes you aware of the utter vulnerability and tenderness of the flesh you are stabbing and carving into, makes you more aware of the delicacy of life and the shocking red warmness of the blood that will flow hot and alive over your own hand."

He launched his attack on Tala, then whirled at the last moment, lunging for Lawri. The tawny-haired girl backed away, green-tinged eyes lit with fear, her own black dagger slipping from her good hand, hitting the wooden floor of the *Val-Sadè* with a soft clatter. Hawkwood halted his advance, black leather armor glistening in the lamplight as he stood still before her.

"Sorry," Lawri mumbled, her face ashen under damp strands of hair. "I did my knife fighting all wrong." She bent and picked up the dagger with her good hand, white dress fluttering in the dim hull as she moved. "I don't think I have it in me to learn the ways of an assassin. I would surely hate to stab another person, even in self-defense. I know I said that I wanted to learn . . . but now?"

Hawkwood sheathed his own two daggers, looking disappointed.

"We must all learn to defend ourselves." Jondralyn left the comfort of the cushioned wood bench she was sitting on. The bench was fixed to the ship's slanting bulkhead. Tala's older sister wore tan leather breeches and a simple black shirt, black eye patch over her missing eye, the scars on her face still red but nearly healed. "You, me, Tala, we all agreed to let Hawkwood teach us how to fight. And we should not give up." Jondralyn stepped up behind Lawri and helped the girl regain the correct grip on the Bloodwood dagger. "Hold it like this, remember, like Hawkwood showed us."

Tala watched as Jondralyn helped Lawri practice the moves Hawkwood had taught them. But Lawri struggled with the lessons. She had from the start. Her heart was not in it, and the strain was starting to get to her. Tala, Lawri, and Jondralyn had been training nonstop ever since Tala had arrived at the *Val-Sadè* two days ago. They were being educated in stealth, thievery, pickpocketing, disguises, sword and dagger, and even poisons by Hawkwood. And unlike Lawri, Tala had enjoyed the training. It was her path to independence. And though Hawkwood was her teacher, he was not her savior. Tala vowed she would never accept a position of dependence on any man ever again—especially if that man was her brother, Jovan, or any man in the church. Everything she learned from Hawkwood was to kill dishonest men like them. And this hidden junk of a ship was the perfect place to learn.

The old pirate vessel was tipped on its side and half-sunk in Memory Bay, yet surprisingly comfortable to live in. Though all the walls were precariously aslant, someone had fitted the tilted ship with level floors and many galleys and rooms full of comforts: cushioned beds, couches, stoves, benches, bookshelves, books, water closets, iron bathtubs, and lanterns hanging in each room. And most peculiarly, under a wooden hatch in the rotted floor of the boat's easternmost galley was a ladder that plunged into the dark. The ladder emptied out into a damp and dripping tunnel burrowing deep under the bay, a twisting tunnel that split off onto a myriad of other passageways, all of which emptied out into various parts of the city, or so Hawkwood claimed.

Is there no part of Amadon immune to secret ways? Tala had thought the first time she had ventured down the ladder. It seemed not only every person, but every place in the city held secrets, including this old sunken ship.

The important thing was she had found the *Val-Sadè* and she was now safe from the horrors of the castle, safe from Glade Chaparral and the grand vicar, and most of all Jovan's rules and restrictions. And Lawri was also safe. Tala's cousin was certainly unable to return to the castle with the silver gauntlet attached to her arm. And, in Tala's estimation, that was a good thing. Mostly the silver gauntlet was like a dead appendage fixed to the end of Lawri's arm. Tala remembered how Lawri's frail fingers had always been listlessly toying with the bandages around her stump. Now her fingers toyed with the mysterious scaled gauntlet as if she were trying to peel the foreign thing off. But the fact was, the gauntlet was melded to her arm by some strange magic. *Or Vallè sorcery!*

"Does it frighten you as it does me?" Lawri asked, noticing Tala staring at her gauntleted arm.

"I don't understand it." Tala gulped, wondering if it was wrong to admit as much out loud.

"The gauntlet sends me visions," Lawri said. "Visions from the underworld, I believe. I'm another person in those dreams, a knight in green-scaled armor with a silver skull mask and a silver whip. . . ." She paused. "And there are *dragons*. *Green dragons*. And I am their eyes. And the Silver Throne at the bottom of the slave quarry. Five holes drilled deep into the marble, colorful lights like a rainbow rising from beneath . . ."

Tala shuddered. *For aren't those visions similar to mine?* She recalled what she had seen in the pool in her mother's bedchamber.

Hawkwood looked at Lawri. "None of us comprehend the full meaning of the gauntlet. If it is sending you dreams, it is best not to heed them, or read too much into them. If only Roguemoore were here, he would likely have information to share."

Tala missed the gruff old dwarf. And Hawkwood was correct: the dwarf would have known about the gauntlet and Lawri's strange visions.

"Speaking of dreams . . ." Jondralyn faced Lawri. "Do you remember our conversation that day on the battlements of Tin Man Square, when we watched the armies of Gul Kana set out for Lord's Point?"

"I might remember some," Lawri said, suddenly wary. "I don't know."

"Well, I've been thinking of that conversation of late," Jondralyn said. "You claimed you would wear a gauntlet of sparkling silver. And that was before you had even lost your arm. Do you remember?"

"I don't know if I said that," Lawri answered. "But I do remember saying that my brother would stand in the center of the arena with two others, everyone cheering. And then Lindholf would just disappear. *Poof!* And he would be gone. That dream came true."

"The hanging!" Tala blurted. "It happened exactly like that."

"What do we make of it?" Jondralyn asked Hawkwood. "For when I was recovering from my injuries, I had many dreams and visions. I saw a girl with a silver claw for a hand in some of those hallucinations. Could it be Lawri I saw?"

"That you dreamt of her hand is no great surprise," Hawkwood said. "Since Lawri found it, I've always believed the gauntlet to be important to the plans of the Brethren of Mia. And perhaps your dreams are proof of that."

"What is the Brethren of Mia?" Lawri asked.

"The Brethren of Mia are a faction of scholars dedicated to ancient secrets," Hawkwood answered.

"And that is all?" Lawri asked.

Jondralyn and Hawkwood exchanged concerned glances. Jondralyn said, "I believe it's time we told both Tala and Lawri all we know. We cannot keep it secret for much longer, not with both living here with us."

Hawkwood nodded. "Sit, Lawri, Tala. Get comfortable."

Lawri sat on the cushioned bench where Jondralyn had previously been sitting. Tala plopped down next to her, watching the looks exchanged between her sister and Hawkwood. *He treats her well,* she thought. *Like an equal.* Tala had been observing every interaction between her sister and the Sør Sevier man ever since coming aboard the *Val-Sadè.* They were clearly in love. They shared secrets.

And they were about to divulge some of those secrets. Hawkwood stood over Lawri and Tala, his chiseled face set with a gravity and earnestness that now made Tala uneasy. Jondralyn stood at his side, a similar stern look on her face.

Hawkwood began, "You girls will both learn things here today that only a select handful of people in the history of the Five Isles have ever known, things only the Brethren of Mia know."

"And you will be sworn to secrecy," Jondralyn added.

"Are you and Jondralyn part of this Brethren of Mia?" Lawri asked, settling the gauntlet over her lap as gently as if it were a pet, brushing her fingers lightly over its polished scales, then digging with her fingernails where the metal met the flesh, digging at some green-blotched skin there.

"Yes," Jondralyn answered. "We are part of the Brethren. And after you and Tala hear what Hawkwood and I have to say, you too will be of the Brethren, considered the truest of friends."

"Well, what is it then?" Lawri asked eagerly. "What is the Brethren of Mia? What are the secrets we cannot tell?"

Hawkwood answered her. "There can be no denying that with Aeros Raijael's destruction of Adin Wyte and Wyn Darrè and his subsequent advance into Gul Kana, Fiery Absolution draws near and some prophecies are close to being fulfilled. Would you not agree, Lawri?"

Lawri swallowed hard. "You think that Aeros' attack on Gul Kana has something to do with my arm, with the gauntlet, with my dreams."

"I will get to that in time," Hawkwood said. "But what I tell you now may be hard for you to hear, confusing even. So if you've any questions, today shall be the time to ask, because we will likely not be talking of these matters again. Understand?"

Lawri nodded. Tala nodded too, intrigued and fearful at once.

"We believe that the angel stones and weapons of the Five Warrior Angels have been found," Hawkwood said bluntly. "*Afflicted Fire, Forgetting Moon, Ethic Shroud, Blackest Heart,* and *Lonesome Crown,* all five of the great and ancient treasures."

Tala recalled the map she and Glade had followed through Purgatory under the Hall of the Dayknights. It had presumably led to the Rooms of Sorrow and some great and ancient treasure. *Could the weapons of the Five Warrior Angels have been hidden down there?*

"What of *The Way and Truth of Laijon?*" she asked. "The scriptures say that weapons and stones were translated into heaven with Laijon at the time of his death. They say that Laijon himself will bring the stones and weapons back with him at the time of Fiery Absolution and that the vicar and quorum of five will rule at his side for all of eternity."

"Much of what *The Way and Truth of Laijon* says about a great many things is false," Hawkwood said. "And most everything that book says about the weapons of the Five Warrior Angels is a lie."

Pale-faced, Lawri did the three-fingered sign of the Laijon Cross over her heart with her good hand.

"Then where are these weapons now?" Tala asked. She suddenly found it hard to breathe. What Hawkwood was saying was not just crazy and improbable, but *blasphemous.* "How are you so certain that *The Way and Truth of Laijon* is false?"

"*The Moon Scrolls of Mia* hold the truth of all things," Jondralyn answered, her good eye resting on Tala. "The Brethren of Mia are tasked with making sure that Fiery Absolution never happens. We are tasked with saving the Five Isles from destruction."

"What are *The Moon Scrolls of Mia?*" Tala asked. "And what do you mean by saving the Five Isles? Do you mean us? Me? You? Hawkwood? *Lawri?*"

"Yes," Jondralyn said. "Us. But we are not alone. There are others. Our own father was one of the Brethren of Mia, Tala. He fought Aeros in Wyn Darrè to buy time for the Brethren of Mia to locate the weapons and stones of the Five Warrior Angels. In fact, everything our father did was to buy time for the rest of the Brethren to find the lost weapons and stones and stave off Fiery Absolution."

Tala felt her brow twist in confusion. Some of what her sister said made a weird kind of sense. She could see her father believing in such fables and tales and holding them secret. But there were other things that were bothersome. She asked, "Who are the others you speak of, the other members of this Brethren of Mia?"

"Roguemoore," Jondralyn said. "And his brother, Ironcloud. The Dayknight, Culpa Barra. Squireck Van Hester." Her eyes narrowed. "Sterling Prentiss."

Sterling Prentiss. Tala's mind reeled. She could picture Sterling's body splayed out naked on the cross-shaped altar in the red-hazed room. And the Prince of Saint Only had been beheaded by the enemy in the arena.

Lawri was breathing hard, sucking down heavy gasps of air, as if her entire body was rejecting everything she was hearing. Tala felt herself also rejecting it too, felt the dread coil around her heart and constrict. "Are you are recruiting me and Lawri to replace the Prince of Saint Only and the Dayknight captain?" she asked. "Are we to be your new members in this Brethren of Mia?"

"No," Jondralyn said, again exchanging glances with Hawkwood. "You are not meant to replace anyone."

"There is more to it than that," Hawkwood said, a penetrating look in his eyes that was shocking. "There is more you need to know about the Brethren of Mia, Tala, and more you must learn about your own family. *The Way and Truth of Laijon* speaks of the return of Laijon during the time of Fiery Absolution. However, *The Moon Scrolls of Mia* speak of the return of all five Warrior Angels. Not just Laijon."

Tala looked at her older sister. "How does this affect our family?"

"The five have been found," Jondralyn answered. "They live amongst us now. The Princess, the Gladiator, the Assassin, the Thief, and the Slave. Each one a descendant of one of the Five Warrior Angels, each one tied to one of the Five Isles by blood, each one ready to bear one of the ancient weapons, each one ready to do his or her part in summoning forth the true heir of Laijon and bringing about his return."

"As *The Moon Scrolls of Mia* have foretold," Hawkwood added.

"But who are they?" Tala asked. "Where are the weapons?"

Hawkwood's answer was swift in coming. "For your own safety, all I will say is that Roguemoore and Val-Draekin have gone off to retrieve the weapons."

"As for who the Five Warrior Angels are," Jondralyn continued, "it's best their identities also remain a mystery for the time being."

"Are you okay?" Tala asked Lawri. Her cousin was still breathing heavily. "What is it, Lawri?"

"I'm just wondering what any of this has to do with my arm." Lawri looked up, fear etched on her face. "Why are you telling me these things if they have nothing to do with my arm?" She held up her silver arm. "I want this beastly thing off me now!"

Jondralyn looked at Hawkwood. "Maybe we've said too much already."

"I can't help but think that gauntlet has a huge part yet to play," Hawkwood said.

"Whatever part it is," Lawri muttered, "it can't be any good. My dreams are so vivid. So wrong. And it frightens me that some of them have come true." She paused a moment, then went on. "Those first few days my hand was missing, not long after Jovan chopped it off, I would sometimes feel it itching. Even though I knew it wasn't there, it would still itch. But I could not scratch it. Sometimes I could even feel my fingers move. But they weren't there *to* move. I would ofttimes reach out to grab something from a table and feel my fingers wrap around the object, even though I had no fingers to wrap around anything." She held up the silver gauntlet, eyes now clouded with pain and confusion. "But the feeling was so real. And now in those rare moments when my mind plays those same tricks on me, the fingers of this gauntlet *will* move. You've all seen it. You've all seen the fingers *move*, right? I am not just imagining things still?"

"We've seen them move," Hawkwood acknowledged.

Lawri let the gauntlet rest on her lap again, petted it again with her free hand as if it were a cat on her lap. "Some days I believe the gauntlet could indeed be a blessing of Laijon, I just don't know how or why. But then I consider my dreams and visions, and I feel there is something evil in it, as if the wraiths have truly claimed me for their own." She looked up at Hawkwood. "And the things you two have said about these *Moon Scrolls* and the Five Warrior Angels sound like blasphemy to me. They sound false to my ears. Wrong according to my Ember Gathering."

Then Lawri looked up at Jondralyn hopefully. "Perhaps I should just take my leave of this ship, go back to the castle, and find myself a noble to marry. Any nobleman would do. He doesn't even have to be cute. Perhaps if I can talk to the grand vicar, he will know what path I should take. This tilted ship is messing with my mind." She dropped her eyes again, looking at no one. "If only I could remember fully the prayer of my Ember Gathering, perhaps the nightmares would end and I could go back to my bedchamber in the castle and fall fast asleep. Sleep with no more dreams attached. Sleep with no more silver arms attached. Sleep forever and end this nightmare altogether." When Lawri looked up at Jondralyn again, tears were forming in the corners of her eyes. "But I can barely recall my Ember Gathering prayers, Jondralyn, let alone the prayers Denarius uttered over me."

"What do you remember of your Ember Gathering?" Tala asked, thinking back to her conversation with Seita on the subject. "What was so special about it?"

Lawri stared angrily at her. "I told you before, I won't speak of it more than I already have." Her green-flecked eyes narrowed to cold slits. "I made a promise. It is sacred to me."

"I'm only trying to help," Tala muttered.

Lawri glared at Tala. "It was the grand vicar's blessings that comforted me when I needed comfort the most. And now you wish me to betray him for your own curiosity."

"I said I was sorry." Tala frowned.

Lawri continued, trembling now. "Just mentioning the Ember Gathering, when I made such a sacred oath not to talk of it, fills me with such cold dread. I can feel the icy presence of the wraiths in the air, more frigid than a Winter Moon's freezing wind. I can feel wraiths heavy and full of shadow waiting to devour me in my dreams." Her trembling disappeared and she stared straight at Tala, conviction in her eyes. "Don't you understand, Tala, speaking of the Ember Gathering is wrong and you have been commanded not to do it, commanded not just by me, but by *The Way and Truth of Laijon*, by the vicar himself in many Eighth Day services?"

To Tala, it suddenly felt as if Lawri was trying to bully her into silence. Angry, she asked, "Did you tell Denarius those things I said about the Ember Gathering in Swensong Courtyard? Did you run to him and tattle on me, Lawri?"

"I've no desire to talk of such things anymore," Lawri snapped at her.

"But you did tell him what I said?"

"Yes," Lawri answered waspishly. "Yes, I did. And you should not have said what you said about the Ember Gathering, Tala. It is a sacred ceremony. I keep repeating how sacred it is and you refuse to listen. And to continually speak of it is a sin. I told the vicar because I was worried for your own salvation. But he reassured me you would one day receive your own purification . . . and all would be forgiven."

Tala shuddered. *My own purification! I first thought the vicar and archbishops were going to rape me in those baths.* The horror of what they had done had not been as egregious as rape, but it was still awful, and Tala thought of it often. *And I did escape the Dayknight sleeping bag on my own.* The claw marks on her flesh were but surface wounds and were healing relatively swiftly, but they were the physical reminder of how foul her "purification" had been. She glared back at Lawri, hatred in her heart. *No. I can't blame Lawri for the sick and twisted sacraments of the vicarship and the quorum of five. . . .*

"I've told Hawkwood of my own Ember Gathering," Jondralyn said, breaking Tala's train of thought. "What rituals were performed in the Ember Gathering are quite okay to talk about, Lawri. It is safe to talk of them here."

"No, it is not." There was real terror in Lawri's feverish, green-flecked eyes. "How could you tell Hawkwood about your own Ember Gathering? How could you tell anyone? You swore an oath. I swore an oath. How could you betray that? The women of Gul Kana are not supposed to betray that oath. It is sacred."

Hawkwood said, "An oath sworn to a bunch of liars is no oath at all. If you cannot tell the truth of your Ember Gathering, then everything you have to say is suspect, everything you say could be a lie. Only those with evil intent would make someone swear an oath of truth over a secret ritual. They require oaths of secrecy to control the minds of the believers, to subjugate and place them into bondage."

Tala recalled her trip into the secret ways, recalled looking down through the crack in the ceiling, recalled looking down on her cousin lying there naked, being blessed with holy oils by the grand vicar. She thought of Jovan being similarly blessed as a child and suddenly realized that what Seita had said was true. *Through the Ember Gathering the church authorities gain control of both your mind and body,* she thought. And just witnessing the distress this conversation was causing Lawri was proof of the control the church had over its patrons, the control it had had since their youth. Tala herself still wondered if it was indeed a sin to even think badly about such sacred rituals, that was how deep her mind and soul had been infected. If she were ever king, she would do away with all such traditions and blessings full of secrecy and ritual and sacrament and save everyone the needless heartache.

"Don't hold too fast to one tenet or belief, Lawri Le Graven,"

Hawkwood said, confirming what Tala was just thinking about. "Such devotion can be dangerous."

"Such devotion is the only path to heaven," Lawri countered.

"Not all devotions are heavenly," Hawkwood said. "Some devotions are full of darkness and death. The making of a Bloodwood through Black Dugal's Sacrament of Souls has a sort of grotesque artistry to it, an unspeakable magnificence, both stunning and heart-wrenching at once, but much like a young woman's Ember Gathering in dastardliness. And Black Dugal's Caste worship him with that same twisted devotion you worship the grand vicar, and all because of the ceremony. You see, much can be learned from those who require oaths of secrecy and blood, and those who follow them. For oaths and secrecy are how Dugal keeps his newly minted children in line. And just like those who partake in an Ember Gathering ceremony, those who fall under Dugal's tutelage are also required to never speak of what they see or hear or do. But you must know, Lawri, I myself have talked of the Sacrament of Souls openly, as Jondralyn has described her own Ember Gathering to me. And despite what oaths we promised, no scythe has ever swept from the heavens and sliced us in half for breaking them, and no bishop has ever cut the hearts from our chests and buried them in a dung-filled grave."

Lawri met Hawkwood's gaze with a hardened gaze of her own. "But you don't understand. It was the Ember Gathering that healed my soul."

Hawkwood knelt before her. "There are many cancerous maladies that can be cured by doctors and medicines and Vallè potions, Lawri. Even the human immune system can reverse many grave illnesses. And the gods and the vicars and the bishops of this world are given quick credit for the miracle. But I will tell you now, not one single blessing of the grand vicar has ever healed anyone." He grasped her hands in his own, grasped both her good hand and her metal one. "Not one single blessing or prayer has ever replaced a limb that has been cut off, Lawri. Not in the entire history of the Five Isles has any prayer or priesthood blessing ever regrown a severed limb."

Lawri jerked her hands away from his, raised her silver arm again, and thrust it in front of his face angrily, rage burning in her eyes. "And how do you know this gauntlet is not the answer to the vicar's prayers and priesthood blessings?"

Hawkwood stood, backing away from her. "The solution to your missing arm may yet come in the form of some Vallè science—"

"No!" Lawri screamed, her voice like a whip crack in the timbered confines of the *Val-Sadè*. "I won't hear any more of this!" She jerked to her feet. "I want to run! I want to run away from you all! I want to run far, far away! I want to run back into my dreams, where there is no underworld and silver rivers carving paths of blood—"

She lurched across the room, crashing into the tilted hull of the ship, her body sliding down the wooden wall until she sank to her knees. "Get me out of here!" she screamed, the front of her body clinging to the hull of the ship, palms of both hands pressed to the wood, fingers splayed wide. The fingertips of her good hand were scratching and tearing at the wooden planks. The hollow, curled fingertips of her gauntleted hand were doing the same, clawing, slashing, ripping, splinters of wood shredding in their wake, the silver hand almost shining with a sickly green light.

"Get me out of here!" Both arms churning, Lawri clawed her way to her feet, leaving a trail of torn and ragged wood under her. Standing now, she swung the gauntlet over her head like a club, metal fingers now clenched into a fist.

A clap of blinding white light flared where the gauntlet met wood. The blow, heavy and thunderous as a sledgehammer, reverberated through the ship loud and full.

She struck the hull again and a ferocious gust of seawater and splintered wood shot back into her chest and face, blasting her straight up and into the lantern and bulkhead above with a fury.

Lawri dropped like a stone, flopping down onto the water-drenched floor with a sickening thud, every stitch of her white dress a soaked ruin. She floundered in the spray as seawater surged upward from the hole in the tilted hull, showering the canted roof above, blankets of water raining down on them all. Jondralyn grabbed Lawri by the back of her dress and pulled her away from the deluge.

"Grab something, Tala!" Hawkwood shouted, water running in torrents down his face and black leathers. "Anything! We've got to plug that hole!" Then he seized her by the shoulders. "There's some lumber and nails in the far galley! Follow me!"

Tala slipped in the ankle-deep water, stumbling to her knees, pain lancing through her legs. Frantic, she crawled over the waterlogged floor, following Hawkwood, glancing one last time into the chaotic galley. Lawri was wrapped in Jondralyn's arms, both of them huddled on the floor in the middle of a storm of cascading waters. The gauntlet attached to Lawri's arm was no longer clenched in a fist. She held it up before her startled pale face.

The gauntlet now gleamed like silver starlight, green light shining from between its clover-shaped scales. And that same green glow was alight in Lawri's two eyes.

Who was the first god, and who created him? Who was the first hero, and what war did he win? Who was the first villain, and who did he betray? History hath no beginning, and that is the one mysterious truth of all.
—THE WAY AND TRUTH OF LAIJON

CHAPTER ELEVEN

NAIL

9TH DAY OF THE FIRE MOON, 999TH YEAR OF LAIJON
MEMORY BAY, EAST OF DIRES WOAD, GUL KANA

G allows Haven chapel, and Nail sat in the front row. He squirmed in his white robes, a raging need to piss consuming his every thought. He would leave, but for the looming presence of Bishop Tolbret and Baron Jubal Bruk glaring down. Both men stood before the chapel's altar. The baron was clad in full battle gear, Dayknight sword with its leather-wrapped hilt and black opal-inlaid pommel at his hip, the bishop in his priestly robes. The chapel seemed an awfully strange place for the baron to be dressed in so much armor, especially during the Ember Lighting Rites. But Nail's need to piss superseded any deep contemplation on the matter.

Bishop Tolbret laid his holy book open atop the altar and thumbed through its ancient, dusty pages. All of Nail's friends sat in white robes on the front bench with him: Stefan Wayland, Zane Neville, and Dokie Liddle.

Shawcroft, Nail's master, was nowhere to be found. But when it came to the Church of Laijon, the man took scant little interest, whereas Nail took comfort in the church and his place within it. He always marveled at the Gallows Haven chapel, dreamed of creating art and sculpture for just such a holy place. In the vaulted apse behind the baron and the bishop was the familiar statue of Laijon, carved of rough-hewn stone. The muscular marble carving was nearly twice the size of a normal man. Laijon wore naught but a loincloth and a wreath of white heather about his head, glints of sunlight sparkling from the chips of silver and quartz in the pale marble stonework. Laijon bore a flawless silver mask in the shape of a skull over his face. He was nailed to an even larger black-painted wooden replica of the Atonement Tree; its twining branches soared, almost reaching the ceiling of the chapel, branching outward to fill the entire space of the vaulted apse, silver dripping from every barbed limb. Five angel stones hovered, suspended by thin, unseen threads over Laijon's masked head. The stones glimmered and gleamed, all but the black one, which seemed strangely out of place amongst the bright opulence of the others. The black stone seemed false. It always had.

It was then that Nail noticed Stefan Wayland was staring right at the black stone with some hint of fear in his eyes. But again, Nail's need to piss was overwhelming any deep contemplation on the matter.

Bishop Tolbret began reading from the Ember Lighting Song of the Third Warrior Angel, near the end of *The Way and Truth of Laijon*—the climactic part of the scriptures. The verse Tolbret read was a recounting of the final day of the Vicious War of the Demons—the final day of the Blessed Mother Mia's pregnancy. Laijon, bleeding from the wound in his neck, had just been nailed, still alive, to the Atonement Tree by the Last Demon Lord. At the end of the passage, Bishop Tolbret closed the large white book and beckoned for the young men to stand.

Nail choked back his nerves and stood with the other boys. He shifted from foot to foot, the need to piss almost driving him to madness now. He turned and scanned the villagers sitting in the pews behind him, locating Ava Shay with the other girls in the choir. She smiled at him sadly. Then Nail caught the eye of Jenko Bruk, who sat in the back row of the chapel. Jenko was smirking as if he knew some secret Nail was not yet privy to. Nail's gaze flew back to Ava again, but her eyes were now focused on Bishop Tolbret, who directed the line of boys toward the altar and ten goblets filled with oil.

Nail stepped forward. His arms were weary, legs leaden. Cramps ached throughout his neck and chest. His entire body was fatigued from working with Shawcroft all week, lingering physical pains garnered from their latest pointless toil along the creek bed, panning for gold.

When the boys were lined up before the altar, Baron Bruk stepped forward. A cloud of apprehension fell over Nail as the man walked around the bishop, his clanking armor echoing through the church. The baron whispered into the bishop's ear, and Tolbret's brow furrowed as he held the holy book up to his chest like a huge white shield.

"Nail will sit out the Ember Lighting," Baron Bruk announced, loudly enough for the whole congregation to hear. Nail felt his face turn a dark shade of red. His eyes crawled around the transept uneasily. The disappointment he'd felt at the baron's pronouncement seemed almost too unfathomable to grasp.

Baron Bruk snatched the holy book from Tolbret's hands. He flipped through the pages, quickly finding what he sought. "I quote from the Acts of the Second Warrior Angel: 'A motherless bastard shall not enter into the Smoke and Fire. Even to the tenth generation shall a motherless bastard not enter into any Ember Lighting or Ember Gathering of Laijon.'" The baron slammed the book shut, and Nail's heart plunged. He kept his gaze trained on the cold gray floor.

I've heard all this before! Nail thought, the pain in his bladder burning. *I've heard a similar scripture somewhere before.* But he couldn't quite place where. Didn't they know that Hawkwood had already told him of his heritage? He remembered Ravenker. *You and your sister were kept from each other for a purpose,* Hawkwood had said. *Your mother is dead. They will say she was Cassietta Raybourne, the younger sister of Ser Torrence Raybourne of Wyn Darrè, and Shawcroft your uncle. They will say you are from Wyn Darrè. They will say your father is King Aevrett Raijael of Sør Sevier, that you are King Aevrett's youngest son. And that only the youngest Raijael can claim ownership of the title Angel Prince.*

But that was all unlikely. It was, as Liz Hen Neville would say, all twaddle. What did Hawkwood know anyway? *What do I know anyway?*

"There is much you don't know." The baron drew his long black Dayknight sword, the weapon slithering from its scabbard with a hiss. "Much." The baron smiled a cruel smile.

Nail pissed himself. The warm liquid stained the front of his white robe yellow. He looked down at the pool of urine growing under him. Stefan, Zane, Dokie, they all laughed. Nail scurried from the chapel, his eyes traveling beyond Ava Shay and Jenko Bruk and the laughing congregation and journeying up, up, up to the three large stained-glass windows inlaid with intricate designs above the front doors of the chapel. In the center window was an ethereal image of Laijon in his silver skull mask and blue dragon-scale armor, the other four Warrior Angels behind him. They all wore equally colorful armor that shimmered in the light, silver whips dangling from their silver-gauntleted hands, an angel stone hanging above each silver-masked head like a halo. The myriad of stones cast ghostlike reflections of red, blue, green, white, and black over the congregation.

But at the moment, to Nail, the colorful light from the windows played upon the laughing worshippers of Gallows Haven like the phantoms the Warrior Angels really were.

**

A clean, cold breeze hit Nail's face, and he jerked awake to the sudden sensation of disorientation and dread. He stared straight up at a sky full of roiling dark clouds. With the motion of the boat upon the waves, he slowly began to recall where he was. The motion also exacerbated his need to urinate. Pain raged through his bladder.

He hauled himself from the bottom of the skiff and stumbled to the sidewall near the prow of the rolling vessel. He went to the place on the boat farthest from the Wyn Darrè girl. Self-conscious, his back turned to everyone, Bronwyn Allen, Val-Draekin, Cromm Cru'x, he braced both knees against the worn sidewall, untied the laces of his pants, and loosed a steam of urine over the edge of the boat and into the sea, relief flooding his entire body.

As he stared down into the wavering waters, he thought he saw floating silver shapes in the deep. But he knew it was just the movement of the boat and the rippling of the sea playing tricks on his mind. Still, he half wondered if there were mermaids down there somewhere, looking up at him. *I can't escape the spying eyes of everyone.* He shuddered, thinking of his journey underwater with the mermaid during Baron Bruk's grayken hunt. It seemed so long ago. Another lifetime. But the creature had almost drowned him that day. Under the water, embraced in her cold clutch, he had seen things, images, fiery symbols; squares, circles within circles, crosses, all emblazoned and glowing in the water like shooting stars. And he had seen *himself*—standing under a large burning tree. With him under the tree was a knight with a brilliant white shield and a horned helm astride a massive white warhorse. A blond girl with glowing green eyes rode on the saddle before the glorious knight, her hand a metal claw. Such a vivid dream, but one that made scant little sense, though the symbols and marks on his own flesh seemed to flare and burn at the mere thought of those underwater visions. He could feel each mark and scar individually: the cross-shaped mark on the back of his hand, the slave mark on the underside of his wrist, the tattoo on his shoulder, and the mermaid's claw marks on his bicep. *What does it all mean?*

When Nail was done urinating, he tied the front of his pants back together, eyes continuing to stare down into the dark waters of the ocean. There *was* something slithering down there in the deep. *Sharks! Merfolk! Or you're just seeing things.*

He looked away, then slumped to the bench just below the sidewall, refusing to acknowledge the dangers he knew lurked below. Thinking back on his dream, he realized he had come so far from his simple life in Gallows Haven. *I'm on a boat with strangers.* The wind picked up and the small ship rose and dipped in the swells. Rain began to fall sideways into his face, the sail above snapping and straining in the sudden gale. Off in the distance Nail could see the waves grow, great black waves they were, boiling up as if from nowhere, threatening to swallow their boat whole.

Cromm stood, sucking on his black rock vigorously, pulling on the ropes, furling up the sail. There was an abrupt shift in the wind and a sharp gust of rain pelted sideways at the oghul. The vessel tossed upon the water. Cromm shouted as one of the hooks tore from its knot, sending the sail billowing and snapping violently in the gale.

With a harsh rending the canvas tore loose, whipping through the air. The bulk of the heavy, wet sail struck Cromm—still gripping the end of one of the ropes—square in the chest, knocking him from the floor of the boat into the sidewall, where he toppled awkwardly into the churning waves. With a tremendous splash, the huge oghul—armor and all—disappeared under the rain-splattered sea, the rope he gripped in one burly hand trailing behind him down into the storm-tossed waters.

Nail stared emptily at the sidewall of the boat where Cromm had vanished, the taut rope he clung to all that remained of the oghul's plunge. Rain lashed the white wood under the straining rope.

Bronwyn Allen rushed to the sidewall, gazing down into the frothing darkness of the water. "I can't see him!" she bellowed. "That armor will sink him!"

Her eyes locked with Nail's. "Help me haul on the rope! He could still be clinging to it down there, trying to climb up!" The normally calloused look in Bronwyn's eyes was now one of pure panic. The burly oghul was her companion, and she was afraid of losing him.

Val-Draekin crawled cautiously along the bottom of the jostling and rolling boat. When he reached the sidewall, he pulled on the rope, helping Bronwyn. But their efforts amounted to nothing. "Help us!" the Wyn Darrè girl screamed at Nail.

The boat dropped and rose violently in the ever-growing waves, churning water splashing over the sidewalls on every side. Nail scrambled from the safety of his bench toward Bronwyn and Val-Draekin. He too seized the rope and, with Bronwyn and Val-Draekin, hauled upward with all his strength.

But it was useless. They all three let go at the same time, gasping.

The rope below jerked back and forth in the water, then went still. Nail waited, wondering if the oghul would resurface on his own. But as the moments passed, he began to realize that even a stout oghul pirate could not survive underwater for long.

Then he saw them. *Merfolk!* Pale shapes hovering just beneath the surface. The rope thrashed about wildly once again, as if the oghul was struggling with it. The rain picked up. Thick droplets splashed the water with more force now. Lightning flashed above, and the surface of the sea tilted and dropped, then boiled up high. Nail pictured his friend Zane Neville's face down there in the deep.

Without thinking, he stripped away what armor might sink him. Dagger gripped firmly in hand, he dove headfirst from the safety of the sailboat, knifing into the storm-tossed ocean. Cold black water immediately punched him in the face with an icy fury that stole his breath. Darkness pressed inward, constricting his body. The marks and scars on his body flared with pain. He raked his way back to the surface, black bubbles and rain churning as his head broke the skin of the sea. He choked. A wave rose up over him and dark water closed in. When his head surfaced again, he could scarcely even see.

Val-Draekin held an oar out to him. But Nail sank below again as another rain-splattered wave rolled over him. He kicked for the surface, his foot striking something hard. Cromm! But his limbs could barely move. The water was so cold. It was like the grayken hunt with Baron Bruk all over again, and he was once more foolishly trying to rescue someone from a violent sea. Wind gusted and the sea rose and fell. His head was above water, then below, then above. Stinging rain clawed at his face. Agony engulfed him as he gazed up at Val-Draekin and Bronwyn, still peering over the side of the skiff at him.

Something grabbed at his foot but his flailing legs and feet were so numb he scarcely felt it. Still, he was pulled below the surface once again by mysterious forces.

Or is Cromm pulling me down, yanking me down toward a cold, watery death? Every muscle in Nail's body screamed in pain. The taut rope was right there in the water next to him, lashing wildly in the storm, scraping against his face. And the hands still grabbed at his feet and legs.

Mermaids! Sharks! The thought of either nearly paralyzed him. And the hands clawing at him persisted.

It was Cromm. The oghul's thick hands were grabbing at him relentlessly. Nail grasped the rope and forced himself down toward the oghul, dagger still miraculously gripped in hand. When he reached Cromm, he immediately started slicing the leather straps holding the heavy plate armor from the oghul's bulky body. The oghul struggled mightily before realizing what Nail was doing. And then he calmed. As he worked, Nail felt his lungs burning. When he cut away the last of the oghul's armor, they both kicked for the surface, following the taut rope up, up, up. As Nail's head broke the black skin of the rolling ocean, lightning struck from above, engulfing Nail in a harsh white brilliance, the scars on his body pulsing light and pain. Cromm jerked violently up from the sea in front of him.

"There they are!" he heard Bronwyn yell.

Lightning struck again, and gleaming ribbons of white light streaked across the roiling sea. Nail took one long breath before a rolling wave swallowed him. When the wave passed over him, he could again once breathe and see.

The pale slender head of a mermaid broke the surface right next to him. And Nail found himself in the grip of utter terror once again. Like the mermaid he had seen before, this one had a delicate chin, thin lips, a thin nose, and eyes that were as wide and blue as the summer sky. She blinked at him. A serrated row of gills stretched and fluttered along her slippery neck. She hissed, and her thin mouth cracked open, revealing sharp white fangs.

Then Cromm's hands were around the mermaid's heaving neck. He twisted hard, squeezing the life from her, snapping her spine. The oghul released his hold on the mermaid and she calmly slid below the black, rain-soaked sea. Cromm crawled the rest of the way up the rope and into the first boat, his brace of knives and armor now lost to the sea.

Once the oghul was safe, he reached back overboard and hauled Nail from the stormy ocean. Nail hugged the bottom of the boat, coughing up what bitter seawater he had swallowed, purging his heaving lungs, feeling a great sodden weariness overtake his entire body. Val-Draekin stared at him with a hint of admiration. Bronwyn looked relieved to see that her oghul partner had not yet perished.

Cromm was grinning from ear to ear. He reached into his mouth and pulled free the black rock he sucked on, pointing at Nail with one thick finger. "That mermaid knew you," he grunted. "Even the merfolk can sense when the marked one is near."

Nail choked on the seawater still lodged in his lungs.

The oghul continued, "The marked one has saved Cromm. And now Cromm is beholden to the marked one and forever in his debt."

Whoso believeth not in Laijon thinks he is wise. What then shall he sin?
Shall he live for today? For he thinketh himself above the law.
For only true obedience to the law leads to righteousness and joy.
—THE WAY AND TRUTH OF LAIJON

CHAPTER TWELVE

AVA SHAY

9TH DAY OF THE FIRE MOON, 999TH YEAR OF LAIJON

SAINT ONLY, ADIN WYTE

The Bloodeye steed that never shied from anything stepped nervously back from Ivor Jace and his flashing sword. Aeros' newest Knight Archaic was trying to teach both Ava Shay and Ser Edmon's young serving girl, Leisel, some fighting moves of his own. But he had nowhere near the skill, or teaching ability, of the Spider, or even Enna Spades. He was wild with a sword.

"Easy, Scowl," Spiderwood said, voice silky and soothing, taking over instruction from Ivor for a moment.

The black stallion's red eyes glinted and flared in the grim light of the stone-walled stable. The stable was nestled atop an outcrop of rock some two-thirds of the way up the northern face of the Mont near the cathedral. The city of Saint Only lay some five hundred feet below, the lofty fortress another two hundred feet above.

The Spider gently stroked the horse's black mane, regaining control of the beast in the wake of Ivor's latest wild swing, his own dark gaze on Ava. The Spider said, "Hold your blade up just a touch more to block Ivor's first blow." The Bloodwood wore black boiled-leather armor under a black cape, hood thrown back, his raven-colored hair seemingly as oily as his stallion's sleek coat. The stable smelled of wet horse, manure, hay, and oats.

Ava lifted the tip of her sword, My Heart, as the Spider had admonished. Enna Spades normally kept the blade for her. But Spades was gone, dead, and the Spider had pulled the weapon from the warrior woman's abandoned gear in the stables, insisting on continuing Ava's training.

She blocked Ivor's first blow, and the next, and even more after that. Her slim ruby-hilted sword took the blows of Ivor's much heavier blade in perfect repetition, foiling his wild and rapid assault, the muscle memory developed through hours of practice finally paying off. Leisel clapped her pleasure, her own small sword now tucked into the slim leather belt around her white shift, her blond hair almost aglow in the dull light of the stable.

The fact was, the Bloodwood's advice had worked, much to the consternation of Ivor Jace, who was doing his utmost to show everyone up. Unlike the dull black leather armor of Spiderwood, Ivor's polished armor gleamed and glimmered in the dim light. He wore the traditional Knight Archaic blue cloak and armor: a silver cuirass over a tunic of shining mail and silver-studded leather greaves and heavy leather boots.

"Ivor clearly relies more on brute strength than skill when he fights," the Spider said. "Most who are unsure of themselves do."

"I reckon I could break you in half with my brute strength." Ivor glowered at the Bloodwood. "That black cloak you wear may protect you from poisons and fire, but not my fists, and certainly not my sword."

"Still, you are untrained in the finer points of fighting."

"You bloody well know I am scarcely even trying here with these girls. I've no wish to hurt any of Aeros' precious little playthings, most especially his most precious princess, Ava Shay." He threw Ava a brief bow and a slick smile. But every smile the tall man gave Ava was slick and full of hidden meaning. "You do not want me to hurt you now, do you, lass?" Ivor's smile widened even more, and in a most distasteful way.

"True," she acquiesced with a forced smile of her own. "I've no wish to be hurt."

She let the slender tip of her blade dip toward the ground, arm weary. My Heart had served her well enough in today's training, and its haft fit snug in her grip. She had named the sword for the heart-shaped ruby fixed atop the hilt. But the truth was, she did not like the fact that Ivor was diminishing her skills by claiming he was not even trying. She wished Aeros hadn't sent the dull-witted knight down here to help.

But it seemed the White Prince was determined to dictate every minute of her day, and who she spent time with and what she wore. He had become more controlling since their arrival at the Mont. He had gifted Ava with many fine gowns and insisted she wear one at all times, as she did even now during her training. Today she was clothed in a pale green affair that clung tightly to her hips and hung all the way down to her ankles. At the moment the gown was cinched at the waist with a crude leather belt given to her by the Spider, a sheath for her sword hooked to her left side. The belt and sheath were likely the closest she would ever come to wearing the garb of a warrior.

And that gave her a wicked, spontaneous thought. She brought her blade to bear, and like lightning she whipped it up and around with a blur, the sharp tip nicking Ivor's knuckles in the process, drawing blood.

The big man jumped back with alarm. "Bloody rotted angels," he cursed, as redness welled up on his hand. Leisel clapped with glee.

Spiderwood also laughed. "Now that is how to kill a man, Ava. Strike when he is either not paying attention or boasting. Strike when he is least expecting it."

"A cheap shot it was." Ivor pressed the back of his hand to his mouth, licking the blood from his knuckles, scowling at the satisfaction he saw on the Spider's face. "Why teach her the trickery of a Bloodwood?"

"Remember, Ava," the Bloodwood said. "Enna Spades and Ivor Jace have taught you to fight the Sør Sevier way and no other. *The Chivalric Illuminations of Raijael* train one only in the basics of sword fighting, brutish slash and parry. But that is all just slow and clumsy nonsense if you fight someone with true skill. That tome of scripture Hammerfiss and Ivor worship does not teach the subtle nuance of real killing. It does not teach you the art of surprise." He grinned. "But I see you have learned that on your own." He turned to Ivor. "See, she used her own initiative."

"Hammerfiss and I are not as oafish as you may think." Ivor gave the Spider a wild, challenging grin. "I will match my blade against yours anytime."

"Perhaps I shall have Ava fight you in my stead," the Spider said, winking at both Leisel and Ava as he calmly stroked Scowl's mane. "I wager she may kill you someday, Ivor. As unskilled as you imagine her to be, I do think she could best even you."

Ivor grunted his disagreement, still sucking the blood from his knuckles.

Ava knew she could not yet best Ivor Jace. But the truth was, her heart had swelled at the Spider's praise. *I did surprise Ivor!* And she took some measure of satisfaction in that. She had drawn his blood the same way she had drawn Aeros' blood that first night of their coupling—the night she had learned the true art of surprise.

Spiderwood reached into the black saddlebag secured to his stallion's flank and produced a leather water skin. "Still icy cold from the well." He unstoppered the skin's wood cork and handed it to Ava. She sheathed her sword and took the water skin, drinking deep, cool water a sweet caress in her throat.

She wondered if the Spider wasn't buying her off with his small offerings and tokens of praise. *Buying me bit by bit.* She watched his dark eyes as she drank. She wanted to trust him. She wanted to trust someone. But it was so hard now that Jenko was dead and Spades was gone. *And I can't believe I ever contemplated trusting her.* But she had. And Enna Spades was the worst monster of them all.

Ivor Jace's eyes sparkled as he watched Ava down the water. *Him I will never trust.* Above Ivor, dust motes glittered down from timbered rafters as the door to the stable swung open with a jar and rattle. Hammerfiss strode in, helm in the crook of his arm, sword clanking at his side. The red-haired giant bowed before Ava and Leisel, then turned to Ivor and the Spider, announcing, "Aeros bids you all to join him in Bruce Hall."

"Bruce Hall?" the Spider asked.

"Ser Jenko Bruk has returned," Hammerfiss said. "Aeros wishes us all to greet him. And he wishes you not tarry."

He's alive! Ava's heart was jumping. *Jenko has returned from the dead!* She tossed the water skin back to the Spider and bounded for the door.

"Whoa." Hammerfiss seized her by the arm. "Don't be too hasty to see your former lover. Aeros wouldn't like that, now would he?"

Ava yanked her arm from his grip.

"Best you follow some paces behind me if you know what's good for you," Hammerfiss advised. "Best act nonchalant about the whole affair, if you take my meaning. Around Aeros, don't look too overjoyed at Jenko's return."

Hammerfiss then took his leave of the stable, leaving Ava be. Ivor and Leisel followed him. Ava unhooked the leather belt and sheath and handed the whole apparatus, along with My Heart, to the Spider. "Can we leave it with your horse?"

"Of course." The Spider took the sword from her graciously, hooking it to Scowl's polished black saddle horn. The ruby in the sword's hilt glowed like the stallion's red eyes.

Then the Bloodwood nodded to her conspiratorially, whispering, "One day you may find that I have stashed the sword somewhere in Aeros' bedchamber. When that day comes, you will know our time to escape is near." And then he bowed to her again and stepped silently from the stable.

**

The cloistered path that wound up the side of the Mont from the stables to the fortress above was somewhat run-down, but not totally decrepit. It was made of garlanded arched trellises of wood that rested on slim columns of stone, weeds and thorny briar growing about the base. It was also lined with apple trees that swayed gently in the wind, their new white summer blossoms pungent with fragrance.

After ten minutes of hiking, Ava still hadn't caught up to the others, though she could still see the Spider on the trail up ahead. Through the vaulted open arches of the cloister's outer wall, Ava had a grand view of the stable and cathedral below and the mostly abandoned and ruined city of Saint Only even farther down the mountain. The Adin Wyte peninsula stretched green and hazy to the north beyond the city, what few survivors from last week's disastrous battle in the channel camped there.

The tall castle of gray stone, jagged battlements, and narrow towers atop the Mont rose up before her, cold and dreary and magnificent. The beacon atop its tallest tower was always burning. Despite all the misery the place held for her, Mont Saint Only was still the grandest structure she had ever seen.

And Jenko Bruk still lives! Her heart thrilled at that news.

Ahead, the Spider had come to a halt on the trail, his eyes now boring into her like black pits. "There is more I must say to you before we reach Bruce Hall. I have done something that will soon undoubtedly put me at irreversible odds with the Angel Prince. And when Aeros discovers my treachery, as I know he will, he will have me flogged again, or perhaps he shall have me choose a duel to pay penance for my sin. And it shall be Hammerfiss who I shall fight." He grasped her by the shoulder, his grip tightening. "And on that day I kill Hammerfiss, I will turn my blade on Aeros Raijael."

Ava couldn't hold back the gasp that escaped her lips. "Why are you telling me this?" she said in a breathless rush.

"Because once Aeros is dead, I shall need your help." His eyes were like tiny pricks of black ice. "And now that Jenko Bruk has returned, I shall need his help too. You must understand, Aeros Raijael's armies are severely weakened, his power diminished, his reign near an end. But there are some prophecies yet to be fulfilled. Once the Angel Prince is vanquished, only the strong shall remain to lead the White Prince's armies to Amadon and usher in Fiery Absolution. And you and Jenko Bruk are strong leaders, the both of you. And it is nearing the time I train you both in the arts of the Bloodwood, for the time of Black Dugal to reveal himself for who he really is and for his Caste to arise from all corners of the Five Isles is nigh."

"What exactly are you saying?" she asked. Ser Edmon Guy Van Hester had also expressed a desire to help her, but that was before he had taken his own life. He claimed he had left her a clue and that he knew every nook and cranny and secret way in the castle. But he had never asked her to help kill Aeros. "What is it exactly that you want from me?"

"As I said before, just look for the sign of My Heart in Aeros' bed-chamber."

"My Heart? How did you know the name of my sword?"

"A Bloodwood always knows."

**

Lately it was always the first thing Ava noticed when entering Bruce Hall—the bulky severed serpent's head Spiderwood had dragged from the ocean, mounted on spikes above the hearth. The gruesome fanged abomination, its long tongue drooping nearly to the floor, overlooked the chamber like a morbid reminder of all that had happened.

Everyone shied away from the demonic-looking monstrosity, most especially the dogs. But Aeros Raijael seemed to think of it as some grand prize. He was now showing the snake head to Jenko Bruk, who was clad in naught but tattered clothes, dirt-stained from hard travel. Several other knights stood at watch nearby, girt with longswords at their waists, their armor glittering, dogs at their feet.

"It's like what I always imagined the beast of the underworld to be," Jenko said, looking up at the serpent head. "Slinking through the water, these snakes. Horrifying. My father and I would spot them once in a while whilst grayken hunting. But I have never had to be in the midst of a battle with one until, well, until the other day."

Hearing Jenko's voice again cut through that fog of grief that had been hovering over Ava for days. And seeing him nearly stopped her heart cold.

When Aeros noticed the group of newcomers, he beckoned everyone toward the serpent head. "Jenko has news. I wanted you all to hear it together, even the Spider." He bowed slightly to Spiderwood. The Bloodwood's eyes glittered icily as he dipped his head in return. Aeros turned back to Jenko Bruk. "Regale us with your tale of survival."

Jenko bowed to the White Prince, a measure of grit in his voice. "As I told you earlier, I recovered your helm and battle-ax from the bottom of the channel. Enna Spades helped me haul both aboard a skiff that she had procured." He paused a moment, swallowing. "But what I did not tell you was that Mancellor Allen has betrayed you."

"Betrayed me?" Aeros asked. "How?"

"Mancellor was also on the skiff with Spades and me and the weapons," Jenko went on. "But in the midst of the battle, we were cut off from the armies of Sør Sevier, forced to seek refuge in Lord's Point. It was in Lord's Point that Ser Mancellor stole the ax and helm. He has fled toward Amadon with both your treasures. Spades has given chase. She pursues him now in hopes of killing him and returning what is rightfully yours. I only returned to Saint Only to deliver unto you this news; otherwise I would be hunting Mancellor alongside Spades."

No! Ava stared at him, breathless and rapt. *He came back for me!* But there was no emotion betrayed in Jenko's face. In fact, he had not even looked at her yet. In that moment, she began to think there was nothing left in her worthy of him.

"So the ax and the helm survived?" Aeros' black-pupiled eyes danced with life for the first time since the battle. "What of the pouch with the stones, Ser Jenko? Did you also find the pouch? Were the angel stones with the ax and helm? For I lost those in the battle too."

"I did not find any pouch or stones," Jenko said, voice now hesitant, amber-colored eyes lowered. "Nor did I see Spades or Mancellor with any such pouch."

Will Aeros now claim that Jenko has failed? Ava recalled Beau Stabler's failure in finding Nail in the Autumn Range and the bloody consequences of that failure. Aeros stared at Jenko darkly. Silence followed.

Then at length Hammerfiss said, "Isn't it grand news that the ax and helm were not lost, my lord Aeros?"

"Grand news indeed," Aeros agreed. He turned to Ivor Jace. "The seabed between here and Lord's Point shall be searched for the pouch holding the stones. Every inch of it. I leave this task to you, Ser Ivor. I want at least half our remaining soldiers out there searching those sands. Daily. The stones will be found."

Ivor's chiseled face twisted in puzzlement. "But the channel tides will sweep us away as soon as we reach the battlefield."

"Then you shall drag boats out there with you," Aeros' harsh voice brooked no argument. "I will have those stones back." His eyes narrowed. "And you know the price for failure."

"As you wish." Ivor bowed stiffly. "We can do naught but follow what orders we're given, my lord."

"There is more truth in that than you know," Aeros said. "For you are but simple creatures, all of you who are not the Angel Prince."

Ivor bowed again, a twitch at the corner of his mouth as he said, "I shall ready the troops, that's if it please my lord."

"On the morrow your search shall begin." Aeros bowed, and Ivor marched from Bruce Hall, his heavy boots echoing through the chamber.

Aeros turned back to Jenko, curiosity etched on his pale face. "And now, pray tell, how did Ser Mancellor overpower Enna Spades and make his escape?"

Jenko said, "We had taken shelter inside an abandoned tavern along the dock district. It was an old and rotten building. When Mancellor made known his intentions to leave, both Spades and I tried to stop him. But in the fight, Spades and I fell through the rotted floor, and Mancellor made his escape. Spades chased after him. And I returned here to you."

Aeros' eyes remained on Jenko as if trying to fathom his depths, as if trying to decide whether all he was hearing was the truth.

"Come now, my lord." Hammerfiss took the White Prince by the arm and led him a few steps away from the serpent head. "Jenko has brought you good news. Why look so glum?"

"You are right." Aeros looked up at the bigger man. "I should not be so melancholy."

"You should not," Hammerfiss agreed.

Aeros bowed to him. "Now I've an assignment for you, Ser Hammerfiss. What soldiers Ivor does not use for his search, you shall start readying for battle. We will launch our armies back into Gul Kana soon."

Aeros then turned to Jenko, smiling. "And you, Ser Jenko Bruk, have earned your spot as my newest Knight Archaic."

And Ava watched in horror as Jenko Bruk bent his knee to the White Prince.

CHAPTER THIRTEEN

CRYSTALWOOD

12TH DAY OF THE FIRE MOON, 999TH YEAR OF LAIJON
IRON HILLS, WYN DARRÈ

The Spud Wagon Inn and Tavern was a dwarven establishment run by a fat little dwarf who also went by the name of Spud Wagon. The inn was a small and clean and efficiently run place, with the best fried breaded chicken Krista Aulbrek had ever tasted. It was also the coziest place she'd ever slept—in spite of having been cuffed and shackled the entire time. Hans Rake had been similarly restrained. Café Colza Bouledogue could not be tied down despite Ironcloud's best attempts. Luckily, the inn accepted dogs. And to his credit, Café Colza had done his utmost not to be a nuisance, which was rare for the dog, and their stay had been pleasant in turn. Borden Bronachell, Tyus Barra, and Ironcloud had all enjoyed a few days' respite from hard travel. But they were all now mounted again and leaving the place behind.

"Our dwarven friends are aware of your route," the dwarf named Spud Wagon informed Ironcloud as their small company saddled up. "And our dwarven friends shall keep anyone following you at bay."

"Black Dugal is crafty," Ironcloud advised. "He may slip by unseen. He may trot on through these hills completely unrecognizable."

"You needn't worry," Spud Wagon said. "I know many a mountain dwarf who is equally as wily as a Bloodwood."

As for southern Wyn Darrè itself, the place was thick with dwarves. But there were few men left in the Iron Hills. Most men in Wyn Darrè had died during the war with the Angel Prince. And what few cathedrals, keeps, and churches between Wynix and the Spud Wagon Inn had been naught but crumbled-down, burnt-out wrecks. Yet the farther east they traveled, the less destruction they saw and the more comfortable the place felt overall. In fact, so used to the bleakness of Sør Sevier, Krista could not believe how green and lush southern Wyn Darrè and the Iron Hills were. She had never seen a forest so thick and alive, trees all in full summer leaf, everything feathery and in blossom and a-shimmer in the hot, humid air.

They rode away from the Spud Wagon in single file, through rolling hills of trees and grass sparkling with sunshine. They were now headed for the southern shores of Sigard Lake to meet with Ironcloud's friend Seabass. The landscape smelled of summer and muggy silence, and their five tall roans glistened with sweat. The blond mute, Tyus Barra, led the way, as he always did.

Tyus was girt with a double-edged shortsword of his own. He wore woolen pants, a black shirt, and a stiff elk-hide jerkin studded with iron loops. Ironcloud was now dressed in studded leather armor, a bulky battle-ax strapped to his back. For the most part, Krista Aulbrek and Hans Rake rode directly behind the dwarf and boy, both of them with hands always cuffed in irons, legs tied to their saddles. They both still wore their sweaty prison rags and their horses were tied to Ironcloud's today, both forced to move at the dwarf's pace. Borden and Ironcloud had mainly let Hans be. Stupid, perhaps. But so far, like Krista and Café Colza, Hans had been a model captive. Still, to be safe, Borden Bronachell brought up the rear, long black sword hooked to a baldric over his back. He now wore solid leather breeches and a white shirt, polished leather armor fit for a king over both, the accoutrements provided by Tyus Barra when they'd originally landed in Wynix. Café Colza followed the processional about fifty feet behind them at all times, spiked collar gleaming around his thick neck, hulking tongue dripping a trail of slobber in his wake.

Over the days, Borden and the dwarf had conversed openly and aplenty, but it was all talk of the Brethren of Mia, the *Moon Scrolls*, and some mysterious bits of parchment called *The Angel Stone Codex*. It was these mysterious writings that Ironcloud was most eager to have his friend Seabass explain. From what Krista had gathered, *The Angel Stone Codex* was a set of ancient Vallè scrolls dating back to the War of Cleansing a thousand years ago, and Seabass had been working tirelessly most of his life trying to plumb its secrets, trying to translate the archaic Vallè script.

Their discussions also revolved around the return of the Five Warrior Angels. Ironcloud talked specifically of his brother, Roguemoore, and a man named Shawcroft and a boy named Nail, hinting that both had some connection to Krista and the ancient weapons of the Five Warrior Angels. The dwarf spoke now and then of a gold coin a Vallè would gift unto one of the Brethren of Mia as foretold in *The Moon Scrolls of Mia*, and claimed that Roguemoore's last letter spoke of just such a Vallè and just such a coin. Borden talked of his children as he had earlier in their journey: Jovan, Jondralyn, Tala, and Ansel. Borden had even mentioned his nephew and niece on more than one occasion: Lindholf and Lawri Le Graven, or "the twins," as he called them. "I wonder if my sister still watches over them."

As they traveled, Krista noticed the blond boy, Tyus Barra, stealing shy glances her way from time to time. He never spoke—he couldn't, and she felt bad for him in a way, knowing that his tongue had been removed at the Battle of Kragg Keep by two of Aeros Raijael's Knights Archaic, Enna Spades and Hammerfiss.

She didn't know why the boy looked at her so. His stolen looks had started at Wynix. And up until their stay at the Spud Wagon, Krista figured she herself had most likely looked a fright. Why any boy would stare at her was beyond comprehension. She'd often longed to simply brush her hair. She thought back to her bedchamber set near the back of Black Dugal's training quarters in Rokenwalder. She remembered her elegant curved-handled hairbrush. Dugal did not want his Bloodwood trainees to have much in the way of possessions. But he did allow them tools to groom themselves, for beauty was the first rule of a Bloodwood. For most of their journey she'd just wanted to be clean. And that was another reason she had enjoyed the Spud Wagon so much. She had been able to take a hot bath and unsnarl her hair—but again, she had had to do both whilst cuffed and shackled. But she had made it work.

She wanted to be clean again. In more ways than just physically. She felt dirty inside. She recalled what Borden Bronachell had said to her on the boat, how she was a killer, the worst kind of human there was. But she did not believe that. *There is good in me.* If she could go back to her Sacrament of Souls and set every single prisoner free, she would. What she had done in the name of training *had* been wrong. Borden was right about that. *But there is still good in me.* In fact, after her experience in the Rokenwalder dungeons, she would set free every prisoner if she could. *For if I was not guilty, who is to say any of them are?*

**

They had spent the entire day on horseback, making slow time, for the road they followed, like every path in the Iron Hills, was an up-and-down, meandering affair.

By early evening, they had ventured into an oak forest that marched along both sides of a winding trail spangled with leaves of green that did not stir in the heavy summer air. The oaks surprised Krista in their size, twice as tall as any birch or pine, and their girth double the span of even the largest wine barrels. Ungainly, large, and crooked, their oaken limbs sprawled haphazardly over the trail, creating a tunnel. Among the forest floor of grass and purple flowers were scattered large boulders, every one luminescent with green moss. Krista thought it the most magical place she'd ever seen.

Their horses were lathered and huffing air by the time Ironcloud finally slowed their gait near a copse of trees circling a glassy clear pond. "We camp here for the night," the dwarf announced. He slid from his saddle and unhooked his bedroll and cooking gear.

Irons about her wrists, Krista placed the side of her face against her mount's neck. It didn't feel the same as Dread, but the touch of the horse against her flesh was some comfort. After a moment, Borden untied her legs and she slid from the horse's back, hobbled straight toward the pond, and knelt down carefully in the grass, leaning her upper body over the water. It wasn't like a hot bath at the Spud Wagon, but it was clean water. She saw herself reflected in the clear pool, long blond hair, pale perfect skin.

But she also saw that shadow in the heart of her eyes that stretched far into her soul, hazy and dark. *What has become of me? Naught but death and murder and assassinations to show for my life.* She dipped her cuffed hands into the pool, breaking up the image she saw below. No matter how hard she tried, Borden Bronachell's words still bothered her. Cupping her palms, she filled them with water and washed her hair, letting the cool water rinse away that dark feeling in her soul. *Can all those awful things Borden Bronachell thinks of me be true?* When she was done washing, she stared into the lush forest across the pond, once again dazzled by the greenery of Wyn Darrè.

She sat there by herself for some time as Tyus Barra gathered wood and Ironcloud started a fire. Her stomach growled as the smell of sizzling bacon eventually wafted over her. Café Colza, drinking from the pond some twenty paces away, also lifted his snot-dripping nose at the delightful aroma. Krista stood and hobbled back to the fire and sat in the grass near Hans Rake, legs crossed before her. Hans was still cuffed and shackled. They would both always remain cuffed and shackled.

Tyus Barra motioned with his hands in Ironcloud's direction, then peered at her owlishly from his spot across the fire, wide-eyed and bashful. The boy and the dwarf had a way of communicating with hand signals that Krista did not understand.

"What did he say?" she asked the dwarf.

Ironcloud stirred the fire under his iron skillet and flipped the bacon, ignoring her question. He had been an uncommunicative asshole to her the entire journey. Krista had known the cruel dwarf as the amiable Squateye for so long that it was strange to think of him as anything else.

"Fine," she mumbled. "Stupid fucking dwarf. I don't care what the mute said then. Just ignore me."

"He said your hair is pretty." Hans' voice was laced with whimsical sarcasm. "He said your hair was pretty and glorious as a dove's feather."

Tyus' face flushed red under his blond hair. Hans flashed him a sly smile. Café Colza waddled up and sat next to Hans. Krista knew that was not what the mute had said.

"Another thing," Hans went on, winking at Krista. "The mute has been leaving flowers atop your bedroll each night as you sleep. He thinks no one notices. But I wake early every morning and pluck the flowers off you and toss them into the woods." He laughed. "Sometimes even piss on them for good measure. A man has to piss a river first thing in the morning, you know."

Tyus Barra's face had flushed an even deeper red, making Krista wonder if the ridiculous story wasn't true. She said, "I would have noticed flowers on my bed. I would have noticed had you woken up and moved them, Hans. Like you, I sleep lightly."

"Not lightly enough." Hans' eyes glittered with mischief as he raised both cuffed hands. "I unhook the irons nightly and wander about at will." He winked at Tyus Barra then. "I could slit the throat of every single one of you if I so wished."

"You are full of lies," Krista scoffed.

"You disappoint me, Crystalwood," Hans said. "Of course I escape each night, else how do you think I keep the sides of my head shaved smooth like I do?" He rubbed both shackled hands through the strip of hair atop his head. "Have you ever tried shaving all shackled up like this? Bloody rotted angels, I should've known your investigative skills were no better than that."

His bold statement about escaping his bonds nightly got no reaction from Borden, who took a seat in the grass near Krista. Ironcloud remained hunched over the fire, cooking, ignoring everyone. The sides of Hans' head indeed looked freshly shaved. *And who knows how many daggers he might still have hidden, despite how thoroughly he was searched?* Hans Rake was a crafty one.

Tyus Barra glanced toward the horses munching grass not far from the pond, then signaled once more to the dwarf, who nodded.

"He wants to know what you named your horse," Hans said. "He saw you rubbing your face all over the thing's neck earlier."

"Sisco," she answered, nodding to the blond mute, glad for a change of subject. "I named him Sisco. And thanks for asking, Tyus."

The mute's quick smile was so pleasant and honest it almost tugged at Krista's heart. "What's your horse's name?" she asked him.

The tongueless boy made several more swift motions with his hands toward her, as if he were tracing waves on the sea. But she could not read his sign language.

"Mud Puddle," Hans blurted. "He named his horse Mud Puddle. Or perhaps Piss Bucket. Or Waves of Piss. Or Dances with Piss."

Tyus Barra frowned, eyes cast to the ground.

Hans laughed at that. "Well then, don't be so sloppy with your hand signals, boy."

"His horse's name is Windwalker," Borden said flatly. "Now leave the poor boy be."

Hans shrugged. "But I've already proved you cannot silence me."

"Don't test us," Ironcloud growled, still fussing with the bacon on the skillet.

"The dwarf speaks." Hans sat back. "You think you can kill me? 'Cause that's what it will take to silence me."

"Yes." Borden's answer was swift in coming. "I think I can kill you."

Hans' eyes narrowed to pinpoints. "Truth is, you all live only on my sufferance. I could have killed you all days ago. And one day perhaps I will. Once I've been granted permission from my master, of course. He follows us like a ghost, he does."

Hans was not shy about saying whatever crossed his mind, even his plans to kill everyone. And Krista wasn't so sure he couldn't do it. In fact, she knew he could. But when she looked at him, she could see his mood had suddenly changed.

There was a haunted look in his eyes. And he was looking right at her. He said, "When that mermaid had me wrapped up in the water, I saw things, Crystalwood. I saw a vision of you, and of Fiery Absolution. I saw Black Dugal and the Skulls. I saw you slay Squateye under a pillar of fire as swift as you please. I saw our Bloodwood cloaks protecting us from the fires of Absolution as they were meant to do."

Ironcloud looked up from the sizzling bacon sharply, his voice rough as a dull saw blade. "Pay no attention to what visions you receive at the touch of a mermaid. For if those creatures get ahold of you long enough, they can fool with your mind, before they rape you bloody."

"Huh, that mermaid wishes." Hans was still watching Krista. "Remember when Dugal took us to the cliffs of Spyke? Remember how he had us jump both feetfirst and headfirst into the sea over and over? Remember how we learned how to control our bodies as we fell from various heights? Remember how we learned how to slice into the water to cause the least amount of pain or damage to our bodies?"

"I remember." Krista nodded. "What of it?"

"I recalled that entire trip whilst in the water with the mermaid," Hans said. "That trip and that training were important. I know it. We will fall from high places, you and I."

"Like the visions of a Vallè maiden," Ironcloud said, "the visions of a mermaid are meant to deceive. Worse than allowing the wraiths to eat at you."

Hans leaned over toward Krista and whispered, his voice velvet soft, smile smooth as red wine. "'Tis not the deceit of mermaids and Vallè maidens we need worry about, but rather the deceptions of Borden and Ironcloud. Every word from their lying mouths is meant to deceive. Meant to *fool* with your mind, Crystalwood. That I promise you. My visions you can trust."

"You're cracked," she said. "Barking mad. One moment you're scared, the next you're naught but a pompous fool." The hunger growing in the pit of Krista's stomach grew and her mouth watered as she watched the bacon cook. She was done with pointless conversation.

"I am not all mad," Hans said, thin lips curling in a mocking sneer. "We used to know him as Squateye. Proof of *Ironcloud's* deception.

Borden Bronachell's, too. I am the only one telling you the truth around here. You need to wake the fuck up and act like a Bloodwood again."

Krista ignored him.

Tyus Barra used sign language again and the dwarf nodded one more time. Then the boy vacated his spot on the grass and drifted toward the horses, opening Ironcloud's saddlebag, searching.

The bulldog next to Hans flopped sideways onto the grass with a loud snore. Hans petted the dog, staring directly at Krista. "I will not deceive you, Crystalwood. Our master follows us, and that is true. I've seen him in the dark watches of the night, talked to him even. Black Dugal but waits for the right moment to make his presence known. You know our master; he has a flair for the dramatic entrance. But he wants you on his side."

Krista stared into the fire, watching the glowing coals.

Tyus Barra returned with a jug and some thin copper plates and copper utensils, then handed a plate to each of them. He took special care in giving Krista the largest one. But every pure and innocent kindness Tyus Barra showed her was like a dagger in the heart. *He knows what kind of killer I am, yet he treats me with utter kindness.* His pureness of heart made her feel guilty. She didn't want the largest plate, or any plate, for that matter. Her appetite was gone.

"We are not being followed," Ironcloud grunted, glaring at Hans. "Quit pretending that we are."

"Café Colza leaves a clear enough trail for Dugal," Hans said. "Hair. Piss. Shit. Slobber. Mucus. Ear wax. Even the bulldog's tears are signs for Dugal to track and trace and follow. My master wishes Crystalwood and me to kill Aeros Raijael as much as you do. And that is why he leaves us be. For now. We are all going in the same direction, after all. We are all traveling toward Aeros Raijael."

"You truly think we want you to kill the White Prince?" Borden asked. "You truly think that is why we are keeping you alive?"

Hans grinned at the man. "Despite your denial, it is a certainty: you wish us to slay the Angel Prince."

"Perhaps we should gag the Bloodwood." Ironcloud's hard eyes met Borden's.

"Of course you wish to stifle the truth," Hans said, glancing at Krista. "They wish to stifle the truth of who you really are, Crystalwood. Do you think they hint around your heritage for nothing? I overheard what Borden said when we were stranded on those boats, that he can show you a better way, that he knows who you really are, that he knows what destiny awaits you. I heard him tell his story, even though I floated thirty paces away. I heard every word. A Bloodwood is trained to listen."

"And what did you hear?" Krista asked.

"I remember it almost word for word," Hans said with confidence. "Seventeen years ago he stole two babes from their mother. Two blond twins who many in the Five Isles would seek to kill. A boy and a girl. For their safety, he disguised them both and hid them where they would *never* be found, for he knew many evil forces sought to slay them. He then dropped hints that the stolen twins were under the care of Ser Torrence Raybourne, king of Wyn Darrè, and his younger brother, Ser Roderic. Both Torrence and Roderic went along with the ruse. Then Borden admitted to having stolen two similar-looking babes, a boy and a girl, babes for the forces of evil to hunt and kill, two children to act as bait whilst the *special* twins remained safe in anonymity. He stole the life from two innocent children. And their lives have been naught but loneliness and hardship ever since. For seventeen years they have been living a lie."

Hans did have a near-perfect memory, and she wasn't at all surprised that he recalled the conversation so well. Ever since Borden had admitted his sins, Krista had oft wondered which of the four kids she was, if any. *Was Ser Aulmut Klingande my real father, as King Aevrett hinted before I knifed him? Was Avril really even my mother?* She had never known Avril. Only through Gault's tender stories and recollections did she know anything of her mother.

Or were Hans and Borden just playing some cruel joke on her?

At the moment, Borden was watching Hans carefully. The dwarf was watching Hans too, skillet no longer over the fire.

"Which of those four children are you, Krista?" Hans asked aloud the very question that plagued her daily. "Or are you really any of them? Or could it all be just a lie, a cruel deception, like a mermaid's dream?"

Why *had* Borden told her? *Is it all just a game?* She knew that Hans didn't know the answers. He was merely poking sticks, trying to get a reaction out of each and every person gathered around the fire.

"Are you really Gault Aulbrek's daughter?" Hans goaded. "Or have you always been fatherless? Are you but a ghost? Or are you naught but a pawn in their grand design, naught but bait to be used in the conspiracies of the Brethren of Mia? For it does seem they are full of grand schemes."

"Pay Hans Rake no mind," Ironcloud said. "He's naught but a gutter rat turned Bloodwood. He just wants everyone to feel like they have as unnoble a heritage as he."

Hans seemed unaffected by the dwarf's insult, eyes fixed on Borden Bronachell, crisp and cool. "I wear my heritage with pride," he said. "I only seek the truth. For I am not Hans Rake. I am Shadowwood, and I am proud to call myself fatherless."

"As should we all call ourselves fatherless," Krista muttered. "As should we all."

It was then that Hans smiled and winked his approval.

*Laijon returned shall be an ensign unto all kingdoms. And he shall be
called the Lord of Fiery Absolution, the Savior of All Mankind, the First
and the Last, the marked one, the Holy Cross, the Slayer of the Beasts, the
Supreme Spirit, the Lord of All Worlds, the preexistent world, this world,
and the next, the Giver of Life and the Bringer of Death, the Father of All
Mourning, the great One and Only. He shall be the King of Slaves.*
—THE WAY AND TRUTH OF LAIJON

CHAPTER FOURTEEN

MANCELLOR ALLEN

13TH DAY OF THE FIRE MOON, 999TH YEAR OF LAIJON

SOUTH OF BETTLES FIELD, GUL KANA

There were eight thieves total, several of them tall, a few of them short, and none of them fat. But all eight blocked the forest road ahead, each one of them brandishing a stumpy shortsword or rusty dagger. The bottom half of their faces were veiled under red bandannas. Mancellor Allen wanted to just push his way through the thieves with his pony, or turn and run. But he wondered if Liz Hen Neville and Dokie Liddle would follow his lead. They all had weapons. The Turn Key Inn & Saloon had provided Mancellor with some old leather armor, a battered gaoler chest plate, a belt, and a fleece-lined sheath and shortsword. Liz Hen and Dokie wore a cobbled-together patchwork of gaoler armor too, each with shortswords girt at their hips. Mancellor knew they were good fighters; he had witnessed their bravery in battle. But could they take on eight thieves?

"There's a reason common folk would rather take the King's Highway and not these back roads." One of the thieves stepped forward, his voice thin and reedy under his bandanna. He was one of the slender ones and had cruel, beady eyes. "The King's Highway is well used and thus well-protected. It is constantly guarded by large groups of armed merchants and many knights of the Silver Throne. The only type of people who take back roads like these are people who are up to no good." He motioned to the seven men behind him with a wave of his sword, then pointed at Mancellor. "People like us."

Mancellor, Liz Hen, and Dokie had slowly traveled east from Lord's Point through the King's Gap toward Amadon for seven days now, crossing dewy fields and cool streams springing crystal and clear from the higher climbs of the Autumn Range, which now rose up behind them to the west. They had passed by a small inn and tavern called the Bloody Stag not an hour ago. It was a lonely little place sitting off to the side of the road, all by itself. The backwoods trail they traveled now was clothed in pine both before and aft. The brisk wind above was blunted by the loftier branches and bore the rich perfume of pine. The dense wood surrounding them had grown dark with both shadow and thieves.

"We aim to take them ponies," the thief said, "and whatever goods you carry in that large sack."

Mancellor gripped the reins of his mount. He didn't want to give over the three ponies. They had carried Liz Hen, Dokie, and himself this far. He also didn't wish to fight. The wound on his right bicep that stretched from the back of his elbow around the front of his arm was not yet healed and still offered much trouble and pain. And above all, he did not wish to see Liz Hen and Dokie hurt. They had been pleasant if not strange travel companions. Their varied conversations could go from the absolute normal to absolutely absurd in the span of a heartbeat. The only negative of their journey was that Liz Hen could at times become impossibly cranky the longer she went without that which she wanted most—food and Blood of the Dragon, the rare drug Mancellor had promised to help her find. Mancellor also didn't want the thieves to have *Lonesome Crown* and *Forgetting Moon*. Both artifacts were secured in the burlap sack tied to the saddle behind him.

"Off the horse," the thief demanded, still eyeing the sack. "Submission is the only way any of you live through this."

"We ain't giving you nothin'!" Liz Hen drew her sword. "You shit-birds can crawl back up into whatever inbred cunt hole you slithered out of."

Mancellor groaned inwardly. A fight seemed inevitable now. But the lead outlaw was laughing at the girl's insult. He pulled the bandanna down around his chin, revealing his thin face. He turned back to his companions. "Did you hear that? She wants us to crawl back into what-ever shit hole—"

A bloody arrow tip suddenly protruded from the man's mouth, teeth spinning to the ground. The thief toppled face-first onto the dirt road with a thud. Similar arrows sprang from the backs and bellies of the seven remaining thieves. None of them could even draw a sword in de-fense before they were falling over dead.

It happened so swiftly that Mancellor had scarcely drawn his own sword. He awaited the next arrow from the dense forest, the one that would claim him. One of the thieves was still alive and moaning on the ground before him, trying to stand. An arrow slammed into the side of his head with a crack, blue fletching quivering.

Mancellor's tense gaze scanned the forest.

Both Liz Hen's and Dokie's ponies shuffled nervously as two men stepped out of the thick woods and undergrowth to their right. The newcomers' faces were not covered. One was young-looking, the other bearded and tall.

"Reckon these three are the fools what sent Praed the signal?" the bearded one asked. "Reckon they the ones been askin' around about us, Llewellyn?" The bearded one sported a frightful smile bursting with murky-looking teeth. He pointed a blue-fletched arrow up at Mancellor.

"They look like fools to me," the shaggy-haired blond named Llewellyn answered. "Beats the rotted dogshite outa me if they the ones what signaled Praed, though." He raised his own arrow to his chin, aimed its gleaming tip at Mancellor's chest, and pulled the bowstring taut.

The one named Llewellyn looked to be no more than a boy, thin and weak, but the sharp arrow centered on Mancellor's chest would pierce his heart just the same.

"Whoever they are," the bearded one continued, lowering his bow, "them robbers was right. They got some mighty nice ponies for the taking, don't they, Llewellyn?"

"Yer right about that, Clive." Llewellyn's arrow remained fixed on Mancellor.

"I want their ponies." Clive smiled.

Mancellor set a gentle heel to his pony's ribs, eyeing the surrounding forest for the rest of their band. He knew of these men, Clive and Llewellyn, two of Praed's crew of outlaws known as the Untamed. They were right: he had summoned Praed.

There had been a fair amount of loose coin in the saddlebags Liz Hen and Dokie had gathered from the Turn Key, enough to buy information from several oghul bloodletters outside Devlin. He purchased information on where Praed and his band of Untamed were camped. Mancellor knew the network of oghul bloodletters could locate Praed. He had learned what secret signals both the bloodletters and Praed answered to from his father, Niklos Allen. He never thought they would come in handy. But they had. He just hoped Praed would recognize him.

Mancellor's father dealt in rare goods out of a humble port north of Ikaboa, the type of rare goods collected and sold mainly by oghul pirates. But one of Niklos Allen's specialties was an extremely scarce drug—Blood of the Dragon. And Praed and his band of Untamed had traded in such goods with Mancellor's father from time to time. Most of the deals had been arranged by an affable oghul named Cromm Cru'x.

Mancellor missed the gruff oghul pirate named Cromm. In fact, just thinking of those long-ago days in Wyn Darrè sent his mind to reeling with both heartache and loss. *What has become of Bronwyn? Did she even survive?* He recalled taking his younger sister up into the wilds north of his hometown north of Ikaboa. It was there, along those white-cliff shores of Wyn Darrè, that he had taught Bronwyn how to shoot a bow. She had been a natural, taking to it immediately, killing most every puffin she had aimed at, even those perched on the highest windswept crags.

It was around that same time that he had tied two white sea-hawk feathers into Bronwyn's hair for her birthday. And his sister had kept those two feathers in her hair until they had practically worn down to nothing. But he always found her more feathers to replace the ones that wore out. And Bronwyn had never gone anywhere without those sea-hawk feathers in her hair. It was a brief, if not sweet, recollection of his former life.

Two more outlaws emerged from the shadows of the pines. One was cloaked and hooded and carried a gleaming sword in hand. The other was a lithe red-haired woman in a forest-green tunic and leggings, a longbow and quiver of arrows with blue-fletched shafts slung over her shoulder. Mancellor new her name was Judi. The cloaked man was Praed, the leader of the Untamed. He was tall and lanky and had dark eyes buried in dark sockets and a thin, menacing face. Dark hair could be seen under the hood pulled up over his head. He grinned a crooked grin with crooked teeth.

It had been five years since Mancellor had last seen this motley crew of thieves. He hoped they still held some goodwill for his long-deceased father, Niklos.

"Look who we found," Llewellyn said to Praed. "The sad lot who've been asking around about us in Devlin, I reckon."

Praed's hollow stare was fixed on Mancellor. "Though he was but a thin teenager last I saw him, this man is from Wyn Darrè, Llewellyn. He's from north of Ikaboa, if I am not mistaken, a friend of the pirate Cromm Cru'x, son of the trader Niklos Allen, brother of Bronwyn Allen."

Mancellor bowed to Praed. "I am most honored that you remember me and my family."

"Rumor is Bronwyn and Cromm vowed to find you," Praed said. "They believe you were captured by the White Prince. So you know, they still trade in Blood of the Dragon and other things, sailing the breadth of the Five Isles, dealing drugs and searching for any word of you."

"Rumor I heard was that he had joined with Aeros Raijael," Judi said.

"I was never 'joined' with Aeros," Mancellor said.

"But your name is Mancellor Allen, correct?" Judi's gaze narrowed.

"Aye, yes." Mancellor bowed in his saddle to the woman. "And it is true that I have been asking about the Untamed among the bloodletters, as my father would have had me do if I needed Blood of the Dragon."

"Blood of the Dragon?" Praed laughed.

"Yes, Blood of the Dragon."

Praed's grin was tight and fierce, crooked teeth no longer visible. "I never figured Niklos Allen's son to be the type to search out Blood of the Dragon."

"I am not at all happy he knew how to find us," Llewellyn said. "No matter who his daddy was."

Clive added, "And I'd cut out his tongue if he ever thought of repeating what he knows to anyone."

"And I'd hold him down while you did it." The red-haired woman named Judi nodded in grim agreement.

Mancellor blanched at the threat. Liz Hen looked at him accusingly, as if she couldn't believe her precious Blood of the Dragon resided with such thugs. But there was also hunger in her eyes.

"Oh, what the addicted won't do for a taste." Praed's cold stare was on Liz Hen.

"Do you have Blood of the Dragon?" she asked boldly.

"I've got what it is you seek, girl, if you but follow me to my lair."

"Your lair?" Dokie asked, trepidation in his voice.

Praed nodded. "It's but a ways down the game trail and into the shadowy wood. Just follow me."

**

A full moon hung overhead by the time they reached the lair of the Untamed.

Mancellor nearly turned his pony and galloped off at the sight. *The ruined abbey from my visions!* During the battle off the shores of Lord's Point, when the mermaid had dragged him under the rising tide, Mancellor had *seen* this place—a skeletal, roofless, floorless, doorless, windowless, and mostly wall-less stone structure of crumbled buttresses choked with twining green ivy, pine, and prickly brush.

"Centuries gone by, it was known as Ten Cairn Abbey," Praed announced.

The leader of the outlaws guided the group on foot toward the abbey, holding the reins of Mancellor's mount. Clive guided Liz Hen's pony, and Llewellyn had the reins of Dokie's. Judi brought up the rear, bow drawn and arrow nocked.

"Long abandoned," Praed went on. "Now 'tis merely a hideout for thieves."

The towering, open-aired stone abbey lay near the base of a sloping hill. A swampy and murky fen of hovering fireflies clogged the very bottom of the ravine beyond the abbey. One bog was larger than the others, ten standing stones arrayed in a circle in the center of black waters, all of them listing to the side. In the faint moonlight, Mancellor could see that the tall leaning stones were carved with squares, circles, crosses, crescent moons, and shooting stars.

"Look, Liz Hen, look." Dokie eyed the standing stones with some trepidation. "Standing stones set at all sorts of angles, none of them aligning north or south."

"What's your point?" Liz Hen grumbled.

To the left of the abbey was a hedgerow and a busted stone fence mottled by rich moss and lichen. The fence wove through the wood from the top of the hill to the dank and ominous marshlands below. To the right was another old wrecked wall, taller than the hedgerow, its crumbling surfaces draped with vine, remnants of one of the lofty abbey's smaller outbuildings. Praed led them past the smaller structure and straight into the center of the roofless abbey, the hooves of their mounts clomping softly in the peat.

Mancellor could clearly see that the abandoned edifice had been built in the typical cross pattern, as had all Gul Kana and Wyn Darrè chapels. It had the typical long nave and chancel and two small transepts on either side. From within, the gaunt ruin was a few hundred paces long and fifty wide. Stone piers and pointed arches rose some twenty feet above on every side; tall, windowless clerestories ascended some fifty feet above those to intermittently join with what few flying buttresses remained standing. That handful of pinnacles high above stretched over the camp like clawed fingers. The snarled trunks of the surrounding pine forest had forced huge cracks in the stone walls, creating natural benches in some places near the foot of the walls. At the very base of the walls of the abbey, the grassy ground was a-litter with large hunks of fallen stone.

Praed and his fellow outlaws hitched the three ponies to a wooden pole sunk near the southernmost wall. Mancellor, Liz Hen, and Dokie dismounted. The outlaws sat upon some of the fallen stones and natural benches, and a fire was soon crackling in front of them, a long shank of stag swiftly sizzling on a spit.

The night was cool and Mancellor groaned as he walked around gingerly, legs stiff, the wound on his arm crying out in pain. Still, he grabbed a horse blanket for himself and one for Liz Hen and Dokie to share. They huddled under the blankets on a length of pine deadfall under one of the pinnacled arches opposite the fire from Praed. Mancellor did not know if he would even be able to sleep in this place—a place straight out of his visions. *Does this mean I am on the path Laijon set me upon?* He felt it within his bones that he was.

"I'm hungry." Liz Hen eyed the cooking meat.

"As am I." Praed smiled. He had gaps between each crooked tooth, which gave his smile a cruel, spiteful twist.

"Best get some food in you." Judi smiled too. "And we must get to know you a little better before Praed shows you the good stuff, the stuff you really want, no?"

"And I wish she'd never even tried the good stuff." Dokie did the three-fingered sign of the Laijon Cross over his heart. Liz Hen elbowed the boy before he could finish the action. "What did you do that for?" Dokie grumbled, pulling the horse blanket back up around his shoulders. An uneasy wind prowled about the abbey.

"That prayer does no good." She glared at him.

"Not a believer in Laijon, are you?" Judi asked her.

A dark look came over Liz Hen's face. She did not answer.

"I never believed in Laijon myself, either," Judi continued. "Seems like a bunch of twatwaddle to me. Raijael too. And those who believe in Mia, demon worshippers all."

Praed had an amused smirk curling at the corners of his mouth. "The Untamed, we are none of us believers in the gods."

"You shouldn't blaspheme any of the gods, Laijon or Raijael." Dokie's fright-filled gaze was now fixed on the large gap in the crumbled abbey. The ten standing stones were silhouetted like dark ship sails against the moonlit bog below. "It's not right to speak ill of the gods," he continued. "And the holy book says Mia is to be revered, never worshipped."

"Mia, Raijael, Laijon," Liz Hen repeated the names. "Prayers to any of them are for the truly demented."

"Stop saying such things," Dokie exclaimed.

But Liz Hen would not be deterred. "Did you know I used to pray for the silliest of reasons, Dokie, asking Laijon for the most trivial of desires: to get a job at the Grayken Spear Inn, to bake the perfect salmon loaf for my pa, to find my favorite copper bracelet I'd lost. And when I got the job or found the bracelet, Laijon be praised. Or, on the other hand, if I burned the salmon, I'd just assume it was Laijon's way of teaching me a lesson—don't build such a big fire in the oven next time, dumb Liz Hen. But it was all folly!"

"How can you call prayer folly?" Dokie asked.

"Don't you see, whilst I was praying for stupid things like lost bracelets and whatnot, Wyn Darrè was at war. Whilst I prayed for trivialities, Wyn Darrè children were in the midst of watching their families being slaughtered. Whilst I prayed for trivialities, Wyn Darrè children were praying for Laijon's intervention. They prayed for Laijon's help whilst stuffing the severed purple guts back into their own mothers' and fathers' torn bellies with their own bloody little hands. And Laijon ignored their horrified pleas. Why? Because, Dokie, because he was busy helping me get a job at the Grayken Spear, helping me find my missing bracelet!"

"God's ways are not our ways," Dokie said.

"But they should be," Liz Hen snapped. "Are you telling me Laijon had no time for little children who cry out for his mercy? Are you saying Laijon has no time for little children getting ass-raped by Sør Sevier swords?"

"I have no idea what god has time for, Liz Hen. I am not the judge of what prayer is more important to Laijon, and neither are you."

"I *should* be the judge," Liz Hen said. "Either all the gods are completely impotent, or they have mixed priorities, or they are just plain cruel. And I for one shall never utter another prayer in their name."

"It pains my heart to hear such," Dokie said. "What would Bishop Godwyn think of you now?"

"Who cares what Godwyn would have thought?" Liz Hen said. "A lot of good belief in Laijon did Bishop Godwyn. He invoked the rules written within *The Way and Truth of Laijon* to his own death."

"He invoked those rules to save you," Dokie said angrily. "Bishop Godwyn was executed in your stead. A selfless sacrifice."

"A foolish sacrifice."

"I see Laijon's hand in all things. Even Godwyn's death!"

"And you are a fool."

Dokie was silent.

"Please share your tale, Liz Hen," Praed said. "I wish to hear of this bishop's sacrifice in your stead."

The girl recounted the story of how she had saved Leif Chaparral during the battle in the Saint Only Channel. How once Leif had discovered she was a female and fighting in his army, he had ordered her to hang. How Hugh Godwyn, a bishop, had stood in proxy for her execution, dying in her stead as was his right to satisfy the law. As she recounted the tale, Mancellor could tell Liz Hen was experiencing a bitter amount of guilt and shame over the event. The chaos of events leading up to Godwyn's sacrifice had clearly shaken her faith to the point of killing it entirely.

"After hearing all that," Praed said, "I am with Dokie. Seems this Bishop Godwyn was an answer to your prayers."

Dokie nodded. "Just like finding Mancellor was an answer to my prayers."

"Many have helped to save us these past few moons, Dokie," Liz Hen said. "And none of them were Laijon. Shawcroft saved us and died.

Culpa Barra and Roguemoore and Val-Draekin and Seita and Stefan and even Nail have fought by our side. And where are they all? Likely dead. And Bishop Godwyn became a bloodletter in effort to save you, Dokie. He was hung by the neck in my stead. And I fail to see Laijon's hand in any of it. 'Twas just the self-sacrifice of humble folk for the lives of their friends. None of the gods ever acted so noble."

"Regardless of your feelings," Dokie said, "you will always be my friend. And I shall still pray when I choose."

"And you shall always be my friend too." Liz Hen's voice dropped to an almost indecipherable mumble. "But the only prayer I wish for is for Beer Mug's return."

"What is Beer Mug?" Judi asked.

"Beer Mug was my brother's dog," Liz Hen answered.

"I've never much liked dogs," Judi said.

"How can a person not like dogs?"

"They're too noisy, for one," Judi answered. "Too rambunctious, for another. Not at all the type of animal for a group of thieves."

"Hey," Llewellyn piped up, round eyes gleaming. "Remember when we were robbing that one manor house in Rokenwalder? Remember that mansion with all the dog-piss stains on the rugs?"

"Oy." Clive pinched his nose. "It stunk something fierce, that place."

"And the lady come home," Llewellyn said. "Caught us scooping up her jewels and good silverware. Remember that, Clive?"

"Aye!" Clive slapped his own leg jovially. "Stupid bitch shouted at us, 'How dare you come in and rob my home!'"

Llewellyn busted up laughing too. "And I shouted back, 'Home! More like a four-hundred-thousand-pence privy for your dog!'"

Clive bellowed. "Ain't never laughed so hard in my life."

"Best insult I ever came up with, that," Llewellyn guffawed. "Sayin' her so-called 'home' was just a big ol' expensive latrine for her dog!"

Praed and Judi were laughing now too.

"Well," Liz Hen huffed. "Regardless of your opinion on manor house privies or dogs, my brother died some time ago, and he had a dog named Beer Mug and I loved him. Beer Mug was lost in the battle off the shores of Lord's Point, lost in the ocean. But he will come back to me, I know it."

Judi shook her head, laughing no more. "I myself am having a hard time believing you were in any battle, much less the battle in the Saint Only Channel!"

"Aye," Clive agreed, stroking his beard in deep contemplation now. "That battle is rumored to have decimated Aeros Raijael's entire army."

"We all were in that battle," Liz Hen answered somberly, motioning to both Mancellor and Dokie, too. "What good that battle did, I don't know. But it does seem that we won, I reckon."

"Gul Kana's victory was sheer accident," Praed said. "'Twas the bloody tide of the Saint Only Channel that took out those armies."

To Mancellor, the entire battle was a farce. For it seemed King Jovan and the grand vicar had been on the side of defeatism from the start. They believed that there was scant point in stemming the dark tide of Aeros Raijael's armies and that allowing Fiery Absolution to come to Gul Kana, as *The Way and Truth of Laijon* foretold, was as it was meant to be. But by sheer accident Leif Chaparral had made short work of all those plans for Fiery Absolution.

He shifted his position on the pine log, injured arm smarting. The horse blanket slid off his shoulder, revealing the Sør Sevier slave brand on his wrist. He caught Praed looking at the mark and then looking away, turning the spit of stag meat.

There was a sudden racket of buzzing from the swamps below. Fireflies by the thousands rose up through the pine trees as one, twinkling and blinking their way into the sky. Mancellor watched through the open roof of the abbey as the bright swirling bugs flew off.

"Look at that," Liz Hen exclaimed, clearly enchanted at the sight.

"On a full Fire Moon, the moths and fireflies will never seek the light of a campfire," Praed said, dark-pitted eyes also focused skyward. "They would rather fly straight up into the black reaches of the heavens, in search of that one round bright orb suspended above." He looked at Liz Hen then, eyes narrowing. "Though they will never reach that which they seek, still they chase it."

Liz Hen's face reddened as she watched the fireflies rise into the sky. The arching buttresses of the abbey were naught but shadowy silhouettes against the thousands of twinkling lights. And the blinking lights disappeared and the fireflies were gone.

"Is it true that you are really thieves?" Dokie broke the silence. "The Untamed? The worst of the worst? Making your way stealing from Rokenwalder dog owners and such?"

"'Tis true," Praed answered. "According to the rules of thievery, I suppose we are thieves."

"Thievery has rules?" Dokie inquired.

"Aye."

"Would you share some of the rules?" Dokie asked.

"Share the rules?" Praed's voice was aghast with mock incredulity. "How can I when the first rule of thievery is never to share the rules of thievery?"

"But I'd be ever so grateful," Dokie plowed on, completely unaware that Liz Hen was again visibly bristling at the conversation. "Thievery intrigues me."

"Bullocks," Liz Hen blurted. "Thievery has never intrigued you."

"I enjoy learning new things," Dokie said. "Gathering information and whatnot." He looked at Praed again. "Like I said, I'd be ever so grateful."

"You'd be ever so grateful?" Praed shrugged with nonchalance. "Well, in that case, how can I not share information with an information gatherer such as yourself?"

"Splendid." Dokie was actually smiling now.

"Most splendid indeed," Praed continued.

"Well, go on," Dokie pleaded.

"I shall." Praed nodded. "The second rule of thievery is to develop both a refinement in manners and a complete disregard for them."

"Refinement in manners?" Liz Hen barked, having none of it.

But Dokie nodded as if he completely understood what was being said. "He claims it's the second rule of thievery," he said. "And I'm inclined to believe him."

"Are you daft?" Liz Hen huffed. "Just look around. They live out here in the woods, you clodpole, not in some vast expensive manor house, sipping cinnamon tea and scrubbing dog piss out of their expensive rugs."

Dokie shrugged. "The third rule?" he asked Praed.

The outlaw looked from Dokie to Liz Hen, then settled on Mancellor. "The third rule is that thievery is not a game to be played with any but those in whom you trust."

"And the fourth?" Dokie asked as if he understood the third.

"To be honest"—Praed again met Dokie's enthusiastic gaze—"there really are no rules to thievery."

"Oh," Dokie muttered. "That is disappointing."

"As I imagine it would be, for you look like you have the makings of a good thief."

"I always thought so myself. And I was enjoying the rules."

Liz Hen punched Dokie hard in the shoulder. "Bloody rotted angels, what are you goin' on about? Why are you even engaging these people in casual conversation?"

Dokie looked at her, a wounded look in his eyes, rubbing his shoulder. "They said they wanted to get to know us, you know, before giving you the good stuff."

"Yes, when do I get the good stuff?" Liz Hen asked.

"You must be patient," Praed said.

"I was once being a lady of some civility and patience," Liz Hen said. "That was before the White Prince sacked Gallows Haven and killed most everyone I know. Before then I tried to avoid all manner of swords and spears and such, mightily I tried. But I have since taken up the blade."

"I can admire that," Praed said.

"Then when do I get a taste of Blood of the Dragon?"

Praed stood, hollow eyes roaming the forest, coming to rest upon their three ponies tethered to the trees just up the hill. His hard gaze narrowed, fixed on the burlap sack tied to the back of Mancellor's mount. "You'll be staying with us for a time, girl," he said, not taking his eyes from the burlap sack. "Make no mistake about that. You will be guests in our camp, if you take my meaning. That is, until you find a way to pay us for the Blood of the Dragon you are about to receive. That is, until the Untamed decide what to do with those precious things you've brought us. In fact, you may just be our guests until Black Dugal comes and claims you as his own."

One must cease trying to control every little thing. Let the rivers of
time flow, let the waters run where they may, for what destiny
is yours shall remain the same and polished from the journey.
THE WAY AND TRUTH OF LAIJON

CHAPTER FIFTEEN
TALA BRONACHELL

13TH DAY OF THE FIRE MOON, 999TH YEAR OF LAIJON

AMADON, GUL KANA

The one-eyed, toothless old man walking Amadon's cobbled streets beside Tala Bronachell sent people a-scurry with horrified looks. *A Bloodwood relies on illusion to survive,* Hawkwood had taught her. And the stooped old man was actually Princess Jondralyn Bronachell in disguise—clothed in a ragged and stained dockside raiment that smelled of seaweed and moldy food. Jondralyn's dirty fingers were curled around a cane she tapped on the cobbles as she shuffled along, barking to everyone in her path, "Out of my way! I make no idle threat!"

A scraggly gray beard and eyebrows covered the princess's rough and wrinkled face. Hawkwood had spread hurion tac paste mixed with birch whiskey over Jondralyn's skin earlier in the day, causing the deep wrinkles. The most disturbing thing about the disguise: Jondralyn's eye patch was absent. She walked the streets with naught but a dark hollow eye socket. It was this cavernous hole in Jondralyn's face and her mad ramblings that startled folks into giving her and Tala a wide berth.

Tala was also in disguise, though her costume was much more tempered. She was dressed as the one-eyed old man's granddaughter. She was shoeless, with dirty calloused feet, tan breeches, and a brown shirt similarly stained and as ripe as Jondralyn's. She wore a wig of scratchy white hair over her sun-worn face. Hawkwood had stuffed the same hurion tac paste into her lower and upper lips. He had even jammed some of the paste into her nostrils and eyelids, all to make her face unrecognizable.

This was the first time Tala and Jondralyn had ventured outside the *Val-Sadè* together since Tala had arrived on the abandoned ship. It was part of their Bloodwood training. Small silver daggers were all Hawkwood had armed them with. He had been teaching them both some tricks with the blades. But for their first journey, he had set them a simple task—to pray at the feet of Laijon.

"We're almost to the temple." Jondralyn's voice was rough and scratchy. Then she shouted to a group of fish merchants gathered on the cobbled street ahead. The merchants scooted out of her way.

Tala's heart thundered as they drew closer to the Temple of the Laijon Statue. The dirty market stalls along the cobbled streets of Amadon rang out with the clatter of trade, barter, and just a touch of danger. *Or is it just because I am a princess in disguise that I feel danger at every corner?* The River Vallè and its aqueducts were near. The riverside district was a haunt of the bloodletters and witches. She shuddered as the rank stench of foul waters grew in the air. These were Bloodwood games of a different sort Hawkwood had set them to.

Over the last few days, Tala had noticed how Hawkwood treated Jondralyn. Despite her sister's real scars and deformities, she could tell the man really did love her. She could tell Jon was in love with him. And the most impressive part was that they seemed to treat each other as equals. She had not heard a cruel word spoken between the two. *If I could have a relationship like that someday too . . .* Sometimes her own heart would flutter in her chest when she watched Jondralyn and Hawkwood's interactions. Other times she wondered if being in a relationship with anyone was the right path for her at all. *Alone is safer, better, less painful than caring for another.* But she did not want bitterness like that to set in and take root.

As Tala and her older sister rounded the next street corner, the Royal Cathedral and the Temple of the Laijon Statue rose up before them. Both grand buildings towered to over three hundred feet high and were constructed of Riven Rock marble. Silver Guards with pikes lined the entrances of both edifices. Tala guided her sister toward the fountain in the center of the temple's outer courtyard, Jondralyn's cane tapping the cobbles. The lively fountain was circled by marble pillars carved with shooting stars, crescent moons, crosses, circles and squares, and other symbols. The temple's stairs and arched entrance were crowded with people, pilgrims and worshippers and flagellants.

We are naught but peasants too, Tala reminded herself. *An old man and his granddaughter come to pray at the feet of the great One and Only.* Tala led Jondralyn though the crowds and carefully up the stairs. Once they were inside the cool shade of the temple's foyer, the clamor of the crowd dissipated. Tala quickly spotted the holy Ember Stone, a round dais at the center of the lobby. She led Jondralyn to it, dabbed at the ash atop the stone basin, brushed the ash over Jondralyn's forehead. They both made the three-fingered sign of the Laijon Cross over their hearts, then proceeded toward the polished doors of the temple's inner dome. A bishop bearing a smoky jar of incense eyed them both with no small amount of distaste. One of the two Silver Guards at the door pulled on a braided rope, and the doors swung soundlessly open.

Tala and Jondralyn shuffled in. The inner temple was silent, the air filled with reverence. But as always, Tala couldn't help but stare straight up through the hundreds of coils of candle smoke to the circular domed ceiling some three hundred feet above. Spear-wielding Silver Guards stood at watch along the curved walls, armor faintly agleam in dark alcoves. Crossbowmen lined the second-story gallery, ring mail also glittering dimly in the shadows. Above the gallery were bright stained-glass windows, sparkling jewel-like as the sun beamed through.

Upon a dais of gray stone in the center of the room was the great

Laijon statue, over five stories tall from head to feet, one muscular
arm held aloft, a silver sword in its hand pointing skyward. A wreath
of heather crowned the statue's head, and intricately carved chain-mail
armor draped its body. The statue's gray dais was ringed by five oxen
with iron cauldrons upon their backs, incense burning within, smoke
swirling above. Each cauldron was resplendent with divine symbols,
symbols carved in black, white, blue, green, and red, representing the
magical angel stones and weapons of the Five Warrior Angels: *Blackest
Heart, Ethic Shroud, Forgetting Moon, Lonesome Crown,* and *Afflicted Fire*—
the Five Pillars of Laijon.

Tala recalled the last time she had been in this vast room, with Glade
Chaparral and Lindholf Le Graven. She had coerced both boys into
accompanying her here to retrieve a note planted by Hawkwood. Of
course it was all a lie; the note had been planted by the Bloodwood assassin as part of an elaborate game, a game Tala considered long over. She
could look up at the Laijon statue now and see the very spot Lindholf
had climbed to so he could retrieve the Bloodwood's note.

*The Bloodwood's game! Where did it lead? Here and back again with noth-
ing gained.* Lawri Le Graven was still under the influence of the poison,
or not, Tala had no way of knowing for certain. But her tawny-haired
cousin now wore a gauntlet permanently attached to her severed arm—a
foreboding silver gauntlet fashioned of some pure Vallè magic. A gauntlet that could punch through the solid timbers of a ship's hull.

And Jondralyn knelt before the statue, leaning on her cane to do so,
pretending to be feeble and half-blind. Tala helped Jondralyn steady herself, noticing one of the Silver Guards moving briskly toward them now.
The guard stopped before Jondralyn and removed his helm, revealing a
head of thinning hair. It was the same Silver Guard who had approached
Tala, Glade, and Lindholf some three moons ago.

"I must ask you both to vacate the temple," the guardsman announced
with a formal air. "Though you've been here but a minute, we've already
many complaints of the stench that hath accompanied you both."

"Stench?" Tala blurted, genuinely offended. She lifting her arm,
smelling her own armpit. Hawkwood had rubbed many foul things over

their clothes before sending them out. The rotten stink nearly knocked her over.

"You would kick out an old man who has traveled so far?" Jondralyn grunted and groveled, keeping her head bowed before the guard. "I have traveled the breadth of Gul Kana to kneel before the great One and Only."

"We've walked clear from Tevlydog together," Tala added, an insolent tone in her voice. "My grandfather has come so far from the north just for this one last chance to offer his soul at the feet of Laijon."

The gray-haired guard's face hardened and his nose twitched with distaste. He gave a quick hand signal to several guardsmen waiting by the door. The guardsmen marched toward him.

"The Val Vallè ambassador and his daughter, Seita, are due here soon," he said. "We must vacate the chamber of all patrons, give the room time to air out before Ambassador Val-Korin arrives. He is liable to complain to the grand vicar if things are not just right. And I've no wish to answer to the grand vicar on what odors one-eyed old beggars from Gavryl have brought in."

"It's Tevlydog we came from," Tala corrected him. "In the north."

Jondralyn took her time standing, groaning as she did so, leaning heavily on her cane. Tala helped steady her. There were tears forming in Jondralyn's one eye, and drool formed over quivering, cracked lips. "But I've walked so far, good ser. Don't empty the chamber now."

"Clean yourself up, old fool." One of the guardsmen grabbed Jondralyn by the arm and pulled her roughly toward the door.

"Leave her be," Tala said. "I mean, leave him be." She cursed the mistake and grabbed Jondralyn by the arm, brushing the guard off, guiding her sister toward the door.

"Foul creatures," the guard sneered as he watched them go.

Tala couldn't believe she'd actually been mistreated by the guards. She wanted to rip away her disguise and give them a tongue-lashing they wouldn't soon forget. But as they passed through the two massive entry doors and into the temple's foyer and then stepped outside, a hush seemed to fall over everything. An entourage of several dozen armed

Vallè marched up the stairs, Val-Korin's bodyguard Val-So-Vreign leading the way.

In the center of the group of Vallè was the ambassador himself, Val-Korin, accompanied by his daughter Seita, both wearing opulent robes of shimmering blue, pendants of gold hanging from glimmering gold chains around their necks.

Tala and Jondralyn were swiftly brushed aside by the entourage. Tala kept ahold of her sister's arm to keep Jondralyn from tumbling down the stairs.

Val-Korin drifted up the stairs, giving Tala and Jondralyn not so much as a passing glance. But when Seita caught Tala's eye, she paused half a heartbeat, then gave her a sly little wink.

**

It was nearing sundown, and the Amadon dock district was still abustle with merchants, burghers, bloodletters, urchins, and traders of every stripe: Vallè, dwarf, oghul, and man. Jondralyn and Tala pushed their way through the press of people. And still none of the crowd knew it was King Jovan's two missing sisters in their midst.

The air was stale and sweaty and smelled of fish, and she wished for just one stray wayward breeze to move the humid stench away from her nose. She cursed Hawkwood for spreading such foulness over her. Though she guessed some of the putridity was coming from Jondralyn, too.

The dock district was abuzz with word from the west. Rumor was that Lord Lott Le Graven had returned, claiming that Leif Chaparral's small army had nearly wiped out Aeros Raijael's forces in what people were calling the Battle of the Saint Only Channel. Aeros Raijael himself might even be dead, rumor was. It seemed everyone was now talking of the battle, describing how the tide had risen and swept away the entire army of the White Prince. Even in her disguise, Jondralyn's face was overcome with shock at the news. Tala didn't know quite what to make of it, wondering if the threat from Sør Sevier was truly over. They traveled on, questions swirling in Tala's mind.

They were about a mile north of the *Val-Sadè* when Jondralyn seized Tala by the arm. "It's Val-Draekin," she hissed. "Up ahead. I swear that is him getting out of that fishing boat tied to the wharf near the crab stalls. See, just beyond all those folk to the left?"

Jondralyn pulled Tala through the throng at a brisker pace, but still doing her utmost to keep up the illusion of a crippled old man. Tala eventually spotted the dark-haired Vallè Jondralyn was referring to. It was Val-Draekin.

He stood on the wharf, wrapping a hefty rope about a wooden pole, securing a small sailboat to the dock. He was clothed in an odd collection of scratched, dented, and ill-fitting armor, with a clunky sword at his hip. Tala was used to seeing Val-Draekin in naught but elegant form-fitting leathers.

Three others were climbing from the sailboat: a young man and a young woman and a huge, burly oghul. The savage-looking brute was massive. He had a flat forehead and a blunt nose and was clad in naught but raggedy tan breeches and a stained shirt. Two long jewel-encrusted teeth protruded from both the top and bottom of the beast's mouth. Tala noticed tiny gems also embedded in the beast's knuckles as he stepped up onto the dock and handed the copper-haired girl next to him an ash-wood Dayknight longbow painted black.

The girl took the bow. A fleece-lined cloak of forest green was draped over her shoulder and a shortsword dangled at her belt. She wore dark breeks and leather boots with thongs wrapped clear up to the knee, and a black quiver full of black arrows hung loose on her back. She was also very pretty, but for her heavily shadowed face. The girl's icy eyes gleamed under black smears of what looked like squid oil that stretched underneath each brow and over each eyelid and down each of her cheekbones. The inky smears made the girl look hard and fearsome, though she couldn't be more than a couple of years older than Tala.

"Help the marked one up," the oghul said to the girl.

The two white feathers in the girl's hair shimmered under the sun-blanched sky as she turned, her harsh gaze falling on the fourth member of Val-Draekin's party, pulling himself out of the sailboat and onto the dock. He was a tall, muscular boy of about seventeen. Handsome, too.

The young man's hair was shoulder length and perfectly blond. He wore a shortsword low on his hip and a patchwork of mismatched armor that fit only slightly better than Val-Draekin's.

"Why didn't you grab the rest of the gear like I asked, Nail?" the copper-haired girl asked the boy.

"Nail," Princess Jondralyn repeated the name, looked at the boy in wonder. "Nail the Slave?" She muttered the last part almost under her breath. Tala had no idea what her sister was mumbling about. Did she know this fellow named Nail?

A lock of blond hair covered the young man's grayish-green eyes as he glared at the girl. But with a natural flick of his head, the strands fluttered easily free. Then, without a word of complaint, the young man named Nail jumped back down into the vessel, grabbed the remaining gear from the bottom of the fishing boat, and hauled it up onto the dock. He had the most arresting face and calm, assured manner Tala had ever seen in anyone her age. As Nail climbed from the boat for the last time, Tala noticed the bright red scar in the shape of a cross on the back of his right hand. His wrist above the scar was wrapped in a strip of tan-colored burlap. *What does he hide under that wrap?*

What does he hide behind those arresting gray-green eyes?

Val-Draekin and his three companions were soon striding down the dock away from Jondralyn and Tala, all four of them disappearing into the thick crowds of the city. "We must follow them," Jondralyn urged. "Before we lose them in the crowds."

Tala and her sister hustled their step, following.

Val-Draekin's motley group traveled but half a block before they stopped at the first blacksmith stand they came to. "I am here to requisition your heaviest armor," the large oghul said to the shop's blacksmith. "I lost mine in the sea."

"Requisition?" the blacksmith questioned. "What does that mean?"

"It means you are going to give Cromm whatever ill-fitting plate armor he may ask for," the girl with the ink-smeared eyes and white feathers in her hair said. On closer inspection, Tala noticed they were tattoos and not smears of squid ink around the girl's eyes.

"And I'll take whatever knives you might have lying about too," the oghul named Cromm added.

"Well, that'll cost you," the blacksmith said.

"We will not pay," Cromm said. "You will give. Like a gift."

"I will give you no such thing."

"You can give Cromm what he asks for," the girl with the ink-smeared eyes said, "or Cromm can suck your neck dry."

The oghul grinned maniacally, the jewels embedded in his teeth aglitter with color.

The girl said, "Cromm does not see this gift-giving thing as so difficult. Do you?"

The blacksmith backed away. "Take what you like."

Cromm and the girl gathered up the ugliest pieces of plate armor and the worst of the knives. Val-Draekin and the blond boy, Nail, watched the entire interaction without emotion. Soon the group of four carried on, leaving the blacksmith's stall behind.

Tala and Jondralyn followed the group into the city. But they had journeyed only a few more twisting and winding blocks when the copper-haired girl stopped and turned. She stared straight at Jondralyn and Tala a moment, then marched straight back toward them. Her hand reached for one of the black arrows in her quiver, and her bow came up too. The girl stood just a few paces from Tala and Jondralyn now. Then, within a heartbeat, she had her arrow nocked and aimed right at Tala's heart.

"Why were you watching us climb from the boat?" she demanded, voice laced with menace, cold eyes like twin pricks of blue flame under the tattoos. "Why are you following us now?"

Tala's heart was racing, eyes fixed on the arrow tip poised at her chest.

"I'm just an old man about my own business," Jondralyn answered the girl, voice gravelly, quavering. "I beg pardon if we've given any offense."

"Bullshit." The girl pulled her bow taut.

Val-Draekin was soon standing at the bow-wielding girl's side. "Put the bow down, Bronwyn," he said.

The girl did not listen, just pulled back on the bowstring more, sighting down the shaft. Nail and the oghul were soon standing behind the Vallè and the girl named Bronwyn, both of them eyeing Jondralyn and Tala harshly.

"Put the bow down, Bronwyn," Val-Draekin said again, peering more closely at both Tala and Jondralyn. "Is that you, Princess Jondralyn?" he asked, then turned his attention toward Tala. "And Tala? Whatever are the two of you doing out in the dock district dressed like this?"

To fall into the dark shadow and vile clutch of false faith and belief is the worst
of all fates, even worse than death, for the dead believeth not.
—The Way and Truth of Laijon

CHAPTER SIXTEEN

NAIL

13TH DAY OF THE FIRE MOON, 999TH YEAR OF LAIJON

AMADON, GUL KANA

Nail had looked on the great city of Amadon in rapt amazement as their fishing boat had made its cautious approach through Memory Bay. As they weighed anchor, the sun was going down over the city, casting a rose-tinted glow against the cloudless sky, the thousands of awe-inspiring buildings, and the lofty castle. It just didn't seem real.

Now Nail followed Val-Draekin, Bronwyn Allen, Cromm Cru'x, and Jondralyn and Tala Bronachell through a musty, dark tunnel beneath the city. The last time he had seen Princess Jondralyn, she had been lying on a litter in the middle of Ravenker, face slashed open and bloody. Culpa Barra had later explained to Roguemoore how the princess had gotten her injuries. Jondralyn had fought an ill-advised duel with one of Aeros Raijael's Knights Archaic, Gault Aulbrek.

Once in the dripping tunnel, Jondralyn had given up the stooped and bent subterfuge of an old man, shedding her wig and beard, revealing her own scarred face. Tala Bronachell was also in disguise. She was shoeless, feet dirty, face sun-worn and tanned, breeches and shirt similarly ragged and as foul-smelling as her sister's. Though once in the tunnel she had also removed most of her disguise, revealing raven-colored locks that tumbled to her shoulders.

Jondralyn led them through the tunnel, lantern in hand, their path winding downward in a slow descent before heading back upward again. The scars crossing the princess's face were pronounced in the lantern light, and whenever Nail saw her face, he found it hard to look away.

This last part of their journey took them up a narrow flight of stairs cut into jagged rock. In fact, the stairway was so narrow Cromm had to slide his bulk through sideways, new stolen armor scraping against the walls. Princess Jondralyn brought them to a locked wooden door at the top of the stone staircase and knocked five times, waited a moment, then knocked five more. The door slowly creaked open and a familiar face was revealed in the dim light above.

Hawkwood!

As Nail climbed the stairs toward the light above, his mind again flew back to Ravenker and Hawkwood's fight with the Bloodwood assassin, Spiderwood. Despite all his conflicting thoughts about what Hawkwood had told him of his parentage, Nail would always be grateful to the man. He was glad to see him again. At the top of the stairs, Nail entered a strange timbered room of slanted walls and flat timbered flooring and flickering lantern light. He suddenly felt disoriented.

Hawkwood gave Nail a look of warm welcome. He wore dark leather armor and no weapons that Nail could see. "I am most pleased to see you, Nail."

"I never got to thank you for saving me in Ravenker," Nail said.

"We've much to talk about," Hawkwood said.

"This place makes my head feel dizzy," Bronwyn said. "What is wrong with the walls?"

"You are inside the *Val-Sadè*," Hawkwood said, "an old pirate ship half-sunk in Memory Bay."

"You mean a Vallè pirate ship?" Cromm crooked his brow.

"Right you are," Hawkwood said. "A Vallè pirate ship." There was a moment of silence as Hawkwood and the oghul took each other's measure. At length Hawkwood addressed Jondralyn and Tala. "Please, divest yourselves of those reeking clothes."

Both princesses took their leave straight away, retreating to distant rooms in the aft of the tilting ship. Hawkwood led the rest of the group down a slanting corridor into a separate, larger room of stout, wide bulkheads and dark rich timber, several lanterns hanging from the tilted roof. He offered the newcomers hot tea and indicated various cushioned benches under the slanting bulkheads for everyone to take rest.

"We have not been properly introduced." Hawkwood bowed to Bronwyn and Cromm as he handed them their tea. "I am Hawkwood." They offered their own names in greeting. Hawkwood turned. "And this is Lawri Le Graven." He motioned to the darkest corner of the room.

Nail had to blink twice to realize the girl was real. For the girl named Lawri was the blond girl straight out of his underwater visions. *A knight with a glowing white shield and horned helm astride a brilliant white stallion, a blond girl on the saddle before him, her hand a metal claw.* Lawri stood there in a long black dress in the shadowy corner of the ship, ashen face and tawny hair ghostlike in the gloom, the flecks in her eyes glowing green. And she had a metal claw for a hand! And she stared right back at Nail, as if she knew him from somewhere long before.

"It's okay, Lawri." Hawkwood beckoned the girl over. "They are friends. And you already know Val-Draekin."

Lawri shyly stepped forward into the light and sat on one of the cushioned benches, resting her silver hand gently atop her lap. Nail was unable to look away from the girl's clawed hand. He sat onto the bench next to Bronwyn and Cromm, sipping his drink, watching as Val-Draekin sat next to the girl. "Pleasure to see you again, Miss Lawri." The Vallè dipped his head to her gracefully. Lawri's lips curled into a halfhearted smile.

"Why do you wear armor on your hand?" Cromm was also looking at the girl's arm in perplexed fascination. "Cromm wonders why such a pretty girl would wear a gauntlet if not in middle of battle?"

"I wear it because it won't come off," Lawri answered. Her green eyes were timid as she took in the large oghul and the copper-haired girl next to him.

Her gaze fell on Nail once again, like she knew him and wanted to say something, but didn't know what. *Does she share the same dream?* Nail couldn't help but study her in fascination. And on closer inspection, it was no simple gauntlet she wore. It was clear that the polished, scaled arm bracers of the silver claw seemed to be molded directly to her flesh just below her elbow. Shards of yellow light from the hanging lanterns appeared to dance in stark, shimmering waves over the armor's scales. There were small holes in the gauntlet's fingertips, as if something was meant to be fastened or screwed into them. *Or something was meant to grow out of them.*

Lawri seemed maybe a year or two younger than he, perhaps his own age even. Pale face and innocent features. But there was a depth of longing and hurt hidden deep within her eyes, her posture, the way she again cradled her silver arm. Her every movement was subtle, demure, full of fear and terror. This girl had been through much. Trials and agonies likely beyond anything he himself had ever faced—which was saying a lot. He found she was still also looking right at him. After a moment, he almost couldn't meet her gaze from the inner pain that flowed from her. *Deep secrets are buried within her.*

"Did you not try and take the gauntlet off your arm?" Cromm pressed the girl.

"Of course she tried." Bronwyn elbowed the oghul hard in the side of his ribs. "What fool wouldn't try? The thing is clearly stuck there."

"Cromm only asks to know the answer." The oghul rubbed his side. "Not to cause embarrassment."

"We've all tried removing it at one point or another," Hawkwood said. "As Bronwyn says, it's somehow attached itself to her permanently, by some Vallè alchemy, I imagine."

"I myself have never seen such a thing," Val-Draekin said. "But star silver is made of many properties and can act in strange ways."

"Star silver?" Hawkwood asked.

"Like Shroud of the Vallè," Val-Draekin said, "an ancient Vallè science. Vallè alchemy, if you will. Rare. The science of the stars."

"Is it made of the same silver we saw in the mines?" Nail asked, remembering the liquid silver Shawcroft told him not to touch in the Roahm Mines, the silver that melted the chairs in Sky Lochs, the silver that had scared him so when he saw it dripping from the barbed whips of the five Skulls. *Silver whips that cut a horse right in half.*

"I do not entirely know what star silver is made of, Nail," Val-Draekin answered.

"Does your hand work under the gauntlet, Law Ree?" Cromm asked, holding up his own arm, wiggling his jewel-encrusted knuckles. "Seems like you cradle it in your lap when you could be crushing things open with it."

"I have no hand under the gauntlet," the girl answered flatly. "King Jovan cut my hand off with Aeros Raijael's sword."

"Now there's a story I'd like to hear." Bronwyn perked up.

"I can crush things with it, though, like you said." Lawri raised the gauntlet. "But only once in a while can I get the fingers to wiggle." The silver fingers of the gauntlet remained stiff and unbending. "Like I said, I have no fingers under the metal."

"Well, Law Ree, you are a most unique human indeed," Cromm said. Then the oghul motioned to Nail with a dip of his gray head. "He is the marked one. And Cromm has brought him to Amadon. You two are alike. The girl with the silver hand is a great omen, just like the marked one."

Lawri looked at him and smiled. He looked away, suddenly self-conscious.

The oghul pulled the black stone from the leather pouch at his belt and slipped it into his lower lip, sucking greedily, eyeing Nail with a slanted gaze. "The marked one seems to care little about Cromm's accomplishments or summations."

"And what are Cromm's accomplishments and summations?" Hawkwood asked.

"Cromm has brought the marked one to Amadon as Hragna'Ar legend tells. And Cromm owes Nail a life debt."

"Indeed." Hawkwood met Nail's gaze.

"You should all be paying more attention to Hragna'Ar," Cromm went on, "especially with the Last Demon Lords in the north. The marked one and the girl with the silver hand should pay attention to these things especially, for Cromm now feels they are all joined. Star silver. Shroud of the Vallè. Blood of the Dragon. The Skulls. It is all of great importance."

"Skulls," Hawkwood said, brow furrowed.

"A Hragna'Ar legend," Cromm answered. "Born anew of Viper and blood sacrifice. Come to follow the marked one to Fiery Absolution, they have."

"That is Hragna'Ar legend, of course," Val-Draekin said. "But I've a different view on the matter of the Skulls." He then gave Hawkwood a brief description of what they had seen in Wroclaw: the silver-faced knights with the saber-toothed lion, the silver whips, the swift death of the fishermen.

"These Skulls," Hawkwood said, "they are mentioned but a few times in *The Moon Scrolls of Mia*. If they've returned, King Jovan should be made aware of them, armies should be sent north."

"What should my brother be made aware of?" Princess Jondralyn stepped into the room. Nail was instantly distracted by the entrance of the tall princess, instantly surprised at how beautiful she was. Even with a black eye patch over her right eye and the raw-looking scar running down the length of her face, she was stunning. Jondralyn now wore leather breeches, knee-high leather boots, and a black leather jerkin over a white shirt, sword hooked to the belt riding low on her hips. Dark hair flowed in rich waves down her back. She commanded the room in a manner even Hawkwood could not, her one eye piercing and keen.

Val-Draekin and Lawri stood and bowed. Nail followed suit and then sat back down. Bronwyn and Cromm stayed seated, clearly unimpressed with royalty.

Val-Draekin answered Jondralyn's question, telling her everything about the Company of Nine and the doomed quest: the finding of *Blackest Heart*, Dokie's injuries in Sky Lochs, Roguemoore's death in the glacier, their separation from Stefan, Culpa Barra, Seita, and *Blackest Heart*, Nail's and his journey under the glacier, their near death and failure to find *Afflicted Fire*, their capture by Hragna'Ar oghuls, their rescue by Bronwyn and Cromm, their journey through Wroclaw and the Skulls, their long sail to Amadon. All of it.

"So Roguemoore is dead?" Jondralyn muttered, her face now a stiff mask of pain.

"Aye." Val-Draekin nodded. "Lost in the glacier."

"He was our leader," Hawkwood said. "There is still much the Brethren of Mia do not know of the Five Warrior Angels and the lost weapons."

Jondralyn looked sick. "So the quest was all a failure, all for naught."

"It would seem so," Val-Draekin confirmed.

Nail felt the disappointment growing in the pit of his own stomach, as if it was all somehow his fault and that any moment someone would turn and blame him.

Then Jondralyn leveled her gaze at Val-Draekin, concern lacing her voice. "I was unaware that the Vallè princess, Seita, had gone to Lord's Point with you."

Val-Draekin nodded. "As I said, Seita was part of the Company of Nine."

"You must know then that Seita returned to court some days ago."

"Returned?" Val-Draekin looked surprised. "What of Culpa Barra?" He looked at Nail, then Bronwyn. "I'm afraid we already know the fate of the Gallows Haven boy Stefan Wayland. The girl and the oghul ran across his corpse. But the manner of his death is still a mystery to us."

"I have not seen Ser Culpa Barra," Jondralyn answered. "But in the time Seita has been back, she has made no mention of the quest. In fact, to explain her long absence at court, she pretended that she had escorted *you* back to Val Vallè."

"Aye," Val-Draekin said, "that was the story Seita agreed to, a valid story to explain her long absence at court."

Jondralyn did not let her piercing gaze fall from Val-Draekin. "I asked you to go to Lord's Point alone."

Val-Draekin said, "And I beg of you, forgive me for not heeding your request, for I did indeed have Seita accompany me against your wishes. You asked a favor of me. You asked that I get word to Roguemoore of your fate. And that I did. To accompany Roguemoore on his quest was a decision Seita and I made together. And I stand by that decision."

Jondralyn looked less than appeased.

"The fact is," Val-Draekin went on, "I was most distraught to lose track of Seita on the quest. But now I am most delighted to hear news of her safety. That Culpa Barra has not also shown up in Amadon with her is concerning indeed. I am sure the Dayknight would have sought you out as soon as possible, Jondralyn. I am most desirous to return to the castle and find out what Seita knows of Culpa's fate, to know if she still has *Blackest Heart*, if they found *Afflicted Fire*. I am also most desirous to inform King Jovan of what we have seen in the north. He must know of the destruction of many villages and towns due to Hragna'Ar raiders. He must know of the presence of the Skulls. We must get word to him. For I imagine they will march on Amadon soon."

"I would gladly speak to the king of the things I have seen in the north," Bronwyn said. "For I fear you are right, those skull-faced knights were naught but pure evil. The king should know. And we should tell him."

"And why would I send you?" Jondralyn's dismissive gaze fell on the bench where Bronwyn and Cromm sat. And at that moment, within Princess Jondralyn Bronachell, Nail saw the same arrogance of station he had seen within Jenko Bruk, within Leif Chaparral, within so many who thought those of lesser station of no account.

Then the princess turned to Val-Draekin. "These are strangers to me. We should not be speaking of such things in front of them—"

"But, alas," Bronwyn cut her off. "You all have already spoken of such things in front of us." There was something most disquieting in her gaze. In fact, there was always something most disquieting in Bronwyn's gaze. Cromm sucked on his rock, glaring up at Jondralyn. "But if it eases your mind," Bronwyn went on, "I think it's all nonsense, this preposterous quest the Vallè recounted. So the fact that I know of it means little."

"All nonsense but for the part where Cromm saved the marked one," the oghul added. "That part is not nonsense."

"Perhaps you should leave," Jondralyn said.

"*Leave?*" Cromm grumbled loudly. "Cromm is not going anywhere."

"What?" Jondralyn glared back at the oghul.

"What Cromm is saying is that he is not going anywhere." Bronwyn's eyes were like white shards of ice under her tattoos. "And neither am I." She stood, her gaze level with Jondralyn's. "We are not leaving until we are duly compensated. Val-Draekin promised us handsome payment for escorting himself and Nail to Amadon."

"Escorting the marked one, you mean," Cromm corrected her.

"Right, the marked one," Bronwyn acknowledged. "And someone will pay us."

"You don't make demands of a princess of Amadon." Jondralyn's face was a rash of red, matching her scars. "Nobody does."

Cromm stood, towering over the princess, sucking loudly on the black stone. "Cromm does not give a damn who he makes demands of. Cromm makes demands and that is that."

"He has a long history of not giving a damn about his demands," Bronwyn added.

Hawkwood stepped between them. "If they were promised payment, Jon, they should receive payment. And then they can make their own way."

"Cromm goes nowhere without the marked one," the oghul stated.

"I did promise them payment," Val-Draekin said. "They did save our lives."

Jondralyn looked at Val-Draekin. "I'm assuming you were expecting the Silver Throne to pay the reward. But you all do realize I've no more access to the royal coffers now than any of you here in this ship. I'm sure Jovan would toss me into Purgatory the moment I stepped back into his court to ask him the favor."

"Well then," Cromm gruffed, drool dripping from one jeweled tooth and down his chin. "Cromm stays right here until he is paid."

Bronwyn's hard eyes narrowed to slits, and her hand went to the black bow strapped over her shoulder—Stefan's bow.

"We haven't any coin with us now," Jondralyn said. "But if Val-Draekin promised you payment, then we shall find payment somehow. So everyone just relax."

"We stay until you do find the coin," Bronwyn said. "Twenty thousand pence should do. And until we have it, we shall be made privy to any conversations you have."

Cromm scooped the black rock from his mouth with one hand and spat a wad of drool against the bulkhead of the ship, the other gnarled hand resting on a dagger at his belt. "Not one coin less than twenty thousand pence." He grinned a wide, toothy grin that made him look a trifle childlike, a trifle insane. But the sharp-edged teeth lining his maw made his intent clear.

"What of Lindholf?" Lawri asked, almost forgotten on the bench. "Does anyone know the fate of my brother?" Her eyes were on Val-Draekin. "He bragged that you and Seita were teaching him how to sneak around, how to be a street thief, a pickpocket. Those things only got him in trouble. I watched him hang in the arena. I saw him vanish in an explosion of fire. I know not if he is dead or alive. What of Lindholf?"

"Lindholf was hung?" Val-Draekin asked, real distress on his normally unreadable face as he stared at Lawri.

"They tried to hang him," Lawri said.

"Some cloaked figure swooped into the arena and rescued him," Jondralyn answered. "Rescued Lindholf, Gault Aulbrek, and the barmaid, Delia."

"Why would anyone want to hang Lindholf?" the Vallè asked.

Jondralyn explained the whole spectacle, starting with duel between Gault Aulbrek and Squireck Van Hester, Prince of Saint Only, and then the hanging of Gault and the two accused of conspiring to assassinate King Jovan. She told him how Lindholf had been found with the barmaid, both of them accused of murdering Sterling Prentiss and plotting to assassinate Jovan. She then described the cloaked figure who swept in over the crowd and down into the arena, a black crossbow in hand, a long white sword strapped on their back, and the burst of flame that hid their escape into the bowels of the arena.

"That is most interesting," Val-Draekin said after reflection, delight almost sparkling in his eyes. "An explosion of fire like you've described can be caused with a few simple Vallè tricks and Shroud of the Vallè spread about. I can see how that would work."

"'Twas a good thing Lindholf escaped." A new voice sounded from behind Nail. "For Lindholf was innocent of all he was accused of."

Nail turned to see Princess Tala Bronachell standing in the slanted doorway. She now wore simple woolen breeches and a dark red shirt of silk that shimmered softly in the lamplight. A black belt circled her thin waist, a sheathed dagger at her hip. "Lindholf was always innocent." She stepped into the room. "Gault and the barmaid should have died, though, in my opinion. They were both uncouth."

"Have you been standing in the doorway long?" Jondralyn asked.

"Long enough," Tala said, her voice calm. "I heard everything, if that is what you are worried about."

Then Tala looked at Nail, simply looked at him now, no expression in her clear gaze. And Nail looked at her, breathless and rapt, not able to look away from her big brown eyes, which seemed to dominate her exquisite face. He felt warmth in those eyes. He felt the beautiful, smooth kindness of her. She held his attention completely.

"Your name is Nail?" she asked, holding out a small hand for him to shake—and he did, their touch soft and brief. Her simple greeting had been genuine and gentle, a little hesitant even, but in a silent, modest way. In fact, her every movement was peaceful.

"Tell the princess it is nice to meet her," Hawkwood urged.

"It—it is. I mean, 'tis very nice to meet you, Princess Tala." He bowed, his nerves finally catching up to him.

He felt his face redden as he smiled at her.

She too smiled and flushed and then looked away.

Some mysteries shall forever go unsolved. Like pirate ships floating
in the void of the stars, only those born of the underworld and
hooked on Shroud of the Vallè can withstand the silver.
—THE MOON SCROLLS OF MIA

CHAPTER SEVENTEEN

STEFAN WAYLAND

13TH DAY OF THE FIRE MOON, 999TH YEAR OF LAIJON

WROCLAW, GUL KANA

A miracle of Hragna'Ar!" Mud Undr'Fut claimed. "The end of humanity."

Stefan Wayland had long since grown inured to the horrors of war. The black saber-toothed lion stood next to him, fierce-looking teeth dripping with blood.

Thousands of human dead lay in scarlet heaps in the oghul army's wake, lumps of severed flesh strewn like trash in the twisted streets and smoking warrens of the destroyed city of Wroclaw. It was a large town the Hragna'Ar oghuls had destroyed, a myriad of cramped gray buildings, dreary storefronts, and other such thatch-roofed dwellings, cut with shadowy alleyways and dingy streets. All of it now burning. Packs of dogs rooted in trash heaps at the edge of the charred city. But they scattered at the sight of the five whip-wielding Aalavarrè Solas. And what few terrified humans fled Wroclaw were cut down without mercy by the Warriors of Hragna'Ar.

The five Cauldron Born treated the oghuls who fought at their side with a reverence bordering on worship. It made sense to Stefan, for like him, the Aalavarrè had been created from Hragna'Ar. "You are oghul, Mud Undr'Fut," Icelyn would say to the small oghul from time to time. "You are sacred. You are of the purest race in all the Five Isles. 'Tis I who should scrub clean the armor and weapons of Mud Undr'Fut, not the other way around." Then Icelyn would look at Stefan. "And you, human, are a test, like the black saber-tooth you call friend."

Stefan was unsure of his place as servant to these strange Cauldron Born. But Mud would have it no other way. The diminutive oghul enjoyed cleaning the armor of all five Cauldron Born. He claimed that for Hragna'Ar to be fulfilled, the Aalavarrè must purge humanity from the Five Isles and he would help how he could, even by shining armor.

"Revenge for our subjugation," Icelyn would oft say. "Humans banished us to the underworld during the War of Cleansing. Now we have returned to slay them all with the help of our friends, the oghul armies of Hragna'Ar."

And this vast oghul army standing behind them was led by Stefan and Mud's master, the Hragna'Ar high priest, Sledg H'Mar. Sledg was a rock-faced and brutishly tall beast with arm and leg muscles like boulders under his spiked leather armor and priestly oghul robes. He stood next to Icelyn now, bloody iron cudgel gripped in hand.

And Mud was never more thrilled to be part of oghul legend, to be part of Hragna'Ar. "As Mud's mother would say, one must notice what beauty there is in the world, and cling to what few positive things there are." And to Mud, going to war with the Aalavarrè Solas was a positive and beautiful thing indeed. "If she could see Mud now, for now her son hunts and chases humans toward Fiery Absolution at the side of the mythical Cauldron Born."

Stefan was numb to it all. Unfeeling. In fact, he was beginning to think he was turning into an oghul himself, unconcerned with the death and destruction of humankind, servant to those who were doing the killing. He felt like he was trapped in some confusing dream.

"Today is the day humans begin to pay the price of their ancestors." Icelyn watched the city burn, the human city that once sat proudly atop a slanting ridgeline of green elms, tree limbs bent and stretched from years in the wind, a city that now ran red with scorch and blood. "Today is the day humans die under our whips of scorch. And soon they shall die under the fires of the dragons."

Next to Stefan, the black saber-toothed lion roared its agreement, the fever of the kill alive within the beast's cruel silver eyes.

"Yes, humans now pay the price of their ancestors!" Sledg H'Mar shouted. "And there shall be no escape for them!"

The air smelled and tasted of scorch and blood and death. And Stefan was starting to realize he didn't even feel the loss of human life dimly. In fact, there was no amount of remorse buried in the sharp valleys of his mind or at the edges of his soul. The deaths of humans didn't even matter. He watched without passion as the remaining humans sought escape, fleeing through the seeping plains of rye, heading for shelter in the thick northern forests of pine. But he knew their flight was futile, for those who attempted escape were hunted and slain. The oghul warriors of Hragna'Ar swiftly saw to their end.

"Our glorious day." With one gauntleted hand, Icelyn removed her silver mask of Skull and surveyed her fellow Aalavarrè, hot silver eyes aglow. "Viper may have done his worst to the Aalavarrè Solas throughout time, thrusting us down to the underworld in restless sleep, all of us naught but a relic of memory. But in the end Viper knew that we were strong, that we would overcome, that we would pass the test. For one does not trifle with the patience of the eternal Viper, the one who carved out the underworld."

The black saber-tooth purred in dark agreement, a deep rumbling purr, silver eyes fixed on the fleeing humans. Icelyn's scorch whip unspooled at her side, silver barbs sizzling in the grass. And to Stefan's ears, Icelyn's next words seemed a long river of rhythmical flowing grace. "Were the five of us Cauldron Born not all resurrected anew by the same Hragna'Ar ritual and sacrifice? Were we not raised from timeless hibernation into the new velvet of the morning? Do we not all wield the scorch, the silver elixir of the stars, the science of negative energy and life, the bender of light, the destroyer of time and the giver, dark matter mixed with starlight? Let us pray that we have done Viper great honor today. Let us pray that the beasts of the underworld embrace our triumph. Let us pray that they shall come to us soon. And once secured, we, the far-wandering dead, shall become that part of the wind that haunts humanity into the eternities. We must cleanse ourselves of all weakness before Viper. Our eternal souls must never cry at the sight of death. We must offer alms of silver scorch and blood sacrifice if our kin ever again wish to shake free the chains of the underworld and walk among the stars with Viper. We must pray. Pray that Viper will hear our words of weakness and make them strength. Pray that the Dragon, our master, shall make his way to us with Shroud of the Vallè. That he shall make his way to us with his vast armies of Vallè and guide us toward Absolution. For Absolution must come and the streets of Amadon must run red with scorch and blood. Though it is difficult to see one's own eternal soul behind the veil of death, like you, my fellow Cauldron Born, I've half-formed ancestral memories—memories of rapture and paradise filled with our immortal ancestors floating inside enormous weaponry made of hot silver and twinkling light, ethereal memories of ancient relatives who could hie unto the stars in the twinkling of an eye to be made one with Viper. And within that eternal bliss they would wage battle at Viper's side amid the eternal mists of heaven, Blood of the Dragon their armament, Dragon Claw their weapon, and the Immortal Lord at their side. The very stars are a part of us. A thousand years ago, during the Vicious War of the Demons, our ancestors forgot this. They became weak and took too easily to the ways of the frail human gods and forgot the song of Viper. Thus they were thrust down into the under-world in their frailty of mind like a star falling from the skies, thousands of our kin, millions. Now we, the five of us here, are of one life, reborn through the blood and harvest of Hragna'Ar, striking out through the corridors of time and into the future with a shining vengeance. We are of one blood with Viper in our search for Laijon reborn and the Dragon Claw, who, once combined, shall be our Immortal Lord resurrected. For we are of one blood with the visionary Vallè maiden with the wrought-iron soul. And like our master, the Dragon, we shall answer to her call and reap destruction all the way to the Burning Tree. For the five of us have not only returned to the Great Above in search of security and peace and Absolution, but also to sow the seeds of turmoil and violence and slaughter."

The speech took Stefan's breath away in its almost nonsensical, garrulous lyricism. But that was just the way these creatures spoke.

"Rogk Na Ark! Rogk Na Ark! Rogk Na Ark! Caldrun Born! Caldrun Born!" Mud's master, Sledg H'Mar, bellowed, in a crude counterpoint to the poetic Aalavarrè.

Sledg's massive iron cudgel was held aloft in one upraised fist. *"Rogk Na Ark! Rogk Na Ark! Rogk Na Ark! Caldrun Born! Caldrun Born!"* the oghul warriors spread out behind the Cauldron Born began to bellow. Their spiked and rusted armor clattered and clanked as they stomped the ground to their chant.

For every last one of them knew, this was the first battle of many more to come. This was the first battle in the Second War of Cleansing, the war to end all of humankind. Soon the dragons would join them in this fight. And for some mysterious reason, Stefan Wayland, reborn of scorch and blood, rode at the vanguard of it.

**

Wroclaw Castle was surrounded by a reeking moat of mossy black water, weed-riddled grass, and pockets of dandelions interspersed between thick briar and nettle. Several spindly trees stood crooked and tall beyond the keep's sparse entry. The bulky gray keep was a gaunt shadow of its former self, but for now served as the living quarters of Stefan Wayland, Mud Undr'Fut, and the Cauldron Born.

The battle for Wroclaw over now, Stefan and Mud sat at the edge of the castle's courtyard, the five Aalavarrè in the gardens behind them.

They all awaited the arrival of the five dragons.

Stefan and Mud ate strips of jerky and bacon, the meat tasteless to Stefan's mouth. But everything tasted different to him now. The black saber-toothed lion stood nearby, once in a while sliding silently over and eating strips of bacon out of Stefan's hand. "You are like brothers," Mud would say. "You and that cat. The toothy beast will take food from only you and no other. Even the Aalavarrè cannot feed it."

And Stefan did feel a kinship to the silver-eyed lion. It was a powerful and scary beast for sure, but it always seemed calm around him. Stefan stood and held forth another strip of bacon. The saber-tooth slipped forward and hesitantly snatched it from his hand. Stefan sat back down again, Mud looking at him in admiration.

It was a miracle Stefan could even sit or stand. He ofttimes felt his legs with his hands to make sure it was all real. He could easily recall the pain of falling through the branches of the pine, hitting the ground, screaming out in terror.

He knew the Vallè healed thrice as fast as humans. But being born again of scorch and blood, one could be healed instantaneously. By drinking the green elixir of life, one could be brought back from the dead. And Mud fed him the green draught daily. It was the only thing that could quench Stefan's constant thirst. Under his skin were emerging faint little silver streaks in his veins, glowing and pulsing silver streaks.

Is it poisoning me, this elixir of life?

"Quite frankly," Mud said, "this castle is the nicest place Mud has ever lived. And one must notice the good things of this world. My mother bestowed that advice upon me not long before she died in the depths of Deadwood Gate. Not a very nice place, Deadwood Gate."

Stefan could agree with that. He felt those cursed mines were playing with his mind still. *Is this all in my head? Am I still crawling through those mines? Has my brain been warped by the wraiths that stalk those caves?* He scratched at his arm, trying to rub away the traces of flowing silver under the skin.

"Mud always tries to appreciate the good things," the small oghul went on. "Like how the golden horizon of rye to the south beyond the castle is always softly a-sway, sparkling motes of dust swimming in the lazy sunset. Mother would have liked that."

Indeed, it was a pretty sight. Even Stefan could appreciate that, especially knowing there was scant beauty to the north and east of the castle, for a massive oghul army had gathered there. It was a ragged throng, bristling with rusted weaponry and harsh, loud grunts.

"Mud's mother would have also loved the sight of that army," Mud continued. "For it is the army of Hragna'Ar. An army readying itself for the beasts of the underworld to arrive."

Mud was a talkative little oghul. He reminded Stefan of his boyhood friend Dokie Liddle—innocent to a fault. Stefan was starting to remember more and more from his previous life. Amidst all the death and slaughter of Hragna'Ar, Stefan did take solace in the vague remembrance of his friends. He wondered where Nail and Val-Draekin were now. He still could not believe they had survived falling into the glacier. And had Dokie lived through the poisons? Things he knew he would likely never find out. *For I am a servant of the Cauldron Born now.*

And as the servants of the Cauldron Born, Stefan and Mud could always be found lingering near the Aalavarrè, performing menial tasks, cleaning, gathering food, and in Mud's case, listening and gathering information for Sledg H'Mar.

"They just squawk their strange poetry and verse at each other all day," was all Mud typically reported to Sledg.

"Poetry and verse?" Sledge had asked during their last meeting, raising his large hand to slap Mud if he did not like the answer. "What kind of poetry?"

"Stuff about Viper and the stars." Mud shrank back. "You hear how they go on and on and on and on and on with their strange talkings. Stuff about their god Viper and the stars and Hragna'Ar and Absolution and Shroud of the Vallè for the dragons."

"Do they talk of their master, the Dragon?"

"Aye, most often."

"Most often?" Sledg slapped Mud across the face, voice rising. "And what is it they say, runt? Don't make me wait. Don't make me ask twice."

"Th-they s-say," Mud stammered, "they s-say that the Dragon, their master, is coming soon with the white powder for the dragons, along with vast armies of the Vallè to fight alongside the oghuls at Fiery Absolution."

"And what do they say about the beasts of the underworld?"

"They seem to be most afraid of the dragons. Unsure."

"As they should be," Sledg snarled.

"As they should be," Mud repeated.

"Do you serve the Cauldron Born as you were asked?" Sledg asked.

"Mud serves them daily."

"How?"

"Mud cleans their gear as you asked. Mud polishes their armor. Mud brushes their cloaks. Mud scrapes the mud from their boots."

Sledg raised his big gray brow. "And what else do you do as their servant?"

"Mud listens to them talk. And Mud reports to you."

"Very well." Sledg nodded. "Never forget your duties to them or to me."

"Yes, my master." Mud bowed. "When it comes to Hragna'Ar warriors, Mud is the least of them all, or so Mud's mother once said."

Stefan hated to see his small oghul friend mistreated by the bigger bully, Sledg. He also wondered what all their talking meant. Since his death in the forest, his life had taken turns and roads most strange. He was a servant to monsters and almost didn't care.

Within the castle courtyard itself, the five Aalavarrè Solas had gathered. Their colorful dragon-scale armor and silver masks of Skull glinted in the setting sun. They all eagerly awaited the arrival of the Hragna'Ar high priest, Sledg H'Mar, and the five scaled beasts born in the depths of Deadwood Gate. They awaited the dragons. As far as Stefan knew, the beasts were simply named the White, the Black, the Green, the Blue, and the Red.

"The beasts do not fully belong to us," Basque-Alia the Blue said from under his silver mask of Skull, crescent-moon designs gleaming on his blue-scaled armor in the fading light. "They await the Shroud to ignite their fires. They will never fully submit to us as long as they are captive."

"Do we risk unchaining them upon our first meeting?" Icelyn the White asked. The black saber-toothed lion lounged in the spindly dry grass nearby, the soft evening sun beaming down on its sleek black fur. "Do we risk unchaining them before our master feeds them the white powder?"

"The beasts of the underworld must remain under chain until

Absolution," Aamari-Laada the Red said, "lest they escape to the skies, never to return."

"I say the beasts must be allowed to roam free before Absolution," Basque-Alia countered. "I say we let them fly free and trust in their desire to return to us."

Anxiety, and no small portion of fear, coursed through Stefan at the thought of finally being in the company of the beasts of the underworld if everything these Cauldron Born were saying was true. For he could hear the distant rumble of the musk oxen and the heavy flat wagons carrying the five chained beasts.

Everyone could hear the wagons.

Aamari-Laada the Red removed his silver mask of Skull and nervously drank from a copper vial, preparing himself. 'Twas Blood of the Dragon the Aalavarrè drank, and he drank deep. Thirst quenched, Aamari-Laada placed the vial on the stone balustrade behind him and placed his silver mask of Skull back over his pale white face.

Mud scurried behind Aamari-Laada to pick up the empty copper vial and whisk it down into the crypts under the castle, down to the deepest parts of the dungeon from whence all such spirits came.

"Once the coverings over their eyes are removed," Basque-Alia said, "the beasts of the underworld shall see open sky and wish to be free. For they have been in the caves for too long. They will wish to fly."

"Perhaps that is as it should be," Sashenya the Black said. "And may Viper be with us."

The black saber-toothed lion lifted its broad head. The five Aalavarrè Solas turned as one, following the black cat's silver gaze. Stefan looked too. Like an approaching storm, the rumble of the wagons carrying the five beasts of the underworld grew in volume, the very ground underfoot shaking.

Stefan soon saw the five massive wooden carts carrying the beasts cresting the rise to the north of Wroclaw Castle. Ponderous and heavy, each cart was pulled by twenty large musk oxen. Huge stone wheels, creaking and turning, sank deep into the peat as the wagons grumbled along, straining musk oxen stepping heavy to the crack of oghul whips, nostrils flared and huffing.

The broad, flat wooden surface of each cart was some twenty feet wide and forty long and at least four feet thick, from what Stefan could tell. Iron bolts the size of tree trunks were drilled deep into every corner. Thick metal chains were fixed to each bolt, and each of the four chains was fixed to the iron collar around each of the beasts' massive scaled necks. The beasts' scaled muzzles were chained shut, rank misty breath huffing from heaving nostrils. Each of their legs was chained to the cart also. Five beasts in all; black, white, blue, green, and red, their eyes covered with thick black canvas blinders strapped to either side of their bulky heads.

Dragons!

The procession of carts was led by Mud's master, the Hragna'Ar high priest, Sledg H'Mar. With great trepidation, Stefan watched the slow progress of the colossal carts, his eyes immediately falling upon the nearest dragon, the scaled monster known as the Red—the very beast he had seen before.

The mines were no delusion. I saw what I saw, and it was real. The dragon was real! The bulk of the creature's sinuous, sleek body was almost too much for the cart to bear. The large circle of iron was heavy around its long scaled neck, four chains drooping to the iron bolts set in the wooden slab. Sheathed in huge scales, the familiar beast was enormous and breathing heavily, jaws straining against the chains holding its mouth shut. Massive corded thews bunched and stretched as the Red shifted its great bulk, forked wings like a huge bat hugging its own body, curved white talons at the joints. A coiled tail of sharp spines and ridges swept the ground behind the cart. A pale white row of sharp horns ran the length of the creature's spine from head to tail; two curving horns, one on either side of its head, matched their ivory color but were much longer and more vicious looking. Crouching on all fours on the wooden slab, clawed feet scratching at the surface, tearing at the wood, the Red looked as if it was preparing to stand, brilliant ruby-colored light aglow under its harsh scarlet knifelike scales. But it was blind. Its eyes, like those of the other four dragons, were now hidden, covered in the black canvas.

Mud had explained the dragons to Stefan some days ago. Like the five Aalavarrè Solas, the five chained beasts had been held down by the arms of sleep in the farthest depths of the underworld, forged anew in caverns so deep they had no bottom, forged in caves and fissures so dark that space and time ceased to exist, forged amid black rivers of boiling waters and molten rock and silver scorch. They had been reborn again of Hragna'Ar and blood sacrifice together with the Aalavarrè to be paired as one. But it was a tenuous pairing at best, Mud had claimed, for the beasts of the underworld were primordial and violent. Unpredictable. Huge and deadly. The only two things the huge scaled beasts seemed to respect was Blood of the Dragon and the silver scorch. And only Shroud of the Vallè could ignite the fires in their bellies.

The flat carts carrying the massive monsters slowed to a stop before a subdued and quailing oghul army, the massive stone wheels crushing the ground underneath. At the behest of Sledg H'Mar, the weary teams of musk oxen were unhooked and led away.

And the five beasts of the underworld were finally presented to the five Cauldron Born in all their enormous scaled glory.

Icelyn broke away from the group of five Aalavarrè Solas first, making her way from the castle courtyard toward the five carts.

The four remaining Aalavarrè Solas followed Icelyn cautiously. Stefan braced himself, stepping from the safety of the castle courtyard toward the huge carts, the black saber-tooth following on his heels, its silver eyes keen and wary. He hoped that what few miracles of Hragna'Ar he had experienced so far were good omens, that he himself would be spared some gruesome, violent death at the mouths of these monsters. For it seemed these creatures were naught but beasts bred for gruesome, violent death.

Sledg H'Mar brought forth another human from the crowd of Hragna'Ar oghuls, a frightened young man in a ragged white shirt and shit-stained tan pants.

Blood and death filled the air. The tension was thick as all eyes watched the oghul high priest lead the terrified human directly before the Red. Stefan felt the sweat grow thick and rank under his own leather armor, for he knew what was likely to come.

He felt his own soul curl inward as the red-scaled dragon stretched forth its chain-wrapped mouth and took one giant sniff of the young man. The beast immediately shifted its great bulk as far away from the human as it could, a low rumble growing deep within its heaving chest. Eyes covered, the dragon could not see what it was smelling, but the huge creature clearly did not approve.

"The Red dislikes the smell of human excrement." Icelyn's voice sounded distant and hollow through the mask of Skull. The scorch whip gripped in her gauntleted hand dripped silver to the ground, sizzling in the grass.

On the cart next to the Red was the White, its scaled chin resting on the flat wood surface, mouth similarly chained, eyes covered. Icelyn ordered the canvas to be removed from the White's eyes. Two eager oghuls leaped up onto the cart and cut the canvas from the white dragon's eyes.

Two merciless pale orbs smoldered and gleamed, pupils long and slitted and burning with pure evil. Now able to see, the White jerked and struggled to free itself, sending the two oghuls scattering from off the jostling cart. The beast's cruel eyes ranged over the landscape of golden rye, fixing on the gray bulk of the castle, before sliding back to Icelyn. The dragon's piercing eyes now followed the tip of Icelyn's whip. The clover-shaped scales along the creature's neck suddenly fluttered and rippled like fish gills. Its mouth was still bound by chains.

The scared human sacrifice in raggedy clothes and shit-stained breeches was marched forth. Icelyn cracked the scorch whip toward the White.

It was a precision strike, and the liquid silver cut through the chains binding the beast's mouth. The white dragon raised its head, chains coiling to the surface of the wooden cart with a clatter. The monster flashed rows of stark white teeth as it opened its mouth, sucking air down into its heaving lungs over and over. Then it roared—a sound almost unbearable to Stefan. He crouched, hands over his ears. Every oghul in the vast Hragna'Ar army also ducked against the sharp noise and pain, holding grubby cracked palms over crooked gray ears. The shit-stained human behind Sledg crouched in terror too, trembling hands over his ears, face grimacing in pain.

Then the white dragon ceased its thunderous cry. Silence. Stillness.

The White shuffled its great bulk back on the cart, chains still holding its legs down. Still, as if confused, the beast tried scooting away from the human as far as it could, as if it deplored both his look and smell.

Icelyn cracked the whip, strands of silver flinging into the air, twinkling against the golden sunset. The White reared away from Icelyn even farther. Chained to the cart still, the dragon could only retreat so far. The beast roared once more, then was silent, a spume of frothy drip trailing from its open and heaving maw. Icelyn took another step forward, scorch whip cracking against the wooden cart, leaving a bright silver trail glinting in the air, silver scorch slicing into the wood with sizzle and smoke.

The white dragon was clearly scared of the whip and the Aalavarrè wielding it. The other four dragons were agitated now too, squirming heavy and loud on the flat cart beds, straining against their iron collars and chains, mouths bound and unable to roar, covered eyes unable to see. But Stefan could see that the chains would not hold the beasts down for long. They would shred the wooden carts if their thrashing continued.

Basque-Alia strode across the field to the farthest cart, the one carrying the Blue. The Aalavarrè soothed the blue dragon with a low whistle and a gentle touch. Scorch whip hooked safe at his hip, Basque-Alia reached both of his gauntleted hands forth, unhooking the iron collar from around the dragon's neck, unhooking the chains from around its heaving jaws, removing its blinders. The creature remained calm throughout.

Then Basque-Alia walked silently away from the cart. The Blue raised its scaled and horned head, stretching its wings, now rippling dark and batlike against the yellow sunset, out to the fullest. The blue-scaled dragon stepped carefully and calmly from the flat perch of the wooden cart, claws digging into the soil as it moved, following Basque-Alia across the grassy plain.

The Aalavarrè turned and looked at the blue dragon. "You are free to hunt, to fly among the clouds and stars," he said, reaching up, rubbing the beast's neck. "But you must return at the beck and call of your master, and I am your master. Know my scent."

Basque-Alia held his armored arm under the beast's heaving nostril. The Blue sniffed, then sat back, eyeing the landscape of oghul warriors. Some small measure of serenity seemed to flow out from the dragon, the feeling reaching out, infecting the other four other agitated beasts, calming them at once.

Basque-Alia reached into the folds of his dark cloak and pulled forth a pouch filled with Shroud of the Vallè. He opened the pouch and reached within, the white powder sifting between his silver-gauntleted fingers. He then beckoned Sledg H'Mar to bring forth the human with the shit-stained breeches.

The oghul priest dragged the screeching man by the shirt collar through the dirt.

The Aalavarrè held one Shroud-coated gauntlet toward the Blue. The dragon dipped its massive sapphire head and sniffed the powder straight down into its huge, heaving nostrils. Thick blue scales rippled like hawk feathers along the beast's neck as it reared back. Head and long horn-lined snout pointing straight up to the sky, it let loose a thunderous roar. A tower of flame shot from its cavernous mouth, and the golden firmament was instantly lit with a blinding fiery orange flame. Shroud mixed with the breath of the dragon created fire—hot, melting fire.

Stefan wanted to retreat back to the safety of the castle's decrepit courtyard. In fact, every oghul warrior of Hragna'Ar jerked back in fear at the sight of the flames spewing out of the Blue's gaping jaws, spears and other weaponry were raised, mutters of concern flowing through each and all.

The human with soiled breeches fell to his knees on the grass, eyes white with fear. The blue dragon's murderous flame and roar ended. Then the beast focused on the frightened man before it, sniffing, hot tongue flickering from between sharp, ivory-colored teeth over the man's face. The man screamed and screamed.

And then the Blue's steaming maw shot forward, massive front teeth snatching the man by the chest, tossing him hard onto the peat. The beast's front paw, claws long and sharp, pinned the man to the ground.

Blood gushed in red sheets over the man's body as the dragon's razorlike teeth deftly stripped the meat from his bones and the guts from his rib cage in one singular mauling pull. The long drip and heavy flow of the man's blood showed stark and red against the blue of the beast's extended jowls and many shimmering scales. The Blue swallowed whole what muscle and innards he had stripped from the man's body.

The white dragon watched, hunger glowing in its own stark eyes. The other dragons could only sense what was going on, their eyes still covered. They strained at their chains, the Green, the Black, and the Red.

As the sun melted away beyond the far horizon, the Blue strode forward, meeting each of the five Aalavarrè Solas stare for stare. Its two piercing orbs were fiery crystal gems of azure that sliced into every one of the Cauldron Born and stripped their eternal souls bare.

Mud Undr'Fut had told Stefan enough of the legends. None of the Aalavarrè would ride these beasts until the one called the Dragon, their master, arrived and breathed more Shroud of the Vallè over them.

Stefan looked at the White. And the white dragon's glowing gaze cut into him. *Free me!* those fiery white orbs seemed to rage in silent communication. *Free me now!* Stefan knew there was nothing he could do. But with the creature's cruel look, he felt he was living within someone else's dream. It was as if the beast was showing him that dream, a dream of a human boy, the least of them all—the marked one.

"We must release them!" Aamari-Laada the Red shouted, the scorch whip unspooling at his side. "Release all the beasts! They must be free. They must come to us of their own accord. Release them! They shall be captive no more."

"Release them!" Raakel-Jael followed, brandishing his whip.

"Release them!" Sashenya cried out.

Icelyn the White nodded, knowing too that it must be done. She struck the remaining chains from the White with her whip of silver. Aamari-Laada, Raakel-Jael, and Sashenya did the same. And once freed, one by one, each dragon unfurled its huge wings, stirring the very air as it leaped toward the sky and freedom.

CHAPTER EIGHTEEN

LINDHOLF LE GRAVEN

14TH DAY OF THE FIRE MOON, 999TH YEAR OF LAIJON

SAVON, GUL KANA

Don't look like no Dayknight to me," the toothless one said.
"Or leastwise not much of one," the bearded fellow added
as he dropped the bundle of wood from the crook of his arm to
the dirt roadway.

"Skinny under that shiny black armor, that I can tell," the toothless
one said. "Thin face of a child, sits the horse awkward, not much of a
fighter, I wager. And the deformities. And are those burns on his face?"

"Not sure," the bearded fellow answered. "But that's some mighty
shiny armor he's wearing. Ain't seen Dayknight armor polished that
sparkly in all my days."

Lindholf Le Graven cursed himself. His armor was shiny. It was
clean. He couldn't scrub the shit smell out of it no matter how hard
he tried. And he scrubbed the armor nightly. He looked at the polished
black Dayknight helmet hooked to the saddle horn between his legs.
And he knew he shouldn't have removed his helm.

Both ruffians carried rusted swords, and their garb was in tatters. Still, they looked cruel enough, and desperate. And the way they stared up at Delia with unblinking eyes made Lindholf more than just a little jittery. Under the black Dayknight armor, his every limb felt weighed down with weariness, drenched in sweat. Delia rode on the dun-colored destrier behind him, vulnerable, clinging to his armored back for protection.

The two men now eyed him greedily, eyed the burlap sack full of ancient weapons balanced on the horse's rump. Lindholf tried to place his arm over the leather pouch of angel stones at his belt. It was clear they were going to attempt to take everything from him: horse, Delia, stones, weapons. Everything.

But doesn't everyone take from Lindholf Le Graven? Lindholf's whole mind was walking the edge of a bitter scream. He did not want to fight off these men. *If I even could.* His very posture, even in full Dayknight armor, spoke of the weakness and uncertainty that lived in his heart. The horse shifted nervously under him. Delia clung to him. "I wish Gault had never left me," she muttered almost under her breath.

Lindholf knew that Delia blamed him for Gault's disappearance. The girl blamed him for everything that had gone wrong, despite his best efforts to get her to Savon. But their journey had been slow. *It wouldn't be taking so long if Gault was still here,* she would groan every night as they bedded down in separate beds.

It had been five days since Gault had abandoned them in the gloomy but furnished cave. After the Sør Sevier man had left, Lindholf and the barmaid had stayed there another two days, the girl complaining the entire time. They eventually packed up and made their way slowly westward toward Savon, Lindholf in his Dayknight armor, Delia on the saddle behind him, and what meager belongings they carried—some small bits of dried food along with *Afflicted Fire, Ethic Shroud,* and *Blackest Heart*—in the cumbersome sack tied to the back of the horse.

"Give us the horse," the toothless man said.

"And the girl, too." The bearded one grinned.

"Gault would have already killed you both by now!" Delia shouted at the two men, her voice like a clap of thunder in Lindholf's ear. "And if Seita were here, you'd all be skinned and gutted like the sorry gutter rats you are! That's if either one of them were here," she finished, voice subdued.

"But the two you speak of ain't here," the toothless ruffian said. "Are they?"

"They ain't," Delia answered. The destrier shuffled under them, Lindholf barely keeping the reins. Then Delia slid from the back of the horse to the ground.

"What are you doing?" Lindholf scowled, reaching back, trying to stop her. She brushed him off, pulling on the sack of weapons, ripping it open. *Afflicted Fire*, *Blackest Heart*, and *Ethic Shroud* all spilled from the bag to the trail.

"Bloody rotted angels. What is all that stuff?" the toothless man exclaimed. "Treasure and loot, for sure!"

Delia picked up the long white sword.

Both anger and fear flooded hot and thick through Lindholf's veins, nearly freezing him solid.

The bearded ruffian pointed his rusty sword at the girl. "I'll be havin' that sword, lassie, same as I'll be havin' you."

"You mean you'll be having this sword up your ass." Delia brandished the weapon in both hands.

Lindholf snapped the reins, bringing the horse between Delia and the two men, blocking their view of her and hers of them.

"Out of our way." The toothless outlaw raised his sword too, grinning.

"You won't hurt her," Lindholf said. "I will stop you."

"*You* will stop *us*?" The bearded man's eyes widened in mockery. "That's very entertaining."

Lindholf drew the black Dayknight sword from the sheath at his hip with all the authority he could muster. The rasp of the blade clearing the sheath echoed through the forest, birds taking flight from flickering leaves above.

The toothless ruffian poked the tip of his rusty sword straight into the chest of Lindholf's horse and pushed, sinking the blade deep, then yanking it free. The startled beast bucked and bellowed, tossing Lindholf backward over its thrashing tail. The black sword flew from his grip as he spun upside down into the briar and bracken and knotty pine branches. The destrier continued bucking and bellowing in pain, stumbling into the forest a few paces. The two ruffians grinned wildly at Delia, their way now clear.

Delia charged forward and ran the entire length of *Afflicted Fire*'s blade, all the way up to its crescent-moon-shaped hilt-guard, through the gut of the bearded thug. When she yanked the sword free, the man folded to the ground, clutching his stomach, howling in pain. Without hesitation, the girl brought the blade sweeping around, striking clean through the neck of the toothless ruffian. The severed head leaped from the man's shoulders into the weeds. His body crumpled into the thorn and weeds near Lindholf, neck spewing a torrent of crimson over green turf and moss.

Lindholf untangled his limbs from the briar patch and scrambled away from the headless corpse. He watched in mute wonder as the shimmering white blade in Delia's grasp soaked up the blood of both men as if eating it, dark red seeping into the white surface, pulsing as it disappeared down into the glowing blade.

"I can't believe it," she muttered. "I can't believe I killed them so easily. It's like something Gault or the Vallè princess would have done. Gault only taught me the two sword moves." She looked up at Lindholf, astonished. "But they worked. They bloody well worked." She started laughing. "This fucking sword is a treasure!"

But one of the men wasn't quite dead. The bearded one moaned, bloody hands clutching the leaking hole in his gut. The joyful look on Delia's face turned instantly savage as she stepped toward the man, menacing white sword in hand.

"Don't," the outlaw pleaded, one arm raised in futile defense as the tip of *Afflicted Fire* entered his heart. Delia left the blade there a moment, letting the sword drink its fill. Then she pulled it free, triumph in her eyes.

There was scant sound but the stir of the leaves above. But soon all Lindholf could hear was the pulse pounding noticeably in his head. A cold certainty that he was losing his mind came creeping over him like a wraith at midnight.

"Pick up the shield and the crossbow," Delia ordered as she called the skittish horse to her. "Stuff them back into the bag and make sure it's tied shut better than before."

Lindholf offered no argument, just did as he was told and gathered the weapons.

Delia went to the dun-colored destrier still standing in the forest a few paces away. "The jab to his chest looks deep but doesn't seem to have struck anything vital," she said, examining the frightened mount. "I don't know why they stabbed him if they aimed to steal him. I guess they were as stupid as they looked. But I wager he'll make it to Savon once I patch him up."

She then turned and glared right at Lindholf. "You know, it's time I took control of my own life. Like Seita once told me I should. No more traveling about making ourselves—or rather making myself—susceptible to rape by whatever toothless vagabond with a turgid prick wanders by." Her eyes narrowed. "And Laijon knows, you ain't no help, Lindholf Le Graven."

**

I ain't no help. As Lindholf trudged along, Delia's insult was all he could think of. *So much killing and death, just for the two of us to stay alive.* He led the injured horse by the bit, Delia plodding along by his side, the weapons of the Five Warrior Angels once again secured in the hastily sewn-together canvas tied to the destrier's back. Delia had used a strip of the canvas to bind the horse's bleeding neck wound. Still it was soaked through and red, for the bleeding hadn't stopped. The horse might die. It was moving slower and slower by the hour.

Even horses die, Lindholf thought. *Why should some men and beasts die so others can live? Is my life worth the death of others? Even a horse?* It was an uncomfortable thought. Everything was uncomfortable. Stifling. Not just his thoughts. The black Dayknight armor was hard to walk in.

Heavy. And he hated the helmet with a passion. But he kept it on now. The childlike look of his face combined with the scars made him easily recognizable. And Savon was near.

As they passed under a latticework of stone aqueducts just outside the city, Lindholf looked up, marveling at the height of the town's stone edifices through the eye slits of his helm. Savon was known for its numerous tall towers, all of them crammed onto the narrow peninsula where the wide and meandering River Vallè met the much smaller and swifter Ridliegh River.

The dripping aqueducts above Lindholf flowed with fresh Sky Lochs water bound for Amadon and all the farm fields that stretched between Eskander, Reinhold, and the Autumn Range to the south. Being from Eskander, Lindholf knew how important those aqueducts were to the farmers in the south. *Structures created by better men than me.*

As they passed under the aqueducts and made their way over the marble-quarried bridge leading into Savon, Lindholf had to face it: Delia had saved herself from the outlaws. She had saved *him*. A frightened barmaid had bested two sword-wielding ruffians, when all he'd done was fall headlong into a briar patch.

With each weary step he took over the dusty bridge, Lindholf was growing more and more disappointed in himself. The whole world was constructed of unfairness and betrayal and disappointment, and he felt he might soon drown under a wave of blackness and despair. He found himself hearkening back to the Riven Rock Quarry, scraping the mashed bodies of Woadson and five other slaves from the hard marble floor with a shovel. The men had all been crushed flat, a terrifying sight he would not soon forget. He still had nightmares of the incident. That slave pit bred naught but nightmares for all who descended into its vast belly. It was also in the bowels of that quarry where Delia had fallen in love with Gault Aulbrek. The Sør Sevier man had saved her from rape at the hands of the other slaves, endearing himself to the barmaid forever. And now Delia blamed Lindholf for Gault's abandoning them. But who was she to cause him such anguish? She was a nobody. *And I am the son of Lord Lott Le Graven.*

A group of three mud-footed peasant women approached, rucksacks slung over their shoulders. They were traveling in the opposite direction over the bridge. They eyed Lindholf, in his dusty black armor, and the injured horse with some apprehension and made sure to give them a wide berth. Delia gave the group a shy smile that seemed to ease the tension as they passed. The waters of the River Vallè drifted calm and dark under them. To the south, Lindholf could see where those lazy waters joined the swifter Ridliegh River.

"The Preening Pintail is a squat wood-and-thatch building at the base of a square stone spire," Delia said. "The spire is tall, if I recall correctly. Every building in Savon is made of stone and tall. And there are hundreds, perhaps thousands of them. I never was good with directions. I doubt I shall remember where it was."

"We haven't any coin anyway," Lindholf said. "We cannot afford an inn. And what did Gault say about staying in such public places?"

"Rutger always wanted me to work for him," Delia said. "Ever since I was a little girl. Coin for our stay will not be a problem. Like I said, we do as I say now."

**

Despite the girl's apprehension in locating the inn, they found the Preening Pintail without any trouble, merely following the main roadway along the southern edge of the Savon peninsula. The roadway was narrow and crowded, tall buildings leaning and hovering over them, some buildings as many as six or seven stories high. Stone towers even double that in height were interspersed here and there along the river's edge.

The Preening Pintail itself was as Delia had described. A wood-and-thatch building under a square tower, a small two-horse stable to the left, the door of the stone tower to the right. The squat inn was two stories tall, the gray tower likely upward of six or seven stories, half-crumbled battlements like rotted teeth lining the top of it on all sides. The door at the base of the tower was wooden and padlocked shut but wide enough that a full-size wagon could easily drive through it.

The front door of the inn itself had a sign over it that read THE

PREENING PINTAIL TAVERN AND INN. But the word *Inn* was half scratched out. Above the sign was a crude painting of what looked like a duck, its bill awkwardly tucked under its wing or rear end.

"Is that duck licking its own asshole?" Lindholf stared up at the sign.

"No," Delia said. "It's preening itself. It's a preening pintail."

"A pintail is a duck?"

"I think."

Lindholf shrugged and hitched the destrier to the rail that ran between the inn and tower. The poor horse looked like it might fold over dead at any moment. He untied the canvas with the weapons, holding it carefully, the tip of the white blade of *Afflicted Fire* poking through the fabric. He did not want to leave the sack and its precious cargo in the middle of the busy roadway atop a near-dead horse.

He followed Delia into the inn, clutching the awkward sack in both hands.

Like the Filthy Horse Saloon, the Preening Pintail was a dark and smoky place, dimly lit with a few flickering torches and hearths of dull red coals. It took a moment for Lindholf's eyes to adjust to the light through the eye slits of his helm. The place had a stale, moldy scent underneath the smoke.

Delia walked up to the bar. "We are in search of the owner."

"You mean Rutger." The fair-haired girl behind the bar eyed Delia with a somewhat hesitant smile, and Lindholf in his black armor with some reservation. The girl's eyes widened when she saw the slave brand on Delia. "The slave mark of Riven Rock. Are you escaped from there? Is this knight your escort to the jail in Ridliegh?"

Delia's hand shot to the swollen black *RR* branded into her neck just below her ear. Her eyes darted up to Lindholf, a hint of worry growing in her grayish-blue gaze. Lindholf noticed that her honey-colored hair was dull in the gloomy light of the tavern, and the dimples and freckles sprinkled over her cheeks blended into the shadow, but the slave brand was the most noticeable thing on her flesh. It stood out. He had a similar brand hidden under the armor on his own neck. Would it stand out too?

"Delia!" an enthusiastic voice called out. A small man approached from out of the darkness of the tavern. He was a mousy fellow, shorter than Lindholf, with a soppy-looking mustache that reeked of ale and lines of age cut across his leathery, freckled forehead and face.

"I'm so happy to see you again, my little Del." The fellow smiled wide at Delia, teeth more rust-colored than his hair. Then he hugged the girl with the same enthusiasm he had called out her name. Delia hugged him back just as tightly.

"How's your father?" the man asked when he pulled away.

"Dead." Delia hung her head. "It's why I am here. I need lodgings."

"I am sorry to hear about your father," the man said hurriedly. Then his beady eyes fell to Lindholf. "A Dayknight escorted you all the way from Amadon? And in such clean armor, too?"

"This is Lindh—" Delia cut herself short. "This is Ser Lin, of Amadon. And yes, he has been my travel companion. He is, or was, an old friend of Father's."

"Rutger." The man held out his hand.

Lindholf shook it. "Ser Lin," he said, playing along with Delia's subterfuge, though his voice sounded both weak and hollow even to his own ears.

"Very nice to make your acquaintance, Ser Lin," Rutger said, and then he turned back to Delia. "I'm afraid I've some bad news: I've no real suitable lodgings. You may have noticed, the 'inn' part was scratched off the sign some time ago. The wood floors in the handful of rooms we used to rent rotted out years ago. I just never got around to replacing them. Those rooms never made me much money anyway, leastwise not the type of money the tavern makes off the booze. So sorry. Lodgings elsewhere in Savon are hard to come by. I'm afraid all I have to offer is a place atop the tower above, where you can squat." He looked right at Lindholf then. "Though I imagine a Dayknight with armor so polished and shiny would be above squatting."

Lindholf had no idea what "squatting" meant in regard to the top of the tower. But it didn't sound pleasant.

"You know, Ser Lin, you can take the helm off if you like," Rutger said. "Any friend of Delia's is a friend of mine. You are just *friends*, right?"

Lindholf didn't answer the question, and he left the helmet on.

"Anyway." Rutger turned again to Delia, smiling. "Atop the tower there is a canopy of sorts to keep out the sun and the rain. And the battlements themselves offer some cover, though they are but knee-high, if that, and crumbled. It's cheap and airy and exposed up there, and you'd have to use the shitter and tub down here." His smile widened. "But it has the best views of Savon and the Ridliegh River below."

"Lovely," Delia said. "But I don't know how long we might stay." Her eyes drifted to Lindholf. "Could be a while."

"No matter," Rutger said.

"How much would it cost us?" Delia asked. "We've not much coin on us now."

"Like I said, no matter. You can stay atop the tower for as long as you'd like, or until you find better accommodations elsewhere." Then he grasped her two hands in his. "The Preening Pintail gets rowdy here most every night. I could use another serving girl in the evenings. I'm sure Luiza would love the help from a nice bonny lass like yourself." He motioned to the girl behind the bar. "That could cover the rent and then some."

He let go of Delia's hands, eyes falling on Lindholf once more, appraising him carefully, as if still trying to see through the armor and helm. "But what I could really use is a knight like yourself to keep the peace, Ser Lin. I mean, a brooding Dayknight a-watch at the door, and I imagine the drunken brawls and knifings on the rowdy nights will go down significantly."

"We'll gladly take the roof of the tower and take the jobs," Delia said quickly before Lindholf could disagree. "We've also a horse needs stabling. It's a warhorse. And it's been recently injured, though not terribly bad, I don't think."

Rutger bowed slightly. "That can be taken care of; the stable is empty. And I've a friend, a part-time ostler of sorts, who can tend to the horse on the morrow." His eyes drifted to the sack of weapons Lindholf carried. He smiled again, murky teeth dull glints in the lamplight. "I hear tell Leif Chaparral destroyed Aeros Raijael's army in Lord's Point. Were you part of that, injured horse and all?"

"No," Lindholf said.

"Shame. It is being called the Battle of the Saint Only Channel. A million knights swept away into the tide, they say. All of them drowned. But I'm sure you know of all that, Ser Lin."

Lindholf remained silent.

"Well, anyway," Rutger said. Then he leaned in toward Delia, voice scarcely above a whisper. "Word is, you got yourself into some trouble in Amadon. A few lads from the Filthy Horse mentioned it not long ago, mentioned you were bound for a hanging in the arena, something about an assassination attempt on the king." He leaned away from her then. "And yet here you are, unhanged." He winked at her. "But I can keep my secrets—if you play your cards right, that is. If things go as planned, you needn't worry about me selling you out. Now let me show you to the top of the tower."

The red-haired man whirled and headed for the front door of the Preening Pintail. Lindholf gulped and looked at Delia. Rutger was pure evil. And Delia seemed to stare at Lindholf with some fear too, but then she followed the man out the door.

Rutger led them back outside past their tethered and injured destrier toward the stone tower. The tower itself rose up over six or seven stories high, at least, and was a mix of light gray and dark gray rock cut at random angles and patterns, crumbling white mortar holding it all together. In the center of the tower was a locked wooden door supported with rusted iron struts and bolts. Rutger slipped a thin iron key into the padlock and swept the door aside just wide enough for the three of them to slip in.

He handed the key to Lindholf. "You'll need the key, and I advise keeping this entrance to the tower locked when you are not using it."

The inside of the tower was hollow from the floor to the wooden-beamed ceiling high above, sun streaming through cracks in the thick girders, dust afloat in the dappled light. A rickety-looking staircase of wood circled the inner walls of the tower all the way up to the timbered roof and a latched door in the ceiling above. The dirt floor of the tower was crammed shoulder high with firewood and coal. There were a few other piles of junk hidden under dusty canvas tarps near the stairs.

"Just climb the stairs," Rutger said. "The roof is yours." Then he motioned back to the street and the destrier. "I'll secure your horse in the stable until my ostler can see to him on the morrow. That wound in his chest looks serious, but I know my guy can fix him up." Then he left them alone.

Delia led the way up the stairs. Lindholf followed, the bulk of his armor scraping the stone walls. The trek up the stairs was long and precarious, and by the time they reached the top, Lindholf was gripping the railing tight, sweating, wishing he could just be rid of the damnable Dayknight armor already. The wooden doorway, set flat in the heavy-trussed ceiling, was already unlatched. Delia pushed against it with her shoulders. It rose up into the sunlight and flopped over onto the floor of the wooden roof above with a thud.

They both stepped out onto the roof of the tower, finding themselves under a sun-bleached canvas canopy held up by four wooden poles that all leaned into each other.

Lindholf's heart froze, not quite knowing why.

Beyond the canopy and the door set in the floor stretched a square timbered rooftop. Crumbled battlements no more than knee-high circled the tower's edge on all sides. Lindholf could hear the bustle of the street behind him and the rustle of the river below. He had a clear view of the city along with hundreds of roofs and towers similar to this one. Tired and sweaty, Lindholf set the sack of weapons down, wondering if they were naught but a curse, wondering if he shouldn't just charge forward and toss the entire lot of them over the battlements and let them sink into the river gurgling below.

Or would it be best if he just ended his own life, tossed himself over the battlements? He still had the means to do just that. Painless means. *It is poisoned,* he remembered Seita saying of the black dagger she had handed him on Rockliegh Isle. *Stick Gault with it, and he will die within moments.*

But he'd failed in killing Gault.

"I'm so tired." Delia settled herself under the canopy, lying down on the wood with a groan that, to Lindholf, seemed exaggerated.

Ignoring her, he walked toward the rim of the tower, his heavy booted feet clomping loud and hollow against the wood-plank rooftop. He stepped slowly then, listening to the soothing sounds of the Ridliegh River lapping against the stone tower below. When he reached the edge, he stepped up onto the knee-high battlement and looked straight down.

It was a long drop to the sparkling waters below, six or seven stories at least. But he was never one to be afraid of heights. He had climbed the Laijon statue, after all. He could throw himself from this ledge easily, without fear.

He turned and looked back at Delia. She was propped up on one elbow and was studying him carefully. And as he stared back at her, he knew why his heart had nearly stopped when he had first emerged from the hatch and stepped onto this rooftop—

—this tower was straight from the visions he'd had in Memory Bay when he'd floundered in the water with the mermaid. The claw marks on his arm suddenly flared in pain, and he found he couldn't breathe as the vision of the tower flooded back.

A knight with dark tattoos under his eyes falling from the roof of a tall tower, Jondralyn Bronachell, two hollow eye sockets, a fierce red-haired warrior woman in black armor and a long white sword, its hilt-guard the shape of a crescent moon.

What happens to the soul of a believer after death? Nothing. Naught
but darkness and the unknown, as before birth. No afterlife. No family.
No Warrior Angels sitting on the heights of the stars. When a believer loses
faith and realizes this truth, his face will become that of a lost and frightened
child. And who wishes to be a child? So the believers pretend to believe, even
though the truth stares them daily in their frightened little faces.
—THE BOOK OF THE BETRAYER

CHAPTER NINETEEN
CRYSTALWOOD

15TH DAY OF THE FIRE MOON, 999TH YEAR OF LAIJON
SIGARD LAKE, WYN DARRÈ

The dawn broke damp with dew and was just a little chilly. The morning was also cloudy and gray, matching Krista Aulbrek's mood perfectly. All the birds and crickets were as subdued as she. Ironcloud guided her mount into the fenced yard of sleeping goats and chickens. Hans Rake's horse was tethered behind her horse, Sisco. Both Bloodwoods were still cuffed and shackled and tied to their mounts.

Café Colza Bouledogue wasn't tethered or shackled to anyone or anything, yet seemed always under hoof. Borden Bronachell brought up the rear. Tyus Barra led their small group through the strange little farmyard nestled in the forest along the southeastern shore of Sigard Lake. The mute boy led them straight toward the tallest and roundest and widest tree Krista had ever seen, the base of it as wide as a small church. The tree was set back against a forest of tall pine, a red barn under its lofty green eaves.

There was a small iron door set smack in the middle of the trunk of the tree, opened wide. A stumpy, red-haired dwarf, puffing on a smoldering hickory-wood pipe, stepped from the doorway and out into the gray light of dawn.

"Seabass!" Ironcloud called out.

Seabass was the shortest, fattest, and most bushy-bearded dwarf Krista had ever seen. He seemed a genial enough dwarf too. The jolly little fellow hustled forward. He snatched the curling pipe from his mouth and immediately greeted them all, even throwing a bright, warm smile to Krista and Hans. He wore a deep-maroon-and-pink-checkered shirt, ruffled at the collar and sleeves. The garish shirt spread over his ample gut, his suspenders holding up dark blue woolen pants. His light brown leather boots curled up at the toes, the entire ensemble making him look like the dwarven jester, Bootleg Jack, who ofttimes entertained for King Aevrett Raijael in Jö Reviens.

When Seabass greeted Ironcloud, he did so with a toothy smile that parted his red beard and stretched across his already wide face like a gleaming white gash. The two dwarves were clearly glad to see each other again.

"How long has it been?" Ironcloud said, sliding from his saddle.

"Too many years." Seabass latched onto his friend in a great big hug. "Too many years."

Krista's knees, hips, and spine creaked like rusty hinges as she slid from Sisco, Tyus Barra holding the horse's bit, keeping her mount steady. A rich tide of red surged over his cheeks whenever she met his gaze. The tongueless boy had been taking care of her and Sisco at every turn with a shy friendliness that annoyed Krista more than helped, though in all their days of travel, they had never spoken. He was mute, after all. The bottom line was, his niceness just made her feel guilty, made her feel bad about herself. She knew she would never be so innocently kind and caring as Tyus Barra. And she let that thought fester. She tried to brush away his helping hands when she could. But then the disappointed look on his face would only make her feel worse. And on top of it all, there were the flowers Hans claimed the mute placed atop her bedroll every night as she slept. Krista had never seen evidence of such efforts herself. But then again, Hans claimed that he himself tossed the flowers into the woods nightly.

Her entire journey from the dungeons in Rokenwalder to this farm had been peculiar beyond words. She'd thought of escape often, figured she could manage it if she really tried. Hans claimed he escaped his cuffs and shackles nightly and met secretly with Black Dugal. Hans claimed their master had followed them into Wyn Darrè. Thing was, Hans' story was actually rather plausible. She knew Hans. And she knew Black Dugal. And she knew the games Bloodwoods liked to play. Yes, she knew she could escape. But something held her back. *What? To figure out what Dugal's game is? To assassinate Aeros Raijael? To follow Borden Bronachell all the way to Amadon? To find out the secrets of her own heritage?*

She let the side of her head rest against Sisco's neck, something she had done each time she dismounted. It gave her solace of a kind. Sisco was not Dread. But horses had a calming effect on her. And Sisco had been a good travel companion across the breadth of Wyn Darrè.

Tyus led both Sisco and Hans Rake's mount away toward the red barn under the massive tree's swooping eaves. Seabass and Ironcloud went with him. Seabass seemed to have a natural rapport with Tyus Barra, the two of them speaking through hand signals as they walked the horses to the barn, the garish dwarf again puffing on his pipe. Café Colza eyed the chickens.

Borden glared at Hans coolly. "We should lock you in the barn too."

"I've been compliant so far," Hans said. "Besides, what makes you think a barn could hold me?"

Borden grunted. "Your agreeableness is what worries me most, frankly."

"That is your problem then." Hans' lips curled back into a sly little smile as he bowed at the waist. "I plan on remaining subservient to you until my master says otherwise. But I shall make sure you are the first to know when I'm ready to cause trouble. Until then, you can just worry about my ever-growing agreeableness."

Krista didn't want to become involved in any arguments at the moment. She just wanted one thing—a bath. Ever since leaving Rokenwalder, it seemed baths were all she could think of. She cast her eyes about the farm. Even a horse trough would suffice if she could find one. They had come across zero quaint inns since leaving the Spud Wagon.

Tyus Barra and the two dwarves eventually emerged from the barn. Seabass led them all to the massive tree trunk in the center of the farm and pulled opened the door, beckoning them to enter. With the door swung wide, Krista felt as if she were looking into the gaping mouth of the tree. They all stepped inside one by one, Borden last. Seabass closed the door before the slobbering Café Colza could follow. The bulldog whimpered on the other side of the door. "That dog eats my chickens, I'll string it up by its eyeballs," Seabass said, the first unkind words from his mouth.

"He won't touch your dirty chickens," Hans said, then clicked his tongue three times. Outside, the dog stopped its whimpering.

Krista was immediately taken with Seabass' humble home. It was as if the entire inside of the tree had been carved out; all the walls and the nooks and crannies smoothed and sanded. Two windows were opposite the door. They were thrown open, letting in plenty of light, white drapes rippling in the breeze. Bookshelves lined the left wall, stuffed with moldering tomes, parchments, wood carvings, and other oddments. A large desk stacked high with parchments sat in front of the sagging shelves. A brick fireplace was set to the right of the windows, a brick chimney rising up, a suspended kettle of steaming food hanging over the fire. Several rocking chairs and one upholstered couch graced the middle of the room, the surface of the couch thick with blankets. A staircase carved of wood led up the right side of the room above the windows and beyond the fireplace to a series of balconies and bed lofts above. A wooden railing traced with dwarven runes lined the staircase all the way up. The ceiling above was flat and carved with what Krista assumed were more dwarf runes. A musty smell of coffee, cigar smoke, damp grain, and fresh cut peppers filled the small space. There was a large round wooden table set with wooden bowls and wooden spoons near the chairs and couch in the center of the room.

It was the coziest space Krista had ever seen, cozier even than the Spud Wagon Inn; so pleasing, in fact, that she never wanted to leave. The more she saw of Wyn Darrè, the more she realized what a harsh and bleak place her homeland of Sør Sevier was. The thought of a simple life studying books and writing in a tree-carved home like this seemed appealing.

Seabass motioned them all to sit at his table. "I shall make you a hearty breakfast you will not soon forget. For we shall talk of dark things. And a good meal will wash down the bad taste left in our mouths once you hear what I have to say."

They all sat. Their host began dropping chopped peppers into the steaming pot over the hearth. "Just let me get the meal to a soft boil, and then we shall have our talk."

"It seems the dwarves are a most peaceful folk," Hans Rake observed, watching the dwarf cook. "We've not been accosted once on our journey through southern Wyn Darrè. No dwarf thieves. No dwarf outlaws to waylay us. This place is not like the wilds of Sør Sevier. Why is that?"

"The dwarves gave up fighting ages ago." Seabass dipped his finger into the broth, tasting. Satisfied, he placed an iron lid over the pot and sat at the table. "We are but peaceful farmers and fishermen now."

"Aeros Raijael's armies did not even attack these lands when he raided his way through Wyn Darrè," Hans stated. "Why is that? Why are the dwarves so insignificant?"

"Not insignificant. Just peaceful."

"You mean already defeated."

"So you know your histories then?"

"I know *The Chivalric Illuminations* speak of the dwarves as having once been fierce fighters, perhaps the fiercest of all. But that was hundreds of years ago."

"And we were," Seabass agreed. "We were the most elite fighters in every way. The great dwarven warriors of old spent their entire lives from cradle to grave training to achieve perfection at one specific skill, be that the war hammer, halberd, battle-ax, or spear, others the bow or mace. We had elite foot soldiers and infantry and mounted cavalry that could ride over any foe. Our archers were unmatched, for they had practiced with the bow since birth. And a dwarf trained to fling a stone with a slingshot could put out the eyes of his enemy at a thousand paces. We also had elite armorers and blacksmiths, who were the best at creating weapons and armor that could not be defeated. And they were passionate about their craft. And we dwarves were unconquerable, for every dwarf soldier had honed his skills with great toil for tens of thousands of hours to become the best at his one singular task. And all of us combined, we made for the most formidable fighting force of all the Five Isles. But that was in ancient times, before dwarven-kind let the softness and the bad ideas of their leaders set in. All it takes is one bad idea to fester and linger and strangle away the greatness and passion in any group."

"What happened?" Hans pressed.

Seabass said, "One dwarf high commander who had risen up through the ranks through family lineage and privilege changed it all with one singular bad scheme."

"What was this bad scheme?" Krista asked, now curious herself. "I mean, what singular idea could destroy the most elite fighting force in the Five Isles?"

"And who was this commander?" Hans asked.

"His name was Longbottom," Ironcloud went on, bitterness in his voice. "And he was a dwarf full of many bad notions and proposals. Foremost of which, he implemented a yearly rotation in the ranks of the army. And he had his many ass-licking minions enforce it upon pain of death."

"Yearly rotation?" Hans questioned. "What is that?"

"In essence, it is what it sounds like. Even if a dwarf had spent his entire life as an archer, he had to rotate out of his post every year and become something new, say, a spearman, or an axman, or even maybe a blacksmith or something else. Overnight we had dwarves who had spent their entire lives learning how to be the best sword fighters in the

Five Isles suddenly forced into retiring their blades for, say, slingshots. Longbottom's grand theory was that every soldier should know a little bit about everything. For if every cavalryman also knew how to shoot a bow or stand a shield wall, and if every spearman knew how to shoe a horse, then we would create a more well-rounded fighting force, a fighting force in which everyone knew everyone else's job and could do it equally."

"I'm no army general," Hans said. "But that sounds ill-advised and preposterous."

"Right," Seabass agreed. "And as you can guess, the entire fighting force was disgruntled by this proposition. But they had no choice. Rotate every year or be named traitor or even be hung. So a generation of dwarf soldiers became somewhat experienced at a lot of things, but they were masters of nothing." Seabass took a long draw on his pipe before continuing. "Like I said, one bad idea. And this nonsense continued for year after year until the dwarven armies became completely ineffectual and decimated by war. In the end, the yearly rotation did naught but breed uncertainty and death, and those few soldiers who remained alive ended up walking away, even knowing they might be hunted down and hung as traitors. They just gladly deserted, thinking a simple life as a farmer was better than being a less-than-average fighter susceptible to being slaughtered by the most mediocre of human or oghul armies. And over time, the desire to achieve greatness of any sort was just plumb bred out of dwarven-kind. We became complacent. We became fine with being mediocre. We became no threat to anyone. We are worthless to Aeros Raijael. We are worthless to ourselves. We are nonthreatening, toothless entities. And the most troubling part is, many historians believe that the idea for the yearly rotation came about due to Longbottom's own pride and laziness. For throughout his life, Longbottom failed in his efforts to become elite at anything. And if he could not be elite at anything, well then, he was determined to make sure that *nobody* was elite at anything. Many believe the yearly rotation was set up by a petty tyrant to keep others languishing in mediocrity."

"Not quite the answer I was expecting," Hans said.

"I'm surprised Black Dugal did not teach you this tidbit," Seabass said. "For I know that Black Dugal is wise to most of history."

Seabass then looked at Ironcloud and Borden. "Which brings me to other matters we need discuss. Dark matters. I know you have both traveled here and suffered much toil to learn more about *The Angel Stone Codex*." He placed his pipe back into his mouth. "But I have most distressful news. I have crimes I must confess to."

A lurking uneasiness stole over Borden Bronachell's face. "What distressful news?" he asked. "What crimes?"

"I burned *The Angel Stone Codex*," Seabass said, eyes downcast.

"*Burned* it!" Ironcloud exclaimed.

"I wished to forget all I'd discovered within those dreadful pages." Seabass kept the pipe clenched between his thick lips as he spoke, almost letting the curling smoke act as a barrier between him and the others. "I desired to wash my hands of the entire thing, for to allow such blasphemous dark words to survive, to possibly fall into the hands of our enemies, into the hands of Black Dugal, would be disastrous. So I burned it before even I myself deciphered all that was within it. I had read enough. I did not want its foul stain in my memory."

Ironcloud and Borden looked sick at the news. Even Krista was surprised and a little sad for them. Since fleeing Rokenwalder, Borden and Ironcloud had spoken of little else but *The Angel Stone Codex*. And now this dwarf claimed to have burned the book. She almost wanted to laugh aloud. Hans was grinning madly. Tyus was nervous in his chair, sensing Ironcloud and Borden's mood.

"I admit, the codex was full of some questionable and dangerous writings," Borden said. "But why destroy it?"

Seabass puffed on his pipe. "All I will say on the matter is that the codex spoke of the underworld as a real place beneath our feet, a vast and deep labyrinth of darkness and rock and silver scorch stretching beneath the entire Five Isles and beyond, stretching outward even to the stars. The underworld is a place that hides the worst sin of humanity."

"What is the worst sin of humanity?" Krista asked.

"Banishing the demons to the underworld." Seabass removed the pipe and leaned both elbows on the table. "To put it simply, I fear that everything the Brethren of Mia have worked for is a lie, a grand deception perpetrated by the Vallè for their own ends. *The Moon Scrolls of Mia. The Way and Truth of Laijon. The Chivalric Illuminations of Raijael.* They are all meant to mislead. I fear the weapons and angel stones we have sought our entire lives are not meant to be wielded by the heirs of the Five Warrior Angels, but rather they are meant to kill them."

He leaned back on his chair, slipping the pipe back between his lips. "What other foul words living inside the codex now survive only within my head, and that is where they shall stay."

**

Krista was naked and alone. Well, almost alone. And almost naked. A thin blue ribbon was tied about her ankle, burning her skin, holding her captive. "You and your friend Hans are both fatherless." Borden Bronachell's voice drifted in from the darkness.

"He is not my friend," Krista muttered, her voice surrounded by a silent, smothering emptiness. Things suddenly shifted, and the depths of the Rokenwalder dungeons rained red lightning, hot and humid. That was how she knew they were no longer in the dungeon but in the underworld, a vast labyrinth that stretched the length of the Five Isles and beyond. "Hans was never my friend," she said.

"What do you mean he was never your friend?" Borden asked. "You're both Bloodwood assassins. Cold-blooded killers. The worst kind of human there is. You both share that honor. You are both *murderers.*" He hissed the word *murderers* as if it were poison air passing through his lips.

"I am no murderer," she said softly.

The blue ribbon vanished. The iron bands now circling her ankles had bit into her skin at first. But those wounds had long since scabbed over and healed.

Yet I am a prisoner. In the underworld. But do I deserve to die?

The bands were two finger-lengths wide, a quarter inch thick, and so tight her feet were in a constant state of numbness. Her hands were free, though, not that that did her any good. She could use them to massage her feet now and then. Get the blood flowing. Two heavy chains, each about five feet in length, anchored her bound feet to the wall behind her, the chains bolted into the solid rock. In the beginning she had tried to dig the bolts out with her fingers, but had only succeeded in grinding her fingernails away, along with the flesh from her fingertips. With the slack in the chains she had some freedom of movement—five feet in either direction; to the right, her food; to the left, her privy, a stone-cold floor that was piling up with rankness. Urine and feces.

She had ceased trying to escape days ago. *Or has it been moons?* Her sense of time had vanished. She spent most of her waking moments lying down, praying.

Praying to who? Dashiell Dugal? Over time it had become difficult to breathe the musty air, and then more difficult to move at all. There was nothing to soften the stony surface beneath her. No clothing, that is, just her bare flesh. Something warmed the stone floor under her. Some deep and hidden pocket of molten rock, or at least that was what she surmised. The underworld was like that. Molten.

Despite the shackles, her feet were the least troublesome; they mostly felt dead, and her awareness of them dwindled to a constant tingling, throbbing ache that every now and then blazed into a searing-hot pain. The rest of her body was a mass of aches and agonies and stiff, cramped muscles, the pain in her gut surging and then subsiding.

King Aevrett's Knight Chivalric had clubbed her good. . . .

Had she been here one week, two, an eternity of weeks? Was Gault Aulbrek worried about her? Was her father looking for her? It seemed unlikely. Krista didn't place much faith in fathers. She didn't place much faith in anything anymore. Her journey to the underworld had been short and painless. She had fallen asleep, and then never woke up. She recalled living in Jö Reviens once, long ago. Of course, that manor house had been a nightmare all its own.

Was the underworld that much different from normal life? In the underworld she lived alone in darkness so black and penetrating she sometimes wondered if she still had eyes. Down here there was naught but the ghost of Borden Bronachell to torment her. Of course, in the underworld, the difference between wakefulness and sleep, torture and normalcy, was slight and mostly indiscernible. And just when the thirst would become unbearable, the demon with the silver eyes and dark cloak would return. Not an oghul or a Vallè, but something else. Of course she only imagined it wore a dark cloak. All she could see of the demon in the darkness were those two evil eyes of silver aglow. Everything else was cloaked in black, a blackness so deep and disturbing it sent shudders through her soul. "Just speak to me," she would plead. "Just tell me what's happening," she would cry. *Just kiss me or rape me. Then I'll know why I'm here in this nightmare. . . .*

But the demon said nothing. It would just stare at her with those smoldering silver eyes. Staring. Staring. Staring. Drinking her in with two flaring, luminescent orbs. They were like two pools of starlight, those two eyes, the only lights Krista would see for days on end, and they wove a sinister spell around her—a hypnotizing spell—the glowing silver orbs somehow keeping her in check, frozen in a stasis of fear and immobility.

Her hands were free, yet she never lashed out in defense of herself. She never fought off the horrors inflicted upon her flesh. On each visit the demon would draw forth a silver whip from the folds of its dark cloak, the snaking weapon unnaturally menacing and hot and wicked to the feel. And feel it she would. The demon's whip would slice deep rivers into her flesh and then the monster would suck the blood from her wounds, its eyes always burning silver, its clawlike fist uncurling over her face, one long and crooked fingernail, the wicked tip a chipped and burnished rust red, stroking her face, slicing open the skin above her eyes, its forked tongue licking out between placid lips, lips that pulled back, baring teeth that were shockingly white and regular, free of stain or blemish, teeth that were straight, strong, and solid—two of them much longer and sharper than the rest. And the demon's nose was neither hooked nor grotesquely mangled, but clean-edged, with a pleasing, smooth chiseled shape. It was a beautiful face, an almost familiar face, with stunning green eyes set above cheekbones that looked as if they had been carved of pure marble. Then the demon's two horrid fangs and pale yellow lips floated down toward her. Her heart hammered as the devil sucked at the blood oozing from her forehead. It sucked and sucked, moaning in pleasure as it drank. When it rose, grinning, its tongue rained frothy ropes of spittle that splashed down onto her flesh, crisscrossing her neck and breasts with a latticework of silver, acid-like foam that burned. And then the monster's face wasted away before her eyes, the cheeks growing gaunt, the eyes sinking into a maggot-eaten skull.

Maggots! The wormlike creatures also glowed silver and screeched with delight as the demon ran its skeletal fingers over her breasts, between her legs and *into* her . . .

. . . no, she would not think of that.

Then maggots poured from the skull. With chilling speed the onrushing worms flashed across her moist, vulnerable skin, burrowing into her flesh, their glowing maws gaping with lionlike roars, slavering for her blood, chewing and digging and eating.

And then the screeching maggots were silenced by the long howl of a dog, and all went quiet—quiet but for the pelting rain, the lonely howl echoing in Krista's ears for a moment. The howl held so much pain. She shook her head clear, reached forward with one free hand, rubbed away the sleek layer of fog built up on the inside of her brain. But the sheets of rain pouring over her naked body still obscured her vision.

"What in the name of all the rotted angels is that dog doing out there?" she asked as the gruesome scene before her became crystal clear. About thirty paces in front of her, pawing ravenously at the ground, was Café Colza Bouledogue, rusted spiked collar around his neck. Soggy clumps of mud were churning up underneath the bulldog as he frantically dug into the earth. One side of the dog's head was a bloody, gaping hole. Its throat was a torn, ragged mess, and the spine over its hind legs was completely chewed away, as if some larger beast had simply taken a bite out of it.

"How is he alive?" Krista was horrified. *My life has turned so strange!*

The dog stopped his digging, then posed like a silver-wolf in the wild, muzzle pointed straight up into the driving rain, and howled again.

Water danced off Café Colza's fur. His short coat glistened and sparkled, and the long, haunted wail shook Krista to her soul.

Then she saw the two arms in the mud. The first arm looked like a small, pale log, palm down, fingers clutching at the earth, thin brown rivulets of water washing from the dead flesh. The second arm was harder to figure; it jutted upward from the ground, the hand reaching awkwardly for the sky, fingers frozen in place, like a filthy white claw digging its way out of the underworld with her.

"Somebody's buried out there," she muttered.

The bulldog snarled, baring wicked fangs, then clamped down on the upthrust hand while all four paws dug into the slick mud, hind legs straining as the stout dog pulled backward. Then, like a submarine slowly rising from a dark sea, a body covered in soupy sludge emerged from the ground. Café Colza's teeth slipped from the hand, tearing flesh from bone, and the dog spun backward into the brown muck. Undaunted, the beast shook the mud from its coat and spiked collar, leaped forward, latched onto the arm again with its bloody jaws, and pulled the stumpy body from the grave.

It was Black Dugal! No. It was Dugal in disguise. It was a Vallè, a Vallè with a face so perfect it could have been chiseled from marble.

And then that perfect face changed before Krista's eyes. *It's Seabass!* her mind screamed. *He is dead. Dead for the secrets he holds!*

Then the dog looked right at Krista and howled.

**

Krista jerked awake, her blanket tossed to the floor, sweating, shivering, staring straight up at the roof of the tree house above her. Her eyes did slowly adjust to the dim light. They had put her on the middle loft with Hans Rake and the tongueless boy, Tyus Barra. Borden Bronachell, Ironcloud, and Seabass slept on the tree-house floor below.

Feet still shackled, Krista rolled onto her side, noticing the lavender rose petals drift to the wood floor under her. A few still clung to her chest. She swiped them away as best she could, hands still bound.

Wide awake, Tyus Barra stared at her, his round orbs stark and white in the dim light. His look made her uncomfortable. *Did he put the flower petals on me?* Beyond Tyus, Hans Rake slept soundly, back to them both. *But does he really sleep?*

They are both creepy, Tyus and Hans. But the mute boy had treated her so well the entire journey. Naught but pureness lived in his heart, and she knew it. He was not trying to be creepy, but just trying his best to be nice in the only ways he knew how. He probably never had an impure thought.

Meanwhile, she was repelled and sickened by the images of her own Sacrament of Souls, frightened by what her own mind could suggest in the way of murder, frightened by what she herself had done in the way of murder. As she looked at Tyus Barra's innocent face, she realized there was certainly some sort of monumental failure in the way her own brain was put together. *How did I allow myself to become this person, this killer? How did I allow myself to be misled, to be brainwashed as Borden Bronachell says? But how does one unravel years of indoctrination? How do those devoted to Laijon and Raijael do the same?*

It was then that Tyus Barra pointed at her feet. She looked down. Whilst she was tossing in her sleep, the leg of her sweaty prison garb had dragged up above her knee, exposing the blue ribbon tied about her ankle. *Gault's ribbon! Always there! No matter what. My father's ribbon!* But in her dream, Borden had claimed she was fatherless.

In the latter days a king shall be made archbishop upon the Silver Throne, one of humble means from Wyn Darrè bearing witness. Therefore watch for curses and war and absolution, for Laijon shall warn everyone night and day with blood and tears.
—The Way and Truth of Laijon

CHAPTER TWENTY
AVA SHAY

17TH DAY OF THE FIRE MOON, 999TH YEAR OF LAIJON
SAINT ONLY, ADIN WYTE

The blue of the ocean was turning deep red as evening sunlight slanted over its smooth surface. The water was almost magical in its blinding, balmy glow. And though a soft, comforting breeze licked at her hair, the Saint Only Channel remained a place of stark death to Ava Shay. She straightened the hem of her fluttering white dress. It clung awkwardly to her hips and legs. So many had been killed down there. Even though the battle had taken place twelve days ago, Ava Shay could not break her gaze from the channel. *But Jenko Bruk still lives!* She took some solace in that.

This perch high on the trellised balcony of the Fortress of Saint Only, which loomed above the channel, was her one place of peace and repose. It was just far enough away from Bruce Hall and the inane conversations of Aeros Raijael below. She oft sought relief from him up here. Though when she asked to leave, he always insisted she have a chaperone. And tonight it was Spiderwood who watched over her. Tall and dark-haired, he stood beside her in his black leather armor and cloak.

She was never left alone. Yet she always felt lonely. Still she sought the most isolated stone grottoes and somber gray alcoves to bide her time. Yes, naught but loneliness filled her days, that and smelly dogs. Lots of them. All of Ser Edmon's dogs still lived in Bruce Hall below. Just thinking of the dogs and she felt sick to her stomach. She looked away from the dizzying watery expanse far below, cramps forming near her lower ribs.

The Bloodwood, sensing her discomfort, handed her his wineskin. She drank deep, appreciative as the liquid calmed her upset stomach, soothed the cramps behind her ribs. His offerings were always genuine and never filled with gross expectation. The Spider was unlike Ivor Jace, who was becoming a constant bother with his gifts. Ivor would slip her gems and trinkets and baubles, his eyes filled with rank lust and danger as he scanned her body. But Ava knew that most gifts came with a price. Ivor was brash for making such bold advances on the mistress of Aeros Raijael. She wished the tall man had not survived the battle that had turned the channel bloody.

"*The Chivalric Illuminations* will record few heroic acts of that war," the Spider said as if reading her thoughts, "and the bards will sing no dirges. In the channel below was Aeros Raijael's greatest defeat, perhaps the greatest defeat in the history of the *Illuminations*. The death of nearly an entire army. And their death is a good thing."

Death could never be a good thing. Ava had watched the battle from this very spot. *Especially the savage death of so many.* She'd watched as the blood of tens of thousands had spread like a red, swirling wave over the sea, engulfing all.

Spiderwood corked the wineskin. "The notion of Laijon and his return and what religion is right and what religion is wrong is near an end," he said, his own heavy gaze cast down to the channel below. "All of this, land and sea, has been fought over for thousands of years, fought over by human, oghul, and Vallè. Like hungry dogs they go at each other, generation after generation. All because of the words written in ancient books, likely written by fools. None of the ancients likely knowing the slightest about heaven or the underworld. It hardly seems fair."

"And that's the truth," Ava muttered more to herself than to the Bloodwood.

The Spider continued, "Would have been better for these Five Isles had humans never arrived. Only when the lost and lonely ship was cast adrift on the Five Isles and humans spilled forth did the notion of waging war over ideas and differing beliefs in a deity catch on with the oghul and Vallè. But it caught on. With a stubborn ferocity. And these past thousand years of religious wars have proven to be the most savage of all."

"I saw the war below," Ava said. "And nothing could be more savage than that."

"A fight for belief is different than a fight for food or property or land or even to defend loved ones. In a fight for belief, the soldier can see himself as god's own avenging sword."

"As Aeros does."

"And as you know, Ava, there lies no restraint in such a notion. For if a man is fighting for his god, then that man can nearly do anything at all: rape, plunder, wetting his sword in the blood of women and their babies. All the basest forms of slaughter are justified and made righteous and noble and worthy of heavenly reward. For one's enemies are by default fighting against your god, the most heinous thing of all. And to kill your religious rival is more than a right, but a divine and holy duty. Because we all believe Laijon is on our side."

"But what can be done against such hate?" Ava asked. For the believers in Raijael truly did hate those of Gul Kana. Ava thought about her own belief in Laijon and how that testimony of his love had sustained her through such hardship. *But was any of it real?* It seemed like she was merely having a conversation with the wind.

"But can you even be a good person if you stand aside and let such savagery and destruction and murder happen?" The Spider's dark gaze roamed over the sea below. "Or should you fight against such immoral beliefs in whatever manner you can?"

He turned, strained red-shot eyes boring down into hers. "Should you fight? Even if that means joining with your enemy for a time, gaining his trust, and then . . ."

"... and then slaying him in the end." Ava finished his thought.

She thought of her sword, My Heart. The Spider had claimed he would hide it in her chamber. It would be his clue that escape was near. But she had yet to find it.

She recalled what the Bloodwood had said to her some days before, that he had done something that would undoubtedly put him at odds with the Angel Prince. And when Aeros discovered his treachery, he would have to atone for his sin via a duel. And once he killed Hammerfiss in the duel, he would turn his blade on Aeros and slay him with the help of Ava and Jenko. He had said some other things about ancient prophecy and how only the strong could lead Aeros' remaining armies to Amadon and Fiery Absolution. He had also mentioned something about training her in the arts of the Bloodwood. *For the time of Black Dugal to reveal himself for who he truly is and for his Caste to arise from all corners of the Five Isles is nigh.*

The dark-haired Bloodwood beside her used to scare her something fierce, but now he was the only one in Aeros' company she felt even slightly at ease around. That used to be Gault Aulbrek she looked to for comfort. Now she could do naught but wonder where he was and if he was even still alive. *He was going to save me....*

"A black kestrel came to me this morning bearing most interesting news," the Spider said. "Black Dugal shall arrive here in Saint Only soon. He shall arrive with two others who can help us, fellow Bloodwoods: the Shadow and the Crystal. Two of my master's most dangerous creations. And then it will be on to Fiery Absolution."

**

The pack of dogs were all spit and snarls and raised hackles. Some of them were eating their own shit in the background, others were dining on the flesh of one of their own, a brown hound killed in the latest dogfight. Hammerfiss and Ivor Jace had cleared space for a dogfighting pit along the back wall of Bruce Hall just underneath the sea-serpent head the Spider had brought Aeros from the battle, the serpent head Aeros had hung on the wall.

Hammerfiss' Knight Archaic cloak was strewn across the floor, as was Ivor's. Both wore naught but their sweat-stained undershirts and leather breeches. Ivor took a long drink from a mug of birch beer. He bellowed in laughter as the remaining dogs tore their dead companion's head clean off.

"I say the burly black shepherd dog will be the last one alive," Hammerfiss said, also downing a mug of beer. The red-haired giant sat at the end of the long wooden table before the Throne of Spears. Several of the smaller dogs lounged on the seat of the throne, nervously watching the cannibalization of their fellow canine.

The White Prince sat quietly at the far end of the table opposite Hammerfiss. He wore a white shirt and a long white cloak tied at the neck. Ivor Jace sat to his left. Jenko Bruk, clad in full Knight Archaic armor, stood stiff and attentive behind Aeros, amber eyes hard and cold.

"These dogfights are savage and wrong," the Spider ventured, pouring himself a mug of beer from the large clay decanter young Leisel had set at the end of the table.

"They all fight," Ivor said. "Until only one is left alive. Do you disapprove?"

"I just said so," the Spider said. "You are drunk."

"Well," Ivor began, lifting his mug to Hammerfiss, "our lord don't want them cluttering up the hall no more."

"So we are getting rid of them," Hammerfiss said. "One bout at a time. And we've of course placed wagers on our favorites." He hoisted his own mug in acknowledgment, nodding to Ivor, then drinking deep. Beer suds matted his thick red beard, dripping from the fetishes tied in his beard down to his shirt. He belched. Ivor laughed. Spiderwood scowled. Ivor gave the Spider a cold stare in turn, arms flexing, bronze skin stretching over his bulging muscles like taut leather over a kettledrum.

The shy court girl, Leisel, drifted to the end of the table with the clay decanter and poured Aeros more beer, then set the jug down. The wispy girl was clothed in naught but a gray shift tied at the waist with a black sash. The garment did not fit her thin form at all, but rather hung awkwardly off her frail frame and limbs. She fussed with her hair, anxious fingers pressing down atop her own head.

Ava oft noticed Leisel struggling with her tawny locks. The girl could never get the one strand of hair at the crown of her head to lie flat. She had the nervous tic of always reaching up and messing with it, making it worse. "I got the most disobedient head of hair in all of Saint Only," the girl said to no one in particular. "I wish my hair was as pretty as Ava Shay's. Perhaps I should just hide it under a bonnet. I think I saw a blue one in the cellar."

Aeros pulled Leisel down onto his lap. "Your hair is divine, young one. Don't you go fretting about it none." She squirmed nervously as he tickled her, and eventually pushed herself away and skittered off toward the wide double doors that led to the kitchen.

The girl wasn't that much younger than Ava, but far too young for one as old as Aeros. Truth was, the interactions between the two set her own nerves on edge. Her eyes darted back toward the pack of growling dogs eating their dead fellow.

"My hair disobeys me sometimes too," Hammerfiss said, "but I pay it no mind. Someone ought to tell the girl that when you die and you're dead, your hair will be perfect always and forever. That is one of the rewards of a good and noble death."

"When you die, you also don't eat," Ivor added.

A glimmer of concern crossed over Hammerfiss' wide face. "What's the glory of the afterlife if there's no food?"

"Nor grog likely." Ivor lifted his mug again.

"No grog in heaven?" Hammerfiss grunted. "But I like drinking. In fact, I like drinking a lot."

"And drinking a lot is the customary thing to do in the here and now." Ivor shrugged. "But in the afterlife, who's to say? With no food or grog, perhaps we'll just drink our own piss and eat our own shit when we die."

Hammerfiss glared at the dogs as if it was their fault heaven stank.

"If I may," Ivor continued, "let's explore the subject from the position of logic. Many of us will be dead soon, and all of us will be dead eventually. A liberating notion, if you ask me, for I, like Leisel, would like to have a perfect head of hair in the afterlife. But the faithful are guaranteed eternal life. So in that sense, neither food nor grog of any sort will be needed for nourishment. Logically speaking."

"Then you likely won't need your penis, either," Spiderwood interjected. "In the afterlife, that is. Logically speaking." A wry smile crept over his lips.

"No hardened cocks in heaven?" Hammerfiss scrunched his eyebrows.

"I see your point, Bloodwood." Ivor raised his mug to the Spider. "I indeed see your point."

"I do not believe this 'no penis in heaven' theory," Hammerfiss said. "In fact, the witches on Suk Skard claim you die and are reborn as some manner of animal, fowl, or fish. Recarnated is what they call it. Born anew with all animalistic reproductive organs fully intact. And that is very forward-thinking, if you ask me."

"Forward-thinking?" The look on Ivor's face was one of sheer incredulity.

"In a manner of speaking," Hammerfiss said.

"Well, I don't wish to be recarnated as an animal."

"You may have no choice, according to the Suk Skard witches."

"Recarnation." Ivor looked contemplative. "If so, I shall attempt to come back recarnated as a warrior in Laijon's army."

"But that is what you already are," Hammerfiss said.

"Most observant of you."

"Fucking rotted angels," Hammerfiss snorted. "Have you not one original thought in your brain? Why don't you make an effort to think outside the normal for once, like the witches of Suk Skard have done?"

"Well, I can't be bothered to keep up with every witch's theory on death," Ivor said. "If that's what you truly believe, recarnation, then I pity you."

"Pity away, but at least I have an open mind."

Ivor took a long drink from his mug, then looked squarely at Hammerfiss. "What are my options in death, according to these forward-thinking witches again?"

"Animal, fowl, or fish," Hammerfiss said. "Those are your options."

"Then I shall recarnate into a house cat," Ivor said proudly.

"A house cat," Hammerfiss laughed.

"Why not?" Ivor straightened his back. "To lie about in blissful leisure in a grand manor house all day sounds most celestial. And yet"—he held up a finger for emphasis—"when things get hairy, I shall scrape and thrash with the best of them. Have you ever seen a house cat defend its territory? Feisty and fierce. Let me just say, you don't wanna get caught up in that kind of merry mayhem."

"A house cat." Hammerfiss was still laughing at the notion.

"Better than a milk cow or some such," Ivor said. "Standing about in your own shit. Waiting for someone to pull on your teat."

"I daresay," the Spider broke in, "this is the most useless conversation I have ever heard."

Hammerfiss glared at the Bloodwood. "If you come back from the dead at all, I guarantee it won't be as some noble warrior, but rather as some Adin Wyte goat or a sea puffin, or perhaps a fat manatee."

"With no tusks," Ivor said.

"Or cock," Hammerfiss added.

The Spider said, "If these Suk Skard witches are right, then I shall make every effort to come back as a stinging viper or rabid bat with the singular goal of giving you two fools rabies—"

"Shut up, all of you!" Aeros slapped the table with the palm of his hand. "All this ridiculous talk of death! I can't take it!"

Leisel walked back into the room, saw that Aeros was angry, and abruptly turned around and stepped lightly back into the kitchen.

Aeros stood, fuming, pointing at each of them. "Don't you realize I've lost nearly my entire army, and here you squawk away like idiots, inferring with all your combined inanity that every one of my dead fighters has been turned into a puffin or some such ridiculousness!" He whirled and pushed past Jenko Bruk, storming from Bruce Hall, long white cloak billowing up like an angry cloud in his wake.

Just the grunts and growls from the dogs eating the last scraps of their dead friend filled the air. *The world has gone mad!* Ava thought. *Madness.*

All madness. Even in conversation, madness. They all stupidly stared at each other, these men; Jenko, Ivor, Hammerfiss, the Spider, and many of the dogs. *A motley crew of idiots indeed.*

Then a huge smile crossed Hammerfiss' face. "My God," he said. "Speaking of death. What a fight the army of Gul Kana gave us in that channel. What a magnificent battle. I revel in the sheer majesty of my own remembrance. Leif Chaparral was a worthy foe indeed. I don't care where I go when I am dead, but that was a beautiful, glorious battle and I shall be happy for having witnessed it, for having fought in it."

Nobody else seemed to agree as the room remained quiet.

The Spider broke the silence. "I told Aeros he should have had spies in Lord's Point. This disaster could have been averted."

"Spies!" Hammerfiss growled. "I've no use for spies! Nor does our Lord Aeros. Especially if they are Bloodwood spies. And that battle was no disaster. It was glorious."

"Aeros relied on Bloodwood spies plenty to locate Shawcroft and Nail," the Spider said.

"I know nothing of that." Hammerfiss scowled. "I war, I don't spy."

Where is Nail now? Ava asked herself. *Have I even forgiven him?* Looking around at Bruce Hall and the strangers who surrounded her, it seemed unlikely she ever could forgive Nail. For here she was surrounded by madness all because of him.

Jenko Bruk was the only one she knew. *But do I really even know him?* She looked at him now, standing at the end of the table in the colors of the enemy. *The boy from Gallows Haven.* But what was different about him now? He always made her feel uncertain, the dark mysteries within him always sparking her curiosity. He had a knack for remaining aloof, even amongst this crowd; nobody knowing what was on his mind, least of all her. At last his eyes met hers, and he looked upon her with both yearning and sadness.

Ivor looked at her too, moved closer, the foul scent of his stained shirt and body odor nearly making her gag. "You know, you should be wary," he whispered in her ear. "Aeros is losing interest in you. He will choose Leisel soon, and then wherever will you be?"

"Leave her alone." Jenko's voice echoed loudly in the hall, amber eyes blazing hatred at Ivor. "She does not wish to speak to you."

"Really?" Ivor asked. "She said no such thing to me. Are you her keeper?"

"Do not whisper in her ear."

"I'm just letting her know that she shall need allies and soon. I merely offer her my services."

"She has allies enough." Jenko stormed around the table toward Ivor, armor clanking loudly with each step, hand on the hilt of his sword.

"I wouldn't come any closer, boy." Ivor squared his shoulders to Jenko. "Lest I slap your face so hard you'll be shittin' teeth for moons on end."

Jenko stopped, stewing, hand still gripping the hilt of his weapon.

"You are smart to stop," Hammerfiss said. "A fight against Ivor is a fight you cannot win, boy."

"Just leave Ava alone," Jenko said. "Just leave us all alone."

Ivor turned his back to Jenko, as if the Gallows Haven boy was of no account. "Let's pick out the next dogs, Ser Hammerfiss. For I am itching for another bloody pit fight. And I say the big brown one wins in the end. He's a brawler, that one."

"Yes, let the tournament resume," Hammerfiss said.

Ava was dumbfounded. Jenko's defense of her had come from no-where. But it had been a failed attempt. He was outnumbered and he knew it. She thought it would warm her heart toward him, but it did not. His defense of her had merely added to the insanity of the day, of the conversations, of everything. She just wanted to flee Bruce Hall, but she knew not where to go. *Aeros' chamber?* But Aeros would be there. She had no idea why the White Prince had chosen her above all the other girls from the hundreds of villages he had destroyed.

It seemed every interaction with this group was getting weirder and far more dangerous, and she sought only escape from the madness, with or without Jenko Bruk or anyone else to protect her.

The last few moments were proof to her: she had to take care of herself from here on out. If she was to escape, if she was to live, she would have to do it on her own.

**

Ava entered the empty bedchamber that she shared with the White Prince, shivering with fever. The cramps behind her ribs had returned, tearing at her insides. It hurt to sneeze. It hurt to cough. It hurt to even breathe. *When do I tell Aeros? Do I ever tell Jenko? Am I even pregnant?*

She lit some of the candles and incense around the bed. Surrounded by the rich scent of pine-pitch and witch hazel, she let her toes settle onto the plush bear rug under her feet. Ser Edmon Guy Van Hester had given her a clue, though it had taken her a while to realize what his final words to her had meant. *I can help you find a way to flee,* he'd said. *I know every nook and cranny and secret passageway in this castle.*

But if there was a secret way from the room, Ava had yet to find it. *Secret doors that lead to secret places,* Edmon had said. *Secret doors that once shut will never again be opened.* She would search one more time. It wasn't often she was alone in the chamber. The candlelit space was large and filled with many dark alcoves and only one window, which was open and faced directly south, overlooking the Mont and sea far below. A chill breeze blew in, stars twinkling in the darkness beyond, creating faint light. No escape lay through the window, though, no escape but for the drop to the rocky shore far below.

A hearth as wide as an oxcart and as high as her head was set against the northernmost wall. She imagined a fire roaring up its chimney. *Can I climb up it and out? Can that be my escape?* She drifted across the room and ducked into the hearth's black belly, looking straight up into the darkness. She could see nothing. No staircase or ladder or even handholds. She cast her gaze about the rest of the chamber. The room itself was gray-walled and complete with grand furniture, including all manner of fine sculptures, burnished ochre and bronze in the dancing candlelight. The sumptuous four-post bed, with a silver canopy and silken hangings, was in the farthest alcove from the window. She had

249

cried herself to sleep atop that bed many a night, face buried in feather pillows.

The walls rose thirty feet or more and the ceiling was a maze of thick, arched stone pillars and buttresses. Most every wall of the room was hung with velvet tapestries and a fair number of decorative spears, all graced with intricate jeweled hafts tied with red ribbons of varying length, spearheads polished and gleaming. Every surface of the room's scrollworked wooden cabinets and shelves was lined with pewter goblets and stone sculptures of curious make.

She searched for over an hour, looking behind every tapestry and bookshelf and under every bear rug, tapping and prodding every gray stone and pillar. There was no secret door, no secret corridor or escape route.

But what else could Ser Edmon have meant? Was this not once his chamber? Surely there is a way out other than the front door or the one window and a drop to the sea below. Sadness possessed her with each minute, the pit in her stomach deepening, the pain intensifying.

With her last vestiges of hope dwindling, she cast one more look around the room, noticing Aeros' chest on the floor near the bed. The gold-filigreed wooden box the White Prince had used to transport the battle-ax and helm, along with the two angel stones, up the western coast of Gul Kana stared back at her as if holding the answer. But those trinkets and artifacts were long gone now.

Ava stepped lightly across the expanse of bear rugs and knelt gently before the chest, her dress sliding up. It was growing tight and uncomfortable around her hips, and something seemed to be grabbing her ribs with fists of iron. She pulled the hem of her dress down, moaning in pain, and examined the chest. With deft fingers she found the box's hidden latch and soundlessly lifted the scrollworked lid with great care. The chest still held a leather satchel—the scrollwork inlays stamped into its rough umber-colored leather were of Vallè design. Ava pulled the satchel from the chest. It had a flap that wrapped up and over the top and a buckle on the side. Ava reached her fingers into the bag and pulled forth a handful of bound scrolls, unrolling them, examining each.

Most were blank. The others made little sense to her. She stuffed them back into the satchel, noticing something odd about the flap of the bag. The leather stitching along one side was loose.

She pulled on the loose thread, unraveling it with care until a secret compartment in the rough leather bag was revealed. She dipped her hand into the narrow pocket and pulled forth a small worn parchment. She read it.

> *The boy now bears the mark of the cross, the mark of the slave, and the mark of the beast. He has bathed in scarlet, bathed in blood.*

Again the words written upon it made scant sense to her. She slipped the parchment back into the secret compartment of the satchel.

"Again she has her hand in secret places."

Ava jerked to her feet at the sound of Aeros' voice, cramps arching through her ribs as the satchel tumbled to the soft bear rug between her feet.

"What is it you've found this time, my princess?" The White Prince stood in the doorway, white shirt open, revealing his pale chest, and his long white cloak tied at the neck, draping from his shoulders to his ankles. The young serving girl Leisel was right behind him, still dressed in her simple gray shift, demure eyes half-hidden behind tawny bangs.

The White Prince drifted coolly into the room and snatched up the satchel, then pulled the slip of parchment from the secret compartment. He read what was written on the paper. "The finding of Laijon made so easy," he muttered, and then met her gaze with those cruel black pupils, pupils—and irises—that cut hard against the paleness of his face. Ava felt as if she were suddenly staring straight into the underworld itself.

Aeros slid the parchment back into the secret compartment and tossed the satchel to the floor. "Spread a little lavender deje over that slip of paper you found and imagine what other things might be revealed." Veins traced blue trails under his ivory skin, and the icy look on his face seemed to peel back her soul. "Or perhaps we would find the secret of

Nail's parentage? Or Shawcroft's instructions on how to find the remaining weapons of the Five Warrior Angels?" He grabbed her chin, forcing her to look straight up at him. "If only your misplaced curiosity had found the pouch's secret compartment moons ago. Fiery Absolution is soon upon us, my princess. Let us hope Enna Spades brings back those things that were lost. She had grown too fond of her little games and cruelties. It is good she is up to something more worthwhile now."

Leisel stepped into the room behind the White Prince. "I've come, as you bade me do, my lord." Her flesh was sallow in the candlelight, accentuating her high cheekbones and pointed chin and large, round eyes.

Aeros shrugged off his cloak and tossed it onto the bed. He rolled up one sleeve of his white shirt, revealing the faint scars of battle. He traced the scars with one languid finger. "According to the *Chivalric Illuminations*, no human, Vallè, dwarf, or oghul can draw the blood of the Angel Prince. It is prophecy. Sacrosanct. Set in the stars and witnessed by angels." He pushed the sleeve of his shirt back down over the injuries, seemingly satisfied. "But the *Illuminations* didn't mention dogs."

He sat down on the edge of the bed. He seemed a little drunk. "Rotted angels, my blood spilt by a damned dog. Now I have to hunt and slay this meddlesome beast, or I imagine some curse is liable to follow me to the very end of my days. Seems almost ridiculous, a dog, the only living thing to have spilt my blood. It's good that Ivor and Hammerfiss are killing all the rotted things. I hate dogs. Only things to have spilled my blood. Dogs."

He's wrong! Ava recalled the first night she had spent in his tent, she recalled slapping him with all her might, splitting his lip. *I've spilled his blood!* But he had healed so fast from that wound, almost instantly. *Does the injury I caused him even count?* She found herself staring at the pristine white sleeve of his shirt, losing herself in the brightness of it.

Aeros said, "Tonight I shall have you soothe me both body and soul."

Heart jumping under aching ribs, Ava glanced up from his shirt-sleeve. But he was not looking at her; his comment had been directed at Leisel. And something inside Ava's heart broke, seeing the unknowing innocence on the young girl's upturned face. The girl offered the White Prince an uncertain smile, bowing courteously.

"Ava was much like you before she bade her old life farewell," Aeros said to Leisel. "But of late she has been having trouble with bad dreams and evil desires, treasonous thoughts. And she should pay them no heed. She must again learn not to tender her opinion, especially on matters not concerning her. She must present herself as clean, not just physically, but in her heart as well—that is, if she desires to have Laijon's will in her life."

He took Leisel by the hand and led her to the bed, pulled back the silk drape, and beckoned her to sit upon the edge of the mattress. "But let us pay no heed to Ava's problems for the moment."

Caution and fear crept up into Leisel's eyes as she let go of his hand.

"Do not fret, young one." Aeros' voice was laced with a sickly charm Ava had never before heard. "Leisel, you are a good and clean girl. Pure. In the flower of your youth. And Laijon has shown me he is very pleased with you, and you are now ready to live the higher order of heavenly law and enter into heavenly session so you can increase your own godliness."

"I do not understand." Leisel's voice was meek. "I know I am clean. I wash myself daily, hands and feet and face, for the mangy dogs in Bruce Hall have such dander. And truth be told, most of the dust is likely just floating dusty motes of their dried shit—"

"Do not be so literal." Aeros placed his finger against her lips. "I look upon your cleanliness and purity with a spiritual eye. You can heal Ava Shay of all her maladies. You and Ava shall administer unto one another, and also unto me, so that you shall both feel my increase within you, the bond of oneness."

Though Ava no longer fought the wraiths that once plagued her soul, she fought the cramps and nausea growing in her gut. Leisel did not deserve this torment any more than Ava had, or anyone had. *She is too young!*

"I am cold." Leisel shivered.

"You are experiencing desire," Aeros said. "The truly pure and innocent grow cold and shiver when their true heart's desire is exposed."

"Is this true?" the girl asked.

"You are alive with heavenly gifts." Aeros stroked Leisel's chin with the back of his languid fingers. "And I shall possess and purify you. For all I do is holy. I place into you the power of the gods and take upon myself your pains and troubles and sins. And I shall bring the oneness of Raijael over you and place a shield of protection around you. For we must all walk in the light of Raijael, and the light of Raijael will grow within us."

Ava didn't know which was worse, the wraiths that once tried to claw their way into her head or the pregnancy in her stomach. There were times, like now, she wished the wraiths would just slink back into her life and steal her away, take her down into forgetful oblivion. *If Enna Spades were here, would she put a stop to this lechery?*

"I shall cleanse and purify you tonight," Aeros said to Leisel.

"I still am not understanding," the girl said. "I am already washed and clean. And I worship Laijon same as everyone does."

"Oh, young Leisel." Aeros lowered his voice to smooth silk, slipped the tip of his pinky finger between the girl's parted red lips. "Let me ask of you then, do you know what a man looks like between the legs?"

**

Ava jerked awake to the sound of Leisel's fierce shrieking. But it was too dark to see. Aeros sprang from the bed and bounded toward the lone flickering candle in the brass candelabra hanging from an iron sconce across the room. With it he lit the other candles.

Leisel was squirming in the middle of the bed next to Ava, scream-ing, kicking at the thick blankets. Her horror-filled visage was streaked with black as she held up similarly black-smeared fingers and hands. She brushed the palms of her hands frantically over the front of her chest, spreading the blackness onto simple gray shift that she wore. "It's every-where!" Leisel scrambled from the bed away from Ava, pointing. "She shit herself with diarrhea!"

And then the smell hit Ava. *Death!* Aeros thrust forth the candelabra, which he now held in hand, eyes widening. It wasn't shit. *It was death!*

Blood, a lake of it, stretched from Ava's belly clear down between her legs, dark and thick. She kicked the bedcovers down around her ankles, revealing more of the rotten scarlet mess soaking her own nightgown. She rolled out of the bed and stood on wobbly legs, trying to make sense of the bloody scene—the smeared white sheets, the blob of blood in the center. A fleshy blob.

And Ava dropped to her knees, clutching the warm slit between her legs. From the marrow of her bones clear out to the surface of her skin she felt ravaged with both fear and sadness and betrayal—betrayal of her own body.

"How is it you've bloodied such fine raiment and bedsheets?" Aeros fumed. "Were you pregnant?"

"I- I-" Ava stuttered, not knowing how to respond. "I d-don't know—"

"How is it you've so carelessly voided my child and smeared it about my very own bed?" Aeros cut her off.

"*Your* child!" she screamed. "Or what about *my* child!"

But screaming aloud like that only sent a stab of pain through her entire body.

"'Twas all the wine you drank!" Aeros hissed. "You're naught but a drunkard. You've slain my child with your all drinking! A child I am just now finding out about!"

He's right! Guilt flooded her. *I killed my own baby!* She looked up. Twilight clouds, somber and raw, stared back at her through the open window. She figured she should just rush over and toss herself out of that window now, let what little remained of herself smash down onto the rocky shoals below.

Where is Enna Spades? Where is Gault Aulbrek? The Spider? Where are my saviors who never came? Where is Jenko Bruk?

War is the great purifier. Like a storm it blows the stagnant calm
from the land of the prosperous. Thus, for a thousand years shall the
heirs of Raijael sow unrest and confusion and slaughter. For a thousand
years they shall bathe in the foolish tears of their enemy.
—THE CHIVALRIC ILLUMINATIONS OF RAIJAEL

CHAPTER TWENTY-ONE
GAULT AULBREK

20TH DAY OF THE FIRE MOON, 999TH YEAR OF LAIJON

SOUTH OF BETTLES FIELD, GUL KANA

S addlebags empty of food, water, or even coin for an inn, Gault
Aulbrek stumbled by accident upon the Untamed camped in the
broken-down stone abbey. He was hungry. It was nearing sundown. And he was surprised to find Mancellor Allen among the outlaws.
The young Wyn Darrè was no longer clad in Sør Sevier livery. He just sat
there in a patchwork of ragtag Gul Kana armor. And from the awkward
way he held his shoulder, Gault could see the boy was injured. Gault was
further amazed when he noticed one of the Untamed, Llewellyn, wearing the magnificent war helm, *Lonesome Crown,* atop his head. The White
Prince had hired the services of the Untamed before. Gault knew their
faces well. The helm Llewellyn wore gleamed in the flickering yellow
light of the fire pit crackling in the center of the decrepit abbey. A stew
pot dangled from a spit over the flame. *Does the shaggy-haired fellow also
have the green angel stone in his pocket?*

Gault's horse stepped softly in the damp pine needles and leaves. So
far no one had noticed his approach. He reined up his mount on the trail

just outside the crumbled abbey wall. A thick buttress crawling with green ivy blocked him from the view of the rest of the Untamed. He swiftly soaked up every detail of the outlaw camp and decaying stone abbey. The towering structure lay at the very end of the game trail at the foot of the hill. Three ponies were grazing not far away, an empty canvas sack draped over the back of one. Overall, the dilapidated abbey was a place of pale, dewy brambles and green tufted grass resting comfortably before a swampy marshland and several ponds glimmering at the bottom of the small dale. Ten tall standing stones stood leaning in a rough circle in the center of the largest of the ponds, fireflies afloat at the base of each stone, thousands of them, lying dormant, awaiting the night.

To the left of the abbey was a hedgerow and a crumbling stone fence that snaked through the wood from the bogs up to the top of the hill behind him. To the right was another stone wall, taller and draped with vine.

Gault leaned forward on his mount to get a better view inside the abbey and a better view of the Untamed. Tree roots had forced cracks in the broken stone wall and created several bumpy carved benches.

Praed, the leader of the outlaws, sat on one of those benches, the hood of his dark cloak thrown over his head, a casual look on his thin face under the cowl.

The massive battle-ax leaning against the rock wall at Praed's side immediately seized Gault's attention. *Forgetting Moon!* The gigantic double-bladed weapon; its curved, gleaming edges and twin pointed horns as sharp as the Dayknight sword at his hip was unmistakable. This was not at all what he had expected after leaving Lindholf and Delia.

More weapons of the Five Warrior Angels to bog me down!

It seemed that since he had left Lindholf and Delia eleven days ago, his every thought was bent on reaching Aeros' army and saving Ava Shay. He had seldom thought of anything else, sometimes letting his mind wander, imagining himself retired on some forgotten farm somewhere in the Five Isles and living out his life in peace. *That's if there are any peaceful places in the Five Isles.* He was only vaguely conscious of his growing sullenness and anger. But as he'd slowly traveled though Gul

Kana, he couldn't help but notice the abundance of bustling farms and orchards, all plentiful with fruit and abloom. Gul Kana was fields of wheat, all a healthy golden haze, the complete opposite of the harsh, rocky climes of the Sør Sevier Nordland Highlands and the stark manner of farming he had been used to as a child. Yes, traveling through this land of plenty had filled him with much bitterness.

He wondered if he should just quietly back his horse up the trail and disappear. The forest road he had followed was far enough north of the King's Highway that he had so far felt safe from discovery. The black Dayknight armor and helm combined with the tall dun-colored destrier he rode frightened most travelers away. He had taken this small detour purely out of hunger, having caught a whiff of whatever was cooking in the stew pot in the center of the abbey. 'Twas his rumbling stomach that had led him down the narrow game trail to this place, a camp full of people he knew, and who likely would know him if he were to remove his helm.

He had somehow stumbled upon the Untamed.

For the last ten years, every soldier worth his salt, be they from Wyn Darrè, Sør Sevier, or Gul Kana, knew the reputation of the Untamed, the most unpredictable set of four thieves and outlaws in all the Five Isles. They were so well-known Aeros Raijael had hired them for their bounty hunting services from time to time. The redhead was named Judi. Clive, the biggest of the four, held a large ceramic jug of wine. The smaller fellow wearing *Lonesome Crown* was Llewellyn—he looked young but was nobody's fool. Praed was their leader. And though they liked to play the part of bungling jesters, Gault knew that with the Untamed, everything was an act of twisted deception. They were deadly.

At the moment, Praed was perched on the stone-carved bench near the fire, the huge dazzling double-bladed battle-ax to his left. Clive and Judi stood opposite the fire from Praed and Llewellyn, their beady eyes agleam under *Lonesome Crown*, lifted the lid of the stew pot and stirred what was inside with a long iron poker.

But there were others in the camp too. Mancellor Allen and two more.

A big girl with cropped red hair wearing similar armor as Mancellor sat to the right of Praed. Gault recognized her as the red-haired girl from Gallows Haven who had forced the daggers into Jubal Bruk's stumps of tar at Enna Spades' behest. He also remembered her name, only because Spades had made such sport of it—Liz Hen. The other was a smaller dark-haired boy in ill-fitting armor standing before the fire. Gault did not know this boy. But it was this diminutive boy who was doing the talking, every eye in the camp focused on him. "I'm just saying I need to dip myself in a creek now and again or my arse gets chafed something fierce."

"What kind of nonsense you spouting now?" Clive asked, cradling the wine jug against his broad chest.

"Dokie has always been mighty particular about the state of his fundament," Liz Hen said.

"She's right," Dokie kept going. "I enjoy keeping all my bodily orifices clean. I'd like to think most everyone else would endeavor to do likewise. For cleanliness' sake anyhow. For comfort's sake too."

"I can respect a man who keeps a clean arsehole," Praed said. "But I wouldn't go dipping myself into that bog. You might have some scaly eel slither right up your urinary meatus."

"What's that?" Dokie looked horrified.

"A medical term coined by a Vallè sawbones ages ago," Praed said.

"It means your pee hole." Clive grinned.

"Bloody rotted angels." Dokie shuddered, doing the three-fingered sign of the Laijon Cross over his heart. "What a nightmare this trip has been."

"Venture into that water, your butt needs to stay puckered," Praed cautioned.

"Enough already," Liz Hen exclaimed. "Talk about Dokie's bum hole always gives me the fidgets."

"I'm just warning Dokie to stay away from those bogs," Praed stated. "Those marsh eels are liable to crawl up his pee hole and eat him alive from the inside out. Turn your little Dokie into naught but a great pile of chewed-upon guts."

"I hear oghul children cut the guts out of humans and eat them like candy," Llewellyn added. "So we best hope there ain't no oghul young'uns about, if Dokie does take a swim. They're liable to eat his innards for a snack."

"Suck on them guts like frozen treats, them oghul young'uns do." Clive took a swig from his ceramic wine jug.

"Why such morbid talk all the time?" Liz Hen asked.

"I enjoy morbid talk," Clive snapped.

"Well, I don't," Liz Hen stated.

"Well, best just shut your piehole about it before you end up in that murky drink." Clive gestured to the pond with a pull of his head.

To Gault, it sounded like one of the many absurd conversations Stabler and Hammerfiss used to have. The horse was growing nervous under him. It was a wonder he hadn't been discovered on the game trail yet. He wasn't that far away from the camp.

Praed faced Dokie, serious now. "Just don't go near them marshes down there."

"I understand about not bathing in the water," the boy said. "But how am I ever gonna draw the pictures carved into the standing stones if I don't get closer? That big pond has a whole circle of ten standing stones. I can't tell from here whether those are shooting stars or crescent moons carved into them."

"Likely both," Praed said.

Clive reached across the fire pit and held forth the wine jug for Dokie. "Drink?"

"Don't drink their wine," Liz Hen snapped at the boy. "You're liable to get liquored up and won't be good to nobody then."

Dokie took the jug and a drink anyway, then wiped his mouth clean. "If you can drink their Blood of the Dragon, Liz Hen, then I can't have a little of their wine?"

Blood of the Dragon! Gault wondered if the outlaws had been feeding the girl that foul brew. Just as the thought crossed his mind, Praed produced a leather pouch from behind his back and slipped his hand into it casually, pulling forth a glass vial. He handed the vial to the Gallows Haven girl.

Liz Hen greedily snatched the vial from his hand and downed the contents in two quick gulps. Gault had seen Spiderwood drink the foul liquid from time to time. It was an addictive substance, and Gault felt sorry for the girl, for he knew she would never shake its cold clutch.

"Ah, now here we go," Llewellyn said, dipping a large wooden spoon into the stew pot. "You are all in luck." The aroma of the cooking food reached Gault, and his stomach rumbled. "No corn cake or carrot pudding and other such useless vittles tonight. Tonight we get a good vegetable cabbage stew, the most rip-roaring tasty of outlaw dishes. First-rate. Beyond excellent."

"Vegetable cabbage stew doesn't sound very outlawish to me," Dokie said.

"Men should not be cooking anyway," Liz Hen huffed. "It ain't right."

"Careful," Clive said. "Else you'll offend young Llewellyn. He took cooking classes once not that long ago in Rokenwalder."

"Why do you think we keep him around?" Judi laughed.

"Cooking class?" Liz Hen scoffed. "As of late, every idiot boy I meet seems to have taken a culinary class of some kind." Llewellyn handed Liz Hen the first wooden bowl, along with a small spoon. The big girl was quick to point out how gruesome it smelled. Undaunted, Llewellyn handed everyone a steaming wooden bowl of stew, the huge helm with its strange white horns balanced awkwardly atop his head the entire time.

"There's no meat in this." Liz Hen scowled, picking through the stew with the spoon. "No meat in a stew is a disgrace."

"As I said, it's a vegetable cabbage stew," Llewellyn exclaimed.

"People want meat in a stew." Liz Hen held up her hand and named off various meats conducive to proper stew making, one finger at a time. "Goat! Codfish! Venison! Cow! Not mashed carrots and taters and sprouts and grassy mulch and Laijon knows what else you gathered off the forest floor."

"How dare you impugn my culinary skills." Llewellyn's face was reddening with rage under *Lonesome Crown*. "I took a class."

"I think the stew is great," Dokie commented, mouth full.

"'Great' is not the word you are looking for," Liz Hen said. "Slightly less than good is what you mean."

Dokie said, "Remember what my father said about how you must treat the waitstaff at any eating establishment."

"But this ain't no eating establishment, you clodpole."

Dokie shrugged, looking up at Llewellyn. "Liz Hen used to serve food at an inn herself once, Ser Llewellyn, an inn the White Prince burned to the ground. She's just upset about it is all. She doesn't know how to act. She's not upset with you or your vegetable cabbage stew."

Liz Hen hung her head, looking duly scolded and ashamed at Dokie's apology to Llewellyn. The camp was silent for a while as everyone spooned mouthfuls of stew. Yes, this conversation was exactly like Hammerfiss and Stabler, arguing about nothing as they oft did. Though Liz Hen and Dokie had shared odd banter with the Untamed, Gault sensed the tension between Mancellor and the outlaws. Though they were not bound hand or foot, it seemed Mancellor Allen, Liz Hen, and Dokie might yet be the unwilling captives of Praed and his merry crew.

A rodent skittered under Gault's mount. Startled, the horse chuffed loudly.

Two wooden bowls hit the ground as Clive and Judi snatched their bows and nocked arrows to the strings, aiming in the darkness toward Gault. With no better plan in mind, Gault set heels to flanks and galloped his destrier right up through the open gap in the wall and straight into the abbey toward their fire.

Dokie scurried to the side. Clive and Judi backed away, arrows aimed at Gault the entire time. Mancellor Allen stood slowly, stiff in his patchwork armor, long cornrows of hair hanging over dark eyes, the familiar black tattoos atop his cheekbones unmistakable. His hand was also on the hilt of his sword.

"I mean you no harm." Gault's mouth was dry and voice hollow beneath the Dayknight helm.

"I doubt you could harm us, Ser Dayknight," Praed said without emotion, judging Gault with a practiced, knowing eye. The head outlaw was lanky. Stray locks of black hair hung from the hood pulled over his head. He had a hard-edged, thin, menacing countenance. And he hadn't moved from his seat on the rock.

Gault dug the spurs into the horse, making sure the destrier under him stomped heavily in the peat and mud. A fully armored Dayknight atop a war charger offered an intimidating presence in any situation, and Gault hoped to establish his dominance. However, this was the Untamed. He'd likely just irritated them with his presence. Clive and Judi still had their arrows trained on him.

"You're churning up the camp, stomping about so!" Llewellyn cried as he guarded the stew pot. Gault calmed the horse with a squeeze of his heels.

"I care not if you are a Dayknight or one of Aeros Raijael's Knights Archaic." Praed relaxed on the stone bench, the cowl of his dark cloak covering his face in even more shadow. "We've no wish to fight you."

"Nor I you." Gault did not like Praed's implication. *Dayknight or Knight Archaic?* Gault knew Praed to be a crafty one. But his stomach was rumbling with hunger now that he was closer to the stew pot and fire. He wanted to eat. "I wandered down the game trail by accident. I shall make my way back to the road soon. My horse is just jittery. He'll calm soon once he gets some food in him."

"We've no food for your horse," Judi said. "Best you just move along."

Llewellyn sneezed loudly, face thin and red under *Lonesome Crown* as he wiped his nose with the back of his hand.

Gault eyed the three ponies tied in the copse of trees just beyond what was left of the abbey's eastern wall. Mancellor's gaze traveled toward the ponies too, brow furrowed; then his eyes returned to the helm on Llewellyn's head and the ax near Praed. His face remained stoic, though his body looked coiled, tense, hand still at the hilt of his sword. Gault wasn't sure he wanted to know Mancellor's story or how one of Praed's fellow outlaws wore *Lonesome Crown*. There was certainly a tale to be told here.

Thing was, he wanted nothing to do with weapons or angel stones. They were a curse in his life. Things had only gone wrong for him since he'd seen the green angel stone and *Lonesome Crown* with Aeros on the Aelathia Plains. "I only wish to sup with you for a while," he said. "Perhaps exchange information, and then I shall be on my way."

Praed spread his arms out wide and welcoming. "Show us your face, Ser Knight, and you are welcome to what delights our humble camp has to offer." He flashed an unbalanced grin, revealing teeth that were crooked and stained. "I am most interested to hear what information a lone Dayknight has. Perhaps you've some news of the three fugitives rumored to have escaped hanging in Amadon? Perhaps 'tis they you search for now?" He gestured to the crumbled abbey and its surroundings. "Rest assured, those fugitives are not hiding in this camp. At least I don't think they are."

Gault was not surprised that the news of his escape had already reached this far west. His destrier shuffled nervously, Dayknight sword clanking against his armor. Gault calmed the horse once again. "You are correct." He gripped the reins. "I've been traveling long and hard, in search of these fugitives you speak of."

"Remove your helm, Ser Knight," Praed said, eyes still cold and less than inviting. "Regale us with your tale of these three vagabonds you hunt."

Once again Gault's eyes drifted to the gleaming battle-ax leaning against the stone wall, then toward *Lonesome Crown* atop Llewellyn's head. Then he let go the reins and with both hands and slipped the black Dayknight helm up and over his head, placing it in the crook of his arm.

Mancellor's eyes narrowed, and Gault could see the conflicting thoughts racing through his head. Liz Hen recognized him too. Her red-hazed eyes widened. She remembered him from the beaches of Gallows Haven.

Praed sized up Gault with cruel, hard eyes, then motioned for Clive and Judi to put away their bows and arrows. They obeyed his order.

"Shall I tell you what I know of the fugitives you hunt, Ser Dayknight?" Praed said. "Shall I tell you what the little birds and pigeons and tiny black kestrels I capture say of the matter? You do know of the little black kestrels and their messages, I assume?"

Gault did not acknowledge the question. He just looked at the man.

Praed continued, "I hear three fugitives were to be hung in the arena. But they escaped in dramatic fashion. Now every Dayknight and Silver Guard not fighting the White Prince in Lord's Point searches for them at the behest of the Silver Throne. Two of the escapees were assassins, caught in an attempt on the king's life: a young noble named Lindholf Le Graven and a barmaid named Delia. The third was the Sør Sevier knight responsible for nearly killing our beautiful Princess Jondralyn. It is believed the three still travel together."

Gault nodded. "Your information is correct."

"Oh, indeed it is." Praed stared at Gault knowingly. "Perhaps for a bounty I can locate one of these fugitives for you, Ser Dayknight. Or perhaps all three of them—that's if they stumble into my camp, anyway." He looked at his companions and laughed. "Now wouldn't that be convenient if one of them just trotted on in here?"

"It's been a while since we worked for a bounty," Clive said, grinning. "But bounty hunting isn't beneath the Untamed. The White Prince paid well for what bounties we brought in, if I recall correctly."

"Indeed you do," Praed said, still staring at Gault. "Folks of obscure origins such as ourselves are quick to spot others on the run like ourselves, others in hiding like ourselves. It's an instinct we have, a sixth sense, if you will."

Gault said nothing.

"You must understand"—Praed issued forth a sigh—"I lied earlier. I am actually not interested in any information. For you know nothing we don't already know. And we've little desire to fight a fully armed and armored Dayknight over a pot of stew. Nor would we even want to fight one of Aeros' Knights Archaic, for that matter, if one were to wander into our camp, that is. I've no doubt we could kill such a knight. But I also know we would suffer our own losses. So it's truly best for everyone if you just move on."

"And if I don't?" Gault asked.

"I think we all know our limitations here," Praed said. "No reason for any of us to act foolishly. There is an inn just up the trail and to the west. Sits on a rutted road next to a bawdy tavern called the Bloody Stag. You can't miss either one. Every traveler looking to avoid the King's Highway seems to stumble upon it at some point or other. I suggest you make your way there. Both the inn and tavern are places where the proprietors and patrons ask few questions of those who enter. You can find stew aplenty there. Trust me."

Gault could see the wisdom in the outlaw's words. He looked at Mancellor. "You can come with me if you'd like."

"My destiny does not lie in that direction," Mancellor answered. "Nor in any direction you go, especially if it's back to the west. I've my own matters to look after now. There are other things that I seek."

"Then I suggest you make your way toward Amadon." Gault grasped the reins tight, turning the destrier with a gentle kick. "And I shall give you some advice. The Preening Pintail in Savon would be a good place to lay your head, for there may be things there that you will find most interesting. Other things that you seek."

And with that, Gault spurred it up the game trail without looking back.

CHAPTER TWENTY-TWO

NAIL

21ST DAY OF THE FIRE MOON, 999TH YEAR OF LAIJON

AMADON, GUL KANA

Val-Draekin and the Silver Guard escort led the ragtag group toward the king. Cromm Cru'x received numerous disapproving stares as he made his way into Sunbird Hall. Still, even though he carried no knives, daggers, or war hammers, he sucked on the black stone, completely unconcerned. Bronwyn Allen was at his side, also weaponless, for weapons were not allowed when seeking assembly with the king.

Jondralyn Bronachell wore a tangled old wig over her raven locks, a ratty beard over her mouth and chin. Her face was sunburned and wrinkled under her beard. And her raw and empty eye socket was exposed. That was enough to make anyone look away. Her tattered breeches and a frayed shirt smelled strongly of the dock district and rotten fish. Her feet were scum-covered and shoeless, whilst her crooked fingers curled around a cane that she tapped on the tile. "Out of my way!" she shouted at everyone. "I make no idle threat!" She was playing the part of a baffled old citizen of Tevlydog.

Tala Bronachell followed her older sister, dressed as the old man's granddaughter. She was also shoeless and dirty, feet bare and calloused, a wig of scratchy white hair over her sun-worn face. She had even stuffed some form of paste into her cheeks and eyelids and nostrils to deform her features.

To Nail it was amazing that they could change the looks of their bodies and faces so completely. The stench wafting from the sisters was enough to get them pitched out of most any building, let alone the most magnificent castle in all the Five Isles. But yet here they were.

Sunbird Hall was unlike any room Nail had ever been in. Large candelabra lined the walls, hundreds of unlit candles sat atop both stone and wooden braziers throughout the room. Black pillars draped in silver and white ribbons flanked each side of the long chamber. Each gap between the pillars was hung with various colorful tapestries depicting Laijon and scenes from *The Way and Truth of Laijon*. Wide double doors leading to the hall's balcony high along the easternmost end of the room were thrown open, letting in a haze of blinding sunlight that illuminated the heavy rafters and arched buttresses above in bright yellow waves.

Their Silver Guard escort led Val-Draekin's group through a modest crowd of royals toward a small structure draped in white sheets. *The Silver Throne?* Jondralyn had told Nail that it had been covered ever since Borden Bronachell's death in Wyn Darrè. A dark-haired man wearing a thin silver crown atop his head sat with casual ease at the head of a long table near the throne, trays of bread and fruit spread out before him, a row of four black-clad Dayknights standing at attention behind him. *Jovan Bronachell!*

The king stood at their approach. He was a tall man, wrapped in a black silken cape fastened at the neck with a clover-shaped brooch of Vallè-worked silver. He wore what looked like shiny decorative ring mail under the cape, and polished leather boots and black leather pants. Nail noticed the familiar blue sword at his hip, Aeros Raijael's sword, Sky Reaver—the blade Hawkwood had taken from Spiderwood in Ravenker. Hawkwood had not come on this venture with them today. He had wisely remained in the *Val-Sadè* with Lawri Le Graven.

Jovan was an imposing figure as he eyed all who had made the journey into the castle one by one. His quick gaze was dismissive of Nail, also passing briefly over Jondralyn and Tala in disguise. Though his cold eyes did linger on Bronwyn and especially on Cromm.

One of their Silver Guard escort stepped from formation and bowed to the king. "We found the Vallè and his friends at the gate, if it please Your Excellency. He claims to have news from the north. And those he brought are witnesses to what he has to report, or so he claims." The guardsman bowed a second time.

"Well met again, Val-Draekin," Jovan said, the timbre of his voice strong and commanding. "How was your visit to Val Vallè?"

"I was there only briefly before heading north." Val-Draekin bowed. "I am afraid I have grave news. The Hragna'Ar raids have become a menace and a plague in the northlands. Places such as Wroclaw and Tevlydog are overrun with marauding oghuls and worse. I urge you to send knights northward before things grow more dire. I've brought these five with me as witnesses to the savagery."

Val-Draekin beckoned Nail, Bronwyn, Cromm, Jondralyn, and Tala forward. The five of them stepped toward the long table and the king, Jondralyn's cane tapping on the tiles. The king took a step back from the group, the aroma of the sisters' filthy clothing finally hitting him. "Make your report quick," he said, wrinkling his face in disgust.

Tala spoke first, bowing, voice reserved and lilting, feigning deference to the king. "I am Ika, fifteen years of age, raised in Tevlydog. And this is my grandfather, Rollo." Tala motioned to Jondralyn, her voice pleading now. "You must extend mercy for us northerners, Your Excellency. We've fled our home, as have most humans in Tevlydog. The oghul raiders from the northern coastlines have spread south like the plague and overrun the city. Please send soldiers of the Silver Throne and other conscripts north to fight them off. Mercenaries, even."

Tala reached grubby hands into her own pockets and pulled out a copper coin, holding it out in the palm of her hand. It was one of the coins with Jondralyn's likeness upon it. "I will even help pay the mercenaries if I can." She held up the coin.

"Mercenaries?" Jovan stepped back, addressing the chamber in general. "The Silver Throne does not lower itself to pay mercenaries. And why would I send soldiers of the Silver Throne to the north when I need them in here Amadon? I even aim to pull all my soldiers from Lord's Point soon, draw all worthy fighters back to Amadon for the fulfillment of . . . other obligations. Why would I waste time on oghuls in the north?"

"Pardon, my lord." Tala performed an awkward curtsy, fingers curling over the coin, hiding it from the king's view. "I am sorry for asking."

He's going to draw all worthy fighters to Amadon for Fiery Absolution? That was what he was going to say. The very notion bothered Nail. One should fight all enemies, not retreat to appease some form of archaic prophecy. Val-Draekin was right: faith and belief in archaic texts sparked the lunacy of men.

"Hragna'Ar is upon us!" Jondralyn smacked the end of her cane against the tile floor, her croaking voice throaty yet pointed in its intent. The princess, though frail-looking in her disguise, gave the impression of courage, her one good eye gleaming in her crooked old face. "You had better do something to stave the flow of oghuls before they reach the borders of this city and harry the walls of your own castle, young man!"

"You, a one-eyed old man who reeks of fish and shit, dare scold me?" Jovan asked. "You should apologize as your kin has apologized. If this is why my lunch has been interrupted—"

"They speak the truth." Bronwyn's ice-blue gaze gleamed under the black-smeared tattoos that stretched over her eyes and down each cheekbone. She wore black breeches and leather boots tied with leather up to her knees, her forest-green cloak draped over one shoulder. She brushed aside the two white feathers tied in her hair. "Hragna'Ar raiders have pillaged nearly every village north of Wroclaw. And they creep farther south by the day. I imagine your city will be overrun with refugees from the north soon."

"And who are you to interrupt your king?" Jovan barked.

"I am Bronwyn Allen of Wyn Darrè," Bronwyn said, spine stiff, "and you are not my king."

Jovan's face flushed red with ire. "Not your king? Any who stand in

Sunbird Hall and draw breath shall refer to me as their king." He gestured to Cromm. "Is this beast one of these dastardly Hragna'Ar savages you are so afraid of?"

"I am Cromm Cru'x." The oghul's voice boomed through the hall, garnering the attention of all. "And I am no Hragna'Ar oghul!" Suddenly realizing that every eye was on him, Cromm smiled, the jewels embedded in his teeth glimmering. He brought his gem-encrusted knuckles together, grinding one rough fist onto one rough palm. "I am a pirate!" he announced proudly, sucking on his black rock.

"A pirate," Jovan said. "And pray tell, why are you *really* here? For a pirate cares for naught but himself."

"I am Cromm Cru'x, and I have brought the marked one forth for Absolution."

Nail's heart was jumping now.

"Marked one?" Jovan asked. "Absolution? What in the bloody rotted underworld are you going on about?" He turned to the Vallè. "What craziness have you brought into my castle, Val-Draekin?"

"Cromm has seen other creatures in the north," Val-Draekin said, bowing. The look in his eyes was stark, haunted. Almost conflicted. "He has seen monsters far worse than Hragna'Ar raiders. I too have seen these creatures. Beasts straight out of our darkest legends."

Murmurs charged through the crowd.

"What creatures?" Jovan pressed. "What monsters?"

"Skulls," Val-Draekin said.

"What do you mean, Skulls?" Jovan questioned.

Val-Draekin bowed again. "That is what mankind called them before all trace of them was wiped out during the Great War of Cleansing."

"What nonsense is this?" Jovan asked.

"An ancient race of Vallè banished to the underworld," Val-Draekin said, his voice grave. "The Aalavarrè Solas. Those who are prophesied to return before Fiery Absolution."

A low murmur and rustle of disapproval echoed throughout the hall.

"What sacrilege is this?" Jovan asked. "I'm sure if Grand Vicar Denarius were here, he would take great issue with such nonsense. It smacks of Mia goddess worship to me and should be counted as blasphemy."

"Not blasphemy," a familiar melodic voice sounded through the depths of the hall. "Not blasphemy at all."

Nail's heart leaped straight into his throat when he turned and saw the Vallè maiden, Seita. She was cloaked and hooded and walked with another Vallè similarly cloaked and hooded into the chamber. When Seita reached the king, she pulled the cowl of her hood back with one hand, thin ears looking sharp as daggers poking through strands of stark icy-white hair. As always, her eggshell-colored face seemed to glow with a delicate inner light of its own. Her almond-shaped eyes met the curious gaze of Val-Draekin with a welcoming glint. Then her green eyes passed over the rest of Nail's group with swift purpose, lingering but a moment on Nail. Then she bowed to him.

Nail was flattered that she bowed to him. But he immediately wished to hear news of Stefan Wayland and Culpa Barra. It was all he could think of, seeing Seita walk so casually into the hall. He hoped the maiden Vallè might even have word of Liz Hen, Dokie, and Bishop Godwyn.

"The Skulls are real." Seita's companion spoke, his voice smooth and pleasant-sounding.

"Real?" Jovan asked in open disbelief. "But how can that be? I have never heard of such, Val-Korin."

"There is much of the ancient War of Cleansing not found in *The Way and Truth of Laijon*," Val-Korin said, pulling back his own hood. On their journey to the Sky Lochs, Nail recalled Seita mentioning her father, the Val Vallè ambassador, by name—Val-Korin. Under his dark cloak, Seita's father wore a long maroon robe embroidered with silver thread at the seams, and a red brass pendant hung about his neck from a slender gold chain. Like Seita, he seemed ever watchful and cautious.

"I shall tell you of the legends surrounding these Skulls in a more private chamber," Val-Korin said to the king before casting his gaze toward Val-Draekin and the others in Nail's group. "The fact that these good folk have traveled so far to relate such news is nothing short of astounding. We shall extend to them all the comforts of the castle." Val-Korin turned back to Jovan. "Should we not?"

"Perhaps," Jovan answered, looking distracted. "Or perhaps they are all full of lies." Then the king looked right at Nail, gaze piercing and strong. "Who are you?"

Nail bowed, offering his name.

"Nail has brought news from the west," Val-Draekin said. "He was there when the White Prince ravaged Gallows Haven."

"Truly?" Jovan asked.

Everyone in Sunbird Hall was looking at Nail now. And Nail found he was looking at Tala, for some reason. She hadn't said a word since the beginning, her eyes constantly alert, focusing on a small boy near the far left wall of the chamber. Ansel, Nail assumed. Her younger brother.

But Nail was even more startled to see who was next to Ansel—Baron Jubal Bruk. The familiar man with the bearded face and sloping forehead sat on a maroon-colored settee, his back propped against the wall. He had no arms or legs, just as Liz Hen had described. Nail only recalled bits and snippets from the time on the beach when Jubal was dismembered. The baron was looking at Nail. *Does he know what has happened to his son? Does he know that Jenko has joined with the enemy, joined with the very monsters who had him dismembered?* But Nail had scant time to dwell on the subject of Jenko and Jubal Bruk. He had to answer the king.

"It is true," he stammered, not knowing what to say. "I was in Gallows Haven when Aeros Raijael first landed. He destroyed the town, then continued north up the coast, destroying every town in his path, leaving few alive, slaughtering all, taking slaves. He is likely almost to Lord's Point by now."

"I know this already," Jovan said. "Leif Chaparral has already destroyed the White Prince's whole army in Lord's Point."

Destroyed the whole army! That couldn't be right. Nail had seen the savagery of Aeros Raijael and his henchmen. Nothing could destroy such evil in such numbers. Did Jondralyn and Tala and Hawkwood already know this and not tell him? There were so many things he needed answered. He looked at Seita. "Where's Stefan?" he blurted, heart in his throat.

Her eyes locked onto his; large, beautiful eyes that suddenly narrowed to thin slits of green. Seita's piercing gaze pulled at him, drew him in, as if searching his thoughts. It was as if she somehow totally knew him with this one singular look, as if she could somehow sense his every want and desire. Nail found himself narrowing his own gaze, refusing to succumb to whatever it was she was doing.

She drew toward him gracefully. Very close. Until they were almost touching, leaning in. "I know not where Stefan is," she whispered in his ear, her hand brushing lightly against his arm. "But he is still alive, I should think. Rest assured, he is alive."

Though Nail's heart soared at the news, he also recalled what Bronwyn and Cromm had told him of Stefan when they had stolen his bow, Gisela. Something was not right, for they had claimed Stefan was dead.

"You're sure he is alive?" he asked. Seita smelled of polished leather, perfume, and fields of heather with a hint of pine. The scent of her was almost intoxicating. Her skin was suffused with light and radiant, as if never touched by the sun. He could almost drown in her gaze. But she offered no more information.

"Enough of this!" Jovan shouted. "Step away from him, Seita! Step away from all of them, the filthy lot!"

The Vallè maiden moved away, leaving Nail feeling hollow.

"They have brought me naught but useless information," Jovan announced dismissively, as if the entire group were of no account to him now. "They have wasted my time and interrupted my lunch. Take them away, Ser Glade. You know of where I speak. Take them there and lock them up until I have sought advice from Denarius on what to do with them and this nonsense information they have saddled me with." He motioned to Glade. "Get them away from my sight."

"With pleasure." One of the four Dayknights who had been standing behind Jovan stepped forward, black helm obscuring his face. The three black-clad knights with him snapped to attention, placing themselves between Nail's group and the king.

**

The Dayknight named Glade Chaparral led the way down the corridor, black helm carried in the crook of his arm. As soon as they were out of Sunbird Hall, Glade had removed the helm, announcing his name with great aplomb, announcing the names of his three Dayknight companions too: Tolz Trento, Alain Gratzer, and Boppard Stockach. They had removed their helms too. All four reminded Nail of Jenko Bruk, confident and swaggering. Hawkwood had warned Nail about Leif Chaparral in Ravenker. And this popinjay named Glade strutting at the head of the line was probably related to the man.

The small group of prisoners was sandwiched in the middle of these four Dayknights and a dozen Silver Guards. There was no room for escape. The long corridor they followed was lined with vast colorful tapestries, crossed spears, and decorative shields. Empty sconces hung at intervals along on the walls, the only light glowing through the stained-glass windows high above, creating a web of colorful light dancing on the stone walls.

Jondralyn and Tala had accomplished nothing by confronting their brother. But that had not been their purpose in entering the castle. This little excursion was part of their training. Hawkwood had encouraged the sisters to venture back into the castle in disguise. If they could fool even their brother, Jovan, they could fool anyone. It was a risk. But Hawkwood was precise in his training and knew the two sisters could pull off the stunt. Besides, he promised he would be following them the entire time, watching, making sure they were safe. Hawkwood reminded Nail of Shawcroft in his attention to detail. But if he was watching them now, Nail had no idea how. The man was a mystery. Was he disguised as a Dayknight? A Silver Guard? A sculpture of Laijon? A bench?

In the depths of the *Val-Sadè*, at the first opportunity they were alone together, Nail had confronted Hawkwood about what the man had revealed of Nail's parentage in Ravenker—that his mother was Cassietta Raybourne and his father King Aevrett Raijael.

"I was full of poisons," Hawkwood had answered. "I have no recollection of that day, and you needn't pay any mind to the mad ramblings of a sick man. Just have faith that your destiny is greater than any of us can ever know."

Nail had been disappointed in the man's response and let the matter drop, knowing Hawkwood had been using his injuries and delirious state to withhold the truth from Nail. And now Nail felt like he had no one to trust once again. And he was a prisoner of King Jovan and being marched down the long corridor to who knew where. Val-Draekin was next to him. Bronwyn and Cromm walked before him, Tala and Jondralyn behind. *This whole venture was a needless and pointless risk.*

Tala looked worried, still gripping the coin she'd offered Jovan tightly in hand. She mouthed to Jondralyn, "They are taking us deeper into the castle," her voice but a whisper. Jondralyn nodded, her one good eye casting about the hall nervously.

"They are taking us toward the holding cells," Jondralyn said.

"And aren't the holding cells the first step toward Purgatory?" Tala asked.

"Who's talking back there!" Glade whirled, face a rash of anger. The procession came to a halt between two tall dark tapestries. "Did I give anyone leave to speak?" he demanded, pushing past his Dayknight companions, handing his helm off to the one named Tolz. Stepping past Bronwyn, Cromm, and Val-Draekin, Glade came face-to-face with Nail. "Is it you who talks, boy?"

Nail glanced at Tala, then Jondralyn. Even under their clever disguises, both of their faces were lined with concern. Tala had been the one talking. But he would never rat her out to Glade or to anyone.

"Yes, it was me who was talking, Ser," Nail said. "I did not realize we were not allowed to speak. It won't happen again. I promise. Just lead us from the castle and we will be on our way."

"Just lead you from the castle?" Glade took a step back, a cocky grin now curling over his face. "As if you give the orders around here."

"I meant no offense." Nail wished he could just slap the insolent smile from the young knight's face. Though he looked stout in his black armor, Glade was shorter and likely skinnier than Nail. *I could take him in a fight.*

Something moved to his left, and Nail's attention was suddenly drawn to one of the dark tapestries hanging against the wall. It was moldering and faded but looked to depict a scene of war and battle, and if he wasn't mistaken, there were silver-skull-faced knights wielding silver whips in the tapestry's center. But something had moved over there. *Perhaps just a breeze.*

"Am I but an inconvenience to you, boy?" Glade said, irritated. "Look at me!" he shouted. "Am I keeping you from some other important engagement you need attend?"

Nail pulled his gaze from the tapestry and stared into Glade's hardened eyes. He could see through the young man's bluster as plain as day. *He is not strong. It is all an act. He's faking it! Trying to look strong in front of his companions. He knows I can take him in a fight.* Nail felt Jondralyn's fingers grab his arm, a warning. Tala's coin hit the floor with a clatter. Glade flinched at the sound.

Embarrassed, Tala snatched the coin from the floor. Her eyes climbed to Glade's face. "Sorry," she uttered, stuffing the coin back into the folds of her ragged clothes.

"Give it here, gutter rat." Glade held out his hand.

Tala pulled the copper coin forth and gave it over with trembling hands.

Glade took it, disgust on his face. "It smells nearly as bad as you." He unsheathed the dagger at his belt with a quick rasp. With the tip of the blade, Glade carved a long scratch into the copper right across Princess Jondralyn's likeness.

"Oh, have I hurt you, my dear?" he asked the coin mockingly. He then held the coin up for all to see, laughing heartily. The Silver Guards and three Dayknights chuckled. Glade held the coin out before Tala. "Stinky little gutter rat, did you know that our lady Jondralyn was a traitor to the Silver Throne?" Glade pretended the coin was a puppet in his hand, making it talk. "Indeed I was a traitor, I was a slutty little whore."

His antics garnered more laughter from the surrounding knights. Glade took their hearty guffaws as a cue to perform some more. "Before my face got sliced up, I joyfully fucked all sorts of courtly nobles," he made the coin talk with the rising voice of a petulant little girl. "But now only dogs and dirty hounds wish to stick their stinky little peckers up my cavernous foul twat."

More laughter as the knights started enjoying the show. Glade continued, making the coin puppet dance before Tala's eyes. "I first fucked a goat," he sang. "But its slippery dong was too small. So I next fucked a warhorse and that fit about right."

He stabbed the tip of the blade straight into the eye on the coin, digging, holding the coin before Tala again. "I even stuffed an entire codfish up my cooch at the same time a crusty old pirate from the arse-end of Adin Wyte licked the scabs from my face, fingering my gaping eyehole with one shit-stained finger—"

Nail punched Glade Chaparral in the face.

With a hollow thud, the young Dayknight folded to the floor in a crumpled heap of black armor, the shiny dagger flopping from his hand, small copper coin rolling away across the stone floor. Nobody moved as Glade sat up, looked at Nail with hazy eyes, then rolled over, unconscious.

Nail's fist ached with both pain and pleasure. Satisfied, he glanced at Tala and Jondralyn, reading nothing but surprise on their disguised faces. Cromm grunted heavily, large hands now balled into fists.

Bronwyn tensed. "Cleary Nail doesn't like little men in armor any more than I," she said, her ink-shaded eyes pointed at the remaining three Dayknights and dozen Silver Guard too. "So come at us, you jabby wee cunts. We are all ready for a fight now."

"To the bloody underworld with you, bitch," Tolz Trento snarled, throwing down both his and Glade's helms, drawing his sword, lunging straight at Bronwyn.

Cromm Cru'x blocked Tolz's charge with his entire body, sending the man hurling back into his two fellow Dayknights, Boppard and Alain. They all three toppled to the floor, helms scattering down the hall.

Bronwyn ripped the sword from the sheath of the nearest Silver Guard. She stabbed him through the thin slit between his chest plate and helm with the tip of the blade before he could even react. The startled knight clutched both hands to his neck as a thick red sheet of blood poured down over his shining silver breastplate.

The remaining eleven Silver Guards had their own blades drawn, not knowing quite what to do. Bronwyn held them off with the bloody sword she had stolen from their companion. Jondralyn brought her cane up, no longer feigning to be a stooped old man. Tala crouched, scooping up Glade's fallen dagger.

Tolz, Boppard, and Alain untangled themselves and charged toward the group, black swords like flashing shadows in the hall. Val-Draekin snatched the sword from the nearest Silver Guard, killed the man swiftly, and whirled to meet the charge of the Dayknights. Cromm batted the helm from another one of the Silver Guards and sank his jeweled fangs into the surprised man's exposed neck. He lifted the knight off his feet, sucking deep. The sword slid from the man's grip and clattered to the floor.

The oghul's sudden bloodletting stopped everyone cold.

Horror filled the corridor. Tolz, Boppard, and Alain backed off, the remaining Silver Guards too, confusion evident in each of their weak-kneed stances.

Nail watched in confusion as the bottom corner of the dark tapestry above him swung away from the wall. Hawkwood emerged from behind the tapestry, his cutlass-like sword in his right hand. "Into the tunnel!" Hawkwood shouted. He snatched Tala by the collar of her roughspun shirt with his left hand and hurled her toward the tapestry. "Into the tunnel, all of you!"

Tala careened toward the wall, sliding her thin body between the thick tapestry and stone, disappearing. Bronwyn was right behind Tala, holding the tapestry out for Jondralyn, who vanished next.

Tolz, Boppard, Alain, and the remaining Silver Guards charged. But Hawkwood had both of his cutlasses now, one in each hand, the swords a silver blur between Nail and the charging knights. Bronwyn dove behind the tapestry, Val-Draekin with her.

"Go, Nail!" Hawkwood shouted as two Silver Guards fell dead at his feet.

Suddenly the corridor was filled with dozens of Silver Guards, all likely alerted by the noise. Cromm pulled long bloody fangs from the neck of the knight in his grip. He dropped the man and flung himself into the hidden tunnel behind the tapestry next.

Nail scrambled toward escape, finding the dark passage beyond the tapestry, a round tunnel. He had to crouch to move forward, sensing the large bulk of Cromm Cru'x trudging along just ahead of him in the dark.

Hawkwood was suddenly in the passageway behind him. Nail heard the sound of a rusty clasp and lock latching closed, and then all was silent.

**

The dark corridor emptied them out into a dimly lit chamber about fifty paces long, walls lined with rows of rotted wooden barrels. Faint rays of sunlight streamed in from thin cracks in the ceiling, dust motes sparkling above.

Hawkwood brought the group to a halt before the staircase at the end of the chamber. The stairs led down into darkness.

"How did you know where to find us?" Jondralyn gasped once the group was gathered together. She had already removed most of her disguise, including the wig and beard. Her face was flushed from exertion. Bronwyn also breathed heavily, as did Cromm.

"I figured there was a slim possibility that Jovan would have you imprisoned whether he recognized you or not. I know the route to the castle's holding cells well, and I know the secret ways. I assured Val-Draekin I would be prepared if you were taken prisoner."

"And you agreed to this scheme?" Jondralyn asked the Vallè.

"We all agreed to the scheme," Val-Draekin said. "I just agreed to the finer details of the scheme."

Jondralyn realized the Vallè was right. Her posture relaxed.

Nail, feeling something wasn't quite right, cast his eyes about the dim chamber, noticing the rows of wooden barrels receding back into the distance from whence they'd come. He watched as the dust floated in the yellow light above. He then looked down at the scuffed and dusty floor that had marked their passing.

Then it hit him.

"Where's Tala?" he asked.

Just as the Vallè heal thrice as fast than a man, they also
give birth thrice as quick. From conception to birth, no more than
three moons for a Vallè babe to be born.
—THE WAY AND TRUTH OF LAIJON

CHAPTER TWENTY-THREE
TALA BRONACHELL

21ST DAY OF THE FIRE MOON, 999TH YEAR OF LAIJON
AMADON, GUL KANA

The altar's cross-shaped capstone lay flat on the floor at Tala Bronachell's feet, just as Hawkwood and Jondralyn claimed to have left it. Tala stared down into the empty stone altar, rays of hazy crimson light cloaking her shoulders. In fact, the red stained glass high above cast the entire room in a deep scarlet haze. The ominous red color stretched over the tapestry of Mia high on the wall behind her, down into the very depths of the altar's bare stone hollow.

This was the room in which Sterling Prentiss had gulped his last breath, blood flowing from his slashed neck—a neck opened by Glade Chaparral's cold blade. This was the room that held secrets. Evil enchantment. Where the silver gauntlet attached to Lawri Le Graven's arm had lain hidden. This was the room where liquid silver had dripped from the ceiling and eaten away the tip of Tala's own finger. There was no trace of that silver drip now, nor any silver left on the capstone. Still, the tip of her finger and fingernail were missing.

Amadon held too many mysteries, too many secrets. And she both hated and feared the castle. The place was still full of heavy monotony, her brother Jovan lording over all, Glade Chaparral brimming with bravado and mock reproof. Nothing had changed. But she still knew the secret ways. And she was once again alone; back in her own element, once again the mistress of her own fate, following her own path. And that path was going to lead her to answers. She was on a real quest now, a quest all her own, a quest not set in motion by some silly Bloodwood game. Today she sought answers for herself. Today was the day she would win the game against her silent tormenter. She had been suspicious of the Val Vallè princess, Seita, for some time now. She cursed herself for not seeing all the clues sooner. Now it was obvious: it was Seita who had been pulling the strings all along. Tala wondered if Jondralyn and the others were searching for her now. She had quietly slipped away just moments after Hawkwood had rescued them, mind resolute to search for answers to all of Seita's deceptions.

She stepped away from the altar, and out the door, and continued on.

**

The narrow corridor she'd chosen emptied her out into Val-Korin's private bedchamber. She slipped quietly from behind the silk curtain hanging behind the Val Vallè ambassador's four-post bed. It was a large, square room, with rugs of deep maroon and dark umber lining the smooth stone floor. To her right were two iron doors—the entryway to the room. Set in the wall to her left was a large stone hearth, a hungry-looking hole of black. Five stone pillars lined each of the four walls, their gray bulk holding up an arched stone ceiling that was adorned with an intricate maze of carvings. Cold sconces were fastened about midway up each pillar, and long, narrow tapestries hung from the stone-cobbled walls between.

The sun cast a golden glow through tall diamond-shaped windows high above. A long wooden table ran down the center of the room. Ceramic vases full of colorful flowers decorated. Every chair, settee, dresser, and wooden surface was overlaid with snowy-white linen, every cabinet and bookshelf held gold goblets and vases of silver and gold. Decorative weapons of every size were propped in dark corners and stony alcoves. It was clear the Vallè ambassador liked to impress with his wealth and luxury. No surface was void of a sparkly trinket or other oddment of some kind.

Tala went straight to the wall tapestries and painted friezes that lined each wall between the pillars. She quickly discovered that behind each tapestry, other than the dust and cobwebs, was a decent-sized alcove built into the wall, a hidden space about chest high with a large shelf that had likely once been used for decorative sculptures or candle stands. She wanted to know if there were any other secret entries and exits to the room.

Satisfied that she was alone, she moved on to the nearest dresser and went through each drawer, searching for any clue about Seita and her many deceptions, not really knowing what she was specifically looking for, but finding only trinkets and gems and pendants and tiny glass baubles and other frivolous nonsense. The tall wooden chest near Val-Korin's bed held naught but silk robes and colorful capes.

Then she found the book-sized pewter jewelry box under Val-Korin's four-post bed. When she pried open the small container's intricately carved lid, something shone green and bright from within. Atop a swath of black silk rested some two dozen marble-sized green orbs, all aglow. A painful shudder, as if icy claws peeled the skin from her back, flooded over her. It was the medicine she had fed Lawri!

Tala picked up one of the little green balls, pinched it between two fingers. The gleaming liquid encased inside the thin, translucent skin of the ball swirled with emerald light. *What foul poison is it?* she asked herself. *What is it I gave Lawri?*

Tala heard voices outside the double chamber doors.

She placed the green marbles back into the pewter box, snapped the lid shut, slid the box back under the bed, and leaped toward the nearest wall tapestry, yanking it aside. Tala deftly scrambled up into the hidden alcove and sat on the shelf sideways, knees pressed up against her chest, letting the tapestry fall back into place behind her.

The door of the chamber opened. Tala sat breathless in the dark stone confine, a trace of light beaming across her face from the tapestry's lone threadbare area. Two people entered the room, the sound of their feet light upon the floor.

"Smells like rot in here," Seita said. "It's putrid."

It's me she smells! Tala suddenly realized her mistake. She had left a stench of rotten fish lingering in her wake. Her disguise was *too* good.

"This castle is a moldering relic compared to the palaces in Val Vallè," Val-Korin said. "The stench comes and goes with the seasons. We're at the end of a hot Fire Moon, and everything in this damnable city stinks."

Seita said, "Soon the we shall rule and all will change to brightness and glory."

"Our armies are ready in Vandivar," Val-Korin said. "They shall soon sail from Val Vallè. You can tell the Dragon, now that we know he lives."

"The Dragon already knows," Seita said. "He still plays his part in all this. But speaking of Vandivar, I do miss Remorse. I shall ride her soon, when Amadon is once again ours."

"Your Bloodeye steed?" Val-Korin asked, a trace of scorn in his voice. "Foul cantankerous mares, all of them."

Bloodeye steed! Tala's mind whirled. Roguemoore had told her about the red-eyed horses the Bloodwoods rode. He had called them Bloodeyes. Tala's suspicions were finally confirmed. *Seita is a Bloodwood!*

"Is Remorse still safe in Vandivar as you say?" Seita asked. "She's been given the best stable, no?"

"She has," Val-Korin answered. "To my regret. I despise the red-eyed beast."

"She's an obedient mare, far tamer than Fear. In fact, Remorse was much more disciplined and fierce in battle than Breita's mare ever was."

"And you've been talking about that damned demon-eyed beast ever since you returned to Amadon." Val-Korin's voice was sharp and biting.

"You've always known that Breita and I would become Bloodwood assassins. So do not criticize who I am now. Am I not allowed to miss my own Bloodeye mare?"

"Well, you miss that horse more than you miss your own sister."

"You must accept the fact that Breita is gone, Father. Remember, the kids from Gallows Haven all saw Fear at the bottom of an elk trap high in the Autumn Range, dead, impaled on spikes. Breita would not leave her horse in that state if she herself were not already dead. It is not the way of a Bloodwood to just walk away from a Bloodeye steed, dead or not."

"I can't help but think she is still alive," Val-Korin said.

"And I've come to accept the truth. Breita is dead."

"You also told me Val-Draekin was dead. Yet I saw him alive and well, just today, less than an hour ago."

Tala pressed her eye to the threadbare patch on the tapestry, trying to see the father-daughter squabble—she could, but barely. Val-Korin stood in the center of the chamber before his daughter, the long table between them. Both their cloaks were draped over the end of the table. The Vallè ambassador wore a maroon robe that hung to his ankles; the pendant of his rank glimmered in the light streaming from above. Seita's back was to Tala. She wore black leather armor; every inch fit snug against her body. Her wintry-white hair glowed in the light.

"I did tell you Val-Draekin was dead," Seita said. "I admit that. I thought he was. I saw him fall into that glacier."

"And yet he lives."

"Yes he lives," Seita admitted. "And that changes many of my plans. Jondralyn is hidden away in the old shipwreck, the *Val-Sadè*. She is with Hawkwood. Perhaps I shall go to them, tell them everything. They should be easy enough to find. Just look for a blind beggar with a cane. 'Twas Jondralyn and Tala who came into Sunbird Hall with Val-Draekin today. Could you not tell?"

Seita saw through our disguise! Tala's heart thudded heavily behind her ribs. *The Bloodwood knows where we hide!* She would have to tell Jondralyn. They would have to move out of the *Val-Sadè*.

"Well, could you not tell, *Father*?" Seita pressed.

Val-Korin's voice was like ice. "You are dodging the issue, my daughter. I am disappointed that you lied to me about Val-Draekin."

"So you really believe I lied to you about Val-Draekin's death?" Seita asked. "Or now that you know he lives, you are again jealous of his place in history? Or you are jealous that plans have once again changed?"

"Under Black Dugal's tutelage, lying becomes second nature to all Bloodwoods," Val-Korin said. "In time they no longer even know when they are telling the truth. They no longer know what is the truth. Do you?"

That could also describe all Vallè, Tala thought, holding her breath. She felt the sneeze tickling her nose, felt her eyes water. She buried her face between her knees.

"I do not like you calling me a liar, Father."

"Shall I list your deceptions, Seita, your shortcomings?"

"Please, I implore you. Let us have it out, once and for all."

"Well," Val-Korin began, "first you bring a counterfeit angel stone back from the north. You tell me Val-Draekin died on the quest. You tell me Lindholf, Delia, and Gault are on Rockliegh Isle, and then I discover they are not. You tell me that Lawri Le Graven's rebirth has been prepared with the Birthloam Tala fed her, and then Lawri also disappears. And lastly I find out you have also lost *Afflicted Fire, Ethic Shroud,* and *Blackest Heart.* Is nothing safe in your care?"

Birthloam? Tala's mind was a ball of confusion. *Is that what I was feeding Lawri?* She began to sweat under her disguise. *Lawri Le Graven's rebirth has been prepared with the Birthloam Tala fed her?* Heart pounding, Tala pressed her face closer to the hole in the tapestry.

"I got foolish with Gault and he overcame me," Seita said. "But the black stone is not my fault. It was missing from the satchel I took from Stefan Wayland. So I put another stone in its place. And what is the difference? Fake stone? Real stone? The legends of their powers are a lie anyway, the scriptures are all false, composed by our ancestors ages ago, all of them meant to deceive humanity for our ends."

"Still, you cannot just shrug it off," Val-Korin said. "What cavalier mistakes you've made and brushed aside were not part of our plan—a plan you yourself acknowledge was set in motion over a thousand years ago. A plan that involves both you and me and every scripture ever penned and each of the weapons of the Five Warrior Angels, and each one of those stones, too."

"You assume too much of what I acknowledge, *Father.*" Seita's voice sounded weary. "And plans can change. Have changed."

"I ask only that you take your destiny seriously."

"I am a Vallè, trained from birth to take *nothing* seriously. Isn't it all a game with us?"

"Don't test me, daughter."

"It is clear you wish it were Breita here instead of me. Her visions were always more lucid than mine, or so you wanted to believe."

"Yes, it should have been Breita here with me so near Fiery Absolution." Val-Korin's voice was laced with bitterness. "But she is not here. And now the task falls to you to carry out the plans of the Vallè, plans that were laid out over a thousand years ago, Seita. You are a Vallè maiden of royal blood. Now that Breita is gone, you are the chosen one, and as much as it pains me to say, this story is now about you."

"You say this story is about me." Seita's tone was now desperate, sad even. "But I feel like it is not being told from my perspective. You do not know what I have gone through. This clairvoyance I was born with. I struggle daily with these dreams, struggle trying to put them all together like a vast puzzle in my head, trying to stay one step ahead of everyone. It's like knowing a storm is coming, yet still reaching up and trying to mold the clouds in the sky to my will in an effort to slow that storm, to redirect it, to halt it if I can. Impossible. And it drives me mad. But who will ever talk to me about my problems? You? Hardly. These visions, they've got to stop. I can't do it anymore, Father. Not without some solid answers. Not without knowing what the hurt and pain is all for. Not without knowing where it is all going. Not without knowing the ultimate secret."

"And what do you think that ultimate secret is?"

"Oh, Father, you know that secret only lies in Black Dugal's head." Seita's voice was so severe in tone that it froze Tala's spine. "Sometimes it seems you forget Breita and I trained under him in Rokenwalder. You forget *who* he really is!"

"Who he really is?" Val-Korin said. "That I have not forgotten. I was never afraid of Dugal or his disguises."

"He is the *father* of us all."

"Yes." Val-Korin's eyes sharpened. "'Twas part of the plan set forth

a thousand years ago. Part of the game. The Hragna'Ar oghuls have fulfilled their part. Dugal fulfills his. And Birthloam has prepared the girl.
Those banished to the underworld shall be brought up from the deep.
And all that combined will be the final redemption of the Five Isles, that
will be our Absolution."

"Oh, there is more to it than that, *Father*. For you have not seen what
I have. You make it sound so simple. But you have not sworn the oaths
that I have sworn. I have touched the Scorch. I am the Seer, the Dreamer
of Dreams. I am the Maiden with the Wrought-Iron Soul, the Princess
Who Shall Crack Open the World."

Sensing a dark change in Seita's voice, Tala pressed her face closer to
the threadbare tapestry. She had understood little of the conversation.
Just another one of Seita's Bloodwood games filled with subterfuge, mis-
direction, and double meaning only the Vallè could understand. When
she peered through the thin fabric of the tapestry, it was a muddled,
cloudy scene she saw, but a scene she would not soon forget.

"I have not quite finished with my Bloodwood training," Seita said
with stark malevolence. "Now that we know Val-Draekin still lives,
my plans have changed and I must end something I should have ended
moons ago."

Val-Korin stepped back from the table, eyes narrowing. "And what is
it you think you must end, my daughter?"

"Your life," Seita said. "For I must now become truly fatherless." The
Vallè princess struck, balance and fluidity in her every move. She leaped
over the table, her black dagger a blur as it sliced deep into Val-Korin's
throat and out the other side. Seita caught her father's limp body before
it hit the floor, cradling his head in her arms as she eased him to the flat,
cold stone between to plush rugs, black dagger still gripped in her hand.

"I have a new master now," she whispered in Val-Korin's ear as she
laid him down gently. "A new father. His name is Black Dugal. The father of us all. And it is his bidding I follow."

"But I was to be by your side at Fiery Absolution," Val-Korin hissed,
blood draining from the corner of his mouth to mix with the flood of

red pumping from his neck. "It was to be me. With Val-Draekin dead, I was to be the Dragon."

"My visions were never about you," Seita said softly, soothingly. "They were always about the true Dragon. 'Twas the one name Roguemoore and Squireck Van Hester guessed correctly. 'Twas the true Dragon who took a similar Bloodwood oath as I, an oath to exist only for the return of the Skulls."

But Val-Korin was dead.

Seita pulled her father's lifeless body into the hollow of the empty hearth across the room, where they both disappeared into the blackness beyond.

CHAPTER TWENTY-FOUR

CRYSTALWOOD

21ST DAY OF THE FIRE MOON, 999TH YEAR OF LAIJON
NEAR LAVENDORIA, WYN DARRÈ

S tooped and crookbacked, the eyeless old man toddled up the
dusty path toward Krista Aulbrek and the others. In his left hand
was a long, smooth cane painted red, its worn tip tapping the road
before him. In his right hand was a large snapping turtle. He held the
turtle up by the tail. The turtle, legs wiggling, jaws biting at the man's
dirty pant legs, looked heavier than the man himself.

At the sight of the old fellow tottering up the road toward them,
Sisco grew intently restless under Krista. She sensed the nervousness
of the others in her group too: Borden Bronachell, Tyus Barra, and
Ironcloud. Hans Rake seemed to be the only one amused by the sight
of the blind man with the snapping turtle in hand. But Hans looked
amused by everything of late, as if he were clued in on some secret joke
that only he and the forests around them were in on.

Ironcloud stopped the group in the middle of the path. They all
watched the old man waddle up. A thick scraggle of gray beard concealed
the bottom half of the eyeless man's face. A dusty white bandanna covered the top of his head. The dry pits where his eyes should have been

stared empty and hollow from under twin bushy gray eyebrows. He wore a green jacket tattered and stained at the cuffs and seams. His dirty roughspun breeches were patched black, brown, and tan, and he wore no shoes. His bare feet were caked in dirt and as calloused as his hands.

The blind man stopped before them. "Who's there?" he asked. His voice was like a rumble of sharp rocks, cracked and throaty, as if he'd spent the bulk of his life smoking the harshest of tobacco. On closer inspection, to Krista, it looked as if both the old man's hands were stained with dried blood. The dark stains on his clothes hinted of blood too. She noticed he was also wearing a string of wolf claws on a stiff rawhide cord around his neck. The jaws of the upside-down turtle squirming in his hand opened wide, then snapped closed, tearing a small chunk from his breeches.

Ironcloud's mount took a nervous step back and chuffed loudly.

"Could hear you five trotting your horses down the road from a mile away," the blind man said. "Noisiest bunch I ever seen."

"*Seen?*" Hans Rake smiled, winking at Krista. "I already like this blind jester."

The old man had a point. They were a noisy bunch. Tyus Barra had led the way, his double-edged shortsword clanking against his belt to the rhythm of his mount's every step. Borden's leather armor creaked and cracked with each step of his horse too. Ironcloud's horse stepped the heaviest and loudest. Krista and Hans traveled in chains that rattled. And Café Colza Bouledogue constantly ran in and out of the woods as if his hair was on fire. Krista had never really appreciated how silent Dread was until clomping the breadth of Wyn Darrè with these companions. Sisco was a good horse but lacked even an ounce of stealth. A Bloodwood on a Bloodeye steed would not make a sound. Yes, Krista missed Dread something fierce.

It had been five days since they had left Seabass' tree house. Once out of the Dwarf Hills, they picked their way across a lamentable wasteland of dust, soot, and poverty. Naught but half-abandoned villages and burnt-out farms dotted the landscape. This part of Wyn Darrè was not lush or green as the Dwarf Hills had been, but rather desolate and dead. Charred buildings lined most every road. They had skirted around Sigard on little-known paths, not wanting any trouble. The major roadways were rife with robbers and outlaws and other degenerates.

Five healthy horses like the ones they rode were a valued commodity in such war-ravaged lands. But so far most desperate folks had stayed well clear of their group. After all, Borden had a long black Dayknight sword hooked to a baldric over his back. And a large battle-ax was strapped to Ironcloud's back too. And Hans likely still had a knife or three still hidden away in his leathers.

"You wouldn't happen to have a scrap of food for an old blind man, would you?" the old man asked.

"Naught but a beggar." Hans chuckled.

"Just a man in need of food."

"Best you bugger off, beggar."

"Better a beggar than a prisoner," the old man said, staring sightlessly in Hans' general direction. "At least I ain't that."

"Gonna use that turtle as some sort of weapon against us, old man?" Hans leaned forward on his mount, chains and shackles around his wrists clinking.

"Food, please, that's all I ask."

Ironcloud pulled a strip of fried bacon from his saddlebag. "You said you heard the five of us?" he asked. "How did you know there were five of us?"

"Spend enough time blind, you learn to read sounds," the man said, turtle squirming in his grip. "I sense there are five of you, all ahorse. One of you is a dwarf. And one of you cannot speak. Now tell me I am wrong in my assumption. You also have a dog."

How would he know one of us is mute? Krista looked at Tyus Barra. He did not return her gaze. She was glad for that. Café Colza waddled up toward the man and began curiously sniffing at the turtle, ignoring the blind man, who attempted to shove him away.

"Can I have that bacon now?" the old man asked.

Borden tossed the man the strip of bacon. It landed in the dusty road. Café Colza sniffed at the meat but left it alone. The sightless man stooped, dirty fingers searching the ground. Once he snatched up the bit of dried meat, he fed it to the turtle. "Ser Snap-a-Lot's been much hungrier than I for some time now."

Upside down, the turtle struggled to eat the bacon, its head retreating up into its thick, mottled shell. "He prefers melon," the old man said.

Hans laughed. "Reckon if a blind man were to keep any type of critter as a pet, makes sense it's a turtle."

The old man grunted and shuffled around the group, the tip of his cane scratching a path through the dirt, turtle swaying in hand. "These roadways are a haunt for thieves and murderers," he advised, almost mumbling to himself. "Best watch yourselves, now. Ever since Aeros Raijael destroyed these lands, it's been naught but cutthroats and robbery. The only safe place left in Wyn Darrè is the Dwarf Hills. Of course, dwarves are naught but lazy vermin. Or perhaps Aeros had the aversion to dwarves. Some folks get the sneezes around a dwarf. Sometimes the staggers. Sometimes they'll stroke right out. Faint. My aunt Sylvia was just such a one, indisposed to all dwarven-kind—"

"I should cut you down for saying such," Ironcloud snapped. "I've scant little need to listen to some doddering old fool besmirch my kin—"

"Don't think I'm some daft fool," the old man turned and snapped right back at the dwarf. "I was once known as Ser Alexander Thork, baron of Thorkell's Landing. The largest port in southeast Wyn Darrè, in case you did not know." The old man seemed to straighten his back for a moment. "That's right, I was once the head of the House of Thork, a barony that had been handed down generation to generation for over a thousand years. Never once was there not a Thork ruling in Thorkell's Landing."

"Until now?" Hans said.

"Until now," Alexander Thork agreed. Though sightless, his face actually turned up in Hans' direction. "'Twas one of Aeros Raijael's henchmen, a knight named Enna Spades, who plucked out my eyes. Now all I see are visions of the torture and dismemberment of my wife and four sons. That bitch forced me to watch their deaths before blinding me." He then looked toward Ironcloud. "I've a right to my opinion on the dwarves. For those lazy farmers did nothing to help stop Aeros Raijael. Nothing."

Ironcloud remained silent.

Krista recalled Seabass telling them how the dwarves used to be fierce fighters.

"The mute who rides with us also suffered at the hands of Enna Spades," Borden Bronachell said, "same as your kin."

"Then I shall at least consider the mute my friend and comrade." Alexander nodded toward Tyus Barra, the tip of his long red cane scratching in the dirt.

Tyus Barra rummaged through his own saddlebag, producing the last roll of sourdough bread Seabass had sent with them before their departure. The tongueless boy urged his mount forward gently and handed the roll of bread to the sightless old man.

"Much obliged." The man nodded, stuffing the bread into the folds of his worn green jacket.

"Have you no flowers to give him?" Hans asked the mute, chuckling. "Or are the flowers just for Crystalwood?"

Tyus Barra blushed and spurred his horse forward.

**

Less than an hour later, Café Colza Bouledogue wandered off the trail. Tyus Barra reined his mount to a complete stop and pointed to the left, where the dog was sniffing along the ground some thirty paces off the beaten path, bulling its way through the grassy bracken, stumpy tail furiously a-wag.

"Idiot dog," Borden said.

Hans Rake whistled, but Café Colza continuing deeper into the trees, spiked collar snagging and pulling on the bracken thickets.

"We must follow him," Hans said.

"Follow him?" Borden exclaimed. "Are you out of your bleeding skull? Idiot dog will come back eventually. No need chasing it into the trees."

The bulldog was still visible in the bracken, growling loudly now, strong jaws and teeth tugging on something in the dirt and briar. Then the dog bounded away into a thicker copse of trees beyond and vanished with a rustle of brush and leaf.

"I think we do need to follow the dog," Ironcloud said, turning his mount off the trail and after the dog.

A whisper-light shiver stole over Krista as they all followed the dwarf. Her eyes were sharp and she could see what the dog was following—a rope of purple intestines that stretched off deeper into the forest. The scene was similar to when the dog had found Ser Aulmut Klingande's intestines on the roadway south of Eark.

They tracked the dog through the trees, following the line of purple guts stretched along the forest floor. They entered a small green clearing to a gruesome but familiar sight. A corpse, tied with thick rope at the ankles, hung upside down from the low-hanging branches of a tall elm. *Seabass!*

Krista recognized the stumpy body of the red-haired dwarf. Seabass was sliced from chin to pubis, stomach pulled wide, the stark hollow of his cavernous gut revealing bone-white ribs and spine and naught else. A scarlet heap of blood and heart and liver and intestines lay under the corpse, steam rising from the fresh-spilled innards. He hung there, both arms dangling. A lit hickory-wood pipe was still smoldering in his purple lips. A thin slip of bloody parchment was pinned to his forehead with a polished black dagger.

"How?" Ironcloud moaned painful and deep. "We left him at his home. How did he get clear out here?"

Nobody had an answer for that question. Café Colza was standing in Seabass' vaporous pile of entrails. The dog jammed his thick head straight into the guts, gnawing and snarling with pleasure.

"Those innards are still warm," Hans observed, eyes narrowing.

Borden Bronachell's own fierce gaze roamed the forest. "He couldn't have been killed more than a few moments ago."

Ironcloud slid silently from his saddle and stepped toward Seabass. He pulled the black dagger free of his friend's forehead, took the parchment pinned there, and read it aloud. "'All who know the secret of the codex shall die. When I next see you, Squateye, only the truly fatherless shall I let live.'" Ironcloud looked up. "It is signed 'Ser Alexander Thork, baron of Thorkell's Landing.'"

"Trust is fleeting," Hans muttered, looking at Krista. "A Sacrament of Souls, sanctioned by Black Dugal himself."

"Are you saying that old man on the road was Black Dugal?" Borden hissed.

"I figured it was obvious," Hans said, grinning. "I told you he has been with us this entire journey."

"Bloody rotted angels," Ironcloud cursed, crumpling up the note.

"A Sacrament of Souls not just sanctioned by our master," Hans said, "but also executed by him." His cruel Bloodwood eyes were now fixed on Krista. "Let me ask you, girl, are you ready to become truly father-less?"

Dragon Claw and rot. One who lies blackened and dead shall be transformed at Fiery Absolution and breathe new life into the beasts of the underworld, and they shall walk up from the underworld upon the bones of the human dead.
—THE ANGEL STONE CODEX

CHAPTER TWENTY-FIVE
LINDHOLF LE GRAVEN

21ST DAY OF THE FIRE MOON, 999TH YEAR OF LAIJON

SAVON, GUL KANA

The morning's swelter and humid air breathed an unhealthy pall over the city of Savon. Lindholf Le Graven could feel the suffocating heat in his bones, sucking all will and ambition from him. The canvas tarp that hung over himself and Delia and the wooden doorway set in the floor of the tower only partially blocked the sun.

"I must return to Amadon," Delia said. "I must go back to my job at the Filthy Horse Saloon. I must find my father. He is still so sick from Seita's poisons. Or so I imagine. Who know what they did with him?"

Lindholf rolled over and looked at her. The girl lay on her back under a thin blanket, another thin pile of blankets between her and the hard wood.

"I cannot take another night working in the Preening Pintail," she continued. "I can't take another day atop this tower or working down in that tavern with Rutger. This is no way to live. This is not my home. I have to leave."

"Are you out of your mind?" Lindholf sat up. "It's madness to think we could go back to Amadon."

BRIAN LEE DURFEE

But she's right, he thought. *This place is miserable!* It didn't help that the two of them had been living like tramps atop an exposed stone tower the last seven days. Or that the tavern owner was getting more and more brazen with Delia every day. Lindholf figured the man would force himself upon the girl any day now.

And what will I do? Am I brave, like Gault?

Rutger was eager to have Delia work with him at all times. Besides being an inn owner, the man was also a tallow chandler. He brought Delia down from the tower daily to help him and Luiza cut wicks and fill molds and make lye from ashes and herbs and flowers and then boil it with fat and all manner of scents. Meanwhile, Lindholf was only allowed to come down from the tower at night and stand his evening post at the door of the tavern, looking menacing in his Dayknight armor. It was a miserable existence. But going back to Amadon was out of the question.

"We cannot go back to Amadon," he said again. "They will be searching for us at the Filthy Horse. Glade, the Dayknights, the Silver Guard, they are all hunting us."

Delia rolled onto her side, the thin blanket no longer covering her body. She wore the outfit Rutger had prepared for her. The tavern owner forced Delia to wear a fetching serving-wench outfit, the skirt and corset designed to show as much leg and cleavage as possible. Lindholf found his own lusty gaze tracing the curve of her hip as she lay there but an arm's length away. Every day she was becoming more and more a distraction to him, driving him crazy. He desired her almost as much as or more than Rutger did. He wanted her almost as much as he wanted Shroud of the Vallè. Delia and the white powder: the lack of both was driving him to madness. He rolled over, looking the other way, looking at his own miserable armor. The black Dayknight greaves and breastplate were hot to the touch. The summer heat seemed to literally leak from the whole pile of polished and clean armor and drag over his whole body. The sack containing the angel stones and unwieldy weapons they'd been lugging about since fleeing Amadon seemed just as hot. *Ethic Shroud, Blackest Heart, Afflicted Fire,* they all seemed to call out to him in their heat.

He sat up and looked out past the long, pointed shadow stretching across the wooden roof, the shadow created by the useless sun-bleached canopy above. He let his gaze roam past the knee-high crumbled battlements of the tower and over the city of Savon, again recalling that he had seen this stone tower and rooftop before, in the dread visions as a mermaid tried to drown him in Memory Bay. The thought made him shudder. *Are we supposed to be here? Is my fate tied to this place? Savon?*

The strange city was spread out before him on all sides; slanted roofs and tall towers rose up everywhere, most of the towers similar to this one, with squatters and beggars making their homes atop them. He could hear the steady hum of the swift-flowing Ridliegh River lapping against the tower below. The clank and clatter and voices of the bustling street behind him were naught but constant reminders of his isolation. Yes, this tower was a most miserable place. Still, for them to return to Amadon was suicide.

"We cannot go back," he said, looking at Delia.

"Who said I wanted you to come with me?" She sat up and adjusted her corselet.

Lindholf's heart plunged into his gut. *She's never wanted me.* Still, just looking at Delia, despite her constant rejections, he felt the desire swell up within him. He wanted her so desperately it was driving him to distraction. Being so near her all the time almost seemed a curse now. He rolled back over, looking at his pile of sun-cooked armor again—black and hard and baking in the heat, the armor still offered more comfort than any sort of human interaction.

The dagger Seita had given him was there too, hidden under the armor. *I was supposed to kill Gault Aulbrek with the poisoned blade and bring all the weapons back to the Vallè princess.* But Gault was gone, and who could he kill now? *I can still use the weapon to murder and can still bring all the weapons back to Seita.* Instant death coated the blade, or so the Vallè claimed.

Lindholf glanced at Delia once again. She had fallen back asleep, covered with the blanket. *Yes, I can still use the dagger on someone.* With that thought, the scars on his body burned. The slave brand from the Riven

Rock Quarry. The cross-shaped mark where Glade had cut him across the back of the wrist. The scars where the mermaid had raked his arm. They all burned when he thought of murder and the dagger. They all burned. Fierce.

The marked one! That was what he ofttimes called himself now. *The marked one, addicted to Shroud of the Vallè, branded for failure.*

**

Smoky and musty-smelling, the Preening Pintail was overflowing with drunks of every stripe tonight: men, women, young, old, all crowded into every corner of the dimly lit tavern, drinking, jostling, flirting, spilling their beers. The buzzing of flies and gnats near the entry gave way only to the raucousness of the patrons dancing in the center of the dirty floor. They danced to the music of a lone fiddler, the thump of boots and feet on the hardwood floor pounding through Lindholf's skull.

He stood his post near the front door of the Preening Pintail, deformed face hidden behind the large black helm, hand resting on the black opal-inlaid pommel of his sword. He stood in obscurity, a black Dayknight statue against the wall. He could feel the small bulk of the leather pouch containing the three angel stones pressing at his hip under the armor. The pouch was tied to his belt. *Ethic Shroud*, *Blackest Heart*, and *Afflicted Fire* were still on the roof of the tower with their bundles of clothing and other meager possessions. The door to the roof of the tower was securely locked, as were the wide double doors at its base.

"Not so rigid, Ser Lin," Rutger would oft say. "We don't want to scare folks off. Your shiny black armor is intimidating enough. Just keep them from knifing each other is all. Seven days on the job and you are still stiff as a board."

Luiza bustled about behind the bar, pouring drinks, whilst Delia walked the floor of the tavern serving them, her ample chest fairly bursting from the top of the tight corselet Rutger made her wear. Rutger also helped with the serving of drinks, but he mainly played host to the guests, joining in their revelry, getting drunker by the moment.

Seven nights at the door and Lindholf had quickly learned that bars like this were full of naught but stupid people and aimless conversation

300

and women being wooed by the dumbest of knaves; men who talked a load of nonsense and drivel, talked loudly and obnoxiously, but talked with a confidence that Lindholf knew he himself could never possess. The men who frequented this tavern clearly offered naught but heartache and lies to the women they wooed, and likely even beatings and abuse in the end.

In fact, Lindholf could almost predict which useless fellow a given girl would leave with. It was never the polite gentleman who won the tavern maiden. It was never the nice man full of compliments and coin who left with the pretty girl. It was always the scoundrel whom the pretty girls favored. It was the rake who offered the women the most perfectly clever of insults who won the evening. The whole nightly routine reminded Lindholf of the lovers' intrigues played out in King Jovan's court. Whether it was a saucy wench in a dirty Savon tavern or a silly court girl in Sunbird Hall, the endgame was the same: all women tended to choose the same type of useless, pompous, peacocking fools. They all chose men like Glade Chaparral. Yes, taverns were a court all their own, but with stakes far more pathetic and meaningless and low. And Lindholf watched it all with complete and utter contempt for everyone. In a tavern filled to the brim with people having a good time, he had honestly never felt so alone.

Delia was at the end of the bar, two mugs of birch beer clutched in her hands. She was conversing with a skinny, gap-toothed young man with short, dark hair. Earrings glistened in both the fellow's ears, and his dark beard was abnormally bushy and long and didn't seem to quite fit his face. Tattoos ran the length of his arms, from his fingertips all the way up and under the frayed sleeves of his beer-stained shirt. He was just the sort of loser the pretty ones adored.

And, unfortunately, Lindholf could hear their conversation.

"Fastest carriage in all of Amadon," the young man said to Delia. His voice was a bit muffled coming from across the noisy tavern, but Lindholf could still hear.

"I could get you from Savon to Amadon in less than two days," the man continued, leaning casually up against the bar, his eyes traveling over Delia's bosoms with little shame. "For the right price I can get you there fast, if you take my meaning. We could leave town right now, even. I mean, you're not the prettiest girl I've offered such a deal to, but—"

A burst of laughter from somewhere deep in the tavern drowned out the man's words, and Lindholf momentarily lost track of the conversation.

He focused on Delia's lips now, trying to read her response. "Along . . . King's Highway?" he thought she asked. "I don't . . . to be seen . . . King's Highway."

"No need we even poke our heads outside the carriage." The young man brushed the back of his tattooed hand over Delia's wrist. "My driver is very discreet. Nobody will even know we are—"

"Do you have a bugle?" A drunken fat man with a round red face was suddenly standing right in front of Lindholf, the stink of his breath overpowering. "A bugle?" he pressed. "Do you have one, Ser Knight of the Shined Black Armor?"

"You can see that I don't." Lindholf turned back to the bar, but Delia and the bearded rake were gone.

"You don't have a bugle?" the man asked again. "We need one to blow in the street at midnight."

"Step back." Lindholf placed a stiff gauntleted hand on the man's chest and gently pushed him back. "I'm the doorman, and you need to remove yourself."

"No need to be disrespectful." The round-faced man glared, then belched loudly. He then stumbled away through the double doors of the tavern and out into the night and the yellow glow of the lamplit cobbled street.

Lindholf cast his gaze back through the smoky, dark tavern. Rutger was laughing heartily with a group of young drunks in the center of the tavern; Luiza was still madly pouring drinks behind the bar. But there was no sign of Delia or the confident young man who'd offered the carriage.

"No bugle?" The fat man with the round red face was back through the double doors, staring at him again. "I've Shroud of the Vallè for sale if you've but one bugle to lend."

Lindholf's mouth watered as he imagined the euphoria of sniffing the white powder up his nose once more. He wasn't so quick to shove the deranged man away a second time. "Shroud of the Vallè?" he asked. "Where?"

"Show me the bugle first," the man demanded greedily.

"Show you the bugle?" Lindholf asked, confused.

"I mean, show me the bugle first."

"I already told you, I haven't a bugle."

"But I need one for midnight."

"Do you have Shroud of the Vallè or not?" Lindholf asked impatiently.

"Well, not with me, no."

Lindholf grasped the man's soft shoulders with his stiff gauntlets and pushed him toward the door. "Then go get it."

"Leave off, good Ser." The fat man shrugged himself away from Lindholf's grip. "Don't order me about so." The man staggered through the doors of the tavern and back into the lamplit street again.

"Don't be thinkin' you're all that." Another man was now standing in front of Lindholf, a bigger man than the last. He was taller than Lindholf and muscular. He had an intimidating shaved head of stiff blond stubble. He wore some armor and a belt studded with links of chain mail and thick boots that rode high up his legs. He carried a wooden shield strapped to his back and a huge broadsword with a leather-wrapped hilt that swayed at his hip. And he had a similarly armed friend just as big and muscular behind him, the second man with blue Suk Skard tattoos covering the entirety of his face, a thick black mustache drooping down on either side of his mouth.

"We've been watching you, Ser *Dayknight*," the first man said. "Watching you all night, standing here at the door all clean and crisp like you own the world. But we see through you."

Lindholf knew he hadn't been standing like he owned anything. Still, it had finally come to this—a drunken confrontation he wasn't sure he could win just by the mere presence of his Dayknight armor. He knew he should ask the two men to leave, but decisive action such as that was meant only for those who never doubted themselves. And Lindholf had doubted himself ever since he agreed to this damnable job.

Ever since he had been born, really.

"Now why would a Dayknight play bouncer at a shit-hole tavern like this?" the man asked, his tattooed friend nodding in agreement. "Unless he ain't a real Dayknight. Where'd you steal that armor from?"

Lindholf could tell by the look in their eyes that these two men were itching for a brawl. *Just once in your life be decisive and stand up for yourself.* He remembered when he had stood up for himself in the corridor of Amadon Castle with Glade Chaparral. He had swum through underground caverns to find *Ethic Shroud* when others dared not. But he had been high on Shroud of the Vallè both times.

He had always met failure with naught but cynicism, resentment, and very little courage. Tala had fought his battles. Gault had fought his battles. Even Delia had fought his battles. As a bouncer, he knew men were bound to challenge him. Dangerous men. Thugs and cutthroats who could fight. *It's time I fight my own battles.*

He had a Bloodwood dagger in his belt that could cause instant death! He was the son of a lord! He breathed deep, gathering his courage.

"Back away," he said, the tenor of his voice low, hopefully intimidating. "I am Ser Lin of Rivermeade, Dayknight of the Silver Throne. I insist you back away."

"And if we don't?" The man laughed, his companion joining him.

The ground seemed to shiver beneath Lindholf's boots. Holding his breath, anger filled him now. The two men were glaring fiercely, sensing his weakness like silver-wolves sniffing out their pray. "You are no Dayknight," the first man said.

"Go!" Lindholf ordered sternly.

"I suppose you think you can make me?" Suddenly the man had a dagger out, and he thrust it threateningly between them. "I will have no problem gutting a fool knight like a wet herring—"

It was instinctive, swift, and crushing. Lindholf's black-armored knee jerked straight up between the man's legs with brutal force. The fellow's eyes bulged in surprise as Lindholf's knee lifted him off the ground. Then the man folded to the floor, gulping for air, dagger tumbling from his grip.

Lindholf drew his sword with a keening hiss that rang out through the tavern. Every eye was on them now. The second man backed off, dragging his friend along the floor in retreat. Lindholf stood a little taller as he watched the men slink back toward the back of the bar. He kept his sword out, eyes scanning the crowd for Delia, hoping she had seen. But he was unable to locate her.

In fact, he didn't see her again that night.

**

After the tavern closed, Lindholf climbed to the top of the tower alone, worried he would find the angel stones and weapons gone. But all of them were still under the canvas tarp where he kept them.

However, Delia's bundle was gone, and what few clothes the barmaid owned were also missing. Both the corselet and skirt Rutger had made her wear in the tavern were hastily scattered over her thin pile of blankets.

Lindholf stripped off his helm and polished Dayknight armor and boots and walked slowly toward the rim of the tower, bare feet padding softly against the wood-plank roof. When he reached the edge, he stepped up onto the crumbled battlement, looking down. Moonlight glinted shards of light off the swift-flowing Ridliegh River, waves lapping against the base of the tower some seven stories below.

He wondered if the fall would kill him, or would the river catch him in its cool embrace and sweep him away, crippled and broken?

He turned. *Or perhaps the cobbled street on the opposite side of the tower would offer an instant death.* But he knew he hadn't the courage for that. He hadn't the courage to stab himself with Seita's poisoned dagger. He hadn't the courage to gather up the weapons and stones and return them to Seita as she had instructed.

He hadn't the courage for anything. The marks on his flesh didn't even burn. *I need a sign,* he thought. *The marked one needs a sign from the gods to guide me!* But he knew Laijon would likely answer no prayer of his.

CHAPTER TWENTY-SIX

GAULT AULBREK

22ND DAY OF THE FIRE MOON, 999TH YEAR OF LAIJON
SOUTH OF BETTLES FIELD, GUL KANA

Gault Aulbrek watched the Dayknight step into the wan light of the Bloody Stag like a saber-toothed lion on the prowl. The knight's polished armor was bathed in shadow, naught but a black silhouette against the open doorway. He instantly knew who it was.

Enna Spades!

Dust from the rutted road clouded behind her, billowing in the bright sun. Then the twin doors of the inn swung closed behind her, and the room was dim.

Sitting alone at one of the few tables near the back of the Bloody Stag, Gault slipped his own Dayknight helm back over his head, hoping he was buried deep enough in the rear of the tavern to remain unnoticed. There were ten other men in the tavern besides himself, each of them armed with a shortsword, dagger, or small cudgel of some kind. And they all regarded the Dayknight who had just entered with the habitual suspicion reserved for newcomers.

Even the two older men at their chess game near the doorway looked up at Spades' entry. Gault had noticed their chess set earlier. It was nice, the intricate pieces all carved of walrus tusk and obsidian. He figured the game had likely been stolen from some manor house nearby and brought to this dingy inn.

The Bloody Stag itself had an air of both heavy use and heavy neglect. Low-slung beams of timber, cobwebs, and dust loomed overhead. Stained, unswept floors strewn with rushes and spittoons stretched the length of the long bar to the right. The place was brimming with the smell of tar and pine-pitch smoke. A large stew pot hung from four rusted chains over a fire pit in the center of the long room. Three bearded wastrels were cooking strips of meat under the pot, the firelight flickering over their face piercings. They too observed Spades' entrance. Two drunk men hunching over mugs of ale at the bar did too.

Spades moved toward the bar like a clot of ominous blackness drifting through the room, her familiar and confident gait fooling all but Gault. She was tall enough to pass for a man. And why would they not believe it was a man in the armor? Things were different here when it came to women and weapons of any kind. Gul Kana was the opposite of Sør Sevier in that regard. In Sør Sevier, women were welcome to any fight—and their armies were double the size for it. Yes, these men would just assume she was a man. But Gault knew she was dangerous enough to best five Dayknights in a fight.

And seeing her again, every bone in his body grew instantly weary with exhaustion, his mind becoming further drained. *What foolish fatigue has come over me?* Ten years in heavy armor marching in war and he had never felt so worn out as he had these last few days, and never more so than now, seeing Enna Spades again.

He had taken rest in the Bloody Stag Inn for the last couple days. Alone in his room above, he would remove the Dayknight armor with blissful pleasure, but when he ventured down into the tavern, he would reluctantly strap it back on, sword with black opal-inlaid pommel always secure at his hip. Everything here was exactly as Praed had described, naught but a single rutted road through a one-building town. The pitch-roofed inn, two stories high, leaned against the tavern, the Bloody Stag.

After their cursory glance at the new Dayknight, most in the tavern had gone back to their own devices, figuring Spades was just another traveling knight like Gault.

"What can I get you, good Ser?" the gray-haired bartender asked the new Dayknight. He had a thin-lipped smile, spittle forming white at the corners of his mouth.

Enna Spades removed her helm. A river of fiery red hair cascaded over her two black shoulder plates in a haphazard sprawl. The bartender's eyes widened as she casually set the Dayknight helm on the polished bar before her. "I'll take a cold drink of water," she said. "The coldest you got. It's hot out there."

All eyes were on her again. One of the old chess players near the doorway halted mid-move, both of them looking at her curiously. Even the wastrels at the stew pot glanced up, brows furrowed. The four burly cardplayers sitting nearest Spades stood and backed away from their table, hostility glaring from dark eyes, hands on the hilts of their short-swords. None of the four wore armor of any sort, but they looked rough and even, Gault dared admit, somewhat competent.

"Best strip out of that armor, lassie," the bartender said with a snarl, his thin smile now gone, eyes incensed. "Else we'll strip it from ya and then take turns fucking ya bloody for disgracing it so."

Spades flicked a glance around the room, then slowly removed her gauntlets, setting each on the bar with a hollow thud. Her bored-looking gaze wavered not once from the bartender's. She pulled a copper coin from a small leather pouch at her belt. She flipped the coin up in the air and caught it casually. She repeated the move heedlessly as she spoke. "I'm searching for a Wyn Darrè man with dark blue tattoos under each eye. I've heard he's been this way. Easy fellow to notice with those tattoos. Easy to track. His trail has led me here. He's likely traveling with a fat redheaded young woman and another smaller boy. Have you seen them?"

"Have I seen them?" the bartender asked. The four husky ruffians who had been playing cards circled around her, swords at the ready. "She asks if I seen them," the bartender repeated.

"That's indeed what I asked." Spades glared at the bartender with a resilient gaze that cut like crystals. "A simple question, really, even for one like you."

"And what happens if I don't answer, lassie?" The bartender pulled a long knife from the sheath at his leather belt, thin lips grinning madly. "Will you toss that coin at me in anger? Clank it off my head and knock me unconscious with it? Or do you aim to draw your sword?" His laugh was like a hoarse croak, echoing through the silent tavern.

The others in the room laughed with him.

"Aye, what happens if I don't answer, lassie?" he repeated, face now still etched with a humorless grin. "What do you aim to do about it?"

"What do I aim to do about it?" Spades set the copper coin flat on the bar directly between her and the bartender. "I aim to paint this shit hole red with the blood of everyone standing here and then burn it to the ground."

Her threat was met with another round of healthy laughs from the four husky cardplayers who had boxed her in. The bartender was now grim-faced, fingers tightening around the knife in his hand. All four men had similar grim smiles.

"Women and little girls ain't allowed to wear armor in Gul Kana," one of the chess players called out from his table. "Women ain't allowed to carry swords. Ain't you heard what happened to Princess Jondralyn Bronachell when she tried playing the soldier like you? Got her face cut off is what she did."

"Cut right off," the bartender followed, casually reaching for a mug behind the bar with his free hand and taking a long drink. "Women ain't supposed to soldier about like that. Not in Gul Kana, anyway."

"Well, I reckon I ain't from Gul Kana," Spades said.

Before the man could so much as swallow his drink, he was staring down the long black Dayknight blade of Enna Spades, the tip of her sword pointed right between his eyes.

One of the cardplayers lunged at her from behind, sword swinging. Spades moved casually aside and spun about, black sword keening through the air, crisp and hard. Her simple backhanded blow sliced the man's neck wide. He doubled over as blood sprayed thick and red across the wood floor at his feet. His sword clattered to the ground as he folded to his knees, clutching at his open throat with both hands.

"Stupid bitch," the bartender growled, leaping over the bar, knife gleaming.

Spades spun again. The tip of her Dayknight blade smashed straight up under the bartender's chin and right out the top of his head. Hair and bone and brains splattered the wall of dishes and mugs behind the bar as Spades ripped the sword free. The man's limp body folded belly-first onto the bar with a wet, bloody thump, then slid slowly backward, disappearing in a crumpled heap behind the bar.

There was naught but silence as Spades turned, setting her stance against the three remaining cardplayers, bloody black sword held up between them.

The two old men by the entry let their chess game scatter as they exited the tavern in mad haste. Sunlight from the swinging doors illuminated the startled faces of the three wastrels at the stew pot. They clearly had no wish to join the fight.

The remaining three cardplayers advanced on Spades, confident still. But her black sword struck like lightning, carving the first man's thick arm from his body in a flash. He cried out in pain, jerking back, weapon and arm hitting the floor, brawny shoulder spurting blood. The two other men leaped forward with angry shouts, blades whistling through the air. Spades also lopped the second attacker's arm off at the shoulder, her follow-through slicing a bloody trail straight across the exposed chest of the third combatant. Both men reeled back, blood gouting from their wounds. Spades ended the first man with a swift stab to the heart. He dropped instantly. She decapitated the second man with a powerful stroke that hummed through the tavern. He too dropped dead. The third man shrank away in terror. But that didn't stop her plunging blade. It entered his left eye and exited the back of his skull, then slid free just as quickly. He slumped face-forward into the lake of scarlet on the wooden floor.

Spades, bloody Dayknight sword still in hand, snatched up the coin she had left on the bar and slipped it back into the small leather pouch at her belt, then eyed the three wastrels at the stew pot in the center of the Bloody Stag.

"Please, lady," one of them cried. "We ain't done nothin'."

"That's your problem," she said darkly, two hands gripping her sword now. "You should have done something. You should have left."

Spades stalked forward and struck the heads from all three without mercy.

She always fought with a remorseless splendor like that, Gault thought. He watched from behind the eye slits of his own helm as she strode back behind the bar, found a rag, and wet it down with a bottle of hard whiskey. She meticulously began to wipe the blood from her sword. From what Gault could see, there was not a drop of blood on her black armor. Sword again sheathed, she rummaged behind the bar, pulling forth two ceramic bowls and two wooden spoons. Leaving her helm on the bar, she stepped carefully over the dead, strode purposefully to the stew pot hanging in the center of the tavern, and filled both bowls with stew. That done, she strolled straight back to where Gault sat hunched in the shadows.

She plopped down on the rickety chair opposite him. "And you, Ser Gault Aulbrek, did not even stand to help a woman in distress." He said nothing. "You seem capable enough to help me anyway," she went on. "For it turns out you're not as armless and legless as Leif Chaparral led Aeros to believe."

Gault removed the helm and placed it on the table next to him. "So Leif claimed Jovan had me tortured and mutilated?"

"Indeed he did." Spades pushed one of the bowls of hot stew across the table. "Aeros was most distressed." She took a timid taste of her own steaming bowl, sipping lightly at the hot broth. "Have some."

"I'd rather not."

"It ain't bad."

"So I see you still carry that coin with Jondralyn's face on it?" He looked around the room at all the dead. "This obsession with the princess of Gul Kana is a sickness. So much killing, and for what? So you slay Jondralyn Bronachell? How many corpses lie in your wake between here and wherever you left Aeros Raijael?"

"More than you can imagine," she answered.

"I can imagine quite a bit."

"All the killing we have done together, Gault Aulbrek, and you are worried about one insignificant tavern full of scum and drunken losers."

"Not particularly. But haven't we done enough killing, the two of us?"

"Not by half." She stirred her stew with the wooden spoon.

"But why kill these folk?"

"We are at war. And they are the enemy. Or have you forgotten that?"

"I am not at war with anyone."

"I am," Spades said. "You see, what I like least in this world is when some ignorant man tells a woman what she can or cannot be. I will kill who I want, when I want, and as many as I want, until I am done. And if any man says different, well, in my opinion, based purely on principle, he shall die. Do you wish to boss me about as the bartender did? Do you wish for me to kill you, too?"

"You couldn't."

She smiled.

Gault counted the number of dead splayed through the tavern, eight total, and that included the three innocent wastrels under the stew pot. Fact was, had there been double that in the tavern, she would have killed them all. To Spades, others existed purely for the amusement it afforded her to slaughter and torture her way through life.

"Aye, look at them. Pathetic lot. They all died for doubting me." She sipped her stew, glancing at the dead and the lake of blood, too. Her creation.

"A lot of people die," Gault said. "Leastwise when you are around."

"Indeed. And Gul Kana seems full to bursting with stupid men thinking they can order me about."

"It's likely the Dayknight armor you wear that sets them off. How did you come by it?"

"Reckon I could ask you the same." She pointed at his armor with her wooden spoon. "Looks like we both have stories to tell." Her eyes finally met his, smoky with desire. "Indeed, we've likely much to catch up on."

Something akin to desire immediately stirred within him. He tried to push it back.

Spades smiled coyly. "You are too stern, Gault." Then her eyes narrowed. "Or perhaps it is Princess Jondralyn Bronachell you desire. Word is that her beautiful face was wrecked. Destroyed by none other than Ser Gault Aulbrek, Knight Archaic of Sør Sevier." She smiled again. "If that isn't the precursor to love, then I don't know what is."

Spades pulled forth a half-dozen Gul Kana coppers from her leather pouch and dumped them onto the table. Each one had a likeness of Princess Jondralyn minted on its surface, each a long scratch through the delicate portrait. "The coin I carried though Wyn Darrè is likely somewhere at the bottom of the Saint Only Channel, buried under sand and guts. But no worries, I've been collecting more in my travels since then." She ran a finger over one of the coins, tracing the scratch over Jondralyn's likeness. "Seems like your handiwork has made quite an impression in Gul Kana, Ser Gault."

"If you desire an apology, you won't get it," he said. "I know you wanted the pleasure of causing Jondralyn's suffering yourself."

Spades shrugged. "I've plenty of time."

"So you lost your favorite coin in the Battle of the Saint Only Channel?" he asked. "I've heard but rumors of that battle, bits and pieces. Sounds as if it did not go well for our Angel Prince at all. Tell me of it."

"The short version: Leif Chaparral kicked our asses." Spades' voice held no emotion. "In my opinion, Aeros got too arrogant once we reached Saint Only. He promoted that idiot of a popinjay, Ivor Jace, to Knight Archaic. Then Aeros carried that ridiculous helm and unwieldy battle-ax into war. The sea itself is what stole his victory, killed most of his army, swept away his precious weapons, perhaps even took his life."

"Aeros is dead?"

"I do not know his fate, truth be told. And I could really care less."

"Interesting."

"Pointless bloody wet chaos is what I remember of that battle. I myself barely escaped to Lord's Point with Jenko Bruk and Mancellor Allen in the end. It was Jenko who pulled *Lonesome Crown* and *Forgetting Moon* from the rising tide." Her eyes focused into narrow hatred. "And 'twas Mancellor Allen who stole the weapons from us in Lord's Point. Jenko Bruk returned to Saint Only and his girl, Ava Shay. And I set off after Mancellor. As for how I am dressed, the Dayknight armor—like you, it seemed the best option, no? Now it is the traitor Mancellor Allen whom I chase."

"Seems clear to me Mancellor was never with us," Gault said. "He was a traitor."

"With *us*?" she asked. "Are *you* with us? Are you still beholden to the Angel Prince?"

But Gault did not answer her. He'd stopped listening after hearing that Jenko had returned to find Ava. *That means she is in Saint Only.* Now Gault had a definite destination. A goal. He recalled the secret ways into the Fortress of Saint Only the Knights Archaic ofttimes used when Aeros' armies had originally taken Adin Wyte. In fact, he knew exactly what bedchamber Aeros would likely claim as his own.

He knew exactly where he would find Ava Shay.

"Well," Spades said impatiently, "are you with us?"

"At the moment, no," he said, lost in a brief vision of what his future life with Ava Shay might be like. "There is a place in the Nordland Highlands, a stretch of plains north of Stone Loring, the only place I ever knew true happiness, the only place I ever felt true joy. I aim to journey back to those plains and find that lone rock in the center of those plains, a jagged outcropping that marks the place I first met my wife, Avril. Perhaps I will build a house there, start a farm, start another family, have my daughter, Krista, join us, and live out my days in calm and peace."

"Look how sentimental you've become." A smile played at the corners of Spades' mouth. "And who is this girl you plan on taking to this farm and marrying. Is it Ava Shay?"

Gault remained silent, knowing he had already spilled too much.

"Only two years with Avril before she died, and you've dwelled on her memory for a lifetime," Spades said. "It consumes you to distraction. It fills you with foolish notions."

"Her memory is all I have."

"Bullshit. What you desire has been written all over your face since I mentioned Ava. She reminds you of Avril, and you are going back to get her. I am not stupid."

"And if I do?"

"The whole of the Five Isles is decimated, Gault. Every place is a ruin. You really think you are going to go off and find Ava Shay and live happily ever after? She is just a kid, same age as your daughter. Plus, and I tell you this for your own good, Ava is a different person now than when you left. Not as innocent. So don't go thinking you can just rush off to Saint Only and sweep her off into your little domestic bliss. You cannot recreate a life you never had. It is a fool's quest you are on."

Her words stung. She could always read him with astonishing accuracy. If he was to be honest with himself, it was a strange pleasure talking with her again, for she could always point out the folly in any plan. But she was wrong this time. He would see his simple dream come to fruition, no matter how small and ridiculous it seemed to her.

Besides, Enna Spades had a mountain of issues of her own.

"And your quest to find Mancellor Allen," he said. "Is it really about saving *Lonesome Crown* and *Forgetting Moon*? Or is it because you know Mancellor will lead you to Jondralyn Bronachell and then eventually to Hawkwood?"

She glared at him. "Don't go thinking me as sentimental as you."

"Oh, I think you are exactly as sentimental as me."

"No." Her voice dropped to no more than a soft breath. "I hate everyone." Their eyes locked. "What are you thinking?" The look in her eyes was again sultry. He again felt the stirrings of desire. "What are you thinking, Gault Aulbrek?"

"Never ask a man what he is thinking," Gault said.

"Why?"

"For he might tell you the truth."

"And what is the truth?"

"You are a killer, Enna Spades. You are a murderer. And you are sad."

"Killer, you say? People generally deserve to be killed."

"Is that why you fight against everything and everyone, because you have such disdain for it all?"

"I fight because it's the only way the world shall know that I have lived. Battle. War. Killing. *The Chivalric Illuminations* record my deeds. Everyone shall remember the name Enna Spades, the greatest warrior in the annals of history. Think of all the millions who have lived and died and done nothing with their lives. I fight against everything and everyone so I shall be *known*."

She stood, unbuckling the black plate armor from off her shoulders, shedding the black bracers from her arms. "Do you *know* me, Gault?"

"Aye." He too stood. "I know you."

Together they stripped off each other's armor, a lake of blood and the scattered dead the only witness to their feverish coupling.

**

The Bloody Stag burned. The fire lit up the night, flames and curling smoke rising into the starless black sky. Spades doused her torch in a nearby horse trough and strode back down the road toward Gault.

As the fire billowed into the night, Gault kept a firm grip on the reins of both their mounts. Spades rode a healthy-looking tall gray palfrey. His own dun-colored destrier was jittery so near the blazing fire. It was not much of a warhorse, in his estimation, so nervous around the fire. But there was no accounting for what horse-training a stolen Gul Kana war charger might or might not have received.

"Well," Gault said as she walked up, the fire raging behind her, "all things considered, I'd say your first-ever visit to the Bloody Stag went well."

Spades laughed. "It was good to see you again too, Gault."

"And here I was wondering how I was going to pay for my stay at the inn." He motioned to the fire. "Looks like you took care of that."

She took the reins of her mount and hauled herself up into the saddle. "No one can ever claim Gault Aulbrek was a low-down thief who skipped out on his tavern debts."

She handed him the torch, and then dug two more from her saddle-bag and handed those to Gault as well. "Take these. You shall need them once you reach Saint Only. Enter the fortress at the base of the Mont. You remember the secret tunnels into the castle, I assume? Use them. Aeros keeps Ava in Ser Edmon's bedchamber."

Gault took the torches and secured them to his mount. He climbed into the saddle, and with a flick of the reins, he pointed its nose west. He glanced back at Spades. "To the east, about an hour up the road, you'll come across a game trail that heads off to the north. Follow it. You'll come to a hedgerow and a crumbled stone fence that will lead you to a swampy clearing at the bottom of a hill. There is an old stone abbey there, naught but a ruin, but impressive nonetheless. The one you seek was there not more than two days ago."

"Mancellor Allen?" she asked.

He nodded. "And the Untamed were with him, as were the ax and helm."

"Splendid," she said. "Most splendid indeed."

"And once you're done with Mancellor, look for the Preening Pintail in Savon. I've a feeling the other three weapons of the Five Warrior Angels may be there."

With a flick of the reins, setting heels to flanks, he galloped down the rutted road toward the west.

Prior to Absolution, an archbishop shall die and rise again, passing through the veil, bathed in heavenly glory. He shall bring back with him a princess most fair. And this shall be a portent and sign, for he shall usher in the return of the Five Warrior Angels, each a servant at his side.
—THE WAY AND TRUTH OF LAIJON

CHAPTER TWENTY-SEVEN
MANCELLOR ALLEN

22ND DAY OF THE FIRE MOON, 999TH YEAR OF LAIJON
SOUTH OF BETTLES FIELD, GUL KANA

I ain't no thief," Dokie Liddle said, abashed.

"You've been slipping your bonds nightly," Clive said, eyes fixed on the frightened face of the Gallows Haven boy. "Your grubby little hands have been in Praed's satchel. You've been takin' Blood of the Dragon that ain't yours. Givin' it to your fat friend over there. Your theft is only adding to a debt you already cannot pay."

"What debt?" Dokie asked.

"All the food we been feeding you. It comes with a price."

Though they were untied during the day, they were tied up nightly. Mancellor Allen, Liz Hen Neville, and Dokie were officially the prisoners of the Untamed. Prisoners in Ten Cairn Abbey. And the days were growing long. And nerves growing frayed.

"Don't listen to any of these fools, Dokie." Liz Hen's bloodshot eyes darted uneasily between each of the Untamed sitting around the fire pit. "They ain't nothin' but a bunch of unwashed assholes, you ask me." Her nervous gaze settled on Clive. "And that one has been givin' me the hairy eyeball ever since we come here."

"I wouldn't *eyeball* you if you was the last girl in Gul Kana." Clive glared at her. "And you're a cunt hair away from me slapping your face. Just one curly red cunt hair away."

"Fuck you and whatever gaping arsehole shit you out," Liz Hen snarled.

"You swear too much." Judi leaned forward, firelight an orange glow on her face.

"I oughta slap the girl a fine lump on the noggin," Clive continued. "Knock her right unconscious, just to get a little peace around here for once."

"Knocking me out won't quiet me," Liz Hen countered.

"Ain't that the truth," Dokie said. "Liz Hen often talks right in her sleep. And when she really gets going, she can yak away even more than when she's awake. A lump on the noggin won't deter her no matter how fine a lump."

"That's right," Liz Hen agreed haughtily. "We Nevilles speak as we please, even in slumber."

"I reckon we've all heard our fill of her sleep talking." Llewellyn spat into the fire. Sparks flew up. "And sleep talking ain't no good in an outlaw camp, you ask me."

"We've all heard her jabber nightly," Judi sneered. "Constant prattling on about someone named Zane and getting lockjaw and the staggers from infected wounds. You're right, Llewellyn, such nightly racket ain't conducive to a good outlaw camp."

"Still doesn't warrant an assault on my face." Liz Hen's red-rimmed eyes narrowed. "And Zane is my brother. And I will talk about him awake or asleep."

"And I'll slap anyone I want," Clive added, "awake or asleep."

"Leave the girl be, Clive," Praed interjected. "I care little if she or her little friend rummages through my things. Blood of the Dragon is a hard addiction, makes one do things untoward."

"I ain't never been untoward," Liz Hen said.

Will it ever end? Mancellor Allen groaned inwardly. It came to this nightly: an angry absurd exchange of words between Liz Hen and the Untamed, their pointless banter interrupted only by the occasional crackle of the fire or snort of the ponies tied in the trees nearby. It was Clive and Judi who goaded the Gallows Haven girl nightly. *And it will never end until Praed and the Untamed hear word from Black Dugal.*

Mancellor knew he could not fight the four outlaws alone. He was not fully healed from the wound he'd suffered in the Battle of the Saint Only Channel, even though Judi had provided several poultices for the injury. The wound stretched up his right bicep from the back of his elbow around the front of his arm and almost up under his armpit. It was still in need of better tending, and he was lucky it was not infected yet.

In many ways the outlaw camp wasn't bad. There was food aplenty. Game wandered into camp daily. And Judi's sourdough bread was the best Mancellor had ever tasted. They were comfortable here. Plus, Liz Hen was sated with all the Blood of the Dragon she needed, mostly because she had Dokie steal extra.

Both *Lonesome Crown* and *Forgetting Moon* rested against the crumbled stone wall nearest to Praed, both artifacts polished and gleaming in the firelight. None of the Untamed knew of the two angel stones in his pocket. Even Liz Hen and Dokie didn't know of the stones. Nobody knew. Mancellor thought of Gault Aulbrek's departing words. *I suggest you make your way toward Amadon. And I shall give you some advice. The Preening Pintail in Savon would be a good place to lay your head, for there may be things there that you will find most interesting. Other things that you seek.* A cryptic message, full of hidden meaning. He knew Gault had not shared the words lightly.

As Mancellor contemplated Gault's words, he watched a black beetle crawl up the lichen-covered wall nearest him, a dense spiderweb stretched across its path. The beetle paused about halfway up the abbey wall, unsure, then proceeded forward, becoming entangled in the intricate web almost immediately, tiny legs whirling in panic. At the sight,

Mancellor's mind traveled back to the Battle of the Saint Only Channel. Beetles had covered the sand before the tide rose up and devoured everything in blood and swirling chaos. He still could not believe he had survived such madness. He couldn't believe he had survived five years in Aeros Raijael's army.

He looked away from the trapped and dying beetle. A hint of dusk was settling over their forest camp now, and with it, the cloudless sky carried the last faint wash of light over the top of the roofless abbey. Fireflies hummed across the nearby bogs and pond, thousands of them clinging to the ten standing stones.

"I've come to know you some these last few days," Praed said to Liz Hen. "And you are a very angry young girl. Vengeful and full of loathing. Why is that?"

"Bloody rotted angels." Liz Hen looked at the man. "What do you expect after all I've been through? The sacking of Gallows Haven. The killing of my parents. The death of my brother. The Battle of the Saint Only Channel. Bishop Godwyn being hung."

Praed shrugged. "Despite all that, you mentioned your distaste for Laijon and your abhorrence of prayer above all else. Have you always been so full of hate?"

"Why is it that anyone who shuns religion is immediately accused of being full of hate?"

"A bitter tone ofttimes laces the words of those who lose their faith."

"Well, if I am bitter, it's because I was taught my whole life the truthfulness of the scriptures." As she talked, her eyes remained focused on the ground. "I was taught of Fiery Absolution and of Laijon's return, only to discover it is all false. And even if it somehow is true, and if Laijon does indeed return with the other Warrior Angels, I think I will kill him. I think I will kill him and torture him and reap upon him a good and hardy dose of the same type pain and suffering he has caused the likes of me."

"And after that rant, you wonder why I think you so full of hate?" Praed chuckled.

"If it's considered hateful to speak the truth, then I guess I am hateful."

"I don't like you talking like that, Liz Hen," Dokie piped up, concern sweeping his countenance. "And I do not like contentious conversations. These last few days, I've oft wondered what happened to your testimony of the truthfulness of Laijon."

"I've reasoned things out in my mind." Liz Hen's voice dropped, a measure of shame evident in her next words. "And Praed is correct; I am angry and vengeful. But one has to be, nowadays, to survive."

Mancellor imagined that in days long past, Liz Hen had invariably been the one who lectured the ignorant and reproached the blasphemers more so than Dokie ever did. *And now look at her transformation. But who am I to critique her notion of vengeance? How am I not worse than her? I've killed in the name of a false god, Aeros Raijael. How have I even kept my faith in Laijon?* It seemed a miracle. For Aeros Raijael had taken a seventeen-year-old boy, captured him, enslaved him, starved him, humiliated him, humbled him, raped him, exhausted him, made him wish he'd never been born, and made him hate. Then Aeros had prayed with him, worshipped with him, made the boy desire to be like him, and most poisonous of all, made the boy desire to belong. *Aeros turned me into what I revile most. A killer. And yet I held on to my faith. And yet I still hope to be forgiven my crimes.*

"I am a student of human nature," Praed went on. "All good thieves become students of human nature eventually. And you fascinate me, Liz Hen Neville. I think we could be good friends, you know, eventually. Comrades, so to speak."

Liz Hen turned up her nose at that. "I'm not the type to go makin' friends with the wrong sort."

"And what is the wrong sort?" Praed asked. "Are we not friends? After this long together, after me sharing my camp, my food, my Blood of the Dragon, are we truly not friends? Am I truly the wrong sort?"

"You bloodsucking oghuls are the very definition of 'wrong sort,'" Liz Hen exclaimed. "And that's the plain fucking truth. And we are not fucking friends, not after a million years we would be friends. I don't care how many *things* you've shared. You are holding me captive."

"Frankly, I'm hurt," Praed said. "We've done naught but open our camp to you in graciousness and good faith."

"Rotted angels," Liz Hen exclaimed. "You tie us up at night. You are naught but killers and thieves. You brag about your murderous exploits daily. Bloody fucking rotted angels, I won't be patronized. Fuck me sideways if I won't."

"Like I said"—Judi sat forward—"the girl swears too much."

"You're right," Clive added. "A woman should not cuss. It's not fair etiquette."

"And this girl does it in such a crude way," Judi said.

"Whereas I myself favor a leisurely tone when swearing," Clive said. "Not the blunt and gruff spewing of random rotted angels, cunts, and fucks."

Judi nodded her agreement. "You've a staggeringly sizable vocabulary of naughty words, Clive. And affectionate toward every last one of them."

"Indeed."

"I can be the most creative cusser once my blood gets to boiling," Llewellyn added. "'Tis a fact. I can swear up a royal bloody fucking storm, as Laijon is my witness I can."

"Why would Laijon witness to that?" Dokie asked the young outlaw.

"It's a manner of speech," Llewellyn said. "Like, 'as Laijon is my witness.'"

"Zane used to say that." Liz Hen looked at Dokie. "Remember?"

"I do miss him," Dokie said. "I do miss Zane."

"I'm not a very sentimental girl"—Liz Hen looked at Praed—"but if Zane were here, I would jump and give him a right proper hug. So. See. I do not hate all things."

Praed met her gaze. "You loved Zane. He was your brother."

"Aye, my brother. I loved my entire family, for that matter."

"And do you love Dokie?" Judi asked. "Have the two of you ever given into lovers' lusts? Have you two ever rutted like craven hound dogs under a pale moonlit night?"

"No!" Liz Hen blurted, startled by the needless detail and frankness of the woman's question.

Judi said, "Vagabonds such as ourselves are allowed to give in to steamy impulse and desire whenever we wish."

Clive added, "I think Liz Hen and Dokie should join the Untamed in an orgy of dirty sweat and naked ass slapping."

"Aye." Judi clapped. "Some nasty hard fucking."

"What?" Liz Hen exclaimed.

"You must free yourself, Liz Hen," Judi said. "Free yourself fully from the shackles that still keep you beholden to Laijon."

"But I'm not still beholden to Laijon." Liz Hen gaped. "And I don't think ass slapping is the answer—"

"A most interesting conversation." A strange new voice sounded from somewhere in the darkness, cutting Liz Hen short.

It was Enna Spades!

Mancellor jerked to his feet, hand on the hilt of his sword, as a fully armed and armored Dayknight on a tall gray palfrey rode through the largest of the crumbled-down openings in the abbey wall, hooves clomping heavily in the peat and briar and straight into their camp. A black helm covered the knight's face, but Mancellor would recognize that voice anywhere.

Clive, Llewellyn, and Judi already had their bows nocked, arrows aimed up at the black knight. Praed stayed seated before the fire.

Spades kept one gauntleted hand on the reins of her horse whilst the other hand reached up and removed the black helm from her head. Red hair flowed like curling flames down her back, framing her porcelain-colored face. Spades' eyes sparkled in the firelight, dangerous and keen, as she hooked the helm to the saddle horn. She looked at Mancellor first, her countenance expressionless. Then her eyes came to rest on the shiny helm and battle-ax near Praed.

"I have no issue with the Untamed," she said, bowing slightly to Praed. "But Mancellor Allen is a deserter, and he has stolen from my lord Aeros Raijael, and I daresay, that pleases me not."

"And I daresay," Praed said, his own dark eyes not wavering from Spades, "what pleases or displeases you is of little concern to me."

"I come to reclaim those items stolen from my lord Aeros and take Mancellor Allen back to the hanging that awaits him."

"Mancellor is a captive of the Untamed," Praed said flatly.

Spades pursed her lips, thin brow furrowed. Mancellor knew that unlike Gault Aulbrek, who had come into camp a few days before her, Spades would throw down and fight until either herself or every member of the Untamed was dead. She would either leave with *Lonesome Crown* and *Forgetting Moon* strapped to the back of her saddle, or die trying. She was just that savage and unyielding. And Mancellor wasn't so sure she couldn't just kill every member of the Untamed herself.

Spades turned her attention from Praed, focusing on Liz Hen and Dokie. "What have we here?" she asked. "Miss Liz Hen Neville and the boy who swam with sharks. Well met again, the both of you."

Mancellor kept his hand on the hilt of his sword. *Lonesome Crown* and *Forgetting Moon* were his main concerns. He felt the leather pouch buried in his pocket, the pouch carrying two angel stones. They felt hot against the side of his hip. He would not let anyone take the weapons that were rightfully his. He would let no man or woman steal his destiny. He had been captive long enough. If Spades fought these thieves, it would be his chance to escape.

"Enna Spades." Praed spoke, his voice casual in tone. "I must confess, you are not the first of Aeros' Knights Archaic wearing Dayknight armor to enter our camp this fine summer. Not but a few days ago Ser Gault Aulbrek graced us with his presence." The outlaw's voice turned cold as he stood and drew his own bow, nocking an arrow. "But Gault had the good sense to turn his mount and ride away. Have you?"

"I must confess"—Spades' gaze was sharp—"good sense has never been one of my better attributes." She was still as a stone atop the horse, both gauntleted hands gripping the reins of the gray palfrey now. Mancellor knew she would not back down from these outlaws. Savagery was in her blood. She was deranged enough to fight them all, and deranged enough to win.

The tip of Praed's arrow was still centered on her armored chest.

He pulled the bowstring taut. Clive, Llewellyn, and Judi began edging around Spades, their arrows also centered on her midsection. Mancellor had witnessed the skill of the four Untamed. He had seen them slay eight thieves in less than a few seconds with just their bows and arrows. *But can their arrows pierce Dayknight armor?* Probably so, at such close range.

Spades cocked her head slightly to the side. "Well, you fools gonna fire those arrows or just—"

They all fired.

Spades yanked the reins of the horse swiftly to the side. Two arrows bounced off her chest-plate armor. One struck deep in the black plate just over her left shoulder. The fourth hit her palfrey in the back of the neck, just below its flaring gray mane.

Spades steadied the injured beast, yanking the arrow free of its neck with one hand. Blood flowed from under the horse's mane, pooling red and warm on the saddle under her. In one smooth motion she flung the bloody arrow at Praed, sending his next shot sailing into the forest beyond the abbey.

Spades drew her sword with a rasp. Clive's, Llewellyn's, and Judi's bows were nocked again and firing too. Spades dropped from her mount, the three arrows flying over her head. She headed straight for Llewellyn, her whirling Dayknight blade knocking the bow from the young outlaw's hand. Llewellyn yelled out in surprise, ducking her next swing, scrambling for his bow.

Mancellor lunged forward and kicked the outlaw's bow away, clubbing Llewellyn over the head with the hilt of his own sword. The boy went down in a heap. The pain in Mancellor's injured arm flared in agony. He pushed the torture to the back of his mind. For all was chaos now.

Dokie sprinted free of the camp, out into the woods toward the ponies. Liz Hen threw herself at Praed in a feverish rage, both hands latching onto the leather satchel at his shoulder, tugging, yanking the leader of the outlaws off-balance. Praed dropped his bow as he grappled with the girl, his quiver of arrows scattering in the peat and fire. A shower of sparks rose heavenward as Liz Hen screamed, "Blood of the Dragon!" She struck the man, clawing at his satchel of drugs.

Mancellor turned just in time to see Spades' next powerful blow take Judi's head off at the neck. Blood spewed high into the air as the woman toppled sideways into the flank of Spades' palfrey. The gray horse bucked and kicked and jumped away. With one powerful leap the horse bolted straight through the opening in the crumbled abbey wall. Judi's severed head hit the ground with a soft thud.

"No!" Clive screamed as he saw Judi fall. His third arrow glanced off the back of Spades' shoulder plate and hummed off into the trees, nearly striking Dokie, who was now untying one of the three ponies from the hitching tree, looking to make his escape.

Spades faced Clive. The bearded outlaw threw down his bow and drew his sword, cruel mouth snarling under his thick beard. "Bitch," he growled, then lunged at her. Spades effortlessly sent his blade spinning away with a quick strike, then rammed the point of her black sword up under his bearded chin, the tip exiting the back of his skull, bloody and white. Clive's heavy body dropped, the force snatching the black sword out of Spades' hands. She twisted to the ground, falling on top of the dead man.

Praed and Liz Hen were still on the ground near the fire pit, grappling for the leather bag of drugs. Liz Hen's great bulk had Praed pinned. The leader of the Untamed was on his stomach, the girl straddling his back. The satchel's strap was wrapped around the man's heaving neck. He fought for breath, his face nearly in the flames, bulging veins popping along his forehead, spit and drool clinging to purple lips.

Llewellyn had recovered himself, grabbing both *Lonesome Crown* and *Forgetting Moon*. With ax and helm in either hand, the young outlaw lurched from the abbey, the weight of the two artifacts burdensome as he ran. Still, he lugged them down the hill toward the pond, its cool black waters still in the moonlight. He tripped and fell, reeds and rushes thrashing under him. But he eventually reached the black slough, hesitant, fireflies now buzzing about his ankles. He turned back, facing the camp. Then an arrow took the young outlaw full in his chest. Llewellyn's eyes widened at the sight of the quivering arrow growing from his body. He turned and wobbled farther out into the pond, knee-deep. Fireflies swirled up into the night, their light twinkling off the surfaces of the battle-ax and helm.

Enna Spades was standing over the body of Clive, the outlaw's bow in hand, a second arrow soon nocked, aimed at Llewellyn. The young outlaw's grip slackened on the heavy helm. *Lonesome Crown* dropped into the pond, its polished shine and curved horns vanishing below the skin of the black water. Spades let the arrow fly. It sank into Llewellyn's chest next to the first one. The young outlaw fell face-first into the pond with a splash, *Forgetting Moon* disappearing beneath the dark water.

Thousands of fireflies exploded into the air like sparks shooting into the night. Llewellyn was dead, one stiff leg sticking straight up out of the black rippling water, which glowed green and blue from under-neath. The carvings on every standing stone in the center of the pond also seemed to shine now with blue and green light; circles, squares, crosses, shooting stars, crescent moons, all magically aglow in the gloom and dark.

Spades dropped Clive's bow and snatched up her Dayknight sword, cruel eyes scanning the outlaw camp. Behind her, Liz Hen bellowed and screamed. Spades whirled and looked down as the big girl, still strad-dling Praed, hauled back on the leather satchel as if reining in a horse, the bag's leather strap cutting a deep furrow into man's straining neck. Praed's last breath hissed out from snot-dripping nostrils as he tried in vain to peel the leather garrote from around his neck. Then his body went slack.

Liz Hen let out one last bellow into the night and loosened her grip. Then she crawled off the dead man, calmly unhooked the satchel from around his neck, opened it, pulled forth a copper vial of Blood of the Dragon, and greedily gulped the contents down. The scent of death was thick in the air. A thousand fireflies lit the night sky.

Dokie came stumbling into their midst, breathing heavily. "The po-nies ran off!" The boy pointed to the east. "I untied 'em to help in our escape, but they all ran off, afraid!"

Spades' gray palfrey was also gone. The forest beyond the blood-soaked abbey was naught but darkness, still and ominous. "No worry." Spades' blood-splattered face, framed in harsh curls of red hair, looked savage in the firelight. "For I am not done with my killing yet." Her sword came up and she set her stance.

"You dirty bitch," Liz Hen snarled, sliding the leather strap of Praed's satchel over her shoulder, standing before Spades. "You wish to fight us after we helped you kill these thieves?" She looked at Dokie and Mancellor as if the very notion was insane. Then her angry eyes flew right back to Spades. "It's girls like you give redheads a bad name."

Mancellor felt the sword in his hands, knowing it would not stop Spades. His own injuries burned with pain. He felt the two angel stones growing hot in the pouch in his pants pocket. The magic in *Forgetting Moon* was the only chance he had! He looked toward the glowing pond. "She'll slay us all if we're not careful," he said, throwing a cautious nod to both Liz Hen and Dokie. "Best run off after those ponies, Dokie, if you aim to save yourself. You too, Liz Hen."

"Bullocks," Liz Hen spat. "I ain't afraid of this bitch no more. I've been in battle. I've killed Sør Sevier knights before, and I can do it again. She won't leave here alive, not if I've anything to say about it."

Spades pointed the tip of her long blade at the big girl's throat, eyes like ice. "I will not be so merciful with you now, pretty Miss Liz Hen, not nearly so merciful as I was in Gallows Haven. I'll kill you, then kill the boy, and then kill Mancellor Allen. Then I will dig the helm and battle-ax out of the quag and go my own way."

"How'd the ax and helm get in the water?" Liz Hen asked, eyes on the pond. Llewellyn's leg was sticking up from the water like a flagpole marking the spot where *Forgetting Moon* and *Lonesome Crown* had fallen. "How'd they get out there?"

"Sunk 'neath that fool of an outlaw who hauled 'em out there." Spades pressed the tip of her sword against Liz Hen's neck. Liz Hen swatted the tip of the sword aside, the back of her hand slapping loud against the flat of the black blade.

The big girl reached down and pulled the sword from the sheath at Praed's belt with a rasp. Now armed, she took a step back, holding her blade up against Spades', iron touching iron. "Dokie," she said, her gaze not breaking from Spades, "run on down to that pond and gather *Forgetting Moon* and *Lonesome Crown*. I will catch up to you after I slay this bitch."

Spades smiled. "You are a different girl from the one I met in Gallows Haven, more foolhardy and brave. And that I can admire. You do realize I could have stabbed you to death ten times over, but I let you live. You amuse me with your misplaced courage."

Liz Hen's eyes narrowed as she took a step forward, her silver blade sliding up the length of Spades' long black sword with a hiss. "Go, Dokie," she said. "Go now."

"I can't just go traipsing into that pond," Dokie exclaimed with alarm. "You heard what Praed said. It's contaminated. I'll get scaled eels up my urinary meatus."

"I don't care what you get up your angel-rotted pee hole," Liz Hen said, still not taking her eyes from Spades. "Get that ax and helm!"

Dokie did the three-fingered sign of the Laijon Cross over his heart, jumped through the bracken and briar and over the crumbled wall of the abbey, and sprinted for the pond. Spades watched him run off.

Seeing that the woman was distracted, Liz Hen swung her sword at the warrior woman with a shout. But Spades parried the blow, backing away, amusement glinting in her eyes. She struck at Liz Hen, black sword sweeping out swift and keen. Liz Hen stumbled to the ground, the sword whistling over her head. Spades swung again. Mancellor lunged forward, blocking her blow with his own sword. His entire body shuddered with the impact, arm and injury singing in pain. Spades shoved him aside and swung again at Liz Hen, downward, an unstoppable stroke, swift and mighty.

A streak of gray bolted from the shadows of the wood—a large gray shepherd dog. It came snarling and bounding through the large gap in the abbey wall, hurling itself straight at Spades. The collision was brunt and brutal. Both Spades and the dog spun to the ground. The sword flew from her grasp, fur and black armor rolling in the brush and green grass.

It was the dog the girl oft spoke of. Large as a silver-wolf. The same dog Mancellor had seen attack Aeros Raijael in the Battle of the Saint Only Channel.

"Beer Mug!" Liz Hen yelled.

Beer Mug regained his footing and tore at Spades' hair. Black gauntlets clubbed at the dog's snout. But the dog dragged the warrior woman through the peat by a clump of her red hair, pulling her away from Liz Hen. Spades punched at the dog again, harder. Beer Mug let go of Spades' hair, spittle flying. The dog's long teeth tore at the woman's face next, sharp white claws raking long scratches in her black arm bracers as she covered her head.

"Eat her fucking face off, Beer Mug!" Liz Hen screeched.

Spades covered her face as the dog savaged her polished arm bracers.

"Eat her face right off!" Liz Hen shouted. "Eat it and swallow it down and shit it back out on the morrow!"

Mancellor stood on wobbly legs, reeling from the pain in his shoulder. He thrust his gaze out toward the pond. A thousand fireflies flickered and hummed. Dokie was out there still, large horned helm atop his head, clothes all a-drip—the boy was dragging the battle-ax from the water with both hands, moving backward, struggling with the weight of the weapon. An azure glow shone bright in the pond, a twisting and curling mist of blue light wrapping around Dokie's arms and the hilt of the ax.

The angel stones in Mancellor's pocket grew hotter against his hip. He flung himself forward, crashing through the shrub and briar and over the crumbled stone wall toward Dokie. He soon found himself shin-deep in black waters much warmer than he imagined they should be. The blue glow still filled the water under Dokie.

Mancellor snatched the ax from the boy's hands and hefted it over one shoulder. It was featherlight. He couldn't imagine why Dokie had been struggling with it so. He grasped the boy by the scruff of his shirt, dragging him from the pond in haste. Dokie held the horned helm atop his head with both hands as they trudged their way to shore.

Liz Hen met them at the edge of the water, and the three of them raced off into the shadowy trees, heading east away from the abbey, a thousand fireflies lighting the way. The snarls and curses of Spades and Beer Mug's fierce fight inside the Ten Cairn Abbey faded as they ran.

**

They were deep into the black wood when they stumbled upon their escaped ponies. The three skittish beasts were standing in a shallow dell, nibbling at the matted grass under hoof. Though jittery, the beasts allowed them to approach.

"Beer Mug!" Liz Hen screeched into the forest behind them. "Beer Mug!"

"Rotted angels, stop shouting like that," Mancellor exclaimed as he tied *Forgetting Moon* to the back of his saddle with a strap of leather. He hooked *Lonesome Crown* to his saddle horn. He still had the angel stones in his pocket. "You're liable to bring every outlaw in this whole bloody forest down on us with all that yelling."

"Beer Mug!" Liz Hen bellowed.

"*Quiet,*" Mancellor hissed as he clutched the pommel of his saddle, hauling himself onto the pony's back, spurring the mount forward.

"But he simply cannot die again." Liz Hen cast a frightened glance into the woods from whence they had come. "We have to wait for him. We can't leave him. We can't let that foul witch kill him."

"There he is!" Dokie called out. And sure enough, the big gray shepherd dog came trotting out of the woods as silent as you please. Blood crusted his muzzle, black and thick.

"He's back," was all Liz Hen said, then burst into tears. "My Beer Mug is back."

*The elect of Laijon oft die young. But in turn, the elect are granted
the right to live with Laijon among the heights of the stars.*
—The Way and Truth of Laijon

CHAPTER TWENTY-EIGHT
TALA BRONACHELL

23RD DAY OF THE FIRE MOON, 999TH YEAR OF LAIJON

AMADON, GUL KANA

Blood oozed from the myriad wounds in the pig's side. The animal hung from a low-hanging beam of timber in the middle of the Filthy Horse Saloon, barbed hook in its gaping mouth. Its curly tail dangled just above the old worn blankets Hawkwood had spread over the saloon's wooden floor near the fire pit.

Nail rammed his sword into the pig's belly with a short, sharp shout, then yanked it free just as swiftly. It was such a clean strike, the pig scarcely swung about or twisted on the rope. The Gallows Haven boy looked proud of his strike.

"Good," Hawkwood acknowledged. Then he turned to Tala. "Thrusting a blade into flesh is different from smacking practice swords against each other over and over, as we've been doing the last few days. A body is soft; muscle and bone and the armor a man wears can catch hold of a blade, jerking it free of your grasp when your foe falls to the ground. One must learn what strength and speed it requires to remove a blade from a dying man's body." He motioned for Tala to step forward.

Nail handed her the sword. Jondralyn and Val-Draekin both rested against the nearby bar; they had previously been sparring with Bronwyn Allen and Cromm Cru'x, who sat at the bar. All four sipped on mugs of birch beer. Lawri Le Graven sat at a separate table alone, hood over her head.

"Remember, speed and strength," Hawkwood advised. "The pig's heart, lungs, intestines, and ribs are mostly in the same position as a human, hanging like that."

Tala hefted the sword in both hands, eyeing the pig as it hung there in the center of the dusky saloon—their new hiding place. The Filthy Horse was dark and empty but for a few rickety chairs and overturned tables. Its thick timbered ceiling and scum-covered wood floor smelled strongly of smoke, abandonment, and ruin. The place was a wreck, the front doors locked and barred, overturned tables placed in front of the doors for good measure. The flags, oars, nets, planks, harpoons, hooks, anchors, and the like that had once gilded the smoke-stained walls had long since been looted.

After the barmaid, Delia, had escaped from the arena with Lindholf Le Graven and Gault Aulbrek, the Filthy Horse Saloon had been searched by almost every Silver Guard and Dayknight in Amadon and then left to rot, loyal patrons too scared to return.

Hawkwood had assured the others that the Filthy Horse was now safe from prying eyes. He deemed it the perfect place to call home now that the *Val-Sadè* had been compromised. For her part, Tala didn't know if she trusted anyone in the saloon, especially not Hawkwood or Val-Draekin. Not after overhearing the conversation between Seita and Val-Korin. *The Bloodwood knew about the* Val-Sadè *all along!* And ever since Tala had returned from Amadon Castle through the secret ways two days ago with the news that Seita knew about the *Val-Sadè*, things had become tense. And that was why they had moved from the wrecked pirate ship to the wrecked saloon. The news about the compromise of the *Val-Sadè* was all she had revealed, all she *could* reveal, for the conversation between Seita and Val-Korin had boggled her mind, confused her. And there were parts of it she simply did not understand.

And besides, who would believe me? Seita murdered her own father! Yes, there was much that confused her. She felt captive to the insanity of her own life. So why try and explain it? Besides, the last time she had revealed a secret—that Jovan and Leif were setting Jondralyn up to be killed—she had just been ignored.

"Well, are you going to strike it or not?" Hawkwood said.

Tala jabbed the sword straight into the pig's belly. The pig spun wildly, and Tala was yanked off her feet and tossed to the floor, losing hold of the sword.

Lying on her back, she watched as the pig twisted on the rope above her. The bloody sword slipped from the pig's midsection and clattered to the old blankets covering the floor. *Tossed on my face by a dead swine!*

Nail held his hand out to her. Tala took it and climbed to her feet. "May I show you something my old master once taught me?" Nail asked her, bowing awkwardly.

Tala thought his awkwardness was cute. It was clear the blond Gallows Haven boy was not used to spending time with royalty. It seemed his face was always flushed with embarrassment. Tala nodded. "Show me."

Nail showed her how to hold the sword and position her feet. She tried but got it wrong. He stepped up behind her, and she felt the warmth of his chest pressed against her back as he leaned in and slid her right foot forward with the side of his own. His hands atop hers were calloused and rough, but no less warm and comforting as he gently wrapped her fingers around the hilt of the sword in just the right position. Now set, she stabbed again. This time the pig remained motionless as she yanked the blade free with scant little effort.

"Nicely done," Hawkwood said. "Nail is a good teacher, no?"

Surprised with herself, Tala nodded at both Hawkwood and the Gallows Haven boy. Nail smiled back, blushing once again.

"Can Cromm cut that pig up for dinner yet?" the burly oghul asked from his seat at the bar. "Cromm is starving and wants to light up that fire pit and have a feast." The oghul sucked hungrily at a rock he always carried in his lip.

"I daresay," Bronwyn said, "when Cromm and I requisitioned the poor beast from the butcher at the edge of the marketplace, we didn't think it would be used for sword practice. You're liable to slice the pig to ribbons. Render it all but useless."

"Cromm is starving," the oghul grunted.

Hawkwood dipped his head to the oghul. "Then it's all yours." He took the sword from Tala. "We shall practice something else whilst the oghul makes his dinner."

Cromm left the bar, pulled a knife from his belt, and cut the pig carcass down. He slung it over his broad shoulder and hauled it away into the kitchen behind the bar. Bronwyn stayed where she was at the bar with Jondralyn and Val-Draekin.

Hawkwood kicked the blankets to the side. He wrapped the blade of Tala's sword in burlap and handed it back to her. He handed her a wooden shield too. He handed Nail a similarly wrapped sword and wooden shield. He directed them to face each other. Tala held up her shield and sword. Nail hefted his own wooden shield to the ready position, sliding his left leg back a pace and raising the sword. Tala mimicked the boy's stance, wondering if the move looked sloppy to Hawkwood. There was always a cool scrutiny in his dark gaze. She stepped back some, unsure of herself, crouching with the rim of her own shield just under her eyes, sword gripped tight in hand.

Nail shifted to the side and struck, his burlap-wrapped sword a thin blur. His blade caught her shield with a bone-jarring thud, sending it tumbling from her stinging hands. Hawkwood beckoned for her to gather it up. She did as instructed and set her stance again.

This time she struck first. But Nail deftly blocked her wild swing with his shield. He swung his own sword, backing her down. Another swing of his weapon and her sword went spinning from her hands this time. "Bloody rotted angels," she cursed.

"Do not become discouraged," Hawkwood said. "You learn from every failure. Even in defeat, you learn how the sword feels in your hands, you learn its weight, you learn the reach of your opponent, you discover how hard he can swing, you learn footwork and what kind of strikes are most apt to throw you or your opponent off-balance. Practice and precision in all things. Stamina, too. You must learn to hold a sword and swing it until your arms grow so weary you cannot carry on. But you always carry on, beyond the point of exhaustion."

Tala again gathered her weapon and shield and set her stance. *Battle is hard. Daunting.* She stepped forward and swung her sword at Nail, one strike after the next in rapid succession, over and over. Nail blocked every blow, thwarting her every attack. He held his shield aloft as if his arm didn't even feel the weight of it. Tala felt as if she was just flailing away for no purpose at all, making a fool of herself. The more she swung, the more she wanted to land a blow. But her arm was growing leaden. But still she pressed her attack. And then Nail's shield dipped down below his chest. She took the opening and struck him in the shoulder. He spun, reeling back, landing awkwardly on his side against the hard wooden floor.

Nail met her gaze, encouragement glinting in his eyes as he picked himself up off the floor. "Excellent move," he said, flicking blond strands of hair from his face. The way he flicked his hair like that was a becoming habit that stirred something within her. She felt herself blush. "'Twas a most excellent move," he repeated.

"No, it was not!" Hawkwood's voice cut through the dark saloon like a dagger. His gaze sliced straight toward Nail. "He dropped his guard on purpose!" Hawkwood snatched the burlap-wrapped sword from Nail's hand. "You do her no favors, letting her win, letting her through your guard like that."

Tala's heart fell in her chest when she saw the look of guilt on Nail's face.

"She has to *earn* each and every win." Val-Draekin rose from his seat at the bar. "Else the training means nothing, else it will get her killed."

Hawkwood glared at Nail. "We all saw what you did, and you cannot gain favor in her eyes by letting her win. When it comes to killing, it isn't like stepping on ants. You both have got to put in your work here. She has to know when she is outmatched and find ways to overcome that."

Was he trying to gain favor? Tala wasn't sure whether she should be flattered or insulted. Everyone tried to gain favor of the Bronachells. It was the one thing she hated about being born into royalty. You never knew the true motives of a person. But she could tell by the look on Nail's face that he was only trying to do a good thing, trying to build some small measure of confidence in her. And Hawkwood had ruined his moment. She grew instantly angry at the Sør Sevier man for embarrassing Nail. And Hawkwood saw that glint of anger in her eyes.

"I only scold you both for your own good," he said. "It takes over ten thousand hours of practice before one becomes proficient in anything. Ten thousand hours of sword craft before one becomes competent enough to fight in a real battle, in a real war. And make no mistake, Tala Bronachell, as a woman, you are severely disadvantaged in *any* fight with a man. Even the most average man is vastly stronger than the most athletic woman. It is a physical fact."

The saloon was filled with an uncomfortable silence. Tala was angry. She expected Jondralyn to tell Hawkwood he was wrong about women. Jondralyn was the type to hate this kind of talk. Yet her older sister remained silent. But Tala could see it was an icy silence, as if Jondralyn were taking each word Hawkwood spoke and burying it deep down within her soul, where it could fester. There was some recent breach in their relationship, and Tala could tell.

"There is only one woman in all the Five Isles who can match the best men in battle," Hawkwood went on. "And her name is Enna Spades, Knight Archaic of the White Prince. And even Spades spent over ten thousand hours practicing in the arts of war before she joined Aeros' army. And in ten years of war she has killed hundreds, if not over a thousand men in single combat, increasing her experience a millionfold. And she is alive today because no one ever, *ever* let her win during practice. She is alive today because no one ever tried to gain her favor."

"Hawkwood is right," Val-Draekin said. "Do it right next time, Nail."

The Gallows Haven boy nodded to the Vallè.

Bronwyn Allen stood, looking at Tala. "I am not good with a blade. I learned that early in life. I am only good with a bow because I have shot well over ten thousand arrows over the span of my life, gathered them up from the dirt, and then shot them ten thousand more times, and so on and so on. I agree with Hawkwood. I am outmatched in most fights. If I ever needed someone stabbed or smashed, I just called on Cromm."

"And Cromm likes to stab and smash." The brutish oghul stepped out of the kitchen, a hock of ham in hand, a wild toothy grin spreading over his face.

"Enough sword practice for the day." Lawri Le Graven pulled her hood back, the gauntlet attached to her arm a dull gleam in the lantern light. "I grow bored with it all." She looked at the oghul with soft green eyes. "I'm hungry. Will you fry me some potatoes to go with that ham?"

The oghul's grin widened. "Cromm would gladly fry potatoes to go with the ham."

**

The night was a vaulted sky, pinpricks of a million crystal stars twinkling in the blackness far above. Tala and Nail lay on their backs in the cool grass of the Filthy Horse Saloon's back courtyard, gazing up into the midnight sky, muscles aching from their day's training. They were alone.

From what Tala could tell, the courtyard had once been enclosed, but the remains of the cloth canopies and tattered and torn tan awnings now drooped sadly over the high stone walls surrounding the yard. Sculptures of naked women holding bowls of fruit and unused brass fountains were set in each corner of the enclosure. A large stone basin overrun with vines and ivy sat in the center, wilted purple flowers surrounding its base. All in all, the courtyard behind the Filthy Horse Saloon felt less depressing than the innards of the saloon itself, and far less stifling than the innards of the *Val-Sadè*.

Muscles sore, mind fatigued, Tala wondered if she could truly go on. She had discovered what it was like never to fall asleep, never to relax, to always know restless solitude and self-pity, to always know extreme loneliness, though she was surrounded by those who claimed to care.

She thought of Seita dragging Val-Korin's body into the black hearth of the chamber. She wondered what effect the Vallè ambassador's disappearance would have on the king's court. *Seita will probably just tell everyone her father went back to Val Vallè.*

"What if I told you I saw Seita kill her own father?" she asked Nail.

"When?" he asked, his voice a soothing sound to all the turmoil in her head.

"When I was in the secret ways of the castle. I snuck into his chamber. Saw her kill him. How could she have done such a thing?" No matter how angry she was at Jovan, she had never thought of killing him. *But Seita was a Bloodwood!* "I could tell my sister what I saw. But she would not believe me."

"I believe you," Nail said, flipping hair out of his eyes. His hair was in a tangle about his head, always falling into his eyes.

"I am so confused," she said. "Should I tell my sister? Should I go back to the castle and tell my brother? Val-Korin said there was an army gathering in Vandivar, about to set sail for Gul Kana."

"I would not trust your brother," he answered swiftly. "I fear he would hold you captive in the castle no matter what information you had for him. We should never have gone there in the first place, despite how good your disguises were. 'Twas a needless and pointless risk."

"You are right," she admitted. "I sometimes question Hawkwood's training methods, sending us into my brother's lair like that. Almost got us all killed. It's almost as if it is all a game with him."

"I think he means well."

"Who would you trust, Nail?"

"I do not know anymore," he answered. "All my friends are lost or dead. I'm learning that Val-Draekin is full of secrets. Hawkwood, too. And who knows what Bronwyn and Cromm are up to? But they seem to want something from me, something beyond payment for their services. Cromm believes I am the marked one. And I don't know what to think of your sister. Jondralyn hasn't said but two words to me."

"That's Jondralyn for you," Tala said. "Her mind is constantly on naught but herself." Voicing that thought aloud made her sad. Just the mention of her sister was a burning reminder of Tala's own want for companionship, of her never having touched the soul of someone, never having anyone touch hers. *Jondralyn is in the saloon behind me and I dare not even go and tell her the truth, that is how little I trust.*

"Seems like your cousin Lawri is the only innocent one among us," Nail said.

But how innocent is she? "It is Lawri I've betrayed the most, I fear."

"I doubt she feels betrayed," Nail said. "You have protected her."

Though she hadn't known him long, the strange boy beside her seemed to know how to say the right things, seemed to like her for who she was. *Or does he too wish me wrapped in frilly brocaded gowns of lace and pastel? Perhaps he hates my leather pants and grubby shirt and terribly mussed-up hair. Or is that just my own insecurity talking?* How could she trust him or anyone if she couldn't even trust her own judgment? She couldn't even take a compliment without twisting it.

"I wish I could sweep all the hurt and distrust from all the Five Isles," she said. "But what can I do? To accomplish such a goal, one would think I need all the help I can muster, but I've no armies like Jovan. I've nothing, just myself."

"Not true," Nail said. "You've a saloon full of castoffs, pirates, and traitors to the Silver Throne who are on your side."

"And even they don't value my opinion all that much. Or believe the things I tell them, or believe the things I have seen. Of course I have not told them everything, just as they have not told me everything. Perhaps I am the one people should not trust."

"Secrets are a dangerous thing."

It was a simple statement, but it silenced her profoundly. Could she trust this boy with her secrets? She sensed an honest tenderness in him, but also reluctance. Not a shy reluctance. No. Not that. It wasn't that he lacked confidence, but rather that his goals, what he truly wanted from life, lay somewhere beyond her. Nail had been on adventures. She had not. Well, perhaps she had been on adventures, but adventures of a different sort. Bloodwood adventures. How would he react to the story of the Bloodwood in the secret ways and all that entailed? The fact was, she did not want to dwell on such matters now. She had to block them from her mind or go mad.

"Tell me of yourself, Nail. Tell me of your childhood. I need something to brighten me up."

"Not much to tell," he said, drawing silent a moment before going on, "Or at least nothing to brighten you up."

"Try," she said. "Think of something."

"I once wanted to design stained-glass windows. There was a time in my life, not long ago really, that I would sketch all day long if I could." He drew silent again. "But that dream is lost to me now."

She was pleasantly surprised at his aspirations. They were honorable goals, and sweet in a way. *An artist.* But she was also saddened that he thought his dream hopeless and lost to him now. "You can still design stained-glass windows if you'd like," she said.

"I also had thoughts of becoming a grayken hunter. But my master would not allow it." He pulled up the sleeve of his shirt to reveal his bicep. His arm was corded with muscle, and she like the shape of it. "Stefan Wayland gave me this tattoo," he said. "Three shark's teeth. Most grayken hunters get a sea serpent or an anchor tattoo. Some get crossed harpoons. Mine is three shark's teeth."

"What's this?" She pointed to the scars below the tattoo.

"A mermaid attacked me." Nail pulled the sleeve of his shirt back down over the tattoo and scars. "Bloody beast tried to drown me too. I fought my way free and saved my friend Zane from the sharks. Baron Jubal Bruk claimed it was the bravest thing he'd ever witnessed."

"You knew Baron Bruk?"

"I was shocked to see him in the castle. Shocked by what Aeros had done to him. Liz Hen told me, but I did not realize his injuries were so horrific. Anyway, yes, I knew him. Baron Bruk *almost* hired me onto his crew. But my master declined. I was *almost* made a free man. I *would* have been a free man."

"You are a free man, Nail. You have done so much with your life, seen so many things I have not. You have lived a life freer than most. Freer than me."

"I've no surname. I don't even know who I'm named after. I have nothing. It's a constant reminder of my own lack."

She had no idea how he must feel as a bastard. She knew how her society was set up. The rulers of cities like Avlonia, Rivermeade, and Lord's Point were titled lords. Large estate owners were titled barons. Peasants and freemen lived in service to these estates. One's station was established by one's lineage. And as a bastard, Nail was relegated to following his master's bidding in all things. But his master was dead, or so he'd claimed. But there were masters of every stripe.

"My brother expected me to be the perfect princess," she said, a touch of sadness in her own voice. "But I would never have been able to live up to his expectations. He's always wished me to be demure and genteel and just like every other brainless court girl he knew. He did not want me to think for myself. He did not want me to be who I wanted to be. Everyone should be free to live how they want. No constraints. No masters. No barons or lords or kings."

"And no bishops," he said.

Tala didn't know quite what to make of that. She had never heard anyone say such a thing out loud. His eyes glowed like pools of cool inviting waters in the starlight. He was looking at her intently, as if searching for something deep within her soul. And she found that she was devouring each detail of his face too. Her breath swelled and grew in her chest. She wanted to reach out and touch him, brush away the locks of hair that almost covered his eyes. It took every effort to stay her hand from doing so.

"What is this?" She pointed to the cross-shaped scar on the back of his hand, looking for another distraction.

"An injury from a lightning strike."

She pointed to the *SS* brand on the underside of his wrist. "And this?"

"A slave brand."

"I'm so sorry." Without thinking, Tala ran her fingers gently over the slave mark, her heart heavy just looking at it. This boy made her contemplative, made her sad. Then she noticed the turtle necklace round his neck. "What is this?"

"It's a reminder."

"Of what?"

"A reminder of the worst thing I've ever done. My deepest sorrow and regret."

"Everyone should be free to live without regret. Perhaps you should be rid of it, the carving, if it is such a harsh reminder of deep sorrow."

"I won't be rid of it. For I hope to one day make right my wrong."

"There are many wrongs I too hope to make right. We should all hope for such."

"You are thoughtful. Smart, too. More so than any girl I have ever spoken with."

And I don't believe him, she thought. Still, his statement once again silenced her profoundly. Nobody had said such a thing to her since her father. His words sharpened her desire to draw nearer to him. This strange boy from Gallows Haven had defended her against Glade in the castle corridor. He had even punched Glade. *If only more people would punch Glade!* Of course Glade was wrapped up in all her lies. Sin and deceit seemed to follow her everywhere. *And will I one day be thrust down into the underworld because of it?* Perhaps the vicar was right to submit her to her purification in the queen's bath.

"Do you believe in *The Way and Truth of Laijon?*" she asked, shifting in the grass. Her arm came to rest against his. An accidental touch. Still she felt the rapture and terror that seized at her chest expand. "Do you believe in Laijon?" she asked again, trying to slow the beating of her heart.

"I know not what to believe anymore," he muttered. "I'm full of doubt when it comes to matters of faith. I do not trust the writings of *The Way and Truth of Laijon.*"

"You are honest, Nail. Most in the king's court would not dare speak against scripture or the church, especially in the presence of royalty."

She couldn't get rid of the image of the queen's bath and her purification at the hands of Denarius. It made her sick. "All my life I have prayed to Laijon. And ofttimes I've felt Laijon's Holy Spirit warm within my bosom, expanding my very soul. But now I wonder if it was all just self-delusion."

"I've often longed to find the warmth of Laijon's spirit within my own heart," Nail said. "But I was never blessed with the gift of faith."

"As the days go on, I wish I could just somehow eradicate all religion, make it punishable by death to teach it to the young. It is a poison." Tala was startled by her own admission, finding her statement completely lacking in compassion.

"I ofttimes feel as if the words in *The Way and Truth of Laijon* have done more harm than good," Nail said.

"I feel so comfortable talking to you. I have never had anyone I could talk to, I mean truly, honestly talk to." She brushed the back of her own fingers against the back of his hand, feeling the warmth of him. Her eyes gazed heavenward. She marveled at her sudden emotions for this strange boy. Glints of starlight twinkled above the courtyard, the vastness of the night sky making her feel so small.

"When you look at the stars, what do you see?" she asked.

Nail's voice was filled with something akin to reverence when he answered. "When I was just a small child, there was a man, a friend of my master, a fellow named Culpa Barra. Perhaps you knew him. He was a Dayknight in Amadon. He traveled with Val-Draekin and me to the Sky Lochs."

"I knew him."

"You did?" His eyes brightened at that.

"Yes. He seemed to be a good man."

"He was," Nail said. "Anyway, one of the things I remember most about my childhood was Culpa telling me of the heavens. He spoke of Laijon and the other Warrior Angels. He claimed those fighters who have died in the service of Laijon are raised into heaven to live among the stars. He spoke of the stars as other worlds like ours, numberless and without end."

"I like this idea of worlds without end," Tala said.

He seemed pleased that she had accepted his story. Somehow that touched her deeply. *Like me, he too has gone his whole life not being believed, not having his voice heard.* She could tell there were deep hurts in him, things he might not ever talk of, things in his heart she would never fathom, things she desperately wanted to pull from him, but things she would likely never know.

Her hand moved up and gently swept the blond locks from his eyes again. He looked at her. And in that moment, it seemed the two of them were stranded alone in the isolation of their shared gaze. It wasn't shyness, awkwardness, or strain between them, but comfort. And within Nail's calm eyes lived the softest place to fall.

She wanted to kiss him. Wondered if she should. If she was brave enough. *Why are boys my weakness?* It seemed so foolish. But she was so lonely. She'd been lonely her entire life. "I need to feel close to someone," she said.

"Do you wish to be close to me?" he asked hesitantly. "I am no royal—"

He was cut short by a deep rumble. The ground moved under them. Nail jerked to his feet, alarmed. There was a faint grinding and clamor of metal gears coming from somewhere beneath them. Tala lurched to her feet too, fingers clutching Nail's hand tight as they both stumbled back from the stone basin in the middle of the yard.

Like the lid of a giant iron pot, the heavy stone in the middle of the yard—along with the ivy clinging to it—slowly rose up at one end, revealing a narrow staircase leading down into some dark hollow under the ground. The void was pitch-black.

Then the yellow shimmer of candle flame rose up out of the hole in the ground. A freckle-faced girl in tattered serving-wench garb climbed up the stairs and into the starlight. She held a tall red candle in her hand. Her own pale visage turned into one of startled amazement when she spotted Tala and Nail.

Tala knew immediately who it was. It was the missing barmaid, Delia.

**

"Where is Lindholf?" Jondralyn asked Delia. "Where is Gault Aulbrek?"

"I came back to find my father," the barmaid stammered, eyes darting around the saloon nervously. "Is he still here? He is the reason I came all the way from Savon." She looked haunted by the journey. "I paid a heavy price for the fastest carriage. I snuck through the tunnels under the city alone, searching for the passage that leads to the saloon. It was no easy trek. I just want my father. That is all."

"We know nothing about your father," Hawkwood said. "This place was emptied out by Silver Guards and Dayknights weeks ago. If your father was here, he is gone now."

Delia looked distressed. She sat nervously at the largest table in the middle of the empty saloon. Everyone was gathered around her: Jondralyn, Hawkwood, Val-Draekin, Tala, Nail, Bronwyn, Cromm, and even Lawri Le Graven, the silver gauntlet attached to her arm visible in the dim glow of the lanterns. The frightened barmaid's eyes seemed to drift between the gauntlet and the burly oghul. Cromm sucked on his black rock as he listened to her story.

"Are Lindholf and Gault in Savon?" Jondralyn asked.

"Gault, he- he left me," the girl stammered. "But- but Lindholf was in Savon when I last saw him two days ago." Her eyes continued to dart around the dark saloon. "Are you sure my father is not here? Last I saw him, he was in one of the back rooms. Before I was thrown into the slave pits . . ." She paused.

"What about Lindholf?" Jondralyn pressed.

"Maybe you're right," Delia said. "Maybe my father isn't here. When we came back to the saloon to get the white shield, he wasn't here then. On the island, the Vallè princess said he was dead, but I did not believe her. He has to be somewhere in the city."

Tala could tell that the girl was rambling, scared. *Or is it an act?* Tala knew the girl could be deceitful.

"The white shield?" Hawkwood asked. "You came *here* to get the white shield?"

"Aye, the shield Lindholf pulled from the Rooms of Sorrow."

"Lindholf?" Hawkwood looked up at Jondralyn. "That explains a lot."

Tala thought of her own journey under Purgatory. *So many secrets I can't even count!* She just didn't know how many lies she could keep straight. *So many secrets I can't even remember them all!*

Hawkwood turned back to Delia. "But how did you know where Lindholf got the shield from?"

"I must find him," Delia blurted, not even listening. "I must find my father."

"You said a Vallè princess claimed your father was dead?" Tala asked, her heart still pounding. "Was it Seita?"

"Aye," the barmaid nodded. "She helped us escape the arena. She had the sword, and the crossbow."

"And the white shield?" Jondralyn asked.

"Gault, Lindholf, Seita, they all insisted the weapons were *Blackest Heart, Afflicted Fire,* and *Ethic Shroud.* Those weapons are all in Savon now. At the Preening Pintail. Lindholf has all the angel stones and weapons in Savon, where I left him."

"*Savon,*" Jondralyn repeated, looking up again at Hawkwood. "Are you sure it was Savon? Tell us all from the beginning."

"Please, I've told you all I know," Delia pleaded. "I must search for my father. And I must sleep in my own bed for a change. I've been dreaming of nothing but that for the last few days. My bed is just down the hall."

The girl shoved herself away from the table, stood, pushed her way past Val-Draekin and Hawkwood, and headed for the back door and the rooms beyond.

"No," Jondralyn exclaimed, reaching for the girl. "Tell us all you know."

"Let her go." Val-Draekin grabbed Jondralyn. "We can get her story on the morrow, when she is better rested. She's clearly out of her mind right now."

Jondralyn watched as the girl disappeared into the dark hallway. "*Savon.*" She repeated the name of the city, turning to Hawkwood. "If the weapons of the Five Warrior Angels are in Savon, we must go there now. We must find Lindholf at the Preening Pintail and get them back."

"Let's not act in haste," Hawkwood said. "We don't even know how much of this girl's story is true."

Jondralyn sat back in a chair, defeated. A dark pall had fallen over the room.

"Several things are now made certain, though," Val-Draekin said. "There are tunnels under this saloon that even we were not aware of. And once again our safety and security are compromised, with this barmaid knowing where we are, who we are, and how to reach us so easily. Like us, she cannot now leave this place and roam about the city. Like us, she is to remain here in this saloon. And she must be watched. As should the courtyard out back. We shall post a watch at the front and back doors."

"We cannot hold her hostage," Jondralyn said. "We don't need her here with us." Tala couldn't have agreed more. She severely disliked the barmaid. Jondralyn insisted, "We cannot all be hostages to this saloon. We *need* to go to Savon."

"It is late," said Val-Draekin. "We shall consider going to Savon on the morrow."

**

But come dawn, Tala awoke to Lawri Le Graven's savage screams.

Tala rushed down the back hallway of the saloon to find her cousin standing in the doorway of Delia's small bedroom. Face blue and bloated, the barmaid hung naked from an exposed beam, a white sheet tied around her elongated neck.

Delia was dead.

CHAPTER TWENTY-NINE

AVA SHAY

24TH DAY OF THE FIRE MOON, 999TH YEAR OF LAIJON
SAINT ONLY, ADIN WYTE

Ava Shay awoke, finding herself in a most luxuriant and familiar bed. Aeros and Leisel were next to her. She was on her back, staring straight up at the dark vaulted ceiling of Aeros Raijael's bedchamber. All she could think of was escape. From the moment she awoke to the moment she fell into blissful sleep.

One day you may find that I have stashed the sword somewhere in Aeros' bedchamber, the Bloodwood had said to her two weeks ago. *When that day comes, you will know your time to escape is near. Just look for the sign of My Heart in Aeros' bedchamber.* And yestermorn she had found her sword, My Heart, hanging behind one of the decorative velvet tapestries, its ruby hilt tied with a string. It dangled high between the back of the tapestry and the cold stone wall, just within arm's reach if she stood on her tiptoes. She left it where it was. It was in a good hiding spot until she needed it.

The Spider had been charged with her training and with keeping her sword. He had hinted that he would leave it for her in the chamber as a sign. *A sign for me to slay Aeros Raijael?* But could she muster the courage to use it against the White Prince? He seemed wise to her subtlety at every turn, even foiling her last attempt on his life with ease.

Still, it was reassuring, knowing the Spider had left her the sword. It meant whatever plans he had made for her escape were underway. She just didn't want to place too much faith in hope. And the death of her baby weighed heavy on her mind. *Was it Jenko's? Or was it the child of the White Prince?* She wanted to vomit at the very notion. *My own body rejected it, killed it. My child!*

Ava rose up in the bed, looking at Aeros and the serving girl, Leisel, their naked bodies entwined in the sheets next to her. *Poor Leisel.* Ava had never seen anyone with such detached numbness about their whole being. It was as if all the depravities Aeros piled upon the young serving girl were simply another daily task for her to complete.

Ava slipped from the bed. Aeros rolled over, one languid hand reaching for hers, seizing her by the wrist. "Where do you go, my princess?" His pale face was ghostlike in the dim light of the chamber. "Where do you sneak off to now?"

"To drink from the basin," she answered. "I wake with a dry mouth."

Aeros rose and sat at the edge of the bed, long arms slung around her waist in a warm embrace as she stood there stiffly. "Speaking of drink," he said, pulling her to him, whispering, so as not to wake Leisel. "I know I was harsh when you lost our baby. I do not blame your addiction to wine and spirits and your drunkenness for that." He cast his black-pupiled gaze about the room. "I blame the Bloodwood."

"You blame the Spider?" she asked, heart atremble, swearing that his eyes now lingered on the tapestry where the Bloodwood had hidden her sword. "What does the Spider have to do with my—my pregnancy?" she asked, heart aching.

If it was Aeros' child, I should be happy. Yet she was miserable. *Because it was Jenko's child.* She knew it in her heart.

"Has the Spider plied you with much drink as of late?" Aeros' gaze was still fixed on the tapestry across the room.

"Not that I recall," she answered. Then she thought back to all the times the Bloodwood had offered her something to drink, *insisted* upon it even.

Her heart almost ceased its beating at the thought. She could feel her own flesh grow cold and pale.

"I have grown lax in my dealings with that man," the White Prince whispered in her ear. "But rest assured, my princess: for what he has done to you, he shall pay dearly."

**

The Spider stood in the middle of Bruce Hall, grooming his horse. Ava studied his face over the oiled black haunches of his Bloodeye steed, Scowl. The Bloodwood's square-jawed face and close-cropped black hair and piercing eyes had frightened her at first, but in time, she had warmed to the assassin. In fact, of all in Aeros' retinue, it was the Bloodwood who had shown her the most kindness.

Kindness in the form of sword training, smooth words, and much drink . . .

But had he really poisoned her? That was the question. Had he killed her baby? And if so, had he not perhaps done her the greatest favor of all?

No, I can't ever think like that.

She walked up to the Spider and brushed the flanks of his Bloodeye steed, feeling scant comfort in the effort, for the black stallion's hair was as coarse and stiff as dry grass. The red-eyed stallion's hide and body was all corded muscle and coiled tension and hardness. *And who knows what those glowing red eyes see?*

"Perhaps you should feed that demon horse a little sip of wine with the delicate combing you give it," Hammerfiss called out to her, his shined battle armor agleam in the hall's torchlight. He sat at the long table with Aeros and Leisel.

Ava stopped brushing the Bloodeye.

"Looks like a wine-drinking horse to me," Hammerfiss continued. "Unlike my Battle-Ax, a stallion hardy enough to take stiff shots of straight whiskey. If the mood struck him anyway, take shots of whiskey by the gallon, he would, Laijon rest his soul. We were two of a kind, Battle-Ax and me. Tough and hard."

"Don't forget brutish and stupid," the Spider added, his black leather armor soundless as he brushed the black stallion where Ava had given up. "A Bloodeye steed is a refined beast, refined like its master, both of us sophisticated killers, subtle and nuanced, appreciating the beauty in their work."

"Beauty in their work," Hammerfiss sneered. "Don't make me laugh. One day we shall see who is truly better at dealing out death, you with your subtlety and nuance, or me and my stupid brute strength. And I imagine our Lord Aeros would look forward to such a grand battle of opposing styles."

The White Prince didn't even acknowledge the large man, preoccupied with some stray lace at the hem of Leisel's simple, stained gray shift. The serving girl sat astraddle the bench in front of Aeros, deadened eyes staring at nothing and everything. Though now and then she would gaze up at Aeros' fine robes and chain mail and blink rapidly, as if it was all her eyes could do to stave off his shimmering white brilliance. Ava glanced down at her own fancy gown. Aeros had been dressing her in more and more elaborate finery—various dresses with layered corsets and trappings that made it nearly impossible to bend or even breathe. *And now he ignores me and gives all his attention to the simple serving girl in dirty peasant garb.* But she would not complain about any lack of attention where Aeros Raijael was concerned. However, she did feel sorry for Leisel. *And I'm complicit in the depravity.* She closed her eyes, trying to block out last evening's decadence. *Yes, I am also to blame, for I do not stop the horrors.*

Ava looked across the chamber toward Jenko Bruk. He stood beneath the severed head of the sea serpent the Bloodwood had slain. The rotting head still hung on the wall above the huge mantel. Jenko's battle armor flickered with shards of torchlight at his every small move. His face had remained impassive throughout the day. Ava had cast her gaze his way often, wondering if he knew that her sword, My Heart, was hidden behind a tapestry in Aeros' chamber. She wondered if he, too, was preparing an assassination attempt with the Spider. After all, the Bloodwood had claimed he had no qualms about bringing Jenko into their plot to escape. But Spiderwood had so far given her no signal other than the hidden sword.

Next to her, the Bloodwood assassin continued brushing Dread as if nothing were out of the ordinary—he brushed the horse daily, it seemed. Even Ol' Man Leddingham hadn't made the serving girls at the Grayken Spear Inn polish the plates and silverware as much as the Bloodwood polished his horse.

"I would like to see a fight between Hammerfiss and the Spider," Ivor Jace shouted from the entryway of Bruce Hall. He led a large white stallion by the bit, the heavy hooves of the horse clomping loudly on the stone floor. It was a white stallion unfamiliar to Ava. He led the horse straight to her. "Would you not care to know who would win such a battle, the Spider or Hammerfiss?" Ivor seemed to be undressing her with his eyes as he asked the question.

She remained silent under his unnerving gaze. The white stallion eyed her with wide, kind eyes. He seemed a good-natured and calm fellow, though his gaze darkened at the sight of the Bloodeye.

"What is this horse you have brought us?" Hammerfiss asked Ivor. "'Tis a glorious young beast."

"For our Lord Aeros!" Ivor announced. "A new white stallion to replace the one that was lost in the channel."

"Look, Aeros, Ivor has gifted you with a new stallion," Hammerfiss announced.

Aeros glanced up. "Splendid-looking thing," he said, then went back to fussing with the hem of Leisel's dirty shift as if he really didn't care about the horse at all.

"'Twas the last such stallion in all of Adin Wyte," Ivor said proudly, trying to get the White Prince's attention again. "His name is Ash, but I reckon our Lord Aeros can name him whatever he likes."

Aeros continued to work on Leisel's shift, not looking up, certainly not looking at the horse.

"His name is Ash," Ivor said again. "But you can name him whatever you like."

"Ash is fine," Aeros said.

Ivor seemed less than thrilled with the White Prince's indifference

354

to the gift, and it showed on his red-flushed face. Anger sparked behind his eyes as he glared down at Aeros and Leisel.

Hammerfiss took the bit of the white stallion from Ivor. "One day we shall fight, the Spider and I, and then we shall be blessedly free of all nuance and subtlety. What say you to that, Ash?" The young stallion chuffed and nickered, unsure of itself under the red gaze of the black Bloodeye.

"Aye, we shall fight one day," the Bloodwood acknowledged Hammerfiss, dark eyes fixed on Ava as he continued, "And on that day, we shall all indeed be free, ready to make our grand escapes from all that hold us captive."

"Yes, we are all captive to your nonsense." Hammerfiss brought the huffing nose of the young stallion right up to the nose of Scowl, the black stallion's eyes now two smoldering sparks of crimson. Ash danced back nervously. But Hammerfiss held him tight, forcing the poor beast closer.

"Best back your horse away," the Spider said coolly, no longer brushing Scowl's stiff coat. "A Bloodeye does not like its personal space encroached on so."

Hammerfiss laughed. "Equines don't have the same 'personal space' issues as us humans. They'll get along just dandy, if introduced properly."

"I wouldn't be so certain," the Spider said.

Both stallions were nose to nose, still as stone.

Then Scowl snapped out with a snarling screech that filled the hall with its piercing sound. Its pointed front teeth were like sharpened daggers, latching onto the nose of the young white stallion. The Bloodeye's frothing jaws clamped down, grinding up the snout of the white stallion, chewing, tearing. Then the black stallion jerked its head and body sharply, once, twice, three times. It thrashed, until the entire front of the white stallion's face was ripped free, leaving naught but a ragged bloody hole. The Bloodeye flung the hunk of severed snout to the floor, where it landed in a wet splat against the cobbles.

Blood spraying, the white stallion jumped and kicked, shrilling in fear and pain, its garbled screams and huffing deep breaths sucking chunks of gore back into its heaving lungs. Hammerfiss tried to snatch the flailing reins out of the air, blood spewing red and hot over his battle armor as he closed with the bucking beast.

Ivor Jace spun away from the savage scene, one strong hand latching onto Ava's arm, pulling her with him. He dragged her about ten paces away from the bloody horse and stopped. The Spider placed one calm hand on the saddle horn of the Bloodeye. But the black stallion was already as calm as the assassin, red eyes like burning coals in its wedge-shaped head, blood and spit drooling from its slathering mouth. A low growl rumbled from deep within its heaving chest.

"Bloody rotted angels!" Aeros rose from the table behind Ava. "May Lady Death take us all, what is this fucking disturbance?"

Hammerfiss finally had the reins of the white stallion in hand. But the poor frightened beast was screaming up an ear-piercing racket, screaming through the torn, gaping hole that remained of its missing snout. It dropped to its front knees, rolled over onto its side, then rolled halfway over onto its back. Blood and bits of frayed flesh smeared the cobbled floor as its legs kicked frantically. And still its unbearably loud screams split the chamber.

"End it!" Aeros bellowed. "Put it down! Kill it now, Hammerfiss! I can't take it!" He clapped both hands over his ears.

Hammerfiss pulled out his sword and stabbed it straight into the heaving chest of the struggling stallion, straight into its heart. And that ended the terror and noise. The white stallion was dead, a thick pool of scarlet spreading out over the floor.

**

Ava had been escorted to Aeros' bedchamber hours ago. Ivor Jace had remained posted in the corridor just outside the door. He had sulked the entire way there, clearly disturbed by the death of the white stallion and Aeros' seeming lack of enthusiasm for his gift. That the whole affair had turned bloody and violent did not surprise Ava. For around the army of Sør Sevier, what affair did not eventually end in violence?

Ava was just glad to be left alone for once. She finally had privacy and was quickly out of her stuffy gown and back into a more comfortable cotton shift. She crept to the tapestry, pulled the bottom of it away from the wall, and looked up, seeing the sword still dangling there above. My Heart. But what would she do with it? The Spider claimed she would know when she saw the clue. But she didn't. *Does he expect me to kill Aeros tonight? Will he come in and help? I've no armor. I may as well be naked.* But the Spider had left the sword. There was that one small reassurance. But it was all so confusing.

And she couldn't shake what Aeros had said earlier that day, the certainty of his words. Had the Bloodwood poisoned her? In her mind's eye she could still see the red globs of her miscarriage on the sheets—an image that would be seared into her mind for as long as she lived.

The door to Aeros' bedchamber swung open. Startled, Ava whirled, letting the tapestry fall back against the gray stone behind her.

"There are no secret passages to or from this chamber." Ivor Jace stepped into the room, letting the door fall softly shut behind him. "There are no holes in the wall behind any of the tapestries, if escape is your aim. There is no way out of this room." He said the last with a note of dread finality. There was something about his posture and stern-faced manner that made her instantly wary.

"You know nothing of my aims." She stepped away from the tapestry, heart leaping in her chest. Then it hit her: he was wearing no armor. Ivor was clothed in naught but leather breeches and a white undershirt and black leather boots. His Dayknight sword was in the sheath at his side, the black belt loose around his hips. Muscles bunched and rippled beneath his thin shirt. He looked even more menacing out of his armor.

"You should not be here," she said, realizing how thin her own clothes were, how exposed she was before him. "Your Lord Aeros would not be happy to find you alone with me so near to being undressed."

But Ivor had an unconcerned, swaggering air about him as he strode farther into the room. He took in the surroundings as if he had never seen them before. "Magnificent how this place cleans up, now that Ser Edmon is no longer in charge. One could literally roll about naked on the floor without becoming infested with fleas and the like. Don't you think, Miss Ava?"

"As I said, your Lord Aeros would be most displeased to find you in here without his permission." She covered her breasts, knowing her shift was so thin he could likely see right through it, as close as he now was.

"Around that little serving girl, Aeros doesn't pay attention to much. Son of a bitch scarcely noticed the white stallion I found for him. I reckon he is still down in Bruce Hall making eyes at Leisel. He will not return for some time now."

"You cannot be so certain."

"I am so certain I doffed my armor and left it piled in the corridor." He hooked his thumbs into his belt, rocked back on his heels. "Hard to move about in such cumbersome attire whilst in the throes of passion. If you take my meaning?"

"Please leave now," she said, warning in her voice.

He smiled with confidence. His hard, sculpted face bore a row of scars across his jaw and neck that reddened as his smile grew. Arrogance laced everything he did at all times. That was the one thing Ava hated about him most. One moment Ivor could be so smooth and eloquent, his manner impeccable; the next moment all his graces vanished into cruel distaste. The worst thoughts flooded her mind.

"He calls you his princess." Ivor kept smiling at her with the utmost self-assurance. "Yet whatever have you been a princess of, that is what I ask? For I imagine you're no princess, but rather like most women, naught but a vain clacking slattern, full of much whining and drama."

His smile widened to an almost foolish-looking width, perfect teeth agleam. He shrugged with nonchalance. "But, unlike most women, at least you are pretty. And so I reckon men will put up with you for a while."

"If you say," she answered with offhand dryness, wishing him gone, but knowing wishes were like prayers that would never be answered.

"Yes, you are a pretty one," he said, smile slowly fading. "A pretty one with a fine tight body, and that is all you are worth to this world."

Ava shrank away from him. His words had their effect. Perhaps if she wasn't so pretty, things would be different for her now. *Well, aren't you just an impossibly pretty little thing?* was the first thing Enna Spades had ever said to her. And her looks had marked her as one belonging to Aeros Raijael from the beginning. *And now I belong to him.* She recalled saying something to Nail along those lines: *What must it be like, always belonging to people?* An image of her dead parents flashed into her mind, her brothers and sisters, too. She remembered how Ol' Man Leddingham had taken her in with kindness and given her a job. *I've never once belonged to myself, but always to others.* Then she realized that in Gul Kana it was the lot of all women to belong to a man.

In war the men either died or became fighters for the enemy, whilst the girls become the prisoners. And the really pretty girls become property. Naught but objects to be raped. The pretty ones always had it the worst. She'd never considered being called pretty a compliment but rather a cynical accusation. But one thing was certain: lust lived in Ivor's eyes, and he was advancing on her now. She stepped back, clutching the fabric of her cotton shift to her flesh.

"Why shy away from me?" he asked, drifting forward, tilting his head, long blond hair like a horse's mane over his left shoulder. "Aeros has sanctioned our coupling. He knows I am here. He wants a break from you. He wants me to fuck you."

"I think not." She darted from his grasping hands.

He pursued, seizing her by the forearm, his grip firm and inescapable.

Terror blazed through every fiber of her being as he pulled her toward him, pressing the great bulk of his muscular chest into hers. It was an odd terror, though, almost comforting in its tense and lingering pain. *Is this what I deserve?*

His eyes burned with desire as he bent to kiss her. She jerked her head to the side, lips and eyes clenched tight. Undaunted, his mouth slid over hers. He licked her face. He ran his sloppy tongue over her cheek and eyelid and up her forehead, growling in gross pleasure as he bit her earlobe.

"Leave her be!" Jenko Bruk bellowed.

Jenko was standing in the doorway. He was encased in full armor, helm in the crook of one arm, longsword at his hip. His Knight Archaic cloak spilled like a blue river over his back and shoulders. "Leave her be!" he shouted a second time, gauntleted hand going to the hilt of his sword.

"Relax." Ivor released his hold on Ava and backed away from her, both hands held up in mock surrender. "We can both have some fun here, Jenko, my lad. No need for anger. I know you wish to rut with your old flame again."

"Remove yourself from this room." Jenko's voice was ice. "Else I tell Aeros your sins."

"'Tell'?" Ivor asked. "Are we little kids here, tattling on each other? What's to 'tell'?"

Ava slid sideways away from the man, trying to go unnoticed. But Ivor drew his sword with a rasp and pointed the blade at her chest, stepping toward her until the tip was hovering between her breasts. "What if I just run her through right now?" he said to Jenko. "Pierce her heart? End her quick? Blame you for her murder?"

Dread coiled over Ava as Ivor leaned in. She could feel the sword's cold tip touch her breastbone. She could see the fear in Jenko's eyes.

"Only a coward would attack another knight who was not properly armored," Ivor said. "And I never pegged you for a coward, Jenko Bruk. How 'bout we take turns fucking her and be friends?"

Jenko's fright-filled gaze was fixed on the sword pointed at Ava's chest. Sweat beaded on his forehead, and he was breathing hard under the layers of armor. Jenko dropped his helm and drew his sword, stepping into the room.

Ava's heart had never been more full of both love and fear.

"Have it your way, fool." Ivor was calm and rigid as a stone, the tip of his blade no longer at Ava's chest, but pointed at Jenko.

Ivor lunged toward Jenko, blond hair flying. His sword was a humming swirl of silver as he struck down upon his foe with might and force. Jenko blocked the blow and reeled back into the open door with a thud, his momentum slamming the door shut. Ivor pressed the attack, another blow hammering down fast and furious. Jenko dropped to the ground, rolling with a clatter of armor. Ivor's sword struck the stone floor where Jenko had just been, sparks flying. Jenko was back on his feet quickly, sword poised and ready.

Ivor did not let up. He struck again, sword striking sword with a loud clash, his bold attack knocking Jenko's sword aside, cutting into Jenko's armor just below the hip. The blow was not deep enough to draw blood, but it left a wicked gash in the armor. The blow nonetheless caused Jenko to shout out in pain as he limped backward, trying to recover. Ivor launched another savage series of strikes. Jenko parried each, but staggered back against the side of Aeros' bed.

It was clear that Jenko would soon be overcome by the bigger man's superior strength. *Jenko is going to die!* Ava turned from the fight. *Unless I help!* She rushed to the tapestry and flung it aside, jumping for My Heart. She latched onto the thin blade and pulled down hard, snapping the string around the hilt that held the sword.

She turned to face the combatants. Ivor was sitting atop Jenko's chest now, trying to press the edge of his longsword down into Jenko's neck with the full weight of his body. Jenko, red-faced and straining under the larger man, held off the sword with two gauntleted hands, desperately trying to keep the blade from slicing open his neck.

Ava lunged forward, the training advice of the Bloodwood foremost on her mind, *That is how to kill a man, strike when he is least expecting it.* She thrust the tip of My Heart between the tangled veil of Ivor's long blond hair and straight into his earhole. She pushed with all the strength she could muster, listening as the blade sank wetly into the man's brain and scraped the other side of his skull. A sound she would never forget. Then she yanked My Heart swiftly back out of his bloody ear.

Ivor's heaving throat sucked in air with a hiss; then blood, red blood, bubbled from between his lips and slid down his chiseled, square chin like drool. His hands let go the sword. Then his hands seemed to claw at Jenko's armor as he slid to the floor in a dripping pool of scarlet, darkness swirling down into his eyes as he rolled over, dead.

I killed him! Ava's mind was a fog of pain and hurt and roiling emotions she just couldn't, at seventeen, fully understand. *I stabbed a man through the ear and now he's dead!* Long-forgotten wraiths boiled up in her soul once more, ready to devour.

"Bloody gracious Mother Mia," Jenko said, trembling in every limb as he sat up, swiping away Ivor's sword. He leaned against Aeros' bed for support. "My life passed before my eyes," he gasped. "I've been naught but a rich man's son and a boastful bully the whole of my existence." His gaze met hers, and he shook his head in disbelief. "It was all I could think of as he pressed that sword down toward my neck, how awful I've been. Funny what a man thinks of as he's dying."

"It's over." Ava felt the tears forming in her eyes.

Jenko's gaze cut into hers. "If not for you, I'd be dead. You saved me, Ava. You saved me."

"No," she found herself crying. "All I did was kill a man."

"And saved me in the process."

"We saved each other."

For some reason, he laughed at that. And at the sound of his laughter, the wraiths instantly vanished from her mind. "We saved each other," she repeated.

"We're certainly an honest pair, ain't we?" he said, still laughing—though it was now the nervous laugh of a man who had just skirted death. She dropped her sword and clung to him, weeping, not knowing what she was doing or what any of it meant, not knowing what to do next, or where to go, or what to say, or if they should hurry and flee. Ava Shay was just glad to be holding Jenko Bruk, even if it was naught but his cold and blood-splattered armor she embraced. They clutched each other tight, both of them crying in exhaustion now.

"Bravo!" Aeros' voice cut through their weeping and tears.

Every bone in Ava's body turned chill.

"Bravo," the White Prince repeated as he stepped into the room, clapping slowly.

All thoughts of flight and escape were instantly swept from Ava's mind. And the heaviest burden yet settled over her heart, for she knew this was the moment both she and Jenko would die at Aeros' hand. For how could they ever explain what had happened?

The White Prince stood in the entrance of the room in all his white armor and finery, sword and daggers at his hip. Then he stepped farther into the room, heading toward them. "Stand." He held one pale hand out for Jenko.

Jenko grasped the offered hand, and the White Prince helped him stand. Ava stood on her own, shivering in fear, Ivor's body at her feet, blood seeping from the hole in his ear. Both Jenko's and Ava's swords were on the stone floor next to the dead man—proof that they had killed him.

Aeros picked up her sword and held it out, examining it, running one finger slowly over the blood-streaked blade. He stepped over Ivor's body toward the bed and rubbed the blood from his finger on the white bedcovering, then cleaned My Heart on the same bedcovering. The task done, Aeros finally broke the silence.

"I imagine you both think me upset by all this."

Ava and Jenko looked at each other, neither saying a word.

"I am not upset." Aeros looked at Jenko. "On the contrary, with this act, you secure yourself in the annals of history and the fulfillment of prophecy, Ser Jenko Bruk. For the *Illuminations* declare that prior to Fiery Absolution there shall be a great division and scattering within the ranks of the Knights Archaic. You merely fought Ivor to protect the honor of my princess, and that is to be commended."

Aeros turned to Ava. "And you merely killed a man who was trying to rape you." He handed My Heart back to her. "It is yours now. Yours to keep. It is now a killer's blade, fully blooded. There shall be no more hiding it in the tapestry. Wear it at your belt, my princess. Wear it whenever and wherever you choose."

Then the White Prince did something he had never done before.

He bowed to them both.

"This all went exactly as I had planned," he said. "And I have been most entertained. Now let us find Leisel, and together we can all clean this mess and then drink ourselves into oblivion."

Only fools find safety in their dreams, in the surety of their faith. For scripture,
like mythology and dreams, is entirely false. For scripture is meant to steal away
the light of understanding and drown one in ignorance and fable.
—THE BOOK OF THE BETRAYER

CHAPTER THIRTY
CRYSTALWOOD

1ST DAY OF THE BLOOD MOON, 999TH YEAR OF LAIJON
KRAGG KEEP, WYN DARRÈ

I can't wait to see my family," Borden Bronachell said, his gaze fixed on the eastern horizon beyond the Kragg Keep Gorge. "Jovan, Jondralyn, Tala, Ansel, they will be most amazed to see me again." He was helping Tyus Barra and a crookbacked old man in stained clothes tie the five brown roans together on the wooden platform that hung precariously over the gorge. Borden still wore the clothing Tyus had provided him weeks ago, leather armor over breeches and a white shirt. His long black Dayknight sword was still hooked to a baldric over his back. "I think I can see Gul Kana from here. I can see the faint haze of my homeland just beyond the five Laijon Towers on the edge of the Aelathia Plains. I think I can see the Fortress of Saint Only."

"Bullocks," Hans muttered.

Though they were no longer mounted, Krista Aulbrek and Hans Rake still had their hands bound with rope. They watched patiently as Borden and Tyus secured the horses to the wooden platform. Ironcloud, clad in studded leather armor, stood just a few paces behind the two Bloodwoods, his battle-ax ready in case they made any false move. Café

Colza Bouledogue sat content at the dwarf's heels, stumpy tail thumping against the dirt.

"And there lies Lord's Point," Borden said, nodding beyond the gorge, hoping Tyus would look. "I think I can see it too."

"He can't see shit," Hans scoffed.

Hans was right. Overhead the clouded sky was slate gray, the air warm and hazy with humidity. And the Aelathia Plains and five Laijon Towers had to be a good fifty miles east of Kragg, and Lord's Point another fifty beyond that.

As part of her Bloodwood training, Krista had studied maps of every location of note in the Five Isles. She could see nothing beyond the extraordinary town of Kragg, some hundred feet across the chasm from where she stood. The shimmering blue bay was two hundred feet below.

She had also studied the unusual layout of the cliff town of Kragg and Kragg Keep and the River Sen, which cut through the middle of both. She had also read about the famous Kragg Bay in the wedge-shaped gorge far below—though standing so close to it now was an exhilarating and frightening experience, for sure. She did not like heights.

Being so near the rim of the cliff, hands bound tight before her, made her gut flutter. It was like being as helpless as a morsel of sugar atop one of Queen Natalia Raijael's pumpkin-spice pies, looking down into the empty wedge-shaped gap where the first piece of pie had been cut and removed. To the north, the sheer cliffs of Kragg Bay widened, opening up to the sea. To the south, the cliffs came tapering together, joining at a point where Kragg Keep rose grim and foreboding above the plateau.

The keep straddled the River Sen. From under the broad castle where the two converging cliffs met emerged the River Sen in the form of a roaring waterfall. The Sen cascaded cool and clear down into the narrow gulf of the bay. The thundering falls created a frothy maelstrom two hundred feet below.

Kragg Keep and the waterfall springing from under it were sights unlike anything she had seen before. It was like a grand painting. The wedge-shaped abyss below had been forged by the ravages of water and wind and then its sides quarried and sculpted into a livable space by the hands of humans. Most of the city of Kragg was carved into the two converging cliff sides. A good portion of the cave dwellings across the ravine were covered in stitched-together hides and canvas that rippled in the breeze. Sheared and chiseled and crafted through the ages, the hundreds of random windows, balconies, buttresses, parapets, cave openings, staircases, and other details staggered Krista's imagination. Her vision and mind could not encompass it all.

The sector of the city on the plateau behind her was naught but desolation: empty streets, run-down shanty dwellings, burnt-out buildings, and yards that at one time had likely been lush and blooming, but were now dusty and dead. Most of the dilapidated buildings boasted broken windows and leaning gates and barred doors; others had lintel-stone entries that led to crumbled courtyards. Like everywhere else in Wyn Darrè, the entire city of Kragg was scarcely more than a dismal ruin now, all but destroyed by the Angel Prince and his armies. Only a small portion of the town's inhabitants remained after Aeros' conquest, most bedecked in nothing more than rags. Wild dogs roamed the near-empty streets.

A handful of hooded beggars and thieves had watched from a distance as Borden and Tyus had marched the five roans onto the platform and begun tying them together with the help of the crookbacked old man. The oldster owned the wooden platform and the twenty mules that would lower the platform to the bay below.

Leaning out over the cliff and the wooden platform was a stout wooden scaffolding attached to a cluster of iron gears and pulleys. A thick, heavy rope stretched up from each of the four corners of the platform to one large iron hook hanging above in the center. The huge hook was connected to a broad iron chain that ran through a series of pulleys high on the scaffolding and then to a giant wooden turning wheel some distance from the crag's rim. The mules were hooked to the wheel.

Along the rim of the crag, to both Krista's left and her right, were at least two dozen other such sets of wooden scaffolding, pulleys, ropes, chains, turning wheels, and platforms.

Far across the gorge, Krista could make out dozens of other sets of scaffolding and apparatuses atop the opposite cliff. She imagined that when Kragg was a viable and booming trade port, every single one of the blocks and pulleys had been utilized daily for hoisting people, horses, oxen, trade goods, and other such heavy cargo from the ships, barges, and other vessels docked below. In fact, a sailing vessel just big enough for Borden, Ironcloud, Tyus, Hans, Krista, and their five mounts awaited them down there. Their ship also belonged to the crookbacked old man.

"Gul Kana," Borden Bronachell said, "my home. Gone for so long, I can almost taste it now."

The old man carried on to the big wheel and his twenty mules. Borden turned and looked back at Tyus Barra, still on the platform. Tyus looked bashfully at Krista. The hilt of the double-edged shortsword at his belt gleamed dully in the light, matching the dullness of his woolen pants and elk-hide jerkin.

Behind Krista the crookbacked old man shouted and cracked a whip. The mules dug in and the large wheel slowly churned to the sound of metal grinding on wood. Tyus and the five roans slowly dropped into the empty air about two feet, and then the old man's mules stopped. The sensation of the sudden descent caused the five roans to nicker, hooves now jittery on the flat wood of the platform.

"She's oiled up and ready for a smooth descent!" the oldster bellowed. "All aboard and down you go!"

Borden Bronachell ordered Krista and Hans to step onto the platform. Krista was hesitant, eyeing the platform and the vast expanse beyond. Hans looked concerned too. The platform itself looked most unsafe—it was completely flat and had zero guardrails or any safety barrier other than the four ropes leading up to the giant iron hook above. The five roans were not tied to anything. They were just tied to each other in the center of the platform.

"On you go," Borden urged.

Krista stepped nervously from the rim of the cliff down onto the precarious wooden platform two feet below.

Hans remained rooted in place. He cast his worried gaze Krista's way. "I've seen this before," he said, the words hissing from his mouth. "This very same platform. This scaffolding. Falling. This cliff and this ravine. The water far below. I saw it all in a vision. When the mermaid held me down under the water. The foul beast filled my head with nightmares, it did. This is what our Bloodwood training in water was for. Our cloaks may be fireproof, but they are not waterproof, Crystalwood. The mermaid would not have shown me these cliffs if . . ."

Krista wondered if Hans had suddenly gone daft. *Visions?* He'd mentioned them before, along with their training—diving off the cliffs of Spyke. But he had never before mentioned anything about Kragg Keep and this gorge.

"On you go," Borden prodded Hans. "Don't make me force you."

Hans looked truly afraid. The five horses nickered again. Krista met the anxious gaze of her roan, Sisco, tied in the middle of the five. She wanted to reach out and reassure the animal that all would be okay. She wanted somehow to let the horse know that these platforms and scaffoldings and pulleys had likely lifted and lowered much heavier loads up and out of the gorge daily. Tyus Barra leaned over and reassured Sisco with a gentle pat and a rub. He held the ends of the reins that drooped from the necks of all five roans. Café Colza barked loudly.

"Bloody beasts of the underworld," Ironcloud cursed.

Tyus pulled his sword from the sheath at his belt, eyes wide, staring at something behind Krista. She turned.

Striding down the center of the dusky street behind Borden and Ironcloud was Black Dugal, his large Bloodeye stallion, Malice, stepping silently behind him. And following Malice was Hans' stallion, Kill, and her own Bloodeye steed, Dread.

Dread! Her heart soared at the sight of her own black mare.

Café Colza barked again, tail wagging furiously. Hans Rake still looked haunted by his visions, as if Dugal's entrance were a part of them.

Self-assured and tall, Krista's master drifted through the dirty ruins of Kragg with a malevolent ease. The bottom of his black cloak dragged over the cobbled street, kicking up dust. His chiseled, gray-bearded face came into focus when he pulled the cowl back from his head. His red-hazed eyes cut through the air straight toward her. Krista stepped farther back onto the platform, scared.

Ironcloud brandished his ax, guarding the platform. Borden Bronachell drew his Dayknight sword, scowling. "I figured we would run into you sooner than this, foul assassin. Or should I call you Baron Alexander Thork?" He brought the tip of his sword up. "You shall pay for the murder of Seabass."

"You got my note, then?" Dugal said, unhooking the dark brooch at the neckline of his heavy cloak and letting the garment drop to the ground. He was clothed in the black leathers of a Bloodwood, thin sword at his belt, hard-angled face grim but beautiful.

And not having seen Black Dugal in some time now, Krista realized just how strikingly *beautiful* her master was, how he shone against the dirt and destruction of Kragg. The hard edges and angles—and even the scars—on his face added to his allure. One scar, shaped like a crescent moon, marked his left cheek. Two scars curved below his right eye and across his face, vanishing under his beard. Another scar sliced through his sooty right brow and up his forehead to become lost in his short-cropped black hair.

Beauty. The first rule of a Bloodwood. Krista also knew of the numerous black daggers—many of them likely coated with all manner of poisons—that were hidden in those sinister black leathers. Yes. Beautiful and sinister. That was Black Dugal.

"Ser Borden Bronachell," Dugal said, voice cool and smooth as silk. "Well met again." The three Bloodeyes behind Dugal stepped back, as if knowing what was to come. He then kicked his cloak aside, creating room, preparing for the fight Krista knew was coming.

Black Dugal had stalked Borden and Ironcloud across the breadth of Wyn Darrè. And, she imagined, for her master, the chase was a measured thing, a tactical hunt to be savored. And now this was that quest's culmination. He would easily slay Borden and the dwarf and free her and Hans. In fact, with just a few words spoken, the conversation had already gone on longer than Krista could have imagined. When it came to dealing in death, Dugal always taught his students, *Be short on words, quick with killing.*

"Does this mean you all ain't goin' down?" the crookbacked old man near the giant wood turning wheel shouted. He was crouching between two of his mules. Black Dugal glared at him. So did the three Bloodeye steeds.

The old man ran off, disappearing into a dusty alley nearby and the small crowd gathered there. Several townsfolk had ventured from their homes, looking on in worry.

Dugal turned back toward the platform, his piercing gaze again on Krista, the dead pits of his red-hazed eyes carving a path through her soul. "Crystalwood, you are so far from home." He pulled two black daggers from hidden folds in his leather armor.

Krista's heart lurched at his words, for there was no companionship in them, rather cold, stark anger. *And the black daggers in his hands?* She sensed Hans' entire body tensing next to her. "Something's not right," she said.

Dugal kept his eyes trained on her, and they narrowed to fierce slits.

"You are not so frightening," Ironcloud growled at the assassin, the heavy ax steady in his two powerful fists. "If it is a fight that you desire, a fight you shall have."

Dugal addressed the dwarf. "My, my, Ser Squateye, does she even know whom you really serve?" The Bloodwood's tone, cold and flat, silenced the dwarf. "Do you even know who you serve, dwarf?"

"I serve the light. I serve Mia," the dwarf said. "Not the dark."

"What does that even mean?" Dugal smiled, raising his daggers. "My blades thirst but have yet to feed, unless you consider Seabass a meal." His smile widened.

"Bastard," Squateye snarled.

Dugal's rigid gaze was on Krista once more. He was unsmiling now. "You could have easily escaped these men, my Crystal. Yet you stayed, knowing they were leading you closer to Gault Aulbrek. And that is your sin. You took back the blue ribbon when it was offered. In your heart, you are not yet fatherless. Even though he was never your kin."

Never my kin? Krista's heart sank, mind whirling. Hans must have seen the ribbon around her ankle when she slept. *The rat! He told Dugal.*

Dugal finally broke his gaze from her and looked at Borden and Ironcloud. "After I slay her, I will need you both alive."

Both daggers spun from Dugal's hands simultaneously. He threw them straight and true. One struck Borden, punching through his polished leather armor, sinking into the left side of his chest just above the heart. The other dagger hit the dwarf in the right shoulder. Ironcloud dropped in a puff of dust, body stiff as a barrel, neck straining, fingers clenched. Borden folded on top of the dwarf, arms and legs stretched out, all four limbs twitching uncontrollably.

Poison! Krista's mind was working fast now. *Spine-pinching gaze!* Dugal had spread spine-pinching gaze, a mixture of poisons that induced immediate paralysis, over the blades. Borden and Ironcloud would remain rigid, incapacitated, for nearly half an hour, before the poison wore off.

Dugal's third dagger was spinning toward her head. Krista flung her hands in front of her face. A reflex. But it saved her. The dagger glanced off the knotted rope that bound her wrists and spun away into the chasm beyond.

Dugal's fourth dagger swiftly followed. But Tyus Barra stepped in front of her, the dagger glancing off the back of his own hand, drawing a thin line of blood, then skittering along the wooden platform under the hooves of the five roans. The boy reeled back in pain, fighting the poison as he staggered away, legs and arms stiffening.

Spine-pinching gaze worked instantaneously, but Tyus had suffered only a superficial blow to the back of his hand. The poison worked best if the dagger entered near the heart or nervous system. The mute appeared mostly in control of his muscles as he turned and drew his sword.

Dugal did not throw a fifth dagger. He drew his sword and ran toward the platform. Krista struggled against the rope binding her hands. All was happening so fast now. She could hear Café Colza barking in front of her. She could hear the five roans whinnying on the platform behind her.

Hans was already free. He'd slipped his bonds quickly. He lunged onto the platform toward Tyus Barra. The mute was strangely chopping with his sword at one of the four ropes holding up the platform—the southeasternmost rope. *Spine-pinching gaze can affect the brain too!*

Krista fought with the ropes around her wrists but could not slip them as Black Dugal lunged onto the platform, his sleek sword sweeping down toward her face.

The platform lurched and jumped, knocking Dugal off his feet, thwarting his blow. He careened into the legs of the five bound roans. Several of the horses fell on top of him, the entire group now sliding toward open air.

Tyus Barra had cut the rope clean through. The platform now listed toward the chasm precariously. The mute's eyes were glazed over with deranged panic. Hans tried to wrestle the sword away from the boy. But Tyus shoved the Bloodwood back. Hans' foot slipped over the edge of the platform and he fell face-first against the surface, scrambling to find purchase on the ever-tilting wood.

Tyus turned from Hans, swinging his blade wildly at the rope that held up the southwesternmost corner of the platform, the corner closest to the cliff face. Krista, seeing what was about to happen, lunged from the platform toward the lip of the plateau.

The mute's third blow sliced through the rope and the platform dropped.

Krista, bound hands stretching forth, barely caught the rim of the cliff with her fingers. She clung to the rock, legs churning for purchase along the sheer cliff face as the entire southern end of the platform swung down, dumping everyone and everything.

The five bound roans swept Black Dugal with them, the entire pile of horses tumbling into thin air, plunging toward the bay two hundred feet below, Krista's master entangled with them. A moment later, with a tremendous splash, the five horses and Black Dugal struck the calm blue waters.

Hans Rake and Tyus Barra clung to the platform as it swung vio-lently beneath Krista, who was still clinging to the lip of the plateau. Then Tyus, nearest to the cliff, lost his grip and fell too. Krista watched in horror as the mute plummeted, striking several balconies and other rocky outcroppings on his way down. The boy's body tore open and broke apart, innards and entrails and ravaged limbs spinning down, rain-ing over Dugal and the horses. Hans fell next. Two hundred feet and he knifed into the bay with hardly a splash.

With her hands still bound, strength giving way, Krista clung to the side of the cliff, stunned, the sounds of Café Colza barking and the three Bloodeyes screaming coming from above. Then the bulldog's barks turned to whimpers, and Krista saw his slobbering face looking straight down at her. The dog was looking straight past her to where Dugal and Hans had disappeared.

The dog began scratching at her straining fingers. *Fuck! Fucking bloody awful beast!* With a burst of energy, Krista managed to swing one leg up and over the lip of the crag. She hauled herself up.

"Get the fuck away from me!" she shouted, pushing Café Colza out of the way as she rolled away from the ledge. Safe. She breathed heavily in both terror and relief.

But the three Bloodeyes were still braying and screaming, sharp and shrill. Krista sat up. All three red-eyed horses were stomping in the dirt and cobbles around Ironcloud. The dwarf was crawling along the ground in strained agony, fighting the poison in his blood. Borden Bronachell still lay on the ground in total paralysis, arms and legs clenched and stiff.

Ironcloud and Borden could wait. Café Colza was at the edge of the plateau, whimpering, bulbous eyes looking over the ledge, nostrils huff-ing wildly. Then the bulldog's stumpy tail started to wag furiously.

Krista crawled back to the rim and looked down. Hans Rake was alive, scrambling up into the sailboat far below, leaning over the side-wall, helping Black Dugal climb aboard. *Both of them were alive!* Hans had warned her to remember their training at the cliffs of Spyke. A trained Bloodwood could survive a long fall into water. However, their cloaks protected them from flame and heat but not drowning.

The fate of the five roans was different. They floated some distance from the boat, slowly sinking one by one beneath the blue skin of the bay. *Sisco!* Her heart went out to the horse. Screeching white gulls circled the dead horses, some picking at the remaining bits of Tyus Barra.

Café Colza's slobbering whimpers had turned to joyful barks.

And then the dog leaped from the ledge.

Krista watched the crazed beast drop like a stone toward the waters below, four legs splayed out as if he were trying to take wing and fly. A breathless moment later he hit the water with a loud slap, the sound of which reached Krista moments later. The water calmed where Café Colza had landed. Then the dog's head breached and he paddled swiftly toward Hans and Dugal and the boat, alive.

Krista dragged herself away from the ledge and scanned the city before her. The three Bloodeyes stood over Ironcloud now, glowing eyes red as blood. Several raggedy-looking villagers had emerged from the ruins of the city streets and were looking at Borden, Ironcloud, and the Bloodeye stallions nervously.

Krista pulled herself to her feet and marched straight toward her own Bloodeye mare. Bound hands outstretched, she touched Dread with trembling fingers. Relief immediately flooded her. *I'm still alive!* She placed the side of her face gently against the Bloodeye's neck, feeling the comforting warmth of the horse she loved flow through her.

Krista remained that way a moment and then stepped around the horse, inspecting the saddle and bedroll. She was confused. *Dugal had prepared for both killing me and keeping me alive!* Her black leather armor was strapped to one of the thin saddlebags. As she stared at it, deep betrayal carved a hole in her heart. *He came to kill me! He betrayed me!* But wasn't Dashiell Dugal, the patron god of assassins, known as the Betrayer? *All men betray.* That was part of the assassin's creed, one of the rules of a Bloodwood.

Krista found a black dagger in the armor and swiftly cut her bonds, letting the rope fall to the dirt and cobbles. She slipped the dagger back into the folds of the leather armor still strapped to the flanks of the horse. Then she placed her left foot in the stirrup and vaulted onto the back of her Bloodeye. Taking the reins in hand, she whirled the mount. *Black Dugal and Hans Rake will find their way back here within a few hours,* she thought. *If not sooner.* She did not wish to be here when they returned.

"Don't . . . leave us." Ironcloud was struggling to stand. But his stiff, squat body was not cooperating. Dugal's Bloodeye, Malice, still stood over the dwarf. The stallion's black coat was lathered in sweat, nostrils huffing and red, eyes blazing with rage.

More townsfolk had ventured out into the open, beggars and thieves, from the look of it. Some of the braver ones approached slowly. They would likely kill Ironcloud and Borden once Krista was gone. Loot their bodies. Take what armor and weapons and coin they could. Krista wanted to ride off and leave them to it . . .

. . . but hesitated. She dismounted and grabbed the black dagger out of her armor again. She found the two lengths of rope that had previously bound her own hands on the dusty cobbles. Snatching the rope up, she went to the dwarf. Malice blocked her path, but she shooed the stallion away with a wave of the dagger. Malice moved over next to Kill, both horses now eyeing the approaching townsfolk.

Krista knelt over Ironcloud, holding the tip of the dagger to the dwarf's eye. "You once pretended to be half-blind, Squateye. I've a mind to make it true."

The dwarf's breathing was heavy, every word a strain. "Do not . . . let the scavengers have us. They will rob us . . . kill us. Stay until we recover. The poison will wear off."

"Why should I?"

"There are . . . things . . . things you must know," the dwarf muttered. "Things you must learn about your own heritage. Only Borden Bronachell can help you. Only Borden can get you into the secret parts of Mont Saint Only. Only Borden can get you to Aeros Raijael. And once you hear the truth from the Angel Prince, you will wish to slay him."

Malice bucked and brayed. A handful of ruffians broke from the larger group of townsfolk and drew near. Krista counted four hard-faced men in stained cloaks and hoods, along with one grinning old woman, all of them toothless and foul. Krista rose to her feet. "Back away!" she demanded.

The ruffians advanced, three of them now grinning. Krista had no patience left. The black dagger spun like lightning from her hand, and its blade sank into the heart of the nearest man. As death's darkness swirled down into his eyes, he toppled over. "Who's next?" she hooted.

The other four ruffians scattered. She turned back to the dwarf. *Where do my loyalties lie?* Surely not with Black Dugal or Hans Rake. Not anymore.

"Do not leave us." Ironcloud's voice was faint.

Borden and the dwarf had never harmed her. They'd kept her alive, in fact. Tyus Barra deserved none of what had happened. *I owe him something, though.* But what? The mute was dead. *I suppose I could save his friends.*

Groaning, Krista knelt over Ironcloud again and began wrapping the ropes around his thick wrists. "Now you and Borden Bronachell shall travel as my captives."

Blue is tranquility and protection. White is cleansing into calcification.
Red is chaotic lust and fire. Black is banishing death and decay. Green
is ferocious, then tamed. Thus shall our heroes be revealed; for they are
the Warrior Angels, each beholden to a stone of their color.
—THE WAY AND TRUTH OF LAIJON

CHAPTER THIRTY-ONE
MANCELLOR ALLEN

4TH DAY OF THE BLOOD MOON, 999TH YEAR OF LAIJON
SAVON, GUL KANA

Liz Hen Neville sat awkwardly atop the pony, the horned war helm, *Lonesome Crown*, perched even more awkwardly on her canted head. "Is that duck licking its own arse?" She gazed up at the sign above the door of the Preening Pintail Tavern and Inn. The word *Inn* had been scratched out.

To Mancellor Allen's untrained artist's eye, it did look as if the painting above the door was of a duck licking its own ass. The battle-ax, *Forgetting Moon*, was strapped to Mancellor's back. He also carried one blue and one green angel stone in a pouch in his pants pocket.

"I can't imagine being able to lick my own arse." Liz Hen straightened her back, pony shifting under her, knocking into Dokie Liddle's. Steadying his mount, Dokie seemed uncomfortable just looking at the duck in the painting. Beer Mug stared up at the sign without opinion.

The evening sun was sinking below the tall buildings to the west, and the light fell dim over the city of Savon. Mancellor dismounted. He hitched his pony to the rail in front of the tavern. Liz Hen and Dokie followed suit. Beer Mug wagged his tail, knowing they were done traveling for the day.

Mancellor took a moment and scanned the roadway. It was busy. But nobody paid them any mind, even with the horned helm glimmering atop Liz Hen's head and the double-bladed ax gleaming away on his back. Everyone went about their business, heads down. Mancellor wasn't sure whether he was relieved or not that they had finally made it to Savon and the Preening Pintail.

They had made their way here to this town purely on Gault Aulbrek's cryptic suggestion. That, and they really had nowhere else to go. And Savon was on the route to Amadon. Mancellor did not know what Gault had meant by, *The Preening Pintail in Savon would be a good place to lay your head, for there may be things there that you will find most interesting. Other things that you seek.* But his advice had at least offered them a destination. It was an inn, and perhaps they could finally sleep in a soft bed rather than on the hard ground. But in a way, he did not look forward to the night.

His dreams had been naught but nightmares ever since leaving Jenko Bruk and Enna Spades in Lord's Point, bloody visions of war and killing that made him fear sleep as much as the war itself. Ofttimes it was as if he were a spectator in the slaughter rather than a participant, watching himself—a loathsome object covered in blood—murder his own countrymen at the side of Aeros Raijael and his Knights Archaic. In these dreams his hands were rubbed raw and blistered from wielding a sword so long, his lips curled open and split in a wicked grin. No, Mancellor did not look forward to the night.

They had reached Savon having followed a narrow roadway toward the western edge of the town, entering the outskirts in late afternoon. They had fled the Ten Cairn Abbey in utmost haste some six days ago, not looking back. Praed and the rest of the Untamed were dead. They knew not if Enna Spades yet lived. But Beer Mug had returned from the fight with the warrior woman with a blood-soaked muzzle. However, Mancellor knew that Spades was likely not that easily vanquished.

The road through Savon had been narrow and crowded, tall buildings leaning this way and that, some as many as seven stories high. Even taller stone towers were thrust up here and there over the landscape of the city, most looking old and abandoned. To the right of the Preening Pintail was one of those tall gray towers, half-crumbled battlements circling its top, a large wooden door at its base. The foreboding tower cast a long shadow over the tavern itself and for some ominous reason filled Mancellor with unease. The two-story tavern and inn was a bulky wood-and-thatch building with a small two-horse stable directly to its left.

Mancellor made sure the battle-ax was secure against his back and the pouch with the angel stones snug in his pocket—a habit he had fallen into ever since taking the stones from Aeros. In fact, ever since Ten Cairn Abbey, whenever he dismounted, he checked the safety of the weapons and stones. The only thing he worried about was the helm on Liz Hen's head. But she insisted on guarding it in her own way. *Easier to wear it on my noggin than carry it around in hand.* And Mancellor had learned early on, it wasn't worth it to argue the point with her.

He took a deep breath, opened the tavern door, and stepped in. Liz Hen, Dokie, and Beer Mug followed. The Preening Pintail was dimly lit. It was hard to see coming from the bright outside. Rubbing his eyes, Mancellor almost walked past the Dayknight. But the knight stuck out his gauntleted hand and stopped him cold.

Mancellor's guard went up immediately. The knight had the most polished armor he had ever seen. It was almost staggering in its shiny cleanliness.

"Dogs ain't allowed." The Dayknight pointed at Beer Mug with one black-gauntleted hand. His voice was hollow behind the helm's black visor. Then the knight stood straighter. "What's that monstrous *thing* on your back?"

Mancellor took a cautious step back, fully conscious now of *Forgetting Moon* strapped over his shoulder.

"You can't just bring a weapon like that in here," the Dayknight said, motioning to the ax. "Stuff like that only invites trouble in a place like this. The crowds can be rough here. And the weird helmet on your friend's head has to go too. The dog, the ax, and the helm. Out. Now."

The knight was firm. Mancellor looked around, eyes now adjusted to the dim light. The shadowy tavern did not appear all that busy, a handful of customers and a serving girl. It was still early evening. Perhaps the rough crowds the knight spoke of arrived later. But the Dayknight was right. The huge and shiny battle-ax and helm were likely liabilities in a place like this. Mancellor found his hand had drifted protectively to the pocket holding the two angel stones.

"Is that paint smeared under your eyes?" the Dayknight asked. "Those markings look familiar to me. Have I seen you somewhere before? Have we met?"

"I doubt it." Mancellor's heart was beating a little faster now. He had met few Dayknights. In all his years of war he had never fought one. Fact was, the Dayknights of Gul Kana had mostly retreated from Wyn Darrè after Borden Bronachell had been killed. Aeros' army had raided up the western coast of Gul Kana north from Gallows Haven and had not seen one single Dayknight other than Leif Chaparral. Sure, there had been plenty of Dayknights fighting during the Battle of the Saint Only Channel. But that was all bloody chaos. *How could one of those knights recognize me now? And why would one of those knights be working as a doorman in a place like this?*

"Who are you?" the Dayknight pressed. "Why are you here?"

"I don't exactly know why we're here," Mancellor answered. "Or where we even are, really."

"You're at the Preening Pintail," the knight said.

Liz Hen removed *Lonesome Crown* and placed it in the crook of her right arm. Her short-cropped hair was aglow in the tavern's flickering torchlight. She ran her fingers through it in frustration. She asked the Dayknight, "Why is the duck on the sign outside licking its own arse?"

"It's preening itself," the Dayknight said.

Liz Hen's brow furrowed. "Preening means to lick one's own arse-hole?"

"No. Preening means . . ." The knight paused. "I don't know what it means. To clean yourself, maybe."

"So the duck is cleaning its own ass?" Dokie piped up, fully engaged in the conversation now.

"It's a preening pintail," the Dayknight answered. "That's all I know."

Liz Hen's brow furrowed even more. "But a pintail is definitely a duck?"

"Aye," the knight said. "Yes. A duck."

"You seem unsure about the whole thing." Liz Hen seemed less than satisfied with the knight's answers. "Besides, it's hard to understand anything you say from under that helm. Can't you take it off and have a normal conversation?"

"Is this a normal conversation for you?" the knight asked.

"Well, the signage is indeed frought with mighty peculiarities. Liz Hen shrugged. "Seems normal to me that one should attempt to suss out its origins."

"Huh?" the knight said.

"Just take off that shiny helm, would you? It's almost blinding me, it's so polished clean, which is weird, 'cause it's black, and this room is dim." She held up one hand over her eyes, squinting. "The lamplight is glaring off it something fierce."

"He ain't allowed to remove his helm." An older man with a leathery, wrinkled face walked up. He held out his hand for Mancellor to shake. Mancellor shook it.

"I'm Rutger. I own the place. And my doorman is right, can't have you carrying an ax like that in here. I don't much like the girl's horned helmet, either. Could poke somebody's eye out." He pointed to Beer Mug. "And for sure that dog has to go."

Rutger had a friendly smile under a droopy mustache but his words brooked no argument. Mancellor was more than reluctant to get into a tussle with either the innkeeper or the Dayknight. He figured they might as well leave.

"Do you know of any lodging that will accept weapons and dogs?" Mancellor asked.

"Well," Rutger said, eyeing Liz Hen up and down. "I'm in need of another serving wench. I've only one left, Luiza. She could use a hand. My last server lit out in the middle of the night not long ago. Lazy bitch. Completely undependable, that one. I could make an exception for your weapons and the dog if the girl is willing to work. Starting tonight."

"I'm a great serving girl." Liz Hen's answer was swift in coming. "Dependable and everything. I'm no lazy bitch. Ain't that the truth, Dokie?"

"She's not lazy at all," Dokie said.

"Splendid." Rutger nodded. "If you take the job, you can take lodging atop the tower with my doorman."

Liz Hen was nearly bursting with joy. Mancellor had never seen her so happy.

"Fact is"—Rutger eyed Mancellor up and down next—"with fall coming soon, things are liable to get much busier around here. I could use a second doorman if you're interested. I imagine we can rustle up some better armor than you got. Maybe even a sword. That ax would scare most customers off." Rutger looked down at Dokie. "Could use a dishwasher, too, and someone to help me with my candles. Laijon knows none of the locals want to work here."

"I can light the candles," Dokie said.

"No," the tavern owner said. "I need help making them."

"Oh." Dokie looked glum.

"I've been dreaming of a serving job ever since the Grayken Spear burned down," Liz Hen said, then crinkled her brow. "Arse-licking ducks aren't befitting a proper tavern sign, though. I'll have to paint over that."

"You'll leave the sign alone," Rutger said flatly.

"The sign remains the same, then," Liz Hen said.

"It's settled." Rutger seemed pleased. "You all can start now. Ser Lin will show you to your new quarters atop the tower. If the dog has trouble with the stairs, it can sleep underneath on the floor near the door."

"Beer Mug has never shied away from stairs," Liz Hen said. "Or glaciers."

"He looks to be a proper stout doggy." Rutger shook her hand, then turned to the Dayknight. "Show them to the tower, Ser Lin."

**

The Dayknight named Ser Lin led them from the tavern and out into the early-evening light. In the street, Ser Lin removed his black helm, holding it in the crook of his arm. Mancellor was startled to see how young the fellow was. Ser Lin also had a scarred and deformed face—as if the entire side of his head had been melted. The flesh covering his left cheek up to his forehead and down his neck was mangled, as were both of his ears. The purpled and yellowish-pale skin was a cracked and flaky mass. The knight's hair was blond and matted. His eyes were dark pits. And it was within those black pupils and irises that Mancellor sensed he somehow knew this man.

"Your ponies can stay in the stable with my horse," Ser Lin said. "But we'll leave them tethered here for now."

The deformed Dayknight led them to the wide door of the square tower, unlocked it, and led them inside. The tower was hollow from floor to ceiling. A steep staircase of dusty wood circled the inner walls of the tower clear to its heavy-timbered roof. The dirt floor was covered with a jumble of canvas-covered junk, wood, and coal. "Smells musty," Liz Hen commented.

"Rutger usually leaves the door unlatched so I can come and go as I want," Ser Lin said, "though I'd rather it be locked." He led them up the stairs, bulky black armor knocking against the stone wall and frail wooden railing. Mancellor found himself gripping the railing as he followed the Dayknight, *Forgetting Moon* heavy on his back. Liz Hen and Dokie gripped the rail too, *Lonesome Crown* still in the crook of Liz Hen's arm. Beer Mug navigated the stairs with ease, bringing up the rear. At the top of the stairs, a wooden doorway was set flat in the wooden ceiling. The Dayknight unlatched the door and pushed it up and over with his shoulders, revealing the clear evening sky above.

Mancellor stepped out onto the roof of the tower, a shudder rippling up his spine. "I've seen this place before," he muttered.

When I was underwater with the mermaid, I saw this very rooftop! Ser Lin was studying him curiously. *And why does this scarred-faced Dayknight look so familiar?*

Mancellor stood under a canvas canopy held up by four wooden poles, all leaning into each other and tied with rope at the top. The sun was going down over the tower's battlements to the west, and he could hear the rushing waters of a river far below. Near the door in the floor he saw Ser Lin's bedroll, along with a few other possessions. Next to the bedroll was a canvas stretched out over the wood, held down at all four corners by several good-sized rocks.

"What's under that canvas?" Liz Hen asked as she and Dokie stepped up into the evening light. Beer Mug bounded up behind her, the dog immediately exploring the entirety of the rooftop, sniffing at the stretched-out canvas curiously.

"You've seen this place before, haven't you?" the Dayknight asked Mancellor.

Mancellor was taken aback by the pointedness of the question and the earnest look on Ser Lin's young face. "This rooftop was in a dream I had once."

"I should let you all know, my name is not Ser Lin," the Dayknight said.

"Who are you?" Liz Hen asked.

"My real name is Lindholf Le Graven," the knight said. "My father is Lott Le Graven, Lord of Eskander." He paused then, as if expecting some sort of reaction. Mancellor, Liz Hen, and Dokie just stared at him. "Before I came here, I once had a dream of this tower too," Lindholf continued. "I was in Memory Bay, floundering in the water. A mermaid attacked me, pulled me beneath the sea. I saw visions in the water. Visions of this tower." He paused again, almost not even breathing, as if contemplating whether or not to say more, whether he *dared* say more. Mancellor could see the struggle within the young knight. Lindholf finally expelled a long pent-up breath. "I had visions of a man with smudges of paint under his eyes, smudges of paint like yours."

A quiet misgiving settled over Mancellor. "You had a vision of me?"

"I've been here in Savon some time now, wondering if I should leave. I've been looking for a sign to stay here in Savon. Praying for a sign." Lindholf held Mancellor's worried gaze. "And you are that sign."

"Me?"

"This place is important. This tower."

"Right," Liz Hen scoffed. "Doesn't look like much of a goin' concern to me." She reached into the folds of her tunic and pulled forth a flask of Blood of the Dragon and took a sip. Redness welled in her eyes. She had been nursing the poison from Ten Cairn Abbey all the way to Savon.

"Do you have any Shroud of the Vallè?" Lindholf asked her.

"What's that?" she replied.

"Nothing. The way you drank your drink just reminded me of it is all," Lindholf answered, pausing a moment. Then he went on. "That helm on your head, is it *Lonesome Crown?*"

Liz Hen nearly spat the red liquid from her mouth. "Why would you ask that?"

"Just a hunch." The young Dayknight turned to Mancellor. "Is that *Forgetting Moon?*" Lindholf didn't wait for an answer. He stepped carefully over to the canvas spread across the floor and kicked two of the rocks holding it down aside with his boot. He then reached down and folded the canvas back. Liz Hen gasped. Dokie stared. Even Beer Mug seemed enraptured by the sight. Mancellor took a step back. *Blackest Heart! Afflicted Fire! Ethic Shroud!* The names of the three remaining weapons of the Five Warrior Angels raced through his mind.

The black crossbow was in the center. The weapon appeared to be fashioned of some manner of wood Mancellor had never before seen. He marveled at its exquisite black string, perfect symmetry, and overall beauty. It had a delicate mechanism that seemed fitted specifically for a rare-sized quarrel.

To the left of the crossbow was a second weapon no less marvelous. It was a sword as pure and white as ice and as long as a man was tall. A bright round ruby was set in its pommel. The weapon's crescent-moon–shaped hilt-guard looked carved of one solid piece of pale bone. Its blade was forged of a mix of silver and translucent ivory and seemed to pulse red light from somewhere within. It was incredible.

"Where is it's sheath?" Mancellor asked. "The blade seems dangerous."

"It didn't come with a sheath," Lindholf said, shrugging. "It's just the way Seita carried it. And Gault too. I try and keep the blade wrapped mostly."

To the right of the black crossbow was the third item—a shield. Like the sword's cross-hilt, the brilliant shield was not fashioned of metal, iron, or even wood, but rather looked to be hewn of the most brilliant piece of walrus tusk or bone in the Five Isles. A glimmering pearl-colored inlay in the shape of a cross stretched across its magical surface.

Lindholf laid three small stones in front of each weapon; a shimmering white stone in front of the shield, a glowing red stone in front of the sword, and a black stone in front of the crossbow.

"Blackest Heart," Dokie muttered almost under his breath. He looked at Liz Hen. "It's the same crossbow I pulled out of that dark crypt in the mines up north."

"I can see that, you clodpole," Liz Hen said. "But why does this strange Dayknight have it now? Why does he have any of it? How did he get *Afflicted Fire* from Deadwood Gate? Seita and Nail and Stefan and the rest went for it." She pointed. "And why does that black stone look like it doesn't belong with the others?"

The girl was right. Whereas the red and white stones looked alive, the black stone looked as dead as a hunk of coal. Not knowing what else to do, Mancellor unstrapped the battle-ax from his back and placed it gently on the wooden slats next to *Ethic Shroud*. Liz Hen followed suit and set *Lonesome Crown* next to *Afflicted Fire*. Mancellor pulled the two angel stones from the pouch in his pocket. He set the blue one before *Forgetting Moon* and the green one before *Lonesome Crown*.

All the weapons and angel stones of the Five Warrior Angels were gathered together in one spot. It seemed like it should be a momentous occasion, yet Mancellor could not summon up the wonder in his heart that the moment must surely deserve. Looking at the deadness of the black angel stone was what caused his misgiving. The very night air he breathed seemed full of ill omen. He felt a stab of guilt knowing that he, like Lindholf, had prayed for a sign. And this was it. He had prayed for all signs to converge at this very place. And now he felt nothing but a deep dread, an ominous foreboding, as if this were the onset of something unimaginably ruinous and bad.

That was when he realized why the young Dayknight with the blond hair and black-pupiled eyes seemed so familiar. If not for the deformed face, Lindholf looked exactly like the Angel Prince, exactly like Aeros Raijael.

CHAPTER THIRTY-TWO
GAULT AULBREK

6TH DAY OF THE BLOOD MOON, 999TH YEAR OF LAIJON

LORD'S POINT, GUL KANA

G ault Aulbrek lingered at the rear of the crowded courtyard atop the dun-colored war charger he had stolen outside Amadon near a moon ago. He still wore the Dayknight armor and helm he had stolen that day too. He desperately wanted to replace the hot black armor and helm with more practical riding attire, but didn't for fear of being recognized as one of the three fugitives being hunted the breadth of Gul Kana.

"Fiery Absolution is upon us!" Ser Leif Chaparral's voice rang out over the courtyard. "That great and glorious day of Laijon's return is nigh!"

The tall Dayknight captain with black-rimmed eyes and long dark hair stood atop a stone podium in the middle of Lord's Point Square. A severely rotted corpse hung limp from the gallows pole behind Leif. Beyond the corpse, the spires of the city's cathedral rose up stark and black against the bright blue sky. Leif was clad in full Dayknight armor and livery, with the silver-wolf-on-a-maroon-field crest over his chest plate. A black sword with a black opal-inlaid pommel hung at his belt.

Two older knights flanked the Dayknight captain on either side. Gault recognized them as Leif's father, Lord Claybor Chaparral of Rivermeade, and Lord Le Graven of Eskander. Lord Claybor was a thick-boned man. He also wore the maroon raiment and silver-wolf crest of Rivermeade. Broad chest puffed out, he looked proud of his son. Lord Lott, on the other hand, was a thin man who wore a perpetually worried expression on his face. He was clothed in the crest of Eskander, a black lion on a yellow field, over his black armor. Gault wondered how much Lord Lott knew of his son, Lindholf, and if that was the cause of his distressed look.

"I have received glorious news from the Silver Throne!" Leif bellowed. A thunderous cheer of anticipation spread through the courtyard, rising over the city, drowning out Leif's voice. The riotous throng was teeming with a mixture of Dayknights, Silver Guards, and countless other soldiers dressed in the colorful armor and regalia representing the breadth of Gul Kana's cities and towns. They were packed shoulder to shoulder amid various townsfolk, banners and spears and swords bristling in the air.

At the break of dawn Gault had entered Lord's Point under the towering gate of the city's outer ring, traveling along the broad avenues and winding side streets of the city. Along the way he had come to appreciate Lord's Point for the beautiful city that it was. Fountains and statues dotted every square and corner, small fenced gardens and flowery porticoes lined every street. The towering spires of the castle and cathedral could be seen from every part of the city. And people were everywhere. Eventually he followed a growing throng of soldiers, shopkeepers, and peasants to the courtyard where Leif had gathered all his Dayknights.

It had been eight days since Gault had left Enna Spades and the burning hulk of the Bloody Stag behind. At first, he had made good time. But then his destrier had gone lame just outside Devlin. Gault had grown fond of the horse, so he was reluctant to abandon it. He settled into another backwoods inn and nursed the beast back to health before carrying on. It had taken him longer than expected to reach this city as a result. But he was in no hurry. He found he was growing more and more hesitant with his plans the closer to Saint Only he got. But now he was in Lord's Point, the Fortress of Saint Only a faint haze on the far horizon.

The roar of the crowd died and Leif continued. "Your king has spoken! The Silver Throne, along with the grand vicar and the quorum of five, have deemed the warriors who fought in the Battle of the Saint Only Channel heroes of our age!" The roar of the crowd rose anew. Leif soaked in the adulation before shouting above them, "Grand Vicar Denarius has claimed that in our defeat of Aeros Raijael, we have helped to usher in Laijon's return! We shall celebrate a great victory over our enemies with great celebration, for we have done our part!" More cheering.

Leif carried on, voice rising above the throng. "King Jovan! Grand Vicar Denarius! The quorum of five! Even Laijon himself! They all now command all our armies to retreat from Lord's Point and make for Amadon. And there we are to prepare for Fiery Absolution! When we go to battle again, it shall be when we again face Aeros Raijael and what remains of his armies at the foot of the Atonement Tree!" The roars died and the crowd grew silent at the news, perplexed that they were being asked to retreat after such a great triumph. Murmurs spread throughout the crowd. And Gault didn't blame them in their dismay, for what soldier wanted to give ground to an enemy they had just defeated?

Leif's voice now echoed in the silence as he shouted, "We all must bear in mind to obey the scriptures! We must fall back for Fiery Absolution to take place at the appointed place and the appointed time! We must all obey the words of *The Way and Truth of Laijon*!" He pointed to the rotting corpse dangling from the gallows pole just behind him. "This is what happens to those who go against the will of the holy book and the grand vicar! This is what happens when one goes against the will of Laijon! This man allowed one of Gul Kana's tender young women to arm herself and fight in the Battle of the Saint Only Channel! And he was hung for his crimes! Will you all be hung for your crimes if you do not do as ordered . . . ?"

Having heard enough of Leif Chaparral, Gault set heels to flanks and guided his horse through the crowd and out of the courtyard.

**

Gault drew his horse up to the shoreline. The heat of the sun made the horizon shimmer. A breeze whispered over the sand. Dust blew by. And the bloody, rotted lumps of the dead stretching out before his dry gaze seemed to writhe and float over the Saint Only Channel. It was low tide. The Battle of the Saint Only Channel had been a moon ago.

It took his eyes a moment to adjust to the gruesome sight. The landscape of the dry channel was a-litter with the torn and scattered remnants of battle. And the stench of the horrific slaughter yet lingered. Every human corpse appeared half-consumed by what carnivorous sea life crept in with the tides. Heaps of dead warhorses and gray mounds of sharks were scattered among the human dead like savage refuse, stark rows of rib cages jutting from the rotted-out flesh. Dead merfolk dotted the landscape too, sinuous forms half-buried in the sand, scales of their normally vibrant tails now lifeless and dull. Heaps of spoiled meat stretched in every direction as far as Gault's eyes could see. What few bits of armor and broken weaponry remained were naught but rusted junk. The stretch of sand had clearly been picked clean of what useful armor and weapons had been left.

Gault had always heard that the view from Lord's Point of both Adin Wyte and Wyn Darrè was the most spectacular in all the Five Isles. And, if not for the battle's carnage spread out before him, he would have believed it. Though he had spent much time in Saint Only, he had never seen its towering Mont and castle from the shores of Lord's Point. Ten miles away the Fortress of Saint Only rose against the far blue horizon. Harsh and foreboding and utterly magnificent, the fortress clung to a pinnacle of rock seven hundred feet above the dry channel, a beacon burning atop its loftiest tower. And through the crystal clear air, Gault could also indeed see Wyn Darrè and the thin soaring slivers of the five Laijon Towers rising needlelike in the far distance. The flames of those towers had been extinguished by Gault and the rest of Aeros' armies moons ago.

He stared across the expanse of sand, hesitant, wondering again if he was on the right path. *Ava Shay is there.* And he had given up the angel stones and weapons of the Five Warrior Angels for her. He had traveled the length of Gul Kana just to rescue her. And now, gazing out across this bitter battlefield, he was having second thoughts.

He knew that at high tide, the ten-mile strip of ocean that separated Saint Only from Lord's Point was normally around fifteen feet deep at the most. But the tide was out, the ocean bare. He had between four and six hours to make his way across the sand to Mont Saint Only, for when the tide did rise, it rose fast. It was this swift-rising tide that had killed near every rotting soul on the sand before him.

I've come this far. Gault spurred the horse to a trot. Onto the vast flat channel he ventured, a lone man on a withered landscape of sunbaked sand and sea-drenched death. He knew his journey must be quick. And as the horse carried him farther into the oppressive reek of the channel, he formulated his plan.

He slowly peeled off his black Dayknight armor, tossing it to the sand under him, glad to be rid of it, knowing he would need it no more. Gault knew the Saint Only fortress. He knew of the secret tunnels and passageways at the base of the Mont that Spades had talked of. And Enna Spades had told him exactly where Aeros would be keeping Ava Shay.

And Laijon gave unto the Warrior Angels the power against unclean
spirits, the power to cast the wraiths from the faithful.
—THE WAY AND TRUTH OF LAIJON

CHAPTER THIRTY-THREE

AVA SHAY

6TH DAY OF THE BLOOD MOON, 999TH YEAR OF LAIJON

SAINT ONLY, ADIN WYTE

A s Spiderwood had predicted, the White Prince summoned everyone to Bruce Hall. Ava Shay wore a simple tan dress to the summoning, no finery or jewels. Today would be the day of her escape from the White Prince. She felt the fear and nervous energy in her every bone. But after killing Ivor Jace, she also felt confident. She even wore My Heart into Bruce Hall with scant fear.

As of late, Aeros had been calling her his Princess with a Blade. The thin weapon was settled firmly within its sheath and the sheath secured to the black leather belt around her waist with a thick white string. She couldn't help but constantly caress the red ruby fixed atop the sword's hilt as she entered the massive hall brimming with nearly a hundred of Aeros' soldiers.

To Ava, it seemed the Spider had responded to the summons with a sharpened purpose of his own. *I have done something that will soon un-doubtedly put me at irreversible odds with the Angel Prince,* he had once said. And today would be the culmination of that reckoning. Today the Spider, Jenko Bruk, and Ava Shay had planned to kill Aeros Raijael.

The Bloodwood had positioned himself and his demon-eyed steed under the moldering serpent's head mounted over the mantel. He stood alone with his arms folded over his black leather armor, a grim look on his chiseled face, some distance from the other hundred knights gathered in the hall. The Bloodeye stallion eyed several nearby hounds, the shaggy remnants of Edmon's collection of dogs that still lingered in the hall.

Jenko Bruk seemed tense, eyes bouncing around the roomful of knights. In shined armor he stood beside Hammerfiss, sword at his hip, helm in the crook of his arm. The red-haired giant was also in full Knight Archaic armor and livery, round iron shield and huge ball mace strapped to his back. The sharpened spikes and barbs of the mace glistened in the torchlight of the hall. Hammerfiss, helm also under his arm, looked ready for a fight. His tattooed face was fierce and determined.

Aeros Raijael, in a white robe and polished chain mail, entered the hall with young Leisel at his side. The slight girl was clothed in a peach-colored gown of silken make, lace at the sleeves and an ornate silver brooch with a blue stone fixed in its center at her neck. Her face was painted in much makeup: thick black eyeliner, dark red lips, and pink blush about her pale cheeks.

The White Prince commanded the room upon entry. He marched confidently through the hall full of knights. Once in the center of the room, he let go of Leisel's hand and stood atop a table. "I've seen many visions!" he announced. "Absolution is nigh! And the weapons of the Five Warrior Angels shall soon return to me!"

The chamber was silent. Ava had heard Aeros speak of visions before. But she had never heard him speak of them openly to anyone else. He continued, "I've received word from my spy across the channel that Leif Chaparral will be pulling all Gul Kana troops from Lord's Point. The armies of Gul Kana will be retreating back to Amadon."

There was a rustle of confused murmurs throughout the crowd.

"They are just giving up?" Hammerfiss scowled.

"Fear not," Aeros continued. "Your lust for battle shall not go unslaked, Ser Hammerfiss. If Leif does abandon Lord's Point, then the armies of Sør Sevier shall leave Saint Only and launch a renewed attack across the channel and continue toward Amadon and Absolution. If what my spy says is true, we shall meet with scant resistance in our trek along the King's Highway and onward to Amadon."

"Doesn't sound like much of a battle to me," Hammerfiss growled.

"Do you truly wish for a fight?" Aeros glared down at Hammerfiss.

"I need blood." Hammerfiss nodded. "You know that I do."

"Then you shall have it," Aeros said, fierce, dark eyes raking the crowd, settling on Spiderwood under the serpent's head. The Bloodwood and the Bloodeye stood as rigid as two oaks in front of the hearth and mantel. The stallion's red eyes glowed in bleak contrast to the dull, dead orbs of the gruesome serpent's head.

"In fact"—Aeros turned back to Hammerfiss—"you shall have your blood today, right here and right now. For there is one bloody bit of business we must settle before launching our might back across the channel."

"And what bloody business is that?" Hammerfiss asked.

"Yes." The Spider drifted into the center of the hall like a dark cloud, the cold gaze of his red-shot eyes cutting through the air, cloak billowing out behind him. "Pray tell, Lord Aeros, what things must needs be settled?"

"I think we all know," Aeros said, the look on his face as stark and unforgiving.

It was all going just as the Spider had told Ava it would. *Today we slay the White Prince!* Ava's grip tightened around the top of her sword. She felt the heart-shaped ruby hot against the palm of her hand. *Today I am free!* Her heart galloped as the Bloodwood faced the White Prince.

"You have betrayed me, brother." Aeros spoke loudly enough for all to hear. "You fed Ava Shay poisons, thus killing my innocent unborn whilst it grew in her womb."

A chill settled over Ava. *The Spider fed me poisons?* Aeros had hinted at it before. It wasn't a question but likely a fact. Her worried gaze flew to the Bloodwood, then to Jenko Bruk, finding he was already studying her carefully, a concerned disquiet flushing his features. *He never knew I was pregnant.* The miscarriage had been the worst moment of her life, seeing so much blood on the sheets. *Have we been betrayed again?* Her eyes hardened as she looked at the Spider. *Has he truly betrayed us?* Her confidence wavered, the roiling emotions in her taking over.

"Nobody has a right to take the life of the unborn," Aeros went on, eyes digging into the Spider, "especially if that unborn is mine."

But you yourself drowned a baby just outside Leifid! Ava wanted to scream the White Prince's hypocrisy to the world. *Every man betrays!* She had watched Aeros take the babe toward the creek. Later watching that same babe floating dead in the water. *But isn't that the way of these fanatics of Raijael?* Ava asked herself. She figured Aeros could call down a disaster from heaven and drown a million babies in a torrential flood and call it righteous, as long as it was written in scripture, as long as enough hypocritical fanatics agreed. *And together they have killed my baby!* She didn't know who she hated more, Aeros or the Bloodwood.

"Do you deny what you have done?" Aeros asked.

"You levy serious accusations," the Spider answered, narrow brows sharpening. "Are you prepared to defend them, brother?"

"Do you deny the accusation?" Aeros followed flatly.

"Do I deny that I murdered *your* baby?" the Bloodwood asked, a vaporous, icy venom in his voice. "What if the baby was Ser Jenko's, or Ser Gault's, or even mine?"

Aeros' pale face twisted in rage. "Today you shall finally suffer my full wrath!"

"And I shall gladly fight you." A black dagger appeared in the Spider's hand. He commanded the attention of all now. "Then I shall fight Hammerfiss. Then I shall fight the next and the next until every knight in this chamber is dead."

"Let me kill him, my lord!" Hammerfiss bellowed, eyes burning with rage. He held the huge ball mace out before him in both hands, its barbs and spikes bristling. "Let me finish the Chivalric Rule of Blood Penance this rat so cowardly snubbed on the beaches of Bedford Bay. Let me bring an end to him now, once and for all!"

"As you wish." Aeros bowed to the large man with an unmistakable courtesy. "Blood Penance must be served. You've my permission to kill him."

The Bloodwood turned to Hammerfiss, dark eyes lancing into the larger man. Brandishing a second dagger, he crouched into a fighting stance. "Today you will suffer the punishment of a bleating cur, and suffer it at my hand. This is a duel long coming."

"Everyone stand back!" Aeros ordered. A circle formed around the combatants. "Let the fight begin!"

The coiled tension in Bruce Hall was thick. Hand on the hilt of her sword, even Ava Shay could feel the weight of this moment deep down in her gut. She had been on the beachhead in Bedford Bay when Aeros had invoked the Chivalric Rule of Blood Penance and the Bloodwood had chosen the flogging at the hands of Hammerfiss rather than the duel. But the Spider would be quick to kill Hammerfiss now. Was she was prepared to fight her way free of this chamber at his side? He said he would throw her a wink when it was time. *But did he poison my child?* A wink and she was to pull her own blade and stick it in Aeros. *Was Jenko ready too?* He looked as anxious as she. Did he also feel the same betrayal that she now felt?

Hammerfiss centered himself before the Bloodwood. "You have proved time and again to be without honor!" he shouted, his tattooed face a rash of red. "Now you shall truly learn how respect is earned in battle with hard steel! One cannot cheat their way into it with sneaky assassin ways! Now it is time you truly pay the butcher's bill!"

The Spider's bloodshot eyes narrowed to cold slits as he deftly flipped both daggers in the air, catching them, doing it again, beckoning the bigger man to attack. "Yes, this day *has* been long in the coming," he said, control infused in his every word as he tossed his daggers. Then he stopped, pointed one black blade at Hammerfiss. "This day has been in the offing ever since you so gleefully and cowardly flogged me when I could not fight back. But now I am in perfect health. And oh how my blades so thirst."

"Then let's fight," Hammerfiss snarled, huge ball mace raised. "Enough jabber."

The Bloodwood slowly began circling the other man, daggers poised. "I shall kill you, Ser Hammerfiss, but not before I quote your own words back to you, words you spoke that day in Bedford Bay, words from the Chivalric Rule of Blood Penance that you so eloquently repeated, 'May this flogging be a gift unto our Lord Aeros,' you said, 'a lord who communes with both Laijon the Father and Raijael the Son.'"

The Spider flicked one of the daggers in the air again, catching it by the blade this time, readying it to throw. "You, Ser Hammerfiss, disgust me. Let the pain I am about to inflict upon you be a reminder of whom it is you serve. And the one whom you serve is the White Prince. And it is time we all escape the false yoke of Raijael."

It was brief, but the Spider winked at Ava on the last word, then nodded toward Jenko Bruk. *The signal!*

A split-second distraction—the wink and nod.

But it was all the opening Hammerfiss needed as his ball mace came thundering down atop the Bloodwood. The wicked, heavy weapon crushed the assassin's head like a melon, continuing downward, pulverizing his neck and shoulders and splitting his body nearly in two pieces. Brains, skin, guts, and black leather armor splattered out in every direction as the two black daggers clattered to the floor.

Ava stared. The amount of blood seemed unreal as the two split pieces of the assassin's smashed body slithered to the cobbles, black cloak fluttering down, covering half the carnage.

For Ava, all hope of escape dissolved into an ocean of grief and despair. *Now that is how to kill a man,* the Spider had once said during her training in the stables. *Strike when he is either not paying attention or boasting. Strike when he is least expecting it.* And the Bloodwood had fallen prey to his own certainty and assertion.

And now their plan to kill Aeros was over.

Hammerfiss swung his bloody mace up and around once more, bringing it crashing down on the dead man again, pounding the macerated corpse further into the cobbled floor. Then the red-haired giant spit on the puddle of black cloak and black leather and mangled flesh and stood back, a crazed grin on his tattooed face, the bangles and fetishes in his beard jangling in triumph.

Near the great hearth, Scowl loosed a violent scream. All the hounds jumped, yelping as the black stallion reared up on hind legs, front hooves pawing at the air, eyes fiery. "Someone grab that horse!" Aeros yelled.

The stallion was lassoed thrice around the neck by three eager Rowdies and brought to bay. The knights held the ropes firm to keep the lathered horse still.

"That stallion is mine!" Hammerfiss marched toward the hearth and the enraged Bloodeye. He dragged the mace along the cobbles behind him, heavy iron tines scraping across the stone and leaving a scarlet trail of gore.

"Everything that was once that foul assassin's is now mine!" The red-haired warrior planted himself before the hearth and mantel and the struggling Bloodeye. Then his fierce eyes found the half-rotted serpent's head mounted on the wall above. He swung the mace at the severed head, knocking it from the wall. The serpent's head thudded to the floor near the Bloodeye, causing the horse to buck and bray again, the three knights trying their utmost to keep the demon-eyed beast under control.

"Everything he once owned is now mine!" Hammerfiss shouted, letting the mace clatter to the floor, and tried to mount Scowl. But the Bloodeye fought against him with a furious bucking and thrashing. "Bloody fuck!" Hammerfiss shouted, and gave up. "I will tame the wild monster, I swear it!"

"And I for one believe you," Aeros said with a casual ease that did not match the bloody chaos surrounding him. Leisel stood at his side, horror etched on her face as she stared at the bloody pile that used to be Spiderwood. It was by far the most emotion Ava had ever seen on the girl's innocent, pale face. She caught the startled gaze of Jenko Bruk and then quickly looked away.

Aeros caught their exchanged glance and chuckled, motioning to the ravaged corpse of the Bloodwood at his feet. "It amuses me to see how drama-like this finally turned out." His eyes burned into Ava's. "Did you really think you could slay me along with a chamber of a hundred knights and then just ride off into the sunset?" He laughed. "Spiderwood was always a fool."

The smell of death hit Ava—death mixed with that scent of polished leather and cloves. The aroma reminded her of that very first time she had ridden on the back of the Spider's horse on the beaches of Gallows Haven. She forced herself to look down at the man's mutilated body. Several of the hounds were now sniffing around the Spider's crushed body, licking at the bloody cobbles, nibbling at some of the scattered lumps of flesh. *Was he ever my friend?*

The hounds began tearing at the assassin's leather armor and skin with more fervor now, growling as they feasted. Ava watched in terror as one of the dogs pulled a bloody string from the pile of flesh with its teeth. It was a leather necklace.

Dangling from one of the dog's teeth—a small birch-wood carving of a beetle. It was the very necklace she had given the Bloodwood a little more than two moons ago.

Any weapon forged of pure dragon bone can shatter iron
and metal with both spark and flame.
—THE MOON SCROLLS OF MIA

CHAPTER THIRTY-FOUR
STEFAN WAYLAND

6TH DAY OF THE BLOOD MOON, 999TH YEAR OF LAIJON

WROCLAW, GUL KANA

The full moon hung high and a million stars glimmered, illuminating the grim surroundings in a wan, ashen light. Stefan Wayland could scarcely look over the landscape without feeling the bile creep up his throat. Hundreds of humans, both male and female, were impaled on towering wooden stakes in every direction around the cauldron of boiling blood as far as his eyes could see.

It was a Hragna'Ar sacrifice to call the five dragons back from the skies.

Some of the humans yet lived, for the wooden stake had somehow followed the contours of their spines from anus to mouth, avoiding all vital organs. He had watched the oghuls impale the people. He had learned how it was done. Now the ones that still lived were writhing and moaning in pain, round eyes pointed skyward, gaping mouths wide in silent screams, their naked chests rising and falling with each pained breath. Dried blood streaked the poles under their clenched and curled feet.

The vast Hragna'Ar army was chanting and howling in the midst of this ghostly forest of pale humanity, their rusted weapons and armor jagged and stark against the gloom of the pallid night. To Stefan, the immensity of the oghuls' roar was like the rushing rivers and plunging waterfalls of the Sky Loch glaciers.

The five Aalavarrè Solas stood together before the cauldron of boiling blood, all of them now staring up into the sky, colorful armor glowing in the night. The black basin before them was suspended above a roaring fire, flame curling up around the bulk of the heavy iron. The saber-toothed lion stood with Stefan, silver eyes roaming the dark.

Stefan didn't know whether he was more disturbed by the hundreds of impaled humans, or the cauldron of boiling blood—human blood drained from the impaled. It was a suppressed memory, but he now recalled his own horrific journey, crawling from a similar boiling cauldron, born anew of scorch and blood and Hragna'Ar. It was just such a sacrificial ceremony as this that had brought him back from the dead. A test, Mud had called it. He had crawled from the cauldron, legs healed, sight and memory covered in a filmy silver haze. He wanted to vomit just thinking of it.

Am I some demon of the underworld? A wraith?

Somehow he knew he was neither, for he had never felt so healthy in his life. He still couldn't believe he could walk after how broken his legs had been. Yes, he was in full health, other than the strange silver veins crawling under his skin. They oft itched and flared in pain, especially when he looked upon the crescent-moon carvings and shooting stars on the colorful dragon-scale armor of the five Aalavarrè Solas.

The Aalavarrè were also Cauldron Born. Stefan wondered if he was connected to them somehow, other than as their servant. The black saber-tooth with the silver eyes and silver teeth was Cauldron Born too. The cat stood beside him now, warm fur brushing against his side. The lion was growing ever more protective and attached to him. *But what does it all mean? The saber-tooth? The cauldron of blood? The silver haze constantly before my eyes?*

I should be with my friends, Nail, Dokie . . .

But he knew he could not leave. *I am tied to the dragons. I can feel it*. But it had been almost a full moon since anyone had seen the five dragons. This new blood sacrifice of Hragna'Ar was meant to call out to Viper and summon their return . . .

. . . and summon their return it had.

For suddenly they arrived. The beasts of the underworld. High above Wroclaw.

Like colorful glowing angels, all five dragons, soaring, sailing. White. Blue. Green. Red. Their great wings split the air, clawing across the starlit sky. Even the black dragon seemed to glow with some unexplainable light against the dark of the sky.

Stefan was once again confused by this new life he found himself living. The saber-toothed lion purred loud at his side. He could feel the rumble deep in its chest.

All the myriad of humble prayers he had uttered to Laijon as a child— and none of them had come true. And it was those simple unanswered prayers that had turned him into an unbeliever. Yet blood sacrifice and oghul chanting could summon dragons.

Each of the five enormous creatures flying above roared with thunderous anticipation and unrest, the intensity of their sound thundering like a shattered anvil across the land, shaking the very ground, nearly drowning out the Hragna'Ar army. *"Caldrun Born! Caldrun Born! Rogk Na Ark! Rogk Na Ark!"* Around the cauldron, thousands of Hragna'Ar oghuls now danced and chanted, *"Rogk Na Ark! Rogk Na Ark! Rogk Na Ark! Caldrun Born! Caldrun Born!"* Their rusted armor bristled and clattered and clanked amongst the forest of the impaled.

And like five resurrected angels the dragons soared, their great wings raking the air, cutting through the clouds, each of them still roaring in riotous thunder.

Stefan couldn't escape the numbing thought that this scene existed in someone else's dream, that it wasn't real, that he himself and the blood-filled cauldron and dragons circling above were no more than a figment of another's mad delusions.

How can it be that I, an insignificant boy from Gallows Haven, am part of such dread and terrible events? He was witnessing the worst parts of *The*

Way and Truth of Laijon come true before his very eyes. At the thought, ideas jumped and hissed in his head. *Deadwood Gate! I am still in those mines and this is all a dream, all delusion, all madness!* Yes, this was Deadwood Gate and his mind was locked away in total darkness, and death stalked him constantly like a poisoned cloud. It felt like he was even starting to form thoughts in the same poetic tongue of the Aalavarrè Solas. And the more time he spent around the five Cauldron Born, the more he believed there were a million universes, a million forms of mind, a million paths to follow.

That's how far gone my mind is.

I have been reborn under a treacherous star!

A voice called out, "Dragons! I can hear their cry. And a glorious cry it is, transforming me with both light and being! In my life before, the only imaginable light was living like flowing silver in my skull, brimming with scant liquid color and movement, naught but blackness folding in on itself deep, deep, deep within the underworld, for years upon years, a thousand years, where everything smelled of ancient dust! Now, having spent so much time meandering like a rootless phantom where such dark reigned eternal, where all threads of silver were doomed to singing in endless night, I can finally see! Yes! We must all of us open our eyes to this miracle of Viper and Hragna'Ar and *see!*"

Stefan thought the musical voice was shouting within his own head. But it was not. It was Icelyn the White, her voice ringing out into the night. "Use your eyes of silver, my fellow Cauldron Born! See what you can with them before they are forever again dimmed! Use this new life in the Great Above for the virtue of our kin and the destruction of our enemy! Hear the call of the Dragon Claw, for scorch and blood and the boiling cauldrons of Hragna'Ar are the mother of the Aalavarrè Solas."

Icelyn approached the cauldron. Aamari-Laada the Red, Raakel-Jael the Green, Sashenya the Black, and Basque-Alia the Blue followed just behind her, each Aalavarrè girt in their colorful dragon-scale armor, scorch whips coiled at their belts, pale faces hidden behind silver masks of Skull. The oghuls' chanting and dancing near the cauldron gave the group of five Aalavarrè a wide berth.

The black saber-toothed lion hissed, flashing long, wicked fangs, muscles along its broad back rippling as it circled around the cauldron, eyeing the glowing coals beneath with impenetrable silver eyes.

Mud Undr'Fut and another blunt-faced oghul in thick leather armor brought forth a middle-aged human male. The Hragna'Ar high priest, Sledg H'Mar, followed behind. He carried a large stone bowl filled with silver scorch.

Mud and the other oghul handled the man roughly, bearing the poor fellow up by his arms, his sandaled feet dragging through the dirt. The man's hollow eyes were partly hidden behind a web of scraggly brown hair. He wore naught but a long white tunic that covered him to his knees, cinched with a belt of thin elk hide.

Another burly oghul in scraps of armor brought forth two wooden oars with flat, broad heads. He carried one in each hand and stood at attention whilst Mud and the blunt-faced oghul hauled the man up to face the cauldron of boiling blood.

The rim of the cauldron was chest-high, and the man looked down into its boiling horrors with wide, fearful eyes.

Icelyn the White pulled her sword and strode forward. "Worry not," she said to the man as she placed the edge of her sword to his neck. "Crane your neck and look up to the sky, look up to the dragons above."

The frightened man did as ordered.

Sledg H'Mar lifted the stone bowl of silver scorch above the man's upturned face. Then the oghul tipped the bowl and a tiny stream of silver poured into the man's left eye. The silver liquid burned the screaming fellow's eye away with sizzle and smoke.

Sledg H'Mar dripped more of the silver scorch into the man's right eye too, burning it away along with half the man's face.

Icelyn stepped back and pulled hard on her sword, opening the man's throat almost to the spine. Blood pumped thick and red from the wound into the cauldron, mixing with the boiling scarlet of a hundred other humans. Sledg H'Mar dumped the remaining scorch into the cauldron, silver swirling with the boiling blood.

The dragons above screeched and roared even louder now, stirring and shaking the air. They circled lower now, great wings blotting out the sun, colorful eyes luminous and glowing and hungry. *The miracles of Hragna'Ar bring the dragons lower!* Stefan's mind raged with both confusion and joy.

Mud and the blunt-faced oghul hauled the dead man up higher, dumping his entire body into the large boiling cauldron, where it sank and disappeared.

The vast sea of Hragna'Ar oghuls chanted, *"Caldrun Born! Caldrun Born! Caldrun Born!"* And, to the rhythm of their booming sound, the blood in the cauldron churned with a life of its own, large welling boils of spitting scarlet and silver curled over the cauldron's rim, spilling down its side in crooked, glowing streams.

The burly oghul with the two broad-headed oars stepped forward. He handed one of the oars to the blunt-faced oghul next to Mud. Then each oghul dipped an oar down into the roiling, burbling blood, stirring. Clouds of steam rose.

The five dragons circling above became more and more agitated, screeching louder now, snapping at each other. Two of the beasts, the Blue and the Green, broke away from the others and grappled in midair, raking with long hind claws. They finally latched onto each other. Twisting and turning, great leathery wings flapping uncontrollably, they plummeted from the sky. Heart in his gut, Stefan watched the two dragons dropped, spinning and tumbling.

The two beasts crashed thunderously to the ground amid impaled humans and the shouts of scattering oghuls. Dust billowed up and the two dragons continued to gnash and claw before they finally broke apart. The Blue towered on hind legs, backing the Green down with a loud roar, wings spread wide and threatening, knocking over more of the impaled dead. The Green cowered, then leaped back up into the sky, great wings flapping in hasty retreat. Silence followed the battle.

The blue dragon faced the cauldron. Basque-Alia removed his mask of Skull. "Come," he said. At the sound of Basque-Alia's voice, the Blue's wings folded inward, large scaled head cocked to the side. The blue dragon then lumbered warily forward, azure dragon scales and muscles rippling with every step, oghul warriors scrambling out of its way. The beast knocked more of the impaled aside, then drew up before Basque-Alia, head held high.

Basque-Alia shed his blue gauntlet, stepped forward, reached out, and stroked the shimmering scales under the beast's neck with the palm of his own pale hand. Stefan wondered if the brave Aalavarrè would attempt to ride the Blue. But the dragon's fierce, glowing eyes were focused on the two oghuls, who had stopped stirring the cauldron of blood, bloody oars held aloft. The dragon roared in the direction of the cauldron. Basque-Alia backed away.

"Continue," Icelyn urged the two oghuls.

The oghuls dipped their oars back into the boiling blood and stirred. All eyes were on the cauldron now as the two oghuls tried to lift a large sack of red viscera and goo from the boiling scorch and blood with the leverage of their two broad oars combined.

Wary, heart thumping in his own chest, Stefan looked on in nervous fascination as a human-sized sack of scarlet viscera emerged from the cauldron under the oars, stretched and heaving and dripping with gore. Indeed, some living thing was moving, slithering within the bloody sack, trying to escape. The two oghuls managed to lift the squirming *thing* over the side of the cauldron.

It flopped to the ground in a red pile of blood, some writhing creature still struggling to escape. *The man they killed, come back to life!* Stefan could not break his gaze away from this new horror, a horror he felt possibly hinted at his own rebirth, his own possible journey from the bloody cauldron. The black saber-tooth grew agitated at his side, baring long fangs, hissing and growling.

Sledg H'Mar stepped forward, drawing a serrated dagger from his belt. He sliced open the squirming sack. And as Stefan had predicted, out spilled the murdered man, pale face streaming with rivulets of blood, mouth and lungs once again heaving for air.

The new Cauldron Born had eyes of silver.

Stefan took a step back. The saber-tooth roared into the night, a horrific sound. The once-dead man screeched in return, stark and shrill, languid fingers clawing at the dirt as he pulled himself free of his bloody birthing sack. But his silver eyes turned almost instantly black, the tips of his fingers, too. The rot that ate at this new Cauldron Born spread like black flickering flame and crooked lightning over the man's pale, silver-veined skin.

Stefan's startled eyes flew to his own silver veins. *What am I?* He thought of the green elixir Mud often fed him. It was the only thing that seemed to quench his constant thirst. *Is it rotting me, too?* He watched as the new Cauldron Born, screaming in great pain now, coiled up and shriveled into a black and twisted corpse, stiff and dead once again. *It is all so wrong!* Stefan's mind screamed over and over and over.

The blue dragon roared its own displeasure. Icelyn the White crouched by the rotting black corpse and sliced both ears from its head. There was no blood, just ash drifting into the air from twin holes. And the blue dragon kept roaring.

Basque-Alia reached out one hand to calm the dragon. The blue beast leaned into his touch, agitated voice now just a low rumble. Basque-Alia then dug into the folds of his dark cloak and brought forth a fistful of Shroud of the Vallè.

He tossed the white powder into the air before the Blue's face and backed away.

The dragon breathed the floating Shroud deep into its heaving lungs. Then *fire!*

Fire, orange and hot, burst from the beast's mouth and nostrils. The funnel of curling flame struck the dead Cauldron Born, burning and twisting the man's corpse into naught but a pile of blackened char and ash.

Silence.

Then the dragon launched itself high into the air, great wings taking flight, stirring the air as it flew away. Stefan watched in both dread and wonder as the great blue beast joined its four companions high above and disappeared into the night.

"It is clear." Icelyn's voice broke the quiet. "Further Hragna'Ar sacrifice is fruitless. We must head south now. We must make haste. We must move the armies of Hragna'Ar toward Absolution. We must prepare ourselves for when the beasts of the underworld are truly ready to claim us as their own. We must ready ourselves for when the remaining hordes of Aalavarrè follow those streams of silver up from the depths of the underworld. We must ready ourselves for when the Dragon, our master, arrives with the armies of all Vallè."

Icelyn turned to the other four Aalavarrè, bowing to them one at a time. "Only we meager five have opened our eyes to crystal vision and borne witness. The stars were not myth. Starlight was real. And the vastness in the Great Above is indeed a brilliant wonder. Viper hath carved out the underworld with great sharp scales of silver and sinew, carved it out with the sole purpose of arising from the deep in anger, marching to the call of the Burning Tree. There is no other way for the millions of Aalavarrè to emerge from the underworld than through Viper, no other way for those banished millions to march up among the bones of the human dead. For 'tis Viper who writes across the sun and the dawn and the rain with lightning and starshine and the shimmering borealis. 'Tis Viper who is our salvation. We must now move toward Fiery Absolution and the cross-shaped altar. We must move toward resurrecting our Immortal Lord."

If someone is mean, then they shall always remain mean. If someone is prideful, then they shall always remain prideful. When someone shows you who they are, you are commanded to believe them. People rarely change. Most will make the same mistakes over and over, be it choosing the wrong relationships, or be it becoming addicted to the alchemy of the Vallè. Most will repeat the same mistakes even unto their death.
—THE WAY AND TRUTH OF LAIJON

CHAPTER THIRTY-FIVE
TALA BRONACHELL

6TH DAY OF THE BLOOD MOON, 999TH YEAR OF LAIJON

AMADON, GUL KANA

It was only midday, but inside the Filthy Horse Saloon, things were dark and muggy. The two flickering sconces added to the saloon's heat, dancing and fooling with Tala Bronachell's already wavering vision in torturous ways. Drowsy, she fought to stay awake. Lawri was already peacefully asleep in the chair next to Tala. She cradled the silver gauntlet in her lap. *The thing is a horror, a misshapen abomination.* Tala didn't even like looking at it.

"We should go to Savon," Jondralyn said. "In fact, we should have departed days ago." Hawkwood, Jondralyn, and Val-Draekin sat at the table opposite Tala.

Jondralyn had been making her case to leave the Filthy Horse Saloon and Amadon for some time now. She'd been arguing the point ever since Delia had arrived with her news of Lindholf and the weapons of the Five Warrior Angels seven days ago.

The saloon was stuffy, and Tala wiped at her brow with a kerchief she had found behind the bar. She wished the place had a proper bath, not just an iron tub in one of the back rooms. Her leather pants and shirt were soaked in sweat. Nail looked miserable from the muggy air too. Blond locks of hair clung to his forehead, matted and damp. The Gallows Haven boy sat next to Tala and Lawri in the center of the dim-lit saloon.

Cromm Cru'x sat next to Bronwyn Allen atop the bar, both of them with their legs dangling over the edge of it. The oghul was clad in sweat-stained leather armor and crude chain mail. His huge square maul rested on the bar at his side. Bronwyn's dark green cloak was thrown over her shoulder. The white feathers in her hair were glimmering wedges in the dim light. Tala wondered if they both wouldn't soon go their own way. They were not taking part in the conversation, spending more and more time alone at the bar away from the others.

Bronwyn and Cromm had carried Delia's stiff body from the Filthy Horse Saloon the very morning they had found the barmaid hanging. Where they had dumped her body, nobody knew. Nobody had asked. Tala had no idea why Delia had hung herself. She hadn't seemed suicidal. Sure, the girl had been upset about her father, but she had shown no signs of true depression. And Tala knew true depression, true hopelessness, for ever since fleeing Amadon Castle, the wraiths assailed her in torrents; like a rustling storm they growled and whispered in her ear, bright and constant and heavy with despair.

"We must go to Savon," Jondralyn pressed.

"Go to Savon?" Val-Draekin questioned. "To what purpose? You've been talking of Savon now for days. Why do you think it's important? Because of what the barmaid who killed herself said?"

"I thought the aim of the Brethren was clear," Jondralyn said, concern in her gaze. "Retrieve the angel stones along with the weapons of the Five Warrior Angels. We must use them to fight Aeros Raijael and stave off Fiery Absolution. We must go to Savon and get them."

Val-Draekin met her concerned look. "No matter how evil you think Aeros Raijael and the marauding armies of Sør Sevier to be, there will always be someone more evil, more full of murder and deception and betrayal."

"What do you mean?" Jondralyn asked, annoyed.

"What if it is all a lie?" Val-Draekin continued. "What if everything Delia told us was a lie? She did hang herself, after all. We cannot interrogate her further."

Jondralyn straightened in her chair. "You think Delia's story of *Afflicted Fire* and *Blackest Heart* and *Ethic Shroud* being in Savon could be false?"

"It is a possibility," Hawkwood said.

Jondralyn glared at Hawkwood. "I say it is a fortuitous boon the girl returned here to this saloon with such crucial information." She leaned toward the Sør Sevier man, a resolute glint in her eye. "When I was sick, in the infirmary, recovering from my injuries, I dreamed of you. I dreamed of Savon. I had a vision that all the weapons of the Five Warrior Angels would be gathered in that city." She shifted forward in her chair. "I am the *Princess*! I shall go to Savon myself if need be. You once believed in me. You once believed we would be together in the end. Do you not still?"

Hawkwood's face remained cold and unreadable in the yellow light of the saloon's sconces.

Val-Draekin took a sip of ale. He met Jondralyn's hardened gaze with one of his own. "What if there were things about *The Moon Scrolls of Mia* that Roguemoore was not privy to, things that he did not tell us?"

"Things like what?" Jondralyn asked.

"Like what if the entire legend of the Five Warrior Angels and their weapons and angel stones is a lie?"

"How can you say that?" Jondralyn asked pointedly, her tone aghast. "After all that we have worked for? After all that the Brethren of Mia have worked for? After all that Ser Roderic Raybourne worked his entire life for? All that my father worked for? After all that the Company of Nine has suffered, all that heartache and pain you yourself and Nail were a part of? How can you even suggest such a thing?"

"I suggest it merely to get you to think," Val-Draekin answered. "So you do not go dragging Hawkwood or anyone else off on some fool's mission to Savon for ancient artifacts that may be useless to us now, that may have always been useless."

It seemed as if the Vallè was baiting Jondralyn now, provoking her ire for some strange purpose of his own. *Like Seita played me!* Tala had heard the conversation between Seita and Val-Korin. Her senses were alert now, for she knew that Val-Draekin wasn't all he presented himself to be. But she also knew that Seita's games ran deep and nothing the Vallè princess said could be trusted.

"Are you suggesting that *The Moon Scrolls of Mia* are false?" Jondralyn asked.

"The Brethren of Mia have made it no secret that they believe all scriptures to be a lie," Val-Draekin said frankly. "Why not the *Moon Scrolls* too?"

"I cannot believe anyone would say this, especially you, Val-Draekin." Jondralyn looked at Hawkwood for reassurance, for confirmation that everything the Vallè was implying was drivel. But Hawkwood said nothing. And with his silence, Jondralyn's face fell into a mask of betrayal. There was a sudden tension in the air between them that Tala had never before seen. And that worried her more than anything yet, for Jondralyn and Hawkwood's relationship had seemed the most solid thing in the beginning, but now even their love was becoming frayed beyond repair.

"It is a simple thing to get humans to believe a lie," Val-Draekin went on. "Just create a myth, a legend, surround it with magical thinking, include the power of suggestion, then add the words 'thus saith Laijon' or 'thus saith Raijael.'"

"This is heretical talk," Jondralyn said.

"I've had this conversation with Nail already," Val-Draekin said, nodding toward the Gallows Haven boy. "You only attach power and significance to the weapons and stones due to the power of suggestion, Jondralyn. You only believe those things Roguemoore told you about yourself because you *want* to believe. You are the *Princess*. But what if he had told you that you were a nobody? What if he suggested that the histories of the Five Isles would never include you? Would you have so readily believed him then? Would you be so ready to run off to Savon in search of magical weapons and angel stones then?"

Val-Draekin toys with her. Tala felt the evilness of it, for she too had been played in the same sinister way. *He is like a Bloodwood. And the Bloodwood toy with everyone.* Seita had told her that she might very well be the last Bronachell standing at Fiery Absolution. *It is all a game with these Vallè, these games of suggestion.* The very light of the saloon was being leeched from the air with every word Val-Draekin spoke.

"Like a sickness, the power of suggestion spreads and grows," Val-Draekin said. "Just look to the Bloodwoods. Fill a young assassin's head with murder and they grow up to be murderous. They won't realize what they do is wrong. They will just think of it as a job. Even when confronted by facts, they will deny. Fill any young person's head with myth and legend and other magical nonsense and lies and they will likely never break the cycle even until their death. Whereas, you fill their heads with truth and logic and they will grow up to be healthy and wise. But that has not happened in the Five Isles. Nor will it ever, for I know the nature of humanity. The Vallè have always known it doesn't matter to humans what the truth is. It matters more to humans what a book of scripture has to say, especially if that book promises eternal life, but eternal life only for those special and chosen few. For that is what humanity yearns to believe in most: ancient words and promises scribbled on ancient parchment by ancient men, promises that they will never have to deliver on. And humanity will believe even unto their own death, or unto the death of those who see things differently than they. Belief destroys everything. Even those pure of heart will kill just to rid themselves of someone who believes differently than they. It is why religion poisons everything. I am only trying to warn you."

"War in the name of the gods." Bronwyn Allen spoke up from her perch at the bar. "Murder in their name? War in their name? What is the difference? 'Tis all death and pain and heartache for many who believe and for many who do not. For my part, I see what you are saying, Ser Vallè. Who knows, perhaps we have all been fools to believe in these gods and these books."

"Aye." Val-Draekin nodded to the Wyn Darrè girl. "Perhaps we have all been fools. Even the Brethren of Mia. I have been contemplating these matters of late. I warn you now, what if you are being played the fool by these ancient writings? What if all humanity has been played a fool? Perhaps we are all looking toward the wrong religion. Even the Vallè. What makes us so certain our truth is the correct truth? What makes us so certain *The Moon Scrolls of Mia* are not just the same hapless drivel that *The Way and Truth of Laijon* is? Or, could it be that the murderous oghuls performing blood sacrifice are truly on the right side of the gods? What if the Hragna'Ar oghuls are right with their dark rituals? What if their dark sacraments actually produce results, unlike our prayers and flagellations?"

"Hragna'Ar *is* true." Cromm Cru'x grunted his approval. "Cromm can drink to that." The oghul lifted his mug. "To Hragna'Ar!" he shouted.

"See." Val-Draekin gestured toward the oghul. "Who is right when we all believe we are right?"

"But I saw the shield," Jondralyn said. "I saw *Ethic Shroud* and the white angel stone. I believe what I believe. I believe my own eyes and my own heart. Despite your best efforts to create doubt within me, I will go on. I will hope. I will not succumb to negativity and doubt. I will find the weapons and stones. And I myself shall prevent the White Prince from conquering all of the Five Isles, I myself will prevent the demons from arising from the underworld again. I myself shall bring about Fiery Absolution. For I am the *Princess*, despite what you may say to the contrary. I know my destiny."

"And what if the destiny of the Princess lies with the Gladiator?" Hawkwood broke in. "Isn't that what Squireck believed? Did he not tell you? It's what he told me in an effort to get me to leave you alone. He showed me the very words in the *Moon Scrolls*. But the *Moon Scrolls* also claim that the Assassin shall watch over the Princess until the end of her days. There is still much we do not know about scripture, Jon."

Jondralyn stood, ignoring Hawkwood, glaring down at Val-Draekin, fire and conviction in her voice. "I saw Savon in my dreams. The weapons of the Five Warrior Angels will be gathered there. I feel it with all my heart. Those weapons are my destiny. I am a proud follower of the Brethren of Mia, like my father was before me, like Squireck and Hawkwood and even you, Val-Draekin. I *believe* in the *Moon Scrolls*. And in those sacred writings of our Blessed Mother Mia, I have the utmost *faith*. I saw Savon in my dreams."

Val-Draekin stayed seated, gazing up at her with a cool calmness. "Dreams are not real, Jondralyn. They are merely distractions."

"I know what I saw," Jondralyn countered.

"You must apply the standard of logic and reason to every question and not fall back on things such as dreams, faith, mysticism, feelings of the heart, burnings in your bosom, or so-called sacred scripture and dogmatic texts."

"But I cannot deny what I have felt. What I have seen. I will not betray the Brethren of Mia. I will not deny *The Moon Scrolls of Mia*."

Val-Draekin sighed. "If you find it honorable to lay claim to blind faith in the antiquated writings of some old man who lived thousands of years ago over your own common sense, then you are the largest type of fool the Five Isles has produced. And if you boast of that faith, know that you are legion. For many boast that they *know* the truth when they do not. Cromm even boasts to know the truth. He won't leave Nail's side because he is so devoted to *his* truth; he is devoted to the marked one of Hragna'Ar legend. And Hragna'Ar is full of bloody ritual and murder, horrid to both you and me. And yet still he believes. What if he is right? Do you deny him his faith?"

"You just called me the greatest fool the Five Isles has ever known?" Jondralyn looked ready to claw the Vallè's face off. She looked at Hawkwood for reassurance. But Hawkwood remained stoic and unreadable. He had offered nothing throughout the entire conversation. And Tala could sense that bothered her sister more than anything Val-Draekin had yet said. *All the fighting and tension!* Tala felt the restlessness surging through her own body, somewhere inside her pounding chest, pressing tighter and tighter.

She recalled her own dreams and visions when the grand vicar rolled her up in the Dayknight sleeping bag and threw her into the queen's bath. *Were those visions real? Is it all somehow connected?* She had seen the Atonement Tree in those visions. She had seen fire and flame and Lawri Le Graven in the clouds sitting the Silver Throne. She had seen the Long Stairs running thick with blood. She had seen a silver gauntlet and the Riven Rock slave quarry, the throne settling onto five black holes punched into the glowing marble . . . and something waiting beneath those holes. She could feel the scars on her arms from when she had escaped the sleeping bag they had stuffed her into. *But dreams are lies, according to Val-Draekin.*

Jondralyn had focused her attention back on Val-Draekin. "Don't presume to tell me what I know and what I don't know. Do not presume that I am a fool for believing in the cause of my father, in the cause of the Brethren of Mia. I saw Lawri punch through the hull of the *Val-Sadè* with that gauntlet. Both Hawkwood and my sister witnessed that too. You cannot tell me that was not magic. You cannot tell me that was just the power of suggestion at work there."

"I sense there could be more than Vallè alchemy at work within that gauntlet." Val-Draekin peered at Jondralyn over his mug of ale. "You still must consider the science of the stars, blue smoke on a battle-ax, the power of suggestion."

"Well, I don't know what any of that means," Jondralyn said, exasperation in her voice. "But I do know what I saw. And I saw the power of that gauntlet. Lawri punched a hole straight through the hull."

"Wood can rot over time," Val-Draekin countered. "Perhaps Lawri struck a weak spot in the ship."

"You deny there is magic in that gauntlet, that her punching through solid wood is some form of miracle?"

"You must come to understand, Jondralyn, when one thinks they see a miracle, if there is any chance of coincidence, no matter how small, then coincidence is the answer to that miracle. Rather than give credit to the supernatural or the gods or the feelings of one's own heart, one must use logic and reason to discover truth. The hull of that ship was rotten. She punched it in exactly the right spot. 'Twas mere happenstance."

Tala was now listening in both perplexed horror and perplexed fascination to the conversation between Jondralyn and the dark-haired Vallè. For what Val-Draekin said did make some sense. Next to her, Nail seemed intent on what the Vallè was saying too, for his face was a stiff mask of concentration in the faint glow of the burning sconces hanging on darkened walls. And as far as Tala could tell, Lawri was still asleep.

"Logic and reason combined do not explain how the gauntlet has attached itself to my cousin," Jondralyn said. "Nor do logic and reason explain how the fingers of the gauntlet can move. For Lawri has *no* arm."

"Indeed," Val-Draekin conceded. "That part of the equation is a mystery even to me. But not all the sciences of the stars are yet known to us Vallè. You people gathered here in this saloon are my friends. I am only trying to warn you of things to come, so that you are not surprised."

"The dragons are coming!" Lawri Le Graven startled everyone with a shout as she jerked awake, nearly tumbling from her chair. "That is what things are to come!"

Tala's heart chilled at the sight of Lawri's wide-open eyes blazing bright and green. Ever since finding Delia dead and hanging, Lawri had been in a stupor, falling into deep trances, retreating to that hidden place in her mind no one could reach.

And when she would wake, she would wake with a start and shout.

Seita said Lawri would spiral into insanity. Tala stared at her sleepy-eyed cousin. *Insanity, or the science of the stars?* Lawri was full of Ember Gathering blessings and Vallè poisons and who knew what else.

"The dragons are coming," Lawri repeated. "The green dragon will soon arrive and I shall be its eyes." Then her own green eyes rolled up in her head.

**

It was midnight; the stars naught but blurry motes above. Tala, unable to sleep, slipped silently into the back courtyard of the Filthy Horse Saloon, hoping to catch some air, hoping to be alone for a while. But she was not alone.

Val-Draekin stood thirty paces from the back door, unaware of her presence. He was on the opposite side of the large stone basin in the center of the yard—the same basin the barmaid Delia had emerged from underneath some many nights ago. He had his back to Tala. A black kestrel was perched on his outstretched arm. He whispered something to the bird and it launched into flight, vanishing into the dark sky beyond the tattered awnings. Val-Draekin unrolled a thin slip of white paper and bent his head to read it.

Senses alert, Tala drifted stealthily through the soft grass toward the stone basin, ducking down behind it, the dark-haired Vallè still unaware that she had entered the yard. Tucking herself in a crouch behind the basin, Tala waited, eyes peering over the rim. A small orange flare of light appeared in the palm of Val-Draekin's hands.

He's burning the note. White powder! She'd seen him use the stuff before.

The Vallè let the burning parchment flutter to the grass. He whirled and stalked toward the back door of the saloon, still oblivious to her presence as she scooted around the basin on all fours, keeping out of sight.

Once Val-Draekin had closed the door behind him, Tala scrambled from behind the basin and swiftly put out the flame with the kerchief from her pocket. The grass was a trifle damp, which slowed the flames consuming the parchment. It was only halfway burnt, mostly around the curled and blackened edges. She could easily decipher most of what was there. It read,

> *As you know, the Aalavarrè Solas roam the north. It is time.*
> *You should go to them now, for they summon you with*
> *sacrifice and blood. What other doors to the underworld may*
> *Hragna'Ar yet still open? And who among us holds the key?*
> *You and Aeros Raijael shall come together again under the*
> *Atonement Tree. I have foreseen seen it. Bloodwood brothers*
> *reuinited. Fire. Lakes of blood. And the bones of the human*
> *dead piled to the heavens. Your destiny awaits you. Remember*
> *your oaths! For you are the Dragon!*

The writing was in the same handwritten script as every note Tala had received from the Bloodwood. From Seita. *And this note is proof that the Vallè princess and Val-Draekin work together in secret combinations.*

Tala sat with her back against the cold stone of the basin, wondering what to do, wondering if she should just destroy the note. She let it crumple in her clenched fingers. *Who do I warn? Who do I tell?* She had said little to anyone about what she had overhead between Seita and Val-Korin, knowing she wouldn't be believed anyway. There was so much about that conversation that was almost daunting, overwhelming; some of it she had even forgotten. And that was what vexed her most. *Could Val-Draekin have killed Delia?* The thought had crossed her mind more than once.

Tala was so lost in dark thoughts that she almost failed to see her older sister padding silently toward her. Jondralyn was clothed in naught but a pair of tan pantaloons and a white shirt. Her sword was hooked to the leather belt at her hip. And her Silver Guard armor was crammed into the canvas sack slung over her shoulder.

"What are you doing?" Tala asked, standing, hiding Val-Draekin's note crumpled in her clenched fist.

"I'm leaving." Jondralyn headed toward the farthest ivy-covered wall and flung the sack of armor up and over the seven-foot stone barrier, where it landed on the other side with a muffled clatter. She began to climb the ivy-choked trellis leaning against the wall.

"Leaving?" Tala went numb all over.

"You mustn't alert the others," Jondralyn said in a rushed whisper as she reached the top of the trellis and wall.

"Are you going back to the castle?" Tala asked.

"No."

"Then where?"

"I must go wherever I must go and do whatever I must do. And that is for me to know and no one else."

"You are going to Savon to find Lindholf and those weapons the barmaid claimed he has," Tala stated, suddenly aware of the situation. "You believe Delia. You believe that our cousin is there with the weapons of the Five Warrior Angels?"

"I've seen it in my dreams," Jondralyn answered, straddling the top of the wall. "And I refuse to deny what I have seen, no matter what Val-Draekin or *Hawkwood* say. Hawkwood once claimed that it was written in *The Moon Scrolls of Mia* that the Princess and the Assassin would be together in the end. But now they say things that contradict all that, that it is all a lie, the scrolls and the scriptures."

"You've been fighting with Hawkwood again?" Tala asked.

"Yes, we fought. He thinks I went to sleep without him in the far room. He stayed in the bar, Val-Draekin with him. I hear what they say when they think I am not listening. They say I am full of foolish whims. They think I have learned nothing from my past mistakes. They think I am brash, impulsive, reckless, crazy."

"And sneaking off to Savon in the middle of the night will prove them wrong?"

Jondralyn did not answer.

"Do you not still love Hawkwood?" Tala asked.

Pain crossed Jondralyn's face. Anger. Regret. Shame. "Even the most wonderful of things can come to a bitter end, Tala. I will not stay with someone who thinks my ideas are crazy."

"So you will just run away?"

"I am not running away. I am going to Savon, to find our cousin and get back the weapons of the Five Warrior Angels."

"You can't go alone." Tala felt a lump growing in her throat, knowing her sister's impulsiveness and pride were going to get her killed. She wondered if she should tell her sister about the note to Val-Draekin she'd found, questioning if it would do any good. "At least let me come me with you."

"No." Jondralyn's answer was quick, firm. "I must make this journey on my own. I must follow my own heart this time. Follow my dreams. My visions. I shall find out for myself what is true and what is not. I shall no longer rely on the words of others or ancient texts. And if what I believe is true, then I shall take the weapons and stones of the Five Warrior Angels and use them to fight our enemies. And I shall not be held back."

Jondralyn's words stung.

"Do you truly think that I will hold you back?" Tala asked.

Without answering, Jondralyn flung herself the rest of the way over the ivy-covered wall and was gone. Tala could hear her muffled foot-steps retreating into the night. She wanted to rush back into the saloon and tell Hawkwood and Val-Draekin that her sister had foolishly run off into the night with naught but her sword and armor for companionship. Hawkwood and Val-Draekin were right to be concerned. Jondralyn had learned nothing from her past mistakes. She was still brash, impulsive, and reckless. Watching her sister so easily disappear was a bitter les-son for Tala. She wondered if people could really change who they fun-damentally were. If Glade Chaparral had changed, it was only for the worse. Had Lindholf changed? Had Lawri? *Have I?* She thought of jump-ing the wall and running after Jondralyn herself.

But Nail stepped out into the courtyard. He walked toward her, hands in the pockets of his brown leather pants. It warmed her heart to see him. "I cannot sleep," he said. "It's too dank and too dark and too hot in that saloon." He looked around the courtyard, flicking blond hair out of his eyes. "Not that this courtyard isn't just as dark. But the air feels cleaner, cooler."

"My sister just left," she said in a rush. "Climbed the wall and just left." She pointed to the ivy-covered trellis Jondralyn had climbed. "She's headed to Savon. She believed the barmaid. She said she will find my cousin and find the weapons and stones and use them to fight Aeros Raijael. She felt it was her destiny."

"And what do you think?"

The question took her aback. She had never had a man ask her what she thought before. "I think my sister is foolish, destiny or not."

"Destiny is naught but blue smoke on a battle-ax," he said.

"What does that mean?" Tala squinted in confusion. "Val-Draekin said that to Jondralyn earlier."

"Nothing, really, just something the Vallè likes to say. I think it means everything is an illusion."

She met Nail's gaze. "I know he is your friend, but I do not fully trust

Val-Draekin. What he was saying to Jondralyn about how all scripture is naught but a fraud."

"That is just the way he talks about everything," Nail said, a haunted look growing in his own eyes. "He is a skeptic, as my master would say. Val-Draekin relies on logic and reason in every decision. Even after we went in search of *Blackest Heart* and *Afflicted Fire*, he always talked about how he never believed in any of it, yet still he and Seita went on the quest just for the fun of it, the thrill of the adventure."

She thought of the note Val-Draekin shared with Seita, with the Bloodwood who had tormented her so. She thought of the conversation she'd overheard between Seita and Val-Korin before Seita killed her father. "I do not trust Seita or Val-Draekin."

Nail straightened his back, flicked the hair out of his eyes once more. "I have faced death and traveled many hard miles with Val-Draekin. I trust him more than anyone. He is a good person."

Nail was so honest with his answers at all times. Never once had he capitulated to what she might want to hear. Tala wanted to hug him for just being truthful with his feelings on the matter of Val-Draekin, even if she knew them to be wrong.

Nail met her gaze. "There is something about Seita, though," he said. "In our journey together to the Sky Lochs, I always felt she was not telling the truth. She lied to Stefan and me about who she was from the start. I, like you, do not trust her."

Something niggled at the back of her mind every time he mentioned Stefan. But in hearing his admission about Seita, she felt a pounding heart. And that was when she told him everything. She told him of the Bloodwood who had stalked her in the secret ways, the games involving Lindholf and Glade, the murder of Sterling Prentiss, the poisons she'd fed Lawri, the journey with Glade under Purgatory, how she found out Seita was a Bloodwood assassin, the conversation she had overheard between Seita and Val-Korin and all that entailed, how the Vallè maiden came to possess *Blackest Heart* and *Afflicted Fire*, how she had lost them to Gault Aulbrek.

She unloaded every burden and secret she had been keeping in.

When it was over, she felt as light as a butterfly floating. Relieved. But Nail looked fraught with both heartache and worry. He looked as if he now carried the weight of the world on his shoulders. She wondered if he believed her. *I need* him to believe me!

"Stefan is truly dead, then," he said, face ashen with pain. "Seita was with Stefan when he died. Bronwyn claimed that she and Cromm came upon Stefan's body and took a black dagger off him, along with his bow, the bow he had named Gisela. But Seita was there when Stefan died."

And then it hit her. What had been bothering her for so long. Why any mention of Stefan struck such a chord in her.

"Stefan and the black stone!" she blurted. "They are part of Seita's story. Before she killed her father, Seita told him that a black stone was missing from the satchel she took from Stefan. She put another stone in its place. A fake stone." She was speaking in a rush now, trying to gather her thoughts. "Val-Korin was upset with Seita because she had replaced the real angel stone with a fake. It is partly why she killed her father, I think, because he kept going on about all her failures, criticizing her."

She grabbed Nail by the shoulders, gazing into his eyes intensely. "What if Bronwyn and Cromm took the stone from Stefan along with the bow?"

"It's possible, I suppose."

"Cromm sucks on a black rock daily."

"You think the oghul has been sucking on one of the angel stones this entire time?" Nail asked. "What made you come so quickly to that conclusion?"

"I don't know. I guess I've been figuring out stupid puzzles for so long now I've developed a knack for it." Then she let go of his arms as another thought stormed into her mind. "Delia claimed she saw a white stone, a red stone, and a black one. Jondralyn should know that it is a fake angel stone she chases. We must go after her."

Then the reality of what she was saying hit her. She leaned against the stone basin, running her hands through her hair in frustration. "But how do we know for sure that Cromm actually has a real angel stone?"

"Well, there is one way to find out," Nail said. "We ask him where he got the black rock. If he got it from Stefan's body, then we know." He turned and headed toward the back door of the saloon. "I will go get him. Wait here."

**

Nail returned to the courtyard with Bronwyn and Cromm. Tala, still at the stone basin, was surprised to see that all three of them were dressed for travel.

Nail wore what few bits of leather armor he had brought with him from the north, plus some other armor Hawkwood had scrounged up for him in the *Val-Sadè*. He carried an old Silver Guard sword at his hip—the blade he had been practicing with.

Though it was a warm night, the fierce-faced Wyn Darrè girl wore her green travel cloak. Her shortsword was at her belt and the quiver of black-hafted arrows was slung over her back. She also carried the black bow in one hand—the bow named Gisela. The oghul wore his thick leather and chain-mail armor, daggers and stilettos once again tucked away in various parts of his belt, boots, and pockets. His square-headed war hammer was strapped to the leather baldric over his shoulder.

Cromm also sucked on the black rock in question. The gray-faced oghul saw Tala staring, jammed two thick fingers between his lips, and plucked the stone out. He dropped it atop the stone basin. It was covered in both slime and spit and a terrible foul stink—bad breath mixed with smoke or something worse, Tala imagined.

"You think it is a star stone Cromm has been sucking on?" the oghul grunted.

"I thought Nail had gone daft when he first asked us," Bronwyn said.

"Can you wipe it off?" Tala asked Cromm.

The oghul snatched the stone back up and rubbed it roughly over his leather armor, then handed it to her. It was still dirty, but it fit warm and perfect in the palm of her hand, though it felt odd holding it, wrong in a way. Not even a flicker or glint of starlight twinkled off its black surface. Overall it was a lifeless object, dark and dusky and rootless and seemingly full of naught but endless despair and death. She shuddered. *Could such an inert and empty thing really be an angel stone?* It still smelled strongly of smoke, either that or something in the city's dock district was burning.

She asked Cromm, "Did you take this stone from Stefan Wayland when you took his bow?"

The blunt-faced oghul cast a concerned glance Bronwyn's way, then looked back at Tala, nodded, and grunted, "Yes. Cromm already told Nail that he did. Told him inside the saloon just now. Cromm not surprised. Most rocks wear out in short time. But this stone keep its shape, no matter how hard I suck. Elsewise I would throw it out long ago."

Tala held out the stone for Nail's inspection. He looked at it with mild disgust, the rancid stench of the thing likely hitting his nose now too.

"Cromm knew protecting the marked one would also lead to great treasure." The oghul snatched the stone from the palm of Tala's hand and thrust it back into his mouth, sucking. But the strong scent of smoke still lingered in the air.

"Let him keep it in his mouth," Bronwyn said. "He likes it. Besides, it's safer there. Ain't nobody looking for an angel stone inside an oghul's mouth." Tala couldn't argue that fact. "Nail also told us that Princess Jondralyn left," Bronwyn went on. "He told us that you wish to find her and tell her about Cromm's stone."

"Aye." Tala nodded.

"Then we will go with you."

Tala looked at Nail apprehensively. Nail shrugged. "I think it would be best if we did not travel alone," he said. "They are both good in a fight. We could use the protection. And they are good at requisitioning supplies and horses, which we will need."

Tala didn't see any harm in having them along. And Nail was right. They would need horses and supplies. "What about Lawri?" she asked.

"Lawri will be safest with Val-Draekin and Hawkwood," Bronwyn said.

Tala couldn't help but agree. "Then let's be off. There is no reason to linger. We need to find my sister. She was heading for Savon. We climb the wall where she did."

Cromm strode toward the ivy-covered wall. The others followed.

Nail climbed the ivy-covered trellis first. His armor and sword scraped against the rock as he slid over to the other side. Bronwyn clambered up the wall behind Nail.

A loud clatter and commotion sounded from the direction of the saloon. The smell of smoke was now heavy in the air.

"It's on fire!" Bronwyn said, standing atop the seven-foot-high stone wall and looking back toward the saloon. Both Tala and Cromm turned. Flames were shooting from the roof of the Filthy Horse. Smoke was pouring from near the top of the saloon's back door. "Bloody Mother Mia," Bronwyn exclaimed, a little louder. "It's burning up."

Lawri! Tala's mind screamed. Her cousin was inside the burning saloon. *I have to save her!* She felt indecision near to panic seize her.

Suddenly the back door burst open, black smoke billowing into the starlit sky. Val-Draekin stumbled out, coughing, choking. He carried Lawri Le Graven in his arms. He set her gently in the grass in front of the stone basin. Lawri was gasping for air, soot smeared over her blue shirt and leather pants.

Tala ran to Lawri and helped her cousin to her feet. The gauntlet attached to Lawri's arm was hot to the touch, and Lawri's eyes glowed green under the mask of soot covering her pale face and tawny hair. "I can't breathe," she wheezed.

The flames shooting from the roof were crackling loud. The air was hot. Val-Draekin was struggling for breath, face black with smoke. He spied Bronwyn and Cromm behind Tala and Lawri. "It looks like you three already made it out," he coughed.

Tala stared at the smoke boiling from the open back door of the saloon. She could feel the heat of the fire consuming the roof against her face. "What's happening?"

"Glade Chaparral and about fifty knights busted through the front door of the saloon," Val-Draekin answered in a rush. "Silver Guards and Dayknights. They attacked Hawkwood and me. Burning sconces were knocked from the wall in the scrum. Set the place alight. Hawkwood held the knights off and I ran into the back rooms and grabbed Lawri. I couldn't find Nail or Jondralyn."

The noise of the fire had turned into a crackling roar. Val-Draekin headed back toward the smoking saloon. "Nail and Jondralyn?" he called back. "Where are they?"

"She's . . . they're . . . still in the saloon," Tala lied.

"I'll find them." Val-Draekin whirled and rushed back into the wall of black smoke pouring from the back door of the building. *I just sent him to his death!* Stunned, Tala just stood there staring at the spot where the Vallè had disappeared, feeling the heat of the fire and smoke blaze against her own flesh. *How many lies are in me? How many will die because of my deception? Sterling Prentiss? Val-Draekin? Numerous prison guards? Where does it end?* She heard the sound of fighting coming from the building now, sword clanking against sword, the shouts of men.

Cromm picked up Lawri and raced toward the ivy-trellised wall. He lifted her up toward Bronwyn. The Wyn Darrè girl knelt on the lip of the wall and pulled Tala's cousin to safety. Lawri dropped over the stone wall to where Nail was waiting on the other side. "I got her!" Tala heard Nail's shout.

Two knights came bursting from the smoke-filled back door of the saloon, a helmetless Dayknight and a soot-covered Silver Guard. The two men stumbled to the grass, falling to their hands and knees before the stone basin, choking for air. The soot-covered face of the helmetless Dayknight looked familiar to Tala.

Glade Chaparral!

Two more helmetless knights burst from the doorway, black smoke billowing out behind them. A black arrow struck the first man right in his gasping mouth, dropping him instantly. A second black arrow sank into the left eye of the next man. He fell in the doorway, half in and half out of the thick wall of smoke.

Bronwyn Allen was standing atop the wall, firing the arrows. Cromm was still at the base of the wall, looking up at her. Glade Chaparral crawled toward the burning building and tried to drag the arrow-shot knight caught in the doorway.

The next two knights attempting to escape the burning saloon tripped over Glade and the dead man, and the next five knights tripped over those two. Soon there was a pile of armored bodies wedged in the doorway, all of them scrambling to stand.

Bronwyn sent arrow after arrow into the pile of struggling knights, ending the struggles of several. Another frantic group of knights stumbled and tripped over the squirming heap already jammed in the doorway. The Wyn Darrè girl was fast with her bow, letting arrow after arrow fly into the pile.

Glade Chaparral, crying out in sheer panic, somehow managed to squirm from beneath the mound of dead men. He crawled out into the grassy yard, armor smoking. Behind him was a logjam of knights in the smoking doorway. Many were already dead from Bronwyn's arrows; the others were desperately trying to scrambling over the pile. Flames, bright and yellow, began to lick out from the top of the narrow doorway. The surge of frantic knights pushing to escape behind the initial mass of men grew intense. More came, trying to shove their way through the blockage of bodies stacking up. It was an ever-growing mound of cooking armor and flesh. The screams were loud and panicked.

And Bronwyn kept firing black arrows into the mass of bodies. Several knights managed to squeeze through the crushing pile, turning, trying to drag their struggling companions from the savage flaming stack. But the heat was too intense, and what lucky few escaped eventually stumbled back into the grassy courtyard near Glade, all struggling for breath, all stamping at the random flames that ate at their own bodies.

The entire saloon was a roaring mass of flame now. The heat against her own flesh was intense. *Hawkwood dead! Val-Draekin dead! Oh, my lies . . .*

Cromm Cru'x grabbed her around the waist, flung her over his broad shoulder, and carried her up the ivy-covered wall.

The last thing Tala saw in the courtyard was Glade Chaparral. He was standing now, smoke still rising from his armor. "I will find you!" he shouted, pointing at her. "I will find you!"

Then Tala dropped into Nail's waiting arms.

Through the Shroud, the five Dragons shall be one with Viper, a chosen Vallè born and bred to awaken those most holy fires within the beasts of the underworld.
—THE BOOK OF THE BETRAYER

CHAPTER THIRTY-SIX
CRYSTALWOOD

7TH DAY OF THE BLOOD MOON, 999TH YEAR OF LAIJON
SAINT ONLY, ADIN WYTE

Krista Aulbrek had come to Saint Only with the sole purpose of assassinating Aeros Raijael. Borden Bronachell led the way through the dark. He carried their only torch. It crackled with bright flame as he guided Krista and the dwarf, Ironcloud, through a series of tapered stone corridors. They were at least half a day's journey into the hidden passageways under Mont Saint Only. The going was smoother now as they scurried through narrow hallways constructed of quarried stone, mortar, and timber. They were in man-made parts of the Mont now, higher up the mountain. Filth and dust clung to everything still, as if the passageways had not been used in years.

For nearly eight hours they had slowly made their way upward through steep, twisting tunnels. The first leg of their journey had been naught but rough-hewn caves, bat-filled crevasses, and slender, rocky passageways choked with spiderwebs, their path always winding upward. They had traveled winding tunnels and secret ways that Borden claimed even Aeros Raijael did not know existed.

The six-day journey from Kragg Keep to Mont Saint Only had been mostly uneventful. But it took Krista some time to get over the senseless death of Tyus Barra. She couldn't stop thinking of the boy's body breaking apart as he fell from the cliffs of Kragg Keep. The mute's actions had likely saved her life that day—cutting the ropes that held the platform, sending Black Dugal and Hans Rake plummeting down into the waters of Kragg Bay with him. She could not have fought them both off. Tyus had gotten rid of them the only way possible.

Krista also couldn't stop thinking of a passage from *The Book of the Betrayer*: *Hath Laijon gifted the world to the wicked, doth he laugh when the good and innocent die.* Tyus Barra had been one of the good and innocent, which, she knew, meant little to the gods. For some reason the innocent boy's death made her more angry with each passing day—so angry she wanted to lash out and create death and misery of her own.

She had treated Borden and Ironcloud with much contempt early on. She would have kept them both tied up and miserable, but she knew nothing of sailing. *A failing of Black Dugal?* Who cared. Dugal was dead to her now.

Truly fatherless.

Early on it had been slow going out of Kragg Keep, dragging Borden and Ironcloud behind her, both of them with their hands bound, nothing but the clothes on their backs, their weapons and armor left in the middle of a dusty road in Kragg, their own two horses somewhere underwater at the bottom of Kragg Bay. They had been her captives for a time. Krista was once again riding her Bloodeye steed. She was beyond happy to be back again with Dread. She was also relieved to once again wear the Bloodwood leathers. She was again at home, various daggers hidden within her armor, poisons, poultices, and other antidotes in the black leather saddlebags strapped to Dread.

But the going had been too slow. To speed their journey, Krista eventually stole two extra ponies from a farmer just outside Kragg. They made better time after that. For two days they had traveled across the isthmus northeast of Pensio Fields, eventually coming upon a wrecked fishing village named Taltos at the tip of the peninsula. In Taltos, Krista had also requisitioned an abandoned sailboat big enough for the Bloodeye and two ponies. She set sail for Mont Saint Only. But not more than a hundred paces from the shore, Krista and her sailboat were hopelessly adrift.

"Untie us and we can sail straight away from here," Borden had said. "You already know we are fine sailors. We sailed from Rokenwalder all the way to Wynix together without trouble."

Despite Borden's offer, Krista stubbornly struggled with the sails and rigging for another half day, all the while drifting into docks and quays and wharves, before she realized she could not control the boat. Sailing was clearly beyond her. She reluctantly untied both Borden and the dwarf, and off they sailed, three days in warm, soft breezes straight to Mont Saint Only without incident or betrayal. He only solace was that she still held all the weapons. She had all the advantage. And she had her poisons.

In the dark of morning, they had left the sailboat moored in a calm, deep hollow under a leaning cliff along the craggy western shore of the Mont, the Bloodeye and the two ponies tethered safely aboard. The hidden recess was one of a few secret entrances to the fortress atop the towering Mont that Borden Bronachell knew of.

And now here they were, at the top of the Mont. Borden brought them to a halt at a dead end in the hallway before a smooth stone wall.

"Beyond lies the bedchamber of Ser Edmon Guy Van Hester," he whispered. "If Aeros Raijael were to stay anywhere in the fortress, it would be here. Bear in mind, this door can only open from this side of the wall. If we all venture into the room and it closes behind us, we will be trapped. One of us should stay behind."

"I'll stay," Ironcloud said. Borden handed the dwarf the torch.

Kneeling, Borden felt along the bottom of the floor where it met the smooth wall. He found the crack he sought, wiggling his finger down into it. There was a faint click, and a doorway revealed itself in the rock wall. The door swung back without a sound, exposing a gaping rectangular hole and a strange, dull pattern of flickering light filtering through the back of a tapestry hanging over the opening on the other side. The bottom lip of the hole was about knee-high and stretched up just above Krista's head. The cavity was about the width of two men.

"There is another similar door on the opposite side of the chamber, also hidden and secret," Borden whispered. He then crouched in the hole and prodded the back of the tapestry with the tip of his finger. "The room is lit with a lantern or torchlight on the other side," he whispered. "Someone may be in the chamber."

"Let me look," Krista said.

Borden backed out of the hole. Krista pulled forth one of her black daggers and climbed into the cavity. Crouching, she stuck the blade into the back of the tapestry, silently slashing a small tear in the fabric, then set her eye to the light streaming through.

She saw a large candlelit room of gray stone walls and many dark alcoves. It was indeed a bedchamber, filled with plush wood furniture and fine bronze sculptures. Every wall was hung with tapestries and long decorative spears with gleaming, jewel-laden hafts tied with red ribbons. Pewter goblets and stone sculptures were placed atop the surface of every wooden cabinet. Bear rugs lined the floor. A large hearth was set against one wall. One window was set high above. It was open, and a blue sky could be seen beyond.

A four-post bed with a silver canopy and white silken hangings was nestled in the alcove directly across from the window. The bed was full of pillows and covered with a white quilt. A slight, blond-haired girl with a perfectly beautiful face sat cross-legged in the center of the bed.

The impossibly pretty girl wore naught but a thin white shirt open down the middle, the fabric scarcely covering her breasts, revealing a strip of pale flesh clear down to her belly button. The lithe girl examined a thin sword that was balanced on her lap. The delicate weapon had a heart-shaped ruby set at the top of its hilt, and its slender blade gleamed and flickered in the candlelight. Even with the sword resting on her lap, the girl appeared the very essence of innocence and purity.

Krista pulled her eye from the hole in the tapestry, climbed from the cavity, and whispered, "The room is empty but for a girl sitting on the bed. She has a sword."

"A sword?"

"Aye, a sword." Krista sheathed her dagger. "She's just a slip of a girl."

"She's likely of no account," Borden said. "Probably one of Aeros' many slave girls. Perhaps she can be of use to us." He glanced back at Ironcloud. "Stay in the tunnel and be wary." Borden crouched in the hole again, swept the tapestry aside, and stepped into the room. Krista followed him.

The blond girl on the bed leaped to her feet, startled, the thin sword in one hand now, its tip between herself and the two intruders. "Who are you?" she gasped.

Borden placed his finger to his lips in a silencing motion. "Shhhh," he hissed. Borden was not armed, nor was he armored. In fact, he looked like a beggar man in the clothes Krista had let him keep. However, he was tall and imposing. Still, the girl kept the tip of her blade up, poised and ready.

She's a brave one, Krista thought as she took in more of the room at a glance. The gray walls rose high around her, thirty feet or more, to a ceiling of arched stone pillars and buttresses. She also noticed a chest on the floor near the bed, a large gold-filigreed wooden box, the type of box in which royals like the Angel Prince kept their most treasured things.

"Lord Aeros will be here soon," the blond girl stated, her sword never wavering. "He will kill you. One of his guards is a very big man. Hammerfiss. He stands guard just outside. One scream from me—"

"But you won't scream," Borden cut her off. "Will you?"

"I"—the girl hesitated, the tip of her sword dropping—"do not rightly know what I shall do."

"What is your name?" Borden stepped lightly across the bear rug toward her. "You've a familiar look about you."

"Ava Shay," the girl answered, backing away, the slit in her white silken shirt revealing the pale, perfect swell of one of her breasts. She clutched the fabric closed with one hand, sword still held out nervously before her in the other, the tip once again steady.

Despite the innocent look of Ava Shay, Krista sensed something dark living within the girl's outwardly placid round eyes. *She hides hurt, pain, deep anger.*

"I am unarmed." Borden held out his hands. "My name is Borden Bronachell. The girl with me is Krista Aulbrek."

Ava Shay's gaze traveled beyond Borden to Krista, her eyes narrowing in dark concern and fear. Krista didn't blame the girl for her fear—she knew how a black-clad Bloodwood assassin looked to even the most jaded of folks, much less to a mostly naked teenaged girl.

Krista flashed the girl a warm smile.

Ava Shay pointed her delicate sword once again at Borden. "The only Borden Bronachell I ever heard of was a king," she said. "And he's dead." Her eyes remained cold slits as she looked at Krista. "And I've heard the name Krista Aulbrek before."

Krista's smile vanished. "Where? When?"

"Aeros and the Spider talked of a girl named Krista," Ava said. "Gault Aulbrek's daughter. They talked often of her—that is, before they betrayed him and let him be captured."

"Captured?" Krista's stomach squeezed hard into a knot. "Gault Aulbrek was captured? By who?"

"He was captured by Leif Chaparral in Ravenker," Ava answered. "Taken to Amadon and . . . and . . ." She trailed off.

"And what?" Krista pressed.

"Killed," the girl answered hesitantly.

"Killed?" Krista's heart froze.

"So I heard," Ava continued. " 'Twas all Aeros and the Spider's doing, the betrayal. But Spiderwood is dead now."

"The Spider is dead too?" Krista asked.

"Are you a Bloodwood assassin?" Ava asked. "Are you like the Spider?"

Krista couldn't even form a coherent thought, let alone answer the girl's questions. *My father is dead?* It didn't seem real. She would need proof before she fully believed such a thing.

"Are you here to avenge Spiderwood?" Ava asked. "Are you here to kill the White Prince? Will you kill him for me?"

"Yes." Krista's heart was heavy with pain, confusion, determination. She bowed to the girl. "I've come to slay Aeros Raijael."

"I am willing to help you." Ava's eyes now glowed like ice sparkling in the sunlight. "What must I do?"

"Have you any other clothes?" Krista asked her.

"In the cabinet."

"Put on something comfortable," Krista ordered her. Ava stepped to the cabinet, opened it, grabbed the nearest garment, a thick blue dress, and slipped it on over her thin shift. "Do you have no pants or anything more suitable for riding?" Krista asked.

"Aeros only provides me with fancy dresses."

Krista looked through the cabinet herself, then took out a pair of shoes and a belt, saying, "At least wear these." Ava put the shoes on, strapped the belt around her waist, slipped the sword into the belt. "You said your Lord Aeros would be here soon?" Krista asked. "Or were you just trying to scare us off?"

"No," Ava said. "Aeros usually comes to the chamber this time of day, he comes for certain . . ." She trailed off, a haunted look in her eyes.

Krista pulled forth another one of her Bloodwood daggers. This particular black blade was coated with a poisonous substance called truth athyra, mixed with Royal Bedlam, a clever little concoction meant to paralyze its victim and strangle their breath away. But not before the victim revealed the truth of every question asked of them.

And Krista had many questions to ask the Angel Prince.

She looked at Borden. "I've the same color hair as Ava. We are about the same size. Do you think I could fool him?"

Borden crooked his mouth in a sly grin. "Yes, you can fool him."

"Aeros likes it when I lie in bed and await his arrival," Ava said, following Krista's line of thinking. "I lie under the covers with my back to him, and he comes up behind me, and . . . and then he . . ."

"Say no more," Krista said. "Wait behind the tapestry with Borden." She looked at Borden, cold calculation in her voice. "I shall slip back behind the tapestry and tap on the door when the deed is done."

If a soldier severs faith with the warriors of Raijael, a soldier
shall never peacefully sleep. For a hero's death is the death
where a soldier accepts his death voluntarily.
—THE CHIVALRIC ILLUMINATIONS OF RAIJAEL

CHAPTER THIRTY-SEVEN
GAULT AULBREK

7TH DAY OF THE BLOOD MOON, 999TH YEAR OF LAIJON
SAINT ONLY, ADIN WYTE

G ault Aulbrek stared at the flat stone wall. He carried one of the
torches he had gotten from Enna Spades in one hand, the long
Dayknight sword in the other. He was barefoot. He was also
dressed in naught but dark leather pants and a raggedy, sweat-stained
cotton shirt. As much as he had hated the sweltering-hot Dayknight
armor, he felt compromised without it. But he'd had to get rid of the
bulky stuff to squeeze through the narrow tunnels far below. He would
gather the armor back up on the return journey. It was the boots he
missed the most.

He had finally reached one of secret entrances to Lord Edmon Guy
Van Hester's bedchamber in the fortress atop Mont Saint Only. He set
down the torch, felt along the bottom of the floor where it met the flat
wall, found the crack where he knew the latch would be. With searching fingers, he released the mechanism. There followed a barely audible
click from somewhere in the wall. The doorway popped open without
a sound and swung back, revealing a square cavity just large enough for
him to slip through. The far side of the hole was covered by a thick

tapestry he knew would be hanging there. Dim light filtered through, barely illuminating the passageway behind him.

Stealth was foremost on his mind now. He had no idea if Edmon's chamber was occupied. Doubts had plagued him all the way up the Mont. *Would Ava Shay even remember me?* He had never felt more afraid in his life. *I have seen ten years of war. Killed thousands in the name of the gods,* he had told Squireck Van Hester in the gladiator arena. And this was the home of the cousin he had so callously slain. He felt the gloom and darkness of the fortress, sensed the wraiths and the ghosts in the cobbled passageways and twisting stairs of the Mont. He felt the ghosts of the thousands who had died at the end of his sword brush cold against his flesh. Those ghosts were icy caresses in the air. *Will rescuing Ava Shay be my absolution?*

He gently pricked a hole in the tapestry with the tip of the Dayknight sword, then peered through the thin slit. It was an opulent bedchamber he gazed upon, still familiar to his eyes. He had been in this room before, some five years ago, when the armies of Sør Sevier had taken the Mont from Lord Edmon and the armies of Adin Wyte. The candlelit chamber still consisted of bear rugs, opulent cabinets, tapestries, sculptures, goblets, and gray stone walls. A large four-post canopied bed was hidden in shadow directly across from the window set high in the wall above.

On the bed, under a snowy quilt, he could see the sleeping form of Ava Shay.

The Gallows Haven girl lay on her side, her back to him, blond tresses spilling over the pillows behind her, gleaming softly in the candlelight. The curve of her hip shifted slightly as she adjusted herself in the bed with a heavy breath.

There was no one else in the room. Sword in hand, Gault cautiously pushed the heavy tapestry away from the wall, just enough that he could slip through the small doorway. He stood fully in the room now. *Ava Shay!* The thudding of his heart slowed. After so much effort he had finally reached this place. He knew he had made the right decision in coming back for her.

He could hear faint breathing, soft sounds that called to him across the chamber. Around him candlelight flickered. Shadows danced in the alcoves as he inched toward her, wanting to wake the Gallows Haven girl with a tender touch. His bare feet felt every crack of the cold stone floor, and then the softness of the bear rugs. The white quilt atop Ava's sleeping form was embroidered with gold and silver needlework.

Gault placed one knee on the bed and reached forward with his free hand, gently pulling the white quilt away. "Ava," he whispered.

The blond girl spun around and a black dagger was buried hilt-deep between his ribs before he knew what happened. *She wears Bloodwood armor!* Gault's mind raced as he stared at the black-clad apparition before him, immediately recognizing who it was.

"Krista." His voice was naught but a distant echo in his own ears. The blond girl's eyes widened in despair as the black dagger slid free of his chest and sweat-stained shirt.

"Father," she muttered.

Then all things faded to black.

CHAPTER THIRTY-EIGHT

AVA SHAY

7TH DAY OF THE BLOOD MOON, 999TH YEAR OF LAIJON
SAINT ONLY, ADIN WYTE

ait behind the tapestry with Borden, Krista Aulbrek had said.
*I shall slip back behind the tapestry and tap on the door when the
deed is done.* And sure enough, in less than half an hour there
came a wild tapping from behind the smooth wall. Ava Shay's hand
tightened around the hilt of her own sword, My Heart.

"Be wary," the dwarf who had introduced himself as Ironcloud said.
Borden Bronachell felt along the crack in the floor for the door release.
Ava wondered if he truly was the real Borden Bronachell, king of Gul
Kana. It didn't seem possible. But she would not know what the real
king looked like. She had been around only a few dwarves in Gallows
Haven, mostly gruff old sailors and traders who visited the Grayken
Spear Inn. Ironcloud was as bearded and gruff and smelly as those few
she'd met.

Borden found the catch, there was a click, and the door swung wide,
revealing Krista Aulbrek's panicked face. "It was Gault, it-it was my

father," she stammered, holding back the tapestry from the opening with one trembling hand, black dagger in the other, the look in her eyes hollow and lost. "I've stabbed him."

Ava could see, over Krista's shoulder, the bald man lying in a heap in the center of the four-post bed. *It is Gault!* Her mind reeled. *Aeros said he was dead!* And then another thought occurred to her. *He came back for me!* And then Ava looked at Krista crouching in the doorway. Truly *saw* her. Aeros and the Spider said she bore a great resemblance to Krista Aulbrek. Ava could clearly see the physical likeness.

"We must get my father down to my horse." Krista spoke in an anxious rush, her face flushed with desperation. "We must get him down to my saddlebags and my poison kit before the toxins from the blade suffocate and kill him. I must get him the antidote."

"Bloody rotted angels," the dwarf cursed. "This could ruin our plan to kill the White Prince."

"Fuck your plan." Krista grabbed the tapestry and ripped down hard. The wall hanging folded to the ground, a plume of dust billowing up. Several decorative spears were knocked from the wall too, both landing silently atop the crumpled tapestry, then rolling off. Krista had two black daggers in hand now. "Help carry my father out of here, *Squateye*," she hissed at the dwarf, "or I will gut you where you stand."

Borden crouched down and stepped through the opening and out into the room beside Krista, beckoning the dwarf to follow. "There is naught we can do now but carry him out of here like she wants."

"Fuck." Ironcloud pushed his way past Ava and squeezed through the opening. Once in the room, the dwarf followed Krista and Borden toward the bed and Gault's inert form.

Smelling smoke, Ava crawled into the opening and leaned her head out into the room, My Heart still in hand. She wondered if she should help with Gault, if she even could help. To her right the fallen tapestry had caught fire, and a handful of lit candles were scattered about. One empty sconce tilted on the wall just above the burning tapestry, dangling, almost ready to drop.

Across the room, the dwarf was hauling Gault from the bed, arms wrapped around the unconscious man's upper torso, thick hands under his armpits. Borden had the bald knight by the legs, and together they lifted him from the bed. Gault's arms hung limp, hands dragging on the stone floor as they shuffled him toward Ava. Krista followed, brandishing black daggers in both hands, a cold look on her face. It was a fierce but desperate look.

Ava wanted to help carry Gault. So many had failed her—but Gault Aulbrek had come back. She slipped back into the room, the tapestry now a raging fire at her side.

Aeros Raijael strode into the chamber through the main door, white cloak billowing out behind him, chain mail underneath shining, longsword at his hip. Young Leisel was right behind him. His eyes widened at the sight of Borden Bronachell and Ironcloud carrying Gault Aulbrek across the room. The longsword came rasping from the sheath at Aeros' side. "What is the meaning of this?" he snarled, cruel eyes sweeping the chamber, sword raised and ready. Everyone stopped what they were doing. Motionless.

"Ava!" Aeros' pale brow furrowed as his gaze fell upon her. She still stood near the secret doorway, flames from the burning tapestry licking up between them.

Ava felt the hilt of My Heart grow hot in her hands. *I know every nook and cranny and secret passageway in this castle,* Edmon Guy Van Hester had once told her. *Secret doors that lead to secret places. Secret doors that once shut will never again be opened.* Ava wondered if this was just such a door, wondered if she shouldn't just close it and leave all the madness behind her.

Hammerfiss, in the gleaming armor and livery of a Knight Archaic, stepped into the room behind Aeros and Leisel. "Oh, yes!" he roared, taking in the scene. "An escape attempt in progress! Action! Adventure! Someone's liable to die a bloody death now!" He hauled the huge spiked mace from over his broad shoulder, grinning.

"Everyone dies a bloody death, Ser Hammerfiss!" Aeros shoved Leisel aside, and launched himself straight at Borden and Ironcloud, sword slicing through the now smoky air. "Let no one live!"

Hammerfiss charged too.

Krista Aulbrek met the White Prince's attack with a keen balance and swiftness Ava had never before seen in any one fighter, not even Enna Spades or the Spider. With just her two black daggers, the blond assassin parried each of Aeros' swift strikes, attacking him just as quickly with lightning-fast slashes of her own, causing him to back away, instantly wary.

Borden dropped Gault's legs, snatched up one of the spears that had previously fallen from its perch in the wall, and blocked Hammerfiss' first blow. The decorative spear shattered under the weight of Hammerfiss' heavy iron mace. Borden dove aside, barely escaping the red-haired giant's second downward strike, which hit the floor, sending splinters of stone spraying up with a thunderous *boom!*

Ironcloud dragged Gault toward Ava and the secret doorway. Ava stepped forward to defend them. The air was heavy with black smoke now, the tapestry before the secret door completely engulfed in flame. Unnoticed, Ironcloud and Ava stamped out a path through the fire and dragged Gault's body up and over the rumpled, blackened tapestry. Together they hauled the bald man into the safety of the dark corridor beyond.

Ava turned and looked back through the opening and into the chamber. More Knights of the Blue Sword came pouring into the room. Jenko Bruk was among them, his own sword drawn, confusion on his face as he took in the smoky scene.

Across the chamber, Aeros pressed his attack, swinging his sword at Krista. She danced lightly over the quilts and pillows scattered atop the four-post bed, aiming for the secret door, giving up the fight. With the entrance of the other knights, Borden had also given up in his fight against the much larger Hammerfiss. Krista scrambled across the room and leaped over the burning tapestry and dove through the secret doorway, knocking Ava aside. Borden was right behind her, launching himself through the rising smoke and flames, tumbling into the corridor behind Ava. Ironcloud leaped forward and grabbed the door with both hands, shoving it closed.

And the last thing Ava Shay saw through the flickering flames was Jenko Bruk's bewildered face. And though she was finally free of the torments of Aeros Raijael, though she was finally rescued, it was the loneliest moment of her life.

Laijon kills who he will kill. Be it the lowliest bastard or the most high king,
be it the innocent, the woman, or the child, the firstborn of the unbeliever or
the last, be it stealing the souls of a thousand in a landslide or deluge, Laijon
kills who he will kill. For he is your god. And your god is good.
—THE WAY AND TRUTH OF LAIJON

CHAPTER THIRTY-NINE

NAIL

10TH DAY OF THE BLOOD MOON, 999TH YEAR OF LAIJON

EAST OF SAVON, GUL KANA

Cromm Cru'x galloped his horse past Nail's, bringing his mount to a steady trot beside Bronwyn Allen. The Wyn Darrè girl rode just ahead of Tala Bronachell and Lawri Le Graven. A severe grunt from Cromm cracked the silence, followed by muffled conversation with Bronwyn.

"We'll have to find our way over the river soon." Bronwyn turned to the others, keeping her horse at a steady trot. "Cromm says there is a contingent of Dayknights following us, and it is gaining ground. He says there are about twenty mounted men total, Glade Chaparral at their head. The boy took off his helm to yell at another knight and Cromm recognized him. We must place the river between them and us."

It was midday and they had been following the southern bank of the River Vallè for some time now.

The oghul whispered something else to Bronwyn. The Wyn Darrè girl glanced back at Nail. "Cromm grows more and more upset that we are taking the marked one farther from Amadon. He thinks this journey

445

is most unwise. Absolution is in the other direction. He wishes to fight Glade and the knights and make our way back to Amadon."

At her words, anger pricked at the edges of Nail's skin. The journey to Savon was to find Jondralyn Bronachell, to let her know that the oghul kept one of the famed angel stones in his mouth. This journey was *because* Cromm stole the stone from Stefan.

"We keep going toward Savon," Tala said forcefully.

Bronwyn set spurs to flanks, urging her mount at a faster clip toward Savon. The four others followed suit. The Wyn Darrè girl led the group down an old rutted trail that skirted a tree-studded ridge along the shores of the River Vallè. The path curved down, wending around old alders and tall elms, and then cut right through a tangle of deadfall and bramble stems. Soon the shore was before them.

Across the burbling river of somber black waters, and peeking over the rim of the alder forest beyond, Nail could just make out the towers of Savon against the far horizon. Even though he could see the city, he knew that Savon was still at least a half day off.

The group of five travelers had made good headway since escaping the Filthy Horse Saloon some four days past, sleeping in hidden valleys and thick groves at night. That they were well-fed and mounted had helped hasten their journey. On the first day of their trek, as dawn rose hazy and pink over the landscape of hedgerows and farm fields west of Amadon, Bronwyn and Cromm had requisitioned five palfreys from a contingent of inattentive Silver Guards camped along the riverbank. The dangerous-looking duo had taken it upon themselves to gather the horses. Tala had desired to help with the endeavor, but Nail had advised against it, letting the princess know that Bronwyn and the oghul had their own way of stealing horses that Tala would not approve of. "I think you'd be surprised at what I may or may not approve of," she had countered, making him feel small. Still, she had heeded his advice and let Bronwyn and Cromm go alone.

The five horses the duo stole came complete with bedrolls and saddlebags that were brimming with food. Lawri Le Graven was especially happy to find hidden at the bottom of one saddlebag two sturdy black cloaks with long, billowing sleeves. Now, despite the heat of midday, the girl hid under the cowl of one of the cloaks. The other was wrapped around the silver gauntlet attached to her arm.

Nail did not know if following Jondralyn to Savon was the best of ideas. But Tala insisted she find her older sister and tell her that Cromm Cru'x had the real black angel stone. And after the destruction of the Filthy Horse Saloon, the five of them had nowhere else to go nor anyone else to follow. Everyone else Nail knew was lost or dead: Shawcroft, Stefan Wayland, Bishop Godwyn, Roguemoore, Hawkwood, Val-Draekin, Liz Hen, Dokie. With their absence, it felt as if something had been torn from him and he would never get it back. It felt wrong, traveling without at least one of them for companionship. *Will I see any of them again? Could Hawkwood or Val-Draekin have survived that fire?* The Filthy Horse Saloon had become a horrific inferno at the end. And without Val-Draekin at his side, what would he do? He had been traveling with the Vallè for so long now it seemed strange to be so suddenly without him. He felt vulnerable.

His mind was a confused maze of random thoughts, worries, and unanswered questions. Seita had lied to him about Stefan and a great many other things. He knew it. *And who really was Val-Draekin?* Tala did not trust the Vallè. *Does she even trust me?*

On the trail ahead, Bronwyn and Cromm reined their mounts up before a rickety old roadhouse crouching on the banks of the river. The ramshackle dwelling of weather-worn wooden slats and wood shingles seemed to be the humble lodgings of a ferryman, for there was a long, flat ferry lazing in the river. It was tied to an old wooden dock near the roadhouse. A rope stretched across the expanse of the River Vallè to a similar dock on the northern shore.

A bearded old man shuffled from the roadhouse. A crooked, gap-toothed smile appeared on his face as he greeted both Bronwyn and the oghul with equal amounts of pleasure. "How may I help you?"

Bronwyn dismounted. "We need passage across the river."

"One copper per horse and rider," the man said.

"And if we ain't got one copper per horse and rider?" Bronwyn asked.

Cromm, still mounted, grinned down at the ferryman, making sure most every long tooth in his mouth was visible to the man.

The ferryman gulped, saying, "I'm sure I can get you across for free today." Bronwyn nodded. "I'll be getting the barge ready," the man said. "Just be a moment is all." Then he scurried off toward the flat ferry tied to the dock.

Cromm still grinned, pleased. Nail could see the bulge in the oghul's lip where he kept the black angel stone. He wondered how Cromm could always remain so jolly when the entire Five Isles seemed so full of hidden treachery and death. And Bronwyn always seemed so unashamedly pleased with herself too. It was as if nothing bothered the pair.

"We should pay the man for his labors." Tala had a scowl on her face.

"With what?" Bronwyn chided. "The coppers that none of us carry?"

"I can at least give him a loaf of bread from my saddlebag," Tala countered. She reached back, folded over the big leather flap of her bag, and rummaged around. As soon as they had left Amadon, the princess's bearing had changed, touched now with a bold certainty of purpose.

Nail found himself staring out at the murmuring, dark river. There was a heron not far away, a stark white shape against the blackness of the waters. The heron was perched on one leg in the shallows of the river, graceful in every move, peaceful in every way. Watching the bird placed him into a trance of sorts. The world around him disappeared, and dark thoughts suddenly closed in. He tried to shut them out, tried to close the doors to his soul and think of better things, imagine better things.

But his wandering mind took over. He found himself peering across a glacier at a woman standing on the far edge, silhouetted against a gaping precipice. She was dressed in black, long tawny hair falling down both sides of her face in straight locks. In her arms was cradled a blond boy. The youngster was shivering from the cold, despite the elk-hide coat wrapped about his small body. Tears filled the woman's eyes. She was weeping. "Who are you?" Nail asked, voice drowned out by the cold hiss and rumble of the roaring glacial river far beneath. *Mother?* he mouthed to himself, the overwhelming sound of rushing waters beating against his skull. Nail could almost feel her warm arms around him. He *wanted* to feel those warm arms holding him. Her son. And then together the woman and boy fell backward into the gleaming white crevasse of the glacier.

"No!" Nail called out.

Lawri Le Graven jumped in her saddle, the cloak wrapped around her gauntleted arm slipping free. It dropped to the ground before she could catch it with her other hand. "Laijon bless me!" she exclaimed. "You scared the breath right out of me, Nail."

Bronwyn and Tala were also looking at him with some irritation.

"Sorry," Nail said, voice hollow and lonely to his own ears. He thought he could still hear his mother's voice calling for him faintly—remnants of the dream.

The old ferryman returned. He stared at the gauntlet attached to Lawri's arm.

Nail slid from his saddle and snatched up the cloak, handing it back to the girl, who swiftly covered her arm. He found that Bronwyn and Cromm were scowling at him. *Like they're so perfect . . .*

In the far distance he heard a soft rumble that swiftly grew, horses' hooves drumming on the turf and peat above the river in the distance.

"Glade and the Dayknights," Bronwyn growled. She turned to the ferryman. "Is that barge ready?" He nodded. "Then let's make haste." Bronwyn set spurs to flanks and galloped her horse down the rutted dirt road and onto the ferry, hooves clattering on the wood. Cromm followed, as did Tala and Lawri. Nail guided his horse to the vessel last. The others dismounted.

"Keep your grips firm on those bridle reins," the ferryman advised, testing the tightness of the thick berthing rope that was tied to a large iron cleat hitch on the dock. The rope stretched through two heavy iron loops on the fore and aft of the ferryman's flat barge and continued on out over the river some two hundred paces to the cleat fixed to the wooden quay on the other side.

With a long wooden pole, the ferryman shoved the barge away from shore, jostling all aboard, horses whinnying nervously, adjusting to keep their feet. Nail held the reins tight as advised. The ferryman jabbed the pole deep into the water, digging, pushing the boat along, the current helping some. But it was slow going.

A contingent of armored Dayknights crested the grassy rise beyond the roadhouse and galloped down to the edge of the shore, hooves gouging the trail, kicking up clods of mud. Cromm was correct in his estimation, as Nail counted at least twenty knights. A bannerman rode at their head bearing a black standard emblazoned with the royal crest of Amadon—a silver tree. The flag snapped in the breeze with dark and ominous threat.

One of the knights spurred his brawny destrier out into the river toward the retreating barge, water splashing and foaming at the warhorse's knees. The knight brought the mount to a stop, then shed his polished black helm, revealing the face of Glade Chaparral. A cruel smile wreathed his face as he called out. "You cannot escape me this time, Tala Bronachell!"

Though the barge was in deeper waters, it was only a stone's throw away from the Dayknights. Nail did not feel safe from threat. Several other Dayknights behind Glade also removed their helms. "Tolz, Alain, Boppard," Tala hissed, rage, red and flaming, crossing her face. "I'd hoped they were killed in the Filthy Horse fire. They will do anything to impress Glade."

The three knights dismounted and unhooked the longbows from their saddlebags.

The ferryman speared his pole into the water with more fervor, pushing, trying to speed their escape. More knights were dismounting now, drawing bows from the stout backs of their war chargers. Lawri looked ashen and scared; her breathing had gone ragged. Nail wiped the sweat from his forehead, wondering if there was anything he could do to comfort the hapless girl.

"Only one way to survive now." Bronwyn threw back her forest-green cloak and drew a dagger from her belt. She looked up into the round eyes of her stolen palfrey, wrapped its reins tightly in her fist. Then she thrust the dagger hilt-deep into the neck of the horse, slashing outward, slicing through hide, tendon, muscle, and jugular vein.

Blood gushed from the open wound as the horse bucked and brayed, gurgling from the throat. Lawri gasped. Tala looked at Bronwyn in horror. Blood sprayed the wooden deck as the horse fell, body thudding against the flat surface of the barge. The dying beast twitched and kicked, crimson pumping over the wood. The remaining horses were jittery now, nervous hooves a-clatter on the wooden surface.

Bronwyn's palfrey tried to rise, but Cromm's thick boot crushed its head with a forceful stomp. The oghul drew a knife and opened the throat of his own mount, then pulled the braying beast by the bridle reins down to the surface of the barge.

Bronwyn and Cromm crouched behind the two dead animals. The Wyn Darrè girl pulled the black bow from off her back and nocked a black arrow. "The rest of you best do the same, kill your horses and hide behind them or get gut shot."

An arrow struck the ferryman right in the center of the chest. The long wooden pole slipped from his grip as he dropped into the river with a splash and disappeared. The barge floundered, unmoving against the rope.

"Kill your horse!" Bronwyn shouted at Nail. "All of you! Take cover!"

Two more arrows buzzed overhead, stirring the air. Bronwyn ducked behind her dead horse. She peered over the bloody bulk of her palfrey and fired, her arrow punching into the mass of Dayknights, twanging off black armor, shattering in the trees beyond.

Two arrows sank into the flanks of Lawri's mount. The startled palfrey jumped and bucked and launched itself from the barge straight into the river and the current quickly pulled the screaming beast under the barge.

A hail of arrows zoomed by. Nail's own horse took a thick-hafted arrow right in the midsection. He let loose the reins as the panicked horse jerked away from him, skidding in pools of scarlet, landing on one haunch with a thud. His horse slid awkwardly into the river with a splash, leaving a smear of blood and water in its wake. Nail dropped, hugging the wooden deck. It was splintered and full of knots and soaking in rivers of scarlet. Arrows whizzed over his head.

Lawri dropped to the deck next to Nail, gauntleted arm smacking the wood hard. He pushed the frightened girl in the direction of Cromm and the cover of the two dead palfreys, arrows now bristling from their bodies. The oghul snatched her by the hood of her cloak and pulled her to him. Bronwyn continued to fire back at the Dayknights from behind the two dead horses.

More arrows ricocheted off the deck in front of Nail and caromed over his head. He rolled away, frantic, looking for any cover. Tala was directly behind him, struggling with her own mount, dagger in hand, stabbing at the horse's neck as best she could. But the screaming palfrey resisted, twisting and bucking, jerking the princess over the bloody deck. Still, Tala stubbornly clung to the reins, wildly stabbing. Nail rose to help her, snatching the reins, wrestling with the stressed beast. The horse took an arrow in the side of the head and dropped instantly dead right on top of Tala.

With the bulk of the horse covering her, Tala cried out. Nail grabbed her under the arms and hauled her from under the dead animal, both of them falling back against a deck awash in blood. The horse was hit with more arrows. Tala appeared uninjured, though her leather pants were streaked with blood. Together Nail and Tala crouched behind her dead palfrey as a hail of arrows continued to punch into its quivering flesh with one wet slap after the next.

The barge hung mid-river, pushing against the taut rope in the current. Bronwyn continued to fire back at the Dayknights from her place of cover. Her arrows dropped only a handful of the enemy's destriers, most bouncing harmlessly off black armor. Glade had retreated from the shallows of the river back onto the bank. He dismounted, drew his sword, and strode the length of the wooden dock toward the rope tied to the iron cleat. With one swift stroke of his black blade he severed the ferry line, and the blood-coated barge was set immediately adrift, its aft end twisting in the current, exposing everyone to a new barrage of Dayknight arrows.

As the barge swung about, Nail and Tala leaped over the dead horse and repositioned themselves on the other side, under far less cover.

Bronwyn, Cromm, and Lawri did the same. The vessel continued to drift downriver. Fortunately, they were slowly being pulled farther away from the Dayknights and across the River Vallè toward the north shore, the rope line now slithering through the twin iron loops on the barge. The rope was still tied to the opposite quay but was quickly snaking its way through the iron loops. They would soon be set adrift to the whims of the river current.

Nail broke from cover and lurched across the barge toward the aft end, grabbing the slick rope as it slithered along the bloody deck. Arrows sailed by as he wrapped the end of the rope around the last iron loop several times before it could slip free of the barge. He then scurried for cover as the vessel plowed through the water, swinging away from the Dayknights, eventually breaking through the willow reeds along the north shore, coming to a stop in a pungent marsh that smelled of damp moss and wet weeds.

"Off the boat!" Bronwyn shouted, jumping off the barge and into the black marsh, pushing her way through the hip-deep water toward the shore. Beyond the banks of marshland sprawled the thick forest of alder Nail had seen from the other shore carpeted with bright grass and bracken and mantled with shimmering green leaves. Cromm hauled Lawri up into his strong, burly arms and leaped from the barge, then began carrying her over his shoulder though the marsh.

Hand in hand, Nail and Tala jumped from the vessel too. The water was drear and chill. But they plowed on, the marsh thick with moss and twiny roots that grabbed at their feet. The bulk of the barge was behind them now, blocking a good portion of the Dayknight arrows. Still, some whizzed by like bees and splashed in the water as the group hobbled toward shore, every step a waterlogged struggle.

Soon the river, choked with reeds and leaves, proved only knee-deep, then ankle-deep. Nail quickly found himself on dry land and sprinting for safety next to Tala, boots and pant legs soaked through, the towers of Savon rising in the far distance.

*Why do faith and the certainty of belief create so much suffering,
spilled blood, and the death of men? And how can we Vallè use it against
humanity? For pride in their faith is their greatest weakness.*
—THE ANGEL STONE CODEX

CHAPTER FORTY

LINDHOLF LE GRAVEN

10TH DAY OF THE BLOOD MOON, 999TH YEAR OF LAIJON

SAVON, GUL KANA

Lindholf Le Graven and Mancellor Allen stood just inside the
Preening Pintail near the front entrance, the dog Beer Mug at
watch behind them. Lindholf was in his full Dayknight armor,
black helmet covering his face and scars. Mancellor was helmetless but
also dressed in what armor he had—a ragtag collection of leather and a
chest plate he had scraped up in Lord's Point after the Battle of the Saint
Only Channel. They were a formidable trio of doormen.

It was early evening now, and the tavern had only two customers—a
couple of affable old blacksmiths, both regulars who typically left before the night crowds poured in and things got rowdy. The mounts of
the two blacksmiths, two piebald ponies, were hitched outside. Liz Hen
Neville was talking to the blacksmiths now, a full pitcher of ale on the
table between them. The men were bantering back and forth and making the red-haired girl giggle. They were good to include her in the jokes.
Rutger did not make Liz Hen wear a low-cut corselet like Luiza wore,
like he had forced Delia to wear.

Liz Hen had been given a long white apron, and she was delighted to have it. In fact, Lindholf had never seen any one person more happily in their element than Liz Hen was, serving patrons in the Preening Pintail Tavern and Inn. She laughed and smiled no matter how busy the tavern was, no matter how late the evenings ran, no matter how rude the customer, no matter how crude the comments about her butchered short haircut. She'd just grin, curtsy, and spout something like, "Oh go impale yourselves on each other's spears, the whole lot of you." She would punch back verbally at whatever group of ruffians insulted her. And the ruffians would always burst into laughter.

"I'm a wicked wench. And thanks for all the laughs!" Liz Hen liked to say before she'd scoot herself back into the kitchen and bring out more rounds of ale.

Indeed, in the six days since Liz Hen had started working for Rutger in the Preening Pintail, she had been the most pleasant and likable girl Lindholf had ever come upon. Though every now and then, she would take a swig of that thick red liquid she was addicted to—Blood of the Dragon, Mancellor called it. And once in a while she would bellow a harsh word or two at Dokie Liddle in the kitchen. It wasn't that she didn't like the boy; she just had a problem with men in kitchens, even if they were but washing dishes and beer steins. In her opinion, which she gave regularly, men had no patience for fine cooking, or dutiful serving, or kitchen cleaning, or really anything at all. If one let her keep going, she could eventually find fault with everything and everyone. The girl could talk a lot. It seemed only the shepherd dog, Beer Mug, was apt to listen to her ramblings for more than ten minutes. But Beer Mug was a good-natured fellow.

Thing was, Lindholf, Mancellor, Liz Hen, and Dokie had come to an understanding that first night together atop the tower. Lindholf related the entire story of the weapons and how he had come into possession of each. *Ethic Shroud* he had found on his own in the catacombs under Amadon. A Vallè maiden named Seita had brought him *Blackest Heart* and *Afflicted Fire* from the north. Gault Aulbrek had stolen them from Seita, and Lindholf and Delia had followed him, regaining the weapons and setting up residence here atop this tower. Delia had left, though.

Mancellor was surprised at Gault Aulbrek's part in getting the weapons out of Amadon, whilst Liz Hen and Dokie seemed at once confused, excited, and distressed at the news of Seita bringing *Blackest Heart* and *Afflicted Fire* from the north. They wondered aloud at the fate of the rest of their Company of Nine. Bishop Godwyn had been hung, but what of Nail, Stefan, Roguemoore, Culpa Barra, and Val-Draekin?

"Did Seita tell you whether Nail and Stefan are alive?" Liz Hen had asked.

"I know nothing of anyone named Nail or Stefan," Lindholf answered. "She mentioned nothing to me about the Company of Nine. Of course, I never asked. I just assumed she had found the weapons herself. I did know Roguemoore and Culpa Barra. If they returned to Amadon with Seita, she did not say. Seita did, however, tell me that Val-Draekin died. He fell into a glacier or some such."

Both Liz Hen and Dokie seemed most distressed by that news. The two youths from Gallows Haven then went on to tell him of their quest to the north with the Company of Nine and how Dokie had found *Blackest Heart*. But that was all they knew of the journey, for Dokie had become poisoned and they had separated from the rest.

Mancellor had disclosed how he had taken the angel stones from Aeros Raijael during the Battle of the Saint Only Channel. He then told the others he had stolen *Lonesome Crown* and *Forgetting Moon* from Enna Spades and Jenko Bruk.

The angel stones and weapons, combined with the dreams Mancellor and Lindholf shared, had bonded the four of them together these last few days. Mancellor considered it divine providence that they were all here in Savon together. They had become a tight group, and Lindholf was glad to have new friends. *In fact, Mancellor, Liz Hen, and Dokie might very well be the only friends I've ever had.* He liked Beer Mug, too.

Today the shepherd dog had found a dark corner near the entry of the tavern to set up camp. Beer Mug reminded Lindholf of one of the big silver-wolves he had once seen on a boar-hunting trip his father had taken him on in the Autumn Range. But Beer Mug was not a rough and wild animal. He was content at his post behind Mancellor and Lindholf.

In fact, to Rutger's delight, the dog had even been of some help in tossing several drunken brawlers from the tavern two nights ago. Seemed a dog as large as a silver-wolf worked mighty wonders in turning disagreeable folk agreeable, especially if it was growling in their general direction.

The last six nights Mancellor had stood proudly next to Lindholf, stoic, almost brooding in his seriousness, the black tattoos under his eyes swallowing up the light. They were rarely challenged. And the weapons and stones of the Five Warrior Angels were safe atop the tower above, though Lindholf found his mind was fixed on them often.

It truly seemed like the stones and weapons were meant for him. The only reservation he felt around his new friends was it seemed that they too regarded the stones and weapons as their own. The stones had become an obsession with him. More so than scrubbing and shining his armor over and over to get rid of the dead knight's stink. He ached to look at the stones nightly. Just as he ached for Shroud of the Vallè. He had a burning need for the white powder that was so fierce it was as if the blood in his veins were doing battle with every other part of him. Some days the white powder was all he could think of, eclipsing even his need for the angel stones. New friends. New purpose. *But will I ever be truly happy now that I've tasted the Shroud?*

Dokie Liddle came wandering out of the kitchen. He had been cooking all day with Rutger. Liz Hen turned from her conversation with the two weathered old blacksmiths to say a curt word to the boy.

Beer Mug's ears perked up as the door to the tavern swung open and a helmeted knight stepped in. The knight wore the full regalia and armor of one of the Amadon Silver Guard. Lindholf's heart beat faster, wondering if it was a knight on the hunt for him. Other than himself, this was the first person he had seen in Savon wearing any sort of official uniform representative of the king in Amadon. But the knight just stood in the doorway, the eye slits of his helm naught but mysterious dark hollows in the dim light of the tavern. "What's a Dayknight doing in here?" the Silver Guard asked with a somewhat familiar voice.

Lindholf's heart sped up even more. "A- a Dayknight can- can be wherever he wants," he stammered.

"Is that you, Lindholf?" The Silver Guard removed his helm, revealing the long hair and scarred face of Jondralyn Bronachell, black eye patch over her right eye.

"M'lady." Lindholf immediately bent his knee to her. Even with the scar slashing across her face, his cousin still was striking to behold, both fierce and beautiful. And she was a princess of Amadon. *And what is she doing here?*

"Stand," Jondralyn ordered. "Delia said you were here at the Preening Pintail."

"Delia?" Lindholf felt his skin flush red at the mention of the barmaid. Clearly she had made it back to Amadon just as she'd desired.

"Stand," Jondralyn repeated, beckoning him to rise. "Please stand up before you draw everyone's attention."

Liz Hen and Dokie were already looking their way. The two old blacksmiths were nursing their mugs, unconcerned. Lindholf took a deep breath and stood, removing his helm. "You saw her?" he asked eagerly. "You saw Delia?"

A bleak look stole over Jondralyn's face, a dark and bleak look that turned swiftly sad, then regretful. "Aye," she muttered almost under her breath, looking away from him as she continued. "I saw her in the Filthy Horse Saloon not more than four days ago. She told me you had—" She stopped herself, shadowy gaze now on Mancellor Allen. "She told me you had something I might—"

"The shield," Lindholf said. "Delia told you I had *Ethic Shroud*; she told you I had the shield and an angel stone."

Jondralyn looked hesitant to answer. She was studying Mancellor with some concern in her gaze.

"Mancellor knows of the weapons of the Five Warrior Angels." Lindholf gestured to the Wyn Darrè man with a nod. "He knows everything, including the story of the shield I found under Purgatory."

Mancellor dipped his head to her. "I'm Mancellor Allen. You are Jondralyn Bronachell, princess of Gul Kana. I recognize you. I saw you in Ravenker, briefly."

"You did?" she said.

"I— I did," Mancellor answered, then fell silent.

Jondralyn studied the Wyn Darrè fellow for a moment, then turned to Lindholf. "You have no idea how much trouble that missing shield has caused me," she said, no small measure of concern in her voice. The conversation felt awkward to Lindholf.

"You're a woman." Liz Hen approached, pushing herself into their midst, gawking at Jondralyn with wide, bloodshot eyes.

"That I am," Jondralyn answered, her worried gaze again roaming the tavern.

"But you're all dressed up in armor," Liz Hen said.

Jondralyn's back stiffened, face darkening with anger. "I wear the livery of the Silver Guard, to be exact. And I wear it with pride."

"And no one has put you to death?" The look on Liz Hen's face was one of pure incredulity.

"They have not," Jondralyn huffed. "They wouldn't dare."

"Splendid." Liz Hen beamed at the answer. "Most splendid indeed. Times must be changing. Leif Chaparral tried to hang me for pretending to be a boy and wearing armor and fighting in the Battle of the Saint Only Channel!"

"*You* fought in the Battle of the Saint Only Channel?" Jondralyn eyed the big, red-haired girl with some skepticism.

"Don't act so alarmed," Liz Hen said. "I'm a big girl. I've donned armor of all kinds. I've used swords and bows and arrows just like a man. I've fought sharks and mermaids and even killed oghuls and at least one Sør Sevier knight that I know of."

"I helped her kill that knight," Dokie piped up. "I also fought in the Battle of the Saint Only Channel."

"As did Beer Mug," Liz Hen added. The shepherd dog drifted over to her side. She gently patted his head. "We are retired fighters, all of us, happily settled in this nice tavern now with respectable jobs, thank you very much."

"Are you Jondralyn Bronachell?" Dokie asked. He held up a copper coin, looking from the image on the coin to the princess's face. "You sure look like her." He slipped the coin back into his pocket. "But for the scars and the missing eye and such, I say you're the spitting image of Jondralyn Bronachell." Dokie elbowed Liz Hen. "I think it's the princess of Gul Kana."

"Well," Liz Hen said, "stands to reckon, only a *princess* can wear armor without getting hanged."

"Are you really Princess Jondralyn?" Dokie asked. "How did you get that scar?"

"Ser Leif Chaparral betrayed me," Jondralyn said. "That is how I got the scar."

"He is a flea-bitten dirty bastard of the rankest order," Liz Hen said.

"He is that," the princess said. Then her attention was again on Lindholf. "You have it still, don't you, *Ethic Shroud*?"

"Not only do I have *Ethic Shroud*," Lindholf said, "but I have all the angel stones and weapons of the Five Warrior Angels."

"Where?" Jondralyn's eyes widened.

"Atop the tower," Lindholf answered.

"What tower? The one just outside? Who watches the weapons then?"

"Nobody. They are safe."

"Can you be sure?" Jondralyn seemed distressed. "You must take me to them."

"We're at work," Lindholf said. "Rutger won't just let us go up there now. If he comes out of that kitchen and sees that we're gone, he'll be more than sore."

"How can you be so worried about a silly tavern job, Lindholf?" Jondralyn asked. "Especially at a time like this?" Her stern gaze searched the tavern once more. "Don't you see, your job is over. You shall show me the weapons and stones. And then you are coming with me back to Amadon."

**

They slipped out of the Preening Pintail without Rutger's permission. Lindholf, Mancellor, Liz Hen, and Dokie led Princess Jondralyn to the roof of the tower. Beer Mug bounded up the stairs last, tail a-wag. The sun had just dipped below the far western horizon, a faint hazy red.

Dokie lit the lanterns. Yellow light poured over the wood-plank roof, throwing long, dancing shadows over the four bedrolls and the tarp covering the weapons of the Five Warrior Angels. The shadows stretched as far as the knee-high crumbled battlement that encircled the stone building. The soothing sound of the Ridliegh River could be heard lapping against the southern base of the tower below. The hum and rustle of those droning waters had lulled Lindholf to sleep many a night. He set his helm aside and pulled the tarp off the five weapons.

"I knew I made the right choice in coming here," Jondralyn said, relief in her voice as she marveled at the glittering magnificence of the five artifacts. "I knew I was right about Savon."

The weapons of lore and legend were spread out before her on the weather-worn planks of the tower, a leather pouch containing the angel stones resting there with them.

Jondralyn shed her helm and gauntlets and picked up *Afflicted Fire* first, examining it carefully, slowly, respectfully. She then picked up the others, studying each: *Blackest Heart, Lonesome Crown, Forgetting Moon, Ethic Shroud*, running her palm over the latter's pearly smooth surface with such a deliberate reverence that it touched Lindholf's heart. He felt a lump growing in his own throat, knowing that he might very well be witnessing something of the divine, even the fulfillment of prophecy, if he dared believe. *One of royal blood holding all five weapons of the Five Warrior Angels.*

Jondralyn knelt and took up the small leather satchel that held the five angel stones. Unstrapping the flap, she reached in and produced two of the stones, one fiery red, the other bright blue. They nestled together in the palm of her hand. She pulled two more from the satchel, one brilliant green and one as white as starlight. The last one she removed from the pouch was black. She cupped all five in her bare hand. "I can feel them vibrate and sing in my hand," she said.

Four of the stones seemed alive with shimmering light and power. The black stone sat lifeless as always, a gloomy black stain next to the others.

"The black one always looks dead to me," Liz Hen said. "As if it doesn't belong with the others."

Jondralyn looked up at the big girl. "They are all magnificent," she said, annoyance in her voice. Then she gently set each stone before the weapon it belonged to: the white stone with *Ethic Shroud*, blue with *Forgetting Moon*, black with *Blackest Heart*, green with *Lonesome Crown*, and the red she laid down last, with *Afflicted Fire*. And the way she knelt and carefully placed the stones, it seemed almost a sacrament.

Lindholf found himself captivated by the simple ritual. With the stones and weapons arrayed before her, the princess was like a giver of hope, a harbinger of things to come. It was as if each stone and each weapon somehow belonged to her, and she to them. With her fierce but beautiful face and sparkling Silver Guard armor, Lindholf could believe Jondralyn Bronachell could very well be one of the Five Warrior Angels returned.

Yes, here atop this lonely tower it seemed as if the princess of Amadon literally began to glow in her armor, more perfect in image and form and splendor than the Laijon statue in Amadon. In fact, Lindholf had never before seen one human look more dignified and ideal. *There is hope at the end of all things.* The lump in his throat was gone and his heart soared. *This is right!* To him this was the beginning, when right overcame all wrongs and betrayals and injustices and the world was made pure. *And I am a part of it. I have done the right things! All my decisions have led me to this place, right here, right now, with the savior of us all, Jondralyn Bronachell.*

The princess stood. She looked at Lindholf. "Delia told me how you both traveled here with *Afflicted Fire*, *Ethic Shroud*, and *Blackest Heart*. It seems divine providence that you and the barmaid chose Savon, for I saw this city in my dreams."

Jondralyn turned to Mancellor, Liz Hen, and Dokie. "But how did *Lonesome Crown* and *Forgetting Moon* get here?"

Mancellor bowed. "I shall tell you, if it please m'lady."

"Tell me," Jondralyn said.

Mancellor Allen launched into his story, starting with his capture in Ikaboa five years before, losing his sister, Bronwyn, being forced to crusade across Wyn Darrè with the armies of Sør Sevier, snatching the angel stones from Aeros Raijael during the Battle of the Saint Only

Channel, then stealing the helm and battle-ax from Jenko Bruk and Enna Spades in Lord's Point, ending with his journey to Savon with Liz Hen and Dokie.

The harrowing tale did not take long to impart, and the princess listened in rapt attention. "You are fearless and you are brave, Ser Mancellor Allen." She turned to Liz Hen and Dokie. "As are the two of you. And if I have anything to say about it, your names shall go down in history as ones most brave and valiant, as good souls who have helped assure Absolution and the return of the Five Warrior Angels."

She seized Mancellor by the arm, her grip firm. "But you mentioned your sister, Bronwyn. I must tell you that I met a girl in Amadon. She had tattoos about her eyes, dark tattoos, much like yours, but covering most of her face. She went by the name of Bronwyn Allen, claimed to hail from Wyn Darrè, though I do not recall if she specified Ikaboa as her home. But she oft talked of her brother, who she lost in the war. Could this Bronwyn be your sister?"

"I do not know, but it could be," Mancellor answered, hope infusing his voice. "Last I saw Bronwyn, she was but a young girl. She had no tattoos as you describe, though she did help tattoo my face before I went off to fight against the White Prince." He motioned to the twin black streaks under his own eyes.

"The Bronwyn I met was good with a bow," Jondralyn went on. "Wore two white feathers in her hair. Traveled with a brute of an oghul named Cromm."

"It is her!" Mancellor exclaimed with exhilaration. "I taught her to shoot with a bow. She had more talent than I ever did. And Cromm Cru'x was a friend of my father. I must get to Amadon and find her! Take me to Amadon. Take me to my sister, I beg of you, m'lady, please."

"I do not know if I could find her again," Jondralyn said. "I left Cromm and your sister in the Filthy Horse Saloon under the care of my sister, Tala. I left the saloon soon after Delia hung herself."

"Soon after Delia *what*?" Lindholf asked, startled, heart in his throat. "How can that be—"

Beer Mug barked. There was a loud noise in the tower below.

"Is Rutger coming up?" Liz Hen asked of no one in particular.

Suddenly a Dayknight emerged. Stepping heavily on the stairs, up from the shadows of the hole in the roof's floor. Atop the tower, the knight stood before them. A black shade. Eye slits of his helm naught but twin pits of darkness. Gripped in the Dayknight's gauntleted right hand was a Dayknight sword, long black blade streaked with blood, ruby drops dripping leisurely to the wood planks beneath its glimmering tip. The new Dayknight casually reached up with his free hand and removed his helm.

Liz Hen gasped aloud. "The red-haired bitch."

Lindholf took a wary step back. It was a woman. A red-haired woman with a pale freckled face of exquisite cold beauty. A blood-soaked cloth was wrapped around her neck. She let her helm drop to the floor with a thud.

"*Enna Spades,*" Mancellor Allen hissed. He drew his own sword with a rasp that cut the night, then crouched, setting his stance, ready to fight.

"You were easy to find." The corners of Enna Spades' mouth twisted into a coy smile. "Not hard to ask around about a man with black tattoos under his eyes." Her cold green eyes fixed on Mancellor, not wavering. "Plus, Gault told me about this place. Made you easy to track, my friend."

"I was never your friend," Mancellor said with venom.

"That's not what your cock said all those many nights. But you always were a fool. Everyone within fifty miles of Savon knew of the doorman with the tattoos working at the Preening Pintail." Spades gave the entire group—including the weapons and angel stones on the floor—a cursory glance, and then she focused on Mancellor. "Who would have guessed, Mancellor Allen of Wyn Darrè would lead me to everything I ever desired."

The pale innocence of the warrior woman's freckled face was disappearing with every calculated word she spoke. Lindholf could sense her savage confidence from across the roof of the tower.

Spades reached up with her free hand and pulled a coin from under the bloodstained cloth wrapped around her neck. The coin glowed copper against the polished blackness of her gauntleted fingers. She studied the coin, comparing it to the face of Jondralyn Bronachell, who stood stiffly across the tower from her.

"The resemblance is uncanny. At least the scar across the coin matches the scar across your face." Spades looked fondly at the coin; then her look soured. "But I shall need it no more." She casually tossed the copper away. Glittering in the lamplight, the coin sailed over the broken-down battlements to the river below.

Spades gripped her Dayknight sword in both hands now. Blood still dripped from the blade as she looked at Mancellor. "Odd, there were no doormen down in the Preening Pintail to protect the place from the likes of me. Rutger seemed most agitated and displeased, you know, before he died. In fact, there is no one left alive down in that horrific little tavern."

Fear crawled through Lindholf's veins. *It's Rutger's and Luiza's blood on her sword.*

Spades' eyes were on Jondralyn. "Apparently I was not the first woman in armor to sully that precious little tavern with my presence tonight. Two idiot patrons down there so rudely made mention that they were most unhappy to see me. I guess I was the second woman in armor to defile their tavern tonight. What they failed to realize is that I left a wake of taverns and inns between here and Lord's Point full of dead men who did not like a woman in armor soiling their dear little drinking holes."

She killed the two old blacksmiths too? Lindholf felt the palm of his own hand grasp the hilt of his own Dayknight sword.

"Don't think I don't know exactly who you are," Liz Hen blurted, fiery red eyes fixed on Spades. "Your words were as smooth and slick as warm pigeon shit back in Gallows Haven, but I'm a different person now, you evil bitch. You saw I did not back down from you in Praed's camp and I won't back down now. I'm not afraid of you or no one."

"Brave of you to say," Spades said. "But the truth is, that dog is the only one of you I fear." She aimed the point of her blood-dripping blade at Beer Mug. "He's the one who chewed up my neck. He's the one who left me for dead."

Lindholf's eyes again fell on the bloody cloth wrapped around Spades' neck.

"But I ain't so easy to kill," the warrior woman said. "Now I aim to slay that fucking dog once and for all. And don't think I won't hesitate to slay the rest of you once I'm done." Her speech was followed by a moment of dark and hollow silence.

Then Dokie said, "You're a real asshole, ain't ya, lady?"

"The third time I meet the boy who swam with sharks." Spades looked at Dokie, admiration in her eyes. "Bravest thing I ever saw."

"Like Liz Hen said, you're a real bitch."

"And here I thought we had a healthy respect for each other after that fight in Praed's camp and after that little incident in Gallows Haven. Now you go calling me an asshole and a bitch. Kind of ruins our relationship, don't you think, really quite destroys the bond we shared?"

"Leave Dokie alone," Liz Hen growled.

"Oh, shut up already," Spades fired back.

But Liz Hen was clearly not the type given to shutting up. "Fuck you!" she blared. "And fuck your papa's big nasty that blew seed into the slimy nether parts of your dirty whore mother."

Spades bowed to the girl in feigned appreciation. "Now that's one inventive, garrulous insult, if I do say so myself. I imagine you are full of a myriad of similar such platitudes, brazen little thing that you are."

Jondralyn bent to pick up the nearest weapon. *Forgetting Moon*. But it was heavy. Frustrated, the princess could do naught but lift the ax's handle, dragging the double blade along the wood-plank floor with a loud scrape, struggling to lift it.

Spades laughed. Then she turned her attention to Lindholf. "You." She beckoned him with a nod. "The one in the shiny armor, you are the only one I do not recognize. Yet I wager there's a story behind that deformed face of yours. A divine *secret*."

Lindholf gripped the pommel of his own sword tighter.

"Yes." Spades' eyes narrowed to cold slits now. "Grip your sword tight, boy." She set her stance. "In fact, you'd all best ready yourselves to fight. And then ready yourselves to die, every last one of you."

She wasted no time and flew straight at Mancellor, black sword slicing through the still of the night. Mancellor scarcely had time to bring his own blade up in defense. Yet he just managed to block her wicked slash, ducking, flinging himself backward, knocking into Dokie, who stumbled and spun toward the crumbled battlement.

Liz Hen had no weapons, but she screamed and flung herself right at Spades, purely reflex, balled fists swinging. The warrior woman elbowed Liz Hen in the face swift and hard, her black armor cracking against Liz Hen's chin and cheekbone, sending the big girl reeling back onto her haunches, lip bloody.

Beer Mug launched himself at Spades, teeth gnashing in a snarling rage. The warrior woman swung out wildly in defense, the flat of her heavy black blade striking the big gray dog across the length of his body. With a yelp of pain, Beer Mug spun into Liz Hen. Both of them tumbled away in a heap.

Frozen in fear, Lindholf stood and watched. Jondralyn tried to lift *Forgetting Moon*, strange tendrils of blue smoke now curling up the haft of the ax.

Spades allowed Mancellor no moment of respite as she was once again on the attack, her sword blazing toward him a second time. The Wyn Darrè man had just recovered from her first jarring blow. He barely dodged her second swing aimed right at his head, trying to counter, his own wild momentum sending him careening away again into Dokie. They both crashed against the broken-down battlement of the tower. Spades lunged after them. Mancellor got his blade up in time to block her third strike. But the force behind her blow sent him reeling back into Dokie again, both of them folding over the battlement, off-balance, nearly falling. Mancellor turned just as Spades kicked. The sole of her heavy boot caught the Wyn Darrè man right in the chest, sending him spinning backward over the battlement and out into the darkness, where he dropped, then vanished from view. A moment later there was a splash as his body landed in the river.

Dokie regained his feet, wide-eyed, looking out over the edge where Mancellor had disappeared. With her free hand, Spades grabbed the small boy by the neck of his shirt and lifted him out over the edge of the tower. "You're the only brave person I ever met in all of Gul Kana," she said, jabbing the tip of her sword up under his chin. "You swam with them sharks like a hero. I respect you too much to kill you. So I shall let you go." Then she dropped him and he disappeared into the darkness.

"No!" Liz Hen screamed as Dokie's body splashed into the dark waters below.

She untangled herself from Beer Mug and jerked to her feet. "He can't be down there in that river alone!" she yelled. "He's afraid of sharks!" Liz Hen barreled across the tower toward Spades. Brushing past the warrior woman, the big girl launched herself over the battlement, knees folded into her chest as she dropped like a boulder into the darkness below. Her splash into the Ridliegh River was the loudest of the three.

Beer Mug stared at the spot where Liz Hen had disappeared, head cocked to the side as if contemplating going after her. He whimpered, took one look at Spades, then dashed toward the opening in the wood floor and scurried down the stairs of the inner tower and was gone.

It had all happened so fast that Lindholf had barely drawn a breath, Dayknight sword impotent in his shaking hand. Jondralyn was still trying to lift *Forgetting Moon*. Thick blue smoke poured from between her fingers, twisted and coiled up her arm, spreading over her chest.

Spades was an ominous black silhouette against the night, bloody sword in hand as she strode toward Jondralyn. She stopped. Her own green eyes were alight in wonder as she stared at Jondralyn and the glowing blue smoke twining up the haft of the battle-ax. Finally Jondralyn lifted *Forgetting Moon* in both hands.

Spades attacked Jondralyn with a swift and vicious swing that crashed down like thunder against the upraised ax. With a boom and burst of blue lightning, Spades' Dayknight blade shattered into a thousand bloody and black shards that pinged and twinkled and scattered over the wood-plank floor. A quivering hilt and black-opal pommel was all that was left in Spades' shaking hands.

Jondralyn managed to keep the battle-ax aloft, the blue light of its smoky surface agleam in her lone startled eye. Spades flung the useless black hilt away and dove for the long white sword, *Afflicted Fire*. The warrior woman seized the sword's ivory-colored hilt and rolled to her feet, ferocious pale face now determined and hard-edged with a seething rage. She set her stance, square to her enemy.

In the center of the tower, Enna Spades and Jondralyn Bronachell faced each other in silence, the princess of Gul Kana bearing the double-bladed battle-ax, *Forgetting Moon*, the fierce red-haired warrior woman wielding *Afflicted Fire*—the bone-white sword with the crescent-moon hilt-guard and pearly blade that Lindholf himself had seen drink the blood of men. *And what can my Dayknight sword do against magic such as that?* he thought. The wrecked remains of Spades' Dayknight sword scattered across the wood-plank floor spoke to that. *But I still have Seita's poisoned Bloodwood dagger.* His hand released its frozen grip on his sword. He reached for the hidden black dirk buried under his armor. *Instant death it held. Seita's poisons still coated its blade.* His fingers curled around the hilt.

"You really believe in the magic, don't you?" Spades' voice cut the silence. "You really do believe in yourself, Jondralyn Bronachell. You believe that the battle-ax is going to save you?"

"I do," Jondralyn answered. "Laijon is with me. Mother Mia, too."

Spades' cold green eyes narrowed. "You really do believe there is some form of divine power in you that makes you better than me, more worthy?"

"The gods have guided me here," Jondralyn said. "Guided me to this place through my dreams, to Savon, to this very tower, to claim what is rightfully mine. The gods deem me the Harbinger, the one to stave off Fiery Absolution and slay Aeros Raijael." Her lone eye narrowed to a hard, cold slit. "The gods shall help me slay you."

Spades offered the princess a curling little smile. "You cannot be better than me through simple dreams and wishful thinking and magic and prayers to your god. That is not real power. Real power comes through hard work and practice and experiencing thousands of battles and thousands of deaths."

Spades then held up the white sword, admiring it, saying, "As I've told many of Aeros' young female slaves, nothing compares to having a sharp blade in your hand and knowing how to wield it. When you can kill as efficiently as a man, that is *strength*. When nobody can defeat you with a blade, that is *power*. There is no more dangerous force in the Five Isles than a woman with a sword. Or a woman willing to use her own mind. Or a woman ready to do whatever she damn well pleases. And *I* am that woman. You, Jondralyn Bronachell, are naught but a dreamer who has put in scant little time or effort to compete on my level."

"Try me," Jondralyn said. "I have been trained by the best. I have been trained by Hawkwood."

Spades swung *Afflicted Fire*. Jondralyn blocked with *Forgetting Moon*. Blue sparks and white thunder roared into the night as both women were flung away from each other, sliding along their backs across the floor of the tower.

Tumbling to a stop, Jondralyn lost her grip on the vibrating *Forgetting Moon*. The ax tumbled and skittered over the wood-plank floor, coming to rest against the tower's crumbled battlement.

Spades also lost her hold on *Afflicted Fire*. She scrambled and caught the white sword before it clattered into the open hole in the floor and tumbled down the stairs and into the black hollows of the tower.

Back on her feet, Jondralyn lunged for *Ethic Shroud* and the five angel stones that were nearer to her than the lost battle-ax. Spades slowly advanced on the princess. Jondralyn scooped up all five stones in one hand, then snatched up the shield by the leather strap hooked to its back. Standing, *Ethic Shroud* protecting the length of her body, the princess held the five angel stones out toward Spades like a weapon, as if some magic would surely jump from them and devour her foe. And magic it was. Blue. Green. Red. White. Colorful shards of light came streaming out from between Jondralyn's quivering fingers. And *Ethic Shroud* shone like pure starlight against her chest, illuminating the entire rooftop with blinding white light.

Enna Spades rushed the princess, *Afflicted Fire* steady in her hands, an icy confidence fixed in her cold eyes. Jondralyn braced herself behind the shield.

And like a strike of lightning, the shimmering white blade of *Afflicted Fire* came arching down, shearing the hand holding the angel stones off at the wrist. Jondralyn's suddenly detached appendage dropped to the wooden floor of the tower with a wet *thump*, spilling the five angel stones from five lifeless fingers—fingers that slowly curled inward on themselves until they were motionless. Blood drained from the raw, severed end of the hand, soaking into the wood, oozing toward the five angel stones.

"Laijon almighty and Mother Mia too." Spades stepped back. "You should have known those weapons and stones weren't gonna be worth a lick of ripe oghul shit in your hands, girl."

Lindholf gaped in horror. He felt his hand gripping the hilt of the Bloodwood dagger. Yet he couldn't bring himself to leap to the aid of Jondralyn. In fact, he felt himself cower back, almost hoping to hide his entire body in the darkness of the night sky behind him, heart pounding with fear. His feet were rooted in place. His whole body immobile. Frozen with cowardice. *It's everything from my dream come true.* He imagined himself back in Memory Bay, a mermaid clawing at his arm. *The visions! Mancellor falling from the tower. A woman in black armor!* Jondralyn could only stare down at what remained of her arm—a stump of an arm that gushed blood over the pure white shield and her own Silver Guard armor.

"Rotted fucking angels," Spades grumbled. "Lady Death take me to the underworld right now, but you're getting everything all bloody." Spades snatched up Jondralyn's bleeding severed hand and tossed it out over the edge of the tower. Lindholf heard the faint but unmistakable wet slap as it lit on the cobbled street below.

Spades then took one step forward and stabbed the tip of *Afflicted Fire* two inches straight into Jondralyn's remaining eye and pulled the blade swiftly back out. The princess screamed in both terror and pain and dropped *Ethic Shroud*, both of her hands frantically clutching at her face, where her lone remaining eye now drained blood.

But she only had one hand to clutch her face with. The handless arm brushed against the side of her face uselessly, pumping blood all over her neck and down her silver chest-plate armor. Jondralyn folded to her knees in agony, crying in desperation now, both arms waving out in vain before her, totally blind.

Spades ignored Jondralyn and her cries. The red-haired warrior woman casually gathered up the angel stones, slipping them one at a time into the leather satchel from whence they came. When she was done, she stretched the tarp out over the wood floor of the tower. She then began gathering up the rest of the weapons, placing them into the middle of the tarp.

Jondralyn rolled over onto her side, writhing in agony, crying aloud, crying for help. Lindholf had to look away. He couldn't go to her. As he watched Spades collect all the weapons of the Five Warrior Angels, he began to truly believe he was something abnormally wicked and slothful, worse than some creature from the underworld. He had done nothing, not one single thing to prevent all that had happened here tonight. *Why? Why did I do nothing? Why do I still do nothing?* He had not lifted a finger. Yet he still felt drained, like an empty water skin made of leather, shriveled and useless. He just couldn't muster up anything in the way of bravery. *It's like I don't even exist, not even to Enna Spades. It's like she can sense that I am not a threat, that I am nothing.*

Spades had ignored him throughout the entire battle. *And that is how useless I am!*

They were all now gathered in the tarp: *Afflicted Fire, Forgetting Moon, Ethic Shroud, Lonesome Crown, Blackest Heart.* Spades folded the canvas over onto itself and hauled the weapons up and over her shoulder. The load was bulky and huge, but she headed for the hole in the floor, carefully taking the stairs, vanishing down into the dark.

Lindholf just stared at the hole. Then he turned and watched Jondralyn squirm in pain. Then, at length, whatever spell of fear that had held him immobile for so long broke and he went to her. He knelt at her side. Grabbed up her one good hand in his. She lay on her back now. Blood covered her entire face.

"It's me," he said. "It's your cousin, Lindholf."

"I can't see," she cried.

"I'm so sorry." He found he was crying too.

"Which hurts worse, the hand or my eye?" She wasn't making any sense, and Lindholf's heart crumbled.

"Why didn't you help me?" Her bloody grip tightened around his own hand. "Why didn't you help me, Lindholf?"

"I don't know," he sobbed. *Jondralyn without eyes. Underwater visions!*

"How can I live as a blind person? How can I live without sight? Why did you not help me, Lindholf?"

"Don't hate me, Jondralyn. Don't hate me. I was scared. I'm scared. I've always been scared. My whole life I've been afraid. I've never been very strong. I have horrible visions. It's the Shroud of the Vallè. It's all I can think of, all the time, it consumes me."

A shadow fell over Lindholf. He whirled and found Enna Spades standing behind him once again, the white sword, *Afflicted Fire*, gripped in her hand. "Shroud of the Vallè?" Spades said. It was a question. She gave him a long, level look, and then continued, "I can get you Shroud of the Vallè. But you need to help me carry the weapons. They are at the bottom of the stairs. But I don't want to lug them clear to Saint Only all by myself."

"I must tend to Jondralyn," Lindholf stammered, wiping at his tear-streaked face with one nervous hand. "She is my cousin."

Spades took *Afflicted Fire* and set its razor tip under Jondralyn's chin.

"Ow, ouch. What's that?" Jondralyn exclaimed as Spades pushed down.

"No." There was terror in the princess's voice as her one good hand clawed at the blade. *"Don't."*

Spades leaned on the sword, driving the blade through Jondralyn's chin and up into her brain. The princess of Amadon went still, her arm falling limp at her side in an ever-widening pool of scarlet.

Afflicted Fire drank her blood. Faint rivulets of red flowed up and into the blade's pulsing and swirling innards. It was as if it were sucking away her very soul. Lindholf shuddered. Then Spades yanked the blade free.

"You needn't tend to her now," she said to him. "Help me carry the weapons back to Saint Only and I shall find you all the Shroud of the Vallè you can sniff up your nose."

"You killed her," Lindholf cried.

"She killed herself."

He couldn't stop the tears. "But it doesn't seem right."

"Oh, spare me the dewy eyes, kid. She's a fair enough mess now and completely dead. So get on your feet. We needn't stick around here. You're coming with me."

"But—"

"You'll do as I say," she growled. "There are more burlap sacks in that junk room downstairs. We can divide up the stuff. Make it easier for the both of us to carry the weapons of the Five Warrior Angels out of this shit-hole town and back to my lord Aeros."

For he who hath known the mind of Laijon hath rejoiced with those who rejoice.
—THE WAY AND TRUTH OF LAIJON

CHAPTER FORTY-ONE

NAIL

10TH DAY OF THE BLOOD MOON, 999TH YEAR OF LAIJON

SAVON, GUL KANA

Even before entering the tavern, Nail had felt an unsettling voice inside his head warning him away. And he wished he *had* stayed away from the Preening Pintail, for death was all that lived within its murky innards. The place was naught but a dank and bloody wreck of overturned tables and upended chairs. And four dead bodies lay in pools of dark scarlet in the main room; three older men and a young serving wench. All four of them crisscrossed with grisly wounds from a sword.

"Fresh slayings," Cromm Cru'x announced after examining the two nearest the front entry. The way the oghul said the word *slayings* sent a shudder through Nail.

"Let's take our leave of this place," Bronwyn Allen advised sternly. "This whole town feels cursed."

"But my sister!" Tala exclaimed, brown eyes roaming the ghostly tavern with worry. "What if she's been hurt?"

"Your sister is not here." Bronwyn's look gave a stern warning. Turning for the door, she beckoned the rest to follow. Lawri Le Graven was the first to heed the Wyn Darrè girl's warning, hustling back out into the cobbled street, her gauntleted arm hidden under one of the two cloaks she always carried. Bronwyn, Cromm, and Tala followed.

Nail exited the building last, stepping warily back into the night. He immediately spotted what looked like a tan leather glove lying in the gutter not far from the entry of the tavern. But he quickly realized what it was—a severed hand cleanly detached at the wrist. There was very little blood, just a smear over the nearest gray cobble. Lawri saw the hand too, and a sick look spread over her pale face. He was sure the gruesome thing had not been there when they had entered the tavern.

"Let's find shelter for the night," Bronwyn said, eyeing the severed hand in disgust, then scanning the street, wary. "And not anywhere near here. Glade Chaparral and his cronies are likely across that river by now. They could easily be in town. We can't afford to run into them again. Not here."

Bronwyn's shadowy eyes settled on two piebald ponies and two black palfreys tethered to a hitching post between the tavern and the tall stone tower to their right.

"We'll need good mounts, too." She headed that way. Cromm followed her.

The door to the tower nearest the tavern suddenly burst open and two helmeted Dayknights spilled out into the street. Heavy canvas bundles were slung over both of the knights' shoulders. One of the knights wore a Dayknight sword at his belt. The other appeared unarmed, though the white hilt of a sword jutted up from the opening of that knight's sack. The hilt-guard was stark and bright and bore the unmistakable shape of a crescent moon. Again an unsettling feeling stole over Nail at the sight of the white sword hilt.

Bronwyn and Cromm stopped. The two knights were closer to the hitching post than they, both heading toward the two black palfreys. "The horse on your left is yours!" one of the knights barked, voice sounding almost familiar to Nail under the helm. "Tie the sack to the saddle with the leathers!"

"I know what to do!" The knight with the black sword clanking at his hip scurried toward the hitching post, his gait unsure under the bulk of the canvas sack. "Just leave me alone!" He hauled his large sack up onto the back of the nearest palfrey and began tying it down. The other Dayknight did likewise, tying his own sack with the white sword in it with more swiftness and assuredness.

"Be quick securing that sack!" the Dayknight with the long white sword ordered the other knight. Then the knight impatiently skirted around the backside of the black palfrey to help his companion tie down the bulky sack. "Leave me be," the other knight snapped. "I've got it."

"Bullshit you've got it!" the other raged. "Let me do it!"

Bronwyn and Cromm watched all this impassively, at the moment neither appearing inclined to approach the two bickering knights, though Bronwyn reached for her bow and pulled it over her shoulder.

The sack was finally tied down and the two palfreys swiftly unhitched. Ironshod hooves clomped heavily on the cobbles, sending hollow echoes into the night. Both knights hauled themselves up into their saddles.

"Lindholf!" Lawri shouted over the clatter of hooves. "Is that you, Lindholf?" Her green-eyed gaze flew back to Tala. "That knight sounds like Lindholf."

One of the Dayknights scooped the black helmet up and off his head, revealing a startled face under ruffled blond hair. It was a young man, likely the same age as Nail, but his pale features were scarred, deformed.

"L-Lawri," the Dayknight stammered, bringing his mount around to face the girl.

"Lindholf!" Lawri ran toward the blond knight, the hood of her cloak flowing back and off her head. The cloak wrapped around her arm unraveled.

The other Dayknight was swiftly between Lindholf and Lawri, the long white sword still in his hand. On closer look, it was the longest, whitest sword Nail had ever seen. His heart quailed at the sight. The magnificent blade shone like a shard of white lightning, cutting open the darkness of the night. The tip of the extended blade was soon pointed at Lawri, who slowed her advance. "Not one step further, lassie," the knight with the white sword said. "The boy comes with me."

Lawri stopped altogether, confused. But her eyes blazed with a strange green light now. And her gauntleted hand was no longer safely hidden from view. Lindholf's eyes widened at the sight of the gauntlet. "What's happened to you, Lawri?" But Lawri just stood there, staring at the long white blade in the other knight's hand.

Tala rushed to her cousin's side, tugging at the girl's cloak in an attempt to pull her away from Lindholf and the Dayknight with the startling white sword. Nail drew his own sword and rushed forward too, imposing himself between the girls and the threatening Dayknight. The knight sat still as a stone atop the palfrey, long white sword still pointed at Lawri, unwavering.

Bronwyn had her bow up and ready, arrow nocked and pointed at the Dayknight threatening Lawri. "We aim to requisition those horses from you, good ser," the Wyn Darrè girl said coolly. "So if you'll just kindly dismount for us and hand them over."

Cromm grinned a frighteningly toothy grin, the hilt of his heavy square maul firmly gripped in two burly hands, the jewels embedded in his knuckles twinkling in the evening light. A few curious onlookers had stopped in the street to watch. But at the sight of the oghul with the iron maul, they ducked out of sight.

"The horses," Bronwyn persisted. "Now. And bear in mind, I ain't one for long conversations, and neither is Cromm. Makes us both a bit testy. Especially when folks hesitate to obey. And you don't wanna see us get testy. So you'd best obey."

The long white sword was no longer pointed at Lawri but at Bronwyn. The Dayknight wielding it said, "I strongly suggest you not go down this path, girl."

"It's only your horses we want." Bronwyn spoke with the same measure of self-assurance. "Not your life."

"Oh, I assure you," the Dayknight with the white sword said, "I am not the one who will be dying tonight. Perhaps I should introduce myself, so you know the name of the one who slices open your belly and walks the very horse you wish to steal right through your own bleeding guts." The Dayknight reached up with one hand and removed the black helm. "I am Enna Spades, Knight Archaic of Sør Sevier and personal bodyguard of Aeros Raijael. And I command you and your oghul to move aside."

It was a freckle-faced, red-haired woman with a bloody bandage wrapped around her neck. Nail recognized her instantly as the woman who had branded him a slave on the beaches of Gallows Haven. It was Enna Spades! And her gaze flicked to his in mutual recognition. Blood raced thick and hot through Nail's veins. This was the woman who had tortured Bishop Tolbret and Baron Bruk and forced Dokie to swim with the sharks. Enna Spades was the most evil person in the entire Five Isles.

The slave brand flared and burned. He tore his gaze from Spades and looked at Lawri Le Graven, felt the heat of her eyes, green and glowing with some power and kinship he felt growing within himself.

"The horse," Bronwyn said, her arrow still aimed right between Spades' eyes. "I will be having it, no matter who you say you are."

"Lindholf," Spades said, keeping her cruel, cold eyes fixed on Bronwyn as she spoke. "Ride away now. I shall be right behind you."

With a snap, Bronwyn let her arrow fly. The white blade came up in Spades' hand. The arrow glanced away with a flash of light, spiraling over the Sør Sevier woman's head in a hissing flurry of sparks. Spades set spurs to flanks and charged her horse straight at Bronwyn, white sword arcing down with keening swiftness.

Cromm lunged between the two women, square iron maul upraised. The white sword met the oghul's huge weapon. With a crack of light and thunder the maul shattered in Cromm's hands, the force of the blow sending the oghul spinning back against the cobbles. Nail covered his eyes from the blinding flash.

"Flee!" Spades yelled at Lindholf. When Nail uncovered his eyes, Spades had reined her palfrey around, long white sword once again poised at Bronwyn. "Go, boy," Spades snarled at Lindholf. "I will be right behind you."

"But my sister," Lindholf said, unsure.

"Go!" Spades yelled. "I'll be right behind you! Go now or I will slay everyone here, including your sister; I will slay her just like I slew Jondralyn atop that tower!"

Lindholf set heels to flanks and disappeared down the dark street.

Slay everyone here, like I slew Jondralyn atop that tower! The words rang hollow in Nail's ear. But Tala looked ill. Her gaze flew to the top of the tower. Then she sprinted for the tower door. Nail followed her.

The last thing he saw before bursting into the tower was Enna Spades whirling her mount and charging off into the night after Lindholf Le Graven.

**

Nail, Tala, and Lawri stood silent, looking down at Jondralyn's body.

The princess of Amadon was in her Silver Guard armor. She lay on her back, face bathed in blood. The wood-plank floor of the tower's roof was soaked black under her body. Jondralyn stared up at nothing, for both her eyes were gone. One eye socket was still hidden under the patch she always wore. The other was a foul pool of blood. There was also a puncture wound under her chin. Her left hand had been chopped neatly off. Nail recalled the severed hand on the cobbled street below.

Ashen-faced, Tala just gazed down at her dead sister, a vacant look in her eyes, fists clenched behind her back. Lawri wiped at the tears streaming down her own cheeks.

Nail had no words for the moment. This was the second time he had seen Jondralyn with gruesome wounds. He recalled seeing the princess similarly sprawled out on a litter in Ravenker. But she had lived through that day. Yet now he was certain she would never move again.

All he wanted to do at the moment was protect Tala from the horrors of the world. But what could he do? What could he say? *Something? Anything?* He settled on nothing. Words forever left on his tongue. He placed his hand on her shoulder, hoping she would at least lean into it. She stepped away. His hand dropped back to his side.

Bronwyn and Cromm came up onto the roof. They looked at Jondralyn briefly, then went straight to the southernmost battlement that circled the tower. Bronwyn propped one foot up on the crumbled stone as she leaned out, casting her gaze over the breadth of Savon.

"We have many decisions," she said. "And we must make haste." She looked back toward Nail, Tala, and Lawri. "Glade Chaparral and his knights are some ten blocks distant and making their way down the main thoroughfare toward us. We will have to leave this tower, and now."

"Or we could stay up here and hope to hide," Cromm said.

"True," Bronwyn agreed. "Glade could just ride on by. But I dare not chance it. If he stops for some reason and searches the tavern below, and finds the dead folk in it, he will surely send his knights up here."

"Cromm is not one for hiding anyway," the oghul said.

"What about my sister?" Tala's voice was meek. "I can't just leave her here."

"We could carry her," Bronwyn said. "Or rather, Cromm could carry her. But that would slow us down. We have to decide soon."

"Stay or leave?" Tala muttered. "Carry her or not? Every path seems cruel and wrong." She turned from her dead sister then, tears now gone, the look in her eyes as hard as stone as she gazed off into the night. Then she buried her face in Nail's chest. And his arms enveloped her.

"Might be the best thing if it's Glade who finds her," Bronwyn said. "He will be forced to take her back to Amadon. Which will likely end his search for us, or so I am thinking. We can tear down these canvas awnings." She looked at Tala. "Cover your sister with them."

"No." Tala broke from Nail's embrace. "Let's go before Glade arrives. There's nothing we can do here."

"We've time to cover her—"

"No." Tala cut Bronwyn short. "We leave her as she lies."

CHAPTER FORTY-TWO
MANCELLOR ALLEN

10TH DAY OF THE BLOOD MOON, 999TH YEAR OF LAIJON
SAVON, GUL KANA

Mancellor Allen climbed a dark winding stairway between crumbled gray stone walls choked with ivy and moss. He was crawling more than climbing, huffing with shallow breaths toward the warm safety of the lamplit streets of Savon twinkling above. Liz Hen Neville and Dokie Liddle were trailing behind him, all three soaked and sodden to the bone, finding themselves unceremoniously washed ashore far downriver from the Preening Pintail.

It was both a good and a bad thing that the Ridliegh River was so deep. Good that the depth of the water cushioned his whirling plunge from the seven-story tower, bad that his armor had pulled him straight down to a bubbling riverbed, muddy and gray with silt. It was the second time heavy armor had almost drowned him. He'd shed the bulky iron plate swiftly enough, launching himself upward through the stiff current with the last bit of strength he had. When his head broke the surface, he had seen Dokie Liddle's flailing body strike the river under the tower with a small splash. A moment later the dark, balled-up bulk of Liz Hen Neville had come plunging down, both arms wrapped around her knees as she struck the water in a tremendous booming spray. Had Enna Spades pushed everyone over the edge? He did not know how Liz Hen and Dokie ended up in the Ridliegh River with him.

Despite the summer weather, there had been a bone-numbing cold-ness to the swift-flowing waters. The Ridliegh River was not like the blood-warmed tides of the Saint Only Channel. When all three of them had surfaced, sputtering for air, Mancellor had swiftly gathered his wits and paddled against the current as best he could, letting the river bring Liz Hen and Dokie to him, helping both gain their bearings.

Clinging together, the three of them had floated away from the tower at the mercy of the black current, the water dragging them past rowboats, wooden docks, stone pilings, porches, balustrades, and even several buildings and towers built right in the river. No matter how hard they tried to find purchase on any of the structures rushing by, the current tore them away. Mancellor had scanned both shores for escape. Though there were fewer buildings, the opposite side of the river looked just as treacherous, lined with large boulders and gnarly trees. Plus, it was a long way off. Luckily, the current eventually swept them into a natural small inlet between two tall buildings.

And that was where they were now, climbing to the safety of the streets above. All three of them soon stood on wobbly legs in the main thoroughfare of Savon, armor lost to the river behind them, their under-clothes adrip. Only a few passersby looked at them strangely for their draggled attire; most just shoved their way past with annoyance.

Mancellor tried to orient himself to his surroundings. "I think the tavern is that way." He pointed to what he thought was the north. His mind was muddled. All he could think of was his underwater visions and the mermaid and being pulled beneath the red waters during the Battle of the Saint Only Channel. *A tower! Falling!* It had come true. He didn't even want to imagine what the rest of his dream had meant. *A gladiator arena. A green dragon. A skull-faced knight. Rivers of silver and blood.*

"I shoulda stayed up there and killed that redheaded bitch," Liz Hen growled, her bloodshot eyes blazing with fury. "I've never met anyone so cruel. I don't need this kind of fucking trouble all the time."

"We have to get back to the tavern." Dokie's darting eyes were round with concern. "What if she's stolen the angel stones and weapons?"

"How did you two end up in the river?" Mancellor asked.

"The lady threw me in," Dokie said.

"And I had to save Dokie from the sharks," Liz Hen said.

Her reason made little sense to Mancellor. "Right, Dokie, we have to get back to the tavern." He headed down the dark street to the north, pushing through the crowd.

Just then Liz Hen let out a wild shriek. Beer Mug burst down the street straight toward them, tail a-wag. His sudden appearance caused Liz Hen to fall to her knees and continue to cry out in joy. The dog raced up to her and licked her face in pure relief.

"Take us back to the tavern," Liz Hen said to the dog.

And Beer Mug led them back.

**

The cobbled street outside the Preening Pintail was empty but for several clumps of steaming horse manure, as if a large contingent of horsemen had just ridden by. There was also a severed hand in the gutter just outside the door of the tavern. And worse, inside the Preening Pintail they found Rutger, Luiza, and the two blacksmiths lying in dark pools of blood. Beer Mug sniffed at the dead bodies with a solemn whimper.

"I loved this job so much." Liz Hen swiped the tears from her redhazed eyes. "I just wanted to stay here and begin a new life." Then her face hardened. "But that red-haired bitch! She ruined it, ruined it like she's ruined everything else in my life." Liz Hen looked around, then growled. "Where is she, Dokie? Where is she?"

"I don't know." Dokie's own eyes were misty. "Up on the tower still, I imagine."

The three of them and Beer Mug hurried back outside. There were no ponies or horses left at the hitching post, and the door to the tower was open wide. Mancellor suddenly felt naked without armor or a weapon. Still, with firm resolve, he marched up the stairs and onto the roof of the tower, Liz Hen, Dokie, and Beer Mug following.

Once at the top, they found that Enna Spades and Lindholf Le Graven were gone, the weapons and angel stones too. But Jondralyn Bronachell remained. At the sight of her face and all the blood, Mancellor knelt and did the three-fingered sign of the Laijon Cross over his heart.

"She's dead," Dokie voiced behind him. "What can we do now?"

"Was that her hand in the dirty gutter below?" Liz Hen asked.

"And her eyes are gone and she's just dead," Dokie mumbled, face empty with pain.

"She didn't deserve it," Liz Hen said.

Dokie's small fists balled up with rage. "Liz Hen is right, everything is ruined." He looked up at Mancellor. "I know what we can do. Let's find the red-haired bitch. She has all the angel stones and weapons and we need to steal them back. We can use them to kill her."

The princess is dead! Mancellor could scarcely let the thought sink in. *And all five weapons of Laijon and all five angel stones are gone!* He felt a sudden thick welling of guilt, sadness, and despair as he moved toward the crumbled-down battlement and stared out over the dark river. He hoped neither Liz Hen nor Dokie could see his eyes. The angel stones had been his destiny. He had stolen them from Aeros Raijael with the help of his god. *Laijon led me here every step of the way, to this place, through all manner of trial and tribulation and suffering . . . and for what?*

"We should take the princess's body to Amadon," Liz Hen said. "Gather her hand from the gutter below. It should go back to Amadon with her."

"*Amadon?*" Dokie's face scrunched up with distaste. "We should hunt the red-haired bitch. We should get back the angel stones and the weapons."

"The angel stones and the weapons are worthless," Liz Hen said. "And the red-haired bitch is long gone. We've no idea where she went. We should take Princess Jondralyn back to her home."

"But what if we get her to Amadon and they think we killed her?" Dokie asked.

Amadon! Mancellor recalled what Jondralyn had told him of Amadon and the Wyn Darrè girl she had left there. *Jondralyn claimed she met my sister in Amadon.*

485

"Liz Hen is right, Dokie," Mancellor said, renewed purpose in his voice. "We shall bear Jondralyn's body back to Amadon. It is the only right thing left for us to do. She must be carried to her home."

"I can tear these awnings down," Liz Hen said. "We can make a litter. We can carry her body in them."

"And let us also hope there is a pony or two left inside Rutger's stables," Mancellor said.

What can we do now? Dokie had asked when they first found the princess's body. *Find our families* was Mancellor's answer to that. Though he did not voice that opinion aloud, for he knew both Liz Hen Neville and Dokie Liddle had no family left. They only had each other. And Beer Mug.

But what could he do now other than find what remained of his family and hold on till the end? If there was a possibility that Bronwyn was in Amadon, then that was where Mancellor Allen would go.

Near the end of all things, humanity shall find seeping scorch and
death climbing up through the rock and dirt, rising like silver waters
up the bore of a well, ascending to overspill its bounds.
—THE WAY AND TRUTH OF LAIJON

CHAPTER FORTY-THREE
AVA SHAY

12TH DAY OF THE BLOOD MOON, 999TH YEAR OF LAIJON
LORD'S POINT, GUL KANA

Ava Shay eased her way out the back door of the Turn Key Inn & Saloon. Alone. To her the saloon was a dark and cheerless place. Five days cooped up in the abandoned building and she needed fresh air. She felt hollow. There was an empty place in her womb where a baby once lived. *Jenko Bruk's child,* she kept telling herself, hoping that just believing would make it true.

Ava stepped lightly across the wood porch and down into the stable yard situated behind the saloon. Krista Aulbrek and her Bloodeye mare, Dread, were already in the yard next to the stable. Krista did not hear Ava's approach. She was talking to her horse.

"I can't believe all the terrible things I have done, Dread. What have we allowed ourselves to become involved in, you and I? So many dead by my hand. So many needlessly slain during my Sacrament of Souls. If I could go back to Amadon and release every prisoner in the Rokenwalder dungeons, I would do it. Penance for my horrific sins."

"Sins," Ava repeated. "We have all of us committed them."

Krista, face registering surprise, turned and looked at Ava. "How much of that did you hear?"

"Not much," Ava lied. "But it is not your fault about Gault."

"When I realized it was my father, I pulled the blade. Yet he still may die. Another death at my hands." The black mare nickered as Krista rested the side of her face against the horse's neck.

"You could never have known it was Gault in that chamber," Ava said. "I was as surprised as you to see him there."

Krista went back to brushing her horse. "In a way, I truly deserve what pain and sorrow I feel now, or the swirl of contradictions running through my head. If not for the Sacrament of Souls, I would not have known how to pull the blade at the last second. Without that foul sacrament I would not know how to miss his beating heart by a hairsbreadth. The contradictions mess with my mind. Have you ever felt so conflicted?"

"Every day," Ava said.

She knew the young Bloodwood struggled with the fact that she had stabbed her own father. Krista Aulbrek wrestled with a lot of inner demons, maybe as many as Ava herself, though the wraiths had not haunted her in a moon or more. *I possess you and I purify you,* Aeros had whispered in her ear. *Everything I do is holy. Everything I do is for your sake. Can you not see? When you lie with me, I place into you the healing power of the gods. Our heavenly sessions are blessed by both Raijael and Laijon. In them, I take upon myself your pains, your troubles, and your sins. I even take the wraiths within you upon myself. I bear your burdens. In time, you will see those wraiths that plague your mind vanish, and your powers to heal flourish. If you have not already.* And now a girl she scarcely knew conversed with her as if they were friends. *As if I can help her, heal her. When it is me who is in need of healing.* Ava thought of her lost baby. The blood on the sheets. "We have all of us committed sins," she repeated. "All of us."

Krista's face was racked with anguish as she continued to brush her horse. *Could I have ever thought I would find another as sad as I?* Ava asked herself. They were the same age, Krista and Ava, seventeen. And, as Krista had once heard Aeros and the Spider say, the two of them did look alike, could even pass as twins. But their appearance and state of depression were where the similarities ended. Krista was a Bloodwood assassin, a coldhearted killer in black leather armor. And Ava was an innocent captive in a simple dress, a captive still longing for freedom.

"Sorry, I have done naught but talk of myself," Krista said.

"That is okay," Ava said.

"I don't know how you lasted so long in the presence of the White Prince," Krista said, looking at Ava now. "What a horror he must have been."

Ava did not answer, did not want to remember. Fact was, she would rather talk of Krista's problems than her own.

"That day," Krista continued, a haunted look in her eye, "when we pulled you out of Aeros' bedchamber, the White Prince and Hammerfiss fought with such ferocious lethal skill to keep you there. Aeros fought so hard for you it scared me. That was the closest I have ever come to death. I must always remember, Bloodwood assassins are not invincible. Those of Black Dugal's Caste can be killed. Of course, I am no longer of Black Dugal's Caste."

Nobody needed to tell Ava Shay that a Bloodwood could be killed. She had witnessed Hammerfiss crush Spiderwood with a mace, turn the man into naught but a puddle of blood and guts and split leather. She had seen a Bloodwood assassin turned into nothing but slop on the cobbles for the dogs to lick clean.

Ava gazed beyond the stables and out over the ocean toward the Fortress of Saint Only—her previous prison. White seagulls sailed above the pure blue channel, outstretched wings tinged with fiery rose against the evening sky. Mont Saint Only rose up dark and gloomy against the blazing red sunset. She wondered if Jenko Bruk looked down upon Lord's Point from one of the keep's many balconies. She wondered if his amber eyes searched for her now. She wondered if he even missed her.

Jenko could have saved her. Gault could have saved her. Mancellor Allen could have saved her. Spiderwood, too. But all had failed. Yet here she was, *saved* at last, sitting in a blue dress in an abandoned inn, her sword, My Heart, her only friend. So many hours and days she had spent dreaming of escape or rescue, and now she was free of her captors, free of the rape and degradation. Yet she still felt so alone.

Could this girl, Krista, be her friend? It seemed not. The girl was distracted by so many problems of her own. *And was it really King Borden Bronachell who helped rescue me?* It was well-known that the king of Gul Kana had died in battle five years ago. *And who is Ironcloud?* The taciturn dwarf seemed casually indifferent to her very presence. The only person in the Turn Key Saloon whom she knew at all was Gault Aulbrek. But he lay unconscious in one of the inn's bedrooms above, nearly dead from the poison of his daughter's black blade.

"I am surprised Borden Bronachell stays here with us," Krista said, focusing again on brushing the sleek black coat of her mare. "He has been free to go his own way since we arrived in Lord's Point. The dwarf, too. Truth be told, I wish they would leave me be. But they still act as if they want something from me. Perhaps I should just kill the both of them and be done with it." There had been a palpable measure of tension between Krista, Borden, and Ironcloud. Ava sensed it daily. It had been obvious ever since their escape from Saint Only.

The barge that had borne the five of them, along with Dread, to the shores of Gul Kana was moored along the wharf just to the south of the Turn Key. They'd come upon the abandoned saloon by accident. Dread had hauled Gault's inert body across her broad, strong back. That was until Gault started retching. Then they had found the first abandoned building they could. To Ava, the entire city of Lord's Point was an eerie place, mostly abandoned.

"Borden has spent long years dreaming of seeing his homeland again," Krista said. "He is so near Amadon now. I am surprised he has not rushed off to rejoin his family. I am inclined to let him do just that, for I fear I am done with my assassin ways. Too many deaths by my hand already. Why add a king to the tally? And you are free to leave too." Krista threw Ava a sidelong look. "You have been a big help in tending to Gault these last few days. But I can watch over my father now."

"I do not mind helping," Ava said. It was the truth. "I expect he shall soon wake. Gault Aulbrek was kind to me when everyone else in Aeros' army was cruel."

"You believe my father returned to Saint Only to rescue you?" Krista asked.

"I asked him to."

Krista smiled wanly. "And he would follow up on any promise." She offered Ava a slight nod. "I can believe that."

"I would like to be here when Gault awakens," Ava said.

"I imagine he would like that," Krista said, brushing her horse.

Ava recalled the conversation she had overheard between the White Prince and Spiderwood in the tent outside Tomkin Sty. *Perhaps Black Dugal has already enlightened the girl to the fact that Gault is not her father,* Aeros had said. And clearly Black Dugal, whoever that was, had not enlightened Krista to that fact. *Part of the Sacrament of Souls is to forsake all one's kin,* Spiderwood had said. *A Bloodwood is to become fatherless and motherless in the eyes of Black Dugal. If he has not already enlightened Krista as to her true parentage, he soon will. Or he may have some other do the telling for him. Dugal can be devious in his purpose.* Aeros and the Spider had also believed that Gault would rush to his daughter's rescue if he ever found out she was to become a Bloodwood. And here she was in her crisp black leathers, brushing her demon-eyed horse. *Gault is not even a full-blooded man of Sør Sevier,* Aeros had said that day. *He should die . . . and he has, of late, exhibited naught but rough lust for other things closest to me.* And Ava knew what other things close to the White Prince Gault had lusted after. *A green angel stone. And me.* How would she ever tell Krista the secrets that she knew about the man she thought was her father?

Ava heard footfalls on the wood porch. Ironcloud marched across the stable yard toward them, stumpy legs and feet kicking up sand and dust in his wake. But Ironcloud was the least talkative of her new companions, and in turn, the most intimidating.

"Gault stirs," the dwarf said on his approach, impassive eyes on Krista. "Borden insists you be there when he wakes."

**

"Only three years," Gault muttered. His eyes were open but his pupils were rolled back in his head. "Avril, my Avril. Only three years we had." The Sør Sevier knight lay on his back in one of the upper rooms of the Turn Key Inn, fluffed pillow under his head, white sheets over his body. Sweat beaded up on his bald head. He was clothed in naught but dark leather pants and a sweat-stained cotton shirt. Ava's heart went out to him, for she knew how he had adored his wife, Avril. He had mentioned her often and with great affection. Borden Bronachell stood over Gault's bed.

"He's been going on about his dead wife ever since he woke," the king said. "Delirious. Rambling. But at least he is speaking. A sign that he is recovering. Slow going as it is."

"He should not be this sick," Krista said, devastated gaze fixed on her father.

"That stuff on your Bloodwood dagger must have been potent," Borden said.

"Truth athyra mixed with Royal Bedlam," Krista answered. "A poison meant to slowly strangle and paralyze, but not before the victim can reveal the truth of whatever question is asked. It should not have made him this ill."

"We did not get him out of the fortress in time," Ironcloud said.

"True, we did not get him to the antidotes in my saddlebags soon enough," the young Bloodwood acknowledged. "I've likely killed my own father. Or perhaps Dugal messed with the potions in my bag. I should have gone through them more carefully."

"It is clear that remnants of the poison still remain in his bloodstream," Borden said. "We *could* ask him questions, get the truth out of him."

"And what truths would he hold?" Ironcloud asked.

"Who knows?" the king said. "But we could find out."

"We should just leave him alone," Krista said. "We should feed him and let him rest, and that is all."

"Is that you, Avril?" Gault stirred. His eyes were open as he struggled to sit. "Or have the wraiths claimed me?"

"No, Father." The young Bloodwood gently lowered him back down onto the pillow. "It's me, Krista, your daughter."

Gault grasped her hands. "My sweet Avril. I've such a clear memory of that day we first met." His eyes widened. "I saw angel stones, Avril. I saw them, and the weapons of the Five Warrior Angels. But I left them with Lindholf and Delia. . . ."

His voice trailed off as he studied Krista's face, confusion in his hazy eyes.

"Lindholf is my sister's son," Borden Bronachell said. "Could Lindholf have the angel stones and weapons? Is that what he is saying? For that could be an interesting boon indeed. Perhaps the truth serum still works within him?" He turned to Krista. "How long does the poison last?"

"Not long," she said crossly, but seemed less than convinced herself. "Not this long, anyway, I don't think."

"We should get him to Amadon as soon as possible," Borden said. "Only my Vallè sawbones has the skill or medicines to cure him now."

"A windswept plain," Gault tried to rise up out of bed again, eyes no longer rolled back and hazed over with poison, but fixed on Krista. "A babe cradled in your arms, Avril. I can still recall the very spot where I found you and your baby."

"It's me," the young Bloodwood said. "Your daughter."

"I found you, Avril," Gault went on. "Found you and your baby."

Krista's fingers tightened around both of her father's hands. "It's me, Krista," she said, voice almost pleading. "I'm here with you now. You are safe."

Ava's heart went out to them both, for Gault Aulbrek was a man whose every secret was becoming exposed, and Krista Aulbrek was a young woman trying to hold fast to the truths about her heritage that she had been told her whole life.

"North of Stone Loring," Gault carried on in his fever dream, eyes fixed on Krista, intense. "A dusky ridge of sharp rock and dry peat. A long, hollow valley. I've oft dreamed of that place." He gripped Krista's arm. "I wish my ashes to be spread there, the one place in the entirety of the Five Isles I ever felt joy, solace. Spread my ashes there, where we met, will you, my love, my Avril? Will you promise?"

"You are not dead yet." Krista's voice cracked.

"You must promise me. You must promise to find that place again."

"But I do not remember. I was just a baby then—"

"Ava Shay!" Gault called out, trying to sit up again, eyes now focused on Ava standing behind Krista. "Is that you, Ava? Or are you a vision of the wraiths? I came back for you?" His head fell back onto the pillow, eyelids drooping. "Ava," he mumbled, eyes closing.

"Do you not see me?" Krista asked of her father, trying to refocus his attention on her. "Do you not see your own daughter right in front of you?"

"I found you and your baby . . ." Gault's voice slowly trailed off. ". . . Ava." And he dropped into unconsciousness again. His body was rigid, motionless.

Ava felt the tears streaming down her face. *He truly came back for me!*

"Why are you crying?" Krista Aulbrek turned back to her. There were no tears in the young Bloodwood's eyes, just a cutting look that seemed to carve a path straight toward Ava. Yet it was an icy look that sliced both ways, for that look Krista threw Ava clearly slashed all the way backward into Krista's own soul too, exposing the piercing and raw wounds of a haunted mind. "He is not your father, Ava. So why do you cry?"

"He treated me well when all the others in Aeros' army did not," Ava said.

The young Bloodwood tore her gaze from Ava's. "He thought I was Avril. He thought I was my mother." Both sadness and confusion sounded in Krista's voice. "He kept saying he found Avril and her baby. What does that mean?"

Nobody answered. Silence filled the room.

"A Bloodwood is like a wild horse," Ironcloud said at length. "A wild horse that must be ridden and kicked, beaten down until forced in the right direction. Now you're closer to knowing the truth of your own heritage, Krista. For Gault could not lie about finding Avril and her baby. And as Black Dugal always said, a Bloodwood must become fatherless."

There was an ancient foul codex claiming a Vallè maiden shall be the fulfillment of all prophecy. But any such ancient codex is bound together with lies. Can demons be angels or angels be demons? And can every mystery posed command a perfect and satisfiying answer?
—The Way and Truth of Laijon

CHAPTER FORTY-FOUR
TALA BRONACHELL

12TH DAY OF THE BLOOD MOON, 999TH YEAR OF LAIJON

EAST OF RIVERMEADE, GUL KANA

Out of the south and west thundered Glade Chaparral and his mounted contingent of twenty armored soldiers. Worn and fatigued from the harried flight out of Savon, Tala Bronachell found herself and her four companions now trapped.

They were also miserable and wet. The two-day chase had led them to this spot atop an arched stone aqueduct straddling the green brush and spindly bracken of a marshy valley some twenty feet below. A driving rain bit into their faces and bled through their clothes as they crouched in the knee-deep trench of rushing waters. The trench was about four paces across and swift. Bronwyn Allen and Cromm Cru'x were huddled together, both peering over the aqueduct's waist-high stone balustrade toward Glade and the approaching Dayknights.

Crouched in the swift waters of the aqueduct, Lawri Le Graven and Nail exchanged a worried, compassionate look. Their shared glance concerned Tala almost as much as, if not more than, the approaching knights. Ever since fleeing Savon, Nail sometimes stared at Tala's cousin as if awaiting a demon to come crawling out of her eyes. And Lawri would ofttimes gaze right back at Nail, emerald flecks in her eyes aglow. There was something growing between the two and Tala couldn't pinpoint exactly what. It wasn't a boyfriend-girlfriend thing, for sure, but rather more like a brother-sister thing.

She tore her gaze from the pair and peered over the balustrade. She looked back down the green slope toward the approaching black-armored knights. It was a sight that froze her heart. The knights galloped under a sky of tumbling gray thunderheads stretching from horizon to horizon, crooked trees of lightning cracking to the ground behind them. It had been a long and harrowing journey to this spot. Glade and his knights had chased Tala and her companions out of Savon, through Rivermeade, to this place, where he had them trapped atop a desolate bit of stone aqueduct arcade some ten miles east of Rivermeade.

As a last resort—their own mounts lost in the River Vallè two days ago—Tala and her companions had climbed onto the series of stone bridges, pipes, and arcading in Rivermeade to escape their enemy. They had followed the maze of aboveground canals to this spot. The move had bought them some time. Half a day at least.

But here the eastern-flowing aqueduct they had followed came to a Y. The southern canal branched off to an inverted siphon that rushed a portion of the channel waters down a chute toward the moors to the south. The other canal veered off to the north, sending that trench of water toward a cavernous hole in the face of a forested hill—a dark tunnel that Bronwyn said likely led to a deep shaft and an underground well. And here they were cornered.

Only Nail, Bronwyn, and Cromm had any weapons to speak of, Nail the Silver Guard sword he had carried from Amadon, Bronwyn Allen her bow. She already had a black-fletched arrow nocked and aimed. Cromm Cru'x had his teeth and powerful muscles, plus the many daggers and knives strapped to his body. His heavy square maul was gone, shattered into a thousand metal shards by *Afflicted Fire* in Savon. He grumbled low in his throat and pulled two of the blades, jewel-encrusted knuckles of each hand gripping the daggers tight.

Tala thought back to the fight that had destroyed Cromm's maul. She had never seen a warrior of such fierce determination as Enna Spades. The red-haired woman had been a marvel in her stolen Dayknight armor and long white sword. *Afflicted Fire! Had Enna Spades and Lindholf Le Graven stolen all the other weapons of the Five Warrior Angels? Had they stolen the five angel stones too?* It was a horrible thought.

But worst of all, Jondralyn was dead. Tala could not wrap her mind around that. In fact, she had mostly tried to block it from her mind. *I left her dead atop some tower in Savon. I never got to tell her the black angel stone was just a fake.* She wondered if that would have even made a difference. *Could the magic of all five stones together have helped save Jondralyn? Who could know the answers to those questions but Laijon? And I am likely a mighty disappointment to him.*

The entire journey had been a waste of time. Tala wondered if she had ever been a good person at all. A noble person. *All the lies I've told!* In some way she knew her older sister's death was her fault. *And Hawkwood and Val-Draekin were likely burnt in the Filthy Horse Saloon due to my deception.* And here she was trapped on a stone aqueduct.

Twenty Dayknights reined up under the arched arcade, the steel-shod hooves of their heavy destriers clomping and sucking in the marshy peat.

Bronwyn Allen rose up, threw back the hood of her green cloak, and set several arrows on the foot-wide stone balustrade in front of her. She pointed her first arrow down at the leader. "We aim to requisition your horses!" she shouted. "All twenty of them! Dismount and turn them over and walk away! Now!"

Tala could hear many of the knights laughing beneath their helms. Several drew their own bows and nocked their own arrows, aiming up at Bronwyn.

"Turn your horses over to us!" Bronwyn bellowed, undaunted. Rain kept pouring down, nearly drowning out her voice.

Glade Chaparral removed his helm. The three knights next to him did the same: Tolz Trento, Alain Gratzer, and Boppard Stockach. Tala's heart roared to life in her chest, hammering with fear at the sight of

Glade. He ran the back side of his black-gauntleted hand over the stub-ble on his face—the beginnings of a dark beard that made him look all the more repulsively cruel in her eyes. Rain splattered his hair and brow. His war charger shifted its weight, and he snapped the reins im-patiently. Watching Glade struggle with the horse, Tala once again won-dered what she had ever seen in him. Yes, he was handsome; even now he looked regal in his black armor, even sopping wet in the driving rain. But the reality was he had chased her nearly halfway across Gul Kana to this place. He had *hunted* her.

Glade got his mount under control and stared up at her, shouting, "Come down from there now, Tala Bronachell! There is no reason any-one else need get hurt!"

"Hurt?" Bronwyn shouted back, laughing. "The only folks getting hurt today are you all, that's if you don't surrender them horses!"

Many of the Dayknights laughed aloud at that.

Glade Chaparral did not laugh. Instead his dark eyes cut into Tala's with cold malice. And Tala became consciously aware of how she must look to him now, dressed in naught but rags. Bedraggled. Uncouth. Homeless. But with that thought, she suddenly took pride in her appear-ance. Fact was, things on this adventure were not like they were at the castle. True, her sister was dead. True, her quest had failed. True, she had to sleep on the cold, hard ground, and hadn't bathed or changed clothes in days. True, she'd worn the same bloodstained leather pants and cot-ton shirt since fleeing Amadon. True, she stank like the oghul Cromm. But for the last week she had been free.

"Dismount and give up your horses now!" Bronwyn yelled again.

Cromm stood up behind her and roared in agreement. "Do as she says!"

More arrows from the Dayknights were aimed up at them.

"If you want my horse"—Boppard Stockach drew his sword, looking up at her, shouting—"come take it from me, bit—!"

Bronwyn's arrow cut Boppard's insult short, punching straight down through his open mouth, burying itself in his throat clear to the black fletching. The Dayknight tried to cough the shaft back up as he slid sideways from his destrier. He hit the sopping peat with a wet *thunk*, neck straight and rigid. A torrent of blood surged from his gaping mouth, coating the nearby briar and bracken. Rain washed the blood away.

"Kill them all!" Glade shouted. The Dayknights behind Glade fired their arrows. Tala dropped behind the stone balustrade, crouching in the stream, arrows sailing over her head. Nail and Lawri crouched with her. Bronwyn rose up from the water and snatched up the arrows she'd left on the rim of the balustrade and fired three in rapid succession down into the crowd of knights, before ducking back down. Tala could hear the bucking and braying of one of the war chargers below.

A half-dozen grappling hooks sailed over the balustrade just west of her near the Y in the aqueduct, their arcing tines catching the trench's foot-wide stone barrier with a loud *clank!* The ropes were pulled taut from below. Tala figured knights were now climbing up the arcade.

"We have to get out of here." Nail drew his sword, eyes roaming their narrow perch back toward to the east, back the way they had come and their quickest retreat. He whirled and eyed the Y in the arcade to the west, just past the six grappling hooks, surveying both branching trenches to the north and south. Rain poured down. His blond hair was plastered to his head. Another volley of arrows sailed overhead. Tala could hear the knights climbing the ropes now.

Cromm shoved his way past Tala, Nail, and Lawri and moved east toward the Y, then seized hold of one of the iron hooks, yanking it free of the stone barrier and tossing it back over the side. He grabbed hold of another hook and tossed it away too. Bronwyn was right behind the oghul, firing arrows down at the Dayknights as she ran, water splashing up around her legs. Two more grappling hooks sailed over the aqueduct to the south beyond the Y junction. Cromm tried to dislodge the remaining hooks, but several Dayknights were already climbing over the foot-wide rim of stone. They dropped down into the southern trench, water swirling up around their knees, swords drawn.

Cromm ducked the wild swing of the first Dayknight, picked the armored man up by his breastplate, and hurled him back over the side. More knights swarmed up the remaining rope lines and into the trench surrounding Cromm and Bronwyn.

Nail moved around Tala and Lawri and rushed down the southern trench to help Bronwyn and the oghul, his sword aimed at the nearest knight, who was in the midst of hauling himself over the rim. Nail's sword cracked against the fellow's armored back, knocking the man to the side. Nail struck again and the knight lost his grip, falling away from the arcade to the ground with a clatter. Nail and Cromm managed to shove three more knights back over the edge. Cromm lumbered farther to the south, tossing more of the grappling hooks back to the ground. Bronwyn was still shooting arrows down into the thick of the knights.

A large knight climbed over the rim and splashed into the knee-high water, gaining his balance. He was big and solid and soon stood sturdy in the trench, towering over Nail. The black-clad knight met Nail's attack with a parry of his own. Sword cracked against sword, sending Nail staggering back. Nail reset his stance and met the brutal assault of the much larger man as best he could, but the knight overpowered him with three quick strikes. Nail barely managed to block each powerful blow as the knight closed in. The knight stepped inside Nail's next swing, grabbed him by the neck, and shoved the Gallows Haven boy against the balustrade. The knight cracked Nail in the face with his armored elbow. Nail's sword spun away into the rain-streaked air. *No!* Tala's heart stopped as Nail toppled backward over the rail and vanished straight down.

"No!" she screamed.

The large Dayknight turned his attention to her and Lawri, stalking down the trench toward them. Tala placed herself between Lawri and the Dayknight. The knight was just a few paces away when he dropped face-first into the rushing stream at Tala's feet with a tremendous splash, arms outstretched before him. One of Bronwyn's black-fletched arrows was jutting straight up from the armor plate covering the knight's back.

Tala peered over the balustrade and saw Nail some twenty feet down among a handful of Dayknights and their braying horses. He was uninjured from the fall and was gathering up his lost sword from the bracken. Weapon in hand, he turned to meet the onrush of knights.

"Grab the sword!" Lawri screamed, latching onto Tala's shoulder with her good hand. Tala whirled, losing sight of Nail. Lawri was pointing at the large Dayknight lying dead in the trench before them. His black sword was right there in front of her, just under the crystal flowing waters. "Grab it!" Lawri screamed again.

Three Dayknights were advancing down the trench toward Tala and Lawri from the east, polished black armor and swords gleaming with ominous intent.

Bronwyn and Cromm were retreating down the narrow aqueduct to the south, the majority of the Dayknights who had climbed up the aqueduct now following them. Bronwyn fired arrow after arrow into their midst. Some of the knights fell.

Realizing she was alone with Lawri now, Tala snatched the dead knight's sword from the water, gripping it in both hands. It was heavy. She lifted it waist-high, facing the three advancing Dayknights, feeling about as ill-prepared for a fight as anyone could.

"Run!" she shouted at Lawri.

Together they turned and ran into the rain, both of them high-stepping over the dead knight in the trench, heading toward the Y, taking the aqueduct to the north and heading away from Bronwyn and Cromm. Side by side Tala and Lawri ran, knee-high water splashing into their faces. The three Dayknights gave chase.

Encumbered by the weighty black sword, Tala soon wore down, unable to catch her breath. Lawri fared no better, her two heavy cloaks, one of which was unraveling from her gauntleted arm, dragging in the water.

The three pursuing knights gained ground quickly, the nearest knight clasping onto the back of Lawri's cloak. "Let me go!" Lawri yelled out, struggling against the man. Then she tripped, tumbling face-first into the trench with a splash, heavy cloak flowing up over the back of her head, the water engulfing her. The knight leaped on top of Lawri, holding her underwater.

"No!" Tala screeched, stopping in the center of the trench and look-ing back, rain drenching her hair and face, eyes wide in terror. The two remaining Dayknights pushed their way past the knight holding Lawri down and lunged for Tala. One was helmetless. It was Glade Chaparral. She whirled and ran down the trench, gripping the black Dayknight sword out in front of her now in both hands. It was almost as if she were following its guiding tip toward the looming black tunnel punched into the thick-forested hill at the far end of the aqueduct. She ran, legs pump-ing through the knee-high waters, muscles burning. But she would not give up. She could sense her two Dayknight pursuers splashing and huff-ing right behind her.

"Stop!" Glade shouted. "Tala, stop!"

But Tala kept running, sodden legs carrying her under green leaves and tree limbs and straight into the rounded entrance of the tunnel. Once underground, the floor of the trench widened. It was also pitched at a slightly steeper angle, the ankle-deep water shallower but flowing at a swifter clip. Tala quickly realized that if she fell, the swift sheet of water might sweep her off into the growing darkness and who knew where.

She slowed her pace, one hand now grasping the stone lip of the balustrade, the other the sword. The foot-wide balustrades of rock cre-ated a small shelf on either side of the tunnel about waist-high. The crude-formed roof of the tunnel curved up over that. And the farther she ventured into the sloping tunnel, the more the light from the entry behind her diminished, darkness swiftly pressing down. Still, the tunnel stretched out before her straight and narrow and long, fading off into a hollow nothingness. *What am I doing? Where am I going?* Tala felt her lungs strain with exertion and her chest expand. The Dayknight sword was a burdensome weight in her left hand, its tip dragging behind her in the water.

"It's too dark, Tala!" Glade shouted.

He and the other Dayknight had ceased pursuing her. She could not hear them splashing behind her anymore. Still, she moved farther away from them into the darkness. "Come out of there, Tala!" Glade shouted, his voice echoing off the water and stone walls.

Tala stopped and cast her gaze back toward the tunnel entry. Two black forms wavered against the distant light. Long swords cut into the light on either side of the shadowy silhouettes.

"I do not wish to hurt you!" Glade's voice drifted toward her once more. "Our only aim is to take you back to Amadon! That is why we followed you all the way here, to take you back to your brother the king! We won't hurt you, neither Alain nor I! Tolz is already helping Lawri up as we speak!"

Tala couldn't see beyond the two shadowy Dayknights. She had no idea whether Tolz was really helping Lawri or not. *I abandoned her!* Tala turned and looked back into the gloom of the watery trench. It was so dark she could scarcely see a thing in front of her. Standing still, she breathed heavily, feeling the big black sword in her grip, wondering what to do. *Nail could be dead! Lawri could be dead! Bronwyn and Cromm, too!* She could feel every beat of her own heart in the wet gloom. She focused on the walls around her, trying to let her eyes adjust to the darkness.

A whisper of wind brushed her face, dragged over her from the right to the left—an uncomfortable little breeze warm to the skin. It seemed to be accompanied by musical voices from somewhere below her. She heard singing. A beautiful, wrenching song. The melody, like the howl of a thousand silver-wolves, echoed down the tunnel, calling out to the latent powers that Tala suddenly felt slept beneath the rock. There were deep rumblings coming from somewhere under the stone floor, answering the song's call. She could sense it; some wicked power she could never understand lived and breathed in this place. She felt it in her soul.

Wraiths! Demons! Dragons! She suddenly felt that the beasts of the underworld were infused within the very soul of the rock around her. They *lived* within the stone. She did the three-fingered sign of the Laijon Cross over her heart and then made a sweeping motion with her hand as if to dispel the poisonous witchcraft she imagined in the air. *Laijon, please, I humbly beg of you, stop this evilness and devilry—*

Her heart leaped up into her throat. Her eyes had adjusted to the darkness just enough. She stood on the very edge of a tremendous drop-off.

The water racing around her ankles plunged over the lip of stone and down into a bottomless nothingness, a shaft so deep she couldn't even hear the water splash into whatever well lay far below.

She could hear only those musical voices of the wraiths, the demons of the underworld calling up to her. Her mind spinning, she reached out and gripped the waist-high balustrade of the aqueduct to her right, steadying herself. *One slip and I am over the edge.* Though the floor of the trench dropped off in front of her, the tunnel itself carried on for another ten paces or so into the darkness, and so did the stone balustrades and their foot-wide rims on either side of the tunnel, until they met in the middle of the wall straight across from her. Glade and Alain were suddenly right next to her.

"Come with us, Tala." Alain reached for her, his hand gentle on her shoulder. She could see into his frightened eyes. Glade also stared warily at the drop-off before her.

Tala jerked away from Alain and climbed out of the water, hauling herself up onto the narrow lip of the stone balustrade that stretched out over the right side of the shaft. She slowly eased her way out over the black hole, her back hugging the wall behind her, Dayknight sword still gripped in one hand.

"Don't be foolish." Glade stood at the edge of the trench, water curling around his booted feet, dropping off into nothingness. "There is nowhere for you to go."

Tala cautiously slid sideways along the stone rim, now well out of either knight's reach. She recalled her journey with Glade under Purgatory, how they had come to a dead end similar to this, naught but water and blackness surrounding them. She could still hear the dread musical hum rising up from below.

"Get her, Alain," Glade commanded. Alain sheathed his sword and clambered up onto the waist-high lip of rock, following her. Tala slid farther away from the Dayknight, her back scraping against the wall. She felt the rough stone with her free hand as she went, her searching fingers gliding over grooves and cracks in the stone, eventually finding a thick iron hook embedded in the wall. Her hand instantly curled around it, grasping it tight. She felt more secure on the dangerous lip of stone now. Across the chasm there was another iron hook—similar to the one she held fast to—embedded in the wall just opposite her. Not that the hook over there mattered, but seeing it proved that her eyes were now adjusted to the dim light of the tunnel.

Alain Gratzer scooted across the same perch as Tala, gradually making his way toward her, steady as he went. Tala lifted her own Dayknight sword. But the weight of the weapon was too much for her one arm to bear; she could barely get the tip of the blade past her knees. Still, she jabbed out with it, pricking the tip of Alain's armored boot.

"Away with your nonsense." Alain kicked the tip of her blade away. "Foolish girl." Then he slipped, armor scraping against stone as he fell. He tried catching himself on the lip of the balustrade but could not. Alain plummeted soundlessly into the darkness.

"Bloody rotted angels!" Glade cried. "You just killed him, Tala! Who knows how deep that shaft is? Who knows where he has fallen to?"

Seeing Alain fall into the pit, Tala was more frightened now than she had ever been in her life. The sword was suddenly a deadweight in her hand. She nearly let it drop into the abyss with Alain. She was in such a panic, she couldn't even seem to grab a breath. *Help me, Laijon.* She uttered a little prayer almost without thinking. *Let Lawri and Nail and the others still be alive! Help me escape this horrible place.* The lesson Val-Draekin had taught her in the *Val-Sadè* about breathing suddenly came to mind. She held her breath and counted to three before expelling it, then filled her lungs, suddenly feeling like she had regained a mastery of her senses.

"Bloody Mother Mia," Glade exclaimed, carefully working his way toward the rim of rock she stood on.

Is he foolish enough to follow Alain? Tala stabbed the tip of the blade down toward him. "Climb up here, Glade, and I will knock you off too, I swear it. You will die just like Alain died."

The whites of Glade's eyes were pools of anger in the dim light. He reversed course, stepping carefully across the trench to the wall opposite her this time, climbing up onto the other balustrade. He eased his way out over the black chasm, his back to the wall like hers, moving slowly, just as she had. Naught but a black emptiness separated them now. His hand searched for the iron hook embedded in the wall. Finding it, he gripped it and drew his sword. "I will stab you," he snarled. "I will stretch across this dark hole and stab you in the heart and watch you fall to your death and there is nothing you can do about it."

"You cannot reach me from there," she said weakly, judging the distance between them, realizing to her horror that if he held fast to that iron hook, he could lean out over the chasm and stretch his sword all the way out and stab her. "You ought not try and kill me," she pleaded. "My brother wants me alive."

"Jovan be damned." Glade set his feet steady and firm atop the foot-wide shelf, gripped the iron hook in one hand, and leaned out over the abyss, sword outstretched before him, its tip aimed right for her chest. "I will just tell Jovan you were killed because of your own stupidity or some such other lie." The tip of his sword pricked her chest.

Gripping the iron hook embedded in the wall with all the strength she had, Tala tried to raise her Dayknight sword in defense. But it was too heavy in her already weary hand. Strained fingers giving out, she lost hold of the hilt and the black weapon tumbled from her grasp, spinning quietly down into the darkness.

Glade grinned as he pushed the tip of his own sword into her flesh. Tala ducked to the side and the tip of his blade sliced across her skin from her chest to shoulder, cutting her. Blood leaked over her chest from the long, ragged cut. The tip of Glade's sword wavered and dropped. He tried to reset his feet, bringing the sword back up for another strike.

Her hand firmly around the iron hook, Tala gritted her teeth in pain. But she did not cry out. She planted both feet solidly again on the precarious shelf of stone, still gripping the iron hook. Glade stabbed out a second time, with much more force now. Tala ducked aside, but the tip of the blade sliced across the top of her shoulder again with a sting and punched a hole through her shirt at the neckline, before ramming into one of the thin cracks in the wall behind her.

Glade, still leaning out over the chasm, tried to pull the sword free. But the blade was wedged deep into the wall behind Tala. It was caught. Glade's body was now suspended precariously over the chasm, left hand on the iron hook behind him, right hand on the sword hilt. Bracing his feet on the balustrade under him, he yanked hard on the hilt a second time, then a third. Nothing.

Tala craned her neck around; she could see that the tip of the sword was lodged at least six inches deep into a thin crack in the stone behind her. She too was caught by the blade.

"Bloody fucking angels!" Glade cursed, and tried again to forcefully yank the weapon free of the wall. His right foot slipped off the balustrade and he lost his grip on the iron hook behind him. He still gripped the hilt of the sword with his right hand, but his left foot was twisted awkwardly under him as he tried to keep his balance. But he was stretched too far over the chasm and his left foot slid from the balustrade too. His whole body twisted as his left hand shot out and grasped the hilt of the sword.

Glade now dangled over the chasm in front of Tala, both hands above his head, gripping the hilt of his Dayknight sword. The length of his blade was all that separated them. His eyes were wide in fear as he stared at Tala. His booted feet kicked in midair. The wriggling weight of his body caused the sword to droop, but its tip remained wedged deep into the wall behind Tala.

Glade calmed himself. "It's a right peculiar situation we're in now, eh, Tala?" Heart hammering in her chest, Tala did not respond. "A peculiar situation that speaks to the strong construction of a Dayknight-forged blade, wouldn't you say?"

Tala jerked to the side, trying to rip her shirt free of the blade pinning her to the wall. Nothing happened; the shirt would not tear away. She let go of the iron hook with her right hand, reached over her left shoulder, and tried unhooking her shirt that way.

Glade let go of the sword hilt above with his right hand. Hanging by just his left hand, he reached out and seized her by the front of her shirt, trying to pull himself toward her. But all he managed to do was yank her away from the wall and completely off the balustrade as her shirt finally tore away from the blade. She clawed desperately at his arm as she fell, grasping onto the black armor, swinging out over the dark abyss, crashing into his body. She was clutching his slick chestplate, sliding down his body, grasping at his ridged waist bucklers, desperately trying to find a handhold on anything. One of her hands finally grasped his belt, the other curled around the sheath that once held his sword—the sword that he now again gripped with both hands around the hilt.

As they hung there, clenched together, suspended over the dark shaft, Tala could feel the sword above her droop and bend, its tip soon to break free of the crack it was wedged in. Frantic, she tried to climb Glade's slick, armored body.

"You're gonna strip the armor right off me, fool." Glade tried to kick her away, knees ramming up into her ribs. But Tala clung to him even tighter now, wrapping her own legs around his ankles, trying to stop his struggle against her. But she could do no more than that. There was nowhere left for her to go. The balustrades before and aft were no longer options. The trench of water spilling over the ledge to her left and plunging down into the chasm was more than several arm's lengths away. And there was naught but dark wall to her right, even farther away than the waterfall.

She looked straight back up at Glade. Teeth clenched and jaw straining, veins bulging along his neck and face and forehead, Glade clung to the trembling hilt of the sword with both hands, his fading strength all that was keeping them both alive.

I am going to die with him here. My once betrothed—

"Tala, reach out."

Lawri Le Graven's voice emerged from the darkness.

"Take my hand!"

Tala looked back. Lawri was crouched on the foot-wide balustrade behind her. Her cousin's face was white as eggshells in the gloom and her eyes glowed bright and green. Lawri grasped the iron hook with her good hand, her gauntleted hand reaching out over the chasm. The silver-scaled gauntlet glowed with an inner emerald light of its own, as if green blood pumped through veins within the scaled metal.

And ivory-colored claws protruded from each of the gauntlet's five fingertips.

And each of the claws was streaked red with blood.

"She's a demon!" Glade cried out, his voice strained with exertion.

"Reach out, Tala." Lawri beckoned with the glowing silver gauntlet. "Take my hand."

Clinging to Glade's belt with her left hand, Tala reached out with her right hand for Lawri and the offered gauntlet. She felt the bloody claws of the gauntlet curl around her wrist, gripping her tight, pulling her away from Glade with a strength and sturdiness she would never have imagined, lifting her to safety. And in the grasp of the claw, Tala saw the demons in her mind's eye, demons of the underworld, thousands, millions, all following rivers of silver, rising up from Riven Rock Quarry over the bones of the human dead. She saw knights with silver Skull faces and sizzling whips of silver-dripping flame, the vision shaking her to her core.

Skulls! Just like Nail and Val-Draekin described!

Then she was safe on the foot-wide stone balustrade with her tawny-haired cousin. Lawri led Tala by the hand back toward the aqueduct's trench of running waters, the silver gauntlet still fastened solid and warm around Tala's wrist.

Once she stood safely in the middle of the aqueduct again, water curling about her ankles, Tala stared at her cousin. And Lawri smiled back at her shyly, looking abashed.

Tala slid her trembling hand free of the silver gauntlet, feeling the warm, red-stained claws run across her cold skin. And then the bloody claws slowly retreated back into the holes in the gauntlet's fingertips as if they had never existed. Tala shuddered, wondering what witchcraft she had just borne witness to.

And Lawri's eyes still glowed green.

Bronwyn Allen and Cromm Cru'x were racing up the tunnel toward them, water splashing at their knees. *Where is Nail?* Tala could not see the Gallows Haven boy behind the Wyn Darrè girl and the oghul. *Is he alive?*

Mind racing, she looked back toward Glade. The young Dayknight still hung there over the chasm, both hands gripping the hilt of his drooping sword. "Help me," he cried.

"Cromm has a length of rope we can throw him," Bronwyn said as she approached. "Unless you'd rather just let him drop into the shaft."

Cromm was already unhooking the rope from his belt, sucking heavily on the black angel stone as he worked.

"Well, what is it?" Bronwyn pressed. "Do we save him? Or shall I put an arrow in him and end it now?"

Tala gazed over the chasm at Glade, saw the utter fear in his widened eyes. His fingers were slipping from the hilt of the sword. She could see the sword droop. It would soon snap. "Help me," he cried again.

"We'll save you only on one condition!" Tala called out.

"Anything!" he yelled back. "Just help me!"

"When we get back to Amadon, you tell the truth about Ser Sterling Prentiss' murder!" she demanded. "You clear Lindholf's name!"

"I'll do it!" he shouted back. "I swear to it, I will tell Jovan I killed Prentiss!"

Cromm tossed the rope over toward Glade, where it landed, draping itself over his shoulder. Cromm braced himself whilst Glade let go of the hilt of the sword with one hand and hastily wrapped the end of the rope around the other hand several times. Secure, Glade let go the sword and swung down under Cromm and the rim of the aqueduct, the water flowing over his body and armor.

Cromm hoisted him up through the waterfall and over the lip of the trench to safety. Drenched and sopping, Glade gasped for breath as Cromm stood him face-first against the wall and tied his hands together behind his back.

Once Glade was bound and captive, Cromm and Bronwyn marched him from the tunnel toward the light, Tala and Lawri following.

Just outside the tunnel they found Tolz Trento lying on his back in the center of the trench, helmetless and dead, cool trench water flowing around him. The Dayknight's cold, wide eyes stared straight up into the rain. It looked like a saber-toothed lion had clawed his neck clear back to the spine; rainwater had washed the wound clean. Pink muscles, pale tendons, frayed brachial and carotid arteries, along with a myriad of ragged purple veins were exposed to the weather.

"He's dead." Glade gulped. "How?"

"He tried to drown me," Lawri said, her eyes green and vacant of emotion. She stepped over the body and continued walking down the trench.

The blood on the claw, Tala thought. *My cousin a cold killer?* She couldn't believe it.

"You killed him!" Glade shouted at Lawri. "He was only trying to save you!"

She turned, green eyes piercing into Glade's. "He was trying to drown me."

"Bloody Mother Mia." Glade stared at the silver gauntlet. In the gray light of the rainstorm he could see it for exactly what it was—a beastly thing attached to her arm. In fact, the normally pale skin of Lawri's arm was now a sickly green color where the silver of the gauntlet met her flesh.

"She's rotting," Glade exclaimed. "I know rot when I see it. She communes with the demons of the underworld. I can see the wraiths living in her!"

Lawri marched back toward Glade. "I know I have no hand under this gauntlet." She held up her silver arm before the soaked and dripping Dayknight. "But it still feels as if I do have a hand, but with fingers sewn together with needle and thread. At times my sewn-together hand underneath feels capable of doing whatever I wish it to do, or being whatever I wish it to be." She looked down at Tolz's mutilated face and neck. "He was trying to drown me." Then she turned and walked away, water swirling about her legs.

Cromm shoved Glade past Tolz's body. Tala and Bronwyn followed. Tala scanned the top of the aqueducts. There were many more dead

Dayknights lying in the trenches, some with crushed skulls, most with black-fletched arrows jutting from their bodies. Bronwyn yanked free what arrows she could and wiped them clean, eyes glinting white shards under her black tattoos.

When they reached the grappling hooks slung over the balustrade, Tala looked over the edge. In the grass and briar twenty feet below the arcade lay more scattered Dayknights in heaps of black armor, dead. Their horses milled about, munching the rain-splatted grass. Tala could not see Nail among the dead.

"We'll have to crawl down these ropes," Bronwyn said.

"What about me?" Glade exclaimed, the dark stubble on his face beaded with rainwater. "My arms are tied behind my back. Unloose me now, or someone will have to carry me."

"Unloose you?" Cromm grunted with a lopsided grin, sucking on the black angel stone with grim determination. Glade quailed at the oghul's severe look.

"Carry you, indeed." Cromm picked the young Dayknight up and dumped him unceremoniously over the side of the aqueduct. Glade's armored body crashed into the brush below. He moaned and squirmed like an upside-down turtle, legs kicking out. But he otherwise looked okay.

Bronwyn was first over the side of the aqueduct, sliding down the rope to the floor of the valley. Cromm motioned for Lawri and Tala to go next. Lawri struggled with only one hand; still, she made it down. Tala went next, followed by Cromm.

Once they were at the bottom, Bronwyn again began gathering her arrows whilst the oghul hauled Glade up and out of the dripping tangle of brush.

Tala immediately went looking for Nail. She found him behind a cluster of spooked destriers, five dead Dayknights arrayed around him. Nail lay face-first on the ground, arms splayed out over his head. What armor he wore was covered in blood. Tala's heart lurched. At first she thought he was dead, until Bronwyn rushed up and rolled him over, and he moaned aloud.

"He doesn't look too hurt," the Wyn Darrè girl said, checking his arms and legs for injuries. "He managed well, killing the knights that remained down here. He took a good whack on the head, though."

A purple bruise marked Nail's forehead under his blond hair.

"Yes, the marked one fought well." Cromm approached, dragging Glade behind him. "I looked down after he fell and saw him fighting with much anger, fighting as one possessed." Nail's eyes flickered open as he tried to sit up. Cromm knelt down and helped hold the Gallows Haven boy up in a sitting position. "Cromm is glad the marked one has made it out of the fight alive." The oghul sucked on his black angel stone, running his thick, bejeweled knuckles over Nail's wet thicket of hair. Cromm looked up at Bronwyn. "We shall now take him back to Amadon and Fiery Absolution."

Bronwyn cast her dark gaze around the valley. "I daresay, we at least got our pick of good horses to speed our travels." She nodded to Cromm. "To Amadon it is, then."

"Not before we go back to Savon," Tala said with resolve. "We go back for Jondralyn. We should never have left her atop that tower. I shall take her back to Amadon and my brother. She shall be buried as a princess of Gul Kana ought to be buried."

"You're bleeding," Nail said, pointing to her arm.

Tala raised her arm. Sure enough, her wrist was drenched in scarlet. Her shirtsleeve was caked to her arm with blood. She slowly, painfully peeled back the sleeve clear to her shoulder, revealing two long cuts, the wounds showing red and angry in the musty air. The cuts intersected in almost the perfect shape of a cross, one cut longer than the other, the wound disappearing beneath her shirt toward her chest.

Bronwyn said, "We should wrap those injuries."

"Aye." Tala nodded, looking up at Nail's frightened gaze. The Gallows Haven boy was staring right at her cross-shapped wounds.

Only starlight and silver can bring forth those true Aalavarrè Solas who were reared in the depths of the underworld. Only Dragon Claw can bring forth the Silver Throne. Only complete and absolute freedom can bring about true loyalty and devotion, even in the beasts of the underworld.
—THE ANGEL STONE CODEX

CHAPTER FORTY-FIVE
LINDHOLF LE GRAVEN

14TH DAY OF THE BLOOD MOON, 999TH YEAR OF LAIJON
EAST OF DEVLIN, GUL KANA

Hedgerows, stone fences, and lush fields lined either side of the dusty road. Lindholf Le Graven's horse moved at an easy stride down the long green hill toward their destination, a large white manor house nestled in the center of a farm on the outskirts of Devlin. Enna Spades was certain they would find what medicines they needed there.

They had both removed their black Dayknight helms some time ago, letting the cool breeze dry the sweat on their brows. Red hair flowed free around Spades' freckled face. The bloody bandage around her neck was stark and white in the sloping sun. She suffered from the bites of Liz Hen's dog, Beer Mug. Infected veins of a sickly green color could be seen twining like tiny serpents up the warrior woman's neck under her chin. Some stray veins even traced green streaks up the sides of her cheeks. Her eyes were rimmed in bruises, her face pallid as bone. Enna Spades was dying.

"Sorry I have not found you any Shroud of the Vallè, Ser Lindholf Le

Graven," she said. Her speech was growing ever more sickly and slurred. She breathed heavily in exertion as she continued talking. "I know I promised you the Shroud. And I've been dreary company these last few days. But you should know, if I do not survive beyond today, I have grown to enjoy your company, Lindholf Le Graven."

She always called Lindholf by his full name. She was respectful that way. *Am I her captive or willing travel companion?* Lindholf asked himself that daily. "You could be somewhere else," he said to her, "eating a hot meal, sleeping in a warm bed, yet here you are with me. Here with all the weapons of the Five Warrior Angels."

"And a festering wound," she added. "Besides, soon there won't be anywhere in the entire Five Isles with hot meals or warm beds. May as well be here with you, right?"

Her wound was growing more serious by the moment. She could hardly stay ahorse the last ten miles. Lindholf had nursed her along. He could tell the Sør Sevier woman continued the journey with naught but the force of her own will and sheer determination. Spades had assured him that if they made it to the manor house, medicines to stave off her infection would be there, along with Shroud of the Vallè for him.

The white sword, *Afflicted Fire*, was also greatly weighing her down. The long weapon was strapped to the baldric hanging over her armored back. The leather strap of the white shield, *Ethic Shroud*, was hooked over her left arm. All of that combined with her Dayknight armor was enough to wear down even the stoutest of knights. However, even in her infirm state, Enna Spades bore them with no complaint. On top of that, the five angel stones rode in the leather pouch at her belt.

It wasn't as if Lindholf was having an easy go of it himself. *Forgetting Moon* was fastened to his back. At times, the battle-ax was heavy beyond belief. At other times, the ax felt as light as a feather. The battle helm, *Lonesome Crown*, and the crossbow, *Blackest Heart*, were in a canvas sack slung over the stout flanks of his mount.

Four days had passed since they had fled Savon, and all that time Lindholf's mind had been reeling from the events he'd witnessed at the Preening Pintail: the death of Jondralyn; seeing Tala Bronachell and

Lawri in the streets under the tower, the silver gauntlet attached to his sister's arm; how he had failed Jondralyn.

Now he was a thief and traitor to his homeland, traveling with one of Gul Kana's greatest enemies in search of drugs. But was Enna Spades his enemy? In the four days he had known her, she had treated him with more kindness and respect than anyone ever had. The fact was, Lindholf knew he liked the woman that first morning they were together after fleeing Savon.

It started at daybreak, before they broke camp. He was scared, lost, nervously polishing his black Dayknight armor with a strip of burlap and rainwater, mindlessly scrubbing every plate and joint for lack of anything else to do, trying to keep his mind on anything but his many failures. He could still remember when Gault Aulbrek had killed the man who once wore the armor he now shined—the man had shit himself and befouled the armor. And Gault had forced Lindholf to clean it, something Lindholf would not soon forget. And ever since then, it seemed as if he cleaned the armor constantly, just to take his mind off horrible things. Horrible and strange things, like how the woman he now traveled with was the woman from his visions. *A fierce red-haired warrior woman in black armor and a long white sword, its hilt-guard the shape of a crescent moon.* That was what the mermaid in Memory Bay had shown him. And he had been polishing the armor over and over as if trying to scrub away a thousand such ill memories.

"Exceptionally shiny, that armor," Spades eventually commented, looking a good deal irritated that he was doing anything at all. But she always looked irritated that first day together. "It's likely the cleanest armor I've ever seen."

"Thanks," he answered, still buffing the armor.

"It wasn't a compliment."

"Oh."

"Only useless ass-lickers shine their boots and armor and other such gear. And what's even worse are the leaders who require such pointless exercises. Did you have some useless captain trick you into polishing your armor like that with false promises of earning rank and accolades just because your boots were the shiniest? Were you one of the ass-lickers who believed such garbage?"

He stopped shining the armor, embarrassed, dejected, confused.

But she threw him a wink and a curling little smile. "If you'd like to duel me over the insult, I'd be fine with that."

She was joking with him. He relaxed.

She went on, "You remind me of an idiot Hound Guard I had the misfortune of talking with after the sacking of Gallows Haven. He'd shined his armor so bright he almost glowed. Don't know if he even lived out the night. Can't even recall his name." She paused, reflecting. "But one cannot be expected to recall the names of every idiot soldier one meets. However, I do recall Ser Angus Mark. He was my captain when I was first recruited into the Rowdies some ten years ago. A man plum full of needless ideas: shine your boots, shine your armor, press your breeches, press your bedsheets, and make your bed at the beginning of every day. He went so far as to claim one could not become a worthwhile soldier if they didn't properly discipline themselves to make their bed each morning, and make it with extreme precision and perfection. And he drilled that frivolous bullshit into us recruits without ceasing. At times he was so focused on the minutiae of his piddly little rules he ignored the more important parts of our training: hard work, practice, swordsmanship, archery, shield work, sparring."

"But I reckon you made your bed until you moved out of his unit?" Lindholf tried to joke back with her. "Like a good little soldier, no?"

"Not quite," she answered. "I deliberately did not make my bed for several days, earning his wrath. Then one morning in our barracks, as he stood over my untidy bed, lecturing me on all my faults as a soldier and a woman in front of all the other Rowdies, I drew my sword and rammed it up under his chin and into his brain. I watched him slip from my sword and fall over backward onto my unmade bed, dark, warm blood pumping from the hole in his neck all over my unpressed sheets. When Aeros heard of the incident he threatened to throw me into the dungeons of Rokenwalder. It wasn't hard to change his mind . . . if you take my meaning. Point is, I despise fancy armor, and I certainly don't number any shiny-armored knights as my friends. So if you aim to get along with me, stop buffing that fucking armor."

Lindholf let the burlap fall to the ground, muttering, "I only clean it because the man who wore this particular set of armor before me shit himself in it when he died."

"Interesting." Spades raised her eyebrow at that. "I was not expecting that excuse. In fact, I can almost admire that reasoning for your precise fastidiousness. I can almost call you friend."

"I've not had a friend in several moons," he said, and then cursed the pathetic tone he heard in his own voice.

"Well, don't look to me to be your friend just yet. I prefer traveling alone. I still haven't decided which will take more energy: carrying all the weapons myself, or having you along as a helper. I seldom like traveling with strange men. I have little to say to most men, when they invariably have much to say to me."

"Because you're so pretty," he blurted. "They desire to talk to you because you are pretty. The White Prince did not throw you into the dungeons because you are pretty. All men become babbling fools around pretty girls."

She laughed. "And I just ain't inclined to pointless conversation. And you are correct, pointless conversation is all most men have to offer when around a pretty girl. It ain't polite for you to say. But I do enjoy your honesty. Men do only talk to me because I am pretty." She winked at him. "It's a curse and burden we pretty folk must bear, no?"

"Well, I'm only talking to you because you're the only one around," he said.

Spades laughed again. "You're more of a scoundrel than you let on."

Lindholf laughed too, relaxing even more now. He enjoyed her conversation and minor teasing. "How long have you been a Dayknight?" he inquired, to be polite. "Where are you from?"

"I ain't a Dayknight." Her eyes narrowed. "Did you not listen to anything I just said?"

"Right." He nodded. "Pointless conversation."

"Avoid pointless questions like that and we should get along just fine."

She winked at him again, smiling. "Besides, you know my Dayknight armor is stolen, just like yours, Ser Lindholf Le Graven." And that was the moment when she had started calling him by his full name.

Lindholf knew he could not escape Enna Spades if he wanted, which he didn't, for he also knew his own lack. He could not steal the weapons and stones from her and go his own way. He knew exactly why he stayed with her. He liked her. She was pretty. And her promise of Shroud of the Vallè consumed his mind at all times.

He felt a fierce need for the white powder. It was like the blood in his veins was doing battle with every other part of him, just awaiting its taste. No. He could not steal the weapons and angel stones. Even sick and near death, Enna Spades was competent enough to track him down. And he *needed* the promised Shroud. And, all things considered, she was a better travel companion than either Gault or Delia had been.

His mind back in the present, craving the white powder, he asked Spades, "Are you sure those in the manor house below have any Shroud of the Vallè?"

"They will." Spades cast a wan smile his way. "I know what oghul lives there. I passed this way once before in search of Mancellor. He was kind enough to have his farrier re-shoe my horse."

"An oghul lives there?" Lindholf questioned.

"The type of oghul who deals in dark oghul magics and secret Vallè alchemy."

"I don't like the sound of that." Lindholf started off toward their destination. It looked like a thriving farm clinging to the outskirts of Devlin, its centerpiece a broad three-story manor house posturing before the dirty town like a jewel. Lush and groomed gardens of rosebushes and ivy marked the entire farm and gated entrance, and the roadway leading up to it.

"Just remember your job at the Preening Pintail," Spades said. Sweat was clinging to her pale forehead. "When we reach the house, stand stiff in your armor at my side, stoic and calm, like the doorman at a tavern. Standing still is exceptional intimidating behavior for any knight, in my view. Plus, we will both keep our helmets on. And above all, keep your mouth shut and let me do the talking. A silent knight can be a forbidding knight. And all I need from you is forbidding. From here on out, silence is to be your virtue, Lindholf Le Graven."

**

The long-nosed, pipe-smoking oghul introduced himself as Gin D'rhu upon their entry into the airy foyer of the manor house. He wore a plush black robe that reached below his knees. The robe had two large breast pockets sewn in with golden thread. Gin D'rhu was barefoot, and the red teardrop tattoo on his cheekbone just below his left eye marked him as—Enna Spades claimed—one who dealt in dark oghul magics and secret Vallè alchemy.

The oghul led them from the foyer down a wide hallway and to the drawing room, two oghul footmen at his side. The footmen wore black pantaloons and wide leather belts with green tunics buttoned over tan shirts. Lindholf had seen four other similarly garbed footmen stationed in the gardens of Gin D'rhu's estate; each of those footmen had also worn wide leather belts girt with shortswords at their hip, hands on hilts. *And who knows how many more such beasts might be crawling around the large manor?* Lindholf thought as he entered the drawing room.

Overall it was a handsome chamber, with many open windows casting wan yellow light into a surprisingly comfortable space full of a myriad of wooden cabinets, bookshelves, tables, bronze sculptures, and woven rugs. Everything about Gin D'rhu and his residence was sophisticated and fine.

"I hope your horse is still well shod, good Ser," Gin D'rhu said, eyes on Spades. "Sit." He beckoned, puffing vigorously on his pipe, cracked, leathery lips pursed about its ivory-colored stem. "The both of you, please sit."

"Your blacksmith did a grand job." Spades stayed standing. Her voice was rough, strained with fatigue and illness under her black Dayknight helm. "But we are here for a different purpose today."

Lindholf stayed standing too, though comfortable seats were aplenty in the large room and he desperately wished to sit.

Spades still carried the five angel stones in a pouch on her belt;

Afflicted Fire and *Ethic Shroud* were strapped to her back. Lindholf also wore *Forgetting Moon* on his back. *Blackest Heart* and *Lonesome Crown* were in the canvas sack slung over his shoulder. Spades dared not leave the stones or weapons with their two mounts, which were tethered to the hitching post just outside the oghul's opulent manor house. And Gin D'rhu seemed unconcerned that they both had carried so much weaponry into his home. *Perhaps he dares not question two fully armed and armored Dayknights knocking at his door.*

Still puffing on his pipe, Gin D'rhu sat on a long, plush velvet couch in the center of the room. A shortsword was on the end table within easy reach. His two burly footmen flanked the couch on either side. "So what can I do for two Dayknights this time?" Gin D'rhu asked.

"We come for medicine this time," Enna Spades said. "I've an infection that needs healing. We've not much coin. But we've brought items to bargain with."

Spades motioned for Lindholf to set the sack containing *Lonesome Crown* and *Blackest Heart* down on the floor before him. He did just that. His heart was pounding at her insinuation that they were going to trade away the weapons, but he was determined to remain silent, mind focused on the Shroud of the Vallè Spades was about to procure. The weapons of the Five Warrior Angels were easily worth the price.

"We've also come for Shroud of the Vallè, if you have it," Spades continued. "And we wish to remain anonymous in the transaction. In fact, we insist."

"Well, I reckon I already know who you are, Ser Knight," Gin D'rhu said with a cordial nod aimed directly at Spades. "I've learned much about you since you passed this way before."

Lindholf figured the long-nosed oghul was just being flippant, or perhaps purposely obtuse, for he'd seemed an odd sort from the moment he and his two footmen had led Lindholf and Spades into the drawing room. Gin D'rhu was not oghul-like at all, leastways not oghul-like in Lindholf's limited experience with the creatures. Other than his pocked gray face and exceptionally long gray nose, his overall royal demeanor was one of utter pipe-smoking sophistication.

"Indeed, I fear I now know exactly who you are, Ser Knight," Gin D'rhu repeated, leaning back on the velvet couch, puffing again on his long, curling pipe. "Though, I imagine, in your modesty you wish to remain anonymous for sure." Gin D'rhu spoke with an eloquence Lindholf had never before heard in an oghul. The two wedge-faced footmen behind Gin D'rhu adjusted their weapons on their fancy belts for effect.

To Lindholf's surprise, Spades removed her Dayknight helm. "You know nothing of me," she said, setting the helm in the crook of her arm. "And that shall be your official answer to anyone who may ask. And trust me: it would not go well for you if you said anything different."

Pipe still in his pursed mouth, Gin D'rhu pulled on it, drawing in deep, then exhaling. Smoke drifted up. Removing the pipe, the oghul casually said, "Oh, you would be surprised what a learned oghul such as myself has discovered about you." His cracked gray lips curled back in a frightening grin, revealing an upper row of startlingly sharp and narrow teeth. "I know most of the goings-on between here and Amadon." Then he winked, the red teardrop-shaped tattoo just below his left eye momentarily disappearing in a wrinkled gray fold. His long nose twitched. The two footmen stiffened their posture at either end of the couch. Lindholf suddenly did not feel safe in this place with these strange oghuls. He kept his own Dayknight helm on. He remained silent.

"Rumor is," Gin D'rhu began, "since last I saw you on my lands in your Dayknight armor there has been a red-haired warrior woman, a demon bitch also in Dayknight armor, burning down taverns and inns and other such places of disrepute between here and Savon. Slaughtering barmen and serving wenches, opening their throats with her sword for not serving a woman in Dayknight armor." The long-nosed oghul set down his pipe and stood. "Or so the rumor is."

"Never heard those stories myself." Spades looked at Lindholf, her green eyes rheumy with sickness. "You?" Lindholf shook his head no, helm rattling on his head.

Gin D'rhu's nose twitched again. "But you are clearly a red-haired warrior woman in Dayknight armor, no?"

"Perhaps that description fits," she answered.

"Have you ever killed anyone?"

"Not yet," Spades replied, mustering a slight little smile.

"How did you come by your injuries?" The oghul gestured to the bandage around her neck, which didn't quite cover the purple swelling and infection.

"A dog bit me," she answered.

Gin D'rhu scowled, his nose no longer twitching. "I've been most deferential to your story thus far. But everything about you seems to be rather disagreeable. Mysterious even. Quite vexing, indeed. You say you want medicine. And I can see the gravity of your injury, and if you wish to survive the night, you shall need the most expensive Vallè alchemy money can buy. It will take all that you have to purchase it."

"So you have circe inviniosa?" Spades' eyes widened in hope. "That should heal me in a day, perhaps less."

"Now that, circe inviniosa, you do not have enough loot to pay for that," Gin D'rhu said. "But we shall see what bargains we can work out." Then he snapped his fingers.

Two more oghul footmen came into the room, weapons not quite hidden under their short brown cloaks, one of them bearing a glass beaker full of the blackest liquid Lindholf had ever seen, coal black, but frosted with an astonishingly pink foam. The footman set the beaker on the end table next to Gin D'rhu's shortsword.

Gin D'rhu looked at Lindholf. "Are you also unwell, Ser Knight?"

Lindholf said nothing. Gin D'rhu produced a small leather pouch from the folds of his black robe. "You must be the one who wants Shroud of the Vallè?" He dangled the pouch in the air. "It is full of the white powder."

Lindholf almost felt his whole body lean forward, sweat beading up on his face under the stifling battle helm.

"The Shroud also comes with a price, Ser Knight." Gin D'rhu gently placed the leather pouch next to the beaker of circe inviniosa. He looked directly at Lindholf as he spoke. "You see, there are oghuls gathering in the north. Hragna'Ar oghuls, to be exact, beasts who work with the Skulls, beasts who would be most anxious to get their hands on your five weapons, the white sword the woman carries, the white shield, that shiny battle-ax on your back, and whatever other trinkets you may be carrying in the canvas sack, plus the five stones I sense are in that leather pouch at your partner's belt. Help me take everything from her and the Shroud is yours."

Spades took a step back, body rigid, green eyes foggy with sickness.

"Oh, yes indeed," Gin D'rhu went on, now looking at Spades. "There are some oghuls who would be most desirous to suck on stones such as those in your pouch. They would be most desirous to fulfill Hragna'Ar legend, stuff those stones down into their filthy lips, and carry them straight to Absolution. Perhaps I am one such oghul."

Lindholf felt his own body stiffen. Gin D'rhu was talking of things like Hragna'Ar legend, which Lindholf did not understand, things that felt blasphemous and wicked. *And how could he possibly know what's in Spades' pouch?* There was some form of witchcraft at work here, and Lindholf was scared.

"Or there is another bloodletting payment we can take, my footmen and I," the oghul said, now eyeing the bandage around Spades' neck. "An infected neck is a rare delight for an old oghul like myself. Well, for any oghul, really. You see, festering warm liquid infection like that can be absolutely divinely euphoric in taste."

Lindholf wanted to vomit. He had seen under the bandage himself, watched as the warrior woman had tried to clean it, watched in horror as she had tried to sear it closed with burning branches from their nightly campfires. He recalled Val-Korin draining the pus and infection from Jondralyn Bronachell's face. And to now find out that such gruesomeness was a rare delicacy to a bloodsucking oghul . . . He felt his slave brand and scars from the mermaid flare up in pain, felt *Forgetting Moon* grow suddenly heavy on his back, rooting him in place as if warning him of danger.

Enna Spades drew *Afflicted Fire* from over her shoulder. She stepped lightly to the side, letting *Ethic Shroud* slip from her other hand to the ground. The four footmen drew their own shortswords, and Gin D'rhu snatched the sword up from off the end table, brandishing it menacingly with a scowl.

Before Lindholf could take his next breath, Spades' white blade flashed under Gin D'rhu's face upward toward the ceiling, slicing through the oghul's long nose. Spades caught the spinning gray lump in her hand before it hit the floor. Then she reached forth and stuffed it into the golden-threaded breast pocket of the oghul's robe.

Stunned, Gin D'rhu stood stiff and still for all of a heartbeat. Then blood welled from the wound down over his mouth and chin, thick and red. The oghul reached up with one gnarled hand to stem the flow, screeching through bloody fingers, "Slay her now!" The four oghul footmen surrounded Spades swiftly.

Spades lunged, the white blade striking out merciless and keen, sweeping off the head of the nearest oghul. Blood sprayed over the other three footmen, who stepped immediately back, surprised. Spades moved quickly. *Afflicted Fire* punched through the astonished face of the second oghul, before chopping off both arms of the third. The armless oghul screamed in terror as the white blade took his head off at the neck. The fourth oghul ran from the room.

Gin D'rhu, noseless and bloody-faced, bellowed for reinforcements. But his cry was cut short as *Afflicted Fire* plunged into his chest, cleaving through his heart and spine and out the back of his robe. The oghul slid open-eyed from the length of the blade, crumpling to a heap on the floor.

Ten more oghuls poured into the chamber, swords drawn, grim looks on their faces. Spades launched herself heedlessly into their midst, the long white blade opening the stomachs of the first five in her way. Purple guts spilled to the floor in piles, and five oghuls clutched at their gaping stomachs. The five other oghuls lost arms and legs and heads just as swiftly and savagely as the others had lost their innards.

In the end, Spades killed them all, and the room was dripping with red. And Lindholf watched in an almost enraptured trance as *Afflicted Fire*'s pearly white surface pulsed with an inner light, with an inner *life*, soaking up the oghuls' blood with each rhythmic beat of its invisible heart.

Swooning on her feet, Spades threw Lindholf a look of cold anger. "The way I feel, all things considered, I would have preferred to settle that in a more congenial way."

"I'd say I would have h-helped," Lindholf stammered. "But I w-would have just been in the way. And you told me to remain still."

"No matter. Things turned out as planned."

"You're the best fighter I've ever seen. And I've been to the arena a lot, seen the best gladiators in all of Gul Kana."

"Gul Kana gladiators are not good fighters," she stated, looking at the long white sword in her grip. "But I'm a decent fighter, even when half delirious."

She held the sword up. *Afflicted Fire* was clean. All trace of blood on its previously slick red surface was gone, mysteriously vanished. Lindholf's mind reeled. Had the warrior woman truly killed all these oghuls, or was it the work of the magical sword?

Spades hooked *Afflicted Fire* to the baldric over her back, snatched up the beaker full of circe inviniosa, and gulped the black liquid down, health infusing her pallid features almost instantaneously. Lindholf stripped off his gauntlets, snatched up the leather pouch holding Shroud of the Vallè, untied it with trembling fingers, took a pinch of the white powder hiding within between two fingers, and greedily sniffed it straight up into his nose. He repeated the process as the much-longed-for pleasure, ecstasy, and euphoria of the Shroud swept over him. Spades cast her green-eyed gaze around the opulent drawing room painted in blood, sizing up the savagery and destruction she had wrought. And as her eyes drank in the scene, she was looking healthier by the moment. She looked at him and said, "A place of such bloody disrepute ought not stand."

And he too was feeling better by the moment. He met her green-eyed stare, saying with the utmost zeal, "Let's burn it to the ground."

Enna Spades smiled at that.

CHAPTER FORTY-SIX
MANCELLOR ALLEN

15TH DAY OF THE BLOOD MOON, 999TH YEAR OF LAIJON

AMADON, GUL KANA

Princess Jondralyn Bronachell's corpse was draped over the back of one of the three piebald ponies huffing for breath behind Mancellor Allen, Liz Hen Neville, and Dokie Liddle. The reins of all three ponies were gripped tight in Liz Hen's balled fist. The piebalds were slow-moving and swaybacked, but they had been the only mounts left in Rutger's small stables next to the Preening Pintail.

"You must open the gate to us!" Mancellor was unarmed, staring straight at the stone guard tower and bulky entry gate of Amadon Castle's outer wall. The summer air was damp, laced with a light rain, heavy with the smell of the city. It was midday and his entire body was wet with sweat under his ragged clothing. "I beg of you, please. Open the gate!"

"I don't think there's anyone up there." Dokie ruffled the soggy gray fur atop Beer Mug's head.

"It's just so big," Liz Hen said, red-hazed eyes gazing upward. "The gate. The castle. Everything in Amadon is just so big."

The Gallows Haven girl was right about that. Even Mancellor had been amazed at the size of the city. Everything in Amadon was huge, and at the moment, wet. Mount Albion and the massive black-and-gray-colored castle rose up before them like a brooding dark thundercloud. Circled by a daunting stone wall and lofty stone guard towers, the castle was a soaring patchwork of outer buildings and makeshift add-on structures, and a myriad of other crenellated battlements, spires, baileys, palisades, barbicans, and causeways, all peppered with flags of silver and black. The sheer grandiose stateliness and splendor of the structures stole Mancellor's breath.

In fact, the awe-inspiring grandeur of Amadon itself was more than he had been expecting. The vast city and its warrens of crooked and cobbled streets and buildings spread out around him as far as his eyes could see, replete with all the illustrious, celebrated landmarks that as a child he had dreamed of one day visiting. The Hallowed Grove and the legendary thousand-year-old Atonement Tree. The prominent Royal Cathedral, shaped like a crown, the sanctuary where the Blessed Mother Mia was buried. The famed Hall of the Dayknights and the ethereal Temple of the Laijon Statue. All of it was *real*, and far more astounding than he had ever imagined. For generations, pilgrims the breadth of the Five Isles had flocked to Amadon to worship at the foot of these magnificent buildings. Mancellor's father had dreamed of just such a pilgrimage. A religious trek that Niklos Allen had never gotten the chance to make, but a journey that Mancellor had made under the most bizarre of circumstances.

When they had passed by the circular, columned gladiator arena, the peculiar nature of Mancellor's journey to this city had set in. For it was then he recalled his visions whilst in the clutches of the mermaid during the Battle of the Saint Only Channel. He had seen himself and Jenko Bruk in that arena, facing a skull-faced knight in green armor. And there was a green dragon in that hazy underwater dream. He shuddered at the thought, knowing that those visions were apt to come true if the events at Ten Cairn Abbey and atop the tower in Savon were any indication.

The pony bearing the covered body of Princess Jondralyn Bronachell shuffled to the side, whinnying. A grubby street urchin ran underfoot, splashing through the puddles.

"Bloody uncooperative nag." Liz Hen held tight to the reins, bringing the pony under control with a hushed whisper. Beer Mug, tail wagging playfully, watched the boy run off into the milling crowd behind them. Liz Hen stroked the wet mane of the pony carrying the princess. Jondralyn was tied securely, if awkwardly, to the back of the poor beast, and wrapped from head to toe in the sodden canvas.

It had taken them five days of hard travel to reach Amadon, each of the ponies taking its turn carrying the princess's body. Her stiff corpse was beginning to smell. Along their journey, Mancellor oft wondered if bringing the princess back to Amadon was the best of plans, be it Laijon's will or not. But deep down, he knew that all things happened for a reason, including this.

"Will they open the damn gate or not?" Liz Hen grumbled.

"You must open the gate to us!" Mancellor called out again.

The distant barking of a dog echoed sharply off the castle wall, and that, mixed with the teeming masses of street merchants and other such vendors and bloodletters filling the marketplace behind them, caused Mancellor to wonder if his voice would ever be heard by the Silver Guards he knew must surely be manning the tower and gate.

"You must open the gate to us!"

"And why is that?" a voice finally sounded from above. "You shouted your demands four times now!" A window in the tower had its wooden shutter swung wide open and a man's head peered down at them. "Who wishes to enter the king's castle?"

"I am Ser Mancellor Allen of Wyn Darrè!"

Still no movement at the gate. Frustrated, Liz Hen reached into the folds of her cloak and pulled forth the vial of Blood of the Dragon she had stolen from Praed. She unstoppered the vial, eyes aglow as she drank the liquid down. "I wish you had never been introduced to that damnable stuff, Liz Hen," Dokie said, an almost desperate concern in his voice. "I wish you'd never started drinking it at all."

"It gives me confidence," Liz Hen said, slipping the vial back into her cloak. She then looked up at the gate. "We have Princess Jondralyn with us!" she screamed. "And she's dead!"

A moment passed. And the gate slowly opened.

**

Sunbird Hall was the largest room Mancellor had ever been in, at least twice the size of Bruce Hall atop Mont Saint Only. It was also blessedly dry. He just wanted to fall down and sleep for a moon or more. Comfortable-looking benches, divans covered in velvet, and bearskin rugs peppered the floor of the chamber. Long wooden tables lined the room. Black pillars flanked lofty walls that were draped with tapestries and hung with large candelabra. Scores of torches and hundreds of candles glittered, causing the room to almost glow. Along the easternmost end of the room was a set of wide double doors perched atop a curving balcony. The doors were thrown open, allowing more light to spread over the crowd. Even as Mancellor entered the hall at the opposite end from the balcony, he could see the storm clouds boiling outside.

The room was full of many nobles, each of them come to see the return of Jondralyn Bronachell. Many Dayknights and Silver Guards stood stiffly at attention. Many noblemen lounged on the soft-cushioned furniture. They stood at Mancellor's, Liz Hen's, Dokie's, and Beer Mug's entrance. Liz Hen guided the pony bearing the covered body of the princess. The piebald's unshod hooves echoed loudly on the stone floor. Their other two ponies had been stabled somewhere below.

Mancellor's eyes traveled to the raised dais in the center of the southern wall. King Jovan Bronachell sat at a table on the dais in a richly jeweled cloak, black cape fastened at the neck with a large silver brooch. A stately-looking older man, round of gut and bald with a strip of brown hair circling the back of his head, sat at the table opposite Jovan. Five similarly dressed men stood behind him. The bald man wore an orange cassock and many gold necklaces about his neck. The stone dais under Jovan's feet was strewn with soft white rugs, and a row of Dayknights in heavy black breastplates and mail stood behind him, their backs against the velvet-draped wall, black longswords hanging under their surcoats.

Behind the king and his knights was a large piece of furniture draped in white sheets. *The Silver Throne!* Mancellor had heard rumors that Jovan would not sit upon the famed throne but rather kept it covered.

Mancellor instantly recognized Ser Leif Chaparral. The dark-eyed man was one of the Dayknights standing at attention behind the king. Leif was glaring at Liz Hen and Dokie like he wanted to kill them.

Jovan stood at the approach of the newcomers, looking positively regal, a thin silver crown circling his head. Mancellor immediately recognized Aeros Raijael's sword, Sky Reaver, at the king's hip. He remembered the Spider losing the blade in Ravenker. Now here it was at King Jovan's side. Mancellor took some small measure of satisfaction in that fact.

"It's Baron Jubal Bruk," Liz Hen whispered pointing toward a dark-eyed armless and legless man on a bench not far from the dais. "Look, Dokie. On that bench. No arms. No legs. My daggers are still stuck in the tar covering his stumps."

Recognition filled Jubal's eyes when he saw Liz Hen, Dokie, and Beer Mug.

Mancellor was surprised to see Jenko Bruk's bearded father lounging on a bench near the king, silver daggers still protruding from the stumps of his arms. Mancellor could still remember Jenko sawing the limbs from his own father that frightful morn in Gallows Haven. *What would the baron think of his son now?* Mancellor wondered if the man even knew his son was fighting for the enemy. An image of Enna Spades flashed into his mind. *I wonder if he knows his son is sleeping with the enemy.*

"And it's Leif Chaparral," Liz Hen hissed, finally recognizing the knight. "Dokie, look, it's that foul knight, the one who hung Bishop Godwyn."

Mancellor soon realized it was Grand Vicar Denarius at the table opposite the king. The five archbishops of Amadon—Vandivor, Donalbain, Spencerville, Leaford, and Rhys-Duncan—were likely the men who stood there behind the grand vicar in robes and necklaces of equal finery.

Overawed, Mancellor dropped to one knee before the vicar and the quorum of five. He did the three-fingered sign of the Laijon Cross over his heart, not quite believing he was seeing the grand vicar with his own eyes.

"Stand, Ser." Jovan's harsh-timbred voice rang through the hall.

"Indeed, rise before us," the grand vicar followed, tone more inviting and laced with a reverent concern. His eyes were fixed on the covered form of Jondralyn atop the pony. "What news have you brought us, good Ser?" he asked Mancellor.

"If it please Your Grace." Mancellor stood but bowed low before the vicar, doing the three-fingered sign of the Laijon Cross over his heart again, his soul brimming, knowing this moment was the culmination of so much perseverance, sacrifice, and faith. A lump grew in his throat as he thought back on his strange and arduous five-year journey to this place, the levels of personal integrity he had forfeited, all the battles he had fought at Aeros Raijael's side just to keep himself alive to reach this place. "You must know, 'tis an honor to be in your presence," he said. "'Tis seldom one such as I can kneel before the grand vicar. I am your servant till the end."

Denarius beckoned him stand with a quick wave of his hand, eyes still lingering on Jondralyn's body. When Mancellor stood, he realized every eye in Sunbird Hall was fixed on the covered body slung over the back of the pony. The king's brow furrowed, his countenance pained, yet skeptical.

"Is it true?" Leif Chaparral stepped up next to Jovan. "Is it the king's sister you have brought us?" His dark-rimmed eyes were fixed on Mancellor, his face a mix of cold fascination and surprise.

"It is her." Liz Hen's red-shot eyes blazed pure anger at the tall Dayknight.

Mancellor knew of the strained history between the two. Leif would have hung the girl in Lord's Point if not for a bishop's intervention. A bishop named Godwyn.

"She's truly dead," Jovan muttered as he stepped from the dais toward the body slung over the pony.

"She was killed in Savon," Mancellor said nervously. "Or at least, that is where we found her body."

Jovan reached forth one tentative hand and tried to pull away the white canvas covering from his sister, struggling with it. Mancellor had wrapped the body tight. "Help me free her, Leif," Jovan beckoned.

The tall Dayknight leaped to his king's aid. Together they folded back the canvas, revealing the armored form of Jondralyn Bronachell. She was folded stomach-down over the swayed back of the pony, feet and legs hanging over the right side of the beast, head and arms dangling over the left. One bare hand along with the long locks of her dark hair hung almost to the floor of Sunbird Hall. Her other hand was shorn at the wrist.

Jovan lifted the hair away from his sister's face. "I cannot tell if it is her," he said, voice atremble now. "The face is all purple and bloated from hanging upside down like this. But she wears an eye patch."

The king stepped back from the body, a dull, faraway stare in his eyes. It was a familiar stare, one that Mancellor had seen before. It was that glazed-over look soldiers ofttimes had after battle, after having witnessed their friends and companions hacked to death in the most gruesome of ways. Hammerfiss called it the thousand-mile gaze. And to Hammerfiss' estimation, a soldier wasn't a soldier until that shocked look was a permanent fixture in their eyes. It was clear to Mancellor: Jovan Bronachell had seen war, and seeing his sister dead like this was swiftly bringing back that trauma.

Leif covered his nose as a gamey, rotten stench wafted through the chamber all at once. "We must lift her from the pony." He summoned a group of Silver Guards standing nearby. "Lift her. Gently. Set her on the floor."

The handful of knights hauled Jondralyn's covered body from the pony's strained back. The princess's body was somewhat stiff and bent in the middle as they placed the wrapped bundle on its side.

Leif knelt by her body. "If this is truly Jondralyn, it does not bode well, especially with the rumors of Vallè warships off the coast up north."

"They are but rumors," Jovan said, irritated. "The stories of those ships are lies."

As Leif cut what remained of the canvas from Jondralyn's armored figure, it swiftly became evident to all that the blood-coated body was indeed that of Princess Jondralyn Bronachell. The black eye patch Jovan spoke of still covered her one eye. Her other eye was naught but a gaping dark hole, and a puncture wound under her chin. As the knights continued to unroll the canvas down the length of her legs, a severed hand spilled out onto the floor. Liz Hen had insisted they gather the hand from the gutter in Savon and wrap it up with her body.

Mancellor heard the sniffles and cries of some of the nobles and their women in the background. It *was* a sad sight. Pale-faced, King Jovan Bronachell turned his back to the chamber, dropped to his knees, and vomited onto the white rug. The sound of his strained retching echoed through Sunbird Hall. This was followed by a deep silence.

"Everything shall be okay, son." Grand Vicar Denarius drifted toward Jovan, placing a comforting hand on the broad back of the king. "None of this is your fault. You needn't blame yourself. Your sister was headstrong and brash. She was as Laijon hath made her. Thus all that has transpired, well, 'tis naught save her own God-willed destiny, 'tis naught save the desires of our Lord the great One and Only. However it was that she hath met her fate, 'twas Laijon's will. In that we shall take our solace."

Liz Hen's brow furrowed and her face darkened. Mancellor knew the girl disliked any talk of Laijon or his will. She stepped toward the pony and picked up the severed hand. With a great deal of reverence, she placed the severed appendage gently next to the princess's body.

Watching her, Leif Chaparral's dark-rimmed eyes narrowed. "What makes you think you can just touch the flesh of royalty?" His question was almost a bark. He stared at the girl with an unflinching self-assurance that reminded Mancellor of Aeros Raijael.

Liz Hen met Leif's self-assured gaze firmly. "It just didn't seem right to leave her hand in a gutter in Savon. We've carried it this far. I don't want to see it sullied. Placing it next to her, I'm only making things right."

"Making things right?" Leif huffed. "Don't think I have forgotten your fat traitorous face, *girl*."

"My traitorous face?" Liz Hen countered, rage washing over her. "I saved your *life* during the Battle of the Saint Only Channel! Bishop Godwyn died because of you!"

"That bishop died because of you!" Leif fired back. "'Twas you who broke the laws of Laijon! The man was hung because of your deception and sins!"

"But I *saved* you in that battle!" Liz Hen growled again.

"You did no such thing!"

"I did exactly such a thing!" she raged. "And Bishop Godwyn also fought at your side, and still you hung him. He fought valiantly at your side, as did I, as did Dokie, as did Beer Mug. We fought against Aeros Raijael and the entire might of his armies."

Her blazing red eyes found Jubal Bruk sitting at the table. "Your son was there too, Baron Bruk! But Jenko fought at the side of the White Prince, wearing the colors of the enemy! He tried to kill me!"

"My son is *alive*?" The baron's voice was gruff and pressing.

"Alive and a traitor!" Liz Hen blurted. "Jenko Bruk is a true traitor to Gul Kana, unlike me and Godwyn and Dokie and Beer Mug, who fought for our homeland."

Horror was etched on Jubal Bruk's face. "Jenko fought for the White Prince?"

"He did. And he was a traitor."

"I cannot believe such of my son."

"The girl is full of lies, Baron Bruk," Leif said. "Everything out of the bitch's fat face is a lie! None of us need listen to her filthy lies!"

"I am no liar." There was dark danger brewing behind Liz Hen's red-shot gaze. Mancellor could sense it. Next to her, Beer Mug could sense the anger too. His hackles were raised. "I fought in the Battle of the Saint Only Channel. And it was I that saved you! I fought the armies of Aeros Raijael in defense of my *homeland* and I *saved* you! Me, a fat-faced girl wielding a sword, saved you!"

"Women do not fight in *my* armies!" Leif gestured to the body on the floor in disgust. "Women do not fight in the armies of Gul Kana. Women do not fight in defense of their homelands or in defense of Laijon. And lying there between us is all the pathetic evidence you need, proof that allowing women in battle is naught but folly in the eyes of your king and in the eyes of your grand vicar, folly in the eyes of your god, Laijon!"

"Folly in the eyes of Laijon?" Liz Hen growled. "Do not speak to me of Laijon!"

"I'll speak to you of whatever I damn well please, you fat shit."

"Fuck you."

"Fuck me?"

"Yes, fuck you and whatever gutter dog pissed you out of its malignant little pee hole, you bitch-made motherfucker."

"Enough!" King Jovan shouted, storming toward Leif and Liz Hen. "Enough bickering and petty fighting!"

Sunbird Hall fell into silence again. Jovan appeared to prowl about the body of his sister like he wished to attack someone with his bare hands. "Everyone just hold your tongues! Can't you see that my sister has been killed?" He turned to Leif. "Can't you see that these good folk have brought her back to us at great peril to themselves? We should be thanking them, offering them the hospitality of the Silver Throne, asking them how they came to know Jondralyn, how they came to find her dead. We should be asking them if they saw her die, saw who killed her."

"Was that red-haired Sør Sevier bitch who likely killed her," Liz Hen said.

"'Red-haired Sør Sevier bitch'?" Jovan met her gaze curiously.

"Aye." She nodded, then stared at Leif, venom in her red-shot eyes. "'Twas a warrior *woman* who likely killed the princess."

"*Likely* killed the princess?" Jovan asked. "Did you not see my sister's murder?"

"No, Ser," Liz Hen replied, eyes still laced with anger as she glared at Leif. "I jumped into the river because Dokie is afraid of sharks, and I missed the whole damn fight. Beer Mug jumped in after me, so he also saw nothing. And Mancellor was already in the river. But I am sure it was that Sør Sevier bitch who done the killing."

"Her name is Enna Spades," Mancellor Allen offered, bowing to the king. "If I may speak, Your Excellency."

"Go on." Jovan motioned to him. "And state your name."

"I am Mancellor Allen," Mancellor continued, nervous now. "Mancellor Allen of Wyn Darrè, at your service." He paused. All eyes were on him now. "The Sør Sevier woman Liz Hen speaks of was none other than Enna Spades, one of Aeros Raijael's famed Knights Archaic."

"I am familiar with the name," Jovan said. "Proceed."

"'Twas Enna Spades who tracked us and the weapons and the angel stones to Savon and killed your sister."

"Weapons and angel stones?" the grand vicar interjected, eyes now fixed on Mancellor with no small measure of intensity.

"Yes," Mancellor answered. "The weapons of the Five Warrior Angels."

"You do realize that what you say smacks of blasphemy," Denarius said. "For the weapons and stones of the Five Warrior Angels were translated into heaven at the time of Laijon's death."

Mancellor shrank under the vicar's cold, crisp gaze. Then he felt a thrill course through his body. *I'm actually sharing words with the prophet of Laijon!* In all his life he had never dreamed of meeting Laijon's mouthpiece in the flesh, let alone becoming engaged in a conversation with the man, especially not about the weapons of the Five Warrior Angels. Then his enthusiasm dimmed at that thought. *How do I convince the prophet of god that I truly have seen the angel stones, that I truly have seen the weapons of the Five Warrior Angels when* The Way and Truth of Laijon *claims it is impossible?*

It stung that the vicar had so casually dismissed his story as blasphemous. But Mancellor knew what he had seen and could not deny it. "You must, um, believe me, Your Grace," he began, stumbling on his words. "Enna Spades followed me—well, rather followed me and Liz Hen and Dokie—to Savon because *she* believed we carried *Lonesome Crown* and *Forgetting Moon* along with two angel stones. I kept the stones in a pouch. I swear it to be true. All of it."

The chamber was silent. The grand vicar furrowed his brow.

"Go on," Jovan finally ordered Mancellor. "How did you come about these weapons and stones?"

Mancellor swallowed back the lump of nervousness growing in his throat. "I stole the weapons and stones from Aeros Raijael during the Battle of the Saint Only Channel. I fled toward Amadon in an effort to bring the weapons and stones to the Silver Throne. Liz Hen and Dokie traveled with me."

"Beer Mug joined us too," Dokie said. "Don't forget that, Mancellor." The dog wagged his tail. Liz Hen patted his head.

"The dog too," Mancellor added. "Enna Spades hunted us the entire way. She tracked us to Savon. In Savon we met a young man by the name of Lindholf Le Graven. Lindholf carried with him what he claimed to be *Ethic Shroud*, *Afflicted Fire*, and *Blackest Heart* along with three angel stones similar in shape and brilliance to the two stones I carried—"

Leif laughed. "This story has officially ventured into the realm of the absurd."

"Shush." Jovan motioned to Leif. "We will hear him out."

"You don't actually believe this tall tale?" Leif asked.

"What I believe is not in question." Jovan's voice was infused with impatience. "The man is recounting the story of my sister's death and I wish to hear it, no matter how outlandish." He looked to Mancellor. "Carry on, Ser."

"Lindholf stayed with us at the Preening Pintail in Savon," Mancellor said. "Your sister, Princess Jondralyn, eventually found us at the Preening Pintail, believing the five weapons and angel stones we had with us were real. She died atop a stone tower above the tavern, trying to guard those weapons. She was killed by Enna Spades."

"And where were you all when my sister was slain?" Jovan asked.

"We were all in the river below the tower," Liz Hen answered. "Including Beer Mug." The dog wagged his tail, hearing his name again.

"Why in the river?" Jovan asked.

"Because Dokie doesn't like sharks," Liz Hen said.

"These are crazy people," Leif said mockingly. "Especially the girl. I knew her in Lord's Point. They are deceivers and liars."

"They are not crazy," the vicar said. "They believe what they say is true. And the news they bring, true or not, is ill tidings indeed. For if Enna Spades takes these five weapons back to Aeros Raijael, *he* may believe that they are real. And having weapons that he believes are the weapons of the Five Warrior Angels will only bolster his confidence. It will speed his advance across the Saint Only Channel and into Gul Kana."

"Yes." Jovan looked at the vicar. "Yes, it will."

"This story proves that Absolution is upon us," Denarius said. "It proves that great and glorious day of Laijon's return is nigh. We should all of us rejoice at what news Ser Mancellor Allen has brought us today. It is all as Laijon wills it."

Jovan looked down on his sister lying in awkward bloodstained repose on the floor at his feet. "We shall thank Ser Mancellor and his travel companions for their bravery and heroism in bringing back my dear sister. In fact, we shall throw a banquet for them, hail them as the heroes that they are."

Mancellor felt the pride swell up inside. He felt the confidence in himself grow, knowing he had done the right thing. All the pain and heartache since being taken captive in Wyn Darrè had led him to this moment. Maybe it wasn't perfect. But it was validation. Laijon had truly watched over him.

Jovan addressed the chamber. "For now we shall honor my sister with the proper funeral rites set aside for those of the kingship. We shall have Val-Gianni and Val-Korin prepare her body, and she shall lie in state in Tin Man Square at the bottom of the Long Stairs. We can all pay homage to her there."

"My father returned to Val Vallè some weeks ago," a silken voice sounded from somewhere in the chamber. "Or did you forget?"

"Seita!" Liz Hen's face was a mask of sheer happiness as her eyes roamed the crowd. Then the most striking Vallè maiden Mancellor had ever seen pushed her way through the throng.

"Seita," Dokie gasped, grin as wide as Liz Hen's. "It's Seita!" Even Beer Mug wagged his tail at the sight of the Vallè maiden.

"You know these people?" Jovan asked Seita.

The Vallè bowed to the king. "'Tis a long story, Your Excellency, perhaps for another time. And yes, they are my friends. But as you say, today is for grieving the loss of our beloved Princess Jondralyn."

Jovan bowed to her. Seita bowed in return. "If it please Your Excellency, I would offer my father's own chamber for my friends to stay in whilst they recover from their travels."

"An admirable idea." Jovan nodded his approval. "I shall leave it up to you to see that all their comforts are met during their stay here at the king's court."

Seita bowed. "Then I should like to take some time and speak with my friends alone, if it please you."

"I leave them to your care," Jovan said.

**

The crowd broke up and Seita led Mancellor, Liz Hen, Dokie, and Beer Mug up the sweeping stairs at the far end of Sunbird Hall and out onto the balcony overlooking Memory Bay. Mancellor was glad to leave the stifling atmosphere of the crowd behind. He breathed deep. The balcony offered air fresh with new rain as a cool breeze sliced up from the bay, moaning over the battlements and towers above. "Let our tour of the castle start here," Seita said, inviting them all to gaze out over Memory Bay.

Leaning against the ivy-strewn balustrade, Mancellor cast his gaze down across the waters. The view before him fell dizzyingly into space far below. The tide crashed foamy water against the rocks and quays at the base of Mount Albion. Ships bobbed in the gray swell and chop. Countless stone towers and outbuildings huddled at the shore, clinging to the craggy base. Mancellor had to admit, even the grand view from the balcony above Bruce Hall atop Mont Saint Only was not as magnificent as this.

"So Enna Spades truly has all five weapons and angel stones?" Seita gazed up at him with captivating green eyes under graceful, slanting eyebrows.

"It's the only conclusion I can draw," Mancellor answered. "She was the last one of us atop the tower, along with Lindholf Le Graven and Jondralyn."

"Interesting," Seita said. Some wan light shone just beneath her pale skin. "But you can regale me with the whole tale at a later time, after you have all rested."

Mancellor studied the thin-eared Vallè. She wore a pair of sleek black breeches and a long black shirt, the hem of which fell almost to her thighs. A thin, silver-colored leather string was tied over the shirt at her waist. A shimmering silver cloak was thrown over her left shoulder, and her flowing blond hair was so icy white it was almost blinding. To Mancellor there was something almost ethereal about Seita, something almost akin to the mermaid who had tried to drown him during the Battle of the Saint Only Channel.

"For my part, I believe the story you told the king," Seita said. "If my father were still in Amadon, he could likely advise us on what course we ought to take, for he is more versed in the lore of the weapons and stones than I. But, alas, Val-Korin has traveled back to Val Vallè on state business. We must make do with what little we know." She looked at Liz Hen. "But until then, you shall surely agree to grow your glorious red hair back out. So I can one day again braid it."

"I would love that," Liz Hen said. "I can't believe you are here in Amadon, after all we went through in the north. I've so many questions."

"And I for you," Seita said.

"Do you know what happened to Nail and Stefan?" Dokie asked. "Do you know where Roguemoore and Culpa Barra are? Lindholf told us Val-Draekin was dead, said he fell into a glacier, said he heard about it from you."

"Aye," Seita answered quickly. "I saw Val-Draekin, Roguemoore, and Nail fall into a glacial crevasse. An icy river swept them away into the dark bowels of the ice. But as for Nail and Val-Draekin, I saw them both briefly in this castle not long ago, though I did not get a chance to talk to either. I fear Roguemoore is dead." Liz Hen looked distressed at the news. "Culpa Barra is dead too," Seita added. "He fell into the silver. It ate half his face."

Liz Hen and Dokie shuddered. Mancellor asked, "What do you mean he fell into the silver? It ate his face?"

"Just know that Culpa Barra died with honor, Ser Mancellor," Seita responded. "And know there are horrors in this world none of us will ever understand." She turned back to Liz Hen and Dokie. "Stefan and I were separated in the north, but I should think he still lives, though I know not where he is."

"Stefan cannot be dead." Liz Hen dropped to her knees, burying her face in the gray fur of Beer Mug's neck. "Everyone is gone and scattered but us."

"Roguemoore and Culpa Barra are tragic deaths." Seita placed her hand on the back of the girl's head. "We have all of us suffered tragic loss."

"And Godwyn, too." Liz Hen wept. "Leif hung the bishop."

"So I heard in the hall below," Seita said.

"I can't believe Stefan is still lost in the north." Dokie's tear-filled eyes were hollow pits of both hurt and pain. "We should find him."

"We all loved Stefan dearly," Seita said. There was genuine regret and pain in her voice as well. "Last I saw of him, he clutched the bow he so loved, the one with Gisela's name carved into it. It was because of Stefan that I escaped the oghuls and Deadwood Gate. It was because of Stefan's bravery that I alone survived to return to Amadon with *Blackest Heart* and *Afflicted Fire*. I dishonored his sacrifice by losing those weapons and angel stones to the gladiator Gault Aulbrek."

"Stefan Wayland was the best of us," Dokie said. "Filled with naught but goodness and kindness. He loved Gisela so much."

"Do not lose heart, Dokie," Seita said. "For I feel all things shall still work out in our favor in the end."

"How do you figure?" Liz Hen asked.

Seita's green eyes brightened. "As the grand vicar said, Enna Spades will take the weapons and angel stones to Aeros Raijael. And he shall bring them to Amadon, he shall bring them to Fiery Absolution, and then, my good friends, we shall steal them back from him." She leaned in and grabbed Dokie by the shoulders. "No, *you* shall steal them back for us, Dokie Liddle, for you are a clever little thief."

"I am?" Dokie asked.

For those ancients who did believe that the soul of every Vallè who hath ever lived did reside within the angel stones, did they believe false sorcery?
—THE WAY AND TRUTH OF LAIJON

CHAPTER FORTY-SEVEN

NAIL

17TH DAY OF THE BLOOD MOON, 999TH YEAR OF LAIJON

AMADON, GUL KANA

Nail had never met a person he despised more than Glade Chaparral. Not even Jenko Bruk. It had been five days since they had captured the Dayknight near Rivermeade, and even in captivity Glade was brash, pompous, egotistical, and unwaveringly entitled.

Glade sat across the worn wooden table from Lawri Le Graven, Tala Bronachell, and Nail. He brooded over his steaming bowl of lamb stew, moaning that it just wasn't spiced enough for his discerning taste, complaining that his ale was rancid too.

They had reached Amadon not more than an hour ago, all of them tired and hungry. Bronwyn Allen and Cromm Cru'x chose the Slaver's Tavern and Inn, a dank little establishment huddled on the western outskirts of Amadon. "We'll be safe here," Bronwyn had said. "Though it is a cheerless place, there are few wandering eyes. Nobody will come looking for Tala or Lawri in a den like this."

Bronwyn and Cromm were just outside the tavern now, making a deal with the driver of a one-horse carriage. When they had arrived, Nail had noticed the buggy in the roadway. The driver of the carriage was an old man with a curling gray mustache that strongly reminded Nail of the curling mustache on Bishop Godwyn. The plan was for Nail and Tala to escort Glade back to the castle, where he would confess his sins against Lindholf Le Graven and confess to murdering Sterling Prentiss. Meanwhile, Bronwyn and Cromm, after arranging for the buggy, would remain at the inn with Lawri.

Nail, done with his own bowl of stew, sipped on his mug of ale, eyes roaming the dark tavern with no small measure of concern. Compared to the Grayken Spear, the Turn Key Saloon, or even the Filthy Horse, the Slaver's Tavern and Inn was a dismal place indeed. The candles flickering in the corner did naught but cast a dull, smoky haze over the bleakness of the place. Worn and stained wood planks lined the sunken floor. There was a dark, brooding hallway at the back of the room. Opposite the bar were a myriad of dark alcoves full of tall tables and tall stools and questionable-looking figures, all of them slouched, cloaked, and hooded, faces hidden in dark shadows.

Nail figured Bronwyn and Cromm fit right into a place like this. Lawri Le Graven did not. Pale and innocent-looking, Lawri's glowing face stuck out from under her own hood like the eastern star, illuminating the gloom. The gauntlet attached to her arm was always hidden under her various cloaks. The olive-green mold growing up her arm from under the gauntlet was becoming more and more noticeable, and she tried to keep it hidden at all times, along with the gauntlet itself.

Nail felt protective of the girl for many reasons and wondered what he could do to keep her comfortable at all times. But Lawri Le Graven was either the shyest girl he had ever met, or she just plain didn't like anyone fussing over her. She was a mystery. There was a deep sadness in her. And perhaps that was what drew him to her. With the gauntlet attached to her arm, she was a strange anomaly. As a bastard, he felt like he could relate.

It was clear that Tala was also concerned for her green-eyed cousin. She had told Nail the story of how Lawri had saved her atop the aqueducts, how Lawri had lifted her up and over the chasm using naught but the strength within the gauntlet. Lawri had also killed one of the Dayknights all on her own, the gauntlet nearly shredding the man's neck clean through. And now rot grew under the gauntlet, and Tala wondered if her cousin wasn't in need of medical attention. But to take the girl back to the castle was too much of a risk.

For his own part, Nail recalled falling from the aqueducts and fighting a handful of knights himself, killing them all. He had fought as if possessed, every single move Shawcroft had taught him in the mines coming to him naturally. He wasn't sure how he felt about killing. It was the first time he had killed anyone. He remembered how much taking a life had bothered his friend Stefan. But to Nail, once he had fallen from that aqueduct, it was either kill or be killed. He was proud of how he had fought, even though he had collapsed in both exhaustion and horror in the end.

That Tala had suffered a wound on her shoulder in the shape of a cross was alarming. He thought back to what Val-Draekin had said about the markings on his own body being nothing but coincidence, and that others could have similar marks. Now he wondered if she had the mark of the beast. Or a slave brand? Both seemed impossible.

After the fight on the aqueducts, they had returned to Savon to gather Jondralyn's body. But bloodstains, black and dark, were all they had found atop the tower above the Preening Pintail. Jondralyn's body was gone. So they had traveled to Amadon empty-handed; empty-handed but for Glade Chaparral, stripped of his Dayknight armor and sword, tied at the wrists, and shackled at the ankles. They had removed the gag from his mouth once they entered the Slaver's Tavern and Inn, much to Nail's chagrin.

Despite how much he hated Glade, if there was one thing Nail had learned, it was that he and Cromm could control Glade with but a stern look. For despite all Glade's arrogance, they were both taller, stronger, and clearly better fighters than Glade.

Bronwyn stepped back into the tavern. "The carriage man has agreed to take you three to the castle. He ain't happy about it. But he will do it. Cromm saw to that."

Nail and Tala stood from the table, Tala urging Glade to also stand. She wrapped Glade up in his cloak and pulled the hood over his features; his shackled hands were hidden too. Tala obscured her face behind her own dark hood. She did not want to be recognized in the streets of Amadon. Together, Tala, Nail, and Glade followed Cromm from the tavern, leaving Bronwyn and Lawri behind. Once outside, Cromm helped them secure Glade into the buggy. Nail climbed in one side, Tala the other. Glade sat between them. The small carriage was a rickety old thing with just enough room for the three of them on the back bench. The driver sat up front, gripping the reins, which led to an old sway-backed horse with a knotted brown mane.

Besides the sword at his hip, Nail had a dagger hidden up the sleeve of his cloak, ready in case Glade acted out. There was an overall sense of dread hovering over this last part of their journey, and Nail wasn't certain they were doing the right thing by going back into Amadon Castle. Cromm grunted at the carriage driver. The man flicked the reins and the horse was off, jostling over the cobbles.

"I'm scared of old wagons," Tala said as she settled back into the cold wooden seat. "I hope this old thing doesn't shake too much. For some reason I'm afraid of falling out and being run over by the wheels." She looked at Nail as their seat creaked and swung under her. The buggy gained speed. "Do you think it's a ridiculous fear I have?"

"Not at all," Nail answered. He reached down with his free hand and grasped the metal bar that secured their seat to the buggy. His effort steadied the swaying seat. He kept his grip firm, making the ride smoother. Tala relaxed some as the carriage trundled through town. In fact, as they journeyed past grubby stone structures and even grubbier alleys, Nail gripped the bar so tightly he began to feel himself sweat. Still, it was enough to steady the ride for Tala.

It was a warm and muggy day. Hot. Blistering even. Gallows Haven could be stifling in the summer, but the ocean breezes blew in from the west, cooling the town some. And it was never very hot up in the higher climes of the Autumn Range, where he spent most of his time mining with Shawcroft. But the cobbled stone streets of Amadon were positively scorching and oppressive. Still, no matter how miserable he felt, he kept the seat still for Tala, gripping the metal bar. Tala eventually noticed his efforts and glanced up at him. Her face flushed red under her hood and she looked away.

Glade noticed the interaction. "I honestly cannot see you two together, you know, as like a couple."

"We are not a couple." Tala glared at Glade from under her cowl.

Glade turned to Nail. "So, are you two, like, a couple, then? 'Cause she's totally wrong for you. I see Lawri Le Graven being more your type, Nail. You share a closeness to her, anyway. I see how you look at her. And her at you."

"You don't see anything of the sort, Glade," Tala snapped. "Just shut up."

"I can't shut up," Glade said. "You know and I know what a weak-willed person I am." He laughed. "Don't you remember how much fun we used to have together, Tala? But now it's you and Nail havin' all the fun, huh? The bastard boy from Gallows Haven."

Tala's eyes darted furtively between Nail and Glade.

"So is he giving you good cock, Tala?" Glade flashed her a sly grin. "Or is he givin' it to Lawri? Have either of you let him wet the ol' noodle? It'd be a shame if he hasn't dipped his pickle. I remember that sweet little honeypot of yours."

"It's always the same lame jokes with you, isn't it, Glade?" Tala's eyes glowed with ire. "I figured without Lindholf around your showing-off days were over. And we killed your new lackeys—what were their names? Tolz? Boppard? Alain? They are all dead now, you know, They can't pretend to laugh at your lame jokes anymore."

Unfazed, Glade looked at Nail. "Too bad I already loosened her up." Tala's eyes were throwing off sparks now. But Glade was still looking at Nail. "Did she tell you about her relationship with Lindholf? Did she tell you how she *loved* her own cousin? I know she hid it from Lawri. But Tala and Lindholf were quite the incestuous pair—"

Tala slapped his face.

Glade cried out in pain, then snarled, "You savage, stinking bitch!"

"What did you just call me?"

"A stinking bitch."

"Keep talking and I'll cut your throat clear to your spine." Tala smoothly produced a small silver dagger from the folds of her cloak and held the tip up to Glade's blinking eye. Glade leaned away from the blade. The dagger sparkled in the sunlight.

Nail was afraid. He looked from the blade to Tala. A deep hatred had seeped into her eyes and smoldered there. Nail had been noticing the subtle but dangerous changes in Tala ever since Jondralyn's death. Tala mostly tried to put on a happy face, but there was a skulking darkness set within her. He could sense it. And now he could see it.

"This is no idle threat, Glade," Tala said. "When we reach the castle, you will apologize for everything you said about Lindholf and tell my brother the truth about Sterling Prentiss' death."

Glade looked visibly shaken by the blade at his eye. Tala pressed the blade up against the skin of his cheek. The buggy jolted to a halt.

"Give me that." The driver half turned in his seat, holding his wrinkled old hand out for the dagger. "I won't have any squabbles on my carriage. Hand over the blade, young lady. This is my carriage, my rules."

Tala slid the dagger back into the folds of her cloak, eyeing the driver with equal parts anger, suspicion, and surprise.

"You kids need to stop bickering," the man said. "It's ridiculous. What with more important things goin' on in the world, Hragna'Ar raids in the north, folks fleeing to Amadon for safety. You're lucky I don't just toss you all over the side and drive off. I would but for that oghul friend of yours, who'd likely hunt me down and suck all the blood from my body. I implore you all, just sit quietly for the rest of the ride."

"I didn't do anything." Glade held up his shackled hands in mock innocence.

The man eyed the shackles nervously. "I don't know what you kids are playing at, but when you get older, you'll all realize how foolish these childish squabbles were. A great man once said, and I quote, 'Anger is oft more harmful than the injury that caused it.' So get control over your anger. If I hear any more trouble from between you three, I will drag you all off my ride, that oghul be damned."

He turned and flicked the reins. The horse resumed its slow trot over the rough cobbles. Nail kept the seat steady for Tala.

**

"And so, my youngest sister returns." Jovan was in Sunbird Hall, awaiting them, long cloak thrown over both shoulders, thin silver crown atop his head. He stood before the long table at the end of the hall. "Tala returns, un-killed by the enemy."

Nail, Tala, and Glade had entered the castle without incident, though they did have to surrender their weapons. Every Silver Guard at the gate had recognized both Tala and Glade. The three of them were escorted straight from the gate to Sunbird Hall. Though, on Tala's order, the guardsmen did not untie or ungag Glade.

Other than Jovan, there were a dozen Dayknights in Sunbird Hall. The grand vicar and five archbishops of Amadon were all there too. Nail had been in this chamber once before with Tala. He had come with Val-Draekin, Jondralyn, Tala, Bronwyn, and Cromm. Both Tala and Jondralyn had been in disguise, confronting Jovan about the threat of Hragna'Ar and the Skulls from the north. Jovan had wanted no part of that and sent them away. But to Nail, that day seemed as if it were moons ago.

"Unlike our brave and foolish Jondralyn, Tala yet lives and breathes," one of the Dayknights nearest the king said as he stepped forward, removing his helm. He was a tall, good-looking fellow with dark-rimmed eyes. Nail had seen the man before in Ravenker. Leif Chaparral was his name. Leif's eyes were snapping with anger. "And she brings my brother, Glade, with her. But she brings my brother bound and shackled with a gag stuffed in his mouth. What disgrace is this, pray tell?"

To Nail's estimation, Leif Chaparral was much like his younger brother, Glade, in his arrogance.

"Easy, Leif," Jovan admonished. "Let my sister explain. Perhaps there is a reason she brings Glade back in chains."

"You already know of Jondralyn's death?" Tala faced her brother. "How?"

"Her body arrived two days ago." It was Leif who answered, voice lacking all compassion, haughty and smug. "She was brought to us by a Wyn Darrè warrior and his two young companions."

"Where is Jondralyn?" Tala asked, eyes still on her brother.

Jovan answered. "Our sister's body has been washed and shrouded and now lies in state at the bottom of the Long Stairs in the Gardens of the Crown Moon in the center of Tin Man Square, in the exact granite crypt graced by our beloved mother, Alana, Laijon rest their souls."

"I wish to see her," Tala said. "Now. Everything else can wait."

"Now?" Jovan exclaimed. "Before you've answered any of my questions?"

"I demand it."

"You will make no demands of me." Jovan's eyes were glittering like a flaming torch as he marched toward her, boots clomping heavily on the tile. "You will make no demands of me, Tala Bronachell. Not now. Not ever!"

"She is my sister!" Tala fired back, undaunted. "It is my right to see her."

Jovan pointed a finger at her forcefully. "You have forfeited what rights you once had! You, who defied me at every turn. You, who disappeared from this castle, your home, without so much as a by-your-leave. You, who have surrendered your place in this court as a princess of Amadon. You have no rights anymore. Not here. Not ever."

"I am a princess of Gul Kana!" Tala fired back. "I am the daughter of Borden Bronachell! I have my rights and you cannot take them away!"

Jovan barked right back at her. "I imagine it was your doing that our sister has died. I imagine you are the cause of her murder."

"You accuse me?"

"You've disobeyed me for too long now, sister!"

"It was you who sent Jondralyn off to die in Ravenker! I heard you and Leif plotting her death. I saw you and Leif kis—"

Jovan slapped her face. "Are you trying to insult me?" he shouted. "Are you trying to shame me in front of the grand vicar, in front of the court? Is that what you are up to, preparing to betray your brother, your king? For I am not as tolerant as I once was."

Tala held her cheek in pain. And rage boiled in Nail's every nerve ending. He did not like seeing any man hit any woman, king or not. He wanted to rush the king and show him just what a real blow to the face felt like. He could feel his fists balling in anger.

Grand Vicar Denarius stepped forward, concern clouding his round face. He placed a thick hand on Jovan's shoulder. "Please, my king, let us not squabble like children, let us not make threats we will regret later." Jovan seemed to calm under the vicar's gentle hand.

"There is still the issue of Glade," Leif said, stepping forward with a limp. "Why is my brother trussed up like some common criminal? What humiliation is this? He is a Dayknight, not some gutter thug."

"Your brother has come to confess." Tala turned to Leif, eyes burning fiercely as she rubbed her face. "Glade has come to confess his crimes."

"Then remove his gag," Leif said, "so he can, as you say, 'confess.'"

Nail felt a tightening in his gut as Tala reached up and yanked the gag down over Glade's chin. "Tell them, Glade. Tell them that Lindholf was innocent all along. Tell them how you killed Ser Sterling Prentiss in the secret ways."

"You think I killed the captain of the Dayknights?" Glade worked his jaw back and forth with a stiff hand. "You're mad if you think I killed that man." He met Tala's gaze coldly. "I never killed Sterling Prentiss. It was proven Lindholf did the deed."

"Proven? How?" Tala's eyes were wide with rage, hurt and betrayal spreading across her ever-reddening countenance. "You promised you would tell the truth if I spared you."

"I promised no such thing." Glade's handsome face divulged nothing behind flat, cold eyes. He glanced at his brother. "I know nothing of what she is talking about. She's mad. Holding me captive. Starving me. It is she who is the murderer. She and her friends ambushed us, killing Alain, Tolz, Boppard, and the rest of my Dayknights."

Nail felt his face tighten dangerously at Glade's dishonesty. "He is lying," he said. "Glade promised Tala he would tell the truth. I was there. I heard him confess to the murder myself. And now he goes back on that promise."

"Who are you?" Jovan asked pointedly. "You've a familiar face, but I cannot place it."

Nail did not know whether that was a good thing or bad. *Should I tell him I am the Angel Prince?* The name raced through Nail's mind, unbidden and swift. *Should I tell him I am Aevrett Raijael's youngest son, born of Cassietta Raybourne of Wyn Darrè?* But he said no such thing out loud. *He does not even remember me from our previous meeting. And why should he? Truth is, I am nobody to him.*

"I'm from Gallows Haven," he answered. "My name is Nail."

"Nail who?" Jovan pressed.

"Just Nail."

Leif Chaparral raised one darkened eyebrow. "So a bastard, then? Proof that your word is worthless in the king's court."

"My word is worth more than Glade Chaparral's." Nail's anger flared anew. He could feel the tattoos and scars burning along his flesh. "I can tell you that. It is Glade's words that are worthless—" Nail stopped speaking, suddenly finding a dozen spears leveled at his throat. Most every Dayknight in the hall had stepped toward him menacingly, pressing him back. There was nothing he could do. He stayed quiet.

"My Dayknights know who is true and who is false," Leif said. He turned to Jovan. "This *bastard* named Nail should be thrown into Purgatory for accusing my brother so. He is unwelcome in our presence."

"Without question," Jovan said.

"I tricked her into bringing me back to the castle," Glade blurted. "Maybe I did tell Tala that I killed Prentiss. But it was no more than a ruse to get her to bring me back."

"He's lying," Tala growled.

The king bowed to Glade. "'Twas a bold yet subtle plan, tricking my sister into escorting you back to the castle. This will stand you in good stead when advancing up the Dayknight ranks."

Glade beamed. And Nail wished he had *Forgetting Moon* in his hands now, wished he could slay them all. As if sensing the treachery in Nail's heart, Jovan nodded to the Dayknights. "Escort this traitor named Nail to Purgatory."

"No!" Tala cried out. "This is not fair—"

"And see that my sister goes with him, as befits a traitor. She shall no longer be a thorn in my side." Jovan turned from his sister. "I do not wish to look upon her face ever again."

"So shall it be done, my lord." Leif Chaparral bent his knee to his king, smiling. "For your rule is always a many-splendored thing."

Dragon Claw shall become like a burnt offering atop the Silver Throne,
a burnt offering to those questing up from the underworld.
—THE ANGEL STONE CODEX

CHAPTER FORTY-EIGHT

LINDHOLF LE GRAVEN

17TH DAY OF THE BLOOD MOON, 999TH YEAR OF LAIJON

FORTRESS OF SAINT ONLY, ADIN WYTE

Lindholf Le Graven and Enna Spades were like two lonely figures under an unbroken sun. The vast stretch of sand between Lord's Point and Mont Saint Only was still a-litter with the dead and the rotting. The Battle of the Saint Only Channel had been some thirty or more days ago. Yet the stench of rot and refuse lingered. Every human corpse was naught but dried, sun-melted mush. Bits and pieces of bone had been scattered by the currents and tides that flooded over the channel nightly. Pale rib cages of dead horses and dead sharks burst up from the sand like giant, sinuous hands, clawing for the sky. Dead merfolk dotted the seabed too, none of them pretty to look upon now, all of them naught but heaps of long-spoiled meat. There was no armor among the dead. No swords. *Had every weapon been scavenged so fast?* Lindholf asked himself. *It would take an army just for that task!* All that remained of the battle was stink and rot and the shrieks of the seagulls and the cawing of the crows.

Spades trotted her sturdy mount ahead of Lindholf, proceeding undaunted toward the towering Mont rising up before them, her horse moving with an assured canter. The stark white sword, *Afflicted Fire*, was tied with two leather thongs to the baldric slung over her armored back, its crescent-moon hilt-guard jutting just over her shoulder. The crossbow, *Blackest Heart*, was also hooked to the baldric on her back. She carried all five angel stones in a leather pouch next to the black Dayknight sword at her hip.

As always, Lindholf was charged with carrying the other three weapons. *Forgetting Moon* was strapped comfortably to his own back. As if it belonged there, it was light and airy, not weighing him down at all. It felt like he could jump up and fly with it. *Ethic Shroud* and *Lonesome Crown* rode in the canvas sack strapped to the back of his horse. Like Spades, he still wore the heavy black armor of a Dayknight. Together with Spades, he heedlessly approached the stronghold of Aeros Raijael.

"You've come a long way with me, Lindholf Le Graven," Spades said, their horses trotting side by side now. "And you've put up scant little fight. You've not tried to steal the weapons or stones, nor have you attempted escape even once. Why is that?"

It was a good question, one that Lindholf had been asking himself ever since leaving Savon. Truth be told, being here now with Enna Spades, riding toward Saint Only, was better than his life before. It was better than being ignored by his cousin Tala Bronachell or bullied by Glade Chaparral.

"I used to get pushed around a lot," he said. "I used to be weak. I was the type who everyone blamed when misfortune struck. Ever since leaving Savon, I have not felt so spineless and powerless as before. With you I do not feel weak."

"A pithy observation, that," Spades said.

"I'm not sure what that means."

"When you are treated like you're weaker for long enough, you start to believe it, Lindholf Le Graven. But I see the potential behind your scars, I see the strength behind your deformities. I see who you really are. And you are by no means weak."

Her compliments silenced him profoundly. Spades spurred her horse forward at a stiffer trot, fiery red hair billowing out behind her. Ever since taking what drugs she needed from the oghul, Gin D'rhu, in Devlin three days ago, Enna Spades had been in healthy high spirits, the wound at her neck almost completely healed over.

Lindholf himself was high on Shroud of the Vallè at all times now, feeling confident and invincible, calm and light atop his horse. And perhaps that was why he enjoyed traveling with Spades. Perhaps it was as simple as that. The white powder made him feel good about anything and everything. After spending his entire life in a perpetual state of uncertainty and fear, he was no longer scared at all. No longer afraid. He'd successfully locked each injustice and humiliation done him deep inside.

Other than that first time of their meeting atop the tower in Savon, Spades hadn't threatened or goaded him once, but had treated him as an equal. And with her kindness, his cares and dreams of Tala Bronachell had receded. In these last few days of travel, he had drifted into a sort of peaceful silence with Spades, a shared silent companionship. Or so he thought. Either way, he had never before felt so alive. Just being with Spades and near the weapons of the Five Warrior Angels made him feel somehow powerful. He was of one purpose with this warrior woman riding across the bleary sea bottom before him. Life had brought him to this point. And he wished to embrace it.

He gazed at the surrounding landscape, overlooking the harshness of the stark stretch of sand and its heaps of rotting meat. He looked beyond all that destruction to Adin Wyte and the Fortress of Saint Only itself, an imposing, towering behemoth of a castle jutting up from the mountain above. Both castle and Mont were a singular majesty almost rivaling Amadon Castle in grandness in and of itself. He looked beyond the towering Mont toward the blue haze of Wyn Darrè in the far distance and the five needle-thin Laijon Towers glinting in the sun. They said that the view from Lord's Point toward Adin Wyte and Wyn Darrè was one of the most celebrated views in all the Five Isles. And Lindholf could believe it. He drank in the sight and with renewed vigor dug his heels into the flanks of his own mount, gathering speed, again catching up to Spades.

"Can I admit something else?" he asked the warrior woman.

"Never ask permission," she said, keeping her eyes focused on the Mont ahead. "Just say what you want and never apologize for it. Unless there is more to gain in the apology. But there rarely is. Basically, do what you want, say what you want, and then deny everything if it looks like your words and actions are getting you into trouble."

That sounded like terrible advice, but still he nodded. "Do you want to know another reason I have not sought escape?"

"Go on."

"Traveling with you, I feel less stress in my life."

"That's quite a statement, really." Spades craned her neck and looked at him squarely. "I must say, I don't often hear that."

"'Tis the truth. And I will not deny it. Unless there is more to gain in the apology."

She smiled at that. "Very well, but most reasonable people find being around me rather stressful."

"And I have never felt more at home."

"You continue to slay me with your pithy observations, Lindholf Le Graven. But in all seriousness, bear in mind, I aim to make you most uncomfortable soon. And you will find out just how uncomfortable I shall make you when you finally meet the Angel Prince. Be warned, you will not like what I aim to say about you when I again sup with Aeros Raijael. In fact, you will think it most cruel what I shall do to you, what I shall say about you. But it will be the best thing for you in the end. And you must remain confident as I discuss you with Aeros, for there is nothing the Angel Prince hates more than when he senses weakness in others. And you must not show weakness before him."

"I only ever feel confident after snorting Shroud of the Vallè. And we stole enough from those oghuls in Devlin that I think I shall manage." Spades looked at him questioningly. He shrugged. "Another one of my pithy observations, I suppose."

"Just remember what I said." Her eyes drifted back toward the lofty fortress atop the Mont. "I see the potential behind your scars, Lindholf Le Graven. I see who you really are."

What is it she thinks she sees in me? Lindholf swallowed hard. *What cruel and uncomfortable things could she say about me to Aeros Raijael?*

Spades slowed her mount. They had finally been spotted.

A dozen Sør Sevier knights galloped out from under the rocky crags of the Mont toward them, charging fast, closing the gap swiftly.

Spades reined her mount up before the twelve knights, Lindholf stopping his own horse at her side. The knights were formidable in their sparkling silver armor under the blue-and-white livery of Sør Sevier, glorious helms of polished silver atop their heads. The leader shed his helm. He had a youthful face and a dark mustache, eyes cold and wary, but firm. "Is it truly you, Enna Spades?"

"Indeed." Spades dipped her head to the knight, meeting his gaze with a firm resolve. "I am Enna Spades, Knight Archaic of our Lord Aeros Raijael, returned from the dead."

"But why do you wear the black armor of a Dayknight? Why do you wear the armor of the enemy?"

"Never mind what armor I wear. For I bear great treasures for our Lord Aeros. And you shall take me to him now, for I hear he also still lives."

The knight's eyes narrowed. "What kind of treasures, if I may ask?"

Spades drew *Afflicted Fire* from over her back, brandishing the great white sword high in the air before the man, letting him drink in its glory. "I bear the greatest kind of treasures our world has ever known," she said. "And I bear all of them."

**

Lindholf and Spades galloped through the open wooden doors straight into Bruce Hall, the hooves of their horses echoing hollowly on the stone floor. Dogs scattered in their wake. Lindholf let his eyes adjust to the dim light, surveying the cavernous chamber. At an initial glance, Bruce Hall seemed about the same size as, yet more stifling, dreadful, and darker than, Sunbird Hall. High above was a vaulted ceiling, where shadows hung heavy in the air. And it smelled of perfume. Lavender and pine, if Lindholf was to guess.

"Hail, Enna Spades!" a hearty voice boomed. "Our fair companion is returned from the dead!"

The declaration came from a dim alcove to the left, where a giant of a man stood near a black stallion with frightful, strident eyes that sparked like glowing coals in the gloom. The large man had a wild thicket of fiery red hair, sparkling fetishes tied into his equally red beard, and blue tattoos spanning his broad face. What looked like the massive rotted head of a sea serpent rested on the floor behind the man and horse. The head was severed at the neck, dull-eyed face droopy and wilted, purple forked tongue splayed out onto the stone floor. The serpent head lay on a pile of strongly scented pine needles, rushes, sprigs of parsley, and herbs.

"Hammerfiss!" Spades called to the man.

"Hail, Enna Spades!" the big red-haired man bellowed again brightly. "Look at me over here. I can't seem to mount this damned Bloodeye steed. Mia-cursed thing won't let me on him. Lady Death take me already, but I've been trying for days now."

"And pray tell, Ser Hammerfiss," Spades hollered back, "why would the Spider let you ride Scowl?" There was a certain delight and elation in her voice when she talked to this man Hammerfiss. A jovial tone that Lindholf had never heard before. She was brimming with joy as she shouted, "Why would the Spider even let you near the dirty black nag?"

"Because I squashed the Spider!" Hammerfiss announced, pointing to the center of the hall. "Squashed him like a bug. Young Leisel perfumes what's left of the black-hearted bastard now."

Both Spades and Lindholf followed the big man's wide gaze. In the center of the hall was a delicate-looking blond girl. She was impossibly pretty and as thin as a blade of grass, with skin the color of cream frosting. Lindholf guessed she was no more than a few years younger than himself. She held an ornate glass decanter of what appeared to be perfume over a sizable heap of black leather piled on the floor at her feet. She was carefully shaking the clear liquid perfume over the mound of leather, and crystal-like droplets sprinkled down like rain from the decanter.

"There, done watering the Bloodwood," the young girl said, placing the stopper back into the large glass ball. "Now he won't stink so much for when my lord Aeros entertains his guests." The girl curtsied to Spades, then cast a curious gaze at Lindholf, her eyes bright and alert. Lindholf sat taller in his saddle. Still, he found he could not breathe under her spell. She was so beautiful and perfect in every way.

Spades assessed the large lump of newly perfumed leather on the floor. "You're not lying, Ser Hammerfiss. You did squash the Spider."

Lindholf finally realized that the dark pile of leather in front of Leisel was actually a dead man in black leather armor, legs splayed out, head pulverized, body split in the middle and crushed down onto itself. Strongly scented pine needles, rushes, and herbs were scattered about the dead man too. Lindholf's horse shied away from the smashed corpse. Gripping the reins tight, he brought the beast under control, now detecting the faint scent of rotted human flesh just beneath the powerful haze of lavender and pine. He noticed that all the dogs in the room gave both the severed serpent head and the perfumed pile of flesh of the Spider a wide berth.

"Black-hearted fool challenged me and my mace to a duel." Hammerfiss sauntered up to Lindholf and Spades. "And as you know, Enna Spades, it's a bad idea to bring naught but silly black daggers to a mace fight."

"I imagine he brought an overabundance of confidence too," Spades chuckled.

"Aye." Hammerfiss grinned. "Whilst he was in the midst of talking about how great and awesome he was, I was already fighting."

"I only wish I could have been here to witness his demise," Spades said.

A door near the hall's great hearth swung wide. Out stepped two armored men—a dark-haired knight clad in the blue-and-white livery of Sør Sevier and a blond knight dressed in gleaming white chain mail and cloak.

"Jenko Bruk." Spades slid from the saddle, nodding to the darker of the two. "And my lord Aeros." She bent her knee to the two approaching men.

The White Prince! Lindholf's mind spun. *Aeros Raijael! The Angel Prince!* He couldn't believe he was looking at the enemy of Gul Kana with his own two eyes. Aeros' skin looked fogged and milky, no color in it at all. The young man walking next to Aeros, Jenko Bruk, was a dark and brooding fellow.

The White Prince swept toward the still-kneeling Spades like a great fierce hawk, white cloak billowing behind him like feathered wings. "I am most happy to see you alive!" He held out his arms wide in greeting.

She stood. "It is good to see you again too, my lord."

Aeros' dark-pupiled eyes were fixed on the crescent-moon hilt-guard of the sword strapped to her back. Jenko Bruk also stared at the weapon greedily. Aeros then noticed Lindholf still ahorse, piercing eyes widening as they fell upon the double-bladed battle-ax hooked to Lindholf's back. *Forgetting Moon.* Jenko was also staring at the ax.

Lindholf found himself shifting in the saddle, almost in an effort to block Aeros' and Jenko's views of the weapon that he had come to know as his own.

Spades' eyes searched the hall beyond Jenko, as if expecting to see someone else with him. There was a flicker of disappointment in her eyes. "Nice to see that you honored your word and returned to Saint Only. I expect you told our lord of Ser Mancellor Allen's betrayal?"

Jenko dipped his head to her. "I did."

"And Jenko is now a Knight Archaic," Aeros announced.

"And young Ava Shay," Spades said. "Where is she?"

Aeros and Jenko exchanged glances. "Ava escaped," Jenko said.

"So Gault Aulbrek saved her?" Spades asked.

"What makes you think it was Ser Gault who saved her?" Aeros asked.

"I know Gault well enough to know that he would travel to the ends of the Five Isles to do just such a thing." Spades looked at Jenko. "Must hurt something fierce, knowing that another man rescued Ava and that you did not."

Gault Aulbrek made it back to Saint Only. Lindholf could still recall the day the Sør Sevier knight had abandoned him and Delia. *But who was this Ava Shay he saved?*

"I'm disappointed in you, Jenko," Spades went on. "I had you pegged as a hero, the type who would have rescued his girl—"

"We need not discuss Ava Shay anymore," Aeros cut her off. "For she is now gone." He looked the warrior woman up and down, settling again on the thin crescent-moon hilt-guard of the white sword jutting over her shoulder. "I implore you, Spades, please regale us with your tales of adventure. Why do you return encased in the black armor of my enemy?" He motioned to Lindholf. "And who is this dour-faced Dayknight with you? And what have you two brought me? For that looks like *Forgetting Moon* on the young knight's back."

Spades drew the sword from over her shoulder. "I bring you *Afflicted Fire*," she said, handing him the weapon. Aeros took the magnificent sword by the hilt, holding it up in two pale hands. He swept the blade to and fro in the dim light of the hall, dark eyes wide in wonder. The blade's porcelain-like surface glowed like a shard of starlight in the gloom.

"I feel some magic in it," he said, voice low and reverent almost to the point of being hushed. "And there is something like magic coursing through my own veins when I hold it. As if this sword were meant for me." He held the blade up high. "It can be naught else but *Afflicted Fire*."

Sword held aloft like that, Aeros was the very image of the Laijon statue in the temple in Amadon. Lindholf could not help but compare the wan translucency of Aeros' ashen skin to the gleaming white surface of the sword. *Aeros is right, 'tis as if man and sword were forged as one.*

Spades produced the crossbow from over her other shoulder. "And tell me this is not *Blackest Heart*."

Aeros broke his gaze from the majesty of the white sword. His greedy dark eyes hungrily soaked in the sight of the black crossbow. "*Blackest Heart*. I must admit, I've never seen a crossbow quite like it."

"Return to Aeros his battle-ax." Spades looked at Lindholf. "And cut the rest of the weapons loose of your saddle." Lindholf dismounted, unhooked the battle-ax from his back. He did not want to hand it over, but he did. Aeros set the white sword down on the nearby table and took the battle-ax from Lindholf.

Forgetting Moon seemed to weigh next to nothing in Aeros' hands too. "I thought I had lost this one at the bottom of the channel. But here it is again."

Jenko stared at the battle-ax too. Lindholf cut loose the canvas sack holding *Ethic Shroud* and *Lonesome Crown* from his saddle. His horse, no longer laden with heavy sacks, seemed relieved. Lindholf set the sack carefully on the ground before the White Prince, undid the leather straps, and pulled the canvas away from the weapons.

"*Lonesome Crown*, returned to you, my lord," Spades announced, motioning with her arms to the open canvas on the floor. "And *Ethic Shroud*."

Aeros placed *Forgetting Moon* on the table next to *Afflicted Fire*. He keenly studied both weapons atop the canvas. "It is indeed *Lonesome Crown*, for 'twas I myself who took it from Torrence Raybourne on the Aelathia Plains." He knelt on one knee and ran nimble fingers over the pearly, gleaming surface of *Ethic Shroud*. "It's as if it were made of the same unrecognizable substance as the sword."

Spades produced the leather satchel holding the five angel stones. She knelt beside Aeros and opened the pouch, letting the five stones pour out onto the canvas beside the two weapons: red, green, blue, white, and black. Together they shone like starlight, illuming the faces of both Spades and Aeros in colorful patterns—all but the black one, which to Lindholf always looked dead as a lump of hard coal.

"They are so beautiful." Leisel spoke with a hushed delicacy. She had drifted up between Spades and Aeros, kneeling too for a closer look. She had eyes so big and round Lindholf thought he could nearly see himself in them. And the young girl's face was flushed with such an innocent loveliness, it filled him with a bliss and contentment he had never before felt. But most pretty faces played tricks on him like that.

"Are they really angel stones?" Leisel asked.

With the question, Lindholf finally realized he was witness to one of the most momentous events in the history of the Five Isles—the gathering and presentation of the angel stones and weapons of the Five Warrior Angels to the White Prince of Sør Sevier.

In times past he would have been horrified by just such a notion, that Aeros Raijael might indeed be Laijon returned. But how else could any of these events be explained? He was either in the wrong place at the wrong time, or he was at the right place at the right time. *Could this have been my destiny all along?*

He was in a strange castle surrounded by naught but strangers, yet he had never before felt so at home. He had never before felt as if he belonged to something. Looking at the circle of faces—Enna Spades, Jenko Bruk, Hammerfiss, the pretty young girl Leisel, the Angel Prince, Aeros Raijael—Lindholf had never felt so content. It felt like he had known these people all his life.

"My last question to you, Spades." Aeros stood, looking at Lindholf. "Who is this Gul Kana fool encased in Dayknight armor? Who is this Gul Kana fool who dared carry my battle-ax upon his back? I know not whether to thank him or slay him."

All the goodwill Lindholf had been feeling toward Aeros Raijael vanished in an instant. He felt small before the man's withering gaze. *"Gul Kana fool," he called me* . . .

"Let me introduce Ser Lindholf Le Graven." Spades bowed to Lindholf. "Ser Lindholf is a Dayknight of Gul Kana, raised as the son of Lott Le Graven, lord of Eskander. 'Twas Ser Lindholf who helped me secure the weapons and stones and bring them back to you. He is no Gul Kana fool. I can assure you of that."

"But he is a Dayknight?" Aeros asked, brow furrowed, skepticism falling over his face. "This *kid* is an actual Dayknight?"

"Aye." Spades winked at Lindholf reassuringly. "He is an actual Dayknight. Raised as the son of a Gul Kana lord. And now, I imagine, he shall be your most loyal servant."

"I've enough loyal servants," Aeros said. "I am in scant need of another. Especially one with such deformities. I wish to be surrounded by those of great quality. Especially when it comes to their physical attributes. This boy will not do. Dayknight or not, lord's son or not, he is a grotesque."

"Well, he is not a lord's son," Spades said. "Not technically, anyway."

"You just claimed he was Lord Lott Le Graven's son," Aeros said.

"I said he was *raised* as Lord Lott Le Graven's son," Spades responded.

"And I imagine he believes he is a Le Graven. As I imagine everyone in Jovan's court believes he is a Le Graven. But I see through the subterfuge. Can you not, my lord?"

Lindholf's heart was suddenly pounding against his ribs with such ferocity he thought it might explode. *What in all the rotted angels is this woman talking about?*

"You aim to confound me," Aeros said. "And you aim to confound the boy, too, for he looks as confused as I. You know I do not like your games, Enna Spades. I like them less than Gault Aulbrek liked them."

A smile played at Spades' lips. "Oh, Gault Aulbrek practically hated my games."

Aeros glared at her with no small measure of impatience. "What are you getting at?"

Spades bowed. "I've a feeling Lindholf is most different from any man you have yet met, my lord Aeros. He is most special, indeed—"

"Special," Aeros cut her off with a mocking grin. "Looks like the exact kind of common Gul Kana dolt who should be rebuffed without ceremony, if not just beheaded on sight."

"Look past his scars," Spades said. "I implore you, look past those scars and see him for who he really is."

"And who is he really?" Aeros demanded. "Speak plainly."

"He is your younger brother, of course," Spades answered. "The lost boy you have been hunting these last ten years."

"Ha!" Hammerfiss' clapping laugh echoed like thunder through the hall. "He looks rather more like a potato than a Raijael. In fact, I think we should call him Lord Potato from now on."

"Aye." Aeros grinned at Hammerfiss. "I deem Ser Lindholf as Lord Potato." Still, despite the frivolity in Aeros' grin, there was a darkness lurking behind the White Prince's gaze.

And Lindholf had never felt more humiliated in his life. Enna Spades was making a mockery of him. She had warned him as they crossed the dry channel that she would.

"He looks exactly like you, Lord Aeros." Spades continued with the ridicule.

"Does he, though?" Aeros snapped waspishly.

"Look at his eyes," Spades went on, undaunted. "Those black pupils, those black irises. No two like them in all the Five Isles."

Everyone was staring at him now. Lindholf's heart was nearly ready to burst in anger, in disgrace, in fear. It thumped hard in his chest. Dread and horror and shame engulfed him. *And to think, not a moment ago I felt so at home with these people.* Utter disappointment hit him like a sledgehammer in the gut, and he knew once and for all that he would never be accepted. Not now. Not ever. Not by anyone. He was a big joke. *Lord Potato.* He could still hear the pure amusement in both Aeros' and Hammerfiss' voices.

"He is your brother, my lord Aeros." Spades carried on with the foolishness.

"This is not the boy who was stolen by Ser Roderic," Aeros snapped. "This is not the Gallows Haven boy Shawcroft hid from us. That boy's name was Nail. It was Nail who I chased across the Five Isles. Not this deformed freak you have brought me."

"Look beyond Lindholf's scars," Spades insisted. "Really *look* at him, and you will see. It is obvious."

Aeros glared at her. "If you feel so strongly about all this, Spades, perhaps I should make him one of my new Knights Archaic. Or perhaps I should deem him the Angel Prince right here and right now and let him lead my armies straight into Gul Kana. Perhaps it will be Lord Potato who ushers in Fiery Absolution in my stead."

"I'm not qualified," Lindholf blurted before he could stop himself. "In fact, I'm about the most unqualified person anywhere for anything."

"A point likely hard to dispute," Hammerfiss said. "Leastwise, just by looking at him, that is."

Lindholf hung his head, feeling the black Dayknight armor constricting around him. It was so hot. He could scarcely breathe. His heart was helplessly trembling. He was panicking now. He had never felt such distress. The girl, Leisel, offered him a tempered smile. It was comforting. But he found himself still gasping for air. Then he found himself falling over backward. As he toppled to the stone floor in a clattering heap of armor, everything went dark.

**

Lindholf had been awake for several hours now; his fainting spell hadn't lasted more than a few minutes. Still, he felt like a Gul Kana fool. *Spades actually thinks I am Aeros Raijael's younger brother. She thinks I am the Angel Prince.* True or not, it was a horrible joke, was what it was, for across the banquet table from Lindholf, Aeros Raijael's black-pupiled eyes were hard as stone. *And he keeps staring at me.* Lindholf just wanted to get drunk and pass out again. He had a full goblet of wine before him, and he was working on it. One had to have goals.

Young Leisel stood behind the White Prince with a ceramic pitcher of red wine. Aeros' goblet was also full. As were Spades' and Jenko's. Hammerfiss, sitting at the end of the table, had already drained his goblet dry and beckoned for seconds. Leisel walked around the table and poured him more. Lindholf drank his wine down swiftly too, then held his goblet out. Leisel refilled it. Yes, Lindholf just wanted to be drunk.

The meal whose remains were now spread out across the table had been amazing: long links of spiced sausage, roasted potatoes, and green spears of fresh asparagus. He hadn't eaten such a meal since he and Spades had left Savon. There was still enough food left on the stone table to feed ten more people. Their long table of food was set some fifty feet from the perfumed corpse of the man named the Spider. The end of the table where they all dined was arrayed with flickering candles.

Aeros had spread out all five weapons of the Warrior Angels across the far end of the table, displaying each angel stone before the weapon it belonged with: the blue with *Forgetting Moon*, the green with *Lonesome Crown*, the red with *Afflicted Fire*, the white with *Ethic Shroud*, and the black with *Blackest Heart*.

Leisel's decanter of perfume had been refilled to the brim and now rested in the middle of the table between the food and the weapons. She had been sprinkling the stuff over the severed serpent head and the dead body in the center of the room off and on. That the dead man had

567

once been a Bloodwood assassin sent a chill up Lindholf's spine. One more reason he just wanted to get drunk. His only solace was that he was once again high on Shroud of the Vallè. Spades had stolen enough of the white powder from the oghul manor house outside Devlin to last him for weeks, if not moons. And the more of it he sniffed, the more he craved it, and the better he felt. *But the powder doesn't stop Aeros Raijael from staring at me nonstop!*

"Are those fresh wounds on your neck?" Hammerfiss asked Spades.

"No." The warrior woman stuffed a hunk of bread into her mouth, chewing as she spoke. "Not fresh wounds at all. Old wounds." The red scars of her injuries were just visible above the neckline of her chain-mail tunic.

Both Spades and Lindholf had changed out of their heavy Dayknight armor for more lightweight attire. Lindholf, like Spades, wore brown pants and a brown leather tunic ringed with chain mail along the sleeves and about the neckline. Jenko Bruk and Hammerfiss still wore most of their Knight Archaic livery, both looking stiff and uncomfortable at the table.

"The wounds look serious," Aeros said, no longer staring at Lindholf. "How did you get them?"

"A big gray shepherd dog."

"My sympathies." A haunted look crossed over Aeros' pale countenance. "I do not like shepherd dogs, myself. Especially the big gray ones."

"They can be a menace," Spades agreed.

"The worst of menaces," Aeros said.

The wide double doors of the chamber's entry swung open with a great groan. Candles flickered on the table as a sharp breeze spilled into Bruce Hall. Two cloaked and hooded horsemen were silhouetted in the early-evening glow of the doorway, their horses black as pitch, eyes blooming with fire-crimson light.

Hammerfiss and Spades stood, weapons ready, as the two horsemen galloped into the chamber and straight toward the banquet table. Jenko rose from the table too, wary hand on the hilt of his sword. Aeros remained seated and calm. The hooves of the black steeds echoed throughout the hall. They were stallions, like the Spider's Bloodeye. And the two cloaked figures atop the red-eyed stallions seemed rooted in blackness. Lindholf noticed a slobbering bulldog with round, bulging eyes following on the heels of the two stallions, a rusted spiked collar around its neck. The strange bulldog got the attention of the other dogs gathered in the hall. All the dogs started barking.

"Shut up!" Hammerfiss roared, and the dogs shut up.

Spades held her sword up before the dark riders. "Not a step farther."

The hooded riders stopped. They both wore black greaves and leather armor under their black cloaks, hoods covering their faces. The shorter of the two black-clad men wore twin black daggers on the right side of his belt, and a crossbow and quiver of arrows were strapped to his back. The taller one wore no weaponry visible about his body.

There was silence in the hall.

"Stand down, Spades," Aeros said with a coolness that set Lindholf's nerves on edge. "For it seems we are graced with a visit from Black Dugal and one of his Bloodwood pets."

Bloodwoods! Lindholf's mind reeled. *Killers like Seita. Killers like the split-open and rotting corpse on the floor not fifty feet away.* Spades scowled as she lowered her weapon. And Lindholf thought he actually heard a growl escape Hammerfiss' throat at the word *Bloodwood.*

Both men slid from their sleek black mounts with a smooth gracefulness that chilled Lindholf's blood. The smaller of the two men threw back his hood, and Lindholf was surprised to see the face of a youth about his own age. But it was a cruel-faced youth. The dangerous-looking fellow had a hooked nose, a square jaw and cheekbones, harsh green eyes tinged with red, and a face brimming with confidence and conceit. His dirty-blond hair was shaved above his ears on both sides of his head and spiked; blue tattoos covered his scalp.

The taller of the two pulled his hood back shortly after the first. This man was much older than his partner but bore a similarly cruel and chiseled face under a gray-streaked beard; his dark eyes were also streaked with red. A scar in the shape of a crescent moon marred his left cheek; two others curled below his right eye and across his face. One scar cut a path through his right brow and up his forehead. Together the two Bloodwoods looked sinister, tortured, and oddly *beautiful*.

The tall one glanced at the weapons and stones spread out on the long stone table. "As I promised you, my lord Aeros, the weapons and stones would all make their way to you in the end."

The man's voice left a cold sensation in Lindholf's gut. *And he looks so familiar.* Lindholf scrutinized the man's face, trying to place where he might have seen him before. He thought back to Aeros holding *Afflicted Fire* aloft earlier, how it had reminded him of the sculpture of Laijon in the temple in Amadon. This Bloodwood had a similar ethereal look, only darker and brooding. *Could they be brothers, Aeros and this man?* Lindholf took a long drink of his wine. *Get drunk! Get drunk as fast as you can!*

Aeros dabbed at the corners of his thin lips with a white kerchief as he stood. "Will you introduce your travel partner? Who is this new member of Black Dugal's Caste? Who is he, Dugal?"

"I am Shadowwood," the young assassin spoke.

"Ha!" Hammerfiss shouted, clapping. He was starting to get drunk too. His clap had startled the bulldog, who scooted under the black stallions. "I recognize the whelp now. The bleating rat voice is unmistakable. It is Hans Rake of Suk Skard." Hammerfiss' joy-filled face turned to Aeros. "Last I saw young Hans he was but a sprout of a boy, not more than five years old, dashing through the moonlit woods chasing fireflies with his sister, Hannah. His blond hair glowed like the eastern star, it was so stark and white under the stars. We used to call him our little blizzard bear. I knew his parents well. His father was a bit of a skulking sneak-thief, if I recall."

"I am fatherless." Hans' response was cold and dry. "And you know nothing of me. And you will not say another word."

"On the contrary," Hammerfiss said. "I know quite a lot about you, boy. And I say whatever the fuck I like."

"Then be warned." A dagger appeared in the youth's hand. "If you say another word about me, I will slice the lying tongue right out of your lying fucking mouth. Then I will cut your heart right out of your fucking chest."

"Seems unduly over-reactionary." Hammerfiss took a step back, hands held up in mock defense. "Please don't hurt me, young rat."

"This is no joke," the youth went on, brandishing the dagger. "Because after you are dead, I will hunt down *your* family and cut their hearts out too. But not before having the ugliest clan of oghuls rape your sisters bloody with their long, spiked dongs. And I'll have them rape your daughters. Your grandmothers, too. You useless, bumbling, fat-faced knight—"

"Wait," Hammerfiss cut him off, holding up but one hand now, an injured tone in his voice. "You think I have a fat face?"

Spades laughed. "The boy knows your measure, Ser Hammerfiss."

"He's insulted my face," Hammerfiss growled. "I do not think that it is fat. Not by any measure."

"Next the boy will be guessing your weight," Spades said. "In fact, we should make a contest out of it. How fat is Hammerfiss' face? How much does he weigh?"

"You think this is a joke too?" Hans glared at the warrior woman. "I will have even more fun slicing you up."

Spades grinned at him. "You're not very good at making friends, are you?"

"*Enough.*" Aeros beckoned both Hammerfiss and Spades to sit back down. They complied, sitting at the banquet table opposite the White Prince. "And stow away your dagger." Aeros glared at Hans Rake.

Black Dugal nodded at the boy. The young assassin slipped the dagger back into his belt, icy, bloodshot eyes on Hammerfiss and Spades the entire time. But Hammerfiss and Spades had gone back to picking at the food on the table as if the young assassin didn't even exist.

Black Dugal looked toward the Spider's black stallion in the alcove. "I see another Bloodeye steed. I see it is left unattended." His eyes wandered the hall. "Where is Spiderwood?"

"He's dead." Hammerfiss swung his legs around, leaning back on the bench, broad back resting against the stone table. He took a long drink from his goblet, then motioned for Leisel to pour him more. He was as drunk as Lindholf wished to be.

"Dead?" Dugal questioned.

"Dead," Hammerfiss said, holding his goblet out as Leisel filled it.

"Dead, how?" Dugal asked.

Hammerfiss smiled. "Something heavy fell upon him." Then he took another long drink.

"What fell on him?" Dugal's roaming eyes found the bloody pile of leather just beyond the banquet table. "What fell on the Spider?" Dugal's voice was cold as he stared at the smashed corpse.

"My mace," Hammerfiss said, bleary eyes planted on Dugal now. "Damnable heavy thing's liable to fall on anyone, even your new little protégé, Hans Rake. Indeed, your mouthy little new rat son may also find his brains splattered all over the floor, just like your old mouthy rat son."

"They are all fatherless," Dugal said. "They are not sons of mine. We are all fatherless, right, Aeros? We are all the children of Dashiell Dugal, we Bloodwoods."

"We are all the children of Dashiell Dugal, we Bloodwoods," Hammerfiss repeated in a mocking, drunken voice. Then he belched long and loud. Hammerfiss' mockery of Dugal was followed by a moment of stiff silence.

The tall Bloodwood glared murder and ice at the red-haired giant. Lindholf felt the tension in the air. He nervously finished his goblet of wine. Leisel was right there to fill it for him again. Then he felt Black Dugal's eyes on him. The man's gaze ran through him like a sharp gust of wind. Even the two black stallions seemed to be staring at Lindholf too, eyes like burning coals. Dugal's gaze lingered but a moment.

He looks so familiar under that beard, under those scars, like Aeros, like the Laijon statue, like me. And with that thought Lindholf felt as if his soul was stripped bare and the buds of truth laid out before him. The answers to everything seemed to hover just at the edge of thought, but unreachable.

"Fact is," Hammerfiss said, finishing his own drink in two gulps, "the Spider still stinks." Now clearly drunk, he turned to Leisel. "Go perfume him, my young darling."

Leisel set the ceramic wine jug on the stone table between two burning candles and took up the full decanter of perfume. The strongly scented liquid sloshed from the glass bottle over her hands and down to the floor as she made her way to the pile of guts and split leather armor that used to be the Spider. She left a glistening, wet trail of perfume from the table to the corpse. Leisel tipped the decanter over the mound of flesh, dousing the heap of gore. Done, she made her way back to the table, dribbling more perfume along the way.

"You spilled most of it on the floor," Aeros said, annoyed.

"The girl usually performs her servanting duties with an eye toward detail," Hammerfiss said drunkenly. "But she's never been too fastidious when perfuming the Spider with perfumes."

Leisel set the decanter down on the stone table and wiped her hands and arms free of perfume with a rag pulled from her apron.

Black Dugal was no longer focused on Lindholf. He was glaring at Aeros now. "Spiderwood should have been afforded more respect than being left to rot in the middle of the room."

"I myself would have preferred burning his body immediately," Hammerfiss said. "So I could have roasted sausages over his flaming corpse."

"A Bloodwood cloak protects from fire," the assassin named Hans said.

Hammerfiss laughed at that. "Oh, really?"

"Why wasn't he given more respect?" Dugal pressed Aeros.

"Aeros wished to burn him," Hammerfiss answered. "But 'twas I who insisted on humiliating him in death, as I humiliated him in life. I like watching little rats rot."

"And for disrespecting the corpse of a Bloodwood, you shall one day die by my knife," Dugal said.

Hammerfiss was clearly not the type to be intimidated by any man. He stood, drunk on his feet, facing Dugal and Hans. "Well, which one of you is gonna stab me first? I am dripping with anticipation, for I would love to squash more poisoned black bugs—"

"Enough!" Aeros shouted. "What's done is done! Spiderwood is dead! What of it?" He glared at Dugal. "Just tell me why you are here!"

It took a moment for Black Dugal to tear his gaze from Hammerfiss, but eventually he did. He addressed Aeros flatly. "Word is Leif Chaparral has abandoned Lord's Point."

"As I have heard," Aeros said. "Excellent tidings indeed. But that does not answer why you are here."

"Leif has withdrawn back to Amadon," Dugal went on. "We all know that his retreat was at the behest of King Jovan. For Jovan, Grand Vicar Denarius, and the quorum of five wish for Absolution and the return of Laijon more than anything. Despite their recent victory, their scripture actually works in our favor, for they are beholden to it, beholden to the fact that Amadon is the prophesied location of Fiery Absolution. They know that the armies of Raijael must make it to Amadon for the return of Laijon. So let us now give them what they yearn for."

"'Us'?" Aeros asked. "Or me?"

"You, of course, my lord Aeros." Dugal's dark gaze fell upon the table and all the weapons and angel stones gathered there. "And now that you have the fabled weapons of the Five Warrior Angels, now that Leif Chaparral has left the way clear, you should bring Absolution unto them. You should unleash Fiery Absolution over Amadon."

At the man's words, Aeros' dark-pupiled eyes were now lit deep from within, aglow with a light and fervor that almost scared Lindholf.

"You know it is the right thing to do," Dugal said. "For you are Angelwood, and it is time for you to face your brother."

"We do have enough horses scrounged up." Aeros stood. "We do have enough men and knights and fighters still left from the battle, enough weaponry and armor retrieved from the ocean bed." He met Dugal's intense stare. "I think we can do it. I think we can make it to Amadon."

"I can drink to that!" Hammerfiss held up his goblet.

But to Lindholf, Dugal's ominous words made the entirety of Bruce Hall feel more than hollow; his words made the chamber feel void of all air and light. He didn't know what to think. *Angel stones! Fiery Absolution! Weapons of the Five Warrior Angels!* It was as if scripture and prophecy were coming to fruition right before his eyes. Jenko Bruk looked confused too. The Gallows Haven boy had been sitting next to Lindholf the entire time. He hadn't said a word. Nor had Lindholf. He took a long drink. *Get drunk. Just get drunk.*

"We shall prepare our armies," Aeros announced to everyone. "And we shall depart on the first day of the Heart Moon."

"I can also drink to that." Hammerfiss still held his goblet aloft. "In fact, I can almost pretty much drink to anything at this point. Had I been born under a different moon in a different age, or even under different circumstances altogether, I reckon I could have made a life out of being drunk. In fact, it is almost a certainty."

The big man toppled back, his drink tumbling from his beefy hand. The goblet hit the stone table with a clatter, spilling the wine, knocking over the candles, and shattering Leisel's large glass decanter of perfume. The candle immediately ignited the spilled wine and perfume, and yellow flame rippled across the entire table near Hammerfiss. The end of the table was a blanket of fire. The spreading fire dripped to the stone bench, then hopped along the floor from puddle to puddle, tracing Leisel's trail of spilled perfume straight toward the mound of flesh that used to be the Spider.

And the pile of black leather—doused in days' and days' worth of flammable fragrance—burst into a great ball of flame. The dark cloak also lit up.

"Ah!" Leisel let loose a sharp and startled scream. All the dogs in the hall, including the slobbering bulldog, scampered into the shadows, and Hans' and Dugal's Bloodeye stallions nickered darkly. The Spider's Bloodeye steed, Scowl, sprinted from the chamber and vanished into the night between the still wide-open doors.

The initial column of fire reached far up into the darkness of Bruce

Hall before it dwindled back down to a dull roar. The remains of the Spider burned under waist-high flames.

"Now isn't that something." Hammerfiss snatched up a metal fork and speared a length of sausage with the tines. He appeared to be in a constant bout of manic gaiety now. "His fancy cloak is sure a-burnin' now." He laughed, clomping toward the burning corpse and holding the fork out over the flames, a large smile spreading over his broad face as he watched the sausage sizzle and pop.

CHAPTER FORTY-NINE
TALA BRONACHELL

21ST DAY OF THE BLOOD MOON, 999TH YEAR OF LAIJON
AMADON, GUL KANA

Tala Bronachell jerked awake to a cold sensation of panic and dread, momentarily disoriented, nightmares swept away into the darkness, unremembered. *Dreaming? Demons? The underworld? The wraiths eating at my brain?* Horrors all. *But I'm okay. I'll be okay.* And then the reality of where she was hit her, and her confidence waned. *How could I have been so stupid as to think Glade would confess?*

She pushed herself up off the cold stone floor of the dungeon cage, the darkness and flickering torchlight combined unfairly disorientating. *How long have I been down in Purgatory?* Here she was, alone in a cage, trying to make sense of emotions that, at sixteen, she could not fully understand. Her life was nothing. Her brother was a disgrace, a man who had betrayed his kingdom. And she was naught but a fugitive in hiding, a prisoner. Everything she believed in now seemed a lie. But the pain was not a lie. *So much pain and betrayal.* But she was not like her cousin Lawri. Other than the mostly healed cross-shaped wound on her shoulder her wounds were not physical. She could not dig at them, bleed away her ache and sorrow and sin. She could not use any physical wounds to release the pain out of her body and into the world. *But what if I could?* She shivered at the thought. *Have the wraiths finally seized my mind, infected my eternal soul?* She could not seem to hold on to one single thought. Everything was random in her mind.

Tala squinted against the glare of the torches hanging from rusted sconces lining the dungeon's walls. She had been here before, in this smothering room of cold stone. But she had been a free person then. Now she was a captive, held in one of two iron cages in the center of the vaulted stone dungeon, thick bars surrounding her on all four sides, the roof above naught but a flat iron slab. She was being held in the same cage that Gault Aulbrek of Sør Sevier had been held in. A hole was cut in the center of the stone floor not three paces from where she lay. She was terrified of that hole, and only dared piss or shit in it when Nail was asleep, his back turned to her.

The Gallows Haven boy was sleeping in a similar cage no more than an arm's reach away from hers. Four fully armed and armored Dayknights stood at attention before the cages, eyes hidden behind the pitch-black slits of their equally black helms. One knight held a large steel shield that stretched from the floor to above his head; the other three held tall spears, their cloverlike blades agleam in the flickering torchlight.

No one escaped the dungeons of Purgatory. The people of Amadon in general accepted it as historical fact. But Tala knew better. *And I will make my escape!*

So Tala knew something that the four guards did not. She knew that she and Nail would be better off left in the cold darkness, alone with only each other for company, rather than being handed open access to their captors. For Tala and Nail had been placed under the Dayknights' direct supervision at the behest of Leif Chaparral and her brother, the king. And that was a mistake, a terrible idea on Leif and Jovan's part.

For in the four days Tala and Nail had been held captive, Tala had quickly found that her Dayknight guards did not always wear their stifling helms nor even all their armor. They were lazy. She got to know their faces, their personalities. Tala had gotten to know all four knights on the day shift and all four on the night shift as well.

She was able to make small talk with them all at will. After all, she was the princess of Amadon, and they were eager to speak with her. And talking with a princess staved off their boredom. Yes, she got to know them all, got them to do her small favors, a cup of water here, an extra biscuit there, an extra blanket for both her and Nail. She had even engaged them in conversations about their families. She knew the names and ages of their children. Knew which knights were still unmarried and which ones had naggy, fat wives whom they hated.

The four men guarding her now were Sers Sagan, Perion, Simmonfall, and Corl. Tala recalled that Ser Sagan enjoyed his life as a newly married man, whereas Ser Perion had married a girl he hated. Tala had talked to them both at length about their recent marriages several nights ago. Ser Simmonfall was an older gentleman with four children. Ser Corl was a single man who desperately wished to get married. Under his helm, Ser Corl had an ugly, thin, pocked face that not many young noblewomen would find attractive. Ser Corl was the one who held the tall shield. These four men made up the night shift crew, who typically arrived in the early evening and departed at dawn. Of course Tala had no idea when dusk and dawn fell other than the coming and goings of the different shifts of four Dayknights.

Early on in her captivity, Tala quickly realized that her daily access to these men could very well be her means of escape. If she manipulated them just right, she could earn her freedom. She was certain she would eventually convince one or all of them to help her and Nail escape. After all, what else did she have to do? And they were easy targets.

At the moment, the four Dayknight guards were standing at attention, helms obscuring their faces, torches crackling with yellow light behind them. But it would not be long until the heat got to them. And then the helms would come off.

And then she would work on them again.

Clank!

Tala's eyes roamed the darkness; she wondered if anyone else had heard the noise. Nail was still asleep in the cage next to her. But there suddenly seemed to be some tension seeping and weaving through the musty air. Tala felt it—a calm before the storm.

Clink!

There it was again. The noise. The four knights looked around, feet rooted in place. They had heard it too.

Clink clank grrrrrhh . . .

There was also a faint grinding noise coming from somewhere all around.

Nail stirred, waking, sitting, rubbing both hands over his eyes and through his tousled blond hair. "What is that?" he muttered, concerned gaze meeting hers.

Tala shrugged.

Grrrrhhh . . . clank . . . grrrr . . .

The noise grew louder, expanding, as if chain rattled against chain. The air in the vaulted chamber seemed to shake with urgent thunder.

Tala stood, gripping the iron bars, casting her own gaze out into the darkness again, moving around the perimeter of her square cage, clinging fast to each bar as she stepped. But she could see nothing in the darkness, not even the hole near the floor across the chamber where she and Glade had escaped this room three moons ago. She recalled that some of the escape hatches and traps on that journey with Glade had made just such a grinding noise as she was hearing now.

Two of the spear-wielding knights removed their helms, Ser Sagan and Ser Perion, the two newlyweds, both of them blond and handsome. They both stared up into the darkness above Nail's iron enclosure. Tala followed their gaze.

A small cage was rattling down toward the top of Nail's confines. The descending cage had a round iron bottom and was held aloft by a long chain that stretched up into the blackness. Two thin legs dangled from the floor of the rickety cage, and two thin arms stretched out from between the iron bars, fingers grasping at the musty air. From her angle, Tala could not see the face of the cage's occupant. Nail was standing, face pressed against the iron bars, looking up, seeing nothing. Ser Simmonfall and Ser Corl removed their helmets too, perplexed looks upon their faces.

"Jellywood has come again!" a voice sounded from the round iron pen as it settled atop the flat metal roof of Nail's cage. Tala saw the thin, emaciated man standing in the small cage. It was the bearded old man named Maizy, the shit-smeared fellow she and Glade had passed by in their journey toward the Rooms of Sorrow. Maizy had dangled over the water-filled tunnel in a similar cage as now. But today he was not covered in his own feces, nor did he smell.

"Yes," Maizy cackled. "Yes, indeed, Jellywood has returned. Jellywood has come again to Purgatory. He has shaken off the mantle of his old life to again take up his old ways. And he has taken up his sneaky old ways indeed."

Maizy cackled and laughed as he swung the rusted door of his cage open and stepped out barefooted atop the solid iron roof of Nail's pen. The old man was garbed in naught but a ragged old loincloth. He continued laughing and cackling. "Indeed, ol' Maizy has taken up his former ways to help his fellow Bloodwood."

Simmonfall rushed forward, pointing his spear up at the old man. "Who are you? How did you get in here? What else is up in that hole in the roof? Who else is up there?" It was a long list of questions, all of them valid. Ser Sagan and Ser Perion stomped up behind Simmonfall, boots heavy on the stone floor, spears also leveled up at the newcomer.

The bearded old man capered about atop Nail's cell, dancing, pale arms and legs akimbo. "Fatherless I am, Jellywood my name. Known as Maizy to the girl in the cage, known as Maizy to the rats that slink about in the dark."

"Come off there!" Simmonfall thrust the clover-shaped tip of his spear at the old man.

Maizy whirled back into his small cage, dodging the blow, crouching. "Now that is no way to treat the friend of a Bloodwood," he said.

"Come down," Simmonfall insisted, the timbre of his voice rising, echoing loudly off the stone walls. "Come down from there now!"

"Oh, no, can't do that." Maizy grinned a gap-toothed grin as his bone-like fingers curled around the bars of his cage. "Jellywood is but a distraction, fools. Naught but a distraction, I says, a distraction." As he spoke, several of the torches burned out completely. The light in the chamber dimmed.

Then Ser Corl toppled forward, landing face-first atop the long shield he'd been holding. The Dayknight hit the hard floor with a tremendous crash, red blood spurting in one long, ropy trail from between his helm and shoulder-plate armor over the rough cobbled stone. Tala let go of the iron bars of her cage and stepped back. Sagan, Perion, and Simmonfall whirled as one, spears thrust out into the still-flickering blackness.

A cloaked figure drifted into the dim yellow light, a curved sword gripped in each gloved hand, hilt-guards naught but rows of spikes. Like a shade thrust up from the underworld, the sword-wielding specter stalked toward the three knights with ominous intent, twin blades a-glimmer in the wavering torchlight, sallow eyes glowing like colorless pools of moonlight in the dusky shadows of the black hood.

The three remaining Dayknights attacked. But the cloaked figure stepped back, disappearing into the dark. Not even a gleam of the phantom's curved swords shone in the blackness—he had simply vanished. Maizy cackled, his aged voice scratching through Tala's frayed nerves. Nail's eyes roamed the darkness of the vaulted cavern.

Sagan, Perion, and Simmonfall nervously scanned the shadows, spears at the ready. Silver light flashed under Ser Simmonfall's neck, and his head toppled from his shoulders. It smacked the stone floor wetly near Nail's cage. Simmonfall's armored body folded over, landing with a thud, blood surging from his gaping neck. His spear rattled on the floor last, a sharp counterpoint to old Maizy's continued cackling. Ser Sagan and Ser Perion gazed out into the blackness in horror, spear tips wavering.

Then another torch dimmed and went dead. With the fading of the light there came another silver flash and Ser Sagan's head spun to the floor, his body dropping cold and hard. Ser Perion whirled, only to take the tip of the shade's curved sword through the center of his face, slicing straight into his brain. Ser Perion slid unceremoniously from the bloody sword to the floor. And Maizy still laughed and cackled.

The cloaked assassin wiped his bloodied blade clean on Ser Perion's black livery and then slowly turned, pulling the cowl back from his face.

It was Hawkwood.

"You killed them" was all Tala could think to say as the horror of what had just happened set in. "They were just guards doing their job. I knew them. I talked to them." *All the numerous knights who have been killed because of me, all who have perished for my lies.*

Hawkwood met her gaze with fierce determination. "If they had not died by my blade, Jovan would have surely slain them anyway, possibly even tortured them."

"Why would he have them tortured or killed?"

"For allowing your escape."

"My escape?"

"Is that not what you were planning?"

It was exactly what I was planning. And he's right, my brother would have had them killed! She recalled the knights Leif and Jovan had killed after she and Glade had gotten lost in Purgatory. *How many more must die for my lies?* She met Hawkwood's intense gaze, unflinchingly. "I suppose you are here to rescue me."

Hawkwood sheathed his blades in the leather baldrics over his back. "I'm here for you and Nail both. When rumor reached me that the princess of Amadon had been thrown into Purgatory, how could I not have come? Am I right, Maizy?"

The old man named Maizy laughed and laughed as he pulled a long iron key out of his dirty loincloth.

**

"I thought you were gone forever." Lawri Le Graven hugged Nail first when he entered the Slaver's Tavern and Inn. She held him tight, then she threw her arms around Tala. "I thought the both of you were lost for good. And then what would I do?" The silver gauntlet was cold against Tala's back. "I would have no one without you, Tala."

"You would have Cromm." The oghul stood right behind her, sucking on the black angel stone. "And Bronwyn."

Lawri slid the gauntlet up under the folded cloak she used to cover it again. Tala noticed the moldy green skin encircling her whole arm now. Where the flesh met the silver was a dark, creeping rot. Lawri's eyes met Nail's bashfully as she continued to arrange the cloak over the gauntlet.

"Are you not pleased with how Cromm has treated you these last four days?" Cromm asked Lawri.

"You treated me most graciously," Lawri said. "As did Bronwyn. I just missed my cousin. I missed Nail."

They all sat at a round wooden table near the rear of the tavern. Tala was glad Lawri was safe and sound, but the fact that her cousin kept stammering and blushing around Nail was bothersome.

Hawkwood finally entered the tavern. The oghul's eyes widened when he saw the Sør Sevier man, as did Bronwyn's. Hawkwood had remained outside, stabling the three horses that had carried him, Nail, and Tala from the dock district. Together the three of them had followed the dirty old man named Maizy up and out of Purgatory through a twisting and turning labyrinth of caverns and narrow stone passageways. The secret ways had emptied them out near the docks. Hawkwood had secured them horses whilst Maizy had retreated back into his secret lair under the city.

"Cromm thought you burnt up in the Filthy Horse fire," the oghul said to Hawkwood as he motioned for everyone to sit.

Hawkwood sat. "I must admit, I almost did die." Pain washed over his normally stoic countenance. "I stayed in that burning building longer than I should have, looking for Jondralyn. And for a time I truly believed that Jondralyn died in that fire. I grieved her loss with great despair." The man stretched his arms over the worn surface of the wooden table, clenching and unclenching his fists, as if trying to gain control of his emotions. Tala sensed the tension and pain within him. Then Hawkwood looked at her with dark, piercing eyes. "I thought my love had perished in the fire with Val-Draekin. But I was wrong."

As the man stared at Tala, a tremendous weight of guilt settled over her like a dark shroud. *It was my lie that sent Val-Draekin back into the burning saloon to save my sister. He must have told Hawkwood that Nail and Jondralyn were still in the tavern.* And it was all a lie. *Everything about me is a lie. And now the Vallè is dead!* She had told so many lies over the last few moons she couldn't even remember them all.

Numb to the world, she slunk back in her own chair, trying to stave off Hawkwood's hard stare. At the moment, she somehow felt like Purgatory was probably the exact right place for a deceitful sinner like her. *Take me back. How many have died because of my lies? Sterling Prentiss? Val-Draekin? Countless Silver Guards and Dayknights?* Yes, Purgatory should be her sentence.

Hawkwood removed his accusing gaze. "Yes, I thought Jondralyn had perished in that fire along with Nail and Val-Draekin. In fact, I believed you all might be dead: Tala, Lawri, all of you. And then I heard a rumor that some Wyn Darrè soldier carried Jondralyn's body from Savon; he bore her into Amadon on the back of a pony and presented her body before King Jovan."

Tala had not seen her sister's body, but not for lack of trying. She had insisted that Jovan take her down the Long Stairs to Tin Man Square and the crypt in the Gardens of the Crown Moon to see the body. Instead she had been taken to Purgatory.

Hawkwood went on, eyes focused on Tala. "Then, not four days ago, I heard another rumor. I heard that Jovan's youngest sister had been thrown into Purgatory. And then I realized there was much I did not know about that fire at the Filthy Horse Saloon." His voice dropped, and Tala almost detected shame in what he said next. "And here I always thought I was the one running things, the one in charge."

Tala wasn't sure she liked seeing these cracks revealed in Hawkwood. He had always been such a rock, the one they all could lean on, the one they all felt safest around. Witnessing him like this made the world feel less safe. *But why should it?* She cursed herself for relying on the confidence of men for her own comfort and safety. She knew she must learn to take care of herself. It was then she realized: she had to finish what Jondralyn had started. It was the only way to make things right, the only way to atone for all her lies. She had to usurp Jovan as leader of Gul Kana.

"Have you heard the other rumors?" Bronwyn asked Hawkwood.

"What other rumors?" the man asked.

"Dark rumors," Bronwyn answered. "The type of rumors that circulate through bleak taverns like this, rumors most evil and foul. Rumors from the north. Rumors that an army of Hragna'Ar oghuls are heading south, that warships sail from Vandivar."

"Not just an army of oghuls," Cromm added, smiling, as if he were thrilled with the news. "No, not just any army of oghuls. But an army of oghuls led by the Skulls, all of them heading toward Absolution." With one finger Cromm dug the black angel stone from his lower lip, holding it out for all to see. "And the dragons come with them."

*'Tis true that the Blessed Mother Mia was trying to hide the angel stones
from the Vallè. For bringing the stones together with Dragon Claw shall
awaken the Great Beneath en masse. For are not the Skulls in tune with the
beasts of the underworld? Will not the Dragon come and lead them?*
—THE MOON SCROLLS OF MIA

CHAPTER FIFTY

STEFAN WAYLAND

23RD DAY OF THE BLOOD MOON, 999TH YEAR OF LAIJON
KASMERE LAKE, GUL KANA

To the west, the oghul army of Hragna'Ar was spread out along the shores of Kasmere Lake, a rippling forest of rusted spears and halberd shafts and flapping, tattered banners. The early night sky was flawlessly clear; scores of stars alight and pricking the black sky, shimmering off the calm surface of the lake like tiny diamonds.

To the east, in front of Stefan Wayland and Mud Undr'Fut and the black saber-toothed lion, was a shimmering lake of another kind. A lake of the dead, iridescent with blood, human limbs, silver scorch, and lifeless pale faces. The stench of seared flesh hung heavy in the air. Wearing her silver mask of Skull, Icelyn the White waded through this gore-filled mere, long, curved dagger slicing the ears from every corpse she passed. Her scorch whip was tied at her hip, hissing silver and dripping.

Stefan drew back from the scene. It happened after every battle just the same, this ritual of mutilation and disfigurement of the dead. Icelyn cutting the ears of the enemy was a way for the dead to remain unrecognizable as either human or Vallè. It made no sense to Stefan. But then again, neither did the scorch whips of the Aalavarrè Solas, strange, evil weapons that had dismembered everyone on this field of battle. No, the liquid silver that could carve through human flesh made no sense to Stefan at all. It was cruel, instant death. It was something from a dream. From a nightmare. And Stefan wondered when his would end.

Am I still crawling through Deadwood Gate, the mines bending my mind to their will? It seemed so, for silver traces of flowing decay still crawled along his flesh. The silver rot followed his veins in lightning-like patterns. He constantly tried to scratch the rot away, but the swirling silver was under his skin, unreachable. A nightmare.

He scratched at it now. To no avail.

The oghul high priest, Sledg H'Mar, drifted out of the dark behind Stefan and Mud Undr'Fut, his priestly robes dragging on the ground. He led two musk oxen, each with a thick rope around its hair-matted neck. The musk oxen lingered silently behind the large oghul, long, sweeping tusks pale in the torchlight.

Sledg H'Mar addressed Mud. "Have you anything to report? Have you taken care of the Cauldron Born as I bade you do?"

Mud nodded toward his master. "Mud reports all to his master, Sledg, and also to the five Cauldron Born. But there is nothing to report now."

"Have you taken care of the Cauldron Born?"

"Mud has taken care of them. And that is how Mud knows his mother would be most proud of her stunted and picked-upon child. To rise from a bullied runt to one of the high priest's personal spies to servant of the Cauldron Born is something even she could not have foreseen, rest her soul."

"Do you polish their armor as I bade you do? Do you polish it even when they have not fought in a battle?"

"Mud does after every battle, my master."

"Their boots?"

"Yes."

"Do you brush their cloaks?"

"Aye."

"Do you brush the saber-toothed cat?"

"Not often."

"And why not?"

"The cat hates being brushed for no reason. The beast only lets Stefan touch it."

"I see." Sledg looked disappointed, glancing at Stefan almost accusingly before looking back at Mud. "How will you handle polishing the dragons themselves if you cannot even clean a cat? For the dragons will need to be washed and scrubbed after battle."

Mud looked horrified. "Shouldn't the dragons clean themselves?"

"No," Sledg H'Mar said. "You shall clean them."

And with that the gruff high priest walked away, leading his two musk oxen down the bloody slope toward the oghul army on the shores of Kasmere Lake.

"Master gives Mud too many menial tasks," Mud said. "Mud is worth more than that. Cannot our master see? Mud is worth more than just a boot cleaner is worth."

"Cleaning a dragon is more than cleaning a boot," Stefan said, shuddering at the thought.

"It is at that." Mud smiled. "Mud shall rethink things now."

Stefan looked toward Kasmere Lake and the sparkling sea of torchlight gleaming off its surface. The saber-toothed lion also studied the lake with flat silver eyes.

"The scene reminds Mud of the many caverns of sparkling quartz found in the farthest reaches of the Deadwood Gate mines," the small oghul said. "Mud remembers those vast and deep dungeons gorged with black waters. Waters that similarly reflected the light. Mud can recall his former life in those mines, when he dreamed of pulling the quartz from the rock and fashioning it into jewels and gems even greater and more brilliant than the angel stones. Yet lofty were the dreams of a young Mud of so small stature. But those days of mining are long behind Mud now. Though mining is the toil of the Hragna'Ar gods." The small oghul looked at Stefan. "Do you know the legend of the marked one?"

"No," Stefan said.

"Mud remembers when his mother first told him the Hragna'Ar

legend of the marked one. 'Like you, Mud, the marked one shall be the least of them,' she said. 'Like you, Mud, the marked one shall be one who is not strong, but rather he shall be one who is likely to be picked on. That is the one you shall seek when the appointed time has come, for you shall seek out the least of them in the midst of the crowds. For there is greatness in you, Mud. Greatness in your bloodline. And you shall one day be a part of Hragna'Ar legend, for you shall bring the marked one forth in the end.' " Mud was still looking at Stefan. "Did you know that about Mud?"

Stefan shook his head no.

"Mud understands your skepticism. For Mud himself was not sure he always believed in those words of his long-dead mother. Every young oghul was told as much. Every young oghul is told that they are destined to escort the marked one to Fiery Absolution. No, Mud himself was not always sure he believed in the words spoken by his mother, but Mud has always remembered them."

The oghul was still looking at Stefan.

"Mud once thought you were the marked one. But you are not. And in a way that makes Mud sad. Are you sad about that?"

Stefan shook his head again. He didn't know anything about the legend of this so-called marked one.

"Even if you are not the marked one, Mud is okay with that. For there is a feeling deep inside Mud's heart that we shall always be together as friends."

Stefan wasn't so sure about that. He missed Nail and Dokie and Beer Mug. He even missed Liz Hen. Those were his real friends. Those were the ones he had fought side by side with. But they were all lost to him. Now he was stuck in this place with these creatures he didn't even believe existed. He was stuck in a silver-hazed dream with seemingly no escape. He was stuck with an oghul and a saber-toothed lion for companions. He wasn't so sure he wasn't dead and living inside a dream.

"Mud's mother died in the fishing village of Tok when Mud was just a pup, no more than knee-high to an Adin Wyte goat," the oghul went on. "And Mud has not grown much since then. Mud's diminutive size bothers him still. But Mud's mother always taught Mud to notice what little beauty there is in the world, and cling to what few positive things there are. So perhaps Mud could believe in her words, that he will be the one to lead the marked one to Absolution. For here Mud is with the Cauldron Born on his way toward Amadon and Fiery Absolution."

Yes, Stefan had heard Mud say quite often how his dear departed mother had always advised her young oghul son to look to the good and positive things in the world.

"Now Mud must go and pick a severed head from the battlefield and suck the blood from it." Mud elbowed Stefan. "Do you also want a severed head to suck on?"

Stefan said no.

**

It was the middle of the night and the one called the Dragon arrived.

Upon the Dragon's arrival, all five of the Cauldron Born marched up the rocky slope, removing their masks of Skull. They bent their knee before him in worship.

Stefan also knew the one called the Dragon—for the Dragon was *Val-Draekin.*

The dark-haired Vallè wore black leather armor under a pitch-black cloak.

Behind him, to the east, a vast army of Vallè warriors stretched off into the darkness, their glorious war chargers dripping in gleaming silver armor. A virtual sea of glimmering spearheads and half-pikes receded into the black of night, silver banners rippling in the soft breeze. Hundreds of thousands of Vallè warriors. It was more fighters in one place than Stefan had ever seen. Both cavalry and footmen, every bit of their scrollworked armor like silver pieces of sculpture, polished and fine. Pale Vallè faces, both male and female, under every magnificent half-helm. Swords that shone. Hilts that sparkled with jewels.

Stefan wondered if it really *was* his friend on the slope above. Could it really be his friend who had led this Vallè army to the shores of Kasmere Lake?

Val-Draekin. The Dragon.

It just couldn't be. Stefan recalled the Company of Nine, and how his Vallè friend had been the most helpful and stalwart and brave of them all, the most optimistic, too. So how could he be the leader of an army of Vallè who meant to join with the armies of Hragna'Ar, their aim, the slaughter of all humankind? Stefan was confused. *Dead and dreaming I am . . .*

"We've a gift for you, master." Icelyn the White drew her arm back and pointed in the direction of Stefan. "One who was found dead now lives."

Val-Draekin's dark eyes lit with joy when he saw Stefan.

"My friend!" the Vallè called out, swiftly making his way down the slope toward Stefan. The saber-tooth grew nervous at Nail's side, a low snarl of warning building in its heaving chest. Stefan placed a comforting hand on the cat's head and the beast relaxed.

Val-Draekin drew Stefan into a warm embrace. Then he backed away, asking, "Can you see me?"

"Of course I can see you," Stefan answered, even more perplexed.

"You are probably wondering why I am here," Val-Draekin said.

"I saw you die in the glacier. I saw that icy river swallow you and Roguemoore and Nail. Yet you live. I saw you and Nail sail away from Wroclaw. I am confused by a lot of things, actually. You come back to life. I come back to life. Or are we both dead?"

Val-Draekin clasped him by the shoulders. "Don't be confused. Yes, Nail and I live. But, alas, Roguemoore did not make it out of the glacier alive. Nail is safe in Amadon, last I saw of him. You should be glad of that."

"What of Liz Hen and Dokie?"

"I do not know their fates."

"What is this army?" Stefan motioned to the mass of Vallè forces stretched out behind Val-Draekin.

"I shall answer all your questions in due time," Val-Draekin said. "We shall have long talks in the coming days, me and you. Just know that, despite even my own doubts, everything has gone exactly as planned and I am glad to see you once more."

Val-Draekin turned to the five Aalavarrè Solas, their stark white faces marbled yellow by the firelight. "Forgive me not coming sooner with the armies of the Vallè," he said to them. "I thank you for your patience, but there was much to take care of in Amadon for the return of the Skulls, for the resurrection of our Immortal Lord."

"Forgiveness is always granted," Icelyn said. "For it was written in the stars since the beginning of time that the Dragon would be right here at this time."

"As you say, so it is." Val-Draekin bowed to the five Cauldron Born. "A glorious sign you were to me that day when I saw you in Wroclaw."

"And you were a glorious sign unto us," Icelyn said. "For we too see the visions that Viper hath sent through the Vallè maiden with the wrought-iron soul, for she is in tune with Hragna'Ar and the one wielding Dragon Claw. 'Tis a glorious day for us all, the original inhabitants of the Five Isles, now gathered to reclaim all the lands stolen from us so long ago, to avenge our banishment into the underworld."

"Where are your dragons?" Val-Draekin asked. "I am most anxious to see them."

"Follow us to the lakeshore," Icelyn said. "And perhaps they will come."

Val-Draekin walked toward the lake with the Cauldron Born.

Stefan turned to Mud. "Why would I not be able to see him?" he asked. "He was right in front of me. Why did Val-Draekin ask me if I could see him?"

The small oghul shrugged. "Many have wondered how the Aalavarrè Solas really see with those silver eyes."

"I don't know what that has to do with me," Stefan said, even more confused.

But Mud didn't hear him. The small oghul was already scampering eagerly after the five Aalavarrè and Val-Draekin, the Dragon.

**

"The five dragons were born of Hragna'Ar and then freed," Icelyn said, looking out over the moon-swept waters of the lake. The five Cauldron Born stood next to Val-Draekin and the Hragna'Ar high priest, Sledg

H'Mar. "Yet the dragons have not returned to the Aalavarrè of their own volition. We have performed more Hragna'Ar blood sacrifices to summon them once again. But I fear they were bred to roam and are now lost to the vastness of the sky."

"They are not lost to me, Icelyn." Val-Draekin pulled forth a small black object from the folds of his leather armor, held it delicately to his lips, and blew into it once, twice, a third time. Then he held the object out for Icelyn to examine. "'Tis a special whistle carved of a Bloodwood tree. Each whistle has its own unique pitch, soundless to our ears. The faint vibrations of similar such whistles can call trained Bloodwood kestrels from the sky from hundreds of miles away. But this whistle is the rarest of all, one of a kind, fashioned by my own hands from the very heart of the Bloodwood Forest, the dying place of the last dragon a thousand years ago. And if legend is to be believed, your dragons have just heard its call; like a sweet melody carried along the drifting winds, your dragons have just heard the last, lost song of their buried ancestors."

"What must we do now?" Icelyn inquired, silver eyes fixed on the Vallè.

"We wait," Val-Draekin answered. "And once all five dragons return to us, you are to ride them to Absolution as their masters."

Mud's master, the oghul high priest, Sledg H'Mar, heard the words of Val-Draekin and led the oghul army in a chant. *"Rogk Na Ark! Rogk Na Ark! Rogk Na Ark!"* 'Twas a glorious sound that thundered and boomed with thousands upon thousands of guttural oghul voices over the breadth of the lake. The glistening Vallè army to the east also took up the chant. Val-Draekin brought the special black whistle back up to his lips and blew into it again, soundless.

The chanting did not last long before every eye was cast skyward, watching the five dragons circling above in the faint light and stars: Black, White, Blue, Green, and Red. One by one the dragons circled lower and lower, each landing with a grand flutter of wings before Val-Draekin, muscles in their huge bodies rippling under sleek, colorful scales as they lowered their heads to him.

The dark-haired Vallè put away the whistle and fearlessly stepped to each dragon, placing his hand lightly on each of their spiked snouts, whispering to them words unheard as he let them sniff the white powder from his glove. Once done, he turned to the five Aalavarrè Solas. "They are now under your command, and they are now yours to ride."

"No one shall ever accuse me of wasting the dawn." Icelyn the White, firstborn of the blood cauldrons of Hragna'Ar, placed the silver mask of Skull over her pale face and strode toward the White. She hauled herself atop the dragon. The White was calm.

Icelyn was followed by Raakel-Jael the Green, Basque-Alia the Blue, Sashenya the Black, and Aamari-Laada the Red. All five Cauldron Born were now astride a dragon, battle armor and dragon scales glowing in unison.

If there was ever a more magical scene in all the Five Isles, Stefan could not imagine what it would be.

Val-Draekin's voice rang out for all to hear, as poetic and lyrical as those of the five Aalavarrè Solas. "The demons of the underworld shall soon arise and reclaim what was taken from them so long ago! They shall come from the grand beginning, where space did not extend and the science of the stars didst reign. They are of the first creation, the generation where gods and matter began to be. They are those who have lived through all eternity. They are those millions lost to the underworld, those who shall rise to the surface in the twinkling of an eye, by the cracking of the world, called forth by Dragon Claw. For they shall heed her call and push through that veil of pure nothingness and dark beneath us, then continue on upward through marble and dust and the cracking of the world, stepping over the bones of the human dead as they continue toward *Afflicted Fire* and that cross-shaped altar to attain pure light and space under the rule of their resurrected Immortal Lord."

And with that said, all five dragons took flight, the five Aalavarrè Solas clinging to their sinuous, scaled backs.

Some say yesterday's wars should not matter, that yesterday's beliefs should not be taken seriously, that yesterday's heroes should be forgotten. But a knight of Raijael is bred to go to war in defense of those beliefs and heroes.
—THE CHIVALRIC ILLUMINATIONS OF RAIJAEL

CHAPTER FIFTY-ONE
GAULT AULBREK

1ST DAY OF THE HEART MOON, 999TH YEAR OF LAIJON
EAST OF DEVLIN, GUL KANA

Safety, comfort, and confidence came to one encased in battle armor, no matter the weather. And Ser Gault Aulbrek's armor was shined and polished now. He was patrolling the harsh landscape of the Nordland Highlands in the silver armor and blue livery of Sør Sevier, longsword girt low on his hip. He sat high and proud and sure atop his roan destrier. The highlands he watched over were naught but jagged mountains and rocky wastes peppered with sparse and gnarled trees, pine and birch leaning crooked against the stiff wind.

At the moment, horse and rider stood upon a dusky ridge of sharp rock and dry peat. Both of them cast their gaze over a long, hollow valley. Both of them watched as a lone cloaked stranger struggled up the hill, one plodding step after the next, bent against the wind, cloak rippling and billowing. After a time, Gault set heels to flanks and guided his horse down the bleak slope at a stiff trot. The cloaked figure watched his approach.

Gault reined his steed up before the stranger. It was a young woman. Her eyes gleamed dully from under her hood, like shimmering pools at the bottom of a well. She clutched her cloak tightly in an attempt to shelter a swaddled baby from the bluster and rage of the growing wind. The infant's sallow face was scarcely visible between the folds of the threadbare blankets. The babe was calm, peaceful, and frail. A newborn.

"Don't take me back to him, Ser," the young woman said, the wind almost taking her words down the slope with it. The cowl of her tattered cloak fell from her face. She was slight and beautiful, unbearably so. Startling. Enchanting. "I beg of you, Ser Knight," she said. "Do not take me back to that monster."

Gault bent low toward her, swooping the young woman and the babe up in one arm, lifting them both onto the saddle before him.

"I'll hold you tight to me," he said, a sudden lull in the wind making his words feel harsh, loud. "You're safe now," he said a bit more softly.

With the young woman and small babe in the saddle before him, the storm-lashed valley was suddenly filled with light and life. The wind seemed less harsh and lonely, and the barren landscape less hollow. Gault had never before felt such elation. If death awaited him behind the next tree, then so be it; he would be dying at the happiest moment of his life. Angels could bury him here and he would care not. For an eternity spent in this very time and place and moment would be an eternity of contentment and joy.

But there was a deepness of sorrow, too, some poison coursing through his veins, for that sacred landscape in the Nordland Highlands was now far gone, an innocent dream left behind. That blissful moment in time had been traded for an unwanted life of war, an unchoreographed, cheerless dance of violence and blood. And all the men he had killed were now spread across a starlit frozen horizon, spread out before his wide-open eyes, exquisite and beautiful in its own terrible way.

What was it he had told his cousin, Squireck Van Hester? *I have seen ten years of war. Killed thousands in the name of the gods.* And now those thousands all stared back at him, the ashen lights of their dead eyes gazing right back at him amongst the twinkling of the frozen stars above. And buried in those myriad of dead expressions, he would never remember Avril's face again. For that unbearable beauty was now cloaked in death and loss, replaced by the images of those thousands who had perished at his hands. *There is no forgiveness for some sins. No absolution . . .*

And as he stared up at the various dead amongst the stars, he heard their murmuring, their whispering, their song. And someone's fingers entwined with his own. A female's hand, half again smaller than his; the feeling was warm and comforting. *Could it be Avril, pulling at him from the crowd of the dead?* But none of it was real. For everyone he once loved was dead. And the murmuring was his own.

Then Ava Shay's thin face floated in the darkness above. The poor, innocent child from Gallows Haven who had been captured and raped by the Angel Prince, come to torment him. *I failed her. . . .*

Or was it Krista's face above? *For I failed her, too. . . .*

Together, Krista and Ava were so similar, yet not.

One pale face staring down at him was etched with tension and unresolved terrors. The other held a worrisome glint of eye, a glint of eye full of a hidden infinite sadness.

Naught but the wraiths. Naught but dreams.

Ava? Krista? Which was which? Who was who? One in blue. One in black.

"Nothing," a gruff voice sounded from nowhere. "No movement out there in the forest. Not a trace. We should be safe here for the night."

Who? Was that me talking? What did I say? Fear enveloped him. Was it the wraiths who had him? He knew his eyes were open. He was on his back, looking up. He rose up on his elbows, letting go the soft hand that held his. He sat all the way up, pushing past the two pale faces, looking out into the darkness in confusion.

A bearded dwarf stood before a crackling campfire, a tall man next to him. The fire seemed a small thing against the surrounding darkness and coldness of the trees. And the black forest rose like fortress walls, walls wrapped in flickering shadow, melding with the black sweep of the sky above. A wagon with a flat wooden bed was hitched to a team of mules behind the dwarf and tall man. Beyond the wagon was a jet-black mare. Rootless and feral was the mare, red glowing eyes.

"Though poisoned, tonight he finally sits," the dwarf said. "Perhaps tonight he will talk sense. Perhaps tonight Ser Gault will be himself again." The dwarf poked the fire with a long stick. Smoke rose from the prodded fire, orange embers floating skyward.

Gault's hands felt the coarseness of the stiff canvas he had been lying on. There was a tattered beggar's cloak of a faded gray—the exact color of clouds on an overcast day—draped over his legs. He was wearing no armor, just dark leather pants and a raggedy sweat-stained cotton shirt. He felt naked with no armor. He felt naked with no weapons. It was a feeling he had never felt before.

"I'd be thrilled to see him stand and travel on his own," the tall man said. "I'm weary of hauling him in and out of that wagon twice daily."

Gault's eyes slowly focused on the tall man. It was King Borden Bronachell of Amadon. *Do I still dream? Borden Bronachell should be dead!* To see the man now in this strange reality just seemed like more fancy delusion, a trick of the mind.

The last thing he recalled was creeping into Aeros Raijael's bedchamber in the Fortress of Saint Only. He remembered his quest to save Ava Shay. He remembered finding her in Aeros' bed. He remembered sneaking up behind her. He remembered her stabbing him in the heart. He remembered his daughter's face in place of Ava Shay's.

"Have you finished your nap, Ser Gault?" the dwarf asked. "You should be well rested—you slept more than two weeks. Pleasant dreams, I hope."

"Not particularly," Gault muttered, gazing through the pall of wood smoke, trying to focus on the mules and the red-eyed horse behind Borden and the dwarf. He wondered where the animals had come from. He wondered where he was.

"Where am I?" he asked.

"We are headed toward Amadon," a girl's voice sounded from behind him. He craned his neck. *Krista!* His mind reeled and he knew he still dreamed. His stepdaughter's small hand clutched his, fingers entwined with his. She wore the black leathers of a Bloodwood. *She can't be!* Fear coiled in Gault's stomach. Real fear. Like he had never felt before. He felt his heart struggling to do its job.

"Krista?" he asked.

"Yes, it is me, Father."

"Is it really you?" he asked, trembling. It was the face of his daughter, older now. And her countenance was as rigidly serene and empty of expression as that of a Bloodwood. He had been separated from her by such a gulf of time he knew not what to say. "Why are you taking me to Amadon? Why are you taking me back to the enemy?"

"You need critical care," Borden Bronachell said. "You need my Vallè healers if you're to survive what foul Bloodwood poisons are in you."

Gault knew he was still dreaming. "Your Vallè healers can't heal me," he said, almost as if daring them to try. Nothing made sense in this dream! *Or is it the wraiths I fight in my head?* "I hate Amadon."

"He's still so sick," another voice said. A female voice. Familiar. Not Krista.

Ava Shay! Gault's mind reeled. He felt so dizzy. The Gallows Haven girl's thin face floated in the darkness before him, her appearance subdued as always, yet still unbearably beautiful. She wore a blue dress, and there was a curious-looking sword with a ruby-colored hilt tucked into the belt at her slim waist. *Did I save her?*

He wanted to stand up and hug her. But the campsite suddenly spun around him and he could not focus on one single thing. He rubbed his hands over his bald head with fingers suddenly gone cold. Avril. Ava. Krista. Avril. Ava. Krista. Three faces spinning, spinning, spinning before him. And then all things again faded to black.

CHAPTER FIFTY-TWO
Mancellor Allen

1st day of the Heart Moon, 999th year of Laijon

Amadon, Gul Kana

Mancellor Allen was once again summoned to Sunbird Hall along with Liz Hen Neville and Dokie Liddle. Beer Mug accompanied them as always, panting from the heat, tail a-wag. Ever since their arrival, Mancellor, Liz Hen, and Dokie had been the toast of the court. Carrying Jondralyn's body back to Amadon had earned them no small measure of status in the eyes of the nobles, King Jovan included. Parties had been thrown in their honor, and Grand Vicar Denarius made it a practice to kiss the back of Liz Hen's hand at their every meeting. That the Silver Throne and the entire court of Amadon Castle hailed them as heroes was final proof to Mancellor that he had followed the true path Laijon had set out for him, that the long suffering at the hands of the White Prince and Enna Spades had been worth it.

Or had it? Sunbird Hall was nearly empty for today's summoning. Something seemed off today. *Is there to be no grand party?* Liz Hen and Dokie glanced around the hollow chamber warily. Even Beer Mug's tail had stopped its wagging.

The only royals present in Sunbird Hall today besides King Jovan were

Leif Chaparral and his brother, Glade, along with five other Dayknights. Grand Vicar Denarius and all five of the archbishops were there too; Vandivor, Donalbain, Spencerville, Leaford, and Rhys-Duncan. All six churchmen were in their most stately of priesthood robes and finery, jewels encircling their wrists. Leif and Glade and the other Dayknights were all clad in their polished black armor, black longswords at their belts.

Mancellor, Liz Hen, and Dokie had just been introduced to Glade Chaparral a day ago. Mancellor did not know the exact details of the young man's story, but apparently Leif's younger brother had brought Princess Tala Bronachell back to Amadon in chains a week ago. According to Seita, the princess had been thrown into Purgatory for crimes that were never made completely clear. Rumor was the princess had already escaped, much to the consternation of the king. Mancellor did not know how much of the story was true, but Glade Chaparral looked as menacing in his black armor as his older brother, Leif.

Jovan was dressed as the other Dayknights were, only he wore a long black cloak over his Dayknight armor and livery, Aeros Raijael's sword, Sky Reaver, at his side.

Nothing was said as Mancellor, Liz Hen, and Dokie were led into the chamber. But the grand vicar moved toward a large silver urn set upon a three-legged table fashioned of rich wood. The urn was filled to the brim with a clear oil. *Consecrated priesthood oil,* Mancellor surmised. He had seen similar oils used by some of the bishops in his hometown in Wyn Darrè. He wondered if some strange ritual had been going on in here before he and Liz Hen and Dokie had been summoned.

Light beamed down on the urn from above. The balcony doors were thrown wide, casting a soft blush of sunlight over the king's long table and the wine goblets lined upon it. Yet the comfort and warmth of that light did naught to dispel Mancellor's sudden sense of uneasiness. He wore his disquiet like a shroud as he gazed up at that balcony and its elaborate balustrade of flowers and ivy honeyed by the sun.

Grand Vicar Denarius walked around the urn toward Liz Hen. He dipped his head and kissed the back of the girl's hand as he always did, eyes fixed on hers. "I know you have had your disagreements with Leif Chaparral in the past," he said. "But you must know that we are all forever your servants, great lady. Especially me."

Liz Hen blushed deeply, returning his bow. The big girl still wore the clothes and armor she had arrived with in Amadon. As did Dokie. Mancellor too.

Mancellor could see the red streaks growing wild in Liz Hen's eyes. Seita had been feeding the girl Blood of the Dragon ever since they had arrived in the castle. And the drug made the girl look half-crazed.

"Why have you summoned us to this meeting, Your Grace?" Liz Hen asked.

"Absolution is nigh, and you are a hero of the realm," Grand Vicar Denarius answered her. "And I have plans for you and Dokie and even Mancellor Allen. But we shall get to that later." He turned to King Jovan. "My little birds tell me that Aeros Raijael and his armies are ready to depart Saint Only on the morrow, on the second day of the Heart Moon. With the news Ser Mancellor brought us of this woman, Enna Spades, taking what she believed to be the weapons of the Five Warrior Angels back to Aeros, I believe the armies of Sør Sevier shall be most eager to advance, and they shall make haste toward Amadon, unhindered. Once they have successfully crossed the Saint Only Channel into Lord's Point, it will not take them long to reach us. And we shall let them come."

"I can still muster soldiers and fight them." Leif Chaparral limped forward. "I've still thousands and thousands of soldiers. I can slow Aeros' advance. I can stop it."

"Save your enthusiasm for a future day, Ser Leif." The grand vicar bowed to the captain of the Dayknights. "Your part in this is over, and you have performed admirably before the eyes of Laijon. You have done all that could have been asked of you and more. Absolution must now come to *us* for the prophecy to be fulfilled. Absolution must come to Amadon, even to the Hallowed Grove and the Atonement Tree itself. It all must now unfold as *The Way and Truth of Laijon* hath foretold."

The vicar paused and did the three-fingered sign of the Laijon Cross over his heart before continuing. "My little birds have also brought news from the north, confirming many of our suspicions. A Hragna'Ar army is marching south toward Amadon, raping and pillaging and burning all in its path. This is evidenced by those in the path of the oghuls now fleeing to the safety of Amadon. Our streets are now teeming with the refugees. The Vallè princess, Seita, claims this is why Ambassador Val-Korin left for his homeland, to ready his armies for what he knows is coming. Make no mistake, the stars are aligning and Fiery Absolution is nigh."

A dark hush fell over Sunbird Hall. The five archbishops did the three-fingered sign of the Laijon Cross over their own hearts, as did Dokie.

"Absolution is coming and we must ready the Silver Throne." Denarius motioned to the large silver urn. "We must consecrate the throne in oil. We must bless it with renewed strength. Then we must remove it from this hall where it has remained shrouded—no, remained *hidden*—these last five years, and then we must place it under the Atonement Tree as *The Way and Truth of Laijon* commands."

"The throne has been covered at my bidding," Jovan said, the timbre of his voice rising, "covered in honor of my father. It has not been 'hidden,' as you say."

"No. It *has* been hidden," the vicar stated plainly. "You know it and I know it and every knight in this hall knows it. You must uncover your shame, Jovan. And you must do it before these three witnesses." Denarius pointed to Mancellor, Liz Hen, and Dokie.

Another dark hush fell over the room, a hush born of tension. There was an uncomfortable silence between the king and the vicar. Jovan's face reddened in anger.

"Welp, looks like you won't be needing me anymore." It was Liz Hen who broke the silence. "You've a lot to do. So we must be taking our leave now, Dokie, Beer Mug, and I. Mancellor too. We are not good witnesses, that I guarantee."

"Nonsense." The vicar's eyes softened as he looked at her. "We shall need all the brave and heroic hands we can get. And I have not yet revealed all I shall require of you and your friends. Who knows what part a great lady such as yourself may yet have to play in the histories of Gul Kana?"

"With all due respect, I'm fairly certain I have no parts to play in the histories of Gul Kana," Liz Hen said. "And Dokie has even less parts than that. And I don't think Beer Mug even cares. Dogs, you know, they don't even know what history is."

Archbishop Spencerville stepped forward, facing the girl. "Our wise vicar is only saying, your part in this war may not yet be over. Laijon has a plan for you, Liz Hen. You must remember your own Ember Gathering. Surely you are of age. You must remember what oaths you swore."

"What oaths I swore?" Liz Hen's face twisted in disgust. "Any oath I swore to liars and deceivers is no oath at all. I remember that foul ceremony well enough."

"You should not speak of your Ember Gathering like that," the vicar said, his voice soft with persuasion, but tinged with a growing anger. "You must regain that lost testimony of Laijon I know you once had when you were younger. Humble yourself and once again become a devout follower of Laijon and his church."

"I don't have enough hate left in my heart to be a good follower of the church or of Laijon," Liz Hen said. "For it seems hate is what is required most when it comes to matters of religion and utmost belief."

"I still believe," Dokie said, a worried look growing on his face. "I feel no hate and I believe in Laijon and in the church."

"How can you still believe?" Liz Hen asked. "After all the horrors we've seen?"

"I've had dreams. I see visions in the standing stones that I sketch. I've had priesthood blessings and other such spiritual experiences too sacred to explain."

"It's all in your head, you clodpole."

"I cannot deny things of the spirit," Dokie said with conviction.

Liz Hen's face drooped with sadness. "I once used to think my brother's spirit was wandering, that he was reaching out for me. But then I realized it was all in my head. That it was impossible. That Zane was dead. That there was nothing left of him. Not even spirit. It was all the conjuring of my own head."

"The visions I experienced are a gift from Laijon," Dokie said. "I *know* they are. And that I can never deny."

"I've received no such gifts," Liz Hen countered. "What makes you more special than I?"

"Your time will come," the vicar answered her. "Laijon will soften your heart, and you too shall feel that same burning testimony that young Dokie feels, that your king feels, that *I* feel, that all true believers feel."

"Do not listen to the vicar, Miss Liz Hen!" a familiar voice sounded from behind Mancellor. He turned to see Seita striding confidently into the hall, her soft leather boots padding faintly on the tile, blond hair glistening in brilliant silvery waves over her shoulders. The Vallè maiden wore studded leather armor of such a black hue it seemed to swallow all light. An equally black belt and a long brace of thin black daggers circled her waist. Mancellor recalled Spiderwood and his black leather armor and thin black knives hidden everywhere. *Is Seita a Bloodwood too?* It seemed unlikely. *Yet the way she's carried herself, the way she's been teaching Liz Hen and Dokie to fight these last few days?* It suddenly dawned on Mancellor: things in Amadon were not all they seemed.

"What ridiculous outfit is this?" King Jovan was also taken aback by the sight of the Vallè in the black armor. "Whatever it is, it is not maidenly."

"Since when have I ever been maidenly?" Seita asked, standing next to Liz Hen. The Vallè bowed to the red-haired girl. "Do not listen to the vicar, Miss Liz Hen, for all gathered here today know that Denarius molests young girls in the Ember Gathering."

Her comment was met with a stunned silence, as if nobody quite knew how to react to such a bold, damning statement. *Why would she so carelessly provoke them?* Mancellor asked himself. A black dagger suddenly appeared in Seita's hand. Everyone stepped back. The Vallè offered the blade hilt-first to Liz Hen. The big girl took it, fingers automatically curling around the hilt of the black weapon. Mancellor's blood curdled at the sight.

"You dare insult the grand vicar?" Leif Chaparral drew his long black sword. "You dare bring a weapon out in his presence?" The six Dayknights behind Leif also drew their weapons, Glade included. He scowled as darkly as his brother.

Jovan also pulled Sky Reaver in a swift motion, the sword singing from its sheath. The king's brow furrowed dangerously as he pointed the weapon straight at Seita. "What is the meaning of this?" he demanded.

Seita ignored him and addressed Liz Hen. "In ancient days the two ceremonies used to be called Ash Gatherings and Ash Lightings. But the word 'ash' sounded too much like 'ass' when certain bishops and vicars performed the rites. You can imagine this created much giggling and ir-reverence amongst the Ash Gathering and Ash Lighting participants. So they changed 'ash' to 'ember' and thusly solved one problem. The other problem was the bishops diddling the young girls during the ceremony, a practice that continues to this day." Seita shrugged. "Apparently mo-lestation isn't as embarrassing as mistakenly saying the word 'ass.' "

Mancellor felt his own blood boil at this Vallè maiden's coarse blas-phemy.

"Do not continue down this path, Vallè scum," Leif growled.

Seita ignored Leif too, addressing Liz Hen again. "And what did you think of your Ember Gathering?" Liz Hen looked mortified by the question. "It's okay," Seita said. "You can speak of it here. Despite what oaths you took otherwise, you are quite safe, and you needn't be afraid. I shall protect you from any lightning bolts that might strike down from heaven."

"I've been struck by lightning before," Dokie interceded. "It's no jok-ing matter." Liz Hen still looked petrified. "You needn't say anything you don't want to, Liz Hen," Dokie admonished, fear set in his eyes. "I implore you, don't betray your sacred oaths."

Liz Hen looked tormented under Dokie's scrutiny, under everyone's scrutiny. The dagger shook in her hand. She looked down at it, per-plexed. It was like she had almost forgotten it was there.

"Our days are numbered," Seita said. "As the scriptures say, Absolution is swift and shall arrive like a thief in the night, Liz Hen. So say what you want to say before you slay one of the archbishops, before it is time for us to go."

"You are frightening the girl with this nonsense," Jovan raged. "I insist you stop."

Seita leaned in to Liz Hen and whispered, "Remember who it is that feeds you Blood of the Dragon." A change came over Liz Hen's countenance. Resolve was what Mancellor saw in her bloodshot eyes now, and she gripped the dagger tight.

"Do you really want to know what I thought of my Ember Gathering?" Liz Hen straightened her spine and looked straight at Denarius. "I thought it was a bunch of inappropriate twaddle when I was standing there bare-ass naked and covered in ash, swearing oaths and promises I didn't fully understand, swearing them to a bishop I scarcely even knew. Strange, because I was always taught that my Ember Gathering was to be the greatest thing of my life, the greatest thing in all of human existence. But it was just weird. And I felt violated. But with all the oaths of secrecy I swore, who could I ever discuss my concerns and fears with?"

"She speaks the unspeakable," Glade Chaparral snarled. "Are we to let this continue?"

"You are right, brother," Leif said. "For this blasphemy she should be killed, hung, beheaded. Right now! That is, if Laijon does not strike her dead himself!"

"Hush." The grand vicar waved them both off with a gesture. "Her words will be forgotten soon enough, for her words are naught but the ramblings of a confused little girl. She shall be forgiven. And that is all."

"'Confused little girl'?" Liz Hen's fingers tightened around the hilt of her dagger. She stepped toward the vicar. "I am not confused. I am not a little girl."

"Not a step farther," Leif warned. Glade moved up beside him, black Dayknight sword menacing in his grip, pointed right at Liz Hen.

"Relax." Denarius gestured for both Leif and Glade to lower their blades. "She will do no one any harm. I shall administer priesthood blessings to her later. I shall gift her comfort of a sort only the grand vicarship can give. She shall soon be set straight in the eyes of Laijon. And she shall soon be forgiven in the eyes of the priesthood. Like Lawri Le Graven before her, Liz Hen Neville is but a confused little girl."

"I already said I am no confused little girl," Liz Hen growled, her thick body coiled with emotion. "I am no confused little girl."

"Be grateful Laijon is still with you," the vicar said. "Despite what misguided words of blasphemy you speak, he is still with you. He is still your Lord."

"I do not know if Laijon was ever my Lord." Liz Hen stood her ground before the vicar. "Or if he is anyone's Lord, for that matter. You must understand I've many doubts on the matter of late. You would too, had you seen the things I have seen. So I doubt any of it is true."

"There is no value in doubt." The vicar softened his voice. "It is like a poisonous mushroom, a word of no significance or worth. In this time of Absolution, a doubter is a stagnant being, content with untruth, unwilling to do the hard work it takes to cultivate great faith and belief, to pay the price of divine discovery no matter what the trial. Doubt substitutes cynicism and ridicule for reason. The doubt planted within you by Seita, the doubt that feeds and grows upon itself and breeds more doubt, is pure evil."

"I am not evil for doubting," Liz Hen countered. "Nor is Seita. I have always done my best to live the tenets of Laijon. That I have fallen into doubt, that I have spoken aloud of my Ember Gathering, does that make me evil?"

Mancellor was conflicted. It seemed things were calming down between the vicar and Liz Hen, like they were having an actual conversation now. There were times in his own life where he'd wanted to shout to the world that he had faith in Laijon, faith enough for both Liz Hen and himself. He was certain that his faith had brought him to this very spot. He could not understand how Liz Hen could see the events of her life leading up to this point in time so vastly differently than he. *We've practically shared the same journey, yet she sees the world entirely opposite of me.*

"You must come to a certain knowledge of Laijon, Liz Hen," Denarius continued. "That is, if you wish to return to the light. You must rid yourself of this doubt in this time of Absolution, shed it from your body, and,

I repeat, come to a certain knowledge of Laijon and his great atonement, else you will be left less than human."

"'A certain knowledge'?" Liz Hen questioned.

"Aye." The vicar nodded. "A certain knowledge, for as I've stated thrice before, doubt is altogether evil."

"No," Liz Hen said emphatically. "I was a rotten person until I gave in to my doubt. I was a rotten person when I was so certain of my belief. I was a rotten person when I knew my faith was noble. It was doubt that saved me from all that rottenness and hate—"

"Such words are poison," Archbishop Spencerville cut her off.

"Such words are the *truth*," Liz Hen fired back.

"Perhaps there truly is no forgiveness for you." Spencerville placed himself between Denarius and Liz Hen. "Must we continue to listen to this girl?" he asked. "My patience has worn thin, Denarius. How can you let her go on?" Spencerville stepped up and thrust his finger up into Liz Hen's face. "You are less than human, girl. You've only a weak female mind to blame for your own rottenness and loss of faith and misplaced doubt. And to break faith with Denarius is to break faith with Laijon. You should beg his forgiveness and not question."

"'Not question'?" Seita repeated with scorn. "We must all have a willingness to question everything and everyone. And anyone who preaches that doubt is wrong and only for the weak-minded is the most sinister and self-serving of souls. Liz Hen is a victim, a victim of falsehoods; blaming her for her own conflicting thoughts is not the answer. It is not Liz Hen's fault that Laijon's words are so unfocused and confusing and contradictory. It is not Liz Hen's fault that the Ember Gathering is so ritualistic and inappropriate and creepy. It is not Liz Hen's fault that this world is on fire and that if Laijon were real he could stop the suffering in the twinkling of an eye. None of it is her fault. So do not blame her for not believing."

"That's right," Liz Hen said, bolstered by Seita's impassioned defense of her. "I will not be blamed for questioning. I will not be called 'less than' for reasoning it out in my own mind and coming to my own conclusions. I will not be called 'less than' or poisonous for purposefully leaving my own faith where it belongs, in the dust under my own feet."

"I name you blasphemer!" Archbishop Spencerville raged. "Your sins are great—"

"Says who?" Liz Hen cut him short.

"Says Laijon!" Spencerville bellowed. "Laijon speaks through the mantle of the vicar!"

"Laijon can speak through my ass!" Liz Hen shouted.

Leif Chaparral's loud laughter echoed through the hall as he imposed himself between Spencerville and the girl. Leif said, "Laijon could indeed speak through the bunghole of a girl. Laijon could even speak through the red puckered anus of an Adin Wyte goat if he so wanted, same as he could speak from the heights of the stars. And all he says is true. For my part, I am sick of listening to this girl!" He held up his sword and looked at Jovan. "I beg of you, grant me permission to slay this blasphemous, fat bitch here and now." His eyes flew to Seita next, the force of his gaze as if it were a spear lancing toward her. "And let me slay the Vallè slut, too."

Liz Hen backed away from Leif, dagger still gripped tight in her hand.

"Where do you go, girl?" Leif snarled.

"As- as I said before," Liz Hen stuttered, "we- we must take our leave, you know, Dokie and I. Beer Mug, and Mancellor too. We- we've been more than a burden on the kingship already." She bowed to the king, the sharp black tip of her dagger now unsteady in her grip. "I do hope our paths cross again." She whirled to run from Sunbird Hall.

And ran smack into Archbishop Spencerville, the entire blade of her black dagger sinking to the hilt in his stomach.

Spencerville's eyes widened in pain. Liz Hen stepped back, pulling the dagger free of the man's gut. "I'm so t- terribly sorry," she stammered.

The archbishop stumbled back, clutching his stomach. Blood welled dark and red from between the man's straining fingers as he backed into the large silver urn. The urn toppled from the table. It shook the hall as it struck the tiles with a thunderous crash, consecrated oil splashing across the floor. Spencerville dropped unceremoniously next to the urn.

He coughed, one great wheezing gasp, blood spurting from between pursed lips. Then his eyes rolled up, whites showing stark and pale.

Stunned, Liz Hen stared down at the scarlet-dripping dagger in her hands. "I seriously do beg everyone's pardon for that."

Vandivor and Rhys-Duncan cried out in horror, both archbishops rushing toward their fallen comrade, nearly slipping in the oil. Archbishop Donalbain performed the three-fingered sign of the Laijon Cross over his heart. Archbishop Leaford bent over and vomited. Mancellor felt sick to his stomach too. The girl would surely hang now.

"He's dying," Vandivor cried, trying to slow the blood.

"Bloody rotted angels." Leif brought his sword up to the ready. Glade was right behind him, sword also poised. "Say the word, Jovan, and I kill her!" Leif shouted. "I will gut her like she gutted Spencerville. If it please Your Excellency, I will gut her good!"

"I didn't do anything," Liz Hen said as Spencerville's blood pooled outward. The wounded man's breaths were growing shallow. "I didn't do anything," she repeated, dagger adrip with red. "I swear it. I did nothing."

Did nothing?" Jovan bellowed, incredulity lacing each word. He pointed the tip of Sky Reaver at the red-haired girl. "You assassinated one of the quorum of five! I hardly call that nothing! I think I shall help Leif in gutting you!"

Beer Mug was suddenly between Liz Hen and the three armed men, hackles raised, spitting and snarling, glistening sharp teeth bared. Leif and Glade stepped back. Jovan did too. The remaining Dayknights drew their black swords. For a moment the only sound in the chamber was the dog's menacing growl.

"I must say," Seita said in mild amusement, two black daggers gripped in her hands, "I've never seen such accidental chaos look so stunningly bloody. A master assassin could not have done better." A look of smug satisfaction was on the Vallè maiden's face as she bowed to Liz Hen.

This is all Seita's doing. Mancellor was angry. The Vallè maiden had practically signed Liz Hen's death warrant.

"You'll hang for this," Leif said, pointing his blade at Liz Hen once more. "And there'll be no bishop to die in your stead this time. That's if I don't gut you first."

Mancellor was stunned they hadn't already gutted Liz Hen. It seemed everyone was still in shock from the suddenness of the accident.

"'Twas but an innocent mistake," Dokie pleaded. "We all saw."

"'Twas no mistake," Grand Vicar Denarius said, looking at Liz Hen. "What have you done, girl?"

"It's an unexplainable matter," Liz Hen stammered, holding the black dagger out for the vicar, almost like a peace offering. "It's an unexplainable mystery. Truly none of my doing. And I beg you make me no part of it."

"Make you no part of it?" Jovan asked. "You've killed him." The king gestured to the remaining Dayknights. "Kill her. And kill the dog, too. But not before I get the first swing."

It all happened so fast, Mancellor wasn't sure he saw everything. Jovan launched himself toward Liz Hen, Sky Reaver slicing toward the girl's head in a streak of blue. Seita danced between the king's arcing blade and Liz Hen, her black daggers countering the king's blow. Sky Reaver twisted from Jovan's hands, the blue sword skipping across the stone floor.

"Grab the king's blade!" Seita yelled at Dokie. Then she spun, blocking both Leif's and Glade's blows, sending both brothers reeling back. Dokie snatched up Sky Reaver from the floor. The Vallè maiden moved with a swift and bold dexterity Mancellor had never before seen, weaving a web of black steel, blocking the advance of the remaining Dayknights, who had set themselves upon her. Beer Mug launched himself at the first Dayknight to engage Seita, and, taking the man down by the calves, together they rolled in a heap of black armor and gray fur.

Seita struck down the next knight in line. "Run for the balcony!" she shouted at Liz Hen. "Climb over the railing once you're outside. There's a rope attached to the balustrade. Climb down the rope to the open hatchway below. It will take you into the secret ways. Don't worry, I will be right behind you."

Liz Hen did not hesitate; she sprinted toward the stairs at the far end of the hall. Dokie followed the girl, Sky Reaver in hand. Seita disengaged from the fight and leaped over the downed knight at her feet, following Liz Hen and Dokie up the balcony stairs. Beer Mug broke away from the Dayknight he was wrestling with and scrambled up the stairs after Seita, Liz Hen, and Dokie.

"Don't let them escape!" Jovan roared. "The boy stole my sword!"

Leif and Glade and the remaining Dayknights burst toward the balcony.

At the top of the stairs, Seita whirled, two Bloodwood daggers spinning through the air. Two Dayknights crumpled to the floor, thin black knives buried hilt-deep in the eye slits of their black helms. Mancellor watched it all, unmoving, stunned at how Seita moved with such cruel elegance.

Outside, atop the balcony, Liz Hen had already found the rope tied to the balustrade. Gripping it, she hefted one leg over the railing and then the other, lowering herself slowly down the rope. Beer Mug watched her descend, a whimper in his throat.

"What about Beer Mug?" Liz Hen cried.

"You'll have to let the dog go if you wish to escape!" Seita pushed the girl down the rope. "Go!"

"No!" Liz Hen screeched.

"Go!" Seita shouted, shoving the struggling girl down the rope.

Leif and Glade reached the top of the balcony. Two more daggers spun from Seita's hands, one glancing off Leif's shoulder plate as he stumbled back down the stairs, the other dagger bouncing off the breastplate of Glade, who staggered to his knees, clutching his chest.

"Go!" Seita shouted at Liz Hen again.

Liz Hen lowered herself down the rope, round, worried face disappearing from sight. Dokie handed Sky Reaver to Seita and followed the big girl over the railing, gripping the rope tight, eyes wide when he saw the gaping drop beyond.

Seita leaped up on the ivy-choked railing of the balustrade, fresh air glazed with calm behind her. She turned to face the remaining knights advancing up the stairs. To Mancellor she made for a formidable black silhouette against the bright azure skies. She held Sky Reaver up taunt-ingly, sun glinting blue shards off its glimmering blade.

"To Absolution!" she shouted, then took one step back, dropping from view.

Beer Mug was left alone on the balcony. He barked and cried, racing back and forth at the foot of the balustrade, knowing to leap over it would be a long fall to the rocky crags below. The first knight up the stairs took a ponderous swipe at the dog with his black sword. Beer Mug dodged the blow, and the sword sparked off the stone railing. The dog lunged at the young knight's legs, knocking the man aside as he raced back down the stairs toward Mancellor.

"Grab him!" Jovan shouted. "Don't let that dog get away!"

Mancellor watched as Beer Mug sprinted past him across the cham-ber and out the front doors of Sunbird Hall, plunging into the depths of the castle, barking as he ran.

"Why did you not stop him?" Jovan looked at Mancellor accusingly.

"I traveled a long way with that dog." Mancellor didn't know whether he would be hanged for his answer, but he said it anyway. "Beer Mug is a friend. He's just a dog. What harm can he do?"

"Idiot." Jovan turned to Leif Chaparral, who was making his way back down the stairs, his brother, Glade, following.

"What the bloody fuck just happened?" the king asked them. "That girl just killed Spencerville. And they made off with my sword. They stole Sky Reaver. And they did so right under your nose, Leif Chaparral. How is this possible? How did this happen?"

"The rope above is cut," Leif said. "We cannot follow them. I can send a man to scale the cliff below to find the hatchway Seita described."

"She betrayed us," Jovan exclaimed, eyes darting around the hall in frustration. "The skinny Vallè bitch."

"I never did like her," Leif said.

"We will hunt them down," Glade said. "Kill them all. I shall get your sword back for you, my king."

Jovan stared back up at the open balcony above. "And what was that nonsense the Vallè shouted?"

"To Absolution," Grand Vicar Denarius answered, eyes locked on the overturned urn of oil. "She shouted, 'To Absolution!'"

"But what does it mean?" Jovan asked.

"It means Seita knows the words in *The Way and Truth of Laijon* more than even you, my king," Denarius snapped, gaze traveling from the urn back down to Archbishop Spencerville. "It means that because of what happened here today, Absolution is now closer than we all can know."

"I don't understand."

"Of course you don't understand, Your Excellency!" the vicar shouted. "In *The Way and Truth of Laijon*, in the Acts of the Second Warrior Angel, it says, and I quote, 'I prophesy unto you, my faithful kin, a most blessed archbishop shall be murdered by means most foul. He shall lie in state with one of royal blood, only to rise again before Fiery Absolution. For only the dead can usher in the return of Laijon.'"

"What are you saying?" Jovan asked.

"I am saying that prophecy has been fulfilled. Spencerville is dead, murdered by means most foul. And now he will search the underworld for the soul of Jondralyn. He shall bring her forth when he arises, and she shall live once more."

It is told that a Vallè maiden of royal blood can see ahead to what the future holds, but her knowledge of the present is never clear.
—The Way and Truth of Laijon

CHAPTER FIFTY-THREE

NAIL

1st day of the Heart Moon, 999th year of Laijon
Amadon, Gul Kana

Seita said we'd find a friend in here." Liz Hen Neville's boister-ous voice cut through the darkness of the Slaver's Inn, startling Nail from his nap. "But she didn't tell us that we would find two friends."

"Both Nail *and* Hawkwood!" Dokie Liddle exclaimed, stepping out from behind Liz Hen, a familiar curved blue sword in his hand.

Nail had been sitting in boredom and half slumber at a table in the farthest corner of the tavern with Hawkwood, Tala, Cromm, Bronwyn, and Lawri, when Liz Hen had come waddling up, Dokie with her.

"Dokie!" Nail shot up from his chair and rushed to his friend, wrap-ping both arms around the smaller boy's shoulders in a most welcome clench. He was overjoyed and could feel the tears forming in his eyes. But he would not cry.

Hawkwood stood from the table and hugged Liz Hen. "Well met, Liz Hen, well met again. I must say it is good to see you."

Liz Hen pulled away from Hawkwood and faced Nail. There was a moment of awkward silence; then she grinned from ear to ear. "I am so happy to see you, Nail. I so feared you were dead, and then Seita told us you lived."

"Your hair is shorter," Nail said.

"Is that all you have to say, you clodpole?" Liz Hen huffed. Then she slugged him in the shoulder. Gently this time, not like she used to, and with the smile growing even wider.

"I am glad to see you, too." Nail leaned in and hugged her.

She blushed in his embrace, squeezing him tight in return. He let her go, and he could see tears in her eyes.

"Where is Beer Mug?" he asked. "Last I saw he was running off across the glacier. But I figured he would find you. Did he?"

"He did," Liz Hen blubbered. "He did. And now he is gone again. Missing."

Nail felt his own heart crawl up into his throat. "What happened?"

"Seita said not to worry," Dokie answered. "She said Beer Mug would find us again. Soon. And I hope he does."

"Seita?" Nail asked. "You've seen her, too?"

"Aye," Dokie continued. "She was just outside. She said go on into the tavern, a very good friend awaits you inside. She said we shouldn't need her until the morning of Fiery Absolution. She said Fiery Absolution is almost upon us. Said it will be here sooner than you think. And then it will be over in the blink of an eye. She snapped her fingers as she said the 'blink of an eye' part. And then she took off."

"I thought she might mean that it was Val-Draekin who awaited us here," Liz Hen said. "I wasn't expecting you and Hawkwood."

"I reckon it could have even been Mancellor awaiting us in here," Dokie said.

"Mancellor?" Bronwyn Allen stood, the whites of her eyes sparking behind black tattoos, brows furrowed in heavy concentration under her green hood. "Did you say 'Mancellor'? That is my brother's name." She pulled the hood back from her tattooed face, the two feathers tied in her hair soft and white against her dark locks. Cromm stood up next to her. A look of fear crossed both Liz Hen's and Dokie's faces at the sight of the towering oghul standing before them, broad back against the wall.

"Who is this Mancellor you name?" Cromm growled.

Dokie raised the curved blue sword up before Cromm. "I have this to kill oghuls with now."

"Please put that blade away." Lawri Le Graven blurted, staring at the blade in Dokie's hand, horror in her eyes. "That blade took my arm." She sat next to Tala, the sleeve of the dark cloak pulled up over the silver gauntlet attached to her arm.

Dokie lowered the blade. "How'd this sword take your arm?"

"Never mind that." Lawri slunk back from him, retreating farther into the shadows of her cloak.

"That's my brother's sword," Tala said, standing and eyeing Dokie warily. "The sword Leif Chaparral gifted him, the one Leif stole from Aeros Raijael."

"And who are you?" Liz Hen asked.

"I am Tala Bronachell."

Dokie did the three-fingered sign of the Laijon Cross over his heart with his free hand and then bowed. "M'lady princess."

Liz Hen stood still as a stone. "Are you really the princess?"

"She is," Nail said, feeling somewhat proud of the esteemed company Liz Hen and Dokie had found him in. "She is Tala Bronachell, princess of Amadon."

Liz Hen stared at Tala, her face a stiff mask of doubt. "She is the princess?"

Cromm Cru'x leaned over the table, gnarled hand offered toward Liz Hen in greeting, the jewels embedded in his knuckles a faint sparkle in the dim light. "I am Cromm Cru'x." His voice was a deep rumble. "Again, who is this Mancellor you speak of?"

Liz Hen did not shake Cromm's hand. Instead she retreated a step, scowling, arms folded over her chest. Then she unfolded her arms and nervously rubbed her neck as if rubbing away a bad memory. The oghul withdrew his hand.

"Cromm senses you have something negative to say to him."

"I've nothing to say," Liz Hen answered.

"But you do," Cromm insisted. "Spit it out, girl."

Liz Hen continued rubbing her neck, looking from Cromm's cold eyes to Nail and then toward Hawkwood and then back. "I, well, I am surprised that you can talk, Ser oghul."

Cromm folded his own large arms over his own broad chest. "So Cromm can talk? What of it?"

"'What of it'?" Liz Hen's eyes darted around the table again. "Well, I beg your pardon for saying, but the only oghuls I ever knew were the grunting and killing kind."

Cromm grinned. "Most oghuls *are* the grunting and killing kind." The jewels in his long fangs sparkled. "Perhaps I shall grunt at you instead. Then kill you—"

"Stop teasing." Bronwyn cut the oghul short. Her brows still furrowed as she studied both Liz Hen and Dokie. "You said the name Mancellor earlier, did you not?"

Liz Hen squinted at the girl, then back at Cromm, as if trying to figure out what exactly was going on, trying to figure if this wasn't some cruel conjurer's trick, a talking oghul in a tavern. She was growing fidgety, both of her hands now trying to cover her flushed neck as she stared at the oghul.

"Yes, Mancellor was his name," Dokie said, keeping the curved blue sword behind his back and out of Lawri's sight. "Mancellor was with us in the castle before we escaped over the balcony. He helped us bring Princess Jondralyn back to Amadon."

"You were with the Wyn Darrè man who brought my sister back from Savon?" Tala asked.

"Aye," Dokie answered. "We were with Mancellor Allen."

Bronwyn exchanged glances with Cromm. "Mancellor Allen?" she repeated.

"Aye." Dokie nodded. "Mancellor Allen of Wyn Darrè. He helped us escape Lord's Point and the Untamed. Helped with Jondralyn. He is a most valiant of knights."

"My brother lives." Bronwyn looked at Cromm.

"So you knew Mancellor?" Dokie asked.

"He was my brother," Bronwyn said. "I mean, he *is* my brother."

Nail could see the tears forming in her eyes. It was odd, as hard as the girl was.

"When did you last see Mancellor?" Cromm asked.

"Earlier today," Dokie answered. "Like we said, in Amadon Castle. Mancellor was there when Liz Hen killed the archbishop."

"Killed the archbishop?" Tala exclaimed.

"Aye." Dokie nodded. "Stabbed him right in the guts."

"Which archbishop?"

"The fat one."

"Spencerville," Tala muttered.

"That's the one." Dokie nodded again.

"It wasn't my fault." Liz Hen's eyes were wide with both horror and fear. She elbowed Dokie hard in the shoulder. "Why did you tell the Princess Tala about the archbishop, you stupid? She'll think bad of me now. She'll think I am some kind of assassin out to slay everyone."

"Nobody will think bad of you, Liz Hen," Hawkwood interjected. "But it sounds like we all have stories to tell. Let us sit and sort things out over some dinner." He motioned to the burly man behind the bar across the room, then glanced at Liz Hen and Dokie. "You two look famished. A bowl of stew would do you some good."

"Stew?" Liz Hen turned up her nose. "From that man?" She was giving the stink eye to the bartender across the tavern. "Don't look like much of a chef to me."

"I'll talk to the bartender about getting you a better meal," Dokie said.

"Talk to the *bartender* about a better meal?" Liz Hen repeated. "Why don't you just talk to a pile of my ripe shit while you're at it, for all the good it will do?"

"What is wrong with this girl who always complains?" Cromm asked.

"I don't always complain," Liz Hen said.

"She doesn't like any tavern food served to her by a man." Dokie shrugged.

The oghul nodded. "That does make some sense to Cromm. I too prefer a woman-cooked meal."

Bronwyn looked at the oghul askance. "Since when has the gender of a cook mattered to you?"

"Cromm is just trying not to tease the girl as you asked." The oghul sat down, leaning his back against the wall. "Cromm is just trying to find common ground. At the moment, Cromm is just an oghul trying to make friends."

"Well," Dokie said, looking up at Hawkwood. "Do you think I could at least ask the bartender if he has an extra parchment and some charcoal? I have been itching to draw again for some time."

"I'm sure he can bring you all the parchment you desire," Hawkwood said, gesturing to the empty chairs at the table. "Let us all sit. Let us all catch up."

**

Stew was served. The stew was good. They all partook but for Lawri Le Graven, who just sat silently. Dokie looked frightened to death of the girl. He was careful to keep the blue sword hidden from her sight. But then the bartender brought Dokie his parchment and charcoal, and the boy began drawing.

Stories were exchanged. Liz Hen gave everyone a quick rundown of all that had happened to them since she and Dokie had parted with Nail atop the Sky Lochs glacier. In turn, Nail related his story to them, leaving out the part about Lawri's silver arm. Liz Hen showed extreme dismay at the fact that the black angel stone had been faked by Seita.

"Stefan is lost," she said with sadness. "Roguemoore dead. Godwyn and Culpa Barra, too. Val-Draekin likely also dead. The weapons and angel stones all lost. And Seita bringing a fake angel stone back from the north? I like her. But clearly Nail and Tala and many others do not trust her. So much for the Company of Nine." She looked at Nail. "It is only we three left: Dokie, me, and you."

Dokie looked up from his drawing. "All I know is that Seita saved our lives many times in the Sky Loch mines. And she saved us in the castle, helped us escape, and brought us here to safety. I do not see how she has betrayed anyone by conjuring up a fake angel stone."

Liz Hen's brow crinkled at that. But she did not counter Dokie's argument.

"How would Seita know that Nail was even here?" Tala asked with real fear in her voice. "She probably knows we are all here. She could betray us to my brother."

"She is a Bloodwood," Hawkwood said. "And Bloodwoods have a way of knowing everything. She will not tell Jovan of our whereabouts, especially considering all the trouble she went through to get Liz Hen and Dokie here safely."

"If only she could have saved Beer Mug, too," Dokie said, then went back to his drawing.

"Despite what Seita said earlier, I fear Beer Mug will never find us again," Liz Hen said, hands fidgeting nervously atop the table. "The more I think about it, the more I realize he is truly gone. Jovan would not have let him live. He is not that type of man. I've worried for that dog this whole journey, and now that I know he is never coming back, I feel almost relieved." Tears were running down her cheeks. "Relieved, yes. And angry, too. I'm so angry. And so sad. And frustrated. And so confused. And lost. I want to fight. To kill. I feel all things bad. No things good."

"You have to make your own reality," Hawkwood said. "For I see that look of both hopeful melancholy and sheer anger on your face, Liz Hen. I recognize it, for I have been there too. It is easy to go through life with your hand balled into a fist, ready to fight, ready to strike out and kill. It's far more difficult opening up those hands to receive, to give, to love."

"But love never lasts," Tala said, saying what Nail was thinking. And then he felt his own mind wander. *Has anyone ever loved me?* In his dreams, yes. Bits and pieces of memory were slowly coming back to him through his dreams. And it all tied back to one singular day upon the Sky Lochs glacier. Not the day when he had fallen through the ice with Roguemoore and Val-Draekin. But rather when he was atop that glacier as a child. All he remembered of that day was his mother holding him. Or maybe it wasn't his mother, but some woman who looked after him. He'd been having many dreams as of late about this woman carrying him over the Sky Lochs glacier. Blood covered her back. Men in dark hoods chased them, horses with red-glowing eyes. Bloodwoods. It was all so similar to the dreams that had haunted him as a child. But these dreams were different. For despite all, these dreams were not the nightmares of old, for the woman in these dreams held him as if she truly did love him, and he basked in her touch. *Was I truly once loved?* When he broke out of his reverie, Hawkwood was still talking to Tala.

"As a Bloodwood, I was empty. Lonely, like most of you at this table. My real name and face had been stripped away, replaced with a false shell named Hawkwood, a man wearing naught but an erroneous mask of lies. But with Jondralyn I found the life I was searching for, with her I felt whole. Where is family, where are my friends, where is my place to call home? I found all that in Jondralyn. Your sister helped shape a purpose and peace in my life I had never before felt, Tala. Love does last."

"You're breaking my heart, Hawkwood," Liz Hen said.

"Mine too," Tala echoed. "Because what you say is not reality. Because Jondralyn died in the end, and your love was still lost. Mine too. If I ever knew it. I went to Savon to save my sister, to tell her the black angel stone she carried was a fake, that none of the weapons would work without the real stone. And that is probably why the weapons didn't work for her."

Cromm Cru'x pulled the real black angel stone from under his bottom lip and set it out on the table in a gray pool of his own spit.

"What's that?" Liz Hen asked. Her hands still nervously fidgeted, moving from atop the table to under it to back on top and over and over.

"The angel stone," Cromm answered.

"You keep the angel stone in your mouth?" Liz Hen was aghast.

"For Cromm it is the safest place," the oghul said.

"'The safest place'?" Liz Hen mimicked sarcastically. "Are you crazy?" Her previous nervousness was gone.

The oghul leaned forward, both heavy elbows resting on the table. "Do you mock Cromm?" he asked.

"Do I mock Cromm?" Liz Hen asked. "Why do you keep saying your own name like that when you speak?"

Cromm's thick brows narrowed sharply.

"You are upsetting him," Bronwyn warned. "Be wary, I'm in no mood for an unscheduled bloodletting."

But Liz Hen plowed on fearlessly. "Well, why does he say his own name every time he talks?"

"My pardon." Cromm sat back, grinning, making sure all his jeweled teeth were exposed. "But Cromm does not speak the human tongue soft and pretty like you, Miss Liz Hen. Cromm speaks how Cromm speaks. With no apologies. For *I* am the oghul who escorts the marked one to Absolution." His eyes found Nail.

"The marked one?" Liz Hen also looked at Nail. "You call Nail 'the marked one'? Why?"

"Because he is the marked one," Cromm answered, nodding to Nail. "He bears the marks. Show her. So she can see that Cromm is not crazy."

Nail saw the look of concern that came over Tala's face. Still, he showed Liz Hen the slave brand on the underside of his wrist and the cross on the back of his hand. He pushed the arm of his shirt up, revealing the tattoo and the scars on his bicep.

"Well, I knew about the slave brand," Liz Hen said. "But how did you get those other scars?"

"From a mermaid."

"How horrid." She looked at him harshly, horrified.

"A mermaid attacked me when I was saving your brother, when I was saving Zane from the sharks on the grayken hunt."

"Oh." Liz Hen grew somber, her face softening. "Oh."

"See," Cromm said. "He is the marked one."

Liz Hen turned to the oghul. "And Cromm thinks those marks mean something?"

"Cromm is certain they do."

"Well, ain't that something interesting indeed."

There was a moment of silence, filled by Dokie's soft scratching of charcoal on parchment. He hadn't looked up from his drawing for a while now, though he seemed to be listening.

Cromm leaned forward on the table, baring his teeth at Liz Hen. "You think you're special, don't you? Don't you?"

"Well," Liz Hen said, "I do believe I have an aura about me."

"You think you have an *aura* about you?"

"We all have auras," Dokie said, shifting the sketch he had been working on, turning it upside down, then going back to work.

"The boy is right," Bronwyn said with a wry smile, winking at the oghul. "Liz Hen does have a bit of an aura, Cromm."

The oghul sat back, grinning. "Cromm sees no *auras*."

"Don't you have even one compliment for the girl?" Bronwyn asked.

"Sure," Cromm said, staring at Liz Hen. "Your hair is like a wild . . . and red . . . What is Cromm meaning to say? Your hair like a flower."

"Flowers make me sneeze," Liz Hen said.

"She's had little luck when sneezing around oghuls." Dokie looked up from his drawing glancing at Nail. "Right? Remember Sky Loch mine?"

Nail nodded.

Cromm was still staring at Liz Hen. "Cromm says past failures should not determine one's future, especially when it comes to sneezing."

"That's preposterous," she said. "Oghuls should not offer up philosophies."

Cromm scowled. "Then forget that nice thing Cromm said about your hair. Cromm should light your head on fire. Make you eat your own ears."

There was a fire igniting in Liz Hen's eyes. "And I should pluck those girly little gems from your knuckles and teeth and cram them up your leathery, large anus."

"No man goes near Cromm's anus."

"And I am no man."

"Could have fooled Cromm." The oghul clenched his fists. "Cromm wagers your mother was as fat and manly as you."

"You dare slur my dear departed mother?" Liz Hen gasped.

"Cromm dares. And Cromm wagers your mother was so fat that if she was to come into this tavern . . . she would order all the food on the menu."

Dokie let out a small chuckle at that. Cromm laughed at his own joke too.

"Order all the food on the menu?" Liz Hen scrunched up her face in disgust. "That didn't even make any sense. Not a lick of sense. And it certainly wasn't funny."

"And you could do better?"

"I could."

"Then show Cromm."

Liz Hen swallowed hard, then fired, "Your mother was so fat that when the Vallè sawbones diagnosed her with skin disease . . . he gave her a hundred years to live."

Silence followed her joke.

"I don't get it." Dokie looked up from his drawing.

"What's not to get?" Liz Hen said. "It's brilliant."

Dokie studied his drawing a moment, then said, "I like the oghul's joke where your mother eats everything on the menu."

"Cromm wins!" Cromm slapped the table, eyes gleaming at Liz Hen. "You're a wicked wench, but thanks for all the laughs."

"Cromm won nothing." Liz Hen slapped the table too.

"Liz Hen is jealous," Cromm laughed. "Because she is less pretty than Cromm."

Liz Hen huffed, "Well, your mother was so ugly—"

"*Enough!*" Bronwyn cut her off with a wave of the hand. "You two idiots can discuss what atrocities you might do to each other and how fat and ugly each other's mothers are at another time." She was staring at Dokie's drawing. "But have none of you been watching what Dokie has been drawing? It is something interesting indeed." She pointed at the parchment in front of Dokie.

Liz Hen was looking at the drawing too. "You drew something similar before. I saw it when I was with Bishop Godwyn, in the cabin in the mountains, right before the oghuls burst in and one of them—" Liz Hen cut herself short, looking at Cromm darkly.

"Anyway," Liz Hen continued. "You have all the Warrior Angels in this drawing too. But you also drew a girl on a throne with a large claw for a hand. Half her skin colored black. As if the claw is burning her. Is it me?"

Nail stared at Dokie's drawing. A tingle of pain raced over the scars and marks on his flesh. It was a simple sketch, five stick figures, each with a weapon: ax, sword, war helm, crossbow, and shield. But there was also a sixth figure, a girl on a throne as Liz Hen had described. And the girl had a claw for a hand. *Like my vision underwater with the mermaid!* The scars from the mermaid flared with pain.

"I always draw a picture similar to this one," Dokie said. "Leastwise ever since I was struck by the lightning."

"Can Liz Hen draw?" Cromm asked. "Can she write? If so, put ink to paper, girl, and write Cromm something nasty."

Liz Hen glared at the oghul. "What do you make of this drawing?" she said, sliding the parchment across the table toward Hawkwood. "Remember when we traveled from the Swithen Wells Trail Abbey down to Ravenker, Dokie mostly just sketched the symbols on the standing stones we passed? But here he's drawn five figures, each with a weapon like the Five Warrior Angels. This person with the crossbow is clearly me, and the figure with the shield is clearly Dokie, I think. But who are the other three? Nail? The one with the ax could certainly be him. Could any of them be you, Hawkwood?"

The Sør Sevier man studied the drawing carefully, brow furrowed. Liz Hen went on, "But who is this sixth figure on the throne with the large claw hand?"

"It's a gauntlet," Lawri Le Graven's soft voice answered. "Not a claw."

All eyes were on Tala's cousin now. Lawri's eyes seemed to glow with an inner light, twinkling like twin emerald stars in the gloomy corner of the tavern.

"It is not a claw in the drawing," Lawri went on. "It's this."

She pulled the cloak back from her arm, revealing the scaled silver gauntlet attached to her arm.

Dokie Liddle scooted his chair back in alarm. "Aye, Laijon save me!" He did the three-fingered sign of the Laijon Cross over his heart. "That gauntlet right there is what I see in my dreams."

"So that's what you meant about the blue sword taking your arm," Liz Hen said.

Lawri nodded.

"But half of your body ain't rotted like in Dokie's drawing," Liz Hen said.

Lawri pulled the cloak off her arm so all could see. Her skin was naught but green patches of rot around the base of the gauntlet. But that wasn't all; glowing emerald streaks twined like crooked lightning up the length of her arm, disappearing under the cloak. Dokie did the three-fingered sign of the Laijon Cross over his heart a second time.

"Bloody rotted angels," Liz Hen exclaimed, a look of pure terror on her face. "What sort of foul witchcraft is this?"

Lawri covered her arm with the cloak and slouched back in her chair, embarrassment flushing over her face. Nail wanted to reach out to the girl, offer her comfort, soothe over Liz Hen's unfeeling reaction. But the scars on his own flesh began to burn with more vigor. He slipped his hand up the sleeve of his shirt, scratching nervously at the mermaid's scars, breathing heavily.

"Blessed Mother Mia and the baby Raijael too," Liz Hen exclaimed, staring at him now. "You're sweating up a storm, Nail. What in the bloody fucking underworld has gotten into you? And just when I thought you were becoming normal again!"

"The scars on my body are burning," he said in a rush, trying to rub the burning sensation away with the palm of his hand, the tips of his fingers, the underside of his wrist. But none of it worked. "I think the pain means something."

"Pain don't mean nothin'," Liz Hen said.

"This pain does," Nail snapped back.

Liz Hen looked at Lawri. "I think a metal hand attached to some noble court girl has more meaning than your arm pain, Nail."

"They may both be ill omens," Hawkwood said. "They may both be ill omens."

CHAPTER FIFTY-FOUR
LINDHOLF LE GRAVEN

8TH DAY OF THE HEART MOON, 999TH YEAR OF LAIJON
KING'S HIGHWAY NEAR RIDLIEGH, GUL KANA

The whole army of Sør Sevier stretched out before Lindholf Le Graven, overflowing the King's Highway like a giant, bristling snake. The horizon was spiked with spears and flags and glittering helms, dust hanging above the entire processional like a moving veil. The march of the horses startled a pheasant and dove into whirring flight. Clouds of flies and gnats pestered everyone and nagged at the exposed flesh of Lindholf's face and arms. He had been given fresh vestments and new leather armor in Saint Only. It was ill-fitting and itchy, but blessedly far less hot than the black plate armor he had worn before. In fact, his stolen Dayknight armor and sword—along with Enna Spades' stolen armor and sword—had been melted by Aeros' master blacksmith into black slag and then fashioned into extra arrowheads for the army. Spades had found Lindholf a new Sør Sevier blade that was shorter, less heavy, and much easier to wield.

Eight days since crossing into Gul Kana and the White Prince's army had thus far met zero resistance. They were nearly a hundred thousand strong, all that was left of Aeros' army after the disastrous Battle of the

Saint Only Channel. They traveled at a good rate, all things considered. That such a vast army could so efficiently set up camp and then tear it down each morn astounded Lindholf.

Over the last eight days, what few travelers, traders, ambling pedestrians, and occasional lone parties of Dayknights that were using the King's Highway moved aside and let them pass. As Aeros had predicted, the way to Amadon was free. And the Sør Sevier army wasted no time. They had not stopped to fight anyone or sack and pillage any town along the way. In fact, as they passed near some of the large towns, droves of people lined the highway, simply watching the enemy army march on by.

Lindholf did not march with the rest of the soldiers. Instead he sat on a long bench at the front of a covered wagon with Aeros Raijael, Jenko Bruk, and the young serving girl, Leisel. Lindholf was on the far right. Jenko next to him in the middle, guiding the team of draught mares pulling the wagon. Jenko's silver Knight Archaic armor was polished and glistening in the sun, his helmet on a hook set in the post behind them. The White Prince, in his own white cloak and glimmering chain mail, sat on the other side of Jenko, young Leisel next to him at the edge of the bench. Leisel wore naught but a tattered white shift tied at the waist with a thin blue string, blond curls peeping out from under a blue bonnet tied to her head. Lindholf could not help but keep looking at the pretty girl.

Lindholf's mount, a roan destrier, trailed behind the wagon with four other roans. The horses were tethered to the hitch, along with a white stallion named Spirit, a beast once ridden by Gault Aulbrek, now meant for Aeros himself.

All the weapons of the Five Warrior Angels traveled in the wagon with them. *Forgetting Moon*, *Blackest Heart*, *Lonesome Crown*, *Ethic Shroud*, and *Afflicted Fire* rode under burlap tarps in the flat space behind Lindholf. The five angel stones were safe in a leather pouch tied securely to Aeros' belt. The White Prince claimed he would not don the weapons until he stood under the Atonement Tree at Fiery Absolution.

The stones and weapons were like a weight clawing at Lindholf's mind. If not for Shroud of the Vallè keeping him calm, he might have tried to steal them for himself. Without the white powder, he quickly found he was consumed with everything rotten and bad about himself. Oh, he knew full well his actions were the direct result of his yearning for Shroud—that poisonous fume smoldering in the center of his dark little heart.

All his life, until Tala had kissed him on the balcony of Sunbird Hall, he had lived with naught but memories of an extraordinarily happy childhood, and that was even despite his scars and deformities. But here, riding beside Jenko Bruk and the White Prince, Lindholf knew he was officially at childhood's end. No more laughter.

I never used to be like this! he thought. *Tala used to call me a joy to be around! Happy. Talkative. Funny.* Yet he hadn't had a funny thought in moons. *You used to be much more lighthearted, Lindholf,* Tala had once said to him in Sunbird Hall. *You could be so clever with your antics.*

The notion that his cousin might still love him was floating round in his wistful imagination. He needed to stop taking part in his own delusions, stop obliging the madness and realize who he really was, a bad person, a drug-addled mope, a failure, a traitor, a person who had watched his own cousin, Jondralyn, die, and then ridden off with her killer. Now he was a silent, brooding outlaw heading toward Fiery Absolution with the enemy of his kingdom. *And you do it well. Silence is to be your virtue.*

And if things couldn't be more desperate, the two Bloodwoods, Black Dugal and Hans Rake, rode their red-eyed stallions just in front of the wagon. The bulldog, Café Colza, padded along under hoof. Lindholf knew there was something hidden under Dugal's scars. Just as he thought there was something hidden under his own. *But what?*

Spades rode beside Hammerfiss at the head of the line, both in the silver armor and dark blue livery of the Knights Archaic, red hair spilling like fire over the back of their armor. Other than the time they spent helping Lindholf with his sword training, Hammerfiss and Spades had kept to themselves for the length of the journey from Saint Only, a fact that was not lost on the White Prince. They both sat regal and tall atop their own dun-colored war chargers. Rumor was, Aeros' five Knights Archaic bodyguards used to all ride brilliant white stallions, until the

Battle of the Saint Only Channel drowned all but one: Gault's old mount, Spirit. A knight named Ivor Jace had saved Aeros, both of them atop Spirit as the powerful beast swam the length of the strait all the way back to Saint Only.

"Ser Jenko Bruk," Aeros said, "you won't so abandon me as Hammerfiss and Spades seem to have done, will you?"

Jenko snapped the reins, face impassive as he urged the team of draught mares along. Their ears flicked against the gnats in the air as the wagon jostled over the dusty road.

"Jenko is taking his job seriously today, Lord Potato." Aeros leaned forward and looked down the bench at Lindholf, smiling. The sun did not even glint off the White Prince's eyes, so hard they were, pupils and irises so black and fathomless. "Jenko is behaving as a true Knight Archaic ought behave. But the truth is, Jenko has become most sullen and untalkative ever since Ava's escape."

Jenko remained untalkative, staring straight ahead.

"Problem is," Aeros continued, "now that Ava Shay is gone, Enna Spades will rut with him no more. What Jenko never realized was that Spades sucked his cock to torture the poor girl, Ava. What Jenko did not realize was that Spades is wildly unpredictable, and not happy unless everyone around her is miserable. But we can all be unpredictable in our own way."

Aeros was wrong about Enna Spades. The warrior woman was the only one who had made Lindholf feel even remotely comfortable and welcome within this group. He had enjoyed his journey from Savon to Saint Only with her. And Spades had secured him more Shroud of the Vallè than he could ever have wished. *So she once fucked Jenko Bruk?* Though Lindholf could see that she was beautiful, he certainly couldn't imagine sex with the woman. And perhaps that was why he liked her so, and why Jenko avoided her and she avoided him. If anyone was unpredictable, it was Aeros Raijael himself. If anyone wasn't happy unless everyone else was miserable, it was the White Prince. And he had a particular knack for picking on Jenko Bruk. Then it dawned on Lindholf just who Jenko Bruk was. *How could I have been so foolishly blind?*

"Was your father Baron Jubal Bruk of Gallows Haven?" Lindholf asked Jenko.

"Jubal Bruk was my father. What of it?"

"You should know that I saw him in Amadon."

"You saw my father?"

"Indeed." Lindholf told Jenko the story of how Leif Chaparral had brought the baron to the castle in a box, legless and armless. He told Jenko how his father had described the sacking of Gallows Haven and how he had relayed Aeros' threats. "He was still alive and living in the castle, last I saw."

"I did not think he would survive," Jenko uttered, his face transforming, as if he were somehow coming to terms with many, many things that had long haunted him.

"And here, according to Dugal, I thought we had all become father-less," Aeros laughed. "And yet Jenko's father still lives."

Jenko sat more rigidly on the bench, staring straight ahead, guiding the draught mares, the wagon jostling and creaking over the dusty path.

"Indeed," Aeros went on, "Jenko is taking his job unusually seriously today. But you did get him talking momentarily, Lord Potato." He winked at Lindholf. "So good on you. But best we make no more mention of Jenko's father. Perhaps we should talk of Ava Shay instead. She was a beauty. And a spirited one in bed for sure." Aeros turned to Leisel. "Even young Leisel saw that much."

Lindholf's heart forgot a couple of beats. The White Prince often picked on Leisel too, and he was particularly cruel about it every time.

"But you needn't worry about sharing my bed any longer," Aeros said to her. "For Ava is gone, and soon shall you be gone too. And then you will have no worries left at all."

"Where will I go?"

"Oh, you shall soon see."

Lindholf felt a stab of fear at Aeros' cryptic tone.

The White Prince was again looking at him. "Young Leisel is the only fair maiden in all the Five Isles who could wear such lowborn stitchery and still look divine. Don't you think, my brother? I mean, you *are* supposedly my brother. Leastwise according to the addled ramblings of Spades. And if you are indeed my brother, would we not have the same taste in young girls? You do like Leisel, no?"

Lindholf stiffened and stared straight ahead now, watching the backs of the draught mares leading the wagon. Aeros had caught him staring at Leisel more than once. Truth was, in the last eight days of traveling with the girl, Lindholf had found her to be so graceful and lithe and pure. She seemed made of air, her every movement like flower petals on the wind. Yes, he liked her. And that was why Aeros tormented him now.

"Well," Aeros pressed. "What say you, *brother*? Do you not fancy her?"

"She is indeed—" He cut himself short, the sudden stinging sweat in his eyes naught but raw misery. He knew he should not say anything further. "She is indeed most beautiful and fair," he said.

"You think me beautiful and fair?" Leisel asked, her pale face now looking across the bench at him. "Why?"

"It is a compliment he pays you," Aeros laughed. "Surely you know that you are exceptionally remarkable and that Lindholf is utterly smitten with you. All other ladies fade from sight when around you, young Leisel."

She sat back against the rattling bench, no longer looking at Lindholf. "I don't think I've ever thought of it like that, Your Excellency."

Aeros laughed again. "The key to your charm is your utmost innocence, young Leisel. Am I not right, Lindholf?"

Lindholf kept his mouth clamped shut this time. He reached into the side pocket of his leather armor and dipped his finger into the Shroud of the Vallè he had hidden there. He leaned away from the others, pretending to spit in the roadway, sniffing the white powder off his finger and up his nose, the drug immediately infusing him with that boldness and confidence he craved.

"See, your beauty has overwhelmed Lindholf," Aeros said, running his fingers up the girl's arm and over her shoulder, touching her chin last. "He can scarcely even look at you. As a prince of Eskander, Lindholf likely grew tired of fumbling with the gowns and finery of the noblewomen. I imagine what he desires most is to get his grubby hands on the filthy raiments of the peasantry, particularly the fetching young peasantry like yourself." Aeros looked at Jenko. "I confessed similar sentiments to Ava Shay when I first met her."

Jenko continued to stare ahead, guiding the horse team.

"Leisel might be a sorceress, she is so fair." Aeros grasped her thin, delicate fingers in his own, bent to touch his lips to the back of her hand. "How else could Lindholf be so bewitched? Ask him if he is bewitched by you, my dear."

"Are you bewitched by me?" Leisel leaned forward and looked over Aeros' and Jenko's laps at Lindholf. "Do you think I am a sorceress?"

Lindholf was embarrassed. The girl was staring right at him with such big and curious eyes. The Shroud of the Vallè had not fully settled over him. His confidence yet waned under Leisel's wide gaze. *I look like nothing more than a flea-bitten beggar next to Aeros Raijael and Jenko Bruk.* It seemed his new clothes and armor were too big for him, which always made him feel shabbier than he truly was.

"Let me steal one last pleasure before I rid myself of you," Aeros said to the serving girl as he slipped his hand down the front of her shift, fondling both of her breasts. Lindholf watched and anger rose like a cold, burning radiance within his soul. *But what can I do? I am not the girl's savior.*

"Before I rid myself of you," Aeros went on, hands still on her breasts, "let me experience one last degradation, young Leisel. For I must become pure again before Absolution. I must become pure again before taking upon myself the weapons of the Five Warrior Angels and claiming my place as Laijon returned, reborn. I must purify myself and none other. So I shall soon be rid of your temptations."

Lindholf rose up on the wobbly floor of the wagon, angry, seeking justice, Shroud of the Vallè spurring his conviction. He could feel the warmth of the white powder, its tempest and wrath, like a thunderstorm flowing hot through his veins, pushing what little confidence he had to the fore. "Don't you speak to her like that!" he raged, gripping the hilt of his new Sør Sevier sword. "Do not touch her!"

"As you wish, Lord Potato." Aeros' voice was flat and expressionless as he slipped his hand out from under Leisel's shirt. "I shall never speak to her again."

The White Prince leaned back, raised one leg, and kicked the girl off the bench. Leisel disappeared from sight and landed in a puff of dust on the roadway below. And the wagon rolled on without her.

"What?" Lindholf exclaimed. "Why?" He whirled and craned his neck, trying to spot her on the roadway behind the still trundling wagon. Clouds of dust kicked up by the greater balance of the army was all he could see, that and heavy warhorses and wagons stretching off into the hazy distance.

Without thinking, Lindholf leaped from his side of the wagon. Landing awkwardly, he tumbled in the dirt, gained his feet, and promptly scurried back the way they'd come.

He spotted Leisel on her hands and knees underneath a team of oxen pulling a heavy cart laden with tent poles and spears. The hulking hooves of the oxen kicked and rolled her into a lone puddle of mud. Lindholf's heart forgot a couple of beats as the wheel of the lumbering cart slowly rolled up the girl's back, crushing her face-first into the muddy mire. He sprinted toward her, whimpering in panic. He reached the girl just as the rear wheel of the wagon rode over her body, pressing her deeper into the small bog until nothing remained but her blue bonnet.

"No!" Lindholf cried out, thinking the wagon had just crushed her. But surprisingly, Leisel pulled herself up from the sludge, brushing herself off with frantic hands, face a mask of grit and brown muck, blond hair a tangled, muddy mess. "I think I'm okay." She met his shocked gaze with an equally shocked gaze of her own.

"Bloody Mother Mia," Lindholf gasped, seizing her by the shoulders, utterly stunned that she wasn't hurt. *The wagon should have smashed her dead!*

"Why did my lord Aeros do that to me?" Leisel asked him. She reached down and snatched her blue bonnet from the mud. "Why did he kick me off the wagon?" She placed the filthy bonnet back on her head. "I thought he loved me."

Lindholf pulled her out of the way of a line of high-stepping destri-ers, grim-faced Knights of the Blue Sword looking down on them both.

"Out of the way!" One of the knights kicked at Lindholf.

Café Colza barked at the knights, biting at the hooves of several of the other war chargers as they rode by. The burly bulldog with the spiked collar was a menace, breaking up the line of riders, causing some of the knights to draw their swords.

"If you hurt Café Colza, I will slice the heads off each one of you." Black Dugal, sitting straight and hale atop his dark stallion, imposed himself between the dog and the line of knights, his every movement as elegant and refined as a cat's. The younger Bloodwood, Hans Rake, was right there by Dugal's side, his own black stallion looking as formidable as Dugal's, eyes like glowing coals. The line of knights rerouted around the two assassins, every knight eyeing the two warily.

Bringing his mount up next to Leisel, Dugal reached down with one arm and lifted the muddy girl up into the saddle before him. "We'll find you and Lindholf a horse of your own," he said to the girl. "But for now, you ride with me."

Dugal looked down at Lindholf. "You are safer with Hans and me. And you shall not soon forget this kindness." Dugal beckoned for Lindholf to climb up onto the Bloodeye behind Hans. "I expect great things from you come Fiery Absolution."

Lindholf hauled himself up into the saddle behind Hans Rake. The sleek muscles of the strange black horse stretched and bunched under his legs. The young Bloodwood set heels to flanks and the stallion took off after Dugal's at a steady pace.

They caught up to the White Prince and Jenko. It was just the two of them on the long bench of the covered wagon now.

"She belongs to you, Lord Potato," Aeros called out as Lindholf and Hans rode by, voice withering in its condescension. "Leisel is your re-sponsibility now, my *brother*."

Hans spurred the Bloodeye past the wagon toward Spades and Hammerfiss.

Amadon, oh, Amadon, what shall await your people after Fiery
Absolution, what shall await but for the lingering stink of ash and
ember along with the blackened hollows of your ruined homes?
—The Way and Truth of Laijon

CHAPTER FIFTY-FIVE
MANCELLOR ALLEN

11TH DAY OF THE HEART MOON, 999TH YEAR OF LAIJON

AMADON, GUL KANA.

Sunbird Hall was empty but for Mancellor Allen, King Jovan Bronachell, Grand Vicar Denarius, and the four remaining archbishops: Vandivor, Donalbain, Leaford, and Rhys-Duncan. It was early morning and there were no Dayknights present other than Leif Chaparral and his younger brother, Glade. It was just the nine of them gathered in the stone-cold vastness of the hall. Sightings of a great oghul army gathering north of the city had caused a tension in Mancellor Allen that he had never before felt. *Absolution is near!* Rumors were the savage horde had destroyed village after village on its way south to Amadon. Rumor was a Vallè army rode with them.

"How many days dead and still their corpses rot in that crypt in Tin Man Square?" Jovan pressed the grand vicar. "You've made me study the scriptures ever since Spencerville's death. As you said, it states in *The Way and Truth of Laijon* in the Acts of the Second Warrior Angel, 'I prophesy unto you, my faithful kin, a most blessed archbishop shall be murdered by means most foul. He shall lie in state with one of royal blood, only to rise again before Fiery Absolution. For only the dead can usher in the return of Laijon.' I've memorized the passages as I've memorized others. 'Prior to Absolution, an archbishop shall die and rise again, passing through the veil, bathed in heavenly glory. He shall bring back with him a princess most fair. And this shall be a portent and sign, for he shall usher in the return of the Five Warrior Angels, each a servant at his side.' And you, Denarius, promised Jondralyn and Spencerville would arise."

"As they shall," the vicar answered curtly. "But we must have patience with Laijon. All things come in time to those who wait."

"But their corpses rot!" Jovan shouted. "How can a rotting corpse rise again?"

"Faith." Denarius stepped away from the large silver urn of consecrated oil he had just placed on the king's main banquet table. He had also placed a large paintbrush, a folded white bedsheet, and a small, rusted iron mallet on the table, all three items brought into Sunbird Hall by Archbishop Rhys-Duncan.

Denarius moved toward the four archbishops, all of them standing stoic in their priestly robes not far from the canvas-covered Silver Throne. They'd purposely positioned themselves in a semicircle around the shrouded throne, as if guarding it.

Jovan continued to press the vicar. "My faith and patience grow thin. Aeros' army draws nearer to Amadon with each passing day. The oghul army is at our very doorstep. What disasters await us? What disasters are we allowing to just wash over Amadon?"

"All is as Laijon wills it," Denarius said with a touch of irritation. "And lest Laijon's plans be undone by your lack of faith, Jovan, I shall prophesy unto you now, the resurrection of Jondralyn and Spencerville is nigh. Even with Aeros' armies on the move from the west, and the oghul armies of Hragna'Ar marching upon Amadon from the north, we must accept the fact that Fiery Absolution has snuck up on us like a thief in the night. Rather than cower in fear at the possibility, or fret over what plot or betrayal has led us to this place in time, we should rejoice that scripture is about to be fulfilled."

The king, face dark and brooding, did not look convinced. His faith was clearly wavering. He wore a simple black shirt tucked into a pair of black pants held up by a black belt. No sword hung at his hip today. The blade Sky Reaver had been stolen by Dokie Liddle during his mad escape with Liz Hen Neville from Sunbird Hall. Mancellor could tell that that entire episode of Liz Hen accidentally killing Spencerville had rattled the king to a great degree. But the scriptures were clear. Spencerville would rise again at Absolution. Jondralyn too. And Mancellor was here in Amadon with the grand vicar himself, bearing witness to history and prophecy.

"How do I know that I am not just letting our enemies march right up to our doorstep unhindered for no good reason?" Jovan asked. "How can I be certain you are right about any of this, Your Grace?"

"Do not ask such pointed questions of the vicarship," Denarius said. "Not on this special day, of all days. Remember, to break faith with the word and bond of the vicar is to break faith with Laijon."

"But we could be wrong. I am full of so much misgiving about Spencerville's death and resurrection. Perhaps I should send Leif and our armies out—"

"Do not let unrighteous doubt overtake you." Denarius cut the king off with a crisp wave of the hand. "You have wholeheartedly believed up until now, up until the last hour, and now you allow skepticism to rear its ugly head in you. Know that Fiery Absolution must happen at the appointed time and at the appointed place. Know that Spencerville searches for your sister in the realm of the dead as we speak. Spencerville is now embarked on a most sacred and divine quest to find her, wash her free of her sin, and then usher her forth at Fiery Absolution and not a moment sooner, both of them bathed in heavenly glory. And you have yet your own part to play, so let your preparation begin."

There was a moment of silence between the vicar and king. *They are truly speaking of resurrection.* Mancellor's mind reeled. He had seen the bodies of both Jondralyn and the vicar lying in state in a crypt in the Gardens of the Crown Moon in the center of Tin Man Square at the bottom of the Long Stairs. The princess's body was indeed rotting, for she had been dead the longest. The archbishop's body was starting to molder. *How can the dead be brought back to life?* It was a thrilling prospect, and with the vicar so close, Mancellor did not doubt it would happen.

"You must remember your place in history," the vicar admonished Jovan, compassion and understanding infusing his voice. "You must show faith before Laijon."

"If you say it"—Jovan bowed to the vicar—"then so shall it be. I shall muster what faith and courage I have. I shall look forward to my sister's return. I shall look toward Absolution with faith in our Lord."

Denarius dipped his head, acknowledging the king's words. The vicar motioned to the four archbishops behind him. They stepped toward the shrouded throne in unison, grasped the bottom hem of the canvas, and pulled the cloth covering from the throne.

"No," Jovan muttered, a look of stunned apprehension on his face.

The royal seat of Gul Kana was revealed for the first time in five years. Mancellor took a step back. For the first time since the death of Borden Bronachell in Wyn Darrè, light and air once again fell upon the throne's sleek exterior in glistening waves. He couldn't help but stare. The throne seemed to be fashioned of one singular, glimmering piece of silver. In the dancing torchlight, the throne's polished silver surface almost seemed to move like shimmering liquid. The smooth seat of the throne was a good bit higher than that of a normal chair, its curving armrests, too. The back of the throne was as high as a man, a five-pointed star set at the top. The throne had five legs. They were also laid out in the shape of a five-pointed star. Legend told that each of the five legs was a representation of one of the Five Warrior Angels holding up the throne, bolstering whichever Bronachell sat upon it. Mancellor Allen was privy to most every story and myth regarding the history of the castle, including the history of the Silver Throne. His father had shared many stories with both him and Bronwyn.

"Bringing back the Silver Throne is not all we must do, Your Excellency," the vicar said to the king. "There is one more thing we must do before Fiery Absolution, one more task we need complete for scripture to be fulfilled."

"And what is that, Your Grace?" Jovan asked, suspicious eyes still on the throne. "Is it to bring back my sword, Sky Reaver, the sword of my enemy?"

After the weapon's theft, Leif had charged his younger brother, Glade, with finding Seita, Liz Hen, Dokie, and Jovan's sword. But the young Dayknight, and the contingent of soldiers in his charge, had been scouring the city to no avail. Mancellor hoped Liz Hen and Dokie would never be found. He wished no ill will on his friends. He knew that if they were found, they would be hung.

"Sky Reaver is another matter altogether," Denarius answered. "I talk of something more vital to the survival of Gul Kana and humanity in general."

"And what is that?"

"It is true that Archbishop Spencerville shall arise from the dead before Fiery Absolution and that Princess Jondralyn shall arise with him. For I blessed Jondralyn that she would come forth during the return of Laijon, clothed in glory, immortality, and eternal life. But until that day, an empty seat remains at my side amongst the quorum of five." Denarius bowed low to Jovan. "And that seat shall be filled by you, my king."

The king's eyes widened. "To fulfill the prophecy in the Revelations of the Fourth Warrior Angel."

"Indeed," the grand vicar answered, and quoted the scripture. "In the latter days a king shall be made bishop upon the Silver Throne, one of humble means from Wyn Darrè bearing witness,'" Mancellor felt the nervousness rise up in his own throat as the vicar tuned to him and confirmed, "And we have the representative soldier from Wyn Darrè right here. One of humble means."

"*Me?*" Mancellor took another step back.

"Peace be unto you, Ser Mancellor Allen," the vicar said. "For this moment is the culmination of your destiny. That is why you, in my foresight, have been summoned to such a special occasion. Will you bear witness to what sacred things are to follow?"

Mancellor gulped, heart hammering. "Yes." He bowed to the grand vicar.

"Most excellent." Denarius bowed in return. "For what happens now will require both strength and great faith from what few of us remain in this room."

The grand vicar stepped toward the banquet table, beckoning Leif and Glade Chaparral to follow him. The vicar turned and faced everyone. "Each of you here will be required to take part in the glory of a special sacrament that has never before been performed in the history of the Five Isles."

Denarius motioned for Leif to pick up the silver urn of oil. He motioned for Glade to grab the large paintbrush and folded white sheet and small, rusted iron mallet.

"Place them before the throne," the vicar ordered. The brothers did as told, setting each item carefully in order on the stone floor before the throne: silver urn, brush, white sheet, rusted mallet. The urn was the heaviest of the items, filled to the brim with what Mancellor surmised were at least two gallons of consecrated oil.

The vicar addressed King Jovan. "Today you shall fulfill prophecy by joining in the righteous brotherhood of the quorum of five. You shall first be stripped of all raiment unto pure nakedness by the brotherhood. Then your flesh shall be bathed in the sacred oils of our priesthood and placed under a pure-white veil, wherein your lungs shall be pressed and purified of all noxious air. And you, Jovan Bronachell, king of Gul Kana, must complete this sacrament in utmost faith and righteousness and trust in your fellow brethren." Denarius stared straight at the king as he asked, "Do you agree?"

"I do." Jovan nodded.

No sooner were the words out of his mouth than the four archbishops—Vandivor, Donalbain, Leaford, and Rhys-Duncan—descended upon the king. They tore at Jovan's clothes with clawing hands, ripping the black shirt from his shoulders, chest, and back, tearing the fabric, shredding it. Jovan, taken off guard, began to fight against the archbishops. It was reactive self-preservation. He punched and kicked.

"You must not resist!" The grand vicar's voice rang loudly through the hall. "You must place all trust in your fellow brethren!"

Jovan breathed heavy from the struggle. Archbishop Vandivor

ripped the belt from around the king's waist and tossed it across the floor. Donalbain and Leaford yanked down the king's pants and under-clothes, revealing his privates. The king covered his exposed parts with one hand, embarrassed, trying to brush the two archbishops away with the other.

"Give in to the sacrament!" Denarius called out. "You think you have known happiness in the past, but you shall never know full joy until you fully embrace all the sacraments of Laijon, until you have gone through your purification."

Jovan, one hand still cupping his groin, let Donalbain and Leaford remove his boots and pull his pants down and toss them aside. The king cowered now, completely naked save for the silver crown atop his head.

The grand vicar was now soaking the large paintbrush in the silver urn of oil. Once Jovan was divested of his clothing, Denarius took the dripping brush and commenced to slather consecrated oil over Jovan's naked form from head to toe, whilst praying.

"Jovan Bronachell, in the name of Laijon and by the power of the priesthood I hold, I, Denarius, grand vicar of the Church of Laijon, con-secrate your body in the name of the great One and Only, even in the name of Laijon. May you retain health in the mind and strength in the marrow and in the bones, and may the power of the priesthood be upon you throughout your purification and throughout eternity."

To Mancellor it looked as if the archbishop were basting the king with butter like a chef basting a plucked Adin Wyte tom turkey, ready-ing him for the fire. Donalbain, Leaford, Rhys-Duncan, and Vandivor began unfolding the white sheet at the foot of the throne.

Done brushing the oil over the king's body, Denarius ordered Jovan to take his seat on the throne. Leif and Glade held Jovan under the arms so he did not slip on the now oil-soaked tile floor. Once the king was sitting naked on the Silver Throne, the Archbishops draped the white sheet over Jovan's body from the top of his head to his lap, cov-ering the nakedness of his upper torso completely, leaving his lower legs exposed.

Donalbain and Leaford stood on one side of the throne whilst

Vandivor and Rhys-Duncan stood on the other. Donalbain and Leaford grabbed one end of the sheet, Vandivor and Rhys-Duncan the other, and then they all four walked around toward the back of the throne, pulling on either end of the sheet as they went, the stretched sheet pressing the upper part of Jovan's body and head against the back of the throne. He squirmed uncomfortably in the oily seat. The four archbishops continued to pull on the sheet wrapped around his upper body. Mancellor could see the king's arms struggle for purchase under the taught fabric. But the strength of the four men pulling on the sheet forced him back into the seat, the white, oily fabric now molding to every contour of his chest and arms, molding around his heaving neck and face and gaping mouth. The king strained for breath.

"You're suffocating him!" Leif called out.

"All is as it should be." Denarius stepped forward. "For this is his purification, his final sacramental anointing into the quorum of five. We must all remain strong as the breath of life leaves his body, we all must remain true to our faith in Laijon, as our great One and Only breathes new life into him."

Leif is right. They are killing him! Mancellor watched Jovan Bronachell heaving for breath under the straining sheet. He felt the bile rise in his throat, nervous now for the king. *They are purposely killing the king!* But before his mind could form any more coherent thoughts than that, the grand vicar began his entreaty and plea to the almighty.

"O great Laijon, hear my prayer!" Denarius held both hands, palms out, toward the vaulted ceiling above. "Hear my prayer, O great One and Only!"

Denarius lowered his hands, motioning Leif and Glade Chaparral forward. "You grab the urn," the vicar ordered Leif. "It should still be about half full of oil. And you, Glade, gather up the mallet and place it in the king's right hand." The two Dayknights did as Denarius bade them whilst the four archbishops kept the sheet tight around Jovan's face and heaving torso.

Glade freed Jovan's right hand from the confines of the sheet and placed the mallet in his straining grip. "I cannot breathe," Jovan gasped, holding the mallet tightly, voice muffled and weak. "I cannot see. I beg of you, release me."

"Don't fight it," the vicar said. "Accept purification, Your Excellency."

"I cannot breathe."

"If you but pray to Laijon, he will deliver you from this death. It is up to your *own* faith now. Do you not remember the many previous purifications at my hand? Do you not recall the purification you asked me to perform on Tala? This is but a similar thing, only harder to endure, for you, like no man before you, will have to speak at the same time your breath is forced from your lungs. But endure it you will, for I have faith in you, my king. Every member of the quorum of five has faith in you. For we too have been similarly purified."

Denarius bent and whispered in Jovan's ear. But all in the hall could hear his words. "Knock the mallet on the arm of the throne when you are told, and repeat after me when spoken to. Do you understand?"

"I do," Jovan gasped, voice still muffled, the sheet still being pulled tight around his mouth by the four archbishops behind him. The king was breathing hard now, chest heaving in and out in panic.

Denarius stood before Jovan, placing his right knee against the exposed and oiled right knee of the king. "Between truth and lie and legend shall be a veil," he said. "Do you have any questions to ask of me, Your Excellency?"

Jovan just sat there, strained breath hissing through the oily fabric. With a nod from Denarius, the four archbishops behind the Silver Throne pulled the sheet tighter around the king's upper body and face.

"Do you have any questions to ask of me?" the vicar repeated. "Tap the throne once with the hammer if you do."

The king raised the mallet and tapped its rusted iron head against the arm of the throne once. It sounded like a door knocker knocking on a hollow door.

"And what is wanted?" Denarius asked, as if indeed Jovan had been knocking on a door and the vicar had just opened it.

"Release me," Jovan pleaded. "I can't breathe."

"Wrong," Denarius said. "When you know, you must repeat all I say unto you, my king."

Denarius then leaned over and whispered into Jovan's ear. But this time nobody could hear but the king. Jovan listened, breathing hard, and then repeated, his mouth and voice straining under the sheet, "Having been true and faithful, I, Jovan Bronachell, king of all Gul Kana, having no way to see through the veil, desire further light and knowledge in the priesthood of Laijon as set forth in *The Way and Truth of Laijon*."

Denarius, knee still pressed against Jovan's knee, answered. "The front leg of the Silver Throne you now sit upon represents the exactness and honor of Laijon in keeping the covenants of the Five Warrior Angels. And that is the secret of the priesthood of Laijon."

Then the grand vicar motioned to Leif. The captain of the Dayknights lifted the urn of oil over Jovan's head and poured. Jovan spat and sputtered under the sheet as the oil slithered down his face, unable to breathe. His struggle lasted a few minutes as the oil soaked into the sheet, seeping into his mouth and down his throat. He gagged and heaved, then his breathing became somewhat normal again, though slow and strained.

The vicar said, "Knock upon the throne twice now, and your next request shall be granted." Jovan coughed, then knocked with the mallet twice. "What is wanted?" Denarius asked, again leaning forward and whispering the answer in the king's ear.

Jovan repeated, voice strained and muffled from the near drowning at the hands of Leif, "Having been true and faithful, I, Jovan Bronachell, king of all Gul Kana, having no way to see through the veil, wish to know the mysteries of godliness."

Denarius answered, "The second leg of the Silver Throne you now sit upon represents the undeviating course toward the eternal life of godliness that awaits you among the heights of the stars. And the mysteries of godliness are as follows: obedience and faith. For they are simple mysteries. And in the stillness of the night will come the wraiths; they will shriek and sing, echoing off one side of your head and the other, but with the mantle of archbishop that you shall soon take upon you, you can stave off such demons with but a simple thought. And only those close to godliness can do such."

Again Denarius motioned to Leif, who lifted the urn of oil over Jovan's head and poured. Jovan struggled and gagged and nearly drowned. Whimpers of humiliation and pain could now be heard from under the sheet. But his breathing eventually steadied.

And the vicar said, "Knock thrice and your next request shall be granted." Jovan knocked three times against the arm of the throne with the mallet. "What is wanted?" the vicar asked. And as Denarius leaned forward and whispered in the king's ear, Mancellor felt some amount of pride that he was being included in such grand history as this, that he was included in scripture and prophecy, that his name would go down in the annals of time as one who had brought Jondralyn's body to Amadon and had witnessed the king of Gul Kana become an archbishop. *Did I ever really even know my religion, or my place within it?* Had every moment of his life led up to this?

Done whispering in the king's ear, Denarius leaned back, and Jovan repeated, "Having been true and faithful, I, Jovan Bronachell, king of all Gul Kana, having no way to see through the veil, wish to now pass through the veil of death unto the other side and enter into the priesthood of Laijon as one of the quorum of five."

Denarius answered, "The third leg of the Silver Throne you now sit upon represents your entrance into the quorum of five. It represents your faith and trust in *The Way and Truth of Laijon*. It represents the power and tokens of Laijon's holy priesthood as given unto the grand vicar and bestowed upon the quorum of five."

For the third time Leif lifted the urn of oil over Jovan's head and poured. And once again oil ran down the sheet, soaking into the king's mouth, clogging his throat. He gagged and heaved and cried out in pain. And still the four archbishops behind the throne hauled tight on the sheet, pressing Jovan's head back against the throne as he struggled to regain his breath.

The vicar said, "Knock now four times and your next request shall be granted." Jovan knocked the mallet on the arm of the throne four times. But this time the knocks were weak and nearly soundless. "What is wanted?" the vicar asked.

"I can't breathe," Jovan tried to cry out, but his hissing voice was but a faint, weak sound. "I will die if we continue." His breaths had slowed.

"You must carry on," the vicar said, knee still pressed against the king's. "It is the only way. You must now knock again, four times."

Jovan knocked again with the mallet, feeble knocks, four times. "What is wanted?" Denarius asked. Again the vicar whispered in the king's ear.

Jovan repeated, "Having been true and faithful, I, Jovan Bronachell, king of all Gul Kana, still having no way to see through the veil, wish to know my place at Fiery Absolution."

The grand vicar answered, "The fourth leg of the Silver Throne you sit upon represents Fiery Absolution, that every knee shall bend and every tongue confess that Laijon has returned, and that you, Jovan Bronachell, are Laijon returned."

Leif lifted the urn of oil over Jovan's head again and poured. Jovan didn't even try to breathe through the oily mask covering his face this time. He just sat still as if holding his breath. In fact, for a moment Mancellor thought the king was dead. But Jovan eventually let out a great gasp and cough, and began breathing again slowly.

The vicar said, "Knock five times and your next request shall be granted."

Jovan knocked with the mallet five times with scant relish or effort. "What is wanted?" the vicar asked. Denarius whispered into Jovan's ear.

The king repeated, voice strained, "Having been true and faithful, I, Jovan Bronachell, king of all Gul Kana, still having no way to see through the veil, wish to know the true names of the five of fellowship."

"And who are the five of fellowship?" the vicar asked, again whispering the answer in Jovan's ear.

The king answered, "The five of fellowship are the Gladiator, Assassin, Thief, Princess, and Slave."

"That is correct," Denarius answered, then whispered into Jovan's ear again.

"And what are their names?" the king asked with his last breath.

The vicar answered, "They are known as the five of fellowship, yea, even the Five Warrior Angels. And their names shall soon be revealed. And they shall join you under the Burning Tree and the veil shall be removed from your eyes."

But Jovan was no longer breathing; the mallet dropped from his hand.

The four archbishops released their hold on the white sheet. It loosened from around Jovan's face. All was silent. Then the king's eyes flew open as he tore the sheet away from his face, gasping for air.

"And thus you are consecrated, Jovan Bronachell," Grand Vicar Denarius called out. "For you shall arise from the Silver Throne as Laijon returned. You shall arise from the throne at Fiery Absolution as the head of the Five Warrior Angels reborn. And you shall take up what weapon and angel stone is rightfully yours and strike down your enemy, that false imposter, Aeros Raijael, and put an end to his slaughter."

CHAPTER FIFTY-SIX

TALA BRONACHELL

12TH DAY OF THE HEART MOON, 999TH YEAR OF LAIJON
AMADON, GUL KANA

The Slaver's Tavern and Inn was nearly empty. Tala Bronachell's group occupied the long table in the darkest corner of the room. Nail sat across from Tala. Next to Nail were Liz Hen Neville, Dokie Liddle, and Hawkwood. Tala sat on the same side of the table as Bronwyn Allen and Cromm Cru'x. Lawri Le Graven was right next to the oghul, all of their backs against the wall.

Lawri was sick and getting sicker. The gauntlet attached to her arm was infecting her with some form of glowing olive-colored rot, spreading up her arm and neck and over her chest. Just the slightest attempt to move the gauntlet caused Lawri to cry out. Cromm, the strongest of them all, had even offered to remove it. But Lawri had declined the offer, horror in her eyes. *If we could just chop it off her! Chop the dreadful gauntlet off above the elbow.* Tala had suggested as much. After all, Lawri had already survived her arm being severed once by Jovan. And Dokie Liddle carried the blue sword, Sky Reaver, at his hip—the very blade that had taken Lawri's arm that first time. But Lawri would not even entertain the suggestion, no matter how much pain she was in. Hawkwood even thought chopping the thing off her arm was a bad idea. Of course all of Lawri's pain circled back to Seita, the Bloodwood assassin, the great betrayer.

Just as Hawkwood had helped Tala and Nail escape Purgatory, Seita had helped Liz Hen and Dokie escape the castle. Tala Bronachell did not know what to think of the newcomers from Gallows Haven, Liz Hen Neville and Dokie Liddle. Dokie was amiable enough, but Liz Hen could go from happy one moment to sad the next. She could go from abashed, twitchy nervousness to outright brazen confidence, all within one spoken sentence. Dokie just drew pictures all day.

For the most part, everyone in the group stayed cloaked and hooded. Except for Liz Hen. "But they might be looking for us," Dokie had tried to reason with her a few days ago. "Jovan's knights might be searching every tavern and saloon in Amadon for a big red-haired girl like you. And remember I stole Sky Reaver from him too."

"Searching for *me*?" had been Liz Hen's snarky reply. "Unlikely." The girl doffed her cloak and hood daily, clearly unconcerned whether anyone saw a large red-haired girl in a saloon. Bronwyn and Cromm had "procured" cloaks for both Liz Hen and Dokie the first day of their arrival. They had even procured new clothes and light leather armor for Tala and Nail, to replace their prison garb. They had also obtained shortswords for Nail, Dokie, and Liz Hen, and a long silver dagger with a fleece-lined sheath for Tala. She wore the blade now at her belt, only halfheartedly listening to the current conversation.

"Beer Mug will take his leave of that castle soon, Dokie," Liz Hen said. "If he has not already."

"He is the leave-taking kind of dog." Dokie looked up from his drawing. "I mean, when he wants to be."

"'When he wants to be'?" Liz Hen asked with some concern.

"Perhaps they are feeding him good food in the castle." Dokie shrugged.

"'Good food'?" Liz Hen looked horrified. "I didn't think of that."

"Sure," Dokie said. "Grilled steaks, grilled codfish, salmon, mutton, and stag and roasted potatoes. Be hard for a dog like Beer Mug to take his leave of good food like that."

"Beer Mug would not betray me," Liz Hen huffed. "Not even for a kingly buffet."

The bartender dropped a plate of fried chicken on the table before Cromm Cru'x. The oghul removed the black stone from his mouth to eat. Picking up the chicken, he said, "Cromm would betray anyone for a kingly buffet."

"Well." Liz Hen eyed the chicken hungrily. "Beer Mug's not like oghul-kind."

"And what is oghul-kind like?" Cromm asked.

"Full of betrayal." Liz Hen's answer was swift in coming. The oghul growled.

"Beer Mug is most certainly *not* full of betrayal," Dokie said. "That I can assure you." He held up his latest drawing in the dim light of the tavern, squinting as he examined it. "But Beer Mug does like a good plate of food."

"So Beer Mug *is* like oghul-kind?" Cromm asked. "Cromm wagers this dog you speak of likes blood, too, no?"

Liz Hen scrunched up her face in disgust. "Perhaps. But Beer Mug is no betrayer."

"Cromm never did say that Beer Mug was full of betrayal. Was you who accused Cromm and all oghul-kind of betrayal."

"Did I?" Liz Hen looked at Dokie questioningly.

"I've honestly lost track of the conversation." Dokie shrugged, focusing on his drawing again. He wore the sword Sky Reaver at his belt. It rattled against the wooden bench.

The world is full of betrayal, Tala thought. It wasn't just oghuls. It was dwarves and Vallè and Glade Chaparral and Jovan and Bloodwood assassins. In fact, if she ever saw Seita again, Tala was apt to knife the Vallè bitch right in the throat. *Everything is the Bloodwood's fault!* Everything wrong with Tala's life was Seita's doing.

"You know nothing of Beer Mug, Cromm Cru'x," Liz Hen said, greedy eyes still fixed on the plate of chicken before the oghul. "Oghuls and shepherd dogs are not in the least similar."

"Cromm begs to differ." The oghul picked up a chicken leg.

"Cromm can beg all he wants," she said.

"Cromm will." The oghul took a huge slobbering bite, sucking all the fried skin and meat from the bone in one gulp.

"Can I at least have a piece of that chicken before it's all gone?" Liz Hen asked.

The oghul handed a chicken breast across the table. Liz Hen took it, then immediately began brushing it clean with the tips of her fingers.

"What do you do?" Cromm asked.

"Your oghul skin is flaky," Liz Hen answered. "It ofttimes gets in the food."

"Cromm does not have flaky skin."

"Cromm does have flaky skin," Liz Hen said, still brushing at the chicken breast. "It's all over the floor under your chair, like a gray carpet of dust."

Cromm looked down at the floor under his chair. When he looked up, his thick brows were narrowed in concern. He picked up a chicken leg in silence, examining it for skin flakes now too.

"You shouldn't have pointed out his flaky skin," Dokie said, no longer studying his drawing. "Sure he is flaky, but why say anything at all?"

Liz Hen took a bite of her newly cleaned chicken breast. "An oghul's got to be told about his flaky skin, otherwise how's he to know?"

Cromm set his chicken leg back down. "Don't you think Cromm can see his own skin falling off his arms and legs? You don't think Cromm is . . . How do you say it . . . ?"

"Self-conscious?" Dokie asked.

"Self-aware," Bronwyn corrected him.

"That is it." The oghul nodded to Dokie. "Cromm's self is very conscious and aware of his skin condition."

"Splendid," Liz Hen said with satisfaction. "Ol' Man Leddingham always said the first step to fixing a problem is acknowledging that there is a problem."

Tala didn't know how much longer she could tolerate the insane conversations between Liz Hen and the oghul. She had a handful of problems herself. And she was doing nothing about any of them. But what could she do alone? It was Hawkwood who claimed they should just lie low here in the inn. But Tala wished to do something. After all, Jondralyn was dead, her brother was readying for Fiery Absolution, Aeros Raijael's army was rumored to be marching upon Amadon from the west, and rumors from the north were that Hragna'Ar oghuls were gathering. And above all, she was a fugitive in her own city. It was a list of problems no one person should have to bear the burden of. *And now we are just supposed to wait here in this saloon? For what? Seita? A Bloodwood assassin to escort us to Fiery Absolution?* For that seemed what everyone was waiting for. It was all madness and insanity. More insane even than a conversation between Liz Hen Neville and Cromm Cru'x.

"Do you know what you are?" Cromm asked Liz Hen.

"What am I?" the red-haired girl answered.

"You are the type who has a bigger and better story than Cromm no matter what Cromm talks about."

Dokie piped up, "You mean she is a one-upper."

"Aye," Cromm huffed. "A one-upper."

"How so?" Liz Hen asked.

"If Cromm tells a story about killing a Sør Sevier knight, then Liz Hen has kilt a dozen Sør Sevier knights. Kilt them as she swims in an ocean. With sharks. And her hair on fire."

"But I have done that," Liz Hen said. "Just not with my hair on fire."

The oghul went on, "Or if Cromm says he is cold, Liz Hen has swung herself through the icy winds whilst over a bottomless crevasse atop a Sky Lochs glacier."

"But I have."

"If Cromm fidgets or scratches at his flaky skin, Liz Hen fidgets more, placing her hands on the table, then off the table, then back on the table, rubs her neck, then stops rubbing, then rubs her neck again, nonstop it is, over and over and endless."

"Well, my fidgeting is your own fault, Cromm," Liz Hen said.

"How so?" the oghul asked.

"Well, when talking to an argumentative oghul, I feel I have no place to put my hands, on or under or near the table—or should I just sit on them? And I rub my neck because . . . Well, anyway, never mind that. Let's just say I remember all too well what happened to Bishop Godwyn in that cabin when the oghuls burst in."

Cromm stared at her blankly, both gnarled elbows on the table now, broad gray chin resting in folded hands. The jewels in his protruding knuckles sparkled and glinted in the faint light of the tavern.

"I don't like it when you look at me like that," Liz Hen said, rubbing her neck.

"Like what?" the oghul asked.

"Like that." Liz Hen pointed. "You are giving me a look."

"Cromm does not give looks," the oghul responded with a grunt. "Cromm's face only contorts and changes when he is sucking on an angel stone."

"It's hard to know what an oghul's facial expressions might mean," Bronwyn broke in. "But you shouldn't be concerned about what looks he gives, Miss Liz Hen. Cromm actually likes you quite a lot, despite his facial expressions."

Bronwyn's own facial expressions were hard to read, save for the perpetual smirk hiding just below the surface of all she said. Or at least that was what Tala thought. The conversations usually got even more weird once Bronwyn joined in.

Dokie looked up from his drawing. "Cromm might not have very lively facial expressions, but he is a trifle, as I would say, bowlegged." He held up the parchment he had been working on. It was a charcoal drawing of an oghul. Tala giggled out loud when she saw the drawing. Then she clapped her hand over her mouth, for it was clear the small boy took his art seriously.

"See. Look." Dokie pointed at various parts of his drawing. "Cromm's head sits too far forward on his shoulders, as if it's liable to fall off at any moment. Cromm's head is what an artist would call ill-proportioned."

Bronwyn laughed. "Astonishing." She turned to Cromm. "It looks just like you."

"It looks nothing like Cromm," the oghul said, thick brows furrowed as he studied the drawing. A low growl was developing somewhere deep in his chest.

Bronwyn turned to Dokie, shrugging. "Best not to get too detailed in your descriptions of Cromm, or any oghul, honestly, especially in matters of portraiture."

"Why not?" Dokie asked.

"Because if the oghul is not fond of the artist's drawing, that oghul can remove all the blood from the artist's body with but two of his oghul teeth."

Dokie turned the drawing facedown on the table. Cromm leaned back in his chair, both burly hands behind his gray head, thick fingers interlaced.

"Clearly, when folks are so cooped up and bored, they start drawing portraits of each other," Bronwyn said. "When that happens, you know it's time to go."

She nodded to her oghul companion. "What say we go a-looking for Mancellor, Cromm? As accommodating as this tavern has been, we've been holed up here long enough. We've come so far. And we are so close now. My brother was last seen in the castle. He is sure to be there still. I say we go back in there and find him."

"Cromm does not think it wise to go back into that castle, as he has said."

"But the Dayknights are not looking for us as they are looking for Hawkwood, Tala, Liz Hen, and the others."

"But Cromm is an oghul, and oghuls are generally not wanted in castles."

"I'm with Bronwyn," Tala interjected. "We've sat around hiding for too long. Fearful. Waiting. For what? We must act. Do something. Jondralyn would not have just sat around like this. My sister would have taken action, even if it meant death."

She glanced at Hawkwood as she said that last part, then dropped her eyes to the table when she saw the moment of pain that crossed his normally stern expression.

"But what are our options?" Nail asked her. "We could return to the castle as Bronwyn suggests and search for her brother, but that would just get us all thrown back into Purgatory, or worse. Or should we head west and search again for the angel stones and weapons of the Five Warrior Angels?"

"I've already been on several quests in search of those Laijon-be-damned weapons and stones," Liz Hen said. "I doubt I'm up for more trekking about."

"And it sounds as if Aeros Raijael has them anyway," Dokie added.

"And he's bringing them to Amadon," Liz Hen said. "If rumors be true, he is nearly here. And Seita said she wanted us to steal them back."

"Aye," Dokie agreed. "She did mention that."

Liz Hen said, "For my part, I am none too thrilled to know that Aeros is bringing the weapons and stones and a hundred thousand bloodthirsty Sør Sevier knights straight into Amadon, with no one to stop him. I've fought his army twice now. I've no wish to do it again."

"Do not worry, Liz Hen," Cromm said. He turned his stiff gaze to Nail. "Aeros is marching his army to Absolution, and the marked one will be ready to meet him on the field of battle under the Burning Tree." Under Cromm's hard scrutiny, Nail's face turned pale. The oghul went on, "And that is why Cromm is satisfied to wait here in this tavern eating chicken and drinking ale. Let Absolution come to Cromm."

Lawri Le Graven pulled the hood back from her own pale face and asked in a hushed whisper, "But will Fiery Absolution come?"

Her question was followed by a moment of silence.

"Yes, Fiery Absolution shall come like a thief in the night," a familiar voice rang out soft and lilting from the darkness of the tavern. It was Seita. Tala's blood curdled at the sound of her voice. "Out of nowhere, all armies shall suddenly gather to that Silver Throne finally placed under that Atonement Tree," Seita said, approaching their table. "That is a direct quote from *The Way and Truth of Laijon*. Revelations of the Fourth Warrior Angel, chapter thirteen, verse thirty-three, to be exact."

"Seita!" Liz Hen jumped up from the table and enveloped the Vallè princess in a huge hug. "You came back!"

All Tala wanted to do was stab the deceitful Vallè bitch in the eye. She curled her fingers around the hilt of her dagger, waiting to pull it and strike. Tala knew the Vallè for what she truly was: a Bloodwood assassin. Naught but evil. Full of betrayal and deception. "You poisoned Lawri." The hissing words spilled out of her clenched mouth unbidden. "You *poisoned* Lawri." Everyone was looking at her now, including Seita.

"No." Seita's cold gaze cut straight into Tala's. "You were the one who fed her the poison, Tala. I did not."

"So you admit she was poisoned."

"Some might say poisoned. Whilst others might say we've merely prepared her for her own destiny, you and I." The Vallè's crisp brow narrowed. "She has been prepared for Absolution, as have you, Tala."

"I want nothing from you"—Tala drew the dagger at her side—"but your death."

"Not today." Seita looked away, as if the threat of the dagger in Tala's hand were of no account. The Vallè princess addressed Hawkwood. "Val-Draekin shall meet us under the Burning Tree. All is as our master planned."

"He might still be your master," Hawkwood said, "but he is not mine. I forsook that life long ago."

Terror and dread burned through Tala's heart at the knowing look shared between the two Bloodwoods.

"So Val-Draekin did not burn up in the Filthy Horse Saloon?" Nail asked. He was at Tala's side, his own sword in hand. There was a pained look on his face, as if he were just now realizing the depth of everyone's deception. "What game have you been playing, Seita?" He turned to Hawkwood. "Are you part of the Vallè's game Val-Draekin spoke of, the game the Vallè have been playing for centuries?"

"And in the end," Seita said, "when it comes to anything involving Val-Draekin, what you thought you saw might not even be what you thought you saw."

Nail brought his sword up, the tip aimed at Seita. "Has everything been a lie? What have you *done*? What is this game?"

"I do not consider it a game," Seita answered. "For I have been fighting against vision and prophecy my whole life, questioning everything about myself with every decision I've ever made. No, this is as real to me as it is to you, Nail. Absolution shall wash away the sins of all humankind. It is no game."

Fear and anger coiled their frigid claws around Tala's spine. *How could we have all been so naive!* She looked around. Everyone was now standing. Lawri Le Graven was the only one who remained seated. She had not looked up once, not even when Tala and Seita had talked about her being poisoned. Lawri's face was hidden in the shadows of her hood. What few other patrons occupying the tavern were watching Tala's group now. Anytime a sword was drawn in a tavern, it was apt to garner attention. And Nail's sword was still pointed at the Vallè princess, the tip just inches from her face.

"Easy, Nail," Hawkwood warned as he reached for the blade.

"No." Seita stopped Hawkwood's hand with her own. "Let him ask his questions. Let him hear the truth." She stared down the length of Nail's sword, undaunted.

"What game do you play?" Nail insisted, cold eyes piercing into hers.

"I do not *play* any game," the Vallè princess answered, her own orbs like shards of green ice. "I live it. And I have been *living* as a queen in this game my whole life, whilst you have been but a pawn. For you are not of my blood, Nail."

Nail blanched at her words.

"Put that sword away," Seita said to him, "before I put it away for you."

"Cromm will not let you harm the marked one," Cromm Cru'x grunted. Bronwyn and the oghul stood, both of them shrouded in darkness across the table from Seita, both tense and ready to fight, Bronwyn with her bow in hand.

"You have it all wrong, you two," Seita said, eyeing the oghul. "One moment the great oghul, Cromm, is relaxing in a tavern, sucking on a black rock; the next he shall be escorting the marked one to Fiery Absolution as he has dreamt of doing his entire life." Bronwyn and the oghul exchanged confused looks. "But the truth is"—Seita gestured to

Lawri, still seated to the left of Cromm—"Your dreams are meaningless, oghul. Lawri is the only one in the Slaver's Inn you need concern yourself with. For she is Dragon Claw, and I have come to fetch her for Fiery Absolution. Lawri Le Graven is the only one of you the Vallè now need. The rest of you can do what you please. You are not needed at Fiery Absolution. None of you." She reached out, gesturing for Lawri to stand.

"You will not touch my cousin." Tala raised her own silver dagger to match Nail's, both blades now pointed at the Vallè princess.

Seita's gaze cut right through both blades, violence in her eyes. "I will not kill you, Tala Bronachell, for like Lawri, I have also enjoyed grooming you. For you were a worthy foe. But you have served your purpose."

Then Seita clapped. And Tala's dagger spun from her hands, clattering under a wooden chair near the bar, sending several onlookers dancing out of the way. The Vallè princess met Tala's startled gaze with a smile.

Nail took a step toward Seita, sword unwavering, backing the Vallè princess down. But Seita's smile was coy as she moved away from him. Then she leaped into the air, twirling, foot striking the sword from Nail's grip. The weapon shot straight into the air, sticking point-first into the ceiling above. Nail looked up at his quivering sword, stunned. Bronwyn now had an arrow nocked and poised. Cromm brandished two long knives.

Seita ignored them as she stepped around the table and held her hand out for Lawri. "Rise," she said. "For I come to fetch you to Fiery Absolution, and we shall tarry no more."

Lawri reached out with her good arm and graciously took the Vallè princess's proffered hand. Seita's delicate fingers curled around Lawri's as she pulled the girl to her feet, guiding her around the table toward the front door.

"The rest of you can follow us to Fiery Absolution if you want," Seita said. "It matters not to me."

All this prophecy—could it be false? Could all this prophecy be the workings of the lord of the underworld himself? Could that lord and his minions be all we thought they were? Or could the very pathways of the underworld, those dark caverns carved out by the slithering scales of Viper, lead to salvation?
—THE BOOK OF THE BETRAYER

CHAPTER FIFTY-SEVEN

CRYSTALWOOD

12TH DAY OF THE HEART MOON, 999TH YEAR OF LAIJON
AMADON, GUL KANA

To the north, beyond the Hallowed Grove, smoke could be seen billowing black and ominous across the far-distant horizon—proof that rumors of a vast army of both oghul and Vallè soldiers descending upon Amadon were true. Just before dusk, farms and forests could be seen burning in the wake of the horde. But night had now fallen, and all that could be seen of that vast army was the soft orange glow of the fires.

The giant Atonement Tree was silhouetted black against the fiery light.

"This is as far as I go," Gault Aulbrek said, placing his cloak on the wagon bench between himself and Ava Shay. "It would be folly for any of you to return to Amadon now. The city is about to be overrun by oghuls from the north and Aeros Raijael's army from the west."

The last few days of travel, Krista Aulbrek's father had sat comfortably atop the wagon bench, wrapped in his gray cloak, leather pants, and raggedy shirt. Color had returned to his flesh, and he no longer looked as sickly and near death as he had. For weeks Krista had worried that her poison was going to kill him. But it had not, and the poison was now almost fully sweated from his system.

"We should not trap ourselves in Amadon." Gault stared fixedly at the backs of Borden Bronachell and the dwarf, Ironcloud. The king of Gul Kana sat at the head of the wagon with the dwarf, reins in his hands pulling against the necks of the team of mules ahead as he slowed their wagon to a halt. Borden had already mentioned that he did not want to venture closer to the Atonement Tree than need be, for many Amadon Silver Guards surrounded it. They were a safe distance from the outer perimeter of the grove now. Borden did not know how the guards would react to his unannounced homecoming, or if they would even believe it was their king returned.

"The tree is so big," Ava Shay said. The Gallows Haven girl's face was both somber and pale against the bright blue of her dress. She wore pants under the dress, and heavier boots she had gathered out of the Turn Key Saloon. Her ruby-hilted sword was tucked into the belt at her waist. She had ridden with Gault in the back of the wagon all the way from Lord's Point, doing her best to nurse him back to health. Krista had to admit, there was magic in Ava's touch when it came to comforting her father during his worst bouts with the poison.

Krista rode her Bloodeye steed, Dread, next to the wagon. She had ridden the black mare every step of the journey, once again at home on her familiar back. The mules leading the wagon huffed with nervousness, smelling the smoke and death in the distance. Dread remained calm. Krista gently rubbed the mare's neck.

"Even if we can survive the coming battle," Gault went on, "I will not be thrown into another Gul Kana prison, or worse, that damnable slave quarry."

"It could be Absolution indeed lies before us, but we will make our way into Amadon," Borden Bronachell said, not looking back at Gault, eyes fixed on the soft orange glow beyond the Atonement Tree. Krista could swear she saw tears glistening in his eyes. Before dusk, as they had

ridden past the slave quarry and watched the fires to the north, the pan-
orama of the city had risen up and spread out before them.

"I'm home." Borden Bronachell had become emotional at the sight.
"To see my daughters again, Jondralyn, Tala. My sons, Jovan, little Ansel."

Krista had marveled at the sheer size of Amadon—the largest city
in Gul Kana, in all the Five Isles. It was not a walled city like those
they had passed in Wyn Darrè. Few towns and hamlets in Gul Kana had
standing walls anymore, or even functional keeps or castles, for that
matter. Gul Kana was not like war-torn Wyn Darrè or the constantly
besieged shores of Sør Sevier and Adin Wyte. No city in Gul Kana had
seen war in a thousand years. No, Amadon was a city with numerous entrance points, only its inner neighborhoods and the castle itself walled
and guarded.

The round, crown-shaped Royal Cathedral dominated the skyline.
It was where the Blessed Mother Mia was buried. Next to the Royal
Cathedral was the almost as tall Temple of the Laijon Statue. Krista had
easily spotted the circular, columned gladiator arena near the ethereal
Hall of the Dayknights. She could just make out the crenellated battlements circling the older part of the city, and below that the warrens of
crooked and cobbled buildings and their crooked and cobbled streets.
And beyond the inner city, completely engulfing the dark skyline, were
the steep cliffs of Mount Albion, set high above the mouth of the River
Vallè and overlooking Memory Bay. Atop the mount was the looming
hulk of Amadon Castle itself, cutting a dark and hollow shape into the
sky; its towering spires, baileys, palisades, barbicans, courtyards, and
connecting causeways were all hewn of black stone and peppered with
flags of silver and black.

To reach the castle, all they needed to do was follow the River Vallè,
and it would take them right to the front gate. Black Dugal had made
Krista memorize everything she could about the city of Amadon. In
fact, Dugal required all his Bloodwoods to study everything about each
of the Five Isles and their major towns, rivers, forests, and mountain
ranges. There were few places within the Five Isles that Krista did not

know something about. And she knew more than she wanted to know about the Hallowed Grove, for Dugal had stressed to her the importance of this illustrious public park located due west of Mount Albion many times.

The park itself clung to the very outskirts of Amadon, the Riven Rock slave quarry a few miles farther to the west. When she had passed by the quarry earlier, Krista had seen her father's eyes burn with both apprehension and anger, his entire body tense. It was a strange thing to witness in him, emotion of any kind. After all, Gault had forever been a distant, awesome figure, who by his sheer existence commanded her complete devotion. But to sense emotion in him now, possibly weakness, was disconcerting. She had watched the poison from her dagger almost claim him. She had seen him fight with the wraiths he thought were in his head. Those things had shaken her. For it made her realize that she herself was not indestructible.

Bloodwoods are not invincible. She needed to keep that in mind when overconfidence set in. Truth was, she had failed to assassinate Aeros Raijael. In fact, in their escape from the Fortress of Saint Only, she had seen her own lack. Hammerfiss and the White Prince had fought her off with such a ferocious and lethal skill it had scared her. Borden, Ironcloud, Ava, Gault, Krista: they had all barely escaped with their lives that day. They had gotten lucky.

Krista glanced at Borden Bronachell sitting at the head of the wagon, reins in hand, staring out at the distant Atonement Tree. There were things to be admired about him. And things she disliked. *He thinks I am a murderer, the worst kind of human there is.* And in a way, she wondered if he was not correct. She had no idea what her own father, Gault, thought of her. She longed to talk with him. But she was scared. And that bothered her. With his poisoning and his long recovery, they had yet to have a meaningful conversation—though he was displeased with her black leather armor and red-eyed horse, that she could tell. But was he displeased with her, or the circumstances she had fallen into? That she did not know. In a way, she wished she could just go back to that day of her Sacrament of Souls and set every prisoner tied to a Bloodwood tree free.

In fact, she would free every prisoner in the dungeons of Rokenwalder if she could. *Good people kill in self-defense.* Though she could not remember his exact words, Borden had once said to her something like that. *Good people kill because they're hungry, or afraid.* Good *people do not kill for the pleasure of it. They do not kill in some Sacrament of Souls.*

At the time his words had stung, but they had also filled her with anger and a deep-rooted need to prove him wrong. *What few I killed deserved to die,* she had countered. *They had justice coming. They were naught but criminals. Prisoners.*

And his answer had silenced her. We *were in the dungeons. Both you and I. Did we deserve to die in some Sacrament of Souls? Does being imprisoned make one man worse than another? Does the prisoner not have hope, or dreams, or potential to change? Or are those imprisoned naught but forgotten souls, condemned to be used in some cruel sacrament?* She had wrestled with those words ever since he had spoken them. And now she stood on the outskirts of the Hallowed Grove. A place of Absolution.

The Atonement Tree *was* big. Krista followed Ava Shay's gaze toward the center of the grove and the massive tree at its center—a pale green monolith in the dim glow of the crescent Heart Moon. Over a thousand years old was the tree, and Krista had learned that not a single leaf had ever rotted or fallen from its lofty heights. The Atonement Tree was always alive and green, even during the starkest of winters. A lush web of ivy peppered with white heather circled the tree's massive trunk, twisting and twining up, up, up, vanishing into the crooked branches and moonlit leaves that soared over five hundred feet above the luxuriant grassy loam.

No more than a dozen other pilgrims and commoners lingered nearby, most of them cloaked Vallè. Like Krista, they were all gazing toward the holy place of Laijon's great sacrifice. A contingent of several hundred Silver Guards was positioned in a circular formation around the perimeter of the park, spears at their shoulders. They guarded over the sacred monument both day and night, allowing only those of the king's court and their retainers close to the tree itself. And closer to the tree were many more Vallè, several dozen at least. Royalty from Val Vallè, Krista assumed. Despite the heat of summer, they were also cloaked.

"See how the leaves look wan and ashen in the light?" Borden Bronachell dipped his head to the tree, speaking to Krista now. "See how the Vallè royals blow into their own hands?"

"Aye," Krista acknowledged. It was true: the entire tree appeared swathed in a dull autumn frost. And the group of Vallè at its base stood with heads angled upward, their cupped hands held aloft.

"Tradition is," Borden continued, "a Vallè will place palms together like that, a white powder called Shroud of the Vallè in hand, and with a swift blow of their breath send the powder into the breeze, where it will ideally float up to meld with the leaves above—leaves as ancient as the tree itself."

"I know what Shroud of the Vallè is," Krista said.

"But did you know that it is this Shroud of the Vallè itself that extends the life of the leaves?" Ironcloud asked her.

She did not answer the question. In fact, she did not answer any question the dwarf posed. She tried to forget that the squat fellow even existed most days. *Squateye? Ironcloud?* She did not trust the dwarf with multiple personalities.

"A thousand years of Vallè royals have followed the tradition," Borden went on, "believing that for one of royal blood to grace the tree with Shroud of the Vallè is to show the gratitude of all Vallè for Laijon's great sacrifice."

Black Dugal had oft spoken of the practice. But Krista had never really believed she would see a Vallè perform such a sacrament until now. She had studied Vallè alchemy, learning that Shroud of the Vallè was a white powder fashioned from the crushed white crystal found within a hidden quarry along the northwestern shores of Val Vallè. The powder was also used as a drug. It was a powerful hallucinogen. When sniffed it produced a euphoric high, though Krista herself had never partaken of it. The white powder could also spark to a quick-burning flame.

Gault climbed out of the back of the wagon, careful not to jostle Ava Shay next to him. His body still appeared weakened by the poison.

"It is here we should turn back," he said, looking at Krista. She remained steady atop her horse, face emotionless.

Gault then offered to help Ava from the cart. But the girl shook her head in refusal. Gault stepped back from the wagon, nodding to her. "As you wish."

Over the course of their journey from Saint Only, Ava Shay had shared with Krista some of the details regarding her relationship with Gault. She claimed Gault had been the only kind one in all of Aeros Raijael's retinue. In fact, she had described Gault's kindness many times, even recounting how she had asked him to help her escape, though it seemed the girl had been holding something back from that story. Krista had become good at reading people, spotting lies and half-truths. And Ava Shay's story seemed scattered with half-truths. Ava had also told Krista of the night she had overheard Aeros and Spiderwood discussing their plans to betray Gault in Ravenker. Again, Krista felt there were parts of that story Ava wasn't completely confessing to.

"You should not be so quick to leave us," Borden said to Gault. He motioned with one arm toward the orange glow to the north. "Absolution is nigh. The armies of Hragna'Ar are upon us. The White Prince is somewhere behind us. Don't tell me we have carried you this far just so you can turn and walk away from history."

"But I can walk away," Gault said. "And that is the important thing. Freedom."

"You are not yet fully well," Borden said. "Some poisons still linger within you."

"The wraiths are within all of us," Gault said.

"My father has no more need of your Vallè healers," Krista said. "He is fine. He suffers from no poison. He suffers not from the wraiths. He is fine and can do as he wishes. Let him leave if he so wants."

"You do not wish to come with me?" Gault asked.

I do, Krista thought. Her stomach was tied in a knot. Her vision blurred. *But I don't.*

"I am your father—"

"No," Borden cut Gault off. "He is not your father, Crystalwood."

Fear further knotted in Krista's stomach. Real fear. She glanced at Gault. He did look ill, still. The black mare suddenly shifted under her, sensing her concern. It seemed Dread was attuned to her every mood. She gained control of the Bloodeye with a flick of the reins.

"That I took a Bloodwood oath to become fatherless does not change the fact that Gault is still my father."

"But he is *not* your father," Borden repeated.

"They do not deserve this," Ava Shay said from from where she sat in the back of the wagon, her thin face floating in the darkness, her voice pleading. "Neither one of them deserves this. Leave them be, I beg of you, King Borden. Just let Gault go if he so wishes. Just let him go in peace."

Krista felt suddenly dizzy atop her horse. *Why does she defend my father?* She and Ava had shared much these past days, but Krista always knew the Gallows Haven girl had been holding information back. *What does she know?* She feared looking at Gault again, feared what she might see there in his face.

"Why do you keep saying he is not my father?" Krista asked Borden, wanting an end to the conversation.

"I keep saying that because it is the truth," Borden said. "He is not your father."

The accusation made Krista flare with anger. She found a black dagger was suddenly in her hand, fingers curling tight around the hilt. She held up the blade between her and Borden. "Keep saying that," she said, voice emotionless, "and I shall carve the eyes out of your face."

"You do not want to fight me," Borden said, his own voice void of emotion or threat, just calm assuredness.

On their journey across the breadth of Wyn Darrè, there seemed to have been a sort of uneasy truce between her and Borden Bronachell, a silent combat of wills. But now it appeared that was over. By pulling her blade, Krista, like all Bloodwoods, had turned a simple conversation into a life-or-death encounter, blood and threat hanging over them all. A black blade revealed meant death was nigh. But Krista also knew Borden was a more than capable fighter in his own right. And in reality, this had been no "simple conversation."

"Tell her the truth, Ser Gault." Borden cast his gaze toward the man. "Tell Krista the truth of her heritage."

Gault looked up at her with a pained expression on his face. And with that one look, furious thoughts came rushing at Krista like an avalanche of mud, trees, and snow. *Who is this man?* Her mind raged. Was this the true face of her father she looked upon, normally as rigidly serene and empty of expression as that of a true Knight Archaic, now so full of grief and sorrow? He had been separated from her for so long that she knew not what to say to him now. They had never really communicated. She just wanted the truth. And with that thought her anger melted away again to fear. But she would not let that fear undo her, bleak as it made her feel. As *The Book of the Betrayer* read, *Live with it, for you cannot undo what has happened.*

"Is what he says the truth?" she asked Gault. "Are you not my father, as he claims?"

With vacant eyes, Gault looked at Borden, saying, "When the poisons are gone from my system, when the wraiths are long gone and I am again at full strength and in my right mind, I shall slay you for this, Borden Bronachell. I shall slay you and the dwarf sitting beside you. Then I shall slay all your kin. And I will make sure they die the most painful of deaths, each and every one. And that is no idle threat."

Gault looked to the ground, then to the sky, his eyes naught but twin hollow caverns. "Are you my daughter?" he asked of no one in particular. "That is the question now, isn't it?" He looked up at her then, still, unblinking. "Borden Bronachell has no way of proving truth or lie to you either way, Krista." He took two steps toward her, gently took the Bloodwood dagger from her, then took her hand in his. It was their first real touch in over five years. He repeated, "Borden has no way of proving the truth or lie to you either way. But I tell you now, it *is* truth he speaks. You are not of my blood. You are not of my loins."

She pulled away from him, her Bloodeye steed shuffling to the side, sensing her stress again. Tears sprang from her eyes, unbidden. She couldn't speak.

"What good ever came of secrets?" Gault asked of no one again, looking down at the black dagger in his hands. "That is why I admit it to you now. And admitting that secrets are bad does not change the fact that

I will slay Borden Bronachell when I am fully healed. But what good has ever come of selfish secrets like the one I've clung to for so long? What good has come of it? That was what this all boils down to. Is one beholden to secrets or the truth? And I am resolved to the truth now. And I beg your forgiveness, Krista, but you and your mother were the loves of my life."

"I don't understand." Her voice was like a whip crack in the night, the lump in her throat replaced by betrayal and rage. "I don't *understand*," she hissed at the man before her.

"When your mother died," he said, "I could not bear to lose you, too. I claimed you as my own, though you were not."

I never knew him. She had so many questions but wanted no more answers. Answers hurt. *Or is it just the truth that hurts?* She couldn't break her gaze from the man before her. *He is so weak.* She suddenly saw him differently now. *Look at him in his hollow despair, making excuses for his lies. How did I not see this before now? They tried to tell me all along.* Borden had tried to tell her. He had once said to her something like, *The perfect king, the perfect soldier, the perfect* father *is only without flaw because he is off fighting for his kingdom,* he'd also said. *The man who is constantly present will never be as perfect as the one who is away, the one who is gone. Any young girl is bound to romanticize her father, especially if he is nobly absent because of a war.* And Gault looked anything but perfect and noble to her now.

As Black Dugal always said, *A Bloodwood must become fatherless.* And she was a Bloodwood; beautiful, silent, and above all, not weak. For that was another rule of being a Bloodwood: never show weakness.

I stole the life from two innocent children, Borden had also confessed. *And their lives have been naught but loneliness and hardship ever since. For seventeen years they have been living a lie.* And Krista now knew for a surety that she was one of those innocent children. *Am I truly fatherless?* she asked herself, appalled at the conflict she sensed growing within herself. She'd been stuck in a world dim and remote, and there was no escaping it now.

Krista found she was still looking down on her father. And what she saw was a broken man. A weak man. An armorless and weaponless man

clothed in naught but raggedy sweat-stained clothes. He was no longer
the gallant and brave knight she remembered from her youth. In fact,
these last few weeks spent with him, he had been naught but a poisoned
man, a sick man, a man in fear of the wraiths, a man in need of tending, a
man who Borden Bronachell and Ironcloud had had to help to the privy
daily. A man unable to care for even himself. *But how can I so easily think
the worst of him? Which one of us has truly been poisoned?*

Gault didn't even meet Krista's eye as he reached forth and snatched
his tattered gray cloak from the back seat of the wagon. He motioned
again for Ava Shay to climb from the cart and join him. But again the
Gallows Haven girl shook her head, uncertainty in her eyes. Gault
wrapped himself in the faded gray cloak. His face vanished within the
cloak's shadowy cowl. Then he turned and walked away from the wagon,
not stopping, not looking back.

Dread shifted all her weight onto her hindquarters, snorting. The
Bloodeye suddenly reared back, nearly spilling Krista to the ground.

Leaning forward, reins loose in hand, Krista held on by clenching
her legs tight to the horse's midsection. When Dread regained all fours,
Krista tugged hard on the reins whilst setting heels to flanks. She gained
quick control of the Bloodeye by turning her in a tight circle.

There was a distant rumble. And the mules hooked to the wagon
also bucked and brayed in panic. Borden and Ironcloud tried to settle
them from atop the wagon. The ground shook. Krista's eyes roamed the
Hallowed Grove and settled on the city of Amadon.

What had moments before been a distant haze of flickering city
lamplight to the south and east was a thunderous torch-bearing army
of soldiers: thousands of foot soldiers, followed by legion after legion
of mounted knights. War chargers pounded the earth at a heavy gait
as they poured from the alleys, streets, and other confines of the city,
rows of mounted cavalry stretching to the left and to the right for miles:
squires, Silver Guards, Dayknights, all of them.

Across the vast expanse between Amadon and the Hallowed Grove
the army marched. They were a polished wave of glittering armor, a sparkling iron-tipped forest of spears, plumed helms, and silver-and-black

banners. This vast army was alive with sound, and moving north and west toward the Hallowed Grove.

"My son," Borden said with both awe and reverence and just a hint of questioning expectation.

"Jovan Bronachell rides at the army's head," Ironcloud said, thick fingers racing nervously through his gnarled beard. "And the grand vicar and archbishops at his side."

In the midst of a thousand advancing torches, Krista could see the leader Borden and Ironcloud were talking about. Even from a great distance, she could tell Jovan Bronachell sat hale and straight atop a black destrier. King Jovan looked like a sturdy, younger version of his father. He rode strong and confident in his black Dayknight armor, dark, shoulder-length hair flowing out behind him.

Behind the king rattled a horse-led wagon. On the two benches behind the driver of the wagon rode a rotund man in the typical burnt-umber cassock of a Gul Kana religious man and a handful of similarly dressed men. Grand Vicar Denarius, Krista surmised, and the Quorum of Five Archbishops of Amadon.

Behind the wagon carrying the vicar was another similar wagon. In the open bed of the second wagon were three long objects wrapped in white canvas. One of the hidden objects was standing on end, taller than a man; the other two were almost of the same shape but laid down on their sides. All were tied to the wagon with rope.

The Vallè royals worshipping under the Atonement Tree moved aside when the king and the two wagons pulled to a stop under the tree. The vast army stretched off into the distance between the Atonement Tree and Amadon to the south and east, staking its claim at Fiery Absolution.

Borden snapped the reins and the wagon began a slow trundle toward the Atonement Tree. "We shall go to them. I shall see my son."

**

Dark of night covered the horizon now. They didn't get far before a small contingent of mounted Silver Guards—those previously stationed around the perimeter of the Hallowed Grove—rode forth and stopped them.

"Only royalty may enter the grove," the lead guard stated as he removed his helm. He was a bright-eyed young knight with wavy blond hair. His gaze was fixed on Borden in somewhat confused recognition. Then his confused stare traveled to Krista, sizing her up in her black leather armor, eyes narrowing to slits at the sight of her red-eyed horse, Dread.

"I am Borden Bronachell," Borden announced. "I ride with Ironcloud of Wyn Darrè and Ava Shay of Gallows Haven, along with Krista of Rokenwalder. We have traveled long and hard to reach Amadon. I ask that you let me pass so I can announce my return to my son, your king, Jovan Bronachell."

The blond knight's mount shuffled back, snorting, kicking up dust, its round brown eyes not leaving the cruel red eyes of Dread. The blond knight gathered control of his mount, guiding it around to again face Borden Bronachell.

"You indeed look like our long-lost king," the blond knight said, doing the three-fingered sign of the Laijon Cross over his heart. "And I would know, for I am Ser Magnus Cornwell, son of Ser Sharp Cornwell. 'Twas King Borden Bronachell himself who knighted me seven years ago when I was but nineteen." The knight dipped his head to Borden. "And you, Ser, I must admit have the look of my former king, though thinner and older." He paused, straightening himself in his saddle, hand on the hilt of his sword now. "But Borden was vanquished in Wyn Darrè. Killed."

"Yes, I was vanquished," Borden said. "But not killed. Rather, I was imprisoned in the darkest dungeons of Sør Sevier. Yet now I have escaped."

The blond knight named Cornwell bowed at the waist, his forehead nearly grazing the mane of his destrier. He raised up. "I believe you. For I prayed you were alive. We shall escort you to King Jovan. Though I believe you, I shall let Jovan make the final determination as to whether you are indeed Borden Bronachell."

**

The canopy of the Atonement Tree soared over Krista into the night sky, every green leaf shimmering under the moonlight and alive with a seemingly individual soul of its own. The dark sky was lit with a thousand torches or more, adding to the tree's overwhelming magical glow. Krista found she was almost gaping straight up at the tree in awe.

On their approach, what few Vallè royals were left worshipping at the tree's edge eyed both her and Dread with disdain. The Vallè pulled their cloaks tighter around their bodies, despite the summer's heat. *Do they not wish to hail the return of the king?*

A team of mounted Dayknights broke from King Jovan's side and galloped toward Borden. One knight drew his sword and spurred his mount before the others, reining up in front of Krista and the wagon and their Silver Guard escort.

"I beg pardon." Ser Magnus Cornwell bowed to this new Dayknight. "But I bring a man who claims to be our lord, Borden Bronachell, returned from the dungeons of Sør Sevier."

The new Dayknight trotted his own war charger up before Borden and Ironcloud sitting in the wagon, the shadowy dark eye slits of his black helm revealing nothing, sword glistening black in his gauntleted hand. Neither Borden nor Ironcloud cowered under the knight's inky gaze. Ava Shay sat alone behind them.

The new Dayknight turned his helmed head toward Krista. She sat comfortable and confident atop her Bloodeye steed just behind the wagon. After a moment the new Dayknight looked away from Krista. He sheathed his sword and reached up and swept off his helm, asking, "Can it truly be?"

"Leif Chaparral." Borden stood slowly in the wagon. "You have the look of a seasoned knight. You are no longer that young man I left in Wyn Darrè."

"Is it truly you, my king?" Leif's dark-rimmed eyes continued to gape at Borden Bronachell.

Borden dipped his head once more. "I heard you were made captain of the Dayknights. Congratulations. I also heard of your victory over the White Prince at the Battle of the Saint Only Channel. A remarkable feat indeed."

"Indeed," Leif repeated, still staring, as if unable to believe who he was seeing atop the wagon. Leif's apprehensive gaze again traveled from Borden to Ironcloud and settled on Ava Shay in the back of the wagon briefly, before moving on to Krista and Dread. Krista immediately detected the fear and suspicion that had crawled up behind Leif's dark-rimmed eyes. She knew she looked ruthless and deadly atop the black horse with the bloodred eyes.

"Using the tidewaters of the channel to your advantage was a brilliant, if not lucky, plan, Ser Leif," Borden said.

The Dayknight's eyes narrowed slightly as they moved from Krista back to Borden. "'Lucky?'" he repeated, a challenge in his voice now.

"Luck is needed in every battle." Borden bowed to him again.

Leif's eyes darkened further. "Do you mock me?"

A second Dayknight reined up next to Leif. He too removed his helm, revealing the face of a young man not much older than Krista herself. This new knight looked like a younger version of Leif Chaparral, hair more naturally curled, eyes less shaded and dark. He too looked around, wary gaze lingering on Krista and Dread but a moment before fixing on Borden. "Is it truly the king?"

"Glade?" Borden asked, eyeing the young man. "Aren't you a bit too young to be a Dayknight? You are not but a year older than Tala, no?"

Leif and Glade glanced at each other, neither answering. An awkward silence filled the space between Borden and the two brothers.

"I earned my place," Glade finally said, sitting proudly atop his horse. "'Twas I who tracked down the ones responsible for the assassination attempt on King Jovan."

"'Assassination attempt?'" Borden questioned.

"You needn't be alarmed," Leif said. "Jovan survived. 'Twas your own nephew, Lindholf Le Graven, who helped the assassin—"

"Lindholf!" Borden cut him off. "How? Where is he? I must know."

"Does it matter?" Leif asked. "He and his accomplice escaped the hangman's noose and fled Amadon with Gault Aulbrek."

Borden and Ironcloud exchanged glances. "Gault was full of secrets from the beginning," the dwarf said. "I am not surprised he mentioned none of this."

Borden turned back to Leif. "Lawri, is she okay?" Borden's face was flushed with worry. "Is my niece safe?"

Glade answered quickly, "Lawri ran off with your daughter Tala."

"Ran off with Tala?"

"Who is it?" came a shout from the torchlit darkness behind Leif and Glade. Jovan Bronachell rode his own mount through the contingent of Dayknights, hair billowing out behind him, a silver crown circling his brow. He reined up between Leif and Glade. "Who dares interrupt the vicar's ceremony?" he demanded, haughty voice laced with anger as he glared at the head of the Dayknights. "Who dares interrupt Fiery Absolution?"

"Look for yourself, my lord." Leif gestured.

Jovan's irritated gaze fell on the wagon. It took a moment, but then it dawned on him who it was. "Father," he muttered, surveying the man's face suspiciously, but not without wonder.

"Son." Borden stepped from the wagon and approached the king.

Dayknights suddenly encircled Jovan, swords drawn, their armored mounts shuffling and jostling to protect him. Leif drew his own sword.

"Move aside." Jovan's voice was shrill and strident as he slid from his horse and pushed his way through the Dayknights.

Leif stopped him. "They say Bloodwood assassins are masters of disguise." His gaze met Krista's then turned back to Jovan. "And this man claiming to be your father travels with a Bloodwood. Just look at her. Isn't it obvious?"

"Move aside, I say!" Jovan pushed his way past Leif. And Leif let him go.

The Dayknights relented too, parting. Jovan stepped stiffly toward his father, stopping short of hugging the man. Both men stared at each other. The resemblance between them was uncanny. Jovan was taller than his father and more sturdily built, although that could be merely the bulk of the Dayknight armor he wore. Borden had increased in size and strength since their escape from Rokenwalder, but he wore no armor like his son. Krista could sense the general aura of uncertainty that filled the air as the two men looked each other over.

It seemed as if Borden wanted to envelop his son in a great big hug. Whereas it seemed Jovan was greeting the moment with a certain degree of caution. Neither of them seemed able to believe what they were seeing. They did not hug. Or even clasp hands.

"This is indeed a grand day for miracles." Another voice spoke from the darkness. Grand Vicar Denarius appeared between Leif's and Glade's horses. Four of the five archbishops of Amadon stepped reverently behind him, heads bowed, hands before their chests as if in prayer.

Borden acknowledged the four archbishops with a bow. The vicar and archbishops wore the simple robes and raiment expected of religious leaders, but with more jewels, bracelets, and gold chains than Krista would have expected. But there were only four of them, not five as she'd been taught. The archbishops were followed by a helmetless knight in strange armor, a knight with long braided hair and streaks of dark blue under his eyes in the fashion of Wyn Darrè.

This strange-looking knight's eyes were curious and wild, and at the moment fixed on Ava Shay. And Ava's eyes were locked onto his. *Do they know each other? Is there some story between them?* More questions Krista would likely never know the answers to.

Denarius gave Krista a dark look, then bowed to Borden. "Not only has tonight brought the Silver Throne to the Hallowed Grove," he said, "but tonight also brings us the return of our long-lost king, Borden Bronachell."

"The Silver Throne?" Borden asked. "It is here?"

Grand Vicar Denarius reached up and snapped his fingers. The cart bearing the three large canvas-covered objects rumbled forward, led by a team of six stout draught mares. The driver forced the cart through the Dayknights, reining up before the grand vicar. The grand vicar then motioned to one of the mounted knights guarding the wagon. The knight dismounted, scrambled aboard the wagon, cut the ropes around the tallest of the objects, and yanked the canvas back.

It was a throne in make and design. *The Silver Throne!* It had five legs and was hewn of one solid piece of polished silver. The shined surface of the throne glittered so brightly in the torchlight it nearly blinded Krista.

The throne sat on a sturdy iron litter that the knights struggled mightily to lift from the wagon. But once they did, they carried the throne and placed it on the grass not twenty paces before the Atonement Tree.

"Not only have we brought the Silver Throne to the Atonement Tree," the vicar said, "but we shall also bear witness to the resurrection of Archbishop Spencerville and the princess."

"What do you mean, the resurrection of Spencerville and 'the princess'?" Borden asked. "What has happened?"

"Jondralyn was killed," Jovan answered with scant emotion. "An emissary of Aeros Raijael likely killed her, if Mancellor Allen is to be believed. But you needn't worry. The vicar shall bring her back to life. We have brought her body to Absolution, brought her and Spencerville in the wagon that carried the Silver Throne."

"*Who* killed Jondralyn?" Borden's confidence in the face of everything finally faltered. "An emissary of Aeros? What emissary?"

"We do not know for sure who killed her," Jovan said. "But she shall live again."

"Show the king his daughter," Denarius ordered the lone man left on the wagon.

The driver of the wagon cut the ropes around the remaining two objects and swept the canvas tarps away in quick succession. They were two long wooden coffins, Vallè-carved symbols and runes gracing their polished mahogany surfaces.

And then the driver opened the lids of both. The stench was ripe. Borden's legs buckled and he dropped to his knees. The two corpses were certainly not easy to look at. Especially Jondralyn's. She was dressed in a long brocaded gown of blue, pearls and jeweled necklaces laid over her chest. But her face was a gaping hollow of blackness and rot. The archbishop's body was wrapped in priestly robes; his face looked more whole.

Borden fell to his knees before the coffins and wept. Jovan stood over his father, no expression on his face.

"Cover the bodies," Denarius ordered the wagon driver. The man did as ordered and the stench subsided.

Borden eventually stood, tears trailing down his cheeks. "What about Ansel? Where is he? Safe in the castle?"

"Ansel is fine, but Tala has betrayed me." Jovan hardened his gaze. "She has run off, Lawri with her, both filled with the same mystical nonsense that turned Jondralyn against me. They are filled with her-esy along with Brethren of Mia witchcraft and other such foolishness, taught to Jondralyn by that traitor, Hawkwood. Yes, Hawkwood and his friend, that demented dwarf, Roguemoore. Jondralyn died for their fool-ishness."

"Foolish was not the way of Roguemoore," Ironcloud said from his perch on the wagon. "Nor the Brethren of Mia."

Jovan ignored the dwarf, glaring at his father accusingly. "The Brethren of Mia continually placed your daughter in harm's way. It is because of the Brethren that Jondralyn died."

"We do not know for certain who took Jondralyn's life in Savon," Denarius said. "'Twas Ser Mancellor Allen here who brought her body back to us and his tale is full of holes."

The vicar motioned to the Wyn Darrè fighter with the tattoos under his eyes and the long hair of carefully pressed braids that dangled like russet ropes over his shoulders, the Wyn Darrè fighter whose gaze still lingered on Ava Shay.

Borden faced Mancellor, bowing. "I am forever in your debt for re-turning my daughter to Amadon, Ser Knight."

"I had help in returning her." Mancellor tore his glance from Ava and bowed to Borden in return. "Two Gallows Haven youths named Liz Hen Neville and Dokie Liddle helped me carry the princess's body from Savon."

"Liz Hen? Dokie?" Ava Shay's voice sounded from behind Ironcloud on the wagon. "You knew them?"

Mancellor's eyes flew back to Ava. "I knew them, yes. They were from Gallows Haven too. Both Dokie and Liz Hen."

"Do not mention Liz Hen's name around me," Jovan snapped harshly. "'Twas she who killed Spencerville."

"Easy, my king." Denarius placed a firm hand on Jovan's arm. "We must be of calm minds now. The girl did not mean to kill Spencerville. All shall be made aright soon enough. He will again be with us. And you shall sit the Silver Throne."

"My father has returned." Jovan yanked his arm from the vicar's grip. "Should he not now sit the Silver Throne? Should he not now usher in Fiery Absolution and the return of Laijon? What need is there of me now?"

"How do you know this man is even your father?" Denarius asked. "Leif is right, the Vallè are known for their tricks. Sør Sevier spies are known for their clever disguises." The vicar's eyes fell on Krista then, taking in the measure of her black leather armor and red-eyed horse, pure revulsion on his face. "For all we know, this is not your father standing before us at all, but rather Black Dugal himself. And even if he is no Bloodwood, even if he is your father, he is still one of the Brethren of Mia."

"Roguemoore always claimed you were a *snake*," Borden hissed at Denarius, hard-edged fury in his eyes, tears for his daughter now gone. "You have clearly poisoned my son against me and the Brethren."

Krista thought of Gault Aulbrek once more. To her, it seemed that today the Hallowed Grove was a place where fathers—blood relation or not—were unwelcome.

There was a sudden loud *Boom!* from the north and everyone jumped, startled.

The ground underneath rumbled and Dread danced to the side.

Horses and war chargers neighed and bucked all around Krista, some spilling knights over backward onto the ground. Krista settled her own horse, brushing the palm of her hand over the mare's sleek neck. She heard the distant grunt and howl of oghuls, her sharpened gaze roaming the fire-lit expanse.

There was another thunderous *Boom!*

An army crested the rise five hundred paces north of the Hallowed Grove, an army of both oghuls and Vallè, thousands upon thousands.

The shined and sculpted armor of the Vallè intermixed with the seething and bristling mass of burly oghuls was a contrast in glamour and grime. The fast-approaching horde was silhouetted against the orange-glowing forests and farms smoldering behind them. Even in the dark, Krista could tell the oghuls were naught but loutish, vulgar beasts, naught but lumbering monsters, whereas the Vallè were glorious warriors all. But together they were formidable allies.

King Jovan's vast army bristled, ready to fight. Dayknights and Silver Guards shouted blood oaths and chanted. But at the behest of Denarius, the king gave no order to charge. Instead Jovan merely watched the enemy advance. And the grand vicar himself watched with a keen eye as the enemy swarmed into the fields north and east of the Atonement Tree, taking their place at Fiery Absolution.

The army of oghuls and Vallè roared and chanted in unison, matching the roars and chants of Jovan's army. The sound was deafening. Many oghuls banged drums, whilst others bashed the butts of their savage mauls and war hammers upon the ground in unison with the drums. *Boom! Boom! Boom!* Thunder rolled.

A great many of the glittering Vallè soldiers were mounted on equally glittering horses, armored in polished silver. A number of the oghuls were mounted too, but not on horses wearing glistening armor. No, the oghuls rode strange beasts with low-swooping horns. Musk oxen.

More and more oghuls and Vallè poured in, and it was soon obvious, the Dayknights and Silver Guards who had come out of Amadon with King Jovan were severely outnumbered. Soon the roars and chanting and beating of drums died down.

And a lone rider on horseback broke from the massive gathering of oghuls and Vallè and rode forward, entering the hallowed space under the Atonement Tree.

As the rider drew near, Krista could tell it was a Vallè, and the horse a simple chestnut sorrel. The Vallè had dark hair and was clothed in black leather armor similar to Krista's. *He's a Bloodwood!*

"Val-Draekin," Jovan Bronachell muttered under his breath as the mysterious Vallè in Bloodwood armor advanced.

**

Leif Chaparral and his brother, Glade, drew their swords and positioned their mounts between Jovan and the approaching Vallè named Val-Draekin.

But the Vallè, refined and poised atop his sorrel, casually drew his mount up before Borden Bronachell and not Jovan.

"Borden Bronachell," Val-Draekin said, voice musical and confident. "You live."

"What has happened to the Brethren of Mia?" Borden glared at the Vallè. "Have you finally betrayed us too, Val-Draekin?"

"Did you expect any different?" Val-Draekin answered. "I am pure Vallè. What did you and Roguemoore think was going to happen, that *The Moon Scrolls of Mia* were speaking to you the truth?"

"You have betrayed the Brethren of Mia with this army you lead," Borden said. "You have betrayed the world."

"You don't know the half of my betrayals," Val-Draekin said. "I have been playing the game of Hragna'Ar my entire life."

More of Jovan's knights gathered around Leif and Glade, weapons drawn, advancing on the Vallè. Val-Draekin whistled, and what Vallè royals had previously gathered in the Hallowed Grove to spread their Shroud of the Vallè threw back their cloaks and drew their own hidden weapons. In a moment they were standing between Val-Draekin and Jovan's knights.

Borden watched, his face grim and impassive. "The Vallè have always been full of surprises. I just did not expect betrayal from every single one of them."

"We've more surprises on the horizon than this." Val-Draekin dismounted, stepped casually toward the Silver Throne, and ran one languid hand over its surface. Then he clicked his tongue and whistled twice.

From the darkness behind the Vallè emerged a young man with flat silver eyes. The boy led a large black saber-toothed lion, two long silver teeth jutting down from its upper jaw. Krista figured the young man was no older than she; his silver eyes almost threw a spell over her. The lion's eyes were also silver pools of swirling magic. Under the saber-tooth's sleek black coat, powerful muscles bunched and coiled with its every graceful move. The fearsome cat sidled up next to Val-Draekin and roared. The terrifying sound was like a punch in the stomach, and Krista found herself recoiling atop her own saddle. Everyone drew back. Even Dread shied away from the murderous-looking beast.

The silver-eyed boy ran his hand over the lion's back, calming it instantly. Done with its threatening cry, the black cat silently eyed everyone with sparkling silver orbs.

"Stefan Wayland?" Ava Shay called out from her seat on the back of Ironcloud's wagon. "Is that you? What's wrong with your eyes?"

"Ava Shay?" The silver-eyed boy looked her way. "Why are you here?"

"You can see me?" Ava asked.

"Yes, I can see you."

Grand Vicar Denarius did the three-fingered sign of the Laijon Cross over his heart. "Demons of the underworld, both the boy and the cat," he muttered, looking at Stefan and the black beast, then straightened, his voice rising as he pointed at Val-Draekin. "You and that foul oghul army you lead shall not steal the glory of Absolution from us!

"Vandivor! Donalbain! Leaford! Rhys-Duncan!" The grand vicar called out each name, beckoning the four archbishops forward. "The Five Isles shall all now bear witness to the power of Laijon and his one true church! It is time to raise the dead!"

The four archbishops knelt before the coffin bearing Princess Jondralyn's corpse and threw open the lid. "Our most dear Laijon." The archbishop named Vandivor led the prayer, the others joining in, their voices rising as one. "We beseech you in your glorious goodness to deliver these armies from the plain of war and reveal yourself to us now in this our moment of Absolution. Hasten the powers of thy kingdom on high, so that what temporary death afflicts both Spencerville and our beautiful princess, Jondralyn Bronachell, may depart their bodies and they may rise again, for the grand vicar hath already promised. The grand vicar has blessed Jondralyn that she shall come forth during the return of Laijon, clothed in glory, immortality, and eternal life—"

The stench of Jondralyn's rotting body was ripe. *Do these archbishops really think the rotting corpse in that coffin will come alive again, rise up and speak, rise up and stave off Absolution?*

Val-Draekin clicked his tongue and the black saber-tooth left Stefan's side and stalked silently toward the coffin holding Jondralyn's corpse and the praying archbishops.

"We ask this of you in true faith and in thy holy name," the four archbishops continued, voices melded together as if in song. "And we grant thee grace and thanks for delivering us so far from the miseries of this sinful, cruel world. And may you consummate our prayer with bliss both body and soul in eternal everlasting glory through you, Laijon, forever and ever, amen—"

And the saber-toothed lion struck, long silver claws snapping out in the darkness like lightning. Wicked and sharp, they tore into the back of Archbishop Vandivor's neck, slicing though flesh and spine, opening the man up right where he knelt. Then the cat's long silver teeth were buried deep in the man's chest.

The other three archbishops screamed in terror, scrambling away. King Jovan leaped to their aid, sword drawn. Borden Bronachell grabbed him firmly by the shoulder. "No!" he shouted. "That beast will kill you, son!"

"Someone must save him!" Jovan shouted to the Dayknights behind him.

The black saber-tooth drew back from the squirming archbishop, silver claws swiping through the air as it exploded toward Donalbain crouching in fear behind the princess's coffin. The cat's crushing paw struck the man's back, slicing him open from the right shoulder clear to his left ribs, tearing through his spine and into his heart. The man's eyes flew open as he slumped to the ground, blood soaking into the dirt and grass, thick and red.

"Save them!" Jovan shouted. "Somebody kill that foul monster!"

A dozen Dayknights along with Leif and Glade, still mounted, rushed to the defense of the two remaining archbishops, long black swords drawn, swinging. The saber-tooth leaped forward, engaging them in the fight without hesitation. Four of the Dayknights fell to the fierce cat fast, deep red gashes in their armor. Their futile attack ended in a frenzy of slashing tooth and claw. Leif's and Glade's mounts bolted from the fray—spooked and terrified they bucked and brayed—the two brothers barely holding on. Four more knights went down. Body parts and bloody armor littered the ground. The cat was too fast, and the remaining four knights backed away.

Leaford and Rhys-Duncan were now on their feet, eyes wide in fear as they tried to stumble away from the blood and horror surrounding Jondralyn's coffin.

But the saber-toothed lion wasn't done. It struck again, silver claws snaking out with both speed and fury, slicing the two men open with merciless ease. They fell to the ground together, pale ribs and purple guts exposed to the night.

Then, as if nothing had happened, the black saber-toothed lion padded casually back toward the silver-eyed boy named Stefan, sitting on blood-splattered haunches by the boy's side, long silver teeth dripping blood to the grass.

The night had grown silent. Leif and Glade gained control of their mounts.

And the air was rank with the pungent taste of blood. It seeped into Krista's nostrils and down her throat, infecting her very soul. The ferociousness of the cat's attack had awoken something buried deep within her—the need to kill.

A diminutive, thin-faced oghul clad in stained oghul garb emerged from the darkness behind Val-Draekin. The strange, mousy oghul was barefooted and carried several threadbare rags in hand. He began cleaning the blood from the sleek black coat of the giant saber-tooth. But the lion seemed annoyed with the cleaning, a low growl sounding from deep within.

"That's enough, Mud," Val-Draekin said to the small oghul. "You are a good servant, but you can step back now. The cat's fur will be bloodied again soon. For the Five Isles shall bow before the might of Hragna'Ar and the Aalavarrè Solas soon." He petted the scrawny oghul atop his thin gray head. "But not before the end, young Mud, not before my armies sing the song of Fiery Absolution."

The mousy oghul leaned into Val-Draekin's comforting hand. The saber-toothed lion now purred loudly. And the silver-eyed boy kept staring at Ava Shay, his head slightly bowed as if embarrassed by all that was happening.

"Bloody Laijon almighty." King Jovan's strained voice cracked the stillness of the night, his legs almost giving out from under him. It appeared to Krista as if he might faint. Leif and Glade slid from their saddles and rushed to his side, holding him up.

"Your fiendish lion killed them all." Denarius faced Val-Draekin, his round face bursting red with rage. "What other demonic horrors have you conjured from the underworld?"

"Is the beast truly of the underworld, Your Grace?" Jovan asked as he clung to Leif and Glade, terror in his dark eyes. "Silver teeth. Silver claws. Silver eyes. What foul sorcery infects it?" His own dark orbs fixed on the silver-eyed boy named Stefan. "And the boy is just like the cat. I should order my army to kill them both." His gaze flew to Val-Draekin. "I should order them to kill you!"

But behind King Jovan, the entire army of soldiers that had poured from Amadon seemed to be in as much shock as he, as if some spell had rendered them immobile. Dayknights who would normally have their bows drawn, arrows nocked, glimmering tips pointed at Val-Draekin and the deadly saber-tooth, sat stone-faced atop their stupefied mounts. *There is some fell magic at work here!* Krista's mind raged. *Some fell Vallè witchcraft!* Even she found it hard to move in her saddle. There was some scent in the air, some Vallè alchemy holding her down, something circling high in the vast darkness above that made the air quiver. Black Dugal had not taught her everything, for this sensation of sorcery encircling her was new.

"I will not let you ruin everything for me!" Jovan shouted at Val-Draekin.

"This is the start of Fiery Absolution," Val-Draekin said, "and it has nothing to do with you, Jovan Bronachell."

"It has everything to do with me!" Jovan roared back. "For I have come to bring back the dead, to summon the return of Laijon—"

"A cat just killed your archbishops," Val-Draekin said. "Killed them as if they were nothing. For that is what they always were. Nothing. As are you, nothing."

Grand Vicar Denarius shouted, "How dare you denigrate and blaspheme—"

"I dared do more than just *blaspheme!*" Val-Draekin snapped, cutting him off. "I just had a beast of the underworld *slay* your most holy of men."

With another click of Val-Draekin's tongue, the black saber-toothed lion stalked forward, now standing directly in front of Denarius, growling low and ominous. The vicar was pale-faced, immobile.

"You are so out of your depth here, Grand Vicar." Val-Draekin glared at both the round-faced vicar and Jovan. "You say you've come to bring back the dead. But do either of you even know how to summon forth the heir of Laijon?"

Jovan had no answer. And Denarius couldn't look away from the huge black saber-toothed lion before him, long silver fangs bared and still bloody.

And then the beast had the vicar by the neck and was pulling the screaming man to the ground. Denarius' bloodcurdling shriek was cut silent as the black cat's furious teeth ripped and tore. In less than a heartbeat the vicar's gurgling throat was naught but shredded flesh. The cat plunged its silver claws into his large belly and ripped. The fat man was soon naught but a pool of blood and slithering purple guts.

"Kill the beast!" Jovan roared. But his army remained still. A moment passed. Leif and Glade managed to draw their swords with a shout. But the cat silenced them both with a hard stare, eyes flat silver.

And from the west came the long braying of horns and the distant beat of thousands upon thousands of galloping hooves.

"The armies of Aeros Raijael," Val-Draekin announced as tens of thousands of advancing warhorses dripping with polished armor advanced through the darkness.

As Krista's gaze took in the coming Sør Sevier army, she could feel Dread tense under her, itching for a fight. As was she. Death. Blood. Killing. But yet she couldn't move, for that strange something was still pressing down on her from above. Some foul entity was up there in the air, circling, waiting, breathing. Whatever it was, it was breeding fear in everything and everyone but Val-Draekin and the saber-toothed lion.

Killing was the only thing that could cleanse her mind now. The bloody slaughter of the archbishops had awoken something in her. She was a trained Bloodwood and wanted the coming fight, *desired* the fight, *needed* the fight. War was on the horizon, and Dread was with her. And what could be better than that? She felt the daggers pressing against her flesh under her leather armor; her fingers itched to let them fly. But she was rooted to her saddle. Transfixed by some unseen angels above.

Every eye was on the army of Sør Sevier, the glimmering form of Aeros Raijael at its head. He rode a white stallion, a giant horned helm crowning his head. He carried a glorious white shield in one hand and an even more glorious white sword in the other. A black crossbow and a large, silver, double-bladed battle-ax were strapped to his back. *He carries the weapons of the Five Warrior Angels!* Krista's mind reeled. *Perhaps it is the spell of the weapons that holds me down!*

"The scriptures are right." Jovan Bronachell did the three-fingered sign of the Laijon Cross over his heart, looking at his father, fear in his eyes. "Like a thief in the night, Fiery Absolution has come, all the armies of the Five Isles converging upon the Atonement Tree, as was written in ages past, as was written in scripture. What do we do now, Father?" There was terror in his voice. "The grand vicar is dead."

"Indeed," Val-Draekin said, dark eyes aglow as he stared at the approaching mass of Sør Sevier warriors. "Indeed, Absolution has come." He smiled mockingly. "And what do we do now that there are no more religious leaders to guide us?"

Krista's narrowed gaze was focused on the two shadowy forms flanking the Angel Prince at the legion's head—Black Dugal and Hans Rake.

On Bloodeye steeds, the two moved in unison, like malevolent, dark mists; they moved as one with their mounts. They rode toward war like

Bloodwoods. Café Colza was with them, the bulldog trotting along behind.

At the sight of Dugal and Hans, the spell was broken.

She could move.

Hate boiled in Krista's blood. She felt a black dagger slip into her hand, fingers naturally wrapping around it, the thrill to kill rising within her, so sweet. She leaned forward and kissed the back of her mare's head. Felt the comfort of Dread under her.

Whatever this "Fiery Absolution" turned out to be, Krista vowed to ruin it for all and everyone.

*The black bark of the Bloodwood trees are like unto the white bark of
the Nordland birch, representing both purification and death. Just
as Fiery Absolution represents both purification and death.*
—THE WAY AND TRUTH OF LAIJON

CHAPTER FIFTY-EIGHT

AVA SHAY

12TH DAY OF THE HEART MOON, 999TH YEAR OF LAIJON
AMADON, GUL KANA

*A*eros Raijael is coming. Ava Shay froze at the sight of the White
Prince galloping toward her on his large white stallion, wielding
the weapons of the Five Warrior Angels. *Aeros is coming and he
is coming for me!* He rode Gault Aulbrek's stallion, Spirit. Ava recognized
the beast even from afar. But it did not matter what horse the White
Prince rode. For at the very sight of him, all such trivial things ceased
to matter to Ava: the vast army of oghuls and Vallè, Mancellor Allen's
return, Stefan Wayland and his silver eyes—whatever devilry that was.
No. None of that mattered. *For Aeros has come for me, a simple slave girl
from Gallows Haven.*

Ava wanted to leap from her seat in the back of the wagon and flee
into the darkness. She did not wish to hide, but to run, and keep running,
far, far away, as far away from this torchlit, demonic Hallowed Grove as
possible. But the reality was, men and oghuls and Vallè surrounded her
in every direction, all with weapons sharp and cruel.

Hemmed in by three armies, there was no escape. Not even below
her or above.

The lower branches of the Atonement Tree stretched over her like an ominous floating roof some thirty feet above. It was a suppressing green canopy that seemed to push down on her with crushing weight, a weight that had held her captive the entire time the grand vicar had been mauled to death by the saber-toothed lion—a huge black beast seemingly conjured up from the underworld. She'd wanted to run then, too, but found that she strangely could not move. But that spell was broken. Now there was just nowhere to go. My Heart was tucked into her belt. The sword was her only comfort. Her only savior. If there was a savior to be had. She didn't think Borden Bronachell or Ironcloud would fight for her. Krista Aulbrek had taught her some fighting skills on their journey from Lord's Point, but Krista seemed the type to take care of herself and only herself. *And the way I treated Gault was distant and cruel.* The man had only ever had her own best interest at heart. *He came back to Saint Only to save me, and I just let him walk away in his most vulnerable moment.* She had seen the pain on his face at her rejection.

And now Aeros returns for me, and it is what I deserve.

The White Prince reined up not thirty paces west of the Atonement Tree and the Silver Throne, his army stretching out behind him. Like the army of oghuls and Vallè to the north, Aeros Raijael's army was a shifting, rustling sea of death. A measureless ocean of silver armor and white surcoats stretching across the torchlit horizon to the west, blue-and-white battle standards fluttering above. Archers made up the front ranks. Battle knights were behind the archers, faces obscured behind the narrow eye slits of their helms, their huge warhorses slathered in blue paint, their half-pikes and halberd staffs thrust toward the black sky.

Ava had traveled with this army. She knew the cruelty of this army. This army was bred for slaughter. This army hungered for blood. The ground shook as the oghul and Vallè army to the north began chanting once again, heavy weaponry pounding the turf to the beat of the Vallè drums and pipes. There was a certain miraculous wonder to all the banners and spearheads stretching out on every dark horizon, north, south, east, and west. Greaves and vambraces of every kind, gleaming hauberks and spearheads, shining coats of mail, shields and armor and weaponry both polished and rusted, all of it surrounding her, all of it lit and flickering in the distance with ever-receding torchlight.

Yes. This was Absolution. The armies of the Five Isles all gathered together for one final battle. Ava recalled Bishop Tolbret reading from *The Way and Truth of Laijon.* *"And on that day of Fiery Absolution, all the armies shall be gathered for Absolution under the Atonement Tree: human, oghul, Vallè, and the like."*

The White Prince motioned for his army to stay. Then he set heels to flanks and rode forward atop the white stallion. To Ava, Aeros looked strange under the bulky horned helm. *Lonesome Crown* didn't fit his head at all. *Blackest Heart* was strapped awkwardly to his back, *Forgetting Moon*, too. Both looked unwieldy. He carried *Ethic Shroud* in his left hand, *Afflicted Fire* in his right. Of all the weapons, the white sword fit him well. It was a long and elegant-looking weapon with a crescent-moon-shaped hilt-guard, its pale coloring matching his skin. Yes, if anything fit Aeros, it was the sword. Ava imagined the five angel stones were in a small pouch somewhere under his armor.

A group of knights, including two dark Bloodwoods on Bloodeye steeds, galloped along at Aeros' side. Ava did not recognize these two new assassins, but their black cloaks and black leather armor were similar to those Spiderwood and Krista wore. One of the assassins had a youthful face under spiked blond hair, blue clan tattoos covering either side of his shaved head. The other assassin was older, his cold, scarred face hidden under dark hair and a neatly trimmed beard. A rough-looking bulldog with a rusted spiked collar followed the Bloodwoods.

Just behind the two Bloodwoods rode Hammerfiss and Enna Spades on black destriers, both in the armor and livery that marked them as the White Prince's Knights Archaic. A large barbed mace was strapped to Hammerfiss' back. Spades had her trusted crossbow. They were helmetless, as was Jenko Bruk, who rode with them on a dappled war charger of his own. He also wore the armor and dark blue cloak of a Knight Archaic. Ava's heart leaped at the sight of her beloved. She remembered Jenko fighting for her in Saint Only, killing Ivor Jace to protect her honor. On that day she had found that there was still good in Jenko Bruk.

Behind Jenko were two more riders, both of them on the same roan destrier: the lissome servant girl, Leisel, and a dough-faced boy about Ava's same age. Leisel sat the saddle in front of the boy. The boy's face was pasty and malformed. Beyond his deformities, the boy had a familiar look. He wore clean leather armor and looked like a smaller version of Nail, or even a more scarred version of Aeros Raijael.

The White Prince's contingent reined up under the Atonement Tree and Silver Throne. Ava sought out Jenko Bruk's amber-colored eyes, immediately seeing the concern for her on his face, the pain buried deep within him. She stood up in the wagon, wanting to go to him. But she remained where she stood, suddenly realizing she was the only one who had moved as the armies surrounding her were silent in their anticipation.

"Looks like we missed most of the fun." Aeros' voice rang out as he eyed the torn and bloody bodies littering the ground between Val-Draekin and King Jovan. His black-pupiled gaze lingered on the saber-toothed lion for a moment before he turned back to Jovan, saying, "Certainly it could not have been Leif Chaparral who caused all this destruction. I admit, the man got lucky during the Battle of the Saint Only Channel, but I do not see him as one who would slay his own grand vicar."

"I will slay you right now if you wish." Leif already had his sword drawn. "I've beaten you once. I can beat you again."

"You may just have a chance to fight me yet, Leif Chaparral," Aeros said. "For Absolution is upon us. And a glorious sight it is."

Again, Ava couldn't help but think the White Prince looked ridiculous with that horned helm balanced atop his head. It was too big for him. Too bulky. Too outlandish.

That thought made her giggle out loud.

She found Aeros was now looking at her with his cruel black eyes. "Ava Shay. You find something funny?"

Everyone gathered under the Atonement Tree was looking at her now. The giggles stopped. Her face flushed. She gathered her composure. "I find you funny, Aeros Raijael. You look like an idiot with that helmet on your head."

His pale face changed as if her words had actually hurt. He had told her himself that he believed he was Laijon reincarnated. *And Ava Shay of Gallows Haven just called him an idiot in front of the entire might of the Five Isles.* She knew she was in shock, traumatized by all that had happened. She felt the giggles returning. *Fiery Absolution, and I cannot stop laughing!* But then she felt her body grow cold, felt herself begin to shiver uncontrollably.

"You do look a fool in that hat," Val-Draekin said to Aeros. "I can see why the girl laughs, my brother. Take the helm off. It does not suit you, Angelwood."

"I shall keep it, Dragonwood," Aeros replied. "For I am Laijon reborn, and these are my weapons." His eyes narrowed. "And do not call me 'brother' again. Though we trained together those many years ago under Black Dugal's care, we were never truly brothers."

"And I see that you have fulfilled the destiny you so desired, Angelwood," Val-Draekin continued. "For indeed you have made it all the way to the Hallowed Grove, all the weapons and angel stones in your possession, the Silver Throne awaiting you at the base of the Atonement Tree."

Aeros motioned to Stefan Wayland and the mousy oghul named Mud. Between them was the black saber-toothed lion. "And I see that you, Dragonwood, have made it here with an army of treacherous creatures, cruel and faithless, demons all. What is this menagerie of fiends?"

"Fiends, yes. But they are not faithless," Val-Draekin said. "As your army shall soon see. For my gathering of both oghuls and Vallè waxes more numerous and powerful as we speak."

"You betray Black Dugal with that army of oghuls behind you," Aeros said. "You betray your own Bloodwood family."

"No," Val-Draekin countered. "You never knew our father's true desires. You've played right into his hands for the last ten years. You never knew what Black Dugal truly wanted from his Bloodwoods, or who Black Dugal truly was."

Aeros looked to the Bloodwood next to him—the older assassin with the dark hair and gray-shot beard who sat comfortably astride his

Bloodeye stallion. "It is true"—the assassin nodded to Aeros—"I did not teach you everything, my lord Aeros. Nor did I require you to swear every Bloodwood vow, for you were not of my blood."

Aeros' dark eyes narrowed even more, almost to a fierce squint. "Have you lied to me in some way, Dugal? Betrayed me?"

"Lies are in my very nature," Black Dugal said, shifting his red-eyed steed away from Aeros, putting space between them. "For I *am* the Betrayer, born and bred of the direct bloodline of Dashiell Dugal, the patron god of all assassins. And I exist only for the return of the Skulls."

Aeros clicked his heels, twisted the reins in his hand, and turned his own white stallion, facing the assassin head-on. "But Dashiell Dugal was a Vallè maiden. And you are no Vallè."

Black Dugal casually lifted the hood of his cloak back up over his head, face now completely concealed in night's shadow. When he pulled the hood of his cloak back down, a different man was revealed.

No, not a man, but a *Vallè*.

Where before there had been a bearded Bloodwood assassin, now there was the most exquisite-looking dark-haired Vallè Ava Shay had ever seen, complete with ears thin and pointed. Black Dugal's once cold and scarred countenance had transformed into a chiseled Vallè face so precise and elegant in its symmetry, it was utterly astonishing. It was a glowing pale face made brighter by the flickering illuminations of a thousand torches.

"Dashiell Dugal was known not only as the Assassin," Black Dugal's voice rang out, "but also as the Betrayer, a master of disguise her entire life. As am I. And no one but my son, Val-Draekin, has ever known my true nature until now."

"Blessed Mother Mia," Borden Bronachell exclaimed. He looked at Ironcloud on the bench in front of Ava. Krista Aulbrek's face darkened as her own Bloodeye mare took two steps back. Even the younger Bloodwood with the spiked blond hair who had accompanied Black Dugal looked surprised at the transformation. The young assassin gripped his reins tight as his Bloodeye steed was suddenly nervous under him.

Enna Spades was the only one who did not look surprised at the revelation. In fact, she had her crossbow aimed, the tip of the bolt pointed right at the long-eared Vallè who had once been a man. "I do not like sorcery," she snarled.

"Or witchcraft," Hammerfiss growled. "And Black Dugal is full of both it seems." The large barbed mace was now a threatening menace in his hands. "The Bloodwoods have betrayed us all. I have always hated them."

"Indeed, you have all been betrayed." Val-Draekin's voice rose. "For Fiery Absolution is the culmination of a game the Vallè have been playing for a thousand years, ever since the Aalavarrè Solas were banished from the Five Isles, ever since they were banished to the underworld."

"None of you listen to this Vallè!" Aeros turned his stallion, Spirit, and pointed *Afflicted Fire* at Val-Draekin. "I am Laijon returned. I possess the weapons of the Five Warrior Angels. You shall all bow to me."

The black saber-toothed lion next to Val-Draekin lowered its head and bared long silver teeth, hissing deep and ominous, flat silver eyes focused on the White Prince. But Aeros kept the sword pointed at Val-Draekin, the clean white blade almost glowing with a burning fire of its own. And the weapon was also humming, a soft whispering melody and whistle sounding in the night, as if the weapon itself were cutting the air with song.

"You shall all bow down before me!" Aeros shouted again for all to hear, sword still aimed at his enemy. "I, Aeros Raijael, am the Supreme Spirit, the Lord of both heaven and the underworld—of all worlds, the preexistent world, this world, and the next, and the ones beyond that! I am the long-awaited return of the great One and Only, whose arrival was foretold by the Warrior Angels long ago! I am the giver of life and the bringer of death, created before the very foundations of the world! I am known by many names: the Father of all Mourning, the Angel Prince, the true and living heir of Laijon, the great One and Only, the King of Slaves! I am an ensign unto all kingdoms! And as the prophecies in *The Chivalric Illuminations* have foretold, I, Aeros Raijael, the heir of Laijon, Mia, and their one and only son, Raijael, have come with my conquering armies to this, the Hallowed Grove, to the very base of the Atonement

Tree, to claim what is rightfully mine: rule and dominion over the entire Five Isles and the destruction of all false doctrines before me! You must now all bow down or die!"

The shield in Aeros' left hand sent shards of light sparking into Ava's eyes, momentarily blinding her. She blinked away the pain cast by *Ethic Shroud*, now noticing the helm on his head, *Lonesome Crown*, no longer a laughing matter, but rather a silver beam of pure luminosity, the tips of both curved horns glimmering like ice. And the sword in his hand was now sheer white fire and flame.

"Bow down or die!" Aeros yelled.

"If you are the true heir of Laijon, the Angel Prince, the last born of Lord Aevrett Raijael, then ride forth and slay me!" Val-Draekin challenged. "Claim your place by killing me, and then let your armies slaughter my armies, then let them slaughter the army of King Jovan. Let it all be as you so dream it. Let Fiery Absolution unfold as you see fit, Angelwood. If that is the way it is to be, then so let it be, my brother."

"Though we trained together in our youth," Aeros hissed, "you were never my brother, as you say." He turned to Black Dugal. "And you were never my father."

"But you are not yet fatherless," Dugal said, the white shard of Aeros' sword reflected in his stallion's glowing red eyes. "Perhaps we should let history repeat itself. Perhaps we should let the one who believes he is Laijon returned fight the Betrayer under the Atonement Tree as once took place in ancient scripture."

"Repeat history?" Aeros laughed. "Me and you?"

"Though you had King Aevrett assassinated," Dugal said, "you are not yet *completely* fatherless."

"And as I said before, you were never my father either."

"You trained as a Bloodwood." A black dagger was suddenly in Dugal's hand. "And as a Bloodwood, I am your father, and I will always be until I am dead." Dugal swung his leg and slid gracefully from the back of his Bloodeye stallion. "Now come and make me dead, my son, my Angelwood. Become truly fatherless."

"You dare fight me whilst I wear the weapons of the Five Warrior

Angels?" Aeros laughed, "Then you are not only the Betrayer but the Fool. For I am Laijon reborn!"

"Then prove yourself now," Dugal said. "Erase me from history. Kill the Betrayer now as Laijon himself failed to kill Dashiell Dugal a thousand years ago."

Aeros Raijael dismounted his white stallion, sword and shield in hand, horned helm still atop his head, battle-ax and crossbow strapped to his back.

He looked toward his Knights Archaic: Hammerfiss, Spades, and Jenko. "Do not interfere. This is my fight, and my fight alone." He palmed the small leather satchel at his belt. "The angel stones guide my weapons."

Hammerfiss nodded. "It shall be the greatest fight recorded in *The Chivalric Illuminations,* and you shall go down in history as Laijon reborn, the one who shall make the streets of Amadon run red with blood."

Aeros Raijael bowed to his knights, then turned to face Black Dugal.

One combatant was dressed all in white, chain mail shimmering in the torchlight, horned helm balanced on his head. The other one was dressed all in black, dark cape thrown back, revealing the cunning fine features of a Vallè. *Afflicted Fire,* the sword of legend, was naught but a pale scar against the dark night and all that separated the fighters. Two black daggers were in Dugal's hands, shadows that seemed to swallow the light cast by the sword.

Black Dugal let his first dagger fly, a black streak of lightning that sparked and thundered against Aeros' upraised shield, *Ethic Shroud.* The dagger spun away into the dirt at the base of the Silver Throne, smoking.

With a flick of his wrist, Dugal loosed his second black blade. It too hit the glowing white shield with a flash of sparks and a hollow sound that shook the air. Undaunted, Aeros effortlessly placed himself in the attack position, turning. With one hand he swung the long white sword up over his head, then brought it crashing down toward Dugal. The ashen blade cut the air with a keening wail as it came slicing down into the dirt where Black Dugal once stood. The Bloodwood now circled Aeros from behind, another black dagger in hand.

"Do you fight with poison on your blades?" Aeros whirled around, the tip of his blade once again between him and his foe. "Do you fight like a trickster, like a Bloodwood coward?"

"You are trained in our ways," Dugal answered, moving sideways, placing the Silver Throne between him and Aeros, wary of the long white sword. "You were once a Bloodwood. And a smart Bloodwood never discloses what is on his blades."

Aeros leaped around the throne and launched another rapid attack, the point of *Afflicted Fire* thrusting straight toward Black Dugal's face. The Bloodwood swept the blade away with a swift swipe of his leather-armored arm, leaving a trail of torn black leather across his forearm. Aeros spun, sword slashing toward the ribs of the Bloodwood this time. Dugal barely jumped away, the tip of the white blade again leaving a ragged tear in the armor along his back. But Aeros wasn't done. His sword again crashed down, white blade glancing off the top of Black Dugal's shoulder, knocking the Bloodwood sideways to the ground. Rolling, the assassin stood, a long gash in his leather armor now, blood leaking from the shoulder wound.

Instead of pressing the attack, Aeros stepped back, creating several paces of separation between Dugal and himself. He seemed annoyed that the Bloodwood had so casually danced aside, annoyed that the white blade hadn't sliced the man completely in half by now.

Aeros angrily tossed *Afflicted Fire* and *Ethic Shroud* aside and swept *Lonesome Crown* from his head. Then he unhooked *Blackest Heart* and tossed it aside too.

Lastly, he pulled the huge double-bladed battle-ax, *Forgetting Moon*, from over his shoulder. He held the huge weapon in both hands, white hair flowing out behind him.

He set his stance, looking better balanced on his feet now, not so weighted down.

"You think those weapons you carry are worth something," Black Dugal said, running his hand over the wound on his shoulder. "You think those angel stones are magic? Let me tell you now: They are useless in your hands. They always have been."

Dugal struck, his dagger lashing out, black blade glancing off the curved edge of the battle-ax with a shower of sparks. He lashed out again, dagger sparking off *Forgetting Moon*'s gleaming edge. The White Prince attacked, swinging the huge ax, its twin blades cutting through the night.

Dugal stepped back and let the massive curved blade slice the air just in front of his face. Aeros was thrown off balance. Dugal ducked low and rammed his dagger straight into the chain mail covering Aeros' stomach. With a wet *thunk* the blade sank deep.

Black Dugal let go of the blade and stepped back.

The black dagger was stuck in Aeros' midsection. Blood, dark and red, soaked the white fabric and chain-mail armor around the hilt.

The White Prince looked down at the hilt protruding from his stomach, stunned, a pained expression on his face. It wasn't an expression of physical pain, but rather pained wonderment at having actually been wounded in battle—something that had never before happened. In fact, the only time Ava Shay had seen blood on Aeros was when she herself had slapped him that first night he had raped her. She had bloodied his lip and he had run off, only to return moments later, fully healed. *But will he heal from this wound too?*

"That one was not poisoned," Dugal said, another dagger in hand. "But who knows about this one?" He leaped forward, naught but a blur of black. Before Aeros could even begin to lift the battle-ax in defense, he was full of five more holes, all bleeding profusely. And Black Dugal struck one final time, a merciless sweeping slash across Aeros' exposed neck, flaying the flesh wide. It was not a deep enough strike to sever an artery, but significant enough to bring blood racing from the wound and over Aeros' chest.

As the White Prince fell, ax still in hand, the entire army of Sør Sevier shifted in their saddles, groans and grumbles and shouts of dismay rippling through the throng. Many weapons were drawn and oaths of vengeance shouted.

"And we shall fight too!" Jovan shouted, drawing his own sword, glaring at Black Dugal. "The armies of Gul Kana shall slay any Bloodwood who stands in our way!" The army that had poured out of Amadon followed the king's pronouncement with cheers and shouts of their own.

But then Aeros rose to his knees, silencing both armies with the bloody palm of his hand upraised. Ava didn't know much about fighting, but with the last handful of strikes, she could tell that Black Dugal had merely been toying with Aeros the entire time.

To drag out the fight? To prolong Aeros' humiliation? What point Dugal was trying to make, Ava could not guess. But at the moment, Aeros looked wholly defeated. *Forgetting Moon* hung useless in his hands, its curved blade biting into the dirt at his feet.

Aeros grabbed the ax up from the grass. Still kneeling, he rested on the thick haft of the weapon, breath wheezing in and out between his lips as blood frothed and bubbled from his neck.

"Have you no fight left in you, Aeros Raijael?" Black Dugal said, bloody dagger still gripped in hand. He walked back and forth before the White Prince now, literally *stalking* the man, with more menace in his stride than that of the black saber-toothed lion. "Have you no fight, White Prince, or are you a disgrace to the name Angelwood?"

Aeros, scarcely able to breathe, still bleeding profusely, hefted the ax, raising it for one last strike. But it slipped from his hands as he again toppled over sideways into the grass and dirt at the foot of the Silver Throne.

His army grew restless, and Ava wondered when they would attack. Her chest hammered. Witnessing her tormenter—her *rapist*—so soundly beaten in battle, so thoroughly humiliated, left scant little pleasure in her heart. But still she wanted him to be dead once and for all.

Aeros rolled onto his back, then half sat up, resting on one elbow, blood oozing through the links of chain mail around his torso, blood welling from his split-open neck.

"Looks like the weapons of the Five Warrior Angels have failed you miserably," Black Dugal said. Then the newly revealed Vallè knelt at the White Prince's side. With his Bloodwood dagger, he cut the leather pouch holding the angel stones from Aeros' belt. Done, he tossed the pouch to Val-Draekin.

The Vallè opened the pouch and pulled forth a simple black stone, black as dull coal. "This one has always been useless." Val-Draekin tossed the black stone to the ground. "Perhaps that is why the weapons did not work to Aeros' advantage." He closed the pouch and slipped it into the folds of his cloak.

"Bloody fuck," Hammerfiss snarled, looking at Enna Spades. "Are we just gonna let them loot our lord's body and throw away the angel stones? I know he asked us not to intervene, but we can't just let this happen. We've come so far. This cannot be."

"Our Lord Aeros is not dead yet." Spades was gazing down at the White Prince bleeding on the ground. She aimed her crossbow, thick quarrel pointed at Dugal. "And we still have an army at our back."

Val-Draekin clicked his tongue.

The black saber-toothed lion standing between Stefan Wayland and the mousy oghul named Mud roared. The lion's enormous rumbling sound lanced through the night, causing every war charger within a hundred paces to shuffle back in fear, including Hammerfiss' and Spades' mounts. Aeros' white stallion bucked and brayed in fear. The huge black cat strode forward and positioned itself in front of Aeros Raijael, who still lay on the ground.

Hammerfiss and Spades settled their mounts, both of them eyeing the saber-tooth warily. Hammerfiss looked like he just might desire to fight the cat with naught but his own hands. Spades, on the other hand, seemed more calculating, as if she were indeed taking the measure of the situation, weighing her options now that Aeros was dying on the ground before her.

The second Bloodwood, the one with the row of spiked hair running down his scalp, spurred his own Bloodeye steed forward, joining Black Dugal. "The White Prince should be nailed to the Atonement Tree," the young Bloodwood said. "If he thinks he is Laijon returned, then we should treat him as Laijon returned and give him the end only a god could appreciate."

"I like your way of thinking, Hans," Black Dugal said.

"I am not yet dead." Aeros reached for the battle-ax still lying in the bloody grass next to him. He grasped it in one hand. "I can still stand and fight." He crawled toward the Silver Throne, trying to pull himself up its slick, silvery surface, straining with the effort, eventually standing on wobbly legs. "I can still fight!" he shouted, using the stout hilt of the ax as a crutch now, trying to steady himself. "I am not dead yet!" And then he flopped back down, sitting unceremoniously on the seat of the throne with a thud, the battle-ax still gripped in his hand.

Aeros Raijael stared out at the bloody ground before him. The remaining weapons of the Five Warrior Angels lay strewn about the ground, the fabled weapons everyone had so worshipped and cherished: *Lonesome Crown*, *Blackest Heart*, *Ethic Shroud*, and *Afflicted Fire*. They were the reason all the armies of the Five Isles were gathered under the Atonement Tree. And now they just lay there. As if they were nothing. Of no concern. Forgotten. Useless, like the black stone that lay there in their midst, the stone Val-Draekin had taken from the pouch and so casually tossed aside. The only weapon not on the ground was the one held limply in Aeros' hand—*Forgetting Moon*.

"He is dying!" a familiar voice called out. "Let me finish him!"

To Ava's surprise—to everyone's surprise—it was Mancellor Allen who strode forward. "Let me finish him!" The Wyn Darrè fighter stepped from behind King Jovan. His sword was drawn. The black streaks tattooed under his eyes made his face seem exceptionally dark and fierce in the torchlight.

"No! Let me finish him!" a second familiar voice rang out. It was Jenko Bruk. "Let me end the White Prince! Let me end him once and for all!" Jenko spurred his mount between Hammerfiss and Spades, giving the saber-toothed lion a wide berth as he circled his horse around Black Dugal, and dismounted before the Silver Throne. He drew his sword too. "Let me be the one who kills Aeros Raijael."

"We shall both kill him!" Mancellor stood next to Jenko. "Together we shall avenge our homelands."

"Traitors." Aeros spat the accusation, *Forgetting Moon* now atop his lap as he sat the Silver Throne. Blood drooled from the corners of his mouth and slithered down his chin. The wound in his neck yawned wide.

"Traitors, the both of you," he wheezed. "After all I did for you, both of you naught but traitors and cowards. You only dare fight me now that I am injured, now that I am not at my full strength. Traitors and cowards, I call you." Aeros straightened in the chair. "Yes, come at me, cowards. Slay me now that I am mostly dead. You shall both be hailed as heroes for sure."

Mancellor and Jenko seemed uncertain. They looked to Black Dugal.

Val-Draekin motioned to the mousy oghul in raggedy garb next to Stefan Wayland. "Find Sledg H'Mar," the Vallè ordered the oghul. "Have him bring a mallet, a large one. And a stake, a long one."

The small oghul nodded and then scurried off into the dark toward the army of oghuls and Vallè stretching off into the distance behind the Atonement Tree.

"I think I know what he has in mind." Black Dugal addressed Jenko and Mancellor. "And I shall let you partake in the fun."

Grim-faced, Mancellor and Jenko looked at each other, then advanced upon the Silver Throne.

"Let him die in peace!" Hammerfiss roared, putting heels to flanks, urging his mount forward. His large mace was gripped tightly in one hand. "Let my lord Aeros die in peace, or I shall slay everyone here!" He pointed at Mancellor and Jenko with his free hand. "And I will start with the both of you!"

The saber-tooth spat and snarled as Hammerfiss' mount drew near the Silver Throne.

"Shoot the damned fucking thing already!" Hammerfiss shouted at Spades, raising his mace. "Kill the damn beast!"

Spades had her crossbow trained on the large black cat. The tip of her bolt followed the saber-tooth's movements as it stalked back and forth before Hammerfiss now. She pointed the tip of the bolt right between the cat's flat silver eyes. The lion hissed at her, long silver teeth glistening in the torchlight.

And then Spades raised up her bow.

"What in the bloody fuck has gotten into you?" Hammerfiss roared. "Kill it!"

"Then what?" Spades shrugged. "Aeros is done. We are on our own now."

"Aeros is not *done!*" Hammerfiss yelled. "He yet lives! And as long as he still draws breath, he is still your lord, he is still Laijon returned."

Spades hooked the crossbow to the baldric slung over her shoulder. "It is over, Hammerfiss."

"Nothing is over!" He charged his mount toward Mancellor and Jenko, barbed mace swinging down. The saber-toothed lion was suddenly in his path. The horse bearing Hammerfiss bucked and reared back on its hind legs, throwing the large man onto his back in the grass, large barbed mace spinning from his hands. He was soon surrounded by a dozen Vallè royals, a dozen silver swords pointed at his bearded neck. The saber-toothed lion stepped calmly through the circle of Vallè royals toward the Sør Sevier knight. Hammerfiss did not move as the large cat sat down in front of him, its gleaming silver fangs inches from his face. Hammerfiss scrambled back on his haunches, then stood slowly and mounted his horse once again. The large cat watched his every move.

Slumping on the Silver Throne now, Aeros Raijael could scarcely breathe. He coughed and blood spewed from his mouth. His lungs gurgled as they fought for air.

Mancellor and Jenko each took the White Prince by an arm, sitting him up straight.

Val-Draekin walked up to Aeros, grabbed the underside of his bloody chin, and lifted his head. They faced each other, the White Prince's eyes glazed, eyelids drooping.

"Angelwood," Val-Draekin began, addressing his old friend, "we assassinated a lot of people together, you and I. We were the two most secret of all Dugal's Caste. But Dugal and I, we always knew you would follow another path than that of the Bloodwood. And indeed, you forsook us. You decided to believe all the scripture and praise written about Aeros Raijael. You began to believe that you were truly the Angel Prince, that you were Laijon returned. And you chose to believe it despite the teachings of *The Book of the Betrayer*, teachings that said *The Chivalric Illuminations* and *The Way and Truth of Laijon* were all false, naught but made-up stories, silly myths penned by the Vallè a thousand years ago. Ancient contradictory legends of faith and belief and promises of heaven and eternal life meant to sow strife and war. And humanity fell for it. As you too eventually fell for it. It was all part of the ancient plan of the Vallè."

Black Dugal spoke to Aeros next. "You were purposefully honed as our instrument in destroying all of humanity, depleting the populations and fighting forces of all the Five Isles, making this day possible for the much smaller army of the oghuls and Vallè. We played upon your vanity and pride to make this day of Fiery Absolution possible. Humanity shall finally suffer the consequences of a thousand years of war. Humanity shall finally suffer the consequences of banishing our true brothers, the Aalavarrè Solas, to the underworld a thousand years ago."

Aeros coughed up blood in response, scarlet trails streaming down his face. Blood now drained thick and red from the gaping wound in his neck. "My horse," he mumbled through bloody lips. "Just don't hurt my horse."

"You are no longer making sense," Black Dugal said. "You mean Gault Aulbrek's horse?" Black Dugal walked over and grabbed Spirit by the reins, marching the white stallion up before Aeros. "Take a long look at it," Dugal said. "For it shall soon belong to another." Then he turned and gazed out into the dark.

The mousy oghul emerged from the blackness, a much larger oghul in priestly robes and armor lumbering along behind him. The stout oghul carried a huge iron mallet in one hand and a long wooden pole in the other, the pole twice as long as a man, its end sharpened to a point.

Val-Draekin leaned into Aeros again. "Your usefulness to the cause of the Bloodwood and Vallè is at an end, my brother. I know we were once close. I know we once trained together. But our friendship was always a fraud. As Dugal said, you and your armies and all your victories were a means to an end. We used you to bring about Fiery Absolution. We used you in a thousand-year game that rewards only the smartest and strongest for their cold calculations and ferocity."

Done with his speech, Val-Draekin backed away.

"Tear off his cape," Black Dugal ordered Mancellor and Jenko. "Lay him flat on the ground. Face in the dirt, legs spread. And hold him steady. He'll want to squirm."

Mancellor and Jenko tore the white cloak from Aeros' back, then lowered him to the bloody grass and kicked his legs apart, holding him fast to the ground.

Ava knew what was coming and wanted to close her eyes, but she couldn't look away. *He's still alive, and so close.* She knew her fears made little sense, considering the state Aeros was in. But she couldn't help it; she was worried he could still somehow hurt her. She would not look away until he was totally dead.

"Sledg H'Mar, bring the stake and the hammer!" Val-Draekin called out. The oghul in the priestly robes stepped forward, sturdy iron mallet in one hand, long wooden pole dragging in the other.

"Do it," Val-Draekin ordered.

The smaller oghul named Mud took the sharp end of the pole and guided it right between the White Prince's spread legs, pressed it firmly up into the center of his rear.

Ava shifted in her own seat on the wagon, uncomfortable and horrified. *He can still hurt me,* she realized, *even with the horror of his death.* Ava knew that if she continued to watch, she would never be able to unsee the horror.

"Aeros Raijael." Black Dugal's voice rang out, echoing loud and clear under the canopy of leafy branches. "You are being impaled for your crimes against the Five Isles. You are being impaled as punishment for your religious fervor in meting out death and destruction. And above all, you are being impaled for discarding your Bloodwood oaths for false myths and lies."

"B-but you said you m-made me do it all." Aeros weak voice was but a bloody whisper.

Dugal turned from Aeros, ignoring him, addressing the crowd in general, his voice somehow carrying over the vast throngs in every direction. "Tonight we rid humanity of what heritage it holds dear! For here at Absolution there is no room for tenderness! Here at Absolution there are no more longings for the past! For tonight humanity shall learn the full art of what we Bloodwoods do!"

Black Dugal then nodded to Sledg H'Mar. The burly gray oghul prepared his heavy iron mallet, lifting it up to his waist, steadying it for the awkward swing to come, large muscles bulging. Mancellor and Jenko gripped Aeros' arms and legs tighter, pressing Aeros' body flat to the ground.

Val-Draekin bent and grabbed a fistful of Aeros' matted hair, pulling the top of the man's head all the way back so his chin rested on the ground, revealing the huge gash in the White Prince's neck. Aeros' mouth was open wide and heaving.

"Hold the stake steady, Mud," Val-Draekin said to the small oghul. "If the pole is allowed to travel straight up the spine and exit the mouth, it will miss all the vital organs. And I want him alive to witness Fiery Absolution."

Val-Draekin nodded to Sledg H'Mar. And the large oghul swung the mallet.

CHAPTER FIFTY-NINE

NAIL

12TH DAY OF THE HEART MOON, 999TH YEAR OF LAIJON

AMADON, GUL KANA

A s promised," Seita said as she led the group from the Slaver's
Inn into the bloody grove under the Atonement Tree, "I give
you Fiery Absolution."

The first thing Nail saw was Aeros Raijael. The base of the long
wooden stake was buried in the cloven soil at the foot of the tree, its
sharpened point jutting slick and red from the White Prince's yawning mouth. Aeros was suspended above the ground, impaled on the pole
from his anus to his gaping mouth. His stiff back was pressed against the
rough bark, arms outstretched to either side of his body, wrists fixed to
the tree with thick iron nails. One glazed eye stared up into the lower
boughs some thirty feet above. The other eye was covered with a coal-
black stone.

Two Bloodwood assassins flanked the White Prince's body, twin
demon-eyed stallions at their sides, grim and dark. A tall white stallion
stood between them, a growling bulldog near the stallion. One of the
Bloodwoods was a stone-faced young man, the sides of his head shaved
and tattooed. The other was a dark-haired Vallè with an exquisitely

pristine, almost perfectly chiseled face. A third Bloodwood—a striking blond girl clad in sleek black leathers—sat astride an even sleeker black mare not far from the tree. At first Nail thought the female assassin was Ava Shay, but then he realized it couldn't be her, for he could not picture Ava on a Bloodeye steed.

Then Nail saw the small barefooted oghul near the black saber-toothed lion and the boy with flat silver eyes standing between them. *Stefan Wayland!*

As he followed Seita into the grove, Nail couldn't believe it was his friend standing with the oghul and lion. *And those eyes, twin silver pools!* Nail wanted to call out to his friend, but the scene before him under the Atonement Tree was too much to take in. *And would Stefan even be able to see me through those witchy silver eyes?* For the boy seemed to be staring into the darkness at nothing. Fact was, Stefan was the last person Nail thought he would see after leaving the Slaver's Tavern and Inn, and he didn't quite know how to react or what to do.

The Vallè princess had guided the group out of Amadon and straight toward the Hallowed Grove: Nail, Tala, Hawkwood, Lawri Le Graven, Bronwyn Allen, Cromm Cru'x, Liz Hen Neville, and Dokie Liddle still carrying Sky Reaver.

Lawri made the journey at Nail's side, cloaked and hooded, the gauntlet attached to her arm hidden from view as Seita guided them down a barren path between the army of oghuls and Vallè.

Legion upon legion of armed and mounted soldiers stretched around the grove in every direction, as far as the eye could see. Dayknights. Silver Guards. Sør Sevier Hounds and Rowdies and Knights of the Blue Sword. Disorganized Hragna'Ar oghuls in spiked and rusted armor. Tight Vallè legions in scrollworked livery and jewel-encrusted mail, splendorous and glittering. It was a sea of men, oghuls, and Vallè unlike anything Nail had ever seen. North, south, east, and west, torchlight kindled off the armor and spearhead of every soldier gathered around the great tree.

And Aeros Raijael was already dead. Impaled on a stake and nailed to the Atonement Tree like the stories of Laijon of old. He not longer looked like the formidable warrior who had so cruelly sacked Gallows Haven. Nail recalled Bishop Tolbret reading from the Ember Lighting Song of the Third Warrior Angel near the end of *The Way and Truth of Laijon*—"*And it came to pass that at the time of final Dissolution, he died upon the tree, nailed thusly, purging all man's Abomination.*"

Am I now the Angel Prince? Nail had never forgotten what Hawkwood had told him of his parentage in Ravenker so long ago. *Was Aeros truly my kin? Am I Laijon returned?* Then he saw the White Prince's strained chest rise and fall with breath. *He is not yet dead!*

"For the last thousand years all history has been driven by the Vallè!" Val-Draekin's voice rang out across the grove, carrying over the multitudes. "All scripture scribed by the Vallè! For without the dreams and machinations of the Vallè, this day of Fiery Absolution would not happen! For our ancestors purposefully preyed upon humanity's willingness to accept ignorance and suffering and ridiculous legends as coming from God."

Seita brought the group from the Slaver's Inn to a halt. And Nail's heart skipped a beat as he gaped at the familiar dark-haired Vallè— Val-Draekin. *He is alive!*

Val-Draekin was the center of all attention. He stood before a five-legged Silver Throne and what Nail assumed were the weapons of the Five Warrior Angels: a blinding-white shield, a sparkling helm with two jutting horns the color of Riven Rock marble, a long white sword with a crescent-moon hilt-guard and a bright red ruby set in its pommel, the crossbow Dokie had hauled from the Sky Loch mines, and the battle-ax he himself had found in the mines above Gallows Haven and carried for so long. All five weapons just lying there, scattered unceremoniously in the bloody grass and dirt behind Val-Draekin.

Nail had just assumed the Vallè had perished in the fire that had consumed the Filthy Horse Saloon. Yet here Val-Draekin was, the center of Fiery Absolution, shouting to a captive throng, shouting to soldiers spread out in every direction, all of them seemingly rooted in place, all of them seemingly unable to look away, as if they were caught in a spell.

"For within each generation there has been an assumption within the

Vallè that the end is near!" Val-Draekin shouted. "And with each generation the Vallè have been encouraging religious strife throughout the Five
Isles! And now here we are, for this is the first generation of Vallè in which
our thousand years of strife we have sown come to fruition! For we shall
soon witness the return of the beasts of the underworld! And they shall
not be the nameless demons humanity has claimed that they were!"

Nail could scarcely concentrate on anything the Vallè was shouting,
for there was still so much to take in. His eyes drifted up the dark broad
trunk of the Atonement Tree, and he stared up toward the tree's lofty
heights above in mute wonder. Over five hundred feet high, he'd been
told, leaves that never died, and every pale green leaf somehow seeming
to distinguish itself from the others, even amongst millions. This was
holy ground. The place of Laijon's death. The place of Laijon's return.
This was where all the armies of the Five Isles were to come together for
that final war, that final ushering in of Fiery Absolution.

And here we are! Nail looked toward Stefan Wayland again, mind reeling. *And here we are! Two boys from Gallows Haven in the middle of Fiery
Absolution, one come with glowing silver eyes, one come as Laijon returned!*

Though Stefan had not seen Nail yet, the ghostly black saber-tooth
next to him had. Horror snuck up Nail's throat as the lion with flat silver
eyes and sharp silver teeth stared straight at him. The ominous creature was similar to the huge black saber-tooth Nail had seen tear the
girl apart on the rocky seashore near Wroclaw. This cat was similar to
the black beast who had accompanied the five skull-faced knights. Nail
wanted Stefan to look his way, if but once. But his friend's silver eyes
remained fixed out into the vast darkness before him.

"Fiery Absolution is retribution for the many Vallè, oghul, and dwarven lives lost over the centuries due to the religions of humanity!" Val-
Draekin still yelled. "Fiery Absolution is retribution for the human
occupation of the Five Isles these last thousand years, retribution for the
physical banishment of our Vallè cousins, the Aalavarrè Solas, to the underworld a thousand years ago, retribution for the occupation the Five
Isles of which humanity never belonged! If there ever was a reckoning,
an absolution, now is the time, and humanity must now pay the price!"

Nail's mind now spun in confusion. He found his heart was hammering in his chest. Hawkwood was standing at his side, staring hollow-eyed at one of the two open coffins on the grass amid a bloody mess of severed body parts, spilled entrails, and the dead. Hawkwood was staring at the rotted corpse of a woman.

Princess Jondralyn?

Tala was staring at the coffin too, tears welling in her eyes.

"Look!" Liz Hen called out. "Look, Dokie, it's Stefan Wayland!"

"What happened to his eyes?" Dokie asked. "He looks sick."

But Stefan could not hear them. Val-Draekin was still shouting over the crowd.

"Look!" Liz Hen called out again. "There's Jenko Bruk!" She pointed.

"And Ava Shay!" Dokie pointed too.

Nail followed Dokie's gaze. And there she was. Ava Shay. Sitting at the back of a wagon not fifty paces away. A dwarf sat at the wagon's helm. *What brought her to this place?* Nail wondered. *What brought any of us to this place?*

And there was Jenko Bruk, just as Liz Hen had said. The baron's son was standing near Ava's wagon in the colors and armor of Sør Sevier. At the sight of Ava Shay, Nail's hand flew to his chest, feeling the turtle carving on the leather thong around his neck, the carving Ava had given him so long ago. He still had it, despite all.

"Mancellor." Bronwyn Allen's voice was a hushed whisper of excitement. She stepped past Nail, the two white feathers in her hair flickering orange and yellow in the torchlight. "It's my brother." She turned and looked at Cromm, who was still standing behind Nail. "It's Mancellor." The Wyn Darrè girl pointed to a familiar-looking long-haired knight with black smears under his eyes, standing next to Jenko Bruk.

Nail recognized the man. It was the Sør Sevier fighter who had attacked him on the beachhead at Gallows Haven and knocked him unconscious, the knight who had helped Jenko steal *Forgetting Moon* from him in Ravenker.

"It is Mancellor," Cromm said.

"Do you think he sees me?" Bronwyn asked.

"He has not looked away from you since we entered the grove," Cromm answered. "He sees you."

The oghul was right. Mancellor's eyes were fixed on his sister with a focused, burning stare. "I should go to him," Bronwyn said.

"Cromm thinks that now is bad timing for family reunions."

Nail thought it a bad idea too. Mancellor was with Sør Sevier, with the enemy. The evil knights Enna Spades and Hammerfiss were right behind him. He remembered that the red-haired woman was a horror. He could feel the slave mark on the underside of his wrist flare with pain. It was Spades who had branded him.

Father? Tala whispered. Her legs and whole body were shaking as she leaned into Nail for support. "Is that my *father* standing with Jovan?" Her hand gripped his tightly.

"I do not know what your father looks like," Nail said.

But there was a bearded man standing near Tala's older brother. Even with the gray-shot beard, the man did look like a thinner, older version of Jovan. The older man and Jovan stood near Leif and Glade Chaparral. None of them had noticed the entrance of Seita or anyone else from the Slaver's Inn, so fixated were they on Val-Draekin and his speech. None of them had noticed but for Glade Chaparral, that is. Glade glared fixedly across the torchlit expanse at Tala.

"I can't believe my father lives," Tala whispered, completely unaware of Glade's intent gaze. Her fingers squeezed Nail's even tighter now. "'Tis either my father or a wraith that I see."

It wasn't a wraith, Nail was certain of that. But he wasn't sure it was Tala's father, either. Borden Bronachell had died five years ago in Wyn Darrè. *But the look in Tala's eyes!* Whoever the bearded man was, it seemed that by simply stepping into the open space under the Atonement Tree, Seita had joined together many long-lost relationships.

But as Cromm had said, this was no time for happy reunions.

Val-Draekin was looking right at Nail. In fact, everyone was.

"And now," Val-Draekin said, "we come to the long-awaited moment when Laijon returned shall reveal himself to the Five Isles and usher in Fiery Absolution!"

Silence followed.

A silence so thick Nail almost couldn't see. Everything went blurry. And he suddenly couldn't breathe, couldn't squeeze the air past the knot in his throat. The marks on his body burned with pain.

Val-Draekin pointed to the Silver Throne, shouting for all to hear, "Will the real heir of Laijon and Raijael step forward and sit the Silver Throne and claim his place at Fiery Absolution?"

Nail's gaze traveled across the grove to Ava Shay, sitting on the back of the wagon. *It must be sad, always belonging to people,* she had once said. *But what will she think now? What will Ava Shay think when she sees that I am no slave, that I am the youngest son of Aevrett Raijael, that I am Aeros' younger brother, that I am the real Angel Prince, that I am Laijon returned? What will she think of me then?*

Val-Draekin shouted once again, "Will the real heir of Raijael step forward?"

Cromm Cru'x placed the black angel stone in Nail's hand. "It is time, marked one." The oghul seized Nail by the arm and pulled him from Tala's grasp.

Nail went with him.

"Not you." Hawkwood grasped Nail by the shoulder and pulled him back. "Not you, Nail. Not you."

"What?" Nail turned, confused.

Cromm growled, thunder in his throat. His eyes were seething with fury, fists balled. "You dare stop Cromm from escorting the marked one to Fiery Absolution?"

Seita stepped from behind Hawkwood. "You may not like what is happening, Nail, but what happens today is the best for everyone and the future of the Five Isles."

"But Cromm says I have the marks. Hawkwood told me that I was—"

"I only told you what people would say you were," Hawkwood cut him off. "Not what you really were."

"What am I, then?" Nail asked.

"Nothing," Hawkwood said.

"He is the *marked one!*" Cromm roared. "And Cromm shall escort him to the Silver Throne!"

"He is right." Nail's mind was spinning. "I read Shawcroft's note. I have the marks. The mark of the cross, The mark of the beast. The mark of the slave."

"You were never truly a slave," Hawkwood said.

"But I've been branded. I can feel the burn marks as we speak."

"Will the real heir of Raijael step forward?" Val-Draekin shouted a third time.

Everyone was still looking at Nail. But for some reason, he felt so small under their withering stares. "I've been branded," he said.

"Perhaps so." Seita moved around Hawkwood and toward Nail. "But there is one here among us who *has* been a slave."

Before Nail knew what the Vallè maiden was doing, Seita deftly swept the black angel stone from his grasp and strode across the bloody field.

Her theft of the stone happened so fast it left Nail stunned.

"What is this?" Cromm glared at Hawkwood. "What is this strange Vallè doing with Cromm's stone?"

Seita marched past Val-Draekin and the Silver Throne and knelt before Stefan Wayland and the small, barefooted oghul clad in dirty rags.

"Seita," Stefan said.

"Aye, it is me." The Vallè handed him the black stone. "I have missed you."

Stefan cupped the stone in his hands, silver eyes curious and gleaming. *"Blackest Heart,"* he whispered.

"It is." Seita stood, her delicate hands on both of Stefan's shoulders. "Since the real heir of Raijael has not stepped forward, it is up to you to show us, Stefan Wayland. For only the pure in heart can show us who is Laijon returned. I have foreseen it. And you shall gift the great One and Only the angel stone in your hand. Then you shall gift Laijon the weapons of the Five Warrior Angels. And then you shall escort our Lord to the Silver Throne. For only the true Laijon returned can usher in Fiery Absolution."

"I don't know if I can," Stefan said.

"We work together," the mousy oghul next to Stefan said. "Remember Mud promised his mother he would escort the marked one. Now is Mud's chance."

"Can I take Mud with me?" Stefan asked.

"We would have it no other way," Val-Draekin answered. "For Mud Undr'Fut is the fulfillment of Hragna'Ar prophecy."

"As you search the crowd," Seita said looking from Stefan to Mud, "remember, Laijon is the least of us."

The oghul's eyes immediately began scanning the throng surrounding them.

Cromm was enraged. "Do these mad Vallè give the scrawny oghul the task that was meant for Cromm?" He swept past Nail and stomped toward Stefan, bellowing, "Do the Vallè steal Cromm's destiny? That is my black rock! You must give it back!"

Val-Draekin clicked his tongue twice. The black saber-toothed lion behind Mud and Stefan stepped forward with a cool saunter of muscle and might, imposing itself between Cromm and the black stone in Stefan's hand. Cromm slowed, breathing heavily, still moving toward Stefan. Bronwyn had her bow out, arrow aimed at the cat. The lion loosed a deep-throated roar, long silver fangs gleaming in the torchlight, silver eyes planted on Cromm. The oghul stopped his advance. Bronwyn's arrow remained pointed at the large cat.

"I wouldn't," Seita called out to the Wyn Darrè girl. There was a black dagger in the Vallè maiden's grip, ready to throw. Val-Draekin had two black daggers in hand.

"I can't move," Cromm said.

"Me either." Bronwyn lowered her bow.

Nail suddenly found that his legs were locked in place too. He felt something stirring in the air above, some foul sorcery.

"The way is yours." Seita turned to Stefan and Mud. "No harm shall come to you now."

Every eye was on the odd pair. Stefan held the black angel stone out before him, cupped in both hands as he stepped forward and scanned the massive armies, silver eyes passing over Cromm, moving past Tala and Hawkwood, lingering on Nail and Tala for but a moment. Then he walked toward Liz Hen Neville and Dokie Liddle, the small oghul on his heels. He reached Liz Hen, the stone held out before him still.

"I ain't takin' it," Liz Hen said, a look of pure bewilderment on her face. "Besides, my feet won't move."

"I was hoping Beer Mug was with you," Stefan said.

"Are you tellin' me you can see with them eyes?" Liz Hen asked.

"What do you mean?" There was confusion on Stefan's face now.

"Beer Mug ain't here." Dokie looked sad to see Stefan, not joyful at all.

Nail was overcome with sadness too. He didn't know if it was really even his friend. There were strange silver streaks running in rivulets under Stefan's pale skin, and his eyes were like pools of liquid silver. They matched the eyes of the saber-toothed lion in their flat luminosity. And most disturbing of all, they were eyes akin to the skull-faced knights Nail had seen in Wroclaw. The Last Demon Lords, Val-Draekin had called them. And now Val-Draekin was conducting Fiery Absolution. *And I am nothing.*

Stefan moved away from Liz Hen and Dokie, Mud right behind him. Stefan's silver eyes lingered but a moment on the hooded form of Lawri Le Graven. He drifted through the crowd glancing at Glade and Leif Chaparral, spending a moment studying the pain-racked faces of Jovan Bronachell and the bearded man Tala had called Father.

Stefan looked toward the armies of Aeros Raijael with some interest now, walking forward, studying Enna Spades, studying Hammerfiss, curious silver orbs scanning the armies behind the two mounted fighters.

Then Stefan and Mud stepped toward the wagon carrying Ava Shay, the oghul's feet treading lightly and carefully. Stefan's gaze was on Bronwyn Allen's brother, Mancellor, now. Then he walked away from the Wyn Darrè man, eyes bouncing between Ironcloud and Jenko Bruk before focusing on Ava Shay.

Then he stopped.

A moment passed, and Nail wondered if his silver-eyed friend wasn't going to hand the black angel stone to Ava.

Then Stefan turned back to Spades and Hammerfiss. Both he and Mud moved as one, stepping purposefully toward the two Sør Sevier warriors. Stefan kept the black stone cupped in his hand, holding it up now at eye level, as if letting it guide his every move. Fierce-eyed, both Spades and Hammerfiss watched Stefan and the oghul approach.

Then they both moved their mounts aside as Stefan and Mud stepped between them toward a third horse bearing a thin, lithesome blond girl. She wore a stained white shift tied with a blue string and a dirty blue bonnet on her head. The innocent-looking girl sat the saddle before a pale young man in simple leather armor. The boy was also blond and seemed to be about Nail's own age. He had a familiar look. It was the deformed, dough-faced boy from Savon. Tala's cousin. Lawri's brother.

"Lindholf," Tala muttered as Stefan held the black angel stone up before the malformed boy. It looked like she wanted to run to her cousin, but she couldn't. Nail still couldn't move his own legs. He didn't even know if blood still flowed in his veins, so numb he was. "Lindholf," Tala muttered again softly.

Lindholf just stared at the offered stone, scared.

The blond girl on the saddle before him lifted her leg and slipped from the horse, landing lightly in the grass. She took the black angel stone from Stefan, holding it up to Lindholf. "I think he means it for you."

"You should not have touched it, Leisel." Lindholf dismounted, real fear in his voice as he stared down at the stone in the girl's hand. "It could still be cursed."

"Fear not, Lindholf Le Graven!" Val-Draekin called out. "The black stone is no longer cursed, for I witnessed Roguemoore lay flesh to it in the Sky Loch mines!"

Lindholf took the stone from Leisel. "It is the *real* angel stone," he said, wonder in his eyes.

Val-Draekin called out again, to Mud this time. "Bring the marked one forth!"

The small oghul stared at Lindholf proudly. "Like Mud's mother once said, you are the least of us." Then he latched onto Lindholf's arm and led him back between Spades' and Hammerfiss' horses toward the Silver Throne. Stefan and Leisel followed.

"He has a burned face," Cromm grumbled, looking back at Nail almost accusingly. Nail recalled the oghul wanting to burn his face to better fulfill the prophecy. *Can this boy, Lindholf, really be Laijon returned? If he is Tala's cousin, then he is not the blood of Aevrett Raijael.* It made scant sense to Nail.

I am the blood of Aevrett Raijael! He felt an urge to step forward, to claim his rightful place. But there was some unseen weight pressing down upon him now, some dark entity in the blackness above that held him rooted in place. He could feel it up there, circling. In fact, nobody, not even one knight in the hundreds of thousands gathered around the Hallowed Grove, had so much as moved since Seita had snatched the black stone from his hand.

Now everyone watched as Mud guided Lindholf to the Silver Throne. Mud began picking up all the weapons of the Five Warrior Angels along the way—*Blackest Heart, Ethic Shroud, Forgetting Moon, Afflicted Fire,* lastly placing *Lonesome Crown* atop his head. He then beckoned Lindholf to sit the Silver Throne. Lindholf sat. Mud then handed Lindholf all the weapons. They all rested awkwardly on the starlted boy's lap. Val-Draekin then handed him a leather pouch. Lindholf opened the pouch and out spilled the remaining angel stones onto his lap too: red, green, blue, and white.

"The King of Slaves!" Val-Draekin stepped back and shouted. "Laijon returned!"

His voice carried like the booming of a hammered anvil across the grove, the very words almost shaking the ground. A deep silence fell over everyone, a silence so deep Nail could hear his own heartbeat pounding in his chest, a silence so deep he could hear the whispers of disappointment and betrayal in his own soul. *I helped find those weapons! This imposter, Lindholf, did not!*

In fact, Lindholf Le Graven looked silly under that horned helm, all the weapons and stones balanced on his lap like so much junk, like so many useless items. The white surfaces of the sword and shield seemed to catch every flicker of torchlight and send it leaping back outward, nearly blinding Nail. Same with the curious curved horns on *Lonesome Crown*. And the angel stones glowed with a light of their own.

And Nail wanted to touch *Forgetting Moon* again so desperately it hurt. *It should be me on the Silver Throne! I am the Heir of Raijael!* Yes, he wanted the battle-ax, but there was something holding him back, holding him from a destiny that had been stolen. *This is all so wrong!* He could feel it, the wrongness and evil of it all.

"We are not yet done," Val Draekin announced, looking back toward Nail.

And Nail felt his heart again beat faster, the scars on his body flare with pain.

"Come." Val-Draekin beckoned.

Nail still could not move. He looked at Tala. She stood stiff and still too, eyes wide in fright. Something was holding them down.

Lawri Le Graven brushed by them then, stepping gently across the grass, face hooded in shadow. She walked straight toward the Silver Throne, the bottom hem of her cloak brushing the grass at her feet.

"Come." Val-Draekin beckoned her forward. "Come and help your twin brother usher in Absolution, Lawri Le Graven. Fight in the coming battle with thine own hand."

Once Lawri stood before the Silver Throne, she reached up and shed the hood of her cloak with both hands—one a hand of flesh and blood, the other naught but a silver gauntlet. Her pale face stood out stark and white in the light of the five weapons and angel stones, her eyes a hazy shade of green.

"Dugal." Val-Draekin beckoned one of the Bloodwood assassins forward.

The dark-eyed Vallè slid from his Bloodeye steed. He took the reins of the white stallion in one hand and walked the tall beast toward Lindholf, a copper flask in his other hand. He handed the flask to Lindholf. "'Tis Blood of the Dragon, and it will summon fiery beasts of the underworld at your command. Drink."

Lindholf stood and took the flask and drank, then handed it back. "You've no Shroud of the Vallè?"

Val-Draekin pulled a small pouch from the folds of his leather armor, a pouch Nail recognized. *Shroud of the Vallè!* Nail had seen Val-Draekin create fire many times with the white powder he carried in that pouch. He opened the pouch and poured some of the white powder into Lindholf's hand. The boy snorted it up his nose, eyes widening in pleasure.

"The horse is yours too," the Vallè named Dugal said, handing the reins to Lindholf. "Its name is Spirit."

Val-Draekin faced Lawri. "Hold out your hand," he said to the girl. She stretched the silver gauntlet forth. "No," Val-Draekin said. "Your real hand."

Lawri did as asked, holding out her good hand.

Val-Draekin poured some of the white powder into the girl's outstretched hand, then placed the pouch back into the folds of his leather armor.

"Now toss the powder as high into the air as you can," Val-Draekin said. "And when the white cloud forms above you, with the gauntlet snap your fingers."

"Snap my fingers?" Lawri questioned.

"You know you can do it," Val-Draekin said. "Only you can usher in Fiery Absolution this way."

Lawri Le Graven tossed the handful of Shroud of the Vallè as high into the air as she could. A hazy billow of white erupted above her, floating momentarily, tendrils wandering higher in the breeze.

Then she lifted the gauntlet and snapped her fingers.

Simple as that.

Fire exploded from the tips of Lawri's silver-scaled fingers, enveloping the drifting Shroud of the Vallè in a flash of orange light and flame. The tree limbs some thirty feet above her instantly ignited, roaring fire racing from branch to branch faster than the eye could see, torrents of fire consuming the fabled leaves of never-fading green. Nail was instantly struck by an astonishing gale of ripping heat that seemed to stretch his skin.

The sudden thunder of rushing and billowing fire and the screams of horror pierced the air. The Hallowed Grove was instantly naught but blinding flame, panic, and chaos, people crouching, hands clenched over their ears.

The spell was broken. Nail grabbed Tala by the hand and ran. Everyone was running. Hundreds of thousands ran in a savage and frenzied retreat from the towering inferno that used to be the Atonement Tree. Hundreds of thousands ran from a five-hundred-foot pillar of fire stretching into the heavens. Flames chased the armies of Jovan Bronachell. Flames chased the armies of Aeros Raijael. And they all fled from it. They fled on foot. They fled on horseback. And they fled in terror.

Val-Draekin's army of oghuls and Vallè chased them, wicked weapons of both rust and shine flashing in the firelight, striking down any human in their way with a bloody ferocity never before seen in battle.

And hand in hand, Nail and Tala also ran, legs churning. They ran by sheer force of will to escape the flame and blood and war. They ran to escape Fiery Absolution.

Then came the shrieks from above, thunderous rumbling sounds of such earsplitting magnitude they caused both Nail and Tala and everyone around to instantly drop to their knees, eyes cast toward a flame-lit sky in pure terror.

Crouching in horror, Nail again felt rooted in place. Stiff. Numb. He clenched Tala's hand tightly and looked skyward, toward whatever held him fast to the ground.

And that was when he saw the beasts of the underworld.

They circled high above the burning tree, five in all, white, black, blue, green, and red, large sinuous wings fanning the lofty inferno. Their heaving lungs gulped down what flame and fire licked skyward from the top reaches of the burning tree. Then their lungs spewed that very flame forth from toothy, jagged maws in searing torrents. The beasts were hungrily drinking in the flame, and then, fueled by its scorching sustenance, they dove down toward the fleeing armies.

Beasts of the underworld! Dragons!

Flames shot from their ragged maws, burning all in their plunging path, serpentlike tails of sharpened spines snaking out behind them. They swooped low, their forked, batlike wings stirring the heated air, wings that fanned out wider than the unfurled sails of the *Lady Kindly*.

Dragons. Red. Blue. Green. Black. White. Diving. Fire spewing from their mouths. Heat lancing across Nail's skin. He looked around and all color had been torn away but for the red glow of fire that now stained the pitch-black of the sky.

Tala let go of Nail's hand and placed both palms over her ears. Nail did the same, for the sounds of the dragons' fiery cries was beyond unbearable. There was nowhere safe to go. Nowhere safe to even look. And he couldn't move anyway. The landscape seethed and boiled with people on fire, raged with oghuls and Vallè, bloodlust sparking in their eyes as their weapons slashed and fell. And when the dragons roared, it seemed nobody but the Vallè and oghuls could move at all. They alone were immune to the paralyzing shriek of the dragons. All Nail could do was stare in horror at the bubbling, panicked faces of those on fire, their skin charred and black and flaming and sloughing off muscle and bone, their clothes and weapons melting.

One of the dragons swooped near, a glowing blue dragon, flame blazing from its open, heaving mouth. It dove so close Nail saw the skull-faced demon that rode upon its back—a silver-masked knight in colorful blue armor, scaled armor that glowed with an azure, cerulean light so bright it almost matched the hideous hue of the blue dragon. And then the shrieking dragon was gone, sailing up into the night.

When Nail looked around, Tala was gone. He risked one last glance toward the Atonement Tree, bile rising in his throat at what he saw, memories of underwater visions from the grayken hunt swirling through his mind, wavering and hazy. The air under the tree was heavy with smoke and red falling embers. Aeros Raijael's burning corpse was still hanging under the large burning tree, arms splayed out in the shape of a cross, flames of crimson light licking over his body.

And strutting before the burning corpse was the glorious white stallion, a knight with a glowing white shield and horned helm sitting in its saddle.

Lindholf Le Graven!

A blond girl was on the saddle before Lindholf.

Lawri Le Graven!

She had *green* glowing eyes!

And in the bloody redness of Fiery Absolution, it looked as if the silver gauntlet attached to her arm had sprouted long, curving claws.

CHAPTER SIXTY

LINDHOLF LE GRAVEN

12TH DAY OF THE HEART MOON, 999TH YEAR OF LAIJON

AMADON, GUL KANA

They fled. Everyone fled before him. All the armies of the Five Isles fled before Lindholf Le Graven. For according to Seita and Val-Draekin, he was Laijon returned, the King of Slaves, as *The Way and Truth of Laijon* had prophesied. *Laijon returned shall be an ensign unto all kingdoms. And he shall be called the Lord of Fiery Absolution, the Savior of All Mankind, the First and the Last, the marked one, the Holy Cross, the Slayer of the Beasts, the Supreme Spirit, the Lord of All Worlds, the pre-existent world, this world, and the next, the Giver of Life and the Bringer of Death, the Father of All Mourning, the great One and Only. He shall be the King of Slaves.*

The White Prince had called Lindholf "Lord Potato."

But who's the one with the stake rammed up his anus now? Lindholf felt his eyes glowing hot with revenge. *Who's the one cooking like a potato on a spit now?* As death and war and slaughter raged in every direction, Lindholf remained untouched, whilst behind him Aeros Raijael burned.

Digging heels into flanks, Lindholf guided the White Prince's

glorious white stallion through swirls of black smoke and hot drifting embers. He moved farther away from the heat of the burning tree.
His twin sister, Lawri, rode in the saddle before him, her back pressed
warmly to his chest, her hand a metal claw.

The five angel stones were in a pouch at Lindholf's belt. In one hand
he carried *Afflicted Fire*; in the other, *Ethic Shroud*. *Forgetting Moon* and
Blackest Heart were both strapped to his back, whilst *Lonesome Crown*
rode atop his head. And together they all weighed less than a feather
pillow. For they all belonged to him now. He knew it. He *possessed* them.
And with them he was invincible. All the scars on his body burned with
glorious power now. For he was the marked one.

And tonight was Fiery Absolution.

Chaos and war swirled around him and above him, glorious colorful
dragons descending from the heights of the stars, their blistering breath
lighting the night afire. Everything burned in red-hot oblivion. Aeros
Raijael burned. The armies of Sør Sevier burned. The armies of Gul Kana
burned. The Atonement Tree burned. And the Silver Throne sat alone,
glowing scarlet embers raining down over it, hot ash brushing its gleaming surface and covering it in black, the tree above naught but a giant
roaring tower of flame.

Lindholf recalled standing on the once crisp grass in the center of
the Hallowed Grove under the towering Atonement Tree not long ago.
A Vallè tradition, Seita had said reverently, blowing white powder up
onto the tree. *To grace the tree with Shroud of the Vallè is to gift the essence of our realm's deep gratitude for Laijon's great sacrifice. For more than
a thousand years the Vallè have worshipped so, sharing the Shroud with the
tree, at this place of our Lord's great sacrifice.* But now Lindholf knew it
was all deception. Generations of Vallè had been preparing the tree for
Fiery Absolution. Preparing it to erupt into a towering column of flame,
preparing it for its thousand-year purpose—to feed the beasts of the
underworld with fire.

And the five dragons above drank that fire in and spat it back out
with searing-hot devastation, their skull-faced masters guiding them in
flights of obliteration and flame, the ground under them naught but

charred stink and ruin. The dragons' dance and savage melody washed over Lindholf in waves, bolstering him, calling to him, the power of the weapons he bore keeping the fire of the beasts at bay.

He thought of his own deformed ears under the magical helm. He'd always thought those burns and scars were a curse. But now they were a blessing, his one and only sustenance. He recalled climbing the statue of Laijon in the temple, discovering the flaw in the statue, the flaw that only he knew of. The chisel marks atop the ears—ears that used to be pointed. Only he knew that the statue was a fraud, that it was no likeness of a human at all. It was the likeness of a Vallè.

But who am I? The King of Slaves? A fraud? Lindholf knew there was no Raijael blood running through his veins. *Unless . . .*

His ears, like the statue of Laijon, were also altered. Deformed. Scarred at birth, he'd been told.

And then he recalled his time in Purgatory.

Do not call me Mother ever again, Mona Le Graven had said when she had come to visit him in that dungeon. *I am not your mother,* she'd hissed. *I can see your lies, Lindholf Le Graven. You disgust me. Look at your face. Your ghastly scarred face. You never were my son.* And with those final words, Mona Le Graven, the woman who Lindholf had known as "Mother," left him alone in the dungeon. And he had folded to the floor, hands desperately clutching the cold iron bars.

You never were my son. Her words echoed in his mind. *Never my son.*

And now Fiery Absolution had come. And it was not the glorious day of Laijon's return that the faithful of Gul Kana—including his mother—had dreamed it would be. No. Fiery Absolution was naught but savage destruction and blood-soaked terror.

And Lindholf Le Graven bore witness as its lord and champion, commanding the fires of Absolution and the beasts of the underworld.

And all fled in terror before him.

When everyone believes they have a divine destiny, be it the followers of Laijon, Mia, or Raijael, someone is bound to be disillusioned. For when every tribe believes they have the one and only truth, someone is certain to be wrong. Thus the problem with scripture and faith and belief and religion and why they all can be justified to whatever end, be it for good, charity, destruction, or war.
— THE BOOK OF THE BETRAYER

CHAPTER SIXTY-ONE
CRYSTALWOOD

13TH DAY OF THE HEART MOON, 999TH YEAR OF LAIJON

AMADON, GUL KANA

Above Krista Aulbrek, the Atonement Tree burned radiant, cast in a hot, fiery glow. The light of the fire and the swirling of the smoke cast shadows that danced and spun around her. The heat from the flames was oppressive, suffocating, collapsing down around her in waves. Voices wailed in pain under the harsh roar of the inferno.

She was surrounded by the chaos of war, flashing weapons and felled bodies swathed in flame. It was Vallè and oghul and man, fighting, dying, burning, oghuls sucking on the necks of the dying and dead. It was overwhelming. It was Absolution.

It was well after midnight now, and so much had happened here tonight it was hard for Krista to take it all in. The end of the White Prince. The return of Laijon. And the Atonement Tree now a towering five-hundred-foot-high torch of flame above her, ignited with the snap of two metal fingers and a sprinkle of Shroud of the Vallè. And dragon fire rent the tortured skies. *Beasts of the underworld!* Bedlam everywhere.

She would sort it out later. The chaos. Now she had to focus on her task—and a Bloodwood's task was killing, for she was a killer above all else.

As the tornado of heat and fire and death spun around her, Krista focused inward, slowing the pounding of her heart, quelling the breath rasping in her chest. Calmed, she hauled herself onto Dread and spurred the Bloodeye toward her foe, Black Dugal. Her former master stood before the Silver Throne under the burning Atonement Tree. He was wrapped in his Bloodwood cloak, a cloak that would protect him from heat and flame.

Seita was with him. *Silkwood*. Krista's sister in Black Dugal's Caste. Hans Rake was there too, the protective cowl of his cloak thrown up over his head. A black saber-toothed lion tore into the body of a fallen Gul Kana knight near Hans, its long fangs bared and bloody. Nailed to the trunk of the tree beyond the ferocious cat was the body of Aeros Raijael, yellow flame licking over his pale melting flesh.

Krista set heels to flanks and aimed Dread toward her master, undaunted by the flaming leaves raining down. She ducked to avoid a falling branch and pressed on. Black Dugal saw her advance and drew a blade from his black leather armor. Hans stood his ground by his master, twin black daggers in his own hands. Seita prepared for her too, setting her stance. The saber-toothed lion looked up, long teeth dripping with scarlet.

Krista pulled two Bloodwood daggers from her own leather armor—poisoned blades. The heat from the roaring firestorm above was intense; she sensed the smoke leaking upward from her black hood and leather armor. A second burning branch fell in front of Dread, and the mare leaped over it. Krista threw her first dagger at Hans. The young Bloodwood raised his own black dagger, blocking hers. Her second dagger flew toward Seita. The Vallè blocked the flying blade. With a keening wail, the dagger spun away into the smoke.

Krista leaped from the saddle and dashed toward Black Dugal, ignoring both Hans and Seita altogether. The master of assassins let his own dagger fly. Krista dodged the spinning blade and struck at him, black dagger a blur in the firelight. Her attack missed as he deftly backed away. The saber-tooth hissed and spat in her direction, lashing out with one long paw. Krista fell backward and the cat's long claws raked across her leather armor, tearing her cloak, the only thing protecting her from the heat. More branches twirled down from above, blazing with fire, one striking her in the shoulder.

Even more branches dropped from above, too many to count now. The black saber-tooth was the first to retreat, bounding around the trunk of the Atonement Tree, vanishing into the orange haze beyond. Black Dugal looked up at the chaotic inferno above and then sprinted after the cat. Hans smiled grimly at Krista and followed his master. Seita met Krista's calm gaze, then launched herself after the others.

Krista gathered her feet and scanned the hellish scene, searching for Dread. The black mare was gone. The reek of burning flesh filled Krista's nostrils. War raged in every direction as the savage Vallè and oghul armies continued their indiscriminate slaughter of Gul Kana and Sør Sevier soldiers. Sprays of dark blood decorated the fiery yellow vapors swirling around her. All Krista could see now were the hundreds and thousands of fleeing knights swathed in fire. The heat from the burning tree above was so intense she could scarcely bear it. Flame even writhed beneath her feet. The only thing protecting her was her Bloodwood cloak, but even that had its limitations.

Ironcloud was guiding the wagon out from under the flaming boughs of the Atonement Tree. Ava Shay was no longer on the wagon. She was gone, burned or dead or fleeing to safety, Krista had no idea. The dwarf sat at the head of the wagon alone, guiding the frightened team of mules through the churning, fiery madness.

Krista aimed herself at the wagon, sprinting now, the deceitful dwarf her new prey. She launched herself up onto the back of the wagon, twin black daggers flashing in the firelight. She buried a black blade into either side of the unsuspecting dwarf's thick neck just below his ears. Ironcloud's burly hands let loose the reins and clutched at the daggers. Then his body folded over sideways, limp. The wagon rumbled to a stop as the dwarf fell back and gazed up at her, the life draining from his eyes.

"You were always worthless, *Squateye*," she snarled his false name as he died. "I should have killed you moons ago."

Krista left the daggers in the dwarf's neck and jumped from the wagon, which was now bristling with flame. With Ironcloud's death, her want to kill was somewhat tempered. Her instinct for survival was now kicking in. She dove underneath the heavy cart as twirling branches spun down around her again. The inferno thundered and roared above. The wagon was on fire now; the mules leading it were burning too, bucking and thrashing and screaming. Krista scuttled out from under the cart's searing clutch and ran, hurling herself into the darkness to escape the blistering heat from above.

Things were not much better away from the Atonement Tree. War still raged in every direction. The remainder of the Hallowed Grove was a mass of savagery and war. Gul Kana Dayknights and Silver Guards fought against Sør Sevier knights, who fought against oghul and Vallè. Burning knights and oghuls fell and died at her feet. Krista leaped over the bodies and tried to get as far away from the tree as she could, dodging sword and spear and arrow as she dashed into the dark. The farther from the tree she ran, the cooler the air became. But beyond the intense heat of the tree was heat of another kind. A dim violet glow filtered through the darkness as the five beasts of the underworld wreaked destruction from above. Flame from the dragons was carving wicked scars of fiery light through the angry, shredded sky.

Still Krista ran, shoving her way through the madness and heat, ducking her way under a dying soldier in the clutches of a burly oghul, the beast's twin fangs buried in the man's neck. A Vallè fighter, resplendent in sparkling armor, rose up before her, long curved sword swinging downward. A burly oghul was right behind the Vallè, gums swollen and ready for blood. Krista pirouetted as she ran, blocking the Vallè's blow with an ease born of timing and practice. The oghul's hammer skimmed off the back of her head, catching the hood of her cloak and sending her reeling. Krista scarcely managed to deflect the beast's second blow and staggered away from the fight. A Sør Sevier knight took off the oghul's head with a longsword. Then the same knight was run through by a sharp Vallè lance head. The knight dropped with a bellow, vomiting blood. Krista felt the slick, balmy droplets of the man's insides dripping from her hair and down her neck.

The Vallè soldier who had killed the knight advanced on her, lance head singing through the air toward her in a flashing arc. Krista ducked and slipped inside the Vallè's guard instinctively, plunging her own dagger into his stomach. The Vallè grunted and pulled away, creating distance, long lance still in hand. The lance head whistled past her face again. She leaned back. He struck with a backhanded blow, the haft of the lance cracking against Krista's ribs, sending her sprawling to the ground. Bare hands glistening with grit, blood, and sweat, she flung a handful of the dirt up into the face of her foe. The spray of dirt startled the Vallè. Krista launched herself at him with pure ferocity, slamming her black blade directly into his throat. When she ripped the blade free, the Vallè fell dead with a gurgle.

The ground under Krista was smoking, blood-sodden, and horrid. A Sør Sevier knight slipped in the muck in front of her, falling, losing his weapon as he landed with a splatter in a pool of scarlet. The heavy hoof of a charging musk ox crushed the knight's skull—helm and all—the oghul atop the beast bellowing in triumph. More oghuls charged toward Krista now. Too many to fight. She whirled and ran.

The heat from the burning Atonement Tree engulfed the Hallowed Grove, the heat from the dragon fire above adding to the misery. Krista's pained and stretched skin craved the mere illusion of something breezy and cool, her eyes yearning for just a hint of blue or green or even white out there somewhere among the frothing sea of fire and darkness and Absolution.

But the only such colors came from the screeching beasts above, five colorful scaled dragons in the sky, each of them diving toward the battlefield, each of them spitting flame, Krista's pained ears forced open to the sinister harmony of their song.

CHAPTER SIXTY-TWO
MANCELLOR ALLEN

13TH DAY OF THE HEART MOON, 999TH YEAR OF LAIJON
AMADON, GUL KANA

F rantic and alone in a jostling sea of panic, Mancellor Allen forced
his way through the crush of people, searching for Jenko Bruk
and Ava Shay, sword gripped tightly in hand. He had become separated from Jenko and Ava in the swirl of pounding hooves and slashing
weapons of the oghul and Vallè armies.

When the Atonement Tree had burst into flame and the beasts of the
underworld had roared overhead, Mancellor and Jenko had hauled Ava
from the back of the wagon. Together, the three of them had fled into the
fearful night, not only to escape the heat of the fire, but also the scorching, fearsome flames of the two dragons above, the Red and the Black.
The two beasts of the underworld were herding the crowd to the west.
And everyone fled before them—Dayknights and Silver Guards of Gul
Kana, the soldiers of Sør Sevier—no one single person safe from the
beasts' fiery slaughter. It was every man for himself in this chaotic mass
of fleeing armies. *It was Fiery Absolution!*

The entire landscape round Mancellor was boiling in panic, war
chargers braying in terror, forced to flee with the flow of humanity,

forced along in every step by the crush of people. Mancellor heard the snap of bowstrings. A hail of Vallè arrows sailed overhead from a dozen mounted archers just ahead. The two dragons above curled away into the darkness, the arrows not hitting home.

One of the mounted Dayknights in front of Mancellor twisted in his saddle and fell with a bloody cry, a spear jutting from his back. More panic ensued. Men were fighting men now. A primal instinct kicked in, and Mancellor ran from the crowd. It was a frantic sprint. His lungs burned and heaved against his chest-plate armor. He could scarcely breathe. Still, he couldn't help but look back in fear, watching as a frothing Vallè war charger bore down on two fleeing Sør Sevier foot soldiers running with him. The Vallè soldier, in sparkling silver armor, struck, glittering spear raking the backs of the fleeing knights, sending them both sprawling, to be swiftly swallowed up by the flowing mass that now fled behind Mancellor. The dragons were once again herding the throng to the west, and Mancellor was caught up in the surge.

An oghul, mounted on a brutish musk ox, charged alongside Mancellor now, long sharp teeth exposed, gums engorged, seeking human blood. The beast's massive ball mace exploded upward in a spray of red as the Gul Kana knight running beside Mancellor was struck down. Mancellor tripped. As he rolled and tumbled, the churning ox hooves beat round him like evil drums, kicking sod into his face and eyes. The musk ox moved on and Mancellor found himself on his knees in a whirling turmoil of shouting soldiers, his sword somehow still in hand. His eyes hardly registered the utter chaos around him except in glimpses: the blur of rusted oghul armor and crude weapons, the flashing of curved Vallè blades, the glimmer of spearheads, the shimmer of the burning Atonement Tree in the distance. He looked up as the red dragon carved long swaths of flame through the throngs of wailing men to his left, the black dragon burning those to his right.

Mancellor scrambled to his feet as another large oghul bore down on him, its corded muscles under spiked armor heaving and strained, a fearsome-looking war hammer in its grip, long murderous teeth exposed under a wild grin. Mancellor ducked as the hammer whooshed overhead. The oghul whirled and swung again, missing Mancellor, who ducked a second time, and the hammer finding the fleeing Gul Kana knight behind him. The knight fell as blood spewed from his crushed face. Mancellor stabbed the oghul and moved on, regaining his bearings, the press of fleeing knights once again forcing him to the west. He cast his gaze about, trying again to locate Ava Shay or Jenko Bruk in the chaos. He saw nothing but frenzy-eyed faces of strangers, that and the fierce grimaces of charging oghuls and the determined cruel eyes of the Vallè.

There was a helmetless Sør Sevier warrior woman running beside him, a Knight of the Blue Sword. The woman lurched along at an unnatural gait, and all Mancellor could see was thick blood on the back of her head. Then she dropped to the ground, moaning in pain. Two other Sør Sevier knights stooped and snatched her up, dragging her along. Mancellor helped the knights pull the injured warrior woman over a crumbled wattle-and-daub barrier. Suddenly an arrow shaft sprouted from the woman's chest. Her eyes glazed over. She was dead. Mancellor and the other two knights let her go and ran. Dark smoke roiled around them. Orange light flared up and waves of heat bore down as the red dragon passed overhead again, flames shooting from its jagged mouth.

Mancellor risked a glance skyward. The dragon's skull-faced rider looked like a demon from the underworld. The dragon spewed fire over the landscape, and the hundreds of fleeing knights behind Mancellor disappeared in billowing balls of flame. Mancellor tried to block out the horrific pain-filled screams of those suddenly engulfed in fire, but he could not escape the screeching symphony of their death. The ruby-colored dragon let loose another wash of flame over the crowd, then swooped up into the darkness above. The black dragon sailed away after the red one, but Mancellor knew they would both come sailing back down out of the darkness soon.

Gulping in the hot and fetid air, Mancellor tottered forward, trying to keep his balance in the crush of people, every muscle in his body groaning in protest. An armored Silver Guard stumbled along beside him, vomiting blood from his mouth, half a dozen Vallè arrows jutting from his chest plate. The silver half-helm bounced around on the fellow's head, blood now pumping from his open, gasping mouth. Still the stalwart knight ran, trying to stay alive like everyone else in the midst of the hacking and slashing and swirling tumult.

A soft wisp of fresh air grazed Mancellor's face as the mass of fleeing Gul Kana and Sør Sevier knights behind him surged forward. They were being forced to the west by the larger oghul and Vallè armies now. Mancellor didn't know how far he had come, but the dirt and grass of the Hallowed Grove had turned to marble, and the burning tree was some distance behind him now, just an orange glow in the corner of his eye.

Still, the farther from the tree he ran, the thicker the crowd seemed to get. In fact, the jostling throng was pushing against him so forcefully he could scarcely move. Mancellor tried to slow his advance, but he was constantly being shoved from behind by the press of people, barely able to move in any direction but forward now. It was continuous. Unrelenting. And all he could do was go with the flow of humanity.

Ahead of him were naught but darkness and the drawn-out screams of the dying. *But what new horror was causing those screams?* He craned his neck for a better view of what was blocking the progress of the crowd. But all he could see were the tops of silver helmets and a dozen or more skeletal silhouettes—empty cages hanging from leaning scaffolding. The odd contraptions stretched to the left and to the right, rising up against the fiery horizon like sentinels.

The Riven Rock slave quarry! He had passed the quarry before when he and Liz Hen and Dokie had brought Jondralyn's body back to Amadon.

The teeming horde of fleeing knights dropped away into nothingness just beyond the line of scaffolding. It was as if the swarm of knights was being forced off the edge of the world, and Mancellor's mind reeled. *We have been herded to our death! We're being driven over the edge of the quarry!* He could hear the horrified screams of those dropping into the quarry ahead.

He tried to back away, but the weight of the shoving crowd behind him imposed its will, forcing him swiftly toward the gaping pit. The two dragons swooped down once again. Several knights tried to fire off arrows, but the thrashing push of the crowd was too much and the arrows flew wide. The spew of dragon fire pushed Mancellor and the crowd closer to the pit. A black cauldron blocked his path, but the surging mass of knights forced him around it and straight toward one of the stout wooden scaffoldings. The contraption leaned precariously out over the quarry and was girt with a number of gears and pulleys. Heavy ropes and chains stretched from the pulleys toward a giant wooden turning wheel at the quarry's rim. Mancellor tried to cling to the ropes and pulleys, but the crowd behind him shoved and shoved, relentless.

The knights in front of Mancellor dropped from sight into the pit, and suddenly he could see across the vast expanse. The slave pit loomed awesome and cavernous before him, stretching over a mile wide in every direction. The opposite edge was lined with a half-dozen scaffoldings between slabs of marble the size of small buildings.

Mancellor tried to slow himself, boots skidding on the marble, sliding toward the edge. But he couldn't fight the weight of the crowd pressing on him from behind. He was forced over the rim of the quarry and into empty air.

He lost hold of his sword as the breath left his lungs and the sensation of falling sank into his guts. *I'm dead,* he thought in dreadful fascination as he fell.

It was a sheer drop. Knights were falling and flailing downward in shiny splendor, screaming on every side, the floor of the quarry a mash of horror and death below, bodies and weapons piling up to the thunderous crunch of armor and bones.

Mancellor crashed heavily into the bristling mound of armored humanity and weaponry stacked halfway up the wall of the quarry. He tumbled down the slope of writhing and dead knights, his entire body absorbing the dissipating energy as he came to a stop. His face and shoulders were forced against the hard marble wall of the cliff whilst armored bodies and weapons rained down atop him, burying him under their crushing weight. Mancellor couldn't tell whether he was injured, but it didn't matter now. He was dead.

As the bodies piled up around him, Mancellor thought of the green-eyed girl with the silver arm. How she had snapped her metallic fingers and the Atonement Tree had burst into flames and Fiery Absolution had begun. Bronwyn had been there with Cromm Cru'x. He had scarcely recognized his younger sister with the black tattoos under her eyes. And now he would die without having reunited with her, the sister who had been lost to him for so many years. Tala Bronachell had also been there. He had recognized the princess from his dreams. When the mermaid had tried to drown him in the Battle of the Saint Only Channel, he had seen Tala's face. But what did it mean, his vision? *A girl I would so desperately love, but could never have?* But once the Atonement Tree had exploded in flame, Mancellor had forgotten all about dreams and visions.

Now here he was, dying, scarcely breathing, death raining down on him.

Then a hand reached out and grabbed his, pulling him up on top of the mountain of bodies and armor. "Keep near the wall and try and stay above the bodies!"

It was Jenko Bruk.

The Gallows Haven boy pushed Mancellor up the ever-growing pile of broken knights. Together they climbed, pressing themselves to the marble cliff, the constant waterfall of knights crashing around them, smashing and tumbling down the growing mountain of both the dead and the living. Hounds. Rowdies. Knights of the Blue Sword. Silver Guards. Dayknights. Some died instantly. Others screamed in pain. All the while, Mancellor and Jenko continued their struggle to stay above the wave of plummeting bodies, pressing themselves as close to the cliff face as possible.

The wall of marble disappeared in front of them. A dark tunnel in the sheer cliff face opened up, and Mancellor and Jenko spilled into the dimly lit marble passageway. They scrambled along the smooth floor as dozens and dozens of busted bodies came spilling in behind them, some alive, most limp and dead.

The falling crush of knights, weapons, and armor outside the tunnel continued to stack up, swiftly covering the entryway of the tunnel, pressing down. A few knights who had survived the fall tried to struggle free of the crush, the weight from above pressing them down. Soon the entry of the tunnel was a mash of flesh and blood and armor, the mass of carnage squeezing into the passageway. Mancellor turned from the horror, eyes scanning the clear tunnel beyond.

Three lit torches flickered in iron sconces some thirty paces or so down the passageway in front of him. It was then he realized there were other survivors in the tunnel besides Jenko and himself. Two knights were standing in the light. One was girt in the colors and bloodstained armor of a Knight of the Blue Sword—a Sør Sevier knight. The other was Liz Hen Neville, her face streaked with red, her armor bloodied.

"Liz Hen!" Mancellor shouted.

"We have to rescue Dokie!" The girl launched herself toward the squirming press of armor, bodies, and blood plugging the entryway of the tunnel behind Mancellor. "He is out there, dying!"

Mancellor grabbed her by the arm and held her back. "It's too dangerous!"

The Sør Sevier knight came up behind her. "She's right! We've got to try and save some of those men!" The knight was helmetless, his face a rash of red under a shock of dark brown hair. "Those men are dying! We can pull some of them free of the pile!"

"They are all dead!" Jenko shouted back. "Crushed!"

"How can you be sure?" Liz Hen grumbled deeply, hacking up a ragged cough. It seemed the fire and smoke from the burning Atonement Tree still lived in her lungs.

The Sør Sevier knight ignored Jenko and strode forward to help a struggling Knight of the Blue Sword soldier from the pile. He pulled on the knight's outstretched arm to no avail. The other man was lodged underneath too much bloody carnage and weight. Cursing in frustration, Jenko stepped toward the mash of bodies, snatched up a Dayknight sword, and stabbed into the panicked face of the half-buried knight.

"You traitor!" The other Sør Sevier knight whirled on Jenko. "You've killed him!"

"I ended his suffering!"

"I've seen you around Aeros! You're the Gallows Haven boy! You are not a full-blooded Sør Sevier man! You've never been nothing more than a traitor!"

"You don't know the half of it." Jenko turned away from the knight, long black sword steady in his grip as he searched the tunnel.

"Answer for your crime!" the knight challenged.

Jenko whirled, his sword flashing in the dim torchlight, cutting deep into the surprised knight's neck. The knight dropped to the ground, holding the wound as he bled out and fell on his back silently.

"Your brain has been baked by all that dragon fire out there, Jenko Bruk," Liz Hen snarled at him. "Seems like this horrible slave pit would be the type of place I would find you. That man is right: you *are* a traitor!"

"Like I said, you don't know the half of it." Jenko glared at her.

"Why kill those men, Jenko, why?" There were tears streaming down Liz Hen's cheeks. "We've got to save Dokie! What's happened to the world?"

"Fiery Absolution happened," Jenko spat back at her, cynicism dripping from his voice. "Fiery Absolution is what happened," he repeated, casting a wary gaze around the passageway, the dull thudding of falling bodies growing more faint behind him.

"Whatever it was, it was a horror for sure," Liz Hen sobbed, eyes fixed on the smashed bodies, armor, and blood jammed into the entrance of the tunnel. "Stefan with silver eyes. Val-Draekin and that huge black cat! The White Prince impaled up the ass. And that fire! So much fire! And dragons! Beer Mug lost and now Dokie too?"

"When did you last see Dokie?" Mancellor grabbed the girl by the shoulders, trying to calm her, to get her to focus. "When did you last see him?"

"I don't know," she blubbered. "I lost him somewhere under the Atonement Tree."

"He likely fled in some other direction then," Mancellor tried to reassure her. "I'm sure he's fine."

"Fine," Jenko laughed. "I doubt anyone out there is *fine*. Those beastly dragons were herding everyone this way, herding us toward this quarry. It's a rare miracle any of us made it into this tunnel."

Liz Hen glared at Jenko. "And I thought you didn't believe in miracles, Jenko Bruk. I thought you didn't believe in the power of Laijon."

"Don't talk to me of belief," Jenko fired back, his face bloodstained and savage in the dim light of the tunnel.

Liz Hen met his gaze with disdain. "You're naught but a Sør Sevier traitor, Jenko Bruk. You still wear their armor. Don't think I haven't forgotten what you did to your father, what you did back in Gallows Haven!"

She shoved her way around Mancellor and launched herself straight at Jenko. She crashed into him, and they stumbled against the smooth marble wall of the tunnel together. She fought to wrestle away his newly found Dayknight sword, smashing her elbow to his face. The sword clattered to the ground as Jenko fell limp, sliding down the marble wall. Liz Hen lunged for the weapon, snatched it up, and turned once more toward Jenko.

"Put the blade down," Mancellor admonished. "You're liable to get us all kilt with that thing in your hands."

"I'm good with a blade." Liz Hen stood over Jenko, Dayknight sword firmly in her possession.

"In your anger, you've a habit of killing folk who don't need to be killed. Remember the archbishop?"

"All people need to be killed nowadays. Especially if they are archbishops or wear Sør Sevier armor."

Jenko groaned and regained his senses.

He sat against the wall a moment, staring up at Liz Hen, then climbed to his feet, dazed, holding the back of his head.

Liz Hen pointed the sleek black sword at him.

He held out his hands in surrender. "I've no fight with you, Liz Hen Neville."

"That doesn't mean I have no fight with you," she answered coldly.

"Nobody is gonna fight anyone." Mancellor stepped between them.

Liz Hen lowered her blade.

"How do you two even know each other?" Jenko asked him.

"We traveled to Amadon together," Mancellor answered. "Liz Hen, Dokie, me, Beer Mug. We carried *Lonesome Crown* and *Forgetting Moon*. We got the weapons all the way to Savon before Enna Spades caught up to us and stole them back. I figured she stole them and took them back to the White Prince. Aeros had them under the Atonement Tree anyway."

"The Atonement Tree," Liz Hen said, a haunted look washing over her face. "What happened under that tree was a complete cluster of outright bum-fuckery and that's for goddamn sure."

Mancellor and Jenko met her wild gaze, nodding their agreement.

"And the bum-fuckery continues," Liz Hen said. "Look at us, Jenko. Look at us, Mancellor. Here we are, lost in a tunnel blocked off by a thousand dead bodies." Her crazed eyes roamed the corridor, focusing one last time on the bubble of mashed and squished bodies blocking the tunnel. "We ain't in Gallows Haven anymore."

"No, we ain't." Jenko looked around too.

"What the fuck do we do now?" Liz Hen asked. "I could really use a swallow of some Blood of the Dragon."

"At least there's these torches." Jenko headed toward one of the three flickering torches hanging in rusted sconces some ways down the corridor. He then walked back toward the mound of crushed bodies, searching, dragging a battle-ax from the bloody pile. He regarded both Mancellor and Liz Hen with a determined look. "I say we follow this tunnel and see if it leads us out of here. Like Liz Hen said, we have to find Dokie."

Jenko's amber-colored eyes were filled with both concern and pain in the torchlight as he met Mancellor's gaze next. "And we have to find Ava Shay."

CHAPTER SIXTY-THREE

NAIL

13TH DAY OF THE HEART MOON, 999TH YEAR OF LAIJON
AMADON, GUL KANA

Nail had lost hold of Tala Bronachell's hand in the fray. He was alone now but for the discarded Dayknight sword he held in his hand. As he ran, he could not block out the dreadful sounds pouring from the throats of the injured and dying. He came to the stark realization that Val-Draekin and Seita had led this attack on humanity from the start. Fiery Absolution had been planned by the Vallè long before Nail had even been born or thought of. As he ran, everywhere he looked, the very ground shuddered with furious sound and fire. Oghul and Vallè banners fluttered over the helms and spear tips of the thousands of fleeing Gul Kana and Sør Sevier soldiers who ran with him.

Val-Draekin's vicious army of oghuls and Vallè thundered outward from the Atonement Tree in every direction, the stomp of their feet and the thundering hooves of their war chargers creating a fearsome noise. As sword crashed against shield, sharp and heavy, men shrieked and roared in both pain and fear, thousands upon thousands of voices raging into the fiery darkness. Horses bellowed in terror, the timbre of their shrieking cries feral and full of bloodcurdling finality. And still Nail ran.

Until he spied the nameless beasts of the underworld above!

Dragons!

Three of the colorful beasts and their fearsome skull-faced riders circled overhead, all of them engaged in destruction. Shrill and thunderous were the cries of the giant beasts. Nail could feel the all-embracing fear welling up around him. Everyone ran. Everyone fled in the face of the dragons.

Nail slowed his pace, exhausted, feeling his own labored wheezing deep down in his heaving lungs. Close to panic, he searched for Tala Bronachell with weary eyes blinking against the glaring shards of light bouncing off the shined armor of the fleeing knights surging all around him. Everything seemed so unreal in its savagery. It seemed a lifetime ago that he had been a simple village boy panning for gold with his master in the Autumn Range. Now he was in the center of Fiery Absolution, in the middle of an ocean of screaming humanity and fire.

Dragon fire raged above. It was so hot. And the unrelenting heat from the blazing Atonement Tree some several thousand paces behind him seared his back. The very ground was on fire, blades of grass flickering orange and yellow at his feet. Sweat trickled down the sides of his face. Still, he searched for any sign of Tala.

Suddenly Bronwyn Allen and Cromm Cru'x were standing beside him. The oghul was almost unrecognizable under all the blood covering his face and arms and armor. He gripped an unwieldy-looking iron shield of oghul make in one hand, a rusted oghul longsword in the other— weapons he had scavenged as Nail had scavenged the black sword he carried.

"You okay?" Bronwyn asked, then began firing arrow after arrow up into the night sky, aimed at the green dragon that sailed overhead. Fire billowed from its mouth, setting knights ablaze just to the south of Nail's position.

Nail followed Bronwyn and Cromm as they pushed their way through the battle, coming to a dip in the landscape where fire no longer licked at their feet. They were soon running on a more level, mud-splattered surface, making their way closer to Amadon. Dayknights and Silver

Guards ran along with them. One of the fleeing knights in front of Nail suddenly sprouted a thick-hafted oghul arrow from his neck under the rim of his helm. The man fell face-forward into the scarlet mire. Oghul arrows rained down everywhere now, thudding against plate armor and shield. Nail and Bronwyn hunkered for cover behind a pile of dead knights.

"We've got to keep going." Cromm's throaty voice echoed over the fray, urging Bronwyn on. "We've got to reach the safety of the city!"

"I've got to go back for Mancellor!" The Wyn Darrè girl turned back toward the still raging Atonement Tree. The heat from the billowing tower of flame could still be felt even at this distance.

"That green dragon is bound to swing back around and come at us!" Cromm called out. "Cromm thinks your brother can look after himself a little while longer!"

Bronwyn's fierce eyes sparked with anger, sweat-soaked hair plastered to her forehead. "I didn't come all the way to this fucking place just to leave my brother the very moment I find him! I will shoot every one of those Laijon-cursed beasts out of the sky if I have to!"

"You will follow Cromm!" the oghul shouted, grabbing the girl by the arm and pulling her away from the pile of knights and cover. Nail followed them into the fray, suddenly finding himself in a blur of Vallè armor and slashing weapons and pounding hooves. He swung at a passing Vallè horseman, his long black blade glancing off the beast's armored neck. The blow staggered Nail, forcing him to his knees. Bloody mud splattered up into his face and eyes, and he lost hold of his sword. Sputtering, he clawed at the ground, searching, hooves of charging warhorses stirring the muck. Latching onto the muddy hilt of the sword, Nail lurched to his feet just as the green dragon passed overhead once more, fire once again blooming from jagged jaws as it screamed its terrible scream. Knights burned. Knights scattered. Knights dropped to their knees, holding their ears in pain. Nail clenched his eyes tight, covering his own ears in an effort to stave off the horror of the dragon's sinister screeching song.

When he looked up, heaps of tortured flesh, both horse and man, littered the muddy landscape, hollow pale eyes staring out from orange flames. The scene was almost too paralyzing to behold; the fiery under-world come to life. All semblance of friend or foe was gone. Everyone fought everyone now as the dragon circled around. Nail hadn't seen real war like this since the siege of Gallows Haven. But that seemed a life-time ago, and it had been nothing like this living hell, this fiery furor and mayhem that leaped and swirled everywhere and in every direction, as far as his eyes could see. And the ever-pressing heat! His throat was parched and unrelenting in its tumult and torture.

"Nail!" Bronwyn's voice called out to him. "Nail, watch out!"

A Vallè fighter rose up in front of him. The fighter was helmetless, pale delicate face streaked red, sword lashing down toward Nail's head. Suddenly blood bubbled from the Vallè's gasping mouth and he dropped his sword.

Hawkwood stood over the dead Vallè, twin curved swords in hand, both blades painted in blood. "We've got to get to the castle."

"Are you sure?" Bronwyn was between them, eyes piercing fierce. "No place is safe from those dragons. Not even the city. Not even the castle."

"It's our only chance," Hawkwood said.

"You seem to know a lot about a lot of things," Bronwyn said. "Why should we trust you? Why should we follow you?" Cromm stood next to her, beady eyes fixed on the Sør Sevier man, a low rumble in his throat.

"In this battle, it is every man for himself!" Hawkwood yelled. "It does not matter who slays who now! If we're to survive, the castle is our only escape! There are tunnels there we can use!"

From out of the smoke, a bull-necked oghul with a wild toothy grin bore down on Hawkwood, huge spiked mace raised high. Cromm stepped in front of the man and met the oghul's charge, ramming his longsword up and under the beast's rusted iron breastplate. The broad-faced creature dropped his mace and slid slowly backward to the ground. A second oghul rose up behind the first one, powerful mace swinging low in a crushing arc toward Cromm's exposed face. Hawkwood struck swiftly with his curved swords, opening up the throat of the second oghul. The monster gasped and spat blood and toppled over dead in a bone-crunching heap and spray of mud. Hawkwood and Cromm silently exchange nods of thanks as more oghuls and Vallè converged upon them.

Stern-faced, Cromm spun around as a gloriously armored Vallè war charger bore down on him. The oghul dropped to his knees, sludge splashing up around his knotted legs as the Vallè warrior's glistening sword sailed high over his head. Hawkwood's curved sword cut the Vallè's steed down at the knees. The warhorse slid to a stop in a blossoming red wave of mud. The Vallè fighter rolled and then stood on wobbly legs. Cromm's heavy longsword clove through the Vallè's midsection. Steaming entrails unraveled from the Vallè's split armor, slithering and coiling at his feet as he fell.

Bronwyn and Nail met the charge of a second mounted Vallè fighter. Nail's high-arching blow was enough to unhorse the Vallè. The riderless horse fell sideways to the ground, one of Bronwyn's arrows jutting from its eye, its lathered body streaked with mud and blood. The Vallè untangled himself from the horse's jerking legs, squirming free, regaining his feet just as another one of Bronwyn's arrows took him full in the face. The Vallè fell dead against his struggling horse and slid to the ground.

"Dear Laijon almighty," Bronwyn muttered, looking to the west, black bow held loosely at her side. The green dragon had landed not far from them. It was stalking through the battlefield toward them now, its skull-faced rider like an emerald jewel on its back, silver whip in hand.

Nail found he could not break his own terrified gaze from the glowing dragon and the skull-faced knight. And the dragon rider seemed to be staring right at him. The dragon itself was enormous, the bulk of its sinuous, scaled body the size of a large house. It was sleek and long and moved on four legs with a graceful ease that belied its tremendous size, hooked feet clawing at the fire-patched ground, raking dead knights in half, raking their guts into a ground already boggy with blood. The scales that sheathed its green body seemed to shimmer with every ominous step it took. A coiled tail of sharpened spines swept the ground in its wake. Huge emerald wings unfurled, and the jagged row of white horns that ran the length of its spine from head to tail seemed to bristle and quake. The swooping horns on either side of its serpentlike head were longer than oghul spears and twice as sharp. And the beast had two shiny green eyes that smoldered and gleamed.

Bronwyn nocked an arrow and sent it sailing toward the dragon. The arrow glanced off the hard green scales just under the dragon's wing. The arrow had garnered the beast's full attention now. It rose up on its hind legs, ready to scream fire over the battlefield. "Retreat!" Hawkwood shouted.

Fire blazed bright and orange from the dragon's toothy maw, setting men and horse alight just in front of Bronwyn and Nail. The teeming mass of flaming knights scattered and fell and died. The green dragon stalked toward Bronwyn and Nail, spiked tail whipping and slashing at the burning bodies on either side. Then the dragon was reined to a stop and the scales along the beast's neck rippled like shimmering jade feathers as the skull-faced rider slid deftly from its back.

The dragon rider circled in front of the beast, sleek green-scaled armor under a dark cape and hood gleaming, long silver whip lined with sparkling silver barbs uncoiling at his side and dripping with evil intent.

Three Dayknights drew up between Nail and the skull-faced knight. The dragon rider cracked the whip out once, droplets of silver flinging into the air as the wicked weapon sliced through the armor of all three men at once. The three men reeled back, all of them severely injured. The skull-faced demon struck again, the whip slicing two of the knights completely in half, disemboweling the third. A fourth Gul Kana knight attacked the dragon. The beast's fiery mouth snapped out, biting the knight in half, swallowing the top of his body whole. A dark river of blood flowed from the beast's mouth as its thick green scales fluttered. The dragon spread its wings once again, its long, sinuous neck and head pointing right at Bronwyn and Nail.

Then the blue and white dragons swooped down over the battlefield, crying out in horrendous song. The dragon rider in green-scaled armor hooked the dripping silver whip to his belt and remounted the green dragon. The dragon roared, fire blooming from its thundering maw straight into the dark night. When the monster's jaws finally clamped shut, it launched itself back into the night, following the blue and white dragons back toward the still raging Atonement Tree.

"Bloody beasts of the underworld," Hawkwood muttered, stepping back, unsteady on his feet, as if he had just awoken from some dark spell. "But if that thing wasn't a horror, I don't know what is."

Nail wasn't sure if the Sør Sevier man was referring to the green dragon or its demonic green rider with the deadly silver whip.

"We are lucky it took off after those other dragons," Bronwyn said.

Nail could still feel the heat from the burning knights scattered about the battlefield. He could still see the towering blaze of the Atonement Tree from the corner of his eye. Battle still raged between himself and the tree, a battle that crawled closer to his position. He cast his gaze toward Amadon once again in search of Tala, hoping.

But all that met his gaze were flames and melted faces, naught but armored and cooked bodies strewn upon the ground in heaps of blackened wreckage. A soft breath of cool air grazed over his face and he savored it, but only for a moment, as he heard Cromm's grunt of dismay.

He turned back toward the Atonement Tree to see what the oghul was looking at. And rising up in the center of the blistering ocean of butchery and gore were Val-Draekin and Seita—the instigators of Fiery Absolution. Black daggers in hand, the two Vallè carved their way through the lashing battlefield with an unobtrusive ease, fighting like dancers, lithe, brutal, and skilled.

Following the two Vallè were Lindholf and Lawri Le Graven, both looking bright and regal atop a magnificent white stallion. The glamour and brilliance of their royal bearing was unmistakable amid the nightmare of slaughter. There was nary a spot of soot or blood upon either one of Tala's twin cousins. They drifted through the darkness and fire of Absolution like a pure river of flowing white light, three dragons soaring above them now: white, blue, and green.

Lawri sat the saddle before her brother, her hand a glowing metal claw. *Lonesome Crown* crowned Lindholf's head, the pale curved horns of the helm matching his pallid skin. *Forgetting Moon* was strapped to his back, along with *Blackest Heart*. The shield, *Ethic Shroud*, was poised in Lindholf's left hand, a glowing white brilliance against the dark stain of Fiery Absolution. In his right hand, Lindholf held the glimmering sword, *Afflicted Fire*.

Even from a distance, Nail marveled at the astonishing sword Tala's cousin carried. It was almost as long as the boy was tall, a bright ruby set within its white pommel. The sword's hilt and cross-guard looked to be fashioned of one long piece of white glimmering bone. Its blade was glittering silver melded together with what appeared to be veins of translucent ivory. The entire weapon seemed to pulse with some red light set deep within, and a white curling mist flowed from Lindholf's hands around the hilt of the weapon and down its long silvery blade.

Blue smoke on a battle-ax, Val-Draekin had called the phenomenon. Nail imagined Lindholf also carried the angel stones. In moments like these, when the weapons and stones were near, Nail normally felt the pain of the scars on his body flare to life. They did not do so now. That feeling was long dead to him.

"That is my bow!" Nail heard a familiar voice cry out.

He whirled and found Stefan Wayland approaching through the darkness, flat silver eyes staring at Bronwyn Allen and the black bow in her hands.

A large black saber-toothed lion strode along beside Stefan, as did the small oghul Nail had seen with Stefan under the Atonement Tree.

"It's the dead boy from Deadwood Gate," Cromm said, a growl of anger rising from somewhere deep in his chest. "What's happened to his eyes? And with him comes the oghul who stole Cromm's glory."

Stefan's metallic eyes were dead as a corpse, twin silver orbs that seemed to shift between Bronwyn and Cromm. Nail could see that his friend was indeed alive, but there was a feral, animal-like bearing about his once innocent face.

"That's my bow you carry!" Stefan snarled at Bronwyn. "You dare touch Gisela with your cursed hands? You dared paint it black?"

Bronwyn clutched the bow protectively to her chest. The large black cat snarled at her, baring dagger-like teeth.

Stefan leaped toward Bronwyn, hands clawing at the bow, instantly latching onto the weapon's black stock, his face a fire-lit mask of rage. Bronwyn wrestled with the silver-eyed boy. "Help me, you bloody fool!" she cried out to Cromm.

The oghul raised his sword and swung at Stefan with a grunt. Nail pushed the oghul aside at the last moment, and the sword missed Stefan's head by a hair.

With a shout, Stefan gave one final jerk and tore the weapon from Bronwyn's grasp. The black bow in hand, lungs huffing loudly for air, Stefan spun and ran off into the night, disappearing into the swirl of battle, the black cat and small oghul following him. "Stefan!" Nail shouted after his friend.

But only the darkness and fire of Absolution called back to him. Val-Draekin, Seita, Lindholf, and Lawri had moved farther to the south. Nail could scarcely see them through the smoke and dark now, though the three dragons still circled above like bright, colorful stars.

Cromm grabbed Nail around the neck. "You hit Cromm."

"He was only trying to save his friend," Hawkwood said, his own blade up against the oghul's throat. "Let Nail go or I kill you where you stand."

Cromm released his hold on Nail, glaring daggers at Hawkwood.

"We've got other problems." Bronwyn pointed.

Nail's attention was suddenly drawn to a lone girl engaged with a dozen oghuls not far away. With the hood of her black cloak thrown back, the girl's face was red from the heat, and she wore Bloodwood leathers. The girl's black armor was painted in scarlet, sodden with blood and ragged junks of torn flesh not her own. Blond hair flowed out behind her like a wild white flag, hair that almost glowed when touched by the surrounding fires. Nail had seen her under the Atonement Tree earlier that evening. She had been there with her Bloodwood steed, but the demon-eyed steed was no longer at her side.

The girl stabbed a black dagger into the oghul that had fallen under her. As she killed the beast, her other weapon flashed upward, deflecting the blows from the other eleven oghuls still fighting her. She whirled from the dead oghul under her and confronted the others with brutal speed. What set this particular girl apart from the hacking, slashing chaos of the surrounding war was her calm demeanor as she fought. She ended the lives of two more oghuls with a detached and cold resolve, then leaped toward the nine remaining and killed two more with a keen swiftness that was startling. Then she calmly set herself to the remaining seven, opening two more oghul necks with her black blade, no emotion on her face, just firm resolve, as if dealing out death were her daily job. *She's even colder than Bronwyn Allen,* Nail thought as the blond Bloodwood slew the five remaining oghuls with little effort.

Then she turned to Nail, her wintry gaze slicing straight through him. "Do you also wish to die?" she asked, the tips of her bloody black daggers pointed at his chest, bloodlust sparking in those crisp eyes as she stalked toward him.

Hawkwood stepped between Nail and the girl. "So you must be Krista Aulbrek," he said to the girl.

She did not answer, eyes narrowing to even fiercer pricks of ice.

"I live and die by the knife," Hawkwood said as if repeating some ritual. "I exist only for the return of the Skulls."

The girl seemed to tense even more; then she lowered her daggers as she said, "And my blade always thirsts."

CHAPTER SIXTY-FOUR

GAULT AULBREK

13TH DAY OF THE HEART MOON, 999TH YEAR OF LAIJON
AMADON, GUL KANA

The Gul Kana and Sør Sevier armies fled in terror from the burning tree and fiery slaughter of the red and black dragons soaring above.

But not Gault Aulbrek. He had refused to be forced toward the slave pit. He had spent enough time in Riven Rock to know that the quarry held naught but misery and death. No. Gault had done his utmost to avoid being swept up in that thrashing, frantic throng. Instead he had made his way toward Fiery Absolution and the thousands of Vallè and oghul warriors charging straight at him.

He would fight, not flee. Earlier, freedom had sounded good. That was until the battle started and the bloodlust rose up once again within him. He was bred for war. It was his life. Always had been. The poison had turned him soft. The wraiths had weakened his mind. He raised his newfound Dayknight sword to face them all, oghul and Vallè, having snatched the discarded weapon from a dead Dayknight moments earlier, a Dayknight he had felled with a brutal punch from his own fist.

The nearest charging oghul coughed out a savage war cry and swung its rusted cudgel at Gault's unprotected head. The oghul moved sluggishly and slowly, and Gault rammed the tip of the black blade up under the beast's rusted iron half-helm and straight into its brain. The burly body dropped to the ground in a heap and the next oghul was upon him. With a vicious backhanded swing, Gault brought the second oghul's charge short, nearly cutting the beast in half, armor and all. Purple guts burst from the oghul's wide-open middle, rusted iron helm spinning from its head.

And with those two kills, Gault felt the last of the poison from Krista's Bloodwood dagger leech from his body. He could feel what sickness and toxins that remained pour out through the sweat beading up on his arms and forehead. He could only decry the fact that he had been so weak with poison for so long, only now finally recovered enough to fight. Yes, it was the surge of battle that had awoken him. The wraiths were gone. The surge of blood pumping through his veins. He wanted a purpose. *Needed* a purpose. And now he had found two. War and death and killing and all those things he had been bred for. And also Krista Aulbrek and Ava Shay. He could still save them.

Sweating heavily, he shed the burden of his tattered gray cloak and snatched up the oghul's fallen helmet. It was heavy and sprouted a row of rusted spikes atop its crown. When he settled the rank-smelling thing over his head, he was surprised at how well he could see through the rusted eye slits of the face visor.

Now to find more armor!

With oghul helm and Dayknight sword, Gault shoved his way toward a dozen bellowing oghuls stabbing and hacking their crude weapons at a group of downed Silver Guards. The savage beasts paid Gault no heed, happily bludgeoning the knights to death and drinking their blood. They paid him no heed until he started killing all of them. Then they fought and lost and died.

Two Vallè fighters rose up in Gault's path next, splendorous and deadly-looking in their intricately scrollworked armor and delicately brocaded silken capes. They stared at him a moment, perplexed, wondering if he was friend or foe under the oghul helm. Battle lust surging through him now, Gault wasted little time, kicking the nearest Vallè in the knee, crippling him, stabbing him in the throat as he fell. He moved with a berserker's rage as he punched the second Vallè in the face, smearing the poor fellow's delicate Vallè nose up into his bleeding eye sockets. A third Vallè fighter rose up behind the second. Gault rammed his black sword through the pale-faced fighter's exposed throat. The Vallè slid off Gault's sword, chin dripping with vomit and spit and blood as he struck the turf.

He searched the battlefield, picked the largest dead Vallè, and dropped to his knees and worked fast, unhooking the bucklers of the dead fellow's sleek silver breastplate. Within moments he had stripped the fey of most of his armor: vambraces, gauntlets, greaves, chest plate. The armor was snug, but it fit fine when he adjusted the bucklers for his broader chest, legs, and arms. Gault left the delicate chain mail, as it was likely too small for his thicker frame.

Gault stood and faced the burning Atonement Tree.

With a Dayknight sword, oghul helm, and Vallè breastplate armor and accoutrements, Gault figured he must really look a sight. But he didn't care. He was an army of one, and everyone would die by his blade today. Not done dressing himself, he snatched up a fallen Sør Sevier battle standard, untied the white flag from the pole, and tied it around his neck, donning the discarded flag of his homeland like a long cape, a blue sword on a white field.

He began his journey anew, killing his way to the Atonement Tree.

**

The tree still stood in the center of the grove, though now it was a twisted and blackened skeleton silhouetted against the coming dawn.

Aeros Raijael hung there, smoldering strips of flesh clinging to his charred and smoking bones. In front of the White Prince, the once glistening Silver Throne was but a useless, ash-covered roost for nothing important at all but fallen branches. The entire floor of the grove around the tree looked like a mottled dark scab streaked with blood, all of it accentuated by the dying glow of faintly pulsing cinders. The air was the hue of ash and rank with the stench of scorched wood and burnt flesh.

Gault had yet to find any sign of Krista or Ava among the tens of thousands of bodies he had come across, though many of the dead were burnt beyond recognition, both horse and man. One bloated destrier lay in front of him now, flames seeming to crawl out of the dead animal from every orifice.

Gault stepped around the smoking horse, trying not to breathe in the fetid air. In fact, in war he stepped with care at all times, wary of the treacherous footing on the deceptively slick ground. For in the sullen, smoky haze that hung over the Hallowed Grove, the blackened ground was boggy with pools of blood and human entrails. It seemed that few Gul Kana or Sør Sevier fighters had escaped the massacre. What few burnt bodies still writhed and moaned, Gault silenced with his sword.

It was a small mercy, and he didn't mind the killing, for nothing built pride in a warrior like killing. And Krista and Ava had stripped him of every ounce of pride he'd once had. He had to prove to himself that he was still a fighter, still a warrior. He had to prove to himself that he was still a *man*, a *hard man* born and bred of a harsh and lonely land. Only then could he die happy. *So be bloody, be brave, be happy, The Chivalric Illuminations* said. *Be bloody, be brave, and do yourself honor, for only in war can one die with admiration and respect. For women as a whole, be they wives or daughters, can only love a man whom they wholly respect.* And Gault had shown his weakness.

But before the end, Ava and Krista would both see him for the warrior he was. It was the only way he could do himself honor. It was the only way he could do Avril honor, Laijon rest her soul.

He had been alone for so long. Ever since Avril's death so many years ago, he had remained isolated, friendless, and alone, living with clenched emotions, living a life engrained in faith and the allure of *The Chivalric Illuminations*, holy writ that had taught him to believe in naught but his own strength. But loneliness was the toughest thing about war. And war led to Absolution. And Gault had to absolve himself of all weakness. He had to be bloody. He had to be brave. He had to do himself honor and be happy.

He could feel the heat from the still smoldering Atonement Tree, an oppressive heat that bullied him mercilessly. The desolate landscape of the Hallowed Grove was parched and hot. Only a small arid breeze pulled at the sweat dripping from his bald head under the rusted helm. Pillars of thick smoke seemed to leech away what little light rose with the morning. As Gault breathed in the stench of charred wood and scorched flesh, he let his gaze range over the battlefield. The white dragon feasted in the distance. The dragon rider was a tall and shiny knight in white-scaled armor that matched the color of the dragon. A silver skull mask covered the knight's face. A whip of silver was coiled at the dragon rider's hip. The knight used a long curved dagger and was liberally slicing the ears from the dead. Gault found himself intrigued by the process.

When he finally looked away, he found he was breathing deeply, his body suddenly weary and begging for relief. But he would make no excuses for himself. The shortness of breath and pain in his bones made him realize he was alive. In fact, despite the weariness, or maybe because of it, Gault felt more alive now than he ever had before. Not since before his first-ever battle in Adin Wyte beside Aeros Raijael had he felt more alive.

With that thought, he looked back toward the burnt husk of the Atonement Tree and the remains of the Angel Prince. *And I used to be one of his five Knights Archaic of Sør Sevier, a vaunted personal guard.* As he looked at his former lord, Gault found that he was glad the man was dead, for that was all Aeros Raijael had ever been, just a *man.*

Though he still wanted to fight, Gault proceeded away from the white dragon, picking his way through the smoking, blood-splashed grove, searching the faces of the dead. He wove his way between the leaning thickets of shattered standards and spear shafts. Oghul, Vallè, and Dayknight arrows lay everywhere. Two oghul shafts jutted from the steel cuirass of an Amadon Silver Guard, two more pierced the ring mail covering his stomach. The broken body of another Gul Kana knight lay in the charred and darkened mud near the boy, his belly splayed open wide. It looked like he had died holding a fistful of his own guts. Another headless Gul Kana knight was folded over the bodies of two Sør Sevier fighters, their helms cocked sideways on their faces, one with a spear embedded in his crotch. A grizzled old Dayknight lay on his back in his black-lacquered armor, legs crushed beneath the weight of his dead war charger, eyes wide and dead and rolled up in the back of his head and glowing up at Gault like twin moons.

It was then that Gault saw the Bloodeye from the corner of his eye— the black horse that belonged to his stepdaughter. The black mare with the eyes of molten fire stared at him from a distance of about fifty paces. Gault approached the beast slowly, not wishing to spook the thing, hoping Krista was nearby, eyes searching.

The oily-looking horse stood over the burnt bodies of several Dayknights, watching Gault's approach with cool confidence. He drew near the beast, reaching out to take its reins. There was no sign of injury on the eerie-looking horse that Gault could see. He grasped the leather reins with his left hand. With his other hand, he removed the spiked oghul helm from his head and placed it gently on the saddle horn.

Gault didn't know why, but he found himself pressing the side of his face against the Bloodeye's sleek black neck. The beast nickered once but did not recoil from his touch. "I don't even know your name," Gault whispered regretfully. He stepped back, stroking the beast's long black mane. "I don't even know what my daughter named you."

The horse regarded him with seemingly cold indifference, red eyes glowing.

"Easy now," Gault said. Then he smoothly mounted the Bloodeye, situating himself on the stiff saddle, which did not quite fit his large, armor-covered body.

He leaned forward, pulled the reins, clicked his tongue. Alone, Gault rode his stepdaughter's Bloodeye mare out of the Hallowed Grove and toward Amadon.

CHAPTER SIXTY-FIVE
TALA BRONACHELL

13TH DAY OF THE HEART MOON, 999TH YEAR OF LAIJON
AMADON, GUL KANA

Cathedral bells pealed over Amadon loud and strong and not
without meaning. The outskirts of the city were a seething
mass of flame, the sky a ceaseless haze of smoke, mocking the
morning sun. The air smelled sickly of roasted meat. And the brilliant
blue dragon and its skull-faced rider rained fire over all. Cottages and
hovels burned below as murderous Vallè and oghuls flooded the streets.

The entire city was roused and awake. Murmurs of the horrors that
had transpired in the Hallowed Grove uncoiled out through the streets.
People emerged from shops and taverns and tenements with looks of
bewilderment and panic. So frightened were they at the sight of all the
fire, of all the blood-covered Vallè and oghul soldiers engaged in riotous
slaughter, and of the blue dragon above, that precious few took notice
of the two Dayknights escorting the harried and bedraggled king of Gul
Kana and his younger sister and long-lost father down the narrow cobbled lanes. Leif and Glade Chaparral were the two Dayknights. Jovan
Bronachell was the king. Tala Bronachell the younger sister. And Borden
Bronachell the long-lost father.

Tala had lost hold of Nail sometime during their panicked flight from under the inferno that was the Atonement Tree. She felt lost without the Gallows Haven boy. He had been her rock these last few days. Now he was gone. *Dead?* She did not know the answer to that but feared the worst. Her uncertainty of Nail's fate was just another horror in a string of horrors that were breeding a dark discontent in her soul. For now she was surrounded by naught but chaos and war and city streets that ran red with blood. Children clutched their mothers, huddling against what shelter they could find, praying they would not perish under the bloodsucking fangs of a rampaging oghul or the fires of the blue dragon above. The dead lay on every corner, innocent men, women, and children, their bodies crumpled and heaped in awkward smoking piles.

A tobacco shop smoldered nearby, but the sweet aroma of burning tobacco was not enough to cover the smell of death. A mangy dog ran past Tala, the severed foot of a child in its teeth. Tala had to look away, her eyes falling on more charred bodies.

Amadon was not the proud city it had been before; rather, now its streets were the ultimate blend of death and bloody disharmony. Still, in the distance, through the drifting haze of smoke, the castle itself seemed untouched. And the castle was their goal. Her father insisted on it. He had to reach the castle.

It had been a shock to Tala's system to see her father, Borden Bronachell, under the Atonement Tree, returned from the dead. In fact, everything under the tree had been a shock. So much had happened tonight that she could not, at sixteen, completely grasp or even deal with effectively. *My father is alive!* He was running right beside her now, fleeing Fiery Absolution with her brother Jovan, with Leif and Glade.

When Tala had lost sight of Nail, her father and brother had somehow found her in the teeming swirl of war. And now they all ran for the castle, Leif and Glade leading them. Tala had no idea why the castle was their destination, other than that it was a familiar place and where her father demanded they go. But in her estimation, everything would soon be destroyed, even the castle.

As she ran, Tala risked a glance backward to see a Gul Kana Silver

Guard following them. Vallè and oghul soldiers were bearing down on the poor knight, all of them wielding weapons that flashed in the orange light of dawn. They killed the knight with ease, rusted weapons hacking at his body. They spotted Tala's group next and advanced.

"Don't look back!" Tala's father urged her onward. "Keep moving forward and don't look back!"

They ran down the cobbled lane side by side, fires on either side. Jovan, Leif, and Glade ran just ahead of them. A large smoking chapel was at the end of the lane. Leif aimed for it and the rest of them followed. But the sound of oghuls in pursuit was growing louder in Tala's ears. The sound of ironshod feet hammering on the cobbles behind Tala sent terror up her spine. Her throat was also clenched in pain, every breath raw, she was so thirsty. She could hear the sound of Vallè horsemen taking up pursuit now too. Fear raced through her veins. Unlike Jovan, Leif, and Glade, Tala wore no armor. She had only a shortsword for defense; it was gripped tightly in hand now, but she scarcely knew how to use it.

Upon reaching the tall wooden door of the church, Leif and Glade slipped through. Jovan followed, black smoke billowing out from the door as he entered. Tala and her father sped for the door. Tala heard a shout to her left and glanced that way. A swirl of black smoke filled the alleyway some twenty paces away. A random Dayknight burst through the dark fog and joined Tala and her father. "Hurry, my king!" the knight shouted at Borden. "The oghuls are right behind you. I will hold them off!"

Tala tripped over a small stone bench that lined the pathway in front of the smoky chapel door. Her father lifted her to her feet and pushed her forward. The Dayknight shoved both Borden and Tala toward the chapel. Oghuls with heavy rusted cudgels and spears swarmed the Dayknight. With a startled shout, the knight whirled and pulled his black sword and swung at the enemy, holding them back as he'd promised.

Tala threw herself through the door and into the church, ducking under the smoke and heat boiling above. The chapel's roof was ablaze.

Her father followed her in, hunched over and limping now, his own sword fixed in the cold, hard grip of his steady hand. Borden turned to help the Dayknight through the doorway, but the black-clad knight was already on his knees and screaming out in pain, oghuls jabbing his armor full of holes with spear tips ragged and rusted. Through the slim opening of the door, Tala watched as the Vallè horsemen closed in on the Dayknight from behind, long glistening halberds striking with deadly precision, slicing the Dayknight's head off at the neck. The decapitated knight fell chest first onto the cobbles and rolled over, severed head spilling from the black helm, blood spurting from the cut tendons and arteries. Tala looked away, sick.

Leif and Glade and Jovan were suddenly at the door with her father. They all four put their shoulders to the mighty door and shoved. A Vallè arrow thudded into the shuddering wood just as the door slammed shut. Tala's father reached up and threw down the wooden latch, barring the door from outside entry, and said, "We haven't much time before they find a way in or before this place burns down around us."

Tala looked around the dark and dismal innards of the chapel as her father guided the group deeper into the grim church. She could hear the crackling of the fire in the rafters and smell the burning timber. Smoke swirled and billowed above her own head. That answered the question of why nobody else had sought shelter here. The place would soon be a raging inferno. She coughed, finding it difficult to breathe. She could feel the crunch of glass and other debris under her feet. The walls were naught but broad smears of black scorch and blistering paint.

"Where are we going?" Leif Chaparral blurted with impatience as he cast his dark-rimmed gaze about the fiery gloom. He had removed his helm. Glade had too. Sweat streaked their faces under matted locks of dark hair.

"We are going to the castle." Borden kept moving, eyes darting about nervously, as if searching for something. "We must see that Ansel is safe. I must see my youngest son. We go to the castle."

"We can't reach the castle from inside this burning church," Leif countered.

"We can," Borden said. "I promise."

"This chapel is completely ruined." Glade's frightened gaze rose to the stained-glass windows above. "That dragon will burn down this entire city." He was clearly scared. "That dragon will crawl in here and slay us, too."

"Pull yourself together, boy," Borden demanded.

The smoke cleared and Tala saw a statue of Laijon rising up before them, smoke streaming up through a massive hole in the chapel's roof, stone and rubble on the floor at the flaming statue's feet. The statue was nailed to the center of an even larger wooden replica of the Atonement Tree. The top of the tree near the rafters had caught fire. Just under the statue was a bishop's altar stone. A faint morning light fell down from the jagged hole in the roof above, illuminating the altar's capstone.

"It's blasphemy!" Glade cried, eyes fixed on the burning tree above. "Such foul desecration. It's like the Atonement Tree, burned by foul flame."

Tala could hear oghul grunts and shouts from outside the chapel now. Then something heavy was banging on the latched wooden door.

"Help me push the altar stone from its base," Tala's father said, leaning his shoulder into the altar stone, shoving. The capstone slid, but not by much. "Help!" he shouted at Leif, Glade, and Jovan.

Leif and Glade helped him shove, putting their shoulders to the stone. Together the three of them slid the capstone off the altar and let it fall to the floor with a crashing thud. Jovan stood and watched, fear in his eyes.

Tala looked down into the altar. Concealed within its hollow depths was a worn wooden ladder, descending straight down into a dark hole.

"How did you know to push that altar stone aside?" Leif's face was a mask of cold puzzlement. "How did you know it was hollow? How did you know there was a ladder down there?"

Borden tossed Leif a cool glance in return. "Every man sworn to the Brethren of Mia knows of the many lost secrets and mysteries that hide under every altar. Just one of the powers of the Brethren of Mia."

"The Brethren of Mia." Leif repeated the words with distaste.

"Down the ladder," Borden advised. "Just go down the ladder, Leif Chaparral, and we can discuss your hatred for the Brethren later."

Leif nodded curtly, glancing at his younger brother with concern as he lifted one leg up over the side of the altar. "Let's just hope *some* mysteries don't lead to dead ends."

"Just go," Borden urged. "We all must go down. I will follow."

Leif lowered himself down into the hole. Jovan followed. Tala's father stepped toward the sculpture of Laijon and snatched up a length of burning wood that had fallen from the flaming tree. "This will make a good torch to light our way." He handed the burning wood to Glade, who descended the ladder after his brother.

Borden helped Tala into the altar next, and down into the darkness she went, the sound of oghuls beating on the chapel's wooden door fading behind her.

**

Their journey was short, the tunnel narrow. There were no random corridors branching off in any direction that Tala could see. This place was not like the secret ways at all, and Tala was surprised by the ease of their journey. She'd figured that every hidden passageway under the city would eventually lead her to Purgatory, or the castle, or even her own bedchamber. Yet this passageway was straight and simple and merely led them to another creaking ladder and up through another stone altar into a second chapel similar to the one they had just fled.

Only this chapel was not on fire.

Once Tala was up from the darkness and out of the tunnel, she felt a sudden reassurance. It was that comfort she always felt when entering one of Amadon's many small chapels—at least ones that weren't on fire. She felt safety residing within the building's great arches, clean gray walls, and bulky grandeur.

Jovan, Leif, and Glade were already poking around the main chamber. In the vaulted apse behind the altar was another gray-hewn statue of Laijon, naught but a loincloth around his waist, a wreath of white heather on his head. This sculpture of Laijon was also nailed to a black wooden replica of the Atonement Tree, its branches reaching toward the ceiling. The altar they had just emerged from lay in front of the statue. Borden took the torch from Glade and tossed it back down the hole.

"We should take a moment and rest here," he said, limping away from the altar. "Those oghuls are too stupid to follow us through the passageways."

Tala didn't know how smart oghuls were or how wise of a choice her father was making. But she needed the rest. The colors of the stained glass at the front of the chapel reflected rainbowlike patterns across her father's face. "We should check our injuries." He sat on a wooden bench, threw off his boot, and examined his ankle.

Tala looked around. At the very front of the chapel, above the large wooden entry door, were bright stained-glass windows inlaid with intricate designs. Those windows threw patterns of twinkling light across the rows of wooden benches. Tala used to glory in the light from stained-glass images. Yet those pretty pictures were naught but harsh falsehoods to her now. In the center window was an image of Laijon, five colorful angel stones hovering magically over his head: white, red, black, green, and blue. Laijon bore a silver battle-ax, *Forgetting Moon*. In the window to the left were two heavenly angels, one bearing a long sword, *Afflicted Fire*, the other wielding a crossbow, *Blackest Heart*. In the window to the right were two other white-robed personages, one wearing a war helm, *Lonesome Crown*, another with a shield over his chest, *Ethic Shroud*. The five angelic images cast gleaming reflections of white, red, black, green, and blue over Leif, Glade, Jovan, and her father. And to Tala it all was false. There never had been a Laijon. And the religions built around that falsehood had done naught but wreak pain and war over the Five Isles for a thousand years. Tala wished she could tear it all down with her own hands, the Laijon statue, the stained-glass windows.

She felt the tip of her finger burning—the missing tip. She recalled the ugliness of the red-hazed room she had discovered in the secret ways. The room with the cross-shaped altar, the room where she had watched Glade murder Sterling Prentiss, the room where Hawkwood had given her the cutlass, the room where she had seen the silver, touched it with her own finger. And now the phantom tip of that finger burned. And the more she thought of that red-hazed room, the more her finger burned, as if that deadly chamber were still calling to her.

As her father continued to examine his ankle, Tala spotted an Ember Stone atop a round dais in one of the small side apses of the chapel. She drifted toward the dais with apprehension in her heart. There was ash in the stone basin set upon the dais. She recoiled, bile rising in her throat at the futility of the weekly ceremony she had once held dear, realizing that she used to spread that ash over her forehead in prayer and then do the three-fingered sign of the Laijon Cross over her heart. Behind the basin of ash, Tala discovered a fountain bubbling crisp waters. Thirsty, she drank.

"That's holy water." Glade's voice echoed through the chapel. "It's blasphemy to drink of it. That water is meant for the bishop of this chapel, meant for prayer."

Tala ignored him. Both Glade and Leif watched her gulp the water, disgust on their faces. "It is because of this very disregard for all things sacred that we have suffered so," Leif said. "'Tis because of blasphemies like drinking holy water that Absolution has come upon us in such horrific ways."

Tala continued to ignore him. The water was cool, and she didn't care about Absolution or anything holy at the moment. She greedily swallowed the precious water down. Her father stepped into the apse with her, boot once more on his foot. He dipped his own hands under the fountain, water pooling in his cupped palms. He cleaned his face of soot and grime, glaring at Leif as he did so, holy water dripping from his brow.

"Blasphemy," Leif muttered, growing angry. Then Borden took a long drink of holy water, as Tala had done. "This is against the laws of Laijon," Leif snarled.

"Oh, stop feigning such gallantry, Leif Chaparral," Borden said, eyeing both Leif and Glade. Tala knew the Chaparral brothers were both lazy, cowardly, and smug. They were everything her father despised, and he was not hiding his feelings.

"You have been mistaken about a great many things, Leif Chaparral," Borden said, his gaze traveling from Leif and resting on Jovan. "You have all been misled about Absolution your whole lives. The Brethren of Mia have always held that Fiery Absolution would be a bitter lesson in despair for humanity. And that is exactly what it has turned out to be."

The room fell silent. Nobody could argue that. To Tala, Fiery Absolution fell somewhere well beyond a mere bitter lesson in despair for humanity. Fiery Absolution had so far been demons and beasts of the underworld come to life with absolute savage and bloody cruelty.

She stretched her neck, then slumped onto a long wooden bench next to the fountain, drained. She couldn't help but stare at her father now that they finally had a moment of quiet. *Is he real? Is it truly him?* He met her adoring gaze. But it was brief, and then he looked away.

Is there any love hidden away beyond those unerring eyes of his? Tala wondered. He seemed so cold now, so distant, and like Jondralyn, so driven with the purpose of the Brethren of Mia. Tala just wanted him to stop for a moment and breathe, stop and acknowledge that Jondralyn was actually dead, show some remorse. Show both her and Jovan that he had never stopped loving them.

At least hug me and let me know that I am still alive in all this madness.

But the very ground under the chapel shook with Fiery Absolution. There was no time for hugs. There was no time to discuss Lawri and her silver hand, or Lindholf and all that had happened to him. *Could my dopey cousin really be Laijon returned?* The very thought was lunacy.

Borden faced Jovan. "I should have introduced you to the Brethren of Mia when you were young, my son. Perhaps all this destruction could have been avoided."

Jovan seemed to recoil inwardly at his father's words. His normally square and rigid jawline had gone slack and sallow. He did not respond to Borden at all, mouth clamped shut, eyes no more than hollow pits of pain and betrayal. He was in shock, Tala realized.

Leif laughed at Borden's statement, saying, "The Brethren of Mia are nothing more than a demonstration in sublime ignorance."

"Mind your tongue, boy," Borden snapped back at him. "Do not take me as weak for my long absence. Do not take me as weak for my current forbearance toward you. I am still king of Gul Kana, and you shall heed me now in all things."

Dually chastised, Leif gazed around the chapel stiffly, not looking at Borden or Jovan or even Glade. Borden looked at his son. "Had you known of the Brethren of Mia, many mistakes could have been averted."

"I only did as Denarius bade me do," Jovan mumbled, staring at the floor. "I always dreamed it would be an honor to take part in Fiery Absolution at the vicar's side, to be part of prophecy and revelation. I only followed what was written in *The Way and Truth of Laijon*. I participated in all the divine rituals Denarius and the quorum of five set me to. Was that not enough for a king of Gul Kana?"

Tala held scant compassion or understanding for her brother's actions these last five years, these five years that her father was believed to have been dead. She found his words and excuses to be hollow and meaningless.

"I am afraid of war," Jovan continued, looking up at his father, tears now streaming down his cheeks. "I have never been very strong, Father. It was not supposed to be like this. Denarius said it was not supposed to be like this." Tears continued to flow as his chin and lips quivered with emotion. "I have never been very strong. I leaned on the vicar for my strength."

"I know," Borden acknowledged. "You never were very strong, son. I tried to hone both you and Leif into warriors whilst we fought in Wyn Darrè, for I could always tell you did not have the heart of a fighter. And I was not surprised that you pulled our armies back to Gul Kana after my capture."

"I could not bear to see death so close," Jovan admitted, still weeping. "I was so afraid in battle. And Denarius promised me so much." As he continued to cry, Tala felt naught but disgust for her brother's weakness.

"You felt a strong sense of duty to Denarius and the quorum of five," Borden said, standing over Jovan now. "I consider that my fault," he said stoically. Tala's father held himself with an air of force and command and maturity that made Jovan's weeping look awkward and childish in comparison. "But as the Brethren discovered, every word written within *The Way and Truth of Laijon* was meant to fool us into making sure Fiery Absolution did indeed happen."

"Nonsense," Leif snarled, face growing grim.

Borden looked at Leif. "None of you are comfortable with this, I know, but I am too old to be bothered with coddling the feelings of grown men. But you all should know, Denarius, the quorum of five, all of you were fooled. Even Aeros Raijael was fooled, blinded by false scripture. That much was made clear by Val-Draekin under the Atonement Tree."

"And Val-Draekin was one of your precious Brethren of Mia," Leif said accusingly. "Why should anyone trust anything you say, old man?"

"The world is burning," Glade interrupted. "Outside the world is on fire. What does any of it matter now?"

Borden nodded. "I am not without blame. For the Brethren failed in their duties too. We were too late in gathering the heirs and weapons of the Five Warrior Angels to stave off this debacle. And now it is too late. Absolution has come. The world burns. As you say, Glade, the world outside is on fire. And it was as Val-Draekin declared, naught but a Bloodwood game meant to destroy humankind."

CHAPTER SIXTY-SIX

AVA SHAY

13TH DAY OF THE HEART MOON, 999TH YEAR OF LAIJON
AMADON, GUL KANA

Ava Shay started her journey at the bottom of the slave quarry with Hammerfiss and Enna Spades. Now the three of them had ascended about halfway up the towering mountain of smoldering corpses. The dead beneath her were crawling with flies, gnats, and crows. Parts of the mound still burned up near the top, lingering fires from the ghastly throats of the dragons that had repeatedly swooped in and burned what knights had survived the fall.

Hammerfiss, Spades, and Ava were not the only ones climbing this grisly mound. Slaves from the quarry were attempting to escape the slave pit up the same exact route as they. And what few knights who had survived the fall and dragon fires like Hammerfiss, Spades, and Ava crawled up the pile too, though most of the surviving knights were burned and injured and would die before reaching the top. Ava's body was battered too, her clothes stained red. Her jaw ached and she tasted blood in her mouth, caustic and raw. Her only consolation—she still had My Heart strapped to her hip. The slender sword with the ruby-embedded hilt had survived the fall and rested safe and snug in its sheath.

Ava scaled the smoking mountain of the dead, breathing heavy gasps of fetid air, body shaking with the effort, her mind naught but a foggy haze of half-remembered terrors. Fiery Absolution had come. Somehow she had escaped from that horror and straight into another. With Mancellor Allen and Jenko Bruk, she had fled from the burning tree and into the dark. She'd run and run, running from the fire of the dragons, following Mancellor and Jenko and the mob of knights from the swirling madness of the Hallowed Grove. But she had lost both Mancellor and Jenko in the chaos.

And then the ground had dropped out from under her. Falling. Falling. Falling through the dark. Her body crashing into the writhing mob of broken and smashed knights with a dull *thunk* that jarred her bones. Then all had gone black.

She did not know how much time had passed before she woke and wiggled from under the layer of dead bodies above her. But what she did know was that it was no longer nighttime and she was climbing a mound of corpses relying on the enemy—Hammerfiss and Enna Spades—to help her in her journey.

Together the three of them scaled the seemingly endless mountain of burnt knights and howling bodies piled against the towering wall of the quarry. It was a grim mountain of humanity, stretching hundreds of feet above and below her and to every side. Thousands of bodies scarlet and sticky and mashed and broken, many with eyes either melted or frozen open in pained disbelief. And the horror of it all, some still lived. Portions of the mound thrashed and quivered under her like the scabbed chest of a giant, flexing and rippling. Muted cries sounded from deep underneath the pile—cries of the suffering underneath her feet. Still Ava climbed, dizzy and sick, flies buzzing about her head, thick and black, ravens and crows circling above. Foul gases and smells wafted up from the burnt sludge of humankind and the slick treachery beneath her feet.

"I can't believe I allowed myself to get pushed into this damnable pit," Hammerfiss growled, standing straight and staring up at the remaining mountain of dead still left to climb. Through the ash and smoke above fluttered the half-burnt blue-and-white banners and cloaks of Sør Sevier, the maroon-and-gray livery of Rivermeade, the yellow and black of Eskander, the black and silver of Amadon, along with the myriad other colors of heraldry representing Gul Kana.

Ava slipped on the burnt face of a Dayknight and slid down the pile. Hammerfiss reached out and snatched her by the hand, slowing her slide. He pulled her up and over a smoking pile of iron plate armor and curled jagged ribs, steadying her as she regained her footing. Numb to every horror beneath her feet, Ava stood quiet and still beside the red-haired man. She stood quietly and glared angrily up the steep slope of bodies slick with blood and black ash. "Will this never end?" Enna Spades muttered, scrambling up the mound below them, her own freckled face a mask of exertion.

"Retreat never has worked in war," Hammerfiss said in consternation. "So why did I let the dragons frighten me so? Frightened me right into this pit, they did. How did I allow such a cowardly fucking travesty?"

"Because they are fucking scary is why." Spades hauled herself up beside Ava and Hammerfiss, steadying herself by grasping Ava's shoulder. "Those dragons herded everyone into this blasted slave pit, then set the whole mound of bodies on fire. Goddamn but weren't those flying snakes a horror?"

"Enna Spades afraid of a dragon?" Hammerfiss chuckled.

"*You* were afraid of a dragon, so don't mock."

"But I'm not as brave as you, m'lady."

"Don't *m'lady* me. Not here. Not now."

"But you *were* afraid of the dragons?"

"I didn't like them at all, that is true," Spades answered. "'Tis why I ran. 'Tis why you ran. 'Tis why all these melted motherfuckers underneath us ran. Those dragons are the exact reason why we all three find ourselves down in this fucking slave pit full of dead people. What a fucking end to this war, no?"

"The last of Aeros' army," Hammerfiss mused as he cast his fierce gaze across the heap of bodies stacked against the marble wall and the vast quarry behind them. "I never thought I would be walking atop such a bloody grim pile of my own comrades. But, alas, what can you do?"

"Piss and moan," Spades said. "Piss. And. Moan."

With that, the two enemy warriors fell silent and Ava swallowed the bile welling in her bleeding mouth. Her past was rife with the memories of many battles sharp and cutting and clear. But it wasn't until now that she fully understood the lure of forgetting, for this was the worst thing she had ever seen, and she wished to forget it immediately. A hundred thousand bodies buried underneath a hundred thousand more. Piled, stacked, crushed and torn asunder, then set aflame by dragon fire. It was death on a staggering scale.

And yet I survived. Somehow I survived. She remembered the fleeing, the falling, and all had gone black. She vaguely remembered squirming free of the pile, Hammerfiss and Enna Spades pulling her from the mound of the dead and into the light. Both Sør Sevier warriors were as battered and bloody as she, yet neither seemed to suffer from any outward injury. Ava's jaw ached and she kept swallowing blood.

"Just spit it out, girl," Hammerfiss said. "Spit the blood out. Quit swallowing it. You're making me sick."

"The girl swallows a little blood from a split lip and that makes you sick?" Spades said. "Look around you, man. Hell. Look under your own feet if you wanna see something disgusting."

"I've seen what's under my feet," Hammerfiss said. "The girl reminds me of a bloodsucking oghul, swallowing her own blood like that. And the sound reminds me of my own mammy feeding on my own pappy's limp cock, me havin' to listen from the—"

"I think we get the idea," Spades cut him off.

"Just spit already," Hammerfiss growled.

Ava spat a ropy stream of red over the hollow eyes of a dead knight beneath her feet. Then she slipped, falling to her butt against the mound of bodies. She thought she might vomit when her hands pressed through the cooked faces of the dead men underneath her. She scrambled up the heap, still gasping for breath in the foul air, trying to push herself to her feet. But her body suddenly froze, wrapped in an impenetrable shield of fear. She couldn't move. She could only stare down at the ash and blood and dead beneath her. She could only stare into melted armor, bodies, and faces of the dead.

"We gotta keep going," Spades said. "The only way out of this fucking pit is up this pile. Keep movin', girl."

Ava looked at the towering mound of bodies rising above. Two Dayknights in black armor ascended the mound of melted bodies not far from them, both men grasping at loose armor and weaponry, one man utilizing the stray stiff limb of a dead soldier protruding from the pile to help in his climb. The other knight kicked loose a blackened helm, which bounced down the heap of bodies and cracked Hammerfiss in the knee before bouncing away down the mountain.

"Bloody fucking shitheads!" the red-haired giant yelled up at the two. "Watch yourselves!" He reached down and snapped the burnt arm off the corpse under him and threw it up the mound of bodies at the two knights. The arm struck the back of one of the men, and he tumbled backward against the mound in a puff of black ash and dust.

Hammerfiss smiled as he looked at Spades, saying, "We catch up to those men and I am tossing them both back down this hill."

"You always were a murderous cunt," Spades said.

"Why, you honey-tongued charmer." Hammerfiss' smile grew. "You truly do know me, don't you?"

"You were never one for charity after a battle," Spades said. "You were always like Gault that way."

Hammerfiss' smile grew even wider. "He was a cold killer."

Ava had never figured Gault Aulbrek as a cold killer. She was not surprised to see these two hardened warriors finding the absurdity in their situation and joking about it. They were both truly crazy.

"I wonder what Gault would have thought of all this?" Spades asked.

"Aye." Hammerfiss nodded, saying the man's name with reverence: "*Gault Aulbrek*. I think he would have found this whole situation as frustratingly humorous and absurd as we do."

"I miss him in battle," Spades said.

"And what a battle this was." Hammerfiss spread his arms wide to encompass all that he was seeing, as if he were king of the entire monstrous ugly mountain. "Fiery Absolution, what a brutal war. What a bloody war. What a beautiful war. What an unexpected slaughter for the ages. I loved it. Just look at this mound of bodies we are crawling upon, Spades. 'Tis a true work of art, is it not? 'Tis the culmination of all my dreams. Indeed, Gault would have loved it."

"Gault would not have been afraid of those dragons," Ava said, the words spewing forth before she could rein them in. "He would not have fallen into this pit, that's for sure."

"She speaks." Spades stared at her.

"She's correct," Hammerfiss said. "We should all be like Gault Aulbrek, fearless in the face of all beasts."

Ava didn't know whether Hammerfiss was mocking her. She also wasn't sure whether Gault would have fought or fled the dragons. The last she had seen of the man, he was walking away, destroyed by both her and his own daughter.

"Unhand me, wench!" a familiar voice sounded from down the slope and slightly to Ava's right.

It was Dokie Liddle. His mousy face was black with soot, and he was stabbing into a squirming pile of half-burnt knights with an elegant blue longsword. The weapon looked almost unwieldy in Dokie's small hands. The whites of the boy's eyes were wild and stark in contrast to his blackened face. Puffs of smoke billowed up under his feet as he stomped at the person beneath him. Two thin quarry slaves stood on the mound above the boy, watching.

"Leave me be!" Dokie shouted, thrusting the sword tip into the mountain of bodies. Ava could see that there was an injured Sør Sevier warrior woman beneath him. The woman was buried up to her waist in the writhing bodies and was struggling to free herself, blood boiling from her mangled lips. Her neck arched like a bow as she grabbed at Dokie's sword, trying to rip it away.

"Bloody fucking slag!" Dokie pushed the point of the blade into her burned face, her half-burnt fingers uncurling from around his blade when he pulled it free.

"You sure kilt the fuck outa that mean bitch, didn't ya, boy," one of the slaves above Dokie said.

"Wench tried to take my sword," Dokie cried. "You seen her. It's all I got. Took it from King Jovan myself."

"What if I try and take the sword from you?" the other slave asked, grinning.

"Get your own sword," Dokie said, concern etched on his face now. "There's plenty lyin' about. You're standin' on a thousand."

"What if I like yours?" the first slave asked.

"Just you try." Dokie straightened, ready for the fight to come.

"Dokie!" Ava shouted. "What are you doing here?"

The slaves turned and looked up at Ava. Dokie looked up at her too. "Ava Shay!" he shouted in response. "What are you doing down here in all this mess? I saw you under the Atonement Tree! I wanted to say hi!"

"I didn't see you!" Ava shouted back. "Shouldn't you be in Gallows Haven?"

"Have you seen Liz Hen?" he called to her. "Have you seen Beer Mug?"

"No!" Ava's gaze darted around quickly, wondering if the big red-haired girl might indeed be lingering somewhere on the mountain of corpses with her shepherd dog.

"Well." Spades sat down on top of a melted Dayknight helm, gazing down the slope of dead bodies toward Dokie. "Aren't you a hard one to kill, Dokie Liddle? And now you have Aeros' sword. Will wonders never cease."

Dokie pointed his sword up at the red-haired warrior woman. "Savage bitch!" he shouted. "This is all your fault somehow, I know it is!"

"How do you figure this is my fault?" Spades asked. "You think I stacked all these dead men here for you to walk on?"

Flames licked up around Dokie's feet as the section of corpses and armor under him began to slide down the slope. Portions of the mountain of flesh were still on fire and moving. The boy scurried away from the sliding bodies and scrambled up the slope toward the two slaves, determination on his face, sword gripped in his sooty little hand. He stabbed out at the first slave and missed, but caught the man by surprise. The slave stumbled back, grabbing his partner's arm. Both slaves fell, tumbling down the slope of bodies like rag dolls. Dokie's stark white eyes focused on Spades next, rage building with each struggling step as he scrambled up the mound toward her.

"I think that boy means to slay you," Hammerfiss chuckled. "And with Aeros' sword no less."

"He's a crafty one, indeed," Spades said. "I make him swim with sharks, and yet here he comes at me moons later looking as rabid as a Spyke Mountain bat." She snatched up a soot-blackened sword from under her feet and stood.

"She'll kill you, Dokie!" Ava shrieked in warning.

But the Gallows Haven boy kept climbing, stabbing the long blue sword straight up at the warrior woman when he reached her. Spades blocked the boy's wild stab, striking the weapon from his hand, sending it skittering and tumbling about twenty feet down the mound.

But Dokie kept coming, lunging at her, ducking her sword, grasping onto her legs, crawling up her armor, beating small fists against her dented breastplate. "Why are you here?" he shouted, tears streaming down his grimy face. "Why aren't you dead?"

Spades tossed her sword away and grabbed him by both of his wrists, holding him tight. "Just calm down, boy!" She wrestled with his arms, gaining control. "Get ahold of yourself. You're lucky you ain't dead. You're lucky I don't pitch you back down this mountain, for fuck's sake."

"Lucky!" Dokie jerked his hands away from the red-haired woman, breaking from her grasp. "Lucky!" he shouted as he plopped down on the mound next to Ava, head between his hands. "How are any of us lucky?"

"We just are," Spades said. "Especially you, Dokie Liddle. Remember, you're the boy who escaped sharks. And then I almost killed you again at Ten Cairn Abbey. Then I tossed you from a tower in Savon. I'm only sparing you now because you entertain and amuse me. You are lucky to be alive."

"I would rather be dead," he sobbed. "I should be buried at the bottom of this cruel mountain."

"One should never envy the dead," Spades said.

Dokie looked up at her. "I would imagine the living have always envied the dead in this quarry."

"The boy's full of philosophy now," Hammerfiss said.

"Well, he's right in one respect," Spades said. "This is no place for the living."

"His whining is annoying me." Hammerfiss scrunched up his face in disgust. "I wish he didn't amuse you. That way we could be rid of him."

"Have a heart." Spades' eyes remained on Dokie. "The boy is distraught."

"*I'm* distraught," Hammerfiss grumbled, looking once again up the pile of bodies toward the rim of the quarry, still some hundred feet above. "We've still halfway to go yet, if we're to ever get out of here."

"Aye," Spades agreed. "It is a long hike."

"What are we going to do?" Dokie was looking at Ava now with a sadness so deep it both shocked and disquieted her. She met his pained gaze with as much sympathy as she could muster. "We've fallen in with the enemy on a pile of the dead, Ava Shay. And even if we climb out of this place, there are still the beasts of the underworld above."

"I wager the power of the dragon does not hold sway over Dokie Liddle," Spades said. "Not the boy who swam with sharks."

"Sharks are not the equal of the beasts of the underworld," Dokie said, tear-filled eyes looking up at Spades as if she were crazy. "You yourself are not even the equal of a fire-breathing demon from the underworld, as evil as you are." He motioned to Hammerfiss. "Nor is he."

"We are your best chance of getting out of this bloody pit alive." Hammerfiss glared down at the boy. "And you are my best chance to get out of here too. For your whiny presence has given me an idea."

"What idea?" Dokie asked.

"I am going to need your help," Hammerfiss said.

"My help?" Dokie faltered.

"Yes, your help. And Ava's too. Now stand up, little man, wipe those tears, and let's climb our asses up and out of this god-awful mess."

"Just let me grab my sword first," Dokie said, looking down the slope of bodies to the blue sword some twenty feet away. "In case you betray Ava and me after we help you."

**

When they reached the top of the mountain of corpses, they found that they were still a good thirty feet below the rim of the quarry. The dead were more burnt and smashed together here at the top. Some were even still on fire, smoldering with hot smoke, melted together into one solid mass of cooked flesh and armor.

"Well, this is bullshit," Hammerfiss grumbled, staring angrily at the flat marble wall rising up before him.

Ava felt her own heart plummet, knowing they had come so far for nothing. The abyss stretched out behind them, and they could not go back down.

"Look at what those two guys are doing." Dokie pointed to the east. "Now, they have the right idea."

Along the fuming ridge some hundred paces away were two helmetless Dayknights stacking dead bodies up in an attempt to make the wall of corpses even higher so they could climb out.

"There is a rope hanging there"—Dokie pointed—"and an iron hook at the end of the rope. Those two knights are trying to reach the rope by stacking more bodies."

"By god, they are indeed." Hammerfiss clapped Dokie on the shoulder. "What say we help them?"

Hammerfiss tromped across the slope of dead toward the two Dayknights, one hand pressed against the marble wall of the quarry as his large feet continued to slip and sink into the gore beneath. Dokie, Spades, and Ava followed, each of them keeping one hand against the wall, for at the top, footing was less stable than ever. Dokie clung to his blue sword with his free hand.

When Hammerfiss reached the two Dayknights, he reached down and pried a dead body from the mash of smoking corpses. He effortlessly tossed the body up onto the shoulder-high pile already created by the two Dayknights. The Dayknights looked annoyed. "Do you want to get out of here or not?" Hammerfiss asked.

The iron hook and rope dangled just out of reach. With just a few more bodies thrown on the stack, someone could climb up and reach the hook. Hammerfiss dragged another body from the blackened slush of blood underfoot and tossed it atop the pile.

"We don't need your help," one of the Dayknights finally said. He was a broad-faced man of near fifty years. "We don't need the help of any Sør Sevier scum."

"Well, this Sør Sevier scum is helping whether you like it or not," Hammerfiss said, glaring at the two men with bottomless eyes. His look brooked no argument.

"Let him help if he wants, Elten," the younger Dayknight said.

"Yes, Elten, let me help." Hammerfiss' cold stare narrowed. "Actually, you know what, Elten? I've a better idea." The big man pulled a sword from the bloody rubble and launched himself at the surprised Dayknight with a shout. Elten died swiftly under Hammerfiss' attack, his head cloven in two. Hammerfiss stabbed the younger Dayknight in the gut and then kicked him down the mountain of copses.

"Why did you kill them?" Dokie asked. "They could have helped us."

"I'd rather feed my scrotum to a trapped badger than climb out of here with the help of those two assholes," Hammerfiss said. "Besides, Elten's body will make the stack even higher." He lifted Elten with scant little effort and placed the dead man atop the stack.

"I think that ought to do it." Hammerfiss admired the stack of dead knights for a moment, then asked Dokie to hand over his sword. Dokie stepped back. "Give it," Hammerfiss insisted. "You can't climb with it in hand." Dokie handed him the weapon. Hammerfiss took it by the hilt and threw it effortlessly up and over the rim of the quarry.

"What did you do that for?" Dokie whined.

"You can have it when you reach the top." Hammerfiss grabbed Dokie by the waist and tossed the boy up onto the pile too.

"Grab the hook and climb out of here," Hammerfiss said. "Once you're up there, find a rope to drop down. And don't even think about leaving us stranded down here, boy."

Dokie jumped up and grabbed the rusted iron hook. He swiftly climbed the remaining twenty feet, both hands gripping the rope, feet against the wall. He quickly made his way up and over the lip of the quarry. A moment later his head peered back over the rim. He fed a thick length of chain slowly down into the pit.

Hammerfiss climbed the chain first. Ava followed second, both feet and hands secure on the links as she climbed. Her ascent went smoothly and she was soon out of the pit and into the light of morning. Spades climbed from the pit last.

As she stood atop the rim of the slave quarry, Ava didn't even want to see the sun. It was like liquid fire pouring more heat over herself and the smoldering pit behind her. Feeling the sun burn hot on her flesh, Ava realized she couldn't even be free of the horror that was Fiery Absolution. A battlefield of dead bodies stretched out before her clear to the Hallowed Grove. Smoke billowed thick from the Atonement Tree. Smoke hung stark and black over Amadon in the far distance. In fact, Ava couldn't even see Mount Albion or the castle through the blackness. *Where is Jenko Bruk? Where is Mancellor Allen? Where is Gault Aulbrek? What do I do now?*

"I've got to go find Liz Hen," Dokie said. Then, without asking anyone, he snatched up his long blue sword and shuffled across the bloody landscape toward the burning city.

> *Doubt is unpleasant, but certainty is absurd. For even the slightest*
> *knowledge of reality is far more useful than even the most certain*
> *knowledge of faith and fantasy. The fact that faith and religion exist and*
> *breed hatred in those who believe different things is not the worst of things,*
> *for faith and religion also breed hatred in those nonbelievers who wish faith*
> *and religion did not exist. They want to kill the believers, and the believers*
> *want to kill them. Thus faith and belief truly poison everything.*
> —THE ANGEL STONE CODEX

CHAPTER SIXTY-SEVEN
LINDHOLF LE GRAVEN

13TH DAY OF THE HEART MOON, 999TH YEAR OF LAIJON
AMADON, GUL KANA

Twisted and black and glowing with embers, the Atonement Tree rose up before Lindholf Le Graven like a monstrous dark skeleton. Aeros Raijael still clung to the burnt husk of the tree; his blackened body naught but a mangle of flame-shredded flesh and cracked bones. Fires burned across the Hallowed Grove and the battle-field beyond, random and haphazard, the smoke forcing back the light of the morning sun. Portions of Amadon burned in the distance.

The white stallion, Spirit, stood silently at Lindholf's side. *Afflicted Fire, Forgetting Moon, Blackest Heart, Lonesome Crown,* and *Ethic Shroud* were all tied to the stallion's saddle. *Fiery Absolution is over and the weapons of the Five Warrior Angels and the five angel stones are mine!* Lindholf thought. *I am the White Prince! I am Laijon returned.* He was high on Shroud of the Vallè and felt invincible.

A commotion drew Lindholf's attention toward Black Dugal's bulldog. The mangy creature named Café Colza was barking up a riot, snarling and spitting right in the face of the saber-toothed lion. The silver-eyed cat hissed, swiping huge black paws at the dog. Café Colza danced away, stumpy little tail gloriously a-wag as if he were involved in some fun game with the cat. The dog's spiked collar gleamed dully in the dim morning as the dog growled and scratched at the ground before the cat. The saber-tooth roared and the air shook with the sheer enormity of the sound. The dog backed away now, wary.

The black cat sniffed the ground where the dog had been, then casually walked across the clearing toward the small oghul named Mud and the boy with the silver eyes, Stefan Wayland. Val-Draekin and Seita were near Stefan. The two Vallè were talking to the Bloodwoods, Black Dugal and Hans Rake. Lindholf did not like the assassins and he never had, not since meeting them in Saint Only.

"What do you think they are talking about?" Lindholf asked.

Lawri Le Graven stepped around Spirit, her frightened eyes on the two Bloodwoods and the two Vallè. She looked fevered and sick, and the mysterious silver gauntlet was still attached to her arm. Young Leisel was right behind her, looking demure as ever. Seeing the lithesome serving girl again, Lindholf could breathe easier. She was a comfort to him for some reason he could not explain. Amongst all the smoking death and destruction, Leisel shone like a doe in a glen filled with heather, her hair wild and bright. Though her face was unusually pale and drawn, her fright-filled eyes glowed like the moon and Lindholf wanted to protect her.

"They will be coming for you soon, brother," Lawri said. "That is what Seita and Val-Draekin are discussing."

"How do you know? I can't hear them. How can you hear them? Who will be coming for me?"

"The demons of the underworld. They have returned from their first attack on the city."

Lindholf eyed her skeptically. It was as if her mind was connected to Vallè's somehow.

"Look." Lawri pointed with her good arm. "The demons come now."

Lindholf turned and peered through the smoke toward where Lawri had pointed. Sure enough, the five skull-faced dragon riders approached him on foot, silver whips coiled at their belts. Their armor-clad bodies were tall and angular in the slanting rays of the morning sun, crescent-moon carvings on their breastplates glimmering in the light. Their stretched shadows seemed to bite jaggedly into the smoldering corpses scattered on the ground. Despite their pale glamour, these five knights somehow remained dark and menacing. Black Dugal called them the Aalavarrè Solas. Lawri's name for them was more fitting—demons of the underworld.

The five dragons soared just above the Aalavarrè, surveying the Hallowed Grove with their colorful glowing eyes, heaving nostrils cease-lessly venting smoke. White. Green. Blue. Black. Red. Lindholf could scarcely peel his eyes from their bright and deadly grandeur. So magnif-icent they were. So horrific. Standing under these five fearsome drag-ons was a moment he would not soon forget. When the five Aalavarrè finally reached Lindholf, the five dragons sped off over the battlefield in search of survivors to roast, their great wings stirring the ash and air.

Watching the beasts swoop and glide was awe-inspiring in a way. He had learned that their blazing brilliant fires were charged with Shroud of the Vallè. He had watched them drink clouds of it in at the moment of Absolution above the Atonement Tree. He had watched Val-Draekin feed them the Shroud since then too. The fire would die inside their bellies without the Shroud. Lindholf could understand. He could not breathe fire like the dragons when he sniffed the Shroud, but the white powder infused him with a confidence he could find no other way.

The Aalavarrè removed their skull-faced masks one at a time. Their feylike faces were thin, pale, and cruel-looking. When the two Vallè and the two Bloodwoods joined them, the five dragon riders knelt before Lindholf as one.

Lawri and Leisel moved back a step, scared.

Black Dugal pulled the hood of his cloak down, revealing the elegant-looking face of a Vallè, ears thin and pointed. Dugal's exquisitely chiseled features were at once pale and cruel and cold and perfect and precise in their symmetry. *A Vallè once disguised as a man!* Though his visage had changed, this Vallè before Lindholf still somehow remained Black Dugal.

And then it dawned on Lindholf why the Vallè still looked so familiar, even though he had spent a lifetime parading as a human. At the moment Black Dugal's peerless Vallè face was surrounded by dancing motes of flame and ash filtering down from the twisted branches of the Atonement Tree. And Dugal's face, framed by such bright sparkling embers, reminded Lindholf of the statue of Laijon in the temple.

It was Black Dugal's squared chin, the sublime lines of his smooth cheekbones, brows, and jaw, along with the subtly aquiline features, that were unmistakable. Lindholf's heart pounded, for only he knew of the hidden blemish on the statue of Laijon. Only he knew of the flaw, because he had once been atop the statue. He alone knew that that glorious likeness of the great One and Only, that holy visage of Laijon that all humankind throughout the breadth of the Five Isles had bowed down before in worship—was a fraud. For he alone had felt the chisel marks atop those ears—ears that used to be pointed, ears that used to be *Vallè*.

And standing before me is a Vallè who spent his life disguised as a human!

It was all coming together for Lindholf now. His mind felt like it was on fire, burning to cinders like the Atonement Tree smoldering behind him. Val-Draekin was right: for centuries humanity had been played for fools. Everything was a deception—the scriptures, the sculptures, the myths, the legends. He felt the tops of his own deformed ears. *And who am I?*

Laijon returned!

As the five Aalavarrè Solas had just done, Black Dugal bent his knee to Lindholf.

Hans Rake, Val-Draekin, and Seita did likewise. But such deference made Lindholf uncomfortable for some reason. Trying to remain cool and confident, he stroked Spirit's soft mane, feeling the markings on his body begin to burn once more, feeling the heat of the angel stones in the pouch at his belt against his flesh.

"I've a charge for you, my lord." Black Dugal stood.

My lord? Lindholf met the Bloodwood's red-streaked gaze. "What is it you wish of me?" he asked.

Dugal gestured to the five Aalavarrè Solas. "You must present the weapons of the Five Warrior Angels to the dragon riders, my lord."

Lindholf felt like he was going to sink into the dirt and ash at his feet, for Dugal's demand was not at all what he was expecting. "I can't give the weapons away, surely?"

"You must offer the weapons to the five Aalavarrè." There was a coolness and a gravity infused in Black Dugal's tone now. "They do not yet belong to you. They shall use them in war. Then return them to you when the time is right."

They do not yet belong to me? Lindholf cast his gaze toward the white sword strapped to Spirit's back, looked at the other weapons hanging there too: *Blackest Heart, Lonesome Crown, Ethic Shroud, Forgetting Moon.* Then he looked at the five dragon riders arrayed before him, focused on the colorful crescent-moon carvings on their breastplates.

They do not yet belong to you, Dugal had confirmed. Lindholf met Seita's gaze but saw no answers there, just pity—and her pitying look stung. "Prophecy uses everyone, Lindholf," she said. "It uses you. It even uses the most well-meaning of Vallè maidens for its ends. Scripture has held an unwholesome power over humankind for generations. Can you imagine the horror humanity must now feel in knowing that the savage oghul rituals of Hragna'Ar were actually God's truth? For only through silver and blood and the green elixir of life can the dead rise again, for in the end it is life renewed. Dugal is right; the weapons are not yet yours, Lindholf. You must show patience."

More Vallè tricks? Lindholf asked himself.

Seita gestured toward the five dragon riders. "Let them end this war with the weapons of the Five Warrior Angels in their own hands. Let them hunt down the last of humanity, let them hunt those cowards who have fled into Amadon. Let them clean up this war, and then the weapons will be given back to you and Lawri. And that is a promise."

Given back to me and *Lawri!* Lindholf felt his mouth twisting as if he had bitten something rotten. Seita's words echoed down a long, empty corridor in his mind, sounding achingly less and less familiar with every hollow echo. "I don't understand."

"You shall in time," Val-Draekin said, turning to Seita. "Has that largest of all Vallè secrets a purpose and a name?"

"It has," Seita answered. "And that name is Absolution. It has been a thousand years since the Aalavarrè Solas have walked abroad. It has been a thousand years since Hragna'Ar ritual and blood sacrifice brought them back. Before that, they were naught but wraiths captive in the underworld. Before that, they were naught but demons passed out of all knowledge and legend. The weapons are a gift of Viper, thrust down from the stars in blood and scorch and silver glory."

The dragon rider in white-scaled armor stepped toward Lindholf, bowing once again, "I am Icelyn the White, firstborn of the blood cauldrons of Hragna'Ar. I trust you know which weapon is mine?"

How would I know? Lindholf felt his heart speed in panic as he stared dumbfounded at the exquisite creature before him. The Aalavarrè's fey-like face was as fine as porcelain and as exquisite as Seita's. Lindholf was unnerved by the twin pools of silver that were the creature's eyes and the gruesome leather thong lined with severed human ears draped over her shoulder. He was also unsettled by the silver whip coiled at the Aalavarrè's belt. "You do know which one I should wield?" Icelyn repeated.

Which one? Lindholf looked at all five weapons secured to Spirit. Shaking, he untied *Ethic Shroud* from the back of the saddle and handed the white shield to Icelyn.

The dragon rider's languid fingers curled tight around *Ethic Shroud*'s glorious surface. "Now this is what the eternal soul was created for." The Aalavarrè held the white shield up for her fellow dragon riders to see. "To take up *Ethic Shroud* and become one with Viper in the long hunt. For it is a hunt uncultivated and raw, shrieking with fiery pain. For it is the song of Viper we sing."

Icelyn's strange pronouncement was meaningless to Lindholf.

The dragon rider in green-scaled armor stepped up to Lindholf next.

"I am Raakel-Jael the Green, second-born of the blood cauldrons of Hragna'Ar. Do you know which weapon I should wield?"

Lindholf removed *Lonesome Crown* from off the saddle horn and handed the helm to the knight in green-scaled armor.

With a tremendous amount of reverence, Raakel-Jael placed the horned helm on his head and turned to the other dragon riders. "Under *Lonesome Crown* I can hear that pure cry of the human dead sail high and loud toward starshine and moonlight. I can hear their cry sail high toward the eternal God of open blue sky, toward Viper."

The third dragon rider stepped forth and bowed before Lindholf, blue-scaled armor shimmering in the light of the rising sun, silver eyes almost aglow in anticipation. "I am Basque-Alia the Blue, third-born of the blood cauldrons of Hragna'Ar. Do you know which weapon I should wield?"

Lindholf unstrapped *Forgetting Moon* from Spirit's back and handed it to the knight in blue. Basque-Alia took the battle-ax, bowed to Lindholf, and turned to his companions. "With this ax in hand, I can now feel myself roaming, stalking, hunting once again with Viper. And a fallow hunt it shall be, to avenge the genocide of the Aalavarrè so long ago, to make extinct the race of man."

Make extinct the race of man! Those words sent a shudder through Lindholf.

The dragon rider in black stepped toward him next, bowing. "I am Sashenya the Black, fourth-born of the blood cauldrons of Hragna'Ar. Do you know which weapon I should wield?"

Lindholf removed the black crossbow from the saddle and handed it to the silver-eyed Aalavarrè. Sashenya took the crossbow, running graceful fingers over its black wooden stock. "My eternal soul now quivers with life and purpose."

The dragon rider in red armor stepped forward last, bowing. "I am Aamari-Laada the Red, fifth-born of the blood cauldrons of Hragna'Ar. And I shall be honored to accept *Afflicted Fire*."

Lindholf handed the knight in red armor the long white sword. The

Aalavarrè took it, examining every inch of the marvelous weapon. Then the pale-faced creature looked at Lindholf with flat silver orbs. "I offer you my allegiance, for you are one of true valor, for you are one with Viper, our Immortal Lord Le Graven."

With the final words of Aamari-Laada, a stillness had settled over the grove. *One of true valor?* Lindholf almost laughed, thinking nothing could describe him less accurately. *Our Immortal Lord Le Graven?*

"What of the angel stones?" He untied the pouch from his belt, loosened its leather straps, and emptied all five of the angel stones into his right hand, glorious colors glowing against his flesh. The stones barely fit in his palm as he held them out toward Black Dugal.

"You keep them, Lindholf," Dugal said. "For the one who wields the stones controls the dragons and their riders. They will do your bidding. For you are Laijon returned, the Immortal Lord Le Graven."

The five Aalavarrè Solas bowed before Lindholf once more.

And in the distance, five dragons roared.

CHAPTER SIXTY-EIGHT
STEFAN WAYLAND

13TH DAY OF THE HEART MOON, 999TH YEAR OF LAIJON

AMADON, GUL KANA

Seita led Stefan Wayland farther out into the smoking battlefield
and away from the Atonement Tree. The black saber-toothed lion
followed. The cat was never far from Stefan. As the three of them
picked their way through the blackened armor and endless piles of the
dead, Stefan tried not to look, but death was everywhere. Knights lay
armless and legless in the mud, their burnt mouths yawning open, revealing dark caverns. Flies and gnats were braving the smoke, lighting
on the bloody bodies and flying off.

Stefan felt like he was walking through some terrible dream, remembering things he had long forgotten. Even though he recalled his previous life as a skeptic when it came to things dealing with *The Way and
Truth of Laijon,* for some reason he had concluded that the little blue
stone Gisela had found at the bottom of the cross-shaped altar had indeed been real. He recalled Gisela being so utterly enraptured by the
stone, such a simple soul, easily entranced with pretty things.

But the glittery blue stone had killed her in the end. Stefan knew it had. Now Gisela was gone. His family was gone. All his friends were gone, likely smoldering and dead heaps on the battlefield. And now Lindholf Le Graven carried the stone as Laijon returned. Stefan knew he had to come to terms with the fact that Fiery Absolution had been real and he himself had played a part in it.

He hugged the black bow closer to his chest. It was the only object tying him to his former life, tying him to Gisela. He had taken the bow back last night during the battle. The thief who had stolen the bow had painted it black. But the paint he didn't mind; he was just glad to have Gisela back, seeking solace in the weapon's familiarity.

After the sacking of Gallows Haven, he had sought solace in Gisela's arms, in her love, for she was all that symbolized the future he dreamed of—hearth and home and a family of his own, their children at his feet. But no matter how hard he tried to hold the bow tight and cherish those thoughts and dreams, all he saw around him was black smoke and the heaping stacks of dead bodies. And he saw it all through a silvery haze of misery and despair, a silvery haze that was fogging his brain more and more each day. Rotting his body, too. He could feel the rot growing in his veins, painful streaks twining under his flesh, trying to peel back his skin. He had to come to terms with his own strange existence too.

If he could cry, he would.

But he knew tears could not escape his eyes now. The sorrow and tears were there, but trapped inside. He glanced down at the silver-eyed cat that followed him, realizing that so much in his life had changed since the sacking of Gallows Haven.

"Stefan." Seita's voice sounded as if from a great distance. "Are you okay?"

He swallowed his pain and reluctantly looked at the Vallè maiden. Seita walked at his side. Close. Very close. He immediately desired to look away, for the Vallè he thought he had once loved was staring at him with bright green eyes brimming with concern. Suddenly the Hallowed Grove seemed cold around him.

He forced his gaze away from hers. "I don't know where you are taking me or whether I should even go with you."

"You do not trust me?" she asked, taking his hand.

Her touch was like lightning against his skin. He drew back and stopped, clutching Gisela tightly to his chest in both hands again.

"Trust me," she repeated, peeling his hand from the bow once more, leading him on. They reached a broad stretch of clear ground blessedly free of twisted corpses and dead snarling faces and bloody spears. They made their way into a small section of the Hallowed Grove that had somehow been miraculously untouched by Fiery Absolution.

They sat together on a stone bench in the center of a patch of un-burned grass, their cold seat overlooking a small dale of green crested by a ridge lined with the ragged silhouettes of more blackened corpses and broken weaponry.

The black saber-tooth sat at Stefan's feet, gazing out over the green grass. The sun beat down on Stefan's neck, yet still he shivered, for the look in Seita's green eyes seemed cold. As she stared at him, he wished he had a cloak he could draw up around his shoulders. Instead he let go her hand and clutched the black bow to his breast again, as if Gisela could keep him warm.

"I feel I must start out by being honest in my objectives," Seita said, settling more comfortably on the stone bench next to him, the palm of her hand straying to his knee now. Her touch was again like ice. He flinched inwardly but did not shift away from her. The large cat sensed his discomfort, gazing up at him with blank silver eyes.

Seita kept her hand where it was, on his knee. "Each of us will have a great role to play in the coming days, Stefan Wayland."

"You killed me." Stefan felt the cold tension in his voice as he stared down into the green blades of grass flickering in the breeze. "My legs were shattered and broken. I could not walk. You did not help me at all. I cannot trust you."

His words were met with silence. Not long ago, Seita had been the one person who had almost made him forget the pain of Gisela. He had loved the Vallè maiden.

And she had betrayed him.

"We are all meant to be here," Seita said, her gaze firm. "You have always been part of the plan, Stefan, your rebirth was a test of Hragna'Ar, a test of a greater resurrection to come. As Culpa Barra once said, ' 'Tis we who are swept up in large and great events, the forces of our times; 'tis we who must now make many important decisions.' "

"Culpa Barra," Stefan muttered, remembering once again the Dayknight's melted face. Seita had rammed her dagger into the side of it. "You murdered him, too."

The Vallè cocked her head, her face impassive. "You were there, Stefan. It was no murder. Culpa Barra asked me to kill him."

Stefan felt his heart tighten. "What is happening to me? I felt myself die after you stuck that dagger into my heart. My legs were broken and now healed. My memories do return, but slowly. I think I remember some things. But not others. I remember the cauldrons. My vision is strange, hazy with silver. Am I reborn? Resurrected through Hragna'Ar ritual, as you say?"

"Yes. You were reborn through the blood cauldrons of Hragna'Ar, a trial run for the oghuls and their blood cauldrons. We call you a successful resurrection, if you will. Just like the saber-tooth that follows you. The lion too was a test."

"Test?" Stefan felt his heart tighten even more, and he gazed down at the silver-eyed cat. "Why?"

"Just be glad you are alive. You have a destiny yet to fulfill."

"What destiny?"

"I do not rightly know." Her eyes darkened. "And I do not wish to speculate, for your fate is now your own."

"Can you not see into the future?"

"On the subject of your fate I have seen no visions."

"What has happened to the world?"

"Fiery Absolution has happened to the world: a reckoning, ancient wrongs once again made right."

"What ancient wrongs?"

"This war is retribution for humans conquering the Five Isles thousands of years ago with their savagery and false belief, interloping into our realm, destroying the lands of the dwarf and the oghul and the Vallè, claiming them as their own, and then relegating the oghul, dwarf, and Vallè to the harsher, unwanted places of the Five Isles. This war is retribution for banishing our cousins, the Aalavarrè Solas, to the underworld in the name of false belief. This war is retribution for humanity's War of Cleansing a thousand years ago."

Stefan recalled Bishop Tolbret's Eighth Day services and the words read from *The Way and Truth of Laijon*. He quoted what he remembered of the sermon: " 'When all demons were banished to the underworld by Laijon and the other Warrior Angels during the Vicious War of the Demons.' "

"Banished, yes," she said. "Though they were not *demons*, as you were taught. They were the Aalavarrè Solas. But you would not know any of that from your scriptures, from what was written in *The Way and Truth of Laijon*. For all the scriptures about Laijon and the Five Warrior Angels were just made-up stories. They were the conjuring of the ancient Vallè, meant to confuse and mislead humanity. All the scriptures taught to you as a youngster were lies, naught but a centuries-long con to get humans fighting against each other, to get humans to kill each other, to get humans to deplete their own armies through religious strife, all so the oghul and Vallè could take back the entirety of the Five Isles stolen from them so long ago. We would never outnumber the humans. But we would outsmart them. 'Twas all a long game played by the Vallè to bring about the return of our cousins, the Aalavarrè Solas. And the five dragon riders are just the beginning of the Aalavarrè's return."

"Are you saying that I was right to be skeptical of my religion when I was younger?" he asked. "Are you saying that I was right to believe it was all a lie?"

Seita nodded. "*The Way and Truth of Laijon, The Chivalric Illuminations of Raijael, The Moon Scrolls of Mia.* All of them full of lies, all of them full of deceptive promises and nonsensical prophecies to drive humanity to war. All of them filled with gross deceptions meant to cause strife, to feed humanity's insatiable hunger for faith and belief, to drive humanity to decimate each other through religious disparity, through holy war and savagery. All scripture is naught but a thousand-year plot of the

Vallè to divide humanity, for my ancestors knew that over time, it would not matter what the truth was; for humanity, it would only matter what those scriptures said. And the centuries-long patience of the Vallè has finally come to fruition."

"But how could generations of humanity have remained so blind to this subtlety?"

"The humans who came to the Five Isles from the Firstlands with their plagues and diseases that killed the Vallè and oghul and dwarf off, also came with a greater sickness, that of faith and belief. Their greatest evil was their belief in an afterlife, their belief in gods. My ancestors observed how those humans would fight each other over these competing notions of god and belief and faith. My ancestors were both mystified and horrified that humans would slay each other over what amounted to bad ideas and silly stories. And then these silly ideas led to the Vicious War of the Demons. Then came the slaying of the dragons and the banishment of our cousins, the Aalavarrè Solas, to the underworld. My ancestors knew they could eventually use this belief and faith in the gods against humanity, culminating in one final Fiery Absolution. And it would be an absolution that humanity would bring upon themselves. Which they have."

Stefan thought of how Nail and every other boy their age in Gallows Haven was so devoted to the church and *The Way and Truth of Laijon*. What Seita said made a perverse sort of sense now, an ugly sort of sense. He recalled his conversation with Culpa Barra after they had escaped the Sky Loch glacier. He recalled how he had said that faith and belief in holy books and moon scrolls had done naught but kill folk and start wars. He had been right, yet Culpa had argued with him on that, tried to shame him for his opinion. *But I was right! Faith and belief in magic weapons and angel stones did naught but launch pointless quests that killed every person dearest to me.*

At the time, Stefan had seen faith and belief as naught but cowardly lies.

And lies were the most dangerous of things.

And the world was full of lies.

And Seita had lied to him many times.

"What is your part in all this?" he asked her. "Why so much death and destruction to bring back five silver-eyed Aalavarrè and five dragons?"

"'Twas oghul sacrifice that brought back the black cat, and you, and the five dragons, and the five Aalavarrè. But we are not done bringing back the dead."

"So this is not the end."

"I am the Vallè maiden who dreamed dreams and saw visions—visions that she was the princess of her people, the Vallè *princess* who would lead armies of Aalavarrè Solas over the bones of the human dead."

"What armies?"

"The armies that are waiting beneath us. The armies that are waiting to rise again."

"The demons of the underworld?"

"The Aalavarrè Solas," she corrected him. "You must stop thinking in terms of your own scripture. They are actually down there, Stefan. Down underneath us awaiting to spring forth from the ground and reclaim the lands they once ruled."

Stefan cast his gaze up to the blue skies. *Why has Laijon cursed us?* Culpa Barra had once asked after Rogemoore, Val-Draekin, and Nail had been lost in the glacier during their search for the weapons of the Five Warrior Angels. *What test from God is this?* He clutched Gisela tighter to his chest, trying to convince himself there was some hope somewhere, trying to convince himself that everything Seita was saying was also a lie.

So many lies in life, what does one ever believe?

"We were fortunate to have found each other once again, Stefan."

"What does it matter?"

"I understand you are frustrated. But the Five Isles will be a much better place after Fiery Absolution, after history has again been made right, now that the angel stones and the weapons of the Five Warrior Angels are finally revealed for the curse and lies that they have always been."

"But why make Lindholf give useless weapons to the dragon riders?"

Stefan had always known the weapons of Laijon and the angel stones were a curse, and not for the reasons the Vallè likely believed them to be. "It's all pointless," he muttered, again remembering his conversation with Culpa Barra. "Everything you Vallè do is a contradiction. For what happens today will likely go down in some made-up religious text, likely to be misinterpreted a thousand years from now. It will all lead to more war and strife. Someone has to end it."

But could that someone be me? He looked at the large black cat with the silver eyes. *You have a destiny yet to fulfill,* Seita had said. Yet nobody seemed to know what that destiny was, not even Seita.

Or should a man make his own destiny, despite the views of others? "Your fate is now your own," she had said.

The five dragons soared above, all five heading toward Amadon and war, their leathery batlike wings stirring the smoke-hazed air. Though they flew high, Stefan could still see that the dragon riders wielded the weapons of the Five Warrior Angels, the ancient artifacts bequeathed to them by Lindholf Le Graven. And Stefan wondered if any of those weapons were even worth a damn. He still suspected that the power of the blue angel stone had cursed Gisela, but the weapons themselves had always seemed useless. The silver whips of the skull-faced Aalavarrè seemed far more deadly.

When the dragons were out of sight, Seita stood, brushing black puffs of ash away from her clothes. "I can't breathe in any more of this flesh-reeking smoke." She gestured to the empty dale before them. "Let us sit in the field. Let us sit in the grass."

Stefan left the comfort of the stone bench and followed the Vallè maiden to the bottom of the sunlit dale. Her blond hair rippled in the breeze, and he felt those stirrings for her in his heart once more. He followed her because she was the only one willing to talk to him about anything anymore. Where was Nail? He had seen Nail with the girl who had stolen Gisela. Where were Dokie and Liz Hen and Beer Mug? He had seen them under the Atonement Tree. They were likely all dead now.

Together Seita and Stefan sat in the cool grass, the fetid smoke of the dead hovering somewhere far above them now. Stefan kept the black bow pressed against his chest, a barrier between himself and the Vallè. The saber-tooth settled in the grass in front of Stefan, silver eyes alert.

"I see you've reclaimed Gisela." Seita eyed the weapon in his hands. "I recognized the bow when I first saw Bronwyn Allen at the Slaver's Inn with Tala and Nail. I knew she had taken it from you, thinking you were dead."

"I was dead," Stefan said. Then he suddenly felt sad for every friend he had ever had, sad for Gallows Haven and every village burned by the White Prince and every dead soldier lying in the Hallowed Grove around him.

"You miss your friends?" she asked.

"I miss"—he paused—"it matters not."

"You miss Gisela?" she said, eyeing the bow still.

They had had this same conversation before not long ago, a few days before he had died. "I don't wish to talk about it. I don't want to be here with you anymore, Seita."

"Do you wish me to leave, then?" She touched his thigh once again. He flinched away.

"What is it you are afraid of, Stefan?" she asked, her pure white hair fluttering in the breeze.

Stefan felt the emotion welling up within him. He had once thought Seita could see into his soul. He felt the tears build in the corner of his eyes—eyes that suddenly flooded with that maddening silver haze. He had once thought his love for her was like a river of pure light. But he saw no light around her now, just a flat silver haze, gray in its translucency.

"I'm rotting inside." He held Gisela out before him, examining the black bow and the black streaks of sickness flowing through the veins in his arms, realizing the rot growing in him was likely some Hragna'Ar curse. "I fear this rot is some form of penance for all the killing I've done."

"You have a tender heart." She reached out, running delicate fingers over a twining streak of rot under his skin. Her touch burned. The saber-tooth sensed his unease and growled at the Vallè.

Ignoring the cat, Seita leaned into him, placing her head on his shoulder, both of her hands wrapping around the black bow, pulling the weapon from him. An image of Gisela's frozen body on the way to the trail to the Swithen Wells Trail Abbey flashed into Stefan's mind.

He drew away from her. "Give the bow back to me."

"Why be afraid?" she asked, clutching the bow to her own chest. "Can't you see that clinging to this love that cannot be replaced is destroying you?"

All Stefan could see was Gisela's frozen pale face on the trail. He stood, towering over the Vallè, silver haze almost completely overtaking his vision. "Give the bow back to me." The saber-tooth stood, hissing low and threatening, silver eyes fixed on the Vallè.

Seita calmly handed the bow up to Stefan. He violently snatched it from her hands and walked away. "Where are you going?" she asked.

"Away from here," he said, stepping lightly up the grassy dale toward the scorched battlefield above, the large black cat following. "Away from here and far away from you, for I fear the next time we meet, one of us will die."

CHAPTER SIXTY-NINE
GAULT AULBREK

13TH DAY OF THE HEART MOON, 999TH YEAR OF LAIJON

AMADON, GUL KANA

Gault Aulbrek rode the Bloodeye mare through the streets of Amadon alone. The horse's eyes glowed with scarlet light in the smoke-filled air. Smears of blood dried on Gault's face and rusted oghul helm, sweat dripping from his brow in the sweltering midmorning heat. Blood also splattered his Vallè armor and Sør Sevier cape. Five dragons and their skull-faced riders circled above, breathing fire over the city. The people of Amadon fled before the dragons in terror, man, woman, and child. Even from a distance, Gault could see the five weapons the dragon riders now bore: *Afflicted Fire, Blackest Heart, Forgetting Moon, Ethic Shroud*, and *Lonesome Crown*.

He took the measure of his grim surroundings. Everything in Amadon was naught but bloody havoc and hopelessness. The cobbles below the mare's hooves were coated in gore and ash. He could smell the blood, coppery and hot. It was an intoxicating smell, and he drank it in. *This is what I was born for, my purpose, blood and war!* Ripe with killer instinct, he had slain everything in his path to reach the center of the city, ending the lives of oghul, Vallè, Dayknights, and Silver Guards. He had even slain Sør Sevier fighters.

He could just make out the bulky silhouette of the gladiator arena above the crumbled, burning rooftops in the distance. He guided the Bloodeye that way. It was a familiar landmark, at least. It seemed like he had lived five lifetimes since he had slain his cousin, Squireck Van Hester, on the sandy floor of that pit. *All the death I have seen. All the death my hands have caused.* He felt guilty for none of those deaths.

He rounded a corner, and a handful of Gul Kana knights fought a handful of oghuls in the street before him, smoking shops and tenements rising up on either side. A Dayknight on a tall brown destrier charged away from the battle, aiming for Gault, sword drawn. Gault spurred the Bloodeye toward the knight. The Dayknight met his charge, black sword swinging high and fast. Gault ducked the blow and stabbed out with his own Dayknight blade as the knight galloped by, opening the war charger's stomach wide. Entrails spilled from the screaming horse as it tumbled violently to the soot-smeared cobbles. The Dayknight was thrown clear, rolling. Gault whirled his own mount, spurring the Bloodeye toward the man a second time. The knight gathered his feet, bracing himself, sword up in defense. Gault struck hard, connecting with the knight's sword arm, nearly severing it. He whirled the Bloodeye and struck the stunned knight once more, a slashing blow across the left shoulder. The man buckled, dropping to his knees. Gault whirled a third time and chopped down, splitting the knight's head. The Bloodeye stomped the man's body, bellowing in heated rage as it did so. The mare was as berserk as he was. They were a good match.

Gault brought the beast under control, recalling a passage from *The Chivalric Illuminations of Raijael: Laijon hath set the faithful soldier on many a path toward destiny!* It was a nice sentiment. But the fact was, he'd killed the man before him with such ease, not because of some divine providence, but because he was the more skilled fighter. And that was that.

He spurred the horse away from the Gul Kana knights still battling with the oghuls. He rounded another corner, finding himself in a much larger and more crowded courtyard between two good-sized chapels. The fighting here was loud and intense under the smoky haze. Dead bodies lay all around; scores of Gul Kana knights were maniacally hacking at the overwhelming force of Vallè and oghul fighters swarming over them, bloodlust in their feverish eyes.

He spotted the king, Jovan Bronachell, and the Dayknight captain, Leif Chaparral, in the midst of the fighting. The duo were desperately battling their way through a rioting sea of braying oghuls near the smaller of the two chapels that lined the yard. Leif's Dayknight sword flashed in the smoky gloom. Jovan's own sword was slick with gore and blood. Leif's younger brother, Glade, was there with them, beating his own blade against the rusted armor of the oghul before him. The oghul fell and Gault saw the princess, Tala Bronachell, her own dagger slashing the air before her, keeping another small oghul at bay. Borden Bronachell was fighting several other oghuls right beside his daughter. He fought with a savagery Gault had rarely seen in a man.

Still, despite their gallant efforts, Jovan's group was swiftly hemmed in against the chapel wall. Gault spurred the Bloodeye that way, in hopes of killing not only the king and his family but also every oghul in the courtyard. Leif was the closest one to him, perhaps twenty paces away now, holding off a group of oghuls. He had lost his Dayknight helm somewhere in the battle. His long dark hair was a bloody tangle, dark-rimmed eyes intense with fear. He'd suffered some injuries already, and his sweat-drenched face was as pale as Riven Rock marble. There was a ragged hole in the black vambrace on his left arm, and blood poured from the battered armor. *The bastard might bleed out before I kill him.* He launched the Bloodeye toward the oghuls fighting Leif.

"Watch out!" Glade shouted to his brother, imposing himself between Leif and Gault's charge, his own face ripe with fear. "Let's send him to the underworld together, Leif!" he shouted, raising his sword.

Gault spurred the Bloodeye steed straight into Glade and the oghuls fighting Leif. Glade tumbled away and the oghuls scattered in a dizzying slurry of rusted weapons and armor. The Bloodeye crashed into Leif, the Dayknight's body sprawling under the horse's pounding hooves. Gault whirled his mount. Leif rose up from behind the horse, scarlet streaming from his wounded arm. Glade hauled himself to his feet too, imposing himself between Gault and his brother once more, sword swinging wildly.

"Smash him, Glade!" Leif yelled.

The Bloodeye danced aside, avoiding Glade's strike. Gault backed the mount away as Glade's sword swung a second time at the exposed legs of the Bloodeye. Gault blocked the blow with a kick of his armored boot. Then he struck down hard with his own sword, knocking the young Dayknight aside. Glade stumbled away, body spinning into a group of oghuls. The bloodthirsty beasts swarmed over him, dragging him to the ground, rusted cudgels and hammers bludgeoning his Dayknight armor. Glade's frantic face burst from the melee briefly, bloody mouth agape, sucking air before he was pulled back down. Jovan, Borden, and Tala Bronachell all leaped to the boy's rescue, pushing their way through the squirming bodies.

Leif, blood streaming from his injured his arm, struck at Gault, his attack sluggish and slow. Gault dodged the lumbering blow, his own blade stabbing down, sinking deep into the Dayknight captain's torn armor. Gault ripped the sword free and Leif folded to the cobbles, dark-rimmed eyes glazed in pain.

"No!" Jovan screamed as he broke from his fight with the oghuls, sword sweeping toward Gault. Jovan's sword spun to the ground as Gault easily parried the blow. Jovan tried dragging Gault from the saddle next. Desperation blazed in the king's eyes as he clawed at both Gault and the Bloodeye. The black mare spun, sending Jovan sprawling away toward Borden and Tala, who were still trying to rescue Glade.

Leif had crawled back up to his knees, blood streaming from many wounds now. He knelt before Gault on the cobbles. Gault swung down at Leif Chaparral one final time, his black sword taking the Dayknight captain's head at the shoulders. Leif's headless body toppled, blood pumping from the severed neck as his legs and feet shuddered and strained. Then his bowels broke in a rush of stink between his legs, brown and red leaking from the joints of his armor.

"No! Leif! No!" Jovan stared in horror at what remained of Leif. Then he faced Gault, snatching up Leif's abandoned Dayknight sword. "You killed him! Who the fuck are you? You bastard!" *They don't know who I am under this rusted oghul helm.*

With a surge of strength, Jovan swung the long weapon at Gault. The Bloodeye reared back, kicking the weapon away from Jovan. The king spun back to the ground once more, landing in a heap.

"You killed my brother!" Glade's bloody blade was now pointed up at Gault. Somehow the boy had risen from the pile of oghuls, though the beasts still wildly hacked at him from behind. Borden and Tala tried to fight the monsters off, but a heavy oghul ax smashed through Glade's Dayknight armor, opening him up in the middle. The boy's guts spilled onto the cobbles. He toppled forward, falling to his knees, eyes wide in both surprise and pain.

Borden and Tala Bronachell stepped back, stunned, horror washing over their faces as they watched the oghuls stomp through Glade's innards, hacking at his kneeling form. Jovan stood too, wild and fearful eyes gazing above the fray as if searching for some new horror.

Five fully armored war chargers shoved their way through the oghuls surrounding Glade, sending the beasts reeling away. Hawkwood was atop the lead destrier, long hair flowing behind him like a banner, curved sword whirling as he struck down the first oghul in his path. A blond-haired youth rode beside Hawkwood, his own weapon slashing at the nearest oghul.

"Nail!" a dark-eyed girl in a forest-green cloak called out to the blond boy. "To your left!" She loosed an arrow at an oghul to Nail's left. The beast dropped to the ground with an arrow quivering in its back. Nail whirled his mount, blond locks sweeping over his eyes. He flicked the hair away, calling out to the girl with the bow, "Thanks, Bronwyn!"

"Cromm!" Bronwyn shouted at a massive oghul on the war charger behind her. "Guard our rear!"

The fourth rider, Cromm, was a brute of an oghul. He fought his own kind with a grim determination, the huge iron maul in his straining fist running slick with oghul brains and blood.

The fifth rider behind Cromm was Gault's own stepdaughter, Krista Aulbrek. Her Bloodwood armor was covered in soot and gore, her black daggers whistling through the smoky air, slicing through oghul flesh with silent ease, opening necks and faces.

Gault urged the Bloodeye away from the fight and watched from a distance.

The number of oghuls surrounding Glade Chaparral swiftly diminished as the beasts fell dead under the weapons of the five newcomers. The girl named Bronwyn could shoot arrows faster than anyone Gault had ever seen. Soon oghuls lay everywhere, arrows sprouting from their bodies, and the fighting died down.

Hawkwood reached out for Jovan, pulling the king up on the saddle behind him. "We've got to get you out of here." The Sør Sevier man whirled his mount. "Grab Borden!" he shouted to Cromm. "Grab Tala!" he called to Nail.

Cromm vigorously hauled Borden Bronachell into the saddle behind him with one strong arm, the thin, bearded man looking startled. Nail reached down and helped the princess onto the back of his destrier.

Clinging to Nail's back, Tala swept her gaze over the courtyard, focusing on the pile of entrails on the cobbles before Glade. The boy was still kneeling in the mashed puddle of his own guts, desperately trying to scream. He began clawing at the cobbles before him with one hand, trying to rake the purple coils of his entrails back into his sagging stomach with the other.

"Bronwyn," Hawkwood called out to the girl. "End his suffering."

Bronwyn drew an arrow and aimed it at the dying boy.

"No!" Tala shouted. "I will do it!" The princess slid from the saddle behind Nail, a short silver dagger in her hand. She knelt before Glade on the gut-strewn cobbles.

"Save me, Tala." His lips pulled back in pain, his voice but a hoarse whisper, eyes bulging in naked terror. "I'm so afraid to die. Can you get me to the castle? Can they fix me there?"

"No, I can't get you to the castle," she said.

His eyes were on the dagger in her hand. "What are you doing then?"

"I'm only doing what is best." Without hesitation Tala rammed the blade straight into the side of Glade's neck, then ripped outward. Blood welled forth thick and red over his chest plate as his face turned yellow. He fell sideways onto the steaming coils of his own entrails, eyes staring lifelessly up at the her.

Tala dropped the dagger and stood, looking down at her handiwork without emotion. Then she turned and hauled herself back up onto the horse. Her face was grim and she did not even look at her brother or father as she settled into the saddle behind Nail.

It was then that Gault realized: if there had been even a drop of innocence left in the world, it was forever gone now. He remembered how Tala had attacked him in Sunbird Hall. She had attacked him in the belief that he was responsible for Jondralyn's grave injuries. He had admired young Tala's courage in defending her older sister. The truth was evident now—the young princess was a killer just like everyone else.

"That's my horse!" Krista's angry shout sliced though the silence. "Dread is my Bloodeye, and I shall have her back!" She stared over the top of her destrier's armored head. The tip of her black dagger was pointed between the horse's alert ears, straight at Gault. "Get off my horse, you mangy sack of shit," she hissed. The look in her eyes was cold, merciless.

Gault's heart failed a beat. *She doesn't recognize me either.* He forced the Bloodeye back another step. He fought against the fear that raked his soul and tore the helmet from his head, resting it on the saddlehorn.

"You!" she shouted, hostility in her voice.

She still hated him. The very thought hurt cold and dreadful, like a dagger plying into his heart, driving stinging bolts of pain through his every nerve ending. He could feel the black mare growing agitated under him, muscles bunching and coiling. He patted the side of the Bloodeye's neck. But the horse flinched away from his touch, blazing red eyes fixed on Krista. The beast would throw him soon. He could feel it.

"Get off the *horse!*" Krista shouted. "Dread is mine! I trained her! I am a Bloodwood! Give her to me!"

Gault sensed something in the air. Something beyond him and his stepdaughter, something sleek and sinuous pulling at his mind. He sensed eyes of pure evil watching him now, and he felt a light-headedness steal over his entire body.

Then a shriek echoed above the courtyard and the air was instantly hot. Fire boiled malicious and orange and blistering overhead. Gault ducked the heat, cringing from the pain of the horrendous noise. A bright blue dragon swooped low over the courtyard, roiling flame a constant stream thundering from its mouth, igniting the buildings to his left. Massive, batlike wings stirred the smoke, covering the bloody dead in the courtyard below in swirling wisps of black soot.

The fire ceased and the dragon sailed high into the sky. Gault could scarcely see the monster's skull-faced rider through the sudden droplets of sweat running from his forehead and down into his eyes. The dragon turned and glided back down toward the courtyard. With another loud cry, the beast landed in the middle of the cobbled yard not fifty paces away from Gault and Krista and the others.

The skull-faced knight in blue armor slid gracefully from the beast's scaled back. A glimmering barbed whip was hooked to the knight's hip, droplets of hissing silver dripping to the cobbles. And strapped to the dragon rider's back was the double-bladed battle-ax, *Forgetting Moon*.

The skull-faced knight reached back with both gauntleted hands and hauled the battle-ax over his shoulder. The blue-clad knight set his stance, cloak flowing out behind in the breeze. The flat silver eyes under the silver mask seemed to scan the entire courtyard at once. The blue dragon rose up behind the blue knight, the two together looking like the indestructible demons of the underworld that they were.

"Let's go!" Jovan's face was stricken with fear. But nobody moved. Jovan set his own heels to the flanks of Hawkwood's destrier hard and sharp, causing the armored destrier to buck. The young king tumbled off the backside of the warhorse and landed in a heap on the hard, bloody stone of the courtyard. Hawkwood remained astride the mount.

The skull-faced knight drifted toward the fallen king, battle-ax gripped in both hands, coiled whip at his belt. Hawkwood backed away from the fallen king.

"Run, Jovan!" Borden called out. "Run!"

Jovan stood, then froze in place, arms hanging at his sides. And the dragon rider struck swift and sure, the curved blade of *Forgetting Moon* slicing through the young king's arm, burying itself deep into the Dayknight armor just above Jovan's hip. The king's arm fell to the cobbles, severed at the elbow.

The skull-faced knight wrenched the ax blade free of Jovan's plate armor and drew back a step, curious.

Nobody moved, not even Jovan.

Jovan dropped to one knee and, with his free hand, picked up his severed arm. He held the limp armored appendage up to his round, surprised eyes.

Tala stared hollow-eyed at her brother, her arms wrapped around Nail, her quivering chin resting on the back of the boy's shoulder. Cromm and Bronwyn sought to retreat, their mounts backing slowly.

"No!" Borden cried out, trying to slide from the horse's back behind Cromm. The oghul reached back with one burly hand and held the man in place.

"No!" Borden fought against the oghul's much stronger grasp.

The blue dragon roared. A terror unlike anything Gault had ever felt before swept through him. He struggled to escape the bitter grasp of fear and repulsion the dragon's ominous scream bred within him. He mustered what strength he could just to urge the Bloodeye mare under him to slowly back away. But the black horse struggled to move. In fact, everyone's mount was huffing for air, jittery and scared. Still the dragon roared.

The knight in blue-scaled armor stood over Jovan, huge silver battle-ax in both hands. And Jovan just knelt there on the cobbles, holding his arm out, blood draining from the wound in his side and the stump of his arm. Then, with one gauntleted hand, the dragon rider reached up and removed the skull-shaped mask covering its face.

Gault found he was staring at some twisted version of a Vallè. The knight's ghostly visage was slender, pale, and fine; chin, lips, nose, and brows seemingly cut of brilliant white marble, though the creature's ears were somehow more thin and pointed than a Vallè's. The feylike demon stared right back at Gault with stony eyes of flat silver, delicate lids blinking slow and purposefully. "Kill that one." The dragon rider pointed with *Forgetting Moon* at Gault.

The dragon roared again, and a soul-shattering pain seemed to burn its way through Gault's heaving chest. His lungs called for air so sharply that all other senses were dulled into complete immobility. He watched as the dragon circled around the pale knight, then stalked forward.

The Bloodeye mare under Gault snorted in terror as the dragon's mouth yawned open with a murderous hiss, fangs bloody and wet, fearsome and sharp.

Then Gault found himself awash in a flame of crimson light as fire pulsed in waves from the dragon's open mouth, setting everything in the courtyard alight.

Gault dug heels to flanks. The horse under him screamed. The Bloodeye mare whirled and bolted down the street in the opposite direction as a searing heat flashed and burned against Gault's skin. All was bright hot oblivion. It felt as if the entire courtyard was folding over onto itself, throbbing with orange light, a blossoming bloody redness that swarmed and slithered with flaming symbols, wavering pockets of illuminated squares and circles within circles and even crosses, all of them a-twinkle, all of them aglitter and glowing in the red-flowing fire.

And as the Bloodeye fled the flaming horror, Gault risked a glance back and saw Krista staring right at him, standing firm in her Bloodwood cloak and hood, the swirling, fiery chaos boiling around her.

CHAPTER SEVENTY
MANCELLOR ALLEN

13TH DAY OF THE HEART MOON, 999TH YEAR OF LAIJON

AMADON, GUL KANA

There's rats everywhere in this tunnel," Liz Hen Neville exclaimed, plopping down against the flat stone wall of the passageway. Jenko Bruk glared at the girl, the flickering torchlight only adding to the angry look of his chiseled face. Liz Hen glared right back at him. "You've been giving me the hairy eyeball ever since we entered these tunnels, Jenko."

The two had been arguing since they had started the journey. This was only their third rest break, and Mancellor Allen was growing weary of their incessant bickering.

"Stop giving me dark looks." Liz Hen stared at Jenko angrily.

"If you wouldn't blabber so much." Jenko sat against the opposite wall.

"I blabber because you give me dark looks."

"If I'm giving you any dark looks, it's purely because I'm tired of hearing your voice, tired of hearing you moan about these tunnels, the darkness, our torches running out, Mancellor's not being bright enough, the rats, your stomach being hungry, your sore back, your sore neck, your sore legs, your sore everything, Blood of the Dragon, whatever that is. I'm just tired. I imagine Mancellor is too."

"Blood of the Dragon is a drink. It soothes my mouth."

"I ought to slap your mouth."

"I ain't afraid of you, Jenko." The girl's eyes narrowed to slits. "You know, since we parted in Gallows Haven, I've killed knights and oghuls too."

"Did you sit on them?"

"I could kill you next."

"By sitting on me?"

"I should have squished you to death when we were held captive in Gallows Haven."

"Please just stop, you two!" Mancellor said, looking down the length of the dark tunnel. Liz Hen was right: his torch was not bright enough. "I can only hear so much of your arguing." He desperately wished he had a water skin. He was thirsty. The dim glow of his flickering torch created a pocket of light around them, burnishing both Jenko's and Liz Hen's faces in a sullen yellow haze. They were a ragged and blood-splattered sight, faces lined with worry and fatigue. Mancellor figured he must look the same, beaten and defeated. "Soon we will have no light," he muttered.

His torch was the last one they had, Liz Hen's and Jenko's having burned out hours ago. They had been wandering this maze of tunnels for what felt like days. Rumor was, even in his homeland of Wyn Darrè, that the tunnels under Amadon were vast, but he had had no idea until now. The unbearable blackness of the accursed passageway was suffocating. The ever-growing darkness bled through the air and into every corner of Mancellor's soul. He feared that once his torch went out, they would be left wandering the endless caverns and corridors like desperate, forgotten ghosts.

The unrelenting upward gradient they had been following was so gentle as to be almost imperceptible, but Mancellor figured they should have surfaced into daylight by now. Jenko had led the way until his torch had burned out. Mancellor had taken over. At every fork in the road, he had chosen the route that seemed to go up. If they came across a staircase or passageway that didn't go up, they doubled back until he found one that did. They bypassed many locked iron grates and empty storage rooms. Water wept from cracks in the wall in some places, and in other places they had to trudge through tunnels running ankle-deep with sewage. Mancellor found he had to breathe through his mouth to avoid the stench in his nose. Despite how much his body craved the water, he dared not drink. It was rough going.

But in a way, Mancellor felt lucky to still be alive. He couldn't help but wonder if something of the divine hadn't intervened as he had fallen into the slave quarry. The fall should have killed him. He should have been crushed in the pile of bodies. Still, somehow he had survived. The Silver Guard shortsword he carried was also one small solace. It was protection of a sort. Jenko still carried the crude oghul battle-ax he had snatched from the passageway floor. And Liz Hen still bore the black Dayknight sword she had found. Jenko was right in that Liz Hen had complained nonstop about her sore neck and back. She was lucky that was all she'd suffered from the fall. Jenko seemed unhurt, or if he was in pain, he did not mention it. Mancellor detected that he himself had only a few injuries, a lightly twisted ankle along with an agonizing pain growing deep within his shoulder.

He wondered if the princess Tala Bronachell had lived through the horror of Fiery Absolution. He had seen her face in his dreams, in his visions when he was drowning in the Saint Only Channel with the mermaid's tail wrapped around him. Delusions. He knew he should not read anything into those visions. *These tunnels are making you crazy. They are full of the wraiths.* The thought struck Mancellor's gut like a hollow drum. "We mustn't tarry here for long," he said, rubbing his hand through his matted tangle of hair. "There are things that hunt us down here."

"Hunt us?" Liz Hen looked worried.

"More like haunt us," he said. "Anyway, my torch is nearly dead, and we've yet to find our way free of this place."

"I can see your torch is almost dead." Liz Hen picked herself up off the cold stone floor. "And I know we haven't found our way out of this place. You needn't point out the obvious."

"We should just keep moving," Mancellor grumbled. "No more breaks."

Jenko stood and they carried onward.

As they trudged on, Liz Hen let the tip of her Dayknight sword scrape along the floor. The noise was irritating, but Mancellor didn't have the energy to tell her to stop, nor, it seemed, did Jenko.

"I need a sandwich," Liz Hen said after a while. "I think I can remember the details of every sandwich I ever ate."

"I bet you could," Jenko said.

"What's that supposed to mean?" Liz Hen asked, and Mancellor feared their arguing would start up anew.

"It means whatever you want it to mean," Jenko snapped.

"Whatever," Liz Hen mumbled, and then went silent.

After a dozen more twists and turns and dark stairways that spiraled down into the darkness and who knew where, they reached a tunnel that widened out to triple the size of any tunnel they had traveled before. This passageway appeared newer, with freshly chiseled walls, and eventually led them to an even wider set of stairs leading up into the blackness. They followed it, climbing. The bitter air of the previous passageways was soon gone. Mancellor breathed in what he thought was fresh air, and his dwindling torch almost seemed to flicker with renewed light.

Upward they went, stair after stair, one belabored step at a time until they came to a pair of heavily barred stone doors. Handing the torch to Liz Hen, Mancellor helped Jenko lift the heavy iron bar. Then they put their shoulders to the stone door and pushed it open just enough for the three of them to slip through.

They were confronted by another set of stairs leading up into a vast darkness. Liz Hen grunted her disappointment at the sight. Still they climbed, for there was no turning back nor anywhere else to go.

"I do believe I am getting tired," Jenko huffed in exasperation.

"I've been tired for a while now," Liz Hen countered. "So don't tell me you're just getting tired now, Jenko, 'cause I won't believe it."

"I've been tired and sore since we started," Mancellor said.

"Do you think we will live the rest of our lives in these horrible tunnels?" Liz Hen asked.

"Laijon have mercy," Jenko said. "But I hope not."

"They say that when you die, your life passes before your eyes," Liz Hen said. "Do you think that will happen to us, Jenko? Even though we will die slowly down here in the dark and have plenty of time to do it, do you think our lives will pass before our eyes? I mean, there won't be a singular 'right before we die' moment. It will happen slowly, I reckon. Still, do you think our lives will pass before our eyes?"

"That's stupid," Jenko said.

"I think it's a thoughtful observation, considering where we are and our likely fate."

"Just die already, would you, and spare us your idiocy."

But Liz Hen carried on, "I think I'm involved in dying right now indeed. Slowly. Dying, dying, dying, just awaiting my life to pass before me."

"Laijon have mercy and take me now," Jenko exclaimed. "Just take me now, please, Laijon just take me now and spare me her jabber."

"Laijon won't have you, Jenko Bruk," Liz Hen said. "No. He won't have one like you at all. Nothing can spare you my jabber."

"Your arguments are always so pointless and asinine," Jenko grumbled.

"My arguments are proof and reassurance that we are not alone in this dark place," Liz Hen huffed. "You should be thanking me, not cursing me, Jenko Bruk."

The conversation fell silent again after that.

It seemed another hour dragged by as they climbed, Mancellor's torch dwindling to just a flicker of red coals now, the darkness pressing in around them as they stumbled over heaps of broken rock piled on the stairs. The light was growing so dim that Mancellor found he was searching the floor with his free hand now, tracing the stairs before him, feeling his way along.

A whisper of a breeze touched the back of his neck, and he saw a sliver of light from the corner of his eye. It was but soft wan light streaming through a cleft in the ceiling just ahead. Still, in the dark, it was a glorious beam of hazy white, slanting down through the dust and over the stairs above.

Mancellor stretched his hand out into the beam.

"We've reached the surface," Liz Hen exclaimed.

Mancellor pressed his face to the ceiling above and peered into the crack from whence the light had sprung. He found himself under another stone door, this one lying flat on top of them. The fissure between the door and the doorjamb was slender, but the light streaming through was almost so blinding it hurt Mancellor's eyes.

Together, he and Jenko braced themselves against the stairs and pushed the stone door up and open with their backs and shoulders, grunting and shoving their way up onto sandy ground and glorious light . . .

. . . and the savage aftermath of Fiery Absolution.

The dead were strewn across the blood-soaked floor of the gladiator arena. Men, women, and children lay everywhere, their guts tossed about in steaming bundles and piles, flies buzzing in and out of their gaping mouths. Rats were busy chewing holes through the exposed privates and anuses of every corpse. Death filled the air with its cloying stench of blood, shit, and human decay. It appeared as if thousands of Amadon's inhabitants had tried to hide in this grand stone structure, to no avail. The stands, the sandy floor of the arena, all of it was covered with the dead.

"They just might be the deadest group of people I ever seen," Liz Hen observed, climbing the remaining stairs into the light, squinting against the harsh sun glaring down above the arena grandstands, her narrow gaze roaming over the smoldering destruction. Ash kicked up and drifted about the grim structure like black snow.

As Mancellor emerged from the dark hole in the center of the arena and stepped farther into the sunlight, the vastness of Amadon's arena engulfed him: lofty columns, crenellated balconies, bulky grandstands, stonework palisades that rose up in a broad circle over stone bleachers. In Mancellor's estimation, the place could easily hold over ten thousand spectators. There were probably that many burned corpses in the stands now. Black-and-silver banners fluttered and snapped in the very wind that stirred the ash.

Mancellor felt the aches and pains that filled his bones and muscles. After so long in the dark, everything here in this gladiator pit seemed to have a heightened intensity about it. The warm breeze caressed his face, rippling the tattered awnings over the arena's larger boxes and suites. *How long were we underground?* he couldn't help but ask himself. *And what new horror have we stumbled upon?*

A rattle of chains echoed through the gladiator pit. Mancellor, Jenko, and Liz Hen whirled to find the giant double doors of the arena opening. Ten Amadon Silver Guards pushed through the crack in the door and ran out into the arena. Fire raged in the city streets behind them before they shoved the door closed.

A green dragon appeared with a thunderous roar, gliding over the top of the arena directly above the doors the Silver Guards had just entered through. The skull-faced demon atop the dragon wore green-scaled armor that glowed as bright as the dragon's luminescent eyes.

"The dragon rider wears *Lonesome Crown!*" Jenko exclaimed. "Look, Mancellor, the dragon rider wears *Lonesome Crown!* I swear that's it!"

To Mancellor, it did look like the horned helm atop the skull-faced knight was *Lonesome Crown.*

Then the dragon roared. Mancellor suddenly could not breathe. And the pain in his ears was intense. It felt like he was swimming, feet no longer touching the sand of the arena. The throbbing sensation rolling through his head was akin to being back in the Battle of the Saint Only Channel, drowning in the swells of the sea. Water folding over him, water pressing inward on his lungs with a stark harshness as the slithery arms and webbed hands of a pale mermaid encircled him, her tail coiling around his legs, her serrated gills heaving as she kept him in her bitter grasp. Pain scorched through his heaving chest as his lungs called for air.

He found himself awash in a flame of crimson light as the dragon soared above the arena, screeching like wild thunder, breathing fire over the dead and dying in the grandstands. Both Jenko and Liz Hen were struggling for air, the same as he. It was as if the dragon held them all spellbound under its flaming cry. And it only got worse.

Mancellor couldn't grasp a breath, mouth open in a silent scream, hands over his ears to block out the fiery shrieks of the dragon above. He prayed to Laijon. His eyes burned with pain while continuous fire, red and hot, blossomed from the dragon as it circled the stands.

Mancellor suddenly couldn't see, and everything was pitched in black. The mermaid returned with her visions, her hazy images fluttering in the air, half-formed images wild and confusing. He again saw *himself* in those visions. Saw himself fighting in a gladiator arena, Jenko at his side. A green dragon. A skull face. A city of snow-stained streets melting in rivers of boiling silver and blood. A young queen on a silver throne. A girl he desperately loved, but could never have . . .

. . . but this reality was different, as strange thoughts crept unbidden into his mind. The snow was black ash and the young girl was *Tala Bronachell!*

Something crashed into him and his visions were ripped away.

"You're facing the wrong direction!" Liz Hen was yelling into his face, spittle flying from her raging mouth. "The dragon is over there! We have to kill it!"

Kill it! Mancellor's mind reeled as he turned, almost drunkenly, and stared.

The dragon had already landed on the floor of the arena.

The skull-faced dragon rider dismounted, *Lonesome Crown* atop his head. The green-clad knight walked toward the group of ten trembling Silver Guards, whip uncoiling in one gauntleted hand, droplets of silver burning into the sand, hissing and smoking in the demon's wake. The skull-faced knight drew the whip back in a flash of silver, striking fast and furious at the ten cowering knights. The flashing weapon sliced into the chest plate of the nearest Silver Guard. Bloody streaks of flesh and viscera instantly washed down the side of the man's armor. The man screamed. The remaining nine knights scattered as the second strike of the silver whip cut the first knight completely in half. The skull-faced knight brought his deadly weapon hissing down against the back of one of the fleeing Gul Kana fighters, barbed silver whip splitting the knight's helm wide. The dead man slid down into the sand.

"We have to fight!" Liz Hen shouted, sweaty hair pressed to her forehead. "We have to kill the dragon and the rider if we're to survive!"

"Are you crazy!" Jenko shouted back at her. "How do we slay such demons?"

"We can't run scared anymore, Jenko Bruk!" She whirled and charged toward the skull-faced knight and the green dragon, Dayknight sword whirling over her head.

"Bloody rotted angels," the Gallows Haven boy swore, hefting the rusted oghul ax, dashing after the girl. "That red-haired bitch won't out-brave Jenko Bruk!"

Without thinking, Mancellor charged after Jenko and Liz Hen, churning legs carrying him across the blood-soaked sand, leaping over the heaps and piles of the dead, dodging the fleeing Silver Guards. *Madness!* his mind screamed with every pained step, knowing this was the moment he would die.

Both the dragon and dragon rider faced Liz Hen, Jenko, and Mancellor. A short burst of flame shot from the beast's mouth. A wave of fire and heat hurled Mancellor against one of the fleeing Silver Guards, knocking them both to the ground. The dragon whirled, launching fire at three knights fleeing in the opposite direction. Mancellor clambered to his feet and joined the attack with Jenko and Liz Hen.

Several of the Silver Guards launched arrows at the dragon. The monster leaped aside, spiked tail whipping out, smashing into Mancellor's shoulder, tossing him into the air. He landed in a spray of sand, sword still gripped in hand. He lost sight of Jenko and Liz Hen, the arena now a swirl of chaos. A handful of the Gul Kana knights were attempting to climb up the side of the arena and escape into the grandstands. The dragon unleashed a long blast of flame their way. The men burned as they tried to lift themselves over the stone railings, one by one dropping to the sand, bodies flaming and dead.

"Help us, you fool!" Jenko screamed.

Mancellor spotted Jenko and Liz Hen, along with one of the Silver Guards, facing off against the skull-faced knight with the silver whip. The dragon rider still wore *Lonesome Crown* atop his head, the sweeping white horns of the helm almost glowing with a magic and power all their own. Liz Hen brandished her Dayknight sword, Jenko the rusted oghul ax. The Silver Guard wielded a long spear. They looked helpless before the skull-faced knight and the dripping silver whip. With a crack and flash, the barbs of the whip sliced the hapless Gul Kana knight in half, bruise-colored guts slithering over the ash-coated sands.

Mancellor lurched toward the fight. But with a roar, the dragon imposed itself between them, blocking the way, its glowing green eyes keen and piercing right at him. Mancellor froze, spellbound. The dragon slithered toward him, nostrils puffing gusts of fetid heat into his face.

A Gul Kana knight attacked the dragon from the side. Then the dragon's long neck craned around as fire burst from its toothy maw, lighting the knight in orange. Mancellor lifted the sword high, bringing it crashing down onto the exposed neck of the dragon. The blade glanced off the green scales. A second Silver Guard ran up and struck the dragon too, a futile blow that snapped his sword.

The dragon turned on both Mancellor and the Gul Kana knight, scales rippling with emerald light. Massive batlike wings spread wide as the beast reared up on two hind legs and lunged forward, forelegs swiping swift as a cat. Huge claws raked the arena floor. Blood, ash, and sand sprayed up into Mancellor's eyes as he reeled backward, falling to the gut-strewn ground once again. Unable to see, he crawled through the gritty sluice of blood and guts and slime in a frantic effort to escape the screaming monster bearing down, awaiting the fire that would consume him.

But the fire never came. Instead Mancellor felt the creature's sharp claws stamp down hard on every side of him. The beast's leathery paw pressed down against his back, pushing him face-first into the sand. With all the strength he could muster, Mancellor fought against the unbearable weight pushing on him from above. He was at the complete mercy of the beast. The Gul Kana knight who had been fighting at his side was pressed under the dragon's other leathery paw. He was trapped like Mancellor—like prison bars, sharp claws dug into the sands on every side of the man. But unlike Mancellor, the other knight was faceup, the full weight of the dragon on his chest.

The dragon's broad snout and steaming nostrils swept over the straining torso of the Gul Kana knight. Then the beast's mouth yawned open with a grumbling low hiss, biting down, then tearing upward, gutting the Silver Guard from neck to pubis, the lancelike teeth deftly stripping all muscle and meat from the man's bones. Mancellor felt the soldier's warm blood sheet across his face as the dragon clawed at the dead knight until naught was left but a mass of flesh and blood. Mancellor's vision blurred and the world seemed to swim away.

"Beer Mug!" Liz Hen shouted with joy as a gray blur streaked across the bloody sands, launching itself toward the face of the green monster. The shepherd dog leaped onto the scaled snout of the dragon, gleaming teeth immediately wrapping around one of the pointed spikes jutting between the beast's glowing green eyes. The dog dangled from the spike, hind legs churning, hind paws digging into the right eye of the dragon for purchase. The dragon screamed and roared and reared back onto its own two back legs, fire spewing from its mouth straight into the air.

With the weight of the dragon's forepaws no longer bearing down on his back, Mancellor shot to his hands and knees and sputtered for air as he scrambled forward, barely able to see through all the blood and grit in his eyes. He aimed toward the blurry forms of Jenko and Liz Hen as the dragon thrashed and roared above, Beer Mug still attached to the spike, hind legs still churning, digging into the gelatinous green eye.

"Kill it, Beer Mug!" Liz Hen yelled. "Kill it!"

Mancellor stood, swiped the grime from his face. The whip-wielding dragon rider was no longer facing off against Jenko and Liz Hen. Instead the skull-faced demon was moving toward the dragon, whip licking out, trying to strike the dog attached to the dragon's face. Glowing green fluids oozed livid and raw from the dragon's right eye. Beer Mug's hind paws still clawed at the wounded orb, which now bled crystallized emerald blood over the sand.

"Kill it!" Liz Hen bellowed again. "Chew those shit-green eyes right out of its shit-green fucking head!" Then, seeing the dragon rider had its back to her, Liz Hen lunged forward and swung her long black sword at the back of the knight's head, knocking *Lonesome Crown* spinning to the sand, staggering the demon. The dragon rider whirled, reaching up with one gauntleted hand and removing the silver skull mask. The pale-faced creature underneath stared at Liz Hen with a steady, sunken animosity in its flat silver eyes.

Jenko struck at the knight from the left. The dragon rider ducked the blow, whip slicing the air, crackling silver cutting into the rusted ax in the boy's hands.

Liz Hen, seeing that the dragon rider was distracted, stabbed the tip of her sword deep into the side of the demon's pale face. Green blood welled from the wound, glowing and bright. The dragon rider was suddenly struggling to stay upright, the silver whip dropping from limp fingers, hissing as it hit the sand. Liz Hen stabbed again, hitting the dragon rider in the throat. The ashen-faced knight fell backward to the ground.

"Fuck you and the hairy crab-crawling asshole that shit you out!" Liz Hen screamed as she stabbed the tip of her sword into the creature's pale face over and over, tears streaming down her face.

"Bloody Mother Mia!" Jenko exclaimed. "You kilt it already, girl!"

Liz Hen ripped her weapon free of the knight's mangled face one last time. "Lady Death take you!" she shouted. Then she spat on the dead demon.

Beer Mug still fought with the dragon. The dog's hind paws dug into the beast's other eye now. The blind monster thrashed and lurched and bellowed like thunder, fire erupting from its mouth, billowing hot and orange into the smoke-laden sky. The dragon's batlike wings unfurled, flapping out of control now, sweeping across the arena floor, stirring sand, ash, and blood over the dead. Then the creature launched itself into the air.

Beer Mug released his hold on the spike and fell to the arena floor. He landed softly in the sand, tail wagging in triumph, muzzle drenched in bright green blood.

Blinded, the dragon flew away, gaining speed, then crashed head-long into the upper tiers of the arena, brick and mortar crumbling with the impact. The beast flopped down the grandstands uncontrollably, tan-colored awnings tangled in its spikes and wings. As the beast tumbled and rolled, it bellowed in frustration and pain, fire from its gaping mouth blackening the rows of stone benches and walls of the arena. The dragon regained its feet and launched itself into the air once again, taking with it the string of tan awnings. Up the creature flew almost drunkenly, weaving wildly into the smoke-clouded sky and out of sight. And the arena was once again calm.

Mancellor dropped to his knees, all the strength having fled from his body.

"Holy shit," Liz Hen exclaimed. "Wasn't that something, make no mistake."

"That's for damn sure," Jenko agreed.

Liz Hen dropped to her knees, suddenly in tears. She buried her round freckled face in Beer Mug's green-stained neck, nuzzling the fur. "You saved us!" She drew her face away from the dog, looking him square in the eyes. "I knew you weren't dead!" She held Beer Mug's head in both of her hands, blubbering now. "I knew you would find us, Beer Mug! I just knew it!"

The dog's tail was a blur of joyfulness as he began licking her face. The girl squealed, pulling away from the dog. "You're covered in green dragon blood!"

The dog cocked his head, a hurt look in his eyes.

"Well, I reckon it ain't poison." She ruffled the dog's blood-covered head. "Besides, it ain't your fault anyway. I hugged you first."

Beer Mug's tail was once again a-wag as she let him lick her. Liz Hen and the dog looked a splendid pair. *One small joy in this bloody horror of a gladiator pit,* Mancellor thought.

"You're one lucky bastard." Jenko reached down to help Mancellor to his feet. "I thought that dragon was going to eat you for sure."

Mancellor stood on shaky legs. "Me too. Bloody thing almost crushed me."

"Rotted angels, but ain't we all lucky?" Jenko stepped toward the dead dragon rider. He reached for the silver whip coiled in the sand.

"Don't!" Mancellor reached out, staying Jenko's hand. "I wouldn't be touching anything made of that silver. I wouldn't touch anything that came out of the underworld, for that matter. Who knows what curses lie upon it?"

It looked like Jenko wanted to pick up the whip and the silver mask lying in the sand near the dead knight. The strange glowing green blood pooled under the dragon rider's body was soaking into the sand. "Mancellor is right," Liz Hen agreed. "That whip will likely melt your face off, Jenko Bruk."

"The silver on the whip looks to have turned solid," Jenko said, kneeling by the weapon, not touching it, though.

"I still wouldn't trust anything that came up from the underworld," Mancellor reiterated.

"You're probably right." Jenko stood. "But that helmet is mine." He stepped over the dead dragon rider, snatched up *Lonesome Crown,* and placed the helm over his head.

"You look like a real gladiator now, Ser Jenko Bruk." Liz Hen climbed to her feet, ruffling the fur atop Beer Mug's head. "You look like a real hero for sure."

"Are you mocking me?" Jenko removed the helm and glared at her. "What do you mean?"

"I mean you look like a gladiator is all," Liz Hen said. "A real hero."

"There ain't no heroes in this war," Jenko said. "And I'm no gladiator."

"This is a gladiator arena, isn't it?" The girl gestured to the vast columned structure surrounding them. "And we just won a fight."

Jenko answered with a dark look.

"Fine," Liz Hen said, shaking her head. "Don't take the compliment. Be a bore. 'Twas Beer Mug that got rid of that dragon anyway. Should be Beer Mug wearing that helmet, not you. Should be Beer Mug claiming the spoils of war instead of you. Should be the dog we name the gladiator." She knelt and snuggled the dog again. "Don't any of us ever underestimate what Beer Mug can do." She looked up at Jenko. "Or perhaps I should claim the spoils of war. I kilt the dragon rider, after all. Together me and Beer Mug chased away a dragon and kilt a dragon rider." She looked at the dog once more, face full of joy. "We've kilt a demon of the underworld, Beer Mug. Me and you. Gladiators. Dokie won't believe it." She glared up at Jenko once more.

Jenko grunted something indecipherable. Then he kicked at the dragon rider's cloak, toeing it open with his boot as if searching for something. "Do you think this dead guy carried one of the angel stones too?"

"If so, they are cursed." Liz Hen scowled. "Just leave that dead demon alone, Jenko Bruk. It's not good to go poking around in the affairs of the underworld."

"But we can't just leave an angel stone here if he has it."

"Oh, yes we can. Those angel stones are cursed, I said."

Jenko ignored her, knelt, and searched the dead knight thoroughly, but found nothing. When he was done, he placed *Lonesome Crown* back on his head and stared at Mancellor. "We should leave this place," he said.

Mancellor agreed. Together, the three of them walked from the arena, Beer Mug bounding along behind.

CHAPTER SEVENTY-ONE

TALA BRONACHELL

13TH DAY OF THE HEART MOON, 999TH YEAR OF LAIJON

AMADON, GUL KANA

Tala Bronachell felt the darkness growing within her. *I killed Glade Chaparral, and I did it coldly and without thought or feeling. Dare I say I did it with joy?*

Dare I say I would like to see more die at my hand?

Death surrounded her, and she wanted more. She wanted vengeance. Tala could tell something had changed within her. She felt the stirrings within her heart, felt the wraiths work their dark magic. She wondered how she could ever be the same again, for to take a life was no small thing. *And I took Glade's with such casual cruelty.*

It was late afternoon, the sun just a faint glow in the smoky haze. Stone statues, hammered and carved into the forms of long-dead saints, rose up above her. The crowns atop the various stone heads of the saints had once been home to pigeons, but like the grass below, they were now blanketed in ash. The tall stone monuments cast long shadows over the tombstone-laden cemetery, and over the dying king.

Jovan Bronachell lay propped up against the feet of one of the saintly gray sculptures, his father desperately trying to stanch the blood welling from his severed arm. Nail was also in the graveyard, helping Borden. Hawkwood was there too. As was the Wyn Darrè girl, Bronwyn Allen, along with the oghul Cromm Cru'x. Krista Aulbrek was a new face, and Tala did not like the looks of the Bloodwood assassin.

Tala's harried and beleaguered group had found the small graveyard after fleeing the courtyard of flame and death. Like Gault Aulbrek, they had fled from the fires of the blue dragon. They had fled through streets strewn with chaos and war to this enclosed cemetery and the seclusion it offered. The entire group had collapsed in exhaustion on the grass, Bronwyn and Cromm leaning against tombstones, Hawkwood and Krista sprawled out on their backs staring straight up at the smoky sky, Nail and Borden tending to Jovan.

An ash-choked brook wound through the center of the graveyard—a once clear stream of cool waters. Tala wished she could drink from it, her mouth was so parched. But everything was so black and hot, including the water.

Beyond the stone fence enclosing the cemetery, Tala's whole world was burning. And it was the gruesome images of the dead children that had scarred her the most. She was lost and felt alone, though many allies still surrounded her. She had so many questions and emotions that, at sixteen, she could not handle.

Leif Chaparral is dead.

Glade is dead!

Borden and Jovan and Ansel were all the family she had left. And Jovan was dying.

Tala just wished something would come swooping out of the sky and pluck her from war's madness. She wished some magic would just whisk her away to safety.

"Where is my Leif?" Tala's brother muttered in delirium.

"He's dead," Borden said, still trying to stop the flow of blood welling from the stump of Jovan's arm with one hand, tying his own belt above the wound with the other to act as a tourniquet.

"How can Leif be dead?" Jovan muttered.

"He just is." Borden cinched the leather belt tight.

Even with his arm strapped, blood still flowed, and Tala knew Jovan would swiftly bleed out. There would be no time to mourn his death. She still could not believe that Leif Chaparral was dead, slain by Gault Aulbrek. That Glade was dead too. She shivered with trauma and guilt. She had hated him so venomously.

Should I feel disgusted with myself? Should I feel angry? Should I feel sad?

No, in war there was no time to mourn the dead. She had read that in one of Jondralyn's adventure books. It made sense now. She couldn't help but wonder what had happened to her cousins. *Where is Lindholf? Where is Lawri?* The last she had seen of the twins, they were atop a brilliant white stallion, leading the charge of Fiery Absolution, five colorful dragons circling over their heads.

"Where is Leif?" Jovan asked again, trying to sit up. "Why did we leave him? We need to go back."

"He's dead," Borden repeated, holding Jovan down. Nail helped him. Tala could see the color bleed from her brother's pallid flesh. With every pump of his heart, Jovan grew more pale and the pool of blood in the grass under his arm spread.

"I love him," Jovan said. "We cannot leave my love to die."

"Leif's already dead," Borden repeated.

"But I love him."

"He was like your brother, I know," Borden said. "You loved him as a brother."

"I was in love with him," Jovan said.

Every time her brother mentioned his love for Leif, a pang of regret and sadness spread through Tala's heart.

"I love him," Jovan said once more, weakly, eyes hazy with tears.

"He is dead," Borden repeated. "You must let him go."

"I cannot. I love him."

"Quiet now," Borden said. "Rest now."

"You do know that he really *was* in love with Leif." Hawkwood sat up, his gaze cutting into Borden's. "Or are you that obtuse?"

Borden's eyes drew down into dark slits. "What do you mean?"

"I mean your son was in a romantic relationship with Leif Chaparral," Hawkwood answered. "His words now are not just the delusional ramblings of a dying man."

Tala's heart stopped, and she felt her face flush as her eyes met Hawkwood's. Even Krista had sat up, attentive. Bronwyn and Cromm were staring at the Sør Sevier man too.

"Why do you goad me now?" Borden hissed. "My son is sorely injured, possibly dying. Why bother me now with nonsense?"

"That is where you are wrong," Hawkwood said, voice nearly a whisper. "It is time for the truth." He looked at Krista, sitting by his side, and then his gaze traveled toward Nail. "It is time we all learn the truth of who we really are." Hawkwood's cutting gaze fell on Tala next. "You know the truth of Jovan and Leif's relationship, do you not? Perhaps you should explain to your father what you have seen."

Tala gulped, saying nothing, sitting still. She knew Hawkwood was a former Bloodwood assassin, possibly even a current Bloodwood. She would give him nothing.

Borden stood and faced Hawkwood on the grass. "I do not appreciate such damning lies being spread about my son in his dying moments."

"Where is Leif?" Jovan cried out. Borden knelt again and wiped the sweat beading up on his son's brow. Nail once again helped to hold Jovan down.

Hawkwood stood, his gaze returning to Tala. "You know the truth of a great many things, don't you, Tala Bronachell? Tell your father the truth."

Tala felt her heart thudding behind her ribs.

"Tell him," Hawkwood pressed, towering over her. "Tell him what you know, what you have seen."

"Leave her alone." Nail, standing over Jovan, had his hand on the hilt of his sword now. "Stop badgering her."

"Stop badgering her?" Hawkwood asked, brow raising. "You would defend her?"

"This is not like you, Hawkwood." Nail's fingers gripped the hilt. "Borden is right: you should not goad any of us, least of all Tala. I appreciate all you have done for me, but can you not just leave us be? You are not acting like the Hawkwood I know."

"And who is the Hawkwood you know?"

"Hawkwood is the honorable man I traveled with from the Swithen Wells Trail Abbey. Hawkwood is the honorable man who trained me in sword fighting. Hawkwood is the honorable man who saved me from the Spider. Hawkwood is the honorable man who rescued me and Tala from Purgatory—"

"That man was always a lie," Hawkwood cut him off. "I have always been the Bloodwood assassin Jovan's court believed me to be." His hardened gaze fell on Krista Aulbrek, still sitting in the grass. "She recognizes me, for Bloodwoods always know their own." Krista's face remained calm, impassive, yet curious.

"Traitor," Borden growled. The tension and anger emanating from him was palpable. He wiped the brow of his son, eyes sparking with rage. "You are naught but a *traitor*."

"Traitor?" Hawkwood shrugged. "Betrayer? I've been called both. I've also been called Lover, by your daughter Jondralyn. Now you shall know me as the Truthsayer. For I know all of your children's secrets. And I know all your secrets too, Ser Borden Bronachell."

Tala suddenly hated Hawkwood. She suddenly hated this man she had once thought so dashing and fair. She recalled her confrontation with him in the secret ways, in the red-hazed room where Sterling Prentiss had died. She recalled all his vague answers and duplicitous ways. Smoke was getting into her eyes, and her vision blurred with tears. "Did you even love my sister?" she blurted. "Or was that a lie, like everything else about you? I trusted you. Jondralyn trusted you. Jondralyn *loved* you."

"I truly loved your sister, Tala." Hawkwood's fierce eyes softened. "That I cannot deny. And I never lied to Jondralyn. Though I did withhold one truth from her. I never admitted to her that I killed your mother, Alana Bronachell. I never told Jondralyn 'twas I who poisoned your mother at Ansel's birth at the behest of Black Dugal."

Tala's heart fell at the man's admission; at the same time rage burned deep.

Borden Bronachell stood, drawing his sword. "You poisoned my wife? You murdered Alana?"

"You've done far worse than murder, Borden Bronachell." Hawkwood faced Tala's father. "And do not pretend that you have not."

"You murdered my *wife*," Borden snarled.

"Shall we go over your sins?" Hawkwood countered. "Shall I tell everyone here how you and Roguemoore and Ironcloud, along with Ser Roderic Raybourne and Ser Torrence Raybourne, stole the twin heirs of Raijael from Cassietta? Shall I tell Nail and Krista how you stole the bastard babes of King Aevrett Raijael and Cassietta Raybourne? Shall I tell how you and your twisted Brethren of Mia stole those bastard babes and hid them in the one place they would never be found?"

Borden's sword came up fast, its tip now aimed at Hawkwood's throat. "You, a betrayer, so blithely throw around false accusations, so blithely dare smear my name?"

"All my betrayals combined do not begin to equal your one great betrayal, Borden Bronachell," Hawkwood said coldly.

"You are naught but a Bloodwood assassin," Borden said. "Naught but a betrayer and a liar."

"Perhaps," Hawkwood said. "But 'tis you and the Brethren of Mia who have betrayed the Five Isles the most. 'Twas the Brethren of Mia who schemed to steal the bastard heirs of Raijael and hide them in plain sight. 'Twas you, Borden Bronachell, who gave those twin babes to your own sister, Mona Le Graven, to raise as her own. 'Twas you, the mighty King Borden Bronachell, who put the flame to the young male child's face in an attempt to twist and deform his flesh so he would be not recognizable. 'Twas you who deformed an innocent babe's face to keep your secrets. 'Twas you who maimed and scarred Lindholf Le Graven."

Tala stopped breathing, picturing the deformities on her cousin's face, the scars Lindholf had lived with his entire life, the scars that had affected everything about him in such agonizing ways. She looked around, seeing the disgust on everyone's faces. Nail and Krista were watching her father and the Sør Sevier man with great interest.

Hawkwood continued, "'Twas you and Ser Roderic Raybourne who schemed to steal two other similar-looking babes to use as bait, two other innocent children stripped from their parents for Aeros and Aevrett Raijael to chase in futility."

"Lies," Borden hissed.

"And chase them they did," Hawkwood went on, "sending assassins like me the breadth of the Five Isles, looking for the man named Shawcroft and the boy he kept. The boy you kidnapped."

Nail was visibly shaking now, hand still on the hilt of his sword. Krista's black leather armor appeared as deadly and sinister as the look on her face; a black dagger was in her hand.

"And the baby girl?" Hawkwood gestured to Krista. "The baby girl you sent north into the wilds of the Nordland Highlands with Ser Aulmut Klingande's young bride, Avril, where she was found and raised by Gault Aulbrek."

"Lies," Borden hissed once more, rage twisting his face into something ugly.

"Two innocent children stolen from their rightful parents to be used in your dark and twisted schemes," Hawkwood said. "All so Lindholf and Lawri Le Graven could remain hidden right in the midst of your own royal court."

Krista Aulbrek glared at Borden. "Was Avril really even my mother?"

By the look of guilt that washed over her father's face, Tala knew the answer.

"Fatherless," Krista muttered, her eyes downcast, head slowly shaking. "And now motherless. Was I even the daughter of Ser Aulmut Klingande as was hinted?" she asked herself. "Who am I?" She turned to Nail. "Who are you?"

Nail, hand resting absently on the hilt of his sword now, looked like he was going to vomit. When Tala noticed a second black dagger in Krista's hands, her heart skipped a beat.

"I think you must admit the truth now, Borden Bronachell," Krista demanded, fingers tightening around the daggers, her eyes cold slits. "You told a similar story to me once before, as we sailed from Sør Sevier to Wyn Darrè. Admit to the world all your dirty schemes while you still draw breath."

Borden looked trapped. To Tala he even looked weak. He did not look like the war hero she always imagined him to be. Tala had never felt such hurt and disappointment. Downhearted, she watched as her father's gaze returned to Jovan; the young king was still struggling for breath, blood still leaking from the stump of his arm.

"Is it true, Father?" Tala finally spoke up, her voice shaking. "Did you burn Lindholf as Hawkwood claims? Did you scar his face? Are Lindholf and Lawri not of our blood? Is this why Lindholf and Lawri rode the white stallion under the Atonement Tree, the weapons of the Five Warrior Angels draped all over them? Are they the heirs of Laijon and Raijael?"

Her father did not even look up at her. Her heart sank further. At that moment, Tala felt as betrayed by Borden Bronachell as she felt betrayed by Hawkwood.

"Tell your daughter the truth," Hawkwood demanded, eyes narrowing in calculation. "She is asking all the right questions. What purpose does it serve you now, to know the truth and keep it from her? What purpose does it serve in your heart? Let your daughter know the truth about her *cousins*. Let Krista and Nail finally know the truth of their own heritage too."

When Tala's father looked up, he did not look at her. Instead he focused on the Bloodwood girl, pain in his eyes. "Hawkwood is right; it serves no purpose to keep secrets from you, Krista Aulbrek. Not now."

"Why even call her by that surname?" Hawkwood interrupted. "For no Aulbrek blood runs through her veins."

Borden cast a pensive gaze into the shadowy sky, as if he was trying to look beyond the smoke, trying to find the truth out there somewhere among the swirling ash. Then he looked back at Krista, or rather, he looked somewhere just beyond her. "It all began with the illicit affair between King Aevrett Raijael of Sør Sevier and Cassietta Raybourne of Wyn Darrè, and the twins born of their brief, but disastrous, coupling.

The affair was short-lived, and all knowledge of the pregnancy was hidden from King Aevrett. On the day of their birth, both of the babes, twins, a boy and a girl, were taken from Cassietta Raybourne by her brothers, Ser Roderic and Ser Torrence Raybourne, the king of Wyn Darrè. With the help of Roguemoore and Ironcloud, the babes were secreted away for their own safety and given to me. For we in the Brethren of Mia knew that if Aevrett ever got wind of their existence, he would have had the babies slain on sight. Aeros was the Angel Prince, and no bastard child born out of wedlock would ever usurp that throne."

Borden's eyes remained fixed somewhere out in the smoky dark haze behind Krista. "That is not the entire truth, actually." He swallowed deeply, as if the next words were hard to speak. "'Twas I, Borden Bronachell, who disguised the bastard children of King Aevrett Raijael and hid them away. 'Twas I alone, Borden Bronachell, king of Gul Kana, leader of the Brethren of Mia, who knew where these children were, promising that the identity of the twins should never be revealed until Fiery Absolution. And those twins were indeed Lindholf and Lawri Le Graven."

Tala sucked down a deep breath, scarcely able to believe what she was hearing. Her stomach had knotted itself into a small ball of pain, a deep-rooted pain that drifted up her throat like bile, stinging and sour. Her mind was but a numb fog, trying to grasp the entirety of her father's story.

Borden's hard eyes pierced into Krista's. "The fact is, I know not who you are, girl, other than that you and Nail were used as bait for Aevrett to chase while Lindholf and Lawri remained safe under my sister Mona's care. Gault Aulbrek's blood is not within you. Nor Cassietta Raybourne's blood. Nor even Aevrett Raijael's blood. Nor any blood that I know of. And King Torrence Raybourne and his brother Ser Roderic are both now dead. Only they knew who you and Nail really came from. You are not kin, you and Nail. That I do know. Other than that, I know nothing."

"Bait?" Krista looked at Nail. The blond boy's soot-stained face was a rash of anger and betrayal. *"Bait?"* she repeated, the word like poison on her tongue.

"Yes, bait," Borden said, face now grave. "Cassietta Raybourne was distraught after her two babies were stripped from her and then spirited away. Before taking her own life, she got word to Aevrett Raijael of the twins' existence. In her final despair, she told him of the children who had been conceived and born and then hidden by the Brethren of Mia. Once King Aevrett found out about the bastard twins, Roguemoore, Ironcloud, and I knew we had to keep their identity a secret until Fiery Absolution. So I came up with a plan. 'Twas my plan. And I will not lay the blame elsewhere."

He focused again on Krista. "At my behest, King Torrence stole you from your real parents. Whoever they were, I do not know. The only guidance I gave Torrence was to make sure that whatever babe he found was a girl and blond and from good and healthy stock. Once you were removed from your home, King Torrence paid a gutter waif named Avril to raise you."

"Removed from my home." Krista's hollow voice sounded distant and disturbed, as if the foggy smoke above was swallowing her words right up. "A gutter waif?"

"Aye," Borden went on. "Also at my behest, King Torrence placed this pretty young waif, Avril, along with the baby, *you*, in the manor house of a rich Rokenwalder noble named Ser Aulmut Klingande. And what I tell you now, I only learned from Ironcloud, or as you prefer to call him, Squateye. Not knowing why she was raising a stranger's child in the house of a Rokenwalder nobleman, Avril did her best with the situation and accepted her lot in life, and also the coin Ser Torrence paid her to go along with the ruse. But Avril was ofttimes beaten and abused by Ser Aulmut. She eventually took you and fled north into the Nordland Highlands, where she met Ser Gault Aulbrek. The two found solace in each other and were eventually married. Avril died shortly thereafter, but not before sending word of her marriage to Gault back to King Torrence Raybourne. Ser Gault Aulbrek raised you as his own, knowing none of your true history. The Brethren of Mia's plans changed, but only slightly, for Avril's death was of little worry to either Torrence or myself. As you grew older, and Gault went off to war, hints were dropped within King Aevrett's court by Roguemoore and Ironcloud and others that the stepdaughter of Ser Gault Aulbrek was in fact one of the twin babes born of his affair with Cassietta Raybourne. That is why Aevrett desired to keep you close. It is why Aevrett's son, Aeros Raijael, the Angel Prince, desired that you become a Bloodwood and slay Aevrett. That also became Black Dugal's conspiracy for you. Or who knows, maybe Dugal knew you were always fatherless."

"*Fatherless.*" Krista's cold eyes drifted from Borden to Tala and back. That piercing look was like a spear to Tala's chest that nearly stopped her heart.

"*Fatherless,*" Krista repeated, a haunted look in her eye. "No. I am not fatherless yet." She slipped one of the daggers back into the folds of her leather armor. She bent and rolled the black leather leggings up around her calf. There was a blue ribbon tied around her ankle. With the black dagger she cut the ribbon free and tossed it into the slow-moving brook, where it floated atop black ash. "Now I am truly *fatherless,*" she said.

"You mentioned another baby besides Krista who was stolen?" Nail asked, flipping blond strands of hair out of his eyes. "A boy to match the twin boy of King Aevrett's loins. Was that really me?"

"Aye." Borden nodded. "King Torrence's younger brother, Ser Roderic Raybourne, was charged with finding a boy to steal, a blond boy of good stock to use as bait for Aevrett's assassins to chase. You knew Ser Roderic as your master, Shawcroft. However, Ser Torrence's younger brother was less enthused at the notion of stealing children. Ser Roderic did not fulfill his duty to the Brethren of Mia for some three years. His wavering and indecision were almost the Brethren of Mia's undoing. For it wasn't until one of Black Dugal's Bloodwood assassins nearly found the real twins that Shawcroft ultimately did his part. He finally found a suitable boy, blond, three years of age, almost an exact match of what young Aeros Raijael looked like. According to Roguemoore and Ironcloud, Ser Roderic stole the boy from a woman in the small Sky

Lochs mining village of Arco. And that boy was you, Nail. And you too were used as a distraction. You were used as bait for Aevrett and Dugal's Bloodwoods to chase for years."

"Shawcroft stole me from a woman in Arco?" Nail asked, brow furrowed in concentration.

It was Hawkwood who answered. "Rumor eventually reached King Aevrett that Ser Roderic was going by the name of Shawcroft and living in the mining town of Arco. Aevrett ordered Black Dugal to send three of his best assassins to find Shawcroft and determine whether the heir of Raijael was indeed with him. I was one of those three assassins, as was my brother, the Spider. When we reached Arco, our third companion, a sly and intelligent young assassin named Snakewood, suspected that Shawcroft had no such child with him. When Shawcroft caught wind that we were in Arco, spying, he finally followed through on his plan to keep up the ruse that he was guarding one of the heirs of Aevrett Raijael. He found a young woman with a blond boy of the right age and began stalking her, with the aim to take her child. We knew he aimed to steal you from her, Nail."

"Shawcroft stole me from a woman in Arco?" Nail repeated, pain filling his eyes.

"It was Snakewood who almost stopped the kidnapping," Hawkwood said. "We had split up, the three of us, each of us looking for Shawcroft. Snakewood came across your master first. They fought, and Shawcroft mortally wounded Snakewood. When Spiderwood and I came upon our dying companion, Snakewood told us that he had found Shawcroft attempting to take the small boy from his mother. He told us how he found Shawcroft fighting with the woman, trying to murder her with a thin boning knife. In his last breaths, Snakewood told us how he had tried to stop the kidnapping, but Shawcroft bested him and fled across the glacier, chasing the injured woman and the boy."

"Shawcroft not only kidnapped me," Nail said, horror washing over his features, "but he also killed my real mother?"

Hawkwood nodded. "The Spider and I followed a trail of blood out onto that glacier. But as for any sign of your mother, she was already gone when we arrived: the smears of blood leading to the edge of the glacier and the loch far below spelled out her fate. We fought with Shawcroft to get you back. But the glacier crumbled down around us and we fell. Shawcroft likely thought we were dead. But the Spider and I survived."

"And you told Dugal and King Aevrett what you knew?" Borden asked. "That Nail was a nobody?"

"No," Hawkwood said. "The Spider and I kept that information to ourselves." He looked at Nail. "We continued to let King Aevrett and the White Prince think you were the real heir and still in Shawcroft's care."

"So you too are full of lies?" Borden accused. "For you kept the same secret as I."

"I am a Bloodwood assassin," Hawkwood said. "As was the Spider. What else would you have us do?"

"You all play games." Bronwyn Allen stood, disgust written all over her dark face. "You sick and twisted shit-stains play games with the lives of others. I ought to slay you all now, rid the world of your wickedness."

Cromm Cru'x grunted angrily as he too stood. "So you are saying that the marked one was never the marked one?"

"Seems so," the Wyn Darrè girl answered, angry eyes fixed on both Hawkwood and Borden Bronachell. "Seems we got two rats in our midst."

"Hrmph," the oghul grunted again. "Cromm greatly bemoans the fact that the marked one was never the marked one and it was these men who fooled him." His fierce eyes turned to Nail. "Cromm always knew you were not the marked one. Yes. Cromm always knew you were nothing."

"He is not *nothing*." Krista's voice cut the silence with intensity. Her black dagger was still gripped in her straining fist. "*I* am not *nothing*."

An awkward silence had fallen over the soot-covered cemetery as everyone stared at the young Bloodwood. Then Krista's gaze met Tala's. "Just because Nail and I are *fatherless* does not make us *nothing*, as you shall soon find out, for my blade thirsts. Now you must prepare to become *fatherless* once again, Tala Bronachell."

The young assassin lunged for Tala's father, black blade stirring the hazy air, slicing toward the man. Nail's reaction was equally as fast, his hand lashing out, catching Krista's wrist just before the tip of her dagger plunged into Borden's exposed chest.

The girl strained against Nail's powerful clutch, angry eyes boring into his. They stood that way a moment, Krista struggling against Nail's strength, the intensity of their eyes almost eating holes into each other. "No more killing," Nail said flatly, wrapping both hands around Krista's wrist now, bending the Bloodwood's arm backward and away from Tala's father.

"But he *stole* our lives." Krista fought against his strength. But Nail was stronger.

"He *stole* our lives," she repeated as Nail forced the tip of the blade away from Borden. "He stole *my* life."

"We only did what we had to, to protect the realm." Borden backed away from the struggling pair. "I stand by every action of the Brethren of Mia."

"And I wish to *end* the Brethren of Mia." Krista still struggled against Nail's powerful grasp. "I only do what I do to avenge myself."

"No more killing," Nail said. "Tala finally has her father back. After so many years, she has him back. At least there is that, and it is a good thing."

"Who cares about the princess or her father?" Krista raged. "What about *my* father? *My* mother? What about *me*? What about Borden Bronachell's lies and murders?"

"Let it go," Hawkwood said. "Justice can be had in other ways, Krista Aulbrek."

"That is not my name!" she shouted, a defeated look washing over her face. She eased her grip on the dagger, letting it fall to the ash-covered grass.

Nail backed away from her then, the dagger lying in the grass between them. The young assassin's pain-filled eyes remained on Nail's, as if asking him why. *Why did you stop me killing him?*

Borden dropped to his knees at Jovan's side, drawing everyone's attention. *"No!"* he cried. Jovan's lifeless body was listing sideways against the foot of the sculpture.

Tala stood there numb and unable to move, so many thoughts and emotions flooding her all at once. *How can he be dead? Our king just slipped away whilst we argued over the bloodline of peasants!* Tala could feel the wraiths once again stirring in her brain. *He cannot be dead!*

But everyone could see, Jovan Bronachell was gone, dead. His dull and sightless eyes stared out into the smoky cemetery, wide and round and searching for nothing.

"No," Borden cried. "What nightmare have I returned to?"

"A nightmare of your own making," Hawkwood said coldly.

Borden touched the side of his son's pale face, sobbing.

"I've had enough of you pathetic people." Krista Aulbrek snatched the black dagger from the ground and stuffed it back into the folds of her armor. "And I'm tired of standing around in other people's grave-yards." She turned and walked away into the cemetery, pushing her way into the haze of dark smoke.

Nail's concerned gaze followed the Bloodwood as she drifted away. Then he stepped toward the ash-covered brook. The blue ribbon Krista had cast aside was hung up on a rocky outcropping in the slow, mean-dering waters. Nail grabbed the ribbon, wiped it clean of grit and ash, and slipped it silently into his pocket. Then he followed Krista Aulbrek into the smoke.

Tala did not want Nail to leave with the other girl, but he did. Lump in her throat, she looked to the sky, again wishing for some magic to come and just whisk her away.

The message we have striven to impart upon you is that man knoweth naught of the true nature of the wraiths of the underworld. They are like silver shadows and blood, rising from the underworld and from cross-shaped tombs to become one Immortal Lord unto the beasts.
—THE WAY AND TRUTH OF LAIJON

CHAPTER SEVENTY-TWO

AVA SHAY

13TH DAY OF THE HEART MOON, 999TH YEAR OF LAIJON
AMADON, GUL KANA

Laijon save us." Dokie Liddle gazed up at the black dragon gliding in lazy circles through the smoky sky, the monster's skull-faced rider surveying the burned city below. "So many dead already and they want more," Dokie said as the dragon circled lower and lower. "Women and children everywhere, all of them dead and burning and no end in sight. When will it all be over? They've won. Everything from Rokenwalder to Amadon is destroyed. What more do they want?"

Ava Shay, Enna Spades, and Hammerfiss stood with Dokie in the blood-smeared cobbled courtyard that skirted the glimmering River Vallè. The burned and dead lay all around, abandoned swords and arrows scattered about. Dozens of slithering merfolk could be seen in the water. Dozens more lined the stone shoreline, sleek and wet, some wielding bone shard daggers, others screeching and hissing as they pulled the human dead from the cobbles and down into the bloody waters. Ava had never seen the gruesome merfolk up close like this before. She recoiled as one long-haired mermaid bit into the flesh of a dead Gul Kana fighter with her savage pointed teeth and began dragging him across the court-yard toward the water.

Ava turned away from the desecration and horror and watched as the black-scaled dragon and its black-clad rider landed in the yard in front of Dokie. The beast looked straight at them through pitch-black eyes and let out a roar that flayed Ava Shay's soul bloody and raw. It seemed the horrors would never end. The skull-faced dragon rider slid from the dragon's sinuous, sleek back, sparkling whip uncoiling at his side, sil-ver dripping from its barbs. A dangerous-looking black crossbow was strapped to the knight's back over a dark cloak.

"That's my crossbow." Dokie pointed. "Bloody bastard has my cross-bow!"

Blackest Heart! Ava had seen the fabled weapon under the Atonement Tree. She shivered, seeing the weapon here again. Murderous merfolk. Dragons. She wanted to run. The black dragon and the skull-faced knight with the silver whip and crossbow were the most frightful sights she had yet seen.

"Well, we should just find another street, Hammerfiss," Spades said, the long black Dayknight sword she had scavenged from the battlefield in her grasp. "Looks like this one is blocked by a dragon on one side and a river boiling with merfolk on the other."

"Bah!" Hammerfiss grunted, eyeing the dragon and the skull-faced knight. "'Tis nothing."

"We cannot fight this beast and its demon rider," Spades stressed. "Plus I've no wish to tangle with those fish men crawling out of the water."

"Bullocks," Hammerfiss growled. The large mace he had snatched from the grip of a dead oghul looked more deadly than ever in his thick, burly fingers. The fetishes tied in his long red beard jingled as he turned back to Spades. "I welcome battle. Hammerfiss of Suk Skard is done fleeing like a frightened rabbit from watery demons and dragons! One dragon already chased me into one slave pit. It won't happen again. Hammerfiss makes his stand here!" A maniacal grin broadened above his quivering beard. "Be bloody! Be brave! Be happy!"

He's mad, Ava thought. *He wants to die in a righteous battle.* Then again,

Spades, Hammerfiss, and every other fighter under Aeros Raijael had always been mad!

"War gets uglier and uglier and more absurd," Spades said as if reading Ava's mind, and she nodded. "As do the people who fight them, especially those warriors who have been at it as long as Hammerfiss."

Judging from the battle lust burning in Hammerfiss' eyes, Ava knew that dying whilst fighting a dragon was the exact glorious way the giant had likely dreamed his entire life of exiting this world. Since climbing from the slave pit, he had probably sought nothing else, fighting his way into Amadon with Enna Spades at his side in hopes of meeting a dragon in battle. *And I willingly followed these crazy people.*

Following the two battle-hardened warriors from Sør Sevier had seemed like the safest course until now. Ever since Fiery Absolution, the four of them, Ava, Dokie, Spades, and Hammerfiss, had spent their journey into the city wide-awake, plodding through the chaotic streets of Amadon, streets strewn with the burning and the dead. Hammerfiss and Spades had led the way, carving their way through the crowds of both frantic citizens and warriors. They spared no one. There was nothing else to do. Nowhere else to go. And no one else to protect them. Ava's only solace was the thin sword, My Heart, at her hip. It would do little to protect her in a real fight against a real dragon, but it was something, and it was hers. She had also found a bow—a discarded Amadon Silver Guard bow and quiver that she had strapped to her back—though she knew little of archery. Now they had reached this place in the middle of Amadon, a burnt and lonely street ending in a cobbled courtyard, a black dragon and its skull-faced rider facing them.

The beast roared again.

It was a roar that shook the very street, and Ava tried to shrink away from the sound, a looming dread clouding her entire mind. Even what merfolk had crawled up from the river took note of the beast's deafening cry.

Hammerfiss shrugged off the earsplitting roar and marched straight toward the dragon, heavy mace in his tightly curled fist. The dragon and the skull-faced knight watched him come.

Spades stepped up behind Dokie. "As I said, war gets more absurd, as do those who fight it." She shoved the boy after Hammerfiss. "Let's not shirk our duty in helping the man slay that monster." Dokie stumbled toward the dragon, Spades pushing him along, saying, "And mind those merfolk too. They are just as ferocious on land as in the sea."

Nearing the end of her strength of will, Ava reluctantly followed.

They were about halfway down the street when six Dayknights spilled from a nearby alley, longbows ready. They dropped to one knee at the same time, drew their bows, and took aim. Ava fell to one knee and shakily nocked the first arrow to the bow she had found. She was terrible with the weapon, but it was her only defense. One of the Dayknights fired at the dragon rider. With a flick of the silver whip, the skull-faced knight sliced the speeding arrow in half. The two pieces skittered across the cobbles behind the dragon.

Hammerfiss charged the dragon rider, huge spiked mace sweeping up and around in a crushing blow aimed right at the demon's head. The skull-faced knight ducked the blow and struck out at Hammerfiss with the whip, cleaving through the heavy iron ball of the mace, sending the red-haired giant reeling back.

Steam curled from the dragon's throat, flat black eyes fixed on Hammerfiss. The red-haired giant hauled himself to his feet and backed away, weaponless. The skull-faced knight hooked the silver whip to its belt and drew *Blackest Heart* from over its shoulder. The dragon rider pulled a thick silver bolt from the folds of its black cloak and fitted it into the crossbow and took careful aim at Hammerfiss.

Spades and Dokie had stopped in the roadway naught but ten paces away from the dragon rider. Ava Shay raised her own bow, pointed the arrow in the direction of the dragon rider, and fired. Her arrow sailed into the air and over the buildings beyond. Cursing, she fumbled to pull another arrow from the quiver strapped to her back.

The dragon rider fired the crossbow at Hammerfiss. The big man dropped to the cobbles and the quarrel zoomed over his head, punched straight through the chest of the Dayknight bowman kneeling behind him, and exited his back, then careened, wobbling, over the cobbled street, and buried itself fletching-deep into the stone building across the courtyard. Stunned, the Dayknight dropped his bow and clutched at the hole in his chest plate. The second silver bolt launched from *Blackest Heart* obliterated the man's helmet and face. One of the merfolk, a male, was already stabbing at the dead man's armor with his thin bone knife. Another of the merfolk began pulling the dead man across the cobbles toward the river.

The remaining Dayknights dropped their bows and drew long black swords; ignoring the merfolk, they rushed the dragon rider at once. Hammerfiss launched himself at the skull-faced knight too, thick hands latching onto *Blackest Heart*. The dragon rider wrestled with Hammerfiss for possession of the crossbow, eventually letting the weapon go as the five Dayknights attacked from the side. Hammerfiss stumbled back, *Blackest Heart* in hand. He swiftly threw the crossbow away and joined in the attack. The skull-faced knight drew the silver whip and met the charge of Hammerfiss and the Dayknights, slicing the first Dayknight in half with a lightning-fast crack of the weapon.

The black dragon roared again, rising on its hind legs, wings spread wide, flame shooting from its gaping mouth high and straight into the air. The remaining four Dayknights backed away, two of them dropping their swords and covering their ears from the pain. The sound was enormous. Hammerfiss also stumbled back, huge hands covering his ears. Spades and Dokie curled away from the sound too. Even the merfolk shrieked in horror.

Farther away from the battle, Ava gritted her teeth and nocked the second arrow into her bow. She took aim at the exposed chest of the black dragon and let the arrow fly. It fluttered away awkwardly, skittering across the cobbles and rolling to a stop at Dokie's feet. Mustering every bit of strength to fight off the terror of the dragon's continuous scream, Ava nocked a third arrow and aimed at the dragon's broad chest once again, this time sending the arrow once again high over the top of the buildings beyond the raging monster.

The black beast dropped down to all fours, quiet now, shimmering wings folding around its great bulky body, black eyes focused on

Hammerfiss and the four Dayknights cowering before the skull-faced knight. With one sweep of its massive scaled paw, the dragon decapitated the nearest Dayknight, sharp claws flinging blood and brains over the courtyard.

The dragon rider's silver whip flashed out and one of the stunned knights fell back, helmet tumbling from his head, neck sliced open from ear to ear, the grinning wound gaping wide as he fell dead. The remaining two Dayknights ran, but they were unable to escape the billowing flame suddenly thundering from the mouth of the dragon. The screaming knights fell, thrashing in the flames. Ava watched in horror as the men burned, fumbling to nock another arrow to her bow.

Hammerfiss stood, facing the beast, weaponless. "Kill me, you bastard!" he shouted, face a rash of red under blue Suk Skard clan tattoos. "Kill me! Your fires will only make me stronger!"

"Idiot!" Spades rushed up and grabbed him by the arm, pulling him away from the dragon and the skull-faced knight. "You're gonna get us all broiled alive!"

As the Dayknights burned, the skull-faced knight turned to Hammerfiss and Spades, silver whip licking out murderously. Spades dodged the knight's first strike, shoving Hammerfiss aside, silver droplets spraying the cobbles where they had just been standing. Ava nocked another arrow. She aimed at the skull-faced knight's armored chest this time, letting the arrow fly. It sailed high through the air, skipping off the black scales just above the dragon's left eye.

"That's the way to do it, Ava Shay!" Dokie shouted. "Aim for the eyes!"

Dokie rushed toward the dragon, snatching up the discarded crossbow, *Blackest Heart*. He grabbed one of the random arrows scattered along the cobbles. He set the arrow into the crossbow's mechanism and aimed the weapon directly up at the dragon's face. Dokie fired *Blackest Heart*. The arrow sliced through the air, disappearing into the center of the dragon's flat black eye.

Every limb of the dragon went instantly limp as it fell heavily to the floor of the courtyard with a tremendous thud, dust billowing up around its sinuous bulk. Like thick black tar, blood oozed from the punctured eye, pooling on the cobbles under the beast's sagging jaw. The dragon slowly tried to rise. Its roar was more of a strained gurgle now as it stumbled awkwardly to the side, wings scraping along the cobbles.

Like an army of ants, dozens of merfolk crawled over the dragon, bone knives stabbing down, prying at black scales as they climbed the bulk of the beast. The dragon screamed in pain as it stood, merfolk clinging to its back and sides and wings. Fire spilled in small molted streams from the dragons slagging jaw. Still the great beast tried to launch itself skyward. But the weight of the clinging merfolk dragged the dragon over the lip of the cobbled courtyard and down into the River Vallè. Hundreds more merfolk boiled up out of the water as the dragon thrashed and spun. But the creatures of the sea took the black beast down, only bloody froth and bubbling water marking its passing.

Stunned, the skull-faced knight stood unmoving, staring at where the dragon had disappeared into the churning river. Taking advantage of the opening, Enna Spades sliced her sword through the dragon rider's black hood and neck, taking the demon's head off just above the shoulders. The skull-faced knight's body folded sideways, black hood fluttering to the ground. When the severed head struck the cobbles, the silver skull mask broke free, revealing the pale face and thin tapered ears of a Vallè—a female Vallè.

Ava tried to catch her breath, drained from the ordeal. The sun pressed through the gritty haze hanging above, the buildings now casting gaunt shadows over the black blood and smoking savagery in the cobbled courtyard. As she walked toward the dead dragon rider, Ava could tell that this Vallè maiden's face was more delicate and refined than any Vallè maiden she had ever seen, the fey's haunting silver eyes staring up at nothing. Black blood oozed from the Vallè's neck, curling over the cobbles like liquid smoke.

Spades gazed down at the strange Vallè too. "Not sure who the fuck you are, demon lady, or where the fuck you came from, but you were no warrior. Without that whip, you were nothing. Without that dragon backing you up, you were weak and easily distracted." She spat on the corpse. "You've clearly not seen enough battles."

Hammerfiss pounded Dokie on the back enthusiastically. "You hit that dragon in its only vulnerable spot. You helped end that foul beast of the underworld good and right, I tell ya. Good. And. Right."

"I suppose I did at that," Dokie responded, in a tone suggesting he thought the big man was barking mad. *Blackest Heart* quivered in his shaking grip. He dropped to his knees in exhaustion.

Spades gazed down at the boy, perplexed. "Me and Hammerfiss are two battle-hardened Sør Sevier warriors, and yet the dragon meets its end at the hands of a Gallows Haven child and a bunch of fish people." She seemed almost put out by the prospect. "It was a lucky shot. You ought to give me that crossbow before you accidentally kill us all with it."

Dokie stood and faced the woman. "I found it." He calmly hooked *Blackest Heart* to his belt. "'Twas me who pulled it from that hideous cave in the Sky Lochs caverns. It was mine then and it's mine again. It's right where it belongs. Try and take it from me and I will beat you over the head with it."

"I think he's serious." Hammerfiss grinned.

"I am serious," Dokie said.

"Fair enough." Spades glared at him. "I've always approved of your bravery and determination, Dokie Liddle. Keep the damn thing if you want."

Ava stepped toward the dragon rider's severed head and set the blackened tip of her thin blade against one of the creature's flat silver eyes. She gently pushed, sinking her slender blade all the way into the dragon rider's brain case. The eye split like an egg yolk, silver streaming down the demon's delicate pale face.

"Are you bloody crazy, girl?" Spades asked.

"What are you doing, Ava?" Dokie asked. "Trying to kill it a second time?"

Ava met Dokie's gaze. He held *Blackest Heart* proudly. A definite change had come over the boy—no longer was this the meek and small boy she knew from Gallows Haven. No. This was someone different standing before her now. Dokie Liddle now looked stern and dangerous and boldly mature. Not only that, but a touch of that heartlessness and steel that lived in Enna Spades' eyes was now in his own.

Ava felt that same heartlessness alive in herself as well. *War gets uglier and uglier and more absurd,* Spades had said. *As do the people who fight them.*

Hammerfiss reached down and snatched up the dragon rider's skull mask. "What a strange thing." Laughing, he set the mask against his own face, gleeful orbs peering out through the twin eye holes.

Then a change washed over his eyes. It was a look of pure horror.

Hammerfiss grasped at the mask frantically with both hands, trying to pull it away from his flesh. But his hands started melting into the depths of the silver mask as his entire head started billowing white smoke.

Ava was hit with the stench of burning flesh as she watched Hammerfiss' broad face morph and change. The silver mask seemed to sink into his skull and eat his flesh away, swiftly dissolving the fetishes tied in his beard. Smoke billowed as his hair caught fire. It seemed like the man was trying to scream, but his voice was buried somewhere deep in the underworld.

"Holy shit," Spades exclaimed, face devoid of emotion as she watched her friend slowly die. Hammerfiss' face was naught but a gaping, boiling mass of scarlet and silver wreckage now. Livid webs of blood bubbled and hissed and ran in crimson streams down the front of his smoking chest. Then the huge man fell sideways onto the cobbles and rolled over onto his back, hands burned away to bloody nubs, face a blood-and-silver-soaked pool of mush. "Holy fucking shit." Spades stared down at him. "But wasn't that something entirely unexpected?"

Ava did not feel so cavalier or unfeeling about what she had just witnessed. *I am in a dream!* She felt the wraiths trying to seep into her brain.

I'm still asleep in my bed in Gallows Haven and none of this has happened. I am simply in a never-ending nightmare.

"Is he dead?" Dokie asked, staring at the remains of Hammerfiss' melted face.

"Yes," Spades said. "He is unmistakably dead, Dokie Liddle. Lady Death take us, boy, but isn't it evident?"

"He shouldn't have touched that mask," Dokie stated.

"Well, no shit," Spades said, shaking her head. "I always said, ain't nothing could kill Hammerfiss but some form of demonic magic. And by Laijon's hairy asshole I was right. This is some demonic magic right here."

Ava stared at Enna Spades. *They fought side by side for years and she doesn't even care he's dead. She makes jokes.* Hammerfiss had been a savage. Still, Ava's heart went out to him. After all, he'd proven a stout traveling companion and a hardy warrior and had never once harmed her directly.

Dokie reached down to grab the silver whip coiled next to the dragon rider.

"Don't!" Ava admonished. Dokie stopped.

"She's right," Spades said. "You're liable to gut yourself or take off an arm with that spindly thing. I'd leave it if I were you. In fact, I wouldn't touch anything silver, 'specially if these dragon riders have handled it first. The stuff is deadly, cursed."

Dokie stepped away from the whip warily, hand gripping *Blackest Heart* protectively. "Looks like the silver on that whip has turned solid anyway."

Spades nodded. "But if you touch it, it might return to life and melt your hand away like it melted Hammerfiss' face."

Dokie turned his attention to the headless corpse of the dragon rider. "Do you think that creature also carries the black angel stone?"

"I wouldn't go rummaging around in its things were I you," Spades said. "Like I said, everything about it is cursed."

Still, Dokie was curious, the toes of his boot kicking at the dragon rider's cloak.

"We should keep moving," Spades said. "We dare not press our luck lingering near these dead demons lest more similar such beasts come sniffing around. And I don't trust those merfolk to stay in the river long." She met Dokie's eyes with cold scrutiny. "And I doubt your luck at killing beasts of the underworld extends beyond the dragon those fish men are eating now."

CHAPTER SEVENTY-THREE
LINDHOLF LE GRAVEN

13TH DAY OF THE HEART MOON, 999TH YEAR OF LAIJON

AMADON, GUL KANA

A ll the dragons and dragon riders had returned but for the
green and the black. Icelyn the White, Basque-Alia the Blue,
and Aamari-Laada the Red returned *Ethic Shroud, Forgetting
Moon,* and *Afflicted Fire* to Lindholf Le Graven, claiming the weapons
were no longer needed and useless in comparison to their whips of silver. Lindholf placed the three weapons on the burnt grass before him,
stunned. The Hallowed Grove smelled of heat and bloat and death and
boiling human blood. *Or perhaps the stench is coming from Lawri's rotting arm.* Either way, the battlefield around the smoldering husk of the
Atonement Tree was still covered in the dead. But legions of oghul soldiers were attempting to pile the bodies for burning.

"I am the eyes," Lawri Le Graven said. She stood by Lindholf, staring
down at the glorious white sword with the crescent-moon hilt-guard,
Afflicted Fire. "I am the eyes. And I will not let those bastards breed me
with that demon."

What does she think is going to happen to her? Lindholf thought.
Something cold and speculative was blossoming in his sister's green

orbs. And that dangerous green light gave Lindholf the chills. The infection in his sister's arm was spreading. Rot was crawling up her pale flesh from under the silver gauntlet, and he was certain her gruesome arm was adding to the overall stench of the battle.

"The beast of the underworld will find me," Lawri continued to babble, "and I shall be its sight. Together we shall find the princess and crack open the world."

"You're talking nonsense." Lindholf looked at her in disgust. The white stallion named Spirit stood behind them. The stout beast seemed to be Lindholf's one and only comfort in all this madness. He found himself constantly stroking the stallion's shoulders and mane. The smoothness of its coat soothed him. In the absence of Shroud of the Vallè, the horse was the only thing that could soothe him. He needed more of the white powder. The dragons were being fed the Shroud all the time; it stoked their fires. But Lindholf was being left out.

"I am the eyes," Lawri continued. "And they will not breed me with a demon in this world or even the next. We shall find the princess, for I shall be its eyes."

"Are you talking about the eyes of one of the dragons?" Leisel asked. Her voice was soft and dreamy. Her manner was sleepy and languid as she moved around the stallion and sat before Lawri on the burnt grass. "Will you truly be the eyes of a dragon?"

"Don't be daft," Lindholf answered the serving girl. "And don't encourage her ravings. My sister is mentally ill and does not need anyone feeding into her delusions."

Leisel shrugged. Her face appeared pensive and tender, pale skin scarcely covering the veins beneath. She looked like Aeros Raijael in a lot of ways. If it wasn't for what goodness she possessed, for what innocence that shone like a golden chalice in her eyes, Lindholf might truly believe part of the White Prince was in her. For the evil of Aeros Raijael had infected everyone. *We should praise his death!* he thought. But the blood and savagery of Fiery Absolution had taken all the joy out of Aeros' demise.

"I *will* be the eyes of a dragon." Lawri's fevered gaze traveled toward the three Aalavarrè Solas, who had gathered together with their dragons some fifty paces away. Black Dugal and Hans Rake were with the three skull-faced knights. The dirty bulldog with the spiked collar was with them too. A black iron cauldron of boiling blood was suspended over a raging fire pit just beyond the dog and the two Bloodwoods. The three dragons, their soot-smeared nostrils gusting smoke, seemed more agitated than normal now that the cauldron boiled. Something was wrong, and some soldiers in both the Vallè and oghul armies were watching the three scaled beasts warily.

Lindholf figured that the return of the three weapons of the Warrior Angels to him had something to do with the fact that the green dragon and the black dragon were missing. Raakel-Jael the Green and Sashenya the Black had also not returned. The three remaining Aalavarrè Solas were also full of nervous energy, same as their dragons. The truth was, to Lindholf, everything about the dragon riders and their beasts was weird and contradictory. One moment the weapons of the Five Warrior Angels were a boon from Viper, the next moment they were useless. None of it made sense to Lindholf.

And are they boiling human blood in a cauldron? Val-Draekin and Seita joined the two Bloodwoods and the three remaining dragon riders before the cauldron.

"Why do the oghuls call Val-Draekin the Dragon?" Leisel asked Lindholf. "It can be so confusing when there are real dragons flying about."

"*Draekin* means 'dragon' in the old forgotten Vallè language," Lindholf said. "Or so Seita told me when I asked her the same question. *Val* is an honorific meaning 'the.' Thus, Val-Draekin. The Dragon. All their names mean something in their ancient language. *Seita* means 'silk,' or so she said. I honestly don't care what they call each other. I can't figure any of them out."

Leisel's face twisted in confusion. "And why do they call you their Immortal Lord? Are you truly Laijon returned?"

Lindholf didn't answer. He didn't know the answer. He looked at the weapons spread out on the burnt grass before him. *Afflicted Fire.*

Ethic Shroud. Forgetting Moon. He reached into his pocket and drew out the five angel stones. He placed them on the ground in front of the weapons. They seemed lusterless, and far less than magical under the black and gray skies. It was late afternoon, yet the sun could not pierce the haze of smoke above. It seemed all of Amadon burned to the south and east.

"They are so beautiful, those stones," a scratchy voice sounded from behind Spirit. "Those precious stones."

Lindholf craned his neck, peering around the white stallion. The diminutive oghul named Mud Undr'Fut was perched atop a pile of dead knights some ten paces beyond the horse. Mud wore ragged leather armor and held a curved dagger in one gnarled fist.

The small oghul slid from the pile of dead knights and slunk forward. Spirit grew nervous at the oghul's approach. "Can I look at the stones?" Mud asked. "Can I look at the weapons, too?" The scrawny fellow's greedy eyes were fixed on the three weapons and five stones.

Then he looked up at Lawri, beady eyes lingering on her hungrily. Lindholf could tell the oghul's gums were swollen and enflamed. The little monster was in need of a bloodletting, and Lindholf's guard heightened. Leisel, clearly frightened of the little oghul, shrank back, even though she probably outweighed the fellow.

"Don't you worry none." Mud eyed the servant girl. "I won't suck on your friend's neck, that I promise. Your friend is filled with some dread disease, and Mud wants no part of it. That gauntlet is making her sick, that is clear. She is much like Stefan, the boy with the silver eyes. She is much like the saber-toothed lion, too. They are all three but a trial and a test for the great resurrection to come."

"What do you mean, great resurrection to come?" Lawri asked.

"Black Dugal has been speaking to the Skulls about it often. The final resurrection. You will see. You will be there. But Mud concerns himself not with these things. Mud will go and find Stefan. He has gone and nobody has seen him. Just like nobody has seen the Green or the Black." The oghul eased closer to Leisel, smiling. "For Stefan was Mud's only friend. So I will find Stefan my friend. Mud cares not for the dragons."

"Don't come any closer to us," Lindholf warned. "Or I will call for Val-Draekin and he will have you slain. He will have Sledg H'Mar skin you alive. I know that none of them like you, not Val-Draekin, not the dragon riders, and most especially not that oghul high priest. And you're babbling naught but nonsense to my sister and it should stop."

Mud drew back, almost hissing, "Please do not tell Sledg H'Mar what I said about finding Stefan. They do not want me looking for him. Especially that Vallè maiden, Seita. She says his usefulness is long over."

"Was Stefan the boy with the silver eyes?" Leisel asked the oghul. "He looked like a demon from the underworld himself with those eyes."

"Aye." Mud nodded vigorously. "Silver eyes, like the cat, the big black cat who has also gone missing." He bowed before Leisel. "And please do not tell Sledg H'Mar what Mud said." Then he pointed toward the three skull-faced knights and the dragons. "Sledg H'Mar is too busy readying the cauldron to worry about Mud anyway. See, look. He pays no concern to Mud, for Hragna'Ar sacrifice starts again."

"Hragna'Ar sacrifice?" Lindholf said.

"It is a sacrifice to summon back their lost kin, Sashenya and Raakel-Jael," Mud said. "It is to be a sacrifice to summon back the two missing dragons, the Green and the Black. Val-Draekin's little whistle no longer summons the beasts as it should."

Lindholf's gaze drifted from Mud toward the three skull-faced knights and their colorful dragons. Val-Draekin, Seita, and the two Bloodwoods watched as the oghul high priest stoked the fires under the cauldron. Smoke billowed from under the black iron pot as the blood bubbled and boiled. Lindholf had heard rumors of the oghuls and their Hragna'Ar rituals his entire life, mostly stories meant to scare little children. He'd never expected to see it himself. He had no idea what to expect, but the swirling red cauldron could only mean dark sorcery.

"Where do you come from?" Lawri asked Mud, drawing Lindholf's attention away from the dark cauldron.

"Mud comes from a place far from here," the oghul responded.

"But who are you?" she asked. "It was you who chose Lindholf and me from the crowd. Just who are you?"

"Mud is a miracle of Hragna'Ar himself." The oghul bowed before her. "Mud has been named the least of us. Mud is of the most pure race in all the Five Isles, according to the Skulls. Mud is the one who helped in the Hragna'Ar births of all five Aalavarrè Solas. 'Twas a task that did Mud's long-dead kin great honor. Hragna'Ar and Fiery Absolution are about the sharing of honor. Mud was the oghul who brought forth the marked one."

"It seems we are all something special." Lawri nodded to the small fellow. "I am named the Eyes of the Dragon."

"Who named you that?" Lindholf asked, wondering who was crazier, the oghul or his sister. "And why do you keep repeating it?"

"The dreams named me." Lawri's eyes returned to the long white sword on the grass at her feet.

A commotion below brought Lindholf's attention back toward the skull-faced knights and their dragons. A dozen more oghuls were dragging four Sør Sevier knights forward, two male and two female. "Hragna'Ar ritual shall begin again." Mud wrung his hands together in anticipation.

Icelyn the White was the first of the Aalavarrè to remove her mask of Skull, revealing her pale white face and delicate fey features. She let the scorch whip unspool in her other hand, the sinister weapon dripping quills of silver to the burnt grass of the grove. The leather strap of human ears that hung over Icelyn's shoulder flickered in the orange light beaming from under the cauldron. "Vibrant in life and yet so pale in death, you humans are!" Her voice was silky and hollow, yet loud enough for all to hear. The four Sør Sevier captives seemed to cower at her words.

Basque-Alia the Blue removed his mask of Skull next. "Humans always die beautifully, my sister." He drifted casually toward the four knights, his own scorch whip uncoiling at his side. "Fiery Absolution has served Viper well."

Aamari-Laada the Red removed his mask of Skull too, his eyes naught but flat silver slates. "Everything has been so bright and clear in this Great Above. Fiery Absolution has been all I could have dreamed, to finally hunt and slay our mortal enemies, to make extinct the race of men, to erase the memory of the War of Cleansing, to divest ourselves of all memory of the underworld and its murderous black depths, to reclaim the Five Isles for Viper once more."

"And to serve again the Dragon." Basque-Alia bowed in the direction of Val-Draekin. "And to one day soon bring scorch and blood together and summon forth our Immortal Lord from that cross-shaped altar."

Icelyn the White hooked her silver mask to her belt and swept her cloak behind her back. One languid hand reached up to the pure white dragon-scale breastplate covering her chest. Her long, delicate fingers traced the shapes of the circles, squares, crosses, crescent moons, and shooting stars that festooned her armor. The palm of her hand eventually came to rest on the spot where her heart would be. "My eternal soul now quivers with despair," she called out loudly. "Though we Aalavarrè are once again roaming, stalking, hunting with Viper, two of us are now lost. Our sister and our brother, Sashenya and Raakel-Jael."

Aamari-Laada stepped toward the black cauldron. "If the dragons yet live, we shall summon them back to us once more." His flat silver gaze fell upon the four Sør Sevier knights. "These humans before us shall shriek with fiery pain, singing the song of Viper, their sacred melody doing Viper honor. And that song shall guide both the Black and the Green to us, their family. So let the ritual begin." Behind the three Aalavarrè Solas the remaining dragons roared; white, blue, and red, fire blooming into the sky.

"They will place the human soldiers into the cauldron of blood next," Mud Undr'Fut said. "Perhaps we shall see a miracle of Viper today, perhaps one or more of the missing dragon riders shall be born anew, as was Stefan of the silver eyes. If so, it will be one more step toward the great resurrection."

Lindholf's mind was in turmoil, not knowing what he was about to witness, but knowing it would be horrible. He was sweating profusely under his armor. *Could this all be some dark dream, some evil nightmare brought on by the wraiths? Am I still in Purgatory? Am I still in Eskander, sleeping peacefully in my own bed?* He certainly hoped so, for as he looked upon the scene below, it seemed he was now on the side of dark oghul sorcery and cold and merciless killers.

Icelyn hooked the silver whip back onto her belt next to her mask, then drew a long silver dagger from the folds of her cloak. As she held the sharp blade up, all four Sør Sevier captives drew back. "'Tis the ancient way of Hragna'Ar," Icelyn said, voice smooth as silk, "to take the ears of the enemy before they die."

Aamari-Laada and Basque-Alia snapped their whips of silver, forcing the first Sør Sevier knight to kneel before Icelyn. He was male and scared. The pale-faced Aalavarrè sliced the ears from the screaming man with cold efficiency. One of the female Sør Sevier soldiers turned and ran. She made it only two steps before Aamari-Laada's scorch whip sliced her legs off at the knees. The fleeing woman fell to the grass, crawling on bleeding stubs. With a flick of his wrist, Aamari-Laada's whip finished the job, decapitating the girl.

"Make them stop," Leisel's timid voice sounded from somewhere behind Lindholf. "Make them stop, please."

"How?" Lindholf didn't even turn to look at the serving girl. "How does one stop such savagery?"

"They made you their leader," Leisel said. "You can stop them. You are Laijon returned. You can do anything."

"Laijon." Lindholf half whispered and half mumbled the word to himself.

Icelyn continue to carve the ears from the remaining three soldiers; even the dead girl with the severed head had the ears stripped from her skull. Dagger dripping blood, Icelyn focused her flat silver eyes on the cauldron of boiling blood. "You must cleanse yourselves of all weakness before Viper," Icelyn said to the three earless soldiers who still lived. "For one's eternal soul must never cry at the sure knowledge of death. We Cauldron Born must offer alms of silver scorch and blood sacrifice if our kin are to return. We must pray. Pray that Viper will hear our words."

"And if our kin and their dragons be dead, so be it," Aamari-Laada added. "For though it is difficult to see behind the veil, we shall be assured that the eternal souls of our lost kin shall be brought up in both rapture and paradise in eternal bliss. And they shall be brought forth in that final glorious morn to dwell with our immortal ancestors. They shall have eternal life within the science of the stars. They shall have eternal life within that enormous weaponry made of hot silver and twinkling light. They shall have eternal life within that ethereal silver machine that shall reach up onto the black skies in the twinkling of an eye. They shall be made one with Viper to wage battle at Viper's side amid the eternal mists of heaven, Blood of the Dragon their armament, Dragon Claw their weapon, and the Immortal Lord their ruler."

Lindholf could make scant little sense of what was being said, but the mystic words frightened him to no end. Behind him, Leisel was crying. "You must stop them, Lindholf, they are going to cook those people."

But all Lindholf could do was stare down at the angel stones and weapons of the Five Warrior Angels spread out on the ash-smeared grass before him. He could scarcely look at the earless Sør Sevier fighters without bile creeping up his throat. Instinctively, he reached up and felt his own deformed ears on either side of his head, shuddering.

The vast Hragna'Ar army encircling the grove was now chanting and howling, rusted weapons pounding the turf in a dark savage rhythm. *"Caldrun Born! Caldrun Born! Rogk Na Ark! Rogk Na Ark!"* Thousands upon thousands of oghuls now chanted, *"Rogk Na Ark! Rogk Na Ark! Rogk Na Ark! Caldrun Born! Caldrun Born!"*

Icelyn stepped toward the cauldron. Aamari-Laada and Basque-Alia followed, scorch whips now coiled at their belts, pale faces once again hidden behind silver masks of Skull. *"Rogk Na Ark! Rogk Na Ark! Rogk Na Ark! Caldrun Born! Caldrun Born!"* the oghul army chanted.

Sledg H'Mar prodded the first of the earless Sør Sevier knights forward. The man looked at the cauldron with fearful eyes, the sides of his face streaked with blood. The oghul high priest lifted the man up by the arms, one leathery hand under each armpit. The rim of the iron cauldron was chest-high, but Sledg H'Mar had no trouble dumping the knight into the large black pot of boiling blood, armor and all.

The soldier immediately sank beneath the bubbling scarlet. His head resurfaced, completely bathed in steaming red. The whites of his two eyes shone round and bright between the angry streaks of smoking blood. The man writhed in pain before dipping below the surface of boiling red once again. Sledg H'Mar effortlessly lifted and dumped the second earless knight into the cauldron, now churning with boiling flesh and blood.

Lawri hummed a soft, strange melody that froze Lindholf's blood. He glanced back and saw his sister, eyes clenched shut, swaying on her feet. Her song grew louder and louder and the oghul chanting stopped. There was a stirring among the remaining three dragons as Icelyn stepped back from the cauldron and cast her gaze toward Lawri. Aamari-Laada and Basque-Alia looked toward her too. Val-Draekin, Seita, the two Bloodwoods, they all watched as Lawri's song grew louder and louder. Her song grew so loud that Spirit began to buck and bray. Lindholf tried to calm the horse.

Then Lawri's song stopped. Her eyes flew open and she stared heavenward. Lindholf looked up too.

The green dragon swooped in low from the smoky sky. It screeched and roared, batlike green wings stirring the air. But the dragon flew aimlessly, as if drunk, weak spits of fire spewing randomly from its gaping maw in all directions.

"The girl sings her own song to Viper!" Icelyn called out. "And the Green has returned!" The vast sea of oghuls renewed their chant, *"Caldrun Born! Caldrun Born! Caldrun Born!"*

Twisting and turning, huge leathery wings flapping wildly, the green dragon plummeted from the sky, slicing through swirls of black smoke, almost out of control. Heart in his gut, Lindholf watched in strange fascination as the massive beast crashed down like an anvil, hammering the land right in front of Seita, Val-Draekin, and the two Bloodwoods. Dust billowed up.

The oghul chanting stopped.

Silence.

Is it dead? Lindholf couldn't imagine anything surviving such a thunderous fall. The cloud of dust and ash drifted away, revealing the green dragon lying in a heap. The beast slowly gathered itself and stood. The emerald scales along its great bulk rippled, and its scaled head was cocked to the side. The beast's eyes were naught but empty glowing sockets of dripping jade. With a loud roar, its wings spread wide and threateningly as it lumbered blindly in the direction of Lindholf and Lawri.

"It can't see," Leisel stated in wonder. "It's blind." Behind Leisel, Lawri's eyes were once again closed tight, a low song still emanating from somewhere deep in her throat. "You were right, Lawri," Leisel said. "The dragon has no eyes."

Lindholf couldn't escape the numbing feeling that he was living in someone else's dream, that everything that had happened wasn't real, that he himself, along with the blood-filled cauldron and green dragon, was no more than a figment of his imagination. Or perhaps they were nightmares brought upon by the wraiths. He wanted to shrink away from the approaching monster, but some dread fascination held him in place as the sightless dragon stopped right before him, nostrils heaving and blowing hot steam up into the already smoke-filled air. Lindholf stared at the monster's huge teeth, which glistened like sharp polished daggers. The murderous beast of the underworld looked to the sky and roared.

Lawri's green eyes snapped open as she stepped around both Leisel and Lindholf. She moved toward the dragon with silent purpose, reaching out her gauntleted hand. The green dragon leaned into her metallic touch, its once powerful roar now just a low rumble. She calmed the beast. "Did they sacrifice those soldiers for us?" Lawri asked the dragon. "Did they sacrifice those soldiers in some fertility ritual for me? Is it part of my Ember Gathering? Is it part of their plan to breed me with immortal creatures from the stars?"

The dragon's empty green eye sockets stared at nothing. Its breath was heavy and hot. Lawri asked it once more, "Did the fey sacrifice those soldiers for us?"

"*Sacrifice?*" Lindholf blurted, horror mounting. "They were enemy soldiers, Lawri, knights of Sør Sevier. They deserved to die. And what makes you think any of this has anything to do with yo—"

"*Shush.*" Lawri's own eyes were glowing green now, boring through the murky air toward his with a flaming green anger. "This has everything to do with me."

"*Everything?*" He felt the meekness in his own voice. "But you're just a girl, not a princess. You are not Laijon returned—"

"I will be your eyes," Lawri cut him off, addressing the dragon once more, her voice rising in volume, her silver gauntlet once again brushing the green scales of the creature's neck. "Yes, I shall see for you. You shall take me to the pale marble of my dreams. And there we shall crack open the world. There we shall help Tala see her future and lead all armies."

"You must take these with you, Lawri." Leisel stepped around Lindholf. She held all five angel stones in the small palm of one of her hands. She held the tall white sword, *Afflicted Fire*, in the other.

"You shouldn't be touching those," Lindholf snapped at the serving girl.

One by one Lawri plucked the angel stones from Leisel's hand and slipped them into a hidden pocket in her dress. Then she took the sword from the serving girl, the long blade seeming to pulse with red veins of twining light as it settled into her silver hand, all five fingers curling around the weapon's hilt. Sword and gauntlet fit together perfectly; the crescent moon of the sword's hilt-guard now glowed with brilliant white light. Lawri's face was illuminated like fine porcelain, the rot living under her skin pulsing with a boiling luminosity all its own.

"I am no one's brood mare," she said to no one in particular.

The ground rumbled and groaned under the dragon's powerful legs as it dipped its sinuous neck toward the girl. It lowered its head almost in supplication.

Without hesitation, Lawri pulled herself up onto the dragon, settling comfortably astraddle the beast's broad scaled spine. Her one good hand gripped the long, pale horn jutting from the dragon's back before her, her gauntleted hand still wrapped protectively around *Afflicted Fire*.

The strangeness of it all seemed like a betrayal to Lindholf. "Give the sword back to me," he uttered, looking up at his twin sister astride the blind dragon. He had recently learned that with enough pain and treachery forced upon you, distrust just became part of your blood, racing through your veins, infecting your heart, staining every part of your being. He knew betrayal when he saw it. But there was nothing he could do.

The dragon launched itself high into the air, great wings flapping once, twice, thrice, as the huge beast took flight, stirring the dark, hazy air as it flew away, Lawri clinging to its back. Like a resurrected angel, the dragon soared, its green leathery wings raking the air, cutting through the smoke and haze above, gaping mouth roaring in riotous song, Lawri guiding it toward Amadon.

Lindholf felt the tears of hurt and betrayal streaming down his face.

"Just let her go," Seita whispered in his ear. The Vallè princess was standing so near to him, Lindholf could feel her hot breath, feel her body pressed into the back of his.

Even through his thick armor, he could *feel* her.

"Just let her go," Seita whispered again. "Everything will be all right, my lord. For I have seen this all in my dreams."

CHAPTER SEVENTY-FOUR
MANCELLOR ALLEN

13TH DAY OF THE HEART MOON, 999TH YEAR OF LAIJON
AMADON, GUL KANA

W hat you doin' with those two bitches?" Liz Hen Neville blurted as Ava Shay, Enna Spades, and Dokie Liddle emerged from the smoke-filled alleyway. Liz Hen was glaring right at Dokie. "What you *doin'* with them two bitches, Dokie Liddle?"

Beer Mug rushed the Gallows Haven boy, tail a-wag. Dokie grinned and ruffled the dog's head. "Good boy! Good boy!" he cried.

Liz Hen rumbled forward and pushed Beer Mug aside. Then she swallowed Dokie up in a tear-filled hug of her own.

Mancellor Allen stared at the crossbow strapped to Dokie's back. It was *Blackest Heart.* Then his gaze fell on Ava and Spades. They both looked like they had traveled to the underworld and back. They returned his gaze with suspicion.

His own group consisted of Jenko Bruk, Liz Hen, and Beer Mug.

They had nearly come to within sight of the gates of Amadon Castle. In fact, they had been making their way over a pile of burned rubble near the ruins of a blackened chapel when they spotted Dokie, Ava, and Spades emerging from the dark alley.

"Were you headed to the castle too?" Dokie asked Liz Hen.

"Seemed the safest place in this god-awful mess, what with the sun goin' down and all."

"I ain't slept in a day and a half," Dokie said. "And all this bloody foul smoke. And so many dead bodies everywhere." He shook his head in exasperation. "It's been rough going since that tree went up in flames last night. Rough, I tell ya."

"You think you've had it rough?" Liz Hen asked. "I fell a hundred feet down into the slave quarry. Had to hike my way out through the tunnels with *Jenko Bruk*."

"I fell into the slave quarry too," Dokie said. "I had to climb up over a mountain of dead knights with *Enna Spades*. And the mountain was burnt. The people was cooked and steaming."

"Well, I had to fight in the arena against a skull-faced knight," Liz Hen countered.

"I watched Hammerfiss' head melt right off his own shoulders when he put a silver skull mask on his *own* face."

"I helped chase off a dragon."

"Well I helped killed a dragon."

Liz Hen took a step back. "You helped kill a dragon?"

"Aye."

"But did you eat its eyes out of its head?"

"No," Dokie answered somewhat sadly.

"Well, Beer Mug ate the eyes right out of a living dragon's *face*."

"What a good dog!" Dokie's eyes lit up. He petted the dog again. Beer Mug's tail had not stopped wagging since he'd seen the boy. It wagged more furiously now.

The two youths from Gallows Haven were so full of joy and talking so rapidly and excitedly it was as if no one else even existed around them. Not Mancellor, not Jenko. Not Ava. Not even Enna Spades.

"How did you help kill a dragon?" Liz Hen asked.

"I shot it in the eye with *Blackest Heart*." Dokie reached up and rattled the crossbow strapped to his back. "Wasn't really all that hard, honestly. The merfolk finished the beast."

"Merfolk?" Liz Hen shuddered. "I remember those foul beasts from when we had to fight in all that water."

"That was a rough day," Dokie said. "Almost as rough as the last few days for sure."

"So you just shot the dragon's eye out easy as that, huh?" Liz Hen asked.

"Well, I wasn't gonna eat the eye out of its skull like Beer Mug."

Liz Hen laughed. "I reckon you're as rough as an old cob now, Dokie Liddle, and I'm thrice that, make no mistake, and Beer Mug's the roughest of us all."

"We're close to being bona fide dragon killers," Dokie said.

"Aye, dragon killers."

They embraced each other once more.

Mancellor was happy for them. After so much savagery and death, it was nice to see just a small moment of triumph and joy between two friends. Three friends, if you counted Beer Mug. He noticed Ava Shay was staring at Jenko Bruk, both of them silent. Spades was looking at everyone with a calculated amusement. Mancellor was surprised she had not said anything yet.

"Is that you, Jenko Bruk?" Dokie asked, finally noticing Jenko. "Is that you under that ghastly helm?"

"Aye." Jenko nodded to the boy, the horned helm riding awkwardly on his head. "It's me, Dokie. And I'm wearing *Lonesome Crown*."

"More triumphs and wonders," Dokie spouted with joy.

"I think it looks ridiculous on his head," Liz Hen said.

There was a moment of silence.

"You're alive," Ava finally muttered, her voice meek as she stared at Jenko. "I can't believe you are alive."

"I can't believe you are." Jenko was staring at her too.

"I am." Ava was crying now. "I am alive. Just barely, it seems. I've seen such terrible things, Jenko."

"We all have." Jenko removed *Lonesome Crown* and handed it to Mancellor. Then he stepped forward and enveloped Ava Shay in his arms. "I will never leave you again."

"Promise?"

"Promise," Jenko answered. "Can you forgive me?"

"Of course I can forgive you." Ava released him, looking him in the eye, seeing the pain on his face. "Why would I not forgive you?"

Jenko stepped back.

"What is wrong?" Ava asked.

"I've done such horrid things," Jenko said. "Against my own conscience, I've obeyed the commands of evil people. How can I ever live with myself? How can I ever be redeemed? How can I expect anyone to love me?"

"Oh, spare us the theatrics," Enna Spades grumbled, the first words she had said. "You took pleasure in most of what you did, Jenko Bruk. You took pleasure in the killing. You took pleasure in my body when it was offered. Don't act so repentant now."

Pain and guilt crawled over Jenko's face. He gripped Ava by both of her shoulders. "I know I am not spotless—"

"You're as guilty as the rest of us," Spades said forcefully. "Don't feign such—"

"Leave him alone," Ava cut her off. She stepped up to Spades, her own face a mask of rage. "He only did what he had to do to survive. As did we all."

Enna Spades drew her sword. "I reckon it's time I take back what is mine then and leave." She pointed with the tip of her sword at the helm in Mancellor's hand. "You stole that helm from me in Lord's Point, if I recall." Her fingers tightened around the hilt of her sword. "And I want it back."

"You should just walk away from here while you still live," Liz Hen said, drawing her own weapon. Dokie had *Blackest Heart* pointed at her chest, an arrow fitted into its mechanism.

"A few bits of luck in battle and you've both developed delusions of grandeur." Spades glared at both Liz Hen and Dokie, the edges of her mouth forming a half smile, a half sneer. "Put those weapons down. I think I shall take *Blackest Heart*, too."

"You ain't takin' nothin'," Liz Hen said, setting her feet, sword poised and ready for battle. "*Blackest Heart* belongs to Dokie. I seen him find it in the mines."

"Hawkwood teach you that stance?" Spades asked, motioning with the tip of her blade to how the girl was standing.

"He did. I learned a lot from Ser Hawkwood. I learned how to kill *you* anyway. I am not the same girl who you forced into sticking knives into Baron Bruk's stumps. I did not back down from you in the outlaw camp and I will fight you now. I have grown to not fear strutting fools such as yourself."

"But you did jump from the tower in Savon to escape my wrath."

Liz Hen's eyes narrowed. "I jumped to save Dokie."

Spades laughed. "You think you're real slick, don't you?"

"Slicker than a court girl's snot rag." Liz Hen's eyes were twin centers of anger now. "See, it doesn't matter what my stance is, because with a word from me, Beer Mug will eat your eyes out faster than he ate the eyes out of that green dragon in the arena. He remembers you. Do you remember Beer Mug?"

The dog imposed himself between Liz Hen and Spades. He growled low and deep as he looked at the Sør Sevier woman, eyes sparkling with danger.

The cocky smile ran away from Spades' face. Her free hand drifted to the scars on her neck.

"That's right," Liz Hen said. "Go, while you still have a throat to breathe with."

Beer Mug arched his spine, hackles raised. His growl grew lower and more murderous. His lips peeled back, revealing glistening fangs, keen and sharp.

Liz Hen smiled—her smile as cocky as Spades' now. "Oh, indeed, Beer Mug remembers you, Enna Spades. He remembers you well."

Spades' worried gaze drifted from Liz Hen to the dog and back. "I'm not done with you yet." She sheathed her sword and cast one last dirty glance at everyone. "I will return and claim what is mine. I *will* have those weapons, mark my words. That dog can't protect you forever, Liz Hen Neville."

Then Enna Spades turned and walked away into the swirling smoke.

Through the power laid upon us by Raijael while he walked amongst us in mortal guise, we shall warn you of false gods and warn you of the day when the seemingly worst beliefs and darkest sorceries turn out to be the truth. For some shall say, "Doth not sacrifice and blood bring forth new life?"
—THE CHIVALRIC ILLUMINATIONS OF RAIJAEL

CHAPTER SEVENTY-FIVE

GAULT AULBREK

13TH DAY OF THE HEART MOON, 999TH YEAR OF LAIJON

AMADON, GUL KANA

As he laid into the enemy with the Dayknight sword, Gault Aulbrek's fiendish energy was focused on just one thing. Death. Death to all, for everyone was his enemy. It was only the youngest of children that he spared. Everyone else died by the edge of his sword. He would not succumb fully to those soft emotions he so despised within himself. Everyone would die, just not the children.

The sun was just dipping below the tops of the crumbled buildings, casting a dull purple haze over a ruined city blanketed in fire and soot. War stretched out in every direction. Amadon was a raw and bloody wreck of chaos, smoldering stone, and broken bodies. Oghuls, knights, and Vallè alike still waged battle in every street, courtyard, and alleyway. They fought and destroyed and razed with glorious savagery. Gault found himself caught in a continuous, primitive havoc of slash and parry and splattered blood.

The flow of war carried him down a scarlet-stained thoroughfare that ended at the main gate of Amadon Castle. Crumbled battlements rose up on either side of the gate, a gate that was thrown wide. Alone but for the Bloodeye steed he rode, Gault fought his way toward the open gate, eyes ablaze, soul aflame, a serene stillness of purpose in every slash and swing. The black mare beneath him felt like an extension of his own body, such a cool fighter it was. *Be bloody, be brave, be happy!* he thought as he killed easily, for nobody was a threat.

Guttural shouts of dismay sounded from the cobbled roadway ahead as one of two flaming church bell towers tumbled to the ground. The bell tower crushed a row of Gul Kana knights who had been holding back a contingent of Vallè fighters. The thunder and billowing dust of the crumbling tower was followed by the screams of the crushed and dying. Several of the surviving Vallè soldiers began stabbing at those Gul Kana knights trapped under the rock and stone. The second bell tower leaned out precariously over the roadway, and Gault did not wish to be under it when it fell. He turned his mount from the dust-choked scene, searching for a quicker route into the castle. But there was dust and smoke and fighting and fire everywhere.

"Nice collection of armor," he heard a familiar voice say. "Are you oghul, Vallè, Dayknight, or Bloodwood, Ser Gault Aulbrek?"

Enna Spades was grinning up at him, blocking his way.

"Move aside," he said.

"You've no wish to fight the enemy with me, Ser Gault?" She stayed rooted in place, eyeing his Bloodeye steed warily, keeping her distance yet still standing in the way. "All the Hounds and Rowdies are dead. The Knights of the Blue Sword too. 'Tis just the two of us left of Aeros' army."

"I fight alone." Gault squinted into the swirling dust and smoke, looking at the roadway beyond her, searching for a new route to the castle.

"Won't you take pity on an old friend?" She held out her arms. "I just got booted out of my last companionship, got kicked right out for not playing nice."

An oghul lurched from the billowing dust toward Spades, drawing his sword with a crisp rasp of rusted iron. Spades saw the warning in

Gault's eyes and turned, stabbing out. The tip of her sword struck the beast in the mouth, splitting its gray face wide. The beast fell at her feet dead. "Bloody fuck," she snarled.

Gault swept the head off the next oghul to spring from the dusty street with a swift strike of his own sword. The Bloodeye stomped on the twitching body once, twice, than backed away. "That horse is a savage," Spades said.

"It is at that."

"Just like old times." Spades winked up at him, bloodlust sparking in her eyes. "Climb off that demon-eyed monster and join me. Let's die glorious deaths destroying this fucking shit hole of a city."

"The oghuls and Vallè and dragons seem to have already done the job of destroying the city."

"There's plenty left to kill." Spades shrugged. "The castle still stands."

Gault could feel the sweat building under his oghul armor now—he did not need anyone crazier than himself at his side. Enna Spades was more rabid than the Bloodeye he rode. Her fierce eyes scanned the roadway, traveling to the massive looming castle at its head. "I say we make for the castle and kill everyone in it. Make Stabler and Hammerfiss and Aeros and all of our dead companions proud."

"Hammerfiss is dead?" he asked. "I figured no man could kill him."

"No man *could* slay Hammerfiss. Yet, alas, he is dead. I watched his face melt into silver jelly right before my own eyes. 'Twas underworld demon magic killed our friend."

Another oghul stumbled out of the dusty cloud behind Spades. She launched herself to the left, sword flashing through the gritty air and cutting down the beast. More oghuls came pouring out of the burning blacksmith shop to Gault's left, rushing to escape the fire, several with arrows already lodged in their backs.

The Bloodeye bucked and brayed, an arrow suddenly buried in its flanks. The mare's hooves clawed the air, and Gault tumbled backward to the cobbled street. He landed heavily on his side, and an oghul jumped on him, burly fists pounding his face. Spades' sword whirled in Gault's defense, striking the head from the beast atop him. Another oghul rose up in the dead one's place, iron maul raised high. Gault's own sword came up instinctively as he blocked the arching blow of the heavy weapon rushing toward his head. He rolled across the cobbles and hauled himself to his feet again, kicking at the oghul's broad face, staggering the beast backward. Spades chopped the oghul's arm off at the shoulder. Blood spewed as both the iron maul and severed arm dropped to the roadway.

Gault looked for the Bloodeye mare, not wanting to lose his horse in the clamor and confusion. He spotted the red-eyed beast bucking and braying in the grit and smoke a few paces away. The horse was stomping the faces of several weaponless oghuls lying on the ground. The arrow was still quivering in the mare's blood-streaked flank, clearly adding to the beast's madness and rage.

"Over there, Bronwyn!" he heard a familiar voice call out.

Hawkwood emerge from the swirl of smoke and dust and war, climbing the rubble of the fallen church tower. A familiar-looking girl was with him—an archer in a dark green cloak with smudges of ink under her eyes. "Shoot those oghuls trying to escape, Bronwyn!" Hawkwood shouted instructions at the girl.

The girl named Bronwyn was firing arrows into the teeming street below with a rapidity Gault had never before seen. A barrel-chested oghul stood with the girl, fighting off any Vallè or oghul fighters that came at her.

Borden Bronachell came up behind the oghul. He was with his daughter Tala. The familiar-looking Gallows Haven boy named Nail was behind Tala, sword flashing in the faces of the charging oghuls. And Gault's stepdaughter, Krista, fought at Nail's side. Their eyes locked and Krista broke away from Nail, barely breaking stride as she headed straight for Gault. "You still have my horse!" she shouted, her face a mask of fury. "I will have Dread back!"

Two oghuls rose up in her path before she could step down off the pile of rubble. An arrow from Bronwyn's bow caught the first oghul in the neck, spinning him around just as his rusted shortsword lashed toward Krista. Another arrow from Bronwyn sank into the chest of the second oghul, dropping him, too. Krista leaped from the rubble. She was almost to Gault when Spades stepped between them.

"I always wanted to kill a Bloodwood," Spades snarled, her blade pointed at Krista. Gault's stepdaughter stopped her charge. Black daggers were suddenly in both of her hands.

"I *hate* Bloodwoods," Spades growled.

Gault could tell that the warrior woman was testing his stepdaughter. Even the way she stood and held her sword was meant as a taunt. She would not kill Krista. Not from this stance anyway. Spades knew that he was right behind her and would defend his stepdaughter. But Krista did not fall for the bait and attack. She remained still, calm, black daggers steady in her hands.

"I have rarely seen such an illustrious collection of Bloodwood scum in one place," Spades went on. "I will kill you and then I will kill your rotted horse and then I will kill Hawkwood."

"Enna Spades," Hawkwood hissed, spotting the warrior woman.

Spades pointed the tip of her sword at Hawkwood. "Betrayer!" Her shout was full of cold fury. Hawkwood met her stare with an icy gaze of his own.

"You will not kill Hawkwood," Krista said to Spades. "You will not kill my horse. And you will not kill me."

"Those are some exquisitely stupid things to believe, girl," Spades answered slyly, keeping her eyes on Hawkwood.

With a flick of her wrists, Krista's black daggers were spinning toward Spades. The red-haired woman ducked the knives and leaped toward the girl, her sword a vicious blur as she caught Krista in the shoulder, opening the Bloodwood armor. The surprising blow sent the young assassin flailing away into the side of the blacksmith shop. Krista's head cracked hard against the stone wall, and she slumped unconscious to the ground. Gault's heart leaped up into his throat as Spades lunged to finish the girl, sword upraised.

But the enraged Bloodeye charged the warrior woman, screaming, red eyes blazing, razorlike hooves raking the air in front of Spades. The warrior woman backed down, her piercing gaze in search of Hawkwood now, spotting him and leaping away.

Gault leaped over smoking rock and stone to help his stepdaughter. The red-eyed mare moved aside, and he knelt at Krista's side. Blood ran thick and red from the split in her shoulder armor. Blood also welled from the top of her skull, soaking her blond hair.

Gault slid his arms beneath her, tried to lift her. But the heavy gauntleted fist of a barrel-chested oghul crashed into his face, the blow sending him reeling away from his stepdaughter in a daze. "Kill him, Cromm!" Bronwyn shouted as she leaped down the pile of rubble toward Gault and the burly oghul. "Smash the Sør Sevier bastard dead!"

The oghul named Cromm glared down at Gault, one jewel-encrusted knuckle pointing forcefully. "Cromm will enjoy drinking the blood pulsing from your veins, Ser Knight. It is not right for you to be wearing oghul armor. You are a desecration to that armor! Cromm will enjoy feasting on the blood pumping through your dying heart."

A thin-faced Vallè in glimmering armor was suddenly between Gault and Cromm. The Vallè's curved sword plowed a deep furrow into the oghul's rusted iron chest plate. Roaring, Cromm swung his iron-spiked fist into the face of the Vallè. Chunks of Vallè teeth, jawbone, and skull spat out in every direction. Then more Vallè attacked Cromm, and Bronwyn joined the fight. Gault immediately turned from Cromm and the Wyn Darrè girl, focusing his attention on his stepdaughter. The Bloodeye mare was still standing watch over her body, bloody arrow still twitching in its flank.

Spades saw him staring down at the girl. "Pay her too much mind and you will die," she said. "Do not let your emotions take you. There is still a war going on. Emotions have no place here."

Borden Bronachell stepped between Gault and Krista, his face a rash of anger, longsword in hand. Tala, Nail, and Hawkwood were right behind the former king, their weapons drawn. They all four looked ready and determined. They were facing their enemy, a knight of Sør Sevier. Gault knew he would have no problem killing three of them, though with Hawkwood, it would not be easy.

Enna Spades, focused on Hawkwood, leaped into the fight, launching herself at the former Sør Sevier man, her former lover. At the same time, Borden rushed Gault, sword swinging low. Gault lunged to the side, blocking the king's blow, returning the attack with a thrust of his own. The tip of his Dayknight sword caught Borden in the mouth, slicing through his teeth and lips. Blood bloomed thick and crimson down the king's chin, neck, and chest.

"No!" Tala screamed, stabbing at Gault with her own blade. Gault knocked the blow aside and shoved the princess away. She rolled to the ground in a puff of dust. Nail attacked him next. Gault kicked the boy in the balls. Nail crumpled. Borden roared, swinging his sword again in a powerful backhanded arc. Gault parried, catching the king's blade just right, yanking it from the man's grip, sending it skittering to the cobbles, where it landed near the flaming door of the blacksmith shop. The king dove for the lost blade and snatched it up, Gault after him. Borden swung again, blade whistling through the smoky air. Gault ducked the blow. Slivers of rock sparked off the smithy wall just over his head. He launched the weight of his body up into Borden's chest, forcing the man backward against the stone wall. The tip of Gault's sword was buried in the man's neck and continued upward until it exited his spine, lodging itself in the mortar of the wall behind. Gault yanked the sword free, slicing most of the man's face in half.

"No!" Tala rushed forward and caught the limp body of her father as he folded over the crumpled form of an already dead oghul. Borden's neck fountained blood to the beat of his heart, painting his daughter's face red. Tala clutched him to her breast, one hand desperately trying to put his wrecked face back together. Nail raced to her side, panicked eyes fixed on the dying king as he tried to help the girl hold her father up.

Seeing the man was dying, Gault turned and rushed to help Spades in her fight with Hawkwood. "He's mine, Gault!" Spades yelled at him as she fought. "Stay away!"

Hawkwood had slipped in a pile of oghul guts, and he was fending off Spades' attack from his knees. He recovered his footing swiftly, driving the warrior woman back, trying to break through her guard. Spades parried with a dogged swiftness of her own. They backed away from each other, glaring. Then Spades' blade swept out like lightning, slitting the leather armor just below Hawkwood's breastbone, drawing the fight's first blood. Hawkwood parried her next rally of blows, scarlet gushing from his chest.

Scenting victory, Spades threw the full weight of her fighting skills at him now. The former Bloodwood was ready for the attack, sidestepping her savage onslaught, answering with a quick jab of his own that sliced open the leather buckler over her left forearm. Spades was undeterred, answering with a more furious rhythm of slashing blows. Hawkwood could do naught but counter the strokes defensively until Spades had knocked the sword from his hand. Hawkwood launched his entire body at her, driving the woman to the blood-covered ground under the larger weight of his own body. For a moment he held the advantage, until Spades threw him off and rolled, hauling herself back up to her feet. She had her blade at his throat in a flash, pinning him on his back, flat against the ground. It seemed everything had fallen into silence around them; the raging war in the background was nothing now.

"I killed her." Spades stood over the former Bloodwood, her former lover, pressing the tip of her blade slowly into his flesh. "I killed your love. I killed Jondralyn Bronachell. And do you want to know how she died?"

Hawkwood stared up at her blankly, the tip of her sword entering his throat.

Spades' eyes narrowed. "I must say, one has not really lived until they've stared down the length of a long white blade and into the eye of one rabid with fear. And rabid with fear Jondralyn was when *Afflicted Fire* took her—"

"I never loved you." Hawkwood's raspy voice pressed through bloody lips, cutting her off. "But I always loved Jon—"

There was a loud *crack!* from above.

The stone chapel's second bell tower tipped ponderously, spilling pebbles and dust over the roadway and over Gault. He dove aside as the tower fell. He reached out and pulled Spades with him. They tumbled to the ground and rolled as the crushing rubble of the bell tower covered Hawkwood and spread out over the roadway, burying Cromm and Bronwyn and the oghuls they fought too. The cobbled street was suddenly awash in a thick, thundering torrent of dust and rumbling stone. And just like that, Hawkwood, Bronwyn, and Cromm were gone, buried under the rubble.

Behind Gault and Spades, the Bloodeye mare kicked and brayed. Gault stood, looking back at his stepdaughter, Krista. She was still slumped against the wall of the blacksmith shop. Tala and Nail were not far away, the princess cradling her father's body in her lap.

Spades stood too, glaring at the billowing cloud of dust. "I need to *kill* him! I need to find him under there and make sure he is dead!"

"Hawkwood is gone." Gault grabbed her. "Buried. He *is* dead."

"No!" she raged, fierce eyes searching the stone rubble and carnage in the street in disbelief. "His death cannot be so easily stolen from me."

The entire roadway was pitched in sudden, deathly silence.

There was a great, powerful roar from above and Gault's eyes turned skyward, ears filled with pain. Spades looked up too, her face still a rash of rage.

A huge green dragon was gliding in slow circles just above them, batlike wings extended, rippling in the smoky air. A blond girl with glowing green eyes rode the beast's emerald-scaled back.

And gripped in the girl's silver-gauntleted hand was the long white sword *Afflicted Fire*.

CHAPTER SEVENTY-SIX

NAIL

13TH DAY OF THE HEART MOON, 999TH YEAR OF LAIJON
AMADON, GUL KANA

The green dragon landed in front of Gault and Spades. Nail remained crouched beside Tala, her father's limp body in her arms. "You stand between me and my cousin," Lawri Le Graven addressed Gault and Spades. The girl sat like a regal queen atop the dragon, aiming the tip of the long white sword down at the two Sør Sevier warriors. "Move aside or you will die."

Gault and Spades exchanged concerned looks, yet remained rooted in place. The dragon's slithering body crept forward through the smoke and haze, its coiled tail stirring the ashy roadway, forked wings unfurling menacingly, curved talons at every joint. As the smoke cleared and the dragon drew nearer the two warriors, Nail saw that the green monster's eye sockets were empty. *It's blind!*

"Move aside or die," Lawri repeated. Her own eyes glowed green; the gauntlet attached to her arm also seemed to glow with silver light. And the bright sword was like a white bolt of lightning in her hand. Nail fought his own trembling heart, feeling the weariness steal upon him.

He had not slept in nearly two days. He had not eaten, either, and his mouth was as parched and dry as the ashy air around him.

The dragon raised its serpentlike head and stretched open its large mouth, brimming with rows of white, razorlike teeth. The beast let out a thunderous roar, and a spout of fire erupted into the smoke-filled sky. The sound was horrific. Nail shrank against the side of the blacksmith shop with Tala Bronachell, both of them cringing against the agony of the beast's unbearable scream. Tala had let go her father, hands now over her ears. Even the Bloodeye mare standing over Krista's inert form lowered its head, glowing red eyes flinching in pain. Sporadic plumes of flame billowed up into the sky. The heat was pulsing and growing in excruciating waves. Then the dragon stopped, spumes of frothy flame trailing from its open jaws. Lawri shifted her position on the beast's back, sword still aimed at the two from Sør Sevier. "The next time it is you two who burn."

Gault and Spades sheathed their weapons and cautiously moved back as the dragon stretched its serpentine neck toward them with ominous intent. Nail could see that the beast was blind, yet it moved as if it could sense where the two Sør Sevier warriors stood. The shadow of the beast stretched over Gault and Spades and moved up the charred wall of the blacksmith shop. The dragon sniffed at the two knights, nostrils puffing ashy air, green scales fluttering and rippling with danger. A roar of flame was once again building from somewhere deep within.

Gault and Spades took their leave, moving with brisk purpose away from the dragon's sightless yet searching gaze, both of them disappearing into the smoke and black haze of Amadon's destroyed streets.

Lawri Le Graven watched them go, her own eyes glowing like fiery green gems, slicing through the gritty air, *Afflicted Fire* in her gauntleted hand, the weapon unwavering and still. She was dying. Nail could see it. Spoiled flesh spread out from under the silver gauntlet and up the girl's arm, disappearing behind her pale dress only to reappear at her neckline. The rotted-black veins spiraled jaggedly up the side of her face like dark bolts of lightning.

She turned to him, her eyes pierced into his. "Help Tala climb onto the dragon, Nail. Help her sit up here behind me on the dragon."

Tala peered out from behind Nail's shoulder. "Why would I climb onto that monster, Lawri?"

"We've somewhere to go, cousin, and only the dragon can take us there."

"Where?" Tala moved past Nail. "Where would you take me?"

"Back to Fiery Absolution. Back to the Atonement Tree."

"Why?"

"Because I am the Eyes of the Dragon and you are the Princess, and this is your sword." Lawri held up *Afflicted Fire*. "Together we shall go back to Fiery Absolution and save the world. I have foreseen it."

"Foreseen it?"

"In my visions. Like a prophecy of old."

"Prophecy?" Tala hissed the word.

"Yes, prophecy," Lawri said. "Like a Vallè maiden of royal blood, I can see the future. I can see your future."

"Fiery Absolution is evidence enough that prophecy leads only to death and suffering."

"The false prophecies of ancient men, yes," Lawri said, beckoning her cousin forward. "But not the prophecies of the living. Not the prophecies of a woman. Not the prophecies within my own heart. And the prophecies and promptings of my own heart will not be so easily disregarded, cousin."

"How can you be so sure you are right?" Tala asked. "After all, you come to me riding one of the beasts of the underworld. What dark sorcery do you follow?"

"The beast speaks to me," Lawri said. "It knows where we must go, cousin. And I am the Eyes of the Dragon and you are the Princess, the Harbinger."

Tala looked back at Nail; she looked past him to her father. Borden Bronachel was sprawled on the dusty ground, face now cast in that unmistakable pallor of death.

"You speak of prophecy," Tala said, turning back to her cousin. "You speak of things you have seen and felt in your own heart. But *I* do not know what to believe anymore."

"The women of this realm have never been listened to, Tala. You can change that. I have foreseen it." Lawri held her good hand out toward her cousin. "But you must come with me for that to happen. You are the Harbinger. You are the Princess who will lead all armies. You are the Princess who shall bring peace to the Five Isles. You must trust me."

"Trust you?" Tala asked.

"I beg of you, trust me, Tala."

"Then answer me one question."

"Anything."

"Was what Seita said about the Ember Gathering ceremony true? Is the ceremony all just secrets and lies as she claimed? Did the grand vicar and archbishops strip you naked and bless your body? Did you stand naked before them as they covered you in ash? Did they bless your stomach and loins that you would be fertile and bear lots of babies? Did you swear an oath to become a servant and concubine of Laijon after death—"

"Stop," Lawri cut her off. "Just stop, Tala. I swore an oath."

"An oath sworn to evil men is no oath at all," Tala said. "Is what Seita said true or not? Was the Ember Gathering as she claimed? Answer me truthfully."

"Tala, no. I cannot."

"How can I trust you if you won't do even that?"

"Please, Tala, no."

"It is the only way I can trust you."

Nail could see the tears welling in Lawri's green eyes, could see the struggle within her. "Yes, it is true," she finally said, crying. "Everything Seita said was true."

"Thank you." Tala bowed to her cousin.

"Laijon help me," Lawri said, "but I feel freer in having confessed it out loud, Tala. Seita was not lying to you, I was."

"Thank you," Tala repeated. "I can trust you now."

"I feel as if a great weight has been lifted from me, admitting the truth."

"There is only freedom in the truth," Tala said. "And there is only bondage in lies."

"Come with me," Lawri implored. "If you trust me now, then you must come."

Tala looked back at her father one last time. "But for Ansel, my family is dead," she muttered. "There is nothing here for me now. Ansel will have to make his own way if he survives." She met Nail's gaze next. "Will you help me onto the dragon, will you lift me up behind my cousin, Nail?"

Nail didn't want to do any such thing. Still, he nodded yes. Together they approached the dragon. It lowered its sinuous head and Nail helped Tala climb up onto the base of the beast's broad neck. Tala settled in behind her cousin. Lawri handed her *Afflicted Fire*. "Hold on to the sword with one hand and me with the other."

The dragon spread its wings, and with a powerful thrust of its hind legs it was aloft, launched into flight, leaving naught but deep claw marks on the ground and wing-stirred ash. Swirls of smoke whispered and curled over Nail as the beast of the underworld disappeared into the sooty blackness above. The evening air took on an almost luminous green tinge in the dragon's wake.

And Nail was once again alone. With the smoke above and the rubble below, it felt like he was cast adrift inside a huge cavern, left to find his own way free. He recalled the glacier. The stifling, smoke-filled roadway was like being trapped under the glacier once more.

Yes, Nail was alone among the dead—alone but for a demon-eyed horse and an unconscious Bloodwood assassin and a very dead Borden Bronachell. Hawkwood was also gone, smashed beneath all the rubble along with Bronwyn and Cromm.

But then Krista Aulbrek's muffled voice let him know he was not completely alone—not yet. The girl was slowly stirring back to life in the dust and ash near the smithy. He knelt at her side, the Bloodeye mare eyeing him nervously. Krista was bleeding from a slash in her black leather armor just below her shoulder. She tried to roll over and sit up, her face and hair a bloody mess. The Bloodeye watched her with concern. Then the girl slumped back against the wall, unconscious once more.

I never had a sister. Nail studied the girl's delicate face. It was matted with scarlet and grime, blood dripping from her chin. Shawcroft had always maintained that he had a twin sister. But Nail had found out that too was a lie. For a brief moment, he had imagined Krista might be his relation, his twin. Yet according to Borden Bronachell and Hawkwood, he shared no blood with this girl. Her hair was blond like his, blond like the first Bloodwood he had ever seen. He recalled the Vallè maiden on the Dead Goat Trail above Gallows Haven. *My blade thirsts,* the strange fey had said, a black dagger suddenly in her hand. A sly smile played on her delicate face, a face that mirrored that of Seita's. *You are not of my blood,* the Vallè Bloodwood had said as if searching his thoughts, slipping the knife back into the folds of her cloak. *Still, they will be coming for you.*

But it was all just part of a grand deception. *The power of suggestion,* Val-Draekin had said. Between what that Bloodwood had said, and what Shawcroft had said, Nail had always thought himself something special. *But my whole life has been a fraud.* He could feel the turtle carving Ava Shay had made dangling around his neck. *It must be sad, always belonging to people,* she had said. Her turtle carving had traveled with him so far, a reminder of the pain she had caused him so long ago, a reminder of the pain the world had doled out over time.

The sun had long since dipped below the rooftops of the city, and it was fast growing dark. The curtain of smoke around Nail had become like a wall of impenetrable shadow. He could hear the screams of the children and the chaos of war out there somewhere in the blackness and fog. Nail wanted no more part of the fighting.

Krista moaned once more. The Bloodeye brayed its concern. Nail looked at both the red-eyed horse and the girl.

Krista Aulbrek had been betrayed just as much as he.

Nail knelt at her side once more, only to have the Bloodeye scream wildly this time. The red-eyed beast pawed at the air before his face with two wild hooves. Nail backed away, eyeing the deranged horse. He could tell the creature was in pain; its black coat was matted with sweat and an arrow quivered in its bleeding flank.

"Easy, girl," he said softly once the beast calmed down. He reached out, stroking the beast's sweating neck. The horse relaxed.

"Will you help me carry her?" He pressed his face into the side of the horse's neck, whispering, "If I lift her onto your back, will you just help me get her to safety? Will you just lead us both out of this nightmare?"

He did not know if the demon-eyed beast understood, but with all the strength his tired and hungry body could muster, Nail reached down and slung Krista's limp form over his shoulder. He then laid her gently over the back of the Bloodeye.

He took the horse by the bit and led it away from the rubble and the dead and out into the swirling black of the smoke-filled road, not knowing in which direction his weary legs were carrying him.

*Silver cannot destroy rock, but rather cause it to shatter with
great thunder. For did not the star of Viper fall from the heavens and
crack open the bones of the world? And like blood flowing from that
fracture, the banished shall rise forth from that pale marble cauldron
of the earth, rising up out of darkness and great tribulation.*
— THE ANGEL STONE CODEX

CHAPTER SEVENTY-SEVEN
LINDHOLF LE GRAVEN

14TH DAY OF THE HEART MOON, 999TH YEAR OF LAIJON

AMADON, GUL KANA

Val-Draekin, Black Dugal, and Hans Rake led the final attack through blood-choked streets of Amadon. Café Colza
Bouledogue ran with them through the smoke, spitting and
snarling. Lindholf followed on the white stallion, Spirit. Leisel sat on
the saddle behind him, one slender arm clutching him tight. Val-Draekin
had given the girl a shortsword and a set of light chain-mail armor,
along with a silver half-helm fit for a Vallè maiden, telling her, "Even the
women fight in our armies." The girl held the sword tight in her other
hand.

Oghul and Vallè banners fluttered over the helms and spear tips of
the thousands of warriors who rode with Lindholf and Leisel. The army
thundered through the destroyed city, creating a fearsome sound, the
very cobbles shuddering under boot and hoof, black ash stirring in their
wake. The burnt and the dead lay everywhere, men, women, and children, the army plowing over their corpses as if they were nothing.

Lindholf Le Graven, near the front of the teeming throng, tried his utmost to ride tall upon Spirit, but with the shield *Ethic Shroud* gripped in one hand, the battle-ax *Forgetting Moon* gripped tightly in the other, and Leisel clinging to his back, it was difficult. The weapons were growing heavier in his grip by the moment. Lindholf felt utterly useless. Sometimes the weapons were light as a feather. Other times they were a burden. They were a burden now.

As the marauding army approached sections of the city still engaged in heavy battle, Lindholf felt the fear welling up within his galloping heart, sheer and all-embracing. He could sense the fear in Leisel, too. Still, he charged forward with the rest of the throng, charged forward into the fading light of day into the smoky night and destruction, blinking against the swirling smoke and ash. He could hear his own labored wheezing echo under the Vallè war helm Val-Draekin had given him. The ill-fitting thing jounced about on his head awkwardly. Sweat poured down the sides of his face. The new Vallè armor he wore was also uncomfortable and hot.

He had to swallow his own instinct to turn around and ride the other way.

He felt so alone.

It seemed a lifetime ago that he had been the simple son of Lott and Mona Le Graven, attending royal functions with his sister, Lawri, without a care in the world. Now he did not know who he was. Now he was charging into war, bearing two of the weapons of the Five Warrior Angels against the very city of his king, beasts of the underworld and their demon riders flying high above.

Seita was not with the army. Everyone else had joined in the attack but her. Even the three remaining Aalavarrè Solas rode on their fearsome dragons above, raining fire down over Amadon. But Seita had gone off in search of Lawri and the green dragon. Lindholf wondered where they had flown off to and whether Seita could really find them. He also wondered about his cousin, Tala Bronachell, and if she still lived. He even wondered about his mother. He wondered if both she and his father knew what a traitor he had become. He wondered if they too were still alive.

I am not your mother, Mona Le Graven had said to him. *You never were my son.* Those two statements still plagued him. *I am the heir of Laijon, Mia, and Raijael, the great One and Only returned!* Under the Atonement Tree, it had all made sense. But now he felt lost and alone. Lawri was gone. Seita was gone. And he certainly did not feel like the heir of anything, not with so much death in every direction.

Yes, he felt so alone.

Still, he charged into Amadon, a vast army of Vallè and oghuls at his side, the young servant girl, Leisel, behind him.

There was a snap of air and one of the mounted Vallè fighters to his left was suddenly sprouting an arrow from his neck, just above the rim of gleaming chest-plate armor. The Vallè fell sideways from his galloping horse onto the cobbles with a crash. More arrows sailed down, fired from the busted and crumbled rooftops above. The rain of arrows glanced off armor and shields all around, some piercing onto Vallè and oghul flesh. There were screams. Some fell dead. Still Lindholf's army plowed on, Val-Draekin, Black Dugal, Hans Rake, and Café Colza leading the charge.

Lindholf could soon hear the clash and shouts of war ahead. Sword crashed against shield, men, and oghul, and Vallè roaring, horses neighing and bellowing, and above it all, dragons spewing flame with blood-curdling shrieks. Soon the horrors of war rumbled and boiled all around him, screams of terror raging from the throats of the injured and dying, hacking and slashing and blood everywhere.

Lindholf reined his stallion to a standstill. The bulk of army behind him charging around him on either side. He sat there shaking and petrified in the saddle, battle-ax and shield wavering heavily in his hands. Leisel clung to him; he could feel her shaking in fear too. "What are you doing?" she asked. "Why have we stopped?"

Café Colza was right in front of Spirit, barking, pawing at the ashy cobbles, hackles raised above his rusted spiked collar. The dog's fierce little eyes were glaring right up at Lindholf and Leisel accusingly, as if scolding them for not joining in on the fight. *Bloody Mother Mia!* Lindholf's mind roiled. His armor felt too tight. Suffocating. *Can even the dogs sniff out my cowardice?* He blinked back the sweat and smoke from his eyes. The night was already hot, made hotter by the fires raging in the buildings all around. The bulldog's eyes glowed red as flame in the swirling chaos.

"We've got to keep going." Val-Draekin had come back. The Vallè reined up beside him, demanding voice echoing from under his helm. "You've got to help with the fight, Lindholf! We do this all for you, my lord, the oghuls, the Vallè, the dragon riders above. We do it all for the return of Laijon and the return of the Skulls. We must reach the cross-shaped altar for the final resurrection."

Lindholf risked a glance backward, hoping Val-Draekin was talking to anyone else but him. *They keep bringing up the cross-shaped altar, final resurrections, the dragon riders—Black Dugal, Val-Draekin. Do they mean the red-hazed room where Sterling Prentiss was murdered by Glade Chaparral? Where Tala pulled the green elixir from his guts? The green potion that brought Lawri back to life?* It made no sense to Lindholf that they should want to go there.

Children ran screaming in every direction now, desperate to stay alive under the savagery of fire and dust and war and the flame of the dragons. It was those screams of the innocent that Lindholf could not shake, that kept him frozen and his mind whirling in confusion.

"Do not drag us down now!" Black Dugal was reined up behind Val-Draekin. "The dragons above carve a path to your throne! The walls to the castle have been breached. You are Vallè prophecy fulfilled, Lindholf Le Graven. Do you not wish to claim your Vallè heritage? You are the direct descendant of the Vallè Laijon and the human Mia. Fey blood runs within you. Act like the warrior you are!"

Act like the warrior you are? They had said as much to Lindholf many times already. But it only confused him further the more he heard it. He looked to the castle looming above the city. That the towering fortress known as Amadon Castle could fall to an oghul and Vallè army was beyond even his comprehension. He almost couldn't breathe, thinking of it. *What am I doing here?* He tore off his helmet, gasping for air.

"Pull yourself together, boy!" Black Dugal yelled, bloodshot eyes ablaze.

"What do you want from me?" Lindholf yelled back.

"We want you to fight!" Dugal shouted. "We want you to fulfill Vallè prophecy and fight!"

"But I can't fight in this bloody awful helm!" Lindholf handed *Ethic Shroud* to Leisel. He tossed the bulky helm angrily to the ground, nearly striking Café Colza. The dog danced away.

"I can't take the heat of these fires!" he cried. "There are dead children in the streets! And the ax and shield are too heavy for me!"

"Then give them to me!" Hans Rake galloped out of the darkness, his black leather armor gleaming with splatters of blood in the firelight. "Give the ax and shield to me and I shall become Laijon returned!

Ashamed, Lindholf glanced down at *Forgetting Moon* resting in one hand across the front of his saddle. He snatched *Ethic Shroud* out of Leisel's hand. "They are mine!" he shouted.

"Then act like they are yours!" Hans yelled back. "Or give them away before you hurt someone with them!"

"That's the point," Black Dugal sneered. "He *needs* to hurt someone with them." He glared at Lindholf. "Do you not wish to slay Borden Bronachell, the man who hid you, the man who burnt you, the man who deformed your face? Are you the Angel Prince or not, lad? You certainly look the part. Now act the part."

Dugal turned to Val-Draekin. "Make a warrior of him, Dragonwood! Do something! Make a killer of him before all we have planned goes for naught!" Dugal whirled his mount and galloped toward the fighting. Hans and the bulldog charged after him.

"Sorry," Lindholf muttered, head hanging. "You've tried to train me in thievery and fighting and I'm just a failure. I always have been. I'm so sorry, Val-Draekin."

"You must ask for no man's pity," Val-Draekin admonished. "You must gather yourself together, Lindholf Le Graven. You have been gifted much. And now you must push on. I promise you, tonight is not the night that you die."

"What does that even mean?"

"Just remember what Seita and I taught you, three deep breaths and patience, and all things will work out."

Then the dark-haired Vallè held out his hand. That fine white powder that Lindholf so desired rested in the palm of his black leather glove. "Perhaps a little of this will breathe some bravery back into you."

Shroud of the Vallè! Lindholf's heart thundered against his ribs.

"Remember, three deep breaths," Val-Draekin said, offering the gift.

Lindholf leaned in and took three deep breaths, sniffing the white powder up his nose. He felt the Shroud's effects almost immediately, felt the confidence swell within.

"Remember, just let the power of *Forgetting Moon* do the work for you," Val-Draekin said. "The more you believe in its power, the lighter the ax shall feel in your hands. Same with the shield."

"Can I leave that blasted helm on the ground at least?" Lindholf asked, his mind clear and alert. "It hinders my vision, suffocates me."

"Leave the helm if you like," Val-Draekin said. "Stick close to me and rely on the power of the battle-ax and all shall be fine. Trust me. But also remember, everything we Vallè do is meant to create a distraction." The Vallè whirled his mount and galloped into the darkness after the two Bloodwood assassins.

With renewed energy and confidence, Lindholf dug his heels into the flanks of Spirit. The stallion charged forward, and once again Lindholf found himself in a swirl of darkness, flame, and pounding hooves. His fierce gaze scarcely noticed the tumult of war all around now: the blur of Vallè armor, the slash and parry of heavy oghul weapons, Dayknights and Silver Guards screaming in pain as they fell bloody to the ground.

Lindholf spotted the oghul high priest, Sledg H'Mar, fighting in the distance. The small oghul, Mud Undr'Fut, was there with the high priest. Mounted Dayknights surrounded the two oghuls. The knights were better fighters, and Sledg H'Mar took a long lance head straight through his chest. He bellowed as he fell. Seeing the high priest die, Mud Undr'Fut scurried off between the churning legs of two Dayknight war chargers and disappeared down the roadway, vanishing into the swirling black smoke.

Lindholf took another deep breath, feeling the Shroud of the Vallè working within his bloodstream, filling him with power and strength. The battle-ax and shield grew lighter in his hands by the second. Sør Sevier and Gul Kana blades appeared to leap and slash at him from every direction now. He swung *Forgetting Moon* at a passing Silver Guard horseman. The sweeping blade bit deep into the man's armor, staggering both horse and rider, knocking the knight from his saddle.

"You got him!" Leisel shouted.

That was all the encouragement Lindholf needed. *Forgetting Moon* felt light as air in his hands now, as did *Ethic Shroud*. It felt like he was in a dream. Then a spear-wielding oghul raked the tip of his weapon across Spirit's flank, forcing the horse to whirl and buck, spilling both Lindholf and Leisel to the bloody cobbles.

Sputtering in surprise, Lindholf scrambled to his feet, still clutching *Forgetting Moon* and *Ethic Shroud*. Leisel lurched to her feet behind him, shortsword still in hand. The girl's eyes grew wide as she gazed upon the bloody wound crossing the entire flank of the white stallion. Still, there was not a spot of blood on either Lindholf or the girl.

The spear-wielding oghul faced them, grinning madly, purple gums curling back revealing sharp oghul fangs. Spirit kicked and brayed, striking the oghul in the face with one flying hoof, splitting the beast's skull wide. The white stallion stirred the ashy cobbles with its continued bucking, the beast's entire hide now awash with blood.

A Sør Sevier knight fell at Lindholf's feet, helmet tumbling from her head—a woman warrior. Her crimson-streaked face was a grimacing mask of pain, blood bubbling from her mouth, gauntleted hands clutching at the gaping wound in her neck. Lindholf hefted *Forgetting Moon* high in one hand and brought the weapon down on the woman's neck. The battle-ax sliced effortlessly through the woman's flesh and spine, its honed edge sparking off the cobblestone underneath. Another injured Sør Sevier fighter stumbled into Leisel, swinging his sword at her. She jabbed her own blade wildly at the knight's helmet. It was a lucky stab, her blade slicing straight into the eye slit of the soldier's helm. The knight dropped, bloody helm sliding from the end of her sword.

"I killed him!" she shouted, amazed, looking up at Lindholf. "Can you believe that? I killed a knight. That's the first one I ever killed. The first person I ever killed."

Lindholf looked down at the severed head of the Sør Sevier woman he had slain. *And that was the first life I've ever taken! How many more will there be?*

Forgetting Moon was unnoticeable in his hand. *Ethic Shroud* felt the same, light and airy. It was as if they belonged in war. The surface of the shield glowed bright and white in the darkness, and some strange glowing blue mist seemed to swirl outward from the surface of the battle-ax. He watched in amazement as the languid mist twirled like blue silken lace up his arm. The magical light of the smoky mist infused him with more strength and confidence. *Trust me!* Val-Draekin had said.

The fire and flame of the three dragons roaring above seemed to sing to Lindholf now. *Forgetting Moon* and *Ethic Shroud* vibrated with magic in his hands. He could feel their power come to life. *A battle-ax for the King of Slaves,* the scripture said.

Lindholf could feel the slave brand burning with righteous fire on his flesh.

Power consumed him.

Black Dugal, Hans Rake, and Val-Draekin emerged from the darkness, all of them watching him now. Lindholf turned to face the onrush of Sør Sevier knights, Dayknights, and Silver Guards fleeing toward the castle.

He met the charge of the first Dayknight with a firm resolve and stalwart confidence he had never before felt. The barrel-chested knight bore down on him fast, huge Dayknight blade aimed at his head. *Forgetting Moon* leaped to life in Lindholf's hand, cutting the charging Dayknight in half, spewing blood and sparks toward the sky from the impact. And still not one drop of red fell upon Lindholf or Leisel.

A second Dayknight fell to *Forgetting Moon* as well, as did a third and a fourth.

With bloodlust in his eyes and blue smoke swirling all around him, Lindholf Le Graven met the charge of all.

"Laijon has returned!" Val-Draekin shouted.

And the dragons above roared their approval.

Let me lay a proverb to your care. 'Tis the heretic who creates the
fire, and those of weak will who keep it stoked and aflame.
—THE WAY AND TRUTH OF LAIJON

CHAPTER SEVENTY-EIGHT
TALA BRONACHELL

14TH DAY OF THE HEART MOON, 999TH YEAR OF LAIJON

AMADON, GUL KANA

It was long past midnight. Smoke clotted the night sky above Lawri Le Graven and Tala Bronachell. The ground circling the Atonement Tree was a-litter with ash and glowing embers. Both Tala and Lawri gazed upon Aeros Raijael's impaled corpse, Lawri's pale face hooded in the shadows of her cowl. All that was left of the White Prince was a twisted and broken skeleton, scraps of blackened flesh clinging to his warped, heat-splintered bones.

Lawri turned away from the Atonement Tree, turned away from the spindly black wretch that used to be Aeros Raijael. She reached up and shed the hood of her cloak with both hands—one hand was healthy flesh, the other hand naught but a glimmering silver gauntlet. Her once delicate features were streaked with rot, and her gaze was lit with glowing swirls of green. Lawri looked sicker than any time before. She moved slowly, unsteady on her feet. Her wandering green eyes eventually found the Silver Throne.

Tala let her own gaze fall upon the ash-covered throne. She gripped the hilt of *Afflicted Fire* tightly in one hand, its razorlike tip digging into the soot somewhere behind her. She remembered how Jovan had kept the Silver Throne shrouded in white sheets. Bile rose up in her throat, thinking of her brother. Jovan was dead, as was her father. She could barely recall their faces, and it had been only hours since their deaths. All the images of her former life were growing fuzzier by the moment. In fact, all her memories had become naught but hazy dreams since she had killed Glade Chaparral.

But it was the journey from Amadon to the Hallowed Grove that had muddied her senses most. It had been a dreamlike, perilous ride through the smoke-filled skies on the scaled back of the huge green dragon. From atop the back of the beast, Tala had seen the extent of the devastation done to Amadon. Atop the back of the dragon, the destruction of the largest city in all the Five Isles was spread out under Tala as far as her eyes could see. The rotund Royal Cathedral had burned. Next to the Royal Cathedral, the Temple of the Laijon Statue had also burned; its roof was cracked open, its walls smashed and crumbled, the great statue of Laijon toppled and lying in the midst of the flaming rubble. Tala remembered Lindholf climbing the statue to get the note from the Bloodwood, the note from Seita. It had all seemed so innocent. *Naught but a game with an assassin. And I enjoyed it. And now I am a killer myself.* She could picture Glade's dying face, the light going out of his eyes.

If not for Lawri and the green dragon swooping down and plucking her from the chaos of Amadon, she would likely be dead now. Dead like Hawkwood and Glade and Leif and Jovan and her father.

She could sense the green dragon behind her now. She could feel the hiss and grumble of its deep breathing, the heavy rustling of its leathery wings. The beast had no eyes, yet Lawri had guided it straight to the Hallowed Grove.

And now here they were. *But what for?*

Lawri brushed by Tala, weaving unsteadily on her feet as she crossed the soot-covered ground toward the Silver Throne, the bottom hem of her cloak brushing over the ash at her feet. Like everything else in the Hallowed Grove, the Silver Throne was blanketed in a thick layer of gritty soot and foul odor.

"As promised"—Lawri swept ash from the silver arm of the throne with her one good hand—"we have been given our final Fiery Absolution, Tala."

"Everyone is dead because of Absolution, Lawri. Can't you see?"

"All is not lost," Lawri said.

"I think it is," Tala said.

"Have faith in me."

"I once had faith in my father," Tala said. "I worshipped everything about Borden Bronachell my whole life, only to find out he was all a lie. The dead are only visible through the flawed eyes of our memories. The living are only seen to disappoint. Or someone once told me. I can't remember who, though. Perhaps I read it in one of Jondralyn's books. I don't know where I heard it, but nothing could be truer. The living only disappoint."

"Are all your thoughts so hopeless?" Lawri asked.

"Seem to be, yes," Tala said, once again studying the rot crawling over her cousin's pale face. *She's almost dead.* "Indeed, all my thoughts are hopeless."

"And I thought I was always the gloomy one." Lawri tried to smile, but the effort only made her look more deranged and ill.

"I don't know who either one of us is anymore," Tala admitted.

"I see hope in the Silver Throne." Lawri brushed more ash from the throne. "I myself might be rotting away, but there is still hope, cousin, hope for Gul Kana."

"I don't see hope anywhere in this foul place."

"You are the Harbinger, Tala, and the Silver Throne is the key. You wield the sword of the crescent moon, and your army lies beneath the five holes in the pale marble. I am the Eyes of the Dragon. And we shall go and retrieve them. I have foreseen it."

"Retrieve what?" Tala asked. "Who?"

"Over the centuries, the slaves did most of the work for us," Lawri said, pointing toward the slave quarry. "They dug deep. Just not deep enough to reach the underworld. And now it is up to me and you to do the rest."

"The rest of what?"

"We are summoning your army up from the underworld, Tala. We are cracking open the world."

Tala's blood turned to ice.

"Come, Tala." Lawri brushed more ash from the throne. "We have one last journey to make, and then all will be made clear. Sit with me on the Silver Throne for a moment, Tala. Just for a moment. And when we are done the dragon shall carry it to Riven Rock. And you shall take this one last journey on the dragon's back with me."

***

Tala gasped aloud when she saw the mountain of smoking bodies piled along the eastern rim of the quarry. *How can so many be dead?* It seemed impossible.

The mountain of burnt knights was just one more horror in a war full of horrors.

Tala and Lawri clung to the blind dragon's sinuous, scaled back as the beast carried the Silver Throne deep down into the western depths of the quarry. The dragon gripped the Silver Throne in sharp curling claws, the heavy relic dangling beneath its feet. The dragon set the throne down gently on the smooth marble of the quarry as it landed, lowering its head for Tala and Lawri to dismount.

Tala slid from the dragon's back and looked around, *Afflicted Fire* still in hand, wondering why she had allowed herself to be brought down here with the Silver Throne. Lawri slid carefully from the dragon's back too and stood next to Tala, leaning into her for support, her own glowing green gaze taking in the strange surroundings.

Though it was the middle of the night, the bottom of the quarry was well lit. The moon and stars reflected pale light off the translucent surface of the marble. There were no other people here. They were all alone, trapped, the dragon their only way out.

If we are to ever come out! Tala thought.

The dragon had emptied them out on a flat surface, a hundred-foot slope descending down into a deeper part of the quarry. To her right was a sheer wall, a spiderweb of ropes leading up to what she imagined were hoists and pulleys balanced on the quarry rim hundreds of feet above. Several wooden buckets hung crooked from the ropes.

The dragon breathed heavily, lungs expanding, scales quivering. Tala had witnessed the destructive power of the dangerous fires living within the beast. She could feel the heat from its body growing. She did not trust the ghastly thing and stepped back.

"The dragon is sick too," Lawri said, reaching forth her good hand, stroking the glowing green scales of the beast. The dragon seemed to melt into her cool touch. "He is growing sicker than me. His eyes are gone. He has not had any Shroud of the Vallè for some time now. His fires are dying and he knows it."

How can any of this be real? Tala thought, watching the interplay between her cousin and the beast of the underworld. One had glowing green scales, the other glowing green eyes. Tala remembered the green elixir she had fed Lawri. *The machinations of the Bloodwood are never-ending, it seems.* Tala knew the shade from the secret ways would forever haunt both her and Lawri.

"You must keep the sword," Lawri said. "No matter what happens to me, you must promise to keep *Afflicted Fire*."

"I promise," Tala muttered less than enthusiastically. She could feel the tears springing into her eyes. She could tell her cousin was trying to tell her something important here. "What is going to happen to you, Lawri? What are we doing down here in this ghastly place?"

Lawri reached into the folds of her cloak with her good hand. She pulled forth a glowing red stone. *An angel stone!* Tala stared at the bright red gem. The ruby atop the pommel of *Afflicted Fire* began to glow too. The reflection of both gems sent twining bolts of glowing scarlet streaking down the length of *Afflicted Fire*'s long, pale blade. Transfixed, Tala reached for the angel stone in Lawri's hand.

"No." Lawri pulled back. "You mustn't touch it, for it is full of curses."

Lawri dropped to her knees and placed the bright red gemstone into a small circular hole someone had bored into the marble beneath her. The angel stone dropped down into the perfectly round fissure, and a red glow emanated from unknown depths.

"Why did you do that?" Tala gasped. "How will we ever get it out now?"

"We're not meant to get it out."

"But what if it was truly an angel stone?"

"I have them all." Lawri crawled forward to another similar circular hole punched in the marble. "Like you and the throne, the stones are part of the key."

Lawri pulled forth another angel stone from her cloak, this one green. She slipped the glowing stone into the round opening and watched it drop. A bright green glow shone up from the hole and onto her face. Lawri shuffled to the next hole, pulled forth a blue stone, dropped it in. She dropped the brilliant white stone into a fourth hole and the black stone into the last. Then Lawri stood in the center of the five colorful holes. Even the black cavity seemed to ooze dark light. The circular fissures had been drilled into the quarry floor in a perfectly symmetrical pentagonal pattern, each about three paces apart and no more.

Tala looked at the Silver Throne sitting just beyond the five holes— the five legs of the Silver Throne, always meant to represent the five pillars of Laijon, would fit perfectly into those holes. With that realization, Tala suddenly found her mind on fire with both confusion and fear. She was suddenly back in her mother's baths with Grand Vicar Denarius and the quorum of five. She was clutching the inside of the sleeping bag as the six men tried to drown her.

Dear Laijon! she had pleaded in the name of the lord for her life to be spared. *I'm dying, please do not let this happen. Oh, dear Laijon, please!* But she had lost that battle.

Be at peace, she had heard a deep voice say, the voice of the great One and Only. *Forgive me of my doubts, my questioning,* she had prayed. *Take me in your arms, dear Laijon. Give comfort to my sinful soul. Forgive me for mocking the Ember Gathering, for I know it is a sacred thing . . .*

Be at peace, the voice had repeated. And then she had seen the light. *White powder and light.* She had seen the Atonement Tree. She had seen fire and flame and Lawri Le Graven in the clouds sitting the Silver

Throne. She had seen a silver gauntlet and the Riven Rock slave quarry and five black holes punched into the glowing marble . . .

. . . and something awaiting her beneath those holes . . .

The key!

The green dragon moved into position behind the throne and lowered the great bulk of its scaled head, then pushed the throne forward, silver legs of the throne screeching against the dusty surface of the marble as it slowly moved.

The dragon pushed the throne across the marble toward the holes.

And with a shuddering clap of thunder, the five legs of the Silver Throne dropped into the five glowing hollows.

Once it was settled, Lawri climbed onto the throne and sat in the center of the silver seat, silver gauntlet resting on her lap. "Now we wait," she said.

The streaks of rot that had been growing up Lawri's neck and now crawled across her pale face had grown darker. "We wait for what?" Tala asked, watching the creeping death spread over her cousin's skin as she spoke. "We wait for *what?*"

"We wait for the underworld to crack open." Lawri's glowing green eyes pierced the night. "We wait for your army to come forth, Tala. We wait for your army to come forth at dawn and walk over the bones of the dead."

Can mortal man be more just and fair than the great One and Only? Can
mortal man be more pure in heart than his savior? For to be pure of heart
can be seen as vanity, but to be pure of soul is vexation for the wraiths.
—THE WAY AND TRUTH OF LAIJON

CHAPTER SEVENTY-NINE

AVA SHAY

14TH DAY OF THE HEART MOON, 999TH YEAR OF LAIJON

AMADON, GUL KANA

"Cromm!" Mancellor Allen called out when their small group of survivors rounded the corner and they saw a broad-faced oghul digging through the mound of smoking rubble under a crumbled church facade.

"Cromm Cru'x! Is it really you?" Mancellor broke from the group, rushing toward the oghul.

"Mancellor!" the oghul bellowed when he saw the young Wyn Darrè emerge from the dark, rushing toward him. "Mancellor Allen! Help Cromm dig Bronwyn from under these rocks!"

"My sister is under there?" Mancellor was now sprinting toward the pile of stone.

Ava Shay could hear someone calling for help under the rubble. Jenko Bruk, Liz Hen Neville, Dokie Liddle, and Beer Mug rushed toward the oghul after Mancellor. Ava followed, weary legs scarcely able to carry her forward.

"She's alive!" Mancellor shouted as he and Cromm struggled to push aside a large block of stone. The rest of the group helped, and the block toppled to the side in a spray of dust. Beneath the rock was a pocket of air in the rubble; the soot-covered face of a girl stared up at them through the dark. Her two grit-covered hands clawed for freedom. Cromm reached down and hauled the girl free of the wreckage and debris.

"Bronwyn," Mancellor exclaimed. "Is it really you? Are you okay?"

"I'm fine, I think." The dust-covered girl hugged Mancellor tightly. The girl's eyes were a rash of black under the dirt and ash, and two white feathers were tied into her hair, though they were dirty, tattered, and torn.

"I can't believe it's really you!" Mancellor cried, squeezing the girl tight.

"I've traveled the entirety of the Five Isles with Cromm, searching for you mostly." Bronwyn drew back from her brother, gazing into his eyes in wide wonder. "I can't believe you are actually here."

"I saw you under the Atonement Tree."

"And I saw you."

"I wanted to go to you. But the fires and the dragons! I never thought I would find you after all that."

"Yet here I am, somehow here I am."

"And here I am too," he exclaimed, arms engulfing her again. "I'm alive. I survived. You survived. We have all survived. Cromm too."

"It's been so long." She clung to her brother.

"You look so much older than I remember." Mancellor pulled away from her again, examining her at arm's length, but still gripping to her shoulders tightly, reluctant to let her go. "What did you do to your eyes?"

"I tattooed them in honor of my brother," she answered, clutching him close again. "I did it for you."

"I prayed for this day of our reunion," Mancellor said, strong arms encircling her again. "Praise be to Laijon and blessed be his name, for his spirit has watched over us both and brought us together once again."

Ava felt a lump growing in her throat, watching them hug and stare at each other and then hug and stare at each other, over and over. A tear rolled down her cheek; she knew how long Mancellor had been a captive and an unwilling fighter in Aeros Raijael's army, how long this girl Bronwyn must have been searching for her brother.

It had been five years since Mancellor had been taken from his sister during the White Prince's initial attack of Wyn Darrè. *Five years!* she thought. *It's been but a handful of moons since Jenko and I were captured in Gallows Haven.* Mancellor had lived the same nightmare as Ava for five years. She cast her gaze into the darkness, seeing the orange glow of the burning city around her. *A nightmare that still goes on.*

She looked at Mancellor and Bronwyn again. The large oghul stood to the side, grinning proudly at the joyful siblings. *Mancellor has found his family again.* All Ava had ever wanted was a family. She couldn't stop her own crying as she watched their reunion. Then she felt Jenko's hand slip into hers, and her tears washed away.

"Who is that?" Liz Hen Neville was weaving through the rubble toward a body lying against the wall, throat slit wide. Beer Mug was right there behind her.

"That's King Borden Bronachell," Bronwyn said. "Gault Aulbrek killed him."

"Borden Bronachell," Liz Hen exclaimed, despair in her tone as she looked down at the dead man. Beer Mug gazed up at the girl, sensing her concern.

All Ava Shay knew was that Borden Bronachell had disappeared in war many years ago. That he was lying here dead in this destroyed city did not surprise her. Nothing surprised her anymore. Flames licked out from under the rubble and over Borden's boots. Ava could feel herself sweat from the heat of the many fires. There was just nowhere to escape the unrelenting heat in the dark, burning city. The fighting had died down some in this destroyed section of Amadon, but clouds of smoke huddled over their small group.

"We were involved in a big fight here," Bronwyn said, looking at Liz Hen. "Before the bell tower fell on us, that is. Nail and Krista Aulbrek were with us, but I do not see them now. I think Hawkwood is buried under here too, but I cannot be sure."

"Hawkwood!" Liz Hen exclaimed. "We have to search for him! Nail, too. What if they are all buried?"

"It would be a waste of time," Bronwyn said. "I'm not sure whether any of them were buried. They could have escaped." She looked at Cromm.

The oghul shrugged broad, dust-covered shoulders. "Cromm did not see where Hawkwood was when the bell tower fell. He did not see where the marked one was when the tower fell. But that black horse with the red eyes is gone too. There are a great many mysteries left to be solved. Cromm thought he even saw a green dragon when he was buried under the stones and rubbles. But Cromm cannot be sure about that, either. Everyone was dead and gone when Cromm crawled from under the fallen bell tower. Other than that, Cromm knows nothing."

The loud rumble of horses' hooves and the thunder of war in the smoky distance grew louder. Ava's heart galloped in her chest once more. War still surrounded them!

"We must leave this place," Mancellor advised. "We must reach the safety of the castle. There are tunnels there. Tunnels we can follow to safety. They are likely our only hope of survival."

"The castle lies this way." Cromm pointed into the smoke and darkness. "Follow Cromm and he shall lead you there."

**

Cromm was right. He led them straight through the smoke and darkness to the gate of the castle and beyond. And hours later, as the fitful light of dawn was settling over Amadon Castle, Ava watched through the hazy morning light as the city burned below. Smoke drifted up the slopes of Mount Albion into the skies.

Though war raged even throughout the castle grounds, Ava's group had met little resistance. A good portion of the spires and battlements crawling up the slopes of Albion were naught but burning rubble now, the destruction caused by the three dragons that still reigned above. Ava knew they were still not safe and likely never would be until they were inside the castle and in the tunnels.

Their small group had reached a large courtyard halfway up the mount that Mancellor had called Tin Man Square. It was a vast, grassy, open space of gardens and sculptures and bulky granite crypts. The square was enclosed on three sides by high stone battlements, and there were three entrances: to the north, west, and east. They had entered through the easternmost entrance. The main garden was named the Gardens of the Crown Moon; it was the place where Jondralyn Bronachell's body had lain in state before Fiery Absolution, or so Mancellor had claimed. The crypt in the center of the garden was set at the bottom of a colossal set of wide marble stairs rising up to the south. The Long Stairs, Mancellor had named them. The almost impossibly long and wide staircase rose some two hundred feet or more up the slope of Mount Albion. At the top was a flat marble platform, punctuated by a long stretch of tall marble columns.

And under the row of columns stood the last of the Gul Kana army: Dayknights and Silver Guards, perhaps several thousand, all of them awaiting the last battle, the final defense of Sunbird Hall. Behind the mass of fighters were passageways that led to the famed Sunbird Hall and other parts of the castle, including the secret tunnels where Ava's group hoped to escape.

Smoke was swiftly filling Tin Man Square, and guttural shouts of dismay sounded from the top of the long staircase, followed by the unmistakable rasp of weapons being ripped free of sheaths. The ominous forms of oghul and Vallè fighters could just be made out through the smoke beyond the gardens and the crypts. The enemy army was pouring in through the gates of the yard to the north and east, banners fluttering. There were thousands of them. Vallè armor twinkled in the dark haze of the smoky dawn. The oghuls began pounding their weapons rhythmically. They gave fullthroated voice to a thunderous chant: *"Rogk Na Ark! Rogk Na Ark! Rogk Na Ark!"*

"Those Dayknights and Silver Guards are gonna come rushing down those stairs," Mancellor said, looking at Jenko Bruk. "They will thunder right over the top of us if we try and reach Sunbird Hall that way."

"So where do we go?" Jenko said. "You are the only one of us who has been in this castle before."

"I didn't stay long here," Mancellor said, nervous gaze scanning the courtyard. "I don't know any other way."

"We've no choice but to fight then," Jenko said. "There is nowhere else to go. The enemy is filling the yard."

Jenko still wore *Lonesome Crown*. He held a long spear comfortably in hand. He had pulled the spear from a pile of dead men. Ava recalled the rumors around Gallows Haven of how good a grayken harpooner Jenko Bruk was. Mancellor drew his own sword with a crisp rasp of steel. Behind him, Cromm brandished the huge rusted maul he had scavenged from the grip of a dead oghul. Bronwyn nocked an arrow into the Dayknight longbow she had also found.

"Bloody fuck," Liz Hen exclaimed as she pulled her sword too. Dokie gripped *Blackest Heart* in his own small hands. Beer Mug growled, also ready to fight.

"Fill as many of the Vallè bastards with arrows as you can." Mancellor nodded to his sister. "It will be an honor to defend this castle with you here today."

Bronwyn nodded at her brother in acknowledgment, the whites of her eyes piercingly clear under the tattoos covering her face.

"I love you," Jenko mouthed silently to Ava. With that one gesture, Ava tried to once again muster what bravery and will she had. She gripped My Heart tightly, expecting that she would die here in this courtyard. She had made peace with that fact.

Arrows rained down into the courtyard from above. Screams and shouts of both Vallè and oghuls rose into the sky. Above the ruckus, Ava could now hear the thunderous clatter of armor and booted feet as the remaining Gul Kana knights descended the Long Stairs. Some were mounted. Most came on foot.

Down the stairs they charged, flooding toward the smoke and haze of Tin Man Square to meet the enemy. The oghuls and Vallè prepared to meet their charge, their own arrows firing up the staircase. Men and chargers fell, tumbling and screaming down the stairway. It was instant chaos as the two armies clashed at the bottom of the stairs not thirty paces in front of Ava's small group.

Mancellor charged toward the fight, Jenko, Bronwyn, and Cromm on his heels, the dark-eyed girl firing arrows into the smoky haze of the battle as she ran. Liz Hen shoved Dokie after them. "Fire that crossbow, idiot!" she shouted as she charged forward. Dokie did the three-fingered sign of the Laijon Cross over his heart and dashed after Liz Hen, firing the crossbow as he ran. Beer Mug followed them.

Ava ran toward the fight last, her own fear at the coming battle primal and raw and all too bloodcurdlingly real. Other than what few things the Spider and Enna Spades had taught her, she knew little of actual fighting. But this was war, and she would soon be in the middle of it. Bronwyn's arrows and Dokie's quarrels had already caused chaos in the flanks of the oghul and Vallè army. Many dropped without even knowing what hit them. Mancellor, Jenko, and Cromm launched themselves at the back of the enemy army, their weapons flashing in the smoky light, cutting down the first oghuls they attacked from behind. Liz Hen was with them, her Dayknight sword stabbing into the back of a Vallè warrior. The Vallè dropped and Liz Hen shouted in triumph.

The unsuspecting Vallè and oghuls turned and launched their own assault, weapons clashing. Mancellor tumbled to the grass of the courtyard under the weight of a charging oghul. Cromm's square iron maul whirled as he struck Mancellor's attacker in the face with a meaty thud. Ava launched herself into the fray at a full sprint, losing sight of Mancellor and Cromm as her own thin sword came up instinctively, blocking the blow of a sleek Vallè dagger aimed at her head. The collision of My Heart with the Vallè's dagger sent her staggering into the back of a brutish oghul. Her hand and arm stung from the impact, but she kept hold of her weapon. Suddenly Jenko was at her side, his spear entering the chest of the Vallè who had attacked her.

I am in a war! Her mind roiled. *I've no armor or war charger or anything to protect me but a thin woman's sword.* It was both exhilarating and horrifying, the sudden splash of blood and noise surrounding her. Cromm's heavy maul pulverized the pale face of a Vallè who struck at her. An arrow from Bronwyn caught another Vallè in the neck, spinning him around just as he swung at Cromm with his sparkling shortsword.

The courtyard was a whirling, disordered roar of metal on metal and screams of the dying. And Beer Mug's fearsome wild barks rose joyously above the overall din. The shepherd dog, muzzle already bloody, ripped into the face of an oghul. The frantic beast tried to shove the dog away with rusted gauntlets. Jenko leaped past Ava, *Lonesome Crown* somehow still balanced on his head, its strange curved horns almost gleaming with pale light. He struck a screaming oghul straight in the face with the butt of his spear, cracking the beast's helm, dropping him cold. Another oghul dove at Jenko. He ducked, one of the horns of *Lonesome Crown* sinking deep into the monster's neck. The oghul fell dead, legs twitching. A dagger flashed before Ava's face. Before she could even register what was happening, Jenko speared the Vallè who had tried stabbing her, then leaped over the dead body, his every move deliberate and skilled, his spear naught but a vicious blur as he slashed the necks of two more oghuls in his way and leaped into the swirling smoke after more. Ava stumbled after him, breathing hard, My Heart feeling heavy in her hands as the chaos and savagery of battle finally sank in. She felt useless, like a liability in the fight.

A thin-faced oghul clambered over a dead Vallè in front of her. The oghul's rusty battle-ax punched a deep red valley into the chest plate of a Dayknight who came running down the stairs to Ava's left. With a roar, the injured Dayknight swung his long pike in a powerful arch. The thin-faced oghul sidestepped the Dayknight's blow and the sharp pike slammed into the face of an unwary Silver Guard, splitting his skull. Chunks of blood and bone and teeth peppered Ava's face. She reeled away, swiping at the bloody grit covering her. Her vision blurred. The entire courtyard was awash in foul torrents of thick smoke and splattering scarlet—the grass was matted and boggy with blood.

Again she swiped her bloody face, trying to clear her eyes. Ava slipped in the sludge and crashed straight into the backside of a large, barrel-chested oghul. She felt her face bounce painfully off the beast's rusted iron armor. The dizzying blow sent her careening across the courtyard in a daze. She fell to her knees. The oghul spun around and charged after her. Through the film of blood covering her eyes, she could just make out the double-bladed battle-ax clutched in the monster's two gauntleted fists.

Ava blinked away the blood and hauled herself upright. She set her feet as Enna Spades and the Spider had taught her. The oghul's gruesome weapon came swinging down. She leaned to the side and let the creature's double-bladed ax skim past her and bury itself deep into the sopping grass. Ava returned the oghul's attack with a thrust of her own. The tip of My Heart entered the narrow eye slit in the oghul's helm, stabbing deep into the creature's brain. Blood bloomed thick and red through the eye slit and the oghul slipped from the tip of her sword. *I killed it!* her mind screamed of its own volition. *I actually killed it!* She couldn't believe what she had done. *I'm a warrior now!*

Another oghul swung a hulking sword at her. The serrated blade sizzled in the air. She ducked just in time and the blade missed. Cromm stepped in and parried swift and hard with his maul, snapping the oghul's sword in half. Cromm then smashed the head of the other beast. He looked at Ava and bellowed, "Don't just stand there, girl, fight!"

Ava thrust up her sword as a Vallè fighter swung at her. The fey's thin blade hit My Heart just right, knocking the weapon from Ava's grip, sending it bouncing across the bloody grass. The slender sword disappeared under the churning feet of the two oghuls Beer Mug had backed up against a stone statue. The Vallè swung again and Ava dove aside, her jerking legs carrying her toward her fallen weapon, outstretched hand reaching for the lost blade under the violent stomping feet of the two oghuls. The Vallè fighter who had knocked the sword away did not relent as he took two long steps toward Ava, keen fey eyes piercing in their murderous intent.

Then the Vallè dropped face-first to the grass in front of her, dead, legs thrashing. Dokie Liddle stood over the fey, *Blackest Heart* gripped in both hands. A thick crossbow quarrel jutted up from the Vallè's back. The small boy met Ava's startled gaze, then bounded away toward Jenko, who was engaged in battle with a group of oghuls near a tall stone statue. Breathing heavily, Ava snatched her thin sword from under the kicking legs of the two oghuls Beer Mug was fighting and lurched toward Jenko.

Then she spotted Cromm from the corner of her eye. The oghul was braced against a separate stone statue, two Vallè arrows lodged in his armor. He fought off a handful of Vallè with his heavy maul. Mancellor fought at his side. He had also taken some injuries. Then he dropped to his hands and knees and vomited up a thick stream of blood, his entire body convulsing in pain. *We're losing!* The thought horrified Ava as she saw Mancellor struggle. She did not want to see her friends die. She stabbed out at the armored stomach of an oghul who rose up from the bloody grass before her. She missed and the oghul lunged at her, a dirty shortsword in hand. Beer Mug tore at the back of the oghul's legs with scarlet-dripping teeth. Ava stabbed the oghul in the neck and it fell.

An arrow bounced off the helm of the Vallè who attacked her next, sending the fey reeling back. Bronwyn had fired the arrow. She was running toward Cromm and Mancellor. Liz Hen was with her. The big girl launched herself straight into a group of charging Vallè, her long black blade flashing mercilessly. Two of the Vallè fell to the ground under her, their necks fountaining blood. A Dayknight stood in front of Ava now, fighting, an enraged Vallè hacking at him with a long spear. The Dayknight fell under the fey's rapid onslaught. Ava's panicked eyes met those of the bloody-faced knight. He looked up to her for help, his own sword clutched in both hands. Ava stabbed her sword into the face of the Vallè spearman. He fell dead at her feet.

"Thanks, lassie," the Dayknight grumbled as he stood and waded off into battle.

The chaos around her was maddening. Ava couldn't keep track of anything or anyone. Smoke and flashing weapons and blood and screaming surrounded her on all sides, bodies pressing in. Then the smoke around her cleared in a huge wave as the blue dragon sailed over the courtyard and marble stairs.

Ava grimaced and clutched the sides of her skull, trying to stave off the ear-piercing pain from the beast's sudden roar. Everyone had stopped fighting as the dragon soared above, all eyes cast to the sky. The dragon sailed over Tin Man Square and disappeared behind the battlements. Ava's head pounded with pain and she looked around.

Something was crawling across the ground toward her. *A dwarf!*

And then she realized who it was. It was Jenko's father. *Baron Jubal Bruk!*

She couldn't mistake the familiar bearded face and sloping forehead. He had silver blades jutting from the tar coating the stumps of his arms. The blades dug into the soft turf as he pulled himself across the ground. Ava couldn't believe what she was seeing. The man was armless and legless, yet still he lived. The last time Ava had seen the baron, Jenko was sawing at his limbs on the blood-scarred beach of Gallows Haven.

"Jenko!" the baron called out as he squirmed along the grass, the stumps of his legs dragging through the bloody slop and gore. "Jenko!" he yelled. "Son!"

"Father!" Jenko spotted his father on the ground.

The entire courtyard was pitched in a sudden, agonizing silence as the blue dragon roared overhead once more, fire billowing from its gaping mouth and over the battlements. The Silver Guard bowmen stationed there burst into screaming flame. The dragon turned and seemed to hang in midair, hovering over Tin Man Square. The skull-faced rider bestride the blue beast eyed the throng below. Then the dragon glided toward the stairs, landing just above Ava. And like a statue, silent and unmoving, the beast remained perched on the stairway as the rider dismounted, whip uncoiling in its blue-gauntleted hand. Sleek drops of silver dripped to the bloody marble as the dragon rider silently drifted down the Long Stairs, dark cloak billowing out behind. The knight's twin silver eyes gleamed in the dim morning light from behind its skull-shaped mask.

Several Dayknights charged up the stairs to meet the demon knight. But when the dragon rider struck with the whip, the sound was a dreadful shrieking sizzle. Silver barbs sliced the legs out from under the nearest Dayknight. The man tipped awkwardly, crying out in horror as he slid down the stairs to the grassy courtyard below, legless, leaving a bloody trail.

The demon with the murderous whip stalked toward its next victim.

And flame surged from the mouth of the dragon.

CHAPTER EIGHTY

GAULT AULBREK

14TH DAY OF THE HEART MOON, 999TH YEAR OF LAIJON

AMADON, GUL KANA

Gault Aulbrek and Enna Spades charged into Tin Man Square
just as the dragon rider in blue struck down the first Dayknight
on the stairs. They had spent the night battling their way up
Mount Albion and into Amadon Castle, killing many. Now it was dawn
and hundreds had likely died at their hands. Gault never counted the
dead.

With blood-smeared weapons at the ready, together he and Spades
rushed into Tin Man Square through a small side entrance trellised with
green vines. Side by side they wove their way through a row of stone
sculptures and into the courtyard. It wasn't long before they were stepping through pools of blood, the entire yard and marble staircase rising
above smelling of dragon-seared death.

The extent of the destruction wrought by the previous battle was
shocking even for Gault Aulbrek to behold. The once lush gardens of
Tin Man Square were trampled, crypts and statues overturned. Amadon

Silver Guards and Dayknights lay sprawled out in twisted, ungainly ways, severed arms and legs and heads scattered like burnt kindling.

Man, oghul, and Vallè had all resumed fighting, all once again hacking away at each other in a symphony of mad havoc. The blue dragon and the skull-faced knight had reached the bottom of the marble staircase now, both of them engaged in the midst of the fighting, dragon fire carving a path through the Gul Kana knights.

Gault and Spades rushed in and fought their way toward the dragon. A black blade came slashing down, angling for Gault's exposed head. He stepped aside and blocked the blow, letting the Dayknight's momentum carry him forward and straight into Spades' reach. Spades ended the knight's life with a swift chop to the back of his neck. The man flopped lifeless to the ground, face splashing in the muck. Another Dayknight came at Gault, a broad-faced helmetless brute who reminded Gault of Hammerfiss. The knight's flying mane of red hair fanned out behind him as he ran, aiming his Dayknight sword low in a sweeping arc at Gault. Once again, Gault stepped back and let the tip of the sword whistle past his face. Then he stabbed out, catching the knight in the throat, driving the blade out the back of the large knight's neck.

Oghuls charged at Gault and Spades next—at least a dozen. Spades blocked the first blow from a heavy spiked mace. The oghul's attack was easily deflected, and Spades lashed out with her own blade. The oghul raised a thick wooden shield. The shield exploded upward in a spray of splintered wood as Spades' blade smashed it, flinging the beast backward into the slop.

A dozen Dayknights joined the battle against Gault and Spades. Gault felt at home attacking both man and oghul, not caring who he killed next, at ease with himself and the world, once again engaged in the thick of battle. The flat of his blade crashed into the nearest Dayknight, armor and bone crunching. A second Dayknight rose up in that one's place. Gault struck the man's helmet from his head. The startled knight's paunchy face was streaked with blood and sweat, long brown hair matted to his scalp. Spades sliced his surprised face in half. An oghul was right behind the fallen Dayknight, corded gray muscles straining under spiked armor. He swung his maul. Spades dropped to her knees, blood and sludge splashing up into her face as she ducked the oghul's swing, the rusted weapon punching through the face of the Dayknight behind her. The knight's body crumpled into the red grass.

Soldiers on horse and foot were coming at them from every direction now. Gault swung his sword, tearing open a Vallè fighter's midsection. The Vallè clutched at his gut, ropes of steaming entrails coiling out from his split stomach. *Be bloody, be brave, be happy!* Gault recited the passage from the *Illuminations* in his head.

Everywhere he looked, the courtyard was streaked with red—man, oghul, Vallè, and horse thrashing and dying. A riderless destrier crashed into him, bucking and braying in pain, its lathered face drenched in blood from a wicked gash between its eyes. The horse's splayed-open nostrils were huffing air. The crazed large horse pushed into Gault, its weight knocking him face-first to the ground. Gagging on the sour taste of grass and blood, Gault swiftly untangled himself from the legs of the horse and squirmed free, regaining his feet. He shoved past the wild beast and forced his way into the rising tide of battle. More and more Dayknights came pouring down the long stairway to the left and into Tin Man Square. Oghuls and Vallè soldiers shoved in from the right.

The blue dragon and its blue-clad rider plied the smoky sky above now, great rivers of boiling flame spilling down into the courtyard.

"The dragon's flying again!" Gault heard a young boy's voice. "Is it coming our way again, Liz Hen? It's coming our way!"

Both Gault and Spades turned to see two familiar young faces.

Spades' hard gaze came to rest on the smaller of the two youths from Gallows Haven. The boy carried the crossbow *Blackest Heart*. A shepherd dog growled at Spades from behind Liz Hen, its muzzle dripping with blood.

"We meet again so soon, Dokie Liddle," Spades snarled with malice. "And this time I will kill that dog if it's the last thing I do in life."

She pointed her bloody blade at the big gray dog.

"You ain't killin' nobody!" Liz Hen raised her own bloodstained sword. "Especially not Beer Mug. Not as long as I draw breath."

"Brave words, girl." Spades flicked the point of her own blade against the tip of Liz Hen's challengingly. "Best you surrender your weapon now."

"Come at us, bitch." Liz Hen scowled, her eyes narrow slits of rage. "I dare you."

Dokie stepped around Liz Hen and the dog, black crossbow in hand, bolt aimed at Spades' chest. Without hesitating, the boy fired. The bolt ricocheted off Spades' upraised blade with a twang, fluttering away into the swarm of oghuls behind her.

"Bloody Mother Mia!" Spades glared at Dokie. Then she swung at the boy, the edge of her blade catching the center of the crossbow, splitting the weapon with a thunderous loud *crack!* that shook the air.

Blackest Heart spun away from Dokie in two separate halves, both pieces landing with a wet spray of blood in the grass. Dokie's eyes widened in shock.

Spades swung at the boy again. At the same time, Liz Hen plowed into the center of Spades' armored chest with the weight of her entire body, sending both of them rolling to the ground, Spades losing her weapon. Liz Hen's fists were a flurry of battering blows. Spades tried to push the big girl off. Beer Mug leaped in and tore at Spades' armored arms and legs.

With one booted foot, Gault kicked the dog away from Spades. He held his sword out, protecting himself from the enraged animal, which had now turned its attention to him. Liz Hen and Spades separated, hauling themselves to their feet, both weaponless. Liz Hen bled from the nose, red bubbles forming around her nostrils. Beer Mug wasted no time and launched himself at Spades once again, going for her throat. Spades scurried back in defense, throwing her armored arms over her face. "Kill her, Beer Mug!" Liz Hen yelled as the dog pulled Spades to the bloody grass. Gault lunged forward and tried to stab at Beer Mug, but the dog was too quick and effortlessly leaped away.

Suddenly Mancellor Allen was there at the dog's side, swinging at Gault with a long sword. A dark-eyed girl was with the Wyn Darrè boy, along with a tall, burly oghul. The oghul had two arrows lodged in his chest plate.

"Let's take him, Bronwyn!" Mancellor yelled at the girl. "We can kill this bastard ourselves!"

"Cromm will smash the fucker!" the oghul roared, advancing.

Gault retreated from the trio of new fighters. But they pursued, relentless, weapons striking out. It was all Gault could do to parry their trio of blows. It would take him a moment to gain back the advantage, but he knew he could. The Wyn Darrè boy looked injured; blood poured from several gashes in his armor. The two arrows lodged in the oghul's chest seemed to have scant effect on slowing the beast. Bronwyn was a scrappy fighter, striking at Gault with the haft of a Dayknight longbow.

A war charger dashed into their midst, separating Gault from the trio of fighters who assailed him. He whirled from Mancellor, Bronwyn, and Cromm to help Spades as more horses thundered by. The warrior woman was still weaponless, still wrestling with Liz Hen. Dokie and Beer Mug had also joined the fight, all of them rolling on the ground. Soon Spades was wrestling with a fourth person—an armless and legless man.

Baron Jubal Bruk!

Gault recognized the baron of Gallows Haven immediately. Jubal Bruk had twin dagger blades jutting from the stumps of both arms, and he was stabbing repeatedly at Spades' exposed face. Spades was doing her utmost to ward off not only the wild blows of the baron, but also the ravaging teeth of Beer Mug and the thudding fists of both Liz Hen and Dokie. Only her armor protected her from serious injury until one of the baron's blades sliced into her left eye, cutting into it deep, cutting it in two. Spades screamed out in pain—a sound Gault had never before heard from her.

Gault reached Spades just in time to see Jenko Bruk and Ava Shay arrive.

He hesitated when seeing the Gallows Haven girl.

Ava Shay was still alive and still in the battle, fair blond hair dripping in blood as she stabbed down at Spades with the thin ruby-hilted blade she had carried from Saint Only. Jenko Bruk carried a lethal-looking spear and wore a familiar horned helm atop his head. *Lonesome Crown!* The first rays of the morning sun peeked up from over the battlements, yellow light glinting off the tips of the strange curved horns of the helm.

He did not want to harm Ava, but Gault launched himself at Jenko with the intent of killing the Gallows Haven boy before he could stab that spear into Spades and finish her. Jenko met his charge with a wild swing of the weapon. There was a jarring crash as sword smashed into spear, and Gault stumbled back. Jenko had always been strong, but now he was a seasoned fighter. Gault swung at him again. Jenko blocked just as swiftly.

Injured, Spades managed to throw Beer Mug off of her and scramble from under the pile of bodies and get to her feet. Baron Bruk was still under her, stabbing futilely at her armored legs. Liz Hen and Dokie crawled away toward the dog. Spades clutched one hand to her left eye, trying to stave the pain. Blood blossomed from the wound and over her fingers. Realizing there was nothing to be done for her injury, she snatched up a fallen sword and rammed it down into the startled face of Baron Bruk. The man clawed at the blade suddenly growing from his split-open face.

Spades yanked the blade free.

Ava Shay backed up, horror falling over her pale features.

Beer Mug barked up a storm, trying to guard the baron now, standing over his squirming body.

"Father!" Jenko cried out as Spades swung at Beer Mug. The dog danced away. Spades then reached down and pulled Baron Bruk along the bloody grass by the back of his collar. Jubal, still alive somehow, could not fight her off, armless and legless as he was. All he could do was use the dagger blades to claw at the bloody yard. "I'll kill you, bitch!" he somehow shouted through his split-open mouth as he was dragged along, stumps flailing. "I will kill you for doing what you did to me!"

"Sure you will." Spades let him go, standing over him now, blood streaming down the left side of her face, nobody within ten paces of them. She stabbed down, burying her blade into Jubal Bruk's heart. When she pulled the weapon from the baron's chest, it was glossy with his blood.

"No!" Jenko cried out, his eyes naught but twin amber slits full of dark rage.

Spades stood above the mutilated body of Baron Jubal Bruk, her red hair flowing out behind her like a ratty red flag of flame. Her left eye was a mutilated mess. There was a fierce bearing about her freckled, blood-splattered face now, a fierce bearing unlike anything Gault had ever seen in her before. Her remaining eye was squinting and icy cold as it cut toward Jenko. "Mancellor Allen stole that helmet from me! Now you wear it! You are naught but a turncoat and thief, Jenko Bruk! And today you shall die like your father just died!"

Jenko lifted his spear, ready to let throw, eyes tightening at the corners. Blood flowing and covering most of her face now, Spades charged. Jenko let the spear fly. It sang through the air, swift and true. Spades knocked the spear aside with a deft flick of her sword. In two strides she was on top of Jenko, her sword swinging down.

Ava Shay launched herself forward, plowing into Spades' side, and they stumbled to the ground in a heap. Spades rolled on top of Ava and sprang to her feet and met Jenko's charge. The boy was coming at her with just his fists. Spades swung her weapon, shouting in fury. She was in a rage. Jenko ducked, and with a *crack!* like thunder, Spades' sword shattered the two curving horns atop *Lonesome Crown*. The helm spun from Jenko's head, the severed horns landing with an unceremonious splat in a patch of bloody grass.

Gault's mind reeled as he stared at the ruined helm. Spades had cut *Blackest Heart* in half not moments ago. Now *Lonesome Crown*. He didn't know what to think—the two fabled weapons destroyed so easily, and by Enna Spades.

The blue dragon landed again on the stairs. The beast and its blue rider moving ominously toward the shattered helm, the beast's azure eyes blazing with malice. The dragon stopped and the dragon rider slid from the monster's scaled back and stalked down the stairway toward Gault, dark cloak sweeping out behind him. Several Dayknights charged the skull-faced knight. The silver coils of the demon's whip snapped forth with a wet hiss, slicing the arm from the first Dayknight. The man's painful shout was sharp and intense. Another strike of the whip and the same knight's head slid neatly from his neck. Silver droplets splattered the ground with a sizzle of white smoke. The dragon rider killed a second Dayknight just as easily.

The blue dragon roared, the tremendous sound looming over the battlefield's lashing butchery and gore. Pain filled Gault's head and he covered his ears. The sheer splendor and brilliance of the dragon's bearing was like the dazzling bravura of a pulsing star. And the dragon rider looked just as brilliant against the sodden scarlet stain of war. A Dayknight horseman charged the dragon. The beast's jagged mouth snapped out, then clamped down, engulfing the horse's front quarters almost entirely. The horse let loose a throaty scream as it was jerked into the air, its twisted, shredded, bloody remains strewn across Tin Man Square. The Dayknight tumbled into the gore-lathered grass, body torn in two. Gault watched in dread fascination as the dragon descended the stairs, searching for more prey. Its huge glowing eyes were a piercing shade of blue. It roared again, the sound casting a spell over the entire courtyard. Its supple scaled neck slithered just above the ground like a snake, weaving back and forth, huge batlike wings unfurling, quivering and sinuous. When it reached the bottom of the marble stairs, the beast's huge claws dug into the soupy crimson grass. The skull-faced knight snapped the deadly silver whip again as if in challenge.

Jenko Bruk was the closest one to the dragon and the demonic knight now. He raised his sword in defense, garnering the dragon rider's attention. Ava Shay stood just behind Jenko, her thin blade held out protectively between them. She faced the dragon and the skull-faced knight with a look of bold fierceness and determination Gault had never before seen within her. Liz Hen and Dokie stepped forward to stand beside their friends, Liz Hen with her bloody sword, Dokie with naught but his balled fists. Beer Mug was with them, bloody muzzle pulled back, glistening teeth bared in a threatening snarl. Mancellor Allen and the dark-haired girl named Bronwyn moved up and stood by Jenko and Ava.

The oghul, Cromm, was with them, two arrows still lodged in his armor. Gault could almost appreciate the bravery of the group, though they were all soon to die.

"Let's get out of here," Spades urged, blood still draining profusely from her ravaged eye socket. "Before this dragon cooks us all."

As if reading her mind, the dragon raised its sleek-scaled head and roared again, louder than ever before. To stave off the pain, Gault fell to his knees and clutched the sides of his skull with both hands. He gulped in the squalid, smoke-filled air, his vision blurring with pain. Spades also tottered forward to her knees, hands over her ears.

And still the dragon roared. Everyone in the courtyard had to cover their ears. Gault tried to stand, but every bone in his body raged in protest, his tortured brain swimming with splintered thoughts and shattered confusion. His head drooped toward the bloody grass in defeat. It was as if the dragon sang for his death, and he couldn't escape the foul melody that saturated the depths of his soul. When the beast finally ceased its roar, a tower of flame and heat bloomed skyward from its gaping maw. Gault stood, relief washing over him. He had never felt such pain as the dragon's cruel sound had caused.

"Let's get the fuck out of here," Spades repeated as the skull-faced knight cracked the silver whip, advancing on the group from Gallows Haven. "That girl ain't worth it, Gault," she said. "That girl ain't worth dying over."

But Gault could not move. He had come so far for Ava Shay and did not wish to see her die.

"Do you have no fear?" The skull-faced knight stepped toward Jenko's group, voice melodious and fine. "Are you not afraid?"

"No," Liz Hen answered. "We are not scared." Though her whole body trembled.

"You should be." The skull-faced knight cracked the whip once more. "Your deaths will do Viper great honor."

"Viper?" Liz Hen asked. "Who is Viper?"

"The lord of all."

"Well, if I could, I would kick this Viper's ass."

"And your attempt would do Viper great honor," the dragon rider said. "For Viper does honor bravery. But you will lose such a fight."

"Well then, fuck this fellow Viper and whatever bloody calloused cunt he slithered out of." Liz Hen's face was florid with rage now. She turned to the shepherd dog. "Get him, Beer Mug. Get him like you got the green dragon."

Beer Mug bolted toward the skull-faced knight. The dragon rider snapped the whip. The dog effortlessly dodged the sinuous weapon and launched himself through the air, powerful teeth latching onto the dragon rider's left forearm, digging deep into the creature's blue-scaled vambrace. The silver whip dropped as Beer Mug's weight pulled the skull-faced knight to the ground. The dragon rider fell on top of the whip, and white smoke billowed up around the two combatants.

"Kill him, Beer Mug!" Liz Hen leaped into the fray. "Tear his fucking arm off!" She kicked the dragon rider's head, knocking the silver skull mask from its head, revealing the creature's bone-white face grimacing in the swirling smoke. She stabbed down with her Dayknight sword, splitting the stretched and pallid face. Blood, blue as the sky, welled up as the demon writhed on the ground, dying, limbs eventually falling limp.

The dragon roared, blue wings flaring high, quivering in rage, blocking the sun. The beast rose up on its hind legs, the talons of its forelegs stretched and bare. It loomed over Liz Hen and the dead knight, its wide mouth open, daggerlike teeth gleaming, flame curling behind its forked blue tongue.

"Run, Liz Hen!" Dokie called out.

Beer Mug and Liz Hen scrambled away from the dead knight as the fire, searing and bright, piled down atop the deceased knight in curling orange waves, the murderous heat sending everyone reeling to escape Tin Man Square.

Once the ashes have gone cold, the banished shall rise again, climbing a scorched mountain of the human dead, making their long journey to the one wielding the white sword and the crescent moon, toward the one meant for greater things.
—The Book of the Betrayer

CHAPTER EIGHTY-ONE

CRYSTALWOOD

14TH DAY OF THE HEART MOON, 999TH YEAR OF LAIJON

AMADON, GUL KANA

The enraged blue dragon rained terror over the courtyard, long neck sweeping from left to right, flame spewing from its mouth, scattering everyone. Thousands of humans and Vallè and oghuls fled before the beast. Those that died instantly in the fire were the lucky ones. The rest could do naught but scream in horror and pain as their own boiling skin slithered from their bones.

Krista and Nail had entered the terror-filled courtyard through a small stone gate dripping with green vines. Krista rode her Bloodeye mare, Dread. She still did not feel whole; the injury to her head still oozed blood. Nail led her horse by the bit, and it was not until they had worked their way around a row of stone sculptures that Krista realized the true horror they had stumbled upon. The vast square was blanketed in an endless array of armored bodies hacked apart and burnt. Human, Vallè, and oghul lay in grassy pools of mush and scarlet for as far as she could see. And the blue dragon was in the middle of it all, roaring and choking out swirling flame.

Then Krista spotted a familiar face near the long marble stairway that rose up to the castle above. Ava Shay was in the mass of knights running toward her, her small, thin sword gripped in hand. The panicked Gallows Haven girl was battered and bloody and looked near exhaustion. She tripped and fell, still clutching her thin weapon. She tried to stand but was roughly shoved back to the ground by the mad horde trying to escape the dragon behind her. Krista lost sight of the girl in the onrush of knights. She urged Nail to lead them back out of the yard before they too were trampled by the frantic knights who now swirled all around them.

Then she spotted Ava Shay once again. Gault Aulbrek, along with several other blood-splattered knights, was helping the girl to her feet. A large red-haired girl in battered armor was also helping, along with a mousy-looking boy and a fierce-looking gray shepherd dog.

Krista's heart skipped a beat, seeing the man who she had once thought of as her father again. She had threatened to kill Gault several times already for riding Dread. He still wore that mishmash of sleek Vallè armor, Sør Sevier cloak, and a rusted oghul helm. He struck down with the long Dayknight sword any fleeing knight who came within striking distance of Ava. Merciless and efficient with the blade, he and the other blood-splattered knights cleared a path for the girl.

But the blue dragon was right behind them now. They all ducked the initial burst of flame, Gault pulling Ava to the ground with him. Both of them rolled across the bloody battlefield as flame washed over where they had all just been standing. Even from where she sat atop her Bloodeye steed, Krista could feel the sweeping heat of the flame.

The beast reared back on two hind legs, wings spreading wide, shimmering with menace. The dragon breathed deep, its heaving lungs preparing to lay waste to Gault and Ava. But Gault shoved Ava away toward the gray shepherd dog and rolled underneath the monster, Dayknight sword stabbing up into the blue scales of the beast's underbelly, the tip of the weapon lodging itself between two stiff scales and snapping off.

Distracted and crying out in pain, the dragon dropped back down onto all fours. Gault barely rolled free, springing to his feet and striking again, the Dayknight blade shattering against the slithering armored neck of the beast. The dragon whipped its head around, a burst of fire blooming along the bloody ground toward Gault.

He leaped aside as murderous flame curled around his legs, the lower half of his body now on fire. Unfazed by the flame, Gault tossed the hilt of the broken sword aside and lunged toward the marble staircase, snatching up a huge iron war hammer half-buried in the muck. The weapon was large and heavy-looking. Still, Gault wielded it with the unnatural rage and exhilaration of a berserker. In one swift move, he brought the tremendous weight of the war hammer high over his head, then brought it crashing down on the sinuous spine of the dragon, shattering the row of ivory-colored spikes lining the beast's neck, cracking blue scales.

The anguished dragon bellowed, stunned now, disoriented, wavering on its feet, stumbling to the side, one of its blue wings bending awkwardly against the marble stairs. Flame sputtered from the monster's gasping lungs and up into the air as its tail lashed out, snapping toward Gault. Legs still on fire, flame crawling up his Vallè armor, Gault wasted no time, swinging the heavy sledge straight down on top of the dragon's head this time, splintering blue scales, opening the beast's skull with an enormous *crack!* like thunder.

The dragon lashed out one last time, daggerlike claws raking down Gault's flaming chest-plate armor. Then the monster's body folded over and fell still, blue liquid oozing from its deformed skull. Wisps of white smoke leaked from the shattered blue scales, heated white smoke that caressed the dragon's corpse and swirled up into the air.

The war hammer slipped from Gault's grasp as he looked down at his own now flaming chest and the cooking ribbons of torn armor and flesh. Then he fell face-forward into the cool bloody grass, flames smothered beneath his body.

**

"These are mortal wounds." Enna Spades rolled Gault Aulbrek onto his back, brushing at the fire licking across his torn Vallè armor. The bald man's chest heaved for breath under scorched and shredded armor. His entire torso was torn to crimson ribbons from his shoulders to his legs, and blood welled thick and fluid from every gash in the rusted armor. The dragon lay dead next to him, its massive skull a misshapen blue lump of splintered scales and shattered spikes and broken bone.

Krista's heart was in her throat. She could only look at the man she had once called father in horror.

"He saved me." Ava Shay knelt down beside the man, took his blackened hand in her own. The Gallows Haven girl looked up at one of the blood-splattered knights who had initially helped Gault pull her to her feet. "He saved us, Jenko."

The brooding knight named Jenko said nothing, just stared at Gault with cool amber eyes. "He saved me," Ava repeated, a hollow look in her own eyes.

"That he did," Spades said, looking up, her face bloody, her one eye looking between Ava and the gore-smeared knight named Jenko. "Gault Aulbrek saw the goodness in you, girl, and you brought out the goodness in him, that is undeniable. I do believe he loved you in a way."

"He's dying," Ava cried.

"Aye, he is," Spades said matter-of-factly. Then she looked at the other blood-covered knight standing near Jenko. "I still wish to kill you, Mancellor Allen, for stealing what was mine in Lord's Point, but alas, I've other matters to attend to now." She looked back down at Gault.

"He's dying," Ava repeated, tears rolling down her cheeks.

Krista felt guilty. The human part of her wanted to go to the man, but the Bloodwood part of her just sat atop Dread, hoping to go unnoticed, hoping he would not know that she was near. Though they had moved forward since Gault had struck the dragon down, she and Nail were still some twenty paces from Spades and the injured man.

"He's dying," Ava said a third time.

"He is," Spades acknowledged. "Now let me have a moment with him, if you would. You shall have your turn in due time."

Ava stood and backed away, burying her face in Jenko's armored shoulder.

Spades placed the palm of one gauntleted hand against the side of Gault's blood-smeared head. "It was an honor to fight with you. But you are on your own now, Ser Gault Aulbrek. This war is lost for the both of us, my comrade, my friend. Our time of glory is done. We are the last of our lord's army, the last of Aeros' Knights Archaic."

Spades stood over the dying man's body, facing the remaining crowd, her left eye a gory mess, her voice harsh and pointed. "This man lived *bloody*! This man lived *brave*! This man lived *happy*! Ser Gault Aulbrek of Sør Sevier exemplified every last code of *The Chivalric Illuminations* like no other before or after."

Spades' crisp one-eyed gaze scanned the crowd, eventually locating Krista atop the Bloodeye. "Honor him." The warrior woman's eye narrowed to a cold slit. "See that your father is laid to rest in all the proper ways. See that he is given a ceremony of fire and ash fitting of one of the greatest warriors whom I ever stood beside."

Spades scanned the rest of the crowd once more. There were hundreds gathered around Gault and the dead dragon now. Krista recognized only some, Ava and the mousy boy and a large red-haired girl and the gray shepherd dog. She knew Bronwyn and the oghul, Cromm, having fought with them briefly in the streets of Amadon.

"Nobody but Ava Shay or Krista Aulbrek touches his body," Spades said. "If my request is not so honored, I will hunt down every last motherfucking one of you withering cunts and make your loved ones watch as I slowly pull your spines straight out of your bleeding little assholes." And with those final words, Enna Spades spared Krista one last scathing look and walked out of Tin Man Square alone.

Krista's eyes fell to Gault Aulbrek. Dread shuffled her feet, feeling her nervousness. Nail calmed the horse with a tug of the bit.

Ava Shay knelt at Gault's side again, her face a mask of fright and pain.

How can he still be alive? Krista's mind reeled. She wanted to go to him, but she knew she would not. The man she'd known as a father for her whole life lay dying and yet she would not comfort him. And she could not break that spell of horror and shame that consumed her.

Nail was looking back at her now. She met his weary gaze. Despite the blood and ragged clothing and armor and the tiredness in his eyes, the blond boy stood hale and straight and proud. *He wants me to go to my father.* Krista's head still spun with fog and pain from the blow she had suffered earlier that morning. But that was no excuse.

The look of urgency in Nail's eyes angered her. She did not want any man saving her or watching over her as Nail was trying to do. Despite all the aches and pains and physical wounds, she realized it was her pride that was injured most. She recalled Nail lifting her atop Dread and leading the horse by the bit through the smoke-choked streets of Amadon and up Mount Albion. He had led her here to this bloody courtyard, to her own absolution. *And now he wants me to go to my dying father.*

But a Bloodwood was fatherless.

Krista looked away from Nail's accusing gaze.

"Krista," Gault called out hoarsely. "Is that you, my daughter?"

Krista could barely bring herself to look. But she did. It was the first words he had spoken since fighting the dragon.

The man she had known as her father lay there in the blood-soaked grass before Ava Shay, Vallè armor sliced to ribbons, chest rising and falling to his struggling breaths. The lower half of his torso was blackened and charred. But his face was whole, his eyes looking straight at her as she sat atop Dread. "Come to me," he said, guttural voice weakening.

Krista's heart was galloping now. She had never been more afraid in her life.

"Shall I help you off the horse?" Nail asked. "Shall I help you to him?"

"I don't need your help," she snapped.

Nail quickly stepped around Dread and grabbed her forearm, his eyes piercing into hers. "The man I knew as my father went by the name of Shawcroft. He was a liar. He never loved me. He only ever loved his religion. He only ever loved the Brethren of Mia and his devotion to the cause. His real name was Ser Roderic Raybourne, prince of Wyn Darrè. You were there in the cemetery, you heard what Borden Bronachell said about me, what he said about the man who raised me. Shawcroft only ever called me 'son' once, and only to manipulate me into doing his will. Shawcroft was a father worth hating." Nail's grip around her wrist tightened as his gaze traveled back to the dying man on the ground. "Gault Aulbrek is not worth hating. He calls you 'daughter' out of *love*. Not out of manipulation. Go to him, Krista. Though he may not be of your blood, honor him. Honor him not because of Spades' threat. Honor him because of his love for you. Forgive him because of his love for you."

"Forgive him?" Krista asked, her heart and soul as numb as the wrist Nail still clenched. "But how does one forgive?"

"One just does," Nail said.

"Would that it were so easy. He was never my father. What do I owe him? He was always off at war. He was only just another man to me."

"He is more than just another man," Nail said forcefully. *"He is more than just another man."*

"No," she countered. "No, he is not."

A lump was building in Krista's throat. She knew that Nail was right. Still, she could not muster the strength to tell Gault how she really felt, that she truly loved him, that she had thought of him constantly whilst he was at war, that she had dreamed of having him by her side. That he was more than just another man to her.

She just couldn't push the words from between her pursed lips.

"I can see your mother, Krista." Gault's gravelly voice weakened, his breath growing raspy. But there was a bright twinkling in his eyes now as he gazed at her. "I can see your mother now." He coughed, blood welling dark and black from between his cracked lips. "I can see Avril. I can see her now. In the Nordland Highlands. On the dusky plain . . . I told you once . . . the only place I ever knew joy . . . I wish to go back . . . be with her there . . . forever—"

—and the twinkle in his eyes was gone. His face fell lax as the life fled his body, bald head lolling to the side.

The only place I ever knew joy.

Krista had heard him say those very words once before, as he had talked in his sleep, after she had accidentally poisoned him.

I wish to go back . . . be there with her forever . . .

Krista wrenched her hand from Nail's grip. She slid from Dread, walked forward, and knelt at Gault's side, knelt at her *father's* side, her blurry gaze trying to focus on his broken and shredded body. She removed her black leather gloves, brushed the back of her hand over the side of his bloody face. Sorrow engulfed her. But she could not cry. She looked across her father's body at the tear-streaked face of Ava Shay. Then she looked down at the man between them.

Who am I? Broken in so many ways. She could only stare in horror at the father she had failed. *Like Borden Bronachell once claimed, I am the worst type of human.*

His body was like ice under her delicate touch. "He's so cold." She looked up at Nail. "Where has he gone? Where is he now?"

"He is nowhere," a familiar voice drifted in from behind her. "Yes, you are now truly *fatherless*, my Crystalwood."

It was Black Dugal. Krista stood, turning slowly, imposing herself between Dugal and Gault's body as her former master emerged from the swirling smoke.

Bloodwood daggers slipped into both of her hands.

She glared at Dugal, she *glared* at the illusory Vallè who had once passed as a man, the sinister Bloodwood assassin so full of wickedness and deception, the creature who had trained her in the dark arts of murder, the evil monster who had turned her heart to stone.

Hans Rake was with Dugal, the young Bloodwood dressed in blood-splattered black armor similar to her own. Café Colza waddled out of the smoke between the two Bloodwoods, slobber and drool dripping from bloody lips and tongue. At the sight of the bulldog, a growl issued forth from deep within the chest of the big gray shepherd dog.

Val-Draekin emerged from the smoke next. He led a tall white stallion. Lindholf Le Graven, the boy with a deformed face, rode the stallion. The pale-faced boy carried a striking white shield, *Ethic Shroud*, in one hand and a huge double-bladed battle-ax, *Forgetting Moon*, in the other. A wispy blond-haired girl rode in the saddle behind him; she bore a shortsword of her own.

The entire might of the enemy army was behind Lindholf, fighters both glorious and crude. Thousands of Vallè and oghul warriors came pouring into Tin Man Square through every entry point. Two dragons—one white and one red—swooped down from the gritty skies, circling the courtyard.

The skull-faced riders bestride the two fiery demons gazed down upon the bloody battlefield as if they wanted the beasts they rode to burn it all again.

Once again, every eye was fixed skyward. As she watched the path of the dragons, guilt washed over Krista. She had scarcely mourned the death of her father before war was upon her again. Both dragons slowed their descent, landing in the bloody slaughter of the courtyard with a rush of hot air and swirling smoke. The red dragon landed to the right of Black Dugal's group, the white one to the left.

The two skull-faced riders dismounted as one. Their white and red armor was agleam in the morning light creeping over the battlements. Both dragon riders removed their silver skull masks, revealing their haunting faces, delicate and pale as bone. Their silver eyes seemed to focus somewhere beyond Krista. She followed their gaze, settling on the dead blue dragon lying just behind her and Gault. The dragon riders pulled the silver whips from their belts, the weapons uncoiled in their grip, silver droplets hissing in the bloody grass.

"Absolution is near its end," Val-Draekin said, voice carrying over the courtyard. "Surrender yourselves. The castle is ours. The Five Isles are now returned to their rightful owners, and those once banished to the underworld shall soon arise to claim their place at our side."

"No." Nail stepped forward alone, sword in hand, meeting the Vallè face-to-face. "I won't surrender, Val-Draekin. I won't let you or your armies or your beasts of the underworld roll over me without a fight. You owe me your life, Val-Draekin. You cannot do this."

"You should have let me die under that glacier with Roguemoore," Val-Draekin said. "You should not have carried me to safety when my leg was injured. Yet you did. Alas, in your goodness and bravery you did. Now all memory of Laijon, Mia, and Raijael shall be swept from the Five Isles so humanity will know they were never real. Go home now, Nail. You are conquered. The prophecies of the Aalavarrè Solas have come to fruition. You thought you were the hero of this tale, but you are not. This story was never about you."

The pale-faced dragon rider in white-scaled armor stepped up beside Val-Draekin. The knight cracked the silver whip inches from Nail's face threateningly. "When humanity banished my ancestors to the underworld a thousand years ago, when the bones of my ancestors were pounded to dust and mixed into the mortar of your cobbled roads and castles, we kept our faith in the stars. For we always knew by the power of Viper that we would take our revenge. The Dragon speaks the truth. Go home, boy, and nothing shall happen to you."

"Icelyn is right," Val-Draekin said. "Take your friends and go home."

Nail set his stance, sword poised in an attack position, the tip of the blade wavering unsteadily before the Vallè's face.

"Do not make this mistake, Nail," Val-Draekin said. "You are no killer."

"Well, I've come to kill you now," Nail said. "I am done with those who have betrayed me."

"This is a fight you cannot win," Val-Draekin said, his tone one of warning. "You are not skilled enough. Use your sword against me, and I shall strike you down."

"I am also done with those who underestimate me."

"Only by chance or distraction could you win, Nail."

"Then I shall take that chance," Nail said, sword no longer wavering in his hands, but steady. "I will die before I give up, even if it means I have to fight this entire army alone."

"But you are not alone, Nail!" a voice called out. "You've got Beer Mug and Dokie Liddle and Liz Hen Neville!" It was the large red-haired girl. She stepped forward with purpose, long black Dayknight sword in hand, the big gray dog on her heels. "Come on, Dokie, let's go!" She beckoned to the small boy behind her. "I called your name too! We are all a part of this fight!"

The boy named Dokie stepped forward with the girl. Ava Shay stood too, drawing the thin sword with the red ruby handle, stepping over

Gault's body and joining Nail. Mancellor and Jenko stepped forward too, as did Bronwyn, Cromm, and every Gul Kana warrior behind them.

Then there came a tremor from above. At the top of the wide marble stairs behind Krista descended hundreds, if not thousands, of Dayknights and Amadon Silver Guards. They came pouring out of the castle in waves, rushing down the long stairway, weapons drawn, the thunder of their descent raining over the courtyard.

"See, Nail!" Liz Hen called out. "This war ain't over yet! Together we shall send Val-Draekin and his army of freaks back to the underworld!"

CHAPTER EIGHTY-TWO
TALA BRONACHELL

14TH DAY OF THE HEART MOON, 999TH YEAR OF LAIJON

AMADON, GUL KANA

It had been the longest night of Tala Bronachell's life. She had not slept in two days. Her cousin, Lawri Le Graven, was dying. And the green dragon was gone. In the heart of the night, the blind beast had launched itself into the air and flown up and out of Riven Rock slave quarry. "Worry not, Tala," Lawri had said as the dragon disappeared up into the starlit skies. "The dragon has served its purpose."

Without the dragon, Tala wondered how they would ever climb back out of this damnable marble pit—or rather, how *she* would ever climb out of the pit.

It was a certainty now: Lawri was nearly dead.

The rancid rot emanating from under the silver gauntlet fixed to Lawri's arm had spread over her entire body. As dawn made its slow crawl over the slave quarry, the extent of the growing rot had been revealed. And as the day progressed, the festering black sickness had increased. The alarming putrefaction and decay had twisted Lawri's once delicate face into a scaly horror of murky black and bloat. A pall of smoke and haze now hung over the quarry, and the air smelled sour and acrid with her coming death.

Putrid air rasped up from Lawri's struggling lungs and through her cracked black lips like rusted chains. The only thing left alive in Tala's cousin were her eyes—vexing eyes of bright glowing green that stared nonstop at Tala.

"Your army will come," Lawri said. The half-blackened fingers of her good hand grabbed Tala's arm. There was still some health left in her good hand, and her grip was strong. "I promise, your army will come. I have seen it in my dreams."

The only thing Tala was sure of was that Lawri Le Graven would soon be dead. *And 'twas me who fed her the green poison!* Ever since she had killed Glade Chaparral, Tala felt she had existed in a perpetual state of shock. Fiery Absolution had destroyed everything in Amadon, including her soul. She wondered if this wasn't some bad dream and she would soon wake. As *The Way and Truth of Laijon* had foretold, Absolution would bring demons and dragons and the streets of Amadon had run red with blood. Fiery Absolution had also brought back her father and revealed him to be a duplicitous, evil man, using innocent people for his own gain, and the gain of the Brethren of Mia. *And here I sit at the bottom of Riven Rock slave quarry!* As absurd as the notion seemed to Tala, she had waited all night down here for Lawri's promised army to reveal itself.

But when the light of morn had finally broken over the quarry, the hellish, pale landscape of the slave pit revealed itself in all its blood and glory. There was no army come to their aid. Instead there rose up a massive mountain of dead knights against the eastern wall of the slave pit. Shiny glints of armor broke through the char and smoke and burnt bodies, armor twinkling like stars. To Tala, the entire mountain of smoking corpses seemed to be a contradiction in both impenetrable blackness and blinding light.

Tala looked down at the tremendously long white sword still gripped in her hand. *Afflicted Fire.* The sharp-looking blade didn't quite gleam or sparkle like a normal metal blade, but rather looked carved of some solid piece of pale bone forged with silver. Crooked veins of translucent red seemed to pulse from somewhere deep within the weapon. The hilt was buffered by an elegant crescent-moon-shaped hilt-guard, and the sword was as long as she was tall. The tip rested against the marble floor of the quarry at the foot of the Silver Throne. A bright ruby was set at the top of the weapon's white pommel. *Afflicted Fire!* She had studied its every intricate detail throughout the night. The weapon did not seem real, like it had come from an entirely different world than the one Tala lived in.

"I would not believe me either, Tala," Lawri interrupted her thoughts. "My entire life, I feel I've lived a strange illusion. I've ofttimes doubted myself. And I can see the doubt in your eyes too, even as you gaze upon the sword of a Warrior Angel. But there is an army beneath us just waiting to rise. The sword is yours. And you *are* the Princess."

"I am no princess." Tala stared at the foreign-looking sword.

"Your army will arise from the pure pale cauldron of the earth," Lawri said, "following streams of silver carved by Viper. It has all been hinted at in scripture. The Silver Throne has always been the key."

Tala looked from the fabled weapon to her dying cousin sitting upon the Silver Throne, a throne with five legs, each leg buried atop an angel stone in five separate holes that had been drilled into the marble . . . who knew how long ago.

She stared at the throne, knowing every word out of Lawri's mouth was naught but the ramblings of someone afflicted and ill. "It is all false, Lawri. Your dreams. The word of God. The scriptures. I've been thinking on it all night. They have been proven all false. Did you not hear Val-Draekin under the Atonement Tree? Did you not hear him say that Fiery Absolution was set in motion thousands of years ago? Set in motion by the Vallè to exploit the human race's greatest weakness. And it is true. It is our weakness to so easily believe in and have blind faith in a God, any God, and to eventually call our God the one true God, and then to fight and kill and enslave any who did not agree in our interpretation of God. The Vallè knew that they could eventually get us to kill each other over our belief in God and a one true religion. They knew it might take thousands of years, but they knew that their only chance to destroy us was if we did most of the work ourselves. They preyed upon the weakness of gods and men. This war is the sole fault of gods and men. The Five Isles are destroyed, vanquished, rubble. Millions have died violent deaths in

Aeros Raijael's bloody crusades and for a Fiery Absolution that our false belief in gods orchestrated. It is an empty land full of naught but ruin that your *Princess* would inherit now."

"You must still believe in something, Tala," Lawri said. Each word was forced from a rotted mouth that was now splitting open at the corners of her lips.

Tala found herself recoiling. "We have all been played for fools," she said, looking away from Lawri's monstrously morphing face. "If I were to have my way, nobody would be allowed to believe in religion or scripture ever again. Faith in such nonsense would be outlawed, for it is altogether evil."

"How can you say such things?" Lawri's eyes were aglow with green light as the cracks branching over her blackened skin split open. "We have seen marvelous and miraculous things, Tala." Pale, pulsing light now seeped forth from underneath her skin.

Tala took another step back. Her cousin was changing right before her eyes.

"Demons and dragons have come to life as scripture foretold," Lawri went on, the cadence of her weakening voice almost prayerlike now, soft and true, as beautiful as she once had been, green light pouring from her skin. "How can you doubt that miracles exist, my dear cousin? For you have seen *dragons*, and you have laid eyes upon the colorful knights that ride them like Warrior Angels from the stars."

"But they are monsters," Tala said, "Beasts of the underworld. Demons."

"The demons of the underworld are not the monsters that we have been taught they were."

"How do you know?"

"They talk to me from beneath." A bright emerald tear burned a trail down Lawri's blackened, cracked cheek, crystallizing. Her breathing slowed. "I am not afraid to die, so why does it feel like I am crying?" Then Lawri's head slumped forward and her body went limp on the throne.

Dead!

Tala could not cry. *Would* not cry. Her heart was hardened, numbed by so much trauma and betrayal and pain. *I fought so hard to keep her alive!* This was just one more absurd, tragic mess in a cluster of absurd, tragic messes she had experienced these last few moons. Tala could not look at the blackened corpse of her cousin any longer. She turned and faced the vast expanse of sunbaked marble surrounding her. She was alone at the bottom of Riven Rock slave quarry. Alone but for Lawri's body.

And for what? Why are we even here? Why am I down here in this goddamn quarry! For nothing. That was the answer. There was nowhere to go. There was no escape. To her, the quarry was a tomb. *I should just curl up and die here with her.* But death would be long in coming, and Tala hadn't the patience for that.

Death will come sooner if I rejoin the battles above. It was faint, but the sounds of war raging through Amadon above still reached her ears, even here so far away.

Alone, Tala walked toward the glimmering dead knights stacked high against the eastern wall, *Afflicted Fire* still gripped in her hand. With the green dragon long gone, there was no way out of the quarry, no way but for climbing the pile of the dead.

**

Hours later, Tala stood on the rim of the quarry and cast her weary gaze toward the smoking city of Amadon in the distance. She could still hear the low hum of war coming from the city. A landscape of twisted and dead bodies stretched out between her and Amadon. There was no other living thing within sight. Black smoke billowed up from the Atonement Tree and the Hallowed Grove.

A sudden breeze, cool as rain, swept across the battlefield as if on bilious dragon wings, heaving over Tala like waves on the ocean. She bent down, legs and arms aching, and picked up *Afflicted Fire*. Before she had climbed out she had tossed the blade up and over the rim of the quarry from the top of the mound of bodies below.

She turned and gazed back down into the slave pit.

It still seemed unreal that she had ascended the towering mountain of the dead and climbed from the quarry all alone. She breathed heavily from the exertion, her body and mind weary from what she had seen, wondering what had possessed her to undertake such a foul and arduous journey with Lawri.

The mountain of burnt knights stretched away below her now, tens of thousands of dead bodies twisted and mashed and smoldering, wide-open eye sockets staring back at her from blistered, fire-scalded faces. Fetid gases and smells drifted from the burnt sludge of bodies in the pit below, and flies buzzed about her head, thick and dark. She had to force back the bile that suddenly crawled up her throat. She had never seen so much death. And the remembrance of those twisted and broken bodies under her feet, all covered in blackened congealed blood and soot, all crawling with flies, gnats, black ravens, and crows, made her want to vomit.

Luckily, there had been an iron hook dangling just within her reach at the pinnacle of the bodies. With both hands she had hurled *Afflicted Fire* up and over the lip of the quarry and then climbed the chain to safety. Now, looking back at the horror, she could still see Lawri's black corpse sitting on the Silver Throne in the far distance below, her tawny hair waving in the breeze. Tala felt the tears mixing with the white marble dust gathering on her cheeks. She wanted to pray for her cousin, but as she looked up into the gloomy, soot-filled sky, she knew there was nobody to answer her prayers.

Anger blossomed in her heart. Anger at Seita for poisoning Lawri. Angry at Jovan for being such a horrible brother and ruler. Anger at Jondralyn for dying. Anger at her father for coming back from the dead and breaking her heart. Anger at Glade for making her take his life.

In fact, ever since she had killed Glade, a darkness had been building within her. A need to kill. A burning need to mete out justice, to right all wrongs as she saw them. Truth was, the darkness had been growing within her long before she had taken Glade's life. It had started in her mother's baths, when the grand vicar had tried to drown her. She could feel the anger and hate take root in her soul and grow. She could feel the scars on her body from that day in the baths. It had been a ritual of subservience. Just like an Ember Gathering. What she had said to Lawri was the truth. If she could have her way, she would kill any who professed allegiance to Laijon, Raijael, or Mia—or any other god, for that matter.

Tears filled her eyes at her own horrible thoughts, and everything looked like a wavering illusion before her. And that too made her mad, her suddenly blurry vision. She wiped away the tears with the back of her hand gripping the long white sword in her other hand, letting her anger flow into it. *Or does it feed on my anger?*

For the weapon suddenly seemed like a living, breathing thing in her hand. Its long, sleek blade pulsed with some mysterious red light once more. Red mists of smoke curled around her fingers, drifting up her arm. She looked away from the demonic sword.

I imagine evil things. Clouds drifted across the smoke-torn sky. She spotted an iron cage to her left. Above the cage, leaning over the pit, was a wood scaffolding and a latticework of gears and pulleys. Chains stretched from the pulleys to a massive wooden turning wheel. There were at least two dozen other such similar sets of cages, scaffolding, pulleys, ropes, chains, stretching off along the rim of the slave pit. For some reason, the strange mechanisms made her mad. *Cages!*

Tala looked back down at the sword in her hands. Red mists still swirled up the length of her arm. She gripped the hilt in both hands, let the strange crimson curls of smoke climb her flesh and become one with it.

But even the weapon and its mystical glow filled her with anger. In fact, it imbued her with more and more rage than she had ever felt before, as if the mysterious red mists were feeding it to her. *Like a Bloodwood poison.*

Loss and pain and utter loneliness engulfed Tala, and she seemed to enter into a realm of total anguish and hurt. She found herself panting, gasping for air. Her fingers clenched the hilt of the pulsing sword with firm resolve, aching from the strain as scarlet mists scaled up her arms. Something very ancient and very fierce welled up within her. Screaming aloud in a savage need for relief and release, Tala hefted the sword over her head. Another violent scream scorched her throat, and she brought the long white blade crashing down against the hard marble along the rim of the slave pit.

White stone splintered as the blade sparked against the marble.

She raised the sword and struck again, then a third time, a fourth.

The wrath that flowed through her was both radiant and bold, spiraling down into an icy shard of rage as she beat *Afflicted Fire* against the rim of the quarry over and over and over. She could feel the sickening force of the pulsing red sword overcome her, filling her head with rushing hot blood. She struck and struck and struck.

And with one last mighty swing of the sword, the ground thundered and cracked open beneath her with a loud, shattering *boom!* And thousands of black crows billowed forth from the corpse-strewn depths of the quarry.

It was just a needle-thin sliver of a crack, but the marble separated in a puff of dust that swirled up around her face.

Then the rift widened to a finger's width. *What have I done?*

Sword now forgotten, Tala stared down at the slim fracture in the marble between her feet, a jagged fault that continued to widen and separate as it traveled toward the rim of the slave pit and then over.

The ground shuddered in an unholy rhythm, throbbing below her like a diseased heart. She looked beyond the crack in the stone beneath her feet, gazed outward into the gaping slave pit beyond the pile of dead bodies, watching as the long, jagged crack continued to spread along the quarry floor like a splinter of jagged lightning and rising dust. The crevice split and raced from beneath the pile of the dead, creating a long, dark gash in the surface of the slave pit clear out to where Lawri Le Graven sat the Silver Throne.

Then the marble beneath the throne began to glow with green, red, blue, and white light as the throne began to shake. Then, with a thunderous tearing sound, the slender gash in the marble cracked wide open under the Silver Throne.

And Lawri's rotted corpse dropped into the chasm, throne and all.

Terror leaped through Tala's veins. She couldn't wrap her head around the fact that her cousin had just been swallowed by the gaping fissure.

Then, from the shimmering dust and blackness of that unholy crag, emerged a thousand pale hands stretching toward the light.

Beware distraction. Let The Way and Truth of Laijon *be your guide. Only through virtue and moral discipline shall you refrain from drinking from the poison wells of philosophy and learning. Distraction can most swiftly lead one away from faith. Distraction of the simplest sort can be the ruin of even the most disciplined. And distraction in battle is most fatal.*
—THE WAY AND TRUTH OF LAIJON

CHAPTER EIGHTY-THREE

NAIL

14TH DAY OF THE HEART MOON, 999TH YEAR OF LAIJON

AMADON, GUL KANA

The sudden jolt nearly knocked Nail off his feet. Still, he managed to keep the tip of his sword pointed at Val-Draekin as the bloody grass of the courtyard rippled and quaked with a distant echo and loud tearing.

Val-Draekin stepped backward to keep his balance.

Vallè and oghul fighters stumbled to the ground as Tin Man Square trembled and shook. The Dayknights and Silver Guards charging down the long marble stairs behind Nail tumbled and rolled in a great clatter of armor. The two Bloodwood assassins at Val-Draekin's side set their stance firm on the ground, whilst the two dragons dug long talons into the mossy grass and roared in unison.

Somehow Lindholf Le Graven and the blond girl managed to stay astride the white stallion, which was bucking and braying.

The ground rumbled to silence and there was a moment of stillness.

Everyone grabbed a breath. Those who had fallen stood. The dragons settled, as did the stallion.

"The underworld has opened!" the dragon rider named Icelyn cried out, pale face rapturous with bliss and joy. "Our brethren have risen, soon to hunt once again with Viper!"

"*Afflicted Fire* has cracked the world?" Val-Draekin turned from Nail, gazing in amazement at the dragon rider in white. "Seita has succeeded in her journey to find Lawri Le Gra—"

And Nail leaped forward and shoved the tip of his sword into the side of Val-Draekin's exposed neck.

The blade bit clean and Nail drove it deep.

Val-Draekin struggled for breath, grasping with one hand at the bloody blade suddenly protruding from under his chin.

It was a surprise attack, nothing Shawcroft had ever taught Nail in the mines, nothing Hawkwood had taught him in the *Val-Sadè*. Instead he had used distraction and surprise, the one move Val-Draekin had taught him.

Nail wrenched the sword violently free and Val-Draekin dropped to his knees, hand clenched tightly to the hole in the side of his neck, trying to stanch the rush of pumping blood.

He was once my friend. He was once my only *friend.*

Nail thought of their journey through the glacier.

Then he hardened his heart.

"You were right." He stared down at the bleeding Vallè, trying to muster his courage as he spoke. "I should never have saved you in that glacier. I should never have carried you across the Sky Lochs on my own back. The Five Isles would have fared better had you perished in those icy tombs with Roguemoore."

The entire enemy army was now staring at Val-Draekin on his knees before Nail.

"He stabbed Val-Draekin!" Lindholf Le Graven muttered as he spurred the white stallion forward. He still held *Forgetting Moon* and *Ethic Shroud* in either hand. The blond girl peered out from behind him with wide, innocent eyes. Lindholf turned to the two Bloodwoods. "A peasant whose name I do not even know tried to *kill* the Dragon. How is that possible?"

"You dare strike Dragonwood?" asked the young assassin with the blue scalp tattoos and the wild row of spiked-blond hair, shooting Nail a sinister sneer. And the look of hate emanating from the red-streaked eyes of the older Vallè Bloodwood named Dugal was palpable. The black daggers in his hands seemed to swallow all light.

"Yes, Hans Rake," the older Bloodwood said, looking down at Val-Draekin still on his knees. "The boy from Gallows Haven has proven to have more daring than we thought."

Lindholf whirled his mount to face Nail. "You very well may have killed Val-Draekin. You very well may have killed the Dragon."

He is the heir of Aevrett Raijael! Nail stared at the misshapen face of Lindholf Le Graven. Beyond the scars and deformed skin, Nail could detect hints of Lawri in his pale features. He could also see the resemblance to Aeros Raijael beyond the scars.

I was to be the heir of Laijon!

Nail raised the tip of his bloodstained blade and aimed it at the boy on the stallion. "I hope I did kill Val-Draekin," he said. "And I'll kill you next."

Lindholf ignored Nail, looking down at Val-Draekin. The light was slowly draining from the Vallè's eyes. Blood poured from between the fingers wrapped around his neck. Then a Bloodwood dagger dropped down into his free hand from a fold in his leather sleeve.

And then Val-Draekin stood. "The Dragon still lives," he said. "And the Dragon will now kill the Nail."

But Val-Draekin never got the chance.

With a great cry that shook the air, the Dayknights and Silver Guards who were flooding down the stairs and into Tin Man Square came pouring around Nail and attacked Val-Draekin and his army of Vallè and oghuls with thunderous noise.

The two dragons roared in response, wings unfurling as they stood on their hind legs menacingly, flames spewing from their mouths, slowing the army's charge.

Battle once again raged around Nail on every side. Silver lightning flashed toward him. He threw himself to the side and rolled across the bloody ground, barely escaping the hiss and sizzle of the barbed silver whip. When he looked up, Icelyn stood over him, ashen face a mask of fury. The dragon rider cracked the whip once again, silver barbs singing through the air like a screaming wraith. Nail dove over the crumpled body of a fallen oghul. The lashing whip sliced the dead beast in half, spraying Nail with blood.

Before the dragon rider could strike again, Nail sprang to his feet and sprinted toward Liz Hen, Dokie, and Beer Mug. The trio had gathered near the corpse of the blue dragon with Krista Aulbrek and her Bloodeye steed. Jenko Bruk, Ava Shay, Cromm Cru'x, Bronwyn Allen, and her brother, Mancellor, were there too.

Oghul and Vallè fighters rushed the staircase, engaging the Dayknights and Silver Guards still pouring down. Nail swung his sword at the nearest charging oghul, his blade glancing off rusted armor. A Bloodwood dagger whistled past his head, the black blade sinking into the chest-plate armor of a charging Silver Guard, dropping the man. But more Silver Guard and Dayknight fighters leaped over their fallen comrade, charging toward the enemy. Nail looked to see where the black dagger had come from and saw Val-Draekin stumbling toward him, one hand clutching his bleeding neck, the other pulling a second dagger from the folds of his cloak.

The chaos of war danced around Nail in brutal savagery. Liz Hen, Dokie, Krista, and the rest of his friends had scattered into the fray, all of them fighting for their own lives now. Nail gripped his sword all the tighter knowing he was alone again; the vast expanse of the courtyard was once again a teeming mass of boiling scarlet mayhem. Val-Draekin hurled the second dagger. Nail whirled and fled, the dagger sailing past his shoulder.

Gul Kana soldiers continued to flood down the staircase. It was a maelstrom of slash and havoc. The air was warm with blood as the screams and shouts of the dying tore at Nail's ears. The two dragons made the most raucous noise of all as they raked and clawed their way through the battle, shredding armor and flesh with their massive teeth and claws. The pale-faced dragon riders cut through the center of the battle too, silver whips flashing. And fighting with the two Bloodwood assassins was Lindholf Le Graven. Tala's cousin sat tall atop the white stallion, *Forgetting Moon* a flashing silver weapon in his hand, *Ethic Shroud* blocking every blow aimed his way. Though his white stallion was streaked with red, there was not a droplet of blood on Lindholf, nor on the blond girl in the saddle behind him.

"Nail!" he heard Liz Hen call out. "Follow us!"

Nail saw Liz Hen, Dokie, and Ava Shay shoving their way up the stairs through the descending flood of Silver Guards and Dayknights. Jenko Bruk was pushing them from behind. "Go! Go! Go!" Beer Mug was with them too.

Bronwyn and Mancellor were engaged in battle with a handful of Vallè fighters at the bottom of the stairs, guarding their retreat. Cromm Cru'x stood at Bronwyn's side, a round spiked ball mace in his hands, the massive weapon glinting in the sun as he brought it crashing down on the head of the nearest Vallè. The gore-covered mace pulverized the head of a second Vallè fighter and then a third. With an opening, Bronwyn and Mancellor broke from the fight and sprinted up the stairs behind Jenko and the others. Cromm followed.

Nail shoved his way up the stairs last. Dayknights and Silver Guards plunged down the blood-soaked stairs above him, whilst oghul and Vallè fighters surged up the vast stairway below him. Nail was suddenly mashed between the armies, unable to move as bodies crushed into him from every side.

He spotted Krista Aulbrek on the grass below. The girl was once again astride the Bloodeye, her own black daggers flashing in the sun as she hacked at both Vallè and oghul. The arrow was still lodged deeply in the lathering mare's flank and blood flowed from the wound.

With one dagger in hand, the other hand still clutching at his neck, Val-Draekin slashed his way toward the girl, focused in his aim. Despite his horrible wound, Val-Draekin fought with a savagery Nail never knew could exist in any one being. Like malevolence flowing, the Vallè's black dagger cut a violent path; his dark eyes were feverish, raw, and aflame. And then Nail saw that the younger Bloodwood assassin named Hans Rake had joined Val-Draekin.

With a sudden surge of energy, Nail launched himself back down the stairs, shoving his way through the crush of oghul and Vallè, shoving his way toward Krista, hoping to help her. But Val-Draekin was upon the girl swiftly, black dagger spinning through the air, sinking into the neck of the Bloodeye mare. The beast shrieked and bucked, nearly throwing the girl. But Krista kept her balance, calming the beast, whirling in her saddle to meet her foe.

Hans Rake struck first, fast and fluent as a cat, his dagger lashing out, opening up another wide gash just below the Bloodeye's exposed neck. Dark crimson froth blossomed from the mare's muscular chest, but the beast did not go down. Instead it kicked out viciously, blocking the attack of Val-Draekin, who struck next, knocking the black dagger from his hand.

"You won't slay me so easily, Hans Rake!" Krista shouted at the young assassin, doing her level best to keep the injured horse under control. Blood poured from the Bloodeye's open chest, and the horse kicked and brayed.

Nail leaped off the last stair and threw himself into the midst of the battle, thrusting his own blade toward the assassin named Hans. The young man dodged the blow with ease, his dagger flashing like lightning, ripping a gash right through Nail's iron breastplate armor.

Staggered by the swiftness of the assassin and the power of the dagger, Nail stumbled back, wide-eyed and stunned. Blood leaked from the tear in his armor, though he felt no pain. Hans Rake turned back toward Krista as if Nail were of no account now.

Then something brushed against Nail's leg. He spun, kicking out. It was the bulldog with the rusted spiked collar. The savage dog's broad mouth was suddenly attached to his ankle, tearing. But Nail felt no pain. It was as if Hans' black dagger had numbed his entire body.

Poison! His mind reeled.

Then he remembered the dog that had attacked Shawcroft during their escape from Gallows Haven. The dog had bitten into the man's artery—and it was that wound that had slowly disabled him. Nail stabbed downward with his sword. The dog leaped back.

"You are outmatched, Nail," Val-Draekin said coolly, advancing on Nail. "You may have surprised me once, but you shall not surprise me again." Even as he clutched the blood-pumping wound at his neck, the Vallè was a striking dark elegance. It seemed like death itself was drifting out of the violent sea of chaos and bloody battle and straight toward Nail. Stricken with fear, he drifted back, limping on the dog-shredded ankle.

Still he felt no pain. *Bloodwood daggers are laced with poison!* was all he could think. Fear raked Nail's soul as he ducked the first dagger Val-Draekin threw. His injured foot slid in the bloody muck and he nearly fell.

The Vallè pulled another dagger and smiled.

He was never my friend, Nail thought. *This was all a game to him!*

From the corner of his eye, he saw Hans strike out at Krista's horse again, slicing a long gash in the mare's flank this time. Krista fought back, whirling the Bloodeye, her blond hair flowing like a banner rippling in the wind, her own black dagger slashing down at Hans' face. The Bloodwood ducked the blade whistling over his head, sinking his sleek black weapon deep into Dread's black-lathered neck. The bleating horse dropped in a swath of bloody spume, falling directly on top of Hans, braying and gasping for life.

Rolling in the gore-sodden grass, the dying horse trapped both Hans and Krista underneath. At the same time, Val-Draekin let another dagger fly. It sank hilt-deep into Nail's shoulder armor. Again Nail did not feel a thing, though scarlet streamed from the wound. He clutched at the dagger's hilt, trying to pull it free. But it was lodged in the armor. What foul taint or poison might be on the horrid blade he dared not guess, but he felt his vision blur and his limbs grow numb.

Val-Draekin threw another dagger. Nail whirled away, the deadly blade raking across the armor covering his flank and spinning away. He still had his sword and turned to fight with it, swinging wildly, his every blow sluggish and slow in comparison to Val-Draekin's swift strikes and parries. Nail sucked in air, tiring as his armor absorbed violent strike after violent strike from Val-Draekin's flashing dagger. Even sorely injured, one hand holding his own throat closed, it seemed the Vallè was merely toying with him now, grinning as he did so. *Yes, it's all a game to him, this battle, these deaths. My death.*

Nail slipped and went down again. He rolled, facing the dying Bloodeye, the mare's once glowing eyes now a dull faded rose. He could see the top half of Krista's body, her legs trapped under the kicking horse. She clawed at Hans' face with her hands and fingers. The bottom half of Hans' torso was trapped too. He fought off the girl's slashing hands with curled fists. Together, they lay in the battle's muck and gore, face-to-face, tearing at each other with bare hands, each trying to get at the other's throat and eyes. The crazed bulldog leaped and danced in joy, nipping at Krista when it could.

Again, Val-Draekin loomed over Nail, pitch-black cloak billowing out behind him, one hand clenching his bleeding neck, black dagger in the other. He pointed the tip of the blade down at Nail, long arm outstretched, black leather armor glistening with blood. "I am a Bloodwood and always was, Nail of Gallows Haven. I have always known who I am. And I have always known who you are. And you were never anything. So prepare to meet the real me, prepare to have your entrails spread across this battlefield. I aim to pull them out one inch at a time, slowly pull them out through your own gaping eye sockets."

There was a flash of steel and suddenly Val-Draekin's arm was gone, hand, dagger, and all—in its place a spewing bloody hole. The startled Vallè looked down at the bubbling red stump of his arm, disbelief and alarm washing over his pale features.

"Your missing arm is courtesy of Jenko Bruk of Gallows Haven, asshole." Jenko yanked the sharp blade of the spear out of the mud at Val-Draekin's feet. He hauled the spear up for another strike, cool amber eyes fixed on the one-armed Vallè. "I know who I am too. And I am the son of Baron Jubal Bruk, and don't you forget."

He jabbed the tip of the spear at Val-Draekin's face.

The Vallè ducked the blow, pulling another dagger from the folds of his black armor with his remaining hand. Blood poured from the stump of Val-Draekin's arm and neck as he parried Jenko's second strike, sweeping the boy's spear up and away, sending the weapon sailing toward Hans and Krista, who were still grappling together underneath the dead Bloodeye.

Weaponless, Jenko charged forward, large balled fist crashing straight into Val-Draekin's delicate nose, connecting. Rage blossomed in the Vallè's dark eyes as he struck out at Jenko with the dagger in his one good hand. A ribbon of blood opened up across Jenko's forehead as he staggered back, wounded and defenseless. Dagger still in hand, Val-Draekin raised his remaining arm to let throw.

And Nail stabbed the Vallè right in the armpit, the tip of his sword slicing through black leather armor and straight into Val-Draekin's rib cage and heart. The Vallè folded over backward, dragging Nail to the bloody grass, still fighting with his good arm as he tried to wrench the sword free. Nail struggled to his feet, hauling with all his might on the hilt of the sword, pulling it loose of the Vallè's body.

Val-Draekin was finally dead, round eyes staring up into the smoky blue sky.

"Thanks," Jenko Bruk muttered. His face was a savage mask of dripping scarlet, blood flowing freely from the wound across his forehead. "That Vallè devil would have likely killed me, even with one arm. How the hell did he even talk with half his throat missing like that?"

"Val-Draekin has always . . . been a mystery." Nail panted for air, gazing in wonder at the baron's son. "You came back to save me."

"Right," Jenko responded. "I came back to save you. What of it?"

Nail knew he was injured, but he felt no pain, his every muscle numb.

"Do you know that girl?" Jenko gestured to Krista, who still clawed at Hans under the dead Bloodeye. "If she is your friend, let's help her."

Together they raced toward Krista. The bulldog had a mouthful of the girl's hair in his slobbering jaws, teeth clamped tight, tugging and pulling at her head. Hans was punching her hard in the face repeatedly, and still she fought.

Jenko kicked the bulldog in the ribs and it danced away. Nail grabbed Krista under the arms and vigorously pulled her from under the dead horse. Hans continued to claw at her. Jenko kicked Hans in the face and the Bloodwood went limp, unconscious.

The bulldog barked and snarled. Nail helped Krista stand. She stared at him in bewilderment, her face bruised and bloody, her hair matted with grass and gore.

"Are you all right?" he asked.

"My horse!" She whirled, gazing down at the stiff black mare *Dread!*

"It's dead!" Jenko yelled forcefully. "We've got to go!"

Krista turned back at Nail, a hollow look in her eyes. Nail wanted to assure her that everything would be fine, but words of comfort seemed pointless now. Blood and death were everywhere. *Do you know that girl?* Jenko's question flashed through his mind. He had only really known Krista for a day. *Do I know her? Or do I merely feel a kinship to her, knowing she was used by the Brethren of Mia same as me?*

The girl knelt by her horse, pressing her face softly against its neck. "Goodbye," she whispered, the clamor of war and the sharp barks coming from the bulldog almost drowning out her voice.

"Let's go, Nail!" Jenko shouted again. "Liz Hen and Dokie should be safely at the top of the stairs by now!" Jenko picked up a fallen sword and shooed the bulldog away with it. "Ava's up there with them. We can escape into the castle!"

Jenko sprinted toward the stairs.

Nail took one final measure of his surroundings, as grim as they were. The dragons were no longer on the ground, but soaring overhead now, the sound of their roars splitting the air. Many Gul Kana knights ignored the pain of their roars and fired arrows up at the wicked beasts. Nail was numb to the sound. Numb to all pain.

He saw that the beasts were riderless.

In fact, the two dragon riders were carving a path through the battle with their silver whips now, heading toward him.

"That's Black Dugal coming with them!" Krista exclaimed with alarm.

Done witnessing the bloody destruction the two dragon riders and Bloodwood assassin had wrought, Nail whirled and followed Jenko up the blood-dripping stairs, Krista Aulbrek on his heels.

**

Thick bloody streaks of slithery flesh and viscera came washing down the long marble staircase. Near the top of the staircase, Bronwyn, Mancellor, and Cromm Cru'x were heavily engaged in battle with a group of three Vallè spearmen. They were a dozen or so steps above Nail. Two of the Vallè fighters rode war chargers, the braying beasts' hooves oft slipping in the gore, almost falling.

Jenko, Krista, and Nail pushed through the frenzied chaos and up the steep stairway toward their friends. Nail risked a glance backward. The bulk of the Vallè and oghul army was still charging up behind them. Black Dugal along with the two dragon riders and their silver whips led the way. Tin Man Square looked so small far below.

Up above, Cromm Cru'x was now wielding a heavy war hammer. The blunt weapon pulverized the white snout of the nearest Vallè destrier. The armored horse bucked and reared, and the Vallè rider tumbled from the beast's back. Mancellor speared the Vallè through the gut as he fell. The Vallè slid down the stairs.

Jenko, Krista, and Nail dodged the falling Vallè, joining Bronwyn, Mancellor, and Cromm in the fight with the remaining two Vallè. Bronwyn's hair was matted against her tattooed face. The white feathers in her hair were soaked red. Nail helped the Wyn Darrè girl pull the second Vallè fighter from the horse. Together they stabbed the soldier and pushed the body down the stairs, letting the charger stomp away. The third Vallè was on foot and chased the now riderless horse.

"Where's Ava?" Jenko shouted at Mancellor.

"With Liz Hen and Dokie!" the Wyn Darrè yelled back. "They already reached the top of the stairs. They could be in Sunbird Hall by now! That big gray shepherd dog was with them!" Nail could see that Bronwyn's brother was clearly injured. Blood drained from the many joints in Mancellor's armor, but he did not seem affected by whatever wounds he had suffered. Nail was numb to his own injuries too, not knowing what Bloodwood poisons might be streaming through his body now.

A fourth Vallè horseman spurred his mount in a mad dash up the stairs toward them, the dun-colored destrier huffing and spitting. The Vallè's spear was aimed straight at Nail, its clover-shaped head dripping with blood. Nail ducked the charge and Bronwyn stabbed the horse in the neck as it galloped by. The charger bucked, throwing the rider, sending him sprawling down the stairway.

The clover-shaped spear tip of a fifth Vallè struck Mancellor from behind. The spear tip slid across his armor, pushing him forward against the stairs. Mancellor whirled and seized the Vallè fighter by the arm, spinning him, snatching the haft of the spear, then wrestling it from one of the fellow's straining hands. The Vallè fighter fell against the stairs. Cromm swung his war hammer down on the spine of the Vallè, crushing the hapless fellow. Bruise-colored guts erupted from the fey's split-open armor.

"This stairway is madness!" Jenko shouted, amber eyes wide and gaping. "Let's find Ava and Liz Hen!"

"I'm with you!" Mancellor yelled as the two dragons attacked the stairway below. The beasts swooped low, raking the stairway with their fire just under Nail. The searing heat and ear-piercing sound was almost paralyzing. Dayknights and Silver Guards dropped their weapons and curled up on the bloody stairs, clutching their ears in pain and terror as the dragons sailed away. Some of the knights attempted to fire arrows up at the retreating dragons, to no avail.

Below Nail the scene was pure savage madness. Black Dugal and the two dragon riders carved their way up the burning stairs. Knights and horsemen fled before them. Lindholf Le Graven rode just behind them, *Forgetting Moon* and *Ethic Shroud* sparkling in his hands. The pale-faced girl still sat the saddle behind him.

Nail and the others whirled from the madness and ran up the stairs, reaching the flat marble landing in just a few strides. But the fighting and chaos on the landing was just as thick and savage as on the stairway below.

Something heavy hit Nail from behind and he lurched across the gut-strewn marble, losing hold of his sword as he fell. A wave of bodies rushed over him as he tried to stand. Both an armored horse and a Dayknight fell on top of him, burying him against the bloody slick surface. He found his muscles straining against the press of the two thrashing bodies.

Then he felt teeth wrap around the armored bracers circling his forearm.

Dog's teeth! It was Beer Mug, sharp teeth digging deeper into his arm bracer, pulling. Liz Hen's blood-splattered face was above the dog. She latched onto his other arm, pulling him free of the fallen horse and rider. Nail crawled to his feet.

"Your sword!" Liz Hen shouted, thrusting the Dayknight blade into his hands. "Dokie and Ava are already in Sunbird Hall. The way lies under the columns!"

Nail gazed up at the massive gray stone columns that rose above. Jenko, Mancellor, Bronwyn, Cromm, and Krista Aulbrek were already charging that way.

A bare-chested oghul rose up behind Liz Hen, bloody maul arcing down. Nail shoved the girl aside and stabbed out with his sword, catching the oghul in its hairy chest just as the maul crashed down where Liz Hen had been. Beer Mug went for the beast's neck, tearing into the oghul's throat. Nail ripped his blade free and the oghul fell. The beast's body was splayed wide, heaving lungs exposed and hissing for air.

"Bloody Mother Mia!" Liz Hen swore. "Bend me over and fuck me in the ass, but this battle is bloody awful and getting more bloody awful by the moment. Let's go!"

As Liz Hen and Beer Mug sprinted after the others toward the castle, Nail risked one last glance down the stairway. The marble stairs ran red with blood and bodies. The blue dragon lay at the bottom, Gault Aulbrek's body next to the beast. Krista's Bloodeye steed lay not far away, also dead. Hans Rake was gone. The last Nail had seen of the young Bloodwood, he'd been unconscious and trapped under the black mare.

Beyond Tin Man Square, the castle battlements were a ruin, and half the structures rising up Mount Albion burned. In fact, all of Amadon was afire. And out beyond the burning city were the Hallowed Grove and the burnt husk of the Atonement Tree, barely visible through the black, ashen haze. Beyond the Hallowed Grove was the slave quarry of Riven Rock, some strange pale light almost shining forth from its depths, some swirling luminosity rising up, cutting through the smoke that hung over all.

Again, the two dragons raked the stairs with fire. Nail ran from the horror and heat of the flames, following Liz Hen and Beer Mug under the tall columns. The girl and the dog dashed under an archway and down a passage. Nail followed. The corridor was instantly cool compared to the bloody stairway, and Nail could see Jenko, Mancellor, Bronwyn, Cromm, and Krista running ahead.

Sounds of fighting echoed in the distance, and a group of Vallè fighters in glimmering armor rounded the corner and crashed headlong into Jenko's group. Mancellor's spear slashed through the air, catching the nearest Vallè in the side of the head, knocking him away. Jenko launched himself toward the next Vallè, his own spear flashing in the dim light of the corridor, cutting into the startled fey's chest plate. Cromm's huge hammer crushed the skull of a third Vallè. Mancellor tumbled to the floor under the weight of two more charging Vallè. Bronwyn's sword whirled with blood as she struck at Mancellor's attackers. Krista's black daggers slashed and flew.

Nail, Liz Hen, and Beer Mug joined the fight at a sprint, Nail's own sword rising instinctively, blocking the rapid strike of a Vallè cutlass aimed at his head. The clash of steel on steel and his own momentum sent him stumbling forward into the back of Cromm. The oghul scarcely noticed him, his war hammer pulverizing the delicate face of another Vallè. A half-dozen more Vallè fighters joined the fray, and the corridor was suddenly a fierce echo of battle cries and metal on metal, Beer Mug's fearsome barks and snarls rising above the overall din. The dog bit into the leg of one of the Vallè nearest Nail, pulling the fighter down, ripping and tearing at the Vallè's shining armor. Krista leaped past Nail, a black dagger spinning from her hand, glancing off an advancing Vallè's helm.

Another dagger was in her hand and she lashed out, slicing the throat of the Vallè fighter, her every move deliberate and catlike, black dagger a vicious blur as she launched herself toward another Vallè.

Nail whirled to help Liz Hen and Dokie, who were engaged in battle on the other side of the passageway. A helmetless, thin-faced Vallè leaped atop a stone bench set against the wall, long Vallè dagger plowing through the air toward Dokie's face. Liz Hen swung her sword down in Dokie's defense. The thin-faced fighter pulled his blow and stepped aside, letting Liz Hen's blade smash the top of the stone bench with a shuddering crash. Splinters of stone flew straight into Dokie's face. The boy spun away, swiping at his eyes. The Vallè struck out at Liz Hen. She blocked the blow, but lost her sword in the effort. Undaunted, she swung at the Vallè with her bare fist. The Vallè fighter ducked the blow and stabbed out with his blade. Nail launched himself into the Vallè's chest, knocking the fighter against the wall. The Vallè recovered and Nail shoved the fellow away, sending him careening across the floor. A second Vallè came at Nail, a serrated cutlass clutched in his balled fist. Nail jerked to the side, dodging the blow, becoming entangled with a third Vallè. They tumbled to the floor. The Vallè scrambled and clutched Nail's chest-plate armor at the neckline, fingers grasping at anything, pulling at the leather thong holding Ava Shay's turtle carving, yanking it free.

Nail felt the necklace that had traveled with him through so many adventures tear loose in the Vallè's hand. Still fighting and punching, the Vallè tossed the trinket away. It landed silently against the wall in a puddle of Vallè blood.

Angry, Nail threw the Vallè off, snatched up his fallen sword, and rose to his feet, setting his stance exactly as Shawcroft had taught him in the mines. The Vallè gathered his weapon too, a shortsword that came swinging toward Nail's face. Nail stepped aside and blocked the attack and then countered with a thrust of his own. The tip of his sword punched through a gap in the Vallè's shoulder-plate armor. Blood bloomed thick and scarlet from the wound as the Vallè cried out. Nail yanked his weapon free and the injured Vallè swung the cutlass in a backhanded arch. Nail parried, but the Vallè's serrated blade caught Nail's sword awkwardly, ripping it from his grip once again, sending it skittering to the floor, where it came to rest on top of the lost necklace.

Nail flung himself after the sword and the Vallè fighter followed, serrated blade whistling overhead. Nail grabbed the turtle necklace and his sword and whirled.

Then the advancing Vallè dropped to the floor in a pool of his own spurting blood, gurgling from a hole in his throat.

Ava Shay stood above the dead Vallè, her slender sword dripping with red, the tip of the blade now poised at Nail's neck, her pain-filled eyes peering out from just beyond the weapon's ruby-inlaid hilt.

Nail could still feel the girl's turtle carving clutched in the palm of his left hand, the hilt of his own weapon clutched in the right. But more importantly, he could feel the tip of Ava's sword press into the flesh of his neck, drawing blood.

"You left me to the tortures of Aeros Raijael," she whispered with cold hatred.

Nail felt the shame fall over him like a dark cloak, pure and real.

"I've longed to kill you, Nail." Ava's voice leaked out through gritted teeth. "In fact, I *dreamed* of it daily."

CHAPTER EIGHTY-FOUR

TALA BRONACHELL

14TH DAY OF THE HEART MOON, 999TH YEAR OF LAIJON
AMADON, GUL KANA

Despite the ethereal scene far below, the smell of the human dead was still a ghastly perfume rising up from the slave pit at Tala Bronachell's feet. She did not know how long she had been standing on the lip of the chasm, watching the army of pale demons emerge from the jagged crack that stretched the length of the quarry floor.

Thousands of them had crawled from the dark crevasse.

Tens of thousands.

Hundreds of thousands.

Young and old. All glorious to behold. From a distance, every one of them looked more like an angel than a demon, their glistening chainmail armor shining starlike under pure white cloaks. To Tala, these demons far below were like sparkling, illuminated crystals, and there seemed to be no end to the number that came rising up from the depths of the underworld. If there were weapons hidden under those snowy white cloaks, Tala could not tell.

The first dozen to emerge from the jagged fissure bore the Silver Throne with them. Lawri's rotted corpse still sat the throne as the demons carried her across the quarry floor toward the mountain of the dead. Tala could scarcely breathe as she watched the scene unfolding below. The long white sword in her hand seemed to swell with heat, pulsing to the same beat as her own heart, curious red mist curling around the hand that gripped the sword's pommel, tendrils drifting up her arm.

"Everything you see is but an illusion," a familiar voice said from behind her. "And you shall forget about it soon."

It was Seita.

Tala froze. Then she mustered up the courage to face the Vallè. She turned with a painful slowness and tried to calm her ragged breathing. Seita stood beside her, green gaze cast down into the quarry. The Vallè princess wore a black cloak with the hood thrown back. She also wore the full black leather armor of a Bloodwood under the cloak.

"Yes, whatever it is you think you see down there in that quarry is but an illusion," Seita repeated. "Soon to be forgotten."

The Vallè's sudden presence added to Tala's unease and confusion.

"This is no illusion," she finally said, glaring at Seita. "How can it possibly be forgotten?"

"Because you shall soon be dead, that sword in your hand will be mine, and your memories will cease to matter. You are in the wrong place at the wrong time, Tala Bronachell, and I will not have you steal my place in these events."

The Vallè princess spoke with such a flat indifference that Tala almost let the words pass unheard. But when the words finally sank in, she backed away from Seita slowly, feeling her fingers curl around the hilt of *Afflicted Fire*. In fact, she found herself gripping the hilt with both hands.

"The sword is mine," Seita said.

"No, it is mine." Tala looked down at the red mist curling up from the blade and around her arms. "The magic living within it belongs to me. 'Twas I who struck the marble. 'Twas I who cracked open the underworld."

"All an illusion." Seita's cool green gaze cut into hers. "Your own *Way and Truth of Laijon* even states, 'Some claim Vallè crystals or shroud mixed with forged iron and silver will glow with a certain light and mist when handled by a mortal man. But the foul tools and weaponry formed of such fey alchemy ought not be trusted nor ever used.' "

"I no longer believe in scripture," Tala said. "So it does you scant little good quoting such nonsense to me."

" 'Tis merely the science of the stars that makes regular objects magical," Seita said, motioning to the sword. " 'Tis merely the science of the stars that makes regular objects feel light as a feather one moment, heavy the next. The oghul and Vallè have always placed trust in the ritual science and miracles of the stars. That is true religion."

Tala raised the blade up between them threateningly.

Seita laughed. "You don't get it, do you?"

"Get what?"

"This story was never about you, Tala Bronachell. It was never about humans. It has always been about the redemption of the Vallè and the return of the Skulls."

"The redemption of the Vallè?" Tala risked another quick glance down into the quarry below and the thousands of sparkling demons rising up from the fissure. "Return of the Skulls?"

"Val-Draekin and I are the chosen of our people," Seita went on. "Val-Draekin is the Dragon and I am the Seer, the Dreamer of Dreams. I have longed for this day to arrive, a glorious day wherein I can usher the banished forth from the underworld. A day wherein my kin are finally released from their long exile. A day wherein my kin shall walk over the bones of the human dead and arise from the dark toward liberty— the culmination of Fiery Absolution. I saw us both here in my dreams, Afflicted Fire between us, the key to all mysteries. I saw us here, me taking the sword from you. And today my prayers and dreams shall be answered."

"Prayers?" Tala asked. "Dreams? So is it all real, or illusion?"

"Only Hragna'Ar and Vallè prophecy were ever real." The Vallè princess held out her hand. "Only the science and rituals of the stars are real. Everything else is false. It was a nice touch, Lawri dumping those angel stones into the five holes down there. But in the end, the gesture was useless, as useless as the stones themselves. Some even believed the five stones to be cursed, that the first to touch them would die. But if anyone did die after touching an angel stone, 'twas merely a coincidence. You see, everything is illusion. Everything is a game. Now give me my sword."

Seita's beauty had once been eerily exquisite to behold, but now Tala was fully aware of the Bloodwood fiend that lurked beneath the beauty. *My tormentor!* Her mind raged. *Since the beginning, this disgusting Vallè princess has tortured me.*

This evil wicked being killed Lawri!

Tala brought *Afflicted Fire* up in one of the many defensive positions Hawkwood had taught her in the *Val-Sadè*. She could feel the sudden magical heat of the sword, a living thing in her hand, the red mist curling up the blade and around her arms. She could almost hear the sword speaking to her, the moaning blade quivering in her grip as she felt the sensation of its power flow into her. She prepared to strike.

"I wouldn't, were I you," Seita warned.

Tala launched her attack, a high swing at Seita's head. The Vallè slipped under Tala's wild swing and grabbed the hilt of the sword, ripping it free of her grasp. With one hand, Seita held the weapon out and away from Tala. A black dagger was in her other hand, the tip of it pointed under Tala's chin.

"My blade thirsts," the Vallè princess said. "But when I stab you this time, it will be no mere warning to keep a bothersome child out of the secret ways. No, this time when I stab you it will be your death, Tala Bronachell."

Tala clapped, striking the front and back of Seita's hand just as the Vallè had once taught her in Greengrass Courtyard. It was a perfect clap.

And the Bloodwood dagger spun away and vanished over the rim of the quarry.

"Clever girl." Seita's thin brows rose in admiration.

Then Seita attacked with savagery, *Afflicted Fire* lashing like black lightning toward Tala's face.

But the long white blade never struck.

Seita's eyes grew wide with pain as *Afflicted Fire* flew from her grip, clattering to the marble not ten paces away. A bright red seepage of froth bubbled from between the Vallè's pale lips as Seita dipped her head, gazing down at the bloody tip of an arrow sprouting from her black leather armor just above her heart. Then she dropped to her knees, looking up at Tala with a startled, sorrow-filled gaze.

Twenty paces behind the Vallè was the boy with the silver eyes and a black longbow, a huge saber-toothed lion lurking at his side. Tala recognized both the boy and the black cat. They had been with Val-Draekin under the Atonement Tree at Fiery Absolution.

The strange silver-eyed boy nocked another arrow to his bow. With the tip of his arrow remaining aimed at the back of the Vallè, he stepped cautiously forward. The boy's flat silver eyes filled Tala with dread, as did the silver eyes of the lion with him. Muscles rippled with brute strength under the cat's shiny black coat.

Tala stepped back, wary of the saber-tooth and its two long teeth, which glimmered with threat. And on closer inspection, the silver-eyed boy appeared to be sick like Lawri, streaks of rot tracing black trails under his pale skin.

The silver-eyed boy stepped cautiously around Seita, arrow now aimed at her face.

"Stefan Wayland," the Vallè princess said as she met his silver gaze, blood flowing from her mouth and down her delicate chin.

Upon hearing the boy's name, Tala remembered Nail talking of his friend from Gallows Haven, Stefan Wayland. But Nail had thought his friend was dead.

But the dead walk once more.

"I see you got Gisela back," Seita said, her eyes on the bow.

The boy said nothing, arrow still pointed at her face.

"This . . . ," Seita muttered, "I did not foresee. Here is where my visions end."

"Your visions were all lies." Stefan stared down at the Vallè.

"My visions have been the only truth in this whole bloody mess." Seita tried to stand but failed, sinking back to her knees, eyes fluttering to stay open. "And now the Gallows Haven boy who confessed that he never wanted to kill . . . has . . . killed me."

Seita folded over onto her side, green eyes open but lifeless now.

The saber-toothed lion sniffed at the Vallè's corpse and hissed. It was a loud, hateful hiss that carried through the air and over the quarry.

"I loved you." Stefan reached down and tore the arrow from her body—a terrible sound. He took care as he wiped the blood from the arrow with a ragged cloth. Then he slipped the arrow back into the quiver strapped to his back.

Then he looked at Tala.

"Be wary," he said, silver-eyed gaze drifting down toward the growing host of gleaming demons in the quarry below. "Some things that spring forth from beneath the dirt and the ground can warp your mind."

"What does that mean?" Tala didn't understand.

"It might all be an illusion," he answered. "Something Culpa Barra taught me. I had to learn that the hard way while lost in the Deadwood Gate mines. Trust no one." He met Tala's shaken, distressed gaze. "And trust nothing, not even your own eyes."

With that, Stefan Wayland clutched the black bow to his chest and walked away, the saber-tooth following. North they went, heading toward the burnt-out farms and villages in the far distance.

Eventually the silver-eyed cat and the silver-eyed boy were like a shimmering vision in the heat, two dark dots disappearing behind the swirls of black battle smoke rising up from the still smoldering corpses that littered the rim of the quarry.

And Seita lay dead at Tala's feet. *My tormentor is gone!* The Vallè's once delicate porcelain skin was now pale as cold candle wax. Seita's bloodstained face and chalky cheeks were fast turning an ashen shade of pink, almost like a painted doll.

A breeze kicked up, blowing the hood of the Vallè's cloak over her face. Tala stepped away from the dead Bloodwood, reached down, and gathered up *Afflicted Fire*. The weapon's hilt now felt cold against the palms of her hands.

She turned back to the slave pit and watched the army of shining demons below, watched them claw their way up the mountain of dead toward her.

It might all be an illusion, the boy had said.

**

But the ethereal, ashen-faced creatures of the underworld were no illusion.

With pale faces and long pointed ears, the unsettling feline look of these Vallè-like demons of the underworld was similar to that of the dragon riders. They all looked regal in their sparkling chain mail and gilded silver breastplates, over which hung cloaks of pure white. They all had a similar symbol on their plate armor: a glowing crescent moon. Each of them carried a curved dagger sheathed at their hip, even the children, the hilts seemingly made of the same marble they had just risen up from.

And like Stefan Wayland and the saber-toothed lion, these creatures from the underworld had eyes of flat liquid silver. Thousands of them stood before Tala along the rim of the slave quarry, male, female, young and old. They gathered around her almost reverently. Thousands more were still climbing the mountain of the dead, pouring up out of the quarry in droves, each of them staring at her with those unnerving silver eyes. Some of them gazed off at the charred expanse of the Hallowed Grove. Whether they were looking at Tala or the bleak surroundings, their flat silver eyes betrayed no emotion.

A dozen of the strange demons carried the silver throne. They set it down before Tala with great reverence.

Tala could scarcely look at her dead cousin. Lawri still sat the throne, the glittering silver gauntlet still attached to her arm. Tala kept her eyes focused on the white demons, her mind reeling with so many questions and emotions and horrors she could not fully understand. Absolution had come to fruition, and she had just witnessed the beasts of the underworld climb up from the depths of the ground as scripture had warned.

"Where are the stars?" One of the demons stepped quietly toward her, voice almost musical in tone. The demon's chain-mail armor rippled like fine silk, yet made no metallic rattle or sound. "Where are the homes of our ancestors, where are the worlds without end?" The creature's silver-eyed gaze turned heavenward, searching.

A second demon knelt, pure white hair billowing in the breeze, one languid hand held up to the sky. "Where art thou, Viper?"

Tala saw the five angel stones cupped there in the creature's delicate white palm, all of them glowing with radiant light.

"The star stones have returned," the demon said. "And we once again offer them to you, Viper."

Tala remained silent, rooted in place, long white sword gripped tightly in hand, heart thundering in her chest.

"We are the Aalavarrè Solas." The first demon also knelt and looked directly up at Tala. Though it was hard to tell what the demon was really looking at, pupil-less eyes so silver and flat. "Where are the homes of our ancestors? Where are the stars?"

It took a moment for Tala to find the words, but she finally answered. "The stars only appear at night."

"What is that then?" The demon pointed at the sun. "Is that a star?"

"No," Tala answered. "It is just the sun."

The creature stared straight at the blazing yellow orb. *"Sun."* The word rolled liquid off the demon's tongue.

"How can you look straight at it?" Tala asked.

"How can you not?" the other demon answered. "For it is glorious beyond description." The creature rose, placing the angel stones back into the folds of the white cloak. All the demons were staring at the sun now, thousands of them looking up all at the same time. *They seem to worship Viper,* Tala thought. *Is the sun their Viper?*

Or is it all illusion still?

"I am Ashure-Ikarii." The first demon bowed to her now. If Tala were to guess, she figured this creature was a male by the tone of its voice, though she could not be sure.

"And I am Yvoirè." The one that carried the angel stones bowed to her too. Tala figured Yvoirè was a female, though, again, she could not be sure.

"I am Tala Bronachell," Tala said, remaining stiff and afraid. She gripped the hilt of *Afflicted Fire* more forcefully. *Is any of this real?*

"You bear the sword," Ashure-Ikarii said, flat silver eyes trained on the blade.

"You have been touched by the scorch," Yvoirè added, eyes fixed on Tala's hand wrapped around the hilt.

"What?" Tala looked down at her own hand, confused.

"The tip of your finger." Yvoirè pointed. "The sure sign of the scorch."

Tala looked down at the missing tip of her finger and shuddered, recalling the red-hazed room in the secret ways and the cross-shaped altar and the dripping silver. She had touched the silver and it had burned away her flesh. It felt like a lifetime ago. She suddenly felt the scars on her arms flare in pain, the scars from when she had escaped Grand Vicar Denarius and the quorum of five in the bathing pools in her mother's chamber. The cross-shaped injury from when she had fought Glade on the aqueduct also burned hot on her flesh. Red mist curled up from the hilt of the sword and up her arm.

"The marks you feel throbbing upon your flesh are of a familiar song," Ashure-Ikarii said.

Tala's blood was ice. "But how do you know?" she muttered.

Ashure-Ikarii once again bowed to her. "Ages ago we were bound into the Great Beneath by the five star stones of magic, and through it all we slumbered. Yet some prophecy we do recall. For our collective memory doth not dwindle completely into the haze of history."

"Huh?" Tala was only growing more confused. "What?"

"Those markings that burn your flesh are portents half recalled through the press of years and prophecy, though the great marble preserved our long silence. We have followed their song. We have come as we were bidden."

"I don't understand any of that," Tala said. "But I do not trust in prophecy. Prophecy leads only to deceit and pain"

"'Twas prophecy that brought us here," Yvoirè said, as if offended. "For we have followed the scorch up through caverns carved by Viper toward Dragon Claw, the girl with the silver-taloned hand. For we have climbed the bones of the human dead, rising onto the burning battle-field to take our place at the side of the one wearing the marks upon her flesh, the maiden with the wrought-iron soul."

"This is no prophecy that I have ever heard," Tala said, bewildered and frightened by every word these creatures spoke.

"We have arisen from the Great Beneath," Ashure-Ikarii added. "'Tis our first step in reaching the stars. 'Tis our first step in finding again our ancestors who dwell there. 'Tis the prophecy we have followed. You are the maiden bearing the crescent-moon sword, the one whom Viper hath sanctified through the scorch."

Their surety filled Tala's heart with horror. But with each cryptic word it all just grew more confusing.

"You are our savior." Yvoirè bowed once again before her. "You are the Seer, the one who shall lead us to Viper, the one who brings peace to the Great Above."

"So it has been written," Ashure-Ikarii said.

Fear took root in Tala's gut. "Written where?" she asked.

"Written in the heights of the stars," Ashure-Ikarii answered. "Written before the ground split asunder and gulped us down into the bowels of the Great Beneath ages ago."

They were going around in circles now, and nothing was growing any clearer. Tala felt the red mist curl up from the sword hilt and around her arms. The sword once again felt alive in her hands. *This is what Seita was fighting for? She was to be the savior the Aalavarrè Solas were looking for, not me. She is the maiden with the wrought-iron soul. She was the Seer!* Though the sun beat down, Tala's blood was like ice.

Do they know I am a fraud?

Thousands of flat silver eyes beamed at her with hope.

They truly believe I am their savior.

Tala's gaze flew to the crumpled form of Seita hidden under the dark Bloodwood cloak not ten paces away. *Lying there, she looks just like another dead soldier in a grim field of dead soldiers.*

The pale-faced demons continued to crawl up from the quarry, tens of thousands now, their numbers ever growing. They all knelt before her now.

Tala finally looked at the blackened corpse listing sideways on the Silver Throne just beyond Yvoirè and Ashure-Ikarii. *Lawri Le Graven. My cousin. Why did they haul you out of the quarry? What madness am I living in?*

"You act as if you were not expecting us," Yvoirè said, concerned. "Were not our Five Warrior Angels transported up the sacrificial portals of Hragna'Ar to help you and the Dragon?"

"Transported up through the *what?*" Tala asked.

"Transported by the power of Viper," Yvoirè answered, looking almost agitated now, flustered, posture growing tense. "Transported by the science of our ancestors, the science of the stars. Have they not risen, the Five Warrior Angels? Have the dragons not been hatched? Were you not expecting us?"

"I . . ." Tala had no idea how to answer Yvoirè. "I did not know what to expect."

"The Five Warrior Angels have prepared the way for our resurrection, elsewise we would not have risen." Ashure-Ikarii stood, his words seeming to ease Yvoirè's rigid stance. He turned his gaze to Lawri on the Silver Throne. "'Tis the resurrection of this one that shall be the key to our survival, the girl with the silver-taloned hand, the girl bearing Dragon Claw. She is the key. The Five Warrior Angels shall have cleared a way to the cross-shaped altar by now."

"What do you mean *her* resurrection?" Tala asked, horrified. They were still talking in circles.

"She is the key," Ashure-Ikarii answered. "The girl with the silver-taloned hand must be placed within the tomb under the scorch within the fortress our ancestors built. She must be bathed in Hragna'Ar, the blood magic of the stars."

Hragna'Ar! Blood magic of the stars! Tala could feel her veins curling in terror.

"You have been touched by the scorch, have you not?" Yvoirè challenged, pointing to her hand and the missing tip of her finger. "You can take us there, to this tomb?"

Tala turned her gaze toward the burning city and the black castle looming above. *Are they really talking about bringing Lawri back to life?*

It had happened before. Tala recalled the green elixir she herself had fed Lawri, the green Bloodwood witchcraft that she herself had pulled from Ser Sterling Prentiss' guts as he lay atop the cross-shaped altar.

The cross-shaped altar? The tomb of Viper? All part of the Bloodwood game!

But could these demons from the underworld really bring Lawri back to life? Tala knew she had to try. She had to find out. She pointed toward Amadon. "The fortress you seek, the fortress your ancestors built, it is there. It grows up the sides of Mount Albion. And I know where the tomb of Viper is."

The two Aalavarrè Solas bowed to her. In fact, every Aalavarrè gathered along the rim of the quarry—hundreds of thousands of them now—bowed to her.

"We are your army now." Ashure-Ikarii stood. "Forever beholden to you." His silver gaze traveled to the city burning in the distance. "Lead us to the castle our ancestors built, lead us to the tomb of Viper."

Gripping *Afflicted Fire* in hand, Tala stepped over Seita's body and led her army of Aalavarrè Solas away from the slave pit.

I am the Harbinger! I am the Leader of all Armies!

I am what Jondralyn never was!

CHAPTER EIGHTY-FIVE
LINDHOLF LE GRAVEN

14TH DAY OF THE HEART MOON, 999TH YEAR OF LAIJON

AMADON, GUL KANA

S pirit hauled Lindholf Le Graven and young Leisel up the Long Stairs. Chaos swarmed around the white stallion. Sword crashed against sword. Men bellowed in terror. Horses brayed in dismay. The constant noise was bloodcurdling and loud.

And through it all, Lindholf Le Graven had to forcefully corral his own panic, had to swallow that ever-present desire to turn and flee the battle. It seemed a lifetime ago that he had been a simple nobleman's son, prancing about Sunbird Hall, acting like a fool, dreaming of pretty court girls, dreaming of his cousin Tala.

But life was no longer so simple.

Fiery Absolution under the Atonement Tree seemed to pale in comparison to the splattered crimson horrors of Tin Man Square and the long bloody stairway stretching above. Nobody was safe from death here. War was the great equalizer, he determined. Even the most skilled fighter was susceptible to the luck and surprise of a lesser soldier. He had watched mere peasant boys slay Val-Draekin. He had borne witness to the slaughter of a dragon and its whip-wielding master.

In fact, he himself had killed . . . and that seemed impossible.

Forgetting Moon rested light in his hand, the battle-ax of legend effortlessly lopping the heads from every knight who opposed him. Dayknights, Silver Guards, his own countrymen died at his hand. It was as if the fabled weapon acted with a mind of its own. And the glorious white shield, *Ethic Shroud*, splintered every arrow launched his way.

If not for the fabled weapons, and the courage Shroud of the Vallè bought him, Lindholf knew he would have fled this war hours ago. In fact, without the white powder, he might have given fuller rein to the fact that everything he was doing was wrong. But seeming was different than being. He was Laijon returned. He had ridden a glorious white stallion named Spirit through Fiery Absolution and through the burning streets of Amadon and not a spot of blood had fallen upon him.

The blond servant girl still rode in the saddle behind him, and he was her protector now. The winsome girl clung to his back, one arm wrapped around his armored chest, the other wielding a shortsword. Leisel was his comfort. She was his strength. The reason he fought. He vowed he would love her forever and she would love him. Tala was an afterthought. And the barmaid Delia was nothing. *What would she think of me now?* Lindholf Le Graven of Eskander had risen above all men.

I am Laijon returned!

He found himself in a whirl of pounding feet and clashing weapons, his troubled gaze scarcely registering the bloody fighting on the sloping stairs all around: the blur of armor, the slashing of weapons, knights screaming hacked and bloody and sliding down the Long Stairs. Oghul and Vallè blades leaped and slashed in every direction.

Lindholf continued fighting, swinging *Forgetting Moon* at a passing horseman as he had a hundred times before in the last few hours, the ax blade glancing off the charger's head and sinking into the Dayknight's chest. The ax was light in his hand as he ripped it free, spurring his own mount onward and upward. Spirit was sure of foot, even on the mash of strewn entrails and slick marble that ran red with blood. Bodies littered the stairs, most mutilated and raw in their death, others wounded and screaming.

An Amadon Silver Guard took a swing at him from below. *Forgetting Moon* leaped to the fight, light as a feather in Lindholf's grasp. The sharp blade of the ax bit into the guardsman's neck. Stunned, the fellow reeled away, helmet tumbling from his head, neck open from ear to ear. The gaping wound grinned back at Lindholf as the man fell backward, dead.

A Dayknight arrow spun past Lindholf and Leisel and buried itself into the chest of the Vallè fighter directly behind them. The stunned fighter fell forward, clutching at the thick shaft growing out of his scrollworked breastplate. The Vallè slid down the stairs headfirst, leaving a wide streak of blood. Lindholf whirled to see what enemy had fired the arrow. It was a Dayknight, several stairs below. The man was balanced on the dead bodies of two oghuls, a second arrow in hand, ready to fire.

Icelyn was right behind the Dayknight. The dragon rider cut the man in half with a snap of the silver whip, the sinuous weapon flashing in the sun. The Dayknight tumbled down the stairs in two separate pieces, entrails unspooling like thick purple eels. With a shout of rage, another Dayknight stepped toward Icelyn, snatching up a discarded lance, swinging it at the dragon rider. Icelyn ducked the blow with smooth elegance, kicking the staff away. Her silver whip sliced into the Dayknight's face and the knight toppled over, legs twitching in death.

There were screams from above, and Lindholf whirled. The dragon rider in red, Aamari-Laada, was perched like a crimson-scaled raptor a dozen stairs above Lindholf. Dayknights cowered and died under his flashing scorch whip. Blood flew in every direction, not one drop hitting Lindholf or Leisel.

"Bloody Mother Mia!" Lindholf exhaled, stunned at the rapidity of the violence.

Soaring above, the two dragons roared, creating a fearsome noise, sheer and all-embracing. The very staircase shuddered under their thunderous sound.

Behind Lindholf, Leisel covered her ears, as did every Gul Kana fighter on the long staircase. Lindholf felt his own labored wheezing and tried to stave off the pain. It was the white powder coursing through his veins that kept him upright. He risked a glance back down the stairway. The Vallè and oghul armies behind him were thinning. Many had died on both sides. The fighting was growing sparse. Lindholf realized that the Vallè's plan to entice humankind into war with false scripture had truly come to fruition: allow man to kill man over differences of belief. Aeros Raijael had conquered the entire Five Isles, thinning the fighting forces of all mankind. It was the only way the much smaller Vallè and oghul armies stood a chance of regaining their lands.

Fiery Absolution.

Even still, the Vallè and oghul armies had suffered devastating losses.

Beyond the bloody slope of marble stairs, Lindholf looked upon the gore-covered courtyard below and the burning city beyond. There was a shining light growing out of the Hallowed Grove in the direction of the slave quarry. It was a strange light, like a ghostly glittering mist was reaching its tentacles from the Hallowed Grove and into the streets of Amadon, seemingly quenching the fires as it flowed. Lindholf squinted against the sunlight, trying for a better look through the smoky haze. But his eyes watered from the smoke, and it seemed the spreading light was but an illusion.

"'Tis the cracking of the world," Black Dugal said. The Bloodwood was on the stairs just above Lindholf and Leisel. "That light that spreads through the city is the cracking of the world and the return of the Skulls."

"What do you mean?" Lindholf asked.

"You shall soon find out," Dugal said. "For Absolution is winding down and a new throne shall soon be prepared for you, our Immortal Lord."

Lindholf looked up. The two dragons circling above had stopped their screaming.

Black Dugal turned back to the fighting, as did Lindholf. He set his sights on finally reaching the marble landing. Icelyn and Aamari-Laada were already on the way, their scorch whips cutting a bloody path to the top.

Lindholf dug his spurs into Spirit's flanks. The stallion huffed loudly, nostrils flaring and ears cocked. Thick muscles bunched under Lindholf and Leisel as the stallion galloped up the blood-splattered stairs.

"I am Laijon returned and I shall claim my throne!" Lindholf shouted, spurring Spirit after Black Dugal and the two pale-faced dragon riders.

Ancient tombs that were lost shall once again be found. Carving scorched paths through the underworld, the Viper shall ascend, bringing malevolence and vice and a Dark Lord to rule over all. So hold Laijon close to your heart, for the serpent rises, that fanged snake full of iniquity and sin.
—THE WAY AND TRUTH OF LAIJON

CHAPTER EIGHTY-SIX

NAIL

14TH DAY OF THE HEART MOON, 999TH YEAR OF LAIJON

AMADON, GUL KANA

Though battle raged in the corridor, everything around Nail ceased to exist. Everything but for Ava Shay's murderous gaze piercing into his. The turtle carving she had given him felt hot in his hand. He wanted to drop it. Forget it ever existed.

"You left me in that tent to die," she said. "You could have saved me."

"I'm sorry." Nail knew his apology was worthless. The sword tip pressing into his flesh was evidence of the hollowness of his confession. "I'm so sorry," he repeated, knowing there was no excuse good enough. He wanted to tell her that he'd regretted that decision ever since he had made it, but the words would not come. "I'm so very, *very* sorry," he muttered a third time, knowing the words were meaningless to her, knowing that his words could not fix the wrong he had done her.

"I was abused in such horrible ways." Tears rolled down her cheeks. "I saw such horrible things." Her face darkened, and she pushed the sword into his flesh. Nail backed away from the blade, his shoulders pressing up against the wall. "I saw such horrible things," she repeated, setting her feet, bracing for the final thrust of the blade.

Nail closed his eyes. He would not fight her.

"We all saw horrible things," Jenko Bruk said.

Nail opened his eyes. The palm of Jenko's hand gently lifted the thin blade away from his neck. The sword slipped from Ava's grip and clattered to the floor as she melted into Jenko's arms, burying her face in his shoulder, cheek pressed against the cold armor. Nail found he had been gripping the turtle carving so tightly his fingers hurt.

"We all saw horrible things," Jenko repeated, holding Ava close. "I not only saw evil things, I did evil things. Against my own conscience, I obeyed the commands of horrible people."

"It's not your fault," Ava cried.

"How can I live with myself?" Jenko asked. "How can I be redeemed?"

"How can any of us be redeemed?"

"Through forgiveness, I suppose," Jenko said.

"I do not know if I can believe in forgiveness."

"We cannot change the past," Jenko said. "We can only accept where we are right now and forgive what wrongs were done us and move on. If anything good can come of this Laijon-forsaken mess, it is that I have changed into a less prideful person. I hold no malice toward Nail, and I can only hope those I have wronged hold no malice toward me."

This wasn't the first time Jenko had saved Nail. They had fought side by side all day. Nail knew he needed to find forgiveness in his own heart too. He stretched forth his hand toward Ava, the turtle carving dangling between tense fingers by the leather thong. "I've worn this ever since you gave it to me. I was wrong to keep it." It was stained with blood now.

Ava broke from Jenko. "I made it for you." She reached out and set the turtle carving back into the palm of Nail's hand, wrapping his fingers around it. Forgiveness was in her eyes now.

The corridor was oddly silent.

"Bloody Mother Mia!" Liz Hen Neville yelled. "Are you three gonna stand there and cry in each other's faces or help in the fight?"

The battle in the hallway was over; Vallè fighters lay scattered in pools of blood. But more Vallè were entering the broad corridor from the direction of Sunbird Hall; oghuls too, bloodlust on their bestial faces as they charged toward them.

Bronwyn, Mancellor, Cromm, Krista, Dokie, and Beer Mug leaped to meet their charge. Ava picked up her sword and then she and Nail and Jenko and Liz Hen followed the others into battle.

In moments the two sides clashed, Nail swinging his sword, blade connecting hard with the armored chest of the first surprised oghul he met. The beast was hurled against the wall. Nail stabbed the tip of his sword into the oghul's thin face. The beast slid down the wall, dead. Nail's sword slashed another oghul across the chest plate. Ava Shay was right behind him, the tip of her thin sword entering the oghul's wide, surprised eye. A third oghul swiped at Ava with a heavy maul. She ducked the blow and Beer Mug tore at the back of the beast's legs, teeth bloody and sharp. Nail launched himself straight into a fourth oghul. The beast fell, clutching his neck, blood bubbling from his yawning mouth. A fifth oghul fell dead under Nail, gauntleted hands clutching at the black dagger in his chest. Krista stood over the unmoving beast. "Watch yourself," she said to Nail. "That fellow almost clobbered you from behind." The girl spun, more black daggers in hand, searching for more of the enemy.

Beer Mug was still tearing at the legs of the third oghul. A sixth oghul with a wild spiked mace bore down on the dog, swinging hard. Nail launched himself at the brute, sending the mace skimming past the dog's head, splintering the stone floor. Nail wrestled with the enraged beast until the oghul shoved him back. Liz Hen stabbed the oghul in the neck just as the oghul struck Nail with one huge fist, flinging him backward into the wall. Liz Hen lunged to his defense, tripped, and disappeared under a swarm of armored Vallè legs. With his war hammer, Cromm crushed the heads of two of the Vallè trampling over Liz Hen. The Gallows Haven girl rose up from the sea of legs, her round face now panicked and streaked with even more blood than before. She swung her sword wildly, matching Cromm blow for blow, swatting the Vallè fighters away—they scattered from the stern-faced oghul and the mad red-haired girl.

"Follow Cromm!" the oghul bellowed at Liz Hen.

"The castle is overrun!" Mancellor shouted. "Sunbird Hall is lost to us! We must flee back to the outside!"

"He's right!" Bronwyn shouted. "There's too many of the enemy in here!"

The corridor was a mass of fighting now. Nail and Krista pushed their way through the thrashing bodies, following Bronwyn, Cromm, and Liz Hen as they pushed past the Vallè and ran. Mancellor, Jenko, Ava, Dokie, and Beer Mug were right behind him.

Together they all raced back toward the marble stairway, Sunbird Hall and the secret ways of Amadon no longer a viable escape. Sucking in air from the long sprint, Nail soon found himself outside once again, under the columns rising high above. But the stretch of marble at the top of the stairway was worse than the corridor they had just fled. Battle still raged the breadth of it, and the surface of the landing ran slick with blood.

In the distance, atop the stairs now, Lindholf Le Graven sat high and proud astride his white stallion, *Forgetting Moon* and *Ethic Shroud* still in hand. The blond girl still sat the saddle behind him. Black Dugal and the two dragon riders were with Lindholf. The silver whips of the pale-faced knights caused the bulk of the mayhem and death.

That and the dragons. Both of them near.

The white dragon bit a Gul Kana knight in half right in front of Nail, tossing the mutilated body into one of the marble columns above. The red dragon shot thunderous gouts of fire from its gaping maw, burning several Dayknight trying to flee back down the stairway. Then both dragons turned their attention to a contingent of a dozen more Dayknights who were lining up to fire their bows, and fire bloomed from the beasts' mouths.

With the attention of the dragons diverted, Liz Hen and Cromm lumbered around them and toward the stairs. "Follow Cromm!" the oghul bellowed. Liz Hen slipped and fell to her knees, bloody sludge splashing into her face. A Vallè cutlass sliced the air above her head. She stabbed at the Vallè with her own sword, missing the mark. Cromm turned to help the girl, his war hammer crushing the Vallè's shining helm in a blossoming spray of red.

Suddenly the young Bloodwood, Hans Rake, rose up on the stairs behind Liz Hen, black daggers clutched in both hands, the blue tattoos on the sides of his shaved head streaked with blood. The bulldog with the spiked collar was with him, barking at everything and everyone.

Liz Hen clambered to her feet. Dokie stumbled toward the girl, Beer Mug at his side. The bulldog with Hans growled at Beer Mug. Hackles rose like spikes on the backs of both dogs. Liz Hen, Cromm, and Dokie faced Hans Rake, weapons ready.

"Leave him for me!" Krista shouted, racing around the dragons next, twin black daggers clutched in her own hands. Nail followed her.

"You do not want Cromm to kill this flea?" the large oghul growled when Krista and Nail reached him, beady eyes glaring at Hans.

"This flea has always been mine," Krista sneered.

Hans grinned confidently in return, daggers twirling in his hands.

"No!" Cromm bellowed. "Cromm will kill this flea!"

In two long strides the huge oghul was on top of the Bloodwood, iron hammer swinging down. Hans ducked Cromm's blow, jamming one of his daggers into a crack in the oghul's rusted armor, the black blade slipping straight into his ribs, lodging deep.

"Cromm!" Bronwyn yelled in dismay.

The oghul's spine arched, war hammer dropping from his gnarled hand to the ground. Hans plunged his other dagger into Cromm's broad face. The oghul struggled and fought to free himself from the assassin's clutch, blood pouring in streaks from his face and thick heavy armor.

"This is my fight," Krista said to Bronwyn and Nail. Then she launched herself at Hans, her own black blades lashing out. Bronwyn ignored Krista and followed the girl's charge, shouting in rage. Hans ducked Krista's initial assault, her momentum carrying her down the stairs behind him. The young Bloodwood rammed his dagger a second time into Cromm's face, then spun to meet Bronwyn's assault. The girl swung her sword at the assassin's head. Hans stepped aside, also letting the Wyn Darrè girl's momentum carry her uncontrollably down the stairs after Krista.

Cromm fell to his knees. "What poison is this?" he snarled, large gray hands swiping at his face and the wounds gushing blood. "It burns!"

Nail leaped into the fight, but the young Bloodwood was too fast, stepping aside and blocking his blow. Nail slid to his knees in a pool of blood, almost sliding down the stairs after Krista and Bronwyn. He jerked to his feet, but the snarling bulldog was now between him and Hans. Beer Mug lunged, teeth raking the bulldog's back. The two dogs squared off, teeth bared.

Blinded by the blood in his eyes, Cromm threw a wild punch at the back of the young Bloodwood's head, huge balled fist glancing off the assassin's shoulder. But the surprise blow was enough to stagger the assassin. In a rising tide of rage, Liz Hen stabbed at Hans, forcing the Bloodwood to retreat down the stairs. Hans threw one of his daggers at the girl. Liz Hen ducked and the black blade missed, sailing out over the stairway. Mancellor and Jenko were rushing toward the fight now, Ava on their heels. Krista and Bronwyn were running back up the stairs toward the fight too, everyone converging on Hans Rake at once. Beer Mug and the bulldog circled each other on the stairs, both of them barking up a storm. Cromm bellowed one last time and blindly charged the assassin.

Hans had more daggers in his hands, both blades striking at once, slicing the oghul's chest armor wide. Cromm fell forward against the Bloodwood, clawing at the young assassin with both gnarled hands, a swell of blood oozing from the gaping slash in his armor. Hans shoved the oghul away. Cromm fell heavily to the gore-smeared stairs, his massive body sliding down and crashing into Krista and Bronwyn.

"Cromm!" Bronwyn Allen yelled, grasping onto the falling oghul. Together they folded against the stairs. "No!" she screamed, seeing his many wounds.

Krista leaped over Bronwyn and Cromm, throwing herself up the remaining stairs at Hans, stabbing at his legs. Hans danced aside, parrying the blows from Mancellor and Jenko as they joined in the fight from above. Nail took a swing at the Bloodwood too, but the fellow was crafty, backing away from the fight easily, throwing daggers as fast as he could. Mancellor, Jenko, and Nail dove out of the way.

Hans retreated down the stairs backward now, deftly wading through the piles of the mutilated dead that littered the marble. For some reason he was giving away the high ground, the bulldog once again snarling at his side. Liz Hen followed the assassin down the stairs, Beer Mug with her, teeth bared and growling at the bulldog.

Hans stopped his retreat and aimed a black dagger at Beer Mug's face, preparing to throw. "I don't wish to kill this dog!" He looked right at Liz Hen. "Nor do I wish to kill any of you. I only want to kill Krista. I only want her to die at the end of my—"

"Fuck you and the pus-leaking twat that spit you out!" Liz Hen shouted. "You ain't killin' nobody! If Beer Mug don't chew your face off, then I will, you black-hearted demon!"

But neither Hans Rake nor the bulldog was looking at Liz Hen or Beer Mug. Instead they were looking at the stairs above.

A soft breeze of fresh air grazed Nail's face as he turned.

Up above was Lindholf Le Graven atop the large white stallion, *Forgetting Moon* and *Ethic Shroud* gripped in either hand, the blond girl still astride the saddle behind him. Black Dugal and the two dragon riders were with Lindholf. The silver whips of the pale-faced knights were dripping with hissing silver.

The red and white dragons had stopped their killing, their hot piercing eyes also gazing down on the scene somewhere down the long stairway beyond Nail, great leatherlike wings unfurling behind them as they rose up on hind legs, fire building in their heaving chests.

"Isn't that your sister down there?" The blond girl astride the saddle behind Lindholf shouted, pointing down the stairs. "Isn't that Lawri on that silver throne?"

Lindholf stared down the bloody stairway beyond Nail and Hans and Beer Mug and everyone, dark-pitted eyes cast clear to the center of Tin Man Square.

"My *sister*," he said.

Heart thudding in his chest, Nail slowly turned and looked for him-self.

And what he saw was nothing less than astonishing.

Tala Bronachell was in the middle of the bloody battlefield below, the long white sword, *Afflicted Fire*, held firmly in her grip.

And behind Tala, pouring into the square like pure light, was what appeared to be a gleaming army of white-cloaked angels.

A dozen of these ethereal, pale-faced creatures bore the Silver Throne on their shoulders. A rotting, blackened corpse sat upon the throne, tawny hair stirring in the breeze, sparkling silver gauntlet attached to one arm.

Lawri Le Graven.

CHAPTER EIGHTY-SEVEN
TALA BRONACHELL

14TH DAY OF THE HEART MOON, 999TH YEAR OF LAIJON

AMADON, GUL KANA

Both rage and sadness consumed Tala Bronachell's soul at what she saw in Tin Man Square. The evidence of faith and true belief was laid out before her in a wash of blood. The dead lay everywhere, hacked and splayed out in grotesque poses. The Gardens of the Crown Moon was destroyed. Sculptures were crushed and shattered and ruined. Broken bodies carpeted the grassy courtyard in guts and gore and draped the Long Stairs leading up to Sunbird Hall.

Scripture and false prophecy and Fiery Absolution had caused so much death.

But today it all ends.

The poison of religion would be cleansed from the world. And Tala Bronachell would be the instrument of that cleansing.

I am the Princess, the Harbinger, the Leader of all Armies!

She could see her cousin, Lindholf Le Graven, atop the Long Stairs, the sunlit silhouette of Amadon Castle and Sunbird Hall towering behind him. He rode a white stallion, *Forgetting Moon* and *Ethic Shroud* in either hand, a thin blond girl on the saddle behind him. Two dragons, one white and one red, along with their pale-faced riders, were at his side. There were Bloodwood assassins up there too, and Tala's heart thundered.

But she calmed her breathing, steeling herself for the long and bloody climb. She had traveled among the dead for so long that she had become inured to the horror. Her trek from the Hallowed Grove into Amadon had been unhindered, yet replete with the smoldering remains of fire and destruction and death.

But the marble stairway rising up between her and Lindholf was a smoking, corpse-strewn gauntlet of blood and guts and body parts unlike anything she had seen before. And the stench was growing in strength.

She stepped forward. Then her heart skipped a beat when she saw Val-Draekin's body among the dead at her feet, dark wisps of hair flickering over his pale face.

Was he too just a pawn in Seita's game, in the legends of Hragna'Ar, in Fiery Absolution? Was he pawn or betrayer? But after a moment's contemplation, Tala felt scant sorrow in her soul for the dead Vallè and stepped over him without looking back, shaking legs carrying her up the Long Stairs.

**

"What have you done with my sister?" Lindholf Le Graven asked as Tala climbed the final stairs and stood before him. Tala's cousin still sat atop the white stallion, the broad blades of *Forgetting Moon* glistening scarlet in his grip, *Ethic Shroud* held protectively before him. Though there was blood smeared over the weapons and splattered over the stallion, there was not a spot of blood on Lindholf. An aura of malevolence and power hung over his countenance, a confidence Tala had never before seen in him. The blond girl peered out from behind his armored back, eyes wide and demure, a bloody shortsword gripped in her own hand. Next to Lindholf and the girl were two dragon riders. Two Bloodwoods stood with them. Unlike the green dragon that had flown Tala and Lawri to the slave quarry, the two dragons looming behind the dragon riders looked large and deadly and ready to kill.

Tala stepped up onto the bloody landing before her cousin. She clenched the hilt of the long white sword, *Afflicted Fire*, feeling its energy burn against the flesh of her palm, mists of red light trailing up her arm. Ashure-Ikarii and Yvoirè flanked her on either side, their pale daggers drawn, silver eyes gazing in awe at the two dragons and their riders stationed just behind Lindholf. The Aalavarrè carrying Lawri set the Silver Throne bearing her body gently on the marble slab between Tala and Lindholf.

"Is she dead?" Lindholf asked. "Why have you carried my sister here dead?"

Tala's eyes wandered over the bloody stairway next, finding the Gallows Haven boy, Nail, standing there amongst all the carnage. She had not seen him since she had climbed up on the blind green dragon and flown away to the Atonement Tree with Lawri. She was glad he still lived. With Nail were Bronwyn, Liz Hen, Dokie, and a big shepherd dog. Two fair-haired girls Tala did not recognize stood beside Nail, one wearing Bloodwood leathers, the other bearing a thin sword with a ruby-studded hilt. Two other blood-streaked warriors stood with Nail, one with harsh Wyn Darrè tattoos under his eyes. The other wore Sør Sevier armor. Both fighters had been under the Atonement Tree at Aeros Raijael's death. A dark-haired girl with dark tattooed eyes, wearing a forest-green cloak, also stood near Nail; a brutish oghul with severe facial injuries leaned on the girl's shoulder. In fact, Nail's entire group looked battle-weary and defeated. Several hundred Dayknights and Silver Guards stood on the stairs below Nail, along with a smattering of oghuls and Vallè fighters. All fighting had stopped upon her approach.

"You must answer me," Lindholf said, garnering Tala's attention once again. "What have you done with my sister?"

Lindholf handed *Forgetting Moon* and *Ethic Shroud* to the girl behind him, then slid from the saddle. He swiftly took the weapons back from the girl and faced the Silver Throne. "What have they done to you, Lawri?" he asked the corpse listing sideways on the throne, tawny hair fluttering in the breeze above a rotted face. "What has Tala done to you, my sister?" Lindholf leaned forward, as if trying to get a better look at the blackened corpse before him. He stared at Lawri a moment, then turned to Tala. "What is this army with you? Where did they come from? Why do they follow you?"

Tala could feel the hilt of *Afflicted Fire* grow hotter in her hand, felt all the scars and marks on her flesh burn. She didn't even know how to answer him, for she wasn't sure herself.

"These are our kin." The dragon rider in white-scaled armor stepped up behind Lindholf. The pale-faced knight held a silver whip, droplets hissing onto the marble. A leather strap hung over the white knight's shoulder, severed and shriveled ears tied to the thong. The dragon rider's ashen face was as graceful and beautiful as Yvoirè's, as beautiful as any fey Tala had seen.

"I am Icelyn." The dragon rider in white bowed before Tala. "But you were not who was expected."

"And who did you expect?" Tala asked, picturing Seita lying dead near the rim of the slave quarry.

"The maiden with the wrought-iron soul, the one who cracked open the world."

"I cracked open the world." Tala held up *Afflicted Fire*.

"'Twas you who brought my people up from their long sleep?" Icelyn asked.

"She is the one," Ashure-Ikarii answered.

Icelyn glanced at Ashure-Ikarii and then bowed once more to Tala. "My scorch whip is forever yours."

The dragon rider in red stepped toward Tala and bowed likewise, introducing himself as Aamari-Laada. "We follow you, leader of armies, the bearer of *Afflicted Fire*."

At the dragon rider's oath of fealty, an expression bleak as winter crossed Lindholf's deformed face. "What do you mean?" he demanded of both of the dragon riders. "I am Laijon returned. I am the White Prince, the youngest son of Aevrett Raijael. It is I who you follow."

But Icelyn and Aamari-Laada ignored him. "Praise be to Viper." Icelyn stepped forward to greet Ashure-Ikarii in a reverent embrace.

"Absolution hath redeemed us. Our long banishment at the hand of man is near an end."

Aamari-Laada stepped forward and embraced Yvoirè. "Grace be to Hragna'Ar and the sacrifice of our kin."

"And grace be to you both for preparing the way," Yvoirè said. "And grace be unto those dragon riders who have perished. For I see there are only two of you here."

"Some have paid the ultimate sacrifice," Icelyn said.

"Grace be unto their dragons, too." Ashure-Ikarii bowed. "We knew your journey through sacrifice and Hragna'Ar would be dangerous, for the science of the stars is not yet fully understood."

"We welcome the Great Above once again," Icelyn said.

And in their odd exchange, Tala felt the world had changed. She felt the hilt of *Afflicted Fire* continue to pulse with both heat and power in her grip, felt the mists curling up from the blade and around her wrists.

Lindholf also saw how the weapon was reacting to her. She saw the confidence draining from his eyes by the moment. "What is the meaning of all this?" he demanded of Icelyn. "I am your leader. Must I repeat, I am Laijon returned. I am the White Prince. I am the heir of Aevrett Raijael. Val-Draekin said under the Atonement Tree that I was the chosen one." But the Aalavarrè Solas stared at him with emotionless eyes of flat silver. "I am the chosen one," Lindholf repeated. "The heir of Aevrett Raijael."

"You were heir to a bunch of Vallè lies and nothing more," Tala said, meeting her cousin's dark-pitted eyes. "Did you not listen to Val-Draekin under the Atonement Tree? Or did you just hear what you wanted to hear? The scriptures were made up, false. *The Way and Truth of Laijon* was only a fantasy."

She gestured coldly to the vast army of Aalavarrè Solas behind her. "'Tis oghul blood sacrifice and Hragna'Ar that has proven true."

"I will not accept such things," Lindholf said. "I know what I know to be true, and that is not Hragna'Ar and bloodletting. *I am the heir of Laijon!*"

If Tala was cold with him before, she was like ice now. "Further belief in Laijon is banned upon pain of death. The Five Isles cannot allow such poisons as faith and belief to ever infect us again. Anyone who continues to believe in such fantasy shall die at my behest." She motioned again to the army behind her. "This is my army and it is now an army of peace. 'Twas I who summoned them from the underworld. They follow me."

"*I am the heir of Laijon!*" Lindholf shouted again. Blue mist swirled from the hilt of *Forgetting Moon* and up his arm. White mist shrouded the shield in a haze of light.

"Only one of you is the leader of all armies." One of the Bloodwoods stepped forward. He was a Vallè, dark-eyed and dangerous.

"I am the leader of all armies," Lindholf addressed the Bloodwood. "You yourself have said as much, Black Dugal. I control the Aalavarrè and the dragons."

"With the cracking of the world, things have now changed for the Aalavarrè," Black Dugal said, glancing at both Lindholf and Tala. "Only one of you can be their Immortal Lord. You must decide who that shall be. Only then will there be peace."

With both hands, Tala hefted *Afflicted Fire* up between her and her cousin. Again, she set her stance and held the white sword in one of the many ways Hawkwood had taught her during her training with Nail in the bowels of the *Val-Sadè*. The blade felt light in her hands and she could sense its magic building. She faced Lindholf, saying, "You will renounce yourself as Laijon returned or you shall die by my sword."

Lindholf looked at the sword, then at her. "You would kill me, your cousin?"

"I will, if it means the end of all war."

"You never did care for me!" Lindholf spat the words at her, pain and venom in his voice. "Nobody has ever cared for me. 'Twas your own father who hid both Lawri and me from the world. Your own father who burnt my face, deformed me. Your entire family has betrayed me at one point or another."

"You're behaving like a spoiled child," Tala said. "Fiery Absolution is over. We can live in peace. All you need do is drop your weapons. We can both forgive each other."

Lindholf leaned *Ethic Shroud* against his hip. Then he jammed his hand into the folds of his cloak. When he tore his hand free, his fingers were coated in white powder. *Shroud of the Vallè!* Tala recognized the substance. Lindholf sniffed the Shroud from his fingers, licking them clean, a renewed glint of confidence in his eyes.

He grabbed the white shield by the strap once more. "I am long past the point of forgiving, long past the point of being pushed around, cousin." He faced her squarely. There was a darkness in his gaze that was less than welcoming; in fact, those beady eyes of his were no longer brimming with innocent love and childish admiration for her. They were full of hatred and malice.

"Despite what you think, Tala, I am the greater one now," he said. "And you shall go to your death knowing that."

Both *Forgetting Moon* and *Ethic Shroud* sparkled with magic in Lindholf's hands.

A sudden red mist hung over Tala's vision and her heart faltered, as she realized the absurdity of the situation she had created. She and her cousin were the two least-skilled fighters here at the end of all things, and yet here they were, about to square off in a duel with weapons out of myth and legend. And to further her doubt, she realized that Lindholf wore armor, yet she had none. *And I haven't eaten or slept for days.* She could feel the weakness overcome her entire body.

Lindholf lunged forward, *Forgetting Moon* singing through the air.

Afflicted Fire came up instinctively, blocking the blow.

Thunder rang in Tala's ears. Sparks flew. And the jarring collision of weapons sent Tala staggering back, arms stinging from the impact. Lindholf scarcely broke stride, heading straight for her again, the battle-ax already slashing toward her once more.

Tala parried with the white blade. Thunder and sparks and she was thrown off balance once again while Lindholf pressed the attack. He rushed her this time. Like Hawkwood had taught her, Tala stepped into her cousin's hurried blow and met it headlong with a swift swing of her own.

Forgetting Moon was turned aside with a hollow clang. Lindholf whirled and shoved her away with the flat of the white shield. *Ethic Shroud* pounded into her shoulder with a jolt like lightning. She stumbled away, spinning, nearly slipping in a patch of blood. She stayed afoot, whirled, and faced her cousin.

Lindholf did not attack. He stared at her sword. In the smoky gloom hanging over the castle, *Afflicted Fire* appeared like a pure gleam of light in her hands, as if made of red and white stardust and flame. Her own eyes widened, marveling at the weapon. The confusion that had caused her so much doubt was suddenly replaced with a crystal clear focus and vision. Tala could feel something from the sword transferring into her, some rush of magic and power.

In one fluid motion she swung the weapon at her cousin, the keen white blade cutting the air swift and merciless. Lindholf met her arcing blow, battle-ax upraised.

Afflicted Fire sliced through *Forgetting Moon*, deafening and bright.

Blue and red sparks shot skyward as the ax shattered.

Thunder vibrated wild and deep.

Lindholf was flung back, *Ethic Shroud* spinning from his grasp. The jagged blue shards of *Forgetting Moon* rained down, cracking loudly against the marble.

The white sword reverberated with a keening song in Tala's clenched fingers as sparks showered around both her and Lindholf. She was alive, painfully alive; the singing sword in her hand was a roaring symphony announcing Absolution's finale, the voices of the all the dead rising above her in a melody of sacrifice and sorrow. Surrounded in colorful sparks and harmony, Tala found that she was possessed of a curious strength that wasn't wholly physical, but all-encompassing.

And with a tearing sound and a wet hiss of air, her backhanded swing of the sword opened her cousin's neck clear to the spine.

Lindholf appeared at once horrified and stunned. He stood there stiffly, blood flooding down in one red sheet from the wound, his white armor finally stained.

Instinctively, letting *Afflicted Fire*'s song guide her hand and seek its own bloody nourishment, Tala stabbed the weapon straight into her cousin's chest. The bloody armor over his heart splintered open as if a bolt of lightning had struck it. The blade sank deep.

Lindholf's black-pitted gaze lifted from the sword in his chest to Tala.

Then he fell sideways, dropping to the bloody marble, rolling onto his back with a deep moan. *I've killed him.* Tala's heart pounded. *I've killed both my cousins and have fallen into complete darkness.*

Lindholf stared up at her, eyes wide. His body twitched as he tried to grab one last breath through his severed throat. Fighting the sorrow in her heart, Tala watched the life bleed from her cousin's dark gaze and fade away. Then he was dead.

And Tala had to look away. She looked at Lawri. And from her cold perch on the Silver Throne, Lawri Le Graven's sightless eyes were somehow fixed on her dead brother.

The marble landing was thrust into a deep silence, everyone having just watched the cousins do battle. Tala looked away from Lawri, staring up into the smoky sky, the markings on her body burning with both guilt and pain now. She could feel *Afflicted Fire* greedily absorb Lindholf's blood, what remained of his life sinking into the blade.

"Why did you have to kill him?" the slender girl astride Lindholf's white stallion asked.

"Who are you?" Tala looked up at the girl.

"Leisel." The girl slid from the saddle and knelt over Lindholf, her face a mask of pale sadness. She reached out and lightly brushed his eyes closed. Then she looked up at Tala once more, asking, "Why did you have to kill him? He was a good and kind person, always so nice to me."

The girl is right. He was *a good and kind person!* A lump built in Tala's throat as she recalled the innocent frivolity of her young cousin. *You used to be much more lighthearted, Lindholf,* she'd said to him in Sunbird Hall not long ago. *Tell me a funny story,* she had pleaded with him that day. *Tell me how you used to tease Lorhand and Lilith. You could be so clever with your antics. I need a laugh.* But he had accused her of being cruel. *Something changed in him that day.* And with that thought, Tala felt her gaze harden as she looked at the lithe blond girl kneeling over her cousin.

Leisel wilted under her stare. "Why did you kill him?" she pleaded.

"He believed he was something that he was not," Tala answered, resentment and anger building within her voice now. "And that is why I killed him. He held faith in falsehoods. And that kind of thinking needs to end. We must now accept reality and stop living lies."

CHAPTER EIGHTY-EIGHT

NAIL

14TH DAY OF THE HEART MOON, 999TH YEAR OF LAIJON
AMADON, GUL KANA

Nail's heart thundered as the white dragon and the red rose up behind Tala Bronachell almost protectively. The young blond girl, Leisel, cowered.

The dragon riders in white and red scaled armor had moved to either side of the Silver Throne, their gleaming whips dripping hissing silver to the bloody marble landing. Black Dugal and Hans Rake moved to either side of the throne too. The bulldog with the spiked collar was with them, beady eyes gazing up at the girl on the throne. Lawri Le Graven's rotted corpse still listed to the side, blond hair fluttering in the breeze. The gauntlet was still attached to her blackened arm, silver glinting in the smoky light.

A vast ominous army of pale-faced Aalavarrè Solas stretched down the length of the bloody stairway and into Tin Man Square and beyond. *Demons of the underworld.* Endless death and slaughter lay everywhere in Amadon, and the entire scene before Nail seemed hopeless to him.

Jenko Bruk, Ava Shay, Liz Hen Neville, Dokie Liddle, Krista Aulbrek, Mancellor, Bronwyn, and Cromm stood with him. Beer Mug too. They were all injured in some way. Nail had lost track of the wounds on his body, all the pains blending into one numb, hazy feeling in his mind. The last few hours and days had been unrelenting and savage, and Nail felt the weariness of it all settling over him like a heavy blanket. He felt light-headed, thoughts running foggy and unclear. He thought he might collapse from pure exhaustion or Bloodwood poison. He had not slept nor eaten in several days.

"Why were you riding with my cousin?" Tala asked Leisel.

"Because he treated me kind," the girl answered, cowering under Tala and the dragons now. *Afflicted Fire* was poised over Leisel's slender neck. "He saved me when the White Prince pushed me from the wagon."

Tala's eyes hardened at the answer. And the sword in her hand now seemed a thing of bright enchantment, beauty, and death. Nail had watched the sallow blade feast on Lindholf's blood, consuming the pulsing redness of his now vanquished life into its swirling pale depths. Now the blade was aimed at Leisel.

"I used to live in the Fortress of Saint Only," the girl continued. "I was a serving girl in Lord Edmon Guy Van Hester's court. I oft tended to what few young children were left in his castle. I also cleaned up after the dogs. And there were a lot of those. And they were oft unfed and very mangy and very dirty. But I did my best."

"Do you believe as Lindholf did?" Tala asked, pointing the tip of *Afflicted Fire* between Leisel's eyes. "Do you believe in Laijon? Do you believe in the scripture?"

Leisel's pale face grew sad, eyes misting with tears. "When he lay with me, the White Prince said he was filling me with his essence. Aeros claimed he was filling me with the essence of both Raijael and Laijon. But I could tell nothing was happening." She swiped the tears from her eyes with the back of her dirty sleeve.

"But do you believe in Laijon?" Tala demanded.

Leisel straightened her posture and stared down the long white blade, meeting Tala's questioning gaze. "To answer your question, no, I do not believe."

Tala lowered the sword. "Then you shall live. And that you cared so much for my cousin Lindholf means much to me. He had few friends. Since you were once a servant, perhaps I shall make you my servant. If my brother Ansel yet lives, you shall watch over him for me. You are an unbeliever like me. And for as long as I draw breath, I do not want Ansel taught anything more about the gods. The days of belief are over."

Tala confronted two bloody Dayknights standing between her and Nail's group. The skull-faced dragon rider in white-scaled armor stepped away from the Silver Throne and moved up behind Tala, scorch whip gripped tightly in hand.

"Do you still hold faith in *The Way and Truth of Laijon*?" Tala asked the first Dayknight before her. "Do you still hold faith in false gods?"

The Dayknight removed his blood-coated helm. The man wore a long curling mustache under dark hair and dark eyes. His black Dayknight armor was streaked with so much splatter and blood it was almost red. "Laijon is real," he said, "and that I cannot deny." There was conviction in his voice as he held his head high and proud.

The dragon rider in white ended the Dayknight's life with a crack of the whip. The man fell dead at Tala's feet, his severed head rolling down the stairs behind him.

"What is the point of this?" the second Dayknight asked, removing his own bloody helm, revealing a sweaty face and fair-colored hair. He was tall and had a look and strength about his bearing that reminded Nail of Culpa Barra. Culpa would not have denied his faith, and it looked as if this man would also hold true to his.

"How does slaying us for our belief help the city we have fought to defend?" he asked. "Our entire history and purpose is tied to *The Way and Truth of Laijon*. The Dayknights were formed by Ser Avard Sansom Bronachell, one of your own kin. Ser Avard formed the Dayknights with the express purpose of defending the faith. Your own father was a Dayknight. Your own brother was a Dayknight." The man's voice was rising in anger. "Where is our king? Where is Jovan Bronachell? Who are you to execute us for our belief? Who are you, a mere girl, to judge us? Do you not know that the vows and *faith* of the Dayknights are entwined with the history of the Five Isles?"

"You want to know about the history of the Five Isles as I see it, the history of *faith*?" Tala's voice rose to meet the scolding tone of the Dayknight. "It is a horrible bloodbath, our history, with just the trickle of hope underlying it, just enough false hope in those scriptures for fools like you to follow, just enough hope for *faith* and belief to spring forth. I shall have all scriptures rooted from these lands and burned, and any and all continued belief in them made punishable by death. For faith is the greatest creation of wicked men; faith is the vile, immoral masterpiece of pure evil. And it ends with me."

"You are a lost soul," the Dayknight said.

"You have been a lost soul the entirety of your life," Tala countered. "Deny Laijon and go home to your family and live out your days in peace."

"I cannot."

With a crack and flash of silver, the knight's body fell into two pieces at Tala's feet, the dragon rider in white standing over the body.

The princess of Amadon moved to Nail next, the dragon rider in white right behind her. Nail looked into her eyes. He could see the pain and conflict building within her, but he could also see the hardness and firm resolve.

This was not the Tala Bronachell that he knew.

She asked him frankly. "Do you, Nail, deny Laijon?"

"You know I lack faith." He wasn't trying to spare his life admitting as much; he was only speaking the truth. "We talked about this very subject many times, Tala. We talked in the *Val-Sadè*, in the courtyard of the Filthy Horse Saloon. You know that I do not believe. But this is not the answer to all your pain, more killing. This is not who you are. This is not the princess I know. Continue down this path of vengeance and you shall become more evil than Aeros, Jovan, Leif, and Glade combined."

"You do not know *who* I am." She stiffened her back. "You can hold whatever opinion you want of me, Nail of Gallows Haven. But I suggest you leave this place and go home now."

"You need help, Tala," he said. "We can still help you slay these demons. They are not your friends. It is not over. This war is *not* over."

"No. This war *is* over, Nail. Go home."

"I will not accept that."

"Go home, Nail. Live out your days in peace."

The dragon rider in white spoke. "I would not so easily let any of these humans go. This boy, Nail, is the one who stabbed the Dragon in the neck during the cracking of the world. He is deceitful. He is the boy who helped killed Val-Draekin, Black Dugal's one and only son. He has thwarted prophecy and must die."

"I am the Princess," Tala said sharply, without looking back at the skull-faced knight. "Do not talk to me of prophecy. I am the leader of all armies and I will allow Nail to go in peace, same as any who deny Laijon."

The dragon rider in white exchanged a quick glance with the dragon rider in red, who still stood near the Silver Throne, then nodded to Tala in acquiescence. "You may do as you please for now, Tala Bronachell. But you have been warned."

Tala stood before Jenko Bruk next. The baron's son was leaning on the bloody haft of a spear, weariness in his amber-colored eyes. "What is your name, soldier?"

"Jenko Bruk."

"Baron Jubal Bruk's son?"

Jenko nodded.

"Do you deny Laijon?" she asked him.

Jenko glared at her icily. Then he spat blood at her feet, almost growling as he spoke. "I say, girl, you and this pale-faced demon offer up an interrogation to your enemies that would make Hammerfiss and Enna Spades proud, though you are more pointed in your purpose than they. Nail is right, what you do now is pure evil."

"That does not answer my question." Tala glared ice right back at him.

Jenko's amber eyes tightened, fingers curling around the spear in his hands. "I hold no allegiance to Laijon or any god."

Tala moved to Ava Shay. "And your name?"

"Ava Shay."

"Do you deny Laijon?"

"I once believed in the power of the wraiths." Ava glared at Tala. "But when the wraiths vanished from my mind, so did my belief in Laijon."

Tala moved to Liz Hen next. Beer Mug growled.

Tala ignored the dog. "Liz Hen Neville, do you deny—"

"Fuck Laijon and the fucking demented minds who conjured him up," Liz Hen cut the princess off. "I know what Val-Draekin said under the Atonement Tree. I know it is all a Vallè game. I've always known. I'm with you, honey, fuck the gods. Fuck them hard and fuck them raw and fuck them all directly in their gaping, shit-stained assholes."

Tala's countenance changed visibly after Liz Hen's harsh denial of Laijon. She looked disturbed by Liz Hen's frank and profanity-laden screed. Still, she continued on, facing Dokie next. "Do you deny Laijon?"

Dokie looked sick to his stomach and refused to answer. Beer Mug whimpered.

"Do you deny Laijon?" Tala pressed.

"Yes," Dokie said nervously. "I do deny." Then he performed the three-fingered sign of the Laijon Cross over his heart.

Liz Hen elbowed him on the ribs. "Idiot," she hissed.

"Sorry." Dokie shot Tala an uneasy look. "A habit is all."

"I mean to break the world of such pointless ritual and habits," Tala said sharply.

Then she moved to Krista. "So you're a real Bloodwood?" Tala asked.

"You know that I am," Krista answered, looking past Tala, eyeing the two pale-faced knights behind the princess and the silver whips. The white dragon slithered up ominously behind the dragon riders, fire-filled lungs straining with hot breath.

"Do you deny Laijon?" Tala asked the assassin.

"I'm a Bloodwood," Krista said. "I owe no fealty to Laijon or Raijael or even to Lady Death. I am no follower of the Brethren of Mia either, as your father was—and as you know, I knew him well. In fact, I reckon I knew your father more than you. And as horrible of a man as Borden Bronachell was, he would not do what you do now, killing people who do not believe as you beli—"

"Do you deny fealty to Laijon?" Tala snapped, contention in her eyes.

Krista's gaze remained fixed on the fearsome white dragon behind Tala. "I'll deny whatever you wish for me to deny. What do I care? I want to live."

"So you deny Laijon?"

"That is what I said," Krista shot back with impatience.

Tala moved to Mancellor Allen next. The Wyn Darrè fighter was suffering more injuries than the rest of them combined. Still, he remained standing.

"Your name, soldier?" she asked.

"Mancellor Allen."

"Do you deny Laijon?" Tala asked him.

"They are using you, m'lady," Mancellor said weakly, motioning to the dragon rider behind her. Nail could tell that just standing was enough to cause Mancellor great pain. But he did not back down from the princess or her question. "They have made you believe you are something that you are not. Same as they did to Lindholf."

"Do you deny Laijon?" Tala pressed a second time.

"Though I know you only from...," Mancellor paused, gulping. "Though I know you only from my dreams, I can see that these demons have cast some spell over you, Tala Bronachell. They have infected you with their evil, with the evil of the underworld."

"What do you mean, you know me from your dreams?"

"I have seen your face in my dreams, m'lady. Beyond that I wish not to say."

"Dreams can be dangerous." Tala seemed visibly disturbed. "Do you deny Laijon?"

Mancellor held his head high. "Laijon is my savior."

"Don't," Bronwyn pleaded, gripping her bow tightly. Cromm leaned against her shoulder, unable to see. But Nail could hear the angry growl growing in his belly.

Bronwyn was staring into her brother's eyes with an intensity and fear Nail had never before seen within her. "Please, Mancellor, just say that you—"

The crack of a silver whip cut the Wyn Darrè girl's plea short. "Do not speak!" the knight in white armor ordered Bronwyn. The dragon rider stepped around Tala, ready to strike Mancellor down.

"No!" Bronwyn shouted, slipping from under the weight of Cromm, brandishing her bow. But she had no arrows. "Somebody give me an arrow!" she shouted, her eyes blazing toward Tala. "I will kill you, make no mistake!"

"Cromm will help you fight!" the oghul shouted, though he was looking in the wrong direction, blind, face burned by the poison of Hans Rake's daggers.

The dragon rider cracked the whip, backing Bronwyn toward the bloody stairs.

"Someone give me an arrow so I can kill the bitch!" the Wyn Darrè girl shouted, eyes still blazing anger at Tala.

The skull-faced knight cracked the whip again. Bronwyn flinched back, nearly stumbling down the slippery stairs in retreat now. The white dragon followed her, mouth stretching open, ready to hit her with murderous flame.

Bronwyn located a stray arrow amongst the carnage on the stairs. She snatched it up and nocked it to her bow, aimed it at Tala's heart. "You will not kill my brother for his belief!"

"It is okay, Bronwyn." Mancellor stepped between his sister and Tala. "I shall gladly die for Laijon."

Nail saw the sudden surprise in Tala's eyes. That Mancellor would step in the way of his own sister's arrow had a profound effect on her. He could see the conflict growing within her. He wished there was something he could do to help her, something he could do to break the spell these wraiths had over her. These demons of the underworld had deemed her their queen, and she could not see the world straight anymore for the power she now wielded.

"Don't let her do this to you," Bronwyn pleaded with her brother. "Don't let her humiliate you like this."

"It is no humiliation to die for my beliefs," Mancellor said. "Lower your bow and Tala will let you live, just like she let Nail and the others live. I know you do not believe in Laijon as I do."

"I cannot allow this, brother," Bronwyn cried. "I cannot allow her to kill you just for your beliefs."

The white dragon roared. Bronwyn cowered, her bow lowered. The dragon rider in white raised the silver whip, ready to strike her down.

"No!" Tala shouted. "Lower your whip! They are right. The wraiths take me! I am so confused! This is not the way!"

Nail could see that pain and conflict and rage were still fighting within her. But by the look now on her face, he knew Tala Bronachell was not completely lost to the evil. There had to be something he could do, for he knew these demons would not let her live long either. She was just some pawn in a larger game they played.

He knew what it was like to be a pawn.

"The Wyn Darrè girl and her brother are right," Tala said. "Killing them is not the way."

"We should not let them live." The dragon rider in white faced Tala.

"Icelyn is right." The Vallè Bloodwood named Black Dugal strode toward Tala, black cloak billowing out behind him. "They will always be a threat to your throne if you let any of them live. Maybe not now. Maybe not today. Maybe not in ten years. But eventually they will try and dethrone you. They are your enemies, and they must all die."

"No," Tala said. "I will let them all go."

"At least let me slay this one," Dugal said, eyeing Krista. "For this one has betrayed me often." Krista glared right back at Dugal, seething hatred in her dark gaze.

"This war is over," Tala said emphatically. "We shall let them all live in peace."

Black Dugal bowed to her crisply. Then he turned to Nail and the others. "Go," he ordered. "Go now."

But Nail did not want to leave Tala Bronachell to these fiends.

Still, he knew he must, as one by one his friends made their way down the long bloody slope of marble stairs in defeat. Jenko, Ava, Liz Hen, Dokie, Beer Mug, Mancellor, Bronwyn, and Cromm.

Krista Aulbrek hesitated with Nail, not taking her eyes off Black Dugal, not quite yet willing or ready to leave.

Nail also met the Bloodwood's hardened gaze, thinking back to that day in Ravenker when he had faced off against the Spider, when Hawkwood had stepped in and saved him, how he had watched two Bloodwood brothers fight over him.

Things had somehow worked out that day. But today it looked like things would be different. Despite her current mercy in letting them live, today a slew of evils from the underworld had claimed Tala Bronachell and she didn't even know it.

Hragna'Ar evil.

Bloodwood evil.

Today the master of Bloodwoods had won, and there was no Hawkwood to step in and save any of them.

With that thought, Nail turned with Krista and walked down the long marble stairs and away from Fiery Absolution, not knowing where he would go or what he would do, not knowing whether peace was really in his future.

For he knew this battle was not yet over.

In time, the squalor of war, all the stench and entrails and lakes of blood and screams of the dead, seep into the dirt. In time, the torture, terror, and agony fade. In time, war takes upon itself a rousing and romantic shape, a pleasing nostalgia bathed in naught but beautiful glory. In time, all things sanctioned of Laijon become righteous. For our fight is to stave off the beasts of the underworld, to prevent those fell demons from rising again from those dark depths at Fiery Absolution. In this we must not fail, lest doom reign over all.
—THE WAY AND TRUTH OF LAIJON

CHAPTER EIGHTY-NINE
TALA BRONACHELL

15TH DAY OF THE HEART MOON, 999TH YEAR OF LAIJON
AMADON, GUL KANA

Peace reigned under Tala Bronachell's rule, though she had ruled for all of half a day and one night and then the start of a second day. She had put an end to Fiery Absolution atop the marble stairway that rose above Tin Man Square less than twenty-four hours ago. War was finally over.

Tala carried *Afflicted Fire* and *Ethic Shroud* with her into the red-hazed room deep within the bowels of Amadon Castle. Ten decorated oghul warriors had followed her into the secret ways. They bore Lawri Le Graven on a white litter, her rotted body covered in a white sheet. The two Bloodwoods, Black Dugal and Hans Rake, came with the oghuls. The dragon riders, Icelyn and Aamari-Laada, along with Yvoirè and Ashure-Ikarii, had also followed. The bulldog Dugal called Café Colza was with them too.

Tala's job was not over yet. Lawri was still dead, and she had to remedy that.

Many things had transpired, and many more were yet to happen. Late last night she had found her younger brother, Ansel, hiding from the sounds of battle under his bed in his own bedchamber. One life spared, and Tala had rejoiced: her family had not been completely vanquished by Absolution. It was just Tala and Ansel now, all that remained of Bronachell royalty. Leisel watched over Ansel now in their mother's bedchamber.

Tala still felt guilt and remorse for the two Dayknights she had killed yesterday for refusing to deny Laijon. That had been a mistake born out of rage and the need to be right. She did not know how she could ever atone for such sins. She thought of all the lies she had told and all the other deaths those lies had caused—many other Dayknights had been put to death under Leif Chaparral's watch for her lies.

But the Five Isles would be different now under her rule, she vowed. It seemed all semblance of truth and reality had been lost in the wake of religion and war. But under her rule, all peoples and races would live in peace: dwarf, oghul, Vallè, and man. The Aalavarrè Solas too. It would take a lot of work, but it could be done.

The streets of Amadon were in the process of being swept free of all blood and death. Those thousands upon thousands risen from the underworld were already busy rebuilding the city, with the help of what humans survived. Yes, the Aalavarrè Solas were once again reclaiming their lands, and doing so in peace.

As Tala entered the red-hazed room, a thrill of excitement crawled up her spine, for her cousin would soon live again. Yvoirè and Ashure-Ikarii had promised her that. The oghuls had borne Lawri's body effortlessly through the secret ways and into this room with the cross-shaped altar, and the ceremony to bring her back to life would soon begin.

Tala scanned the familiar ruby-hazed chamber, and she shivered in both worry and anticipation. Things here in this room had changed since yesterday, when she had shown both Yvoirè and Ashure-Ikarii through the secret ways to the altar. The room looked the same in that it still had a high, vaulted ceiling and was flanked with rows of wooden benches, with a cross-shaped altar in the center. The difference was, the room was clean. Set high on one white-plastered wall was a tall stained-glass window of deep red, the glass washed clean, bright red light beaming through. The grit and smoke stains that had previously covered the benches and white walls had been washed off. What ash and bone fragments had once littered the floor were now gone. Even the intricately woven tapestry of Mother Mia against the wall opposite the window seemed to glow with renewed radiancy. It was clear that the Aalavarrè had scoured every nook and cranny of the chamber clean. Still, seeing the room sparkle under a renewed red light did not make the place any less unnerving than before. This had been a place full of much darkness for Tala in the past.

She felt herself shivering, not because the room was cold and clean and without blemish, but for the anticipation and excitement and, yes, even some dread, growing in her own heart. This was to be the place of Lawri's resurrection. And what scared her most were the changes made to the cross-shaped altar itself. Its capstone had been removed. Blood filled its cross-shaped hollow. Whose blood was in the altar, Tala did not know. But the city was full of the still-warm bodies of hundreds of thousands of dead soldiers.

Once everyone had settled into the room, finding their places standing around the altar, all was silent.

And that was when Tala noticed something *odd* about the tapestry above. Or something new. Or rather something she had not previously noted. Before, she had believed the tapestry to be naught but a beautifully stitched likeness of the Blessed Mother Mia. She recalled her father saying that the worshippers of Raijael in Sør Sevier never referred to Mia by name, but rather called her Lady Death. Yet Tala did not want to think of her father's explanation now. The tapestry was clearly not an image of Mother Mia. It was an image of something else entirely.

It was the likeness of neither a man nor a woman but something in between, or both. And the personage's face glowed with some inner white light, ears as finely tapered and delicate as the Aalavarrè's themselves.

And on one of the personage's arms was a silver gauntlet.

How had she not noticed that detail before? Or had the tapestry been swapped for another? That seemed unlikely, as the artwork looked the same as she remembered, but for those few small differences. Perhaps the recent cleaning had made the silver on the arm more apparent.

And then the ceremony began.

"Only through silver and blood and the green elixir of life can the dead rise again," Icelyn the White said as she stepped to the cross-shaped altar. The row of severed ears dangling from the leather thong over her shoulder always sent an extra shiver of apprehension up Tala's spine. She wished the dragon rider would just be rid of them.

"For Hragna'Ar is life renewed," Icelyn continued, "and we are here at the tomb of Viper for true Absolution." The dragon rider turned to the oghuls bearing Lawri's litter. "Harsh and beautiful these humans are in death. May we honor them that."

Yvoirè, Ashure-Ikarii, and Aamari-Laada the Red bowed in unison. Black Dugal and Hans Rake looked on in rapt interest.

"Has the tomb of Viper been prepared?" Icelyn asked the oghul warriors. "Have Hragna'Ar and the blood magic of the stars been summoned?"

The ten oghuls grunted yes.

"My eternal soul now quivers with life and purpose." Aamari-Laada the Red reached one gauntleted hand up to the red-scaled breastplate covering his chest, armored fingers caressing the many circles, squares, crosses, crescent moons, and shooting stars etched there. "We have roamed and stalked and hunted once again with Viper. And a fallow hunt it was, to become one with Viper and make extinct the race of man, to avenge the genocide visited upon the Aalavarrè so long ago, to erase the memory of the War of Cleansing, to make right that Vicious War of the Demons, to rid ourselves of all memory of the underworld and its black depths, to serve again the Dragon, our Vallè master, and bring about Fiery Absolution."

There was a lot in Aamari-Laada's odd recital that did not sit well with Tala. She felt her hands gripping both *Afflicted Fire* and *Ethic Shroud* tighter, and she thought to herself, *It's just part of the ritual. A prayer to the stars. And when it is over, Lawri will once again be whole.* She recalled how the very same green elixir of life Icelyn spoke of had filled Lawri's lungs with breath once before—a green elixir she herself had pulled from the guts of Sterling Prentiss as he lay upon this very same altar.

"May the Dragon rest at Viper's side." Aamari-Laada knelt before the cross-shaped altar. "May Val-Draekin rest with Raakel-Jael, Basque-Alia, and Sashenya in the heights of the stars. And let them all live there with the knowledge that we have fulfilled our destiny, fulfilled prophecy, that our kin have risen from the underworld and taken back the entirety of the Five Isles from humanity, taken back the precious lands stolen from us so long ago." The dragon rider removed his mask of Skull. Reaching over the lip of the altar, he placed the silver mask reverently atop the thick pool of blood.

Tala watched in both fascination and terror as the skull mask disappeared down into thick swirls of blood. It vanished as if being drawn down into the depths of the underworld itself. She clenched *Afflicted Fire* and *Ethic Shroud* even more tightly in hand, once again feeling the scars on her body begin to burn.

"May Val-Draekin fly amongst the heights of the stars with the glorious knowledge of our triumph." Icelyn knelt and removed her silver mask too, letting it sink down into the cross-shaped pool of blood.

Then Black Dugal drifted forward, facing Tala. "Where is the maiden with the wrought-iron soul?"

"The who?" Tala asked, confused, gripping her weapons even more.

"Where is Seita?"

"Dead." The word slipped from Tala's tongue before she could rein it in.

"And you knew this all along?" Dugal's face was like stone, dark Vallè eyes unreadable. Tala wished she had kept her mouth shut.

"May Seita fly amongst the heights of the stars with the Dragon." Aamari-Laada stood, facing Tala, silver eyes burning into hers.

"May she live with Viper." Icelyn stood too, glaring at Tala.

And then the door to the chamber swung open and ten Vallè noblemen entered the room, several of them bearing Lindholf Le Graven's body on a white litter similar to Lawri's, a white sheet covering his body, covering all but his face and head.

"What is this?" Tala asked. "Why have they carried Lindholf in here?"

Black Dugal just looked at her, his stare stark and raw.

Icelyn and Aamari-Laada knelt once again before the altar.

In fact, every Aalavarrè in the chamber was kneeling as the oghuls and Vallè brought the twins forth, reverently removing the white sheets from their bodies. Lindholf still wore his armor, his deformed face pale, the wound across his throat still gaping and red. Lawri still wore her dress, and the silver gauntlet was still attached to her arm, though her dried and blackened skin was almost too grotesque to look upon.

The oghuls lifted Lawri from the litter first and gently placed her into the blood-filled basin of the altar, letting her rotted body slowly sink beneath the thick scarlet. The Vallè then hefted Lindholf's body, armor and all, laying him atop his sister in the altar's cross-shaped hollow.

As Lindholf's body settled down below the dark crimson surface, the pool of blood itself overflowed the stone. Like a red storm rising, blood oozed over the rim of the altar and down the rough sides, curling around the tiny carvings at the altar's base—carvings of beasts of the underworld. And as the rivulets of red dripped and curled down the altar, those beastly carvings began to glow. Beneath that sinuous blood the carvings glowed with a silver light as dazzling and pure as fire. Tala felt her own veins pounding to the galloping of her heart.

The ten oghuls and ten Vallè backed away from the altar and knelt around the room, facing the altar. Yvoirè stood next. The Aalavarrè brought forth the five angel stones from the folds of her white cloak, all the stones now glowing more brightly than Tala had ever seen them glow before. They illuminated the red-hazed chamber in a rainbow of light. Yvoirè placed the stones into the altar. They also sank, their bright life swallowed up in blood.

Sweat sheathed Tala's forehead as she felt something stirring within the altar, a hollow whispering melody, no more than a lonely breath and hiss.

"Who hears that pure cry of the human dead sail high and loud toward starshine and moonlight?" Icelyn the White asked. "For I hear it. I hear that cry. And it sails high toward Viper, the one who carved out the underworld, the one who sits upon the heights of the stars with the Dragon, our master. Together they shall bring forth the dead this day. Together they shall send us our Immortal Lord."

Icelyn stood, then slipped the leather thong from off her shoulder, that ghastly thing strung with the severed ears of the human dead. Tala shuddered as Icelyn placed the strap of shriveled ears into the blood of the altar. And like Lawri and Lindholf and the five angel stones before, the ears were soon swallowed up.

Black Dugal still faced Tala. "You must sacrifice the sword and the shield."

"What?" Tala's voice cracked.

"Place *Ethic Shroud* over the altar first," the Bloodwood instructed.

Icelyn was running one gauntleted hand over the crescent-moon design on her white armor. Aamari-Laada the Red was doing the same.

"The cross on the shield matches the cross of the altar," Black Dugal said. "And once you have placed the shield over the altar, you must then take *Afflicted Fire* and lay it over the shield. The altar, the shield, and the sword are three crosses combined. Only then can Hragna'Ar be complete under the shape of the crescent moon."

Icelyn beckoned Tala forward, saying, "'Tis the last part of the ritual. 'Tis your final part in this story, to call forth the scorch from above and set your dear cousins free."

Final part in this story! Tala could only imagine Lawri alive once more. She felt herself shaking as she placed the pearly white shield over the center of the cross-shaped altar. *Ethic Shroud* settled over the stone rim like a capstone, almost creating a seal with the blood. Tala placed *Afflicted Fire* over *Ethic Shroud*, careful to align the crescent-moon hilt-guard of the long white sword with center of the cross engraved into the shield.

Once she was done, she stepped back, trembling in both anticipation and fear, for the low whispering song emanating from the blood-filled hollow of the altar seemed to deepen and grow into a low familiar rhythm: *"Hragna'Ar, Hragna'Ar, Hragna'Ar."*

Black Dugal and Hans Rake looked at each other and smiled.

And then the ten oghuls began to chant to the bloody cadence. *"Rogk Na Ark! Rogk Na Ark! Rogk Na Ark!"* Their deep booming voices echoed sharp and harsh off the chamber walls. The ten Vallè noblemen and the four Aalavarrè Solas joined the chant, which went on for some time. *"Rogk Na Ark! Rogk Na Ark! Rogk Na Ark!"* before they all went silent and looked up toward the ceiling as one.

Tala looked up too. Scared.

But there was nothing above but a red-hazed blackness and the dying echoes of *Rogk Na Ark! Rogk Na Ark!*

And then she saw it. The silver. The shooting star falling from the dark.

As she watched the glittering silver star drop down straight toward the altar, Tala felt the tip of her own missing finger burn, remembering that this was where she had touched the deadly silver herself—the silver that could cut through flesh and armor like it was air.

And with that thought, she recalled something Seita had said right before her death. *I will not have you steal my place in these events.*

The maiden with the wrought-iron soul!

With a crack of thunder, the silver droplet splashed against the crescent-moon hilt-guard of the white sword, and the entire room fell dark.

Tala found herself in total blackness.

Silence.

Then a light appeared in the room, increasing in brightness until the chamber was lit up as if the midday sun were right there beside the altar. Tala recoiled, blinking back the painfully harsh brilliance. When her eyes adjusted to the light and she wiped away the tears, she saw the personage standing in the air before the altar, feet not touching the floor, a personage bearing both *Afflicted Fire* and *Ethic Shroud* in hand.

Lawri!

No . . .

Lindholf!

It was Lawri, just as pretty as ever, even more so. But it was Lindholf, too.

It was some monstrous, angelic construct of them both, and the radiance of their face was truly like lightning.

The altar-born personage that was both Lawri and Lindholf wore armor of the most exquisite whiteness—a whiteness and brilliance beyond anything Tala had ever before seen. The twins' flat silver eyes were the only two things punching any sort of faint hollow in the vivid radiance and luster of their being.

"Our Immortal Lord," Icelyn announced to the room.

The thing that was both Lawri and Lindholf set foot on the ground and the stone floor shook, then settled.

It was then that Tala saw the silver gauntlet on the left arm of the brilliant white monster was still there. And the fingers of the gauntlet were wrapped around the hilt of *Afflicted Fire*. And growing from the tips of those fingers were long white claws that looked as sharp as the teeth of a saber-toothed lion.

Then there was *Ethic Shroud* in the creature's other hand. The five angel stones, now embedded into the cross-shaped surface of the shield, began to glow: red, green, blue, white, and black. The white stone was fixed at the top of the cross, the red stone at the bottom, the blue and green stones on either arm of the cross, and the black stone naught but a hollow pit at the cross's gleaming center.

"You are *not* the maiden with the wrought-iron soul," the glowing personage that was both Lawri and Lindholf said, creeping closer to Tala. "And you never were."

"Lawri? Lindholf?" Tala uttered in disbelief. *What dark sorcery is this?* She couldn't wrap her mind around what devilry she was seeing.

"You let your friends all live when you should have slain them for their belief," the creature that was her twin cousins said. "You are weak, false, an imposter, and in time I shall hunt down all those that you let escape. I shall hunt their posterity too, lest their descendants once again rise against me, lest their kin once again thrust me and my kin down into the underworld."

"Lawri?" Tala repeated, confused, trying to back away. "Lindholf?"

"Neither," the altar-born creature answered, "and both."

"But how—"

"You killed us, Tala," they cut her off sharply, and Tala Bronachell felt the tip of *Afflicted Fire* pressing into her chest just above her heart, pricking the skin. She saw her own blood on the sword, fading into the brilliant white blade. It was as if the sleek, murderous weapon was drinking up her entire soul. The angel stones embedded in the shield still glowed with unnatural bright light.

"Please," she whispered, "Lindholf, Lawri, please, no—"

A shadow covered the stained glass above, darkening the room, and all eyes flew to the window, including Tala's.

With a shout, oghul and Vallè weapons were brought to bear. Silver whips uncoiled in both Aamari-Laada's and Icelyn's hands. Yvoirè and Ashure-Ikarii drew long marble-colored daggers of their own. Black Dugal and Hans Rake looked up, black daggers dropping into their hands. The bulldog eyed the window too, growling softly.

Even the creature that was both Lawri and Lindholf turned to see what had blocked the light, the pressure of *Afflicted Fire* easing against Tala's chest.

A dark silhouette was perched menacingly on the ledge of the window. The mysterious figure was cloaked in a black hood, black leather armor glinting underneath, black daggers poised in both hands. Bright red light filtered around the faceless apparition, casting haunting shadows over the room.

"So everything has come to pass." The newcomer's voice was sensuous, liquid, and above all fearless. "So everything has all played out as Val-Draekin foresaw. In a way, it is a shame your one and only son is no longer here to see the fruits of his dark labors and various Vallè games, Black Dugal."

Hearing that sensuous voice, shards of ice lanced up Tala's spine.

Could it be Seita somehow come back to life? *Could it be that the Bloodwood continues to torment me in the secret ways, even now?* It was beyond comprehension.

I saw her die with my own eyes.

"Looks as if the prophecies of *The Book of the Betrayer* have come to pass, Black Dugal," the cloaked figure said. "Your Immortal Lord has been reborn, resurrected, a grotesque of Hragna'Ar, a Dark Lord born out of cauldrons of blood, a Dark Lord to rule the Five Isles for all time and all eternity, a Dark Lord to subjugate all of humanity, just as Dashiell Dugal, the patron god of all assassins, foresaw."

The creature that was both Lawri and Lindholf hissed at the dark figure in the window. The tip of *Afflicted Fire* was no longer pointed at Tala's chest, but up at the dark stranger.

"Reveal yourself!" Icelyn demanded, scorch whip uncoiling in her hand. "Who dares interrupt this ceremony? Who are you?"

"I dare. And I am your death," the dark figure said, calmly pulling the hood back, revealing the familiar face underneath.

Hawkwood!

Tala's mind reeled. She had also seen him die with her own eyes. She had seen the bell tower crush the man. He should be dead.

"You cannot fight the scorch, stranger," Icelyn said, the silver whip hissing in her hand, impatience growing in her voice.

"I am a Bloodwood assassin," Hawkwood said calmly. "And this Bloodwood does not die so easily. Your whip does not scare me, Cauldron Born, for I know its secrets."

Icelyn snapped the silver weapon. The sinister crack of the whip echoed like thunder in the room.

Then Black Dugal laughed, harsh laughter that echoed through the chamber like a rasp of a dull and rusted saw blade. "Oh, my dear Hawkwood. We will kill you swiftly, for you are one man against many. This room is full of your enemies. And all of them stronger than you, my son."

"That is where you are mistaken," Hawkwood said. "For I am not your son, I am fatherless. And I am not alone."

"I see no one with you." Black Dugal looked around the room and shrugged.

"Oh, but the secret ways are a many-splendored thing," Hawkwood said. "For as you know, they are the haunt of the Bloodwoods, and this room will soon be full of my friends. My *real* friends, that is. My friends from Gallows Haven and Wyn Darrè and Sør Sevier, who dug me out from under a pile of rubble not long ago."

With a tremendous *boom!* the door to the chamber shattered open.

Cromm Cru'x stood in the entryway, roaring wild and savage, brutish face and eyes covered in bandages, huge war hammer in hand.

Nail, Liz Hen, Dokie, Jenko, Ava Shay, Krista Aulbrek, Mancellor and Bronwyn Allen, along with a snarling gray shepherd dog came rushing into the room from behind the huge oghul, weapons flashing.

The hilt of Hawkwood's black dagger was suddenly growing out of Icelyn's flat silver eye. The Aalavarrè fell dead, white armored body dropping with a crash, white cloak smoking as it came to rest over the snaking silver whip. Just as swiftly, a second black dagger pierced the left eye of Aamari-Laada. The dragon rider folded over his companion, silver whip disappearing under his red-armored body. The eerie weapon sizzled and sparked between the red and white scaled armor of the two dragon riders.

Four daggers sliced up through the red-hazed air toward Hawkwood, glimmering like four black flashes of lightning. Dugal's and Hans Rake's impeccable aim was immediate and true. But Hawkwood struck all four spinning blades aside with one flashing swipe of a dagger pulled from his cloak. All four of the Bloodwood blades rained down to the chamber floor with a clatter.

The stench of burning metal overtook the chaotic chamber, the silver whips still sizzling under the two dead dragon riders. The battle raged throughout the room as Nail's group attacked the ten oghul warriors and ten Vallè noblemen. The creature that was both Lawri and Lindholf hissed and spat at all the sudden noise and fighting in the crowded chamber, weapons clashing and ringing, the loud barks of the two dogs echoing throughout the room.

Hawkwood dropped silently from the window ledge, black cloak billowing, twin black daggers in hand. Landing softly, he wasted no time, leaping over the stone altar, his first dagger stabbing straight out with a powerfully aimed thrust, thin blade piercing through Yvoirè's chest. The Aalavarrè's entire body clenched in pain as her sword slipped from fingers gone limp. With his free hand, Hawkwood blocked two more Bloodwood daggers thrown his way. At the same time he twisted his own blade roughly, ripping it free of Yvoirè's chest in a wild swing that flung ropes of blood over the newly scrubbed walls. The Aalavarrè fell backward over the bodies of Icelyn and Aamari-Laada, blood bubbling from her mouth.

With a haunting shout, Ashure-Ikarii struck at Hawkwood with his marble-colored dagger. But Hawkwood was too fast; a second black dagger whipped out, opening the Aalavarrè's throat. Ashure-Ikarii reeled backward against the cross-shaped altar, sword clattering to the floor.

"No!" the *thing* that was both Lawri and Lindholf howled as Hawkwood launched himself at Black Dugal and Hans Rake, engaging them in a battle, black daggers flying in the red-hazed light. Krista Aulbrek leaped to Hawkwood's aid, and the fight between the Bloodwoods was on.

"No!" the *thing* that was both Lawri and Lindholf howled again, lurching toward the fray. Tala launched herself into the chest of the altar-born monster before it could reach the Bloodwoods. Together they fell to the floor hard, knocking the wind from Tala as both *Afflicted Fire* and *Ethic Shroud* tumbled from the creature's grasp.

Tala kicked the shield away and grabbed for the hilt of the long white sword. The creature grasped the hilt at the same time, the powerful fingers of the silver gauntlet clamping painfully over Tala's hand, the sharp white claws digging into her skin. They battled for the weapon as they rolled and careened across the floor, tripping several of the oghul and Vallè noblemen still engaged with Nail's group.

The foreign light radiating from the altar-born monster nearly blinded Tala. Still she fought and rolled, until she found herself pressed against Icelyn's smoking cloak, the glowing silver of the scorch whip mere inches from her eyes. The silver weapon gleamed and shivered, murderous to behold at such close range. Tala forced herself to roll in the other direction, hands still wrapped around the hilt of *Afflicted Fire*.

The altar-born creature rolled with her, the metal scales of the silver gauntlet cutting into the flesh of both her hands, the long white claws drawing blood too. Tala gritted her teeth to stave off the pain, clenching her eyes shut from the bright light radiating from the armor and skin of the creature that used to be her twin cousins. With a powerful jerk, Tala gained possession of the weapon and lurched to her feet, hands shredded and bloody. She aimed *Afflicted Fire* down at the altar-born fiend. The glowing personage rolled, snatching up *Ethic Shroud*, holding it over its chest protectively as it lay on its back, gazing up at her through flat silver eyes.

"*Cousin, spare us,*" the creature pleaded, blistering white light from the shield blazing up into Tala's eyes. The beautiful hints of Lawri that had once existed within the demon's features were now gone. Tala recoiled in horror, scarcely able to keep her eyes open from the pain of the light emanating from the shield. She could hear the sounds of fighting and dying in the chamber around her, but her attention was focused on the creature below her. "*Spare us, cousin,*" the demon cried again, trying to struggle from under the shield.

It was a pathetic plea in Tala's ears, and she tried to end the ghastly creature's life, aiming a swift downward stab toward the heart. But the tip of the sword sparked against the top edge of the blinding white shield, nearly knocking Tala to her knees.

She kept her balance, but the monster grabbed the blade with the silver gauntlet, claws scraping along the sword's surface with a shriek. The beast tried to wrench the weapon from Tala's grasp. With a shout, Tala twisted the sword free of the creature's gauntleted hand and stabbed downward once more. The tip of *Afflicted Fire* glanced off the shield once again in a shower of sparks and white flame.

The creature still lived and fought, spitting and hissing in rage as it swung the gauntlet out wildly once more, claws raking past Tala's eyes, barely missing the top of her head. Tala jerked backward out of harm's way, gripping the long white sword tightly, breathing heavily, gathering strength, senses alert. Fighting raged around her. The shouts of oghuls and dogs. She had to ignore it all and concentrate on the danger before her.

The cauldron-born monster tossed *Ethic Shroud* aside, hauled itself up on hands and knees, and hissed at her once again, *"Give us the sword."* The demon came at Tala, crawling forward, long white claws of the gauntlet dragging ominously against the stone.

Tala retreated. A Vallè nobleman fell dead just behind her and she tripped. She stumbled backward, losing her grip on *Afflicted Fire* as she fell, the sword trapped under her when she landed. Sitting on the flat of the white blade, Tala felt her back press up against the cross-shaped altar and she could retreat no farther, the clash and shouts of battle still swirling around her. There was blood splashed everywhere, a caustic stench. She had no idea how Nail's group or the Bloodwoods were faring; her focus was strictly on the creature that used to be Lawri and Lindholf, her eyes fixed on the long, sharp claws growing out of the silver gauntlet, now coming toward her.

"The sword is ours," the altar-born creature snarled, its face no longer beautiful like Lawri's but twisted in furious rage. Tala couldn't even breathe. Her eyes blurred with tears. The smell of blood was overwhelming. She coughed and heaved, but nothing came out. *"Give us the sword, cousin,"* the demon hissed, silver gauntlet reaching forth, long razorlike claws stretching out, seemingly growing longer. And when those sharp claws curled around her throat and squeezed, Tala knew she was dead.

Then the blood-slavered jaws of the big gray shepherd dog were wrapped around the creature's arm just above the gauntlet, tearing through the monster's pale flesh, a mixture of silver and blood oozing though his teeth.

"Kill it, Beer Mug!" Liz Hen bellowed, standing between Tala and the creature now. "Tear the fucking monster's arm right the fuck off!"

The Cauldron Born's shriek was ear-piercingly shrill as the dog wrenched and tore, shredding flesh and bone, stripping the gauntlet free with one powerful jerk. *"NOO!"* the *thing* that used to be Lawri and Lindholf howled as the dog named Beer Mug continued to chew at what remained of the monster's de-gloved arm. The dog was in a rage, tearing and pulling and dragging the creature across the floor and away from Tala, a mixture of silver and blood trailing in smears and splatters.

"Destroy it, Beer Mug!" Liz Hen shouted. "Kill the ghastly fucker!"

Tala glanced down at the gauntlet that was no longer attached to her cousin's arm. It lay in twisting pools of silver and blood, long white claws retreating into the silver-scaled fingertips. She couldn't believe her cousin was finally free of the gauntlet.

But the *thing* fighting Beer Mug was no longer her cousin. With that realization, Tala jerked to her feet. She hefted *Afflicted Fire* in both hands and stalked toward the screeching thing that used to be her twin cousins. The ferocious shepherd dog was biting the creature's face now, ripping and tearing.

"Call your dog off!" Tala shouted to the red-haired girl.

"Beer Mug!" the girl yelled. "Enough!"

The dog backed away, tail wagging, mouth dripping silver and blood.

The creature hissed and spat, pale face mangled, silver and blood draining from the stump of its arm. Without hesitation, Tala raised the sword high over her head and swept the white blade downward with all the strength and speed she could muster.

Afflicted Fire bit through the demon's neck with a flash of light and a cry of thunder. The keen and merciless blade cut the head off cleanly above the shoulders.

The creature's armored body dropped to the floor heavily, shaking the ground. And the severed head landed with a thud at Tala's feet, faceup. Still wary, Tala pointed the tip of her blade at the head and watched as the light slowly faded from the monstrous fiend's silver eyes.

It's dead!

She pulled the blade up and away and squinted against the red light of the room, devastated beyond redemption. *I only ever wanted to save her life. I only ever wanted to see Lawri happy.* Now her cousin was naught but a headless monster at her feet, dead forever, and gone.

"We gotta help the others!" Liz Hen was screaming in her face.

Afflicted Fire glowing with white light in her bloody hand, Tala snatched up *Ethic Shroud* and faced the room.

Nail's group had slain a good portion of the oghul warriors and Vallè noblemen, and it looked like they now had the advantage. But the battle between the four Bloodwoods under the tapestry was a bloody affair.

Café Colza chewed and clawed at the heels of Hawkwood and Krista Aulbrek as they desperately tried to fight off their attackers. They were losing the battle. Black Dugal and Hans Rake fought with a deadly, malevolent skill Tala had never before seen. Their daggers whipped and flashed like thunder, striking both Hawkwood and Krista with relentless ease, slicing their leather armor to bloody ribbons.

"Get that ratty bulldog!" Liz Hen yelled, and Beer Mug dove toward Café Colza, teeth clamping around the spiked iron collar. Beer Mug yanked the other dog away, and both rolled under the stone benches, fur and spittle flying.

Tala threw herself into the fight with the same reckless vigor Beer Mug had, *Afflicted Fire* and *Ethic Shroud* weightless in her hands, the bloody tip of the white sword racing high above her with all the deadly speed and power of a silver scorch whip.

The streaking blade caught Black Dugal in the left side of the neck and carried through to the right, decapitating the unsuspecting Bloodwood in one swift stroke.

Black Dugal tumbled headless into Hans Rake, blood bursting from his severed neck, coating the younger Bloodwood from head to toe.

Hawkwood and Krista reeled back, stunned.

Tala advanced on the wide-eyed young assassin, *Afflicted Fire* blazing with light in one hand, *Ethic Shroud* shining in the other.

Hans Rake took one look at Tala bearing down.

"Bugger this," he exclaimed, and launched himself across the room away from her. He scrambled straight up the stone wall, grabbed the stone rim of the stained-glass window, and pulled himself up onto the ledge. He cast one last look down into the red-hazed room, whirled and shattered the red-paned glass with his black dagger, and dove out into blue sky and nothingness.

A singular beam of light spilled into the chamber below, illuminating the room in white. Still, the chamber was painted in blood, and the sound of dogs fighting under the bench was a distraction. But in the new warm glow, Tala gazed around the room.

All the Vallè noblemen were dead. And Nail's group had killed all but one of the oghuls. Hawkwood and Krista turned from Dugal's head-less corpse and let their daggers fly. The remaining oghul dropped dead, black daggers buried in either eye.

Nail, Jenko, Ava, Liz Hen, Dokie, Bronwyn, and Mancellor all lived, each of them splattered with blood and breathing heavily. Cromm still stood near the door he had smashed, bloody war hammer in hand, face and eyes wrapped in bandages.

The noise and racket of the two dogs still fighting under the bench echoed throughout the chamber.

"Beer Mug!" Liz Hen yelled. "Stop toying with that dog! Kill him or let him go!"

The growling and snarling immediately ceased, and Beer Mug's blood-matted head poked up from behind the stone bench, eyes wide and curious.

Café Colza scrambled from under the bench and bolted across the room and over the dead toward the stone wall under the smashed win-dow. The frantic and bloody bulldog tried climbing the wall same as Hans Rake, paws clawing at the stone to no avail. The dog gave up; its beady eyes scanned the room, spotting Cromm Cru'x standing near the smashed open door. Then Café Colza shot across the room one last time and disappeared through the open door and into the secret ways.

The room was finally still.

"Is it over, Bronwyn?" Cromm asked. "Cromm cannot see."

"It's over," Bronwyn said, relief in her voice.

But Tala felt no relief. Her gaze traveled from Bronwyn to Mancellor; they had both suffered many injuries in this battle, but still stood near each other, love for each other in their eyes. Jenko and Ava and Dokie stood just under the tapestry, piles of Vallè noblemen dead at their feet. Nail stood by himself, his own sword dripping with blood. Beer Mug si-dled up next to Liz Hen, tail a-wag, both of them standing over the dead dragon riders and two Aalavarrè. Hawkwood and Krista moved silently around the cross-shaped altar and away from Black Dugal's headless corpse, as if they truly thought the Bloodwood assassin would spring to life again.

Tala's gaze followed the new beam of white light streaming in from above their heads, followed it to where it lit on the deformed corpse that used to be her twin cousins.

Ethic Shroud dropped from her bloody fingers and clattered to the floor. Then she folded to her knees, the sword, *Afflicted Fire*, a scarcely noticeable object in her hands anymore.

Lawri is dead! Lindholf is dead! I failed miserably.

She wept, every emotion pouring from deep within her soul and out into the room. She wept, not caring who heard or what happened to her next.

Everyone I ever loved is dead!

The once red-hazed room had fallen silent—silent but for her own labored sobs.

Stone of ages, cleft for thee. Beware, a cross-shaped altar is naught
but an island surrounded by death and filled with blood.
—THE WAY AND TRUTH OF LAIJON

CHAPTER NINETY

NAIL

15TH DAY OF THE HEART MOON, 999TH YEAR OF LAIJON

AMADON, GUL KANA

R est easy, Tala." Hawkwood broke the silence. "Things are now as
they should be. It is over."

Tala Bronachell gazed up at the Sør Sevier man and swiped away her tears with one hand, *Afflicted Fire* gripped in the other. *Ethic Shroud* lay on the blood-coated floor at her knees.

Her eyes hardened to cold slits the longer she glared up at Hawkwood. He stood on the opposite side of the dripping red altar from her, his black cloak and armor cut to shreds and glistening with blood. Krista Aulbrek stood near him, bleeding from many wounds, her armor also sliced to ribbons.

The armless and headless creature that used to be both Lindholf and Lawri laying in the beam of light was a mangled mess, the scaled gauntlet curled in a dark ruby pool swirling with silver. In fact, the entirety of the small white chamber was dripping in savagery and blood.

"They came back to save you," Hawkwood said to Tala. "The war is over. All of these people came back to save you."

"I am not worthy of saving," Tala said, still glowering at Hawkwood, more tears flowing. She swiped at them again to no avail, her injured fingers just smearing her face with blood. "I am not worth saving. Not me. You have all wasted your time. The wraiths possess me."

"You are in shock," Hawkwood said. "You have been through a harrowing experience, Tala. Put down the sword and let us talk."

"I don't wish to talk. I wish to be left alone. Do you not understand?"

"We understand—"

"No you don't!" she shouted. "Can't you see I just killed my own cousins, *again*? I've killed them both. I keep killing them over, and over, and over. I keep killing *her*. I keep killing Lawri no matter how many times she is brought back to life."

Tala pointed the long white sword at Hawkwood, tears streaming down her face, cutting crisp trails through the smeared blood. "I just want to be alone."

Nail's heart ached. He wanted to reach out to her. He wanted to talk to her as they had talked in the courtyard of the Filthy Horse Saloon. Those talks were the only times he had ever felt anyone had understood him without judgment. And he was sure she had felt the same way. But she seemed like such a different person now, completely damaged and unreachable. He wanted to take that long white sword from her and tell her she was safe.

"Tala," he said softly. "We are here for you. We need to get you out of this room. We all need to get out of this room. This is no place for any of us to be."

"Then go," she said, her eyes hard and brittle. "I just want to be alone."

Hawkwood nodded to Nail and the others.

Nail understood.

They all understood.

One by one they exited the grim room, bloody weapons still gripped in their hands. Only Nail looked back at Tala with a hint of worry in his gaze.

*The only way peace and happiness can be had is if we
do unto others as we would have done unto us.*
—THE WAY AND TRUTH OF LAIJON

CHAPTER NINETY-ONE
TALA BRONACHELL

15TH DAY OF THE HEART MOON, 999TH YEAR OF LAIJON
AMADON, GUL KANA

O nce the others had filed out of the room, Tala Bronachell
stood, keeping the tip of *Afflicted Fire* pointed across the blood-
dripping altar at Hawkwood. "Why do you stay?" she asked. He
said nothing.

"In the graveyard, you admitted to killing my mother," she said "You
are a Bloodwood and you are evil. You murdered Alana Bronachell."

"That is true," Hawkwood said, holding his own bloody black daggers out in surrender, the altar still separating them. "I will not lie to
you. I am a Bloodwood, fatherless and alone. But I do not consider myself altogether evil."

"What are you doing here?"

"Making amends for killing your mother, if you will let me."

"It is not me who you should make your appeal to."

"I can only do right by Alana and Jondralyn by appealing to you, by
helping you, by dedicating myself to you and your protection. It is written in the Moon Scrolls that the Assassin shall watch over the Princess
until the end of her days."

"Did you love my sister?"

"You have asked that before, and the answer has not changed. Jondralyn Bronachell changed my life. She was my life. I loved her. And I will always love her. But I did wrong by Jondralyn. I doubted her, and that is why she ran off to Savon alone. I will have to live with that mistake my entire life now."

For some reason the answer calmed Tala. She breathed in deep, once, twice, three times. Truth be told, she was glad to see him here. He *had* saved her. She lowered her weapon. "I saw you die. I saw the bell tower crush you."

"Aye." He nodded, his posture relaxing. "That bell tower is likely what saved me from Enna Spades, or she would have killed me for sure. I was trapped under heavy stone in a pocket of rubble. 'Twas that blinded oghul, Cromm, who lifted the heaviest of the stones off me, lifted me free of the rubble. Luck has always followed me in that way, as it follows you, Tala Bronachell."

"Luck?" Tala looked at the scattered dead, her gaze circling the blood-smeared room; every surface was spattered in red, bathed in red light. "What luck is this?"

"Naught but luck and circumstance and haphazard coincidence have found us both here in this room at this time," Hawkwood answered. "Luck and the help of our friends. When I found out it was you who had cracked open the world and not Seita, I knew we still had a chance. I would never have escaped the rubble if not for Nail. I don't know how long I lay under all that rock, unconscious. But 'twas Nail's idea to come back for me, to see if I was still alive. He remembered how I had helped the two of you escape from Purgatory. 'Twas Nail who convinced the others that if I was alive, I could help them through the secret ways and back to you. And they followed him. They came to help you, knowing they might die fighting against those deadly silver whips, knowing they might have to fight Bloodwoods. Or even dragons. 'Twas Nail who did not give up on you, Tala. We are both lucky that he thought of our well-being, even until the end."

"I didn't even thank him," Tala said. "I dismissed him without thought."

"It is forgivable. You can thank him properly later. You can thank them all when you've recovered. You were traumatized by the fight, from witnessing the cauldron-born monster your twin cousins became, from killing both Lawri and Lindholf. But it is all over now, Tala. The madness of war. The madness of prophecy. The madness of Fiery Absolution. The madness of Hragna'Ar and the underworld. It is all over and you should rest easy. You have won. You are the Princess. You have prevailed."

"But there are a million Aalavarrè Solas awaiting us outside, a million demons of the underworld awaiting their . . . awaiting their *Immortal Lord*."

"And *you* shall be that lord." Hawkwood stepped around the altar toward her. "Our final absolution shall be to invite the Aalavarrè back to live with us in peace."

"But they know I am false."

"The Aalavarrè who are awaiting their Immortal Lord will believe no such thing. They already think of you as their savior, the one who cracked the world. They will follow you."

"I hardly see how that will be possible."

"Just believe in yourself."

"Believe in myself?" Tala cast her gaze around the room once more. "Look at this mess. How can any of it ever be explained?"

"I shall clean up the dead here. It will be as if they never existed."

Tala looked at the remains of her cousins, the silver gauntlet lying in a pool of silver and blood. She shuddered. "If you truly wish to help me, then make sure you throw them into the altar too, that gauntlet and that creature both. Seal them up for all time and all eternity. And then see that this altar is destroyed. Then see that this room is sealed and also forgotten."

"So it shall be done."

Tala focused her attention on the two dragon riders, the hilts of twin black daggers jutting from their eyes. "Their silver whips shall be sealed away into the altar too," she said.

Hawkwood nodded.

"What happens when I exit this room and enter Sunbird Hall? They are expecting their Immortal Lord to be born again."

"You shall tell the Aalavarrè Solas awaiting you in Sunbird Hall that their two kin that lie here dead and the two dragon riders sacrificed themselves upon the altar of Viper. They will not ask about Black Dugal for they do not care. They shall believe you, for you will be their Immortal Lord."

"But I am nothing," Tala said. "And should I start my rule off with lies?"

"Worry not." Hawkwood drifted around the altar and picked up *Ethic Shroud*. He handed her the shield. At her touch, the five angel stones embedded in *Ethic Shroud*'s surface seemed to glow with renewed light. "Take the shield and the sword. The demons of the underworld await you. And you shall rule over them. And you shall not be afraid, for I shall be at your side. You shall rule over all the Five Isles in peace. The oghul and Vallè armies have been depleted in this war. They were outnumbered at Fiery Absolution. They only succeeded through surprise and the strength and fear of the dragons."

Tala held the shield in one hand, the sword in the other, studying both. She felt less than confident. "The dragons?" She looked up. "Will I have to slay them too?"

"Without their riders and without Shroud of the Vallè, the dragons will go their own way. Nobody will stop them."

"Go their own way? That sounds less than promising . . . and just a little sad." She thought of the green dragon that had carried her and Lawri to the quarry. "They are beautiful in their own way."

"I imagine the dragons will live wherever they like. And I also imagine many men will rise up thinking themselves dragon slayers. They *can* be killed. But you needn't be the one to kill them."

"Let's hope they live forever."

"They are bred to kill. They will be a menace for sure. They will be hunted their entire lives. Eventually they will be slain."

His every answer seems to make sense, she thought. *But I feel so powerless, still. So many mysteries yet unanswered!*

"With *Afflicted Fire* and *Ethic Shroud*, you have power," Hawkwood said, as if reading her mind. "The Aalavarrè Solas are now free of the underworld, and that is a good thing. And 'twas you who freed them, 'twas you who cracked open the world, not Seita. Black Dugal's plans to pervert Fiery Absolution have been foiled, and now he is dead. The dreams and machinations of the Vallè and the prophecies of Hragna'Ar and their dark sorceries led us all to the Atonement Tree, and *you* have stepped in the way and led us here, to this final absolution right here in this room. You are Laijon returned. You are the Immortal Lord. The Harbinger. The Leader of All Armies. You are whatever you want to be, Tala Bronachell. You take control of history now. Unlike the dead scattered at our feet, who would have brought horror unto the Five Isles, you are a good person, the only one capable of ruling the Five Isles in peace."

"But I am *not* a good person." Tala thought of the two Dayknights that Icelyn had killed for not denying Laijon; she thought back on all the lies she had told, all the many deaths those lies had caused. Her mind had become like a black and bottomless well, revealing nothing and hiding everything decent about herself. "I am not a good person, Hawkwood. And you should not claim that I am. I accused you of being murderous and evil, but it is I who is murderous and evil. It is I who has killed. It is I who has murder in her heart. It is I who is guilty of telling lies, guilty of betrayal. It is I who is possessed of the wraiths."

"Remember, for what sins you imagine lay heavy upon you, there is always atonement." His eyes focused on hers. There was kindness there. He smiled. And with that one gesture all her apprehension faded away. In that one moment she trusted him utterly. This was why her sister had loved him. He was strong and sure and confident.

"The truth will always makes us free," he went on. "I spent my youth believing that murder was my calling, for it was all I had been taught, that following the tenets of Dashiell Dugal, the Betrayer, the Angel Warrior known as the assassin, the patron god of the Bloodwoods, was my life's goal. But when I finally realized the truth, that everything about Black Dugal's Caste was built upon the power of suggestion, my life changed. I realized that my entire persona and ego had rested solely upon ancient fables, myths, and false histories, dangerous writings meant to make me believe I was more important to the world than I really was. Once I figured that out, once I figured out my *real* place in this world, I finally understood myself. It was a true cleansing. I could finally love myself. I could finally love others. I finally knew I was meant for better things. And I could finally face the realities of this world and absolution. Reality is the truth, far better than faith or belief or fantasy."

"But what about all this?" Tala motioned to the bloody room. "Demons of the underworld? *Afflicted Fire? Ethic Shroud?* There must have been some truth in those fantasies penned by the Vallè, for the *reality* and *truth* of their words lie before us. There must have been some truth in *The Way and Truth of Laijon.*"

"That is the clever wickedness of the ones who pen such evil as the scriptures. Truth mixed with lies until nobody knows where reality falls, until no man can trust another. Now how does one face the fact that there is truth in the rituals of Hragna'Ar and the science of the stars? How do we wrap our minds around things that we do not yet understand?"

"There shall be no worship of me," she said, her voice almost a whisper. "That will be forbidden. I will rule as a person, not a religious figure. I will be no one's 'Immortal Lord.'"

"You must rule in peace." Hawkwood nodded.

"But how?" She looked up at him, knowing there was disbelief in her own gaze. "I still have no faith or belief in myself."

"Do you remember when we fled to that cemetery with your father and brother?" he asked. "Do you remember when I told Nail of his heritage, when I told him of my days as a young Bloodwood assassin, when I told him the story of my fight with Ser Roderic Raybourne on the edge of the glacier?"

"I remember some of it, yes," Tala answered. Her brow furrowed as she thought back to that horrific night just days ago when she'd discovered her father's many betrayals and sins.

"There is one specific thing about that fight with Ser Roderic that I never shared with anyone but Jondralyn." His eyes narrowed. "Do you wish to hear that secret?"

Tala nodded in anticipation.

"Ser Roderic—or rather, Shawcroft, as we called him then—had won the fight. My brother the Spider had fallen from the glacier, and I dangled by one hand from a dagger lodged in the ice. And as I looked up with utmost panic into Ser Roderic's eyes, I saw compassion there. He said that he knew who I was. He said that I was meant for greater things. Then he knocked the dagger from the ice and I fell."

Hawkwood drew back, tears welling in the corner of his eyes as he continued, "Those were the first positive words anyone had ever spoken to me. It was a small thing, really, said by a duplicitous man. But I clung to those words through the years, always believing I was indeed meant for greater things. That is why I eventually left the darkness of Black Dugal's Caste. That is why I accepted the love of your sister, even though I felt as if I did not deserve it. And that is why I shall be your protector until the end of your days, Tala Bronachell. I shall be your protector and I shall help you rebuild your kingdom, for those are things your sister would have wanted of me. And I've always desired to honor Jondralyn. For I know I was always meant for greater things. And I know that *you* are meant for even greater things than I."

> *The power to create. The power to destroy. One need only look to the*
> *Crystal and the Nail. Both thrive deep within the soul and conflictions*
> *of men. For humanity breathes deep the silence of history gone by. 'Tis in*
> *the nature of man to always rebuild after the devastation of savagery and*
> *war, even under the yoke of a great conqueror, even until a thousand years*
> *and that next inevitable and terrible conflict tear it all down again.*
> —THE ARCHAIC ILLUMINATIONS OF
> AULBREK THE GAULT

EPILOGUE ONE

AVA SHAY

13TH DAY OF THE CROWN MOON, 999TH YEAR OF LAIJON

GALLOWS HAVEN, GUL KANA

Ava Shay traveled down the Roahm Mine Trail with Jenko Bruk. She held his hand, their fingers tightly entwined. Jenko's other hand gripped the leather reins as he led their two gray geldings to the ledge overlooking Gallows Haven.

Far below, Ava's new world was a small one, but a most welcome one. The town was vacant and restful, and she would relish her quiet place within it. Along the coastline to the south, as far as her eyes could see, between the craggy Autumn Range rising up behind her and the brilliant blue ocean below, her entire world was spread out before her.

A new world.

And an old.

Gallows Haven. *Home.* Baron Jubal Bruk's manor house and farm were still down there below, and that was where Jenko was taking her.

Beer Mug's tail spun up a storm as he pranced in joyful circles around Liz Hen Neville and Dokie Liddle. It was obvious that the big gray shepherd dog remembered the village below and was eager to complete their long journey from Amadon and explore his home once more.

Both Liz Hen and Dokie sat atop dun-colored ponies to the left of Jenko. They too looked down upon Gallows Haven, but with a sad anticipation of their own. For the village still showed all the signs of its destruction by the White Prince's armies.

Behind Liz Hen and Dokie were a small family of Aalavarrè Solas walking their horses, a man and a wife and two pale younglings, their silver eyes agleam as they studied their new home below. Beer Mug was now licking the hand of one of the Aalavarrè, tail a-wag, nose occasionally pointing down below as if proud to show the alien creatures their new home. The Aalavarrè ruffled the fur on the dog's head and smiled. Beer Mug had made fast friends with the Aalavarrè Solas along their journey. Queen Tala Bronachell had decreed that all races would rebuild the Five Isles together. She had sent diverse groups consisting of dwarf, oghul, Vallè, Aalavarrè, and man to help rebuild every destroyed village in Adin Wyte, Wyn Darrè, and Gul Kana.

Ava Shay still could not believe the demons of the underworld were real and that she would be starting a new life with them in her very own village. Not only that, but two oghuls trailed behind the Aalavarrè, both male and both fairly young. The smelly beasts sat atop a rickety wooden cart pulled by two swayback ponies, the cart laden with all manner of smelly oghul garbage. Near the cart, one very thin and tall Vallè maiden rode a very thin and tall white palfrey. The Vallè still wore her bright Vallè armor and carried a long, curved sword. She was a widowed warrior, her husband killed under the Atonement Tree at Fiery Absolution. Her sharp gaze rested on the town below with some hesitation.

This ragtag group of strangers had traveled from Amadon with Ava, Jenko, Liz Hen, and Dokie, to help rebuild Gallows Haven. It had taken their small party almost a full moon to travel south from Amadon through Eskander and Reinhold and Swithen Wells and over the Autumn Range.

They had been in no real hurry to reach this spot, but now that they were here, Ava felt a certain thrill at starting life over in peace.

She recalled the flat boulder just up the trail where she and Nail had sat not that long ago, her whittling a small wooden duck whilst Nail sketched the scene below. Stefan Wayland had been practicing with his bow behind them on the trail. She recalled the pale-faced Vallè maiden on the Bloodeye steed.

My blade thirsts, the Vallè had said, producing a Bloodwood blade from the folds of her cloak, addressing Nail. *You are not of my blood. Still, they will be coming for you.* The words had been cryptic, and Nail had denied knowing what the Vallè Bloodwood meant. But Nail and everyone who knew him had eventually come face-to-face with what those words had meant.

That day had been the first time Ava had seen a Vallè up close. That day had been the beginning of her nightmare, for not long after that, the White Prince had sacked the town and Ava had been captured.

How many moons ago was it?

Ava had lost count of the days. But it mattered little now. Jenko had forgiven Nail, even if she had not fully done so. Still, she would try and forget him, even though she wondered daily where he was, even though she had helped him rescue Hawkwood, even though she had fought by his side in the end, even though they had slain oghuls and Vallè together in that red room with the altar. Even after all that, she did not know if she could totally forgive him.

There was just still so much trauma and conflict coursing through her veins. The horrible things she had seen. The horrible things she had endured. Aeros Raijael and the rape. And still she couldn't stop blaming Nail. When she had first seen him in that corridor in Amadon Castle, she had aimed her sword at him with the intent to kill. Only Jenko had stopped her. There were so many horrors that would live forever in her mind.

And what about Stefan Wayland? What had become of him? *Silver-eyed like the demons of the underworld!* It was all too much to fret over now. She had to place it all behind her. The important thing was, she could make a new start.

She was home again and drank in the peaceful scene below. Though the town had been destroyed, new growth and greenery still flourished. Meadows, fields, woodlands, rock fences, and hedgerows lined the farms both north and south of Gallows Haven. The burnt-out chapel and abandoned keep north of town looked tiny from so high up, but their familiarity bred warmth in her soul.

With a lump growing in her throat, she located the familiar shape of her thatch-roofed home near the center of town, mostly obscured under a large oak. The house was small and she shared it with her five younger siblings before they had been killed by Aeros Raijael's armies. She'd had a good life living there alone with her brothers and sisters near the now-burned Grayken Spear Inn. Ol' Man Leddingham had put her and her five siblings up in the house shortly after her parents had died. An illness had taken her mother. And her father had been killed in a logging accident above Tomkin Sty. Would they ever have believed the terrors their daughter had seen? Now Ava's family was Jenko Bruk, and the meager number of oghuls, Aalavarrè, and Vallè who had traveled with her were naught but strangers.

Her gaze reluctantly traveled north of town to the horrors of the battlefield. Gentle rippling waves rolled in from the west, lapping up against the shoreline. The remnants of Aeros' slaughter still littered those shores. What corpses had not washed out to sea still lined the sands, naught but rags and twisted crow-picked skeletons.

"I will clean it up," Jenko said. "You won't have to look at the dead for long. Or smell them either. That I promise. I shall clean out the chapel, too, and rebuild the Grayken Spear Inn just for you. And build myself a ship. And folks from the breadth of the Five Isles will flock to what we have created, and the town shall thrive once more."

"Do you really think so?" she asked.

"I fully agree with Tala Bronachell," he said. "We should rebuild, and I am glad she sent these travelers with us." He motioned to the Aalavarrè family, the Vallè maiden, and the two oghuls behind them. "We shall all rebuild."

"Sounds like a lot of work," Liz Hen said. "Despite the extra hands."

Jenko turned and met her gaze. "Against my own conscience, I obeyed the command of evil people. I've bullied those weaker than me. I've often wondered how I could ever live with myself. How could one such as me be redeemed? Rebuilding and following the dreams of our queen, Tala, seems the only way."

Liz Hen frowned. "You do realize she nearly had every single one of us sliced in half for not renouncing Laijon. You do realize she barely said thanks when we came back and saved her."

"We are none of us perfect," Jenko said. "We have none of us walked in her shoes. And she did thank us in her own way before she sent us back home. For my part, I shall forgive her and move on and rebuild."

"Well, we ain't always been the closest of friends." Liz Hen favored Jenko with a smile. "But I do admire your renewed purpose and aspirations. It's almost heroic."

"We'll never be heroes," Jenko said. "Just people who stayed alive."

Liz Hen's gaze drifted back down to the destroyed village. "Seems like a god-awful lot of work fixin' that place up, though."

"We are not the first people in history to have their lands destroyed," Jenko said. "We're not the first to lose a war and our village in such devastating bloody fashion. We can rebuild this place, our home. Even in loss, there can be hope."

"But such an awful lot of work," Liz Hen repeated with a sigh. "I feel like I've just been through a massive shit-mix of lunatic fuckery I don't wish to repeat."

Liz Hen was right, Ava realized. Jenko's plans were ambitious. But she was resolved to support him in whatever endeavor he set himself to and help him along the way. She too wished to see Gallows Haven alive again. And a life with Jenko Bruk was all she had ever wanted. "I will help you," she said, leaning into his broad shoulder.

"And I will help you too," Dokie said eagerly. "I also want to see Gallows Haven back the way it was. You can count on me."

Liz Hen squinted at Dokie. "Have you ever even done any hard work?"

"None that I can own up to," Dokie said. "But I aim to help Jenko nonetheless."

Jenko nodded his thanks at the grinning boy. "And so we return to our homes, Dokie Liddle, beaten but not broken. In fact, your words of support make me feel as tall as a Warrior Angel myself."

Dokie's grin widened. "We return to our home like Five Warrior Angels."

"But there are only four of us here from Gallows Haven," Jenko said.

Beer Mug barked.

"You're right, good boy," Liz Hen said, patting the top of the dog's head from her perch atop the pony. "There are five of us here from Gallows Haven. We are Five Warrior Angels returned."

EPILOGUE TWO

MANCELLOR ALLEN

8TH DAY OF THE ARCHAIC MOON, 999TH YEAR OF LAIJON

NORTH OF IKABOA, WYN DARRÈ

*T*his is where I belong.

Mancellor Allen breathed deep the coastal air. The breeze gathered strength as he gazed out over the tiny Wyn Darrè port he used to call home. Being so near sea and the familiar harbor again, he just wanted to jump straight from his horse and right into the cool waters, scrub himself clean of all the dirt and grit and carnage and evil he had experienced the last five years.

The port consisted of no more than a handful of frail, thatch-roofed huts huddled within a windblown inlet of water-worn cliffs. A rickety dock stretched out into the choppy blue waves in the hamlet's center.

As his mount wended its way down the boulder-strewn slope toward the harbor, Mancellor watched a small white fishing boat struggle toward the quay. One lone fisherman still eking out a living in a long-destroyed land sat at the paddles.

Bronwyn, riding ahead, reached the spindly dock first, water lapping

against the wooden posts. She dismounted, fell to her knees, and kissed
the ground. Mancellor reined up behind his sister, legs sore from long
riding, body still aching from the many wounds he'd suffered in battle.
He remained in his saddle, soaking in the glory of all he saw.

Things would begin anew for him here now.

He could not summon forth any good memories of the last five years.
He could not recall any good memories in his entire life, for that matter;
all good remembrances had been swept away by his myriad of sins. He
had killed in the name of the White Prince, and he oft wondered how he
could ever live with that. The only consolation was that he had held fast
to his faith and belief in Laijon and had not denied his savior in the end.
Still, despite his unwavering faith, Mancellor was unsure of himself, unsure of where he fit into this new world, unsure of where he might fit in
the afterlife when his time came.

Behind Mancellor, Cromm Cru'x slid from his mount, his wide feet
thudding heavy on the peat. "Has Cromm come home?" the oghul asked.

"Yes, Cromm has come home," Mancellor answered.

The oghul was blind from Hans Rake's poisoned daggers, his broad
gray face still scarred from the injuries he'd suffered at the Bloodwood's
hand. Cromm had remained stolidly good-natured despite his lack of
vision. He had even helped in digging Hawkwood from the rubble and
saving Tala Bronachell in the end.

In fact, the oghul was in high spirits, for twenty oghul widows, their
husbands slain during Fiery Absolution, dismounted their own sway-
backed ponies behind him, twenty oghul widows Cromm had person-
ally chosen by the feel of his own hands, twenty oghul widows he'd
chosen to join him here in Wyn Darrè. "Yes, Cromm has come home and
Cromm is legend!" the oghul bellowed.

Cromm's harem of twenty oghul females were not the only ones who
had journeyed here with Mancellor and Bronwyn. A family of dwarves,
a family of Vallè, and around a dozen Aalavarrè Solas had made the journey here too. All of them were tasked with helping Mancellor, Bronwyn,
and Cromm rebuild the port. They had all traveled here as part of Tala

Bronachell's decree that all the races of the Five Isles live together in peace, that they all help in rebuilding the Five Isles in the wake of Fiery Absolution and Aeros Raijael's destructive crusade.

Mancellor vowed that one day he would go back and find the queen. He would hope that she would remember him. But for now, he would relish his time here in the place he had once known as home.

As he watched Bronwyn scurry down the dock and help the lone fisherman tether his boat to safety, Mancellor felt the tears well up in his eyes.

Yes, this is where I belong.

*Let the Scroll of Spades regale you with tales of faith and heroism
and Ash of a Thousand Years, a pirate girl born of the sea, heir of the
Bastards, and enemy of the Skulls and their Immortal Lord. Let us
tell you how she shall take up her weapons of chrome and white powders
and go in search of the Crystal and the Nail. Let us tell you how she
shall save the Five Isles from those prophesied invaders from the Firstlands,
those foreign conquerors with their silver machines and science of the stars.*
—THE BOOK OF THE BASTARDS

EPILOGUE THREE

NAIL

1ST DAY OF THE LONESOME MOON, 999TH YEAR OF LAIJON

NORDLAND HIGHLANDS, SØR SEVIER

It was near dusk, and Krista Aulbrek held a torch aloft. The hood of her black cloak was thrown back, revealing a face of sadness and regret.

To Nail, the torch flame combined with the dipping sun made the girl's blond hair look like molten gold. She stood before him on the boulder-strewn ridgeline, a shoulder-high bier of weather-faded dead-fall in front of her. Nail had helped her gather the wood. The body of Gault Aulbrek lay atop the pyre, a dark blanket covering it from feet to neck. Only his bald head was uncovered, the sun angling off the ridges of his strong jaw and peaceful face.

They had packed his body in salt and charcoal for the journey to this faraway place. He was well-preserved and still looked like he had in life. It had taken them over two moons to reach this dusky ridge near Stone

Loring in the Nordland Highlands. Nail and Krista had ridden two roan palfreys the length of Gul Kana and Adin Wyte, a dun-colored draught mare pulling Gault's body on a solid flat-bedded cart behind them. The three mounts stood on the ridge not far from Krista and Nail, all three horses gusting thick puffs of breath into the crisp air.

The scent of coming winter lay heavy on the land. The northern climes of Sør Sevier were vast, and Nail felt dwarfed by the endless plateaus of rock and tundra, all of it frosted in snow. The saddleback where they had constructed Gault's bier was mostly windswept and barren, though there were some boulders scattered here and there, each of them cloaked in umber-colored lichen and a light dusting of snow. A handful of the boulders were thick and squat, but most towered toward the sky, all of them casting shadows of lush purple and blue over the snowy bramble. Beyond the ridge rose similar rolling hills cloaked in snow and pine and towering aspen, leafless and gray.

"He wished his body to be brought here," Krista said, holding the torch near the pyre, hesitant. "The only place he ever knew joy, the ridge where he met Avril. I hope we found the right spot."

"I'm sure we have," Nail added. "This is also where he met you, though you were just a babe."

Krista remained rigid before the pyre, her back to him.

"You were lucky to have such a father," Nail said.

"I should have been kinder to him in those last moments," she said. "I do regret that. I hope I have repaid that unkindness by bringing him here."

"You do him great honor," Nail said. "And that is all that can be done."

Krista was still deeply hurt after finding out from Borden Bronachell that Gault Aulbrek and Avril were not her real parents. Nail had tried consoling her during their journey from Amadon. Though he had never known the man, from what he could glean of Krista's stories, Gault Aulbrek had loved her as his own.

She had shown some appreciation for his perspective on the matter; after all, he was a bastard like her. They both had their heritage stolen by the Brethren of Mia and for the same foul purposes. Neither of them had ever met a blood relative. *And Shawcroft claimed I had a twin sister.* But that was also a lie. There was a brief moment in time when Nail thought Krista might be that long-lost sister. But it wasn't to be so. Nail knew less about his heritage now than ever before.

"'Tis a pyre to parents neither of us knew," Krista said as if reading his mind. She held the torch near the wood, hesitant. "Why was I not kinder to him in the end?" She turned back to Nail, pain in her eyes. "Am I a bad person?" she asked. "Borden Bronachell said I was the worst type of person, a murderer. Do you think I am a bad person, Nail?"

"Borden Bronachell was the worst type of person," Nail said. "I would not grant credence to his words. He was a liar, and I still wonder if we should have listened to anything he said."

During their journey to this place, Nail had tried to forget about Borden and Tala and Val-Draekin and everything to do with Amadon. It was a failed adventure, their search for the weapons of the Five Warrior Angels. *And I once thought we were heroes, but we did nothing and accomplished even less.* Everyone in the Five Isles had either suffered or died. It was only by chance that they had saved Tala Bronachell. He could only hope that Jenko, Ava, Liz Hen, and Dokie had made it back to Gallows Haven.

But who knows what the world holds for any of us now?

"I just don't feel like I'm a very good person," Krista muttered, eyes cast to the cold ground between them.

The fact that Krista had shown such devotion in carrying Gault's body so far was all Nail needed to know about who she was as a person. Though she put on a tough facade, Nail could tell that she cared about her father deeply.

Nail had seen the loneliness in her soul and promised to do his best to heal it, though she was the one person who claimed to need no help. She was like him in that regard, for he also needed no help, or so he told himself.

Her face hard as stone, Krista turned back to the wooden bier. Her voice was steady as she spoke. "Forgive me, Ser Gault Aulbrek, for treating you so poorly in the end. I hope you can now rest in peace, here in this place you once knew joy."

But she did not place the torch into the bier.

Instead her cool gaze traveled out beyond Gault's pyre toward the far ridge.

"Someone comes." She drew a black dagger from the folds of her black leather armor with her free hand and moved deftly around the pyre.

Nail followed, throwing his cloak back, unsheathing his own sword.

A dark, hooded figure meandered through a sparsely wooded valley in the far distance, eventually proceeding up the rutted trail toward them. A bulldog was with the mysterious newcomer, the stunted dog bounding through the snow-covered bramble thickets. *"Hans Rake,"* Krista hissed. "Be ready, Nail. He's come to kill us."

Nail braced himself for a fight. He remembered Hans' viciousness from Tin Man Square and the red-hazed room. He recalled that the Bloodwood had vanished up through the shattered window at the end. The bulldog had also escaped that grim room.

When the cloaked figure and the bulldog were about fifty paces away, Krista yelled, "Come no farther, Hans!"

The figure stopped. The dog stopped too, beady eyes and rusted spiked collar gleaming dully in the fading sunlight. Nail could feel the lingering pain in his ankle where the dog had bit him, an injury that he had largely ignored as he fought in Amadon, but an injury that lingered now.

"My name is not Hans," the hooded figure called back in a familiar voice, pulling back the hood.

It was Enna Spades.

"I mean you no harm," Spades said, holding out her empty hands. A black eye-patch covered her left eye. "I've merely come to pay my respects to Gault Aulbrek."

"Just stay away," Krista said.

"Why would I do that?" Spades said. "It's an exemplary day for a funeral, is it not? I knew if you survived, you would bring him here."

"How do I know you are really Enna Spades?" Krista's eyes were on the bulldog. "Those who travel with Café Colza are known to be deceivers."

"Is that the little monster's name?" Spades glanced down at the bulldog. "I've just been calling him the Asshole."

"You are Hans Rake in disguise," Krista said, sure of herself. "You are Shadowwood."

Spades laughed. "A Bloodwood scorned is hard to shake. Hans Rake is hunting you, I am sure. So I can see why you would be nervous. Yes, I imagine Shadowwood is still out there somewhere, and if he's like every Bloodwood I've ever known, he will hold a grudge until the end of time, or the end of you, whichever comes first. Yes, you should be on your guard and watch for his return. But let me ask you, was this Hans Rake a talented enough assassin to disguise himself as Enna Spades?"

"Likely not," Krista answered.

"Exactly." Spades's countenance hardened. "Someone such as myself just might take umbrage at such a rotten trick. Trust me, had any Bloodwood tried to pass himself off as Enna Spades, I would have already found that Bloodwood and slain him. For Bloodwoods are weak and easily slain."

Krista remained still.

"Do I call you Krista or Crystalwood?" Spades asked.

Krista did not answer.

"Right." Spades' one eye looked up at the girl in seemingly lazy regard. "I forgot, silence is the second rule of the Bloodwood. Right after beauty."

Still, Krista said nothing.

"Well, then." The red-haired warrior woman walked toward Krista and Nail, hands still held out in a gesture of peace. "Hither comes Enna Spades and no other."

When Spades reached the boulder-studded summit, she paused to catch her breath, then faced the bier and bent her head in homage to Gault. Despite the reverence she showed the dead, there was no warmth about her bearing. Spades' raw beauty cut like a weapon each time Nail saw her. Even the black eye-patch did not diminish her overall charisma. He could see the sparkle of armor underneath her cloak, the hilt of a sword. He kept his hand on the hilt of his own sword.

Krista kept the black dagger in hand. She held the torch in the other, watching closely as Spades bowed before Gault's body.

The bulldog sniffed at the bier. Annoyed, Krista kicked at it and it backed away.

"Ser Gault Aulbrek was the only man I ever respected," Spades said, turning toward Krista. "He cared for you deeply, that I do know."

The annoyance on Krista's face intensified.

"I must say, this bier made of sticks and deadfall does do him honor," Spades said blithely. "When you light it, *The Chivalric Illuminations* speak of how his soul shall take wing with the smoke of the holy pyre and rise into heaven to dwell in the service of Raijael. A ritual ceremony . . . though Gault believed none of it in the end."

"Did you come to pay homage or just piss me off?" Krista asked.

"I came to keep the promise I made in Amadon, that I would slay anyone who did not lay Gault to rest with honor. I am but following up on that promise."

"Is this bier honor enough for you then?"

Spades nodded. "I have paid my respects, and I shall soon leave you alone in your grief." Then her hardened gaze roamed the stark landscape. "But what will you do once he is burnt and gone, Krista Aulbrek? Where will you go?"

"What does it matter to you?"

Spades shrugged, her mouth curling into a wry little smile. "I've been so busy being devious, I haven't had time to make plans of my own. I reckon I'm just trying to live vicariously through you."

Krista did not seem to be amused.

Spades turned to Nail. "And where will you go, Nail? Will you venture back to Gallows Haven and be with your friends? Will you become a mercenary in search of the three dragons now loose on the countryside? Will you join the great hunt for the White and the Red and the Green, those monsters that do naught but menace every farm, village, and child?

That Tala Bronachell let those beasts live is odd indeed. Will you become a dragon slayer like so many now wish to become? Will you venture into that gaping crack of River Rock Quarry and explore those deep caverns from whence the demons arose? Will you search for those underground cities made of jewels and gemstones that many adventurers claim to have found?" She paused, her sharp gaze dancing with mischief. "Or will you go off in search of the boy with the silver eyes?"

Nail pictured his friend and those unsettling silver eyes. He had thought of Stefan Wayland daily, but with much sadness and confusion, wondering about his fate.

"Rumor is there is a boy with silver eyes and a black longbow wandering Gul Kana," Spades continued. "Stories have taken root throughout the realm, tales of this silver-eyed boy who helps those in need, protecting the innocent, killing outlaws and ne'er-do-wells, generally being a do-gooder in a lawless land."

Nail wondered if the warrior woman was mocking his friend.

"Well, anyway," Spades went on, "since the thought of fire-breathing dragons scares even me, I've no wish to become a dragon slayer. Instead I have a real powerful urge to join up with this silver-eyed hero, this Stefan Wayland. They say a large black saber-toothed lion fights at his side. Together they wreak terror in every thief and outlaw camp in Gul Kana."

She paused, a reflective look washing over her pale features. "Just talking about the subject gets me to thinking. I conjecture and maintain that I could be of some use to this silver-eyed cat and the silver-eyed boy in their exploits. 'Twould give me a purpose anyway." She looked down at Café Colza. "And I reckon an odd adventure such as that would really tickle the fancy of a dog like you, too." The bulldog barked, tongue lolling from its open mouth, slobbering lips adrip with strings of drool.

Spades continued, "They say a small oghul announcing himself as Mud Under Foot travels with Stefan and the saber-tooth. Should be easy enough to find, what with them announcing themselves everywhere. What say you, Café Colza, are you in for a wild escapade, chasing villains with a silver-eyed boy? It's either that or become dragon slayers. But the horror stories of those dragons on the loose, roaming the countryside, wrecking villages and farms and eating children . . . I don't know. Which is it?"

The dog barked again, small curling tail a-wag.

"Then it's settled." Spades looked back to Krista. "We go in search of Stefan Wayland and his silver-eyed cat. After all, the Five Isles are soon going to be a most dangerous place. They say Tala Bronachell is letting these demons of the underworld, these Aalavarrè Solas, live amongst us in peace. They say that Hawkwood has become her bodyguard, advising her in all things. But we all know this peace won't last. The Aalavarrè Solas are bred for revenge, bred to kill, and Hawkwood was bred to betray."

"I have faith in Tala Bronachell," Krista said.

"Ah, yes, we should all bow to Tala Bronachell," Spades said mockingly. "Fallen angel so eager to kill. I heard she requires all her subjects to burn all scripture. Sounds like a winning plan and something Hawkwood would gladly enforce."

"Hawkwood is an honorable man," Krista said. "Their plan to integrate the Five Isles is a good one."

"Our new ruler of the Five Isles is a fool," Spades said. "For now the Aalavarrè are studiously rebuilding the castle and city of Amadon and the rest of the Five Isles into a celestial realm of glory. But how long will that last? They may live under Tala's rule for a time, they may leave humanity alone for a time, maybe even for several generations, but they will eventually enslave mankind and reclaim the entirety of the Five Isles. But who is to say, perhaps it is their right to reclaim their home, take back the native lands stolen from them so long ago. And who could blame them in their triumph? Perhaps that is our part in this tale and nothing more. We are not the heroes of this story, we humans. We humans would be better off seeking the Firstlands from which we sprang."

"If the Firstlands were ever even a real place," Krista said.

"Indeed," Spades said. "Who is to know what history taught us was ever real? Doubt and cynicism are both good things when it comes to things of faith and belief. One thing I learned while fighting alongside

Aeros Raijael is that your ideologies will always let you down, especially the harder you cling to them. Whether you're beholden to belief or beholden to nonbelief, they both will fail you. And that is a bitter poison we all must swallow. There may be peace now, but centuries from now, religion will be built up once again. Legends and myths and faiths will be built anew over the events and wars we have just fought. And future wars against the Aalavarrè Solas will be waged in the name of these new faiths and beliefs. Wars may very well be fought in your name, Krista Aulbrek. They may very well be fought in Nail's name. They may well be fought in Gault's name. Perhaps even in mine. Our stories of today will be written down and twisted in the name of someone's future ideology."

"What makes you so sure?" Nail finally spoke up.

"I'm not sure of anything," Spades answered, another wry smile growing on her face. "But can you imagine someone reading something like *The Scroll of Spades*, or *The Archaic Illuminations of Aulbrek the Gault*, or the *Book of the Bastards*, and marching off to war because of the words written therein?"

"I cannot," Nail said. "For who would write such nonsense?"

"Only someone truly immoral and vile," Spades answered with a wink of her good eye. "Only someone purely evil." And with those final words, Enna Spades bowed one last time to Gault Aulbrek atop the pyre and walked down the snowy, boulder-strewn slope.

Nail watched the warrior woman stride confidently into the sunset, the slobbering bulldog on her heels. The palpable tension that had been in the air with her presence was slowly dissipating. It was not until she vanished into the dark shadows of the distant trees that Nail let out a long, pent-up breath. Krista's torch had nearly burned down to nothing. A weak flame still flickered. She needed to light the pyre soon.

"I used to carry a blue ribbon with me always," she said. "Gault's last gift to me. I wish I had it now. I secretly wore it around my ankle, even during my Bloodwood training. But I threw it away in Amadon. I tossed it away in a stupid fit of rage. I did wrong by Gault in so many ways. I wish I had that ribbon now."

"You mean this ribbon?" Nail pulled the blue ribbon from the folds of his cloak, the blue ribbon she had tossed in the ash-filled creek in Amadon.

"Where did you get that?" she asked, brow furrowed.

"I snatched it from the creek before we left that cemetery in Amadon."

"Why?"

"I did not like seeing you throw it away like that." He pulled Ava's turtle carving from around his neck. "This small carving saw me through many adventures, even though the one who gave it to me grew to hate me and even sought my death. We made our peace, and I am glad I still have it as a remembrance of more innocent days." He held the blue ribbon out for her. "I thought you might wish to have your ribbon back someday."

She took it, face expressionless as she slipped it into the folds of her own dark cloak. Then she thrust the flickering torch into the center of the bier, sparking the kindling and dry thatch, watching it catch flame.

She took a step back and stood near Nail, closer than she had ever stood before. The fire swiftly took hold and soon began to crack and roar, sending smoke curling up into the crisp evening sky. "I may not be a good person," she said. "But I have done the right thing today."

"Yes, you have," Nail said, feeling suddenly melancholy and very lost, the weight and weariness of the last year falling over him like a shroud. "And now that I've helped you see your father off, where will I go?"

Krista slipped her hand into his. "We will find somewhere."

The End of The Five Warrior Angels Trilogy

AFTERWORD

Before I ever signed with a literary agent or signed a book contract, The Five Warrior Angels was plotted out as a five-book epic fantasy series, each book much, much smaller than the three books that you hold in your hands now. At least that was the plan floating around in my head ever since I was thirteen years old and had the first germ of a story idea. At least that was the plan whilst I was merely dreaming of getting published. At least that was the plan I would talk about with my friends, on social media, on YouTube, on Goodreads, on my website, and even in some interviews I gave during the initial stages of writing . . . all before I was published.

But then I signed a three-book contract with Saga Press and had to slightly reimagine my plans. And by "reimagine" my plans, I mean I had to either hustle my way into a contract for two more books or cram five smaller fantasy novels into three very, very LARGE fantasy novels . . . and then hope my editor didn't freak out . . . because I already knew I wasn't going to cut any of the story.

So after some initial back-and-forth between myself and my agent, and then some more back-and-forth between myself and my editor at Saga, it was decided that we should do three epic (and I mean EPIC) large books. Let's throw ourselves onto the shelf with Robert Jordan and George R. R. Martin and Brandon Sanderson and just go BIG! And that is what we have now, three enormous books. And I must say I couldn't be more pleased with the result, because not one single part of the story was cut to cram all my plotlines into three larger books (well ... except for one sex scene in *Forgetting Moon*, but that cut was for the best. Trust me!).

Anyway, I just want to give one more last shout-out to my amazing editor, Joe Monti, for allowing me, a new writer, to pen such MASSIVE TOMES without even batting an eye. In fact, Joe even suggested I add EXTRA scenes here and there, that's how cool he is!

APPENDIX

Seasonal Moons of the Five Isles

A year is 360 days.
There are fifteen moons (months) per year.
A moon (month) is twenty-four days long.
A week is eight days long. There are three weeks per moon (month).

Afflicted Moon . . . . Winter
Blackest Moon
Shrouded Moon
Mourning Moon
Ethic Moon . . . . Spring
Angel Moon
Fire Moon
Blood Moon . . . . Summer
Heart Moon
Crown Moon
Thunder Moon . . . . Fall
Archaic Moon
Lonesome Moon
Forgetting Moon
Winter Moon . . . . Winter

Five Tomes of Ancient Writings

The Way and Truth of Laijon
The Chivalric Illuminations of Raijael
The Moon Scrolls of Mia
The Book of the Betrayer
The Angel Stone Codex

Five Weapons of Laijon

Forgetting Moon: battle-ax. Angel stone: blue for the Slave.
Blackest Heart: crossbow. Angel stone: black for the Assassin.
Lonesome Crown: helm. Angel stone: green for the Gladiator.
Ethic Shroud: shield. Angel stone: white for the Thief.
Afflicted Fire: sword. Angel stone: red for the Princess.

TIMELINE OF EVENTS LEADING UP TO *THE FORGETTING MOON*

5000–6000 Years Before—Humans arrive on the shores of Gul Kana.

1000 Years Before—Thousand Years' War of the humans, dwarves, oghuls, and Vallè begins.

Year Zero—Laijon is born.

18th Year of Laijon—Laijon is thrown into the slave pits.

19th Year of Laijon—Rise of the Five Warrior Angels and rise of the Demon Lords.

20th Year of Laijon—Laijon unites all races against the Fiery Demons and Demon Lords (some call this the War of Cleansing, some call it the Vicious War of the Demons).

21st Year of Laijon—Death of Laijon and banishment of all demons to the underworld.

21st Year of Laijon—Raijael, son of Laijon, is born to the Blessed Mother Mia.

22nd Year of Laijon—Church of Laijon formed by the last three Warrior Angels in Amadon.

40th Year of Laijon—Raijael banished from the church and flees Amadon to Sør Sevier.

40th Year of Laijon—Raijael begins his twenty-year war to reclaim his crown as Laijon's heir.

60th Year of Laijon—Death of Raijael in war, after having conquered Adin Wyte and Wyn Darrè.

200th Year of Laijon—The Church of Laijon retakes Adin Wyte in war from Sør Sevier.

220th Year of Laijon—The Church of Laijon retakes Wyn Darrè in war from Sør Sevier.

300th–400th Years of Laijon—Sør Sevier slowly retakes Adin Wyte and Wyn Darrè in war.

500th–900th Years of Laijon—The Church of Laijon reclaims Adin Wyte and Wyn Darrè.

900th Year of Laijon—The Brethren of Mia formed by a secret group of scholars.

900th–985th Years of Laijon—Battles continue between Sør Sevier, Adin Wyte, and Wyn Darrè.

985th Year of Laijon—Shawcroft fights two Bloodwood assassins atop a Sky Lochs glacier.

986th Year of Laijon—Shawcroft and the boy, Nail, arrive in Deadwood Gate.

989th Year of Laijon—Sør Sevier launches its final crusade against Adin Wyte.

994th Year of Laijon—Adin Wyte conquered by Sør Sevier.

994th Year of Laijon—Shawcroft and the boy, Nail, arrive in Gallows Haven.

994th Year of Laijon—Sør Sevier launches its final crusade against Wyn Darrè.

997th Year of Laijon—Squireck Van Hester slays Archbishop Lucas in Amadon.

999th Year of Laijon—Wyn Darrè conquered by Sør Sevier.

999th Year of Laijon—Sør Sevier prepares for the Final Battle of Absolution against Gul Kana.

CHARACTERS in
The Lonesome Crown

ROKENWALDER, SØR SEVIER

Crest: the Blue Sword of Raijael
Colors: blue sword on a white field
KING AEVRETT RAIJAEL: King of Rokenwalder and Sør Sevier.
QUEEN NATALIA RAIJAEL: wed to Aevrett. From Kayde, Sør Sevier.
AEROS RAIJAEL: 28, the Angel Prince. Son of Aevrett.
SPIDERWOOD: Aeros' Knight Archaic bodyguard. A Bloodwood
    assassin.
HAMMERFISS: Aeros' Knight Archaic bodyguard.
BEAU STABLER: Aeros' Knight Archaic bodyguard.
ENNA SPADES: 27, Aeros' Knight Archaic bodyguard.
GAULT AULBREK: 38, Aeros' Knight Archaic bodyguard.
AVRIL AULBREK: wed to Gault. Mother of Krista.
KRISTA AULBREK: 17, Crystalwood. Bloodwood assassin. Gault's
    stepdaughter.
AGUS AULBREK: Gault's father. Lord of the Sør Sevier Nordland
    Highlands.
EVALYN AULBREK: Gault's mother. Sister to Edmon Guy Van Hester
    of Saint Only.
MARCUS GYLL: a Rowdie.
PATRYK LAURENTS: a Rowdie.
BLODEVED WYNSTONE: a Rowdie.
RUFIC BRADULF: Hound Guard captain.
KARLOS: a Hound Guard.
ALVIN: a Hound Guard.
BLACK DUGAL: head of the Bloodwood assassins.

CHARACTERS

MANCELLOR ALLEN: 22, Knight of the Blue Sword. From Wyn
 Darrè.
HANS RAKE: Shadowwood. Bloodwood assassin.
AULMUT KLINGANDE: a Rokenwalder noble.
SOLVIA KLINGANDE: Wed to Aulmut.
DAME PORTEA: head laundress in Aevrett's palace.
BOGG: warden of the dungeons of Rokenwalder.
SQUATEYE: dwarf gaoler and cohort of Bogg.

GALLOWS HAVEN, GUL KANA

BARON JUBAL BRUK: Baron of Gallows Haven and owner of the
 Lady Kindly.
JENKO BRUK: 18, Baron Jubal Bruk's son.
BRUTUS GROVE: works for Baron Jubal Bruk.
OL' MAN LEDDINGHAM: owner of the Grayken Spear Inn.
AVA SHAY: 17, works at the Grayken Spear Inn.
TYLDA EGBERT: 16, works at the Grayken Spear Inn.
POLLY MOTT: 16, works at the Grayken Spear Inn.
GISELA BARNWELL: 15, Maiden Blue of the Mourning Moon
 Feast.
SHAWCROFT: also known as Ser Roderic Raybourne.
NAIL: 17, a bastard boy under the care of Shawcroft.
STEFAN WAYLAND: 17, friend of Nail.
DOKIE LIDDLE: 17, friend of Nail.
ZANE NEVILLE: 17, Liz Hen's brother.
LIZ HEN NEVILLE: 19, Zane's sister.
BISHOP TOLBRET: bishop of Gallows Haven chapel.
BISHOP HUGH GODWYN: bishop of the Swithen Wells Trail
 Abbey.

CHARACTERS

AMADON, GUL KANA

Crest: the Atonement Tree
Colors: the silver Atonement Tree on a black field
Silver Guard. Silver Throne.

KING BORDEN BRONACHELL: former king of Amadon and Gul Kana.

QUEEN ALANA BRONACHELL: wed to Borden. Sister of Mona Le Graven.

JOVAN BRONACHELL: 28, Borden's son. King of Amadon and Gul Kana.

JONDRALYN BRONACHELL: 25, Borden's daughter.

TALA BRONACHELL: 16, Borden's daughter.

ANSEL BRONACHELL: 5, Borden's son.

DAME MAIRGRID: tutor to Tala and Ansel.

SER STERLING PRENTISS: Dayknight captain.

SER LARS CASTLEGRAIL: Commander of the Silver Guard.

SER TOMAS VORKINK: Steward of Amadon Castle.

SER LANDON GALLOWAY: Chamberlain of Amadon Castle.

SER TERRELL WICKHAM: Stable marshal of Amadon Castle.

SER OSTEN NORTHANGER: Blacksmith of Amadon Castle.

DAME VILAMINA: old kitchen matron of Amadon Castle.

DAME NELS DOUGHTY: new kitchen matron of Amadon Castle.

GRAND VICAR DENARIUS: Grand vicar in Amadon. Holy Prophet of Laijon.

ARCHBISHOP VANDIVOR: Quorum of the Five Archbishops in Amadon.

ARCHBISHOP DONALBAIN: Quorum of the Five Archbishops in Amadon.

ARCHBISHOP SPENCERVILLE: Quorum of the Five Archbishops in Amadon.

ARCHBISHOP LEAFORD: Quorum of the Five Archbishops in Amadon.

ARCHBISHOP RHYS-DUNCAN: Quorum of the Five Archbishops in
   Amadon.
SER CULPA BARRA: 28, a young Dayknight.
TATUM BARRA: Ser Culpa Barra's father.
DELIA: barmaid at the Filthy Horse Saloon.
GEOFF: patron of the Filthy Horse Saloon.
SHKILL GHA: an oghul. Gladiator.
ANJK BOURBON: an oghul. Gladiator trainer.
G'MELLKI: an oghul.
ROGUEMOORE: dwarf ambassador from Ankar.
HAWKWOOD: from Sør Sevier.
SER TOLZ TRENTO: a young Silver Guard.
SER ALAIN GRATZER: a young Silver Guard.
SER BOPPARD STOCKACH: a young Silver Guard.
HIGGEN: slave at Riven Rock Quarry.
WOADSEN: slave at Riven Rock Quarry.
MAIZY: a nobody.
SER SAGAN: a Dayknight guard.
SER PERION: a Dayknight guard.
SER CORL: a Dayknight guard.
SER SIMMONFALL: a Dayknight guard.
SER MAGNUS CORNWELL: a young Silver Guard.

ESKANDER, GUL KANA

Crest: the Saber-Toothed Lion
Colors: black lion on a yellow field
Lion Guard. Lion Throne.
LORD LOTT LE GRAVEN: Lord of Eskander. Lion Throne.
MONA LE GRAVEN: Wed to Lott. From Reinhold. Sister of Alana
   Bronachell.
LINDHOLF LE GRAVEN: 17, Lott's son, twin to Lawri.
LAWRI LE GRAVEN: 17, Lott's daughter, twin to Lindholf.

CHARACTERS

LORHAND LE GRAVEN: 12, Lott's son, twin to Lilith.
LILITH LE GRAVEN: 12, Lott's daughter, twin to Lorhand.

RIVERMEADE, GUL KANA

Crest: the Wolf
Colors: gray wolf on a maroon field
Wolf Guard. Wolf Throne.
LORD CLAYBOR CHAPARRAL: Lord of Rivermeade. Wolf Throne.
LESIA CHAPARRAL: Wed to Claybor. Sister of Nolan Darkliegh.
LEIF CHAPARRAL: 28, Claybor's son.
SHARLA CHAPARRAL: 23, Claybor's daughter.
JACLYN CHAPARRAL: 21, Claybor's daughter.
GLADE CHAPARRAL: 17, Claybor's son.

STANCLYFFE, GUL KANA

MARDGOT: Stanclyffe street merchant.
S'IST RUNK: an oghul, Stanclyffe street merchant.

WROCLAW, GUL KANA

SLEDG H'MAR: an oghul, Hragna'Ar high priest.
MUD UNDR'FUT: an oghul, slave of Sledg H'Mar, servant to the
   Aalavarrè Solas.

AVLONIA, GUL KANA

Crest: white with silver overlay
Colors: silver overlay on a white field

Marble Guard. Marble Throne.
LORD NOLAN DARKLIEGH: Lord of Avlonia.
ELYNOR DARKLIEGH: Wed to Nolan. Edmon Guy Van Hester's
  sister.
LESIA CHAPARRAL: Nolan's sister. Wed to Claybor Chaparral.

LORD'S POINT, GUL KANA

Crest: Blue of the Ocean
Color: blue
Ocean Guard. Ocean Throne.
LORD KELVIN KRONNIN: Lord of Lord's Point.
EMOGEN KRONNIN: Wed to Kelvin.
BEATRIZ VAN HESTER: Kronnin's sister. Wed to Lord Edmon Guy
  Van Hester.
RAYE KRONNIN: Kronnin's baby daughter.
SER REVALARD AVOCET: one of the Ocean Guard.
PRAED: leader of the Untamed, a small gang of roaming thieves.
LLEWELLYN: part of the Untamed.
CLIVE: part of the Untamed.
JUDI: part of the Untamed.
DERRY RICHRATH: owner of the Turn Key Inn & Saloon.
OTTO: worker in the Turn Key Inn & Saloon.

BAINBRIDGE, GUL KANA

Crest: Purple Stag
Colors: Purple Stag on a black field
BARON BRENDER WAYLAND: Uncle of Stefan Wayland.

SAINT ONLY, ADIN WYTE

Crest: two Crossed Spears
Colors: two white crossed spears on a field of red
Spear Guard. Throne of Spears.
KING EDMON GUY VAN HESTER: King of Saint Only and Adin
    Wyte.
QUEEN BEATRIZ VAN HESTER: Wed to Edmon. From Lord's Point.
SQUIRECK VAN HESTER: 28, Edmon's son. Prince of Saint Only.
    Gladiator.
EVALYN AULBREK: Edmon's sister. Wed to Lord Agus Aulbrek of Sør
    Sevier.
ELYNOR DARKLIEGH: Edmon's sister. Wed to Lord Nolan Darkliegh
    of Avlonia.
ELYSE KOHN-AGAR: Edmon's sister. Wed to Lord Nigel Kohn-Agar
    of Agonmoore.
SER IVOR JACE: warden of Mont Saint Only.
LEISEL: a servant girl.

DEVLIN, GUL KANA

GIN D'RHU: an oghul, a merchant.

SAVON, GUL KANA

RUTGER: owner of the Preening Pintail.
LUIZA: barmaid at the Preening Pintail.

CHARACTERS

WYN DARRÈ

Crest: the Black Serpent
Colors: black serpent on a yellow field
Serpent Guard. Serpent Throne.
KING TORRENCE RAYBOURNE: King of Wyn Darrè.
QUEEN BIANKA RAYBOURNE: Wed to Torrence. From Morgandy,
 Wyn Darrè.
KAROWYN RAYBOURNE: 19, Torrence's daughter.
SER RODERIC RAYBOURNE: Torrence's brother. Known as
 Shawcroft.
CASSIETTA RAYBOURNE: Torrence's sister.
MANCELLOR ALLEN: 22, Knight of the Blue Sword in Aeros Raijael's
 army.
BRONWYN ALLEN: 18, Mancellor's younger sister.
NIKLOS ALLEN: Mancellor and Bronwyn's father.
CROMM CRU'X: oghul pirate.
IRONCLOUD: dwarf from Ankar. Brother of Roguemoore.
SEABASS: dwarf from Sigard Lake.
TYUS BARRA: Ser Culpa Barra's younger cousin. Mute.
SPUDWAGON: dwarf. Owner of the Spud Wagon Inn and Tavern.

VAL VALLÈ

VAL-KORIN: Val Vallè ambassador.
SEITA: Val-Korin's younger daughter.
BREITA: Val-Korin's older daughter.
VAL-DRAEKIN: a mysterious Vallè.
VAL-SO-VREIGN: bodyguard of Val-Korin.
VAL-GIANNI: Vallè healer (sawbones).
VAL-CE-LAVEROC: a gladiator.
VAL-RIEVAUX: a gladiator.

THE ALAVARRÈ SOLAS

ICELYN THE WHITE: a Skull. Firstborn of the blood cauldrons of
   Hragna'Ar.
RAAKEL-JAEL THE GREEN: a Skull. Second-born of the blood caul-
   drons of Hragna'Ar.
BASQUE-ALIA THE BLUE: a Skull. Third-born of the blood cauldrons
   of Hragna'Ar.
SASHENYA THE BLACK: a Skull. Fourth-born of the blood cauldrons
   of Hragna'Ar.
AAMARI-LAADA THE RED: a Skull. Fifth-born of the blood cauldrons
   of Hragna'Ar.

FEATURING

BEER MUG: the most badass dog in the Five Isles.
CAFÉ COLZA BOULEDOGUE: kind of an asshole, a real son of a
   bitch.

ABOUT THE AUTHOR

BRIAN LEE DURFEE is an artist and writer raised in Fairbanks, Alaska, and Monroe, Utah. He has done illustrations for Wizards of the Coast, Tolkien Enterprises, Dungeons & Dragons, Humane Society Wildlife Land Trust (Denali National Park), and many more. His art has been featured in *SPECTRUM: Best in Contemporary Fantastic Art #3* and *Writers of the Future, Vol. 9*. He won the Arts for the Parks Grand Canyon Award and has a painting in the permanent collection of the Grand Canyon Visitor Center—Kolb Gallery. Brian is the author of the fantasy series Five Warrior Angels. He lives in Salt Lake City.